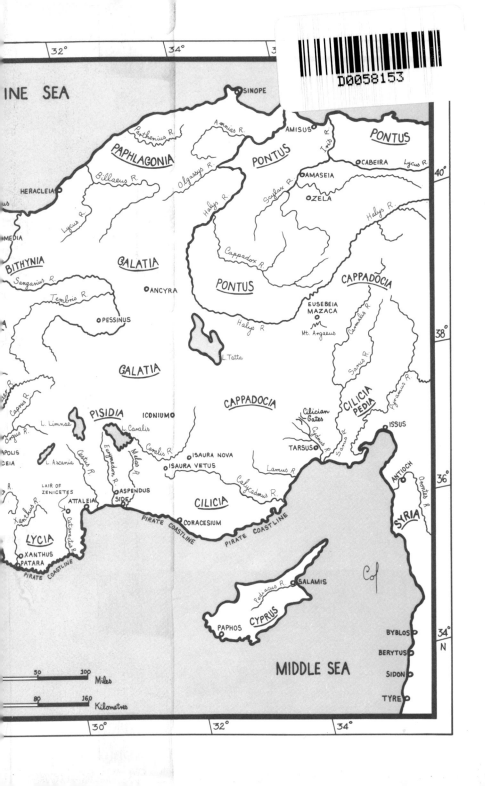

INE SEA

32° 34°

PAPHLAGONIA

SINOPE

Parthenius R.
Amnias R.
AMISUS
Iris R.
PONTUS

PONTUS
CABEIRA *Lycus R.*
40°

Billaeus R.
Olgassys R.
AMASEIA
Scylax R.
ZELA

HERACLEIA
Lycus R.

MEDIA

BITHYNIA
Halys R.
Cappadox R.
CAPPADOCIA

GALATIA
Sangarius R.
ANCYRA
PONTUS
EUSEBEIA
MAZACA
Melas R.
38°

Tembris R.
PESSINUS
Halys R.
Mt. Argaeus
Carmalis R.

L. Tatta
Saros R.

GALATIA
CAPPADOCIA
**CILICIA
PEDIA**
Pyramus R.

Caprus R.
PISIDIA
ICONIUM
Cilician
Gates
Cydnus R.
ISSUS

Orgas R.
L. Limnae
L. Caralis
Saros R.
ANTIOCH
36°

POLIS
CEIA
L. Ascania
Caralis R.
ISAURA NOVA
TARSUS
Orontes R.

Castus R.
Eurymedon R.
Melas R.
ISAURA VETUS
Lamus R.
SYRIA

LAIR OF
ZENICETES
ASPENDUS
CILICIA
Calycadnus R.

Xanthus R.
ATTALEIA
SIDE
CORACESIUM
PIRATE COASTLINE
PIRATE COASTLINE

LYCIA
Cataractes R.
PIRATE COASTLINE

XANTHUS
PATARA
Patoecus R.
SALAMIS
Cof

PIRATE COASTLINE
PAPHOS
CYPRUS
BYBLOS
34°
N

50 100
Miles
MIDDLE SEA
BERYTUS

80 160
Kilometres
SIDON

TYRE

30° 32° 34°

Karen C. Gomes

FORTUNE'S
FAVORITES

by Colleen McCullough

Tim
The Thorn Birds
An Indecent Obsession
A Creed for the Third Millennium
The Ladies of Missalonghi
The First Man in Rome
The Grass Crown

FORTUNE'S FAVORITES

Colleen McCullough

It is the policy of William Morrow and Company, Inc., and its imprints and affiliates, recognizing the importance of preserving what has been written, to print the books we publish on acid-free paper, and we exert our best efforts to that end.

ISBN 0-688-09370-1

Printed in the United States of America

For Lieutenant Colonel the Reverend A. Rebecca West
Femina Optima Maxima
The world's greatest woman

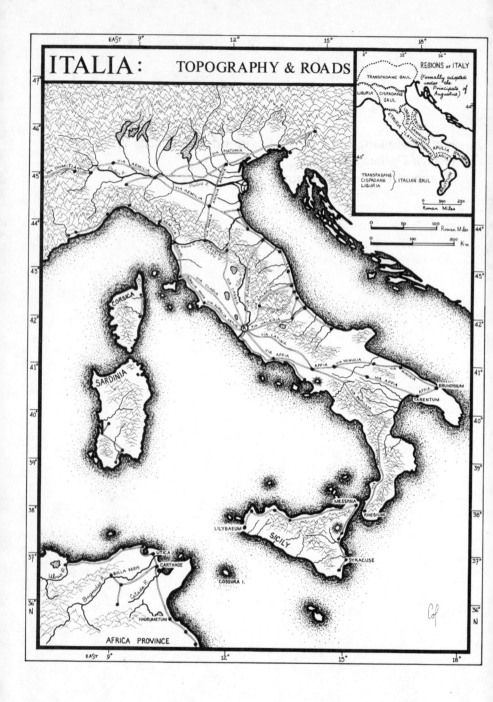

ITALIA: TOPOGRAPHY & ROADS

REGIONS OF ITALY
(Formally adopted under the Principate of Augustus)

TRANSPADANE GAUL
LIGURIA — CISPADANE GAUL
ETRURIA
UMBRIA — PICENUM
LATIUM — SAMNIUM
CAMPANIA
APULIA — CALABRIA
LUCANIA
BRUTTIUM

TRANSPADANE
CISPADANE ⎱ ITALIAN GAUL
LIGURIA

Roman Miles

Roman Miles

Km

VIA DOMITIA
VIA AEMILIA
VIA POSTUMIA
VIA AEMILIA
Padus R.
VIA AEMILIA

CORSICA

SARDINIA

VIA CLODIA
VIA AEMILIA
VIA VALERIA
VIA LATINA
VIA APPIA
APPIA
VIA MINUCIA
VIA APPIA
APPIA
MINUCIA
BRUNDISIUM
TARENTUM

MESSANA
RHEGIUM

LILYBAEUM
SICILY
SYRACUSE

COSSURA I.

ULUS
UTICA
BULLA REGIS
CARTHAGE
Bagradas R.
Catada R.
HADRUMETUM

AFRICA PROVINCE

EAST 9°   12°   15°   18°

LIST OF MAPS
AND ILLUSTRATIONS

MAPS
The Roman Near East (with particular reference
    to the movements of Caesar and Verres)   *front endpapers*
Italia: Topography and Roads   6
Northern Italy and South-Central Italian Gaul   46, 130, 516
East-Central Italy   50
Ofella's Siege of Praeneste; Sulla's Occupation of
    Via Latina   144
Route of Samnites to Colline Gate of Rome   153
The Hellespont, the Propontis, the Thracian
    Bosporus, Bithynia, Mysian Asia Province,
    and Lesbos   366
The East (with emphasis upon the conquests of
    Tigranes)   416
Pompey's Route Across the Alps   540
The Spains   546
The Wanderings of Spartacus 73–71 B.C.   711
Southwestern Italy   725

ILLUSTRATIONS
Nicomedes III Epiphanes Philopator   8
Young Pompey   30
Lucius Cornelius Sulla Felix   186
Quintus Caecilius Metellus Pius   272
Lucius Licinius Lucullus   404
Gaius Julius Caesar   454
Quintus Sertorius   536
Marcus Licinius Crassus   606
The Consul Pompey   746
The Well of the Comitia   841
Aurelia's Insula   865
Roman Magistrates   873
Shape of Toga   899
Triclinium   903
Some Events in the History of Rome Prior to
    The First Man in Rome   *back endpapers*

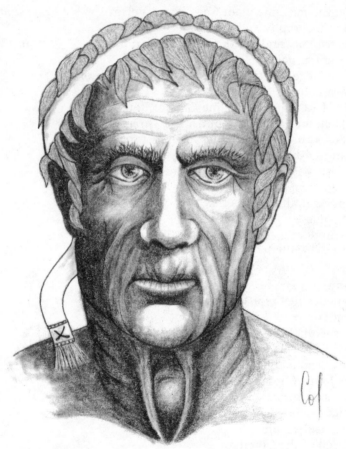

NICOMEDES III EPIPHANES PHILOPATOR

SYNOPSES

It is my intention that *Fortune's Favorites* be read with full enjoyment as a complete, free-standing novel, without the necessity of having previously read *The Grass Crown* or *The First Man in Rome*. The synopses below provide a brief summary of those two books for the reader's convenience and enhanced enjoyment.

EVENTS CHRONICLED IN *THE FIRST MAN IN ROME*

The year is 110 B.C. More by accident than design, the Republic of Rome has begun to acquire her territorial empire, a process of expansion that has placed increasingly intolerable strains upon an antique constitution. This constitution had been designed to regulate the affairs of a small city-state and protect the interests of its ruling class, embodied still in 110 B.C. by the Senate.

The true profession of Rome was war, which she conducted superbly and had come to rely upon in order to maintain growth and a thriving economy; she also kept the various other nations within Italy in a subordinate position by denying their peoples the Roman citizenship and parity in commerce.

But the voice of the People had become louder, and a series of political demagogues like the Brothers Gracchi had arisen with the avowed intention of depriving the Senate of its power. Power was to be transferred to the People in the persons of a slightly lower echelon of Roman citizens, the knights, who were primarily wealthy businessmen. (Agitation for social change in the ancient world was never undertaken on behalf of the poor, but rather took the form of a struggle between the landed aristocracy and the commercial plutocracy.)

*　*　*

In 110 B.C. the forty-seven-year-old **Gaius Marius** was a relative nobody from the little Latin district of Arpinum. Thanks to his superlative military ability, he had managed to rise as far as the second-most-important position in elected government, the praetorship, and had accumulated vast riches. But Marius hungered to be consul (the top office), though he knew that his obscure birth and ancestry would not permit of his rising so high. The consulship belonged to the landed aristocrats of ancient family who had never grubbied their hands with making money in a commercial marketplace.

Then a chance meeting with an impoverished patrician (the most august class of these aristocrats) senator, **Gaius Julius Caesar** (grandfather of the great Caesar), enabled Marius to improve his chances of attaining the consulship. In return for funding the careers of old Caesar's two sons and providing a dowry for the younger of old Caesar's two daughters, Marius was given the elder daughter, **Julia,** in marriage. Thus ennobling Marius's family and greatly enhancing his electoral image.

Now married to Julia, in 109 B.C. Marius and his letter-writing friend **Publius Rutilius Rufus** went off to wage war against King Jugurtha of Numidia. But Marius was not the commander-in-chief; this position had gone to the aristocrat Metellus (who would later call himself **Metellus Numidicus** to commemorate his war against Numidia, but whom Marius called by a far more derogatory name, **Piggle-wiggle**). With Metellus Numidicus was his twenty-year-old son, **Metellus Pius** the **Piglet.**

The war in Africa went slowly, as Metellus Numidicus was not a very effective general. In 108 B.C. Marius asked to be released from his post as senior legate so that he could return to Rome to run for election as one of the two consuls for 107 B.C. Metellus Numidicus refused to let him go, so Marius through letters waged a campaign of complaint and criticism in Rome against his superior's conduct of the war. Eventually his campaign was successful, and Metellus Numidicus was forced to release Marius from service in Africa.

However, before Marius left Africa, the Syrian prophetess Martha foretold that Marius would be consul of Rome an unprecedented seven times and would be called the Third Founder of Rome; but she also told him that his wife's nephew named Gaius would be the greatest Roman of all time. This child was as yet unborn. Marius believed in the prophecy implicitly.

Returned to Rome, Marius was elected the junior of the two consuls for 107 B.C. He then used the legislative body called the Plebeian Assembly to pass a law stripping command of the war against Jugurtha of Numidia from

Metellus Numidicus Piggle-wiggle; that same command was given to him instead.

However, his chief problem was a source of troops. The six legions Metellus Numidicus had commanded in Africa were now earmarked for the use of the other consul of 107 B.C. Italy was literally without recruitable men to serve in Rome's armies: too many men had died uselessly in battle over the preceding fifteen years, thanks to a series of utterly incompetent generals of impeccably aristocratic background. And the important friends of Metellus Numidicus, outraged at Marius's taking the war against Jugurtha away from him, now ganged up to prevent Marius's finding new soldiers.

But Marius, an iconoclastic thinker, knew of a source of troops as yet untapped—the *capite censi* or Head Count, which was the propertyless lowest class of Roman citizens—and resolved to find his army among the Head Count. A revolutionary concept!

Rome's soldiers had always been required to own land and have sufficient wealth to fund their armaments and gear out of their own purses; it was this class of fairly prosperous farmers that had supplied Rome with her soldiers for centuries. Now these men had almost ceased to exist, and their small-holdings had come into the ownership of men in the Senate or the top ranks of knight-businessmen. Vast ranches called *latifundia* which ran on slave labor had come into being, thus depriving free men of employment.

When Marius said he was going to recruit his soldiers from the Head Count, the furor was unimaginable. Fought every inch of the way by the senatorial aristocrats and many of the knight-businessmen as well, Marius went ahead and got his way through the Plebeian Assembly, then passed a further law in that body obliging the Treasury of Rome to fund the arming and equipping of his pauper legionaries.

When Marius sailed back to Africa he took with him six full legions of pauper troops the Senate deemed incapable of valor or loyalty. Also with him was his quaestor (a junior magistrate responsible for finances), one **Lucius Cornelius Sulla.** Sulla had just married **Julilla,** the younger daughter of old Caesar, and was therefore Marius's brother-in-law.

Sulla was almost the complete opposite of **Marius.** A handsome aristocrat of irreproachably patrician ancestry, he had been disqualified from entry into the Senate because of his extreme poverty—until a series of cunning murders enabled him to inherit the estates of his mistress, Nicopolis, and his stepmother, Clitumna. Ambitious and utterly ruthless, Sulla too believed in his destiny. But his first thirty-three years had been spent in a most ignoble world of theatrical riffraff, and had left Sulla possessed of a dangerous secret;

in a Rome whose citizens were adamantly opposed to homosexuality, Sulla now began to claw his way upward suppressing his love for a Greek actor, **Metrobius,** at this time still an adolescent.

It took Marius almost three years to beat Jugurtha of Numidia, though the actual capture of the King was effected by Sulla, now one of Marius's legates and his most trusted right-hand man. So different in their natures and backgrounds, the two men nonetheless got along together very well. Marius's Head Count army distinguished itself in battle, thus leaving its senatorial critics with nothing to say.

While Marius and Sulla were engaged in the African war, a new threat to Rome had come upon the scene. A vast collection of Germanic peoples (the Cimbri, the Teutones and the Cherusci/Marcomanni/Tigurini) had migrated to Gaul (modern France) and inflicted several disastrous defeats upon Rome's armies, led by aristocratic incompetents who refused to co-operate with men they considered beneath them.

Without his knowledge, Marius was elected consul for the second time and given command of the war against the Germans; despite the opposition of Metellus Numidicus and **Marcus Aemilius Scaurus** Princeps Senatus (the Leader of the House), everyone in Rome had come to believe that Marius was the only man capable of defeating the Germans, hence this extraordinary and completely unsought second consulship.

Accompanied by Sulla and the seventeen-year-old **Quintus Sertorius** (a cousin of Marius's), in 104 B.C. Marius led his men of the Head Count—now seasoned veterans—to Gaul-across-the-Alps, there to await the coming of the Germans.

But the Germans didn't come. While Marius occupied his troops in public works, Sulla and Sertorius disguised themselves as Gauls and went off to discover what the Germans meant to do. In 103 B.C. Marius was again elected consul. And due to the efforts of a tribune of the plebs, **Lucius Appuleius Saturninus,** Marius was elected consul for the fourth time in 102 B.C. It was in that year the Germans came—and just in time. Marius's senatorial enemies were preparing to oust him for good.

Thanks to some successful spying by Sulla and Sertorius, Marius had been warned of a startling German strategy, for the Germans had produced a thinking leader, King Boiorix. He split his colossal mass of people into three divisions and embarked upon a three-pronged invasion of Italy. One division, the Teutones, was to journey down the river Rhodanus (the Rhone) and enter Italy across the western Alps; another division, the Cimbri (led by

Boiorix himself), was to invade central northern Italy through the alpine pass now known as the Brenner; the third division, motley in composition, was to cross the eastern Alps into Italy and advance toward modern Venice. Then all three divisions would unite to invade the Italian peninsula and conquer Rome.

Marius's consular colleague in the year 102 B.C. belonged by blood to the Caesars; his name was **Quintus Lutatius Catulus Caesar,** and he was a haughty aristocrat with an inflated idea of his own ability but no real military talent, as Marius knew.

Electing to remain where he was in the neighborhood of modern Aix-en-Provence to intercept the German Teutones, Marius was obliged to leave interception of the German Cimbri to Catulus Caesar (the third division of Germans gave up and went back to Germania long before they were due to cross the eastern Alps). Endowed with an army of twenty-four thousand men, Catulus Caesar was ordered by the Senate to march north to intercept the Cimbri. But Marius, not trusting him, sent Sulla to him to be his second-in-command; Sulla's orders were to do everything in his power to keep Catulus Caesar's precious troops alive despite the worst blunders Catulus Caesar might make.

In late summer of 102 B.C. the Teutones, fielding over one hundred thousand men, reached Marius's position; the strength of his army was about thirty-seven thousand men. In a battle conducted with genius, Marius slaughtered the undisciplined and unsophisticated Teutones; the survivors scattered and the threat to Italy from the west was no more.

However, at about the same moment as Marius was extirpating the Teutones, Catulus Caesar, Sulla and their small army had penetrated up the alpine valley of the Athesis (now the Adige) River. There they encountered the Cimbri, just emerged from the Brenner Pass. Because there was no room to maneuver the legions, Sulla insisted that Catulus Caesar retreat; Catulus Caesar adamantly refused. So Sulla instigated a mutiny and brought the army safely into the Po Valley, quartering it in Placentia (now Piacenza) while the two hundred thousand men of the Cimbri—together with their women, children and animals—overran the eastern Po Valley.

Elected consul for the fifth time thanks to his resounding victory over the Teutones, in 101 B.C. Marius brought the bulk of his army to northern Italy and combined it with the army of Catulus Caesar; the force now numbered fifty-four thousand men. And at the height of summer the final battle against the Germans was fought on the field of Vercellae near the foot of the western

Alps. Boiorix was killed and the Cimbri annihilated. Marius had saved Italy and Rome from the Germans, who were to remain an utterly spent force for the next fifty years.

However, Metellus Numidicus, Scaurus Princeps Senatus, Catulus Caesar and the rest of Marius's enemies were no less his enemies because Marius was now being hailed the Third Founder of Rome and was able to get himself elected consul for the sixth time, in 100 B.C.

That year saw the turmoil shift from the battlefield to the Forum Romanum, which became the scene of bloody riots and frenzied political demagoguery. Marius's adherent Saturninus had managed (with the aid of his confederate Glaucia and the murder of a tribune of the plebs) to be elected a tribune of the plebs for the second time, and through this office (famous for its radicals and demagogues) sought to secure land grants for Marius's veteran soldiers of the Head Count.

This was the one bad thing about enlisting propertyless men in the legions; owning nothing and receiving little by way of pay, these men when Rome had finished with their military talents had to be rewarded. Marius had promised them grants of land—but not in Italy. His aim was to spread Roman culture and habits throughout the mushrooming empire of provinces (in which Rome owned great tracts of public land) by settling his Head Count soldier veterans abroad. In fact, the vexed question of granting Rome's public lands to veterans of the lower classes was ultimately to contribute enormously to the downfall of the Republic of Rome, for the Senate, shortsighted and antipathetic, consistently refused to co-operate with Rome's generals by willingly granting land. This meant that as time went on, these veterans of the Head Count were to find it expedient to adhere first to their generals (because their generals wanted to give them land) and only after that to Rome (because, embodied in the person of the Senate, Rome was reluctant to give them land).

Senatorial opposition to Saturninus's two land bills was obdurate and violent, though he did not entirely lack support among the upper classes. The first land bill succeeded, but the second land bill was passed only after Marius forced the members of the Senate to swear an oath to uphold it. Metellus Numidicus could not be persuaded to take this oath, and voluntarily went into exile after paying a huge fine—the penalty for not swearing.

But Scaurus Princeps Senatus had tricked the politically less talented Marius during the debates about the second land bill by making Marius admit there was a possibility that both of Saturninus's land bills were invalid. Until that moment totally loyal to Marius, Saturninus now turned against Marius as well as against the Senate, and began to plot the downfall of both.

Unfortunately for Marius, his health chose this moment to break down; a small stroke forced him to retire from political life for some months, during which Saturninus intrigued.

The harvest was due to arrive in Rome in the autumn, but a Mediterranean-wide drought blighted it. For the fourth year in a row Rome's populace faced high grain prices and an acute lack of grain. This gave Saturninus his chance. He decided to become the First Man in Rome: not as consul but as tribune of the plebs, in which position he could control the huge masses of people who now gathered each day in the Forum Romanum to protest against the coming winter's privation. It was not the lowest classes Saturninus was wooing when he introduced his grain law to provide State-funded grain; he was actually wooing the merchants and trade guilds whose businesses were threatened because the lowest classes would not eat well. The votes of the lowest classes were worthless, but the votes of the merchants and trade guilds carried enough weight for him—with their support—to overthrow both the Senate and Gaius Marius.

More or less recovered from his stroke, Marius called a meeting of the Senate for the first day of December of 100 B.C. to see what could be done to stop Saturninus, who now planned to run for a third term as a tribune of the plebs, while his friend Glaucia ran for consul. Neither candidacy was precisely illegal, but both were highly disapproved of because they flouted custom.

Matters came to a head during the consular elections when Glaucia murdered another candidate. Marius convened the Senate, which passed its Ultimate Decree (a form of martial law); the Senate and its supporters went home to get their arms, and battle was joined in the Forum Romanum. Saturninus and Glaucia had thought that the lowest classes, threatened with starvation, would rise up in revolt. But the lowest classes were not willing to do so. Quietly they went home instead. Using Sulla as his right-hand man, Marius defeated the consequently limited forces Saturninus had at his disposal. Saturninus sought asylum in the temple of Jupiter Optimus Maximus, but was forced to surrender when Sulla cut off the water supply to the Capitol.

Glaucia committed suicide, but Saturninus and the rest of his close friends were imprisoned in the Senate House until they could be tried for treason— a trial everybody in the Senate knew would fracture Rome's already tottering constitutional framework. Sulla solved the problem by secretly leading a small band of young aristocrats onto the roof of the Senate House, from which vantage point they killed Saturninus and his friends by bombarding them with tiles torn from the roof.

Saturninus's grain law was repealed, but Marius—now fifty-seven years old—had to face the fact that his political career had ground to a halt. Consul six times, it seemed he would never fulfill the prophecy by being consul a seventh time. But Sulla hoped to be elected praetor in a year's time. He decided he would therefore have to withdraw from Marius, now politically odious, in order to preserve his own career.

During these ten years, the private lives and loves of Marius and Sulla fared differently.

Marius's marriage to Julia prospered. They had a son born in 109 B.C., their only child, who was called **Young Marius.** Old Caesar died, but not before he saw both his sons firmly placed for future political and military eminence. His younger son, Gaius, married a rich and beautiful daughter of the Famous Family Aurelius Cotta, one **Aurelia,** and sensibly the young couple took up residence in Aurelia's apartment house in the Subura, a district of Rome in evil repute. They had two girls, and finally in 100 B.C. a son (the great Caesar) who was of course, as Marius immediately recognized, the child of the prophecy—the greatest Roman of all time. Marius resolved that he would try to foil this part of his cherished foretelling.

Sulla's marriage to old Caesar's younger girl, Julilla, was not a happy one, mostly due to Julilla's febrile and overly dramatic nature. Two children were born of it, a daughter and a son. Loving Sulla obsessively, Julilla was aware she did not hold all of Sulla's heart, though she had no idea of his true sexual inclinations. Unhappiness prompted her to drink, and as time went on she became completely dependent upon her wine.

Then a rare event took place; the young Greek actor Metrobius came to visit Sulla in his house. Sight of Metrobius broke down Sulla's resolve never again to become physically involved with him. Unbeknownst to them, Julilla witnessed their lovemaking. And immediately committed suicide. Later on Sulla married a charming and childless widow of excellent family, one **Aelia,** to provide his children with a mother.

Scaurus Princeps Senatus had a son who was guilty of cowardice while serving with the army of Catulus Caesar in northern Italy. Disgusted, Scaurus disowned the young man, who committed suicide. Whereupon Scaurus, now close to sixty years of age, promptly married his son's fiancée, the seventeen-year-old daughter of Metellus Numidicus's older brother; she was known as **Dalmatica.** No one asked her what she thought of this union.

And young **Marcus Livius Drusus,** eminently aristocratic son of a famous man, in 105 B.C. arranged a double wedding; he married the sister of his best friend, the patrician **Quintus Servilius Caepio,** while Caepio married Drusus's sister, **Livia Drusa.** Drusus's union was childless, but Caepio and

Livia Drusa produced two girls, the elder of whom, **Servilia,** was to grow up to be the mother of Brutus and the mistress of the great Caesar.

EVENTS CHRONICLED IN *THE GRASS CROWN*

The year is 98 B.C., almost two years after the events which closed *The First Man in Rome*—but two years of relative uneventfulness.

Sulla was absolutely bored by the charm and goodness of his second wife, **Aelia,** and plagued by his hunger for two other people—the young Greek actor **Metrobius** and the nineteen-year-old wife of **Marcus Aemilius Scaurus** Princeps Senatus, **Dalmatica.** But as ambition and a sense of destiny still ruled every other passion in Sulla, he steadfastly refused to see Metrobius or to begin an affair with Dalmatica.

Unfortunately Dalmatica was not so self-disciplined, and made a public spectacle of herself by advertising her unrequited love for Sulla. Scaurus, humiliated, demanded that Sulla quit Rome to stop the gossip, but deeming himself guiltless and Scaurus unreasonable, Sulla refused. He intended to seek election as praetor, which meant he had to stay in Rome. Well aware Sulla was innocent, old Scaurus nonetheless blocked his election as a praetor— and confined Dalmatica to her house.

Thwarted in his political career, Sulla decided to go to Nearer Spain as the legate of its warlike governor, Titus Didius. Scaurus had won. Before he left, Sulla made advances to **Aurelia,** wife of Gaius Julius Caesar, and was rejected; furious, he went to see **Metellus Numidicus** (just returned from exile) and murdered him. Far from blaming Sulla for his father's death, **Metellus Pius** the **Piglet** continued to admire and trust him.

The family Caesar was prospering. Both of old Caesar's sons, Sextus and Gaius, had advanced under Marius's patronage, though this meant Gaius was away from home most of the time. His wife, Aurelia, managed her apartment house and efficiently saw to the welfare and education of her two daughters and her precious little son, **Young Caesar,** who from a very early age demonstrated startling intelligence and ability. The one aspect of Aurelia which caused misgivings in all her relatives and friends was her liking for Sulla, who visited her because he admired her.

Still in political eclipse, **Gaius Marius** took his wife, **Julia,** and his son, **Young Marius,** on a long holiday to the east, there to visit various parts of Anatolia.

Having reached Cilician Tarsus, Marius learned that King **Mithridates** of Pontus had invaded Cappadocia, murdered its young monarch, and put one of his own many sons on its throne. Leaving wife and son in the care of nomads, Marius rode virtually alone for the Cappadocian capital, where fearlessly he confronted King Mithridates of Pontus.

Captious and cunning, Mithridates was a curious mixture of coward and hero, braggart and mouse; he commanded vast forces and had expanded his kingdom mightily at the expense of all his neighbors save Rome. By forging a marital alliance, Mithridates had arrived at complete agreement with **Tigranes,** the King of Armenia; the two kings planned to unite, defeat Rome, and end in ruling the world between them.

All of these vaunting plans disintegrated when Mithridates met Marius, a solitary figure who yet had the confidence to order the King of Pontus out of Cappadocia. Though he could have had Marius killed, instead Mithridates clipped his tail between his legs and took his army back to Pontus, while Marius rejoined his wife and son and resumed his holiday.

Matters in Italy were coming to a head. Rome was suzerain over the various semi-independent nations which made up the checkerboard of peninsular Italy. Her Italian Allies, as they were called, had long existed in an unequal partnership with Rome, and were well aware Rome considered them inferiors. They were called upon to provide and pay for soldiers whom Rome used in her foreign wars, yet Rome had ceased to reward the Italian Allies with gifts of the Roman citizenship, and denied Italians parity in trade, commerce, and all the other benefits accruing to full Roman citizens. The leaders of the various Italian peoples were now clamoring with increasing vigor and resolution for equal status with Rome.

Marcus Livius Drusus had a friend, **Quintus Poppaedius Silo,** who was an Italian of high estate; the leader of his people, the Marsi, Silo was determined to see all the Marsi become full Roman citizens. And Drusus sympathized with him. A great Roman aristocrat of enormous wealth and political clout, Drusus was sure that with his assistance the Italians would gain the longed-for franchise and equality.

But matters within Drusus's own family were to undermine Drusus's resolve. His sister, **Livia Drusa,** was unhappily married to Drusus's best friend, **Quintus Servilius Caepio** (Caepio had taken to physically abusing her); then she met **Marcus Porcius Cato,** fell in love with him, and began an affair. Already the mother of two girls, Livia Drusa became pregnant by Cato and bore a son who she managed to convince Caepio was his child. Then her eldest girl, **Servilia,** accused Livia Drusa of infidelity with Cato, and precipitated a family crisis. Caepio divorced Livia Drusa and disowned all three children; Drusus and his wife stood by her. Livia Drusa then married Cato and gave him two more children, Porcia and **Young Cato** (the future Cato Uticensis). While all this was going on, Drusus had struggled to convince the Senate of the justice of Italian claims to the citizenship, but after Livia Drusa's scandal he found his task far more difficult, thanks to Caepio's sudden and bitter enmity.

In 96 B.C. Drusus's wife died. In 93 B.C. Livia Drusa died. Her five children passed fully into Drusus's care. In 92 B.C. Cato died. Only the estranged Caepio and Drusus were left.

Though considered too old for the office, Drusus decided the only way to obtain equality for the Italians was to become a tribune of the plebs and coax the Plebeian Assembly into granting the franchise against obdurate opposition from the Senate. An impressively patient and intelligent man, he did very well. But some of the senatorial diehards (including Scaurus, **Catulus Caesar** and Caepio) were absolutely determined he would not succeed. On the very eve of victory, Drusus was assassinated in the atrium of his own house. The time was late in 91 B.C.

The five children of Livia Drusa plus his own adopted son, Drusus Nero, witnessed the horror of his lingering death. Only Caepio was left to those young people, but Caepio refused to have anything to do with them. So they passed into the care of Drusus's mother and his younger brother, **Mamercus** Aemilius Lepidus Livianus. In 90 B.C. Caepio died, and in 89 B.C. Drusus's mother died. Now only Mamercus remained. When his wife refused to shelter the children Mamercus was forced to leave them to grow up in Drusus's house. He put them in the charge of a spinster relative and her formidable mother.

Sulla had returned from Nearer Spain in time to be elected urban praetor for 93 B.C. In 92 B.C. (while Drusus struggled to bring about the franchise for all of Italy) Sulla was sent to the east to govern Cilicia. There he discovered that Mithridates, emboldened by five years of Roman inertia, had once again invaded Cappadocia. Sulla led his two legions of Cilician troops into Cappadocia, ensconced them inside a superbly fortified camp, and proceeded to run military rings around Mithridates, despite the King's overwhelming superiority in numbers. For the second time Mithridates was forced to look a solitary Roman in the eye and hear himself curtly ordered to go home. For the second time Mithridates clipped his tail between his legs and took his army back to Pontus.

But the son-in-law of Mithridates, King Tigranes of Armenia, was still at large and intent upon war. Sulla led his two legions to Armenia, becoming the first Roman to cross the Euphrates on a military mission. On the Tigris near Amida, Sulla found and warned Tigranes; then on the Euphrates at Zeugma he hosted a conference between himself, Tigranes and ambassadors from the King of the Parthians. A treaty was concluded whereby everything to the east of the Euphrates was to remain the concern of the Parthians and everything to the west of the Euphrates was to become the concern of Rome. Sulla was also the subject of a prophecy by a famous Chaldaean seer: he would be the greatest man between Oceanus Atlanticus and the Indus River, and would die at the height of his fame and prosperity.

With Sulla was his son by the dead **Julilla**. This boy—in his middle teens—was the light of Sulla's life. But after Sulla's return to Rome (where he found the Senate indifferent to his deeds and to his magnificent treaty), Young Sulla died tragically. The loss of the boy was a terrible blow to Sulla, who severed the last vestige of his relationship with the Caesars, except for his sporadic visits to Aurelia. On these visits he now encountered her son, Young Caesar, who impressed Sulla.

The Italian War broke out with a series of shattering defeats for Rome. At the beginning of 90 B.C. the consul Lucius Caesar took over the southern theater of war (in Campania), with Sulla as his senior legate. The northern theater (in Picenum and Etruria) was commanded by several men in turn, all of whom proved to be woefully inadequate.

Gaius Marius hungered to command the northern theater, but his enemies in the Senate were still too strong. He was forced to serve as a mere legate, and to suffer many indignities at the hands of his commanders. But one by one these commanders went down in defeat (and, as in the case of Caepio, died), while Marius plodded on training the troops, very raw and timorous. Waiting his chance. When it came he seized it immediately, and in association with Sulla (loaned to him) won for Rome the first significant victory of the war. Then on the day following this victory Marius suffered his second stroke—far worse than his first—and was forced to withdraw from the conflict. This rather pleased Sulla, for Marius refused to take Sulla seriously as a general, though Sulla generaled all the victories in the southern theater—always in the name of someone else.

In 89 B.C. the war took a better turn for Rome, especially in the southern theater. Sulla was awarded Rome's highest military decoration, the Grass Crown, by his troops before the city of Nola, and most of Campania and Apulia were subjugated. The two consuls of 89 B.C., Pompey Strabo and a Cato, fared very differently. Cato the Consul was murdered by Young Marius to avoid a military defeat; Marius procured his son's freedom by bribing the commander left in charge, **Lucius Cornelius Cinna.** Cinna, an honorable man despite this bribe, was to remain Marius's adherent ever after—and Sulla's enemy.

The senior consul of 89 B.C., **Pompey Strabo,** had a seventeen-year-old son, **Pompey,** who adored his father and insisted on fighting at his side. In 90 B.C. they had besieged the city of Asculum Picentum, wherein the first atrocity of the Italian War had taken place. With them was the seventeen-year-old **Marcus Tullius Cicero,** a most inept and unwilling warrior whom Pompey sheltered from his father's wrath—and contempt. Cicero was never afterward to forget Pompey's kindness, which dictated much of his political orientation. When Asculum Picentum fell in 89 B.C., Pompey Strabo executed every male inhabitant and banished every female and child with no more than the clothes they wore on their backs; the incident stood out in the annals of a terrible war.

But by 88 B.C., when Sulla was finally elected consul with a Quintus Pompeius Rufus as his colleague, Rome was victorious in the war against her Italian Allies. Not without yielding much she had gone to war to prevent: the Italians were—in name at least—given the full Roman franchise.

Sulla's daughter by Julilla, **Cornelia Sulla,** was very much in love with her cousin Young Marius, but Sulla forced her to marry the son of his colleague in the consulship; she bore this young man a girl, **Pompeia** (later the second wife of the great Caesar), and a boy.

Now ten years old, Young Caesar was sent by his mother to help his Uncle Marius recover from the effects of that maiming second stroke, and eagerly learned whatever he could from Marius about the art of war. Well aware of the prophecy, Marius's exposure to the boy only reinforced his determination to curtail Young Caesar's future military and political career.

Angered by an innocuous remark made by his boring wife Aelia, Sulla suddenly divorced her—for barrenness. Old Scaurus had died, so Sulla then married his widow, Dalmatica. Most of Rome censured Sulla for his conduct toward Aelia (who was much admired), but Sulla didn't care.

Knowing that Rome was fully occupied in her war against the Italian Allies, King Mithridates of Pontus invaded the Roman province of Asia in 88 B.C. and murdered every Roman and Italian man, woman and child living there. The death toll was eighty thousand, plus seventy thousand of their slaves.

When Rome heard the news of this mass slaughter, the Senate met to discuss who would lead an army to the east to deal with King Mithridates. Deeming himself recovered from his stroke, Marius shouted that the command against Mithridates must be given to him. A peremptory demand which the Senate wisely ignored. Instead, that body awarded the command to the senior consul, Sulla. An affront Marius did not forgive; Sulla now joined the list of his declared enemies.

Understanding that he was capable of defeating Mithridates, Sulla accepted the command with great content, and prepared to leave Italy. But the Treasury was empty and Sulla's funds far too slender, even after much public land around the Forum Romanum had been sold to pay for his army; the wealth Sulla needed to pay for his war was to come from plundering the temples of Greece and Epirus. Sulla's army was relatively tiny.

In that same year, 88 B.C., another tribune of the plebs of enduring fame arose—**Sulpicius.** A conservative man, he turned radical only after the King of Pontus slaughtered the inhabitants of Asia Province—because he realized that a foreign king had not made any distinction between a Roman and an Italian—he had killed both. Sulpicius decided the Senate was to blame for Rome's unwillingness to grant the full citizenship to all Italians, and decided the Senate would have to go. There could be no difference between a Roman and an Italian if a foreign king could find no difference. So Sulpicius proceeded to pass laws in the Plebeian Assembly which expelled so many men from the Senate that it could no longer form a quorum. With the Senate rendered impotent, Sulpicius then proceeded to boost the electoral and political power of the new Italian citizens. But all this took place amid bloody riots in the Forum Romanum, and the young husband of Sulla's daughter, Cornelia Sulla, was killed.

Riding high, Sulpicius then allied himself with Marius and got the Plebeian Assembly to pass another law—a law stripping the command in the war against Mithridates from Sulla and awarding it to Marius instead. Almost seventy years old and crippled by disease he might be, but Marius was not about to let anyone else go to war against Mithridates—especially Sulla.

Sulla was in Campania organizing his army when he heard of the new legislation and his own disqualification. He then made a momentous decision: he would march on Rome. Never in her six hundred years of existence had any Roman done that. But Sulla would. His officers refused to support him except for his loyal quaestor, **Lucius Licinius Lucullus,** but his soldiers were fervently on his side.

In Rome no one believed Sulla would dare to make war upon his own homeland, so when Sulla and his army arrived outside the city walls, panic ensued. Unable to lay their hands on professional soldiers, Marius and Sulpicius were forced to arm ex-gladiators and slaves to resist Sulla. Who entered the city, trounced the motley opposition, took over Rome, and drove Marius, Sulpicius, Old Brutus and a few other men into flight. Sulpicius was caught before he could leave Italy and beheaded. Marius, after a terrible ordeal in the town of Minturnae, succeeded with Young Marius and the others in reaching Africa, where after many adventures they sheltered among the veterans Marius had settled on Cercina.

As virtual owner of Rome, Sulla's worst act was to fix the head of Sulpicius on the rostra in the Forum Romanum in order to terrify (among others) Cinna into obedience. He repealed all of Sulpicius's laws and put laws of his own into effect. These laws were ultra-conservative, aimed at fully restoring the Senate and discouraging future tribunes of the plebs with radical ideas. Satisfied that he had done what he could to shore up traditional Republican government, Sulla finally departed for the east and the war against Mithridates in 87 B.C. But not before marrying his widowed daughter to Mamercus, brother of the dead Drusus and custodian of the orphaned children.

The exile of Marius, Young Marius, Old Brutus and their companions lasted about a year. Sulla had attempted one final measure to shore up his hastily drafted emergency constitution—he tried to have men loyal to himself elected consuls for 87 B.C. In the case of the senior consul, Gnaeus Octavius Ruso, he did succeed; but the pernickety electors returned Cinna as the junior consul, and Sulla knew this man belonged to Marius. So he tried to secure Cinna's loyalty to the new constitution by making him swear a sacred oath to uphold it—an oath Cinna nullified as he swore it by holding a stone in his hand.

As soon as Sulla had sailed for the east in spring of 87 B.C., strife broke out in Rome. Cinna abrogated his worthless oath and openly opposed Gnaeus Octavius and his ultra-conservative backers—men like Catulus Caesar, Publius Crassus, Lucius Caesar. Cinna was ejected from Rome and outlawed, but the ultra-conservatives failed to make military preparations. Cinna did not; he raised an army and laid siege to the city. Marius promptly returned from exile and landed in Etruria, where he too raised an army and marched to the aid of Cinna and his confederates **Quintus Sertorius** and **Gnaeus Papirius Carbo.**

The ultra-conservatives, desperate, sent to Pompey Strabo in Picenum and begged that he come to their rescue, as he had not disbanded his army of loyal vassals. Accompanied by his son Pompey, Pompey Strabo marched to Rome. But once he arrived there he did nothing to bring on a battle against Cinna, Marius, Carbo and Sertorius. All he did was to sit in a huge, insanitary camp outside the Colline Gate and antagonize the inhabitants of Rome's northern hills by polluting their water and causing a frightful epidemic of enteric fever.

The Siege of Rome ground on for some time, but eventually a battle took place between Pompey Strabo and Sertorius. It came to no conclusion, for Pompey Strabo fell ill with enteric fever and collapsed. Shortly afterward he died. Aided by his friend **Cicero,** young Pompey prepared to bury his father; but the people of the devastated northern hills of Rome stole the body, stripped it naked, tethered it behind an ass, and dragged it through their streets. After a frantic search Pompey and Cicero found it. The outraged Pompey then quit Rome to take his father's body and army back to Picenum.

Bereft of Pompey Strabo's army, Rome was incapable of further resistance, and surrendered to Cinna and Marius. Cinna entered the city at once. Whereas Marius refused to do so, stating that he was still officially an outlaw and would not move from the protection of his camp and soldiers until Cinna had not only repealed the decree of outlawry, but had succeeded in having Marius elected consul for the prophesied seventh time. Sertorius also refused to enter the city, but not because of events; the cousin of Marius, he had realized that Marius was mad, his brain eroded by that second stroke.

Understanding that every soldier would if pushed serve Marius ahead of himself, Cinna had no choice other than to see himself and Marius "elected" consuls for the year 86 B.C., now only days away. And on New Year's Day Marius entered Rome as consul for the seventh time; the prophecy was fulfilled. With him he brought five thousand ex-slaves fanatically devoted to his cause.

A bloodbath ensued, the like of which Rome had never seen. Quite demented, Marius ordered his ex-slaves to slaughter all his enemies and many of his friends; the rostra bristled with heads, including those of Catulus Caesar, Lucius Caesar, Caesar Strabo, Publius Crassus, and Gnaeus Octavius Ruso.

Gaius Julius Caesar, father of Young Caesar, returned to Rome in the midst of the carnage to find himself summoned to see Marius in the Forum Romanum. There he was informed by Marius that his thirteen-year-old son was to be made the *flamen Dialis,* the special priest of Jupiter Optimus Maximus, principal deity of Rome. For the crazed old man had found the perfect way to prevent Young Caesar from enjoying a political or military career. Young Caesar would never now surpass Gaius Marius in the annals of Rome. The *flamen Dialis* was forbidden to touch iron, ride a horse, handle a weapon or see the moment of death (as well as a host of other taboos); he could never fight on a battlefield or stand for election to curule executive office. Because at the moment of inauguration and consecration the *flamen*

Dialis had to be married to another patrician, Marius ordered Cinna (a patrician) to give his seven-year-old younger daughter, **Cinnilla,** to Young Caesar as his wife. The two children were immediately married, after which Young Caesar was formally made *flamen Dialis,* and his wife Cinnilla *flaminica Dialis*.

Scant days into his seventh consulship, Gaius Marius was felled by a third and terminal stroke. He died on the thirteenth day of January. His cousin Sertorius then killed the huge band of ex-slaves, and the bloodbath was over. Cinna took a Valerius Flaccus as his consular colleague to replace Marius, and began the process of soothing a shaken Rome. Now *flamen Dialis* and a married boy, Young Caesar contemplated a dreary and disappointing future as the lifelong servant of Jupiter Optimus Maximus.

A CHRONICLE OF EVENTS BETWEEN 86 B.C. AND 83 B.C.

Finding his feet, **Cinna** took control of a much-reduced Senate; while he repealed some of Sulla's laws, he did not repeal all, and the Senate was allowed to continue to exist. Under his aegis, the Senate formally stripped the absent **Sulla** of his command against King **Mithridates** and authorized the other consul, Flaccus, to take four legions to the east and relieve Sulla. Flaccus's senior legate in this enterprise was Fimbria, a savage and undisciplined man who yet inspired affection in his soldiers.

But when Flaccus and Fimbria reached central Macedonia they decided not to turn south into Greece (where Sulla was lying with his army); instead they continued to march across Macedonia toward the Hellespont and Asia Minor. Quite unable to control Fimbria, Flaccus found himself subordinate to his subordinate. Quarreling and disaffected, they reached Byzantium, where the final and fatal falling-out took place. Flaccus was murdered and Fimbria assumed the command. He crossed into Asia Minor and commenced—very successfully—to war against King Mithridates.

Sulla had become bogged down in Greece, which had welcomed the generals and armies of Mithridates and now hosted a huge Mithridatic force. The city of Athens had defected, so Sulla besieged it; after bitter resistance it fell. Sulla then won two stunning victories around Lake Orchomenus in Boeotia.

His legate **Lucullus** had assembled a fleet and also inflicted defeats upon Pontus. Then Fimbria trapped Mithridates in Pitane and sent to Lucullus to help him capture the King by blockading the harbor. Haughtily Lucullus refused to work with a Roman he considered not legally appointed. The result was that Mithridates escaped via the sea.

By the summer of 85 B.C. Sulla had expelled the Pontic armies from Europe, and himself crossed into Asia Minor. On August (Sextilis) 5, the King of Pontus agreed to the Treaty of Dardanus, which required that he retire inside his own borders and stay there. Sulla also dealt with Fimbria, whom he pursued until Fimbria in despair committed suicide; forbidding Fimbria's troops ever to return to Italy, Sulla incorporated them into a standing army for use in Asia Province and Cilicia.

Sulla was very well aware that King Mithridates was by no means a spent force when he tendered the Treaty of Dardanus and obliged the King to retire. However, he was also aware that if he remained in the east much longer, he would lose all chance of regaining what he considered as his rightful position in Rome. His wife **Dalmatica** and his daughter **Cornelia Sulla** had been forced to flee to join him under the escort of **Mamercus;** his house had been looted and burned down; his property had been confiscated (except that Mamercus had managed to conceal most of it); and his status was now that of an outlaw stripped of Roman citizenship and under interdiction. As was true of his followers; many of the members of the Senate had also fled to join him, unwilling to live under Cinna's administration. Among the refugees were **Appius Claudius Pulcher, Publius Servilius Vatia,** and **Marcus Licinius Crassus,** the latter from Spain.

Thus Sulla had no choice but to turn his back on Mithridates and return to Rome; this he planned to do in 84 B.C., but a very serious illness compelled him to linger in Greece for a further year, fretting because his extended absence gave Cinna and his confederates more time to prepare for war. War there was bound to be—Italy was not big enough to contain two factions so obdurately opposed to each other—and so unwilling to forgive and forget for the sake of peace.

So too did Cinna and Cinna's Rome understand that war with Sulla on his return was inevitable. When Cinna learned of the death of his consular colleague, Flaccus, he took a new and much stronger man as junior consul, **Gnaeus Papirius Carbo.** Together with their pliant Senate, they decided that Sulla must be opposed before he reached Italy, still exhausted from the Italian War. With the object of stopping Sulla in western Macedonia before he could cross the Adriatic Sea, Cinna and Carbo began to recruit a huge army which they shipped to Illyricum, just to the north of western Macedonia.

But recruitment was slow, especially in the fief of the dead **Pompey**

Strabo, Picenum. Thinking his personal attendance would attract more volunteers, Cinna himself journeyed to Ancona to supervise the enlistments. There Pompey Strabo's son **Pompey** paid Cinna a visit, apparently toying with the idea of joining up. However, he did not. Shortly afterward Cinna died in Ancona in circumstances shrouded with mystery. Carbo took over Rome and control of the Senate, but decided that Sulla would have to be allowed to land in Italy. The war against him would have to be fought on Italian soil after all. Back came the troops from Illyricum, and Carbo laid his plans. After securing the election of two tame consuls, Scipio Asiagenus and Gaius Norbanus, Carbo went to govern Italian Gaul, and placed himself and his section of the army in the port city of Ariminum.

The stage was set. Now read on. . . .

PART ONE

from APRIL 83 B.C.
until DECEMBER 82 B.C.

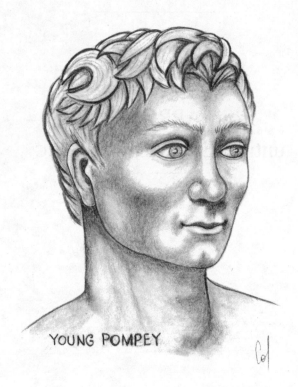

YOUNG POMPEY

Though the steward held his five-flamed lamp high enough to illuminate the two recumbent figures in the bed, he knew its light had not the power to waken Pompey. For this, he would need Pompey's wife. She stirred, frowned, turned her head away in an effort to remain asleep, but the vast house was murmuring beyond the open door, and the steward was calling her.

"*Domina! Domina!*"

Even in confusion modest—servants did not make a habit of invading Pompey's bedchamber—Antistia made sure she was decently covered before she sat up.

"What is it? What's the matter?"

"An urgent message for the master. Wake him and tell him to come to the atrium," barked the steward rudely. The lamp flames dipped and smoked as he swung on his heel and left; the door closed, plunging her into darkness.

Oh, that vile man! He had done it deliberately! But she knew where her shift lay across the foot of the bed, drew it on, and shouted for a light.

Nothing woke Pompey. Provided with a lamp and a warm wrap, Antistia finally turned back to the bed to discover him slumbering still. Nor did he seem to feel the cold, lying on his back uncovered to the waist.

She had tried on other occasions—and for other reasons—to kiss him awake, but never could. Shakes and pummels it would have to be.

"What?" he asked, sitting up and running his hands through his thick yellow thatch; the quiff above his peaked hairline stood up alertly. So too were the blue eyes surveying her alert. That was Pompey: apparently dead one moment, wide awake the next. Both soldiers' habits. "What?" he asked again.

"There's an urgent message for you in the atrium."

But she hadn't managed to finish the sentence before he was on his feet and his feet were shoved into backless slippers and a tunic was falling carelessly off one freckled shoulder. Then he was gone, the door gaping behind him.

For a moment Antistia stood where she was, undecided. Her husband hadn't taken the lamp—he could see in the dark as well as any cat—so there was nothing to stop her following save her own knowledge that probably he wouldn't like it. Well, bother that! Wives were surely entitled to share news important enough to invade the master's sleep! So off she went with her little lamp barely showing her the way down that huge corridor flagged and walled with bare stone blocks. A turn here—a flight of steps there—and suddenly she was out of the forbidding Gallic fortress and into the civilized Roman villa, all pretty paint and plaster.

Lights blazed everywhere; the servants had busied themselves to some effect. And there was Pompey clad in no more than a tunic yet looking like the personification of Mars—oh, he was wonderful!

He might even have confided in her, for his eyes did take her presence in. But at the same moment Varro arrived in startled haste, and Antistia's chance to share personally in whatever was causing the excitement vanished.

"Varro, Varro!" Pompey shouted. Then he whooped, a shrill and eldritch sound with nothing Roman in it; just so had long-dead Gauls whooped as they spilled over the Alps and took whole chunks of Italy for their own, including Pompey's Picenum.

Antistia jumped, shivered. So, she noticed, did Varro.

"What is it?"

"Sulla has landed in Brundisium!"

"Brundisium! How do you know?"

"What does that matter?" demanded Pompey, crossing the mosaic floor to seize little Varro by both shoulders and shake him. "It's here, Varro! The adventure has begun!"

"*Adventure?*" Varro gaped. "Oh, Magnus, grow up! It's not an adventure, it's a civil war—and on Italian soil yet again!"

"I don't care!" cried Pompey. "To me, it's an adventure. If you only knew how much I've longed for this news, Varro! Since Sulla left, Italy has been as tame as a Vestal Virgin's lapdog!"

"What about the Siege of Rome?" asked Varro through a yawn.

The happy excitement fled from Pompey's face, his hands fell; he stepped back and looked at Varro darkly. "I would prefer to forget the Siege of Rome!" he snapped. "They dragged my father's naked body tied to an ass through their wretched streets!"

Poor Varro flushed so deeply the color flooded into his balding pate. "Oh, Magnus, I do beg your pardon! I did not—I would not—I am your guest—please forgive me!"

But the mood was gone. Pompey laughed, clapped Varro on the back. "Oh, it wasn't your doing, I know that!"

The huge room was piercingly cold; Varro clasped his arms about his body. "I had better start for Rome at once."

Pompey stared. "Rome? You're not going to Rome, you're coming with me! What do you think will happen in Rome? A lot of sheep running around bleating, the old women in the Senate arguing for days—come with me, it will be much more fun!"

"And where do you think you're going?"

"To join Sulla, of course."

"You don't need me for that, Magnus. Climb on your horse and ride off. Sulla will be glad to find you a place among his junior military tribunes, I'm sure. You've seen a lot of action."

"Oh, Varro!" Flapping hands betrayed Pompey's exasperation. "I'm not going to join Sulla as a junior military tribune! I'm going to bring him three more legions! I, Sulla's *lackey*? Never! I intend to be his full partner in this enterprise."

This astounding announcement broke upon Pompey's wife as upon Pompey's friend and houseguest; aware that she had gasped, almost voiced her shock aloud, Antistia moved quickly to a place where Pompey's eyes would not encounter her. He had quite forgotten her presence and she wanted to hear. Needed to hear.

In the two and a half years she had been his wife, Pompey had left her side for more than a day on only one occasion. Oh, the loveliness of that! To enjoy his undivided attention! Tickled, chided, rumpled, ruffled, hugged, bitten, bruised, tumbled . . . Like a dream. Who could ever have imagined it? She, the daughter of a senator of mere middle rank and barely sufficient fortune, to find herself given in marriage to Gnaeus Pompeius who called himself Magnus! Rich enough to marry anyone, the lord of half Umbria and Picenum, so fair and handsome everyone thought he looked like a reincarnation of Alexander the Great—what a husband her father had found for her! *And* after several years of despairing that she would ever find a suitable husband, so small was her dowry.

Naturally she had known why Pompey had married her; he had needed a great service from her father. Who happened to be the judge at Pompey's trial. That had been a trumped-up affair, of course—all of Rome had known it. But Cinna had desperately needed vast sums to fund his recruitment campaign, and young Pompey's wealth was going to provide those vast sums. For which reason had young Pompey been indicted upon charges more correctly directed at his dead father, Pompey Strabo—that he had illegally appropriated some of the spoils from the city of Asculum Picentum. Namely, one hunting net and some buckets of books. Trifling. The catch lay not in the magnitude of the offense, but in the fine; were Pompey to be convicted, Cinna's minions empaneled to decide the size of the penalty were at perfect liberty to fine him his entire fortune.

A more Roman man would have settled to fight the case in court and if necessary bribe the jury; but Pompey—whose very face proclaimed the Gaul in him—had preferred to marry the judge's daughter. The time of year had been October, so while November and December wore themselves away,

Antistia's father had conducted his court with masterly inaction. The trial of his new son-in-law never really eventuated, delayed by inauspicious omens, accusations of corrupt jurors, meetings of the Senate, agues and plagues. With the result that in January, the consul Carbo had persuaded Cinna to look elsewhere for the money they so desperately needed. The threat to Pompey's fortune was no more.

Barely eighteen, Antistia had accompanied her dazzling marital prize to his estates in the northeast of the Italian peninsula, and there in the daunting black stone pile of the Pompey stronghold had plunged wholeheartedly into the delights of being Pompey's bride. Luckily she was a pretty little girl stuffed with dimples and curves, and just ripe for bed, so her happiness had been undiluted for quite a long time. And when the twinges of disquiet began to intrude, they came not from her adored Magnus but from his faithful retainers, servants and minor squires who not only looked down on her, but actually seemed to feel free to let her know they looked down on her. Not a great burden—as long as Pompey was close enough to come home at night. But now he was talking of going off to war, of raising legions and enlisting in Sulla's cause! Oh, what would she do without her adored Magnus to shield her from the slights of his people?

He was still trying to convince Varro that the only proper alternative was to go with him to join Sulla, but that prim and pedantic little fellow— so elderly in mind for one who had not been in the Senate more than two years!—was still resisting.

"How many troops has Sulla got?" Varro was asking.

"Five veteran legions, six thousand cavalry, a few volunteers from Macedonia and the Peloponnese, and five cohorts of Spaniards belonging to that dirty swindler, Marcus Crassus. About thirty-nine thousand altogether."

An answer which had Varro clawing at the air. "I say again, Magnus, grow up!" he cried. "I've just come from Ariminum, where Carbo is sitting with eight legions and a huge force of cavalry—and that is just the beginning! In Campania alone there are sixteen other legions! For three years Cinna and Carbo gathered troops—there are *one hundred and fifty thousand* men under arms in Italy and Italian Gaul! How can Sulla cope with such numbers?"

"Sulla will eat them," said Pompey, unimpressed. "Besides, I'm going to bring him three legions of my father's hardened veterans. Carbo's soldiers are milk-smeared recruits."

"You really are going to raise your own army?"

"I really am."

"Magnus, you're only twenty-two years old! You can't expect your father's veterans to enlist for you!"

"Why not?" asked Pompey, genuinely puzzled.

"For one thing, you're eight years too young to qualify for the Senate. You're twenty years away from the consulship. And even if your father's men would enlist under you, to ask them to do so is absolutely illegal. You're a private citizen, and private citizens don't raise armies."

"For over three years Rome's government has been illegal," Pompey countered. "Cinna consul four times, Carbo twice, Marcus Gratidianus twice the urban praetor, almost half the Senate outlawed, Appius Claudius banished with his imperium intact, Fimbria running round Asia Minor making deals with King Mithridates—the whole thing is a joke!"

Varro managed to look like a pompous mule—not so very difficult for a Sabine of the *rosea rura,* where mules abounded. "The matter must be solved constitutionally," he said.

That provoked Pompey to outright laughter. "Oh, Varro! I do indeed like you, but you are hopelessly unrealistic! If this matter could be solved constitutionally, why are there one hundred and fifty thousand soldiers in Italy and Italian Gaul?"

Again Varro clawed the air, but this time in defeat. "Oh, very well, then! I'll come with you."

Pompey beamed, threw his arm around Varro's shoulders and guided him in the direction of the corridor which led to his rooms. "Splendid, splendid! You'll be able to write the history of my first campaigns—you're a better stylist than your friend Sisenna. I am the most important man of our age, I deserve to have my own historian at my side."

But Varro had the last word. "You must be important! Why else would you have the gall—good pun, that!—to call yourself Magnus?" He snorted. "The Great! At twenty-two, The Great! The best your father could do was to call himself after his cross-eyes!"

A sally Pompey ignored, busy now with steward and armorer, issuing a stream of instructions.

And then finally the vividly painted and gilded atrium was empty save for Pompey. And Antistia. He came across to her.

"Silly little kitten, you'll catch a chill," he scolded, and kissed her fondly. "Back to bed, my honey cake."

"Can't I help you pack?" she asked, sounding desolate.

"My men will do that for me, but you can watch."

This time the way was lit by a servant bearing a massive chandelier;

fitting herself into Pompey's side, Antistia (still clutching her own little lamp) walked with him to the room where all his war gear was stored. An imposing collection. Fully ten different cuirasses hung from T-shaped poles—gold, silver, steel, leather strapped with *phalerae*—and swords and helmets hung from pegs on the walls, as did kilts of leather straps and various kinds of padded underpinnings.

"Now stay there and be an absolutely darling little mouse," Pompey said as he lifted his wife like a feather and put her atop a couple of big chests, her feet dangling clear of the floor.

Where she was forgotten. Pompey and his menservants went through every item one by one—would it be useful, was it going to be necessary? Then when Pompey had ransacked the other trunks scattered around the room, he carelessly transferred his wife to a different perch in order to ransack her original seat, tossing this and that to the waiting slaves, talking away to himself so happily that Antistia could cherish no illusions he was going to miss his wife, his home, or civilian life. Of course she had always known that he regarded himself first and foremost as a soldier, that he despised the more customary pursuits of his peers—rhetoric, law, government, assemblies, the plots and ploys of politics. How many times had she heard him say he would vault himself into the consul's ivory chair on his spear, not on fine words and empty phrases? Now here he was putting his boast into practice, the soldier son of a soldier father going off to war.

The moment the last of the slaves had staggered away under armloads of equipment, Antistia slid off her trunk and went to stand in front of her husband.

"Before you go, Magnus, I must speak to you," she said.

Clearly this he regarded as a waste of his precious time, but he did pause. "Well, what is it?"

"How long are you going to be away?"

"Haven't the slightest idea," he said cheerfully.

"Months? A year?"

"Months, probably. Sulla will eat Carbo."

"Then I would like to return to Rome and live in my father's house while you're gone."

But he shook his head, clearly astonished at her proposal. "Not a chance!" he said. "I'm not having my wife running round Carbo's Rome while I'm with Sulla in the field against the selfsame Carbo. You'll stay here."

"Your servants and other people don't like me. If you're not here, it will go hard for me."

"Rubbish!" he said, turning away.

She detained him by stepping in front of him once more. "Oh, please, husband, spare me just a few moments of your time! I know it's a valuable commodity, but I am your wife."

He sighed. "All right, all right! But quickly, Antistia!"

"I *can't* stay here!"

"You can and you will." He moved from one foot to the other.

"When you're absent, Magnus—even for a few hours—your people are not kind to me. I have never complained because you are always kind to me, and you've been here except for the time you went to Ancona to see Cinna. But now—there is no other woman in your house, I will be utterly alone. It would be better if I returned to my father's house until the war is over, truly."

"Out of the question. Your father is Carbo's man."

"No, he is not. He is his own man."

Never before had she opposed him, or even stood up to him; Pompey's patience began to fray. "Look, Antistia, I have better things to do than stay here arguing with you. You're my wife, and that means you'll stay in my house."

"Where your steward sneers at me and leaves me in the dark, where I have no servants of my own and no one to keep me company," she said, trying to appear calm and reasonable, but beginning to panic underneath.

"That's absolute rubbish!"

"It is not, Magnus. It is not! I don't know why everyone looks down on me, but everyone does."

"Well, of course they do!" he said, surprised at her denseness.

Her eyes widened. "Of course they look down on me? What do you mean, of course?"

He shrugged. "My mother was a Lucilia. So was my grandmother. And what are you?"

"That is a very good question. What am I?"

He could see she was angry, and it angered him. Women! Here he was with his first big war on his hands, and this creature of no significance was determined to stage her own drama! Did women have no sense at all? "You're my first wife," he said.

"*First* wife?"

"A temporary measure."

"Oh, I see!" She looked thoughtful. "A temporary measure. The judge's daughter, I suppose you mean."

"Well, you've always known that."

"But it was a long time ago, I thought it had passed, I thought you loved me. My family is senatorial, I'm not inappropriate."

"For an ordinary man, no. But you're not good enough for *me*."

"Oh, Magnus, where do you get your conceit from? Is that why you have never once finished yourself inside me? Because I'm not good enough to bear your children?"

"Yes!" he shouted, starting to leave the room.

She followed him with her little lamp, too angry now to care who heard. "I was good enough to get you off when Cinna was after your money!"

"We've already established that," he said, hurrying.

"How convenient for you then, that Cinna is dead!"

"Convenient for Rome and all good Romans."

"You had Cinna murdered!"

The words echoed down the stone corridor that was big enough to allow the passage of an army; Pompey stopped.

"Cinna died in a drunken brawl with some reluctant recruits."

"In Ancona—your town, Magnus! *Your* town! And right after you had been there to see him!" she cried.

One moment she was standing in possession of herself, the next she was pinned against the wall with Pompey's hands about her throat. Not squeezing. Just about her throat.

"Never say that again, woman," he said softly.

"It's what my father says!" she managed, mouth dry.

The hands tightened ever so slightly. "Your father didn't like Cinna much. But he doesn't mind Carbo in the least, which is why it would give me great pleasure to kill him. But it won't give me any pleasure to kill you. I don't kill women. Keep your tongue behind your teeth, Antistia. Cinna's death had nothing to do with me, it was a simple accident."

"I want to go to my father and mother in Rome!"

Pompey released her, gave her a shove. "The answer is no. Now leave me alone!"

He was gone, calling for the steward; in the distance she could hear him telling that abominable man that she was not to be allowed to leave the precincts of the Pompey fortress once he was off to his war. Trembling, Antistia returned slowly to the bedroom she had shared with Pompey for two and a half years as his *first* wife—a temporary expedient. Not good enough to bear his children. Why hadn't she guessed that, when she had wondered many times why he always withdrew, always left a slimy puddle for her to clean off her belly?

The tears were beginning to gather. Soon they would fall, and once they did she would not be able to stop them for hours. Disillusionment before love has lost its keenest edge is terrible.

There came another of those chilling barbarian whoops, and faintly Pompey's voice: "I'm off to war, I'm off to war! Sulla has landed in Italy, and it's war!"

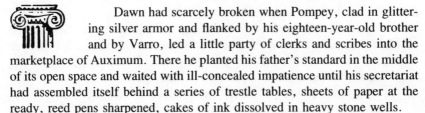 Dawn had scarcely broken when Pompey, clad in glittering silver armor and flanked by his eighteen-year-old brother and by Varro, led a little party of clerks and scribes into the marketplace of Auximum. There he planted his father's standard in the middle of its open space and waited with ill-concealed impatience until his secretariat had assembled itself behind a series of trestle tables, sheets of paper at the ready, reed pens sharpened, cakes of ink dissolved in heavy stone wells.

By the time all this was done, the crowd had gathered so thickly that it spilled out of the square into the streets and lanes converging upon it. Light and lithe, Pompey leaped onto a makeshift podium beneath Pompey Strabo's woodpecker standard.

"Well, it's come!" he shouted. "Lucius Cornelius Sulla has landed in Brundisium to claim what is rightfully his—an uninterrupted imperium, a triumph, the privilege of depositing his laurels at the feet of Jupiter Optimus Maximus inside the Capitol of Rome! At just about this time last year, the other Lucius Cornelius—he cognominated Cinna—was not far away from here trying to enlist my father's veterans in his cause. He did not succeed. Instead, he died. Today you see me. And today I see many of my father's veterans standing before me. I am my father's heir! His men are my men. His past is my future. I am going to Brundisium to fight for Sulla, for he is in the right of it. How many of you will come with me?"

Short and simple, thought Varro, lost in admiration. Maybe the young man was correct about vaulting into the consul's curule chair on his spear rather than on a wave of words. Certainly no face he could discern in that crowd seemed to find Pompey's speech lacking. No sooner had he finished than the women began to drift away clucking about the imminent absence of husbands and sons, some wringing their hands at the thought, some already engrossed in the practicalities of filling kit bags with spare tunics and socks, some looking studiously at the ground to hide sly smiles. Pushing excited children out of the way with mock slaps and kicks, the men shoved forward to cluster about those trestle tables. Within moments, Pompey's clerks were scribbling strenuously.

From a nice vantage spot high on the steps of Auximum's old temple of Picus, Varro sat and watched the activity. Had they ever volunteered so lightheartedly for cross-eyed Pompey Strabo's campaigns? he wondered. Probably not. That one had been the lord, a hard man but a fine commander; they would have served him with goodwill but sober faces. For the son, it was clearly different. I am looking at a phenomenon, Varro thought. The Myrmidons could not have gone more happily to fight for Achilles, nor the Macedonians for Alexander the Great. They *love* him! He's their darling, their mascot, their child as much as their father.

A vast bulk deposited itself on the step next to him, and Varro turned his head to see a red face topped by red hair; a pair of intelligent blue eyes were busy assessing him, the only stranger present.

"And who might you be?" asked the ruddy giant.

"My name is Marcus Terentius Varro, and I'm a Sabine."

"Like us, eh? Well, a long time ago, at any rate." A horny paw waved in the direction of Pompey. "Look at him, will you? Oh, we've been waiting for this day, Marcus Terentius Varro the Sabine! Be he not the Goddess's honeypot?"

Varro smiled. "I'm not sure I'd choose that way of putting it, but I do see what you mean."

"Ah! You're not only a gentleman with three names, you're a learned gentleman! A friend of his, might you be?"

"I might be."

"And what might you do for a crust, eh?"

"In Rome, I'm a senator. But in Reate, I breed mares."

"What, not mules?"

"It's better to breed the mares than their mule offspring. I have a little bit of the *rosea rura,* and a few stud donkeys too."

"How old might you be?"

"Thirty-two," said Varro, enjoying himself immensely.

But suddenly the questions ceased; Varro's interlocutor disposed himself more comfortably by resting one elbow on the step above him and stretching out a Herculean pair of legs to cross his ankles. Fascinated, the diminutive Varro eyed grubby toes almost as large as his own fingers.

"And what might your name be?" he asked, falling into the local vernacular quite naturally.

"Quintus Scaptius."

"Might you have enlisted?"

"All Hannibal's elephants couldn't stop me!"

"Might you be a veteran?"

"Joined his daddy's army when I was seventeen. That was eight years ago, but I've already served in twelve campaigns, so I don't have to join up anymore unless I might want to," said Quintus Scaptius.

"But you did want to."

"Hannibal's elephants, Marcus Terentius, Hannibal's elephants!"

"Might you be of centurion rank?"

"I might be for this campaign."

While they talked, Varro and Scaptius kept their eyes on Pompey, who stood just in front of the middle table joyfully hailing this man or that among the throng.

"He says he'll march before this moon has run her course," Varro observed, "but I fail to see how. I admit none of these men here today will need much if any training, but where's he going to get enough arms and armor? Or pack animals? Or wagons and oxen? Or food? And what will he do for money to keep his great enterprise going?"

Scaptius grunted, apparently an indication of amusement. "He do not need to worry about any of that! His daddy gave each of us our arms and armor at the start of the war against the Italians; then after his daddy died, the boy told us to hang on to them. We each got a mule, and the centurions got the carts and oxen. So we'd be ready against the day. You'll never catch the Pompeii napping! There's wheat enough in our granaries and lots of other food in our storehouses. Our women and children won't go hungry because we're eating well on campaign."

"And what about money?" asked Varro gently.

"Money?" Scaptius dismissed this necessity with a sniff of contempt. "We served his daddy without seeing much of it, and that's the truth. Wasn't any to be had in those days. When he's got it, he'll give it to us. When he hasn't got it, we'll do without. He's a good master."

"So I see."

Lapsing into silence, Varro studied Pompey with fresh interest. Everyone told tales about the legendary independence of Pompey Strabo during the Italian War: how he had kept his legions together long after he was ordered to disband them, and how he had directly altered the course of events in Rome because he had not disbanded them. No massive wage bills had ever turned up on the Treasury's books when Cinna had them audited after the death of Gaius Marius; now Varro knew why. Pompey Strabo hadn't bothered to pay his troops. Why should he, when he virtually owned them?

At this moment Pompey left his post to stroll across to Picus's temple steps.

"I'm off to find a campsite," he said to Varro, then gave the Hercules sitting next to Varro a huge grin. "Got in early, I see, Scaptius."

Scaptius lumbered to his feet. "Yes, Magnus. I'd best be getting home to dig out my gear, eh?"

So everyone called him Magnus! Varro too rose. "I'll ride with you, *Magnus.*"

The crowd was dwindling, and women were beginning to come back into the marketplace; a few merchants, hitherto thwarted, were busy putting up their booths, slaves rushing to stock them. Loads of dirty washing were dropped on the paving around the big fountain in front of the local shrine to the Lares, and one or two girls hitched up their skirts to climb into the shallow water. How typical this town is, thought Varro, walking a little behind Pompey: sunshine and dust, a few good shady trees, the purr of insects, a sense of timeless purpose, wrinkled winter apples, busy folk who all know far too much about each other. There are no secrets here in Auximum!

"These men are a fierce lot," he said to Pompey as they left the marketplace to find their horses.

"They're Sabines, Varro, just like you," said Pompey, "even if they did come east of the Apennines centuries ago."

"Not quite like me!" Varro allowed himself to be tossed into the saddle by one of Pompey's grooms. "I may be a Sabine, but I'm not by nature or training a soldier."

"You did your stint in the Italian War, surely."

"Yes, of course. And served in my ten campaigns. How quickly they mounted up during that conflagration! But I haven't thought of a sword or a suit of chain mail since it ended."

Pompey laughed. "You sound like my friend Cicero."

"Marcus Tullius Cicero? The legal prodigy?"

"That's him, yes. Hated war. Didn't have the stomach for it, which my father didn't understand. But he was a good fellow all the same, liked to do what I didn't like to do. So between us we kept my father mighty pleased without telling him too much." Pompey sighed. "After Asculum Picentum fell he insisted on going off to serve under Sulla in Campania. I missed him!"

In two market intervals of eight days each Pompey had his three legions of veteran volunteers camped inside well-fortified ramparts some five miles from Auximum on the banks of a tributary of the Aesis River. His sanitary dispositions within his camp were faultless, and care of them rigidly policed. Pompey Strabo had been a more typical product of his rural origins, had known only one way to deal with wells, cesspits, latrines, rubbish disposal, drainage: when the stink became unbearable, move on. Which was why he had died of fever outside Rome's Colline Gate, and why the people of the

Quirinal and Viminal, their springs polluted from his wastes, had done such insult to his body.

Growing ever more fascinated, Varro watched the evolution of his young friend's army, and marveled at the absolute genius Pompey showed for organization, logistics. No detail, regardless how minute, was overlooked; yet at the same time the enormous undertakings were executed with the speed only superb efficiency permitted. I have been absorbed into the very small private circle of a true phenomenon, he thought: he will change the way our world is, he will change the way we see our world. There is not one single iota of fear in him, nor one hairline crack in his self-confidence.

However, Varro reminded himself, others too have shaped equally well before the turmoil begins. What will he be like when he has his enterprise running, when opposition crowds him round, when he faces—no, not Carbo or Sertorius—when he faces Sulla? That will be the real test! Same side or not, the relationship between the old bull and the young bull will decide the young bull's future. Will he bend? *Can* he bend? Oh, what does the future hold for someone so young, so sure of himself? Is there any force or man in the world capable of breaking him?

Definitely Pompey did not think there was. Though he was not mystical, he had created a spiritual environment for himself that fitted certain instincts he cherished about his nature. For instance, there were qualities he knew he owned rather than possessed—invincibility, invulnerability, inviolability— for since they were outside him as much as inside, ownership seemed more correct than possession. It was just as if, while some godly ichor coursed through him, some godly miasma wrapped him round as well. Almost from infancy he had lived within the most colossal daydreams; in his mind he had generaled ten thousand battles, ridden in the antique victor's chariot of a hundred triumphs, stood time and time again like Jupiter come to earth while Rome bowed down to worship him, the greatest man who had ever lived.

Where Pompey the dreamer differed from all others of that sort was in the quality of his contact with reality—he saw the actual world with hard and sharp acuity, never missed possibility or probability, fastened his mind leech- like upon facts the size of mountains, facts as diminutive as one drop of clearest water. Thus the colossal daydreams were a mental anvil upon which he hammered out the shape of the real days, tempered and annealed them into the exact framework of his actual life.

So he got his men into their centuries, their cohorts, their legions; he drilled them and inspected their accoutrements; he culled the too elderly from his pack animals and sounded blows on the axles of his wagons, rocked them, had them driven fast through the rough ford below his camp. Everything would be perfect because nothing could be allowed to happen that would show him up as less than perfect himself.

Twelve days after Pompey had begun to assemble his troops, word came from Brundisium. Sulla was marching up the Via Appia amid scenes of hysterical welcome in every hamlet, village, town, city. But before Sulla left, the messenger told Pompey, he had called his army together and asked it to swear an oath of personal allegiance to him. If those in Rome had ever doubted Sulla's determination to extricate himself from any threat of future prosecutions for high treason, the fact that his army swore to uphold him—even against the government of Rome—told all men that war was now inevitable.

And then, Pompey's messenger had gone on to say, Sulla's soldiers had come to him and offered him all their money so that he could pay for every grain of wheat and leaf of vegetable and seed of fruit as he moved through the heartland of Calabria and Apulia; they would have no dark looks to spoil their general's luck, they would have no trampled fields, dead shepherds, violated women, starving children. All would be as Sulla wanted it; he could pay them back later, when he was master of the whole of Italy as well as Rome.

The news that the southern parts of the peninsula were very glad to welcome Sulla did not quite please Pompey, who had hoped that by the time he reached Sulla with his three legions of hardened veterans, Sulla would be in sufficient trouble to need him. However, that was clearly not to be; Pompey shrugged and adapted his plans to the situation as it had been reported to him.

"We'll march down our coast to Buca, then head inland for Beneventum," he said to his three chief centurions, who were commanding his three legions. By rights these jobs should have gone to high-born military tribunes, whom he could have found had he tried. But high-born military tribunes would have questioned Pompey's right to general his army, so Pompey had preferred to choose his subordinates from among his own people, much though certain high-born Romans might have deplored it had they known.

"When do we move?" asked Varro, since no one else would.

"Eight days before the end of April," said Pompey.

Then Carbo entered the scene, and Pompey had to change his plans yet again.

From the western Alps the straight line of the Via Aemilia bisected Italian Gaul all the way to the Adriatic Sea at Ariminum; from Ariminum another excellent road skirted the coast to Fanum Fortunae, where began the

Via Flaminia to Rome. This gave Ariminum a strategic importance only equaled by Arretium, which dominated access to Rome west of the Apennines.

It was therefore logical that Gnaeus Papirius Carbo—twice consul of Rome and now governor of Italian Gaul—should put himself, his eight legions and his cavalry into camp on the fringes of Ariminum. From this base he could move in three directions: along the Via Aemilia through Italian Gaul toward the western Alps; along the Adriatic coast in the direction of Brundisium; and along the Via Flaminia to Rome.

For eighteen months he had known Sulla would come, and that of course would be Brundisium. But too many men still lingered in Rome who might when the time came side with Sulla, though they declared themselves completely neutral; they were all men with the political clout to overthrow the present government, which made Rome a necessary target. And Carbo also knew that Metellus Pius the Piglet had gone to earth in Liguria, bordering the western Alps of Italian Gaul; with Metellus Pius were two good legions he had taken with him out of Africa Province after Carbo's adherents had ejected him from Africa. The moment the Piglet heard that Sulla had landed, Carbo was certain he would march to join Sulla, and that made Italian Gaul vulnerable too.

Of course there were the sixteen legions sitting in Campania, and these were much closer to Brundisium than Carbo in Ariminum; but how reliable were the consuls of this year, Norbanus and Scipio Asiagenus? Carbo couldn't be sure, with his own iron will removed from Rome herself. At the end of last year he had been convinced of two things: that Sulla would come in the spring, and that Rome would be more inclined to oppose Sulla if Carbo himself were absent from Rome. So he had ensured the election of two staunch followers in Norbanus and Scipio Asiagenus and then given himself the governorship of Italian Gaul in order to keep an eye on things and be in a position to act the moment it became necessary. His choice of consuls had been—in theory anyway—good, for neither Norbanus nor Scipio Asiagenus could hope for mercy from Sulla. Norbanus was a client of Gaius Marius's, and Scipio Asiagenus had disguised himself as a slave to escape from Aesernia during the Italian War, an action which had disgusted Sulla. Yet were they strong enough? Would they use their sixteen legions like born generals, or would they miss their chances? Carbo just didn't know.

On one thing he had not counted. That Pompey Strabo's heir, mere boy that he was, would have the audacity to raise three full legions of his father's veterans and march them to join Sulla! Not that Carbo took the young man seriously. It was those three legions of veterans worried Carbo. Once they reached Sulla, Sulla would use them brilliantly.

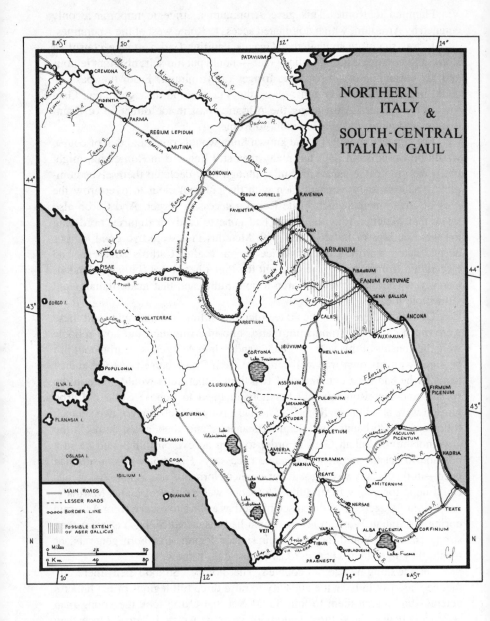

It was Carbo's quaestor, the excellent Gaius Verres, who had brought the news to Carbo of Pompey's projected expedition.

"The boy will have to be stopped before he can start," said Carbo, frowning. "Oh, what a nuisance! I'll just have to hope that Metellus Pius doesn't move out of Liguria while I'm dealing with young Pompeius, and that the consuls can cope with Sulla."

"It won't take long to deal with young Pompeius," said Gaius Verres, tone confident.

"I agree, but that doesn't make him less of a nuisance," said Carbo. "Send my legates to me now, would you?"

Carbo's legates proved difficult to locate; Verres chased from one part of the gigantic camp to another for a length of time he knew would not please Carbo. Many things occupied his mind while he searched, none of them related to the activities of Pompey Strabo's heir, young Pompeius. No, what preyed upon the mind of Gaius Verres was Sulla. Though he had never met Sulla (there was no reason why he ought, since his father was a humble backbencher senator, and his own service during the Italian War had been with Gaius Marius and then Cinna), he remembered the look of Sulla as he had walked in the procession going to his inauguration as consul, and had been profoundly impressed. As he was not martial by nature, it had never occurred to Verres to join Sulla's expedition to the east, nor had he found the Rome of Cinna and Carbo an unendurable place. Verres liked to be where the money was, for he had expensive tastes in art and very high ambitions. Yet now, as he chased Carbo's senior legates, he was beginning to wonder if it might not be time to change sides.

Strictly speaking, Gaius Verres was proquaestor rather than quaestor; his official stint as quaestor had ended with the old year. That he was still in the job was due to Carbo, whose personal appointee he had been, and who declared himself so well satisfied that he wanted Verres with him when he went to govern Italian Gaul. And as the quaestor's function was to handle his superior's money and accounts, Gaius Verres had applied to the Treasury and received on Carbo's behalf the sum of 2,235,417 sesterces; this stipend, totted up with due attention to every last sestertius (witness those 417 of them!), was intended to cover Carbo's expenses—to pay his legions, victual his legions, assure a proper life-style for himself, his legates, his servants and his quaestor, and defray the cost of a thousand and one minor items not able to be classified under any of the above.

Though April was not yet done, something over a million and a half sesterces had already been swallowed up, which meant that Carbo would have to ask the Treasury for more before too long. His legates lived extremely well, and Carbo himself had long grown used to having Rome's public resources at his fingertips. Not to mention Gaius Verres; he too had stickied his hands in a pot of honey before dipping them deeply into the moneybags. Until now he had kept his peculations unobtrusive, but, he decided with fresh insight into his present position, there was no point in being subtle any longer! As soon as Carbo's back was turned to deal with Pompey's three legions, Gaius Verres would be gone. Time to change sides.

And so indeed Gaius Verres went. Carbo took four of his legions—but no cavalry—the following dawn to deal with Pompey Strabo's heir, and the sun was not very high when Gaius Verres too departed. He was quite alone save for his own servants, and he did not follow Carbo south; he went to Ariminum, where Carbo's funds lay in the vaults of a local banker. Only two persons had the authority to withdraw it: the governor, Carbo, and his quaestor, Verres. Having hired twelve mules, Verres removed a total of forty-eight half-talent leather bags of Carbo's money from the banker's custody, and loaded them upon his mules. He did not even have to offer an excuse; word of Sulla's landing had already flown around Ariminum faster than a summer storm, and the banker knew Carbo was on the march with half his infantry.

Long before noon, Gaius Verres had escaped the neighborhood with six hundred thousand sesterces of Carbo's official allowance, bound via the back roads first for his own estates in the upper Tiber valley, and then—the lighter of twenty-four talents of silver coins—for wherever he might find Sulla.

Oblivious to the fact that his quaestor had decamped, Carbo himself went down the Adriatic coast toward Pompey's position near the Aesis. His mood was so sanguine that he did not move with speed, nor did he take special precautions to conceal his advent. This was going to be a good exercise for his largely unblooded troops, nothing more. No matter how formidable three legions of Pompey Strabo's veterans might sound, Carbo was quite experienced enough to understand that no army can do better than its general permits it to. Their general was a kid! To deal with them would therefore be child's play.

When word of Carbo's approach was brought to him, Pompey whooped with joy and assembled his soldiers at once.

"We don't even have to move from our own lands to fight our first battle!" he shouted to them. "Carbo himself is coming down from Ariminum to deal with us, and he's already lost the fight! Why? Because he knows I'm in command! You, he respects. Me, he doesn't. You'd think he'd realize The Butcher's son would know how to chop up bones and slice meat, but Carbo is a fool! He thinks The Butcher's son is too pretty and precious to bloody his hands at his father's trade! Well, he's wrong! You know that, and I know that. So let's teach it to Carbo!''

Teach it to Carbo they did. His four legions came down to the Aesis in a fashion orderly enough, and waited in disciplined ranks for the scouts to test the river crossing, swollen from the spring thaw in the Apennines. Not far beyond the ford, Carbo knew Pompey still lay in his camp, but such was his contempt that it never occurred to him Pompey might be in his own vicinity.

Having split his forces and sent half across the Aesis well before Carbo arrived, Pompey fell on Carbo at the moment when two of his legions had made the crossing, and two were about to do so. Both jaws of his pincer attacked simultaneously from out of some trees on either bank, and carried all before them. They fought to prove a point—that The Butcher's son knew his trade even better than his father had. Doomed by his role as the general to remain on the south bank of the river, Pompey couldn't do what he most yearned to do—go after Carbo in person. Generals, his father had told him many times, must never put the base camp out of reach in case the battle didn't develop as planned and a swift retreat became necessary. So Pompey had to watch Carbo and his legate Lucius Quinctius rally the two legions left on their bank of the Aesis, and flee back toward Ariminum. Of those on Pompey's bank, none survived. The Butcher's son did indeed know the family trade, and crowed jubilantly.

Now it was time to march for Sulla!

Two days later, riding a big white horse which he said was the Pompeius family's Public Horse—so called because the State provided it—Pompey led his three legions into lands fiercely anti-Rome a few short years earlier. Picentines of the south, Vestini, Marrucini, Frentani, all peoples who had struggled to free the Italian Allied states from their long subjection to Rome. That they had lost was largely due to the man Pompey marched to join— Lucius Cornelius Sulla. Yet no one tried to impede the army's progress, and some in fact came asking to enlist. Word of his defeat of Carbo had outstripped Pompey, and they were martial peoples. If the fight for Italia was lost, there were other causes; the general feeling seemed to be that it was better to side with Sulla than with Carbo.

Everyone's spirits were high as the little army left the coast at Buca and headed on a fairly good road for Larinum in central Apulia. Two eight-day market intervals had gone by when Pompey's eighteen thousand veteran soldiers reached it, a thriving small city in the midst of rich agricultural and pastoral country; no one of importance in Larinum was missing from the

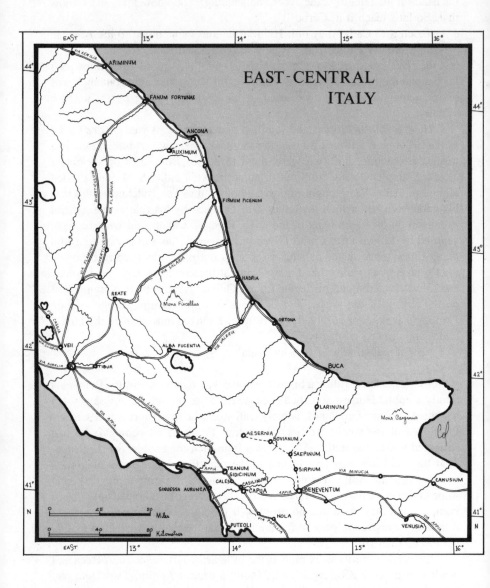

delegation which welcomed Pompey—and sped him onward with subtle pressure.

His next battle lay not three miles beyond the town. Carbo had wasted no time in sending a warning to Rome about The Butcher's son and his three legions of veterans, and Rome had wasted no time in seeking to prevent amalgamation between Pompey and Sulla. Two of the Campanian legions under the command of Gaius Albius Carrinas were dispatched to block Pompey's progress, and encountered Pompey while both sides were on the march. The engagement was sharp, vicious, and quite decisive; Carrinas stayed only long enough to see that he stood no chance to win, then beat a hasty retreat with his men reasonably intact—and greater respect for The Butcher's son.

By this time Pompey's soldiers were so settled and secure that the miles swung by under their hobnailed, thick-soled *caligae* as if no effort was involved; they had passed into their third hundred of these miles with no more than a mouthful or two of sour weak wine to mark the event. Saepinum was reached, a smaller place than Larinum, and Pompey had news that Sulla was now not far away, camped outside Beneventum on the Via Appia.

But first another battle had to be fought. Lucius Junius Brutus Damasippus, brother of Pompey Strabo's old friend and senior legate, tried to ambush the son in a small section of rugged country between Saepinum and Sirpium. Pompey's overweening confidence in his ability seemed not to be misplaced; his scouts discovered where Brutus Damasippus and his two legions were concealed, and it was Pompey who fell upon Brutus Damasippus without warning. Several hundred of Brutus Damasippus's men died before he managed to extricate himself from a difficult position, and fled in the direction of Bovianum.

After none of his three battles had Pompey attempted to pursue his foes, but not for the reasons men like Varro and the three *primus pilus* centurions assumed; the facts that he didn't know the lay of the land, nor could be sure that these were not diversions aimed at luring him into the arms of a far bigger force, did not so much as intrude into Pompey's thoughts. For Pompey's mind was obsessed to the exclusion of all else with the coming meeting between himself and Lucius Cornelius Sulla.

Visions of it unrolled before his sightless dreaming eyes like a moving pageant—two godlike men with hair of flame and faces both strong and beautiful uncoiled from their saddles with the grace and power of giant cats and walked with measured stately steps toward each other down the middle of an empty road, its sides thronged with every traveler and every last inhabitant of the countryside, an army behind each of these magnificent men, and every pair of eyes riveted upon them. Zeus striding to meet Jupiter. Ares striding to meet Mars. Hercules striding to meet Milo. Achilles striding to meet Hector. Yes, it would be hymned down the ages so loudly that it would put Aeneas and Turnus to shame! The first encounter between the two colossi of this world, the two suns in its sky—and while the setting sun was still hot and still strong, its course was nearing an end. Ah! But the rising sun! Hot and strong already, yet with all the soaring vault before it in which to grow ever hotter, ever stronger. Thought Pompey exultantly, Sulla's sun is westering! Whereas mine is barely above the eastern horizon.

He sent Varro ahead to present his compliments to Sulla and to give Sulla an account of his progress from Auximum, the tally of those he had killed, the names of the generals he had defeated. And to ask that Sulla himself venture down the road to meet him so that everyone could witness his coming in peace to offer himself and his troops to the greatest man of this age. He didn't ask Varro to add, "or of any other age"—*that* he was not prepared to admit, even in a flowery greeting.

Every detail of this meeting had been fantasized a thousand times, even down to what Pompey felt he ought to wear. In the first few hundred passes he had seen himself clad from head to foot in gold plate; then doubt began to gnaw, and he decided golden armor was too ostentatious, might be labeled crass. So for the next few hundred passes he saw himself clad in a plain white toga, shorn of all military connotations and with the narrow purple stripe of the knight slicing down the right shoulder of his tunic; then doubt gnawed again, and he worried that the white toga would merge into the white horse to produce an amorphous blob. The final few hundred passes saw him in the silver armor his father had presented to him after the siege of Asculum Picentum had concluded; doubt did not gnaw at all, so he liked that image of self best.

Yet when his groom assisted him into the saddle of his big white Public Horse, Gnaeus Pompeius (Magnus) was wearing the very plainest of steel cuirasses, the leather straps of his kilt were unadorned by bosses or fringes, and the helmet on his head was standard issue to the ranks. It was his horse he bedizened, for he was a knight of the eighteen original centuries of the First Class, and his family had held the Public Horse for generations. So the horse wore every conceivable knightly trapping of silver buttons and medallions, silver-encrusted scarlet leather harness, an embroidered blanket beneath a wrought and ornamented saddle, a clinking medley of silver pendants. He looked, Pompey congratulated himself as he set off down the middle of the empty road with his army in rank and file behind him, like a genuine no-

nonsense soldier—a workman, a professional. Let the *horse* proclaim his glory!

Beneventum lay on the far side of the Calor River, where the Via Appia made junction with the Via Minucia from coastal Apulia and Calabria. The sun was directly overhead when Pompey and his legions came over the brow of a slight hill and looked down to the Calor crossing. And there on this side of it, waiting in the middle of the road upon an unutterably weary mule, was Lucius Cornelius Sulla. Attended only by Varro. The local populace!—where were they? Where were Sulla's legates, his troops? Where the travelers?

Some instinct made Pompey turn his head and bark to the standard-bearer of his leading legion that the soldiers would halt, remain where they were. Then, hideously alone, he rode down the slope toward Sulla, his face set into a mask so solid he felt as if he had dipped it in plaster. When he came within a hundred paces of the mule, Sulla more or less fell off it, though he kept his feet because he threw one arm around the mule's neck and fastened his other hand upon the mule's long bedraggled ear. Righting himself, he began to walk down the middle of the empty road, his gait as wide-based as any sailor's.

Down from his clinking Public Horse leaped Pompey, not sure if his legs would hold him; but they did. Let one of us at least do this properly, he thought, and strode out.

Even at a distance he had realized that this Sulla bore absolutely no resemblance to the Sulla he remembered, but as he drew ever closer, Pompey began to discern the ravages of time and awful malaise. Not with sympathy or pity, but with stupefied horror, a physical reaction so profound that for a moment he thought he would vomit.

For one thing, Sulla was drunk. That, Pompey might have been able to forgive, had this Sulla been the Sulla he remembered on the day of his inauguration as consul. But of that beautiful and fascinating man nothing was left, not even the dignity of a thatch of greyed or whitened hair. This Sulla wore a wig to cover his hairless skull, a hideous ginger-red affair of tight little curls below which two straight silver tongues of his own hair grew in front of his ears. His teeth were gone, and their going had lengthened his dented chin, made the mouth into a puckered gash below that unmistakable nose with the slight crease in its tip. The skin of his face looked as if it had been partially flayed, most of it a raw and bloody crimson, some few places still showing their original whiteness. And though he was thin to the point of scrawniness, at some time in the not too distant past he must have grown enormously fat, for the flesh of his face had fallen into crevices, and vast hollow wattles transformed his neck into a vulturine travesty.

Oh, how can I shine against the backdrop of this mangled piece of human wreckage? wailed Pompey to himself, battling to stem the scorching tears of disappointment.

They were almost upon each other. Pompey stretched out his right hand, fingers spread, palm vertical.

"Imperator!" he cried.

Sulla giggled, made a huge effort, stretched out his own hand in the general's salute. "Imperator!" he shouted in a rush, then fell against Pompey, his damp and stained leather cuirass stinking foully of waterbrash and wine.

Varro was suddenly there on Sulla's other side; together he and Pompey helped Lucius Cornelius Sulla back to his inglorious mule and shouldered him up until he sprawled upon its bare and dirty hide.

"He would insist on riding out to meet you as you asked," Varro said, low-voiced. "Nothing I could say would stop him."

Mounted on his Public Horse, Pompey turned, beckoned his troops to march, then ranged himself on the far side of Sulla's mule from Varro, and rode on into Beneventum.

"I don't believe it!" he cried to Varro after they had handed the almost insensible Sulla over to his keepers.

"He had a particularly bad night last night," Varro said, unable to gauge the nature of Pompey's emotions because he had never been privy to Pompey's fantasies.

"A bad night? What do you mean?"

"It's his skin, poor man. When he became so ill his doctors despaired of his life, they sent him to Aedepsus—a small spa some distance from Euboean Chalcis. The temple physicians there are said to be the finest in all Greece. And they saved him, it's true! No ripe fruit, no honey, no bread, no cakes, no wine. But when they put him to soak in the spa waters, something in the skin of his face broke down. Ever since the early days at Aedepsus, he has suffered attacks of the most dreadful itching, and rips his face to raw and bleeding meat. He still eats no ripe fruit, no honey, no bread, no cakes. But wine gives him relief from the itching, so he drinks." Varro sighed. "He drinks far too much."

"Why his face? Why not his arms or legs?" Pompey asked, only half believing this tale.

"He had a bad sunburn on his face—don't you remember how he always wore a shady hat whenever he was in the sun? But there had been some local ceremony to welcome him, he insisted on going through with it despite his illness, and his vanity prompted him to wear a helmet instead of his hat. I presume it was the sunburn predisposed the skin of his face to break down," said Varro, who was as fascinated as Pompey was revolted. "His whole head looks like a mulberry sprinkled with meal! Quite extraordinary!"

"You sound exactly like an unctuous Greek physician," said Pompey, feeling his own face emerge from its plaster mask at last. "Where are we housed? Is it far? And what about my men?"

"I believe that Metellus Pius has gone to guide your men to their camp. We're in a nice house not far down this street. If you come and break your fast now, we can ride out afterward and find your men." Varro put his hand kindly on Pompey's strong freckled arm, at a loss to know what was really wrong. There was no pity in Pompey's nature, so much he had come to understand; why therefore was Pompey consumed with grief?

That night Sulla entertained the two new arrivals at a big dinner in his general's house, its object to allow them to meet the other legates. Word had flown around Beneventum of Pompey's advent—his youth, his beauty, his adoring troops. And Sulla's legates were very put out, thought Varro in some amusement as he eyed their faces. They all looked as if their nursemaids had cruelly snatched a delicious honeycomb from their mouths, and when Sulla showed Pompey to the *locus consularis* on his own couch, then put no other man between them, the looks spoke murder. Not that Pompey cared! He made himself comfortable with unabashed pleasure and proceeded to talk to Sulla as if no one else was present.

Sulla was sober, and apparently not itching. His face had crusted over a little since the morning, he was calm and friendly, and obviously quite entranced with Pompey. I can't be wrong about Pompey if Sulla sees it too, thought Varro.

Deeming it wiser at first to keep his gaze concentrated within his immediate vicinity rather than to inspect each man in the room in turn, Varro smiled at his couch companion, Appius Claudius Pulcher. A man he liked and esteemed. "Is Sulla still capable of leading us?" he asked.

"He's as brilliant as he ever was," said Appius Claudius. "If we can keep him sober he'll eat Carbo, no matter how many troops Carbo can field." Appius Claudius shivered, grimaced. "Can you feel the evil presences in this room, Varro?"

"Very definitely," said Varro, though he didn't think the kind of atmosphere he felt was what Appius Claudius meant.

"I've been studying the subject a little," Appius Claudius proceeded to explain, "among the minor temples and cults at Delphi. There are fingers of power all around us—quite invisible, of course. Most people aren't aware of them, but men like you and me, Varro, are hypersensitive to emanations from other places.''

"What other places?'' asked Varro, startled.

"Underneath us. Above us. On all sides of us,'' said Appius Claudius in sepulchral tones. "Fingers of power! I don't know how else to explain what I mean. How can anyone describe invisible somethings only the hypersensitive can feel touching them? I'm not talking about the gods, or Olympus, or even *numina*. . . .''

But the others in the room had lured Varro's attention away from poor Appius Claudius, who continued to drone on happily while Varro assessed the quality of Sulla's legates.

Philippus and Cethegus, the great tergiversators. Every time Fortune favored a new set of men, Philippus and Cethegus turned their togas inside out or back to the right side again, eager to serve the new masters of Rome; each of them had been doing it for thirty years. Philippus was the more straightforward of the two, had been consul after several fruitless tries and even became censor under Cinna and Carbo, the zenith of a man's political career. Whereas Cethegus—a patrician Cornelius remotely related to Sulla—had remained in the background, preferring to wield his power by manipulating his fellow backbenchers in the Senate. They lay together talking loudly and ignoring everybody else.

Three young ones also lay together ignoring everybody else—what a lovely trio! Verres, Catilina and Ofella. Villains all, Varro was sure of it, though Ofella was more concerned about his *dignitas* than any future pickings. Of Verres and of Catilina there could be no doubt; the future pickings ruled them absolutely.

Another couch held three estimable, upright men—Mamercus, Metellus Pius and Varro Lucullus (an adopted Varro, actually the brother of Sulla's loyalest follower, Lucullus). They patently disapproved of Pompey, and made no attempt to conceal it.

Mamercus was Sulla's son-in-law, a quiet and steady man who had salvaged Sulla's fortune and got his family safely to Greece.

Metellus Pius the Piglet and his quaestor Varro Lucullus had sailed from Liguria to Puteoli midway through April, and marched across Campania to join Sulla just before Carbo's Senate mobilized the troops who might otherwise have stopped them. Until Pompey had appeared today, they had basked in the full radiance of Sulla's grateful approval, for they had brought him two legions of battle-hardened soldiers. However, most of their attitude was founded in the who of Pompey, rather than in the what or even in the why.

A Pompeius from northern Picenum? An upstart, a parvenu. *A non-Roman!* His father, nicknamed The Butcher because of the way he conducted his wars, might have achieved the consulship and great political power, but nothing could reconcile him and his to Metellus Pius or Varro Lucullus. No genuine Roman, of senatorial family or not, would have, at the age of twenty-two, taken it upon himself—absolutely illegally!—to bring the great patrician aristocrat Lucius Cornelius Sulla an army, and then demand to become, in effect, Sulla's partner. The army which Metellus Pius and Varro Lucullus had brought Sulla automatically became his, to do with as he willed; had Sulla accepted it with thanks and then dismissed Metellus Pius and Varro Lucullus, they would perhaps have been angered, but they would have gone at once. Punctilious sticklers, both of them, thought Varro. So now they lay on the same couch glaring at Pompey because he had used the troops he had brought Sulla to elicit a top command neither his age nor his antecedents permitted. He had held Sulla to ransom.

Of all of them, however, by far the most intriguing to Varro was Marcus Licinius Crassus. In the autumn of the previous year he had arrived in Greece to offer Sulla two and a half thousand good Spanish soldiers, only to find his reception little warmer than the one he had received from Metellus Pius in Africa during the summer.

Most of the chilly welcome was due to the dramatic failure of a get-rich-quick scheme he and his friend the younger Titus Pomponius had engineered among investors in Cinna's Rome. It had happened toward the end of the first year which saw Cinna joined with Carbo in the consulship, when money was beginning rather coyly to appear again; news had come that the menace of King Mithridates was no more, that Sulla had negotiated the Treaty of Dardanus with him. Taking advantage of a sudden surge of optimism, Crassus and Titus Pomponius had offered shares in a new Asian speculation. The crash occurred when word came that Sulla had completely reorganized the finances of the Roman province of Asia, that there would be no tax-gathering bonanza after all.

Rather than stay in Rome to face hordes of irate creditors, both Crassus and Titus Pomponius had decamped. There was really only one place to go, one man to conciliate: Sulla. Titus Pomponius had seen this immediately, and gone to Athens with his huge fortune intact. Educated, urbane, something of a literary dilettante, personally charming, and just a trifle too fond of little boys, Titus Pomponius had soon come to an understanding with Sulla; but finding that he adored the atmosphere and style of life in Athens, he had chosen to remain there, given himself the cognomen of Atticus—Man of Athens.

Crassus was not so sure of himself, and had not seen that Sulla was his only alternative until much later than Atticus.

Circumstances had conspired to leave Marcus Licinius Crassus head of his family—and impoverished. The only money left belonged to Axia, the widow not only of his eldest brother, but also the widow of his middle brother. The size of her dowry had not been her sole attraction; she was pretty, vivacious, kindhearted and loving. Like Crassus's mother, Vinuleia, she was a Sabine from Reate, and fairly closely related to Vinuleia at that. Her wealth came from the *rosea rura*, best pasture in all of Italy and breeding ground of fabulous stud donkeys which sold for enormous sums—sixty thousand sesterces was not an uncommon price for one such beast, potential sire of many sturdy army mules.

When Axia's husband, the eldest Crassus son, Publius, was killed outside Grumentum during the Italian War, she was left a widow—and pregnant. In that tightly knit and frugal family, there seemed only one answer; after her ten months of mourning were over, Axia married Lucius, the second Crassus son. By whom she had no children. When he was murdered by Fimbria in the street outside his door, she was widowed again. As was Vinuleia, for Crassus the father, seeing his son cut down and knowing what his fate would be, killed himself on the spot.

At the time Marcus, the youngest Crassus son, was twenty-nine years old, the one whom his father (consul and censor in his day) had elected to keep at home in order to safeguard his name and bloodline. All the Crassus property was confiscated, including Vinuleia's. But Axia's family stood on excellent terms with Cinna, so her dowry wasn't touched. And when her second ten-month period of mourning was over, Marcus Licinius Crassus married her and took her little son, his nephew Publius, as his own. Three times married to each of three brothers, Axia was known ever after as Ter-tulla—Little Three. The change in her name was her own suggestion; Axia had a harsh un-Latin ring to it, whereas Tertulla tripped off the tongue.

The glorious scheme Crassus and Atticus had concocted—which would have been a resounding success had Sulla not done the unexpected regarding the finances of Asia Province—shattered just as Crassus was beginning to see the family wealth increase again. And caused him to flee with a pittance in his purse, all his hopes destroyed. Behind him he left two women without a male protector, his mother and his wife. Tertulla bore his own son, Marcus, two months after he had gone.

But where to go? Spain, decided Crassus. In Spain lay a relic of past Crassus wealth. Years before, Crassus's father had sailed to the Tin Isles, the Cassiterides, and negotiated an exclusive contract for himself to convey

tin from the Cassiterides across northern Spain to the shores of the Middle
Sea. Civil war in Italy had destroyed that, but Crassus had nothing left to
lose; he fled to Nearer Spain, where a client of his father's, one Vibius
Paccianus, hid him in a cave until Crassus was sure that the consequences of
his fiscal philandering were not going to follow him as far as Spain. He then
emerged and began to knit his tin monopoly together again, after which he
acquired some interests in the silver-lead mines of southern Spain.

All very well, but these activities could only prosper if the financial
institutions and trading companies of Rome were made available to him again.
Which meant he needed an ally more powerful than anyone he knew personally: he needed Sulla. But in order to woo Sulla (since he lacked the charm
and the erudition possessed so plentifully by Titus Pomponius Atticus) he
would have to bring Sulla a gift. And the only gift he could possibly offer
was an army. This he raised among his father's old clients; a mere five cohorts,
but five well-trained and well-equipped cohorts.

His first port of call after he left Spain was Utica, in Africa Province,
where he had heard Quintus Caecilius Metellus Pius, he whom Gaius Marius
had called the Piglet, was still trying to hold on to his position as governor.
He arrived early in the summer of the previous year, only to find that the
Piglet—a pillar of Roman rectitude—was not amused by his commercial
activities. Leaving the Piglet to make his own dispositions when his government fell, Crassus went on to Greece, and Sulla, who had accepted his gift
of five Spanish cohorts, then proceeded to treat him coldly.

Now he sat with his small grey eyes fixed painfully upon Sulla, waiting
for the slightest sign of approval, and obviously most put out to see Sulla
interested only in Pompey. The cognomen of Crassus had been in the Famous
Family of Licinius for many generations, but they still managed to breed true
to it, Varro noted; it meant thickset (or perhaps, in the case of the first Licinius
to be called Crassus, it might have meant intellectually dense?). Taller by far
than he looked, Crassus was built on the massive lines of an ox, and had
some of that animal's impassive placidity in his rather expressionless face.

Varro gave the assembled men a final glance, and sighed. Yes, he had
been right to spend most of his thoughts upon Crassus. They were all ambitious, most of them were probably capable, some of them were as ruthless
as they were amoral, but—leaving Pompey and Sulla out of it, of course—
Marcus Crassus was the man to watch in the future.

Walking back to their own house alongside a completely sober Pompey,
Varro found himself very glad that he had yielded to Pompey's exhortations
and attached himself at first hand to this coming campaign.

"What did you and Sulla talk about?" he asked.

"Nothing earthshaking," said Pompey.

"You kept your voices low enough."

"Yes, didn't we?" Varro felt rather than saw Pompey's grin. "He's no fool, Sulla, even if he isn't the man he used to be. If the rest of that sulky assemblage couldn't hear what we said, how do they know we didn't talk about them?"

"Did Sulla agree to be your partner in this enterprise?"

"I got to keep command of my own legions, which is all I wanted. He knows I haven't given them to him, even on loan."

"Was it discussed openly?"

"I told you, the man is no fool," said Pompey laconically. "Nothing much was said. That way, there is no agreement between us, and he is not bound."

"You're content with that?"

"Of course! He also knows he needs me," said Pompey.

Sulla was up by dawn the next morning, and an hour later had his army on the march in the direction of Capua. By now he had accustomed himself to spurts of activity that coincided with the state of his face, for the itching was not perpetually there; rather, it tended to be cyclic. Having just emerged from a bout and its concomitant intake of wine, he knew that for some days he would have a little peace—provided he did absolutely nothing to trigger another cycle. This required a rigid policing of his hands, which could not be permitted to touch his face for any reason. Not until a man found himself in this predicament did he understand how many times his hands would go to his face without volition, without any awareness. And here he was with the weeping vesicles growing harder as they struggled to heal, and all the tickles, tingles, tiny movements of the skin that healing process involved. It was easiest on the first day, which was today, but as the days went on he would tend to forget, would reach up to scratch a perfectly natural itch of nose or cheek—and the whole ghastly business could start again. *Would* start again. So he had disciplined himself to get as much done as possible before the next outbreak, and then to drink himself insensible until it passed.

Oh, but it was difficult! So much to do, so much that had to be done, and he a shadow of the man he had been. Nothing had he accomplished without overcoming gigantic obstacles, but since the onset of that illness in Greece over a year ago he constantly found himself wondering why he bothered to continue. As Pompey had so obviously remarked, Sulla was no fool; he knew he had only a certain time left to live.

On a day like today, of course, just emerging from a bout of itching, he did understand why he bothered to continue: because he was the greatest man in a world unwilling to admit that. The Nabopolassar had seen it in him on the banks of the river Euphrates, and not even the gods could delude a Chaldaean seer. To be great beyond all other men, he understood on a day like today, meant a far greater degree of suffering too. He tried not to smile (a smile might disturb the healing process), thinking of his couch companion on the previous evening; now there was one who didn't even begin to comprehend the nature of greatness!

Pompey the Great. Trust Sulla to have discovered already by what name he was known among his own people. A young man who actually thought that greatness did not have to be worked at, that greatness had been given him at birth and would never not be there. I wish with all my heart, Pompeius *Magnus,* thought Sulla, that I could live long enough to see who and what will bring you crashing down! A fascinating fellow, however. Most definitely a prodigy of some sort. He was not the stuff of a loyal subordinate, so much was sure. No, Pompey the Great was a rival. And saw himself as a rival. Already. At twenty-two. The veteran troops he had brought with him Sulla knew how to use; but how best to use Pompey the Great? Give him plenty of free rein to run with, certainly. Make sure he was not given a task he couldn't do. Flatter him, exalt him, never prick his monumental conceit. Give him to understand that he is the user, and *never* let him see that he is the one being used. I will be dead long before he is brought crashing down, because while I am alive, I will make sure no one does that to him. He's far too useful. Too . . . Valuable.

The mule upon which Sulla rode squealed, tossed its head in agreement. But, ever mindful of his face, Sulla did not smile at the mule's sagacity. He was waiting. Waiting for a jar of ointment and a recipe from which to make further jars of ointment. Almost ten years ago he had first experienced this skin disease, on his way back from the Euphrates. How satisfying that expedition had been!

His son had come along, Julilla's son who in his adolescence had turned out to be the friend and confidant Sulla had never owned before. The perfect participant in a perfect relationship. How they had talked! About anything and everything. The boy had been able to forgive his father so many things Sulla had never been able to forgive himself—oh, not murders and other necessary practicalities, they were just the things a man's life *forced* him to do. But emotional mistakes, weaknesses of the mind dictated by longings and inclinations reason shouted were stupid, futile. How gravely Young Sulla had listened, how completely had he, so short in years, understood. Comforted. Produced excuses which at the time had even seemed to hold water. And

Sulla's rather barren world had glowed, expanded, promised a depth and dimension only this beloved son could give it. Then, safely home from the journey beyond the Euphrates and Roman experience, Young Sulla had died. Just like that. Over and done with in two tiny little insignificant days. Gone the friend, gone the confidant. Gone the beloved son.

The tears stung, welled up—no! No! He could not weep, must not weep! Let one drop trickle down his cheek, and the itchy torment would begin. Ointment. He must concentrate upon the idea of the ointment. Morsimus had found it in some forgotten village somewhere near the Pyramus River of Cilicia Pedia, and it had soothed, healed him.

Six months ago he had sent to Morsimus, now an *ethnarch* in Tarsus, and begged him to find that ointment, even if he had to search every settlement in Cilicia Pedia. Could he but find it again—and, more importantly, its recipe—his skin would return to normal. And in the meantime, he waited. Suffered. Became ever greater. Do you hear that, Pompey the Great?

He turned in his saddle and beckoned to where behind him rode Metellus Pius the Piglet and Marcus Crassus (Pompey the Great was bringing up the rear at the head of his three legions).

"I have a problem," he said when Metellus Pius and Crassus drew level with him.

"Who?" asked the Piglet shrewdly.

"Oh, very good! Our esteemed Philippus," said Sulla, no expression creasing his face.

"Well, even if we didn't have Appius Claudius along, Lucius Philippus would present a problem," said Crassus, the abacus of his mind clicking from *unum* to *duo,* "but there's no denying Appius Claudius makes it worse. You'd think the fact that Appius Claudius is Philippus's uncle would have kept him from expelling Appius Claudius from the Senate, but it didn't."

"Probably because nephew Philippus is some years older than uncle Appius Claudius," said Sulla, entertained by this opinion.

"What exactly do you want to do with the problem?" asked Metellus Pius, unwilling to let his companions drift off into the complexities of Roman upper-class blood relationships.

"I know what I'd like to do, but whether or not it's even possible rests with you, Crassus," said Sulla.

Crassus blinked. "How could it affect me?"

Tipping back his shady straw hat, Sulla looked at his legate with a little more warmth in his eyes than of yore; and Crassus, in spite of himself, felt an uplift in the region of his breast. Sulla was deferring to him!

"It's all very well to be marching along buying grain and foodstuffs from the local farmers,'' Sulla began, his words a trifle slurred these days because of his lack of teeth, ''but by the end of summer we will need a harvest I can ship from one place. It doesn't have to be a harvest the size of Sicily's or Africa's, but it does have to provide the staple for my army. And I am confident that my army will increase in size as time goes on.''

''Surely,'' said Metellus Pius carefully, ''by the autumn we'll have all the grain we need from Sicily and Africa. By the autumn we will have taken Rome.''

''I doubt that.''

''But why? Rome's rotting from within!''

Sulla sighed, his lips flapping. ''Piglet dear, if I am to help Rome recover, then I have to give Rome a chance to decide in my favor *peacefully*. Now that is not going to happen by the autumn. So I can't appear too threatening, I can't march at the double up the Via Latina and attack Rome the way Cinna and Marius descended upon her after I left for the east. When I marched on Rome the first time, I had surprise on my side. No one believed I would. So no one opposed me except a few slaves and mercenaries belonging to Gaius Marius. But this time is different. Everyone expects me to march on Rome. If I do that too quickly, I'll never win. Oh, Rome would fall! But every nest of insurgents, every school of opposition would harden. It would take me longer than I have left to live to put resistance down. I can't afford the time or the effort. So I'll go very slowly toward Rome.''

Metellus Pius digested this, and saw the sense of it. With a gladness he couldn't quite conceal from those glacial eyes in their sore sockets. Wisdom was not a quality he associated with any Roman nobleman; Roman noblemen were too political in their thinking to be wise. Everything was of the moment, seen in the short term. Even Scaurus Princeps Senatus, for all his experience and his vast *auctoritas,* had not been wise. Any more than had the Piglet's own father, Metellus Numidicus. Brave. Fearless. Determined. Unyielding of principle. But never wise. So it cheered the Piglet immensely to know that he rode down the long road to Rome with a wise man, for he was a Caecilius Metellus and he had a foot in both camps, despite his personal choice of Sulla. If there was any aspect of this undertaking from which he shrank, it was the knowledge that—try though he might to avoid it—he would inevitably end in ruining a good proportion of his blood or marital relations. Therefore he appreciated the wisdom of advancing slowly upon Rome; some of the Caecilii Metelli who at the moment supported Carbo might see the error of their ways before it was too late.

Of course Sulla knew exactly how the Piglet's mind was working, and let him finish his thoughts in peace. His own thoughts were upon his task as he stared between the mournful flops of his mule's ears. I am back in Italy and soon Campania, that cornucopia of all the good things from the earth, will loom in the distance—green, rolling, soft of mountain, sweet of water. And if I deliberately exclude Rome from my inner gaze, Rome will not eat at me the way this itching does. Rome will be mine. But, though my crimes have been many and my contrition none, I have never liked so much as the idea of rape. Better by far that Rome comes to me consenting, than that I am forced to rape her. . . .

"You may have noticed that ever since I landed in Brundisium I have been sending written letters to all the leaders of the old Italian Allies, promising them that I will see every last Italian properly enrolled as a citizen of Rome according to the laws and treaties negotiated at the end of the Italian War. I will even see them distributed across the full gamut of the thirty-five tribes. Believe me, Piglet, I will bend like a strand of spider's web in the wind before I attack Rome!"

"What have the Italians to do with Rome?" asked Metellus Pius, who had never been in favor of granting the full Roman citizenship to the Italians, and had secretly applauded Philippus as censor because Philippus and his fellow censor, Perperna, had avoided enrolling the Italians as Roman citizens.

"Between Pompeius and me, we've marched through much of the territory which fought against Rome without encountering anything beyond welcome—and perhaps hope that I will change the situation in Rome concerning their citizenships. Italian support will be a help to me in persuading Rome to yield peacefully."

"I doubt it," said Metellus Pius stiffly, "but I daresay you know what you're doing. Let's get back to the subject of Philippus, who is a problem."

"Certainly!" said Sulla, eyes dancing.

"What has Philippus to do with me?" asked Crassus, deeming it high time he intruded himself into what had become a duet.

"I have to get rid of him, Marcus Crassus. But as painlessly as possible, given the fact that somehow he has managed to turn himself into a hallowed Roman institution."

"That's because he has become everybody's ideal of the dedicated political contortionist," said the Piglet, grinning.

"Not a bad description," said Sulla, nodding instead of trying to smile. "Now, my big and ostensibly placid friend Marcus Crassus, I am going to ask you a question. I require an honest answer. Given your sad reputation, are you capable of giving me an honest answer?"

This sally did not appear even to dent Crassus's oxlike composure. "I will do my best, Lucius Cornelius."

"Are you passionately attached to your Spanish troops?"

"Considering that you keep making me find provisions for them, no, I am not," said Crassus.

"Good! Would you part with them?"

"If you think we can do without them, yes."

"Good! Then with your splendidly phlegmatic consent, my dear Marcus, I'll bring down several quarry with the same arrow. It is my intention to give your Spaniards to Philippus—he can take and hold Sardinia for me. When the Sardinian harvest comes in, he will send all of it to me," said Sulla. He reached for the hide flask of pale sour wine tied to one horn of his saddle, lifted it, and squirted liquid expertly into his gummy mouth; not a drop fell on his face.

"Philippus will refuse to go," said Metellus Pius flatly.

"No, he won't. He'll love the commission," said Sulla, capping the birdlike neck of his wineskin. "He'll be the full and undisputed master of all he surveys, and the Sardinian brigands will greet him like a brother. He makes every last one of them look virtuous."

Doubt began to gnaw at Crassus, who rumbled deeply in his throat, but said no word.

"Wondering what you'll do without troops to command?"

"Something like that," said Crassus cautiously.

"You *could* make yourself very useful to me," said Sulla in casual tones.

"How?"

"Your mother and your wife are both from prominent Sabine families. How about going to Reate and starting to recruit for me? You could commence there, and finish among the Marsi." Out went Sulla's hand, clasped the heavy wrist of Crassus. "Believe me, Marcus Crassus, in the spring of next year there will be much military work for you to do, and good troops—Italian, if not Roman—for you to command."

"That suits me," said Crassus. "It's a deal."

"Oh, if only everything could be solved so easily and so well!" cried Sulla, reaching once more for his wineskin.

Crassus and Metellus Pius exchanged glances across the bent head of silly artificial curls; he might say he drank to ease the itching, but the truth appeared more to be that nowadays Sulla couldn't go for very long without wetting his whistle. Somewhere down the nightmare alley of his physical torments, he had embraced his palliative with a permanent and enduring love. But did he know it? Or did he not?

Had they found the courage to ask him, Sulla would have told them readily. Yes, he knew it. Nor did he care who else knew it, including the fact that his deceptively weak-looking vintage was actually strongly fortified. Forbidden bread, honey, fruit and cakes, little in his diet did he truly like. The physicians of Aedepsus had been right to remove all those tasty things from his food intake, of that he had no doubt. When he had come to them, he knew he was dying. First he had endured an insatiable craving for sweet and starchy things, and put on so much weight that even his mule had complained about the burden of carrying him; then he began to experience numbness and tingling in both feet, burnings and pains too as time went on, so that the moment he lay down to sleep, his wretched feet refused to let him. The sensations crept into his ankles and lower legs, sleep became harder and harder to find. So he added a heavy, very sweet and fortified wine to his customary fare, and used it to drug himself into sleeping. Until the day when he had found himself sweating, gasping—and losing weight so quickly that he could almost see himself disappearing. He drank flagons of water one after the other, yet still was thirsty. And—most terrifying of all!—his eyes began to fail.

Most of that had disappeared or greatly eased after he went to Aedepsus. Of his face he wouldn't think, he who had been so beautiful in his youth that men had made absolute fools of themselves, so beautiful after he attained maturity that women had made absolute fools of themselves. But one thing which had not disappeared was his need to drink wine. Yielding to the inevitable, the priest-physicians of Aedepsus had persuaded him to exchange his sweet fortified wine for the sourest vintages available, and over the months since, he had come to prefer his wine so dry it made him grimace. When the itch was not upon him he kept the amount he drank under some sort of control, in that he didn't let it interfere with his thought processes. He just drank enough to improve them—or so he told himself.

"I'll keep Ofella and Catilina with me," he said to Crassus and Metellus Pius, stoppering up the flask again. "However, Verres is the epitome of his name—an insatiably greedy boar. I think I will send him back to Beneventum, for the time being at least. He can organize supplies and keep an eye on our rear."

The Piglet giggled. "He might like that, the honey-boy!"

This provoked a brief grin in Crassus. "What about yon Cethegus?" he asked, legs aching from hanging down limply; they were very heavy legs. He shifted his weight a little.

"Cethegus I shall retain for the moment," said Sulla. His hand strayed toward the wine, then was snatched away. "He can look after things in Campania."

* * *

Just before his army crossed the river Volturnus near the town of Casilinum, Sulla sent six envoys to negotiate with Gaius Norbanus, the more capable of Carbo's two tame consuls. Norbanus had taken eight legions and drawn himself up to defend Capua, but when Sulla's envoys appeared carrying a flag of truce, he arrested them without a hearing. He then marched his eight legions out onto the Capuan plain right beneath the slopes of Mount Tifata. Irritated by the unethical treatment meted out to his envoys, Sulla proceeded to teach Norbanus a lesson he would not forget. Down the flank of Mount Tifata Sulla led his troops at a run, hurled them on the unsuspecting Norbanus. Defeated before the battle had really begun, Norbanus retreated inside Capua, where he sorted out his panicked men, sent two legions to hold the port of Neapolis for Carbo's Rome, and prepared himself to withstand a siege.

Thanks to the cleverness of a tribune of the plebs, Marcus Junius Brutus, Capua was very much disposed to like the present government in Rome; earlier in the year, Brutus had brought in a law giving Capua the status of a Roman city, and this, after centuries of being punished by Rome for various insurrections, had pleased Capua mightily. Norbanus had therefore no need to worry that Capua might grow tired of playing host to him and his army. Capua was used to playing host to Roman legions.

"We have Puteoli, so we don't need Neapolis," said Sulla to Pompey and Metellus Pius as they rode toward Teanum Sidicinum, "and we can do without Capua because we hold Beneventum. I must have had a feeling when I left Gaius Verres there." He stopped for a moment, thought about something, nodded as if to answer his thought. "Cethegus can have a new job. Legate in charge of all my supply columns. That will tax his diplomacy!"

"This," said Pompey in disgruntled tones, "is a very slow kind of war. Why aren't we marching on Rome?"

The face Sulla turned to him was, given its limitations, a kind one. "Patience, Pompeius! In martial skills you need no tuition, but your political skills are nonexistent. If the rest of this year teaches you nothing else, it will serve as a lesson on political manipulation. Before ever we contemplate marching on Rome, we have first to show Rome that she cannot win under her present government. Then, if she proves to be a sensible lady, she will come to us and offer herself to us freely."

"What if she doesn't?" asked Pompey, unaware that Sulla had already been through this with Metellus Pius and Crassus.

"Time will tell" was all Sulla would say.

They had bypassed Capua as if Norbanus inside it did not exist, and rolled on toward the second of Rome's consular armies, under the command of Scipio Asiagenus and his senior legate, Quintus Sertorius. The little and very prosperous Campanian towns around Sulla did not so much capitulate as greet him with open arms, for they knew him well; Sulla had commanded Rome's armies in this part of Italy for most of the duration of the Italian War.

Scipio Asiagenus was camped between Teanum Sidicinum and Cales, where a small tributary of the Volturnus, fed by springs, provided a great deal of slightly effervescent water; even in summer its mild warmth was delightful.

"This," said Sulla, "will be an excellent winter camp!" And sat himself and his army down on the opposite bank of the streamlet from his adversary. The cavalry were sent back to Beneventum under the charge of Cethegus, while Sulla himself gave a new party of envoys explicit instructions on how to proceed in negotiating a truce with Scipio Asiagenus.

"He's not an old client of Gaius Marius's, so he'll be much easier to deal with than Norbanus," said Sulla to Metellus Pius and Pompey. His face was still in remission and his intake of wine was somewhat less than on the journey from Beneventum, which meant that his mood was cheerful and his mind very clear.

"Maybe," said the Piglet, looking doubtful. "If it were only Scipio, I'd agree wholeheartedly. But he has Quintus Sertorius with him, and you know what that means, Lucius Cornelius."

"Trouble," said Sulla, sounding unworried.

"Ought you not be thinking how to render Sertorius impotent?"

"I won't need to do that, Piglet dear. Scipio will do it for me." He pointed with a stick toward the place where a sharp bend in the little river drew his camp's boundary very close to the boundary of Scipio's camp on the far shore. "Can your veterans dig, Gnaeus Pompeius?"

Pompey blinked. "With the best!"

"Good. Then while the rest are finishing off the winter fortifications, your fellows can excavate the bank outside our wall, and make a great big swimming pool," said Sulla blandly.

"What a terrific idea!" said Pompey with equal sangfroid, and smiled. "I'll get them onto it straightaway." He paused, took the stick from Sulla and pointed it at the far bank. "If it's all right with you, General, I'll break down the bank and concentrate on widening the river, rather than make a separate swimming hole. And I think it would be very nice for our chaps if I roofed at least a part of it over—less chilly later on."

"Good thinking! Do that," said Sulla cordially, and stood watching Pompey stride purposefully away.

"What was all that about?" asked Metellus Pius, frowning; he hated to see Sulla so affable to that conceited young prig!

"He knew," said Sulla cryptically.

"Well, I don't!" said the Piglet crossly. "Enlighten me!"

"Fraternization, Piglet dear! Do you think Scipio's men are going to be able to resist Pompeius's winter spa? Even in summer? After all, our men are Roman soldiers too. There is nothing like a truly pleasurable activity shared in common to breed friendship. The moment Pompeius's pool is finished, there will be as many of Scipio's men enjoying it as ours. And they'll all get chatty in no time—same jokes, same complaints, same sort of life. It's my bet we won't have to fight a battle."

"And he understood that from the little you said?"

"Absolutely."

"I'm surprised he agreed to help! He's after a battle."

"True. But he's got my measure, Pius, and he knows he will not get a battle this side of spring. It's no part of Pompeius's strategy to annoy me, you know. He needs me just as much as I need him," said Sulla, and laughed softly without moving his face.

"He strikes me as the sort who might prematurely decide that he doesn't need you."

"Then you mistake him."

Three days later, Sulla and Scipio Asiagenus parleyed on the road between Teanum and Cales, and agreed to an armistice. About this moment Pompey finished his swimming hole, and—typically methodical—after publishing a roster for its use that allowed sufficient space for invaders from across the river, threw it open for troop recreation. Within two more days the coming and going between the two camps was so great that,

"We may as well abandon any pretense that we're on opposite sides," said Quintus Sertorius to his commander.

Scipio Asiagenus looked surprised. "What harm does it do?" he asked gently.

The one eye Sertorius was left with rolled toward the sky. Always a big man, his physique had set with the coming of his middle thirties into its final mold—thick-necked, bull-like, formidable. And in some ways this was a pity, for it endowed Sertorius with a bovine look entirely at variance with the power and quality of his mind. He was Gaius Marius's cousin, and had inherited far more of Marius's personal and military brilliance than had, for instance, Marius's son. The eye had been obliterated in a skirmish just before the Siege of Rome, but as it was his left one and he was right-handed, its loss had not slowed him down as a fighter. Scar tissue had turned his pleasant face into something of a caricature, in that its right side was still most pleasant while its left leered a horrible contradiction.

So it was that Scipio underestimated him, did not respect or understand him. And looked at him now in surprise.

Sertorius tried. "Asiagenus, think! How well do you feel our men will fight for us if they're allowed to get too friendly with the enemy?"

"They'll fight because they're ordered to fight."

"I don't agree. Why do you think Sulla built his swimming hole, if not to suborn our troops? He didn't do it for the sake of his own men! It's a trap, and you're falling into it!"

"We are under a truce, and the other side is as Roman as we are," said Scipio Asiagenus stubbornly.

"The other side is led by a man you ought to fear as if he and his army had been sown from the dragon's teeth! You can't give him one single little inch, Asiagenus. If you do, he will end in taking all the miles between here and Rome."

"You exaggerate," said Scipio stiffly.

"You're a fool!" snarled Sertorius, unable not to say it.

But Scipio was not impressed by the display of temper either. He yawned, scratched his chin, looked down at his beautifully manicured nails. Then he looked up at Sertorius looming over him, and smiled sweetly. "Do go away!" he said.

"I will that! Right away!" Sertorius snapped. "Maybe Gaius Norbanus can make you see sense!"

"Give him my regards," Scipio called after him, then went back to studying his nails.

So Quintus Sertorius rode for Capua at the gallop, and there found a man more to his taste than Scipio Asiagenus. The loyalest of Marians, Norbanus was no fanatical adherent of Carbo's; after the death of Cinna, he had only persisted in his allegiance because he loathed Sulla far more than he did Carbo.

"You mean that chinless wonder of an aristocrat actually has concluded an armistice with *Sulla*?" asked Norbanus, voice squeaking as it uttered that detested name.

"He certainly has. And he's permitting his men to fraternize with the enemy," said Sertorius steadily.

"Why did I have to be saddled with a colleague as stupid as Asiagenus?" wailed Norbanus, then shrugged. "Well, that is what our Rome is reduced to, Quintus Sertorius. I'll send him a nasty message which he will ignore, but I suggest you don't return to him. I hate to think of you as a captive of Sulla's—he'd find a way to murder you. Find something to do that will annoy Sulla.''

"Eminent good sense," said Sertorius, sighing. "I'll stir up trouble for Sulla among the towns of Campania. The townspeople all declared for Sulla, but there are plenty of *men* who aren't happy about it." He looked disgusted. "Women, Gaius Norbanus! *Women!* They only have to hear Sulla's name and they go limp with ecstasy. It's the women decided which side these Campanian towns chose, not the men."

"Then they ought to set eyes on him," said Norbanus, and grimaced. "I believe he looks like nothing human."

"Worse than me?"

"A lot worse, so they say."

Sertorius frowned. "I'd heard something of it, but Scipio wouldn't include me in the treating party, so I didn't see him, and Scipio made no reference to his appearance." He laughed grimly. "Oh, I'll bet that hurts him, the pretty *mentula*! He was so vain! Like a woman."

Norbanus grinned. "Don't like the sex much, do you?"

"They're all right for a poke. But I'll have none to wife! My mother is the only woman I have any time for at all. Now she is what a woman ought to be! Doesn't stick her nose into men's affairs, doesn't try to rule the roost, doesn't use her *cunnus* like a weapon." He picked up his helmet and clapped it on his head. "I'll be off, Gaius. Good luck convincing Scipio that he is wrong. *Verpa!*"

After some thought, Sertorius decided to ride from Capua toward the Campanian coast, where the pretty little town of Sinuessa Aurunca might just be ripe for a declaration against Sulla. The roads everywhere in Campania were free enough from trouble; Sulla had not attempted any blockades aside from a formal investment of Neapolis. No doubt he would shortly put a force outside Capua to keep Norbanus in, but there had been no sign of it when Sertorius visited. Even so, Sertorius felt it advisable to stay off the main roads. He liked the sensation of a fugitive existence; it carried an extra dimension of real life with it, and reminded him slightly of the days when he had posed as a Celtiberian warrior of some outlandish tribe in order to go spying among the Germans. Ah, that had been the life! No chinless wonders of Roman aristocrats to placate and defer to! Constant action, women who knew their place. He had even had a German wife, sired a son by her without once ever feeling that she or the boy hampered him. They lived in Nearer

Spain now, up in the mountain stronghold of Osca, and the boy would be—how time flew!—almost a man. Not that Quintus Sertorius missed them, or hankered to set eyes upon this only child. What he missed was the life. The freedom, the sole ruling excellence, which was how a man acquitted himself as a warrior. Yes, those were the days. . . .

As was his invariable habit, he traveled without any kind of escort, even a slave; like his cousin, dear old Gaius Marius, he believed that a soldier ought to be able to care for himself completely. Of course his kit was back in Scipio Asiagenus's camp and he would not go back for it—or would he? Come to think of it, there were a few items he would sorely miss: the sword he normally used, a shirt of chain mail he had picked up in Further Gaul of a lightness and workmanship no smith in Italy could match, his winter boots from Liguria. Yes, he would go back. Some days would elapse before Scipio would fall.

So he turned his horse around and headed back toward the northeast, intending to swing beyond Sulla's camp on its far side. And discovered that some distance in his rear a small party was proceeding along the rutted track. Four men and three women. Oh, women! Almost he reversed direction once more, then resolved to pick up speed and hasten by them. After all, they were heading seaward, he was now going back toward the mountains.

But as they loomed larger he frowned. Surely the man in their lead was familiar? A veritable giant, flaxen-haired and massive of thews, just like thousands more German men he had known—Burgundus! Ye gods, it was! Burgundus! And behind him rode Lucius Decumius and his two sons!

Burgundus had recognized him; each man kicked his horse in the ribs and rode to a meeting, with little Lucius Decumius flogging his beast to catch up. Trust Lucius Decumius not to miss a word of any conversation!

"What on earth are you doing here?" Sertorius asked after the hand-shakes and the backslappings were over.

"We're lost, that's what we're doing here," said Lucius Decumius, glaring at Burgundus balefully. "That heap of German rubbish *swore* he knew the way! But do he? No, he do not!"

Years of exposure to Lucius Decumius's never-ending spate of (quite well meant) insults had inured Burgundus to them, so he bore them now with his usual patience, merely eyeing the small Roman the way a bull eyed a gnat.

"We're trying to find the lands of Quintus Pedius," said Burgundus in his slow Latin, smiling at Sertorius with a liking he felt for few men. "The lady Aurelia is going to fetch her daughter to Rome."

And there she was, plodding along upon a stout mule and sitting absolutely straight, not a hair out of place nor a single smear of dust upon her fawn traveling robe. With her was her huge Gallic serving maid, Cardixa, and another female servant Sertorius did not know.

"Quintus Sertorius," she said, joining them and somehow assuming command.

Now she was a woman! Sertorius had said to Norbanus that he prized only one of the breed, his mother, but he had quite forgotten Aurelia. How she managed to be beautiful as well as sensible he didn't know; what he did know was that she was the only woman in the entire world who was both. Added to which, she was as honorable as any man, she didn't lie, she didn't moan or complain, she worked hard, and she minded her own business. They were almost exactly the same age—forty—and had known each other since Aurelia had married Gaius Julius Caesar over twenty years earlier.

"Have you seen my mother?" Sertorius asked as she prodded her mule to lead them slightly apart from the rest of her party.

"Not since last year's *ludi Romani,* so you would have seen her yourself since I have. But she'll be down to stay with us again this year for the games. It's become a regular habit."

"Old horror, she never will stay in my house," he said.

"She's lonely, Quintus Sertorius, and your house is such a lonely place. If she stays with us she's in the midst of a bustle, and she likes that. I don't say she'd like it for longer than the games last, but it's good for her once a year."

Satisfied on the subject of his mother, whom he loved very much, he turned his mind to the present predicament.

"Are you really lost?" he asked.

Aurelia nodded, sighed. "I fear we are. Wait until my son hears about it! He'll never let me live it down. But he cannot leave Rome, being *flamen Dialis,* so I had to trust in Burgundus." She looked rueful. "Cardixa says he can lose himself between the Forum and the Subura, but I confess I thought she was being pessimistic. Now I see she didn't exaggerate in the slightest!"

"And Lucius Decumius and his boys are useless too."

"Outside the city walls, completely. However," she said loyally, "I could not ask for more caring and protective escorts, and now that we've met you, I'm sure we'll arrive at Quintus Pedius's in no time."

"Not quite in no time, but certainly I can put you on your way." His one good eye studied her thoughtfully. "Come to fetch your chick home, Aurelia?"

She flushed. "Not exactly. Quintus Pedius wrote to me and asked me to come. Apparently both Scipio and Sulla are camped on the borders of his land, and he felt Lia would be safer elsewhere. But she refused to leave!"

"A typical Caesar," said Sertorius, smiling. "Stubborn."

"How right you are! It really ought to have been her brother come— when *he* tells them to do this or do that, both his sisters jump! But Quintus Pedius seems to think I will do. My job is not so much to fetch my chick home, as to persuade my chick to come home."

"You'll succeed. The Caesars may be stubborn, but it isn't from the Caesars that your son gets his air of command. That he gets from you, Aurelia," said Sertorius. He looked suddenly brisk. "You'll understand when I tell you that I'm in a bit of a hurry. I'm going your way for a part of your journey, but I won't be able to escort you to Quintus Pedius's door, unfortunately. For that you'll have to apply to Sulla. He's camped squarely between where we are at the moment and Quintus Pedius's door."

"Whereas you are on your way to Scipio," she said, nodding.

"I wasn't," he said frankly, "until I realized I had too much gear back in his camp that I didn't want to part with."

The large purple eyes surveyed him tranquilly. "Oh, I see! Scipio doesn't meet the test."

"Did you think he could?"

"No, never."

A small silence fell; they were riding now back the way both had come, and the rest of Aurelia's party had fallen in behind them without a word.

"What will you do, Quintus Sertorius?"

"Make as much trouble for Sulla as I can. In Sinuessa, I think. But after I fetch my gear from Scipio's camp." He cleared his throat. "I can take you all the way to Sulla. He'd never try to detain me if I came on business like this."

"No, just take us as far as some spot from which we can find his camp without getting lost." Aurelia heaved a small and pleasurable sigh. "How nice it will be to see Lucius Cornelius again! It is four years since he was last in Rome. He always visited me just after he arrived, and just before he left. A kind of tradition. Now I have to break it, and all because of one stubborn daughter. Still, it doesn't matter. The important thing is that Lucius Cornelius and I will set eyes upon each other again. I have missed his visits dreadfully."

Almost Sertorius opened his mouth to warn her, but in the end he didn't. What he knew about Sulla's condition was hearsay, and what he knew about

Aurelia was hard fact. She would prefer to make her own discoveries, of that he was sure.

So when the earth-and-timber ramparts of Sulla's camp began to trace lines across the rolling Campanian horizon, Quintus Sertorius bade his cousin-in-law a grave goodbye, geed up his horse and departed.

A new road led across the fields toward the ramparts, worn already by a ceaseless progress of supply carts and shod hooves; there could be no excuse for getting lost.

"We must have passed right by it," said Lucius Decumius, scowling. "Hid from view by the size of your arse, Burgundus!"

"Now, now," said Aurelia calmly, "stop quarreling, do!"

And that was the end of the conversation. An hour later the little band of riders paused before the gate while Lucius Decumius demanded to see the general, then entered a world very strange and new to Aurelia, who had never been anywhere near an army camp in her entire life. Many were the glances she received as they paced down the broad high street which led as straight as a spear shaft toward the tiny aperture of another gate in the far distance. Perhaps three miles lay between, she realized, amazed.

Halfway along the Via Principalis there reared the only piece of raised ground within the camp; an obviously artificial knoll upon which stood a large stone house. The big red general's flag was flying to indicate that the general was in, and the red-haired duty officer seated at his table under an awning stood up awkwardly when he saw that the general's visitor was a woman. Lucius Decumius, his sons, Burgundus, Cardixa and the other female servant remained by the horses as Aurelia walked sedately up the path toward the duty officer and the sentries who flanked him.

Because she was completely wrapped in voluminous fine fawn wool, all young Marcus Valerius Messala Rufus the duty officer could see was her face. But that, he thought, catching his breath, was quite enough. As old as his mother, yet the most *beautiful* woman! Helen of Troy hadn't been young either. For the years had not dimmed Aurelia's magic; she still turned all heads whenever she appeared outside her own apartment.

"I would like to see Lucius Cornelius Sulla, please."

Messala Rufus neither asked for her name nor thought to warn Sulla of her advent; he simply bowed to her and gestured with his hand toward the open door. Aurelia entered, smiling her thanks.

Though the shutters were wide to let in air, the room was shadow-filled, especially in the far corner where a man was bent over his desk writing busily by the light of a big lamp.

Her voice could be no one else's: "Lucius Cornelius?"

Something happened. The bowed shoulders stiffened, hunched up as if to ward off some frightful blow, and the pen and paper skittled across the surface of the table, so violently were they thrust away. But after that he sat without moving, back to her.

She advanced a few paces. "Lucius Cornelius?"

Still nothing, but her eyes were becoming used to the gloom and took in the sight of a head of hair which did not belong to Lucius Cornelius Sulla. Little ginger-red curls, quite ridiculous.

Then he heaved himself around as if convulsing, and she knew it was Lucius Cornelius Sulla only because he looked at her out of Lucius Cornelius Sulla's eyes. Unmistakably his eyes.

Ye gods, how could I do this to him? But I didn't know! If I had known, a siege tower could not have dragged me here! What is my face saying? What does he see in my expression?

"Oh, Lucius Cornelius, how good to see you!" she said in exactly the right tones, covered the rest of the distance to his desk, and kissed him on both poor scarred cheeks. Then she sat down on a folding chair close by, tucked her hands in her lap, gave him an unselfconscious smile, and waited.

"I didn't intend ever to see you again, Aurelia," he said, not taking his eyes from hers. "Couldn't you wait until I got to Rome? This is a departure from our normal habit I didn't expect."

"Rome seems to be the hard way for you—an army at your back. Or perhaps I sensed this would be the first time you did not come to visit. But no, dear Lucius Cornelius, I'm not here for any guessable reason. I'm here because I'm lost."

"Lost?"

"Yes. I'm trying to find Quintus Pedius. My silly daughter won't come to Rome and Quintus Pedius—he's her second husband, which you won't know—doesn't want her anywhere near two firmly encamped armies." It came out quite cheerfully and convincingly, she thought. It ought to reassure him.

But he was Sulla, so he said, "Gave you a shock, didn't I?"

She did not attempt to dissemble. "In some ways, yes. The hair, principally. Yours is gone, I presume."

"Along with my teeth." He bared his gums like an ape.

"Well, we all come to it if we live long enough."

"Wouldn't want me to kiss you now the way I did a few years ago, would you?"

Aurelia put her head to one side, smiled. "I didn't want you to kiss me that way even then, though I *did* enjoy it. Far too much for my own peace of mind. How you hated me!''

"What did you expect? You turned me down. I don't like women turning me down.''

"I do remember that!''

"I remember the grapes.''

"So do I.''

He drew a deep breath, squeezed his eyelids together. "I wish I could weep!''

"I am glad you can't, dear friend,'' she said tenderly.

"You wept for me then.''

"Yes, I did. But I won't weep for you now. That would be to mourn for a vanished reflection gone a long way down the river. You're here. I rejoice at that.''

He got up at last, an old tired man. "A cup of wine?''

"Yes, indeed.''

He poured, she noticed, from two separate flagons. "You wouldn't like the urine I'm forced to drink these days. As dry and sour as I am.''

"I'm pretty dry and sour myself, but I won't insist upon tasting your choice if you don't recommend that I do.'' She took the simple cup he handed her and sipped gratefully. "Thank you, it's good. We've had a long day looking for Quintus Pedius.''

"What's your husband about, to leave you to do his job? Is he away yet again?'' asked Sulla, sitting down with more ease.

The luminous eyes grew glassily stern. "I have been a widow for two years, Lucius Cornelius.''

That astonished him. "Gaius Julius, dead? He was as fit as a boy! Was he killed in battle?''

"No. He just died—suddenly.''

"Yet here I am, a thousand years older than Gaius Julius, still hanging on to life.'' It came out sounding bitter.

"You're the October Horse, he was just the middle of the field. A good man, and I liked being married to him. But I never thought him a man who *needed* to hang on to life,'' said Aurelia.

"Just as well perhaps that he didn't. If I take Rome, it would have gone hard for him. I presume he would have elected to follow Carbo.''

"He followed Cinna, for Gaius Marius's sake. But Carbo? That I do not know.'' She changed the subject, growing used now to the way he looked, who had been as beautiful as Apollo. "Is your wife well, Lucius Cornelius?''

"When I last heard. She's still in Athens. Gave me twins last year, a boy and a girl.'' He chuckled. ''She's afraid they're going to grow up to look like her Uncle Piggle-wiggle.''

''Oh, poor little things! But that's nice, to have children. Do you ever wonder about your other twins, the boys your German wife had? They'd be young men now.''

''Young Cherusci! Taking scalps and burning Romans alive in wicker cages.''

It was going to be all right. He was calmer, less tormented. Of all the fates she had imagined might have been lying in wait for Lucius Cornelius Sulla, the loss of his special and unique attraction had not been among them. And yet he was still Sulla. His wife, she thought, probably loved him just as much as she ever had when he looked like Apollo.

For some time they talked on, slipping back through the rolling years as they exchanged information about this one and that one; he, she noticed, liked to talk about his protégé, Lucullus, and she, he noticed, liked to talk about her only son, who was now called Caesar.

''As I remember, young Caesar was scholarly. Being *flamen Dialis* ought to suit him,'' said Sulla.

Aurelia hesitated, seemed about to say something, then apparently said a different something: ''He has made a tremendous effort to be a good priest, Lucius Cornelius.''

Frowning, Sulla glanced at the window nearest to him. ''I see the sun is westering, that's why it's so dim in here. Time to get you on your way. I'll have some cadets act as guides—Quintus Pedius is not far beyond my camp. And you may tell your daughter that if she stays, she's a fool. My men are not ravening beasts, but if she's a true Julia she'll be a sore temptation, and one cannot forbid the troops to drink wine when they're in a permanent camp in Campania. Take her to Rome at once. I'll provide an escort for you as far as Ferentinum on the day after tomorrow. That will see you safely out of the clutches of both the armies encamped hereabouts.''

She rose. ''I have Burgundus and Lucius Decumius, and dear Lucius Decumius's sons as well. But I would appreciate an escort if you can truly spare the men. Is there no battle imminent between you and Scipio?''

Oh, how sad, never to see that wonderful Sullan smile again! The best he could do these days was a grunt that didn't disturb the scabs and scars of his face. ''That idiot? No, I don't foresee a battle,'' he said, standing in his doorway. He gave her a little push. ''Now go, Aurelia. And don't expect me to visit you in Rome.''

Off she went to join her waiting escort, while Sulla began to issue instructions to Messala Rufus. And in no time, it seemed, they were riding down the Via Praetoria toward yet another one of the four gates into Sulla's enormous camp.

One look at her face had not encouraged any of her companions to speak to her, so Aurelia was accorded the much-needed peace of finishing her journey inside her own thoughts.

I have always liked him, even though he became our enemy. Even though he is not a good person. My husband was a genuinely good person, and I loved him, and was faithful to him with my mind and my body. Yet—I know it now, though I did not until now—some little bit of me did I give to Lucius Cornelius Sulla. The bit my husband did not want, would not have known what to do with. We only kissed that once, Lucius Cornelius and I. But it was as beautiful as it was black. A passionate and engulfing mire. I did not yield. But ye gods, how I wanted to! I won a victory of sorts. Yet—did I perhaps lose a war?

Whenever he walked into my comfortable little world, a gale blew in around him; if he was Apollo, he was also Aeolus, and ruled the winds of my spirit, so that the lyre at my core hummed a melody my husband never, never heard. . . . Oh, this is worse than the grief of death and utter parting! I have looked upon the wreckage of a dream that was as much mine as his, and he knows it, poor Lucius Cornelius. But what courage! A lesser man would have fallen upon his sword. His pain, his pain! Why am I feeling this? I am busy, practical, unimaginative. My life is sifted out and very satisfying. But now I understand what bit of myself has always belonged to him; the bird bit, that might have lifted in soaring spirals singing its heart out while all the earth below burned away to an unimportant nothing. And no, I am not sorry I kept my feet upon the earth, never soared. It suits the way I am. He and I would never have known a moment's peace. Oh, I bleed for him! I weep for him!

And because she rode in front of all save the party of Roman officers who led the way, her people did not see Aurelia's tears any more than they had seen Lucius Cornelius Sulla, the wreckage of a dream.

The patient and protesting letter Gaius Norbanus sent to Scipio Asiagenus did nothing to avert Scipio's self-inflicted disaster; yet no one was more astonished than Scipio Asiagenus when, having decided after all to give battle, he discovered that his troops would not fight for him. Instead, his eight legions deserted en masse to Sulla.

In fact, even when Sulla stripped him of his consular insignia of office and sent him packing under the escort of a squadron of cavalry, Scipio Asiagenus was still incapable of appreciating Rome's predicament. Quite tranquilly and complacently he went off to Etruria and began to recruit another army from among the enormous number of Gaius Marius's clients who lived there. Gaius Marius might be dead, but his memory would never fade. Whereas Scipio Asiagenus was merely a passing presence.

"He doesn't even understand that he broke a solemn truce," said Sulla, looking puzzled. "I know the Scipiones are on the way down, but that one—! He's not worthy of the name Cornelius Scipio. If I take Rome, I'll execute him."

"You should have executed him when you had him," said the Piglet, a little waspishly. "He's living to be a nuisance."

"No, he's the poultice I'm applying to Etruria's boil," said Sulla. "Draw the poison out, Pius, while there's only one head to deal with. Don't leave it to become a carbuncle."

More wisdom, of course; Metellus Pius grinned. "What a wonderful metaphor!"

Though the month was still Quinctilis and summer not yet over, Sulla moved no more that year. With Scipio's departure the two camps were joined cozily together, and Sulla's hoary centurions began working upon the young and inexperienced troops who had belonged to Carbo's Rome. Fear of Sulla's veterans had operated upon them more powerfully than had the more friendly aspects of fraternization; the slight exposure of scant days had revealed to them a kind of soldier they didn't know—hardbitten, weathered, completely professional. Definitely not the sort of men any raw recruit could confidently face on a field of battle. Desertion had seemed the better alternative.

The defection of Sinuessa Aurunca under the influence of Quintus Sertorius could be no more than a pinprick; Sulla did invest it, but only to use it as a training ground for Scipio's army, not to starve it out or storm its forbidding ramparts. He was not interested in any task which caused mass loss of life that year. Sinuessa's most useful purpose was to contain the extremely able Quintus Sertorius. Holed up there, he was useless to Carbo, who could indeed have used him to better purpose.

Word came from Sardinia that Philippus and his Spanish cohorts had seized power easily. He would be able to send the entire harvest of Sardinia: and in due time the grain ships arrived in Puteoli, there to unload for Sulla's benefit, having encountered no war galleys or pirates en route.

Then winter came early, and was an unusually severe one. To split the size of his more than doubled forces, Sulla sent some cohorts off to invest Capua as well as Sinuessa and Neapolis, thus compelling other parts of Campania than Teanum to help feed his troops. Verres and Cethegus proved capable victuallers, even devised a method of storing fish caught in the Adriatic in bins of packed-down snow; fish lovers who could never get enough of it fresh, Sulla's soldiers reveled in this unexpected treat, and the army surgeons found themselves coping with case after case of bone-in-the-throat.

All of which was of no importance to Sulla, who had picked at some of the scabs on his healed face, and started the itching again. Everyone who came into contact with him had begged him to let them fall off naturally, but that restless temperament couldn't wait; when they began to lift and dangle, he picked.

The outbreak was a very bad one, and (perhaps because of the cold? wondered Varro, pressed into service because he had revealed a scientific curiosity) raged without let for three full months. Three months of a sodden, genuinely lunatic Sulla, who moaned and scratched, screamed and drank. At one stage Varro bound his hands to his sides to keep them from his face, and though—like Ulysses tied to the mast while the Sirens sang—he was willing enough to endure this confinement, at the same time he implored to be freed. And of course succeeded eventually in freeing himself. To scratch again.

It was at the turn of the year that Varro despaired, went to warn Metellus Pius and Pompey that he doubted whether Sulla would recover by the spring.

"There's a letter for him from Tarsus," said Metellus Pius, who was resigned to keeping Pompey company through the winter; Crassus was among the Marsi, and Appius Claudius and Mamercus were in charge of siege operations elsewhere.

Varro looked alert. "Tarsus?"

"That's right. From the *ethnarch* Morsimus."

"Is there a jar?"

"No, just a letter. Can he read it?"

"Definitely not."

"Then you'd better read it, Varro," said Pompey.

Metellus Pius looked scandalized. "Really, Pompeius!"

"Oh, Piglet, stop being so sanctimonious!" said Pompey wearily. "We know he's been hoping for some magic salve or other, and we know he'd charged Morsimus with finding it. Now there's news of some sort, but he can't read. Don't you think—for *his* sake, if for no one else's—that Varro ought to see what Morsimus has to say?"

So Varro was allowed to see what Morsimus had to say.

Here is the recipe, which is the most I can do for you, dear Lucius Cornelius, my friend and patron. It seems the salve has to be freshly prepared more often than the length of a journey from the Pyramus of Cilicia Pedia all the way to Rome would permit. So you must seek out the ingredients and make it for yourself. Luckily none of the ingredients is exotic, though many of them apparently are hard to extract.

The cure has to come from a sheep, or sheep. First you take a fleece of absolutely raw wool, and set someone to scraping the fibers with an instrument sharp enough to crush them, yet not sharp enough to cut them through. You will find that on the edge of your *strigilis* a substance builds up—rather oily, but having the consistency of cheese curds. You must scrape until you have a great mound of this—many fleeces, was how my source put it. Then you soak the substance in warm water— *warm,* not hot!—though it cannot be too cool either. The best test is a fingertip in the water—it should feel hot, but by no means unbearable. The substance will partially melt into a layer which floats on top. That layer is the part you want, in measure a full beaker.

Then you take a fleece with its hide attached, making sure some fat adheres to the back of the hide—the animal must have been freshly slaughtered, as indeed all must have been—and you boil it. The fat you obtain from this you must render twice over, and then you must reserve a full beaker of it.

The fat of a sheep, so said my source, needs some special fat from inside the beast also, for sheep fat is very hard, even in a warm room. My source—the smelliest and most detestable of crones, not to mention the most rapacious of creatures!—said this internal fat must be plucked from amid the harder fat on top of the sheep's kidneys, and mashed. Then it must be melted in warm water, as with the scrapings from the wool. You must lift off the layer which forms on top of the water, in the amount of two thirds of a beaker. To this, add one third of a beaker of bile freshly drawn from the sheep's gallbladder immediately after its slaughtering.

After which, you mix all the ingredients together gently, but thoroughly. The ointment is rather hard, but not as hard as the rendered fat on its own. Smear it on at least four times a day. I warn you, dear Lucius Cornelius, that it stinks disgustingly. But my source insists that it be used without the addition of perfumes or spices or resins.

Please let me know if it works! The vile old crone swears it was she who made that original jar you used with such success, though I myself am in some doubt.

Vale from Morsimus.

Off went Varro to marshal a small army of slaves, and set the slaves to find a flock of sheep. After which, in a little house close by the more solid building in which Sulla lived, he hovered anxiously between cauldrons and toiling scrapers, insisting upon personally inspecting every carcass and every kidney, insisting that he personally test the temperature of all the water, measuring meticulously and driving the servants to the point of exasperation with his fusses and clucks and tches. For perhaps an hour before his ointment factory commenced work he fretted and fumed over the size of the beaker; and then, at the end of the hour, he saw the truth, and laughed until he cried. Provided his beakers were all the *same* size, what did size matter?

One hundred sheep later (the bile and the rendered-down fat came from only two sheep, but the little bit of fat on top of the kidneys and the scrapings from the wool were painfully slow in accumulating), Varro found himself with a fairly large porphyry jar of ointment. As for the exhausted slaves, they found themselves with a hundred largely untouched carcasses of delicious mutton, and counted their labors well done for the chance of a full belly of roasted meat.

The hour was late, and Sulla, so his attendant whispered, was asleep on a couch in his dining room.

"Drunk," nodded Varro.

"Yes, Marcus Terentius."

"Well, I think that's probably good."

In he went on tiptoe, and stood for a moment looking down at the poor tortured creature Sulla had become. The wig had fallen off and lay with its gauze interior gaping; many thousands of hairs had gone into its manufacture, each one painstakingly knotted onto that base of gauze. To think that it took longer to make than my ointment! Varro thought, and sighed, shook his head. Then, very delicately, he applied his salve-caked fingers to the bleeding mess of Sulla's face.

The eyes snapped open at once, pain and terror shrieking from beneath their wine-blinded glaze; the mouth opened, the lips stretched to show gums and tongue. Yet no sound did he emit.

"It is the ointment, Lucius Cornelius," Varro whispered. "I have made it to the exact recipe. Can you bear it if I try to smear some on?"

Tears welled, pooled in the sockets of Sulla's eyes because he lay flat on his back. Before they could overflow from each outer corner, Varro had dabbed them away with a piece of softest cloth. Still they welled. Still Varro dabbed.

"You mustn't weep, Lucius Cornelius. The salve has to be applied to *dry* skin. Now lie quietly, and close your eyes."

So Sulla lay quietly, eyes closed. After a few reflexive jerks because his face was being touched, he made no other protest, and slowly the tension oozed out of him.

Varro finished, took a lamp with five flames and held it up to view his handiwork. A clear, watery fluid was popping up in beads wherever the skin had broken down, but the layer of ointment seemed to have tamed the bleeding.

"You must try not to scratch. Does it itch?" Varro asked.

The eyes remained closed. "Yes, it itches. But I've known it to itch far worse. Tie my hands to my sides."

Varro did that. "I'll come back toward dawn and smear some more on. Who knows, Lucius Cornelius? Perhaps by dawn the itching will have gone away." Then he tiptoed out.

At dawn the itch was still present, but to Varro's clinically detached gaze Sulla's skin looked—what was the word?—*calmer*. On went more ointment; Sulla asked that his hands remain tied. But by nightfall, three applications later, he announced that he thought he could refrain from scratching if Varro loosed his bonds. And four days after that, he told Varro that the itching was gone.

"The stuff works!" cried Varro to Pompey and the Piglet, afire with the satisfaction of a vindicated physician, for all that he was no physician, nor wanted to be.

"Will he be able to command in the spring?" asked Pompey.

"Provided that the stuff continues to work, probably well before the spring," said Varro, and bustled off with his porphyry jar to embed it in the snow. Kept cold, it would last longer, though Varro's hands stank of what he suspected was the rancid version of it. "Truly he is *felix*!" said Varro to himself; he meant, of course, that Sulla had luck.

When the onset of that cold and early winter brought snow to Rome, many of those who lived there saw the freeze as an ill omen. Neither Norbanus nor Scipio Asiagenus had returned after their respective defeats, nor did cheering news come of their subsequent activities; Norbanus was now under halfhearted siege in Capua, while Scipio drifted around Etruria recruiting.

Toward the end of the year, the Senate thought about convening to debate what its—and Rome's—future held. Numbers were down to about a third of Sulla's original fairly plump body of men, between those who had streamed to join Sulla in Greece, and this latest outpouring anxious to align itself with Sulla now he was back in Italy. For despite the protestations of a group of senators who insisted upon calling themselves neutral, everyone in Rome from highest to lowest knew very well that the lines were drawn. All of Italy and Italian Gaul were not large enough to accommodate Sulla and Carbo in peaceful coexistence; they stood for opposite values, systems of government, ideas of where Rome ought to go. Sulla stood for the *mos maiorum*, the centuries-old customs and traditions which embodied the landed aristocrats as leaders in peace and war, whereas Carbo stood for the commercial and business leaders—the knights and the *tribuni aerarii*. As neither group would agree to share an equal dominance, one or the other would have to win dominance by means of another civil war.

That the Senate even toyed with the idea of meeting was due only to the return of Carbo from Italian Gaul, summoned from Ariminum by the tribune of the plebs Marcus Junius Brutus, he who had legislated the status of a fully Roman city for Capua. They met in Brutus's house on the Palatine, a place with which Gnaeus Papirius Carbo was very familiar; he and Brutus had been friends for many years. It was besides a discreeter location than Carbo's house, where (so rumor had it) even the boy who cleaned out the chamber pots was taking bribes from several people interested in knowing what Carbo was thinking of doing next.

That Brutus's house was free from corrupt servants was entirely thanks to Brutus's wife, Servilia, who ran her establishment more stringently by far than Scipio Asiagenus had his army. She tolerated no kind of misbehavior, seemed to have as many eyes in her head as Argus, and as many ears as a colony of bats. The servant who could outwit or outgeneral her did not exist, and the servant who was not afraid of her lasted scant days.

So it was that Brutus and Carbo could settle to their very private conversation in complete security. Except, of course, for Servilia herself. Nothing happened or was said in her house that she did not know about, and this very private conversation was not conducted out of her hearing, she made sure of that. The two men were inside Brutus's study with the doors shut, and Servilia crouched outside on the colonnade beneath the one open window. A cold and uncomfortable place for an eavesdropper, but Servilia thought that of little consequence compared to what might be said inside the cozy room.

They began with pleasantries.

"How is my father?" asked Brutus.

"He's well, sends you his regards."

"I'm surprised you can put up with him!" burst from Brutus, who stopped, obviously shocked at what he had said. "I'm sorry. I didn't mean to sound angry. I'm really not angry."

"Just somewhat bewildered that I can put up with him?"

"Yes."

"He's your father," said Carbo in tones of comfort, "and he's an old man. I understand why you might find him a trouble. However, he isn't to me. It's as simple as that. After Verres absconded with what was left of my governor's allowance, I had to find a replacement quaestor anyway. Your dad and I have been friends ever since he returned with Marius from exile, as you well know." Carbo paused, probably to pat Brutus on the arm, thought the eavesdropper cynically; she knew how Carbo handled her husband. He then went on. "When you married, he bought you this house so he wouldn't be underfoot. What he didn't count on was the loneliness of living by himself after you and he had been—well, bachelors together might be the best way to put it—for so long. I imagine he made a nuisance of himself, and may have annoyed your wife. So when I wrote and asked him to be my new proquaestor, he accepted with alacrity. I see no need for guilt in you, Brutus. He's happy where he is."

"Thank you," said Brutus with a sigh.

"Now what's so urgent I had to come in person?"

"The elections. Since the desertion of everyone's friend, Philippus, morale in Rome has plummeted. No one will lead, no one has the courage to lead. That's why I felt you had to come to Rome, at least until after the elections. I can find no one well qualified who wants to be consul! No one qualified wants to hold *any* position of importance, for that matter," said Brutus nervously; he was a nervous man.

"What about Sertorius?"

"He's a stickler, you know that. I wrote to him in Sinuessa and begged him to stand for the consulship, but he declined. For two reasons, though I had expected only one—that he is still a praetor, and ought to wait the customary two years before being consul. I had hoped to talk him over that hurdle, and might have, had it been his only reason. The second reason I found impossible."

"What was his second reason?"

"He said Rome was finished, that he refused to be consul in a place full of cowards and opportunists."

"Elegantly put!"

"He would be governor of Nearer Spain, he said, and take himself right away."

"*Fellator!*" snarled Carbo.

Brutus, who did not like strong language, said nothing to this, and apparently had nothing further to say on any subject, as nothing was said for some time.

Exasperated, the listener on the colonnade applied her eye to the ornate lattice of the shutter, and saw Carbo and her husband sitting one on either side of Brutus's desk. They might, she thought idly, have been brothers— both very dark, both rather homely of features, and neither particularly tall nor particularly well built.

Why, she had asked herself often, had Fortune not favored her with a more impressive-looking husband, one she could be sure would shine politically? Of a military career for Brutus she had abandoned hope early, so politics it must be. But the best Brutus could think of was to legislate to give Capua the status of a Roman city. Not a bad idea—and certainly it had saved his tribunate of the plebs from utter banality!—but he would never be remembered as one of the great tribunes of the plebs, like her Uncle Drusus.

Brutus had been Uncle Mamercus's choice, though in himself Uncle Mamercus was mind and body Sulla's man, and had been in Greece with Sulla at the time it became necessary to find a husband for the eldest of his six wards, Servilia. They were all still living in Rome under the chaperonage of a poor relation, Gnaea, and her mother, Porcia Liciniana—a terrifying woman! Any guardian, no matter how geographically removed from his wards he might happen to be, need have no worry about the virtue and moral status of a child living under the thumb of Porcia Liciniana! Even her daughter, Gnaea, just grew plainer and more spinsterish as the years passed.

Thus it had been Porcia Liciniana who had received the suitors for Servilia's hand in marriage as her eighteenth birthday approached, and Porcia Liciniana who had transmitted relevant information about the various suitors to Uncle Mamercus in the east. Together with penetrating remarks about virtue, morality, prudence, temperance, and all the other qualities she considered desirable in a husband. And though Porcia Liciniana had never once committed the gross solecism of expressing an outright preference for one suitor above any other, those penetrating remarks of hers did sink into Uncle Mamercus's mind. After all, Servilia had a huge dowry and the felicitude of a splendid old patrician name, and was, Uncle Mamercus had been assured by Porcia Liciniana, not unattractive in her person besides.

So Uncle Mamercus took the easy way out; he chose the man Porcia Liciniana had hinted about most heavily. Marcus Junius Brutus. Since he was a senator in his early thirties, he was deemed old enough to be beyond youthful follies and indiscretions; he would be the head of his branch of the family when Old Brutus died (which could not be too far away, said Porcia Liciniana); and he was a wealthy man of impeccable (if plebeian) ancestry.

Servilia herself did not know him, and even after Porcia Liciniana informed her of her impending marriage, she was not allowed to meet Brutus until their wedding day arrived. That this antique custom was levied upon her was not due to the daunting Porcia Liciniana; it was rather the direct outcome of a childhood punishment. Because she had served as her estranged father's spy in the household of her Uncle Drusus, her Uncle Drusus had sentenced her to a form of domestic imprisonment: she was never to be allowed to have her own room or any vestige of privacy within his house, and never to be allowed to leave that house unless accompanied by people who would police her smallest step or expression. And all that had been years and years before she reached marriageable age, and every adult in her life at that time—mother, father, aunt, uncle, grandmother, stepfather—was long dead. But still the rule continued to be enforced.

No exaggeration then to say that Servilia was so anxious to marry and be gone from Uncle Drusus's house that she would hardly have cared who her husband was. To her, he had come to represent liberation from a detested regimen. But on learning his name, she had closed her eyes in profound relief. A man of her own class and background rather than the country squire she had expected—the country squire her Uncle Drusus during his lifetime had more than once threatened would be her husband when she grew up. Luckily Uncle Mamercus could see no advantage in marrying his niece below her station—nor could Porcia Liciniana.

Off to the house of Marcus Junius Brutus she went, a new and very thankful bride, and with her went her enormous dowry of two hundred talents—five million sesterces. What was more, it would remain hers. Uncle Mamercus had invested it well enough to ensure her a good income of her own, and directed that upon her death it should go to her female children. As her new husband, Brutus, had plenty of money of his own, the arrangement concerning her dowry did not disappoint him. Indeed, it meant that he had acquired a wife of the highest patrician aristocracy who would always be able to pay for her own upkeep—be it slaves, wages for slaves, clothing, jewelry, houses, or other expenses she incurred, she would have to pay for them herself. His money was safely his!

Aside from freedom to go where she pleased and see whomever she pleased, marriage for Servilia turned out to be a singularly joyless affair. Her husband had been a bachelor too long, no mother or other woman in his house; his ways were set, and did not include a wife. He shared nothing with her—even, she felt, his body. If he asked friends to dinner, she was told to absent herself from the dining room; his study was forbidden to her at all times; he never sought her out to discuss anything of any kind with her; he never showed her anything he bought or acquired; he never requested her company when he visited any of his country villas. As for his body—well, it was just a thing which from time to time visited her room and excited her not at all. Of privacy, she suddenly found she had far more than the long years without privacy now made comfortable or welcome. As her husband liked to sleep alone, she didn't even have someone else in the cubicle where she slept, and found the silence horrifying.

So it was that marriage turned out to be merely a variation on the theme which had dogged her almost from infancy: she was important to no one, she mattered to no one. The only way she had managed to matter was by being nasty, spiteful, vicious, and this side of herself every servant in the house knew to his or her cost. But to her husband she never showed this side of herself, for she knew he did not love her, and that therefore divorce was never far away. To Brutus, she was unfailingly pleasant. To the servants, she was unfailingly hard.

Brutus did his duty, however. Two years a wife, Servilia fell pregnant. Like her mother, she was properly formed for bearing children, and suffered not a bit. Even labor was not the nightmare agony she had been led to believe; she brought forth her son within seven hours on an icy March night, and was able to revel in him when he was given to her, washed and sweet.

Little wonder then that baby Brutus expanded to fill every vacant corner of his mother's love-starved life—that she would not let any other woman give him milk, and cared for him entirely herself, and put his crib in her own sleeping cubicle, and from his birth was wrapped in him to the exclusion of all else.

Why then did Servilia bother to listen outside the study on that freezing day late in November of the year Sulla landed in Italy? Certainly not because her husband's political activities interested her for his sake. She listened because he was the father of her beloved son, and she had made a vow that she would safeguard her son's inheritances, reputation, future welfare. It meant she had to keep herself informed about *everything*. Nothing must escape her! Especially her husband's political activities.

Servilia didn't care for Carbo, though she acknowledged that he was no lightweight. But she had correctly assessed him as one who would look after his own interests ahead of Rome's; and she wasn't sure that Brutus was clearheaded enough to see Carbo's deficiencies. The presence of Sulla in Italy worried her deeply, for she was possessed of a genuinely political mind, and could see the pattern of future events more acutely than most men who had spent half a lifetime in the Senate. Of one thing she was sure; that Carbo didn't have sufficient strength in him to hold Rome together in the teeth of a man like Sulla.

She took her eye away, presented her ear to the lattice instead, and sank to her knees on the painfully cold terrazzo floor. It was beginning to snow again—a boon! The flakes formed a veil between her muffled body and the hive of domestic activity at the far end of the peristyle garden, where the kitchens were, and servants pattered back and forth. Not that fear of detection concerned her; Brutus's household would never have dared question her right to be anywhere she liked in any kind of posture. It was more that she liked to appear to Brutus's household in the light of a superior being, and superior beings did not kneel outside a husband's window to eavesdrop.

Suddenly she tensed, pressed her ear closer. Carbo and her husband were talking again!

"There are some good men among those eligible to run for praetor," Brutus was saying. "Carrinas and Damasippus are as capable as they are popular."

"Huh!" from Carbo. "Like me, they let a hairless youth beat them in battle—but unlike me, they at least had been warned that Pompeius is as ruthless as his father, and ten times as crafty. If Pompeius stood for praetor, he'd win more votes than Carrinas and Damasippus put together."

"Pompeius's veterans carried the day," said Brutus in a reasonable tone.

"Maybe. But if so, then Pompeius let them do their job without interference." Impatient, it seemed, to leap into the future, Carbo now changed the subject. "Praetors are not what concern me, Brutus. I'm worried about the consulship—thanks to your predictions of gloom! If necessary, I'll stand for consul myself. But whom can I take for a colleague? Who in this wretched city is capable of shoring me up rather than dragging me down? There will be war in the spring, nothing is surer. Sulla's not been well, but my intelligence sources say he'll face the next campaigning season in high fettle."

"Illness was not his only reason for hanging back this past year," said Brutus. "We've heard rumors that he's stayed inert to give Rome the chance to capitulate without a war."

"Then he stayed inert in vain!" said Carbo savagely. "Oh, enough of these speculations! Whom can I take as my fellow consul?"

"Have you no ideas?" asked Brutus.

"Not a one. I need someone capable of firing people's spirits—someone who will inspire the young men to enlist, and the old men to wish they could enlist. A man like Sertorius. But you say flatly that he won't consent."

"What about Marcus Marius Gratidianus, then?"

"He's a Marius by adoption, and that's not good enough. I wanted Sertorius because he's a Marius by blood."

There was a pause, but not of a helpless kind; hearing an indrawn breath from her husband, the listener outside the window stiffened to absolute stillness, determined not to miss a single word of what was coming.

"If it's a Marius you want," said Brutus slowly, "why not Young Marius?"

Another pause ensued, of the thunderstruck variety. Then Carbo said, "That's not possible! *Edepol,* Brutus, he's not much more than twenty years old!"

"Twenty-six, actually."

"He's four years too young for the Senate!"

"There's no constitutionally official age, in spite of the *lex Villia annalis.* Custom rules. So I suggest you have Perperna appoint him to the Senate at once."

"He's not his father's bootlace!" cried Carbo.

"Does that matter? Does it, Gnaeus Papirius? Really? I admit that in Sertorius you would have found your ideal member of the Marii—no one in Rome commands soldiers better, or is more respected by them. But he won't consent. So who else is there except Young Marius?"

"They'd certainly flock to enlist," said Carbo softly.

"And fight for him like the Spartans for Leonidas."

"Do *you* think he could do it?"

"I think he'd like to try."

"You mean he's already expressed a wish to be consul?"

Brutus laughed, something he was not prone to do. "No, Carbo, of course not! Though he's a conceited sort of fellow, he's not actually very ambitious. I simply mean that I think if you went to him and offered him the chance, he'd jump at it. Nothing so far in his life has presented him with any opportunity to emulate his father. And in one respect at least, this will give him the opportunity to surpass his father. Gaius Marius came late into office. Young Marius will be consul at a younger age even than Scipio Africanus. No matter how he fares, there's fame in that for him."

"If he fares half as well as Scipio Africanus, Rome stands in no danger from Sulla."

"Don't hope for a Scipio Africanus in Young Marius," warned Brutus. "The only way he could prevent Cato the Consul from losing a battle was to stab him in the back."

Carbo laughed, something he did often. "Well, that was a bit of luck for Cinna at least! Old Marius paid him a fortune not to press a charge of murder."

"Yes," said Brutus, sounding very serious, "but that episode should point out to you some of the difficulties you'll face with Young Marius as your colleague in the consulship."

"Don't turn my back?"

"Don't turn your best troops over to him. Let him prove he can general troops before you do that."

There came the noise of chair legs scraping; Servilia got to her feet and fled to the warmth of her workroom, where the young girl who did the nursery laundry was enjoying a rare chance to cuddle baby Brutus.

The flare of scorching jealousy leaped inside Servilia before she could control it; her hand flashed out, cracked so hard against the girl's cheek that she fell from her perch on the crib, and in so doing, dropped the baby. Who didn't reach the floor because his mother swooped to catch him. Then, clasping him fiercely to her breast, Servilia literally kicked the girl from the room.

"Tomorrow you'll be sold!" she shrieked down the length of the colonnade enclosing the peristyle garden. Her voice changed, she merely shouted now: "Ditus! Ditus!"

The steward, whose flowery name was Epaphroditus but was usually addressed as Ditus, came at the run. "Yes, *domina*?"

"That girl—the Gaul you gave me to wash Baby's things—flog her and sell her as a bad slave."

The steward gaped. "But *domina,* she's excellent! Not only does she wash well, she's absolutely devoted to Baby!"

Servilia slapped Epaphroditus quite as hard as she had the girl, then demonstrated that she knew how to use a choice obscenity. "Now listen to me, you pampered, over-fed Greek *fellator*! When I give you an order you'll obey it without a word, let alone an argument! I don't care whose property you are, so don't go whining to the master, or you'll rue it! Now fetch the girl to your office and wait for me. You like her, so you won't flog her hard enough unless I'm there to see it."

The crimson mark of her hand standing out on his face was complete to its fingers, but it didn't provoke the terror in him that her words did. Epaphroditus bolted.

Servilia didn't ask for another maid; instead, she herself wrapped baby Brutus warmly in a fine wool shawl, and carried him down to the steward's office. The girl was tied down and a weeping Epaphroditus forced, under the basilisk glare of his mistress, to flog her until her back turned to bright red jelly and gobbets of her flesh flew everywhere. Incessant screams erupted from the room into the snow-muffled air, but the snow could not muffle those screams. Nor did the master appear to demand what was going on, for Brutus had gone with Carbo to see Young Marius, as Servilia had guessed.

Finally Servilia nodded. The steward's arm fell. She walked up to inspect his handiwork closely, and looked satisfied. "Yes, good! She'll never grow skin back on that mess again. No point in offering her for sale, she wouldn't fetch a single sestertius. Crucify her. Out there in the peristyle. She'll serve as a warning to the rest of you. And don't break her legs! Let her die slowly."

Back to her workroom Servilia marched, there to unwrap her son and change his linen diaper. After which she sat him on her lap and held him out at arm's length to adore him, leaning forward occasionally to kiss him tenderly and talk to him in a soft, slightly growling voice.

They made a sufficiently pretty picture, the small dark child upon his small dark mother's knee. She was a beautiful woman, Servilia, endowed with a firmly voluptuous figure and one of those little pointed faces which have an air of many secrets in a stilly folded mouth and thickly lidded, hooded eyes. The child, however, owned only his infant's beauty, for in truth he was plain and rather torpid—what people called a "good baby" in that he cried hardly at all and made no fusses.

And so when he came home from the house of Young Marius did Brutus find them, and listened without comment to the coldly narrated story of the negligent laundress and her punishment. As he would never have dared to interfere with Servilia's smoothly efficient domestic arrangements (his house had never run as well before he married her, so much was sure), he made no alterations to his wife's sentence, and when his steward came to him later at his summons, did not remark upon the snow-smothered figure tied lolling to a cross in the garden.

"Caesar! Where are you, Caesar?"

He came strolling barefooted out of what used to be his father's study, a pen in one hand and a roll of paper in the other, wearing no more than a thin tunic. Frowning, because his mother's voice had interrupted his train of thought.

But she, swaddled in layer upon layer of exquisitely fine home-woven woolen fabric, was more concerned with the welfare of his body than the output of his mind, and said testily, "Oh, why will you ignore the cold? You do, you know! And no slippers either! Caesar, your horoscope suggests that you will suffer a terrible illness at about this time in your life, and you're aware it does. Why do you tempt the lady Fortune to touch the line of that

evil aspect and bring it into being? Horoscopes are commissioned at birth to
ensure that potential risks can be prevented from becoming real. *Be good!*''

Her perturbation was absolutely genuine—and he knew it—so he gave
her the smile for which he was already famous, a kind of unspoken apology
that did not threaten his pride.

"What is it?" he asked, resigned the moment he set eyes on her to the
fact that his work would have to wait; she was clad for going out.

"We've been sent for to your Aunt Julia's."

"At this time of day? In this weather?"

"I'm glad you've noticed the weather! Not that it prompts you to dress
sensibly," said Aurelia.

"I do have a brazier, Mater. In fact, I have two."

"Then go into the warmth and change," she said. "It is freezing in
here, with the wind whistling down the light well." Before he turned to go,
she added, "Best find Lucius Decumius. We're *all* asked."

That meant both his sisters, which surprised him—it must be a very
important family conference! Almost he opened his mouth to assure his mother
that he didn't need Lucius Decumius, that a hundred women would be safe
under his protection; then he shut it. He wouldn't win, so why try? Aurelia
always knew how she wanted things done.

When he emerged from his rooms he was wearing the regalia of the
flamen Dialis, though in weather like this he wore three tunics beneath it,
woolen breeches to below his knees, and thick socks inside a pair of baggy
boots without straps or laces. His priest's *laena* took the place of another
man's toga; this clumsy double-layered garment was cut on the full circle,
contained a hole in its middle through which he poked his head, and was
richly colored in broad stripes of alternating scarlet and purple. It reached to
his knees and completely concealed his arms and hands, which meant, he
thought ruefully (trying to find some virtue in his detested *laena*), that he did
not need to wear mittens in this icy storm. Atop his head sat the *apex,* a
close-fitting ivory helmet surmounted by a spike upon which was impaled a
thick disc of wool.

Since officially becoming a man, Caesar had adhered to the taboos which
hedged the *flamen Dialis* around; he had abandoned military practice on the
Campus Martius, he allowed no iron to touch his person, he wore no knots
or buckles, said hello to no dog, had his footwear made from the leather of
an animal killed accidentally, and ate only those things his role as *flamen
Dialis* permitted. That his chin displayed no beard was because he shaved
with a bronze razor; that he had managed to wear boots when his priestly
clogs were impractical was only because he had personally designed a style

of boot to fit well without using the normal devices which made it snug around ankle and calf.

Not even his mother knew how deeply he loathed his lifelong sentence as Priest of Jupiter. When he had become a man at half-past fifteen, he had assumed the senseless shibboleths of his flaminate without a murmur or a look, and Aurelia had heaved a sigh of relief. The early rebellion had not lasted. What she couldn't know was his true reason for obeying: he was a Roman to his core, which meant he was committed absolutely to the customs of his country, and he was inordinately superstitious. He *had* to obey! If he did not, he would never obtain the favor of Fortune. She would not smile upon him or his endeavors, he would have no luck. For despite this hideous lifelong sentence, he still believed Fortune would find a way out for him— *if* he did his best to serve Jupiter Optimus Maximus as his special priest.

Thus obedience did not mean reconciliation, as Aurelia thought it did. Obedience only meant that with every passing day he hated being *flamen Dialis* more. And hated it most because under the law there could be no escape. Old Gaius Marius had succeeded in shackling him forever. Unless Fortune rescued him.

Caesar was seventeen, would not be eighteen until another seven months had elapsed; but he looked older, and he carried himself like a consular who had also been censor. The height and the broad shoulders helped, of course, allied as they were to a gracefully muscular frame. His father had been dead for two and a half years, which meant he had come very early into his title of *paterfamilias,* and now wore it naturally. The extreme good looks of his boyhood had not faded, though they had become more manly—his nose, thank all the gods, had lengthened to a form properly, bumpily Roman, and saved him from a prettiness which would have been a great burden to one who so ardently desired to be everything a man should be—soldier, statesman, lover of women without suspicion that he was also a lover of men.

His family was assembled in the reception room, garbed for a long, cold walk. Except, that is, for his wife, Cinnilla. At eleven years of age she was not considered adult enough to attend these rare gatherings of the clan. However, she was present, the only small and dark member of the house; when Caesar entered, her pansy-black eyes flew to his face just as they always did. He adored her, moved to her now and swept her off her feet to hold her in his arms, kissing her soft pink cheek with his eyes closed the better to inhale the exquisite perfume of a child kept clean and balmed by his mother.

"Doomed to stay home?" he asked, kissing her cheek again.

"One day I'll be big enough," she said, showing dimples in her enchanting smile.

"Indeed you will! And then you'll be more important than Mater, because you'll be the mistress of the house." He put the child down, smoothed his hand over her mass of waving black hair, and winked at Aurelia.

"I won't be the mistress of this house," she said solemnly. "I'll be the *flaminica Dialis,* and mistress of a State house."

"True," he said lightly. "How could I have forgotten?"

Out into the driving snow he went, up past the shops which nestled in the outer wall of Aurelia's apartment house, to the rounded apex of that triangular building. Here was located what appeared to be a tavern, yet was not; it was the headquarters of the College of Crossroads Brethren who supervised the well-being and spiritual life of the crossroads outside its double doors, especially the towerlike shrine to the Lares and the big fountain which now flowed sluggishly amid a tumble of ethereally blue icicles, so cold was this winter.

Lucius Decumius was in residence at his usual table in the back left-hand corner of the huge, clean room. Grizzled these days but face as unlined as ever, he had recently admitted his two sons to membership, and was training them in all the multifarious activities of his college. So they sat one on either side of him like the two lions which always flanked a statue of Magna Mater—grave, tawny, thick-maned, yellow-eyed, claws furled. Not that Lucius Decumius in any way resembled Magna Mater! He was little, skinny, and anonymous-looking; his sons took after their mother, who was a large Celtic lady from the Ager Gallicus. To no one unacquainted with him did he seem what he actually was—brave, tortuously subtle, amoral, enormously intelligent, loyal.

The three Decumii brightened when Caesar walked through the door, but only Lucius Decumius rose. Threading his way between the tables and benches, he reached Caesar, stood on tiptoe and kissed the young man on the lips more fondly than he did either of his sons. It was the kiss of a father, though it was given to someone whose only connection with him lay tangled amid the cords of his not inconsiderable heart.

"My boy!" he crowed, and took Caesar's hand.

"Hello, dad," Caesar answered with a smile, lifted Lucius Decumius's fingers and pressed them against his cold cheek.

"Been sweeping out some dead man's house?" asked Lucius Decumius, in reference to Caesar's priestly regalia. "Nasty weather for dying! Have a cup of wine to warm you, eh?"

Caesar grimaced. He had never managed to cultivate a real liking for wine, try though Lucius Decumius and his brethren had to instill it in him. "No time, dad. I'm here to borrow a couple of the brethren. I have to take my mother and sisters to the house of Gaius Marius, and she doesn't trust me to do it on my own, of course.''

"Wise woman, your mother," said Lucius Decumius with a look of wicked glee. He beckoned to his sons, who rose at once and came to join him. "Togs on, lads! We're going to take the ladies to the house of Gaius Marius.''

No resentment of their father's obvious preference for Gaius Julius Caesar colored the emotions of Lucius Decumius Junior or young Marcus Decumius; they simply nodded, clapped Caesar on the back in great affection, and went off to find their warmest clothing.

"Don't come, dad," said Caesar. "Stay here out of the cold."

But that didn't suit Lucius Decumius, who allowed his sons to dress him much as a doting mother might have dressed her toddling offspring. "Where's that oaf Burgundus?" he asked as they spilled out into the swirling snow.

Caesar chuckled. "No use to anyone at the moment! Mater sent him down to Bovillae with Cardixa. She might have started breeding late, but she's produced one baby giant every year since she first set eyes on Burgundus. This will be number four, as you well know."

"You'll never be short of bodyguards when you're consul."

Caesar shivered, but not from the cold. "I'll never be consul," he said harshly, then lifted his shoulders and tried to be pleasant. "My mother says it's like feeding a tribe of Titans. Ye gods, they can eat!"

"Good people, but."

"Yes, good people," said Caesar.

By this time they had reached the outer door of Aurelia's apartment, and collected the womenfolk. Other aristocratic ladies might have elected to ride in litters, especially in such weather, but not the Julian ladies. They walked, their progress down the Fauces Suburae somewhat eased by the Decumius sons, who shuffled ahead to blaze a path through the accumulating snow.

The Forum Romanum was utterly deserted, and looked odd bled of its vividly colored columns and walls and roofs and statues; everything was marble-white, seemed sunk in a deep and dreamless sleep. And the imposing statue of Gaius Marius near the rostra had a bank of snow perched on either bushy eyebrow, masking the normally fierce glare of his dark eyes.

Up the Hill of the Bankers they toiled, through the vast portals of the Fontinalis Gate, and so to the door of Gaius Marius's house. As its peristyle garden lay at the back of the mansion, they entered straight into the foyer, and there peeled off outer garments (save for Caesar, doomed to wear his regalia). Lucius Decumius and his sons were taken away by the steward,

Strophantes, to sample some excellent food and wine, while Caesar and the women entered the atrium.

Had the weather been less unnaturally cold, they might have remained there, since it was well past dinnertime, but the open rectangle of the *compluvium* in the roof was acting like a vortex, and the pool below it was a twinkling crust of rapidly melting snowflakes.

Young Marius appeared then to welcome them and usher them through into the dining room, which would be warmer, he said. He looked, thought Caesar warily, almost afire with happiness, and the emotion suited him. As tall as Caesar (who was his first cousin), he was more heavily built, fair of hair and grey of eye, handsome, impressive. Physically far more attractive than his father, he yet lacked that vital something which had made of Gaius Marius one of the Roman immortals. Many generations would go by, Caesar reflected, before every schoolchild ceased to learn about the exploits of Gaius Marius. Such would not be the lot of his son, Young Marius.

This was a house Caesar loathed visiting; too much had happened to him here. While other boys of his age had been heedlessly frittering away their time playing on the Campus Martius, he had been required to report here every day to act as nurse/companion to the aged and vindictive Gaius Marius. And though he had swept strenuously with his sacred broom after Marius died here, that malign presence still lingered. Or so Caesar thought. Once he had admired and loved Gaius Marius. But then Gaius Marius had appointed him the special priest of Jupiter, and in that one stroke had rendered it impossible for Caesar ever to rival him. No iron, no weapons, no sight of death—no military career for the *flamen Dialis*! An automatic membership in the Senate without the right to stand for election as a magistrate—no political career for the *flamen Dialis*! It was Caesar's fate to be honored without earning that honor, revered without earning that reverence. The *flamen Dialis* was a creature belonging to the State, housed and paid and fed by the State, a prisoner of the *mos maiorum,* the established practices of custom and tradition.

But of course Caesar's revulsion could never endure past the moment in which he set eyes upon his Aunt Julia. His father's sister, the widow of Gaius Marius. And, differently from his mother, the person in the world he loved the most. Indeed, he loved her more than he did his mother, if love could be classified as a simple rush of sheer emotion. His mother was permanently grafted to his intellect because she was adversary, adherent, critic, companion, equal. Whereas Aunt Julia enfolded him in her arms and kissed him on the lips, beamed at him with her soft grey eyes innocent of the faintest condemnation. Life for him without either one was unthinkable.

Julia and Aurelia elected to sit side by side on the same couch, ill at ease because they were women, and women did not recline on couches. Forbidden by custom to lie comfortably, they perched on the edge with their feet dangling clear of the floor and their backs unsupported.

"Can't you give the women chairs?" asked Caesar of Young Marius as he shoved bolsters behind his mother and his aunt.

"Thank you, nephew, we'll manage now you've propped us up," said Julia, always the peacemaker. "I don't think the house has enough chairs for all of us! This is a conference of women."

An inalienable truth, acknowledged Caesar ruefully. The male element of this family was reduced to two men: Young Marius and Caesar. Both only sons of dead fathers.

Of women, there were more. Had Rome been present to see Julia and Aurelia side by side, Rome would have enjoyed the spectacle of two of her most beautiful women encompassed in one glance. Though both were tall and slim, Julia owned the innate grace of the Caesars, whereas Aurelia moved with brisk, no-nonsense economy. One, Julia, had softly waving blonde hair and widely opened grey eyes, and might have posed for the statue of Cloelia in the upper Forum Romanum. The other, Aurelia, had ice-brown hair and a quality of beauty which had, in her youth, caused her to be likened to Helen of Troy. Dark brows and lashes, a pair of deeply set eyes many of the men who had tried to marry her had insisted were purple, and the profile of a Greek goddess.

Julia was now forty-five years old to Aurelia's forty. Both had been widowed in distressing though very different circumstances.

Gaius Marius had died of his third and most massive stroke, but only after launching and pursuing an orgy of murder no one in Rome would ever forget. All his enemies had died—and some of his friends—and the rostra had bristled with the heads as thickly as pins in a cushion. With this sorrow, Julia lived.

Aurelia's husband, loyal to Cinna after the death of Marius—as was only fitting in one whose son was married to Cinna's younger daughter—had gone to Etruria to recruit troops. One summer morning in Pisae he had bent over to lace up his boot, and died. A ruptured blood vessel in his brain was the conclusion reached at postmortem; he was burned on a pyre without a single member of his family present, and his ashes were then sent home to his wife. Who did not even know her husband was dead when Cinna's messenger came to present her with the funerary urn. How she felt, what she thought, no one knew. Even her son, made head of his family a month short of his fifteenth birthday. No tear had she shed that anyone had seen, and the look on her face had not changed. For she was Aurelia, fastened up inside herself, apparently more attached to her work as landlady of a busy insula than to any human being save for her son.

Young Marius had no sisters, but Caesar had two older than himself. Both of them looked like their Aunt Julia; there were strong echoes of Aurelia in Caesar's face, but not in either of his sisters'.

Julia Major, called Lia, was now twenty-one years old, and carried the faintest suggestion of something careworn in her expression. Not without reason. Her first husband, a penniless patrician by name of Lucius Pinarius, had been the love of her heart, so she had been allowed—albeit reluctantly—to marry him. A son had arrived less than a year later, and shortly after that happy event (which did not turn out to have the hoped-for sobering effect on Lucius Pinarius's character or behavior), Lucius Pinarius died in mysterious circumstances. Murder by a confederate was thought likely, but no proof could be found. So Lia, aged nineteen, found herself a widow in such an impoverished state that she had been obliged to return to live under her mother's roof. But between her marriage and her widowhood the identity of the *paterfamilias* had changed, and she now discovered that her young brother was not nearly as softhearted or malleable as her father had been. She must marry again, said Caesar—but a man of *his* choosing, for, "It is clear to me," he said to her dispassionately, "that, left to your own devices, you will pick another idiot."

Quite how or where Caesar had found Quintus Pedius, no one knew (though some suspected a collaboration with Lucius Decumius, who might be a seedy little man of the Fourth Class, but who had remarkable contacts), but home he came with Quintus Pedius, and betrothed his widowed oldest sister to this stolid, upright Campanian knight of good but not noble family. He was not handsome. He was not dashing. At forty, he was not even very young. But he was colossally rich and almost pathetically grateful for the chance to marry a lovely and youthful woman of the most exalted patrician nobility. Lia had swallowed, looked at her fifteen-year-old brother, and graciously accepted; even at that age, Caesar could put something into his face and eyes that killed argument before it was born.

Luckily the marriage had turned out well. Lucius Pinarius might have been handsome and dashing and young, but as a husband he had been disappointing. Now Lia discovered that there were many compensations in being the darling of a rich man twice her age, and as time went on she grew very fond of her uninspiring second husband. She bore him a son, and was so settled into her delightfully luxurious life on her husband's estates outside Teanum Sidicinum that when Scipio Asiagenus and then Sulla had established camps in the neighborhood, she flatly refused to go home to her mother, who would, she knew, regulate her exercise, her diet, her sons and her life to suit her own austere ideas. Of course Aurelia had arrived in person (after, it seemed, an unexpected meeting with Sulla—a meeting about which she had said little beyond mentioning it), and Lia had been bundled to Rome. Without her sons, alas; Quintus Pedius had preferred to keep them with him in Teanum.

Julia Minor, called Ju-Ju, had been married in the early part of this year, not long after her eighteenth birthday. No chance that she would be allowed to pick someone unsuitable! Caesar did the picking, though she had railed against his high-handed usurpation of a task she felt herself fully able to perform. Of course he won. Home he came with another colossally rich suitor, this time of an old senatorial family, and himself a backbencher senator content to stay on the back benches. He hailed from Aricia, just down the Via Appia from the Caesar lands at Bovillae, and that fact made him Latin, which was one cut above mere Campanian. After setting eyes on Marcus Atius Balbus, Ju-Ju had married him without a murmur; compared to Quintus Pedius he was quite reasonable, being a mere thirty-seven, and actually handsome for such an advanced age.

Because Marcus Atius Balbus was a senator, he owned a *domus* in Rome as well as enormous estates at Aricia, so Ju-Ju could congratulate herself on yet one more advantage over her elder sister; she at least lived more or less permanently in Rome! On that late afternoon when all the family was summoned to the house of Gaius Marius, she was beginning to be heavy with child. Not that her pregnancy had prevented her mother from making her walk!

"It isn't good for pregnant women to coddle themselves," said Aurelia. "That's why so many of them die in childbirth."

"I thought you said they died because they ate nothing but fava beans," Ju-Ju had countered, wistfully eyeing the litter in which she had made the journey from her husband's house on the Carinae to her mother's apartment building in the Subura.

"Those too. Pythagorean physicians are a menace."

One more woman was present, though by blood she was not related to any of the others—or at least, not closely related. Her name was Mucia Tertia, and she was Young Marius's wife. The only daughter of Scaevola Pontifex Maximus, she had been called Mucia Tertia to distinguish her from her two famous cousins, the daughters of Scaevola the Augur.

Though she wasn't precisely beautiful, Mucia Tertia had disturbed many a man's sleep. A muddy green in color, her eyes were abnormally far apart and thickly fringed by black lashes which were longer at the outer corners of her eyes, thereby accentuating the distance between them; though she never said so, she deliberately trimmed her lashes shorter at the inner corners of her eyes with a tiny pair of ivory scissors from Old Egypt. Mucia Tertia was well aware of the nature of her unusual attractions. Her long, straight nose somehow managed not to be a disadvantage, even if the purists did think there ought to be some sort of bump or break in it. Again, her mouth was far from the Roman ideal of beauty, being very wide; when she smiled, she showed what seemed like a hundred perfect teeth. But her lips were full and sensuous, and she had a thick, creamy skin which went well with her dark red hair.

Caesar for one found her alluring, and at half-past seventeen was already highly experienced in sexual matters. Every female in the Subura had indicated willingness to help such a lovely young man find his amatory feet, and few were deterred when they discovered Caesar insisted they be bathed and clean; the word had gone out very quickly that young Caesar was equipped with a couple of mighty weapons, *and* knew how best to use them.

Most of the reason Mucia Tertia interested Caesar lay in a certain quality of enigma she owned; try as he might, she was one person he couldn't see to the bottom of. She smiled readily to display those hundred perfect teeth, yet the smile never originated in her extraordinary eyes, and she gave off no clues of gesture or expression as to what she really thought.

She had been married for four years of apparent indifference, as much on Young Marius's side as on hers. Their conversation together was pleasantly chatty but quite formal; they never exchanged those glances of secret understanding most married couples did; no move did either make to touch the other, even when no one was looking; and they had no children. If the union *was* genuinely devoid of feeling, Young Marius for one certainly did not suffer; his philanderings were common knowledge. But what about Mucia Tertia, of whom no whisper had ever circulated concerning indiscretion, let alone infidelity? Was Mucia Tertia happy? Did she love Young Marius? Or did she hate him? Impossible to tell, and yet—and yet—Caesar's instincts said she was desperately unhappy.

The group had settled down, and every eye was now fixed on Young Marius, who perversely had elected to sit upon a chair. Not to be outdone, Caesar too drew up a chair, but far removed from where Young Marius sat in the hollow of the U formed by the three dining couches; he sat behind his mother's shoulder, on the outside of the U, and so could not see the faces of his most beloved women. To him, it seemed more important by far to look at Young Marius, Mucia Tertia, and the steward Strophantes, who had been asked to attend and who stood near the doorway, having quietly refused Young Marius's invitation to seat himself.

Wetting his lips—an unusual sign of nervousness—Young Marius began to speak. "Earlier this afternoon, I had a visit from Gnaeus Papirius Carbo and Marcus Junius Brutus."

"That's an odd combination," said Caesar, who didn't want his cousin to flow on without interruption; he wanted Young Marius a little flustered.

The look Young Marius flashed him was angry, but not angry enough to fluster his thinking. A start only.

Then Caesar found his ploy foiled. Said Young Marius, "They came to ask me if I would stand for the consulship in conjunction with Gnaeus Carbo. I said I would."

The stir was general. Caesar saw amazement on the faces of his sisters, a sudden spasm in his aunt's spine, a peculiar but unfathomable look in Mucia Tertia's remarkable eyes.

"My son, you're not even in the Senate," said Julia.

"I will be tomorrow, when Perperna puts me on the rolls."

"You haven't been quaestor, let alone praetor."

"The Senate is willing to waive the usual requirements."

"You don't have the experience or the knowledge!" Julia persisted, her voice despairing.

"My father was consul seven times. I grew up surrounded by consulars. Besides, you can't call Carbo inexperienced."

Asked Aurelia, "Why are we here?"

Young Marius shifted his earnest and appealing gaze from his mother to his aunt. "To talk the matter over between us, of course!" he said, a little blankly.

"Rubbish!" said Aurelia bluntly. "Not only have you made up your mind already, but you've also told Carbo you'll run as his colleague. It seems to me that you've dragged us out of our warm house just to listen to news the city gossip would have brought to our ears almost as quickly."

"That's not so, Aunt Aurelia!"

"Of course it's so!" snapped Aurelia.

Skin bright red, Young Marius turned back to his mother, a hand extended to her in appeal. "Mama, it's *not* so! I know I told Carbo I'd stand, but—but I *always* intended to listen to what my family had to say, truly! I can change my mind!"

"Hah! You won't change your mind," said Aurelia.

Julia's fingers fastened upon Aurelia's wrist. "Be quiet, Aurelia! I want no anger in this room."

"You're right, Aunt Julia—anger is the last emotion we want," said Caesar, inserting himself between his mother and his aunt. From this new vantage spot he stared at his first cousin intently. "Why did you say yes to Carbo?" he asked.

A question which didn't fool Young Marius for a moment. "Oh, give me credit for more intelligence than that, Caesar!" he said scornfully. "I said yes for the same reason you would have, if you didn't wear a *laena* and an *apex*."

"I can see why you'd think I would have said yes, but in actual fact I never would have. *In suo anno* is the best way."

"It's illegal," said Mucia Tertia unexpectedly.

"No," said Caesar before Young Marius could answer. "It's against the established custom and even against the *lex Villia annalis,* but it's not exactly illegal. It could only become prosecutably illegal if your husband usurped the position against the will of Senate and People. Senate and People can legislate to nullify the *lex Villia*. And that is what will happen. Senate and People will procure the necessary legislation, which means the only one who will declare it illegal is Sulla."

A silence fell. "That is the worst of it," said Julia, voice faltering. "You'll be in the field against Sulla."

"I would have been in the field against Sulla anyway, Mama," said Young Marius.

"But not as the inaugurated representative of Senate and People. To be consul is to accept ultimate responsibility. You will be leading Rome's armies." A tear trickled down Julia's cheek. "You'll be the focus of Sulla's thoughts, and he is the most formidable man! I don't know him as well as your Aunt Aurelia does, Gaius, but I know him quite well enough. I've even liked him, in the days when he used to take care of your father—he did, you know. He used to smooth over the little awkwardnesses which always seemed to happen around your father. A more patient and perceptive man than your father. A man of some honor too. But your father and Lucius Cornelius share one very important factor in common—when all else fails, from constitution to popular support, they are—or should that be were?—both capable of going to whatever lengths are necessary to achieve their aims. That's why both of them have marched on Rome in the past. And that is why Lucius Cornelius will march on Rome again if Rome takes this course, elects you consul. The very fact of your election will tell him that Rome intends to fight him to the end, that there can be no peaceful resolution." She sighed, wiped the tear away. "Sulla is why I wish you'd change your mind, dear Gaius. If you had his years and background, you might possibly win. But you do not. You cannot win. And I will lose my one and only child."

It was the plea of a reasonable and mature adult; Young Marius was neither, and his face as he listened to this heartfelt speech only set. His lips parted to answer.

"Well, Mater," said Caesar, getting in first, "as Aunt Julia says, you know Sulla better than any of the rest of us! How do you feel about it?"

Little discomposed Aurelia, and she had no intention of telling them the details of her last discomposure: that awful, tragic encounter with Sulla in his camp. "It is true, I do know Sulla well. I've even seen him within the last six months, as all of you know. But in the old days I was always the last person he saw before he left Rome, and the first person he saw when he came back. Between his goings and his comings, I hardly saw him at all. That is typical of Sulla. At heart he's an actor. He can't live without drama. And he knew how to make an otherwise innocuous situation pregnant with meaning. That's why he chose to see me at the moments he did. It invested my presence in his life with more color, more significance. Instead of a simple visit to a lady with whom he liked to talk of relatively unimportant things, each visit became a farewell or a reunion. He endowed me with portent, I think it would be fair to say that."

Caesar smiled at her. "You haven't answered my question, Mater," he said gently.

"Nor I have," said that extraordinary woman without alarm or guilt. "I will proceed to do so." She looked at Young Marius sternly. "What you must understand is that if you face Sulla as the inaugurated representative of the Senate and People—that is, as consul—you will endow yourself with portent as far as Sulla is concerned. Your age combined with the identity of your father Sulla will use to heighten the drama of his struggle to achieve dominance in Rome. All of which is scant comfort to your mother, nephew. For her sake, give up this idea! Face Sulla on the field as just another military tribune."

"How do you feel?" asked Young Marius of Caesar.

"I say—do it, cousin. Be consul ahead of your year."

"Lia?"

She turned troubled eyes toward her Aunt Julia and said, "Please don't do it, cousin!"

"Ju-Ju?"

"I agree with my sister."

"Wife?"

"You must go with your fortune."

"Strophantes?"

The old steward sighed. "*Domine,* do not do it!"

With nods that rocked his upper body gently, Young Marius sat back on his chair and flung an arm along its tall back. He pursed his mouth, blew through his nostrils softly. "Well, no surprises, at any rate," he said. "My female relatives and my steward exhort me not to step out of my time and status and imperil my person. Perhaps my aunt is trying to say that I will also imperil my reputation. My wife puts it all on the lap of Fortune—am I one of Fortune's favorites? And my cousin says I must go ahead."

He got to his feet, a not unimposing presence. "I will not go back on my word to Gnaeus Papirius Carbo and Marcus Junius Brutus. If Marcus Perperna agrees to enroll me in the Senate, and the Senate agrees to procure the necessary legislation, I will declare myself a candidate for the consulship."

"You haven't really told us why," said Aurelia.

"I would have thought that was obvious. Rome is desperate. Carbo can find no suitable colleague. So where did he turn? To the son of Gaius Marius. Rome loves me! Rome needs me! That is why," said the young man.

Only the oldest and loyalest of retainers would have found the courage to say what Strophantes did, speaking not only for the stricken mother, but for the father who was dead: "It is your father Rome loves, *domine*. Rome turns to you because of your father. Rome doesn't know you, except that you are the son of the man who saved her from the Germans, who won the first victories in the war against the Italians, and who was consul seven times. If you do this thing, it will be because you are your father's son, not because you are yourself."

Young Marius loved Strophantes, as the steward well knew; considering its implications, he took the steward's speech very well. His lips tightened, that was all. When Strophantes was done, he merely said, "I know. It is up to me to show Rome that Young Marius is the equal of his dear old dad."

Caesar looked at the floor, said nothing. Why, he was asking himself, didn't the crazy old man give the *laena* and *apex* of the *flamen Dialis* to someone else? I could do it. But Young Marius never will.

And so toward the end of December the electors in their Centuries met upon the Campus Martius in the place called after a sheepfold, and voted in Young Marius as senior consul, with Gnaeus Papirius Carbo as his junior colleague. The very fact that Young Marius polled far higher than did Carbo was an indication of Rome's desperation, her fears as well as her doubts. However, many who voted genuinely felt that *something* of Gaius Marius must have rubbed off on his son, and that under Young Marius victory against Sulla was a strong possibility.

In one respect the electoral results had highly gratifying consequences; recruitment, especially in Etruria and Umbria, accelerated at once. The sons and grandsons of Gaius Marius's clients flocked to join the son's legions, suddenly much lighter of heart, full of new confidence. And when Young Marius visited the enormous estates of his father, he was hailed as a savior, feted, adored.

Rome turned out in festive mood to see the new consuls inaugurated on the first day of January, and was not disappointed. Young Marius went through the ceremonies displaying a transparent happiness which endeared him to the hearts of all who watched; he looked magnificent, he smiled, he waved, he called out greetings to familiar faces in the crowd. And, since everybody knew where his mother was standing (beneath the stern statue of her late husband near the rostra), everybody saw the new senior consul leave his place in the procession in order to kiss her hands and her lips. And gesture a brave salute to his father.

Perhaps, thought Carbo cynically, the people of Rome needed to have Youth in power at this critical moment. Certainly it was many years since a crowd had given full-throated approval to a consul on his first day in office. Today it did. And by all the gods, Carbo finished his thought, hope that Rome did not come to regret her electoral bargain! For so far Young Marius's attitude had been cavalier; he seemed to assume as a matter of course that everything would just fall into his lap, that he would not need to work, that all the battles of the future were already safely won.

The omens were not good, though nothing untoward had been witnessed by the new consuls during their night watch atop the Capitol. What boded ill was an absence—an absence of such moment that no one could forget or ignore it. Where the great temple of Jupiter Optimus Maximus had reared on the highest point of the Capitoline Hill for five hundred years, there now existed only a heap of blackened, unrecognizable detritus. On the sixth day of Quinctilis of the year just ended, a fire had begun inside the Great God's house, and burned for seven long days. Nothing was left. Nothing. For the temple had been so old that no part of it save its podium was made of stone; the massive drums of its plain Doric columns were as wooden as its walls, its rafters, its interior paneling. Only its great size and solidity, rare and costly colors of paint, glorious murals and plenteous gilding had served to make it look a fitting abode for Jupiter Best and Greatest, who lived only in this one place; the idea of Principal Jupiter setting up house on top of the highest mountain—as Greek Zeus had done—was quite unacceptable to any Roman or Italian.

When the ashes had cooled sufficiently for the priests to inspect the site, disaster had piled on top of disaster. Of the gigantic terracotta statue of the God made by the Etruscan sculptor Vulca during Old Tarquin's reign as King

of Rome, there was no trace. The ivory statues of Jupiter's wife, Juno, and
his daughter Minerva had vanished too; as had the temple's eerie squatters,
Terminus the Boundary and Juventas of Youth, who had refused to move out
when King Tarquin had commenced the building of Jupiter Optimus Maximus's home. Law tablets and records of unparalleled antiquity had gone, as
had the Sibylline Books and many other prophetic documents upon which
Rome relied for godly guidance in times of crisis. Innumerable treasures made
of gold and silver had melted, even the solid gold statue of Victory given by
Hiero of Syracuse after Trasimene, and another massive statue in gilded bronze
of Victory driving a *biga*—a two-horsed chariot. The tortured lumps of admixed metals found among the detritus had been gathered up and given to
the smiths for refining, but the ingots the smiths had smelted (which went
into the Treasury beneath the temple of Saturn against the time when they
would be given to artisans to make new works) could not replace the immortal
names of the original sculptors—Praxiteles and Myron, Strongylion and Polyclitus, Scopas and Lysippus. Art and History had gone up in the same flames
as the earthly home of Jupiter Optimus Maximus.

Adjacent temples had also suffered, particularly that of Ops, who was
the mysterious guardian of Rome's public wealth and had no face or person;
the temple would have to be rebuilt and rededicated, so great had been the
damage. The temple of Fides Publica was badly hurt too. The heat of the
nearby fire had charred all the treaties and pacts fixed to its inside walls, as
well as the linen swaddle around the right hand of an ancient statue thought—
only thought!—to be Fides Publica herself. The other building which suffered
was new and made of marble, and therefore required little beyond fresh paint;
this was the temple to Honor and Virtue erected by Gaius Marius to house
his trophies of war, his military decorations and his gifts to Rome. What
perturbed every Roman was the significance of the distribution of the damage:
Jupiter Optimus Maximus was the guiding spirit of Rome; Ops was Rome's
public prosperity; Fides Publica was the spirit of good faith between Romans
and their gods; and Honor and Virtue were the two principal characteristics
of Rome's military glory. Thus every Roman asked himself and herself: was
the fire a sign that Rome's days of ascendancy were over? Was the fire a sign
that Rome was finished?

So it was that on this New Year's Day the consuls were the first ever
to enter office unhallowed by the shelter of Jupiter Best and Greatest. A
temporary shrine had been erected beneath a canopy at the foot of the blackened old stone podium upon which the temple used to stand, and here the
new consuls made their offerings, swore their oaths of office.

Bright hair hidden by his close-fitting ivory helmet, body hidden by the suffocating folds of his circular *laena*, Caesar the *flamen Dialis* attended the rites in his official capacity, though he had no active role to play; the ceremonies were conducted by the chief priest of the Republic, the Pontifex Maximus, Quintus Mucius Scaevola, father of Young Marius's wife.

Caesar stood there experiencing two separate and conflicting foci of pain: one, that the destruction of the Great Temple rendered the special priest of Jupiter religiously homeless, and the other, that he himself would never stand in purple-bordered toga to take office as consul. But he had learned to deal with pain, and throughout the rituals disciplined himself to stand straight, tall, devoid of expression.

The meeting of the Senate and the feast held afterward had been shifted from Jupiter Optimus Maximus to the Curia Hostilia, home of the Senate and a properly inaugurated temple. Though by age Caesar was disbarred from the interior of the Curia Hostilia, as *flamen Dialis* he was automatically a member of the Senate, so no one tried to stop his entering, and he listened impassively to the short, formal proceedings which Young Marius as senior consul got under way quite creditably. The governorships to commence in twelve months' time were apportioned out by lot to this year's praetors and both the consuls, the date of the feast of Jupiter Latiaris on the Alban Mount was determined, and other movable days of public or religious nature were also fixed.

As there was little the *flamen Dialis* could eat among the bountiful and expensive food offered after the meeting concluded, Caesar found an inconspicuous spot and set himself to listen to whatever conversations drifted past him as men sorted out their preferred couches. Rank dictated the positions of some, like those holding magistracies, priesthoods, augurships, but the bulk of the senators were at liberty to distribute themselves among cronies and settle to partake of viands the bottomless purse of Young Marius had provided.

It was a thin gathering, perhaps no more than a hundred strong, so many senators had fled to join Sulla, and by no means all of those present to witness the inauguration of the consuls were partial to the consuls or their plans. Quintus Lutatius Catulus was there, but no lover of Carbo's cause; his father, Catulus Caesar (who died during Marius's bloodbath) had been an implacable enemy of Marius's, and the son was cut from the same cloth, though not as gifted or educated. That, reflected the watching Caesar, was because his father's Julian blood had been diluted in the son by his mother, a Domitia of the Domitii Ahenobarbi—Famous Family stock, but not famous for intellect. Caesar didn't like him, a prejudice of looks; Catulus was weedy and undersized, and had his mother's Domitian red hair as well as her freckles. He was married to the sister of the man who reclined next to him on the same couch, Quintus Hortensius, and Quintus Hortensius (another noble stay-in-Rome neutral) was married to Catulus's sister, Lutatia. Still in his early thirties, Quintus Hortensius had become Rome's leading advocate under the rule of Cinna and Carbo, and was held by some to be the best legal mind Rome had ever produced. He was quite a handsome man, his taste for life's little luxuries was betrayed by a sensuous lower lip, and his taste for beautiful boys by the expression in his eyes as they rested upon Caesar. A veteran of such looks, Caesar extirpated any ideas Hortensius might have been forming by sucking his mouth in ridiculously and crossing his eyes; Hortensius flushed and turned his head immediately to look at Catulus.

At that moment a servant came to whisper to Caesar that his cousin demanded his presence at the far end of the room. Rising from the bottom-tier step where he had huddled himself to look, Caesar slopped in his backless clogs to where Young Marius and Carbo lay, kissed his cousin on the cheek, then perched himself on the edge of the curule podium behind the couch.

"Not eating?" asked Young Marius.

"There's not much I can eat."

"S'right, I forgot," mumbled Young Marius through a mouthful of fish. He swallowed it, and pointed to the huge platter laid out on the table in front of his couch. "There's nothing to stop you having some of that," he said.

Caesar eyed the partially dismembered carcass with distinct lack of enthusiasm; it was a licker-fish of the Tiber. "Thank you," he said, "but I never could see any virtue in eating shit."

That provoked a chuckle from Young Marius, but couldn't destroy his enjoyment in consuming a creature which thrived upon the excrement flowing out of Rome's vast sewers; Carbo, Caesar noted with amusement, was not so strong-stomached, for his hand, which had been in the act of reaching out to tear off a chunk of licker-fish, suddenly grabbed at a tiny roast chicken instead.

Of course here Caesar was more noticeable, but prominence carried considerable reward; he could see many more faces. While he exchanged idle badinage with Young Marius, his eyes were very busy skipping from man to man. Rome, he thought, might be pleased enough at the election of a twenty-six-year-old senior consul, but some of the men present at this feast were not pleased at all. Especially Carbo's minions—Brutus Damasippus, Carrinas, Marcus Fannius, Censorinus, Publius Burrienus, Publius Albinovanus the Lucanian . . . Of course there were some who were highly delighted, like Marcus Marius Gratidianus and Scaevola Pontifex Maximus—but they were both related to Young Marius, and had, so to speak, a vested interest in seeing the new senior consul do well.

The younger Marcus Junius Brutus appeared behind Carbo's end of the couch. He was greeted, Caesar noticed, with unusual fervor; Carbo did not normally indulge in rapturous welcomes. Seeing it, Young Marius weaved away in search of more convivial company, leaving Brutus to take his place. Brutus nodded in passing to Caesar, without displaying any interest in him. That was the best thing about being *flamen Dialis;* he interested nobody because he was so politically insignificant. Carbo and Brutus proceeded to talk openly.

"I think we can congratulate ourselves on an excellent ploy," said Brutus, digging his fingers into the disintegrating carcass of the licker-fish.

"Huh." The chicken, barely nibbled, was thrown down with a grimace of distaste; Carbo took bread.

"Oh, come now! You ought to be elated."

"About what? *Him?* Brutus, he's as hollow as a sucked egg! I've seen enough of him during the past month to know that, I do assure you. He may hold the *fasces* for the month of January, but it's I will have to do all the work."

"You didn't expect that to be different, surely?"

Carbo shrugged, tossed the bread away; since Caesar's remark about eating shit, his appetite had vanished. "Oh, I don't know. . . . Maybe I'd hoped to see him grow a little sense. After all, he is Marius's son, and his mother is a Julian. You'd think those facts would be worth something."

"They're not, I take it."

"Not your granny's used handkerchief. The most I can say about him is that he's a useful ornament—he makes us look very pretty, and he sucks in the recruits."

"He might command troops well," said Brutus, wiping his greasy hands on the linen napkin a slave passed to him.

"He might. My guess is he won't. I intend to take your advice in that area, certainly."

"What advice?"

"To make sure he isn't given the best soldiers."

"Oh." Brutus flipped the napkin into the air without bothering to see whether the silent servant hovering near Caesar managed to catch it. "Quintus Sertorius isn't here today. I had at least hoped he'd come to Rome for this occasion. After all, Young Marius is his cousin."

Carbo laughed, not a happy sound. "Sertorius, my dear Brutus, has abandoned our cause. He left Sinuessa to its fate, made off to Telamon, enlisted a legion of Etrurian clients of Gaius Marius's, and sailed on the winter winds for Tarraco. In other words, he's taken up his governorship of Nearer

Spain very early. No doubt he hopes that by the time his term is over, there will be a decision in Italy.''

''He's a coward!'' said Brutus indignantly.

Carbo made a rude noise. ''Not that one! I'd rather call him strange. He's got no friends, haven't you ever noticed it? Nor a wife. But he doesn't have Gaius Marius's ambition, for which we all ought to thank our lucky stars. If he did, Brutus, he'd be senior consul.''

''Well, I think it's a pity he's left us in the lurch. His presence on the battlefield would have made all the difference. Aside from anything else, he knows how Sulla fights.''

Carbo belched, pressed his belly. ''I think I'm going to retire and take an emetic. The young cub's prodigious assortment of food is too rich for my stomach.''

Brutus assisted the junior consul from the couch and led him off toward a screened corner of the hall behind the podium, where several servants tended an array of chamber pots and bowls for those in need.

Flicking a scornful glance at Carbo's back, Caesar decided he had heard the most important conversation likely to take place at this consular inaugural feast. He kicked off his clogs, picked them up, and quietly stole away.

Lucius Decimius was lurking in a sheltered corner of the Senate House vestibule, and appeared at Caesar's side the moment he had fully emerged from the doorway. His arms were full of more sensible garments—decent boots, a hooded cloak, socks, a pair of woolen breeches. Off came the regalia of the *flamen Dialis*. Behind Lucius Decimius loomed an awesome personage who took *apex*, *laena* and clogs from Lucius Decimius and stuffed them into a drawstringed leather bag.

''What, back from Bovillae, Burgundus?'' asked Caesar, gasping with the cold as he struggled to pull on a laceless boot.

''Yes, Caesar.''

''How goes it? All well with Cardixa?''

''I am the father of another son.''

Lucius Decimius giggled. ''I told you, Pavo my peacock! He will have given you a whole bodyguard by the time you're the consul!''

''I will never be consul,'' said Caesar, and looked out at the shrouded end of the Basilica Aemilia, swallowing painfully.

''Rubbish! Of course you'll get there,'' said Lucius Decimius, and reached up his mittened hands to cup Caesar's face. ''Now you just stop all that gloomy business! There's not nothing in the whole world will stop you once you make up your mind to it, hear me?'' Down came the hands, one of them gesturing impatiently at Burgundus. "Go on, you great German lump! Clear a path for the master!"

It went on as it had begun, that terrible winter, and seemed as if it would never end. The seasons were in fair company to the calendar after some years of Scaevola as Pontifex Maximus; he, like Metellus Dalmaticus, believed in keeping date and season in harmony, though the Pontifex Maximus between them, Gnaeus Domitius Ahenobarbus, had allowed the calendar to gallop ahead—it was ten days shorter than the solar year—because he despised finicky Greek habits, he had said.

But finally in March the thaw set in, and Italy began to believe that warmth would return to countryside and house. Asleep since October, the legions stirred, woke into activity. Braving the deep snow of early March, Gaius Norbanus issued out of Capua with six of his eight legions and marched to join Carbo, who was back in Ariminum. He went straight past Sulla, who chose to ignore him; on the Via Latina and then the Via Flaminia, Norbanus could manage to move despite the snow, and soon reached Ariminum. His arrival plumped out Carbo's forces there to thirty legions and several thousand cavalry, an enormous burden for Rome—and the Ager Gallicus—to carry.

But before leaving for Ariminum, Carbo had solved his most pressing problem: where the money to keep all these troops under arms would come from. Perhaps it was the melted gold and silver from the burned temple of Jupiter Optimus Maximus stored as ingots in the Treasury gave him the idea, for certainly he commenced by seizing them, leaving in their stead a promissory note that Rome owed her Great God so many talents of gold and so many talents of silver. A large number of Rome's temples were rich in their own right, and since religion was a part of the State and run by the State, Carbo and Young Marius took it upon themselves to "borrow" the money held in Rome's temples. In theory this was not unconstitutional, but in practice it was abhorrent, a solution to financial crises which was never put into effect. But out of the temple strong rooms came chest after chest after chest of coins: the single sestertius which was given at the birth of a Roman citizen's male or female child to Juno Lucina; the single denarius which was given upon maturation of a Roman citizen male child to Juventas; the many denarii donated to Mercury after a businessman wetted his laurel bough at the sacred fountain; the single sestertius which was given at the death of a Roman citizen to Venus Libitina; the sesterces which were donated by successful prostitutes to Venus Erucina—all this money and much more was commandeered to fund Carbo's war machine. Bullion too was taken, and any gold or silver temple gift not felt to be an artistic loss was melted down.

The stammering praetor Quintus Antonius Balbus—not one of the noble Antonii—was given the job of minting new coins and sorting out the old. Sacrilegious many may have deemed it, but the value of the haul was staggering. Carbo was able to leave Young Marius in charge of Rome and the campaign in the south, and journey to Ariminum with an easy mind.

Though neither camp was aware it shared something in common, both Sulla and Carbo had made a similar resolution—that this was one civil war would not wreck Italy, that every mouthful of provender for man and beast involved in the hostilities must be paid for in hard cash, that the amount of land ruined by army maneuvers must be kept to an absolute minimum. The Italian War had brought the whole country to the brink of extinction; the country could not afford another war like it, especially so soon. And this, both Sulla and Carbo knew.

They were also aware that the war between them lacked in the eyes of ordinary people the nobility of purpose and ironclad reason which the Italian War had possessed in abundance. That had been a struggle between Italian states which wanted to be independent of Rome, and Rome which wanted the Italian states kept in a certain degree of vassalage. But what was this new conflict really all about? Simply, which camp would end in ruling and owning Rome. It was a struggle for ascendancy between two men, Sulla and Carbo, and no amount of propaganda either camp put out could really disguise that fact. Nor were the ordinary people of Rome and Italy fooled. Therefore the country could not be subjected to extreme hardship, nor the economic well-being of the Roman and Italian communities diminished.

Sulla was borrowing from his soldiers, but the only ones Carbo could borrow from were the gods. And always at the back of each man's mind there loomed an awful dilemma: how, when the struggle was over, could the debt be paid back?

None of this impinged upon the thoughts of Young Marius, the son of a fabulously wealthy man never brought up to care about money, be it the money to pay for some expensive personal trifle, or the money to pay the legions. If old Gaius Marius had talked to anyone about the fiscal side of war, it had been to Caesar during those months when Caesar had helped him recover from his second stroke. To his son, he had hardly talked at all. For by the time he had needed his son, Young Marius was of an age to be seduced more by the charms of Rome than by his father. To Caesar—nine years younger than his cousin—fell the lot of Gaius Marius's reminiscences. And Caesar had listened avidly to much the arrival of his priesthood had rendered worse than useless.

When the thaw set in after the middle of March, Young Marius and his staff of legates moved from Rome to a camp outside the little town of Ad Pictas on the Via Labicana, a *diverticulum* which avoided the Alban Hills and rejoined the Via Latina at a place called Sacriportus. Here on a flat alluvial plain eight legions of Etrurian and Umbrian volunteers had been encamped since early winter, under as strict and intensive a training program as the cold made possible. Their centurions were all Marian veterans, and good at training, but when Young Marius arrived toward the end of March, the troops were still very green. Not that Young Marius cared; he genuinely believed that the greenest recruit would fight for him the way hardened soldiers had fought for his father. And he faced the task of stopping Sulla with unimpaired confidence.

There were men in his camp who understood far better than Young Marius the enormity of that task, but not one of them tried to enlighten their consul-commander. If taxed for a reason why, each one would probably have answered that beneath all his bluster, Young Marius did not have the internal resources to cope with so much truth. The figurehead, Young Marius must be cherished and protected, kept together.

When intelligence reports arrived to inform him that Sulla was preparing to move, Young Marius cheered. For Sulla it seemed had detached eleven of his eighteen legions along with all save a few squadrons of cavalry, and sent this big force under the command of Metellus Pius the Piglet toward the Adriatic coast and Carbo in Ariminum. Which left Sulla with seven legions only, a smaller force than Young Marius owned.

"I can beat him!" he said to his senior legate, Gnaeus Domitius Ahenobarbus.

Married to Cinna's elder girl, Ahenobarbus was committed to Carbo's side despite a natural inclination in Sulla's direction; he was very much in love with his beautiful red-haired wife, and sufficiently under her thumb to do whatever she wished. The fact that most of his close relatives were either sternly neutral or with Sulla he contrived to ignore.

Now he listened to Young Marius in jubilant mood, and felt a much greater degree of unease; perhaps he ought to start thinking of how and where to flee if Young Marius didn't make good his boast and beat the old red fox, Sulla.

On the first day of April, Young Marius in high fettle moved his army out of camp and marched through the ancient pylons at Sacriportus onto the Via Latina, heading southeast toward Campania and Sulla. He wasted no time, for there were two bridges to cross within five miles of each other, and he wanted to be clear of them before he encountered the enemy. No one offered him any advice as to the prudence of marching to meet Sulla rather than remaining where he was, and though he had traveled the Via Latina dozens of times, Young Marius did not have the kind of mind which remembered terrain or saw terrain in military terms.

At the first bridge—spanning the Veregis—he remained behind while his troops marched across in high spirits, and suddenly realized that the ground was better for fighting around the pylons of Sacriportus than in the direction he was going. But he didn't stop. At the second bridge—across the bigger, more torrential stream of the Tolerus—it finally dawned on him that he was steadily moving into country where his legions would find it difficult to maneuver. His scouts arrived to tell him that Sulla was ten miles down the road and rapidly passing the town of Ferentinum, whereupon Young Marius panicked.

"I think we'd better go back to Sacriportus," he said to Ahenobarbus. "I can't hope to deploy the way I want to in this country, and I can't get past Sulla to more open ground. So we'll face him at Sacriportus. Don't you think that's best?"

"If you think so," said Ahenobarbus, who was well aware of the effect an order to face about and retreat would have on these green troops, but decided not to say a word. "I'll give the command. Back to Sacriportus."

"At the double!" cried Young Marius, his confidence oozing away moment by moment, and his sense of panic increasing.

Ahenobarbus looked at him, astonished, but again elected to say nothing. If Young Marius wanted his army exhausted by some miles of run-trot-walk retreat, why should he argue? They couldn't win anyway.

So back to Sacriportus the eight legions proceeded at the double, the thousands of young soldiers growing more bewildered as their centurions exhorted them to pick up their heels and *move*! Young Marius too became infected with this desperate hurrying, and rode among the ranks urging them on—without once thinking to inform them that they were not in retreat, merely moving to better ground on which to fight. The result was that both troops and commander arrived on that better ground in no mental or physical condition to make proper use of it.

Like all his peers, Young Marius was tutored as to how to fight a battle, but until now he had simply assumed his father's acumen and skill would automatically swirl into his mind; but at Sacriportus, with legates and military tribunes all clustered about him looking at him to receive orders, he couldn't think, he couldn't find one single iota of his father's acumen and skill.

"Oh," he said finally, "deploy the legions in checkered square—eight men deep on each side of each square, and keep two legions in line behind to serve as reinforcements."

They were not adequate orders, but no one tried to force better orders out of him, and his thirsty, panting troops did not find their flagging spirits cheered by an address from Young Marius; instead of attempting to speak to them, he rode off to one side of the field and sat upon his horse with his shoulders hunched and his face betraying the depth of his dilemma.

Discerning Young Marius's unadventurous battle plan from the top of a ridge between the Tolerus and Sacriportus, Sulla sighed, shrugged, and sent his five legions of veterans into action under the elder Dolabella and Servilius Vatia. The two best legions from Scipio Asiagenus's old army he held in reserve under Lucius Manlius Torquatus, while he himself remained on the ridge, attended by a squadron of cavalry deputed to form a messenger corps and carry the general's instructions to the battlefield at the gallop if a change in tactics should become necessary. With him was none other than old Lucius Valerius Flaccus Princeps Senatus, the Leader of the House; Flaccus had made up his mind during the worst of the winter, and quit Rome for Sulla halfway through February.

When he saw Sulla's army approaching, Young Marius underwent a return of his calm, though not of his optimism, and assumed personal command of his left wing without having any real idea of what he was doing or what he ought to do. The two armies met in midafternoon of that shortish day, and before the first hour was over the Etrurian and Umbrian farm boys who had enlisted so enthusiastically for Young Marius were fleeing the field in all directions away from where Sulla's veterans were chopping them into pieces with effortless ease. One of the two legions Young Marius had kept in reserve deserted en masse to Servilius Vatia, and stood quietly while the slaughter of their confederates went on scant paces away.

It was the sight of that defected legion finished Young Marius. Remembering that the formidable fortress town of Praeneste lay not far to the east of Sacriportus, he ordered a retreat into Praeneste. With something tangible to do, he fared better, and contrived to evacuate the troops of his left wing in reasonable order. Commanding Sulla's right, Ofella took after Young Marius with a swiftness and savagery Sulla, watching from his ridge, applauded heartily. For ten miles Ofella harried and harassed, cut off stragglers and cut them up, while Young Marius endeavored to save as many as he could. But when at last the enormous gates of Praeneste closed behind him, only seven thousand of his men had managed to stay with him.

Young Marius's center had perished on the field almost to the last man, but his right wing, led by Ahenobarbus, succeeded in breaking off hostilities and making a run for Norba. This ancient stronghold of the Volsci, fanatically loyal to Carbo's cause, stood atop a mountain twenty miles to the southwest, and gladly opened the gates in its impregnable walls to receive Ahenobarbus's ten thousand men. But not to receive Ahenobarbus! Wishing his devastated soldiers the best of luck for the future, Ahenobarbus continued on for the coast at Tarracina and there took ship for Africa, the farthest place from Italy he could bear to think of with equanimity.

Unaware that his senior legate had slipped away, Young Marius was satisfied with his Praenestian shelter; from this city Sulla would find it extremely difficult—if not impossible—to dislodge him. Some twenty-three miles from Rome, Praeneste occupied the heights of a spur of the Apennines, a site which had enabled it to withstand many assaults on its frowning walls through the centuries before Young Marius availed himself of its defenses. No army could take it from behind, where the outcrop on which it stood joined higher, more precipitous mountains; yet it could be provisioned from this direction, which made it impossible to starve out. Of springs there were aplenty within the citadel, and in vast caverns below the mighty shrine to Fortuna Primigenia for which Praeneste was most famous, there lay many *medimni* of wheat and oil and wine, other imperishable foods like hard cheeses and raisins, as well as apples and pears from the previous autumn's picking.

Though its roots were Latin enough and its version of that language proudly held by its citizens to be the oldest and purest, Praeneste had never allied itself with Rome. It fought on the side of the Italian Allies during the Italian War, and still held defiantly that its citizenship was superior to Rome's—Rome was a parvenu place! Its fervent espousal of Young Marius was therefore logical enough; he seemed to the people of Praeneste the underdog facing Sulla's vengeful might, and being his father's son besides, was warmly welcomed. As thanks, he pressed his soldiers into forming forage parties and sent them out along the snake-paths behind the citadel to procure as much food as possible. Praeneste now had many extra mouths.

"By summer Sulla will have moved on from sheer necessity, and then you can leave," said the city's chief magistrate.

A prophecy not to bear fruit; less than a market interval after the battle of Sacriportus, Young Marius and the inhabitants of Praeneste witnessed the beginnings of a siege investment too monumental to be anything less than iron determination to see Praeneste fall. The tributaries which ran off the spur in the direction of Rome all entered the Anio River, whereas those which ran off the spur in the opposite direction all eventually entered the Tolerus River: Praeneste was a watershed. And now, with a speed the imprisoned onlookers found incredible, a great wall and ditch began to grow from the Anio side of the spur all the way around to the Tolerus side. When these siegeworks were completed, the only way in or out of Praeneste would be the snake-paths through the mountains behind. Provided, that is, that they were left unguarded.

The news of Sacriportus flew to Rome before the sun had set upon that fatal day—but very secretly. General dissemination would have to wait upon hearsay. It came by special courier from Young Marius himself, for the moment he was inside Praeneste he dictated a hasty letter to Rome's urban praetor, Lucius Junius Brutus Damasippus. It said:

All is lost south of Rome. We must hope that Carbo in Ariminum wages the sort of war Sulla will not be able to deal with, if only because he grossly lacks Carbo's numbers. Carbo's troops are far better than mine were. Mine's lack of proper training and experience unsettled them so much they could not hold for an hour against Sulla's old retainers.

I suggest you try to prepare Rome for a siege, though that may be impossible in a place so huge and so divided in its loyalties. If you think Rome will refuse to undergo siege, then you must expect Sulla within the next market interval, for there are no troops to oppose him between here and Rome. Whether he intends to occupy Rome, I do not know. What I hope is that he intends to bypass it in favor of attacking Carbo. From what I have heard my father say about Sulla, it would be like him to be forming a pincer to crush Carbo, using Metellus Pius as his other jaw. I wish I knew. I do not know. Except that it would be premature for Sulla to occupy Rome at this time, and I do not see Sulla making that mistake.

It may be some time before I can leave Praeneste, which has taken me in willingly—its people have a great affection for Gaius Marius, and have not refused to succor his son. Rest assured that as soon as Sulla moves on to deal with Carbo, I will break out and come to Rome's aid. Perhaps if I am in Rome myself, her people will agree to withstand siege.

Further to that, it occurs to me that the time has come to destroy every last nest of Sullan vipers within our beloved city. Kill them all, Damasippus! Do not allow sentiment to soften your resolve. Living men who might decide to support Sulla will make it impossible for Rome to resist him. But if the great ones who might make trouble for us are dead, then all the little ones will knuckle under without demur. Every man who might be of military help to Carbo must leave Rome now. That includes you, Damasippus.

Here follow a very few names of Sullan vipers which spring to mind. I know I have missed dozens, so think of them all! Our Pontifex Maximus. The elder Lucius Domitius Ahenobarbus. Carbo Arvina. Publius Antistius Vetus.

Brutus Damasippus followed orders. During the short-lived but comprehensive program of murder old Gaius Marius had perpetrated before he died, Quintus Mucius Scaevola the Pontifex Maximus had been stabbed, for no good reason anyone could discover. His would-be assassin (that Fimbria who had gone off with Flaccus the suffect consul to relieve Sulla of his command against King Mithridates, then murdered Flaccus) could produce no better excuse at the time than to laugh that Scaevola deserved to die. But Scaevola had not died, though the wound was severe. Tough and doughty, the Pontifex Maximus was back on his feet and about his public duties within two months. Now, however, there was to be no escape. Father-in-law of Young Marius though he was, he was cut down as he tried to seek asylum in the temple of Vesta. Of treachery to Young Marius he was quite innocent.

The elder Lucius Domitius Ahenobarbus, consul not long after his brother the reforming Pontifex Maximus, was executed in his home. And no doubt Pompey the Great would have beamed his full approval had he known that his father-in-law's blood need not now stain his own hands; Publius Antistius was murdered too, and his wife, demented with grief, took her own life. By the time Brutus Damasippus had worked his way through those he considered might endanger Carbo's Rome, some thirty heads adorned the rostra in the lower Forum Romanum; men who called themselves neutral (like Catulus, Lepidus and Hortensius) bolted the doors of their houses and refused to venture out in case one of Brutus Damasippus's minions decided they must die too.

His work done, Brutus Damasippus fled from Rome, as did his fellow praetor Gaius Albius Carrinas. Both of them joined Carbo. The minting praetor, Quintus Antonius Balbus, also left Rome at this time, but commanding a legion of troops; his task was to go to Sardinia and wrest that island off Philippus.

Strangest defection of all, however, was that of the tribune of the plebs Quintus Valerius Soranus. A great scholar and a known humanitarian, he found himself unable to condone this slaughter of men not even proven to be affiliated in any way with Sulla. But how to make a public protest which would impress the whole city? And how could one man destroy Rome? For Quintus Valerius Soranus had come to the conclusion that the world would be a better place if Rome ceased to exist. After some thought, he arrived at his solution. He went to the rostra, climbed upon it, and there, surrounded by the dripping trophies of Brutus Damasippus, he screamed aloud the secret name of Rome.

"*AMOR!*" he cried, again and again.

Those who heard and understood ran with hands clapped over their ears away from his voice. Rome's secret name could *never* be uttered aloud! Rome and all she stood for would fall down like a shoddy building in an earthquake. Quintus Valerius Soranus himself believed that implicitly. So having told air and birds and horrified men Rome's secret name, Soranus fled to Ostia wondering why Rome still stood upon her seven hills. From Ostia he sailed for Sicily, a marked man to both sides.

Virtually bereft of government, the city did not fall down or fall apart. People went about their affairs as they always did; the neutral noblemen popped their heads from out of their front doors, sniffed the air, sallied out, said nothing. Rome waited to see what Sulla would do.

Sulla did enter Rome, but quietly, and without his army at his back to protect him.

There was no compelling reason why he should not enter Rome, but very many compelling reasons why he should. Matters like his imperium—and whether or not he relinquished it in the moment he crossed the sacred boundary of the *pomerium* into the city—he cared little about. Who was there in this rudderless Rome to gainsay him, or accuse him of illegalities, or religiously impugn him? If he came back to Rome it would be as Rome's conqueror and master, with whatever powers he needed to make all right concerning his past career. So he stepped across the *pomerium* without a qualm, and proceeded to give the city back some semblance of government.

The most senior magistrate left in Rome was one of the two brothers Magius from Aeclanum, a praetor; him Sulla put in charge, with the aediles Publius Furius Crassipes and Marcus Pomponius to assist him. When he heard about Soranus's uttering the secret name of Rome aloud he frowned direfully and shuddered, though the bristling fence of speared heads around the rostra he eyed with perfect equanimity, only ordering that they be taken down and given the proper rites. He made no speeches to the people, and called no meeting of the Senate. Less than a full day after he entered he was gone again, back to Praeneste. But behind him he left two squadrons of cavalry under the command of Torquatus—to assist the magistrates to maintain order, he said blandly.

He made no attempt to see Aurelia, who had wondered; when she heard that he was gone again she presented an indifferent front to her family, especially to Caesar, who *knew* his mother's meeting with Sulla outside Teanum had been fraught with all kinds of significance, but knew she wasn't going to enlighten him.

The legate in charge of the investment of Praeneste was the defector Quintus Lucretius Ofella, whose orders had come directly from Sulla.

"I want Young Marius penned up in Praeneste for the rest of his days," Sulla had said to Ofella. "You'll build a wall thirty feet high all the way from the mountains behind on the Anio side to the mountains behind on the Tolerus side. The wall will contain a sixty-foot fortified tower every two hundred paces. Between the wall and the town you will dig a ditch twenty feet deep and twenty feet wide, and you will fix *stimuli* in its bottom as thick as reeds in the shallows of the Fucine Lake. When the investment is completed, you will station camps of men to guard every little track which leads from behind Praeneste across the high Apennines. No one will get in, and no one will get out. I want that arrogant pup to understand that Praeneste is now his home for as long as he has left to live." A sour smile twisted the corners of Sulla's mouth, a smile which would have displayed those ferally long canines in the days when he had had teeth; it was still not a pretty phenomenon. "I also want the people of Praeneste to know that they have Young Marius for the rest of his life, so you will have heralds inform them of that fact six times a day. It is one thing to succor a lovely young man with a famous name, but quite another to realize that the lovely young man with the famous name has brought death and suffering into Praeneste with him."

When Sulla moved on to Veii to the north of Rome, he left Ofella behind with two legions to carry out the work. And work they did. Luckily the area was rich in volcanic tufa, a curious stone which cut as easily as cheese, yet hardened to the consistency of rock after it was exposed to the air. With this to quarry, the wall went up at mushroom pace, and the ditch between it and Praeneste deepened daily. Earth from the ditch was piled into a second wall, and in the large No Man's Land which existed inside these siegeworks no tree or object tall enough to serve as a battering ram was left standing. On the mountains behind the town, every tree was also felled between the back walls and the camps of men who now guarded the snake-paths and prevented the Praenestians foraging.

Ofella was a hard taskmaster; he had a reputation to make with Sulla, and this was his chance. Thus no one paused to rest, or so much as had the time to complain about a sore back or aching muscles. Besides, the men too had a reputation to make with Sulla; one of the legions was the one which had deserted Young Marius at Sacriportus, and the other had belonged to Scipio Asiagenus. Loyalty was suspect, so a well-built wall and well-excavated ditch would show Sulla they were worthy. All they had to work with were their hands and their legionary's digging tools; but there were over ten thousand pairs of hands and more than sufficient tools, and their centurions taught them the shortcuts and knacks in building siegeworks. To organize a task of such monumental size was no great trouble to Ofella, a typical Roman when it came to methodical execution.

In two months the wall and ditch were finished. They were over eight miles in length and bisected both the Via Praenestina and the Via Labicana in two places, thereby interrupting traffic on both these roads and rendering them useless beyond Tusculum and Bola. Those Roman knights and senators whose estates were affected by the fortifications could do nothing save glumly wait for the siege to be over—and curse Young Marius. On the other hand, the smallholders of the region rejoiced as they eyed the tufa blocks; when the siege was over the wall would come down and they would have an inexhaustible supply of material for field fences, buildings, barns, byres.

At Norba the same sort of exercise went on, though Norba did not require such massive siegeworks. Mamercus had been sent there with a legion of new recruits (dispatched from Sabine country by Marcus Crassus) to reduce it, and settled to his task with the dour and understated efficiency which had successfully carried him through many a perilous situation.

As for Sulla, at Veii he divided the five legions he had left between himself and Publius Servilius Vatia. Vatia was to take two of them and march into coastal Etruria, while Sulla and the elder Dolabella took the other three up the Via Cassia toward Clusium, further inland. It was now the beginning of May, and Sulla was very well pleased with his progress. If Metellus Pius and his larger section of the army acquitted themselves equally well, by autumn Sulla stood an excellent chance of owning all of Italy and all of Italian Gaul.

And how were Metellus Pius and his forces doing? Sulla had heard little about their progress at the time he himself started up the Via Cassia toward Clusium, but he had a great deal of faith in this loyalest of adherents—as well as a lively curiosity as to how Pompey the Great would fare. He had quite deliberately given Metellus Pius the larger army, and deliberate too were his instructions that Pompey the Great should have the command of five thousand cavalry he knew he would not need in his own maneuvers through more settled and hillier terrain.

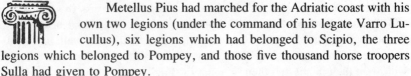

Metellus Pius had marched for the Adriatic coast with his own two legions (under the command of his legate Varro Lucullus), six legions which had belonged to Scipio, the three legions which belonged to Pompey, and those five thousand horse troopers Sulla had given to Pompey.

Of course Varro the Sabine traveled with Pompey, a ready and sympathetic ear (not to mention a ready and sympathetic pen!) tuned to receive Pompey's thoughts.

"I must put myself on better terms with Crassus," said Pompey to him as they moved through Picenum. "Metellus Pius and Varro Lucullus are easy—and anyway, I quite like them. But Crassus is a surly brute. More formidable by far. I need him on my side."

Astride a pony, Varro looked a long way up to Pompey on his big white Public Horse. "I do believe you've learned something during the course of a winter spent with Sulla!" he said, genuinely amazed. "I never thought to hear you speak of conciliating any man—with the exception of Sulla, naturally."

"Yes, I have learned," admitted Pompey magnanimously. His beautiful white teeth flashed in a smile of pure affection. "Come now, Varro! I know I'm well on my way to becoming Sulla's most valued helper, but I *am* capable of understanding that Sulla needs other men than me! Though you may be right," he went on thoughtfully. "This is the first time in my life that I've dealt with any other commander-in-chief than my father. I think my father was a very great soldier. But he cared for nothing aside from his lands. Sulla is different."

"In what way?" asked Varro curiously.

"He cares nothing for most things—including all of us he calls his legates, or colleagues, or whatever name he considers judicious at the time. I don't know that he even cares for Rome. Whatever he does care for, it isn't material. Money, lands—even the size of his *auctoritas* or the quality of his public reputation. No, they don't matter to Sulla."

"Then what does?" Varro asked, fascinated with the phenomenon of a Pompey who could see further than himself.

"Perhaps his *dignitas* alone," Pompey answered.

Varro turned this over carefully. Could Pompey be right? *Dignitas!* The most intangible of all a Roman nobleman's possessions, that was *dignitas*. His *auctoritas* was his clout, his measure of public influence, his ability to sway public opinion and public bodies from Senate to priests to the Treasury.

Dignitas was different. It was intensely personal and very private, yet it extended into all parameters of a man's public life. So hard to define! That, of course, was why there was a word for it. *Dignitas* was . . . a man's personal degree of impressiveness . . . of glory? *Dignitas* summed up what a man was, as a man and as a leader of his society. It was the total of his pride, his integrity, his word, his intelligence, his deeds, his ability, his knowledge, his standing, his worth as a man. . . . *Dignitas* survived a man's death, it was the only way he could triumph over death. Yes, that was the best definition. *Dignitas* was a man's triumph over the extinction of his physical being. And seen in that light, Varro thought Pompey absolutely correct. If anything mattered to Sulla, it was his *dignitas*. He had said he would beat Mithridates. He had said he would come back to Italy and secure his vindication. He had said that he would restore the Republic in its old, traditional form. And having said these things, he would do them. Did he not, his *dignitas* would be diminished; in outlawry and official odium there could be no *dignitas*. So from out of himself he would find the strength to make his word good. When he had made his word good, he would be satisfied. Until he had, Sulla could not rest. Would not rest.

"In saying that," Varro said, "you have awarded Sulla the ultimate accolade."

The bright blue eyes went blank. "Huh?"

"I mean," said Varro patiently, "that you have demonstrated to me that Sulla cannot lose. He's fighting for something Carbo doesn't even understand."

"Oh, yes! Yes, definitely!" said Pompey cheerfully.

They were almost to the river Aesis, in the heart of Pompey's own fief again. The brash youth of last year had not vanished, but sat now amid a branching superstructure of fresh, stimulating experiences; in other words, Pompey had grown. In fact, he grew a little more each day. Sulla's gift of cavalry command had interested Pompey in a type of military activity he had never before seriously considered. That of course was Roman. Romans believed in the foot soldier, and to some extent had come to believe the horse soldier was more decorative than useful, more a nuisance than an asset. Varro was convinced that the only reason Romans employed cavalry was because the enemy did.

Once upon a time, in the days of the Kings of Rome and in the very early years of the Republic, the horse soldier had formed the military elite, was the spearhead of a Roman army. Out of this had grown the class of knights—the Ordo Equester, as Gaius Gracchus had called it. Horses had been hugely expensive—too expensive for many men to buy privately. Out of that had grown the custom of the Public Horse, the knight's mount bought and paid for by the State.

Now, a long way down the road from those days, the Roman horse soldier had ceased to exist except in social and economic terms. The knight—businessman or landowner that he was, member of the First Class of the Centuries—was the horse soldier's Roman relic. And still to this day, the State bought the eighteen hundred most senior knights their horses.

Addicted to exploring the winding lanes of thought, Varro saw that he was losing the point of his original reflection, and drew himself resolutely back onto thought's main road. Pompey and his interest in the cavalry. Not Roman in manpower anymore. These were Sulla's troopers he had brought from Greece with him, and therefore contained no Gauls; had they been recruited in Italy, they would have been almost entirely Gallic, drawn from the rolling pastures on the far side of the Padus in Italian Gaul, or from the great valley of the Rhodanus in Gaul-across-the-Alps. As it was, Sulla's men were mostly Thracians, admixed with a few hundred Galatians. Good fighters, and as loyal as could be expected of men who were not themselves Roman. In the Roman army they had auxiliary status, and some of them might be rewarded at the end of a hard-won campaign with the full Roman citizenship, or a piece of land.

All the way from Teanum Sidicinum, Pompey had busied himself going among these men in their leather trousers and leather jerkins, with their little round shields and their long lances; their long swords were more suitable for slashing from the height of a horse's back than the short sword of the infantryman. At least Pompey had the capacity to think, Varro told himself as they rode steadily toward the Aesis. He was discovering the qualities of horsemen-soldiers and turning over the possibilities. Planning. Seeing if there was any way their performance or equipage might be improved. They were formed into regiments of five hundred men, each regiment consisting of ten squadrons of fifty men, and they were led by their own officers; the only Roman who commanded them was the overall general of cavalry. In this case, Pompey. Very much involved, very fascinated—and very determined to lead them with a flair and competence not usually present in a Roman. If Varro privately thought that a part of Pompey's interest stemmed from his large dollop of Gallic blood, he was wise enough never to indicate to Pompey that such was his theory.

How extraordinary! Here they were, the Aesis in sight, and Pompey's old camp before them. Back where they had begun, as if all the miles between had been nothing. A journey to see an old man with no teeth and no hair, distinguished only by a couple of minor battles and a lot of marching.

"I wonder," said Varro, musing, "if the men ever ask themselves what it's all about?"

Pompey blinked, turned his head sideways. "What a strange question! Why should they ask themselves anything? It's all done for them. *I* do it all for them! All they have to do is as they're told." And he grimaced at the revolutionary thought that so many as one of Pompey Strabo's veterans might *think*.

But Varro was not to be put off. "Come now, Magnus! They are *men*— like us in that respect, if in no other. And being men, they are endowed with thought. Even if a lot of them can't read or write. It's one thing never to question orders, quite another not to ask what it's all about."

"I don't see that," said Pompey, who genuinely didn't.

"Magnus, I call the phenomenon human curiosity! It is in a man's nature to ask himself the reason why! Even if he is a Picentine ranker who has never been to Rome and doesn't understand the difference between Rome and Italy. We have just been to Teanum and back. There's our old camp down there. Don't you think that some of them at least must be asking themselves what we went to Teanum for, and why we've come back in less than a year?"

"Oh, they know *that*!" said Pompey impatiently. "Besides, they're veterans. If they had a thousand sesterces for every mile they've marched during the past ten years, they'd be able to live on the Palatine and breed pretty fish. Even if they did piss in the fountain and shit in the cook's herb garden! Varro, you are such an original! You never cease to amaze me—the things that chew at you!" Pompey kicked his Public Horse in the ribs and began to gallop down the last slope. Suddenly he laughed uproariously, waved his hands in the air; his words floated back quite clearly. "Last one in's a rotten egg!"

Oh, you child! said Varro to himself. What *am* I doing here? What use can I possibly be? It's all a game, a grand and magnificent adventure.

Perhaps it was, but late that night Metellus Pius called a meeting with his three legates, and Varro as always accompanied Pompey. The atmosphere was excited: there had been news.

"Carbo isn't far away," said the Piglet. He paused to consider what he had said, and modified it. "At least, Carrinas is, and Censorinus is rapidly catching him up. Apparently Carbo thought eight legions would be enough to halt our progress, then he discovered the size of our army, and sent Censorinus with another four legions. They'll reach the Aesis ahead of us, and it's there we'll have to meet them."

"Where's Carbo himself?" asked Marcus Crassus.

"Still in Ariminum. I imagine he's waiting to see what Sulla intends to do."

"And how Young Marius will fare," said Pompey.

"True," agreed the Piglet, raising his brows. "However, it isn't our job to worry about that. Our job is to make Carbo hop. Pompeius, this is your purlieu. Should we bring Carrinas across the river, or keep him on the far side?"

"It doesn't really matter," said Pompey coolly. "The banks are much the same. Plenty of room to deploy, some tree cover, good level ground for an all-out contest if we can bring it on." He looked angelic, and said sweetly, "The decision belongs to you, Pius. I'm only your legate."

"Well, since we're trying to get to Ariminum, it makes more sense to get our men to the far side," said Metellus Pius, quite unruffled. "If we do force Carrinas to retreat, we don't want to have to cross the Aesis in pursuit. The report indicates that we have a huge advantage in cavalry. Provided that you think the terrain and the river will allow it, Pompeius, I would like you to spearhead the crossing and keep your horse-troopers between the enemy and our infantry. Then I'll wheel our infantry on the far bank, you peel your cavalry back out of the way, and we'll attack. There's not much we can do in terms of subterfuge. It will be a straight battle. However, if you can swing your cavalry around behind the enemy after I've engaged him from the front, we'll roll Carrinas and Censorinus up."

No one objected to this strategy, which was sufficiently loose to indicate that Metellus Pius had some talent as a general. When it was suggested that Varro Lucullus should command Pompey's three legions of veterans, thereby allowing Pompey full license with his cavalry, Pompey agreed without a qualm.

"I'll lead the center," said Metellus Pius in conclusion, "with Crassus leading the right, and Varro Lucullus the left."

Since the day was fine and the ground was not too wet, things went very much as Metellus Pius had planned. Pompey held the crossing easily, and the infantry engagement which followed demonstrated the great advantage veteran troops bestowed upon a general in battle. Though Scipio's legions were raw enough, Varro Lucullus and Crassus led the five veteran legions superbly, and their confidence spilled over onto Scipio's men. Carrinas and Censorinus had no veteran troops, and went down without extending Metellus Pius too severely. The end result would have been a rout had Pompey managed to fall upon the enemy rear, but as he skirted the field to do so, he encountered a new factor. Carbo had arrived with six more legions—and three thousand horse to contest Pompey's progress.

Carrinas and Censorinus managed to draw off without losing more than

three or four thousand men, then camped next to Carbo a scant mile beyond
the battlefield. The advance of Metellus Pius and his legates ground to a halt.

"We will go back to your original camp south of the river," said Metellus
Pius with crisp decision. "I would rather they think us too cautious to proceed,
and I also think it behooves us to keep a fair distance between us and them."

Despite the disappointing outcome of the day's conflict, spirits were high
among the men, and quite high in the command tent when Pompey, Crassus
and Varro Lucullus met their general at dusk. The table was covered with
maps, a slight disorder indicating that the Piglet had been poring over them
closely.

"All right," he said, standing behind the table, "I want you to look at
this, and see how best we can outflank Carbo."

They clustered around, Varro Lucullus holding a five-flamed lamp above
the carefully inked sheepskin. The map displayed the Adriatic coastline between Ancona and Ravenna, together with inland territory extending beyond
the crest of the Apennines.

"We're here," said the Piglet, finger on a spot below the Aesis. "The
next big river onward is the Metaurus, a treacherous crossing. All this land
is Ager Gallicus—here—and here—Ariminum at the northward end of it—
some rivers, but none according to this difficult to ford. Until we come to
this one—between Ariminum and Ravenna, see? The Rubico, our natural
border with Italian Gaul." All these features were lightly touched; the Piglet
was methodical. "It's fairly obvious why Carbo has put himself in Ariminum.
He can move up the Via Aemilia into Italian Gaul proper—he can go down
the Sapis road to the Via Cassia at Arretium and threaten Rome from the
upper Tiber valley—he can reach the Via Flaminia and Rome that way—he
can march down the Adriatic into Picenum, and if necessary into Campania
through Apulia and Samnium."

"Then we have to dislodge him," said Crassus, stating the obvious.
"It's possible."

"But there is a hitch," said Metellus Pius, frowning. "It seems Carbo
is not entirely confined to Ariminum anymore. He's done something very
shrewd by sending eight legions under Gaius Norbanus up the Via Aemilia
to Forum Cornelii—see? Not far beyond Faventia. Now that is not a great
distance from Ariminum—perhaps forty miles."

"Which means he could get those eight legions back to Ariminum in
one hard day's march if he had to," said Pompey.

"Yes. Or get them to Arretium or Placentia in two or three days," said
Varro Lucullus, who never lost sight of the overall concept. "We have Carbo

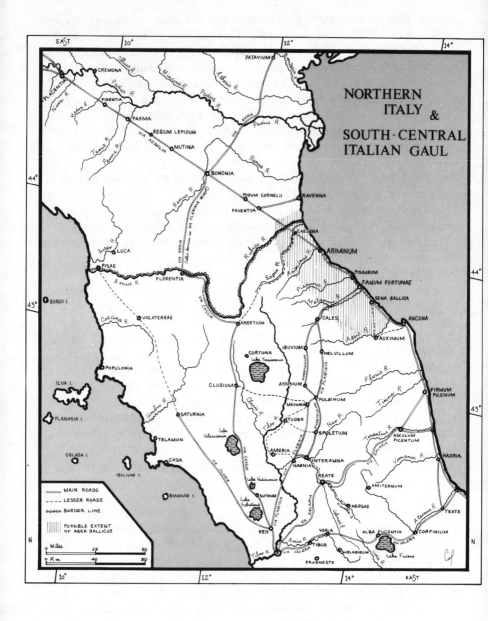

himself sitting on the other side of the Aesis with Carrinas and Censorinus—
and eighteen legions plus three thousand cavalry. There are eight more legions
in Forum Cornelii with Norbanus, and another four garrisoning Ariminum in
company with several thousand more cavalry.''

"I need a grand strategy before I go one more inch," said Metellus Pius,
looking at his legates.

"The grand strategy is easy," said Crassus, the abacus clicking away
inside his mind. "We have to prevent Carbo's recombining with Norbanus,
separate Carbo from Carrinas and Censorinus, and Carrinas from Censorinus.
Prevent every one of them from recombining. Just as Sulla said. Fragmen-
tation.''

"One of us—probably me—will have to get five legions to the far side
of Ariminum, then cut Norbanus off and make a bid to take Italian Gaul,"
said Metellus Pius, frowning. "Not an easy thing to do."

"It *is* easy," said Pompey eagerly. "Look—here's Ancona, the second-
best harbor on the Adriatic. At this time of year it's full of ships waiting on
the westerlies to sail for the east and a summer's trading. If you took your
five legions to Ancona, Pius, you could embark them on those ships and *sail*
to Ravenna. It's a sweet voyage, you'd never need to be out of sight of land,
and there won't be any storms. It's no more than a hundred miles—you'll
do it in eight or nine days, even if you have to row. If you get a following
wind—not unlikely at this time of year—you'll do it in four days." His hand
stabbed at the map. "A quick march from Ravenna to Faventia, and you'll
cut Norbanus off from Ariminum permanently."

"It will have to be done in secret," said the Piglet, eyes shining. "Oh,
yes, Pompeius, it will work! They won't dream of our moving troops between
here and Ancona—their scouts will all be to the north of the Aesis. Pompeius,
Crassus, you'll have to sit right where we are at the moment pretending to
be five legions stronger until Varro Lucullus and I have sailed from Ancona.
Then you move. Try to catch up to Carrinas, and make it look serious. If
possible, tie him down—and Censorinus as well. Carbo will be with them at
first, but when he hears I've landed at Ravenna, he'll march to relieve Norbanus. Of course, he may elect to stay in this neighborhood himself, send
Carrinas or Censorinus to relieve Norbanus. But I don't think so. Carbo needs
to be centrally located."

"Oh, this is going to be tremendous fun!" cried Pompey.

And such was the contentment in the command tent that no one found
this statement too flippant; even Marcus Terentius Varro, sitting quietly in a
corner taking notes.

* * *

The strategy worked. While Metellus Pius hustled himself, Varro Lucullus and five legions to Ancona, the other six plus the cavalry pretended to be eleven. Then Pompey and Crassus moved out of the camp and crossed the Aesis without opposition; Carbo had decided, it seemed, to lure them toward Ariminum, no doubt planning a decisive battle on ground more familiar to him.

Pompey led the way with his cavalry, hard on the heels of Carbo's rear guard, cavalry commanded by Censorinus, and nipped those heels with satisfying regularity. These tactics irritated Censorinus, never a patient man; near the town of Sena Gallica he turned and fought, cavalry against cavalry. Pompey won; he was developing a talent for commanding horse. Into Sena Gallica the smarting Censorinus retreated with infantry and cavalry both—but not for long. Pompey stormed its modest fortifications.

Censorinus then did the sensible thing. He sacrificed his horse, made off through the back gate of Sena Gallica with eight legions of infantry, and headed for the Via Flaminia.

By this time Carbo had learned of the unwelcome presence of the Piglet and his army in Faventia; Norbanus was now cut off from Ariminum. So Carbo marched for Faventia, leaving Carrinas to follow him with eight more legions; Censorinus, he decided, would have to fend for himself.

But then came Brutus Damasippus to find Carbo as he marched, and gave him the news that Sulla had annihilated the army of Young Marius at Sacriportus. Sulla was now heading up the Via Cassia toward the border of Italian Gaul at Arretium, though all the troops he had were three legions. In that instant, Carbo changed his plans. Only one thing could be done. Norbanus would have to hold Italian Gaul unaided against Metellus Pius; Carbo and his legates must halt Sulla at Arretium, not a difficult thing to do when Sulla had but three legions.

Pompey and Crassus got the news of Sulla's victory over Young Marius at just about the same time as Carbo did, and hailed it with great jubilation. They turned westward to follow Carrinas and Censorinus, each now bringing eight legions to Carbo at Arretium on the Via Cassia. The pace was furious, the pursuit determined. And this, decided Pompey as he headed with Crassus for the Via Flaminia, was no campaign for cavalry; they were heading into the mountains. Back to the Aesis he sent his horse-troopers, and resumed command of his father's veterans. Crassus, he had discovered, seemed content to follow his lead as long as what Pompey suggested added up to the right answers inside that hard round Crassus head.

Again it was the presence of so many veterans made the real difference; Pompey and Crassus caught up to Censorinus on a *diverticulum* of the Via Flaminia between Fulginum and Spoletium, and didn't even need to fight a battle. Exhausted, hungry, and very afraid, the troops of Censorinus disintegrated. All Censorinus managed to retain were three of his eight legions, and these precious soldiers he determined must be saved. He marched them off the road and cut across country to Arretium and Carbo. The men of his other five legions had scattered so completely that none of them afterward were ever successfully amalgamated into new units.

Three days later Pompey and Crassus apprehended Carrinas outside the big and well-fortified town of Spoletium. This time a battle did take place, but Carrinas fared so poorly that he was forced to shut himself up inside Spoletium with three of his eight legions; three more of his legions fled to Tuder and went to earth there; and the last two disappeared, never to be found.

"Oh, wonderful!" whooped Pompey to Varro. "I see how I can say bye-bye to stolid old Crassus!"

This he did by hinting to Crassus that he should take his three legions to Tuder and besiege it, leaving Pompey to bring his own men to bear on Spoletium. Off went Crassus to Tuder, very happy at the thought of conducting his own campaign. And Pompey sat down before Spoletium in high fettle, aware that whoever sat down before Spoletium would collect most of the glory because this was where General Carrinas himself had taken refuge. Alas, things didn't work out as Pompey had envisaged! Astute and daring, Carrinas sneaked out of Spoletium during a nocturnal thunderstorm and stole away to join Carbo with all three of his legions intact.

Pompey took Carrinas's defection very personally; fascinated, Varro learned what a Pompeian temper tantrum looked like, complete with tears, gnawed knuckles, plucked tufts of hair, drumming of heels and fists on the floor, broken cups and plates, mangled furniture. But then, like the nocturnal thunderstorm so beneficial to Carrinas, Pompey's thwarted rage rolled away.

"We're off to Sulla at Clusium," he announced. "Up with you, Varro! Don't dawdle so!"

Shaking his head, Varro tried not to dawdle.

It was early in June when Pompey and his veterans marched into Sulla's camp on the Clanis River, there to find the commander-in-chief a trifle sore and battered of spirit. Things had not gone very well for him when Carbo had come down from Arretium toward Clusium, for Carbo had nearly won the battle which developed out of a chance encounter, and therefore could not be planned. Only Sulla's presence of mind in breaking off hostilities and retiring into a very strong camp had saved the day.

"Not that it matters," said Sulla, looking greatly cheered. "You're here now, Pompeius, and Crassus isn't far away. Having both of you will make all the difference. Carbo is finished."

"How did Metellus Pius get on?" Pompey asked, not pleased to hear Sulla mention Crassus in the same breath.

"He's secured Italian Gaul. Brought Norbanus to battle outside Faventia, while Varro Lucullus—he'd had to go all the way to Placentia to find asylum— took on Lucius Quinctius and Publius Albinovanus near Fidentia. All went splendidly. The enemy is scattered or dead."

"What about Norbanus himself?"

Sulla shrugged; he never cared very much what happened to his military foes once they were beaten, and Norbanus had not been a personal enemy. "I imagine he went to Ariminum," he said, and turned away to issue instructions about Pompey's camp.

Sure enough, Crassus arrived the following day from Tuder at the head of three rather surly and disgruntled legions; rumor was rife among their ranks that after Tuder fell, Crassus had found a fortune in gold and kept the lot.

"Is it true?" demanded Sulla, the deep folds of his face grown deeper, his mouth set so hard its lips had disappeared.

But nothing could dent that bovine composure. Crassus's mild grey eyes widened, he looked puzzled but unconcerned. "No."

"You're sure?"

"There was nothing to be had in Tuder beyond a few old women, and I didn't fancy a one."

Sulla shot him a suspicious glance, wondering if Crassus was being intentionally insolent; but if so, he couldn't tell. "You are as deep as you are devious, Marcus Crassus," he said at last. "I will accord you the dispensations of your family and your standing, and elect to believe you. But take fair warning! If ever I discover that you have profited at the expense of the State out of *my* aims and endeavors, I will never see you again."

"Fair enough," said Crassus, nodding, and ambled off.

Publius Servilius Vatia had listened to this exchange, and smiled now at Sulla. "One cannot like him," he said.

"There are few men this one does like," said Sulla, throwing his arm around Vatia's shoulders. "Aren't you lucky, Vatia?"

"Why?"

"I happen to like you. You're a *good* fellow—never exceed your authority and never give me an argument. Whatever I ask you to do, you do." He yawned until his eyes watered. "I'm dry. A cup of wine, that's what I need!"

A slender and attractive man of medium coloring, Vatia was not one of the patrician Servilii; his family, however, was more than ancient enough to pass the most rigorous of social examinations, and his mother was one of the most august Caecilii Metelli, the daughter of Metellus Macedonicus—which meant he was related to everybody who mattered. Including, by marriage, Sulla. So he felt comfortable with that heavy arm across his back, and turned within Sulla's embrace to walk beside him to the command tent; Sulla had been imbibing freely that day, needed a little steadying.

"What will we do with these people when Rome is mine?" asked Sulla as Vatia helped him to a full goblet of his special wine; Vatia took his own wine from a different flagon, and made sure it was well watered.

"Which people? Crassus, you mean?"

"Yes, Crassus. And Pompeius Magnus." Sulla's lip curled up to show his gum. "I ask you, Vatia! *Magnus!* At his age!"

Vatia smiled, sat on a folding chair. "Well, if he's too young, I'm too old. I should have been consul six years ago. Now, I suppose I never will be."

"If I win, you'll be consul. Never doubt it. I am a bad enemy, Vatia, but a stout friend."

"I know, Lucius Cornelius," said Vatia tenderly.

"What do I do with them?" Sulla asked again.

"With Pompeius, I can see your difficulty. I cannot imagine *him* settling back into inertia once the fighting is over, and how do you keep him from aspiring to offices ahead of his time?"

Sulla laughed. "He's not after office! He's after military glory. And I think I will try to give it to him. He might come in quite handy." The empty cup was extended to be refilled. "And Crassus? What do I do with Crassus?"

"Oh, he'll look after himself," said Vatia, pouring. "He will make money. I can understand that. When his father and his brother Lucius died, he should have inherited more than just a rich widow. The Licinius Crassus fortune was worth three hundred talents. But of course it was confiscated. Trust Cinna! He grabbed everything. And poor Crassus didn't have anything like Catulus's clout."

Sulla snorted. "Poor Crassus, indeed! He stole that gold from Tuder, I know he did."

"Probably," said Vatia, unruffled. "However, you can't pursue it at the moment. You need the man! And he knows you do. This is a desperate venture."

The arrival of Pompey and Crassus to swell Sulla's army was made known to Carbo immediately. To his legates he turned a calm face, and made no mention of relocating himself or his forces. He still outnumbered Sulla heavily, which meant Sulla showed no sign of breaking out of his camp to invite another battle. And while Carbo waited for events to shape themselves, tell him what he must do, news came first from Italian Gaul that Norbanus and his legates Quinctius and Albinovanus were beaten, that Metellus Pius and Varro Lucullus held Italian Gaul for Sulla. The second lot of news from Italian Gaul was more depressing, if not as important. The Lucanian legate Publius Albinovanus had lured Norbanus and the rest of his high command to a conference in Ariminum, then murdered all save Norbanus himself before surrendering Ariminum to Metellus Pius in exchange for a pardon. Having expressed a wish to live in exile somewhere in the east, Norbanus had been allowed to board a ship. The only legate who escaped was Lucius Quinctius, who was in Varro Lucullus's custody when the murders happened.

A tangible gloom descended upon Carbo's camp; restless men like Censorinus began to pace and fume. But still Sulla would not offer battle. In desperation, Carbo gave Censorinus something to do; he was to take eight legions to Praeneste and relieve the siege of Young Marius. Ten days after departing, Censorinus was back. It was impossible to relieve Young Marius, he said—the fortifications Ofella had built were impregnable. Carbo sent a second expedition to Praeneste, but only succeeded in losing two thousand good men when Sulla ambushed them. A third force set off under Brutus Damasippus to find a road over the mountains and break into Praeneste along the snake-paths behind it. That too failed; Brutus Damasippus looked, abandoned all hope, and returned to Clusium and Carbo.

Even the news that the paralyzed Samnite leader Gaius Papius Mutilus had assembled forty thousand men in Aesernia and was going to send them to relieve Praeneste had no power now to lift Carbo's spirits; his depression deepened every day. Nor did his attitude of mind improve when Mutilus sent him a letter saying his force would be seventy thousand, not forty thousand, as Lucania and Marcus Lamponius were sending him twenty thousand men, and Capua and Tiberius Gutta another ten thousand.

There was only one man Carbo really trusted, old Marcus Junius Brutus, his proquaestor. And so to Old Brutus he went as June turned into Quinctilis, and still no decision had come to him capable of easing his mind.

"If Albinovanus would stoop to murdering men he'd laughed and eaten with for months, how can I possibly be sure of any of my own legates?" he asked.

They were strolling down the three-mile length of the Via Principalis, one of the two main avenues within the camp, and wide enough to ensure their conversation was private.

Blinking slowly in the sunlight, the old man with the blued lips made no quick, reassuring answer; instead, he turned the question over in his mind, and when he did reply, said very soberly, "I do not think you can be sure, Gnaeus Papirius."

Carbo's breath hissed between his teeth; he trembled. "Ye gods, Marcus, what am I to do?"

"For the moment, nothing. But I think you must abandon this sad business before murder becomes a desirable alternative to one or more of your legates."

"Abandon?"

"Yes, abandon," said Old Brutus steadily.

"They wouldn't let me leave!" Carbo cried, shaking now.

"Probably not. But they don't need to know. I'll start making our preparations, while you look as if the only thing worrying you is the fate of the Samnite army." Old Brutus put his hand on Carbo's arm, patted it. "Don't despair. All will be well in the end."

By the middle of Quinctilis, Old Brutus had finished his preparations. Very quietly in the middle of the night he and Carbo stole away without baggage or attendants save for a mule loaded down with gold ingots innocently sheathed in a layer of lead, and a large purse of denarii for traveling expenses. Looking like a tired pair of merchants, they made their way to the Etrurian coast at Telamon, and there took ship for Africa. No one molested them, no one was the slightest bit interested in the laboring mule or in what it had in its panniers. Fortune, thought Carbo as the ship slipped anchor, was favoring him!

Because he was paralyzed from the waist down, Gaius Papius Mutilus could not lead the Samnite/Lucanian/Capuan host himself, though he did travel with the Samnite segment of it from its training ground at Aesernia as far as Teanum Sidicinum, where the whole host occupied Sulla's and Scipio's old camps, and Mutilus went to stay in his own house.

His fortunes had prospered since the Italian War; now he owned villas in half a dozen places throughout Samnium and Campania, and was wealthier than he had ever been: an ironic compensation, he sometimes thought, for the loss of all power and feeling below the waist.

Aesernia and Bovianum were his two favorite towns, but his wife, Bastia, preferred to live in Teanum—she was from the district. That Mutilus had not objected to this almost constant separation was due to his injury; as a husband he was of little use, and if understandably his wife needed to avail herself of physical solace, better she did so where he was not. However, no scandalous tidbits about her behavior had percolated back to him in Aesernia, which meant either she was voluntarily as continent as his injury obliged him to be, or her discretion was exemplary. So when Mutilus arrived at his house in Teanum, he found himself quite looking forward to Bastia's company.

"I didn't expect to see you," she said with perfect ease.

"There's no reason why you should have expected me, since I didn't write," he said in an agreeable way. "You look well."

"I feel well."

"Given my limitations, I'm in pretty good health myself," he went on, finding the reunion more awkward than he had hoped; she was distant, too courteous.

"What brings you to Teanum?" she asked.

"I've an army outside town. We're going to war against Sulla. Or at least, my army is. I shall stay here with you."

"For how long?" she enquired politely.

"Until the business is over one way or the other."

"I see." She leaned back in her chair, a magnificent woman of some thirty summers, and looked at him without an atom of the blazing desire he used to see in her eyes when they were first married—and he had been all a man. "How may I see to your comfort, husband? Is there any special thing you'll need?"

"I have my body servant. He knows what to do."

Disposing the clouds of expensive gauze about her splendid body more artistically, she continued to gaze at him out of those orbs large and dark enough to have earned her an Homeric compliment: Lady Ox-eyes. "Just you to dinner?" she asked.

"No, three others. My legates. Is that a problem?"

"Certainly not. The menu will do you honor, Gaius Papius."

The menu did. Bastia was an excellent housekeeper. She knew two of the three men who came to eat with their stricken commander, Pontius

Telesinus and Marcus Lamponius. Telesinus was a Samnite of very old family who had been a little too young to be numbered among the Samnite greats of the Italian War. Now thirty-two, he was a fine-looking man, and bold enough to eye his hostess with an appreciation only she divined. That she ignored it was good sense; Telesinus was a Samnite, and that meant he hated Romans more than he could possibly admire women.

Marcus Lamponius was the paramount chieftain from Lucania, and had been a formidable enemy to Rome during the Italian War. Now into his fifties, he was still warlike, still thirsted to let Roman blood flow. They never change, these non-Roman Italians, she thought; destroying Rome means more to them than life or prosperity or peace. More even than children.

The one among the three Bastia had never met before was a Campanian like herself, the chief citizen of Capua. His name was Tiberius Gutta, and he was fat, brutish, egotistical, as fanatically dedicated to shedding Roman blood as the others.

She absented herself from the *triclinium* as soon as her husband gave her permission to retire, burning with an anger she had most carefully concealed. It wasn't fair! Things were just beginning to run so smoothly that the Italian War might not have happened, when here it was, starting all over again. She had wanted to cry out that nothing would change, that Rome would grind their faces and their fortunes into the dust yet again; but self-control had kept her tongue still. Even if they had been brought to believe her, patriotism and pride would dictate that they go ahead anyway.

The anger ate at her, refused to die away. Up and down the marble floor of her sitting room she paced, wanting to strike out at them, those stupid, pigheaded men. Especially her own husband, leader of his nation, the one to whom all other Samnites looked for guidance. And what sort of guidance was he giving them? War against Rome. Ruination. Did he care that when he fell, everyone attached to him would also fall? Of course he did not! He was all a man, with all a man's idiocies of nationalism and revenge. All a man, yet only half a man. And the half of him left was no use to her, no use for procreating or recreating.

She stopped, feeling the heat at the core of her all this anger had caused to boil up. Her lips were bitten, she could taste a little bead of blood. On fire. On fire.

There was a slave. . . . One of those Greeks from Samothrace with hair so black it shone blue in the light, brows which met across the bridge of his nose in unashamed luxuriance, and eyes the color of a mountain lake . . . Skin so fine it begged to be kissed . . . Bastia clapped her hands.

When the steward came, she looked at him with her chin up and her bitten lips as plump and red as strawberries. "Are the gentlemen in the dining room content?"

"Yes, *domina.*"

"Good. Continue to look after them, please. And send Hippolytus to me here. I've thought of something he can do for me," she said.

The steward's face remained expressionless; as his master Mutilus did not care to live in Teanum Sidicinum, whereas his mistress Bastia did, his mistress Bastia mattered more to him. She must be kept happy. He bowed. "I will send Hippolytus to you at once, *domina,*" he said, and did many obeisances as he extricated himself carefully from her room.

In the *triclinium* Bastia had been forgotten the moment she departed for her own quarters.

"Carbo assures me that he has Sulla tied down at Clusium," Mutilus said to his legates.

"Do you believe that?" asked Lamponius.

Mutilus frowned. "I have no reason to think otherwise, but I can't be absolutely sure, of course. Do you have any reason to think otherwise?"

"No, except that Carbo's a Roman."

"Hear, hear!" cried Pontius Telesinus.

"Fortunes change," said Tiberius Gutta of Capua, face shining from the grease of a capon roasted with chestnut stuffing and a skin-crisping glaze of oil. "For the moment, we fight on Carbo's side. After Sulla is defeated, we can turn on Carbo and every other Roman and rend them."

"Absolutely," agreed Mutilus, smiling.

"We should move on Praeneste at once," said Lamponius.

"Tomorrow, in fact," said Telesinus quickly.

But Mutilus shook his head emphatically. "No. We rest the men here for five more days. They've had a hard march, and they still have to cover the length of the Via Latina. When they get to Ofella's siegeworks, they must be fresh."

These things decided—and given the prospect of relative leisure for the next five days—the dinner party broke up far earlier than Mutilus's steward had anticipated. Busy among the kitchen servants, he saw nothing, heard nothing. And was not there when the master of the house ordered his massive German attendant to carry him to the mistress's room.

She was kneeling naked upon the pillows of her couch, legs spread wide apart, and between her glistening thighs a blue-black head of hair was buried; the compact and muscular body which belonged to the head was stretched across the couch in an abandonment so complete it looked as if it belonged to a sleeping cat. In no other place than where the head was buried did the two bodies touch; Bastia's arms were extended behind her, their hands kneading the pillows, and his arms lolled alongside the rest of him.

The door had opened quietly; the German slave stood with his master in his hold like a bride being carried across the threshold of her new home, and waited for his next instructions with all the dumb endurance of such fellows, far from home, almost devoid of Latin or Greek, permanently transfixed with the pain of loss, unable to express that pain.

The eyes of husband and wife met. In hers there flashed a shout of triumph, of jubilation; in his an amazement without the dulling anodyne of shock. Of its own volition his gaze fell to rest upon her glorious breasts, the sleekness of her belly, and was blurred by a sudden rush of tears.

The young Greek's utter absorption in what he was doing now caught a change, a tension in the woman having nothing to do with him; he began to lift his head. Like two striking snakes her hands locked in the blue-black hair, pressed the head down and held it there.

"Don't stop!" she cried.

Unable to look away, Mutilus watched the blood-gorged tissue in her nipples begin to swell them to bursting; her hips were moving, the head riding upon them. And then, beneath her husband's eyes, Bastia screeched and moaned the power of her massive orgasm. It seemed to Mutilus to last an eternity.

Done, she released the head and slapped the young Greek, who rolled over and lay faceup; his terror was so profound that he seemed not to breathe.

"You can't do anything with *that,*" said Bastia, pointing to the slave's diminishing erection, "but there's nothing wrong with your tongue, Mutilus."

"You're right, there isn't," he said, every last tear dried. "It can still taste and feel. But it isn't interested in carrion."

The German got him out of the room, carried him to his own sleeping cubicle, and deposited him with care upon his bed. Then after he had completed his various duties he left Gaius Papius Mutilus alone. No comment, no sympathy, no acknowledgment. And that, reflected Mutilus as he turned his face into his pillow, was a greater mercy than all else. Still in his mind's eye the image of his wife's body burned, the breasts with their nipples popping out, and that head—that head! That head . . . Below his waist nothing stirred, could never stir again. But the rest of him knew torments and dreams, and longed for every aspect of love. *Every* aspect!

"I am not dead," he said into the pillow, and felt the tears come. "I am not dead! But oh, by all the gods, I wish I were!"

* * *

At the end of June, Sulla left Clusium. With him he took his own five legions and three of Scipio's; he left Pompey in command, a decision which hadn't impressed his other legates at all. But, since Sulla was Sulla and no one actively argued with him, Pompey it was.

"Clean this lot up," he said to Pompey. "They outnumber you, but they're demoralized. However, when they discover that I'm gone for good, they'll offer battle. Watch Damasippus, he is the most competent among them. Crassus will cope with Marcus Censorinus, and Torquatus ought to manage against Carrinas."

"What about Carbo?" asked Pompey.

"Carbo is a cipher. He lets his legates do his generaling. But don't fiddle, Pompeius! I have other work for you."

No surprise then that Sulla took the more senior of his legates with him; neither Vatia nor the elder Dolabella could have stomached the humiliation of having to ask a twenty-three-year-old for orders. His departure came on the heels of news about the Samnites, and made Sulla's need to reach the general area around Praeneste urgent; dispositions would have to be finished before the Samnite host drew too near.

Having scouted the whole region on that side of Rome with extreme thoroughness, Sulla knew exactly what he intended to do. The Via Praenestina and the Via Labicana were now unnegotiable thanks to Ofella's wall and ditch, but the Via Latina and the Via Appia were still open, still connected Rome and the north with Campania and the south. If the war was to be won, it was vital that all military access between Rome and the south belong to Sulla; Etruria was exhausted, but Samnium and Lucania had scarcely been tapped of manpower or food resources.

The countryside between Rome and Campania was not easy. On the coast it deteriorated into the Pomptine Marshes, through which from Campania the Via Appia traveled a mosquito-ridden straight line until near Rome it ran up against the flank of the Alban Hills. These were not hills at all, but quite formidable mountains based upon the outpourings of an old volcano which had cut up and elevated the original alluvial Latin plain. The Alban Mount itself, center of that ancient subterranean disturbance, reared between the Via Appia and the other, more inland road, the Via Latina. South of the Alban Hills another high ridge continued to separate the Via Appia from the Via Latina, thus preventing interconnection between these two major arteries all the way from Campania to a point very near Rome. For military travel the more inland Via Latina was always preferred over the Via Appia; men got sick when they marched the Via Appia.

It was therefore preferable that Sulla station himself on the Via Latina—

but at a place where he could, if necessary, transfer his forces rapidly across to the Via Appia. Both roads traversed the outer flanks of the Alban Hills, but the Via Latina did so through a defile which chopped a gap in the eastern escarpment of the ridge and allowed the road to travel onward to Rome in the flatter space between this high ground and the Alban Mount itself. At the point where the defile opened out toward the Alban Mount, a small road curved westward round this central peak, and joined the Via Appia quite close to the sacred lake of Nemi and its temple precinct.

Here in the defile Sulla sat himself down and proceeded to build immense fortified walls of tufa blocks at each end of the gorge, enclosing the side road which led to Lake Nemi and the Via Appia within his battlements. He now occupied the only place on the Via Latina at which all progress could be stopped from both directions. And, his fortifications completed within a very short time, he posted a series of watches on the Via Appia to make sure no enemy tried to outflank him by this route, from Rome as well as from Campania. All his provisions were brought along the side road from the Via Appia.

By the time the Samnite/Lucanian/Capuan host reached the site of Sacriportus, everyone was calling this army "the Samnites" despite its composite nature (enhanced because remnants of the legions scattered by Pompey and Crassus had tacked themselves on to such a strong, well-led force). At Sacriportus the host chose the Via Labicana, only to discover that Ofella had by now contained himself within a second line of fortifications, and could not be dislodged. Shining from its heights with a myriad colors, Praeneste might as well have been as far away as the Garden of the Hesperides. After riding along every inch of Ofella's walls, Pontius Telesinus, Marcus Lamponius and Tiberius Gutta could discern no weakness, and a cross-country march by seventy thousand men with nowhere positive to go was impossible. A war council resulted in a change of strategy; the only way to draw Ofella off was to attack Rome herself. So to Rome on the Via Latina the Samnite army would go.

Back they marched to Sacriportus, and turned onto the Via Latina in the direction of Rome. Only to find Sulla sitting behind his enormous ramparts in complete control of the road. To storm his position seemed far easier than storming Ofella's walls, so the Samnite host attacked. When they failed, they tried again. And again. Only to hear Sulla laughing at them as loudly as had Ofella.

Then came news at once cheering and depressing; those left at Clusium had sallied out and engaged Pompey. That they had gone down in utter defeat was depressing, yet seemed not to matter when compared to the message that

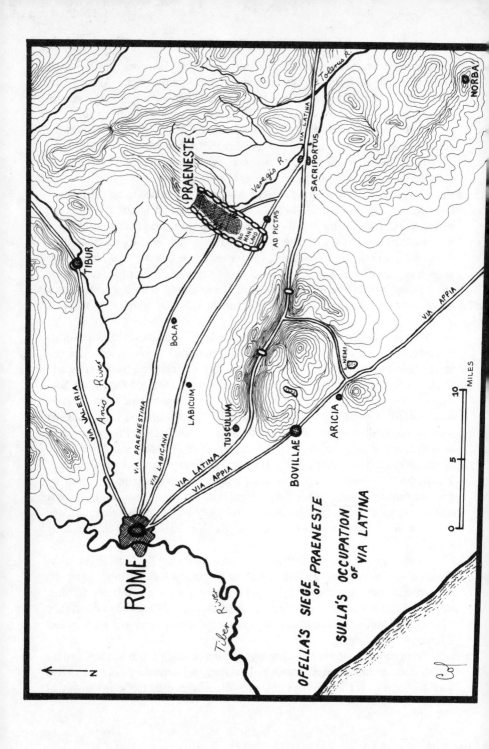

OFELLA'S SIEGE OF PRAENESTE

SULLA'S OCCUPATION OF VIA LATINA

the survivors, some twenty thousand strong, were marching south under Censorinus, Carrinas and Brutus Damasippus. Carbo himself had vanished, but the fight, swore Brutus Damasippus in his letter to Pontius Telesinus, would go on. If Sulla's position were stormed from both sides at once at the exact same moment, he would crumble. *Had* to crumble!

"Rubbish, of course," said Sulla to Pompey, whom he had summoned to his defile for a conference as soon as he had been notified of Pompey's victory at Clusium. "They can pile Pelion on top of Ossa if they so choose, but they won't dislodge me. This place was made for defense! Impregnable and unassailable."

"If you're so confident, what need can you have for me?" the young man asked, his pride at being summoned evaporating.

The campaign at Clusium had been short, grim, decisive; many of the enemy had died, many were taken prisoner, and those who got away were chiefly distinguished for the quality of the men who led their retreat; there had been no senior legates in the ranks of those who surrendered, a great disappointment. The defection of Carbo himself had not been known to Pompey until after the battle was over, when the story of his nocturnal flight was told with tears and bitterness to Pompey's men by tribunes, centurions and soldiers alike. A great betrayal.

Hard on the heels of this had come Sulla's summons, which Pompey had received with huge delight. His instructions were to bring six legions and two thousand horse with him; that Varro would tag along, he took for granted, whereas Crassus and Torquatus were to remain at Clusium. But what need had Sulla for more troops in a camp already bursting at the seams? Indeed, Pompey's army had been directed into a camp on the shores of Lake Nemi and therefore adjacent to the Via Appia!

"Oh, I don't need you here," said Sulla, leaning his arms on the parapet of an observation tower atop his walls and peering vainly in the direction of Rome; his vision had deteriorated badly since that illness in Greece, though he disliked owning up to it. "I'm getting closer, Pompeius! Closer and closer."

Not normally bashful, Pompey found himself unable to ask the question he burned to ask: what did Sulla intend when the war was over? How could he retain his authority, how could he possibly protect himself from future reprisals? He couldn't keep his army with him forever, but the moment he disbanded it he would be at the mercy of anyone with the strength and the clout to call him to account. And that might be someone who at the present moment called himself a loyal follower, Sulla's man to the death. Who knew what men like Vatia and the elder Dolabella really thought? Both of them were of consular age, even if circumstances had conspired to prevent their becoming consul. How *could* Sulla insulate himself? A great man's enemies were like the Hydra—no matter how many heads he succeeded in cutting off, there were always more busily growing, and always sporting bigger and better teeth.

"If you don't need me here, Sulla, where *do* you need me?" Pompey asked, bewildered.

"It is the beginning of Sextilis," said Sulla, and turned to lead the way down the many stairs.

Nothing more was said until they emerged at the bottom into the controlled chaos beneath the walls, where men busied themselves in carrying loads of rocks, oil for burning and throwing down upon the hapless heads of those trying to scale ladders, missiles for the onagers and catapults already bristling atop the walls, stocks of spears and arrows and shields.

"It is the beginning of Sextilis?" Pompey prompted once they were out of the activity and had begun to stroll down the side road toward Lake Nemi.

"So it is!" said Sulla in tones of surprise, and fell about laughing at the look on Pompey's face.

Obviously he was expected to laugh too; Pompey laughed too. "Yes, it is," he said, and added, "the beginning of Sextilis."

Controlling himself with an effort, Sulla decided he had had his fun. Best put the young would-be Alexander out of his misery by telling him.

"I have a special command for you, Pompeius," he said curtly. "The rest will have to know about it—but not yet. I want you well away before the storm of protest breaks—for break, it will! You see, what I want you to do is something I ought not to ask of any man who has not been at the very least a praetor."

Excitement growing, Pompey stopped walking, put his hand on Sulla's arm and turned him so that his face was fully visible; bright blue eyes stared into white-blue eyes. They were now standing in a rather pretty dell to one side of the unsealed road, and the noise of so much industry to front and back was muted by great flowering banks of summer brambles, roses and blackberries.

"Then why have you chosen me, Lucius Cornelius?" Pompey asked, tones wondering. "You have many legates who fit that description—Vatia, Appius Claudius, Dolabella—even men like Mamercus and Crassus would seem more appropriate! *So why me?*"

"Don't die from curiosity, Pompeius, I will tell you! But first, I must tell you exactly what it is I want you to do."

"I am listening," said Pompey with a great show of calm.

"I told you to bring six legions and two thousand cavalry. That's a respectable army. You are going to take it at once to Sicily, and secure the coming harvest for me. It's Sextilis, the harvest will begin very soon. And sitting for the most part in Puteoli harbor is the grain fleet. Hundreds upon hundreds of empty vessels. Ready-made transports, Pompeius! Tomorrow you will take the Via Appia and march for Puteoli before the grain fleet can sail. You will bear my mandate and have sufficient money to pay for the hiring of the ships, and you will have a propraetorian imperium. Post your cavalry to Ostia, there's a smaller fleet there. I've already sent out messengers to ports like Tarracina and Antium, and told all the little shipowners to gather in Puteoli if they want to be paid for what would under normal circumstances be an empty voyage out. You'll have more than enough ships, I guarantee you."

Had he once dreamed of a meeting between himself and an equally godlike man called Lucius Cornelius Sulla? And been crushed to abject misery because he had found a satyr, not a god? But what did the look of a man matter, when he held in both hands such a store of dreams? The scarred and drunken old man whose eyes were not even good enough to see Rome in the distance was offering him the whole conduct of a war! A war far away from interference, against an enemy he would have all to himself . . . Pompey gasped, held out his freckled hand with its short and slightly crooked fingers, and clasped Sulla's beautiful hand.

"Lucius Cornelius, that's wonderful! Wonderful! Oh, you can count on me! I'll drive Perperna Veiento out of Sicily and give you more wheat than *ten* armies could eat!"

"I'm going to need more wheat than ten armies could eat," said Sulla, releasing his hand; despite his youth and undeniable attractions, Pompey was not a type who appealed to Sulla physically, and he never liked to touch men or women who didn't appeal to him physically. "By the end of this year, Rome will be mine. And if I want Rome to lie down for me, then I'll have to make sure she's not hungry. That means the Sicilian grain harvest, the Sardinian grain harvest—and, if possible, the African grain harvest too. So when you've secured Sicily, you'll have to move on to Africa Province and do what you can there. You won't be in time to catch the loaded fleets from Utica and Hadrumetum—I imagine you'll be many months in Sicily before you can hope to deal with Africa. But Africa must be subdued before you can come home to Italy. I hear that Fabius Hadrianus was burned to death in the governor's palace during an uprising in Utica, but that Gnaeus Domitius Ahenobarbus—having escaped from Sacriportus!—has taken over and is holding Africa for the enemy. If you're in western Sicily, it's a short distance from Lilybaeum to Utica by sea. You ought to be able to wrap up Africa. Somehow you don't have the look of a failure about you.''

Pompey was literally shivering in excitement; he smiled, gasped. ''I won't fail you, Lucius Cornelius! I promise I will never fail you!''

''I believe you, Pompeius.'' Sulla sat down on a log, licked his lips. ''What are we doing here? I need wine!''

''Here is a good place, there's no one to see us or listen to us,'' said Pompey soothingly. ''Wait, Lucius Cornelius. I'll fetch you wine. Just sit there and wait.''

As it was a shady spot, Sulla did as he was told, smiling at some secret joke. Oh, what a lovely day it was!

Back came Pompey at a run, yet breathing as if he hadn't run at all. Sulla grabbed at the wineskin, squirted liquid into his mouth with great expertise, actually managing to swallow and take in air at the same time. Some moments elapsed before he ceased to squeeze, put the skin down.

''Oh, that's better! Where was I?''

''You may fool some people, Lucius Cornelius, but not me. You know precisely where you were,'' said Pompey coolly, and sat himself on the grass directly in front of Sulla's log.

''Very good! Pompeius, you're as rare as an ocean pearl the size of a pigeon's egg! And I can truly say that I am very glad I'll be dead long before you become a Roman headache.'' He picked up the wineskin again, drank again.

''I'll never be a Roman headache,'' said Pompey innocently. ''I will just be the First Man in Rome—and not by mouthing a lot of pretentious rubbish in the Forum or the Senate, either.''

''How then, boy, if not through stirring speeches?''

''By doing what you're sending me off to do. By beating Rome's enemies in battle.''

''Not a novel approach,'' said Sulla. ''That's the way I've done it. That's the way Gaius Marius did it too.''

''Yes, but I'm not going to need to snatch my commissions,'' said Pompey. ''Rome is going to give me every last one on her very knees!''

Sulla might have interpreted that statement as a reproach, or even as an outright criticism; but he knew his Pompey by this, and understood that most of what the young man said arose out of egotism, that Pompey as yet had no idea how difficult it might be to make that statement come true. So all Sulla did was to sigh and say, ''Strictly speaking, I can't give you any sort of imperium. I'm not consul, and I don't have the Senate or the People behind

me to pass my laws. You'll just have to accept that I will make it possible
for you to come back and be confirmed with a praetor's imperium.''

"I don't doubt that."

"Do you doubt anything?"

"Not if it concerns me directly. I can influence events."

"May you never change!" Sulla leaned forward, clasped his hands
between his knees. "All right, Pompeius, the compliments are over. Listen
to me very carefully. There are two more things I have to tell you. The first
concerns Carbo.''

"I'm listening," said Pompey.

"He sailed from Telamon with Old Brutus. Now it's possible that he
headed for Spain, or even for Massilia. But at this time of year, his destination
was more likely Sicily or Africa. While ever he's at large, he is the consul.
The *elected* consul. That means he can override the imperium of a governor,
commandeer the governor's soldiers or militia, call up auxiliaries, and generally make a thorough nuisance of himself until his term as consul runs out.
Which is some months off. I am not going to tell you exactly what I plan to
do after Rome is mine, but I will tell you this—it is vital to my plans that
Carbo be dead well before the end of his year in office. *And it is vital that I
know Carbo is dead!* Your job is to track Carbo down and kill him. Very
quietly and inconspicuously—I would like his death to seem an accident. Will
you undertake to do this?''

"Yes," said Pompey without hesitation.

"Good! Good!" Sulla turned his hands over and inspected them as if
they belonged to someone else. "Now I come to my last point, which concerns
the reason why I am entrusting this overseas campaign to you rather than to
one of my senior legates." He peered at the young man intently. "Can you
see why for yourself, Pompeius?''

Pompey thought, shrugged. "I have some ideas, perhaps, but without
knowing what you plan to do after Rome is yours, I am most likely wrong.
Tell me why.''

"Pompeius, you are the *only* one I can entrust with this commission! If
I give six legions and two thousand horse to a man as senior as Vatia or
Dolabella and send that man off to Sicily and Africa, what's to stop his
coming back with the intention of supplanting me? All he has to do is to
remain away long enough for me to be obliged'to disband my own army,
then return and supplant me. Sicily and Africa are not campaigns likely to
be finished in six months, so it's very likely that I will have had to disband
my own army before whoever I send comes home. I cannot keep a permanent

standing army in Italy. There's neither the money nor the room for it. And the Senate and People of Rome would never consent. Therefore I must keep every man senior enough to be my rival under my eye. Therefore it is you I am sending off to secure the harvest and make it possible for me to feed ungrateful Rome.''

Pompey drew a breath, linked his arms around his knees and looked at Sulla very directly. "And what's to stop *me* doing all of that, Lucius Cornelius? If I'm capable of running a campaign, am I not capable of thinking I can supplant you?''

A question which plainly didn't send a single shiver down Sulla's spine; he laughed heartily. "Oh, you can think it all you like, Pompeius! But Rome would never wear you! Not for a single moment. She'd wear Vatia or Dolabella. They have the years, the relations, the ancestors, the clout, the clients. But a twenty-three-year-old from Picenum that Rome doesn't know? Not a chance!''

And so they left the matter, walked off in opposite directions. When Pompey encountered Varro he said very little, just told that indefatigable observer of life and nature that he was to go to Sicily to secure the harvest. Of imperium, older men, the death of Carbo and much else, he said nothing at all. Of Sulla he asked only one favor—that he might be allowed to take his brother-in-law, Gaius Memmius, as his chief legate. Memmius, several years older than Pompey but not yet a quaestor, had been serving in the legions of Sulla.

"You're absolutely right, Pompeius,'' said Sulla with a smile. "An excellent choice! Keep your venture in the family.''

The simultaneous attack on Sulla's fortifications from north and south came to pass two days after Pompey had departed with his army for Puteoli and the grain fleet. A wave of men broke on either wall, but the waves ebbed and died away harmlessly. Sulla still owned the Via Latina, and those attacking from the north could find no way to join up with those attacking on the south. At dawn on the second morning after the attack, the watchers in the towers on either wall could see no enemy; they had packed up and stolen off in the night. Reports came in all through that day that the twenty thousand men belonging to Censorinus, Carrinas and Brutus Damasippus were marching down the Via Appia toward Campania, and that the Samnite host was marching down the Via Latina in the same direction.

"Let them go,'' said Sulla indifferently. "Eventually I suppose they'll come back—united. And when they do come back it will be on the Via Appia. Where I will be waiting for them.''

By the end of Sextilis, the Samnites and the remnants of Carbo's army had joined forces at Fregellae, and there moved off the Via Latina eastward through the Melfa Gorge.

"They're going to Aesernia to think again," said Sulla, and did not instruct that they be followed further. "It's enough to post lookouts on the Via Latina at Ferentinum, and the Via Appia at Tres Tabernae. I don't need more warning than that, and I'm not going to waste my scouts sending them to sneak around Samnites in Samnite territory like Aesernia."

The action shifted abruptly to Praeneste, where Young Marius, restless and growing steadily more unpopular within the town, emerged from the gates and ventured out into No Man's Land. At the westernmost point of the ridge, where the watershed divided Tolerus streams from Anio streams, he began to build a massive siege tower, having judged that at this point Ofella's wall was weakest. No tree had been left standing to furnish materials for this work anywhere within reach of those defending Praeneste; it was houses and temples yielded up the timber, precious nails and bolts, blocks and panels and tiles.

The most dangerous work was to make a smooth roadway for the tower to be moved upon between the spot where it was being built and the edge of Ofella's ditch, for these laborers were at the mercy of marksmen atop Ofella's walls; Young Marius chose the youngest and swiftest among his helpers to do this, and gave them a makeshift roof under which to shelter. Out of harm's reach another team toiled with pieces of timber too small to use in constructing the tower, and made a bridge of laminated planking to throw across the ditch when it came time to push the tower right up against Ofella's wall. Once work upon the tower had progressed enough to create a shelter inside it for those who labored upon building it, the thing seemed to grow from within, up and up and up, out and out and out.

In a month it was ready, and so were the causeway and the bridge along which a thousand pairs of hands would propel it. But Ofella too was ready, having had plenty of time to prepare his defenses. The bridge was put across the ditch in the darkest hours of night, the tower rolled heaving and groaning upon a slipway of sheep's fat mixed with oil; dawn saw the tower, twenty feet higher than the top of Ofella's wall, in position. Deep in its bowels there hung upon ropes toughened with pitch a mighty battering ram made from the single beam which had spanned the Goddess's *cella* in the temple of Fortuna Primigenia, who was the firstborn daughter of Jupiter, and talisman of Italian luck.

But it was many a year before tufa stone hardened to real brittleness, so the ram when brought to bear on Ofella's wall roared and boomed and pounded in vain; the elastic tufa blocks shook, even trembled and vibrated, but they held until Ofella's catapults firing blazing missiles had set the tower on fire, and driven the attackers hurling spears and arrows fleeing with hair in flames. By nightfall the tower was a twisted ruin collapsed in the ditch, and those who had tried to break out were either dead or back within Praeneste.

Several times during October, Young Marius tried to use the bridged ditch filled with the wreckage of his tower as a base; he roofed a section between Ofella's wall and the ditch to keep his men safe and tried to mine his way beneath the wall, then tried to cut his way through the wall, and finally tried to scale the wall. But nothing worked. Winter was close at hand, seemed to promise the same kind of bitter cold as the last one; Praeneste knew itself short of food, and rued the day it had opened its gates to the son of Gaius Marius.

The Samnite host had not gone to Aesernia at all. Ninety thousand strong, it sat itself down in the awesome mountains to the south of the Fucine Lake and whiled away almost two months in drills, foraging parties, more drills. Pontius Telesinus and Brutus Damasippus had journeyed to see Mutilus in Teanum, come away armed with a plan to take Rome by surprise—and without Sulla's knowledge. For, said Mutilus, Young Marius would have to be left to his fate. The only chance left for all right-thinking men was to capture Rome and draw both Sulla and Ofella into a siege which would be prolonged and filled with a terrible doubt—would those inside Rome elect to join the Samnite cause?

There was a way across the mountains between the Melfa Gorge and the Via Valeria. This stock route—for so it was better termed than road— traversed the ranges between Atina at the back of the Melfa Gorge—a wilderness—went to Sora on the elbow of the Liris River, then to Treba, then to Sublaquaeum, and finally emerged on the Via Valeria a scant mile east of Varia, at a little hamlet called Mandela. It was neither paved nor even surveyed, but it had been there for centuries, and was the route whereby the many shepherds of the mountains moved their flocks each summer season between pastures at the same altitude. It was also the route the flocks took to the sale yards and slaughterhouses of the Campus Lanatarius and the Vallis Camenarum adjoining the Aventine parts of Rome.

Had Sulla stopped to remember the time when he had marched from Fregellae to the Fucine Lake to assist Gaius Marius to defeat Silo and the Marsi, he might have remembered this stock route, for he had actually followed a part of it from Sora to Treba, and had not found it impossible going. But at Treba he had left it, and had not thought to ascertain whereabouts it

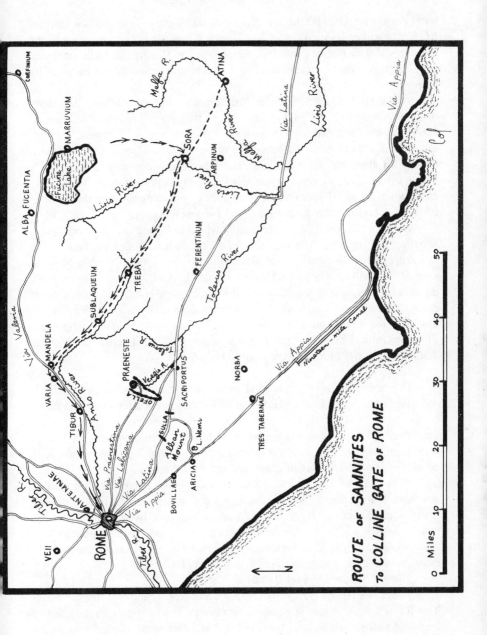

ROUTE of SAMNITES
to COLLINE GATE of ROME

went north of Treba. So the one chance Sulla might have had to circumvent Mutilus's strategy was overlooked. Thinking that the only route open to the Samnites if they planned to attack Rome was the Via Appia, Sulla remained in his defile on the Via Latina and kept watch, sure he could not be taken by surprise.

And while he sat in his defile, the Samnites and their allies toiled along the stock route, secure in the knowlédge that they were passing through country whose inhabitants had no love of Rome, and well beyond the outermost tentacles of Sulla's intelligence network. Sora, Treba, Sublaquaeum, and finally onto the Via Valeria at Mandela. They were now a scant day's march from Rome, a mere thirty miles of superbly kept road as the Via Valeria came down through Tibur and the Anio valley, and terminated on the Campus Esquilinus beneath the double rampart of Rome's Agger.

But this was not the best place from which to launch an attack on Rome, so when the great host drew close to the city, Pontius Telesinus and Brutus Damasippus took a *diverticulum* which brought them out on the Via Nomentana at the Colline Gate. And there outside the Colline Gate—waiting for them, as it were—was the stout camp Pompey Strabo had built for himself during Cinna's and Gaius Marius's siege of Rome. By nightfall of the last day of October, Pontius Telesinus, Brutus Damasippus, Marcus Lamponius, Tiberius Gutta, Censorinus and Carrinas were comfortably ensconced within that camp; on the morrow they would attack.

The news that ninety thousand men were occupying Pompey Strabo's old camp outside the Colline Gate was brought to Sulla after night had fallen on the last day of October. It found him a little the worse for wine, but not yet asleep. Within moments bugles were blaring, drums were rolling, men were tumbling from their pallets and torches were kindling everywhere. Icily sober, Sulla called his legates together and told them.

"They've stolen a march on us," he said, lips compressed. "How they got there I don't know, but the Samnites are outside the Colline Gate and ready to attack Rome. By dawn, we march. We have twenty miles to cover and some of it's hilly, but we have to get to the Colline Gate in time to fight tomorrow." He turned to his cavalry commander, Octavius Balbus. "How many horses have you got around Lake Nemi, Balbus?"

"Seven hundred," said Balbus.

"Then off you go right now. Take the Via Appia, and ride like the wind. You'll reach the Colline Gate some hours before I can hope to get the infantry there, so you've got to hold them off. I don't care what you have to do, or how you do it! Just get there and keep them occupied until I arrive."

Octavius Balbus wasted no time speaking; he was out of Sulla's door and roaring for a horse before Sulla could turn back to his other legates.

There were four of them—Crassus, Vatia, Dolabella and Torquatus. Shocked, but not bereft of their wits.

"We have eight legions here, and they will have to do," said Sulla. "That means we'll be outnumbered two to one. I'll make my dispositions now because there may not be the time for conferences after we reach the Colline Gate."

He fell silent, studying them. Who would fare best? Who would have the steel to lead in what was going to be a desperate encounter? By rights it ought to be Vatia and Dolabella, but were they the *best* men? His eyes dwelt upon Marcus Licinius Crassus, huge and rock-solid, never anything save calm—eaten up with avarice, a thief and a swindler—not principled, not ethical, perhaps moral. And yet of the four of them he had the most to lose if this war was lost. Vatia and Dolabella would survive, they had the clout. Torquatus was a good man, but not a true leader.

Sulla made up his mind. "I will move in two divisions of four legions each," he said, slapping his hands on his thighs. "I will retain the high command myself, but I will not command either division. For want of a better way to distinguish them, I'll call them the left and the right, and unless I change my orders after we arrive, that is how they'll fight. Left and right of the field. No center. I haven't enough men. Vatia, you will command the left, with Dolabella as your second-in-command. Crassus, you'll command the right, with Torquatus as your second-in-command."

As he spoke, Sulla's eyes rested upon Dolabella, saw the anger and outrage; no need to look at Marcus Crassus, he would not betray his feelings.

"That is what I want," he said harshly, spitting out the words because they shaped themselves poorly without teeth. "I don't have time for argument. You've all thrown in your lots with me, you've given me the ultimate decisions. Now you'll do as you're told. All I expect of you is the will to fight in the way I command you to fight."

Dolabella stood back at the door and allowed the other three to precede him; then he turned back. "A word with you alone, Lucius Cornelius," he said.

"If it's quick."

A Cornelius and a remote relation of Sulla's, Dolabella was not from a branch of that great family which had managed to acquire the luster of the Scipiones—or even of the Sullae; if he had anything in common with most of the Cornelii, it was his homeliness—plump cheeks, a frowning face, eyes a little too close together. Ambitious and with a reputation for depravity, he and his first cousin, the younger Dolabella, were determined to win greater prominence for their branch of the family.

"I could break you, Sulla," Dolabella said. "All I have to do is make it impossible for you to win tomorrow's fight. And I imagine you understand that I'll change sides so fast the opposition will end in believing I was always with them."

"Do go on!" said Sulla in the most friendly fashion when Dolabella paused to see how this speech had been received.

"However, I am willing to lie down under your decision to promote Marcus Crassus over my head. On one condition."

"Which is?"

"That next year, I am consul."

"Done!" cried Sulla with the greatest goodwill.

Dolabella blinked. "You're not put out?" he asked.

"Nothing puts me out anymore, my dear Dolabella," said Sulla, escorting his legate to the door. "At the moment it makes little odds to me who is consul next year. What matters at the moment is who commands on the field tomorrow. And I see that I was right to prefer Marcus Crassus. Good night!"

The seven hundred horsemen under the command of Octavius Balbus arrived outside Pompey Strabo's camp about the middle of the morning on the first day of November. There was absolutely nothing Balbus could have done had he been put to it; his horses were so blown that they stood with heads hanging, sides heaving and white with sweat, mouths dripping foam, while their riders stood alongside them and tried to comfort them by loosening girths and speaking soft endearments. For this reason Balbus had not halted too close to the enemy—let them think his force was ready for action! So he arranged it in what appeared to be a charge formation, had his troopers brandish their lances and pretend to shout messages back to an unseen army of infantry in their rear.

It was evident that the attack upon Rome had not yet begun. The Colline Gate stood in majestic isolation, its portcullis down and its two mighty oak doors closed; the battlements of the two towers which flanked it were alive with heads, and the walls which ran away on either side were heavily manned. Balbus's arrival had provoked sudden activity within the enemy camp, where soldiers were pouring out of the southeastern gate and lining up to hold off a cavalry onslaught; of enemy cavalry there was no sign, and Balbus could only hope that none was concealed.

Each trooper on the march carried a leather bucket tied to his left rear saddle horn to water his horse; while the front rank carried on with the farce of a coming charge and an invisible army of foot soldiers behind, other troopers ran with the buckets to various fountains in the vicinity and filled them. As soon as the horses could safely be watered, Octavius Balbus intended that the business should be finished in short order.

So successful was this mock show of aggression that nothing further had happened when Sulla and his infantry arrived some four hours later, in the early afternoon. His men were in much the same condition as Balbus's horses had been; exhausted, blown, legs trembling with the effort of marching at the double across twenty miles of sometimes steep terrain.

"Well, we can't possibly attack today," said Vatia after he and Sulla had ridden with the other legates to inspect the ground and see what sort of battle was going to develop.

"Why not?" asked Sulla.

Vatia looked blank. "They're too tired to fight!"

"Tired they may be, but fight they will," said Sulla.

"You can't, Lucius Cornelius! You'd lose!"

"I can, and I won't," said Sulla grimly. "Look, Vatia, we have to fight today! This war has got to end, and here and now is where and when it *must* end. The Samnites know how hard we've marched, the Samnites know the odds are in their favor today more than on any other day. If we don't offer battle today, the day they believe they have their best chance of winning, who knows what might happen tomorrow? What's to stop the Samnites packing up in the night and vanishing to choose another venue? Disappearing perhaps for months? Until the spring, or even next summer? Next autumn? No, Vatia, we fight today. Because today the Samnites are in the mood to see us dead on the field of the Colline Gate."

While his soldiers rested, ate and drank, Sulla went among them on foot to tell them in a more personal way than the usual speech from a rostra that somehow they had to find the strength and the endurance to fight. That if they waited to recover, the war might go on and on. Most of them had been with him for years and could be said in truth to love him, but even the legions which had belonged to Scipio Asiagenus had felt his hand for long enough to know themselves his men. He didn't look like the wonderful, godlike being to whom they had offered a Grass Crown outside Nola all those campaigns ago, but he was *theirs*—and hadn't they grizzled and wrinkled and grown a bit creaky in the joints too? So when he went among them and asked them to fight, they lifted laconic hands and told him not to worry, they'd fix the Samnites.

A bare two hours before darkness, battle was joined. The three legions which had belonged to Scipio Asiagenus comprised the major part of Sulla's left division, so while he did not assume command of the left, Sulla elected to remain in its area of operation. Rather than bestride his customary mule, he chose to mount a white horse, and had told his men that he would do so. That way they would know him, see him if he came to their part of the fight. Choosing a knoll which gave him a fair perspective of the field, he sat upon the white animal watching the conflict develop. Those inside Rome, he noted, had opened the doors of the Colline Gate and raised the portcullis, though no one issued out to participate in the battle.

The enemy division facing his left was the more formidable, for it was composed entirely of Samnites and commanded by Pontius Telesinus, but at forty thousand it was less numerous—some kind of compensation, thought Sulla, touching his groom with a foot, the signal for the fellow to lead his horse onward. No rider, he didn't trust this white force of nature, and had preferred that it be led. Yes, his left was falling back, he would have to go there. On lower ground, Vatia probably couldn't see that one of his worst problems was the open gate into the city; as the Samnites pushed forward stabbing and slashing upward with their short infantry swords, some of Vatia's men were slipping through the gate rather than standing and holding.

Just before he entered the melee, he heard the sharp smack of his groom's hand on the horse's shoulder, had the presence of mind to lean forward and grab its mane in both hands as it took off at a gallop. One glance behind showed him why; two Samnite spearmen had launched their weapons simultaneously at him, and he ought to have fallen. That he had not was thanks to the groom, who had made the horse bolt. Then the groom caught up and hung on to the creature's plumy tail; Sulla came to a halt unscathed and still in the saddle.

A smile of thanks for his groom, and Sulla waded into the thick of the battle with his sword in his hand and a small cavalry shield to protect his left side. He found some men he knew and ordered them to drop the portcullis—which, he noted in some amusement, they did with scant regard for those beneath it at the time it fell. The measure worked; having nowhere now to retreat, Scipio's legions stood and held while the single legion of veterans began the slow and steady job of pushing the enemy back.

How Crassus and the right were faring, Sulla had no idea; even from his knoll they had been too far away for him to supervise, and he had known his left was his weakness from the beginning. If anybody could cope, it was Crassus and the four veteran legions under his command.

Night fell but the fight went on, aided by thousands of torches held on high by those atop Rome's walls. And, gaining its second wind, Sulla's left took heart. He himself was still among it, cheering Scipio's frightened men on, doing his share of hand-to-hand combat because his groom, splendid fellow, never allowed the horse to become an encumbrance.

Perhaps two hours later, the Samnite host opposing Sulla's left broke and retreated inside Pompey Strabo's camp, where they proved too exhausted to keep Sulla out. Hoarse from shouting, Sulla and Vatia and Dolabella urged a finish, and their men cut the Samnites to pieces within the camp. Pontius Telesinus fell with his face split in two, and the heart went out of his men.

"No prisoners," said Sulla. "Kill the lot, with arrows if they clump together and try to surrender."

At that stage in a battle so bitterly fought, it would have been more difficult to persuade the soldiers to spare their foes, so the Samnites perished.

It was only after the rout was complete that Sulla, now back on his trusty mule, found time to wonder about the fate of Crassus. Of the right division there was no sign; but nor was there sign of an enemy. Crassus and his opponents had vanished.

About the middle of the night a messenger came. Sulla was prowling through Pompey Strabo's old camp making sure the still bodies lying everywhere were well and truly dead, but paused to see the man, hoping for news.

"Are you sent from Marcus Crassus?" he asked the man.

"I am," said the man, who did not look downcast.

"Where is Marcus Crassus?"

"At Antemnae."

"Antemnae?"

"The enemy broke and fled there before nightfall, and Marcus Crassus followed. Another battle took place in Antemnae. We won! Marcus Crassus has sent me to ask for food and wine for his men."

Grinning widely, Sulla shouted orders that the requested provisions be found, and then, riding upon his mule, accompanied the train of pack animals up the Via Salaria to Antemnae, just a few miles away. There he and Vatia found the reeling town trying to regain its breath, having played involuntary host to a battle which had made a wreck of it. Houses were burning fiercely, bucket brigades toiled to prevent the fires from spreading, and everywhere the bodies sprawled in death, trampled underfoot by panicked townsfolk striving to save their own lives and belongings.

Crassus was waiting on the far side of Antemnae, where in a field he had gathered the enemy survivors.

"About six thousand of them," he said to Sulla. "Vatia had the Samnites—I inherited the Lucanians, the Capuans, and Carbo's remnants. Tiberius Gutta fell on the field, Marcus Lamponius I think escaped, and I have Brutus Damasippus, Carrinas and Censorinus among the prisoners.''

"Good work!'' said Sulla, showing his gums in the broadest of smiles. "It didn't please Dolabella and I had to promise him a consulship next year to get him to go along, but I *knew* I'd picked the right man in you, Marcus Crassus!''

Vatia swung his head to stare at Sulla, aghast. *"What?* Dolabella demanded that? *Cunnus! Mentula! Verpa! Fellator!''*

"Never mind, Vatia, you'll get your consulship too,'' soothed Sulla, still smiling. "Dolabella will do no good by it. He'll go too far when he goes to govern his province and he'll spend the rest of his days in exile in Massilia with all the other intemperate fools.'' He waved a hand at the pack animals. "Now where do you want your little snack, Marcus Crassus?''

"If I can find somewhere else to put my prisoners, here, I think,'' said the stolid Crassus, who didn't look in the least as if he had just won a great victory.

"I brought Balbus's cavalry with me to escort the prisoners to the Villa Publica at once,'' said Sulla. "By the time they're moving, it will be dawn.''

While Octavius Balbus rounded up the exhausted enemy who had survived Antemnae, Sulla summoned Censorinus, Carrinas and Brutus Damasippus before him. Defeated though they were, none of them looked beaten.

"Aha! Think you're going to fight again another day, eh?'' Sulla asked, smiling again, but mirthlessly. "Well, my Roman friends, you are not. Pontius Telesinus is dead, and I had the Samnite survivors shot with arrows. Since you allied yourselves with Samnites and Lucanians, I hold you no Romans. Therefore you will not be tried for treason. You will be executed. Now.''

Thus it was that the three most implacable foes of the whole war were beheaded in a field outside Antemnae, without trial or notice. The bodies were thrown into the huge common grave being dug for all the enemy dead, but Sulla had the heads put in a sack.

"Catilina, my friend,'' he said to Lucius Sergius Catilina, who had ridden with him and Vatia, "take these, find the head of Tiberius Gutta, add the head of Pontius Telesinus when you get back to the Colline Gate, and then ride with them for Ofella. Tell him to load them one by one into his most powerful piece of artillery, and fire them one by one over the walls of Praeneste.''

Catilina's darkly handsome face brightened, looked alert. "Gladly, Lucius Cornelius. May I ask a favor?''

"Ask. But I don't promise.''

"Let me go into Rome and find Marcus Marius Gratidianus! I want his head. If Young Marius looks on his head too, he'll know that Rome is yours and his own career is at an end."

Slowly Sulla shook his head—but not in refusal. "Oh, Catilina, you are one of my most precious possessions! How I do love you! Gratidianus is your brother-in-law."

"*Was* my brother-in-law," said Catilina gently, and added, "My wife died not long before I joined you." What he did not say was that he had been suspected by Gratidianus of murdering her in order to pursue another liaison more comfortably.

"Well, Gratidianus would have to go sooner or later anyway," said Sulla, and turned away with a shrug. "Add his head to your collection if you think it will impress Young Marius."

Matters thus tidily disposed of, Sulla and Vatia and the legates who had accompanied them settled down with Crassus and Torquatus and the men of the right division to a jolly feast while Antemnae burned and Lucius Sergius Catilina went happily about his grisly business.

Seeming not to need sleep, Sulla rode thereafter back to Rome, but did not enter the city. His messenger sent on ahead summoned the Senate to a meeting in the temple of Bellona on the Campus Martius. En route to Bellona, he paused to make sure the six thousand prisoners were assembled in the grounds of the Villa Publica (which was close to the temple of Bellona), and issued certain orders; after that he completed his journey, and dismounted from his mule in the rather desolate and unkempt open space in front of the temple always called "Enemy Territory."

No one of course had dared not to answer Sulla's summons, so about a hundred men waited inside. They all stood; it did not seem the right thing to do to wait for Sulla seated on their folding stools. A few men looked serenely comfortable—Catulus, Hortensius, Lepidus—and some looked terrified—a Flaccus or two, a Fimbria, a minor Carbo—but most bore the look of sheep, vacuous yet skittish.

Clad in armor but bareheaded, Sulla passed through their ranks as if they did not exist and mounted the podium of Bellona's statue, which had been added to her temple after it became very fashionable to anthropomorphize even the old Roman gods; as she too was clad for war, she matched Sulla very well, even to the fierce look on her too-Greek face. She, however, owned a kind of beauty, whereas Sulla had none. To most of the men present, his appearance came as an absolute shock, though no one dared to stir. The wig of orange curls was slightly askew, the scarlet tunic filthy, the red patches on his face standing out amid remnants of near-albino skin like lakes of blood on snow. Many among them grieved, but for differing reasons: some because they had known him well and liked him, others because they had at least expected the new Master of Rome to look a fitting master. This man looked more a ruined travesty.

When he spoke his lips flapped, and some of his words were hard to distinguish. Until, that is, he got under way, when self-preservation stimulated his audience to total comprehension.

"I can see I'm back not a moment too soon!" he said. "The Enemy Territory is full of weeds—everything needs a fresh coat of paint and a good wash—the stones of the road bases are poking through what's left of the surface—laundresses are using the Villa Publica to hang out their washing— a *wonderful* job you've been doing of caring for Rome! Fools! Knaves! Jackasses!"

His address probably continued in the same vein—biting, sarcastic, bitter. But after he yelled "Jackasses!" his words were drowned by a hideous cacophony of noises from the direction of the Villa Publica—screams, howls, shrieks. Bloodcurdling! At first everyone pretended they could still hear him, but then the sounds became just too alarming, too horrifying; the senators began to move, mutter, exchange terrified glances.

As suddenly as it had begun, the din died away.

"What, little sheep, are you frightened?" jeered Sulla. "But there's no need to be frightened! What you hear is only my men admonishing a few criminals."

Whereupon he scrambled down from his perch between Bellona's feet and walked out without seeming to see a single member of the Senate of Rome.

"Oh dear, he's really *not* in a good mood!" said Catulus to his brother-in-law Hortensius.

"Looking like that, I'm not surprised," said Hortensius.

"He only dragged us here to listen to that," said Lepidus. "Who was he admonishing, do you imagine?"

"His prisoners," said Catulus.

As proved to be the case; while Sulla had been speaking to the Senate, his men had executed the six thousand prisoners at the Villa Publica with sword and arrow.

"I am going to be extremely well behaved on all occasions," said Catulus to Hortensius.

"Why, in particular?" asked Hortensius, who was a far more arrogant and positive man.

"Because Lepidus was right. Sulla only summoned us here to listen to the noise of the men who opposed him dying. What he *says* doesn't matter one iota. But what he *does* matters enormously to any of us who want to live. We will have to behave ourselves and try not to annoy him.''

Hortensius shrugged. ''I think you're overreacting, my dear Quintus Lutatius. In a few weeks he'll be gone. He'll get the Senate and the Assemblies to legalize his deeds and give him back his imperium, then he'll return to the ranks of the consulars in the front row, and Rome will be able to get on with her normal business.''

''Do you really think so?'' Catulus shivered. ''How he'll do it I have no idea, but I believe we're going to have Sulla's unnerving eyes on us from a position of superior power for a long time to come.''

Sulla arrived at Praeneste the following day, the third one of the month of November.

Ofella greeted him cheerfully, and gestured toward two sad men who stood under guard nearby. ''Know them?'' he asked.

''Possibly, but I can't find their names.''

''Two junior tribunes attached to Scipio's legions. They came galloping like a pair of Greek jockeys the morning after you fought outside the Colline Gate and tried to tell me that the battle was lost and you were dead.''

''What, Ofella? Didn't you believe them?''

Ofella laughed heartily. ''I know you better than that, Lucius Cornelius! It will take more than a few Samnites to kill you.'' And with the flourish of a magician producing a rabbit out of a chamber pot, Ofella reached behind him and displayed the head of Young Marius.

''Ah!'' said Sulla, inspecting it closely. ''Handsome fellow, wasn't he? Took after his mother in looks, of course. Don't know who he took after in cleverness, but it certainly wasn't his dad.'' Satisfied, he waved the head away. ''Keep it for the time being. So Praeneste surrendered?''

''Almost immediately after I fired in the heads Catilina brought me. The gates popped open and they flooded out waving white flags and beating their breasts.''

''Young Marius too?'' asked Sulla, surprised.

''Oh, no! He took to the sewers, looking for some way to escape. But I'd had all the outflows barred months before. We found him huddled against one such with his sword in his belly and his Greek servant weeping nearby,'' Ofella said.

''Well, he's the last of them!'' said Sulla triumphantly.

Ofella glanced at him sharply; it wasn't like Lucius Cornelius Sulla to forget anything! ''There's still *one* at large,'' he said quickly, then could have bitten off his tongue. This was not a man to remind that he too had short-comings!

But Sulla appeared unruffled. A slow smile grew. "Carbo, I suppose you mean?"

"Yes, Carbo."

"Carbo is dead too, my dear Ofella. Young Pompeius took him captive and executed him for treason in the agora at Lilybaeum late in September. Remarkable fellow, Pompeius! I thought it would take him many months to organize Sicily and round up Carbo, but he did the lot in one month. *And* found the time to send me Carbo's head by special messenger! Pickled in a jar of vinegar! Unmistakably him." And Sulla chuckled.

"What about Old Brutus?"

"Committed suicide rather than tell Pompeius whereabouts Carbo had gone. Not that it mattered. The crew of his ship—he was trying to raise a fleet for Carbo—told Pompeius everything, of course. So my amazingly efficient young legate sent his brother-in-law off to Cossura, whence Carbo had fled, and had him brought back to Lilybaeum in chains. But I got three heads from Pompeius, not two. Carbo, Old Brutus, and Soranus."

"Soranus? Do you mean Quintus Valerius Soranus the scholar, who was tribune of the plebs?"

"The very same."

"But why? What did he do?" asked Ofella, bewildered.

"He shouted the secret name of Rome out loud from the rostra," said Sulla.

Ofella's jaw dropped, he shivered. *"Jupiter!"*

"Luckily," lied Sulla blandly, "the Great God stoppered up every ear in the Forum, so Soranus shouted to the deaf. All is well, my dear Ofella. Rome will survive."

"Oh, that's a relief!" gasped Ofella, wiping the sweat from his brow. "I've heard of strange doings, but to tell Rome's secret name—it passes all imagination!" Something else occurred to him; he couldn't help but ask: "What was Pompeius doing in Sicily, Lucius Cornelius?"

"Securing the grain harvest for me."

"I'd heard something to that effect, but I confess I didn't believe it. He's a kid."

"Mmmm," agreed Sulla pensively. "However, what Young Marius didn't inherit from his father, young Pompeius certainly grabbed from Pompeius Strabo! And more besides."

"So the kid will be coming home soon," said Ofella, not very enamored of this new star in Sulla's sky; he had thought himself without rival in that firmament!

"Not yet," said Sulla in a matter-of-fact tone. "I sent him on to Africa to secure our province for me. I believe he is at this moment doing just that." He pointed down into No Man's Land, where a great crowd of men stood abjectly in the chilly sun. "Are they those who surrendered bearing arms?"

"Yes. In number, twelve thousand. A mixed catch," said Ofella, glad to see the subject change. "Some Romans who belonged to Young Marius, a good many Praenestians, and some Samnites for good measure. Do you want to look at them more closely?"

It seemed Sulla did. But not for long. He pardoned the Romans among the crowd, then ordered the Praenestians and Samnites executed on the spot. After which he made the surviving citizens of Praeneste—old men, women, children—bury the bodies in No Man's Land. He toured the town, never having been there before, and frowned in anger to see the shambles to which Young Marius's need for timber to build his siege tower had reduced the precinct of Fortuna Primigenia.

"I am Fortune's favorite," he said to those members of the town council who had not died in No Man's Land, "and I shall see that your Fortuna Primigenia acquires the most splendid precinct in all of Italy. But at Praeneste's expense."

On the fourth day of November, Sulla rode to Norba, though he knew its fate long before he reached it.

"They agreed to surrender," said Mamercus, tight-lipped with anger, "and then they torched the town before killing every last person in there— murder, suicide. Women, children, Ahenobarbus's soldiers, all the men of the town died rather than surrender. I'm sorry, Lucius Cornelius. There will be no plunder or prisoners from Norba."

"It doesn't matter," said Sulla indifferently. "The haul from Praeneste was huge. I doubt Norba could have yielded much of use or note."

And on the fifth day of November, when the newly risen sun was glancing off the gilded statues atop the temple roofs and that fresh light made the city seem less shabby, Lucius Cornelius Sulla entered Rome. He rode in through the Capena Gate, and in solemn procession. His groom led the white horse which had borne him safely through the battle at the Colline Gate, and he wore his best suit of armor, its silver muscled cuirass tooled with a scene representing his own army offering him his Grass Crown outside the walls of Nola. Paired with him and clad in purple-bordered toga rode Lucius Valerius Flaccus, the Princeps Senatus, and behind him rode his legates in pairs, including Metellus Pius and Varro Lucullus, who had been summoned from Italian Gaul four days earlier, and had driven hard to be here on this great occasion. Of all the ones who were to matter in the future, only Pompey and Varro the Sabine were not present.

His sole military escort was the seven hundred troopers who had saved him by bluffing the Samnites; his army was back in the defile, tearing down its ramparts so that traffic on the Via Latina could move again. After that, there was Ofella's wall to dismember and a vast stockpile of building material to dump in several fields. Much of the tufa block had been fragmented in the demolition, and Sulla knew what he was going to do with that; it would be incorporated into the *opus incertum* construction of the new temple of Fortuna Primigenia in Praeneste. No trace of the hostilities must remain.

Many people turned out of doors to see him enter the city; no matter how fraught with peril it was, no Roman could ever resist a spectacle, and this moment belonged to History. Many who saw him ride in genuinely believed they were witnessing the death throes of the Republic; rumor insisted that Sulla intended to make himself King of Rome. How else could he hang on to power? For how—given what he had done—could he dare relinquish power? And, it was quickly noted, a special squad of cavalry rode just behind the last pair of legates, their spears held upright; impaled on those lances were the heads of Carbo and Young Marius, Carrinas and Censorinus, Old Brutus and Marius Gratidianus, Brutus Damasippus and Pontius Telesinus, Gutta of Capua and Soranus—and Gaius Papius Mutilus of the Samnites.

Mutilus had heard the news of the battle at the Colline Gate a day after, and wept so loudly that Bastia came to see what was the matter with him.

"Lost, all lost!" he cried to her, forgetting the way she had insulted and tormented him, only seeing the one person left to whom he was bound by ties of family and time. "My army is dead! Sulla has won! Sulla will be King of Rome and Samnium will be no more!"

For perhaps as long as it would have taken to light all the wicks of a small chandelier, Bastia stared at the devastated man upon his couch. She made no move to comfort him, said no words of comfort either, just stood very still, eyes wide. And then a look crept into them of knowledge and resolution; her vivid face grew cold and hard. She clapped her hands.

"Yes, *domina*?" asked the steward from the doorway, gazing in consternation at his weeping master.

"Find his German and ready his litter," said Bastia.

"Domina?" the steward asked, bewildered.

"Don't just stand there, do as I say! At once!"

The steward gulped, disappeared.

Tears drying, Mutilus gaped at his wife. "What is this?"

"I want you out of here," she said through clenched teeth. "I want no part of this defeat! I want to keep my home, my money, my life! So out you go, Gaius Papius! Go back to Aesernia, or go to Bovianum—or anywhere else you have a house! *Anywhere* but this house! I do not intend to go down with you."

"I don't believe this!" he gasped.

"You'd better believe it! Out you go!"

"But I'm *paralyzed,* Bastia! I am your husband, and I'm paralyzed! Can't you find pity in you, if not love?"

"I neither love you nor pity you," she said harshly. "It was all your stupid, futile plotting and fighting against Rome took the power out of your legs—took away your use to me—took away the children I might have had—and all the pleasure in being a part of your life. For nearly seven years I've lived here alone while you schemed and intrigued in Aesernia—and when you did condescend to visit me, you stank of shit and piss, and ordered me about—oh no, Gaius Papius Mutilus, I am done with you! Out you go!"

And because his mind could not encompass the extent of his ruin, Mutilus made no protest when his German attendant took him from the couch and carried him through the front door to where his litter stood at the bottom of the steps. Bastia had followed behind like an image of the Gorgon, beautiful and evil, with eyes that could turn a man to stone and hissing hair. So quickly did she slam the door that the edge of his cloak caught in it and pulled the German up with a jerk. Shifting the full weight of his master to his left arm, the German began to tug at the cloak to free it.

On his belt Gaius Papius Mutilus wore a military dagger, a mute reminder of the days when he had been a Samnite warrior. Out it came; he pressed the top of his head against the wood of the door and cut his throat. Blood sprayed everywhere, drenched the door and pooled upon the steps, soaked the shrieking German, whose cries brought people running from up and down the narrow street. The last thing Gaius Papius Mutilus saw was his Gorgon wife, who had opened the door in time to receive the final spurt of his blood.

"I curse you, woman!" he tried to say.

But she didn't hear. Nor did she seem stricken, frightened, surprised. Instead, she held the door wide and snapped at the weeping German, "Bring him in!" And inside, when her husband's corpse was laid upon the floor, she said, "Cut off his head. I will send it to Sulla as my gift."

Bastia was as good as her word; she sent her husband's head to Sulla with her compliments. But the story Sulla heard from the wretched steward compelled by his mistress to bring the gift did not flatter Bastia. He handed the head of his old enemy to one of the military tribunes attached to his staff, and said without expression, "Kill the woman who sent me this. I want her dead."

And so the tally was almost complete. With the single exception of Marcus Lamponius of Lucania, every powerful enemy who had opposed Sulla's return to Italy was dead. Had he wished it, Sulla could indeed have made himself undisputed King of Rome.

But he had found a solution more to the liking of one who firmly believed in all the traditions of a Republican *mos maiorum,* and thus rode through the middle of the Circus Maximus absolutely free of kingly intent.

He was old and ill, and for fifty-eight years he had done battle against a mindless conspiracy of circumstances and events which had succeeded time and time again in stripping from him the pleasures of justice and reward, the rightful place in Rome's scheme of things to which birth and ability entitled him. No choice had he been offered, no opportunity to pursue his ascent of the *cursus honorum* legally, honorably. At every turn someone or something had blocked him, made the straight and legal way impossible. So here he was, riding in the wrong direction down the length of the empty Circus Maximus, a fifty-eight-year-old wreck, his bowels knotted with the twin fires of triumph and loss. Master of Rome. The First Man in Rome. Vindication at last. And yet the disappointments of his age and his ugliness and his approaching death curdled his joy with the sourest sadness, destroyed pleasure, exacerbated pain. How late, how bitter, how warped was this victory. . . .

He didn't think of the Rome he now held at his mercy with love or idealism; the price had been too high. Nor did he look forward to the work he knew he had to do. What he most desired was peace, leisure, the fulfillment of a thousand sexual fantasies, head-spinning drunken binges, total freedom from care and from responsibility. So why couldn't he have those things? Because of Rome, because of duty, because he couldn't bear the thought of laying down his job with so much work undone. The only reason he rode in the wrong direction down the length of the empty Circus Maximus lay in the knowledge that there was a mountain of work to be done. And he had to do it. There was literally no one else who could.

He chose to assemble Senate and People together in the lower Forum Romanum, and speak to both from the rostra. Not with complete truth—was it Scaurus who had called him politically nonchalant? He couldn't remember. But there was too much of the politician in him to be completely truthful, so he blandly ignored the fact that it had been he who pinned up the first head on the rostra—Sulpicius, to frighten Cinna.

"This hideous practice which has come into being so very recently that I was urban praetor in a Rome who did not know of it"—he turned to gesture at the row of speared heads—"will not cease until the proper traditions of the *mos maiorum* have been totally restored and the old, beloved Republic rises again out of the ashes to which it has been reduced. I have heard it said that I intend to make myself King of Rome! No, *Quirites,* I do not! Condemn myself to however many years I have left of intrigues and plots, rebellions and reprisals? No, I will not! I have worked long and hard in the service of Rome, and I have earned the reward of spending my last days free of care and free of responsibilities—free of Rome! So one thing I can promise you, Senate and People both—I will not set myself up as King of Rome, or enjoy one single moment of the power I must retain until my work is over."

Perhaps no one had really expected this, even men as close to Sulla as Vatia and Metellus Pius, but as Sulla went on, some men began to understand that Sulla had shared his secrets with one other—the Princeps Senatus, Lucius Valerius Flaccus, who stood on the rostra with him, and did not look surprised at one word Sulla was saying.

"The consuls are dead," Sulla went on, hand indicating the heads of Carbo and Young Marius, "and the *fasces* must go back to the Fathers, be laid upon their couch in the temple of Venus Libitina until new consuls are elected. Rome must have an *interrex,* and the law is specific. Our Leader of the House, Lucius Valerius Flaccus, is the senior patrician of the Senate, of his decury, of his family." Sulla turned to Flaccus Princeps Senatus. "You are the first *interrex*. Please assume that office and acquit yourself of all its duties for the five days of your interregnum."

"So far, so good," whispered Hortensius to Catulus. "He has done exactly what he ought to do, appoint an *interrex*."

"*Tace!*" growled Catulus, who was finding it difficult to understand every word Sulla was saying.

"Before our Leader of the House takes over the conduct of this meeting," Sulla said slowly and carefully, "there are one or two things *I* wish to say. Rome is safe under my care, no one will come to any harm. Just law will be returned. The Republic will go back to its days of glory. But those are all things which must come from the decisions of our *interrex,* so I shall not dwell upon them any further. What I do want to say is that I have been well served by fine men, and it is time to thank them. I will start with those who are not here today. Gnaeus Pompeius, who has secured the grain supply from

Sicily, and has thereby guaranteed that Rome will not be hungry this winter ... Lucius Marcius Philippus, who last year secured the grain supply from Sardinia, and this year had to contend with the man who was sent against him, Quintus Antonius Balbus. He did contend with Antonius, who is dead. Sardinia is safe. . . . In Asia I left three splendid men behind to care for Rome's richest and most precious province—Lucius Licinius Murena, Lucius Licinius Lucullus, and Gaius Scribonius Curio. . . . And here standing with me are the men who have been my loyalest followers through times of hardship and despair—Quintus Caecilius Metellus Pius and his legate, Marcus Terentius Varro Lucullus—Publius Servilius Vatia—the elder Gnaeus Cornelius Dolabella—Marcus Licinius Crassus . . ."

"Ye gods, the list will be endless!" grumbled Hortensius, who loathed listening to any man save himself speak, especially one whose rhetoric was as unskilled as Sulla's.

"He's finished, he's finished!" said Catulus impatiently. "Come on, Quintus, he's calling the Senate to the Curia, he'll tell these Forum fools no more! Come on, quickly!"

But it was Lucius Valerius Flaccus Princeps Senatus who took the curule chair, surrounded only by the skeletal body of magistrates who had remained in Rome and survived. Sulla sat off to the right of the curule podium, probably about where he ought to have ordinarily placed himself in the front row of consulars, ex-censors, ex-praetors. He had not, however, changed out of his armor, and that fact told the senators that he was by no means relinquishing his control of the proceedings.

"On the Kalends of November," said Flaccus in his wheezing voice, "we almost lost Rome. Had it not been for the valor and promptness of Lucius Cornelius Sulla, his legates, and his army, Rome would now be in the power of Samnium, and we would be passing under the yoke just as we did after the Caudine Forks. Well, I need go no further on that subject! Samnium lost, Lucius Cornelius won, and Rome is safe."

"Oh, get *on* with it!" breathed Hortensius. "Ye gods, he's growing more senile every day!"

Flaccus got on with it, fidgeting a little because he was not comfortable. "However, even with the war over, Rome has many other troubles to plague her. The Treasury is empty. So are the temple coffers. The streets are thin of business, the Senate thin of numbers. The consuls are dead, and only one praetor is left of the six who commenced at the beginning of the year." He paused, drew a deep breath, and launched heroically into what Sulla had ordered him to say. "In fact, Conscript Fathers, Rome has passed beyond the point where normal governance is possible. Rome must be guided by the most able hand. The *only* hand capable of reaching out and drawing our beloved Lady Roma to her feet. My term as *interrex* is five days long. I cannot hold elections. I will be succeeded by a second *interrex* who will also serve for five days. He will be expected to hold elections. It may not lie in his power to do so, in which case a third *interrex* will have to try. And so on, and so forth. But this sketchy governance will not do, Conscript Fathers. The time is one of the acutest emergency, and I see only one man present here capable of doing what has to be done. But he cannot do what has to be done as consul. Therefore I propose a different solution—one which I will ask of the People in their Centuries, the most senior voting body of all. I will ask the People in their Centuries to draft and pass a *lex rogata* appointing and authorizing Lucius Cornelius Sulla the Dictator of Rome.''

The House stirred; men looked at each other, amazed.

''The office of Dictator is an old one,'' Flaccus went on, ''and normally confined to the conduct of a war. In the past, it has been the Dictator's job to pursue a war when the consuls could not. And it is over one hundred years since the last Dictator was put into power. But Rome's situation today is one she has never experienced before. The war is over. The emergency is not. I put it to you, Conscript Fathers, that *no elected consuls* can put Lady Roma back on her feet. The remedies called for will not be palatable, will incur huge resentments. At the end of his year in office, a consul can be compelled to answer to the People or the Plebs for his actions. He can be charged with treason. If all have turned against him he may be sent into exile and his property confiscated. Knowing himself vulnerable to such charges in advance, no man can produce the strength and resolution Rome needs at this moment. A Dictator, however, does not fear retribution from People or Plebs. The nature of the office indemnifies him against all future reprisals. His acts as the Dictator are sanctioned for all time. He is not prosecutable at law on any charge. Bolstered by the knowledge that he is immune, that he cannot be vetoed by a tribune of the plebs or condemned in any assembly, a Dictator can utilize every ounce of his strength and purpose to put matters right. To set our beloved Lady Roma on her feet.''

''It sounds wonderful, Princeps Senatus,'' said Hortensius loudly, ''but the hundred and twenty years which have elapsed since the last Dictator took office have spoiled your memory! A Dictator is proposed by the Senate, but must be appointed by the consuls. We have no consuls. The *fasces* have been sent to the temple of Venus Libitina. A Dictator cannot be appointed.''

Flaccus sighed. ''You were not listening to me properly, Quintus Hortensius, were you? I told you how it could be done. By means of a *lex rogata* passed by the Centuries. When there are no consuls to act as executives, the

People in their Centuries are the executive. The only executive, as a matter of fact—the *interrex* must apply to them to execute his only function—which is to organize and hold curule elections. The People in their tribes are not an executive. Only the Centuries.''

"All right, I concede the point," said Hortensius curtly. "Go on, Princeps Senatus."

"It is my intention to convoke the Centuriate Assembly at dawn tomorrow. I will then ask it to formulate a law appointing Lucius Cornelius Sulla the Dictator. The law need not be very complicated—in fact, the simpler it is, the better. Once the Dictator is legally appointed by the Centuries, all other laws can come from him. What I will ask of the Centuries is that they formally appoint and authorize Lucius Cornelius Sulla the Dictator *for however long it may take him to fulfill his commission;* that they sanction all his previous deeds as consul and proconsul; that they remove from him all official odium in form of outlawry or exile; that they guarantee him indemnity from all his acts as Dictator at any time in the future; that they protect his acts as Dictator from tribunician veto and any Assembly's rejection or negation, from the Senate and People in any form or through any magistrates, and from appeal to any Assembly or body or magistrates."

"That's better than being King of Rome!" cried Lepidus.

"No, it is simply different," said Flaccus stubbornly; he had taken some time to get into the spirit of what Sulla wanted from him, but he was now well and truly launched. "A Dictator is not answerable for his actions, but he does not rule alone. He has the services of the Senate and all the Comitia as advisory bodies, he has his Master of the Horse, and he has however many magistrates he chooses to see elected beneath him. It is the custom for consuls to serve under the Dictator, for instance."

Lepidus spoke up loudly. "The Dictator serves for six months only," he said. "Unless my hearing has suddenly grown defective, what you propose to ask of the Centuries is that they appoint a Dictator with no time limit to his office. Not constitutional, Princeps Senatus! I am not against seeing Lucius Cornelius Sulla appointed the Dictator, but I am against his serving one moment longer than the proper term of six months."

"Six months won't even see my work begun," said Sulla without rising from his stool. "Believe me, Lepidus, I do not want the wretched job for one single day, let alone for the rest of my life! When I consider my work is finished, I *will* step down. But six months? Impossible."

"How so?" asked Lepidus.

"For one thing," Sulla answered, "Rome's finances are in chaos. To right them will take a year, perhaps two years. There are twenty-seven legions to discharge, find land for, pay out. The men who supported the lawless regimes of Marius, Cinna and Carbo have to be sought out and shown that they cannot escape just punishment. The laws of Rome are antiquated, particularly with regard to her courts and her governors of provinces. Her civil servants are disorganized and prey to both lethargy and cupidity. So much treasure, money and bullion were robbed from our temples that the Treasury still contains two hundred and eighty talents of gold and one hundred and twenty talents of silver, even after this year's profligate waste. The temple of Jupiter Optimus Maximus is a cinder." He sighed loudly. "Must I go on, Lepidus?"

"All right, I concede that your task will take longer than six months. But what's to stop your being reappointed every six months for however long the job takes?" asked Lepidus.

Sulla's sneer was superlatively nasty without his teeth, despite the fact that those long canines were missing. "Oh, yes, Lepidus!" he cried. "I can see it all now! Half of every six-month period would have to be spent in conciliating the Centuries! Pleading, explaining, excusing, drawing pretty pictures, pissing in every knight-businessman's purse, turning myself into the world's oldest and saddest trollop!" He rose to his feet, fists clenched, and shook both of them at Marcus Aemilius Lepidus with more venom in his face than most men there had seen since he had quit Rome to go to war with King Mithridates. "Well, comfortable stay-at-home Lepidus, married to the daughter of a traitor who did try to set himself up as King of Rome, *I will do it my way or not at all!* Do you hear me, you miserable pack of self-righteous stay-at-home fools and cravens? You want Rome back on her feet, but you want the undeserved right to make the life of the man who is undertaking to do that as miserable and anxious and *servile* as you possibly can! Well, Conscript Fathers, you can make up your minds to it right here and now— Lucius Cornelius Sulla is back in Rome, and if he has a mind to it, he can shake her rafters until she falls down in ruins! Out there in the Latin countryside I have an army that I could have brought into this city and set on your despicable hides like wolves on lambs! I did not do that. I have acted in your best interests since first I entered the Senate. And I am still acting in your best interests. Peacefully. *Nicely.* But you are trying my patience, I give all of you fair warning. I will be Dictator for as long as I need to be Dictator. Is that understood? Is it, Lepidus?"

Silence reigned absolutely for many long moments. Even Vatia and Metellus Pius sat white-faced and trembling, gazing at the naked clawed monster fit only to screech at the moon—oh, how could they have forgotten what lived inside Sulla?

Lepidus too gazed white-faced and trembling, but the nucleus of his terror was not the monster inside Sulla; he was thinking of his beloved Appuleia, wife of many years, darling of his heart, mother of his sons—and daughter of Saturninus, who had indeed tried to make himself King of Rome. Why had Sulla made reference to her in the midst of that appalling outburst? What did he intend to do when he became Dictator?

Sick to death of civil wars, of economic depression and far too many legions marching endlessly up and down Italy, the Centuriate Assembly voted in a law which appointed Lucius Cornelius Sulla the Dictator for an unspecified period of time. Tabled at *contio* on the sixth day of November, the *lex Valeria dictator legibus scribundis et rei publicae constituendae* passed into law on the twenty-third day of November. It contained no specifics beyond the time span; as it bestowed virtually unlimited powers upon Sulla and also rendered him unanswerable for a single one of his actions, it did not need specificity. Whatever Sulla wanted to enact or do, he could.

Many in the city fully expected a flurry of activity from him the moment his appointment as Dictator was tabled, but he did nothing until the appointment was ratified three *nundinae* later, in accordance with the *lex Caecilia Didia*.

Having taken up residence in the house which had belonged to Gnaeus Domitius Ahenobarbus (now a refugee in Africa), Sulla did, it seemed, little except walk constantly through the city. His own house had been wrecked and burned to the ground after Gaius Marius and Cinna had taken over Rome, and he walked across the Germalus of the Palatine to inspect its site, poke slowly among the heaps of rubble, gaze over the Circus Maximus to the lovely contours of the Aventine. At any time of day from dawn to dusk he might be seen standing alone in the Forum Romanum, staring up at the Capitol, or at the life-size statue of Gaius Marius near the rostra, or at some other among the numerous smaller statues of Marius, or at the Senate House, or at the temple of Saturn. He walked along the bank of the Tiber from the great trading emporium of the Aemilii in the Port of Rome all the way to the Trigarium, where the young men swam. He walked from the Forum Romanum to every one of Rome's sixteen gates. He walked up one alley and down another.

Never did he display the slightest sign of fear for life or limb, never did he ask a friend to accompany him, let alone take a bodyguard along. Sometimes he wore a toga, but mostly he just wrapped himself voluminously in a more easily managed cloak—the winter was early, and promised to be as cold as the last. On one fine, unseasonably hot day he walked clad only in his tunic, and it could be seen then how *small* he was—though he had been a well-made man of medium size, people remembered. But he had shrunk, he was bent over, he crabbed along like an octogenarian. The silly wig was always on his head, and now that the outbreaks on his face were under control he had taken once more to painting his frost-fair brows and lashes with *stibium*.

And by the time one market interval of the Dictator's wait for ratification was over, those who had witnessed his awful rage in the Senate but had not been direct objects of it (like Lepidus) had begun to feel comfortable enough to speak of this walking old man with some degree of contempt; so short is memory.

"He's a travesty!" said Hortensius to Catulus, sniffing.

"Someone will kill him," said Catulus, bored.

Hortensius giggled. "Or else he'll tumble over in a fit or an apoplexy." He grasped at his brother-in-law's toga-swaddled left arm with his right hand, and shook it. "Do you know, I can't see why I was so afraid! He's here, but he's not here. Rome doesn't have a hard taskmaster after all—very peculiar! He's cracked, Quintus. Senescent."

An opinion which was becoming prevalent among all classes as every day his uninspiring figure could be seen plodding along with wig askew and *stibium* garishly applied. Was that powder covering up his mulberry-hued scars? Muttering. Shaking his head. Once or twice, shouting at no one. Cracked. Senescent.

It had taken a great deal of courage for such a vain man to expose his aged crudities to general gaze; only Sulla knew how much he loathed what disease had done to him, only Sulla knew how much he yearned again to be the magnificent man he was when he left to fight King Mithridates. But, he had told himself, shunning his mirror, the sooner he nerved himself to show Rome what he had become, the sooner he would learn to forget what the mirror would have shown him had he looked. And this did happen. Chiefly because his walks were not aimless, not evidence of senility. Sulla walked to see what Rome had become, what Rome needed, what he had to do. And the more he walked, the angrier he became—and the more excited, because it was in his hand to take this dilapidated, threadbare lady and turn her into the beauty she used to be.

He waited too for the arrival of some people who mattered to him, though he didn't think of himself as loving them, or even needing them—his wife, his twins, his grown-up daughter, his grandchildren—and Ptolemy Alexander, heir to the throne of Egypt. They had been waiting patiently for many months under the care of Chrysogonus, first in Greece, then in Brundisium, but by the end of December they would be in Rome. For a while Dalmatica would have to live in Ahenobarbus's house, but Sulla's own residence had recently begun rebuilding; Philippus—looking brown and extremely fit—had arrived from Sardinia, unofficially convoked the Senate, and browbeaten that cowed body into voting nonexistent public funds to give back to Sulla what the State had taken away. Thank you, Philippus!

On the twenty-third day of November, Sulla's dictatorship was formally ratified, and passed into law. And on that day Rome awoke to find every statue of Gaius Marius gone from the Forums Romanum, Boarium, Holitorium, various crossroads and squares, vacant pieces of land. Gone too were the trophies hung in his temple to Honor and Virtue on the Capitol, fire-damaged but still habitable for lifeless suits of enemy armor, flags, standards, all his personal decorations for valor, the cuirasses he had worn in Africa, at Aquae Sextiae, at Vercellae, at Alba Fucentia. Statues of other men had gone too—Cinna, Carbo, Old Brutus, Norbanus, Scipio Asiagenus—but perhaps because they were far fewer in number, their going was not noticed in the same way as the disappearance of Gaius Marius. He left a huge gap, a whole grove of empty plinths with his name obliterated from each, herms with their genitalia hammered off.

And at the same time the whispers increased about other, more serious disappearances; *men* were vanishing too! Men who had been strong and loud in their support of Marius, or Cinna, or Carbo, or of all three. Knights in the main, successful in business during a time when business success was difficult; knights who had gained lucrative State contracts, or loaned to partisans, or enriched themselves in other ways from affiliations to Marius, to Cinna, to Carbo, or to all three. Admittedly no senator had puffed out of existence, but suddenly the total of men who had was big enough to be noticed. Whether because of this public awareness or as a side effect of it, people now saw these men vanishing; some sturdy-looking private individuals, perhaps ten or fifteen in number, would knock upon a knight's street door, be admitted, and then scant moments later would emerge with the knight in their midst, and march him off to—no one knew where!

Rome stirred uneasily, began to see the peregrinations of her wizened master as something more than just benign excursions; what had been quite amusing in a saddened way now took on a more sinister guise, and the innocent eccentricities of yesterday became the suspicious purposes of today and the terrifying objectives of tomorrow. He never spoke to anyone! He talked to himself! He stood in one place for far too long looking at who knew what! He had shouted once or twice! What was he really doing? *And why was he doing it?*

Exactly in step with this growing apprehension, the odd activities of those innocuous-looking bands of private persons who knocked on the street doors of houses belonging to knights became more overt. They were now noticed to stand here or there taking notes, or to follow like shadows behind an affluent Carboan banker or a prosperous Marian broker. The disappearing men disappeared with increasing frequency. And then one group of private persons knocked upon the street door of a *pedarius* senator who had always voted for Marius, for Cinna, for Carbo. But the senator was not marched away. When he emerged into the street there was a flurry of arms, the sweep of a sword, and his head fell to the ground with a hollow *thock!,* and rolled away. The body lay emptying itself of blood down the gutter, but the head disappeared.

Everyone began to find a reason for drifting past the rostra to count the heads—Carbo, Young Marius, Carrinas, Censorinus, Scipio Asiagenus, Old Brutus, Marius Gratidianus, Pontius Telesinus, Brutus Damasippus, Tiberius Gutta of Capua, Soranus, Mutilus. . . . No, that was all! The head of the backbencher senator was not there. Nor any head of any man who had vanished. And Sulla continued to walk with his idiotic wig not quite straight, and his brows and lashes painted. But whereas before people used to stop and smile to see him—albeit smiled with pity—now people felt a frightful hole blossom in their bellies at sight of him, and scrambled in any direction save toward him, or bolted at a run away from him. Wherever Sulla now was, no one else was. No one watched him. No one smiled, albeit with pity. No one accosted him. No one molested him. He brought a cold sweat in his wake, like the wraiths which issued from the *mundus* on the *dies religiosi.*

Never before had one of the great public figures been so shrouded in mystery, so opaque of purpose. His behavior was not *normal.* He should have been standing on the rostra in the Forum telling everyone in magnificent language all about his plans, or throwing rhetorical sand in the Senate's eyes. Speeches of intent, litanies of complaint, flowery phrases—he should have been *talking*! To someone, if not everyone. Romans were not prone to keep their counsel. They talked things over. Hearsay ruled. But from Sulla, nothing. Just the solitary walks which acknowledged no complicity, implied no interest. And yet—all of it *had* to be emanating from him! This silent and uncommunicative man was the master of Rome.

On the Kalends of December, Sulla called a meeting of the Senate, the first such since Flaccus had spoken. Oh, how the senators hurried and scurried to the Curia Hostilia! Feeling colder even than the air, pulses so rapid heartbeats could not be counted, breathing shallow, pupils dilated, bowels churning. They huddled on their stools like gulls battered by a tempest, trying not to look up at the underside of the Curia roof for fear that, like Saturninus and his confederates, they would be felled in an instant by a rain of tiles from above.

No one was impervious to this nameless terror—even Flaccus Princeps Senatus—even Metellus Pius—even military darlings like Ofella and panders like Philippus and Cethegus. And yet when Sulla shuffled in he looked so harmless! A pathetic figure! Except that he was ushered in by an unprecedented twenty-four lictors, twice as many as a consul was entitled to—and twice as many as any earlier dictator.

"It is time that I told you of my intentions," Sulla said from his ivory seat, not rising; his words came out in jets of white vapor, the chamber was so cold. "I am legally Dictator, and Lucius Valerius, the Leader of the House, is my Master of the Horse. Under the provisions of the Centuriate law which gave me my position, I am not obliged to see other magistrates elected if I so wish. However, Rome has always reckoned the passing of the years by the names of the consuls of each year, and I will not see that tradition broken. Nor will I have men call this coming year 'In the Dictatorship of Lucius Cornelius Sulla.' So I will see two consuls elected, eight praetors elected, two curule and two plebeian aediles elected, ten tribunes of the plebs elected, and twelve quaestors. And to give magisterial experience to men too young to be admitted into the Senate, I will see twenty-four tribunes of the soldiers elected, and I will appoint three men to be moneyers, and three to look after Rome's detention cells and asylums."

Catulus and Hortensius had come in a state of terror so great that both sat with anal sphincters clenched upon bowel contents turned liquid, and hid their hands so that others would not see how they shook. Listening incredulously to the Dictator announcing that he would hold elections for all the magistracies! They had expected to be pelted from the roof, or lined up and beheaded, or sent into exile with everything they owned confiscated—they had expected anything but this! *Was* he innocent? Did he not know what was going on in Rome? And if he did not know, who then was responsible for those disappearances and murders?

"Of course," the Dictator went on in that irritatingly indistinct diction his toothlessness had wrought, "you realize that when I say elections, I do not mean *candidates*. I will tell you—and the various Comitia!—whom you will elect. Freedom of choice is not possible at this time. I need men to help me do my work, and they must be the men *I* want, not the men whom the electors would foist on me. I am therefore in a position to inform you who will be what next year. Scribe, my list!" He took the single sheet of paper from a clerk of the House whose sole duty seemed to be its custodian, while another secretary lifted his head from his work, which was to take down with a stylus on wax tablets everything Sulla said.

"Now then, consuls . . . Senior—Marcus Tullius Decula. Junior—Gnaeus Cornelius Dolabella—"

He got no further. A voice rang out, a togate figure leaped to his feet: Quintus Lucretius Ofella.

"No! No, I say! You'd give our precious consulship to *Decula*? No! Who is Decula? A nonentity who sat here safe and sound inside Rome while his betters fought for you, Sulla! What has Decula done to distinguish himself? Why, as far as I know he hasn't even had the opportunity to wipe your *podex* with his sponge-on-a-stick, Sulla! Of all the miserable, malicious, unfair, unjust tricks! Dolabella I can understand—all of your legates got to know of the bargain you made with him, Sulla! But who is this Decula? What has this Decula done to earn the senior consulship? I say no! No, no, no!"

Ofella paused for breath.

Sulla spoke. "My choice for senior consul is Marcus Tullius Decula. That is that."

"Then you can't be allowed to have the choice, Sulla! We will have candidates and a proper election—and I will stand!"

"You won't," said the Dictator gently.

"Try and stop me!" Ofella shouted, and ran from the chamber. Outside a crowd had gathered, anxious to hear the results of this first meeting of the Senate since Sulla had been ratified Dictator. It was not composed of men who thought they had anything to fear from Sulla—they had stayed at home. A small crowd, but a crowd nonetheless. Pushing his way through it without regard for the welfare of anyone in his path, Ofella stormed down the Senate steps and across the cobblestones to the well of the Comitia and the rostra set into its side.

"Fellow Romans!" he cried. "Gather round, hear what I have to say about this unconstitutional monarch we have voluntarily appointed to lord over us! He says he will see consuls elected. But there are to be no candidates—just the two men of his choice! Two ineffectual and incompetent idiots—and one of them, Marcus Tullius Decula, is not even of a noble family! The first of his family to sit in the Senate, a backbencher who scrambled into a praetorship under the treasonous regime of Cinna and Carbo! Yet *he* is to be senior consul while men like me go unrewarded!"

Sulla had risen and walked slowly down the tesselated floor of the Curia to the portico, where he stood blinking in the stronger light and looking mildly interested as he watched Ofella shouting from the rostra. Without drawing attention to themselves, perhaps fifteen ordinary-looking men began to cluster together at the foot of the Senate steps right in the path of Sulla's eyes.

And slowly the senators crept out of the Curia to see and hear what they could, fascinated at Sulla's calm, emboldened by it too—he wasn't the monster they had begun to think him, he couldn't be!

"Well, fellow Romans," Ofella went on, voice more stentorian as he got into stride, "I am one man who will not lie down under these studied insults! I am more entitled to be consul than a nonentity like Decula! And it is my opinion that the electors of Rome, if offered a choice, will choose me over both of Sulla's men! Just as there are others they would choose did others step forward and declare themselves candidates!"

Sulla's eyes met those of the leader of the ordinary-looking men standing just below him; he nodded, sighed, leaned his weary body against a convenient pillar.

The ordinary-looking men moved quietly through the thin crowd, came to the rostra, mounted it, and laid hold of Ofella. Their gentleness was apparent, not real; Ofella fought desperately, to no avail. Inexorably they bent him over until he collapsed on his knees. Then one of them took a handful of hair, stood well back, and pulled until head and neck were extended. A sword flashed up and down. The man holding the hair staggered despite his wide stance in the moment when his end parted company with the rest of Ofella, then whipped the head on high so all could see it. Within moments the Forum was empty save for the stunned Conscript Fathers of the Senate.

"Put the head on the rostra," said Sulla, straightened himself, and walked back into the chamber.

Like automatons the senators followed.

"Very well, where was I?" asked Sulla of his secretary, who leaned forward and muttered low-voiced. "Oh, yes, so I was! I thank you! I had finished with the consuls, and I was about to commence on the praetors. Clerk, your list!" And out went Sulla's hand. "Thank you! To proceed. . . . Mamercus Aemilius Lepidus Livianus. Marcus Aemilius Lepidus. Gaius Claudius Nero. Gnaeus Cornelius Dolabella the younger. Lucius Fufidius. Quintus Lutatius Catulus. Marcus Minucius Thermus. Sextus Nonius Sufenas. Gaius Papirius Carbo. I appoint the younger Dolabella *praetor urbanus,* and Mamercus *praetor peregrinus.*"

A truly extraordinary list! Clearly neither Lepidus nor Catulus, who might at a proper election have expected to come in at the top of the poll, was to be preferred to two men who had actively fought for Sulla. Yet there they were, praetors when loyal Sullans of senatorial status and the right age had been passed over! Fufidius was a relative nobody. And Nonius Sufenas was

Sulla's sister's younger boy. Nero was a minor Claudius of no moment. Thermus was a good soldier, but so poor a speaker he was a Forum joke. And just to annoy all camps, the last place on the list of praetors had gone to a member of Carbo's family who had sided with Sulla but failed to distinguish himself!

"Well, you're in," whispered Hortensius to Catulus. "All I can hope for is that I'm on next year's list—or the year after that. Ye gods, what a farce! How can we bear him?"

"The praetors don't matter," said Catulus in a murmur. "They'll all flog themselves to shine—Sulla isn't fool enough to give the wrong job to the wrong man. It's Decula interests me. A natural bureaucrat! That's why Sulla picked him—had to, given that Dolabella had blackmailed him into a consulship! Our Dictator's policies will be meticulously executed, and Decula will love every moment of the execution."

The meeting droned on. One after another the names of the magistrates were read out, and no voice was raised in protest. Done, Sulla handed his paper back to its custodian and spread his hands upon his knees.

"I have said everything I want to say at this time, except that I have taken due note of Rome's paucity of priests and augurs, and will be legislating very soon to rectify matters. *But hear this now!*" he suddenly roared out, making everyone jump. "There will be no more elected Religious! It is the *height* of impiety to cast ballots to determine who will serve the gods! It turns something solemn and formal into a political circus and enables the appointment of men who have no tradition or appreciation of priestly duties. If her gods are not served properly, Rome cannot prosper." Sulla rose to his feet.

A voice was raised. Looking mildly quizzical, Sulla sank back into his ivory chair.

"You wish to speak, Piglet dear?" he asked, using the old nickname Metellus Pius had inherited as his father's son.

Metellus Pius reddened, but got to his feet looking very determined. Ever since his arrival in Rome on the fifth day of November, his stammer— almost nonexistent these days—had steadily and cruelly worsened. He knew why. Sulla. Whom he loved but feared. However, he was still his father's son, and Metellus Numidicus Piggle-wiggle had twice braved terrible beatings in the Forum rather than abrogate a principle, and once gone into exile to uphold a principle. Therefore it behooved him to tread in his father's footsteps and maintain the honor of his family. And his own *dignitas*.

"Luh-Luh-Lucius Cornelius, wuh-wuh-will you answer wuh-wuh-one question?"

"You're stammering!" cried Sulla, almost singing.

"Truh-truh-true. Suh-suh-suh-sorry. I will try," he said through gritted teeth. "Are you aware, Luh-Luh-Lucius Cornelius, that men are being killed and their property confiscated thruh-thruh-throughout Italy as well as in Rome?"

The whole House listened with bated breath to hear Sulla's answer: did he know, was he responsible?

"Yes, I am aware of it," said Sulla.

A collective sigh, a general flinching and huddling down on stools; the House now knew the worst.

Metellus Pius went on doggedly. "I uh-uh-uh-understand that it is necessary to punish the guilty, but no man has been accorded a truh-truh-trial. Could you cluh-cluh-clarify the situation for me? Could you, for instance, tuh-tuh-tuh-tell me whereabouts you intend to draw the line? Are *any* men going to be accorded a trial? And who says these men have committed treason if they are nuh-nuh-not tried in a proper court?"

"It is by my dictate that they die, Piglet dear," said the Dictator firmly. "I will not waste the State's money and time on trials for men who are patently guilty."

The Piglet labored on. "Then cuh-cuh-can you give me some idea of whom you intend to spare?"

"I am afraid I cannot," said the Dictator.

"Then if yuh-yuh-yuh-you do not know who will be spared, can you tell me whom you intend to punish?"

"Yes, dear Piglet, I can do that for you."

"In which case, Luh-Luh-Lucius Cornelius, would you please share that knowledge with us?" Metellus Pius ended, sagging in sheer relief.

"Not today," said Sulla. "We will reconvene tomorrow."

Everyone came back at dawn on the morrow, but few looked as if they had enjoyed any sleep.

Sulla was waiting for them inside the chamber, seated on his ivory curule chair. One scribe sat with his stylus and wax tablets, the other held a scroll of paper. The moment the House was confirmed in legal sitting by the sacrifice and auguries, out went Sulla's hand for the scroll. He looked directly at poor Metellus Pius, haggard from worry.

"Here," Sulla said, "is a list of men who have either died already as traitors, or who will die shortly as traitors. Their property now belongs to the State, and will be sold at auction. And *any* man or woman who sets eyes upon a man whose name is on this list will be indemnified against retaliation if he or she appoints himself or herself an executioner." The scroll was handed to Sulla's chief lictor. "Pin this up on the wall of the rostra," said

Sulla. "Then all men will know what my dear Piglet alone had the courage to ask to know."

"So if I see one of the men on your list, I can kill him?" asked Catilina eagerly; though not yet a senator, he had been bidden by Sulla to attend meetings of the Senate.

"You can indeed, my little plate-licker! *And* earn two talents of silver for doing so, as a matter of fact," said Sulla. "I will be legislating my program of proscriptions, of course—I will do nothing that has not the force of law! The reward will be incorporated into the legislation, and proper books will be kept of all such transactions so that Posterity will know who in our present day and age profited."

It came out demurely, but men like Metellus Pius had no trouble in discerning Sulla's malice; men like Lucius Sergius Catilina (if in truth they discerned Sulla's malice) obviously did not care.

The first list of proscribed was in the number of forty senators and sixty-five knights. The names of Gaius Norbanus and Scipio Asiagenus headed it, with Carbo and Young Marius next. Carrinas, Censorinus and Brutus Damasippus were named, whereas Old Brutus was not. Most of the senators were already dead. The lists, however, were basically intended to inform Rome whose estates were confiscate; they did not say who was already dead, who still alive. The second list went up on the rostra the very next day, to the number of two hundred knights. And a third list went up the day after that, publishing a further group of two hundred and fifteen knights. Sulla apparently had finished with the Senate; his real target was the Ordo Equester.

His *leges Corneliae* covering proscription regulations and activities were exhaustive. The bulk of them, however, appeared over a period of a mere two days very early in December, and by the Nones of that month all was in a Deculian order, as Catulus had prophesied. Every contingency had been taken into account. All property in a proscribed man's family was now the property of the State, and could not be transferred into the name of some scion innocent of transgression; no will of a man proscribed was valid, no heir named in it could inherit; the proscribed man could legally be slain by any man or woman who saw him, be he or she free, or freed, or still slave; the reward for murder or apprehension of a proscribed man was two talents of silver, to be paid by the Treasury from confiscated property and entered in the public account books; a slave claiming the reward was to be freed, a freedman transferred into a rural tribe; all men—civilian or military—who after Scipio Asiagenus had broken his truce had favored Carbo or Young Marius were declared public enemies; any man offering assistance or friendship to a proscribed man was declared a public enemy; the sons and grandsons of the proscribed were debarred from holding curule office and forbidden to repurchase confiscated estates, or come into possession of them by any other means; the sons and grandsons of those already dead would suffer in the same way as the sons and grandsons of those listed while still living. The last law of this batch, promulgated on the fifth day of December, declared that the whole process of proscription would cease on the first day of the next June. Six months hence.

Thus did Sulla usher in his Dictatorship, by demonstrating that not only was he master of Rome, but also a master of terror and suspense. Not all the days of itching agony had been spent in mindless torment or drunken stupor; Sulla had thought of this and that and many things. Of how he would achieve mastery of Rome; of how he would proceed when he became master of Rome; of how he would create a mental attitude in every man and woman and child that would enable him to do what had to be done without opposition, without revolt. Not soldiers garrisoning the streets but shadows in the mind, fears which led to hope as well as to despair. His minions would be anonymous people who might be the neighbors or friends of those they sneaked up on and whisked away. Sulla intended to create a climate rather than weather. Men could cope with weather. But climates? Ah, climates could prove unendurable.

And he had thought while he itched and tore himself to raw and bloody tatters of being an old and ugly and disappointed man given the world's most wonderful toy to play with: Rome. Its men and women, dogs and cats, slaves and freedmen, lowly and knights and nobles. All his cherished resentments, all his grudges grown cold and dark, he detailed meticulously in the midst of his pain. And took exquisite comfort from shaping his revenge.

The Dictator had arrived.

The Dictator had put his gleeful hands upon his new toy.

PART TWO

from DECEMBER 82 B.C.
until MAY 81 B.C.

LUCIUS CORNELIUS SULLA FELIX

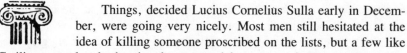 Things, decided Lucius Cornelius Sulla early in December, were going very nicely. Most men still hesitated at the idea of killing someone proscribed on the lists, but a few like Catilina were already showing the way, and the amount of money and property confiscated from the proscribed was soaring. It was money and property, of course, which had directed Sulla's footsteps down this particular path; from *somewhere* had to come the vast sums Rome would need in order to become financially solvent again. Under more normal circumstances it would have come out of the coffers of the provinces, but given the actions of Mithridates in the east and the fact that Quintus Sertorius had managed to create enough trouble in both the Spains to curtail Spanish incomes, the provinces could not be squeezed of additional revenues for some time to come. Therefore Rome and Italy would have to yield up the money—yet the burden could not be thrust upon the ordinary people, nor upon those who had conclusively demonstrated their loyalty to Sulla's cause.

Sulla had never loved the Ordo Equester—the ninety-one Centuries of the First Class who comprised the knight-businessmen, but especially the eighteen Centuries of senior knights who were entitled to the Public Horse. Among them were many who had waxed fat under the administration of Marius, of Cinna, of Carbo; and these were the men Sulla resolved would pay the bill for Rome's economic recovery. A perfect solution! thought the Dictator with gleeful satisfaction. Not only would the Treasury fill up; he would also eliminate all of his enemies.

He had besides found the time to deal with one other pet aversion—Samnium, and this in the harshest way possible, by sending the two worst men he could think of to that hapless place. Cethegus and Verres. And four legions of good troops.

"Leave nothing," he said. "I want Samnium brought so low that no one will ever want to live there again, even the oldest and most patriotic Samnite. Fell the trees, lay waste the fields, destroy the towns as well as the orchards"—he smiled dreadfully—"and lop off the head of every tall poppy."

There! That would teach Samnium. And rid him of two men with considerable nuisance value for the next year. *They* would not be back in a hurry! Too much money to be made above and beyond what they would send to the Treasury.

It was perhaps well for other parts of Italy that Sulla's family arrived in Rome at this moment to restore to him a kind of normality he had not realized he needed as well as missed. For one thing, he hadn't known that the sight of Dalmatica would fell him like a blow; his knees gave under him, he had to sit down abruptly and stare at her like a callow boy at the unexpected coming of the one unattainable woman.

Very beautiful—but he had always known that—with her big grey eyes and her brown skin the same color as her hair—and that look of love that never seemed to fade or change, no matter how old and ugly he became. And she was there sitting on his lap with both arms wound about his scraggy neck, pushing his face against her breasts, caressing his scabby head and pressing her lips against it as if it was that glorious head of red-gold hair it used to flaunt—his wig, where was his wig? But then she was tugging his head up, and he could feel the loveliness of her mouth enfold his puckered lips until they bloomed again. . . . Strength flowed back into him, he rose lifting her in the same movement, and walked with her in triumph to their room, and there dealt with her in something more than triumph. Perhaps, he thought, drowning in her, I am capable of loving after all.

"Oh, how much I have missed you!" he said.

"And how much I love you," she said.

"Two years . . . It's been two years."

"More like two thousand years."

But, the first fervor of that reunion over, she became a wife, and inspected him with minute pleasure.

"Your skin is so much better!"

"I got the ointment from Morsimus."

"It's ceased to itch?"

"Yes, it's ceased to itch."

After which, she became a mother, and would not rest until he accompanied her to the nursery, there to say hello to little Faustus and Fausta.

"They're not much older than our separation," he said, and heaved a sigh. "They look like Metellus Numidicus."

She muffled a giggle. "I know. . . . Poor little things!"

And that set the seal upon what had been one of the happiest days of Sulla's life; she *laughed* with him!

Not knowing why Mama and the funny old man were clutching each other in paroxysms of mirth, the twins stood looking up with uncertain smiles until the urge to join in could no longer be resisted. And if it could not be said that Sulla grew to love them in the midst of that burst of laughter, he did at least decide that they were quite nice little people— even if they did look like their great-uncle, Quintus Caecilius Metellus Numidicus Piggle-wiggle. Whom their father had murdered. What an irony! thought their father: is this some sort of retribution the gods have visited upon me? But to believe that is to be a Greek, and I am a Roman. Besides which, I will be dead long before this pair are old enough to visit retribution on anyone.

The rest of the new arrivals were also well, including as they did Sulla's grown daughter, Cornelia Sulla, and her two children by her dead first husband. The little girl Pompeia was now eight years old and completely absorbed in her beauty, of which she was very aware. At six years of age the little boy Quintus Pompeius Rufus bade fair to living up to his last name, for he was red of hair, red of skin, red of eye, red of temper.

"And," asked Sulla of his steward, Chrysogonus, whose task it had been to look after the family, "how is my guest who cannot cross the *pomerium* into Rome?"

A little thinner than of yore (it could not have been an easy job to shepherd so many people of different and distinct natures, reflected Sulla), the steward rolled his expressive dark eyes toward the ceiling and shrugged.

"I am afraid, Lucius Cornelius, that he will not agree to remain outside the *pomerium* unless you visit him in person and explain exactly why. I tried! Indeed I tried! But he deems me an underling, beneath contempt—or credibility."

That was typical of Ptolemy Alexander, thought Sulla as he trudged out of the city to the inn on the Via Appia near the first milestone where Chrysogonus had lodged the haughty and hypersensitive prince of Egypt, who, though he had been in Sulla's custody for three years, was only now beginning to be a burden.

Claiming to be a refugee from the court of Pontus, he had turned up in Pergamum begging Sulla to grant him asylum; Sulla had been fascinated. For he was none other than Ptolemy Alexander the Younger, only legitimate son of the Pharaoh who had died trying to regain his throne in the same year as Mithridates had captured the son, living on Cos with his two bastard first cousins. All three princes of Egypt had been sent to Pontus, and Egypt had fallen firmly into the grasp of the dead Pharaoh's elder brother, Ptolemy Soter nicknamed Lathyrus (it meant Chickpea), who resumed the title of Pharaoh.

From the moment he set eyes on Ptolemy Alexander the Younger, Sulla had understood why Egypt had preferred to be ruled by old Lathyrus the Chickpea. Ptolemy Alexander the Younger was womanish to the extreme of dressing like a reincarnation of Isis in floating draperies knotted and twisted in the fashion of the Hellenized goddess of Egypt, with a golden crown upon his wig of golden curls, and an elaborate painting of his face. He minced, he ogled, he simpered, he lisped, he fluttered; and yet, thought Sulla shrewdly, beneath all that effeminate facade lay something steely.

He had told Sulla a tale of three hideous years spent as a prisoner at the court of one who was the most militant of heterosexuals; Mithridates, who genuinely believed womanish men could be "cured," had subjected young Ptolemy Alexander to an endless series of humiliations and degradations designed to disenchant the poor fellow of his chosen proclivities. It had not worked. Thrown into bed with Pontine courtesans and even common whores, Ptolemy Alexander had been able to do no more than hang his head over the edge of the bed and vomit; forced to don armor and go on route marches with a hundred sneering soldiers, he had wept and collapsed; beaten with fists and then with lashes, he had only betrayed the fact that he found such treatment highly stimulating; set on a tribunal in the marketplace of Amisus in all his finery and paint, and there subjected to rains of rotten fruit, eggs, vegetables and even stones, he had dumbly endured without contrition.

His chance had come when Mithridates began to reel under Sulla's competent conduct of the war with Rome, and the court disintegrated. Young Ptolemy Alexander had escaped.

"My two bastard cousins preferred to remain in Amisus, of course," he lisped to Sulla. "The atmosphere of that abominable court has suited *them* beautifully! They both went into marriage eagerly—to daughters of Mithridates by his part-Parthian, part-Seleucid wife, Antiochis. Well, they can keep Pontus and all of the King's daughters! I hate the place!"

"And what do you want of me?" Sulla had asked.

"Asylum. Shelter within Rome when you return there. And, when Lathyrus Chickpea dies, the Egyptian throne. He has a daughter, Berenice, who is reigning with him as his Queen. But he cannot marry her, of course—he could only marry an aunt, a cousin, or a sister, and he has none of any available. In the natural way of things Queen Berenice will survive her father. The Egyptian throne is matrilineal, which means the king becomes the king through marriage to the queen or to the eldest-born princess of the line. I am the only legitimate Ptolemy left. The Alexandrians—who have the sole say in the matter since the Macedonian Ptolemies established their capital there rather than in Memphis—will want me to succeed Lathyrus Chickpea, and will consent to my marrying Queen Berenice. So when Lathyrus Chickpea dies I want you to send me to Alexandria to claim the throne—with Rome's blessing."

For some moments Sulla considered this, eyeing Ptolemy Alexander in amusement. Then he said, "You may marry the Queen, but will you be able to get children by her?"

"Probably not," said the prince with composure.

"Then is there any point to the business?" Sulla smirked at his own pun.

Ptolemy Alexander apparently did not see the point. "I want to be Pharaoh of Egypt, Lucius Cornelius," he said solemnly. "The throne is rightfully mine. What happens to it after my death is immaterial."

"So who else is there in line for the throne?"

"Only my two bastard cousins. Who are now the minions of Mithridates and Tigranes. I was able to escape when a messenger came from Mithridates that all three of us were to be sent south to Tigranes, who is extending his kingdom in Syria. The purpose of this removal, I gather, was to keep us from Roman custody if Pontus should fall."

"Your bastard cousins may not be in Amisus, then."

"They were when I left. Beyond that I do not know."

Sulla had put his pen down and stared with cold goat's eyes at the sullen, bedizened person before him. "Very well, Prince Alexander, I will grant you asylum. When I return to Rome you may accompany me. As to your eventual assumption of the Double Crown of Egypt—best perhaps to discuss that when the time comes."

But the time had not yet come when Sulla trudged out to the inn at the first milestone on the Via Appia, and he could now foresee certain difficulties anent Ptolemy Alexander the Younger. There was a scheme in the back of his mind, of course; had it not occurred to him on the occasion of his first meeting with Ptolemy Alexander he would simply have sent the young man to his uncle Lathyrus Chickpea in Alexandria, and washed his hands of the whole affair. But the scheme had occurred to him, and now he could only hope that he lived long enough to see it bear fruit; Lathyrus Chickpea was much older than he was, yet apparently still enjoyed the best of health. Alexandria had a salubrious climate, so they said.

"However, Prince Alexander," he said when he had been shown into the inn's best parlor, "I cannot house you at Rome's expense for however many years it will take your uncle to die. Even in a place like this."

Outrage flared in the dark eyes; Ptolemy Alexander drew himself up like a striking snake. "A place like this? I'd rather be back in Amisus than remain in a place like this!"

"In Athens," said Sulla coldly, "you were housed royally at the expense of the Athenians, purely due to your uncle's gifts to that city after I was obliged to sack a part of it and did some little damage. Well, that was the prerogative of Athens. You cost *me* nothing. Here you're likely to cost me a fortune Rome cannot spare. So I'm offering you two choices. You may take ship at Rome's expense for Alexandria, and make your peace with your uncle Lathyrus Chickpea. Or you may negotiate a loan with one of this city's bankers, hire a house and servants on the Pincian or some other acceptable place outside the *pomerium,* and remain until your uncle dies.''

It was difficult to tell if Ptolemy Alexander lost color, so heavy was his maquillage, but Sulla rather fancied that he did; certainly the fight went out of him.

''I can't go to Alexandria, my uncle would have me killed!''

''Then negotiate a loan.''

''All right, I will! Only tell me how!''

''I'll send Chrysogonus to tell how. He knows everything.'' Sulla had not sat down, but he moved now to the door. ''By the way, Prince Alexander, under no circumstances can you cross the sacred boundary of Rome into the city.''

''I shall die of boredom!''

Came the famous sneer. ''I doubt that, when it's known you have money and a nice house. Water always finds its level. Alexandria is a long way from Rome, and I must assume that you will be its lawful king the moment Lathyrus Chickpea dies. Which neither you nor I can know until word reaches Rome. Therefore, as Rome will tolerate no ruling sovereign within her boundary, you must stay outside it. I mean that. Flout me, and you won't need to go to Alexandria to meet a premature death.''

Ptolemy Alexander burst into tears. ''You're a horrible, hateful person!''

Off went Sulla down the road to the Capena Gate, giving voice to an occasional neigh of laughter. What a horrible, hateful person Ptolemy Alexander was! But—how very useful he might prove to be if only Lathyrus Chickpea had the grace and good sense to die while Sulla was still the Dictator! And he gave a little skip of pleasure at the thought of what he was going to do when he heard that the throne of Egypt was vacant.

Oblivious to the fact that his laughter and his skip and that crabbed gait had become portents of terror to every man and woman who chanced to see him, whose mind was in fabled Alexandria.

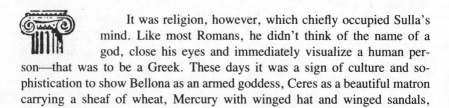 It was religion, however, which chiefly occupied Sulla's mind. Like most Romans, he didn't think of the name of a god, close his eyes and immediately visualize a human person—that was to be a Greek. These days it was a sign of culture and sophistication to show Bellona as an armed goddess, Ceres as a beautiful matron carrying a sheaf of wheat, Mercury with winged hat and winged sandals,

because a Hellenized society was superior, because a Hellenized society despised more numinous gods as primitive, unintellectual, incapable of behavior as complex as human behavior. To the Greeks, their gods were essentially human beings owning superhuman powers; they could not conceive a being more complex than a man. So Zeus, who was king of their pantheon, functioned like a Roman censor—powerful but not omnipotent—and handed out jobs to the other gods, who took delight in tricking him, blackmailing him, and behaving a bit like tribunes of the plebs.

But Sulla, a Roman, knew the gods were far less tangible than the Greeks would have them: they weren't humanoid and they didn't have eyes in their heads or hold conversations, nor did they wield super*human* powers, nor go through the integration and differentiation of thought processes akin to a man's. Sulla, a Roman, knew that the gods were specific forces which moved specific events or controlled other forces inferior to themselves. They fed on life-forces, so they liked to be offered living sacrifices; they needed order and method in the living world as much as they did in their own, because order and method in the living world helped maintain order and method in the world of forces.

There were forces pervaded storage cupboards and barns and silos and cellars, liked to see them full—they were called Penates. There were forces kept ships sailing and crossroads together and a sense of purpose among inanimate objects—they were called Lares. There were forces kept the trees right-thinking, obliged them to grow their branches and leaves up into the air and their roots down into the earth. There were forces kept water sweet and rivers going from on high all the way down to the sea. There was a force gave a few men luck and good fortune, but gave most men less, and a few men nothing—it was called Fortuna. And the force called Jupiter Optimus Maximus was the sum total of all other forces, the connective tissue which bound them all together in a way logical to forces, if mysterious to men.

It was clear to Sulla that Rome was losing contact with her gods, her forces. Why else had the Great Temple burned down? Why else had the precious records gone up in smoke? The prophetic books? Men were forgetting the secrets, the strict formulae and patterns which channeled godly forces. To have the priests and augurs elected disturbed the balances within the priestly colleges, obviated the delicate adjustments only possible when the same families filled the same religious positions time out of mind, forever and ever.

So before he turned his energies toward rectifying Rome's creaky institutions and laws, he must first purify Rome's *aether,* stabilize her godly forces and allow them to flow properly. How could Rome expect good fortune when a man could be so lost as to what was fitting that he could stand and holler out her secret name? How could Rome expect to prosper when men plundered her temples and murdered her priests? Of course he didn't remember that he himself had once wanted to plunder her temples; he only remembered that he had not, though he was going to fight a true enemy. Nor did he remember quite how he had felt about the gods in those days before illness and wine had made a shambles of his life.

In the burning of the Great Temple there was an implicit message, so much he knew in his bones. And it had been given to him to halt the chaos, correct the present drift toward utter disorder. If he did not, then doors supposed to be shut would fly open, and doors supposed to be open would slam shut.

He summoned the priests and augurs to him inside Rome's oldest temple, Jupiter Feretrius on the Capitol. So ancient that it had been dedicated by Romulus and was built of tufa blocks without plaster or decoration, it had only two square columns to support its portico, and it contained no image. On a plain square pedestal of equal age there rested a straight electrum rod as long as a man's hand and arm to the elbow, and a silica flint brooding black and glassy. The only light admitted to its interior came through the door, and it smelled of incredible age—mouse droppings, mildew, damp, dust. Its one room was a mere ten feet by seven feet, so Sulla was grateful for the fact that neither the College of Pontifices nor the College of Augurs was anywhere near full membership.

Sulla himself was an augur. So too were Marcus Antonius, the younger Dolabella and Catilina. Of priests, Gaius Aurelius Cotta had been in the college the longest; Metellus Pius was not far behind, nor Flaccus the Master of the Horse and Princeps Senatus, who was also the *flamen Martialis*. Catulus, Mamercus, the Rex Sacrorum Lucius Claudius of the only branch of the Claudii with the first name of Lucius—and a very uneasy pontifex, Brutus the son of Old Brutus, who clearly wondered if and when he was going to be proscribed.

"We have no Pontifex Maximus," Sulla began, "and our company is thin. I could have found a more comfortable place for us to meet, but I suspect a little discomfort may not be displeasing to our gods! For some time now we have thought of ourselves ahead of our gods, and our gods are unhappy. Dedicated in the same year as our Republic was born, our temple of Jupiter Optimus Maximus did not burn down by accident. I am sure it burned down because Jupiter Best and Greatest feels the Roman Senate and People have cheated him of his due. We are not so callow and credulous that we subscribe to barbarian beliefs in godly wrath—bolts of lightning that strike us dead or pillars that squash us flat are *natural* events—they merely indicate a man's personal ill luck. But portents do indicate unhappy gods, and the burning of our Great Temple is a terrible portent. If we still had the Sibylline Books we might discover more about it. But the Sibylline Books burned, along with our *fasti* of the consuls, the original Twelve Tables, and much else.''

There were fifteen men present, and not enough room to allow a proper arrangement of speaker and audience; Sulla just stood in their midst and spoke in normal tones. ''It is my task as Dictator to return Rome's religion to its old form, and to make all of you work toward that end. Now I can enact the laws, but it is up to all of you to implement them. On one point I am adamant, for I have had dreams, I am an augur, and I *know* I am right. Namely, I will invalidate the *lex Domitia de sacerdotiis* which our Pontifex Maximus of some years ago, Gnaeus Domitius Ahenobarbus, took so much pleasure in foisting upon us. Why did he? Because he felt his family had been insulted and himself overlooked. Those are reasons founded in personal pride, not in a true religious spirit. I believe Ahenobarbus Pontifex Maximus displeased the gods, especially Jupiter Best and Greatest. So there will be no more elections for Religious. Not even for the office of Pontifex Maximus.''

''But the Pontifex Maximus has always been elected!'' cried Lucius Claudius the Rex Sacrorum, astonished. ''He is the High Priest of the Republic! His appointment *must* be democratic!''

''I say, no. From now on, he too will be chosen by his fellow members of the College of Pontifices,'' said Sulla in a tone which brooked no argument. ''I am right about this.''

''I don't know. . . .'' Flaccus began, then trailed off when he met Sulla's awful eyes.

''I *do* know, so that will be the end of it!'' Sulla's gaze traveled from one distressed face to another, and quelled all further protest. ''I also think it is displeasing to our gods that there are not enough of us to go around, so I intend to give each priestly college—most of the minor as well as the major—fifteen members each instead of the old ten or twelve. No more of this squeezing two jobs in for every one man! Besides, fifteen is a lucky number, the fulcrum upon which thirteen and seventeen—the unlucky ones—turn. Magic is important. Magic creates pathways for the godly forces to travel. I believe that numbers have great magic. So we will work magic for Rome's benefit, as is our sacred duty.''

''Perhaps,'' ventured Metellus Pius, ''wuh-wuh-we could set up only wuh-wuh-one candidate for Pontifex Maximus? That wuh-wuh-way, we could at least have an election process.''

''There will be no election process!'' Sulla spat.

Silence fell. No one so much as shifted a foot.

After some time had passed Sulla began to speak again. "There is one priest who sits ill with me, for a number of good reasons. I refer to our *flamen Dialis*, the young man Gaius Julius Caesar. Upon the death of Lucius Cornelius Merula he was chosen to be Jupiter's special priest by Gaius Marius and his bought-and-paid-for minion, Cinna. The men who chose him alone are ominous enough! They contravened the usual selection process, which ought to involve the entire gamut of colleges. Another reason for my disquiet concerns my own ancestors, for the first Cornelius to be cognominated Sulla was *flamen Dialis*. But the burning of the Great Temple is by far the most ominous reason. So I began to make enquiries about this young man, and have learned that he flatly refused to observe the regulations surrounding his flaminate until he assumed the *toga virilis*. His behavior since has been orthodox, as far as I can find out. Now all this could well have been a symptom of his youth. But what *I* think is not important. What does Jupiter Optimus Maximus think? *That* is important! For, my fellow priests and augurs, I have learned that Jupiter's temple fire finally went out two days before the Ides of Quinctilis. On that exact same day of the year, the *flamen Dialis* was born. An omen!"

"It could be a good omen," said Cotta, who cared about the fate of this particular *flamen Dialis*.

"Indeed it could," said Sulla, "but that is not for me to say. As Dictator, I feel free to determine the method whereby our priests and augurs are appointed, I feel free to abolish the elections. But the *flamen Dialis* is different. All of you must decide his fate. All of you! Fetials, pontifices, augurs, the priests of the sacred books, even the *epulones* and the *salii*. Cotta, I am putting you in charge of the investigation, as you are the longest-serving pontifex. You have until the Ides of December, when we will meet again in this temple to discuss the religious position of the present *flamen Dialis*." He looked at Cotta sternly. "No word of this must get round, especially to young Caesar himself."

Home he went, chuckling and rubbing his hands together in transports of delight. For Sulla had thought of the most wonderful joke! The kind of joke Jupiter Optimus Maximus would find a terrific boost to his force pathways. An offering! A living sacrificial victim for Rome—for the Republic, whose High Priest he was! He had been invented to supplant the Rex Sacrorum, ensure that the Republic outranked the Kings, all of whom had been Rex Sacrorum as well as King. Oh, a superb joke! he cried to himself, literally crying—with laughter. I will offer the Great God a victim who will go consenting to the sacrifice, and continue to sacrifice himself until his death! I will dower the Republic and the Great God with the best segment of one man's life—I will offer up his suffering, his distress, his pain. And all with his consent. Because he will never refuse to be sacrificed.

The next day Sulla published the first of his laws aimed at regulating the State religion by fixing them to the rostra and the wall of the Regia. At first the rostra perusers presumed it was a new proscription list, so the professional bounty hunters clustered quickly, only to turn away with exclamations of disgust: it turned out to be a list of the men who were now members of the various priestly colleges, major and minor. Fifteen of each, somewhat haphazardly divided between patricians and plebeians (with the plebeians in the majority), and beautifully balanced between the Famous Families. No unworthy names on this list! No Pompeius or Tullius or Didius! Julii, Servilii, Junii, Aemilii, Cornelii, Claudii, Sulpicii, Valerii, Domitii, Mucii, Licinii, Antonii, Manlii, Caecilii, Terentii. It was also noted that Sulla had given himself a priesthood to complement the augurship he held already—and that he was the only man to hold both.

"I *ought* to have a foot in both camps," he had said to himself when contemplating doing this. "I am the Dictator."

The day after, he published an addendum containing only one name. The name of the new Pontifex Maximus. Quintus Caecilius Metellus Pius the Piglet. Stammerer extraordinary.

The people of Rome were beside themselves with horror when they saw that frightful name upon the rostra and the Regia—the new Pontifex Maximus was *Metellus Pius*? How could that be? What was wrong with Sulla? Had he gone quite mad?

A shivering deputation came to see him at Ahenobarbus's house, its members consisting of priests and augurs, including Metellus Pius himself. For obvious reasons he was not the deputation's spokesman; his tongue stumbled so these days that no one was willing to stand there shifting from one foot to the other while the Piglet strove to articulate his thoughts. The spokesman was Catulus.

"Lucius Cornelius, *why*?" wailed Catulus. "Are we to have no say about this?"

"I duh-duh-duh-don't wuh-wuh-wuh-*want* the juh-juh-job!" the Piglet stuttered painfully, eyes rolling, hands working.

"Lucius Cornelius, you can't!" Vatia cried.

"It's impossible!" shouted son-in-law Mamercus.

Sulla let them run down before he answered, no flicker of emotion on his face or in his eyes; it was no part of his joke ever to let them see that it was a joke. They must always think him earnest, serious. For he was. He was! Jupiter had come to him in a dream last night and told him how much he appreciated this wonderful, perfect joke.

They ran down. An apprehensive silence fell, save for the soft sound of the Piglet's weeping.

"Actually," said Lucius Cornelius Sulla in conversational tones, "as the Dictator I can do anything I want. But that is not the point. The point is that I dreamed Jupiter Optimus Maximus came to me and asked specifically for Quintus Caecilius as his Pontifex Maximus. When I woke I took the omens, and they were very propitious. On the way to the Forum to pin my two pieces of parchment up on the rostra and the Regia, I saw *fifteen* eagles flying from left to right across the Capitol. No owl hooted, no lightning flashed."

The deputation looked into Sulla's face, then at the floor. He was serious. So, it seemed, was Jupiter Optimus Maximus.

"But no ritual can contain a mistake!" said Vatia. "No gesture, no action, no *word* can be wrong! The moment something is performed or said wrongly, the whole ceremony has to start all over again!"

"I am aware of that," said Sulla gently.

"Lucius Cornelius, surely you can see!" cried Catulus. "Pius stutters and stammers his way through every statement he makes! So whenever he acts as Pontifex Maximus, we are going to be there *forever*!"

"I see it with crystal clarity," said Sulla with great seriousness. "Remember, I too will be there forever." He shrugged. "What can I say, except that perhaps this is some extra sacrifice the Great God requires of us because we haven't acquitted ourselves as we ought in matters pertaining to our gods?" He turned to Metellus Pius to take one of the spasming hands in both his own. "Of course, Piglet dear, you can refuse. There is nothing in our religious laws to say you can't."

The Piglet used his free hand to pick up a fold of toga and employ it to wipe his eyes and nose. He drew in a breath and said, "I will do it, Lucius Cornelius, if the Great God requires it of muh-muh-me."

"There, you see?" asked Sulla, patting the hand he held. "You almost got it out! Practice, Piglet dear! *Practice!*"

The first paroxysm of laughter was welling dangerously close to eruption; Sulla got rid of the deputation in a hurry and bolted to his study, where he shut himself in. His knees gave way; he collapsed onto a couch, wrapped his arms round his body and howled, the tears of mirth pouring down his face. When he couldn't breathe properly he rolled onto the floor and lay there shrieking and gasping with his legs kicking in the air, hurting so much he thought he might die. But still he laughed, secure in the knowledge that the omens had indeed been propitious. And for the rest of that day, whenever the Piglet's expression of noble self-sacrifice flashed before his mind's eye, he doubled over in a fresh paroxysm; so too did he laugh again whenever he remembered the look on Catulus's face, and Vatia's, and his son-in-law's. Wonderful, wonderful! Perfect justice, this Jupiterian joke. Everyone had received exactly what everyone deserved. Including Lucius Cornelius Sulla.

On the Ides of December some sixty men—members of the minor as well as the major priestly colleges—tried to squash into the temple of Jupiter Feretrius.

"We have paid our respects to the god," said Sulla. "I do not think he will mind if we seek the open air."

He sat himself on the low wall which fenced off the old Asylum from the parklike areas of ground swelling easily up on either side to the twin humps of Capitol and Arx, and gestured to the rest to sit on the grass.

That, thought the desperately unhappy Piglet, was one of the oddest things about Sulla: he could invest small things with huge dignity, then—as now—reduce huge things to complete informality. To the Capitoline visitors and tourists—to the men and women who arrived panting at the top of the Asylum steps or the Gemonian steps, taking a shortcut between Forum Romanum and Campus Martius—they must look like a strolling philosopher and his pupils, or an old country daddy with all his brothers, nephews, sons, cousins.

"What have you to report, Gaius Aurelius?" asked Sulla of Cotta, who sat in the middle of the front row.

"First of all, that this task was very difficult for me, Lucius Cornelius," Cotta replied. "You are aware, I suppose, that young Caesar the *flamen Dialis* is my nephew?"

"As indeed he is also my nephew, though by marriage rather than blood," said the Dictator steadily.

"Then I must ask you another question. Do you intend to proscribe the Caesars?"

Without volition Sulla thought of Aurelia, and shook his head emphatically. "No, Cotta, I do not. The Caesars who were my brothers-in-law so many years ago are both dead. They never really committed any crimes against the State, for all they were Marius's men. There were reasons for that. Marius had helped the family financially, the tie was an obligatory gratitude. The widow of old Gaius Marius is the boy's blood aunt, and her sister was my first wife."

"But you have proscribed both Marius's and Cinna's families."

"That I have."

"Thank you," said Cotta, looking relieved. He cleared his throat. "Young Caesar was but thirteen years old when he was solemnly and properly consecrated as the priest of Jupiter Optimus Maximus. He fulfilled all the criteria save one: he was a patrician with both parents still living, but he was not married to a patrician woman with both parents still living. However, Marius found him a bride, to whom he was married before the ceremonies of inauguration and consecration. The bride was Cinna's younger daughter."

"How old was she?" Sulla asked, snapping his fingers at his servant, who promptly handed him a peasant's wide-brimmed straw hat. Having adjusted it comfortably, he looked out slyly from under it, truly an old country daddy.

"She was seven."

"I see. A literal marriage of children. Faugh! Cinna *was* hungry, wasn't he?"

"Quite so," said Cotta uncomfortably. "Anyway, the boy did not take kindly to his flaminate. He insisted that until he put on the toga of manhood he would pursue the customary activities of a noble Roman youth. So he went to the Campus Martius and there did his military exercises. He fenced, shot arrows, cast spears—and revealed a talent for whatever he was called upon to do. I am told he used to do something remarkable—he would ride a very fleet horse at the full gallop with both hands behind his back—and no saddle! The old fellows of the Campus Martius remember him well and deem his flaminate a shame in view of his natural aptitude for soldiering. For his other behavior, my source is his mother—my half sister, Aurelia. According to her, he did not adhere to the stipulated diet, he pared his nails with an iron knife, had his hair cut with an iron razor, and wore knots and buckles."

"What happened when he donned the *toga virilis*?"

"He changed radically," said Cotta, considerable surprise in his voice. "The rebellion—if indeed it had been rebellion—ceased. He had always performed his religious duties with scrupulous care, but then he put on his *apex* and *laena* permanently, and adhered to all the prohibitions. His mother says he liked his role no better, but had become reconciled."

"I see." Sulla kicked his heels softly against the wall, then said, "It begins to sound quite satisfactory, Cotta. What conclusion have you come to about him and his flaminate?"

Cotta frowned. "There is one difficulty. Did we have the full set of prophetic books available to us, we might have been able to elucidate the matter. But we do not, of course. So we have found it impossible to form a conclusive opinion. There appears to be no doubt that the boy is legally the *flamen Dialis,* but we are not so sure from the religious viewpoint.''

"Why?"

"It all hinges upon the civic status of Caesar's wife. Cinnilla, they call her. Now twelve years of age. Of one thing we are absolutely positive—the flaminate *Dialis* is a dual entity which involves wife as much as it does husband. She has her religious title of *flaminica Dialis,* she is under the same taboos, and she has her own religious duties. If she does not fulfill the religious criteria, then the whole flaminate is in doubt. And we have come to the conclusion that she does not fulfill the religious criteria, Lucius Cornelius.''

"Really? How have you reached that conclusion, Cotta?" Sulla kicked the wall harder, thought of something else. "Has the marriage been consummated?"

"No, it has not. The child Cinnilla has lived with my sister and my sister's family since she married young Caesar. And my sister is a very proper Roman noblewoman," said Cotta.

Sulla smiled briefly. "I know she's proper," he said.

"Yes, well . . ." Cotta shifted uneasily, remembering the debates which had raged in the Cotta household about the nature of the friendship between Aurelia and Sulla; he was also aware that he was about to criticize one of Sulla's new proscription laws. But in he plunged bravely, determined to get it over and done with. "We think Caesar is the *flamen Dialis,* but that his wife is not the *flaminica.* At least, that is how we have interpreted your laws of proscription, which, in the matter of under-age children of the proscribed, do not make it clear whether these children are subject to the *lex Minicia.* Cinna's son was of age when his father was proscribed, therefore his citizenship was not in question. But what about the citizen status of under-age children, especially girls? Does your law intend judgment under the *lex Minicia,* or—as with conviction and exile by a court—does the father's loss of citizenship extend only to himself? That is what we had to decide. And given the severity of your laws of proscription in relation to the rights of children and other heirs, we came to the conclusion that the *lex Minicia de liberis* does apply.''

"Piglet dear, what do you have to say?" asked the Dictator demurely, entirely ignoring the implication of a legislative cloudiness. "Take your time, take your time! I have nothing else to do today.''

Metellus Pius flushed. "As Gaius Cotta says, the law of a child's citizen status does apply. When one parent is not a Roman citizen, the child cannot be a Roman citizen. So Caesar's wife is not a Roman citizen and cannot therefore be the *flaminica Dialis* under religious law.''

"Brilliant, brilliant! You got that out without a single mistake, Piglet!"
Drum, drum, went Sulla's heels. "So it is all my fault, eh? I left a law up
to interpretation instead of spelling every detail out."

Cotta drew a deep breath. "Yes," he said heroically.

"That is all very true, Lucius Cornelius," said Vatia, adding his mite.
"However, we are fully aware that our interpretation may be wrong. We
respectfully ask for your direction."

"Well," said Sulla, sliding off the wall, "it seems to me that the best
way out of this dilemma is to have Caesar find a new *flaminica.* Though he
must have been married *confarreatio,* in the eyes of both civil and religious
law a divorce is possible. It is my opinion that Caesar must divorce Cinna's
daughter, who is not acceptable to the Great God as his *flaminica.*"

"An annulment, surely!" said Cotta.

"A divorce," said Sulla firmly. "Though all and sundry may swear that
the marriage is not consummated—and though we could have the Vestals
examine the girl's hymen—we are dealing with Jupiter Best and Greatest.
You have pointed out to me that my laws are open to interpretation. In fact,
you have gone so far as to interpret them—without coming to consult with
me before making your decision. Therein lies your mistake. You should have
consulted me. But since you did not, you must now live with the consequences.
A *diffarreatio* divorce."

Cotta winced. "*Diffarreatio* is a dreadful business!"

"I weep to see your pain, Cotta."

"Then I shall inform the boy," said Cotta, mouth set.

Sulla put out his hand. "No!" he said, quite sharply. "Say nothing to
the boy, nothing at all! Just tell him to come to my house tomorrow before
the dinner hour. I prefer to tell him myself, is that clear?"

"And so," said Cotta to Caesar and Aurelia a short time later, "you
must see Sulla, nephew."

Both Caesar and his mother were looking strained, but saw the visitor
to the door without comment. After her brother had gone Aurelia followed
her son into his study.

"Do sit, Mater," he said to her gently.

She sat, but on the edge of the chair. "I don't like it," she said. "Why
should he want to see you in person?"

"You heard Uncle Gaius. He's starting to reform the religious orders,
and he wants to see me as *flamen Dialis.*"

"I do not believe that," said Aurelia stubbornly.

Worried, Caesar put his chin on his right hand and looked at his mother searchingly. His concern was not for himself; he could cope with whatever was to come, he knew that. No, it was for her, and for all the other women of his family.

The tragedy had marched on inexorably from the time of the conference Young Marius had called to discuss his seeking the consulship, through the season of artificially induced joy and confidence, through the downslide of the terrible winter, to the yawning pit which had been the defeat at Sacriportus. Of Young Marius they had seen practically nothing once he had become consul, and that included his mother and his wife. A mistress had come on the scene, a beautiful Roman woman of knightly forebears named Praecia, and she monopolized every spare moment Young Marius could find. Rich enough to be financially independent, she was at the time she caught Young Marius in her toils already thirty-seven years old, and not of a mind for marriage. There had been a marriage in her eighteenth year, but only to obey her father, who had died shortly thereafter; Praecia had promptly embarked upon a series of lovers, and her husband had divorced her. Which suited her very well. She settled to the kind of life she most liked, mistress of her own establishment as well as mistress to some interesting nobleman who brought his friends, his problems and his political intrigues to her dining couch and bed, and thus enabled her to combine politics with passion—an irresistible combination to one of Praecia's leanings.

Young Marius had been her biggest fish and she had grown quite fond of him, amused at his youthful posturings, fascinated by the power inherent in the name Gaius Marius, and pleased at the fact that the young senior consul preferred her to his mother, a Julia, and his wife, a Mucia. So she had thrown her large and tastefully decorated house open to all Young Marius's friends, and her bed to a small, select group who formed Young Marius's inner circle. Once Carbo (whom she loathed) had left for Ariminum, she became her paramour's chief adviser in all things, and fancied that it was she, not Young Marius, who actually ran Rome.

So when the news came that Sulla was about to depart from Teanum Sidicinum, and Young Marius announced that it was more than time he left to join his troops at Ad Pictas, Praecia had toyed with the idea of becoming a camp follower, accompanying the young senior consul to the war. It had not come to pass; Young Marius found a typical solution to the problem she was becoming by leaving Rome after dark without telling her he was going. However, not to repine! Praecia shrugged, and looked about for other game.

All this had meant that neither his mother nor his wife had been given the opportunity to bid him farewell, to wish him the luck he would certainly need. He was gone. And he was never to come back. The news of Sacriportus had not spread through Rome before Brutus Damasippus (too much Carbo's man to esteem Praecia) had embarked upon his bloodbath. Among those who died was Quintus Mucius Scaevola Pontifex Maximus, the father of Young Marius's wife, and a good friend to Young Marius's mother.

"My son did this," Julia had said to Aurelia when she came to see if there was anything she could do.

"Nonsense!" Aurelia had answered warmly. "It was Brutus Damasippus, no one else."

"I have seen the letter my son sent in his own writing from Sacriportus," Julia had said, drawing in her breath on something far worse than a sob. "He couldn't accept defeat without this paltry retaliation, and how can I expect my daughter-in-law to speak to me again?"

Caesar had huddled himself in a far corner of the room and watched the faces of the women with stony concentration. How could her son have done this to Aunt Julia? Especially after what his mad old father had done at the end? She was caught inside a mass of sorrow like a fly in a chunk of amber, her beauty the greater because she was static, her pain all within and quite invisible. It didn't even show in her eyes.

Then Mucia came in; Julia shrank away, averted her gaze.

Aurelia had sat bolt upright, the planes of her face sharp and flinty. "Mucia Tertia, do you blame Julia for your father's murder?" she demanded.

"Of course not," said Young Marius's wife, and pulled a chair over so that she could sit close enough to Julia to take her hands. "Please, Julia, look at me!"

"I cannot!"

"You must! I do not intend to move back to my father's house and live with my stepmother. Nor do I intend to seek a place in my own mother's house, with those frightful boys of hers. I want to stay here with my dear kind mother-in-law."

So that had been all right. Some kind of life had gone on for Julia and Mucia Tertia, though they heard nothing from Young Marius walled up in Praeneste, and the news from various battlefields was always in Sulla's favor. Had he been Aurelia's son, reflected Aurelia's son, Young Marius would have drawn little comfort from dwelling upon his mother while the days in Praeneste dragged on interminably. Aurelia was not as soft, not as loving, not as forgiving as Julia—but then, decided Caesar with a smile, if she had been, he might have turned out more like Young Marius! Caesar owned his mother's detachment. And her hardness too.

Bad news piled on top of bad news: Carbo had stolen away in the night; Sulla had turned the Samnites back; Pompey and Crassus had defeated the men Carbo had deserted in Clusium; the Piglet and Varro Lucullus were in control of Italian Gaul; Sulla had entered Rome for a period of hours only to set up a provisional government—and left Torquatus behind with Thracian cavalry to ensure his provisional government remained a functioning government.

But Sulla had not come to visit Aurelia, which fascinated her son sufficiently to try a little fishing. Of that meeting his mother had found thrust upon her outside Teanum Sidicinum she had said just about nothing; now here she was with her calm unimpaired and a tradition broken.

"He ought to have come to see you!" Caesar had said.

"He will never come to see me again," said Aurelia.

"Why not?"

"Those visits belong to a different time."

"A time when he was handsome enough to fancy?" the son snapped, that rigidly suppressed temper suddenly flashing out.

But she froze, gave him a look which crushed him. "You are stupid as well as insulting! Leave me!" she said.

He left her. And left the subject severely alone thereafter. Whatever Sulla meant to her was her business.

They had heard of the siege tower Young Marius built and of its miserable end, of the other attempts he made to break through Ofella's wall. And then on the last day of October there came the shocking news that ninety thousand Samnites were sitting in Pompey Strabo's camp outside the Colline Gate.

The next two days were the worst of Caesar's life. Choking inside his priestly garb, unable to touch a sword or look on death at the moment it happened, he locked himself in his study and commenced work on a new epic poem—in Latin, not in Greek—choosing the dactylic hexameter to make his task more difficult. The noise of battle came clearly to his ears, but he shut it out and struggled on with his maddening spondees and empty phrases, aching to be there and in it, admitting that he would not have cared which side he fought on, as long as he fought. . . .

And after the sounds died away during the night he came charging out of his study to find his mother in her office bent over her accounts, and stood in her doorway convulsed with rage.

"How can I write what I cannot do?" he demanded. "What is the greatest literature about, if not war and warriors? Did Homer waste his time on flowery claptrap? Did Thucydides deem the art of beekeeping a suitable subject for his pen?"

She knew exactly how to deflate him, so she said in cool ledgerish tones, "Probably not," and returned to her work.

And that night was the end of peace. Julia's son was dead—all of them were dead, and Rome belonged to Sulla. Who did not come to see them, or send any message.

That the Senate and the Centuriate Assembly had voted him the position of Dictator everyone knew, and talked about endlessly. But it was Lucius Decumius who told Caesar and young Gaius Matius from the other ground-floor apartment about the mystery of the disappearing knights.

"All men who got rich under Marius or Cinna or Carbo, and that be no accident. You're lucky your *tata* has been dead for enough years, Pimple," Lucius Decumius said to Gaius Matius, who had borne the unflattering nickname of Pustula—Pimple—since he had been a toddler. "And your *tata* too, probably, young Peacock," he said to Caesar.

"What do you mean?" asked Matius, frowning.

"I means there's some awful discreet-looking fellows walking round Rome pinching rich knights," the caretaker of the crossroads college said. "Freedmen mostly, but not your average gossipy Greek with boyfriend troubles. They're all called Lucius Cornelius something-or-other. My Brethren and I, we calls them the Sullani. Because they belongs to *him*. Mark my words, young Peacock and Pimple, they do not bode no good! And I safely predicts that they are going to pinch a lot more rich knights."

"Sulla can't do that!" said Matius, lips compressed.

"Sulla can do anything he likes," said Caesar. "He's been made Dictator. That's better than being King. His edicts have the force of law, he's not tied to the *lex Caecilia Didia* of seventeen days between promulgation and ratification, he doesn't even have to discuss his laws in Senate or Assemblies. And he cannot be made to answer for a single thing he does—or for anything he's done in the past, for that matter. Mind you," he added thoughtfully, "I think that if Rome isn't taken into a very strong hand, she's finished. So I hope all goes well for him. And I hope he has the vision and the courage to do what must be done."

"That man," said Lucius Decumius, "has the gall to do anything! Anything at all."

Living as they did in the heart of the Subura—which was the poorest and the most polyglot district in Rome—they found that Sulla's proscriptions had not the profound effect on life that they did in places like the Carinae, the Palatine, the upper Quirinal and Viminal. Though there were knights of the First Class aplenty between the far poorer Suburanites, few of them held a status above *tribunus aerarius,* and few the kind of political contacts which imperiled their lives now that Sulla was in power.

When the first list had displayed Young Marius's name second from the top, Julia and Mucia Tertia had come to see Aurelia; as these visits were usually the other way around, their advent was a surprise. So was news of the list, which had not yet spread as far as the Subura; Sulla had not kept Julia waiting for her fate.

"I have had a notice served on me by the urban praetor-elect, the younger Dolabella." Julia shivered. "Not a pleasant man! My poor son's estate is confiscate. Nothing can be saved."

"Your house too?" Aurelia asked, white-faced.

"Everything. He had a list of everything. All the mining interests in Spain, the lands in Etruria, our villa at Cumae, the house here in Rome, other lands Gaius Marius had acquired in Lucania and Umbria, the wheat *latifundia* on the Bagradas River in Africa Province, the dye works for wool in Hierapolis, the glassworks in Sidon. Even the farm in Arpinum. It all belongs now to Rome and will, I was informed, be put up for auction."

"Oh, Julia!"

Being Julia, she found a smile and actually made it reach her eyes. "Oh, it isn't all bad news! I was given a letter from Sulla which authorizes payment out of the estate of one hundred silver talents. That is what he assesses my dowry at, had Gaius Marius ever got round to giving me one. For, as all the gods know, I came to him penniless! But I am to have the hundred talents because, Sulla informs me, I am the sister of Julilla. For her sake, as she was his wife, he will not see me want. The letter was actually quite gracefully phrased."

"It sounds a lot of money—but after what you've had, it's nothing," said Aurelia, tight-lipped.

"It will buy me a nice house on the Vicus Longus or the Alta Semita, and yield me an adequate income besides. The slaves of course are to go with the estate, but Sulla has allowed me to keep Strophantes—I am so glad about that! The poor old man is quite crazed with grief." She stopped, her grey eyes full of tears—not for herself, but for Strophantes. "Anyway," she continued, "I will manage very comfortably. Which is more than the wives or mothers of other men on the list can say. They will get absolutely nothing."

"And what about you, Mucia Tertia?" asked Caesar. "Are you classified as Marian or Mucian?" She displayed no sign of grief for her husband, he noted, or even self-pity at her widow's status. One knew Aunt Julia grieved, though she never showed it. But Mucia Tertia?

"I am classified as Marian," she said, "so I lose my dowry. My father's estate is heavily encumbered. There was nothing for me in his will. Had there been something, my stepmother would try to keep it from me anyway. My own mother is all right—Metellus Nepos is safe, he is for Sulla. But their two boys must be thought of ahead of me. Julia and I have talked it over on the way here. I am to go with her. Sulla has forbidden me to remarry, as I was the wife of a Marius. Not that I wish to take another husband. I do not.''

"It's a nightmare!'' cried Aurelia. She looked down at her hands, inky-fingered and a little swollen in their joints. "It may be that we too will be put on the list. My husband was Gaius Marius's man to the end. And Cinna's at the time he died.''

"But this insula is in your name, Mater. As all the Cottae stand for Sulla, it should remain yours,'' Caesar said. "I may lose my land. But at least as *flamen Dialis* I will have my salary from the State and a State house in the Forum. I suppose Cinnilla will lose her dowry, such as it is.''

"I gather Cinna's relatives will lose everything,'' Julia said, and sighed. "Sulla means to see an end to opposition.''

"What of Annia? And the older daughter, Cornelia Cinna?'' asked Aurelia. "I have always disliked Annia. She was a poor mother to my little Cinnilla, and she remarried with indecent haste after Cinna died. So I daresay she'll survive.''

"You're right, she will. She's been married to Pupius Piso Frugi long enough to be classified as Pupian,'' said Julia. "I found out a lot from Dolabella, he was only too anxious to tell me who was going to suffer! Poor Cornelia Cinna is classified with Gnaeus Ahenobarbus. Of course she lost her house to Sulla when he first arrived, and Annia wouldn't take her in then. I believe she's living with an old Vestal aunt out on the Via Recta.''

"Oh, I am so glad both my girls are married to relative nobodies!'' Aurelia exclaimed.

"I have a piece of news,'' said Caesar, to draw the women's attention away from their own troubles.

"What?'' asked Mucia Tertia.

"Lepidus must have had a premonition of this. Yesterday he divorced his wife. Saturninus's daughter, Appuleia.''

"Oh, that's terrible!'' cried Julia. "I can bear the fact that the ones who fought against Sulla must be punished, but why must their children and their children's children suffer too? All the fuss about Saturninus was so long ago! Sulla won't care about Saturninus, so why should Lepidus do that to her? She's borne him three splendid sons!''

"She won't bear him any more,'' Caesar said. "She took a nice hot bath and opened her veins. So now Lepidus is running around sobbing rivers of grief. Pah!''

"Oh, but he was always that sort of man,'' said Aurelia with scorn. "I do not deny that there must be a place in the world for flimsy men, but the trouble with Marcus Aemilius Lepidus is that he genuinely believes he has substance.''

"Poor Lepidus!" sighed Julia.

"Poor Appuleia," said Mucia Tertia rather dryly.

But now, after what Cotta had told them, it seemed that the Caesars were not to be proscribed. The six hundred *iugera* at Bovillae were safe, Caesar would have a senatorial census. Not, he reflected wryly as he watched the snow pouring down the light well like a powdery waterfall, that he needed to worry about a senatorial census! The *flamen Dialis* was automatically a member of the Senate.

As he watched this sudden appearance of real winter, his mother watched him.

Such a nice person, she thought—and that is *my* doing, no one else's. For though he has many excellent qualities, he is far from perfect. Not as sympathetic or forgiving or tender as his father, for all that he has a look of his father about him. A look of me too. He is so brilliant in so many different ways. Send him anywhere in this building and he can fix whatever is wrong— pipes, tiles, plaster, shutters, drains, paint, wood. And the improvements he has made to our elderly inventor's brakes and cranes! He can actually write in Hebrew and Median! And speak a dozen languages, thanks to our amazing variety of tenants. Before he became a man he was a legend on the Campus Martius, so Lucius Decumius swears to me. He swims, he rides, he runs, all like the wind. The poems and plays he writes—as good as Plautus and Ennius, though I am his mother and should not say so. And his grasp of rhetoric, so Marcus Antonius Gnipho tells me, is without peer. How did Gnipho put it? My son can move stones to tears and mountains to rage. He understands legislation. And he can read anything at a single glance, no matter how bad the writing. In all of Rome there is no one else who can do that, even the prodigy Marcus Tullius Cicero. As for the women—how they pursue him! Up and down the Subura. He thinks I do not know, of course. He thinks I believe him chaste, waiting for his dear little wife. Well, that is better so. Men are strange creatures when it comes to the part of them makes them men. But my son is not perfect. Just superlatively gifted. He has a shocking temper, though he guards it well. He is self-centered in some ways and not always sensitive to the feelings and wants of others. As for this obsession he has about cleanliness—it pleases me to see him so fastidious, yet the extent of it he never got from me or anyone else. He won't look at a woman unless she's come straight from a bath, and I believe he actually inspects her from the top of her head to the spaces between her toes. In the Subura! However, he is greatly desired, so the standard of cleanliness among the local women has risen hugely since he turned fourteen. Precocious little beast! I always used to hope my husband availed himself of the local women during those many years he was away, but he always told me he didn't, he waited for me. If I disliked anything in him, it was that. Such a burden of guilt he shifted to me by keeping himself for me, whom he rarely saw. My son will never do that to *his* wife. I hope she appreciates her luck. Sulla. He has been summoned to see Sulla. I wish I knew why. I wish—

She came out of herself with a start to find Caesar leaning across his desk snapping his fingers at her, and laughing.

"Where were you?" he asked.

"All over the place," she answered as she got up, feeling the chill. "I'll have Burgundus give you a brazier, Caesar. It is too cold in this room."

"Fusspot!" he said lovingly to her back.

"I don't want you confronting Sulla with a sniffle and a thousand sneezes," she said.

But the morrow brought no sniffles, no sneezes. The young man presented himself at the house of Gnaeus Ahenobarbus a good summer hour before the winter dinnertime, prepared to kick his heels in the atrium rather than run the risk of arriving too late. Sure enough, the steward—an exquisitely oily Greek who subjected him to subtle come-hither glances—informed him that he was too early, would he mind waiting? Conscious of crawling skin, Caesar nodded curtly and turned his back on the man who would soon be famous, whom all Rome would know as Chrysogonus.

But Chrysogonus wouldn't go; clearly he found the visitor attractive enough to pursue, and Caesar had the good sense not to do what he longed to do—knock the fellow's teeth down his throat. Then inspiration struck. Caesar walked briskly out onto the loggia, and the steward disliked the cold too much to follow him. This house had two loggias, and the one where Caesar stood making crescent patterns in the snow with the toe of his clog looked not down onto the Forum Romanum, but back up the Palatine cliff in the direction of the Clivus Victoriae. Right above him was the loggia of another house which literally overhung the house of Ahenobarbus.

Whose house? Caesar wrinkled his brow, remembered. Marcus Livius Drusus, assassinated in its atrium ten years ago. So this was where all those orphaned children lived under the arid supervision of . . . Who? That's right, the daughter of that Servilius Caepio who had drowned coming back from his province! Gnaea? Yes, Gnaea. And her dreaded mother, the ghastly Porcia Liciniana! Lots of little Servilii Caepiones and Porcii Catones. The wrong

Porcii Catones, of the branch Salonius. Descendants of a slave—there was one now! He was leaning over the marble balustrade, a painfully thin boy with a neck long enough to give him a resemblance to a stork, and a nose large enough to show even at this distance. A lot of lank, reddish hair. No mistaking Cato the Censor's brood!

All of these thoughts indicated one thing about Caesar his mother had not catalogued during her reverie: he adored gossip and forgot none of it.

"Honored priest, my master is ready to see you."

Caesar turned away with a grin and a cheerful wave up to the boy on Drusus's balcony, hugely amused when the wave was not returned. Young Cato was probably too amazed to wave back; there would be few in Sulla's temporary dwelling with the time to make overtures of friendship to a poor little storky boy who was the descendant of a Tusculan squire and a Celtiberian slave.

Though he was prepared for the sight of Sulla the Dictator, Caesar still found himself shocked. No wonder he hadn't sought Mater out! Nor would I if I were he, thought Caesar, and walked forward as quietly as his wooden-soled clogs permitted.

Sulla's initial reaction was that he looked upon a total stranger; but this was due to the ugly red-and-purple cape and the peculiar effect the creamy ivory helmet created, of someone with a shaven skull.

"Take all that stuff off," said Sulla, and returned his gaze to the mass of papers on his desk.

When he looked up again the priestling was gone. In his place there stood his son. The hairs bristled on Sulla's arms, and on the back of his neck; he emitted a sound like air oozing out of a bladder and stumbled to his feet. The golden hair, the wide blue eyes, the long Caesar face, all that height . . . And then Sulla's tear-clouded vision assimilated the differences; Aurelia's high sharp cheekbones with the hollows beneath and Aurelia's exquisite mouth with the creases in the corners. Older than Young Sulla had been when he died, more man than boy. *Oh, Lucius Cornelius, my son, why did you have to die?*

He dashed the tears away. "I thought you were my son for a moment," he said harshly, and shivered.

"He was my first cousin."

"I remember you said you liked him."

"I did."

"Better than Young Marius, you said."

"I did."

"And you wrote a poem about him after he died, but you said it wasn't good enough to show me."

"Yes, that's true."

Sulla sank back into his chair, his hands trembling. "Sit, boy. There, where the light is best and I can see you. My eyes are not what they used to be." Drink him in! He is sent from the Great God, whose priest he is. "Your uncle Gaius Cotta told you what?"

"Only that I had to see you, Lucius Cornelius."

"Call me Sulla, it's what everybody calls me."

"And I am called Caesar, even by my mother."

"You are the *flamen Dialis.*"

Something flashed through the disquietingly familiar eyes—why were they so familiar, when his son's had been much bluer and sprightlier? A look of anger. Pain? No, not pain. Anger.

"Yes, I am the *flamen Dialis,*" Caesar answered.

"The men who appointed you were enemies of Rome."

"At the time they appointed me they were not."

"That's fair enough." Sulla picked up his reed pen, which was encased in gold, then put it down again. "You have a wife."

"I do."

"She's Cinna's daughter."

"She is."

"Have you consummated your marriage?"

"No."

Up from behind his desk Sulla got to walk over to the window, which gaped wide open despite the freezing cold. Caesar smiled inwardly, wondering that his mother would have said—here was another who didn't care about the elements.

"I have undertaken the restitution of the Republic," said Sulla, looking out the window straight at the statue of Scipio Africanus atop his tall column; at this altitude, he and tubby old Scipio Africanus were on the same level. "For reasons I imagine *you* will understand, I have chosen to begin with religion. We have lost the old values, and must return to them. I have abolished the election of priests and augurs, including the Pontifex Maximus. Politics and religion in Rome are inextricably intertwined, but I will not see religion made the servant of politics when it ought to be the other way round."

"I do understand," said Caesar from his chair. "However, I believe the Pontifex Maximus must be elected."

"What you believe, boy, does not interest me!"

"Then why am I here?"

"Certainly not to make smart remarks at my expense!"

"I apologize."

Sulla swung round, glared at the *flamen Dialis* fiercely. "You're not a scrap afraid of me, boy, are you?"

Came the smile—the same smile!—the smile which caught at heart and mind together. "I used to hide in the false ceiling above our dining room and watch you talking to my mother. Times have changed, and so have all our circumstances. But it's hard to be afraid of someone you suddenly loved in the moment you found out he was not your mother's paramour."

That provoked a roar of laughter, laughter to drive away a fresh spring of tears. "True enough! I wasn't. I did try once, but she was far too wise to have me. Thinks like a man, your mother. I bring no luck to women, I never have." The pale unsettling eyes looked Caesar up and down. "You won't bring any luck to women either, though there'll be plenty of women."

"Why did you summon me, if not to seek my advice?"

"It's to do with regulating religious malpractices. They say you were born on the same day of the year that Jupiter's fire finally went out."

"Yes."

"And how did you interpret that?"

"As a good omen."

"Unfortunately the College of Pontifices and the College of Augurs do not agree with you, young Caesar. They have made you and your flaminate their most important business for some time now. And have concluded that a certain irregularity in your flaminate was responsible for the destruction of the Great God's temple."

The joy flooded into Caesar's face. "Oh, how glad I am to hear you say that!"

"Eh? Say what?"

"That I am not the *flamen Dialis*."

"I didn't say that."

"You did! You did!"

"You've misinterpreted me, boy. You are definitely the *flamen Dialis*. Fifteen priests and fifteen augurs have arrived at that conclusion beyond a shadow of a doubt."

The joy had died out of Caesar's face completely. "I'd rather be a soldier," he said gruffly. "I'm more suited for it."

"What you'd rather be doesn't matter. It's what you are that does. And what your wife is."

Caesar frowned, looked at Sulla searchingly. "That's the second time you've mentioned my wife."

"You must divorce her," said Sulla baldly.

"Divorce her? But I can't!"

"Why not?"

"We're married *confarreatio*."

"There is such a thing as *diffarreatio*."

"Why must I divorce her?"

"Because she's Cinna's brat. It turns out that my laws pertaining to proscribed men and their families contain a minor flaw in regard to the citizen status of children under age. The priests and augurs have decided that the *lex Minicia* applies. Which means your wife—who is *flaminica Dialis*—is not Roman or patrician. Therefore she cannot be *flaminica Dialis*. As this flaminate is a dual one, the legality of her position is quite as important as yours. You must divorce her."

"I won't do that," said Caesar, beginning to see a way out of this hated priesthood.

"You'll do anything I say you must, boy!"

"I will do nothing I think I must not."

The puckered lips peeled back slowly. "I am the Dictator," said Sulla levelly. "You will divorce your wife."

"I refuse," said Caesar.

"I can force you to it if I have to."

"How?" asked Caesar scornfully. "The rites of *diffarreatio* require my complete consent and co-operation."

Time to reduce this young pest to a quivering jellyfish: Sulla let Caesar see the naked clawed creature which lived inside him, a thing fit only to screech at the moon. But even as the creature leaped forth, Sulla realized why Caesar's eyes were so familiar. They were like his own! Staring back at him with the cold and emotionless fixity of a snake. And the naked clawed creature slunk away, impotent. For the first time in his life Sulla was left without the means to bend another man to his will. The rage which ought by now to possess him could not come; forced to contemplate the image of himself in someone else's face, Lucius Cornelius Sulla was powerless.

He had to fight with mere words. "I have vowed to restore the proper religious ethics of the *mos maiorum*," he said. "Rome will honor and care for her gods in the way she did at the dawn of the Republic. Jupiter Optimus Maximus is displeased. With you—or rather, with your wife. You are his special priest, but your wife is an inseparable part of your priesthood. You must separate yourself from this present unacceptable wife, take another one. You must divorce Cinna's non-Roman brat.''

"I will not," said Caesar.

"Then I must find another solution."

"I have one ready to hand," said Caesar instantly. "Let Jupiter Best and Greatest divorce *me*. Cancel my flaminate.''

"I might have been able to do that as Dictator had I not brought the priestly colleges into the business. As it is, I am bound by their findings.''

"Then it begins to look," said Caesar calmly, "as if we have reached an impasse, doesn't it?''

"No, it does not. There is another way out.''

"To have me killed.''

"Exactly.''

"That would put the blood of the *flamen Dialis* on your hands, Sulla.''

"Not if someone else has your blood on his hands. I do not subscribe to the Greek metaphor, Gaius Julius Caesar. Nor do our Roman gods. Guilt cannot be transferred.''

Caesar considered this. "Yes, I believe you're right. If you have someone else kill me, the guilt must fall on him.'' He rose to his feet, which gave him some inches over Sulla. "Then our interview is at an end.''

"It is. Unless you will reconsider.''

"I will not divorce my wife.''

"Then I will have you killed.''

"If you can," said Caesar, and walked out.

Sulla called after him. "You have forgotten your *laena* and *apex*, priest!''

"Keep them for the next *flamen Dialis*.''

He forced himself to stroll home, not certain how quickly Sulla would regain his equilibrium. That the Dictator had been thrown off balance he had seen at once; it was evident that not too many people defied Lucius Cornelius Sulla.

The air was freezing, too cold for snow. And that childish gesture had cost him protection from the weather. Not important, really. He wouldn't die of exposure walking from the Palatine to the Subura. More important by far was his next course of action. For Sulla would have him killed, of that he had absolutely no doubt. He sighed. It would have to be flight. Though he knew he could look after himself, he had no illusions as to which of them would win did he remain in Rome. Sulla. However, he had at least a day's grace; the Dictator was as hampered by the slowly grinding machinery of bureaucracy as anyone else, and would have to squeeze an interview with one of those groups of quite ordinary-looking men into his crowded schedule; his foyer, as Caesar had quickly assessed, was filled with clients, not paid assassins. Life in Rome was not a bit like a Greek tragedy, no impassioned instructions were roared out to men straining like hounds at the leash. When Sulla found the time he would issue his orders. But not yet.

When he let himself into his mother's apartment he was blue with cold.

"Where are your clothes?" asked Aurelia, gaping.

"With Sulla," he managed to say. "I donated them to the next *flamen Dialis*. Mater, he showed me how to be free of it!"

"Tell me," she said, and got him to sit over a brazier.

He told her.

"Oh, Caesar, why?" she cried at the end.

"Come, Mater, you know why. I love my wife. That's first of all. All these years she's lived with us and looked to me for the kind of care neither father nor mother was willing to give her, and thought me the most wonderful aspect of her little life. How can I abandon her? She's Cinna's daughter! A pauper! Not even Roman anymore! Mater, I don't want to die. To live as the *flamen Dialis* is infinitely preferable to death. But there are some things worth dying for. Principles. The duties of a Roman nobleman you instilled in me with such uncompromising care. Cinnilla is my responsibility. I *can't* abandon her!" He shrugged, looked triumphant. "Besides, this is my way out. As long as I refuse to divorce Cinnilla, I am unacceptable to the Great God as his priest. So I just have to keep on refusing to divorce her."

"Until Sulla succeeds in having you killed."

"That's on the lap of the Great God, Mater, you know it is. I believe that Fortune has offered me this chance, and that I must take it. What I have to do is stay alive until after Sulla dies. Once he's dead, no one else will have the courage to kill the *flamen Dialis,* and the colleges will be forced to break my priestly chains. Mater, I do not believe Jupiter Optimus Maximus intends me as his special *flamen*! I believe he has other work for me. Work of better use to Rome."

She argued no more. "Money. You'll need money, Caesar." And she ran her hands through her hair, as she always did when she was trying to find mislaid funds. "You will need more than two talents of silver, because that's the price of a proscribed man. If you're discovered in hiding, you'll need to pay considerably more than two talents to make it worth an informer's while to let you go. Three talents ought to give you a purchase price plus enough to live on. Now can I find three talents without talking to bankers? Seventy-five thousand sesterces . . . I have ten thousand in my room. And the rents are due, I can collect them tonight. When my tenants hear why I need it, they'll pay up. They love you, though why they should I don't know—you're very difficult and obstinate! Gaius Matius might know how to get more. And I imagine Lucius Decumius keeps his ill-gotten gains in jars under his bed. . . ."

And off she went, still talking. Caesar sighed, got to his feet. Time to organize his flight. And he would have to talk to Cinnilla before he left, explain.

He sent the steward, Eutychus, to fetch Lucius Decumius, and summoned Burgundus.

Old Gaius Marius had bequeathed Burgundus to Caesar in his will; at the time Caesar had strongly suspected that he had done so as a last link in the chain of *flamen Dialis* with which he had bound Caesar hands and feet. If by any chance Caesar should not continue to be Jupiter's special priest, Burgundus was to kill him. But of course Caesar—who owned a great deal of charm—had soon made Burgundus *his* man, helped by the fact that his mother's gigantic Arvernian maidservant, Cardixa, had fastened her teeth into him. A German of the Cimbri, he had been eighteen when he was captured after the battle of Vercellae, and was now thirty-seven to Cardixa's forty-five. How much longer she could go on bearing a boy a year was one of the family jokes; their total at the moment was five. They had both been man-umitted on the day Caesar put on his toga of manhood, but this formal rite of being freed had changed nothing save their citizen status, which was now Roman (though of course they had been enrolled in the urban tribe Suburana, and therefore owned worthless votes). Aurelia, who was both frugal and scrupulously fair, had always given Cardixa a reasonable wage, and thought Burgundus was worthy of good money too. They were believed to be saving this for their sons, as their living was provided for them.

"But you must take our savings now, Caesar," Burgundus said in his thickly accented Latin. "You will need them."

His master was tall for a Roman, two inches over six feet, but Burgundus was four inches taller and twice as wide. His fair face, homely by Roman standards because its nose was far too short and straight and its mouth too wide, looked its normal solemn self when he said this, but his light blue eyes betrayed his love—and his respect.

Caesar smiled at Burgundus, shook his head. "I thank you for the offer, but my mother will manage. If she doesn't—why, then I will accept, and pay you back with interest."

Lucius Decumius came in accompanied by a swirl of snow; Caesar hastened to finish with Burgundus.

"Pack for both of us, Burgundus. Warm stuff. You can carry a club. I will carry my father's sword." Oh, how good to be able to say that! *I will carry my father's sword!* There were worse things than being a fugitive from the Dictator's wrath.

"I knew that man meant trouble for us!" said Lucius Decumius grimly, though he didn't mention the time when Sulla had frightened him almost witless with a look. "I've sent my boys home for money, you'll have enough." A glare buried itself in Burgundus's back. "Listen, Caesar, you can't go off in this sort of weather with only that big clod! The boys and I will come too."

Expecting this, Caesar gave Lucius Decumius a look which silenced protest. "No, dad, I can't allow that. The more of us there are, the more likely I am to attract attention."

"Attract attention?" Lucius Decumius gaped. "How can you not attract attention with that great dolt shambling along behind you? Leave him at home, take me instead, eh? No one ever sees old Lucius Decumius, he's a part of the plaster."

"Inside Rome, yes," Caesar said, smiling at Decumius with great affection, "but in Sabine country, dad, you'd stick out like dog's balls. Burgundus and I will manage. And if I know you're here to look after the women, I'll have a lot less to worry about while I'm away."

As this was the truth, Lucius Decumius subsided, muttering.

"The proscriptions have made it more important than ever that someone be here to guard the women. Aunt Julia and Mucia Tertia have no one except us. I don't think they'll come to any harm up there on the Quirinal, everyone in Rome loves Aunt Julia. But Sulla doesn't, so you'll have to keep watch on them. My mother"—he shrugged—"my mother is herself, and that's as bad as it is good when it comes to dealing with Sulla. If things should change— if, for instance, Sulla should decide to proscribe me, and because of me, my mother—then I leave it to you to get my household out." He grinned. "We've put too much money into feeding Cardixa's boys to see Sulla's State end up making a profit on them!"

"Nothing will happen to any of them, little Peacock."

"Thanks, dad." Caesar bethought himself of another matter. "I must ask you to hire us a couple of mules and get the horses from the stables."

This was Caesar's secret, the one aspect of his life he kept from everyone save Burgundus and Lucius Decumius. As *flamen Dialis* he couldn't touch a horse, but from the time when old Gaius Marius had taught him to ride he had fallen in love with the sensation of speed, and with the feel of a horse's powerful body between his knees. Though he wasn't rich in any way except his precious land, he did have a certain amount of money which was his, and which his mother would not have dreamed of managing. It had come to him in his father's will, and it enabled him to buy whatever he needed without having to apply to Aurelia. So he had bought a horse. A very special horse.

In all ways but this one Caesar had found the strength and self-denial to obey the dictates of his flaminate; as he tended to be indifferent to what he ate the monotonous diet did not cost him a pang, though many a time he had longed to take his father's sword out of the trunk in which it reposed and swing it around his head. The one thing he had not been able to give up was his love of horses and riding. Why? Because of the association between two different living creatures and the perfection of the result. So he had bought a beautifully made chestnut gelding as fleet as Boreas and called it Bucephalus, after the legendary horse of Alexander the Great. This animal was the greatest joy in his life. Whenever he could sneak away he would walk to the Capena Gate, outside which Burgundus or Lucius Decumius waited with Bucephalus. And he would ride, streaking down the towpath along the Tiber without regard for life or limb, swerving around the patient oxen which drew the barges upriver—and then, when that ceased to be interesting, he would head off across the fields taking stone walls in his stride, he and his beloved Bucephalus as one. Many knew the horse, nobody knew the rider; for he trousered himself like a mad Galatian and wore a Median scarf wound round head and face.

The secret rides also endowed his life with an element of risk that he didn't yet understand he craved; he merely thought it tremendous fun to hoodwink Rome and imperil his flaminate. While he honored and respected the Great God whom he served, he knew that he had a unique relationship with Jupiter Best and Greatest; his ancestor Aeneas had been the love child of the goddess of love, Venus, and Venus's father was Jupiter Optimus Maximus. So Jupiter understood, Jupiter gave his sanction, Jupiter knew his earthly servant had a drop of divine ichor in his veins. In all else he obeyed the tenets of his flaminate to the best of his ability; but his price was Bucephalus, a communion with another living creature more precious to him by far than all the women in the Subura. On them, the sum was less than himself. On Bucephalus, the sum was more.

Not long after nightfall he was ready to leave. Lucius Decumius and his sons had trundled the seventy-six thousand sesterces Aurelia had managed to scrape up in a handcart to the Quirinal Gate, while two other loyal Brethren of the college had gone to the stables on the Campus Lanatarius where Caesar kept his horses and brought them the long way round, outside the Servian Walls.

"I do wish," said Aurelia without displaying a sign of her terrible inward anxiety, "that you'd chosen to ride a less showy animal than that chestnut you gallop all over Latium."

He gasped, choked, fell about laughing; when he could, he said, wiping his eyes, "I don't believe it! Mater, how long have you known about Bucephalus?"

"Is that what you call it?" She snorted. "My son, you have delusions of grandeur not in keeping with your priestly calling." A spark of amusement glittered. "I've always known. I even know the disgracefully long price you paid for it—fifty thousand sesterces! You are an incorrigible spendthrift, Caesar, and I don't understand where you get that from. It is certainly not from me."

He hugged her, kissed her wide and uncreased brow. "Well, Mater, I promise that no one but you will ever keep my accounts. I'd still like to know how you found out about Bucephalus."

"I have many sources of information," she said, smiling. "One cannot but, after twenty-three years in the Subura." Her smile dying, she looked up at him searchingly. "You haven't seen little Cinnilla yet, and she's fretting. She knows something is amiss, even though I sent her to her room."

A sigh, a frown, a look of appeal. "What do I tell her, Mater? How much, if anything?"

"Tell her the truth, Caesar. She's twelve."

Cinnilla occupied what used to be Cardixa's room, under the stairs which ascended to the upper storeys on the Vicus Patricius side of the building; Cardixa now lived with Burgundus and their sons in a special room it had amused Caesar to design and build with his own hands above the servants' quarters.

When Caesar entered on the echo of his knock, his wife was at her loom diligently weaving a drab-colored and rather hairy piece of cloth destined to form a part of her wardrobe as *flaminica Dialis,* and for some reason the sight of it, so unappealing and unflattering, smote at Caesar's heart.

"Oh, it isn't fair!" he cried, swept her off her stool into his arms and sat with her on his lap in the one place available, her little bed.

He thought her exquisitely beautiful, though he was too young himself to find her burgeoning womanhood attractive in itself; he liked females considerably older than he was. But to those who have been surrounded all their lives by tall, slender, fair people, a slightly plump mite of night-dark coloring held an irresistible fascination. His feelings about her were confused, for she had lived inside his house for five years as his sister, yet he had always known she was his wife, and that when Aurelia gave her permission he would take her out of this room and into his bed. There was nothing moral in this confusion, which might almost have been called a matter of logistics; one moment she was his sister, the next moment she would be his wife. Of course all the eastern kings did it—married their sisters—but he had heard that the family nurseries of the Ptolemies and the Mithridatidae resounded with the noises of war, that brothers fought sisters like animals. Whereas he had never fought with Cinnilla, any more than he had ever fought with his real sisters; Aurelia would not have let that kind of attitude develop.

"Are you going away, Caesar?" asked Cinnilla.

There was a strand of hair drifting across her brow; he smoothed it back into place and continued to stroke her head as if she were a pet, rhythmic, soothing, sensuous. Her eyes closed, she settled into the crook of his arm.

"Now, now, don't go to sleep!" he said sharply, giving her a shake. "I know it's past your bedtime, but I have to talk to you. I'm going away, that's true."

"What is the matter these days? Is it all to do with the proscriptions? Aurelia says my brother has fled to Spain."

"It has a little to do with the proscriptions, Cinnilla, but only because they stem from Sulla too. I have to go away because Sulla says there is a doubt about my priesthood."

She smiled, her full top lip creasing to reveal a fold of its inside surface, a characteristic all who knew Cinnilla agreed was enchanting. "That should make you happy. You'd much rather not be the *flamen Dialis*."

"Oh, I'm still the *flamen Dialis*," said Caesar with a sigh. "According to the priests, it's you who are wrong." He shifted her, made her sit upright on the edge of his knees so he could look into her face. "You know your family's present situation, but what you may not have realized is that when your father was pronounced *sacer*—an outcast—he ceased to be a Roman citizen."

"Well, I do understand why Sulla can take away all of our property, but my father died a long time before ever Sulla came back," said Cinnilla, who was not very clever, and needed to have things explained. "How can he have lost his citizenship?"

"Because Sulla's laws of proscription automatically take away a man's citizenship, and because some men were already dead when Sulla put their names on his proscription lists. Young Marius—your father—the praetors Carrinas and Damasippus—and lots of others—were dead when they were proscribed. But that fact didn't stop their losing their citizen rights."

"I don't think that's very fair."

"I agree, Cinnilla." He ploughed on, hoping that he had been dowered with the gift of simplifying. "Your brother was of age when your father was proscribed, so he retains his Roman status. He just can't inherit any of the family property or money, nor stand as a curule magistrate. However, with you, it's quite different."

"Why? Because I'm a girl?"

"No, because you are under age. Your sex is immaterial. The *lex Minicia de liberis* says children of a Roman and a non-Roman must take the citizenship of the non-Roman parent. That means—at least according to the priests— that you now have the status of a foreigner."

She began to shiver, though not to weep, her enormous dark eyes staring into Caesar's face with painful apprehension. "Oh! Does that mean I am no longer your wife?"

"No, Cinnilla, it does not. You are my wife until the day one of us dies, for we are married in the old form. No law forbids a Roman to marry a non-Roman, so our marriage is not in doubt. What *is* in doubt is your citizen status—and the citizen status of all the other children of a proscribed man who were under age at the time of proscription. Is that clear?"

"I think so." The expression of frowning concentration did not lighten. "Does that mean that if I give you children, they will not be Roman citizens?"

"Under the *lex Minicia,* yes."

"Oh, Caesar, how terrible!"

"Yes."

"But I am a patrician!"

"Not any longer, Cinnilla."

"What can I do?"

"For the moment, nothing. But Sulla knows that he has to clarify his laws in this respect, so we will just have to hope that he does so in a way which allows our children to be Roman, even if you are not." His hold tightened a little. "Today Sulla summoned me and ordered me to divorce you."

Now the tears came, silently, tragically. Even at eighteen Caesar had experienced women's tears with what had become boring regularity, usually turned on when he tired of someone, or someone discovered he was intriguing elsewhere. Such tears annoyed him, tried his sudden and very hot temper. Though he had learned to control it rigidly, it always flashed out when women produced tears, and the results were shattering—for the weeper. Whereas Cinnilla's tears were pure grief and Caesar's temper was only for Sulla, who had made Cinnilla cry.

"It's all right, my little love," he said, gathering her closer. "I wouldn't divorce you if Jupiter Optimus Maximus came down in person and ordered it! Not if I lived to be a thousand would I divorce you!''

She giggled and snuffled, let him dry her face with his handkerchief. "Blow!" he commanded. She blew. "Now that's quite enough. There's no need to cry. You are my wife, and you will stay my wife no matter what."

One arm stole round his neck, she put her face into his shoulder and sighed happily. "Oh, Caesar, I do love you! It's so hard to wait to grow up!"

That shocked him. So did the feel of her budding breasts, for he was wearing only a tunic. He put his cheek against her hair but delicately loosened his hold on her, unwilling to start something his honor wouldn't let him finish.

"Jupiter Optimus Maximus doesn't have a person to come down in," she said, good Roman child who knew her theology. "He is everywhere that Rome is—that's why Rome is Best and Greatest."

"What a good *flaminica Dialis* you would have made!"

"I would have tried. For you." She lifted her head to look at him. "If Sulla ordered you to divorce me and you said no, does that mean he will try to kill you? Is that why you're going away, Caesar?"

"He will certainly try to kill me, and that *is* why I'm going away. If I stayed in Rome, he would be able to kill me easily. There are too many of his creatures, and no one knows their names or faces. But in the country I stand a better chance." He jogged her up and down on his knee as he had when she had come first to live with them. "You mustn't worry about me, Cinnilla. My life strand is tough—too tough for Sulla's shears, I'll bet! Your job is to keep Mater from worrying."

"I'll try," she said, and kissed him on his cheek, too unsure of herself to do what she wanted to do, kiss him on his mouth and say she was old enough.

"Good!" he said. He pushed her off his lap and got to his feet. "I'll be back after Sulla dies," he said, and left.

When Caesar arrived at the Quirinal Gate he found Lucius Decumius and his sons waiting. The two mules were panniered with the money evenly divided between them, which meant neither was carrying anything like a full load. There were no leather moneybags in evidence; instead, Lucius Decumius had put the cash in false compartments lining what looked like—and were!— book buckets stuffed with scrolls.

"You didn't make these in a few hours today," Caesar said, grinning. "Is this how you shift your own loot around?"

"Go and talk to your horse—but first, a word in your ear. Let Burgundus lift the money," Lucius Decumius lectured, and turned to the German with such a fierce look upon his face that Burgundus took an involuntary step backward. "Now see here, lout, you make sure when you lifts those buckets that you makes it seem like you was lifting feathers, hear me?"

Burgundus nodded. "I hear, Lucius Decumius. Feathers."

"Now put all your other baggage on top of them books—and if the boy takes off like the wind, you hang on to them mules no matter what!"

Caesar was standing at his horse's head, cheek against cheek, murmuring endearments. Only when the rest of the baggage had been tied onto the mules did he move, and then it was to allow Burgundus to toss him into the saddle.

"You look after yourself, Pavo!" shrilled Lucius Decumius into the wind, eyes tearing. He reached up his grubby hand.

Caesar the cleanliness fanatic leaned down, took it, and kissed it. "Yes, dad!"

And then they were gone into the wall of snow.

Burgundus's mount was the Caesar family steed, and almost as expensive as Bucephalus. A Nesaean from Median bloodstock, it was much bigger than the horses of the peoples around the Middle Sea. Nesaeans were few and far between in Italy, as they could be used for nothing else than bearing oversized riders. Many farmers and traders had eyed them longingly, wishing they could be employed as beasts of burden or attached to heavy wagons and ploughs because they were both speedier and more intelligent than oxen. But, alas, when yoked to pull a load they strangled; the forward movement pressed the harness against their windpipes. As pack animals they were useless too; they ate too much to pay their way. An ordinary horse, however, could not have taken Burgundus's weight, and though a good mule might have, on a mule Burgundus's feet literally skimmed the ground.

Caesar led the way toward Crustumerium, hunched down in the lee of Bucephalus's head—oh, it was a cold winter!

They pressed on through the night to put as much distance as possible between themselves and Rome, and paused only when the next night threatened. By then they had reached Trebula, not far from the crest of the first range of mountains. It was a small place, but boasted an accommodation house which also served as the local tavern, and was therefore noisy, overcrowded, and very hot. The general atmosphere of dirt and neglect did not please Caesar in the least.

"Still, it's a roof and a sort of a bed," he said to Burgundus after inspecting a room upstairs where they were to sleep—along with several shepherd dogs and six hens.

Of course they attracted a considerable amount of attention from their fellow patrons, who were all locals there to drink wine; most would be fit to stagger home again through the snow, but some (so Mine Host confided) would spend the night wherever they happened to be lying when they fell over.

"There's sausages and bread," said Mine Host.

"We'll have both," said Caesar.

"Wine?"

"Water," said Caesar firmly.

"Too young to drink?" Mine Host demanded, not pleased. His profit was in the wine.

"My mother would kill me if I took a single sip."

"What's wrong with your friend, then? He's old enough."

"Yes, but he's mentally retarded, and you wouldn't want to see him with a bit of wine in him—he pulls Hyrcanian bears apart with his hands, and did in two lions some praetor in Rome thought he was going to show at the games," said Caesar with a straight face; Burgundus just looked vacant.

"Oooer!" said Mine Host, and retreated quickly.

No one ever tried to bother Caesar when he had Burgundus for company, so they were able to sit in the most peaceful part of that turbulent room and watch the local sport, which mostly seemed to consist in plying the drunkest youngster there with more wine and speculating upon how much longer he would manage to keep it down.

"Country life!" said Caesar, slapping at his bare arm. "You'd never think Rome was close enough for these yokels to vote every year, would you? Not to mention that their votes count because they belong to rural tribes, whereas canny fellows up to every political trick but unfortunate enough to own Rome as their birthplace have votes that are worthless. Not right!"

"They can't even read," said Burgundus, who could these days because Caesar and Gnipho had taught him. His slow smile dawned. "That's good, Caesar. Our book buckets are safe."

"Quite so." Caesar slapped at his arm again. "The place is full of mosquitoes, wretched things!"

"Come in for the winter," said Burgundus. "Hot enough to boil eggs in here."

An exaggeration, but the room was certainly unbearably hot, a combination of the bodies jammed into a confined space and a huge fire which roared away inside a thick stone box let into the side of the room; though the box was open at the top to let the smoke out, no cold could compete with several logs as big around as a man's waist sending great tongues of flame into the smoke hole; clearly the men of Trebula, literally with timber to burn, disliked being cold.

If the dark corners were full of mosquitoes, the beds were full of fleas and bugs; Caesar spent the night on a hard chair and quit the place thankfully at dawn to ride on. Behind him he left much speculation as to why he and his giant servant were abroad in such weather—and what class of man he was.

"Very uppish!" said Mine Host.

"Proscriptions," suggested Mine Host's wife.

"Too young," said a rather urban-looking fellow who had arrived just as Caesar and Burgundus were departing. "Besides, they'd have looked a lot more frightened if Sulla was after them!"

"Then he's on his way to visit someone," said the wife.

"Very likely," said the stranger, looking suddenly unsure. "Might bear investigating, though. Can't mistake the pair of them, can you? Achilles and Ajax," he ended, displaying a morsel of education. "The thing that struck me was the horses. Worth a fortune! There's money there."

"Probably owns a bit of the *rosea rura* at Reate," said Mine Host. "It's where the horses come from, I'll bet."

"He has a look of the Palatine about him," said the newcomer, whose thoughts were now definitely suspicious. "One of the Famous Families, in fact. Yes, there's money there."

"Well, if there is it's not with him," said Mine Host, disgruntled. "Know what they had on those mules? Books! A dozen great buckets of books! I ask you—*books*!"

Having battled worsening weather as they climbed higher into the ranges around the Mons Fiscellus, Caesar and Burgundus finally arrived in Nersae a full day later.

The mother of Quintus Sertorius had been a widow for over thirty years, and looked as if she had never had a husband. She always reminded Caesar of the late, much-lamented Scaurus Princeps Senatus, for she was little and slight, incredibly wrinkled, very bald for a woman, and owned one remarkable focus of beauty, a pair of vivid green eyes; that she could ever have borne a child as massive as Quintus Sertorius was hard to imagine.

"He's all right," she said to Caesar as she loaded her old and well-scrubbed table with goodies from her smokehouse and her larder; this was country living, everyone sat on chairs at a table to eat. "Didn't have any trouble setting himself up as governor of Nearer Spain, but he's expecting big trouble now that Sulla has made himself Dictator." She chuckled gleefully. "Never mind, never mind, he'll make life harder for Sulla than that poor boy of my cousin Marius's. Brought up too soft, of course. Lovely lady, Julia. But too soft, and my cousin Marius was too much away when the boy was growing up. That was true of you too, Caesar, but *your* mother wasn't soft, was she?"

"No, Ria," said Caesar, smiling into her eyes.

"Anyway, Quintus Sertorius likes Spain. He always did. He and Sulla were there when they went poking about among the Germans years ago. He's got a German wife and son in Osca, he tells me. I'm glad for that. Otherwise there'll be no one after he goes."

"He ought to marry a Roman woman," said Caesar austerely.

Ria emitted a cracked laugh. "Not him! Not my Quintus Sertorius! Doesn't like women. The German one got him because he had to have a wife to get inside the tribe. No, doesn't like women"—she pursed her lips and shook her head—"but doesn't like men either."

The conversation revolved around Quintus Sertorius and his deeds for some time, but eventually Ria talked herself out on the subject of her son, and got down to what Caesar must do.

"I'd gladly have you myself, but the connection is too well known, and you're not the first refugee I've had—my cousin Marius sent me the king of the Volcae Tectosages, no less—name was Copillus. Very nice man! Quite civilized for a barbarian. They strangled him in the Carcer after my cousin Marius triumphed, of course. Still, I was able to make a nice little nest egg out of taking care of him for my cousin Marius all those years. Four, I think it was. . . . He was always generous, my cousin Marius. Paid me a fortune for that job. I would have done it for nothing. Company, Copillus was. . . . Quintus Sertorius is not a homebody. Likes to fight." She shrugged, slapped her knees briskly, got down to business. "There's a couple I know live in the mountains between here and Amiternum. They'd be glad of some extra money, and you can trust them—I say that in truth. I'll give you a letter for them, and directions when you're ready to go."

"Tomorrow," said Caesar.

But she shook her head. "Not tomorrow! Not the day after, either. We're in for a big storm and you won't be able to find the road or know what's underneath you. The German there would be under the ice in a river before he even knew there *was* a river! You'll have to stay with me until the winter sets."

"Sets?"

"Gets its first nasty storms over and the freeze sets in. Then it's safe to travel, everything is solid ice. Hard on the horses, but you'll get there. Make the German go first, his horse's hooves are so big the creature won't slip much and will break the surface for your dainty creature. Fancy bringing a horse like that up here in winter! You have no sense, Caesar.''

He looked rueful. "So my mother told me.''

"She has sense. Sabine country folk are horse folk. That pretty animal is noticed. Just as well where you're going there's no one to notice.'' Ria grinned, revealing a few black teeth. "But you're only eighteen, after all. You'll learn!''

The next day proved Ria right about the weather; the snow continued unabated until it piled up in massive drifts. Had Caesar and Burgundus not got to work and shoveled it away, Ria's cozy stone house would soon have been snowed in, and even Burgundus would not have been able to open the door. For four more days it snowed, then patches of blue sky began to appear; the air grew much colder.

"I like the winter up here,'' said Ria, helping them pile straw warmly in the stables. "In Rome, a cold one is a misery, and we're going through the cold winter cycle this decade. But up here at least it's clean and dry, no matter how cold.''

"I must get away soon,'' said Caesar, dealing with hay.

"Considering the amounts your German and his nag eat, I will be glad to see you away,'' said Sertorius's mother between grunts. "Not tomorrow. Perhaps the day after. Once it's possible to travel between Rome and Nersae you won't be safe here. If Sulla remembers me—and he should, he knew my son very well—then he will send his hirelings here first.''

But Ria's guests were not destined to leave. On the night before the start was planned, Caesar began to ail. Though it was indeed far below freezing outside, the house was well warmed through in country fashion, braziers against its thick stone walls and good stout shutters to keep out every wind. Yet Caesar was cold, and grew colder.

"I don't like this,'' Ria said to him. "I can hear your teeth. But it's been going on too long to be a simple ague.'' She put her hand upon his forehead and winced. "You're burning up! Have you a headache?''

"Bad,'' he muttered.

"Then you're not going anywhere tomorrow. Look to it, you German lump! Get your master into his bed.''

In his bed Caesar remained, consumed with fever, racked by a dry cough and a perpetual headache, and unable to keep any food down.

"*Caelum grave et pestilens,*'' said the wisewoman when she came to see the patient.

"It isn't a typical ague," said Ria stubbornly. "It's not quartan and it's not tertian. And he doesn't sweat."

"Oh, it's the ague, Ria. The one without a pattern."

"Then he'll die!"

"He's strong," said the wisewoman. "Make him drink. I can give you no better advice. Water mixed with snow."

Sulla was preparing to read a letter from Pompey in Africa when the steward Chrysogonus came to him looking flustered.

"What is it? I'm busy, I want to read this!"

"*Domine*, a lady wishes to see you."

"Tell her to buzz off."

"*Domine*, I cannot!"

That took Sulla's mind off the letter; he lowered it and stared at Chrysogonus in astonishment. "I didn't think there was anyone alive could defeat you," he said, beginning to be amused. "You're shaking, Chrysogonus. Did she bite you?"

"No, *domine*," said the steward, who had absolutely no sense of humor. "However, I thought she might kill me."

"Oh! I think I have to see this lady. Did she give you a name? Is she mortal?"

"She said, Aurelia."

Sulla extended his hand and watched it. "No, I'm not in a pother yet!"

"Shall I bring her in?"

"No. Tell her I don't want to see her ever again," Sulla said, but did not pick up Pompey's letter; his interest in it had waned.

"*Domine*, she refuses to go until she's seen you!"

"Then have the servants carry her out."

"I tried, *domine*. They wouldn't lay a finger on her."

"Yes, that would be right!" Sulla huffed, closed his eyes. "All right, Chrysogonus, send her in." And when Aurelia marched in he said, "Sit down."

She sat, the glaring winter light bathing her without mercy, once more showing Sulla's wreckage how powerless perfect bones could render time. In his general's quarters at Teanum the light had been so bad he hadn't really seen her properly, so now he looked his fill. Too thin, and that ought to have made her less beautiful; instead it made her more, and the rosy flush which used to suffuse her lips and cheeks had faded away to leave her skin marmoreal. The hair had not greyed, nor had she yielded to a wish to bring back her youth by softening the style in which she wore it; it was still scraped back from her face into an uncompromising bun on the nape of her neck. And the eyes were so lovely, set in thick black lashes beneath feathered black brows. They gazed at him sternly.

"Come about your boy, I suppose," he said, leaning back in his chair.

"I have."

"Then speak! I'm listening."

"Was it because he looks so like *your* son?"

Shaken, he could not continue to meet her gaze, stared at Pompey's letter until the pain of that barb had dissipated. "It was a shock when I first set eyes on him, but no." His eyes came back to hers, cold and goatish.

"I liked your son, Lucius Cornelius."

"And this is no way to get what you want, Aurelia. My boy died a long time ago. I've learned to live with it, even when people like you try to make capital out of it."

"So you do know what I want."

"Certainly." He tipped the chair back, not easy with the backward-curving legs of a sturdy Roman-designed version. "You want me to spare your son. Even though mine was not spared."

"You can hardly blame me or my son for that!"

"I can blame anyone I like for anything I like! I am the Dictator!" he shouted, beads of foam at the corners of his lips.

"Rubbish, Sulla! You don't believe that any more than I do! I am here to ask you to spare my son, who does not deserve to die any more than he deserved to be made *flamen Dialis.*"

"I agree, he's not the right type for the job. But he's got it. You must have wanted it for him."

"I did not want him to be *flamen Dialis,* any more than my husband did. We were told. By Marius himself, in between his atrocities," Aurelia said, lifting her lip just enough to indicate her disgust. "It was also Marius who told Cinna to give my son his daughter. The last thing Cinna wanted was to see Cinnilla made *flaminica Dialis!*"

Sulla changed the subject. "You've given up wearing those lovely colors you used to like," he said. "That bone thing you have on doesn't even begin to do you justice."

"Oh, rubbish again!" she snapped. "I am not here to please your discriminating eye, I'm here to plead for my son!"

"It would please me very much to spare your son. He knows what he has to do. Divorce Cinna's brat."

"He won't divorce her."

"Why not?" shouted Sulla, leaping to his feet. *"Why not?"*

A little color crept into her cheeks, reddened her lips. "Because, you fool, you showed him that she's his way out of a job he loathes with all his being! Divorce her, and remain the *flamen Dialis* for the rest of his life? He'd rather be dead!"

Sulla gaped. "What?"

"You're a fool, Sulla! A fool! He'll never divorce her!"

"Don't you criticize me!"

"I'll say what I like to you, you evil old relic!"

A peculiar silence fell, and Sulla's rage trickled away as fast as Aurelia's gathered. He had turned to the window, but now he turned back to stare at her with something more on his mind than anger or the ordeal she had become.

"Let's start again," he said. "Tell me why Marius made your son the *flamen Dialis* if none of you wanted it."

"It has to do with the prophecy," she said.

"Yes, I know about that. Consul seven times, Third Founder of Rome— he used to tell everyone."

"But not all of it. There was a second part he told to no one until his mind was failing. Then he told Young Marius, who told Julia, who told me."

Sulla sat down again, frowning. "Go on," he said curtly.

"The second part of the prophecy concerned my son. Caesar. Old Martha foretold that he would be the greatest Roman of all time. And Gaius Marius believed her about that too. He saddled Caesar with the flaminate *Dialis* to prevent his going to war and enjoying a political career." Aurelia sat down, white-faced.

"Because a man who cannot go to war and cannot seek the consulship can never shine," said Sulla, nodding. He whistled. "Clever Marius! Brilliant! Make your rival the *flamen Dialis* and you've won. I didn't think the old beast was so subtle."

"Oh, he was subtle!"

"An interesting story," Sulla said then, and picked up Pompey's letter. "You can go, I've heard you out."

"Spare my son!"

"Not unless he divorces Cinna's daughter."

"He will never do that."

"Then there is no more to be said. Go away, Aurelia."

One more try. One more try for Caesar. "I wept for you once. You loved that. Now I find myself wanting to weep for you again. But you wouldn't love these tears. They would be to mourn the passing of a great man. For now I see a man who has diminished inside himself so much that he's reduced to preying upon children. Cinna's daughter is twelve years old. My son is eighteen. Children! Yet Cinna's widow strolls brazenly through Rome because she's someone else's wife, and that someone else belongs to you. Cinna's son is left penniless, with no alternative than to leave his country. Another child. While Cinna's widow thrives. Not a child." She sneered at him, made a derisory sound. "Annia is a redhead, of course. Is that some of her hair on your naked old pate?"

After which sally she swung on her heel and walked out.

Chrysogonus came bustling in.

"I want someone found," said Sulla, looking his nastiest. "Found, Chrysogonus, not proscribed and not killed."

Dying to know what had transpired between his master and that extraordinary woman—they had a past together, nothing was surer!—the steward heaved an inward sigh; he would never know. So he said very smoothly, "A private transaction, is it?"

"That's as good a way of putting it as any! Yes, a private transaction. Two talents reward for the fellow who locates one Gaius Julius Caesar, the *flamen Dialis*. Who is to be brought to me with not so much as one hair of his head disturbed! Make sure they all know, Chrysogonus. No man kills the *flamen Dialis*. I just want him here. Understand?"

"Of course, *domine*." But the steward made no move to go. Instead he coughed delicately.

Sulla's eyes had drifted back to Pompey's letter, but he lifted his head at this. "Yes?"

"I have prepared the outline you wanted, *domine,* at the time I first asked you if I might be appointed the bureaucrat in charge of administering the proscriptions. I have also found a deputy steward for you to interview, in the event that you should agree to allow me to administer the proscriptions."

The smile was not nice. "You really believe you can cope with two jobs, do you? *If* I give you a deputy steward."

"It is best if I do both jobs, *domine,* truly. Read my outline. It will show you conclusively that I do understand the nature of this particular administrative task. Why put some Treasury professional in the job when he'd prove too timid to seek clarification of his problems from you personally, and would be too mired in Treasury methods to take advantage of the more commercial aspects of the job?"

"I'll think about it and let you know," said Sulla, picking up Pompey's hapless letter yet again. Impassively he watched the steward bow his way out of the room, then grinned sourly. Abominable creature! Toad! Yet that, he reflected, was what administration of the proscriptions required—someone absolutely abominable. But trustworthy. If the administrator were Chrysogonus, Sulla could be sure that disastrous liberties would not take place. No doubt Chrysogonus would make a fat profit for himself somewhere, but no one was in a better position than Chrysogonus to know that it would go very ill with him if he made his profit in any way which would reflect personally on Sulla. The business end of the proscriptions had to be conducted in a positive cloud of respectability—sale of properties, disposal of cash assets, jewelry, furniture, works of art, stocks and shares. It was impossible for Sulla to administrate all of this himself, so someone would have to do it. Chrysogonus was right. Better him than a Treasury bureaucrat! Put one of those fellows on the job and nothing would ever get done. The work had to proceed expeditiously. But no one could be given the opportunity to say that Sulla himself had profited at the State's expense. Though Chrysogonus was a freedman now, that made him no less Sulla's creature; and Chrysogonus knew his master would have no qualms about killing him if he erred.

Satisfied that he had solved the chief dilemma of the proscriptions, Sulla returned to pore over Pompey's letter.

Africa Province and Numidia are both pacified and quiet. The task took me forty days. I left Lilybaeum at the end of October with six legions and two thousand of my horse, leaving Gaius Memmius in charge of Sicily. I did not consider there was any need to garrison Sicily. I had already begun to assemble ships when I first arrived in Sicily, and by the end of October there were more than eight hundred transports on hand. I always like to be well organized, it saves so much time. Just before I sailed, I sent a messenger to King Bogud of Mauretania, who keeps his army these days in Iol, not so far away as Tingis. Bogud is now ruling from Iol, and has put a minor king, Ascalis, in Tingis. All these changes are because of the strife in Numidia, where Prince Iarbas has usurped King Hiempsal's throne. My messenger instructed King Bogud to mount an invasion of Numidia from the west immediately, no excuses for delay. My strategy was to have King Bogud push Iarbas eastward until he encountered me and I could roll him up.

I landed my men in two divisions, one half at Old Carthage, the second half at Utica. I commanded the second division myself. The moment I stepped ashore, I received the submission of seven thousand of Gnaeus Ahenobarbus's men, which I took as a good omen. Ahenobarbus decided to give battle at once. He was afraid that if he did not, more of his men would desert to me. He deployed his army on the far side of a ravine, thinking to ambush me as I marched through. But I went up on a high crag and saw his army. So I did not fall into his trap. It began to rain (winter is the rainy season in Africa Province) and I took advantage of the fact that the rain was beating into the eyes of Ahenobarbus's soldiers. I won a great battle and my men hailed me imperator on the field. But Ahenobarbus and three thousand of his men escaped unharmed. My men were still hailing me imperator on the field, but I stopped them by saying they could do that later. My men saw the truth of this and stopped hailing me imperator on the field. We all rushed to Ahenobarbus's camp and killed him and all his men. I then allowed my men to hail me imperator on the field.

I then marched into Numidia, Africa Province having surrendered all insurgents still at large. I executed them in Utica. Iarbas the usurper went to earth in Bulla Regis—a town on the upper Bagradas River— having heard that I was approaching from the east and Bogud from the west. Of course I got to Bulla Regis ahead of King Bogud. Bulla Regis opened its gates the moment I arrived, and surrendered Iarbas to me. I executed Iarbas at once, and also another baron called Masinissa. I reinstated King Hiempsal on his throne in Cirta. I myself found sufficient time to hunt wild animals. This country abounds in wild game of every description, from elephants to very large cattle-looking things. I write this from camp on the Numidian plain.

I intend to return soon to Utica, having subdued the whole of North Africa in forty days, as I have already stated. It is not necessary to garrison our province there. You may send a governor without fear. I am going to put my six legions and two thousand horse on board my ships and sail for Tarentum. I will then march up the Via Appia to Rome, where I would like a triumph. My men have hailed me imperator on the field, therefore I am entitled to a triumph. I have pacified Sicily *and* Africa in one hundred days and executed all your enemies. I also have some good spoil to parade in my triumph.

By the time Sulla had worked out what Pompey said, he was weeping with laughter, not sure whether the missive's artless confidences amused him more than its arrogance, or the imparting of information like winter being the rainy season and Bulla Regis being on the upper Bagradas—*surely* Pompey knew that Sulla had spent years in Africa and had single-handedly captured King Jugurtha? At the end of a mere forty days Pompey knew *everything*. How many times had he managed to say that his troops had hailed him imperator on the field? Oh, what a hoot!

He pulled forward some paper and wrote to Pompey; this was one letter he didn't intend to dictate to a secretary.

What a pleasure to get your letter, and thank you for the interesting facts you impart about Africa. I must try to visit it someday, if for no other reason than to see for myself those very large cattle-looking things. Like you, I do know an elephant when I see one.

Congratulations. What a speedy young chap you are! Forty days. That, I think, is the length of time Mesopotamia was inundated a thousand years ago.

I know I can take your word for it that neither Africa nor Sicily needs to be garrisoned, but, my dear Pompeius, the niceties must be observed. I therefore command you to leave five of your legions in Utica and sail home with only one. I do not mind which one, if you have a favorite among them. Speaking of favorites, you are certainly one of Fortune's favorites yourself!

Unfortunately I cannot allow you to celebrate a triumph. Though your troops hailed you imperator on the field many times, triumphs are reserved for members of the Senate who have attained the status of praetor. You will win more wars in years to come, Pompeius, so you will have your triumph later, if not sooner.

I must thank you too for the speedy dispatch of Carbo's eating, seeing, hearing and smelling apparatus. There is nothing quite like a head to convince a man that another man has bitten the dust, to use a phrase of Homer's. The force of my contention that Carbo was dead and Rome had no consuls was immediately apparent. How clever of you to pop it in vinegar! Thank you too for Soranus. And the elder Brutus.

There is just one small thing, my dear Pompeius. I would have preferred that you had chosen a less public way to dispose of Carbo, if you were determined to do it in such barbaric fashion. I am beginning to believe what people say—scratch a man from Picenum, and reveal the Gaul. Once you elected to set yourself upon a tribunal with *toga praetexta* and curule chair and lictors, you became Rome. But you did not behave like a Roman. Having tormented poor Carbo for hours in the hot sun, you then announced in lordly tones that he did not deserve a trial, and was to be executed on the spot. Since you had housed and fed him atrociously for some days prior to this distressingly public hearing, he was ill. Yet when he begged you to allow him to retire and relieve his bowels in private before he died, you denied him! He died, so I am told, in his own shit but very well.

How do I know all this? I have my sources. Did I not, I doubt I
would now be Dictator of Rome. You are very young and you made the
mistake of assuming that because I wanted Carbo dead, I had no time
for him. True enough in one way. But I have all the time in the world
for the consulship of Rome. And the fact remains that Carbo was an
elected consul at the time he died. You would do well to remember in
future, young Pompeius, that all honor is due to the consul, even if his
name is Gnaeus Papirius Carbo.

On the subject of names, I hear that this barbaric episode in the
agora of Lilybaeum has earned you a new name. A great benefit for one
of those unfortunates with no third name to add a little luster, eh, Pompeius No Third Name? *Adulescentulus carnifex*. Kid Butcher. I think
that is a wonderful third name for you, Kid Butcher! Like your father
before you, you are a butcher.

To repeat: five of your legions will remain in Utica to await the
pleasure of the new governor when I find time to send one. You yourself
are at liberty to come home. I look forward to seeing you. We can have
a nice chat about elephants and you can educate me further on the subject
of Africa and things African.

I ought too to convey my condolences upon the death of Publius
Antistius Vetus and his wife, your parents-in-law. It is hard to know
why Brutus Damasippus included Antistius among his victims. But of
course Brutus Damasippus is dead. I had him executed. Yet in private,
Pompeius Kid Butcher. In private.

And that, thought Sulla as he finished, is one letter I really did enjoy
writing! But then he began to frown, and he sat thinking about what he ought
to do with Kid Butcher for some time. This was one young man who would
not easily let go of something once he had it in the center of his gaze. As he
did this triumph. And anyone who could set himself up in all state in the
public square of a non-Roman town, complete with lictors and curule chair,
then behave like a complete barbarian, was not going to appreciate the nuances
of triumphal protocol. Perhaps even then in the back of his mind he knew
that Kid Butcher was cunning enough to go after his triumph in ways which
might make it hard to go on refusing the triumph; for Sulla started plotting.
His smile grew again, and when his secretary came in, the man breathed an
involuntary sigh of relief to see it; he was in a good mood!

"Ah, Flosculus! In good time. Sit yourself down and take out your
tablets. I am in a mood to behave with extraordinary generosity to all sorts
of people, including that splendid fellow Lucius Licinius Murena, my gov-

ernor of Asia Province. Yes, I have decided to forgive him all his aggressions against King Mithridates and his transgressions against me when he disobeyed my orders. I think I may need the unworthy Murena, so write and tell him that I have decided he is to come home as soon as possible and celebrate a triumph. You will also write to whichever Flaccus it is in Gaul-across-the-Alps, and order him to come home at once so as to celebrate a triumph. Make sure to instruct each man to have at least two legions with him. . . ."

He was launched, and the secretary labored to keep up. All recollection of Aurelia and that uncomfortable interview had vanished; Sulla didn't even remember that Rome had a recalcitrant *flamen Dialis*. Another and far more dangerous young man had to be dealt with in a way almost too subtle—almost, but not quite. For Kid Butcher was very clever when it came to himself.

The weather in Nersae had, as Ria predicted, set into real winter amid days of clear blue skies and low temperatures; but the Via Salaria to Rome was open, as was the road from Reate to Nersae, and the way over the ridge into the Aternus River valley.

None of which mattered to Caesar, who had slowly worsened day by day. In the earlier, more lucid phase of his illness he had tried to get up and leave, only to discover that the moment he stood upright he was assailed by an uncontrollable wave of faintness which felled him like a child learning to walk. On the seventh day he developed a sleepy tendency which gradually sank to a light coma.

And then at Ria's front door there arrived Lucius Cornelius Phagites, accompanied by the stranger who had seen Caesar and Burgundus in the accommodation house at Trebula. Caught without Burgundus (whom she had ordered to cut wood), Ria was powerless to prevent the men entering.

"You're the mother of Quintus Sertorius, and this fellow asleep in bed here is Gaius Julius Caesar, the *flamen Dialis,*" said Phagites in great satisfaction.

"He's not asleep. He can't be woken," said Ria.

"He's asleep."

"There is a difference. I can't wake him, nor can anyone else. He's got the ague without a pattern, and that means he is going to die."

Not good news for Phagites, aware that the price on Caesar's head was not payable if that head was not attached to its owner's breathing body.

Like the rest of Sulla's minions who were also his freedmen, Lucius Cornelius Phagites had few scruples and less ethics. A slender Greek in his early forties—and one of those who had sold himself into slavery as preferable to eking out a living in his devastated homeland—Phagites had attached himself to Sulla like a leech, and had been rewarded by being appointed one of the chiefs of the proscription gangs; at the time he arrived to take custody of Caesar he had made a total of fourteen talents from killing men on the lists. Presentation of this one to Sulla still alive would have brought that total to sixteen talents, and he didn't like the feeling that he was being cheated.

He did not, however, enlighten Ria as to the nature of his commission, but paid his informer as he stood beside Caesar's bed and then made sure the man departed. Dead was no good for his income in Rome—but perhaps the boy had some money with him. If he was clever enough, thought Phagites, he might be able to prise that money out of the old woman by pitching her a tale.

"Oh well," he said, taking out his huge knife, "I can cut off his head anyway. Then I'll get my two talents."

"You'd better beware, *citocacia!*" shrilled Ria, standing up to him fiercely. "There's a man coming back soon who'll kill you before you can jump if you touch his master!"

"Oh, the German hulk? Then I tell you what, mother, you go and get him. I'll just sit here on the edge of the bed and keep the young master company." And he sat down beside the inanimate figure in the bed with his knife pressed against Caesar's defenseless throat.

The moment Ria had gone scuttling out into the icy world crying for Burgundus, Phagites walked to the front door and opened it; outside in the lane there waited his henchmen, the members of his decury of ten.

"The German giant's here. We'll kill him if we must, but some of us will have broken bones before we do, so no fighting him unless we can't avoid it. The boy is dying, he's no use to us," Phagites explained. "What I'm going to try to do is get whatever money there is out of them. But the moment I do, I'll need you to protect me from the German. Understood?"

Back inside he went, and was sitting with his knife held to Caesar's throat when Ria returned with Burgundus. A growl came rumbling up from Burgundus's chest, but he made no move toward the bed, just stood in the doorway clenching and unclenching his massive hands.

"Oh, good!" said Phagites in the most friendly way, and without fear. "Now I tell you what, old woman. If you've got enough money, I might be prepared to leave this young fellow here with his head still on his shoulders. I've got nine handy henchmen in the lane outside, so I can go ahead and cut this lovely young neck and be out in the lane quicker than your German could get as far as this bed. Is that clear?"

"Not to him, it isn't, if you're trying to tell Burgundus. He speaks not one word of Greek."

"What an animal! Then I'll negotiate through you, mother, if that's all right. Got any money?"

She stood for a short while with her eyes closed, debating what was the best thing to do. And being as practical as her son, she decided to deal with Phagites first, get rid of him. Caesar would die before Burgundus could reach the bed—and then Burgundus would die—and she too would die. So she opened her eyes and pointed to the book buckets stacked in the corner.

"There. Three talents," she said.

Phagites moved his soft brown eyes to the book buckets, and whistled. "Three talents! Oh, very nice!"

"Take it and go. Let the boy die peacefully."

"Oh, I will, mother, I will!" He put his fingers between his lips, blew piercingly.

His men came tumbling in with swords drawn expecting to have to kill Burgundus, only to find the scene a static one and their quarry one dozen buckets of books.

"Ye gods, what weighty subjects!" said Phagites when the books proved difficult to lift. "He's a very intelligent young fellow, our *flamen Dialis*."

Three trips, and the book buckets were gone. On the third time his men entered the room Phagites got up from the bed and inserted himself quickly among them. "Bye-bye!" he said, and vanished. There was a sound of activity from the lane, then the rattle of shod hooves on the cobblestones, and after that, silence.

"You should have let me kill them," said Burgundus.

"I would have, except that your master would have been the first to die," said the old woman, sighing. "Well, they won't be back until they've spent it, but they'll be back. You're going to have to take Caesar over the mountains."

"He'll die!" said Burgundus, beginning to weep.

"So he may. But if he stays here he will surely die."

Caesar's coma was a peaceful one, undisturbed by delirium or restlessness; he looked, Ria thought, very thin and wasted, and there were fever sores around his mouth, but even in this strange sleeping state he would drink whenever it was offered to him, and he had not yet been lying immobile for long enough to start the noises which indicated his chest was clogging up.

"It's a pity we had to give up the money, because I don't have a sled, and that's how you'll have to move him. I know of a man who would sell me one, but I don't have any money now that Quintus Sertorius is proscribed. I wouldn't even have this house except that it was my dowry.''

Burgundus listened to this impassively, then revealed that he could think. "Sell his horse," he said, and began to weep. "Oh, it will break his heart! But there's nothing else."

"Good boy, Burgundus!" said Ria briskly. "We'll be able to sell the horse easily. Not for what it's worth, but for enough to buy the sled, some oxen, and payment to Priscus and Gratidia for your lodging—even at the rate *you* eat.''

It was done, and done quickly. Bucephalus was led off down the lane by its delighted new owner, who couldn't believe his luck at getting an animal like this for nine thousand sesterces, and wasn't about to linger in case old Ria changed her mind.

The sled—which was actually a wagon complete with wheels over which polished planks with upcurving ends had been fixed—cost four thousand sesterces and the two oxen which pulled it a further thousand each, though the owner indicated that he would be willing to buy the equipage back in the summer for four thousand sesterces complete, leaving him with a profit of two thousand.

"You may get it back before then," said Ria grimly.

She and Burgundus did their best to make Caesar comfortable in the sled, piling him round with wraps.

"Now make sure you turn him over every so often! Otherwise his bones will come through his flesh—he hasn't enough of it left, poor young man. In this weather your food will stay fresh far longer, that's a help, and you must try to give him milk from my ewe as well as water," she lectured crabbily. "Oh, I wish I could come with you! But I'm too old."

She stood looking over the white and rolling meadow behind her house until Burgundus and the sled finally disappeared; the ewe she had donated in the hope that Caesar would gain sufficient sustenance to survive. Then, when she could see them no more, she went into her house and prepared to offer up one of her doves to his family's goddess, Venus, and a dozen eggs to Tellus and Sol Indiges, who were the mother and father of all Italian things.

The journey to Priscus and Gratidia took eight days, for the oxen were painfully slow. A bonus for Caesar, who was hardly disturbed by the motion of his peculiar conveyance as it slid along the frozen surface of the snow very smoothly, thanks to many applications of beeswax to its runners. They climbed from the valley of the Himella where Nersae lay beside that swift stream along a road which traversed the steep ascent back and forth, each turn seeing them a little higher, and then on the other side did the same thing as they descended to the Aternus valley.

The odd thing was that Caesar began to improve almost as soon as he began to chill a little after that warm house. He drank some milk (Burgundus's hands were so big that he found it agony milking the ewe, luckily an old and patient animal) each time Burgundus turned him, and even chewed slowly upon a piece of hard cheese the German gave him to suck. But the languor persisted, and he couldn't speak. They encountered no one along the way so there was no possibility of shelter at night, but the hard freeze continued, giving them days of cloudless blue skies and nights of a heaven whitened by stars in cloudy tangles.

The coma lifted; the sleepiness which had preceded it came back, and gradually that too lifted. In one way, reasoned the slow alien mind of Burgundus, that seemed to be an improvement. But Caesar looked as if some awful underworld creature had drained him of all his blood, and could hardly lift his hand. He did speak once, having noticed a terrible omission.

"Where is Bucephalus?" he asked. "I can't see Bucephalus!"

"We had to leave Bucephalus behind in Nersae, Caesar. You can see for yourself what this road is like. Bucephalus couldn't have managed. But you mustn't worry. He's safe with Ria." There. That seemed better to Burgundus than the truth, especially when he saw that Caesar believed him.

Priscus and Gratidia lived on a small farm some miles from Amiternum. They were about Ria's age, and had little money; both the sons who would have contributed to a greater prosperity had been killed during the Italian War, and there were no girls. So when they had read Ria's letter and Burgundus handed them the three thousand sesterces which were all now remaining, they took in the fugitives gladly.

"Only if his fever goes up I'm nursing him outside," said Burgundus, "because as soon as he left Ria's house and got a bit cold, he started to get better." He indicated the sled and oxen. "You can have this too. If Caesar lives, he won't want it."

Would Caesar live? The three who looked after him had no idea, for the days passed and he changed but little. Sometimes the wind blew and it snowed for what seemed like forever, then the weather would break and snap colder again, but Caesar seemed not to notice. The fever had diminished and the coma with it, yet marked improvement never came, nor did he cease to have that bloodless look.

Toward the end of April a thaw set in and promised to turn into spring. It had been, so those in that part of Italy said, the hardest winter in living memory. For Caesar, it was to be the hardest of his life.

"I think," said Gratidia, who was a cousin of Ria's, "that Caesar will die after all unless he can be moved to a place like Rome, where there are doctors and medicines and foods that we in the mountains cannot hope to produce. His blood has no life in it. That's why he gets no better. I do not know how to remedy him, and you forbid me to fetch someone from Amiternum to see him. So it is high time, Burgundus, that you rode to Rome to tell his mother."

Without a word the German walked out of the house and began to saddle the Nesaean horse; Gratidia had scarcely the time to press a parcel of food on him before he was away.

"I wondered why I hadn't heard a word," said Aurelia, white-faced. She bit her lip, began to worry at it with her teeth, as if the stimulus of some tiny pain would help her think. "I must thank you more than I can say, Burgundus. Without you, my son would certainly be dead. And we must get him back to Rome before he does die. Now go and see Cardixa. She and your boys have missed you very much."

It would not do to approach Sulla again by herself, she knew. If that avenue hadn't worked before the New Year, it would never work now, four months into the New Year. The proscriptions still raged—but with less point these days, it seemed, and the laws were beginning to come; great laws or terrible laws, depending upon whom one spoke to. Sulla was fully occupied.

When Aurelia had learned that Sulla had sent for Marcus Pupius Piso Frugi several days after their interview, and learned too that he had ordered Piso Frugi to divorce Annia because she was Cinna's widow, she had dared to hope for Caesar. But though Piso Frugi had obeyed, had divorced Annia with alacrity, nothing further happened. Ria had written to tell her that the money had been swallowed by one who was named for the size of what he could swallow, and that Caesar and Burgundus were gone; but Ria had not mentioned Caesar's illness, and Aurelia had allowed herself to think all must be well if she heard nothing at all.

"I will go to see Dalmatica," she decided. "Perhaps another woman can show me how to approach Sulla."

Of Sulla's wife, who had arrived from Brundisium in December of last year, Rome had seen very little. Some whispered that she was ill, others that Sulla had no time for a private life, and neglected her; though no one whispered that he had replaced her with anyone else. So Aurelia wrote her a short note asking for an interview, preferably at a time when Sulla himself would not be at home. This latter request, she was careful to explain, was only because she did not wish to irritate the Dictator. She also asked if it was possible for

Cornelia Sulla to be there, as she wished to pay her respects to someone she had once known very well; perhaps Cornelia Sulla would be able to advise her in her trouble too. For, she ended, what she wished to discuss was a trouble.

Sulla was now living in his rebuilt house overlooking the Circus Maximus; ushered into a place which reeked of fresh, limey plaster and all kinds of paints and had that vulgar look only time erases, Aurelia was conducted through a vast atrium to an even vaster peristyle garden, and finally to Dalmatica's own quarters, which were as large as Aurelia's whole apartment. The two women had met but had never become friends; Aurelia did not move in the Palatine circle to which belonged the wives of Rome's greatest men, for she was the busy landlady of a Suburan insula, and not interested in tittle-tattle over sweet watered wine and little cakes.

Nor, to do her justice, had Dalmatica belonged to that circle. For too many years she had been locked up by her then husband, Scaurus Princeps Senatus, and in consequence had lost her youthful appetite for tittle-tattle over sweet watered wine and little cakes. There had come the exile in Greece— an idyll with Sulla in Ephesus, Smyrna and Pergamum—the twins—and Sulla's awful illness. Too much worry, unhappiness, homesickness, pain. Never again would Caecilia Metella Dalmatica find it in her to cultivate an interest in shopping, comedic actors, petty feuds, scandal and idleness. Besides which, her return to Rome had been something in the nature of a triumph when she found a Sulla who had missed her into loving her more than ever.

However, Sulla did not confide in her, so she knew nothing of the fate of the *flamen Dialis;* indeed, she didn't know Aurelia was the mother of the *flamen Dialis.* And Cornelia Sulla only knew that Aurelia had been a part of her childhood, a link to the vague memory of a mother who had drunk too much before she killed herself, and to the vivid memory of her beloved stepmother, Aelia. Her first marriage—to the son of Sulla's colleague in his consulship—had ended in tragedy when her husband died during Forum riots at the time of Sulpicius's tribunate of the plebs—and her second marriage— to Drusus's younger brother, Mamercus—had brought her great contentment.

Each of the women was pleased at how the others looked, and as each was held one of Rome's great beauties, it was fair to deduce that they all felt they had weathered the corroding storms of time better than most. At forty-two, Aurelia was the oldest; Dalmatica was thirty-seven, and Cornelia Sulla a mere twenty-six.

"You have more of a look of your father these days," said Aurelia to Cornelia Sulla.

The eyes too blue and sparkling to be Sulla's filled with mirth, and their owner burst out laughing. "Oh, don't say that, Aurelia! My skin is perfect, and I do not wear a wig!"

"Poor man," said Aurelia, "it's very hard for him."

"It is," agreed Dalmatica, whose brown beauty was softer than Aurelia remembered, and whose grey eyes were much sadder.

The conversation passed to mundanities for a little while, Dalmatica tactfully steering it away from the more uncomfortable topics her stepdaughter would have chosen. Not a natural talker, Aurelia was content to contribute an occasional mite.

Dalmatica, who had a boy and a girl by her first husband, Marcus Aemilius Scaurus, as well as the twins, was preoccupied with her eldest, Aemilia Scaura.

"The prettiest girl!" she said warmly, and looked happy. "We think she's pregnant, but it's a little early to be sure."

"Whom did she marry?" Aurelia asked; she never kept up with who married whom.

"Manius Acilius Glabrio. They'd been betrothed for years, Scaurus insisted. Traditional ties between the families."

"He's a nice fellow, Glabrio," said Aurelia in carefully neutral tones; privately she considered him a loudmouthed and conceited son of a far better father.

"He's a conceited loudmouth," said Cornelia Sulla flatly.

"Now, now, he wouldn't suit you, but he does suit Aemilia Scaura," said Dalmatica.

"And how is dear little Pompeia?" asked Aurelia quickly.

Cornelia Sulla beamed. "Absolutely ravishing! She's eight now, and at school." Because she was Sulla's daughter and had much of his detachment, she went on to say, "Of course she *is* abysmally stupid! I'll count myself fortunate if she learns enough Latin to write a thank-you note—she'll certainly never manage to learn any Greek! So I'm very glad she's going to be a beauty. It's better that a girl's beautiful than brilliant."

"It certainly is when it comes to finding a husband, but a decent dowry helps," said Aurelia dryly.

"Oh, she'll have a decent dowry!" said Pompeia's mother. "*Tata* has grown to be enormously rich, and she'll inherit a bit from him as well as from the Pompeii Rufi—who have quite changed their tune since I was a widow living in their house! Then they made my life a misery, but now I bask in reflected light from *tata*. Besides, they're afraid he might proscribe them."

"Then we'll have to hope that Pompeia finds a very nice husband," said

Dalmatica, and looked at Aurelia in a more serious way. "It is delightful to see you and I hope I can now count on you as a much-needed friend, but I know you didn't come merely to pay your respects—you're too renowned as a sensible woman who minds her own business. What is this trouble, Aurelia? How may I help you?"

The story came out, told in that unsensational and unvarnished style Aurelia had made her own. She could not fault her audience, who listened in complete silence.

"We must do something," said Dalmatica when the tale was told. She sighed. "Lucius Cornelius has too many things on his mind, and I'm afraid he's not a very *warm* person." She shifted, looked uncomfortable. "You were his friend for many years," she said awkwardly. "I can't help thinking that if you could not influence him, I stand little chance."

"I trust that isn't true," said Aurelia stiffly. "He did come to see me from time to time, but I do assure you there was nothing untoward between us. It was not my so-called beauty that drew him. Unromantic though it may sound, what drew him was my common sense."

"I believe that," said Dalmatica, smiling.

Cornelia Sulla assumed control. "Well, it's all a long way down the river," she said briskly, "and it can't influence what we need today. You're quite right, Aurelia, when you say you can't try to see *tata* on your own again. But you *must* try to see him—and the sooner, the better. He's between laws at the moment. It will have to be a formal delegation. Priests, male relatives, Vestal Virgins, you. Mamercus will help, I'll talk to him. Who are Caesar's closest relatives not on the proscription lists?"

"The Cottae—my three half brothers."

"Good, they'll add luster to the delegation! Gaius Cotta is a pontifex and Lucius Cotta is an augur, which gives them a religious importance too. Mamercus will plead for you, I know. And we'll need four Vestal Virgins. Fonteia, because she is the Chief Vestal. Fabia. Licinia. And Caesar Strabo's daughter, Julia, of Caesar's own family. Do you know any of the Vestals?"

"Not even Julia Strabo," said Aurelia.

"Never mind, I know them all. Leave it to me."

"What can I do to help?" asked Dalmatica, a little overawed at so much Sullan efficiency.

"Your job is to get the delegation an appointment to see *tata* tomorrow afternoon," said Cornelia Sulla.

"That may be easier said than done. He's so busy!"

"Nonsense! You're too humble, Dalmatica. *Tata* will do anything for you if you ask him. The trouble is that you hardly ever ask, so you have no idea how much he loves to do things for you. Ask him at dinner, and don't be afraid," said Sulla's daughter. To Aurelia she said, "I'll get everyone here early. You can have some time with them before you go in."

"What should I wear?" asked Aurelia, preparing to go.

Cornelia Sulla blinked. So did Dalmatica.

"I only ask," said Aurelia apologetically, "because he commented on my clothes last time I saw him. He disliked them."

"Why?" demanded Cornelia Sulla.

"I think he found them too drab."

"Then wear something colorful."

So out of the chest came dresses Aurelia had put away years ago as too undignified and skittish for an aristocratic Roman matron. Blues? Greens? Reds? Pinks? Lilacs? Yellows? In the end she decided upon layers of pink, darkest underneath, and shading through to a gauzy overlay of palest rose.

Cardixa shook her head. "All giddied up like that, you look just as you did when Caesar's father came to dinner at your uncle Rutilius Rufus's. And not a day older!"

"Giddied up, Cardixa?"

"You know, like one of those Public Horses on parade."

"I think I'll change."

"No you won't! You don't have time. Off you go at once. Lucius Decimius will take you," said Cardixa firmly, pushing her out the door onto the street, where, sure enough, Lucius Decimius waited with his two sons.

Since Lucius Decimius had enough sense to hold his tongue about Aurelia's appearance and his sons no tongues at all, the long walk to the far side of the Palatine proceeded in silence. Every moment Aurelia waited for word to come from Priscus and Gratidia that it was too late, that Caesar was dead, and every moment that this word did not come was one more blessing.

Somehow the news had got round the insula that Caesar was at death's door; little gifts kept arriving, everything from bunches of flowers from the Cuppedenis Markets to peculiar amulets from the Lycians on the fifth floor and the mournful sounds of special prayers from the Jewish floor. Most of Aurelia's tenants had been with her for years, and had known Caesar since he was a baby. Always an alert, insatiably curious, chatty child, he had wandered from floor to floor experimenting with that dubious (his mother thought it very dubious) quality he possessed in abundance, charm. Many of the women had wet-nursed him, fed him tidbits from their national dishes, crooned to him in their own languages until he learned what the crooning meant, then sang their songs with them—he was extremely musical—and taught himself to pick away at peculiar stringed instruments, or blow through all kinds of pipes and flutes. As he grew older, he and his best friend, Gaius Matius from the other ground-floor flat, extended their contacts beyond the insula and into the Subura at large; and now the news of his illness was getting around the Subura too, so the little gifts kept arriving from further and further afield.

How do I explain to Sulla that Caesar means different things to different people? That he has the most intense Romanness about him, yet is also a dozen different nationalities? It is not the priest business matters most to me, it is what he is to everyone he knows. Caesar belongs to Rome, but not to Rome of the Palatine. Caesar belongs to Rome of the Subura and the Esquiline, and when he is a great man he will bring a dimension to his office no other man could, simply because of the breadth of his experience, of his life. Jupiter only knows how many girls—and women as old as I am!—he's slept with, how many forays he's gone on with Lucius Decumius and those ruffians from the crossroads college, how many lives he touches because he is never still, never too busy to listen, never uninterested. My son is only eighteen. But I believe in the prophecy too, Gaius Marius! At forty my son will be formidable. And I hereby vow to every god there is that if I have to journey to the Underworld to bring back the three-headed dog of Hades, I will, to see that my son lives.

But of course when she got to Sulla's house and was ushered into a room stuffed with important people, she did not have all that eloquence at her command, and her face was closed upon her thoughts; she simply looked austere, severe. Daunting.

As Cornelia Sulla had promised, there were four Vestals, all of them younger than she was; having entered at seven or eight, a Vestal left the Order after thirty years, and none of these, including the Chief Vestal, was yet due to retire. They wore white robes with long sleeves gathered in fine folds by a longitudinal rib, more white drapes over that, the chain and medal of a Vestal's *bulla,* and on their heads crowns made of seven tiers of rolled wool, over which there floated fine white veils. The life, which was female-oriented and virginal—though not sequestered—endowed even the youngest of Vestals with a massive presence; no one knew better than they that their chastity was Rome's good luck, and they radiated consciousness of their special status. Few of them contemplated breaking their vows, as most of them grew into the role from a most malleable age, and took enormous pride in it.

The men were togate, Mamercus with the purple border he could now wear thanks to his position as *praetor peregrinus,* and the Cottae, too young yet for purple-bordered togas, in plain white. Which meant that Aurelia in her gradations of pink was by far the most colorful of them all! Mortified, she felt herself stiffen into stone, and knew that she would not do well.

"You look magnificent!" breathed Cornelia Sulla in her ear. "I had quite forgotten how absolutely beautiful you are when you decide to bring the beauty out. You do, you know. You shut it up as if it didn't exist, and then suddenly—there it is!"

"Do the others understand? Do they agree with me?" Aurelia whispered back, wishing she had worn bone or beige.

"Of course they do. For one thing, he is the *flamen Dialis*. And they think he's terrifically brave, to stand up to the Dictator. No one does. Even Mamercus. I do, sometimes. He likes it, you know. *Tata,* I mean. Most tyrants do. They despise weaklings, even though they surround themselves with weaklings. So you go in at the head of the delegation. And stand up to him!"

"I always have," Caesar's mother said.

Chrysogonus was there, smarming with exactly the correct amount of oil to the various members of the delegation; he was beginning to get a reputation as one of the chief profiteers of the proscriptions, and had become enormously rich. A servant came to whisper in his ear, and he bowed his way to the great double doors opening into Sulla's atrium, then stood back to let the delegation enter.

Sulla waited for them in a sour mood rooted in the fact that he knew he had been tricked by a parcel of women, and angry because he hadn't been able to find the steel to resist them. It wasn't fair! Wife and daughter pleaded, cajoled, looked sad, made him aware that if he did this futile thing for them, they would be eternally in his debt—and if he did not, they would be very put out. Dalmatica wasn't so bad, she had a touch of the whipped cur in her that Scaurus no doubt had instilled during those long years of imprisonment, but Cornelia Sulla was his blood, and it showed. Termagant! How did Mamercus cope with her and look so happy? Probably because he never stood up to her. Wise man. What we do for domestic harmony! Including what I am about to do.

However, it was at least a change, a diversion in the long and dreary round of dictatorial duties. Oh, he was bored! Bored, bored, bored . . . Rome always did that to him. Whispered the forbidden blandishments, conjured up pictures of parties he couldn't go to, circles he couldn't move in. . . . Metrobius. It always, always came back to Metrobius. Whom he hadn't seen in—

how long? Was that the last time, in the crowd at his—triumph? Inauguration as consul? Could he not even remember that?

What he could remember was the first time he had seen the young Greek, if not the last. At that party when he had dressed up as Medusa the Gorgon, and wore a wreath of living snakes. How everyone had squealed! But not Metrobius, adorable little Cupid with the saffron dye running down the insides of his creamy thighs and the sweetest arse in the world . . .

The delegation came in. From where he stood beyond the huge aquamarine rectangle of the pool in the middle of the vast room, Sulla's gaze was strong enough to absorb the entire picture they made. Perhaps because his mind had been dwelling upon a world of theater (and one particular actor), what Sulla saw was not a prim and proper Roman delegation but a gorgeous pageant led by a gorgeous woman all in shades of pink, his favorite color. And how clever, that she had surrounded herself by people in white with the faintest touches of purple!

The world of dictatorial duties rolled away, and so did Sulla's sour mood. His face lit up, he whooped in delight.

"Oh, this is wonderful! Better than a play or the games! No, no, don't come an inch closer to me! Stand on that side of the pool! Aurelia, out in front. I want you like a tall, slender rose. The Vestals—to the right, I think, but the youngest can stand behind Aurelia, I want her against a white background. Yes, that's right, good! Now, fellows, you stand to the left, but I think we'll have young Lucius Cotta behind Aurelia too, he's the youngest and I don't think he'll have a speaking part. I do like the touches of purple on your tunics, but Mamercus, you spoil the effect. You should have abandoned the *praetexta*, it's just a trifle too much purple. So you—off to the far left." The Dictator put his hand to his chin and studied them closely, then nodded. "Good! I like it! However, *I* need a bit more glamor, don't I? Here I am all alone looking just like Mamercus in my *praetexta*, and just as mournful!"

He clapped his hands; Chrysogonus popped out from behind the delegation, bowed several times.

"Chrysogonus, send my lictors in—crimson tunics, not stodgy old white togas—and get me the Egyptian chair. You know the one—crocodiles for arms and asps rearing up the back. And a small podium. Yes, I must have a small podium! Covered in—purple. Tyrian purple, none of your imitations. Well, go on, man, hurry!"

The delegation—which had not said a word—reconciled itself to a long wait while all these stage directions were seen to, but Chrysogonus was not chief administrator of the proscriptions and steward to the Dictator for nothing. In filed twenty-four lictors clad in crimson tunics, the axes inserted in their *fasces,* their faces studiously expressionless. On their heels came the small podium held between four sturdy slaves, who placed it in the exact center at the back of the pool and proceeded to cover it neatly with a tapestry cloth in the stipulated Tyrian purple, so dark it was almost black. The chair arrived next, a splendid thing of polished ebony and gilt, with ruby eyes in the hooded snakes and emerald eyes in the crocodiles, and a magnificent multihued scarab in the center of the chair back.

Once the stage was set, Sulla attended to his lictors. "I like the axes in the bundles of rods, so I'm glad I'm Dictator and have the power to execute within the *pomerium*! Now let me see. . . . Twelve to the left of me and twelve to the right of me—in a line, boys, but close together. Fan yourselves away so that you're nearest to me next to me, and dribble off a bit into the distance at your far ends. . . . Good, good!" He swung back to stare at the delegation, frowning. "That's what's wrong! I can't see Aurelia's feet, Chrysogonus! Bring in that little golden stool I filched from Mithridates. I want her to stand on it. Go on, man, hurry! Hurry!"

And finally it was all done to his satisfaction. Sulla sat down in his crocodile and snake chair on the Tyrian purple small podium, apparently oblivious to the fact that he should have been seated in a plain ivory curule chair. Not that anyone in the room was moved to criticize; the important thing was that the Dictator was enjoying himself immensely. And that meant a greater chance for a favorable verdict.

"Speak!" he said in sonorous tones.

"Lucius Cornelius, my son is dying—"

"Louder, Aurelia! Play to the back of the *cavea*!"

"Lucius Cornelius, my son is dying! I have come with my friends to beseech you to pardon him!"

"Your friends? Are all these people your friends?" he asked, his amazement a little overdone.

"They are all my friends. They join with me in beseeching you to allow my son to come home before he dies," Aurelia enunciated clearly, playing to the back row of the *cavea,* and getting into her stride. If he wanted a Greek tragedy, he would get a Greek tragedy! She extended her arms to him, the rose-colored draperies falling away from her ivory skin. "Lucius Cornelius, my son is but eighteen years old! He is my only son!" A throb in the voice there, it would go over well—yes, it was going over well, if his expression was anything to go by! "You have seen my son. A god! A Roman god! A descendant of Venus worthy of Venus! And with such courage! Did he not have the courage to defy you, the greatest man in all the world? And did he show fear? No!''

"Oh, this is wonderful!" Sulla exclaimed. "I didn't know you had it in you, Aurelia! Keep it coming, keep it coming!''

"Lucius Cornelius, I beseech you! Spare my son!'' She managed to turn on the tiny golden stool and stretched out her hands to Fonteia, praying that stately lady would understand her part. "I ask Fonteia, Rome's Chief Vestal, to beg for the life of my son!''

Luckily by this the rest were beginning to recover from their stupefaction, could at least try. Fonteia thrust out her hands and achieved a distressed facial expression she hadn't used since she was four years old.

"Spare him, Lucius Cornelius!'' she cried. *"Spare him!"*

"Spare him!'' whispered Fabia.

"Spare him!'' shouted Licinia.

Whereupon the seventeen-year-old Julia Strabo upstaged everyone by bursting into tears.

"For Rome, Lucius Cornelius! Spare him for Rome!'' thundered Gaius Cotta in the stentorian voice his father had made famous. "We beg you, spare him!''

"For Rome, Lucius Cornelius!'' shouted Marcus Cotta.

"For Rome, Lucius Cornelius!'' blared Lucius Cotta.

Which left Mamercus, who produced a bleat. "Spare him!''

Silence. Each side gazed at the other.

Sulla sat straight in his chair, right foot forward and left foot back in the classical pose of the Roman great. His chin was tucked in, his brow beetled. He waited. Then: "No!''

So it began all over again.

And again he said: "No!''

Feeling as limp and wrung out as a piece of washing—but actually improving in leaps and bounds—Aurelia pleaded for the life of her son a third time with heartbroken voice and trembling hands. Julia Strabo was howling lustily, Licinia looked as if she might join in. The beseeching chorus swelled, and died away with a third bleat from Mamercus.

Silence fell. Sulla waited and waited, apparently having adopted what he thought was a Zeus-like aspect, thunderous, regal, portentous. Finally he got to his feet and stepped to the edge of his small Tyrian purple podium, where he stood with immense dignity, frowning direfully.

Then he sighed a sigh which could easily have been heard in the back row of the *cavea,* clenched his fists and raised them toward the gilded ceiling's splendiferous stars. "Very well, have it your own way!" he cried. "I will spare him! But be warned! In this young man I see many Mariuses!"

After which he bounced like a baby goat from his perch to the floor, and skipped gleefully along the side of the pool. "Oh, I needed that! Wonderful, wonderful! I haven't had so much fun since I slept between my stepmother and my mistress! Being the Dictator is no kind of life! I don't even have time to go to the play! But this was better than any play I've ever seen, and I was in the lead! You all did very well. Except for you, Mamercus, spoiling things in your *praetexta* and emitting those peculiar sounds. You're stiff, man, too stiff! You must try to get into the part!"

Reaching Aurelia, he helped her down from her (solid) gold stool and hugged her over and over again. "Splendid, splendid! You looked like Iphigenia at Aulis, my dear."

"I felt like the fishwife in a mime."

He had forgotten the lictors, who still stood to either side of the empty crocodile throne with wooden faces; nothing about this job would ever surprise them again!

"Come on, let's go to the dining room and have a party!" the Dictator said, shooing everybody in the chorus before him, one arm about the terrified Julia Strabo. "Don't cry, silly girl, it's all right! This was just my little joke," he said, rolled his eyes at Mamercus and gave Julia Strabo a push between her shoulder blades. "Here, Mamercus, find your handkerchief and clean her up." The arm went round Aurelia. "Magnificent! Truly magnificent! You should always wear pink, you know."

So relieved her knees were shaking, Aurelia put on a fierce frown and said, her voice in her boots, " 'In him I see many Mariuses!' You ought to have said, 'In him I see many Sullas!' It would have been closer to the point. He's not at all like Marius, but sometimes he's awfully like you."

Dalmatica and Cornelia Sulla were waiting outside, utterly bewildered; when the lictors went in they hadn't been very surprised, but then they had seen the small podium go in, and the Tyrian purple cloth, and the Egyptian chair, and finally the gold stool. Now everyone was spilling out laughing— why was Julia Strabo crying?—and Sulla had his arm around Aurelia, who was smiling as if she would never stop.

"A party!" shouted Sulla, pranced over to his wife, took her face between his hands and kissed her. "We're going to have a party, and I am going to get very, very drunk!"

It was some time later before Aurelia realized that not one of the players in that incredible scene had found anything demeaning in Sulla's impromptu drama, nor made the mistake of deeming Sulla a lesser man because he had staged it. If anything, its effect had been the opposite; how could one not fear a man who didn't care about appearances?

No one who participated ever recounted the story, made capital out of it and Sulla at dinner parties, or tittle-tattled it over sweet watered wine and little cakes. Not from fear of their lives. Mostly because no one thought Rome would ever, ever believe it.

When Caesar arrived home he experienced the end results of his mother's one-act play at once; Sulla sent his own doctor, Lucius Tuccius, to see the patient.

"Frankly, I don't consider Sulla much of a recommendation," Aurelia said to Lucius Decumius, "so I can only hope that without Lucius Tuccius, Sulla would be a lot worse."

"He's a Roman," said Lucius Decumius, "and that's something. I don't trust them Greeks."

"Greek physicians are very clever."

"In a theory-etical way. They treats their patients with new ideas, not old standbys. Old standbys are the best. I'll take pounded grey spiders and powdered dormice any day!"

"Well, Lucius Decumius, as you say, this one is a Roman."

As Sulla's doctor emerged at that moment from the direction of Caesar's room, conversation ceased. Tuccius was a small man, very round and smooth and clean-looking; he had been Sulla's chief army surgeon, and it had been he who sent Sulla to Aedepsus when Sulla had become so ill in Greece.

"I think the wisewoman of Nersae was right, and your son suffered the ague without a pattern," he said cheerfully. "He's lucky. Few men recover from it."

"Then he *will* recover?" asked Aurelia anxiously.

"Oh, yes. The crisis has long passed. But the disease has left his blood enervated. That's why he has no color, and why he is so weak."

"So what does we do?" demanded Lucius Decumius pugnaciously.

"Well, men who have lost a lot of blood from a wound show much the same symptoms as Caesar," said Tuccius, unconcerned. "In such cases, if they didn't die they gradually got better of their own accord. But I always found it a help to feed them the liver of a sheep once a day. The younger the sheep, the quicker the recovery. I recommend that Caesar eat the liver of a lamb and drink three hen's eggs beaten into goat's milk every day."

"What, no medicine?" asked Lucius Decumius suspiciously.

"Medicine won't cure Caesar's ailment. Like the Greek physicians of

Aedepsus, I believe in diet over medicine in most situations," said Lucius Tuccius firmly.

"See? He's a Greek after all!" said Lucius Decumius after the doctor had departed.

"Never mind that," said Aurelia briskly. "I shall adhere to his recommendations for at least a market interval. Then we shall see. But it seems sensible advice to me."

"I'd better start for the Campus Lanatarius," said the little man who loved Caesar more than he did his sons. "I'll buy the lamb and see it slaughtered on the spot."

The real hitch turned out to be the patient, who flatly refused to eat the lamb's liver, and drank his first mixture of egg-and-goat's-milk with such loathing that he brought it up.

The staff held a conference with Aurelia.

"*Must* the liver be raw?" asked Murgus the cook.

Aurelia blinked. "I don't know. I just assumed it."

"Then could we send to Lucius Tuccius and ask?" from the steward, Eutychus. "Caesar is not an eater—by that I mean that the sheer taste of food does not send him into ecstasies. He is conservative but not fussy. However, one of the things I have always noticed is that he will not eat things with a strong smell of their own. Like eggs. As for that raw liver—pew! It stinks!"

"Let me cook the liver and put plenty of sweet wine in the egg-and-milk," pleaded Murgus.

"How would you cook the liver?" Aurelia asked.

"I'd slice it thin, roll each slice in a little salt and spelt, and fry it lightly on a very hot fire."

"All right, Murgus, I'll send to Lucius Tuccius and describe what you want to do," said the patient's mother.

Back came the message: "Put what you like in the egg-and-milk, and *of course* cook the liver!"

After that the patient tolerated his regimen, though not with any degree of affection.

"Say what you like about the food, Caesar, I think it is working," was his mother's verdict.

"I know it's working! Why else do you think I'm eating the stuff?" was the patient's disgruntled response.

Light broke; Aurelia sat down beside Caesar's couch with a look on her face that said she was going to stay there until she got some answers. "All right, what's the real matter?"

Lips pressed together, he stared out the open window of the reception

room into the garden Gaius Matius had made in the bottom of the light well.
"I have made the most wretched business out of my first venture on my
own," he said at last. "While everybody else behaved with amazing courage
and daring, I lay like a log with nothing to say and no part in the action. The
hero was Burgundus, and the heroines you and Ria, Mater."

She hid her smile. "Perhaps there's a lesson to be learned, Caesar.
Perhaps the Great God—whose servant you still are!—felt you had to be
taught a lesson you've never been willing to learn—that a man cannot fight
the gods, and that the Greeks were right about hubris. A man with hubris is
an abomination."

"Am I really so proud you think I own hubris?" he asked.

"Oh, yes. You have plenty of false pride."

"I see absolutely no relevance between hubris and what happened at
Nersae," said Caesar stubbornly.

"It's what the Greeks would call hypothetical."

"I think you mean philosophical."

Since there was nothing wrong with her education, she did not acknowl-
edge this quibble, simply swept on. "The fact that you own an overweening
degree of pride is a grave temptation to the gods. Hubris presumes to direct
the gods and says that a man is above the status of men. And—as we Romans
know!—the gods do not choose to show a man he is above himself with what
I might call a personal intervention. Jupiter Optimus Maximus doesn't speak
to men with a human voice, and I am never convinced that the Jupiter Optimus
Maximus who appears to men in dreams is anything more than a figment of
dreams. The gods intervene in a natural way, they punish with natural things.
You were punished with a natural thing—you became ill. And I believe that
the seriousness of your illness is a direct indication of the degree of your
pride. It almost killed you!"

"You impute a divine vector," he said, "for a disgustingly animal event.
I believe the vector was as mundanely animal as the event. And neither of
us can prove our contention, so what does it matter? What matters is that I
failed in my first attempt to govern my life. I was a passive object surrounded
by heroism, none of which was mine."

"Oh, Caesar, will you *never* learn?"

The beautiful smile came. "Probably not, Mater."

"Sulla wants to see you."

"When?"

"As soon as you're well enough, I am to send to him for an appointment."

"Tomorrow, then."

"No, after the next *nundinae*."

"Tomorrow."

Aurelia sighed. "Tomorrow."

He insisted upon walking without an attendant, and when he discovered Lucius Decumius lurking some paces behind him, sent his watchdog home with a firmness Lucius Decumius dared not defy. "I am tired of being cosseted and clucked over!" he said in the voice which frightened people. "Leave me alone!"

The walk was demanding, but he arrived at Sulla's house far from exhausted; now definitely on the mend, he was mending rapidly.

"I see you're in a toga," said Sulla, who was sitting behind his desk. He indicated the *laena* and *apex* disposed neatly on a nearby couch. "I've saved them for you. Don't you have spares?"

"Not a second *apex*, anyway. That one was a gift from my wonderful benefactor, Gaius Marius."

"Didn't Merula's fit?"

"I have an enormous head," said Caesar, straight-faced.

Sulla chuckled. "I believe you!" He had sent to Aurelia to ask if Caesar knew of the second part of the prophecy, and having received a negative answer, had decided Caesar wouldn't hear it from him. But he fully intended to discuss Marius. His thinking had swung completely around, thanks to two factors. The first was Aurelia's information about the circumstances behind Caesar's being dowered with the flaminate *Dialis,* and the second was his one-act play, which he had enjoyed (and the party which had followed) with huge gusto; it had refreshed him so thoroughly that though it was now a month in the past, he still found himself remembering bits and pieces at the most inappropriate moments, and had been able to apply himself to his laws with renewed energy.

Yes, the moment that magnificent-looking delegation had walked into his atrium so solemnly and theatrically he had been lifted out of himself— out of his dreary appalling shell, out of a life devoid of enjoyment and lightness. For a short space of time reality had utterly vanished and he had immersed himself inside a sparkling and gorgeous pageant. And since that day he had found hope again; he knew it would end. He knew he would be released to do what he longed to do, bury himself and his hideousness in a world of hilarity, glamor, idleness, artificiality, entertainments, grotesques and travesties. He would get through the present grind into a very different and infinitely more desirable future.

"You made a thousand mistakes when you fled, Caesar," said Sulla in a rather friendly way.

"I don't need to be told. I'm well aware of it."

"You're far too pretty to disappear into the furniture, and you have a natural sense of the dramatic," Sulla explained, ticking his points off on his fingers. "The German, the horse, your pretty face, your natural arrogance— need I go on?"

"No," said Caesar, looking rueful. "I've already heard it all from my mother—and several other people."

"Good. However, I'd be willing to bet they didn't give you the advice *I* intend to. Which is, Caesar, to accept your fate. If you are outstanding— if you can't blend into the background—then don't hare off on wild excursions which demand you can. Unless, as I once did, you have a chance to masquerade as a rather terrific-looking Gaul. I came back wearing a torc around my neck, and I thought the thing was my luck. But Gaius Marius was right. The thing was noticeable in a way I didn't want to be noticed. So I gave up wearing it. I was a Roman, not a Gaul—and Fortune favored me, not an inanimate hunk of gold, no matter how lovely. Wherever *you* go, you will be noticed. Just like me. So learn to work within the confines of your nature *and* your appearance." Sulla grunted, looked a little astonished. "How well-meaning I am! I hardly ever give well-meaning advice."

"I am grateful for it," said Caesar sincerely.

The Dictator brushed this aside. "I want to know why you think Gaius Marius made you the *flamen Dialis.*"

Caesar paused to choose his words, understanding that his answer must be logical and unemotional.

"Gaius Marius saw a lot of me during the months after he had his second stroke," he began.

Sulla interrupted. "How old were you?"

"Ten when it started. Almost twelve when it finished."

"Go on."

"I was interested in what he had to say about soldiering. I listened very intently. He taught me to ride, use a sword, throw a spear, swim." Caesar smiled wryly. "I used to have gigantic military ambitions in those days."

"So you listened very intently."

"Yes, indeed. And I think that Gaius Marius gained the impression that I wanted to surpass him."

"Why should he?"

Another rueful look. "I told him I did!"

"All right, now to the flaminate. Expound."

"I can't give you a logical answer to that, I really can't. Except that I believe he made me *flamen Dialis* to prevent my having a military or a political career,'' said Caesar, very uncomfortably. ''That answer isn't all founded in my conceit. Gaius Marius was sick in his mind. He may have imagined it.''

''Well,'' said Sulla, face inscrutable, ''since he's dead, we'll never know the real answer, will we? However, given that his mind was diseased, your theory fits his character. He was always afraid of being outshone by men who had the birthright. Old and great names. His own name was a new one, and he felt he had been unfairly discriminated against because he was a New Man. Take, for example, my capture of King Jugurtha. He grabbed all the credit for that, you know! *My* work, *my* skill! If I had not captured Jugurtha, the war in Africa could never have been ended so expeditiously and finally. Your father's cousin, Catulus Caesar, tried to give me the credit in his memoirs, but he was howled down.''

Not if his life depended upon it would Caesar have betrayed by word or look what he thought of this astonishing version of the capture of King Jugurtha. Sulla had been Marius's legate! No matter how brilliant the actual capture had been, the credit had to go to Marius! It was Marius had sent Sulla off on the mission, and Marius who was the commander of the war. And the general couldn't do everything himself—that was why he had legates in the first place. I think, thought Caesar, that I am hearing one of the early versions of what will become the official story! Marius has lost, Sulla has won. For only one reason. Because Sulla has outlived Marius.

''I see,'' said Caesar, and left it at that.

Scuffling a little, Sulla got out of his chair and walked across to the couch where the garb of the *flamen Dialis* lay. He picked up the ivory helmet with its spike and disc of wool, and tossed it between his hands. ''You've lined it well,'' he said.

''It's very hot, Lucius Cornelius, and I dislike the feel of sweating,'' said Caesar.

''Do you change the lining often?'' Sulla asked, and actually lifted the *apex* to sniff its interior. ''It smells sweet. Ye gods, how a military helmet can stink! I've seen horses turn up their noses at the prospect of drinking from a military helmet.''

A faint distaste crossed Caesar's face, but he shrugged, tried to pass it off. ''The exigencies of war,'' he said lightly.

Sulla grinned. ''It will be interesting to see how you cope with *those,* boy! You're a trifle precious, aren't you?''

''In some ways, perhaps,'' said Caesar levelly.

The ivory *apex* bounced onto the couch. ''So you hate the job, eh?'' Sulla asked.

"I hate it."

"Yet Gaius Marius was afraid enough of a boy to hedge him round with it."

"It would seem so."

"I remember they used to say in the family that you were very clever—could read at a glance. Can you?"

"Yes."

Back to the desk: Sulla shuffled his papers and found a single sheet which he tossed at Caesar. "Read that," he said.

One glance told Caesar why. It was execrably written, with such a squeezing together of the letters and absence of columns that it really did look like a continuous, meaningless squiggle.

"You don't know me Sulla but do I have something to tell you and it is that there is a man from Lucania named Marcus Aponius which has a rich property in Rome and I just want you to know that Marcus Crassus had this man Aponius put on the proscription list so he could buy the property real cheap at auction and that is what he did for two thousand sesterces—A Friend." Caesar finished his effortless translation and looked at Sulla, eyes twinkling.

Sulla threw back his head and laughed. "I thought that's what it said! So did my secretary. I thank you, Caesar. But you haven't seen it and you couldn't possibly have read it even if you had seen it."

"Absolutely!"

"It causes endless trouble when one cannot do everything oneself," Sulla said, sobering. "That is the worst feature about being Dictator. I have to use agents—the task is too Herculean. The man mentioned in there is someone I trusted. Oh, I knew he was greedy, but I didn't think he'd be so blatant."

"Everyone in the Subura knows Marcus Licinius Crassus."

"What, because of his little arsons—the burning insulae?"

"Yes—and his fire brigades which arrive the moment he's bought the property cheaply, and put the fire out. He's becoming the Subura's biggest landlord. As well as the most unpopular. But he won't get his hands on my mother's insula!" vowed Caesar.

"Nor will he get his hands on any more proscription property," said Sulla harshly. "He impugned my name. I warned him! He did not listen. So I will never see him again. He can rot."

It was awkward listening to this: what did Caesar care about the troubles a dictator had with his agents? Rome would never see another dictator! But he waited, hoping Sulla would eventually get to the point, and sensing that this roundabout route was Sulla's way of testing his patience—and probably tormenting him too.

"Your mother doesn't know it and nor do you, but I didn't order you killed," the Dictator said.

Caesar's eyes opened wide. "You didn't? That's not what one Lucius Cornelius Phagites led Ria to believe! He got off with three talents of my mother's money pretending to spare me when I was ill. You've just finished telling me how awful it is to have to use agents because they get greedy. Well, that's as true of the bottom as it is of the top."

"I'll remember the name, and your mother will get her money back," said Sulla, obviously angry, "but that is not the point. The point is that I did not order you killed! I ordered you brought before me alive so I could ask you exactly the questions I have asked you."

"And then kill me."

"That was my original idea."

"And now you've given your word that you won't kill me."

"I don't suppose you've changed your mind about divorcing Cinna's daughter?"

"No. I will never divorce her."

"So that leaves Rome with a difficult problem. I can't have you killed, you don't want the job, you won't divorce Cinna's daughter because she's your way out of the job—and don't bother trying to give me high-flown explanations about honor and ethics and principles!" Suddenly a look of incredible old age came into the ruined face, the unsupported lips folded and flapped, worked on themselves; he was Cronus contemplating eating his next child whole. "Did your mother tell you what transpired?"

"Only that you spared me. You know her."

"Extraordinary person, Aurelia. Ought to have been a man."

Caesar's most charming smile dawned. "So you keep saying! I must admit I'm rather glad she wasn't a man."

"So am I, so am I! Were she a man, I'd have to look to my laurels." Sulla slapped his thighs and leaned forward. "So, my dear Caesar, you continue to be a trouble to all of us in the priestly colleges. What are we going to do with you?"

"Free me from my flaminate, Lucius Cornelius. You can do nothing else save kill me, and that would mean going back on your word. I don't believe you would do that."

"What makes you think I wouldn't break my word?"

Caesar raised his brows. "I am a patrician, one of your own kind! But more than that, I am a Julian. You'd never break your word to one as highborn as I.''

"That is so.'' The Dictator leaned back in his chair. "We of the priestly colleges have decided, Gaius Julius Caesar, to free you from your flaminate, just as you have surmised. I can't speak for the others, but I can tell you why *I* want you freed. I think Jupiter Optimus Maximus does not want you for his special *flamen*. I think he has other things in mind for you. It is very possible that all of the business about his temple was his way of freeing you. I do not know for sure. I only feel it in my bones—but a man can do far worse than to follow such instincts. Gaius Marius was the longest trial of my life. Like a Greek Nemesis. One way or another, he managed to spoil my greatest days. And for reasons I do not intend to go into, Gaius Marius exerted himself mightily to chain you. I tell you this, Caesar! If *he* wanted you chained, then *I* want you freed. I insist upon having the last laugh. And you are the last laugh.''

Never had Caesar conceived of salvation from this unlikely quarter. Because it had been Gaius Marius who chained him, Sulla would see him freed. As he sat there looking at Sulla, Caesar became unshakably convinced that for no other reason was he being released. Sulla wanted the last laugh. So in the end Gaius Marius had defeated himself.

"I and my colleagues of the priestly colleges are now of the opinion that there may have been a flaw in the rituals of your consecration as *flamen Dialis*. Several of us—not I, but enough others—were present at that ceremony, and none of them can be absolutely certain that there was not a flaw. The doubt is sufficient given the blood-soaked horror of those days, so we have agreed that you must be released. However, we cannot appoint another *flamen Dialis* while you live, just in case we are mistaken and there was no flaw.'' Sulla put both palms down on his desk. "It is best to have an escape clause. To be without a *flamen Dialis* is a grave inconvenience, but Jupiter Optimus Maximus is Rome, and he likes things to be legal. Therefore while you live, Gaius Julius Caesar, the other *flamines* will share Jupiter's duties among them.''

He must speak now. Caesar moistened his lips. "This seems a just and prudent course,'' he said.

"So we think. It means, however, that your membership in the Senate ceases as of the moment the Great God signifies his consent. In order to obtain his consent, you will give Jupiter Optimus Maximus his own animal, a white bull. If the sacrifice goes well, your flaminate is over. If it should not go well—why, we will have to think again. The Pontifex Maximus and the Rex Sacrorum will preside''—a flicker of antic mirth came and went in the pale cold eyes—"but you will conduct the sacrifice yourself. You will provide a feast for all the priestly colleges afterward, to be held in the temple of Jupiter Stator in the upper Forum Romanum. This offering and feast are in the nature of a *piaculum*, to atone for the inconveniences the Great God must suffer because he will have no special priest of his own."

"I am happy to obey," said Caesar formally.

"If all goes well, you are a free man. You may be married to whomsoever you choose. Even Cinna's brat."

"I take it then that there has been no change in Cinnilla's citizen status?" asked Caesar coolly.

"Of course there hasn't! If there had been, you'd wear the *laena* and *apex* for the rest of your life! I'm disappointed in you, boy, that you even bothered to ask."

"I asked, Lucius Cornelius, because the *lex Minicia* will automatically extend to apply to my children by my wife. And that is quite unacceptable. *I* have not been proscribed. Why should *my* children suffer?"

"Yes, I see that," said the Dictator, not at all offended at this straight speaking. "For that reason, I will amend my law to protect men like you. The *lex Minicia de liberis* will apply only to the children of the proscribed. If any of them are lucky enough to marry a Roman, then their children will be Roman." He frowned. "It should have been foreseen. It was not. One of the penalties of producing so much legislation so quickly. But the way in which it was drawn to my attention put me publicly in a ridiculous position. All your fault, boy! And your silly uncle, Cotta. The priestly interpretation of my laws anent the other laws of Rome already on the tablets must stand for the children of the proscribed."

"I'm glad for it," said Caesar, grinning. "It's got me out of Gaius Marius's clutches."

"That it has." Sulla looked brisk and businesslike, and changed the subject. "Mitylene has revolted from Roman tribute. At the moment my proquaestor Lucullus is in the chair, but I have sent my praetor Thermus to govern Asia Province. His first task will be to put down the revolt of Mitylene. You have indicated a preference for military duty, so I am sending you to Pergamum to join Thermus's staff. I expect you to distinguish yourself, Caesar," said Sulla, looking his most forbidding. "On your conduct as a junior military tribune rests the final verdict about this whole business. No man in Roman history is more revered than the military hero. I intend to exalt all such men. They will receive privileges and honors not given to others. If you win accolades for bravery in the field, I will exalt you too. But if you do not do well, I will push you down harder and further than Gaius Marius ever could have.''

''That's fair,'' said Caesar, delighted at this posting.

''One more thing,'' said Sulla, something sly in his gaze. ''Your horse. The animal you rode while *flamen Dialis,* against all the laws of the Great God.''

Caesar stiffened. ''Yes?''

''I hear you intend to buy the creature back. You will not. It is my dictate that you will ride a mule. A mule has always been good enough for me. It must also be good enough for you.''

The like eyes looked a like murder. But—oh no! said Gaius Julius Caesar to himself, you won't trap me this way, Sulla! ''Do you think, Lucius Cornelius, that I deem myself too good for a mule?'' he asked aloud.

''I have no idea what you deem yourself too good for.''

''I am a better rider than any other man I have ever seen,'' said Caesar calmly, ''while you, according to reports, are just about the worst rider ever seen. But if a mule is good enough for you, it is certainly more than good enough for me. And I thank you sincerely for your understanding. Also your discretion.''

''Then you can go now,'' said Sulla, unimpressed. ''On your way out, send in my secretary, would you?''

His little flash of temper sent Caesar home less grateful for his freedom than he would otherwise have been; and then he found himself wondering if such had not been Sulla's purpose in stipulating that final rather picayune condition about a mule. Sulla didn't want his gratitude, didn't want Aurelia's son in any kind of cliental bondage to him. A Julian beholden to a Cornelian? That was to make a mockery of the Patriciate. And, realizing this, Caesar ended in thinking better of Lucius Cornelius Sulla than he had when he left that man's presence. He has *truly* set me free! He has given me my life to do with what I will. Or what I can. I will never like him. But there have been times when I have found it in me to love him.

He thought of the horse Bucephalus. And wept.

''Sulla is wise, Caesar,'' said Aurelia, nodding her full approval. ''The drains on your purse are going to be considerable. You must buy a white bull without flaw or blemish, and you won't find such for less than fifty thousand. The feast you have to provide for all of Rome's priests and augurs will cost you twice that. After which, you have to equip yourself for Asia. And support yourself in what I fear will be a punishingly expensive environment. I remember your father saying that the junior military tribunes despise those among them who cannot afford every luxury and extravagance. You're not rich. The income from your land has accumulated since your father died, you've not had any need to spend it. That is going to change. To buy back your horse would be an unwelcome extra. After all, you won't be here to ride the beast. You must ride a mule until Sulla says otherwise. And you can find a splendid mule for under ten thousand.''

The look he gave his mother was not filial, but he said no word, and if he dreamed of his horse and mourned its permanent passing, he kept those things to himself.

The piacular sacrifice took place several days later, by which time Caesar had readied himself for his journey to take up duty under Marcus Minucius Thermus, governor of Asia Province. Though the feast was to be held in the temple of Jupiter Stator, the ritual of atonement was to take place at the altar erected below the steps which used to lead up to the temple of Jupiter Optimus Maximus on the Capitol.

Togate (his *laena* and *apex* had been given to the priests for storage until they could be laid to rest in Jupiter's unbuilt new temple), Caesar himself led his perfect white bull from his house down the Fauces Suburae and the Argiletum. Though he could have got away with tying ribbons around its splendid horns, Caesar now demonstrated his disregard for economy by having the animal's horns covered in thick gold foil; around its neck garlands of the most exotic and costly flowers were thrown, and a wreath of perfect white roses sat between its horns. Its hooves too were gilded, its tail wound round with cloth-of-gold ribbons intertwined with flowers. With him walked his guests—his uncles the Cottae, and Gaius Matius, and Lucius Decumius and his sons, and most of the Brethren of the crossroads college. All were togate. Aurelia was not present; her sex forbade her attending any sacrifice to Jupiter Optimus Maximus, who was a god for Roman men.

The various colleges of priests were clustered waiting near the altar, and the professionals who would do the actual killing were there too—*popa*, *cultarius*, slaves. Though it was the custom to drug the sacrificial animal beforehand, Caesar had refused; Jupiter had to be given every opportunity to indicate pleasure or displeasure. This fact was immediately apparent to everyone; the pure white bull, not a mark or blemish on it, was brisk of eye and step, and swished its tail importantly—obviously it liked being the center of attention.

"You're mad, boy!" whispered Gaius Aurelius Cotta as the waiting crowd grew larger and the steeply sloping Clivus Capitolinus began to level out. "Every eye is going to be on this animal, and you haven't drugged him! What are you going to do if he refuses to behave? It will be too late by then!''

"He won't misbehave," said Caesar serenely. "He knows he carries my fate. Everyone must see that I bow unreservedly to the will of the Great God." There came a faint chuckle. "Besides, I'm one of Fortune's favorites, I have luck!''

Everyone gathered around. Caesar turned aside to the bronze tripod holding a bowl of water and washed his hands; so did the Pontifex Maximus (Metellus Pius the Piglet), the Rex Sacrorum (Lucius Claudius), and the other two major *flamines, Martialis* (the Princeps Senatus, Lucius Valerius Flaccus) and *Quirinalis* (a new appointee, Mamercus). Bodies and clothing now ceremonially pure, the participating priests lifted the folds of toga lying across their shoulders and draped them over their heads. Once they had done so, everyone else followed.

The Pontifex Maximus moved to stand at the altar. "O mighty Jupiter Optimus Maximus—if you wish to be addressed by this name, otherwise I hail you by whatever name it is you wish to hear—receive your servant, Gaius Julius Caesar, who was your *flamen* and now wishes to atone for his wrongful appointment, which he wishes to point out to you was not of his doing!" cried the Piglet without a single stammer, and stepped back with a glare of fury aimed at Sulla, who was managing to keep a straight face; this flawless performance had cost the Piglet days of remorseless practice more grueling than military drills.

The professional priestlings were stripping the bull of its flowers and gold foil, patting the latter carefully into a rough ball, and paid no attention to Caesar, who now stepped forward and placed his hand upon the moist pink nose of his offering. The ruby-dark eyes surrounded by long thick lashes as colorless as crystal watched him as he did so, and Caesar felt no tremor of outrage in the white bull at his touch.

He prayed in a voice pitched much higher than his natural one, so that every word would travel. "O mighty Jupiter Optimus Maximus—if you wish to be addressed by this name, otherwise I hail you by whatever name it is you wish to hear—you who are of whichever sex you prefer—you who are the spirit of Rome—accept, I pray, this gift of your own sacred animal which I offer you as an atonement for my wrongful appointment as your *flamen*. It is my prayer that you release me from my vows and grant me the opportunity to serve you in some other capacity. I submit myself to your will, but offer you this best and greatest and strongest living thing in the knowledge that you will grant me what I ask because I have offered you exactly what I ought."

He smiled at the bull, gazing at him, it seemed, with insight.

The priestlings stepped forward; Caesar and the Pontifex Maximus turned to one side and each took a golden chalice from a tripod, while the Rex Sacrorum took up a golden bowl of spelt.

"I cry for silence!" thundered Caesar.

Silence fell, so complete that the distant noises of busy activity in the Forum arcades of shops floated clearly on the warm and gentle breeze.

The flautist put his instrument made from the shinbone of an enemy to his lips, and began to blow a mournful tune intended to drown out these sounds of Forum business.

As soon as the flute began the Rex Sacrorum sprinkled the bull's face and head with spelt, a thistledown shower which the beast seemed to take as rain; its pink tongue came out and sopped up the granules of fine flour on its nose.

The *popa* moved to stand in front of the bull, his stunning hammer held loosely by his side. "*Agone?* Do I strike?" he asked Caesar loudly.

"Strike!" cried Caesar.

Up flashed the hammer, down to land with perfect precision between the bull's mild and unsuspecting eyes. It collapsed on its front knees with an impact heavy enough to feel through the ground, its head outstretched; slowly the hindquarters subsided to the right, a good omen.

Like the *popa* stripped naked to the waist, the *cultarius* took the horns in both his hands and lifted the bull's limp head toward the sky, the muscles in his arms standing out ribbed and sinewy, for the bull's head weighed more than fifty pounds. Then he lowered his burden to touch the cobbles with its muzzle.

"The victim consents," he said to Caesar.

"Then make the sacrifice!" cried Caesar.

Out came the big razor-sharp knife from its scabbard, and while the *popa* hauled the bull's head into the air, the *cultarius* cut its throat with one huge deep slice of his knife. The blood gushed but did not spurt—this fellow knew his job. No one—even he—was spattered. As the *popa* released the head to lie turned to the right, Caesar handed the *cultarius* his chalice, and the *cultarius* caught some of the blood so accurately that not a drop spilled down the side of the vessel. Metellus Pius gave his chalice to be filled in turn.

Avoiding the steady turgid crimson stream which flowed away downhill, Caesar and the Pontifex Maximus walked to the bare stone altar. There Caesar trickled the contents of his cup, and said, "O mighty Jupiter Optimus Maximus—if you wish to be addressed by this name, otherwise I hail you by whatever name it is you wish to hear—you who are of whichever sex you prefer—you who are the spirit of Rome—accept this offering made to you as an atonement, and accept too the gold from the horns and hooves of your victim, and keep it to adorn your new temple.''

Now Metellus Pius emptied his cup. ''O mighty Jupiter Optimus Maximus—if you wish to be addressed by this name, otherwise I hail you by whatever name it is you wish to hear—I ask that you accept the atonement of Gaius Julius Caesar, who was your *flamen* and is still your servant.''

The moment Metellus Pius had clearly enunciated the last syllable of his prayer, a collective sigh of relief went up, loud enough to be heard above the sad tweetling of the *tibicen*.

Last to offer was the Rex Sacrorum, who sprinkled the remnant of his spelt into the starred splashes of blood on the altar. ''O mighty Jupiter Optimus Maximus—if you wish to be addressed by this name, otherwise I hail you by whatever name it is you wish to hear—I bear witness that you have been offered the life-force of this best and greatest and strongest victim, and that all has been done in accordance with the prescribed ritual, and that no error has been made. Under the terms of our contractual agreements with you, I therefore conclude that you are well pleased with your offering and its donor, Gaius Julius Caesar. Furthermore, Gaius Julius Caesar wishes to burn his offering whole for your delectation, and does not wish to take any of it for himself. May Rome and all who live in her prosper as a result.''

And it was over. Over without a single mistake. While the priests and augurs unveiled their heads and began to walk down the slope of the Clivus Capitolinus toward the Forum, the priestlings who were professional sacrificers began to clean up. They used a hoist and cradle to winch the huge carcass off the ground and deposit it upon the pyre, then set a torch to it amid their own prayers. While their slaves worked with buckets of water to wash away the last traces of blood upon the ground, a peculiar aroma arose, a mixture of delicious roasting beef and the costly incenses Caesar had bought to stuff among the brands in the pyre. The blood on the altar would be left until after the bull had burned away to bony ashes, then it too would be scrubbed. And the ball of gold was already on its way to the Treasury, where it would be marked with the name of its donor and the nature and date of the occasion.

The feast which followed in the temple of Jupiter Stator on the Velia at the top of the Forum Romanum was at least as successful as the sacrifice; as Caesar passed among his guests exhorting them to enjoy themselves and exchanging pleasantries, many eyes assessed him that had never so much as noticed him before. He was now by virtue of rank and birth a contender in the political arena, and his manner, his carriage, the expression on his handsome face, all suggested that he bore watching.

"He has a look of your father about him," said Metellus Pius to Catulus, still flushed with the well-being which stemmed from a ceremony executed without one improperly pronounced word.

"He should," said Catulus, eyeing Caesar with an instinctive dislike. "My father was a Caesar. Such a pretty fellow, isn't he? I could suffer that. But I'm not sure I can suffer his awful conceit. Look at him! Younger by far than Pompeius! Yet he struts as if he owned the world."

The Piglet was disposed to find reasons. "Well, how would you feel in his shoes? He's free of that terrible flaminate."

"We may rue the day we let Sulla instruct us to free him," said Catulus. "See him over there with Sulla? Two of a kind!"

The Piglet was staring at him, mildly astonished; Catulus could have bitten off his tongue. For an indiscreet moment he had forgotten his auditor was not Quintus Hortensius, so used was he to having his brother-in-law's ear permanently ready to listen. But Hortensius was not present, because when Sulla had informed the priestly colleges who were the new members, he had excluded the name of Quintus Hortensius. And Catulus considered Sulla's omission quite unforgivable. So did Quintus Hortensius.

Unaware that he had offended Catulus, Sulla was busy getting some information from Caesar.

"You didn't drug your animal. That was taking a colossal chance," he said.

"I'm one of Fortune's favorites," said Caesar.

"What leads you to that conclusion?"

"Only consider! I have been released from my flaminate—before that I survived an illness men usually die from—I evaded your killing me—and I am teaching my mule to emulate a very aristocratic horse with marked success."

"Does your mule have a name?" asked Sulla, grinning.

"Of course. I call it Flop Ears."

"And what did you call your very aristocratic horse?"

"Bucephalus."

Sulla shook with laughter, but made no further comment, his eyes roaming everywhere. Then he extended an arm. "You do this sort of thing remarkably well for an eighteen-year-old."

"I'm taking your advice," said Caesar. "Since I am unable to blend into the background, I decided that even this first banquet in my name should not be unworthy of it."

"Oh, arrogant! You really are! Never fear, Caesar, it is a memorable feast. Oysters, dug-mullets, licker-fish of the Tiber, baby quail—the menu must have cost you a fortune."

"Certainly more than I can afford," said Caesar calmly.

"Then you're a spendthrift," said Sulla, anything but.

Caesar shrugged. "Money is a tool, Lucius Cornelius. I don't care whether I have it or not, if counting up a hoard is what you believe to be the purpose of money. I believe money must be passed on. Otherwise it stagnates. So does the economy. What money comes my way from now on, I will use to further my public career."

"That's a good way to go bankrupt."

"I'll always manage," said Caesar, unconcerned.

"How can you know that?"

"Because I have Fortune's favor. I have luck."

Sulla shivered. "*I* have Fortune's favor! *I* have luck! But remember—there is a price to pay. Fortune is a jealous and demanding mistress."

"They're the best kind!" said Caesar, and laughed so infectiously that the room went quiet. Many of the men present took that memory of a laughing Caesar into the future with them—not because they suffered any premonitions, but because he had two qualities they envied him—youth and beauty.

Of course he couldn't leave until after the last guest was gone, and that was not until many hours later; by then he had every last one of them assessed and filed away because he had that kind of mind, always storing up whatever it encountered. Yes, an interesting company, was his verdict.

"Though I found none I was tempted to make a friend of," he said to Gaius Matius at dawn the next day. "Sure you don't want to come with me, Pustula? You have to serve in your ten campaigns, you know."

"No, thank you. I have no wish to be so far from Rome. I will wait for a posting, and hope it's Italian Gaul."

The farewells were genuinely exhausting. Wishing he might have dispensed with them, Caesar endured them with what patience he could muster. The worst feature of it was the many who had clamored to go with him, though he had steadfastly refused to take anyone save Burgundus. His two body servants were new purchases—a fresh start, men with no knowledge of his mother.

Finally the goodbyes were over—Lucius Decumius, his sons and the Brethren of the crossroads college, Gaius Matius, his mother's servants, Cardixa and her sons, his sister Ju-Ju, his wife, and his mother. Caesar was able to climb on his inglorious mule and ride away.

PART THREE

from JANUARY 81 B.C.
until SEXTILIS (AUGUST) 80 B.C.

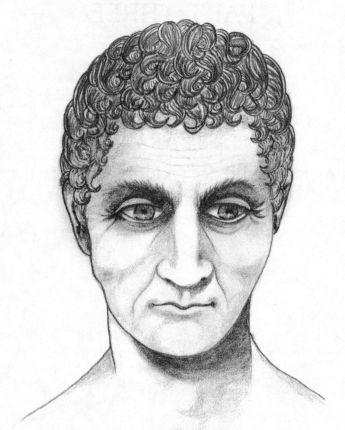

QUINTUS CAECILIUS METELLUS PIUS

Not two months had gone by when Sulla decided that Rome had adjusted satisfactorily to the presence of his proscriptions. The slaughter was only marginally more subtle than Marius's slaughter during the few days of his seventh consulship; the streets of Rome didn't run with quite so much blood, and there were no bodies piled in the lower Forum Romanum. The bodies of those killed in Sulla's proscriptions (the victims were forbidden funeral rites and interment) were dragged with a meat hook under the sternum to the Tiber, and thrown in· only the heads were piled in the lower Forum Romanum, around the perimete · of the public fountain known as the Basin of Servilius.

As the amount of property gathered in for the State by the administrator, Chrysogonus, accumulated, a few more laws came into being: the widow of a man proscribed could not remarry, and the wax masks of Gaius Marius and Young Marius, of Cinna or his ancestors, or of any proscribed man and his ancestors, could not be displayed at any family funeral.

The house of Gaius Marius had been sold at auction to the present Sextus Perquitienus, grandson of the man who had made that family's fortune, and next door to whom Marius had erected his house; it now served as an annex for art works to the Perquitienus residence, though it was not incorporated in it.

At first the auctions Chrysogonus conducted saw the estates of the proscribed knocked down to successful bidders at a fair market price, but the amount of money to buy was not great, so that by the time the tenth auction occurred, the prices being realized were dropping rapidly. It was at this moment that Marcus Crassus began to bid. His technique was shrewd; rather than set his heart on the best property on the agenda, he chose to concentrate upon less desirable estates, and was able to pick them up for very little. The activities of Lucius Sergius Catilina were more feral. He concentrated upon informing Chrysogonus of traitorous talk or actions, and thus succeeded in having his elder brother Quintus proscribed, after which he ensured that his brother-in-law Caecilius was proscribed. The brother was sent into exile, but the brother-in-law died, and Catilina applied to the Dictator for a special law to inherit, arguing that in neither case was he named in the will, nor was he a direct heir—both men had male children. When Sulla acceded to his request, Catilina became rich without needing to spend a single sestertius at the auctions.

It was in a dually chilly climate, therefore, that Sulla celebrated his triumph on the last day of January. Ordinary Rome turned out en masse to do him honor, though the knights stayed home, apparently on the theory that should Sulla or Chrysogonus see their faces, they might wind up on the next proscription list. The Dictator displayed the spoils and tributes of Asia and King Mithridates with every tricky device conceivable to camouflage the fact that his conclusion of the war had been as hasty as it was premature, and that in consequence the booty was disappointing considering the wealth of the enemy.

On the following day Sulla held an exposition rather than a triumph, displaying what he had taken from Young Marius and Carbo; he was careful to inform the spectators that these items were to be returned to the temples and people they had been taken from. On this day the restored exiles—men like Appius Claudius Pulcher, Metellus Pius, Varro Lucullus and Marcus Crassus—marched not as senators of Rome, but as restored exiles, though Sulla considerately spared them the indignity of having to don the Cap of Liberty, normally the headgear of freedmen.

The taming of Pompey proved to be more difficult than reconciling Rome to the proscriptions, as Sulla learned the day before he held his triumph. Pompey had ignored his instructions from the Dictator and sailed with his whole army from Africa to Italy. The letter he sent Sulla from Tarentum informed Sulla that his army had refused to let him sail without every last one of his loyal soldiers coming along, and he claimed to have been powerless to prevent this mass embarkation (without explaining how it was that he had gathered sufficient ships to fit five extra legions and two thousand horses on board); at the end of his missive he again asked to be allowed to celebrate a triumph.

The Dictator sped a couriered letter to Tarentum in which for the second time he denied Pompey this mouth-watering triumph. The same courier carried back a letter from Pompey to Sulla apologizing for the refractory behavior of his army, which he protested yet again he could not control. Those naughty, naughty soldiers were *insisting* their darling general be allowed his well-deserved triumph! If the Dictator were to continue his negative attitude, Pompey was very much afraid his naughty, naughty soldiers might take matters into their own hands, and elect to march to Rome. He himself would— of course!—do *everything* in his power to prevent this!

A second letter was galloped from Sulla down the Via Appia to Tarentum, containing a third refusal: NO TRIUMPH. This proved to be one refusal too many. Pompey's six legions and two thousand cavalry troopers set out to march to Rome. Their darling general came along with them, protesting in another letter to Sulla that he was only doing so in order to prevent his men taking actions they might later have cause to regret.

The Senate had been privy to every episode in this duel of wills, horrified at the presumption of a twenty-four-year-old knight, and had issued a *senatus consultum* to back every one of Sulla's orders and denials. So when Sulla and the Senate were informed that Pompey and his army had reached Capua, resistance hardened. The time was now nearing the end of February, winter storms came and went, and the Campus Martius was already crowded because other armies were sitting on it—two legions belonging to Lucius Licinius Murena, the ex-governor of Asia Province and Cilicia, and two legions belonging to Gaius Valerius Flaccus, the ex-governor of Gaul-across-the-Alps. Each of these men was to triumph shortly.

Hot on the heels of the inevitable letter ordering Pompey to halt at Capua (and informing Pompey that there were four battle-hardened legions occupying the Campus Martius), the Dictator himself left Rome in the direction of Capua. With him were the consuls Decula and the elder Dolabella, Metellus Pius the Pontifex Maximus, Flaccus Princeps Senatus the Master of the Horse, and an escort of lictors; no soldiers traveled with them to protect them.

Sulla's letter caught Pompey before he could leave Capua, and the news that four battle-hardened legions were encamped outside Rome shocked him into remaining where he was. It had never been Pompey's intention to go to war against Sulla; the march was a bluff purely designed to obtain a triumph. So to learn that the Dictator had four battle-hardened legions at his immediate disposal broke upon Pompey like a torrent of ice-cold water. He himself knew he was bluffing—but did Sulla know it? Of course not! How could he? To Sulla, this march would look like a repeat of his own from Capua in the year that he had been consul. Pompey flew into an absolute funk.

So when the news came that Sulla in person was approaching without an army to back him, Pompey scrambled frantically to ride out of his camp and up the Via Appia—also without his army to back him. The circumstances of this meeting bore some resemblance to their first encounter at the ford across the Calor River. But today Sulla was not drunk, though inevitably he was mounted upon a mule. He was dressed in the purple-bordered *toga praetexta* and preceded by twenty-four lictors shivering in crimson tunics and brass-bossed black leather belts, with the ominous axes inserted in their bundles of rods. In Sulla's wake there followed thirty more lictors—twelve belonging to Decula, twelve to the elder Dolabella, and six to the Master of the Horse, who had a praetor's rank. So the occasion was more dignified and impressive than had been that at the Calor crossing. More in tune with poor Pompey's original fantasies.

But there could be no arguing that Pompey had grown in stature during the twenty-two months which had elapsed since his original meeting with Sulla; he had conducted one campaign in conjunction with Metellus Pius and

Crassus, another in Clusium with Sulla and Crassus, and a third in complete command abroad. So now he didn't quibble about wearing his best gold-plated suit of armor, and flashed and glittered quite as much as did his gaily caparisoned Public Horse. The Dictator's party was coming up on foot; unwilling to look more martial, Pompey dismounted.

Sulla was wearing his Grass Crown, an unkind reminder that Pompey as yet had not managed to win one—had not managed to win a Civic Crown, for that matter! Silly wig and all, scar-spattered face and all, the Dictator still contrived to look every inch the Dictator. Pompey was quick to note it. The lictors moved twelve to either side of the road, thus permitting the tanned young man in his gold-plated armor to walk between their files toward Sulla, who had halted and arranged his party so that he stood a few feet ahead of the others, but was not isolated from them.

"*Ave*, Pompeius Magnus!" cried Sulla, right hand lifted.

"*Ave*, Dictator of Rome!" cried Pompey, transported with joy. Sulla had actually called him in public by the third name he had given himself—he could now officially be Pompey the Great!

They kissed on the mouth, something neither man enjoyed. And, the lictors preceding as always, turned slowly to walk in the direction of Pompey's camp, the others following on.

"You're prepared to admit I'm Great!" said Pompey happily.

"The name has stuck," said Sulla. "But so has Kid Butcher."

"My army is determined that I triumph, Lucius Cornelius."

"Your army has absolutely no right to make that determination, Gnaeus Pompeius Magnus."

Out flew both powerful, freckled arms. "What can I *do*?" he cried. "They won't take a scrap of notice of me!"

"Rubbish!" said Sulla roundly. "Surely you realize, Magnus, that throughout the course of four letters—if you count the original one you received in Utica—you have demonstrated that you are not competent enough to control your troops?"

Pompey flushed, drew his small mouth in even smaller. "That is not a fair criticism!" he exclaimed.

"It most certainly is. You have admitted its truth yourself in no less than three letters."

"You're deliberately failing to understand!" said Pompey, red-faced. "They're only behaving like this because they *love* me!"

"Love or hate, insubordination is insubordination. If they belonged to me, I'd be decimating them."

"It's a harmless insubordination," Pompey protested lamely.

"No insubordination is harmless, as you well know. You are threatening the legally appointed Dictator of Rome."

"This is not a march *on* Rome, Lucius Cornelius, it's just a march *to* Rome," labored Pompey. "There is a difference! My men simply want to see that I receive what is due to me."

"What is due to you, Magnus, is whatever I, as Dictator of Rome, decide to give you. You are twenty-four years old. You are not a senator. I have agreed to call you by a wonderful name which could only be improved by degree—Magnus can go to Maximus, but nowhere else—unless it be diminished to Parvus—or Minutus—or even Pusillus," said Sulla.

Pompey stopped in the middle of the road, faced Sulla; the party behind somehow forgot to stop until they were well and truly close enough to hear.

"I *want* a triumph!" said Pompey loudly, and stamped a foot.

"And I say you can't have one!" said Sulla, equally loudly.

Pompey's broad, temper-reddened face grew beetling, the thin lips drew back to reveal small white teeth. "You would do well to remember, Lucius Cornelius Sulla, Dictator of Rome, that more people worship the rising than the setting sun!"

For no reason any of the enthralled listeners could determine, Sulla burst out laughing. He laughed until he cried, slapping his hands helplessly on his thighs and quite losing control of the many folds of toga draped upon his left arm; it began to fall away and drag upon the ground. "Oh, very well!" he gasped when he could speak at all. "Have your triumph!" And then, still shaken by fresh guffaws, he said, "Don't just stand there, Magnus, you great booby! Help me pick up my toga!"

"You are a complete fool, Magnus," said Metellus Pius to Pompey when he had an opportunity to speak in private.

"I think I've been very clever," said Pompey smugly.

Still not consul though he had entered into his late forties, the Piglet had aged well; his curly brown hair was frosted with white at the temples and his skin bore none but attractive lines at the corners of his brown eyes. Even so, next to Pompey he paled into insignificance. And he knew it. Not so much with envy as with sadness.

"You've been anything but clever," the Piglet said, pleased to see the brilliant blue eyes widen incredulously. "I know our master considerably better than you do, and I can tell you that his intelligence is greater than both of ours put together. If he has a failing, it is only a failing of temperament—

not of character! And this failing doesn't affect the brilliance of his mind one iota. Nor does it affect the consummate skill of his actions, as man or as Dictator.''

Pompey blew a derisive noise. ''Oh, Pius, you're not making any sense! Failing? What failing of Sulla's can you possibly mean?''

''His sense of the ridiculous, of course. Better to cuh-cuh-call it that than a sense of huh-huh-huh-humor.'' The Piglet floundered, his own disability recollected, and stopped for a few moments to discipline his tongue. ''I mean things like his appointing me the Pontifex Maximus when I stumble over my words. He can never resist that kind of joke.''

Pompey contrived to look bored. ''I have no idea where you are going, Pius, or what it has to do with me.''

''Magnus, Magnus! He's been having a laugh at your expense all along! That's what it has to do with you. He *always* intended that you should triumph—what does he care about your age or your knight's status? You're a military hero, and he raises them to all kinds of exalted heights! But he wanted to see how much it meant to you, and how far you'd go to get it. You should never have risen to his bait. Now, he has you properly assessed and tucked away in his mental accounting system. He knows now that your courage is *almost* the equal of your self-esteem, not to mention your ambition. Almost. But not quite. He knows now that at the bitter end, Magnus, you won't stick the course.''

''What do you mean, I won't stick the course?''

''You know perfectly well what I mean.''

''I was marching on Rome!''

''Rubbish!'' The Piglet smiled. ''You were marching *to* Rome. You said so yourself. And I believed you. So did Sulla.''

Confounded, Pompey glared at his critic, not sure what he ought to— what he *could* say. ''I got my triumph.''

''Yes, you did. But he's making you pay a price for it you wouldn't have had to pay if you'd behaved yourself.''

''Price? Price?'' Pompey shook his head like a large and angry animal confused by teasing. ''Today, Pius, you seem quite determined to speak in riddles!''

''You'll see,'' said the Piglet, no less obscure.

And Pompey did see, but not until the day of his triumph. The clues were there; excitement clouded his perceptions, was the trouble. The date of his triumph was set at the twelfth day of March. On the sixth day of March,

Gaius Flaccus, the ex-governor of Gaul-across-the-Alps, triumphed for victories over rebellious Gallic tribes; and on the ninth day of March, Murena, the ex-governor of Asia Province, triumphed for victories in Cappadocia and Pontus. So by the time that the day of Pompey's triumph came round, Rome had had enough of victory parades. A few people turned out, but not a crowd; after Sulla's magnificent two-day extravaganza Flaccus had been mildly interesting, Murena somewhat less so, and Pompey hardly at all. For no one knew his name, no one was aware of his youth or beauty, and no one could have cared less. *Another* triumph? Ho hum, said Rome.

However, Pompey wasn't particularly worried as he set off from the Villa Publica; word would fly and the people would come running from all directions when they heard the style of this particular triumph! By the time he turned the corner from the Circus Maximus into the Via Triumphalis, all of Rome would be there to see. In almost every respect his procession was a standard one—first the magistrates and senators, then musicians and dancers, the carts displaying spoils and the floats depicting various incidents from the campaign, the priests and the white male sacrificial victims, the captives and hostages, and then the general in his chariot, followed by his army.

Even Pompey's garb was correct—the purple toga solidly embroidered with gold, the laurel wreath upon his head, the palm-embroidered tunic with the massive purple stripe. But when it came to painting his face red with *minim,* he balked. It was vital to his plans that Rome should see his youth and beauty, the face of an individual. His likeness to Alexander the Great. If his face were to be reduced to a brick-red blob, he might be anyone of any age. Therefore, no *minim!*

This barefaced presentation was not the major difference between Pompey and every other triumphing general; that lay in the animals which drew the antique four-wheeled triumphal chariot in which Pompey rode. Instead of the customary matched white horses, he was using four enormous male African elephants he had personally captured in Numidia. Four mahouts had worked every day since—in Utica and Tarentum, on the Via Appia, at Capua—to tame the recalcitrant pachyderms sufficiently to persuade them to act as beasts of slight burden. No easy feat, yet accomplished. Thus Pompey was able to set off in a triumphal chariot towed by four elephants. His companion in the car did not drive, simply held on to a set of ornate reins attached to the flashy trappings worn by these fabulous creatures. The elephants were under the control of the mahouts, each one sitting between a pair of massive, wrinkled grey shoulders more than ten feet off the ground. Once word spread—and it would, very quickly!—crowds would line the route of the parade just to see this remarkable sight—the New Alexander drawn by the very animals Rome regarded as most sacred. *Elephants!* Gigantic elephants with ears the size of sails and tusks seven feet long!

The path of the parade led from the Villa Publica on the Campus Martius to a narrow roadway lined with villas and apartment houses that wound around the base of the Capitoline Hill and approached the Servian Walls below the sharp cliffs at the hill's western end; here was the Porta Triumphalis, through which the parade passed into the city itself. As Pompey's was the third triumph within six days, senators and magistrates were thoroughly fed up with the whole procedure, so this first contingent was thin of company and inclined to be brisk. Taking their cue from the leaders, the musicians, dancers, carts, floats, priests, sacrificial victims, captives and hostages also moved quickly. Trundling along at the leisurely pace of four elephants harnessed two abreast, Pompey soon fell behind.

The chariot came to the Triumphal Gate at last, and stopped dead. The army—minus swords and spears but carrying staves wrapped in laurels—also stopped. Because the triumphal car was so old it belonged to Etruscan times and had been ceremonial from the beginning, it was much lower to the ground than the classical two-wheeled war chariot still employed by some outlandish tribes of Gauls; Pompey couldn't see what was happening over the majestic but tousled rumps of the pair of elephants in front of him. At first he merely fretted and fumed a little; then when the halt became tediously long, he sent his driver forward to see what was the matter.

Back came the driver, looking horrified. "Triumphator, the elephants are too big to fit through the gate!"

Pompey's jaw dropped. He felt a prickling in his skin, beads of sweat popping out on his forehead. "Nonsense!" he said.

"Truly, Triumphator, it is so! The elephants are too big to fit through the gate," the driver insisted.

Down from the chariot in all his glory descended Pompey to run, trailing gold and purple garments, in the direction of the gate. There the mahouts belonging to the two leading pachyderms were standing looking helpless; thankfully they turned to Pompey.

"The opening is too small," said one.

While on his way to the gate, Pompey had been mentally unharnessing the beasts and leading them through the aperture one at a time to the far side, but now he saw what he had not been able to see from the chariot; it was not a question of width, but of height. This opening—the only one by which the triumphal parade was permitted to travel—was wide enough to allow an army to march through eight abreast, even to allow the entry of a chariot drawn by four horses abreast, or a huge float; but it was not high enough to pass the head of an old and mighty African tusker, as the masonry above it which burrowed into the cliff of the Capitoline Hill began at about the height of these elephants' shoulders.

"All right," said Pompey confidently, "unharness them and lead them through one at a time. Just make them bend their heads right down."

"They're not trained to do that!" said one mahout, aghast.

"I don't care whether they're trained to shit through the eye of a needle!" snapped Pompey, face beginning to look as if it had been painted with *minim* after all. "Just do it!"

The leading elephant refused to bend his head.

"Pull on his trunk and make him!" said Pompey.

But no amount of pulling on his trunk or sitting on his glorious curving tusks would persuade the beast to bend his head; instead, he became angry. His unrest began to infect the other three, two of whom were still attached to the chariot. They began to back away, and the chariot began to threaten the lionskin-clad band of Pompey's standard-bearers immediately behind.

While the mahouts continued to battle to obey him, Pompey stood articulating every horrific profanity in a ranker soldier's vocabulary and producing threats which reduced the mahouts to glassy-eyed jellies of fear. All to no avail. The elephants were too big and too unwilling to be brought through the gate.

Over an hour had gone by when Varro came through the gate to see what had gone wrong. He, of course, had been walking with the other senators at the very front of the parade.

One look was enough. A terrible urge invaded Varro to lie down in the road and howl with laughter. This he could not do—not, one glance at Pompey's face told him, if he wanted to live.

"Send Scaptius and some of his men to the Stabulae to get the horses," said Varro crisply. "Come, Magnus, abandon these tantrums and *think*! The rest of the parade has reached the Forum, and no one knows why you're not following. Sulla is sitting up on Castor's podium fidgeting more and more, and the caterers for the feast in Jupiter Stator are tearing their hair out!"

Pompey's answer was to burst into tears and sit down on the dirty cobbles in all his triumphal finery to weep his heart out. Thus it was Varro who sent the men for horses, and Varro who supervised the unhitching of the elephants. By this the scene had been complicated by the arrival of several market gardeners from the Via Recta, armed with shovels and barrows, and determined to appropriate what was known to be the best fertilizer in the world. Stepping unconcernedly between the gigantic legs of the pachyderms, they busied themselves scooping up piles of dung the size of wheels of cheese from Arpinum. Only urgency and pity kept Varro's mirth at bay as he shouted and shooed, finally saw the mahouts get their charges under way toward the Forum Holitorium—no one could have driven them back the way they had come, with six legions congesting the roadway.

In the meantime the front half of the parade had ground to a halt in the Forum Romanum opposite the imposing Ionic facade of the temple of Castor and Pollux—upon which, high up, sat Sulla with his Master of the Horse, the two consuls, and some of his family and friends. Courtesy and custom said that the triumphator must be the most important man in his parade as well as at his feast, so these august men did not participate in the parade, nor would they attend the feast afterward.

Everyone was restless; everyone was also cold. The day was fine, but a bitter north wind was blowing, and the sun in the depths of the lower Forum not strong enough to melt the icicles hanging from temple eaves. Finally Varro returned, took the steps of Castor's two at a time, and bent to whisper in Sulla's ear. A huge gust of laughter assailed all the suddenly curious men; then, still laughing, Sulla got to his feet and walked to the edge of the podium to address the crowd.

"Wait a little longer!" he shouted. "Our triumphator is coming! He decided he'd improve the look of his parade by using elephants to draw his car instead of horses! But the elephants wouldn't fit through the Porta Triumphalis, so he's had to send for horses!" A pause, and then (quite audibly), "Oh, how I wish I'd been there to see it!"

General titters followed that announcement, but only the men who knew Pompey—Metellus Pius, Varro Lucullus, Crassus—roared their amusement.

"You know, it isn't wise to offend Sulla," said Metellus Pius to those around him. "I've noticed it time and time again. He has some sort of exclusive claim on Fortune, so he doesn't even have to exert himself to see a man humiliated. The Goddess does it for him. Sulla is her favorite person in the world."

"What I can't understand," said Varro Lucullus, frowning, "is why Pompeius didn't measure the gate beforehand. Give him his due, he's usually very efficient."

"Until his daydreams overpower his good sense," said Varro, arriving breathless; he had run all the way from the Triumphal Gate as well as up Castor's steps. "His mind was so set on those wretched elephants that it never occurred to him anything could go wrong. Poor Magnus, he was shocked."

"I feel sorry for him, actually," said Varro Lucullus.

"So do I, now I've proved my point to him," said Metellus Pius, and looked closely at the panting, scarlet-faced Varro. "How is he taking it?"

"He'll be all right by the time he gets to the Forum," Varro said, too loyal to describe the bout of tears.

Indeed, Pompey carried the rest of his triumphal parade with grace and dignity, though there could be no denying, even in his mind, that the two-hour fracture in its middle relegated it to the level of a very pedestrian triumph. Nor had many people lined the route to see him; what were horses compared to old men elephants, especially the plodding bay mediocrities which were all Scaptius could find?

It was not until he entered the temple of Jupiter Stator, in which his feast was laid out, that he fully understood how funny the men who mattered thought his elephantine fiasco was. The ordeal had actually begun on his way down from the Capitol after the triumph itself had concluded, when he found a group of people clustered about the base of Scipio Africanus's encolumned statue, laughing hilariously. The moment he drew near, however, everyone cleared a path to make sure he saw what some Forum wit had chalked upon the plinth in huge letters:

> "Africanus up here in the air
> Found elephants worthy of prayer.
> Kid Butcher, precocious young shit,
> Found elephants just wouldn't fit!"

Inside Jupiter Stator it was even worse. Some of his guests contented themselves by putting a heavy emphasis on the word "Magnus" when they addressed him by it, but others feigned a slip in pronunciation which turned him into "Magus"—a ludicrous wise man from Persia—or punned deliciously on "Manus"—hand—to imply everything from his being on hand to smarm to Sulla, to smarming to Sulla by using his hand. A very few remained courteous, like Metellus Pius and Varro Lucullus; a few were Pompey's own friends and relatives, who made matters worse by waxing indignant and offering to fight the mockers; and some, like Catulus and Hortensius, were conspicuous by their absence.

Pompey did make a new friend, however; none other than the Dictator's long-lost nephew, Publius Cornelius Sulla, who was introduced to him by Catilina.

"I didn't realize Sulla had a nephew!" said Pompey.

"Nor did he," said Publius Sulla cheerfully, and added, "Nor did I until recently, for that matter."

Catilina began to laugh. "It's no less than the truth," he said to Pompey, now obviously confused.

"You'd better enlighten me," said Pompey, glad to hear a shout of laughter that was not directed at him.

"I grew up thinking I was the son of Sextus Perquitienus," Publius Sulla explained. "Lived next door to Gaius Marius all my life! When my grandfather died and my father inherited, neither of us suspected the truth. But my father was friendly with Cinna, so after the proscription lists started going up on the rostra, he expected to see his name at the top of every new one that came out. And worried so much that he fell over dead."

This was announced with such careless insouciance that Pompey correctly assumed there was no love lost between father and son—not a surprise, considering that old Sextus Perquitienus (and Publius Sulla's father) had been detested by most of Rome.

"I'm fascinated," Pompey said.

"I found out who I was when I was going through a chest of old documents belonging to my grandfather," said Publius Sulla. "I unearthed the adoption papers! Turned out my father had been adopted by my grandfather before my uncle the Dictator was born—he never knew he had an older brother. Anyway, I thought I had better take the papers to Uncle Lucius the Dictator before someone put *my* name on a proscription list!"

"Well, you do have a look of Sulla about you," Pompey said, smiling, "so I suppose you didn't have much trouble convincing him."

"No trouble at all! Isn't it the most wonderful luck?" asked Publius Sulla happily. "Now I have all the Perquitienus wealth, I'm safe from proscription, and I'll probably inherit a share of Uncle Lucius the Dictator's millions as well."

"Do you think he'll groom you as some kind of successor?"

A question which sent Publius Sulla into slightly wine-soaked giggles. "*I?* Succeed *Sulla?* Ye gods, no! I, my dear Magnus, have no political ambitions whatsoever!"

"Are you in the Senate already?"

Catilina stepped into the breach. "We're both summoned by Sulla to attend meetings of the Senate, though he hasn't made us senators officially— yet. Publius Sulla and I just had a feeling you might need some young and friendly faces here today, so we came along to sample the eats and cheer you up."

"I'm very glad you did come," said Pompey gratefully.

"Don't let these haughty sticklers for the *mos maiorum* grind you down," said Catilina, clapping Pompey on the back. "Some of us were really delighted to see a young man triumph. You'll be in the Senate very soon, I can promise you that. Sulla intends to fill it with men whom the haughty sticklers do not approve of!''

And suddenly Pompey saw red. ''As far as I'm concerned,'' he said through his teeth, ''the Senate can disappear up its own fundamental orifice! I know what I intend to do with my life, and it does *not* include membership in the Senate! Before I'm done with that body—or enter it!—I mean to prove to it that it can't keep an outstanding man from any office or command he might decide he wants—as a knight, not a senator!''

One of Catilina's darkly slender eyebrows flew up, though Publius Sulla seemingly missed the significance of this remark.

Pompey gazed around the room, then beamed, his flash of temper gone. ''Ah! There he is! All alone on his couch too! Do come and eat with me and my brother-in-law Memmius! He's the best of good fellows!''

''You should be eating with all the haughty sticklers who unbent enough to come today,'' said Catilina. ''We'll quite understand, you know, if you join Metellus Pius and his friends. You leave us with Gaius Memmius and we'll be as happy as two elderly Peripatetics arguing about the function of a man's navel.''

''This is *my* triumphal feast, and I can eat with whomsoever I like,'' said Pompey.

At the beginning of April, Sulla published a list of two hundred new senators, promising that there would be more in the months to come. The name at the top was that of Gnaeus Pompeius Magnus, who went to see Sulla immediately.

''I will not enter the Senate!'' he said angrily.

Sulla gazed at his visitor, astonished. ''Why? I would have thought you'd be breaking your neck to get in!''

The anger fled; self-preservation came to the fore as Pompey realized how Sulla would see this extraordinary departure from what Sulla thought of as Pompey's normal self; after all, he had been at some pains to build a certain image for Sulla. Cool, Magnus! Cool down and think this thing out. Find a reason Sulla will believe because it fits his idea of me. No! No! Give him a reason that fits his idea of himself!

''It's all to do,'' said the young man, gazing at Sulla in wide-eyed earnestness, ''with the lesson you taught me over that wretched triumph.'' He drew a breath. ''I've had a good think since then, Lucius Cornelius. And I realize I'm too young, not educated enough. Please, Lucius Cornelius, let me find my own way into the Senate in my own good time. If I go in now,

I'll be laughed at for years." And that, thought Pompey, is very true! I'm not joining a body of men who will all smirk every time they set eyes on me. I'll join that body of men when their knees shake every time they set eyes on me.

Mollified, Sulla shrugged. "Have it your own way, Magnus."

"Thank you, I really would prefer to. I'll wait until I've done something they'll remember over elephants. Like a decent and conscientious quaestorship when I'm thirty."

That was a little too much; the pale eyes were now frankly amused, as if the mind behind them was reaching deeper into Pompey than Pompey wanted. But all Sulla said was, "A very good idea! I'll remove your name before I take my list to the Popular Assembly for ratification—I am going to have all my major laws ratified by the People, and I'll start with this one. But I want you in the House tomorrow just the same. It's fitting that all my legates of the war should hear the beginning. So make sure you're there."

Pompey was there.

"I will begin," said the Dictator in a strong voice, "by discussing Italy and the Italians. In accordance with my promises to the Italian leaders, I will see that every last Italian entitled is enrolled as a citizen of Rome in the proper way, with an equal distribution across the full spectrum of the thirty-five tribes. There can be no more attempts to cheat the Italian people of full suffrage by burying their votes in only a few selected tribes. I gave my word on the matter, and I will honor my word."

Sitting side by side on the middle tier, Hortensius and Catulus exchanged a significant glance; neither was a man who favored this massive concession to people who were not, when it was all boiled down, a Roman's bootlace.

Sulla shifted a little on his curule chair. "Regretfully, I find it impossible to honor my promise to distribute Rome's freedmen across the thirty-five tribes. They will have to remain enrolled in urban Esquilina or Suburana. I do this for one specific reason: to ensure that a man who owns thousands of slaves will not at any time in the future be tempted to free large numbers of them and thus overload his own rural tribe with freedman clients."

"Clever old Sulla!" said Catulus to Hortensius.

"Not much escapes him," said Hortensius under his breath. "It sounds as if he's heard that Marcus Crassus is going heavily into slaves, doesn't it?"

Sulla went on to discuss towns and lands. "Brundisium, a city which treated me and my men with the honor we deserved, will be rewarded by becoming exempt from all customs and excise duties."

"Phew!" said Catulus. "That little decree will make Brundisium the most popular port in Italy!"

The Dictator rewarded some districts but punished many more, though in varying degree; Praeneste suffered perhaps worst, though the lesser Sulmo was ordered razed to the ground, and Capua went back to its old status as well as losing every last *iugerum* of its lands to swell the Roman *ager publicus*.

Catulus only half-listened after Sulla began to drone an endless list of town names, to find himself rudely jerked back to the present by Hortensius's elbow in his ribs. "Quintus, he's talking about you!" said Hortensius.

" . . . Quintus Lutatius Catulus, my loyal follower, I hereby give the task of rebuilding the temple of Jupiter Optimus Maximus on the Capitol." The puckered lips drew back to display gum, and a derisive, spiteful gleam flickered in Sulla's eyes. "Most of the funds will come out of income generated from our new Roman *ager publicus,* but I also expect you, my dear Quintus Lutatius, to supplement this source from the depths of your private purse."

Jaw dropping, Catulus sat filled with an icy fear, for he understood that this was Sulla's way of punishing him for staying safely in Rome under Cinna and Carbo all those years.

"Our Pontifex Maximus, Quintus Caecilius Metellus Pius, is to restore the temple of Ops damaged in the same fire," Sulla went on smoothly. "However, this project must be entirely funded from the public purse, as Ops is the manifestation of Rome's public wealth. However, I do require that our Pontifex Maximus shall rededicate that temple himself when the work is finished."

"That ought to be stammering good fun!" said Hortensius.

"I have just published a list containing the names of two hundred men I have elevated to the Senate," Sulla continued, "though Gnaeus Pompeius Magnus has informed me that he does not wish to join the Senate at this time. His name has been deleted."

That caused sufficient sensation to stir the whole House; all eyes turned to Pompey, who sat alone near the doors looking very comfortable with himself, and smiling demurely.

"I intend to add a further hundred or so men to the Senate in the future, which will bring total membership up to about four hundred, so many senators have we lost over the past decade."

"You wouldn't think he'd killed any of them, would you?" asked Catulus of Hortensius with a snap. How could he possibly find the huge sums he suspected would be required of his private purse in order to rebuild the Great Temple?

The Dictator proceeded. "I have tried to find my new members of the Senate from among senatorial families, though I have included knights of hitherto unsenatorial family, provided their bloodlines do the Senate honor.

You will find no mushrooms growing on my list! However, in relation to one kind of new senator, I pass over all qualifications, from the completely unofficial census of one million sesterces to a suitable family background. I am referring to soldiers of exceptional valor. I intend that Rome should honor all such men as she did in the days of Marcus Fabius Buteo. Of recent generations we have entirely ignored the military hero. Well, I will see an end to that! If any man should win a Grass Crown or a Civic Crown, no matter who or what his antecedents, he will automatically enter the Senate. In this way, the little new blood I have permitted the Senate will at least be brave blood! And I would hope that there will be fine old names among the winners of our major crowns: it should not be left to newcomers to earn accolades as our bravest men!"

Hortensius grunted. "That's a fairly popular edict."

But Catulus could get no further than the financial burden Sulla had laid upon him, and merely rolled a pair of piteous eyes at his brother-in-law.

"One further thing, and I will dismiss this assemblage," Sulla said. "Each man on my list of new senators will be presented to the Assembly of the People, patrician as well as plebeian, and I will require of that body that he be voted in." He got to his feet. "The meeting is now concluded."

"How am I going to find enough money?" wailed Catulus to Hortensius as they hurried out of the Curia Hostilia.

"Don't find it," said Hortensius coolly.

"I'll have to!"

"He's going to die, Quintus. Until he does, you'll have to adopt delaying tactics. After he dies, who cares? Let the State find every sestertius of the money."

"It's all due to the *flamen Dialis*!" said Catulus savagely. "He caused the fire—let him pay for the new Great Temple!"

The fine legal mind of Hortensius found issue with this; its owner frowned. "You'd better not be heard saying that! The *flamen Dialis* cannot be held responsible for a mischance phenomenon unless he has been charged and tried in a court of law, as with any other priest. Sulla hasn't explained why the young fellow has apparently fled from Rome, but he hasn't proscribed him. Nor has a charge been laid against him."

"He's Sulla's nephew by marriage!"

"Exactly, my dear Quintus."

"Oh, brother-in-law, why do we bother with all this? There are times when I long to gather up all my money, sell my estates, and move to Cyrenaica," said Catulus.

"We bother because we have the birthright," said Hortensius.

* * *

New senators and old gathered two days later to hear Sulla announce that he intended to abolish the election of censors, at least for the time being; the way he would reorganize the State's finances, he explained, would make it unnecessary to call for contracts, and no census of the people would be of value for at least another decade.

"At that point you may re-examine the matter of censors," said the Dictator grandly. "I do not presume to legislate the censors completely out of existence."

He would, however, do something special for the men of his own order, the Patriciate. "Over the centuries which have passed since the original plebeian revolt," he said, "patrician rank has come to mean very little. The only advantage a patrician possesses over a plebeian these days is that he can assume certain religious offices barred to plebeians. I do not consider this worthy of the *mos maiorum*. A man born a patrician goes back to before the Kings in a clean, clear line. The mere fact that he exists shows that his family has served Rome for more than half a millennium. I think it fair in light of this that the patrician must enjoy *some* special honor— minor perhaps, but exclusive to him. I am therefore going to allow the patrician to stand for curule office—both praetor and consul—two years ahead of the plebeian."

"What he means, of course, is that he's looking after his own," said the plebeian Marcus Junius Brutus to his wife Servilia, a patrician.

Servilia had found her husband slightly more communicative in these peril-fraught days. Ever since the news came that her father-in-law had died off Lilybaeum as a result of the Dictator's house pet Pompey's cleaning-up operations, Brutus had lived on a hairline. Would his father be proscribed? Would he be proscribed? As the son of a proscribed man he could inherit nothing, would lose everything; and if he himself were proscribed, he would lose his life. But Old Brutus's name had not been among the forty proscribed senators, and no more senatorial names had been published since that first list. Brutus hoped the danger was over—but he couldn't be sure. *No one* could be sure! Sulla dropped hints.

That he was less aloof toward Servilia was due to his sudden appreciation of the fact that it was probably his marriage to her that had kept the Marcus Junius Brutus name off Sulla's lists. This new honor Sulla was providing for patricians was just one more way in which Sulla was saying that the patrician was special, due more honors than the richest and most powerful plebeian of a consular family. And among the Patriciate, what name was more august than Servilius Caepio?

"It is a pity," said Servilia now, "that our son cannot have patrician status."

"My name is sufficiently old and revered for our son," said Brutus stiffly. "We Junii Bruti are descended from the founder of the Republic."

"I've always found it odd," said Servilia coolly, "that if that is really so, the present-day Junii Bruti are not patrician. For the founder of the Republic certainly was. You always talk of an expedient adoption into a plebeian family, but a plebeian family called Junius Brutus must have been descended from a slave or a peasant belonging to the patrician family."

This speech, which Brutus felt himself obliged to swallow, was one more indication that Servilia was no longer a silent and compliant wife. Her fear of divorce had lessened, and her sense of power had correspondingly grown. The child in the nursery, now two years old, meant everything to her. Whereas the child's father meant nothing. That she intended to preserve her husband's status was purely because of her son. But that didn't mean she had to bow and scrape to Brutus as she had in the days before the old man's treason had threatened everything.

"Your younger sister will do superbly," said Brutus with a slight tinge of malice. "A patrician married to another patrician! She and Drusus Nero can't go wrong."

"Drusus Nero is a plebeian," said Servilia haughtily. "He may have been born a Claudian, but my uncle Drusus adopted him. He is a Livian, with rank no greater than yours."

"I predict he'll prosper all the same."

"Drusus Nero is twenty years old, and has about a medicine spoon of intelligence. Why, our son is more capable at two!" said Servilia tartly.

Brutus eyed her warily; it had not been lost upon him that his wife's attachment to little Brutus was phenomenal. To say the least. A lioness!

"Anyway," said Brutus pacifically, "Sulla will continue to tell us what he means to do the day after tomorrow."

"Have you any idea what he's going to do?"

"Not until the day after tomorrow."

The day after tomorrow saw Sulla tackling elections and elected offices with an expression on his face that did not brook argument. "I am tired of haphazard electoral scrambles," he said, "and will legislate a proper procedure. In future, all elections will be held in Quinctilis, which is five to six months earlier than an elected man takes office. During the waiting period, the curule men will assume a new importance in the House. Consuls-elect will be asked to speak immediately after consuls in office, and praetors-elect immediately after praetors in office. From now on the Princeps Senatus, ex-censors and consulars will not speak until after the last praetor-elect. It is a plain waste of the House's time to listen to men who have passed beyond office ahead of men occupying it or in transition toward occupying it.''

All eyes had turned to Flaccus Princeps Senatus, sharply demoted by this edict, but he sat blinking gently, apparently not at all put out.

Sulla continued. ''The curule elections in the Centuriate Assembly will be held first, on the day before the Ides of Quinctilis. Then will follow the elections for quaestors, curule aediles, tribunes of the soldiers and other minor positions in the Assembly of the People ten days before the Kalends of Sextilis. And finally the plebeian elections in the Plebeian Assembly will be held on a date between two and six days before the Kalends.''

''Not too bad,'' said Hortensius to Catulus. ''We'll all know our electoral fates well before the end of the year.''

''And enjoy a new prominence,'' said Catulus, pleased.

''Now to the offices themselves,'' said Sulla. ''After I've personally finished adding the names of new senators to this distinguished body, I intend to close the door. From then on, the only entrance will be through the office of quaestor, which a man will stand for in his thirtieth year, no earlier. There will be twenty quaestors elected each year, a sufficient number to offset senatorial deaths and keep the House plump. There are two minor exceptions which will not affect overall numbers: a man elected tribune of the plebs who is not already a senator will continue to enter the Senate through this office. And a man who has been awarded the Grass Crown or the Civic Crown will be promoted to the Senate automatically.''

He shifted a little, looked at his mute flock. ''I will see eight praetors elected every year. A plebeian man will not be able to seek election as praetor until his thirty-ninth year, but a patrician man two years sooner, as already said. There will be a two-year wait between a man's election as praetor and his election as consul. No man will be able to stand for consul unless he has already been praetor. And I will restate the *lex Genucia* in the strongest terms, making it impossible for any man—patrician or plebeian!—to stand for consul a second time until after ten full years have elapsed. I will have no more Gaius Mariuses!''

And that, everyone thought, was an excellent thing!

But when Sulla introduced his legislation to cancel the powers of the tribunes of the plebs, approval was not so general or so strong. Over the centuries of the Republic, the tribunes of the plebs had gradually arrogated more and more legislative business unto themselves, and turned that Assembly which contained only plebeians into the most powerful of the lawmaking bodies. Often the main objective of the tribunes of the plebs had been to handicap the largely unwritten powers of the Senate, and to render the consuls less essential.

"That," said Sulla in tones of great satisfaction, "is now all finished with. In future, tribunes of the plebs will retain little except their right to exercise the *ius auxilii ferendi*."

A huge stir; the House murmured and moved restlessly, then frowned and looked bleak.

"I will see the Senate supreme!" Sulla thundered. "To do that, I must render the tribunate of the plebs impotent—and I will! Under my new laws, no man who has been a tribune of the plebs will be able to hold any magistracy after it—he will not be able to become aedile or praetor or consul or censor! Nor will he be able to hold office as a tribune of the plebs for a second time until ten years have elapsed. He will be able to exercise the *ius auxilii ferendi* only in its original way, by rescuing an individual member of the Plebs from the clutches of a single magistrate. No tribune of the plebs will be able to call a law threatening the Plebs as a whole a part of that right! Or call a duly convened court a part of that right."

Sulla's eyes rested thoughtfully upon, oddly enough, two men who could not hold the office of tribune of the plebs because they were patricians—Catilina and Lepidus.

"The right of the tribune of the plebs to veto," he went on, "will be severely curtailed. He will not be able to veto senatorial decrees, laws carrying senatorial approval, the right of the Senate to appoint provincial governors or military commanders, nor the right of the Senate to deal with foreign affairs. No tribune of the plebs will be allowed to promulgate a law in the Plebeian Assembly unless it has been authorized first by the Senate in passing a *senatus consultum*. He will no longer have the power to summon meetings of the Senate."

There were many glum faces, quite a few angry ones; Sulla paused rather stagily to see if anyone was going to protest audibly. But no one did. He cleared his throat. "What do you have to say, Quintus Hortensius?"

Hortensius swallowed. "I concur, Lucius Cornelius."

"Does anyone not concur?"

Silence.

"Good!" said Sulla brightly. "Then this *lex Cornelia* will go into law forthwith!"

"It's horrific," said Lepidus to Gaius Cotta afterward.

"I couldn't agree more."

"Then why," demanded Catulus, "did we lie down under it so tamely?

Why did we let him get away with it? How can the Republic be a genuine Republic without an active and properly constituted tribunate of the plebs?"

"Why," asked Hortensius fiercely, taking this as a direct criticism of his own cowardice, "did *you* not speak out, then?"

"Because," said Catulus frankly, "I like my head right where it is—firmly attached to my shoulders."

"And that about sums it up," said Lepidus.

"I can see," said Metellus Pius, joining the group, "the logic behind it—how clever he's been! A lesser man would simply have abolished the office, but not he! He hasn't tampered with the *ius auxilii ferendi*. What he's done is to pare away the powers added on in later times. So he can successfully argue that he's working well within the framework of the *mos maiorum*—and that has been his theme in everything. Mind you, I don't think this can possibly work. The tribunate of the plebs matters too much to too many."

"It will last as long as he lives," said Cotta grimly.

Upon which note, the party broke up. No one was very happy—but on the other hand, nor did anyone really want to pour his secret thoughts and feelings into another man's ear. Too dangerous!

Which just went to show, thought Metellus Pius as he walked home alone, that Sulla's climate of terror was working.

By the time Apollo's games came round early in Quinctilis, these first laws had been joined by two more: a *lex Cornelia sumptuaria* and a *lex Cornelia frumentaria*. The sumptuary law was extremely strict, even going so far as to fix a ceiling of thirty sesterces per head on ordinary meals, and three hundred per head on banquets. Luxuries like perfumes, foreign wines, spices and jewelry were heavily taxed; the cost of funerals and tombs was limited; and Tyrian purple carried an enormous duty. The grain law was reactionary in the extreme. It abolished the sale of cheap grain by the State, though Sulla was far too shrewd to forbid the State to sell grain; his law just said that the State could not undercut the private grain merchants.

A heavy program, by no means ended. Perhaps because the onerous task of preparing all this legislation had been going on without let since just after Sulla's triumph, the Dictator decided on the spur of the moment to take a few days off and attend the *ludi Apollinares,* celebrated during early Quinctilis. The events held in the Circus Maximus were not what he wanted to see, of course; he wanted to go to the plays, of which a good ten or eleven had been scheduled in the temporary wooden theater erected within the space of the Circus Flaminius on the Campus Martius. Comedy reigned. Plautus, Terence and Naevius were well represented, but there were several mimes listed too, and these were always Sulla's favorites. True comedy contained written lines which could not be deviated from, but the mime was just a stock situation upon which the cast and its director extrapolated their own lines, and played without masks.

Perhaps it was his interlude with Aurelia's delegation led to his whole-hearted participation in the plays put on during Apollo's games; or perhaps the fact that one of his ancestors had founded Apollo's games made him decide he must show himself; or was it a need to set eyes upon the actor Metrobius? Thirty years! Could it really be that long? Metrobius had been a lad, Sulla celebrating his thirtieth birthday in bitter frustration. Since his entry into the Senate three years afterward, their meetings had been few and far apart, and filled with torment.

Sulla's decision to deny that part of himself had been considered, obdurate, firmly based in logic. Those men in public life who admitted to—or succumbed to—a preference for their own sex were damned for it. No law compelled them to retire, though there were several laws on the tablets, including a *lex Scantinia* which demanded a death penalty; mostly they were not used, for there was a certain tolerance in fair men. The reality was more subtle, need not even retard the public career if the man was able. It consisted in amusement, contempt, liberal applications of wit and pun and sarcasm, and it diminished a man's *dignitas* drastically. Some men who ought to be his peers would always regard him as their inferior because of it. And that to Sulla made it something he couldn't have, no matter how badly he wanted it—and he wanted it badly. His hopes were pinned on his eventual retirement—after which, he told himself, he didn't care one iota what men said of him. He would come into his own, he would grab eagerly at a personal reward. His accomplishments at his retirement would be tangible and formidable, his *dignitas* accumulated over the length of his public career too cemented to be diminished by an old man's last sexual fling.

But oh, he longed for Metrobius! Who probably wouldn't be interested in an old and ugly man. That too had contributed to his decision to go to the plays. Better to find out now than when the time came to retire. Better to feast his worsening eyes upon this beloved object while he could still see.

There were several companies taking part in the festival, including the one now led by Metrobius, who had changed from acting in tragedies to formal comedy some ten years ago. His group was not scheduled to perform until the third day, but Sulla was there on the first and second days, devoted to mime, and enjoyed himself enormously.

Dalmatica came with him, though she couldn't sit with the men, as she could at the Circus; a rigid hierarchy had been established in the theater, plays not being quite approved of in Roman society. Women, it was felt, might be corrupted if they sat with men to watch so much immorality and nudity. The two front rows of seating in the semicircular, tiered *cavea* were reserved for members of the Senate, and the fourteen rows just behind had used to be reserved for the knights of the Public Horse. This privilege had been conferred on the senior knights by Gaius Gracchus. And it had afforded Sulla intense pleasure to take it away. Thus all knights were now forced to battle for seats among their inferiors on a first-come, first-served basis. The few women who attended sat right up the top at the back of the *cavea;* they could hear well enough, but had difficulty in seeing anything titillating on the stage. In formal comedy (such as Metrobius played), no women were included in the fully masked cast, but in the mimes from Atella female roles were played by women, and nobody was masked; quite often, nobody was clothed.

The third day's play was by Plautus, and a favorite: *The Vainglorious Soldier*. The starring role was taken by Metrobius—how foolish! All Sulla could see of his face was the grotesque covering with its gaping mouth curving up in a ridiculous smile, though the hands were there, and the neat, muscular body looked well in its Greek armor. Of course at the end the cast took their bows with masks off; Sulla was finally able to see what the years had done to Metrobius. Very little, though the crisp black hair was exquisitely sprinkled with white, and there was a deepening fissure on either side of the straight, high-bridged Greek nose.

He couldn't weep, not there in the very middle of the front row upon his cushioned section of the wooden seat. But he wanted to, had to fight not to. The face was too far away, separated from him by the vacant half-moon of the orchestra, and he couldn't see the eyes. Oh, he could distinguish two black pools, but not what they held. Not even whether they rested on him, or on some current lover three rows behind. Mamercus was with Sulla; he turned to his son-in-law and said, voice a little constricted,

"Ask the man who played the *miles gloriosus* to come down, would you? I have a feeling I used to know him, but I'm not sure. Anyway, I'd like to congratulate him in person."

The audience was vacating the temporary wooden structure, and the women present were wending their way toward their spouses if they were respectable women, or trolling for business if they were prostitutes. Carefully escorted by Chrysogonus—and very carefully avoided by those in the audience who recognized them—Dalmatica and Cornelia Sulla joined the Dictator and Mamercus just as Metrobius, still in armor, finally arrived before Sulla.

"You did very well, actor," said the Dictator.

Metrobius smiled to reveal that he still had perfect teeth. "I was delighted to see you in the audience, Lucius Cornelius."

"You were a client of mine once, am I right?"

"Indeed I was. You released me from my cliental obligations just before you went to the war against Mithridates," said the actor, eyes giving nothing away.

"Yes, I remember that. You warned me of the charges one Censorinus would try to bring against me. Just before my son died." The wrecked face squeezed up, straightened with an effort. "Before I was consul, it was."

"A happy chance that I could warn you," said Metrobius.

"A lucky one for me."

"You were always one of Fortune's favorites."

The theater was just about empty; weary of these continuing platitudes, Sulla swung to face the women and Mamercus.

"Go home," he said abruptly. "I wish to talk with my old client for a while."

Dalmatica (who had not been looking well of recent days) seemed fascinated with the Greek thespian, and stood with her eyes fixed on his face. Then Chrysogonus intruded himself into her reverie; she started, turned away to follow the pair of gigantic German slaves whose duty it was to clear a path for the Dictator's wife wherever she went.

Sulla and Metrobius were left alone to follow too far behind for anyone to think they belonged to the same party. Under normal circumstances the Dictator would have been approached by clients and petitioners, but such was his luck that no one did approach.

"Just this stroll," Sulla said. "I ask nothing more."

"Ask what you will," said Metrobius.

Sulla stopped. "Stand here in front of me, Metrobius, and see what time and illness have done. The position hasn't changed. But even if it had, I am no use to you or to anyone else except these poor silly women who persist in—oh, who knows? Pitying me, in all probability. I don't think it can be love."

"Of course it's love!" He was close now, close enough for Sulla to see that the eyes still held love, still looked at him with tenderness. And with a dynamic kind of interest unspoiled by disgust or revulsion. A softer, more personal version of the way Aurelia had looked at him in Teanum Sidicinum. "Sulla, those of us who have once fallen under your spell can never be free of you! Women or men, there is no difference. You are unique. After you, all others pale. It's not a matter of virtue or goodness." Metrobius smiled. "You have neither! Maybe no great man is virtuous. Or good. Perhaps a man rich in those qualities by definition is barred from greatness. I have forgotten all my Plato, so I am not sure what he and Socrates have to say about it."

Out of the corner of his eye Sulla noticed Dalmatica turn back to stare in his direction, but what her face displayed he could not tell at the distance. Then she went round the corner, and was gone.

"Does what you say mean," asked the Dictator, "that if I am allowed to put down this present burden, you would consider living with me until I die? My time grows short, but I hope at least some of it will be mine alone to spend without consideration of Rome. If you would go with me into retirement, I promise you would not suffer in any way—least of all financially."

A laugh, a shake of the curly dark head. "Oh, Sulla! How can you buy what you have owned for thirty years?"

The tears welled, were blinked away. "Then when I retire, you will come with me?"

"I will."

"When the time comes I'll send for you."

"Tomorrow? Next year?"

"Not for a long while. Perhaps two years. You'll wait?"

"I'll wait."

Sulla heaved a sigh of almost perfect happiness: too short, too short! For he remembered that each time he had seen Metrobius on those last occasions, someone he loved had died. Julilla. His son. Who would it be this time? But, he thought, I do not care. Because Metrobius matters more. Except for my son, and he is gone. Only let it be Cornelia Sulla. Or the twins. Let it not be Dalmatica! He nodded curtly to Metrobius as if this had been the most trivial of encounters, and walked away.

Metrobius stood watching his retreating back, filled with happiness. It was true then what the little local gods of his half-remembered home in Arcadia said: if a man wanted something badly enough, he would get it in the end. And the dearer the price, the greater the reward. Only when Sulla had disappeared did he turn back toward the dressing rooms.

Sulla walked slowly, completely alone; that in itself was a seldom experienced luxury. How could he find the strength to wait for Metrobius? Not a boy any longer, but always *his* boy.

He could hear voices in the distance and slowed even more, unwilling that anyone should see his face just yet. For though his heart hoped and acknowledged a premonitory joy, there was anger in him because of this joyless task he still must finish, and fear in him that it might be Dalmatica to die.

The two voices were louder now, and one of them floated high above the other. He knew it well. Odd, how distinctive a man's voice was! No two alike, once one got past superficial similarities of pitch and accent. This speaker could be no one save Manius Acilius Glabrio, who was his step-daughter Aemilia Scaura's husband.

"He really is the outside of enough," said Glabrio now, in tones both forceful and aristocratically languid. "Thirteen thousand talents his proscriptions have put into the Treasury, and he *boasts* of it! The truth is, he ought to hang his head in shame! The sum should have been ten times as much! Properties worth millions knocked down for a few thousands, his own wife the proud owner of fifty millions in big estates bought for fifty thousands— it's a disgrace!"

"I hear you've profited yourself, Glabrio," said another familiar voice— that belonging to Catilina.

"A trifle only, and not more than my due. Frightful old villain! How dared he have the audacity to say the proscriptions would end on the Kalends of last month—the names are still going up on the rostra every time one of his minions or his relatives covets another luscious slice of Campania or the seashore! Did you notice him remain behind to have a chat to the fellow played the vainglorious soldier? He can't resist the stage—or the riffraff who strut across it! That goes back to his youth, of course, when he was no better than the most vulgar strumpet who ever hawked her fork outside Venus Erucina's! I suppose he's worth a laugh or two among the pansies when they get together to see who is on which end today. Have you ever seen a daisy chain of pansies? Sulla's seen plenty!"

"Be careful what you say, Glabrio," said Catilina, sounding a little uneasy. "You too could wind up proscribed."

But Glabrio laughed heartily. "Not I!" he cried gleefully. "I'm part of the family, I'm Dalmatica's son-in-law! Even Sulla can't proscribe a member of the family, you know."

The voices faded as the two men moved off, but Sulla stayed where he was, just around the corner. All movement had stilled in him, and the ice-cold eyes glowed eerily. So that was what they said, was it? After all these years too . . . Of course Glabrio was privy to much Rome was not—but clearly Rome would soon be privy to everything Glabrio imagined or knew. How much was idle gossip, how much the opportunity to read documents and papers filed away year by year? Sulla was in the throes of collecting all his written evidence against the day of his retirement, for he intended to author his memoirs, as Catulus Caesar had done ten years earlier. So there were plenty of bits and pieces lying around, it wouldn't have taken any great talent to unearth them. Glabrio! Why hadn't he thought of Glabrio, always in and out of his house? Not every member of that privileged visiting circle was a Cornelia Sulla or a Mamercus! Glabrio! And who else?

The ashes of his anger at having to continue to hold Metrobius at arm's length tumbled onto a fresh conflagration within Sulla's mind and fueled it sourly, relentlessly. So, he thought as he picked up his feet and began to walk again, I cannot proscribe a member of my own family, eh? I cannot, he's right about that. Yet—need it be proscription? Might there not be a better way?

Round the corner he came, straight into the arms of Pompey. Both men stepped back, reeling a little.

"What, Magnus, on your own?" asked Sulla.

"Sometimes," said Pompey, falling into step alongside the Dictator, "it's a pleasure to be alone."

"I heartily concur. But don't tell me you tire of Varro!"

"Too much Varro can be a pain in the *podex,* especially when he starts prating on about Cato the Censor and the old ways and when money had real value. Though I'd rather hear Varro on those topics than on invisible fingers of power," grinned Pompey.

"That's right, I'd forgotten he was a friend of poor old Appius Claudius's," said Sulla, rather glad that if in his present mood he had to collide with anyone, it had turned out to be Pompey. "I wonder why we all think of Appius Claudius as so old?"

Pompey chuckled. "Because he was born old! But you are out of touch, Sulla! Appius Claudius is quite eclipsed these days. There's a new man in town—name of Publius Nigidius Figulus. A proper sophist. Or do I mean Pythagorean?" He shrugged casually. "No use, I never can keep one sort of philosopher distinct from all the others."

"Publius Nigidius Figulus! It's an old and hallowed name, but I hadn't heard of the genuine article raising his head in Rome. Is he a bucolic gentleman, perhaps?"

"Not a hayseed, if that's what you're asking. More a gourd half-full of peas—rattle, rattle . . . He's a great expert on Etruscan soothsaying, from lightning to livers. Knows more lobes in that organ than I know figures of speech."

"How many figures of speech do you know, Magnus?" asked Sulla, highly diverted.

"Two, I think. Or is it three?"

"Name them."

"*Color* and *descriptio*."

"Two."

"Two."

They walked on in silence for a moment, both smiling, but at different thoughts entirely.

"So how does it feel to be a knight when they don't have special seats at the theater anymore?" demanded Sulla.

"I'm not complaining," said Pompey blithely. "I never go to the theater."

"Oh. Where have you been today, then?"

"Out to the Via Recta. Just for a good walk, you know. I get very hamstrung in Rome. Don't like the place."

"On your own here?"

"More or less. Left the wife behind in Picenum." He pulled a sour face.

"Not to your liking, Magnus?"

"Oh, she'll do until something better comes along. Adores me! Just not good enough, is all."

"Well, well! It's an aedilician family."

"I come from a consular family. So ought my wife."

"Then divorce her and find a consular wife."

"Hate making small talk, to women or their fathers."

At that precise moment a blinding inspiration came to Sulla, who stopped dead in the middle of the lane leading from the Velabrum to the Vicus Tuscus just below the Palatine. "Ye gods!" he gasped. "Ye gods!"

Pompey stopped too. "Yes?" he asked politely.

"My dear young knight, I have had a brilliant idea!"

"That's nice."

"Oh, stop mouthing platitudes! I'm thinking!"

Pompey obediently said nothing further, while Sulla's lips worked in and out upon his toothless gums like a swimming jellyfish. Then out came Sulla's hand, fixed itself on Pompey's arm.

"Magnus, come and see me tomorrow morning at the third hour," he said, gave a gleeful skip, and departed at a run.

Pompey remained where he was, brow furrowed. Then he too began to walk, not toward the Palatine but toward the Forum; his house was on the Carinae.

Home went Sulla as if pursued by the Furies; here was a task he was really going to enjoy performing!

"Chrysogonus, Chrysogonus!" he bellowed in the doorway as his toga fell behind him like a collapsing tent.

In came the steward, looking anxious—something he did quite often of late, had Sulla only noticed. Which he didn't.

"Chrysogonus, take a litter and go to Glabrio's house. I want Aemilia Scaura here at once."

"Lucius Cornelius, you came home without your lictors!"

"Oh, I dismissed them before the play began—sometimes they're a wretched nuisance," said the Dictator impenitently. "Now go and pick up my stepdaughter!"

"Aemilia? What do you want her for?" asked Dalmatica as she came into the room.

"You'll find out," said Sulla, grinning.

His wife paused, stared at him searchingly. "You know, Lucius Cornelius, ever since your interview with Aurelia and her delegation, you've been different."

"In what way?"

This she found difficult to answer, perhaps because she was reluctant to provoke displeasure in him, but finally she said, "In your mood, I think."

"For better or for worse, Dalmatica?"

"Oh, better. You're—*happy*."

"I am that," he said in a happy voice. "I had lost sight of a private future, but she gave it back to me. Oh, what a time I'm going to have after I retire!"

"The actor fellow today—Metrobius. He's a friend."

Something in her eyes gave him pause; his carefree feeling vanished immediately, and an image of Julilla lying with his sword in her belly swam into his mind, actually blotted Dalmatica's face from his gaze. Not another wife who wouldn't share him, surely! How did she know? What could she know? Did they *smell* it?

"I've known Metrobius since he was a boy," he said curtly, his tone not inviting her to enquire further.

"Then why did you pretend you didn't know him before he came down from the stage?" she asked, frowning.

"He was wearing a mask until the end of the play!" Sulla snapped. "It's been a good many years, I wasn't sure." Fatal! She had maneuvered him to the defensive, and he didn't like it.

"Yes, of course," she said slowly. "Yes, of course."

"Go away, Dalmatica, do! I've frittered away too much of my time since the games began, I have work waiting."

She turned to go, looking less perturbed.

"One more thing," he said to her back.

"Yes?"

"I shall need you when your daughter arrives, so don't go out or otherwise make yourself unavailable."

How peculiar he was of late! she thought, walking through the vast atrium toward the peristyle garden and her own suite of rooms. Touchy, happy, labile. Up one moment, down the next. As if he had made some decision he couldn't implement at once, he who loathed procrastination. And that fine-looking actor . . . What sort of place did he occupy in Sulla's scheme of things? He mattered; though how, she didn't know. Had there been even a superficial resemblance, she would have concluded that he was Sulla's son—such were the emotions she had sensed in her husband, whom she knew by now very well.

Thus it was that when Chrysogonus came to inform her that Aemilia Scaura had arrived, Dalmatica had not even begun to think further about why Sulla had summoned the girl.

Aemilia Scaura was in her fourth month of pregnancy, and had developed the sheen of skin and clearness of eye which some women did—no bouts of sickness here! A pity perhaps that she had taken after her father, and in consequence was short of stature and a little dumpy of figure, but there were saving echoes of her mother in her face, and she had inherited Scaurus's beautiful, vividly green eyes.

Not an intelligent girl, she had never managed to reconcile herself to her mother's marriage to Sulla, whom she both feared and disliked. It had been bad enough during the early years, when her brief glimpses of him had shown someone at least attractive enough to make her mother's passion for him understandable; but after his illness had so changed him for the worse she couldn't even begin to see why her mother apparently felt no less passionately about him. How could any woman continue to love such an ugly, horrible old man? She remembered her own father, of course, and he too had been old and ugly. But not with Sulla's internal rot; though she had neither the perception nor the wit thus to describe it.

Now here she was summoned into his presence, and with no more notice than to leave a hasty message for Glabrio in her wake. Her stepfather greeted her with pats of her hand and a solicitous settling on a comfortable chair—actions which set her teeth on edge and made her fear many things. Just what was he up to? He was jam-full of glee and as pregnant with mischief as she was with child.

When her mother came in the whole business of hand pats and solicitous settlings began all over again, until, it seemed to the girl, he had arranged some sort of mood and anticipation in them that would make whatever he intended to do more enjoyable to him. For this was not unimportant. This was going to matter.

"And how's the little Glabrio on the way?" he asked his stepdaughter, nicely enough.

"Very well, Lucius Cornelius."

"When is the momentous event?"

"Near the end of the year, Lucius Cornelius."

"Hmmm! Awkward! That's still a good way off."

"Yes, Lucius Cornelius, it is still a good way off."

He sat down and drummed his fingers upon the solid oaken back of his chair, lips pursed, looking into the distance. Then the eyes which frightened her so much became fixed upon her; Aemilia Scaura shivered.

"Are you happy with Glabrio?" he asked suddenly.

She jumped. "Yes, Lucius Cornelius."

"The truth, girl! I want the truth!"

"I am happy, Lucius Cornelius, I am truly happy!"

"Would you have picked somebody else had you been able?"

A blush welled up beneath her skin, her gaze dropped. "I had formed no other attachment, Lucius Cornelius, if that's what you mean. Manius Acilius was acceptable to me."

"Is he still acceptable?"

"Yes, yes!" Her voice held an edge of desperation. "Why do you keep asking? I am happy! I am happy!"

"That's a pity," said Lucius Cornelius Sulla.

Dalmatica sat up straight. "Husband, what is all this?" she demanded. "What are you getting at with these questions?"

"I am indicating, wife, that I am not pleased at the union between your daughter and Manius Acilius Glabrio. He deems it safe to criticize me because he is a member of my family," said Sulla, his anger showing. "A sign, of course, that I cannot possibly permit him to continue being a member of my family. I am divorcing him from your daughter. Immediately."

Both women gasped; Aemilia Scaura's eyes filled with tears.

"Lucius Cornelius, I am expecting his child! I cannot divorce him!" she cried.

"You can, you know," the Dictator said in conversational tones. "You can do anything I tell you to do. And I am telling you that you will divorce

Glabrio at once.'' He clapped his hands to summon the secretary called
Flosculus, who entered with a paper in his hand. Sulla took it, nodded dis-
missal. "Come over here, girl. Sign it."

Aemilia Scaura sprang to her feet. "No!"

Dalmatica also rose. "Sulla, you are unjust!" she said, lips thin. "My
daughter doesn't want to divorce her husband."

The monster showed. "It is absolutely immaterial to me what your
daughter wants," he said. "Over here, girl! And sign."

"No! I won't, I won't!"

He was out of his chair so quickly neither woman actually saw him
move. The fingers of his right hand locked in a vise around Aemilia Scaura's
mouth and literally dragged her to her feet, squealing in pain, weeping frantically.

"Stop, stop!" shouted Dalmatica, struggling to prise those fingers away.
"Please, I beg of you! Leave her be! She's with child, you can't hurt her!"

His fingers squeezed harder and harder. "Sign," he said.

She couldn't answer, and her mother had passed beyond speech.

"Sign," said Sulla again, softly. "Sign or I'll kill you, girl, with as
little concern as I felt when I killed Carbo's legates. What do I care that
you're stuffed full with Glabrio's brat? It would suit me if you lost it! Sign
the bill of divorcement, Aemilia, or I'll lop off your breasts and carve the
womb right out of you!"

She signed, still screaming. Then Sulla threw her away in contempt.
"There, that's better," he said, wiping her saliva from his hand. "Don't
ever make me angry again, Aemilia. It is not wise. Now go."

Dalmatica gathered the girl against her, and the look of loathing she
gave Sulla was without precedent, a genuine first. He saw it, but seemed
indifferent, turned his back upon them.

In her own rooms Dalmatica found herself with an hysterical girl on her
hands and a huge burden of anger to deal with. Both took some time to calm.

"I have heard he could be like that, but I've never seen it for myself,"
she said when she was able. "Oh, Aemilia, I'm so sorry! I'll try to get him
to change his mind as soon as I can face him without wanting to tear his eyes
out of his head."

But the girl, not besotted, chopped the air with her hand. "No! No,
Mother, no. You'd only make things worse."

"What *could* Glabrio have done to provoke this?"

"Said something he ought not have. He doesn't like Sulla, I know that.
He keeps implying to me that Sulla likes men in ways men shouldn't."

Dalmatica went white. "But that's nonsense! Oh, Aemilia, how could

Glabrio be so foolish? You know what men are like! If they do not deserve that slur, they can behave like madmen!''

"I'm not so sure it is undeserved," said Aemilia Scaura as she held a cold wet towel to her face, where the marks of her stepfather's fingers were slowly changing from red-purple to purple-black. "I've always thought there was woman in him."

"My dear girl, I've been married to Lucius Cornelius for almost nine years," said Dalmatica, who seemed to be shrinking in size, "and I can attest that it is an infamy."

"All right, all right, have it your own way! I don't care what he is! I just hate him, the vile beast!"

"I'll try when I'm cooler, I promise."

"Save yourself more of his displeasure, Mother. He won't change his mind," said Aemilia Scaura. "It's my baby I'm worried about, it's my baby matters to me."

Dalmatica stared at her daughter painfully. "I can say the same thing."

The cold wet towel fell into Aemilia Scaura's lap. "Mother! You're pregnant too?"

"Yes. I haven't known for very long, but I'm sure."

"What will you do? Does he know?"

"He doesn't know. And I'll do nothing that might provoke him to divorce me."

"You've heard the tale of Aelia."

"Who hasn't?"

"Oh, Mother, that changes everything! I'll behave, I'll behave! He mustn't be given any excuse to divorce you!"

"Then we must hope," said Dalmatica wearily, "that he deals more kindly with your husband than he has with you."

"He'll deal more harshly."

"Not necessarily," said the wife who knew Sulla. "You were first to hand. Very often his first victim satisfies him. By the time Glabrio arrives to find out what's the matter, he may be calm enough to be merciful."

If he wasn't calm enough to be merciful, Sulla was at least drained of the worst of his anger at Glabrio's indiscreet words. And Glabrio was perceptive enough to see that blustering would only make his situation more perilous.

"There is no need for this, Lucius Cornelius," he said. "If I have offended you, I will strive mightily to remove the cause of that offense. I wouldn't put my wife's position in jeopardy, I assure you."

"Oh, your ex-wife is in no jeopardy," said Sulla, smiling mirthlessly.

"Aemilia Scaura—who *is* a member of my family!—is quite safe. But she cannot possibly stay married to a man who criticizes her stepfather and spreads stories about him that are manifest lies."

Glabrio wet his lips. "My tongue ran away with me."

"It runs away with you very often, I hear. That is your privilege, of course. But in future you'll let it without the insulation of claiming to be a member of my family. You'll let it and take your chances, just like everyone else. I haven't proscribed a senator since my first list. But there's nothing to stop my doing so. I honored you by appointing you to the Senate ahead of your thirtieth birthday, as I have a great many other young men of high family and illustrious forebears. Well, for the moment I will leave your name among the senators and will not attach it to the rostra. Whether in future I continue to be so clement depends on you, Glabrio. Your child is growing in the belly of my children's half sister, and that is the only protection you have. When it is born, I will send it to you. Now please go."

Glabrio went without another word. Nor did he inform any of his intimates of the circumstances behind his precipitate divorce. Nor the reasons why he felt it expedient to leave Rome for his country estates. His marriage to Aemilia Scaura had not mattered to him in an emotional way; she satisfied him, that was all. Birth, dowry, everything as it ought to be. With the years affection might have grown between them. It never would now, so much was sure. A small twinge of grief passed through him from time to time when he thought of her, mostly because his child would never know its mother.

What happened next did nothing to help heal the breach between Sulla and Dalmatica; Pompey came to see the Dictator the following morning, as directed.

"I have a wife for you, Magnus," said Sulla without delay.

There was a quality of sleepy lion about Pompey that stood him in good stead when things happened he wished to think about before acting or speaking. So he took time to ingest this piece of information, face open rather than guarded; but what was going on inside his mind he did not betray. Rather, thought Sulla, watching him closely, he just rolled over in some metaphorical sun to warm his other side, and licked his chops to remove a forgotten morsel from his whiskers. Languid but dangerous. Yes, best to tie him to the family— he was no Glabrio.

Finally, "How considerate of you, Dictator!" said Pompey. "Who might she be?"

This unconscious grammatical betrayal of his Picentine origins grated, but Sulla did not let it show. He said, "My stepdaughter, Aemilia Scaura.

Patrician. Of a family you couldn't better if you looked for a millennium. A dowry of two hundred talents. And proven to be fertile. She's pregnant to Glabrio. They were divorced yesterday. I realize it's a bit inconvenient for you to acquire a wife who is already expecting another man's child, but the begetting was virtuous. She's a good girl.''

That Pompey was not put off or put out by this news was manifest; he beamed foolishly. "Lucius Cornelius, dear Lucius Cornelius! I am delighted!''

"Good!'' said Sulla briskly.

"May I see her? I don't think I ever have!''

A faint grin came and went across the Dictator's face as he thought of the bruises about Aemilia Scaura's mouth; he shook his head. "Give it two or three market intervals, Magnus, then come back and I'll marry you to her. In the meantime I'll make sure every sestertius of her dowry is returned, and keep her here with me.''

"Wonderful!'' cried Pompey, transported. "Does she know?''

"Not yet, but it will please her very much. She's been secretly in love with you ever since she saw you triumph,'' lied Sulla blandly.

That shot penetrated the lion's hide! Pompey almost burst with gratification. "Oh, glorious!'' he said, and departed looking like a very well-fed feline indeed.

Which left Sulla to break the news to his wife and her daughter. A chore he found himself not averse to doing. Dalmatica had been looking at him very differently since this business had blown up out of a tranquillity almost nine years old, and he disliked her disliking him; as a result, he needed to hurt her.

The two women were together in Dalmatica's sitting room, and froze when Sulla walked in on them unannounced. His first action was to study Aemilia Scaura's face, which was badly bruised and swollen below her nose. Only then did he look at Dalmatica. No anger or revulsion emanated from her this morning, though her dislike of him was there in her eyes, rather cold. She seemed, he thought, ill. Then reflected that women often took refuge in genuine illnesses when their emotions were out of sorts.

"Good news!'' he said jovially.

To which they gave him no reply.

"I have a new husband for you, Aemilia.''

Shocked, she looked up and at him with tear-reddened, dull eyes. "Who?'' she asked faintly.

"Gnaeus Pompeius Magnus.''

"Oh, Sulla, really!" snapped Dalmatica. "I refuse to believe you mean it! Marry *Scaurus's daughter* to that Picentine oaf? *My* daughter, of Caecilius Metellus blood? I will not consent!"

"You have no say in the matter."

"Then I wish Scaurus were alive! He'd have plenty to say!"

Sulla laughed. "Yes, he would, wouldn't he? Not that it would make any difference in the end. I need to tie Magnus to me with a stronger bond than gratitude—he doesn't have a grateful bone in his body. And you, step-daughter, are the only female of the family available at the moment."

The grey shade in Dalmatica's skin deepened. "Please don't do this, Lucius Cornelius! *Please!*"

"I'm carrying Glabrio's baby," whispered Aemilia Scaura. "Surely Pompeius wouldn't want me?"

"Who, Magnus? Magnus wouldn't care if you'd had sixteen husbands and had sixteen children in your nursery," said Sulla. "He knows a bargain when he sees one, and you're a bargain for him at any price. I give you twenty days to heal your face, then you'll marry him. After the child is born, I'll send it to Glabrio."

The weeping broke out afresh. "Please, Lucius Cornelius, don't do that to me! Let me keep my baby!"

"You can have more with Magnus. Now stop behaving like a schoolgirl and face facts!" Sulla's gaze went to Dalmatica. "That goes for you as well, wife."

He walked out, leaving Dalmatica to do what she could to comfort her daughter.

Two days later, Pompey informed him by letter that he had divorced his wife, and would like a firm wedding date.

"I plan to be out of town until the Nones of Sextilis," said Sulla in his answer, "so I think two days after the Nones of Sextilis seems propitious. You may present yourself in my house at that time, not before."

Hercules Invictus was the god of the triumphing imperator and held sway over the Forum Boarium, in which lay the various meat markets, and which formed the large open space in front of the starting-post end of the Circus Maximus. There he had his Great Altar, his temple, and there too his statue, naked save on the day a general held his victory parade, when it was dressed in triumphal robes. Other temples to other aspects of Hercules also dotted the area, for he was the patron god of olives, of merchant plutocrats, and of commercial voyages personally placed under his protection.

On the feast day of Hercules Invictus, announced Sulla in a citywide proclamation, he would dedicate one tenth of his private fortune to the god, as thanks for the god's favor in all his martial endeavors. A huge stir of anticipatory pleasure went through the populace, as Hercules Invictus had no temple funds, so could not keep the moneys donated to him; they were spent in his and the triumphing general's name on providing a public feast for all free men in Rome. On the day before the Ides of Sextilis—this being the god's feast day—five thousand tables of food would be laid out, each table catering for more than a hundred hungry citizens (which was not to say that there were half a million free males in Rome—what it did say was that the donor of the feast understood that it was hard to exclude spry grannies, determined wives and cheeky children). A list of the location of these five thousand tables was appended to the proclamation; a formidable exercise in logistics, such an occasion was very carefully planned and executed so that the participants by and large remained in their own districts, did not clog the streets or overflow into rival regions and thereby cause fights, public disturbances, crime waves and riots.

The event set in train, Sulla left for his villa at Misenum with his wife, his daughter, his children, his grandchildren, his stepdaughter, and Mamercus. Dalmatica had avoided him ever since the dissolution of Aemilia Scaura's marriage to Glabrio, but when he did see her in passing, he had noticed that she looked ill. A holiday beside the sea was clearly called for. This entourage was augmented by the consul Decula, who drafted all Sulla's laws for him, and by the ubiquitous Chrysogonus.

It was therefore some days after they had settled into seaside living before he found the leisure to spend a little time with his wife, still tending to avoid him.

"There's no point in holding things like Aemilia against me," he said in reasonable but unapologetic tones. "I will always do what I have to do. You should know that by now, Dalmatica."

They were sitting in a secluded corner of the loggia overlooking the water, cooled by a gentle zephyr wind and shaded by a judiciously planted row of cypresses. Though the light was not harsh, it revealed that several days of healthier air had not served to improve Dalmatica's ailment, whatever it might be; she looked drawn and grey, much older than her thirty-seven years.

"I do know it," she said in answer to this overture of peace, but not with equanimity. "I wish I could accept it! But when my own children are involved, it's different."

"Glabrio had to go," he said, "and there was only one way to do that—sever him from my family. Aemilia is young. She will get over the blow. Pompeius is not such a bad fellow."

"He is beneath her."

"I agree. Nonetheless, I need to bind him to me. Marriage between him and Aemilia also drives home to Glabrio that he dare not continue to speak out against me, when I have the power to give Scaurus's daughter to the likes of a Pompeius from Picenum." He frowned. "Leave it be, Dalmatica! You don't have the strength to withstand me."

"I know that," she said, low-voiced.

"You're not well, and I'm beginning to think it has nothing to do with Aemilia," he said, more kindly. "What is it?"

"I think—I think . . . "

"Tell me!"

"I'm going to have another child."

"Jupiter!" He gaped, recovered, looked grim.

"I agree it isn't what either of us wants at this time," she said wearily. "I fear I am a little old."

"And I am far too old." He shrugged, looked happier. "Oh well, it's an accomplished thing, and we're equally to blame. I take it you don't want to abort the process?"

"I delayed too long, Lucius Cornelius. It wouldn't be safe for me at five months. I didn't notice, I really didn't."

"Have you seen a doctor or a midwife?"

"Not yet."

He got up. "I'll send Lucius Tuccius to you now."

She flinched. "Oh, Sulla, please don't! He's an ex-army surgeon, he knows nothing about women!"

"He's better than all your wretched Greeks!"

"For doctoring men, I agree. But I would much rather see a lady doctor from Neapolis or Puteoli."

Sulla abandoned the struggle. "See whomever you like," he said curtly, and left the loggia.

Several lady physicians and midwives came to see her; each agreed she was run down, then said that as time went on and the baby in her womb settled, she would feel better.

And so on the Nones of Sextilis the slaves packed up the villa and the cavalcade set off for Rome, Sulla riding ahead because he was too impatient to dawdle at the snail's pace the women's litters made inevitable. In conse-

quence he reached the city two days ahead of the rest of his party, and plunged
into the last-moment details concerning his coming feast.

"Every baker in Rome has been engaged to make the bread and the
cakes, and the special shipments of flour are already delivered," said Chrysogonus smugly; he had arrived in the city even earlier than Sulla.

"And the fish will be fresh? The weather is scorching."

"All taken care of, Lucius Cornelius, I do assure you. I have had a
section of the river above the Trigarium fenced off with nets, and the fish
are already swimming there against the day. A thousand fish-slaves will
commence to gut and cook on the morning of the feast."

"The meats?"

"Will be freshly roasted and sweet, the guild of caterers has promised.
Sucking pigs, chickens, sausages, baby lambs. I have had a message from
Italian Gaul that the early apples and pears will arrive on time—five hundred
wagons escorted by two squadrons of cavalry are proceeding down the Via
Flaminia at this moment. The strawberries from Alba Fucentia are being
picked now and packed in ice from the Mons Fiscellus. They will reach Rome
the night before the feast—also under military escort."

"A pity people are such thieves when it comes to food," said the
Dictator, who had been poor enough and hungry enough in his youth to
understand, for all he pretended otherwise.

"If it were bread or porridge, Lucius Cornelius, there would be no need
to worry," soothed Chrysogonus. "They mostly steal what has a novel taste,
or a season."

"Are you sure we have enough wine?"

"There will be wine *and* food left over, *domine*."

"None of the wine's vinegary, I hope!"

"It is uniformly excellent. Those vendors who might have been tempted
to throw in a few air-contaminated amphorae know well who the buyer is."
Chrysogonus smiled reminiscently. "I told every one of them that if we found
a single amphora of vinegar, the lot of them would be crucified, Roman
citizens or no."

"I want no hitches, Chrysogonus. No hitches!"

But the hitch when it came bore no connection (or so it seemed) to the
public feast; it involved Dalmatica, who arrived attended by every wisewoman
Cornelia Sulla could find as they passed through the towns on the Via Appia.

"She's bleeding," said Sulla's daughter to her father.

The relief on his face was naked. "She'll lose the thing?" he asked
eagerly.

"We think she may."

"Far better that she does."

"I agree it won't be a tragedy if she loses the baby," said Cornelia Sulla, who didn't waste her emotions on anger or indignation; she knew her father too well. "The real worry is Dalmatica herself, *tata.*"

"What do you mean?"

"She may die."

Something darkly appalled showed in his eyes, just what his daughter couldn't tell; but he made a movement of distress, shook his head violently. "He *is* a harbinger of death!" he cried, then, "It is always the highest price! But I don't care, I don't care!" The look of amazement on Cornelia Sulla's face brought him back to his senses, he snorted. "She's a strong woman, she won't die!"

"I hope not."

Sulla got to his feet. "She wouldn't consent to see him before, but she will now. Whether she wants to or not."

"Who?"

"Lucius Tuccius."

When the ex-army surgeon arrived in Sulla's study some hours later, he looked grave. And Sulla, who had waited out those hours alone, had passed from horror at what always seemed to happen after he saw Metrobius, through guilt, to resignation. As long as he didn't have to see Dalmatica; for he didn't think he could face her.

"You don't bear good tidings, Tuccius."

"No, Lucius Cornelius."

"What exactly is wrong?" Sulla asked, pulling at his lip.

"There seems to be a general impression that the lady Dalmatica is pregnant, and that is certainly what she thinks," said Lucius Tuccius, "but I doubt the existence of a child."

The crimson patches of scar tissue on Sulla's face stood out more starkly than usual. "Then what does exist?"

"The women speak of haemorrhage, but the loss of blood is too slow for that," said the little doctor, frowning. "There is some blood, but mixed with a foul-smelling substance I would call pus were she a wounded soldier. I diagnose some kind of internal suppuration, but with your permission, Lucius Cornelius, I would like to obtain some further opinions."

"Do whatever you like," said Sulla sharply. "Just keep the comings and goings unobtrusive tomorrow—I have a wedding to see to. I suppose my wife cannot attend?"

"Definitely not, Lucius Cornelius."

Thus it was that Aemilia Scaura, five months pregnant by her previous husband, married Gnaeus Pompeius Magnus in Sulla's house without the support of anyone who loved her. And though beneath her veils of flame and saffron she wept bitterly, Pompey set himself the moment the ceremony was over to soothing and pleasing her, and succeeded so well that by the time they left, she was smiling.

It ought to have been Sulla who informed Dalmatica of this unexpected bonus, but Sulla continued to find excuse after excuse as to why he couldn't visit his wife's rooms.

"I think," said Cornelia Sulla, upon whom his communication with Dalmatica had devolved, "that he can't bear to see you looking so ill. You know what he's like. If it's someone he doesn't care about he is utterly indifferent. But if it's someone he loves, he can't bring himself to face the situation."

There was a smell of corruption in the big airy room where Dalmatica lay, reinforced the closer a visitor came to the bed. She was, Cornelia Sulla knew, dying; Lucius Tuccius had been right, no baby was growing inside her. What was pushing her poor laboring belly into a travesty of pregnancy no one seemed to know, except that it was morbid, malign. The putrid discharge flowed out of her with sluggish remorselessness, and she burned with a fever no amount of medicine or care seemed to cool. She was still conscious, however, and her eyes, bright as two flames, were fixed on her stepdaughter painfully.

"I don't matter," she said now, rolling her head upon her sweat-soaked pillow. "I want to know how my poor little Aemilia got on. Was it very bad?"

"Actually, no," said Cornelia Sulla, with surprise in her voice. "Believe it or not, darling stepmother, by the time she left to go to her new home, she was quite happy. He's rather a remarkable fellow, Pompeius—I'd never more than seen him in the distance before today, and I had all a Cornelian's prejudice against him. But he's terribly good-looking—far more attractive than silly Glabrio!—and turned out to have a great deal of charm. So she started out in floods of tears, but a few moments of Pompeius's telling her how pretty she was and how much he loved her already, and she was quite lifted out of her despond. I tell you, Dalmatica, the man has more to him than ever I expected. I predict he makes his women happy."

Dalmatica appeared to believe this. "They do tell stories about him. Years ago, when he was scarcely more than a child, he used to have congress with Flora—you know who I mean?"

"The famous whore?"

"Yes. She's a little past her prime now, but they tell me she still mourns the passing of Pompeius, who never left her without leaving the marks of his teeth all over her—I cannot imagine why that pleased her, but apparently it did! He tired of her and handed her over to one of his friends, which broke her heart. Poor, silly creature! A prostitute in love is a butt."

"Then it may well be that Aemilia Scaura will end in thanking *tata* for freeing her from Glabrio."

"I wish he would come to see me!"

The day before the Ides of Sextilis arrived; Sulla donned his Grass Crown and triumphal regalia, this being the custom when a man of military renown sacrificed on the Ara Maxima in the Forum Boarium. Preceded by his lictors and heading a procession of members of the Senate, the Dictator walked the relatively short distance from his house to the Steps of Cacus, and down them to the empty area in which the meat markets were normally located. When he passed by the statue of the god—today also clad in full triumphal regalia—he paused to salute it and pray. Then on he went to the Great Altar, beyond which stood the little round temple of Hercules Invictus, an old plainly Doric structure which enjoyed some fame because inside it were located some frescoes executed by the famous tragic poet Marcus Pacuvius.

The victim, a plump and perfect cream-colored heifer, was waiting in the care of *popa* and *cultarius*, chewing her drugged cud and watching the frenzied pre-banquet activity within the marketplace through gentle brown eyes. Though Sulla wore his Grass Crown, the rest of those assembled were crowned with laurel, and when the younger Dolabella—who was urban praetor and therefore in charge of this day's ceremonies—began his prayers to Hercules Invictus, no one covered his head. A foreigner within the sacred boundary, Hercules was prayed to in the Greek way, with head bare.

Everything proceeded in flawless fashion. As donor of the heifer and celebrant of the public feast, Sulla bent to catch some of the blood in the *skyphos,* a special vessel belonging to Hercules. But as he crouched and filled the cup, a low black shape slunk like a shadow between the Pontifex Maximus and the *cultarius,* dipped its snout into the growing lake of blood on the cobbles, and lapped noisily.

Sulla's shriek of horror ripped out of him as he leaped back and straightened; the *skyphos* emptied as it fell from his nerveless hand, and the wizened, stringy Grass Crown tumbled off his head to lie amid the blood. By this the panic was spreading faster than the ripples on the crimson pool at which the black dog, starving, still lapped. Men scattered in all directions, some screaming thinly, some hurling their laurels away, some plucking whole tufts from their hair; no one knew what to do, how to end this nightmare.

It was Metellus Pius the Pontifex Maximus who took the hammer from the stupefied *popa* and brought it crashing down upon the dog's working head. The cur screeched once and began to whirl in a circular dance, its bared teeth snapping and gnashing, until after what seemed an eternity it collapsed in a convulsing tangle of limbs and slowly stilled, dying, its mouth spewing a cascade of bloodied foam.

Skin whiter than Sulla's, the Pontifex Maximus dropped the hammer to the ground. "The ritual has been profaned!" he cried in the loudest voice he had ever produced. "*Praetor urbanus,* we must begin again! Conscript Fathers, compose yourselves! And where are the slaves of Hercules, who ought to have made sure no dog was here?"

Popa and *cultarius* rounded up the temple slaves, who had drifted off before the ceremony got under way to see what sort of goodies were being piled upon the readied tables. His wig askew, Sulla found the strength at last to bend over and pick up his blood-dabbled Grass Crown.

"I must go home and bathe," he said to Metellus Pius. "I am unclean. In fact, all of us are unclean, and must go home and bathe. We will reassemble in an hour." To the younger Dolabella he said, less pleasantly, "After they've cleared away the mess and thrown the carcass of the heifer and that frightful creature into the river, have the *viri capitales* lock the slaves up somewhere until tomorrow. Then have them crucified—and don't break their legs. Let them take days to die. Here in the Forum Boarium, in full sight of the god Hercules. He doesn't want them. They allowed his sacrifice to be polluted by a dog."

Unclean, unclean, unclean, unclean: Sulla kept repeating the word over and over as he hurried home, there to bathe and clothe himself this time in *toga praetexta*—a man did not have more than one set of triumphal regalia, and that one set only if he had triumphed. The Grass Crown he washed with his own hands, weeping desolately because even under his delicate touch it fell apart. What remained when finally he laid it to dry on a thick pad of white cloth was hardly anything beyond a few tired, limp fragments. My *corona graminea* is no more. I am accursed. My luck is gone. My luck! How can I live without my luck? Who sent it, that mongrel still black from its journey through the nether darknesses? Who has spoiled this day, now that Gaius Marius cannot? Was it Metrobius? I am losing Dalmatica because of him! No, it is not Metrobius. . . .

So back to the Ara Maxima of Hercules Invictus he went, now wearing a laurel wreath like everyone else, his terrified lictors ruthlessly clearing a path through the crowds gathering to descend on the feast once it was laid out. There were still a few ox-drawn carts bringing provisions to the tables, which created fresh panics as their drivers saw the cavalcade of approaching priests and hastened to unyoke their beasts, drive them out of the way; if one ox plopped a pile of dung in the path of priests, the priests were defiled and the owner of the ox liable to be flogged and heavily fined.

Chrysogonus had obtained a second heifer quite as lovely as the first, and already flagging from the drug the frantic steward had literally rammed down its throat. A fresh start was made, and this time all went smoothly right to the last. Every one of the three hundred senators present spent more time making sure no dog lurked than in paying attention to the ritual.

A victim sacrificed to Hercules Invictus could not be taken from the pyre alongside the god's Great Altar, so like Caesar's white bull on the Capitol, it was left to consume itself among the flames, while those who had witnessed the morning's dreadful events scurried home the moment they were free to do so. Save for Sulla, who went on as he had originally planned; he must walk through the city wishing the feasting populace a share of his good fortune. Only how could he wish them that when Fortune's favoritism had been canceled out of existence by a black mongrel?

Each made of planks laid on top of trestles, five thousand tables groaned with food, and wine ran faster than blood on a battlefield. Unaware of the disaster at the Ara Maxima, more than half a million men and women gorged themselves on fish and fruit and honey cakes, and stuffed the sacks they had brought with them full to the top so that those left at home—including slaves—might also feast. They greeted Sulla with cheers and invocations to the gods, and promised him that they would remember him in their prayers until they died.

Night was falling when he finally returned to his house on the Palatine, there to dismiss his lictors with thanks and the news that they would be feasted on the morrow in their precinct behind the inn on the corner of the Clivus Orbius.

Cornelia Sulla was waiting for him in the atrium.

"Father, Dalmatica is asking for you," she said.

"I'm too tired!" he snapped, knowing he could never face his wife, whom he loved—but not enough.

"Please, Father, go to her! Until she sees you, she won't abandon this idiotic notion your conduct has put into her head."

"What idiotic notion?" he asked, stepping out of his toga as he walked to the altar of the Lares and Penates on the far wall. There he bent his head, broke a salt-cake upon the marble shelf, and laid his laurel wreath upon it.

His daughter waited patiently until this ceremony was done with and Sulla turned back in her direction.

"What idiotic notion?" he asked again.

"That she is unclean. She keeps saying she's unclean."

Like stone he stood there, the horror crawling all over him, in and out and round and round, a wormy army of loathesome sensations he could neither control nor suffer. He jerked, flung his arms out as if to ward off assassins, stared at his daughter out of a madness she had not seen in him in all her life.

"Unclean!" he screamed. *"Unclean!"*

And vanished, running, out of the house.

Where he spent the night no one knew, though Cornelia Sulla sent parties armed with torches to look for him amid the ruins of those five thousand tables, no longer groaning. But with the dawn he walked, clad only in his tunic, into the atrium, and saw his daughter still waiting there. Chrysogonus, who had remained with Cornelia Sulla throughout the night because he too had much to fear, advanced toward his master hesitantly.

"Good, you're here," said Sulla curtly. "Send to all the priests—minor as well as major!—and tell them to meet me in one hour's time at Castor's in the Forum."

"Father?" asked Cornelia Sulla, bewildered.

"Today I have no truck with women" was all he said before he went to his own rooms.

He bathed scrupulously, then rejected three purple-bordered togas before one was presented to him that he considered perfectly clean. After which, preceded by his lictors (four of whom were ordered to change into unsoiled togas), he went to the temple of Castor and Pollux, where the priests waited apprehensively.

"Yesterday," he said without preamble, "I offered one tenth of everything I own to Hercules Invictus. Who is a god of men, and of men only. No women are allowed near his Great Altar, and in memory of his journey to the Underworld no dogs are permitted in his precincts, for dogs are chthonic, and all black creatures. Hercules is served by twenty slaves, whose main duty is to see that neither women nor dogs nor black creatures pollute his precincts. But yesterday a black dog drank the blood of the first victim I offered him, a frightful offense against every god—and against me. What could I have done, I asked myself, to incur this? In good faith I had come to offer the god a huge gift, together with a sacrificial victim of exactly the right kind. In good faith I expected Hercules Invictus to accept my gift and my sacrifice. But instead, a black dog drank the heifer's blood right there at the foot of the Ara Maxima. And my Grass Crown was polluted when it fell into the blood the black dog drank.''

The ninety men he had commanded to attend him stood without moving, hackles rising at the very thought of so much profanation. Everyone present in Castor's had been at the ceremony the day before, had recoiled in horror, and then had spent the rest of that day and the night which followed in wondering what had gone wrong, why the god had vented such displeasure upon Rome's Dictator.

"The sacred books are gone, we have no frame of reference," Sulla went on, fully aware of what was going through the minds of his auditors. "It was left to my daughter to act as the god's messenger. She fulfilled all the criteria: she spoke without realizing what she said; and she spoke in ignorance of the events which occurred before the Great Altar of Hercules Invictus.''

Sulla stopped, peering at the front ranks of priests without seeing the face he was looking for. "Pontifex Maximus, come out before me!'' he commanded in the formal tones of a priest.

The ranks moved, shuffled a little; out stepped Metellus Pius. "I am here, Lucius Cornelius.''

"Quintus Caecilius, you are closely concerned in this. I want you in front of the rest because no man should see your face. I wish I too had that privilege, but all of you must see *my* face. What I have to say is this: my wife, Caecilia Metella Dalmatica, daughter of one Pontifex Maximus and first cousin of our present Pontifex Maximus, is''—Sulla drew a deep breath— "unclean. In the very instant that my daughter told me this, I knew it for the truth. My wife is unclean. Her womb is rotting. Now I had been aware of that for some time. But I did not know that the poor woman's condition was offensive to the gods of men until my daughter spoke. Hercules Invictus is a god of men. So too is Jupiter Optimus Maximus. I, a man, have been entrusted with the care of Rome. To me, a man, has been given the task of helping Rome recover from the wars and vicissitudes of many years. Who I am and what I am matters. And *nothing* in my life can be unclean. Even my wife. Or so I see it today. Am I right in my assumption, Quintus Caecilius, Pontifex Maximus?''

How much the Piglet has grown! thought Sulla, the only one privileged to see his face. Yesterday it was the Piglet took charge, and today it is only he who fully understands.

"Yes, Lucius Cornelius," said Metellus Pius in steady tones.

"I have called all of you here today to take the auspices and decide what must be done," Sulla went on. "I have informed you of the situation, and told you what I believe. But under the laws I have passed, I can make no decision without consulting you. And that is reinforced because the person most affected is my wife. Naturally I cannot have it said that I have used this situation to be rid of my wife. I do not want to rid myself of my wife, I must make that clear. To all of you, and through you, to all of Rome. Bearing that in mind, I believe that my wife is unclean, and I believe the gods of men are offended. Pontifex Maximus, as the head of our Roman religion, what do you say?"

"I say that the gods of men are offended," said Metellus Pius. "I say that you must put your wife from you, that you must never set eyes upon her again, and that you must not allow her to pollute your dwelling or your legally authorized task."

Sulla's face revealed his distress; that was manifest to everyone. "I love my wife," he said thickly. "She has been loyal and faithful to me. She has given me children. Before me, she was a loyal and faithful wife to Marcus Aemilius Scaurus, and gave him children. I do not know why the gods of men require this of me, or why my wife has ceased to please them."

"Your affection for your wife is not in question," said the Pontifex Maximus, her first cousin. "Neither of you needs to have offended any god, of men or of women. It is better to say that her presence in your house and your presence in her life have in some unknown way interrupted or distorted the pathways whereby divine grace and favor are conducted to Rome. On behalf of my fellow priests, I say that no one is to blame. That we find no fault on either your side, Lucius Cornelius, or on your wife's side. What is, is. There can be no more to be said."

He spun round to face the silent assemblage, and said in loud, stern, unstammering voice, "I am your Pontifex Maximus! That I speak without stammer or stumble is evidence enough that Jupiter Optimus Maximus is using me as his vessel, and that I am gifted with his tongue. I say that the wife of this man is unclean, that her presence in his life and house is an affront to our gods, and that she must be removed from his life and his house immediately. I do not require a vote. If any man here disagrees with me, let him say so now."

The silence was profound, as if no men stood there at all.

Metellus Pius swung back to face the Dictator. "We direct you, Lucius Cornelius Sulla, to instruct your servants to carry your wife, Caecilia Metella

Dalmatica, out of your house and convey her to the temple of Juno Sospita, where she must remain until she dies. On no account must you set eyes upon her. And after she has been taken away, I direct the Rex Sacrorum and the *flamen Martialis* in lieu of the *flamen Dialis* to conduct the purification rites in Lucius Cornelius's house.''

He pulled his toga over his head. ''O Celestial Twins, you who are called Castor and Pollux, or the Dioscuri, or the Dei Penates, or any other name you might prefer—you who may be gods or goddesses or of no sex at all—we have come together in your temple because we have need of your intercession with the mighty Jupiter Optimus Maximus—whose off-spring you may or may not be—and with the triumphator Hercules Invictus. We pray that you will testify before all the gods that we are sincere, and have striven to right whatever wrong it is that has been done. In accordance with our contractual agreements, which go back to the battle at Lake Regillus, we hereby promise you a sacrifice of twin white foals as soon as we can find such a rare offering. Look after us, we beg you, as you have always done.''

The auspices were taken, and confirmed the decision of the Pontifex Maximus. The clear morning light, which struck the interior of the temple through its open doorway, turned suddenly darker when the sun moved toward its zenith, and a chill breath of some strange wind came whistling softly in the sunlight's stead.

''One final matter before we go,'' said Sulla.

The feet stilled at once.

''We must replace the Sibylline Books, for though we have the Book of Vegoe and Tages still safe in the temple of Apollo, that work is unhelpful in any situation wherein foreign gods are involved, as is Hercules Invictus. There are many sibyls throughout the world, and some who are closely connected to the Sibyl of Cumae who wrote her verses on palm leaves and offered them to King Tarquinius Priscus so long ago. Pontifex Maximus, I wish you to depute someone to organize a search throughout the world for the verses which were contained in our prophetic books.''

''You are right, Lucius Cornelius, it must be done,'' said Metellus Pius gravely. ''I will find a man fit for the purpose.''

The Dictator and the Pontifex Maximus walked back to Sulla's house together.

''My daughter won't take it kindly,'' said the Dictator, ''but if she hears it from you, she may not blame me for it.''

''I am very sorry for this mess.''

''So,'' said Sulla unhappily, ''am I!''

Cornelia Sulla did believe her father, a fact which surprised her as much as it did him.

"Insofar as you're able, Father, I think you do love her, and I don't think so badly of you that I credit you with wanting to be rid of her."

"*Is* she dying?" asked Metellus Pius, smitten with a qualm because it had been his idea to place Dalmatica in the temple of Juno Sospita for however much longer she had to live.

"Very soon now, Lucius Tuccius says. She's full of a growth."

"Then let us get it over and done with."

Eight sturdy litter-bearers took Dalmatica from her sickbed, but not in dignified silence; the forbearance with which Sulla's wife had conducted her life to date vanished in the moment she was informed of the priests' decision, and realized she would never see Sulla again. She screamed, she wept, she shrieked his name over and over and over as they carried her away, while Sulla sat in his study with his hands over his ears and the tears coursing down his face. One more price to pay. But did he have to pay it for Fortune's sake—or for the sake of Metrobius?

There were four temples in a row outside the Servian Walls in the vegetable markets: Pietas, Janus, Spes, and Juno Sospita. Though this Juno was not one of the primary goddesses who looked after gravid women, she was simultaneously a warrior offshoot of the Great Mother of Pessinus, Juno of Snakes from Lanuvium, Queen of Heaven, and Savior of Women. Perhaps because of this last aspect in her makeup, it had long been the custom for women safely delivered of a child to bring the afterbirth to Juno Sospita and leave it in her temple as an offering.

At the time of the Italian War, when money had been short and temple slaves few, the Metella Balearica who had been wife to Appius Claudius Pulcher had dreamed that Juno Sospita appeared to her complaining bitterly that her temple was so filthy she couldn't live in it. So Balearica had gone to the consul, Lucius Caesar, and demanded that he help her scrub it out. They had found more than rotting placentas; the place was green and runny with the detritus of dead women, dead bitches, dead babies, rats. Herself pregnant at the time she and Lucius Caesar had performed their stomach-turning labor, Caecilia Metella Balearica had died two months later after giving birth to her sixth child, Publius Clodius.

But the temple had been beautifully kept ever since; the offered afterbirths were placed in an ooze-proof basket and taken away regularly to be ritually burned by the *flaminica Dialis* (or, in these days, by her designated replacement), and no temple floor was cleaner or temple interior sweeter-smelling. Cornelia Sulla had prepared a place for Dalmatica's bed, to which the litter-bearers transferred her in an agony of terror, men brought into a woman's precinct. She was still crying out for Sulla, but weakly, near her end, and seemed not to recognize her surroundings.

A painted statue of the goddess stood upon a plinth; she wore shoes with upturned toes, brandished a spear, and faced a rearing snake, but the most striking aspect of her image was the real goatskin draped about her shoulders, tied at her waist, and with its head and horns perched atop the goddess's dark brown hair like a helmet. There beneath this outlandish creature sat Cornelia Sulla and Metellus Pius, each holding one of Dalmatica's hands to help her surmount the mortal barriers of pain and loss. The wait was one of hours only, a spiritual rather than a physical ordeal. The poor woman died still asking to see Sulla, apparently deaf to the reasonable answers both Cornelia Sulla and Metellus Pius gave her.

When she was dead the Pontifex Maximus had the undertakers set up her *lectus funebris* inside the temple, as she could not be taken home to lie in state. Nor could she be displayed; she sat in the traditional upright position completely covered by a black, gold-edged cloth, hedged in by the keening professional mourners, and had for her background that strange goddess with goatskin and rearing snake and spear.

"When one has written the sumptuary law," said Sulla afterward, "one can afford to ignore it."

As a result, Caecilia Metella Dalmatica's funeral cost one hundred talents, and boasted over two dozen chariot-borne actors who wore the ancestral wax masks of the Caecilii Metelli and two patrician families, Aemilius Scaurus and Cornelius Sulla. But the crowd which thronged the Circus Flaminius (it had been decided that to bring her body inside the *pomerium* would be imprudent, given her unclean status) appreciated so much luster less than they did the sight of Dalmatica's three-year-old twins, Faustus and Fausta, clad in black and carried by a black-festooned female giant from Further Gaul.

On the Kalends of September the real legislating began, an onslaught of such dimensions that the Senate reeled.

"The present law courts are clumsy, time-consuming and not realistic," said Sulla from his curule chair. "No comitia should hear civil or criminal charges—the procedures are too long, too liable to political manipulation, and too influenced by the fame or popularity of the accused—not to mention his defending advocates. And a jury which might be as large as several thousand electors is as unwieldy as it is injudicious."

Having thus neatly disposed of a trial process in one of the Assemblies, Sulla went on. "I will give Rome seven permanent standing courts. Treason, extortion, embezzlement, bribery, forgery, violence, and murder. All of these except the last one involve the State or the Treasury in some way, and will be presided over by one of the six junior praetors, according to the lots. The murder court will try all cases of murder, arson, magic, poison, perjury, and a new crime which I will call judicial murder—that is, exile achieved through the agency of a court. I expect that the murder court will be the busiest, though the simplest. And I will see it presided over by a man who has been aedile, though not yet praetor. The consuls will appoint him.''

Hortensius sat horrified, for his greatest victories had been fought in one of the Assemblies, where his style and his ability to sway a big crowd had made of him a legend; juries of the size staffing a court were too intimate to suit him.

"Genuine advocacy will die!" he cried.

"What does that matter?" asked Sulla, looking astonished. "More important by far is the judicial process, and I intend to take that off the Assemblies, Quintus Hortensius, make no mistake about it! However, from the Assembly of the People I will seek a law to sanction the establishment of my standing courts, and by the provisions of that law all three Assemblies will formally hand over their juridical duties to my standing courts.''

"Excellent!" said the historian Lucius Cornelius Sisenna. "Every man tried in court will therefore be tried by the consent of the Assemblies! That means a man will not be able to appeal to an Assembly after the court has delivered its verdict.''

"Exactly, Sisenna! It renders the appeal process null and void, and eliminates the Assemblies as judges of men.''

"That is disgusting!" shouted Catulus. "Not only disgusting, but absolutely unconstitutional! Every Roman citizen is entitled to an appeal!''

"Appeal and trial are one and the same, Quintus Lutatius,'' said Sulla, "and part of Rome's new constitution.''

"The old constitution was good enough in matters like this!''

"In matters like this history has shown us all too clearly that the provisions of the old constitution led to many a man who ought to have been convicted getting off because some Assembly was persuaded by some trick rhetoric to overturn a legal court decision. The political capital made out of such Assembly trials and appeals was odious, Quintus Lutatius. Rome is too big and too busy these days to be mired down in customs and procedures invented when Rome was little more than a village. I have not denied any man a fair trial. I have in fact made his trial fairer. And made the procedure simpler.''

"The juries?" asked Sisenna.

"Will be purely senatorial—one more reason why I need a pool of at least four hundred men in the Senate. Jury duty was a burden, and will be a burden when there are seven courts to staff. However, I intend to reduce the size of juries. The old fifty-one-man jury will be retained only in cases of the highest crimes against the State. In future jury size will depend on the number of men available to sit, and if for any reason there is an even number of men on a jury, then a tied decision will count as an acquittal. The Senate is already divided into decuries of ten men, each headed by a patrician senator. I will use these decuries as the jury base, though no decury will be permanently seconded to duty in one particular court. The jury for each individual trial in any court will be selected by lot *after* the trial date has been set."

"I like it," said the younger Dolabella.

"I hate it!" cried Hortensius. "What happens if my decury is drawn for jury duty while I myself am occupied in acting for a defendant in another trial?"

"Why, then you'll just have to learn to fit both in," said Sulla, smiling mirthlessly. "Whores do it, Hortensius! You ought to be able to."

"Oh, Quintus, shut your mouth!" breathed Catulus.

"Who decides the number of men to staff a particular jury?" asked the younger Dolabella.

"The court president," said Sulla, "but only to a limited extent. The real determination will depend upon the number of decuries available. I would hope to see a figure between twenty-five and thirty-five men. Not all of a decury will be seconded at once—that would keep jury numbers even."

"The six junior praetors will be each given presidency of a court by lot," said Metellus Pius. "Does that mean the old system will still prevail to decide who will be urban and who foreign praetor?"

"No, I will abolish giving urban praetor to the man at the top of the poll, and foreign praetor to the man who comes in second," said Sulla. "In future, all eight jobs will be decided purely by the lots."

But Lepidus wasn't interested in which praetor would get what; he asked the question he already knew the answer to, just to make Sulla say it. "You therefore intend to remove all court participation from the knights?"

"Absolutely. With one brief intermission, the control of Rome's juries has rested with the knights since the time of Gaius Gracchus. That will stop! Gaius Gracchus neglected to incorporate a clause in his law which allowed a corrupt knight juror to be prosecuted. Senators are fully liable under the law, I will make sure of that!"

"So what is left for the urban and foreign praetors to do?" asked Metellus Pius.

"They will be responsible for all civil litigation," said Sulla, "as well as, in the case of the foreign praetor, criminal litigation between non-Romans. However, I am removing the right of the urban and foreign praetor to make a judgment in a civil case himself—instead, he will pass the case to a single judge drawn by lot from a panel of senators and knights, and that man will act as *iudex*. His decision will be binding on all of the parties, though the urban or foreign praetor may elect to supervise the proceedings."

Catulus now spoke because Hortensius, still red-faced and angry at Sulla's gibe, would not ask. "As the constitution stands at the moment, Lucius Cornelius, only a legally convoked Assembly can pass a sentence of death. If you intend to remove all trials from the Assemblies, does this mean you will empower your courts to levy a death sentence?"

"No, Quintus Lutatius, it does not. It means the opposite. The death sentence will no longer be levied at all. Future sentences will be limited to exiles, fines, and/or confiscation of some or all of a convicted man's property. My new laws will also regulate the activity of the damages panel—this will consist of between two and five of the jurors chosen by lot, and the court president."

"You have named seven courts," said Mamercus. "Treason, extortion, embezzlement, bribery, forgery, violence, and murder. But there is already a standing court in existence for cases of public violence under the *lex Plautia*. I have two questions: one, what happens to this court? and two, what happens in cases of sacrilege?"

"The *lex Plautia* is no longer necessary," said Sulla. He leaned back, looking pleased; the House seemed happy at the idea of having criminal procedures removed from the comitia. "Crimes of violence will be tried either in my violence court or in the treason court if the magnitude is great enough. As for sacrilege, offenses of this nature are too infrequent to warrant a standing court. A special court will be convened when necessary, to be presided over by an ex-aedile. Its conduct, however, will be the same as the permanent courts—no right of appeal to the Assemblies. If the matter concerns the unchastity of a Vestal Virgin, the sentence of being buried alive will continue to be enforced. But her lover or lovers will be tried in a separate court and will not face a death sentence."

He cleared his throat, continued. "I am nearly done for today. First of all, a word about the consuls. It is not good for Rome to see the consuls embroiled in foreign wars. These two men during their year in office should be directly responsible for the welfare and well-being of Rome and Italy, nothing else. Now that the tribunes of the plebs have been put in their proper place, I hope to see the consuls more active in promulgating laws. And secondly, conduct within the Senate itself. In future, a man may rise to his feet to speak if he so wishes, but he will no longer be permitted to stride up and down the floor as he does so. He must speak from his allocated place, either seated or standing. Noise will not be tolerated. No applause, no drumming of feet, no calls or outcries will be tolerated. The consuls will levy a fine of one thousand denarii upon any man who infringes my new standards of conduct within the House.''

A small group of senators clustered below the Curia Hostilia steps after Sulla had dismissed the meeting; some of them (like Mamercus and Metellus Pius) were Sulla's men to the last, whereas others (like Lepidus and Catulus) agreed that Sulla was at best an evil necessity.

''There's no doubt,'' said the Piglet, ''that these new courts will take a great burden off the legislating bodies—no more fiddling about trying to induce the Plebeian Assembly to enact a special court to try someone, no more worrying about some unknown knight taking a bribe—yes, they are good reforms.''

''Oh come, Pius, you're old enough to remember what it was like during the couple of years after Caepio the Consul gave the courts back to the Senate!'' cried Philippus. ''I was never not on some jury or other, even during the summer!'' He turned to Marcus Perperna, his fellow censor. ''You remember, surely.''

''Only too well,'' said Perperna with feeling.

''The trouble with you two,'' said Catulus, ''is that you want the Senate to control juries, but you complain when it's your turn to serve. If we of the Senate want to dominate the trial process, then we have to be prepared to take the pain along with the pleasure.''

''It won't be as difficult now as it was then,'' said Mamercus pacifically. ''There are more of us.''

''Go on, you're the Great Man's son-in-law, he pulls your strings and you howl like a dog or bleat like a sheep!'' snapped Philippus. ''There *can't* be enough of us! And with permanent courts there will be no delays—at least back then we could hold things up by getting the Assemblies to dither about for a few market intervals while we had a holiday. Now, all the president of a court has to do is empanel his jury! And we won't even know in advance whether we'll be sitting on it, so we won't be able to plan a thing. Sulla says the lots won't be drawn until after the trial date has been set. I can see it now! Two days into a lovely summer laze by the sea, and it's off back to Rome to sit on some wretched jury!''

''Jury duty ought to have been split,'' said Lepidus. ''Keep the important courts for the Senate—you know, extortion and treason. The murder court could function properly on knight jurors—it would probably function properly if its juries were drawn from the Head Count!''

''What you mean,'' said Mamercus acidly, ''is that juries trying senators should be composed of senators, whereas juries trying the rest of the world on charges like witchcraft or poisoning are not important enough for senators.''

''Something like that,'' said Lepidus, smiling.

''What I'd like to know,'' said the Piglet, deeming it time to change the subject a little, ''is what else he plans to legislate.''

''I'd be willing to bet it won't be to our advantage!'' said Hortensius.

''Rubbish!'' said Mamercus, not a bit dismayed at being called Sulla's puppet. ''Everything he's done so far has strengthened the influence of the Senate and tried to bring Rome back to the old values and the old customs.''

''It may be,'' said Perperna thoughtfully, ''that it is too late to go back to the old ways and the old customs. A lot of what he's abolished or changed has been with us long enough to deserve being lumped in with the rest of the *mos maiorum*. These days the Plebeian Assembly is like a club for playing knucklebones or dice. That won't last because it *can't* last. The tribunes of the plebs have been Rome's major legislators for centuries.''

''Yes, what he did to the tribunes of the plebs isn't at all popular,'' said Lepidus. ''You're right. The new order of things in the Plebeian Assembly can't last.''

On the Kalends of October the Dictator produced new shocks; he shifted the sacred boundary of Rome exactly one hundred feet in the vicinity of the Forum Boarium, and thus made Rome a little bit larger. No one had ever tampered with the *pomerium* after the time of the Kings of Rome; to do so was considered a sign of royalty, it was an un-Republican act. But did that stop Sulla? Not in the least. He would shift the *pomerium,* he announced, because he now declared the Rubico River the official boundary between Italy and Italian Gaul. That river had been so regarded for a very long time, but the last formal fixing of the boundary had been at the Metaurus River. Therefore, said Sulla blandly, he could justifiably be said to have enlarged the territory of Rome within Italy, and he would mark the event by moving Rome's *pomerium* an infinitesmal hundred feet.

''Which as far as I'm concerned,'' said Pompey to his new (and very pregnant) wife, ''is splendid!''

Aemilia Scaura looked puzzled. ''Why?'' she asked.

She did a lot of asking why and might thus have irritated a less egotistical man, but Pompey adored being asked why.

"Because, my darling little roly-poly girl who looks as if she has swallowed a giant melon whole"—he tickled her tummy with a leer and a wink—"I own most of the Ager Gallicus south of Ariminum, and it now falls officially into Umbria. I am now one of the biggest landowners in all Italy, if not the very biggest. I'm not sure. There are men who own more land thanks to their holdings in Italian Gaul, like the Aemilii Scauri—your *tata*, my delectable wee pudding—and the Domitii Ahenobarbi, but I inherited most of the Lucilian estates in Lucania, and with the southern half of the Ager Gallicus added to my lands in Umbria and northern Picenum, I doubt I have a rival inside Italy proper! There are many going around deploring the Dictator's action, but he'll get no criticism from me."

"I can't wait to see your lands," she said wistfully, putting her hand on the mound of her abdomen. "As soon as I am able to travel, Magnus—you promised."

They were sitting side by side on a couch, and he turned to tip her over with a gentle push in just the right place, then pinched her lips painlessly between his fingers and kissed her all over her ecstatic face.

"More!" she cried when he finished.

His head hung over hers, his impossibly blue eyes twinkled. "And who's the greedy little piggy-wiggy?" he asked. "The greedy little piggy-wiggy should know better, shouldn't she?"

She fell into cascades of giggles, which provoked him to tickle her because he liked the sound of them so; but soon he wanted her so badly that he had to get up and move away.

"Oh, bother this wretched baby!" she cried crossly.

"Soon, my adorable kitten," he managed to say cheerfully. "Let's get rid of Glabrio before we try for our own."

And indeed Pompey had been continent, determined that no one, least of all Aemilia Scaura's stiff and haughty Caecilius Metellus relatives, should be able to say that he was not the most considerate and kindest of husbands; Pompey wanted badly to join the clan.

Learning that Young Marius had made an intimate of Praecia, Pompey had taken to visiting her sumptuous house, for he deemed it no comedown to sample someone else's leavings provided that the someone else had been famous, or stuffed with clout, or awesomely noble. Praecia was, besides, a sexual delight sure to please him in ways he knew very well Aemilia Scaura would not when her turn came. Wives were for the serious business of making babies, though poor Antistia had not even been accorded that joy.

If he liked being married—which he did—it was because Pompey had the happy knack of knowing how to make a wife besotted. He paid her

compliments galore, he didn't care how silly what he said might sound were
Metellus Pius Pontifex Maximus to overhear (he just made very sure he never
said things like that in the hearing of Metellus Pius Pontifex Maximus), and
he maintained a jolly, good-tempered attitude which disposed her to love
him. Yet—clever Pompey!—he allowed *her* to have moods, to weep, to carp
a trifle, to chastise him. And if neither Antistia nor Aemilia Scaura knew that
he manipulated them while they thought they did the manipulating, then that
was all for the good; all parties were satisfied, and strife was nonexistent.

His gratitude to Sulla for bestowing Scaurus Princeps Senatus's daughter
upon him knew almost no bounds. *He* understood that he was more than good
enough for Scaurus's daughter, but it also reinforced his positive opinion of
himself to know that a man like Sulla considered him good enough for
Scaurus's daughter. Of course he was quite aware that it suited Sulla to bind
him by a tie of marriage, and that too contributed to his positive opinion of
himself; Roman aristocrats like Glabrio could be thrown aside at the Dictator's
whim, but the Dictator was concerned enough about Gnaeus Pompeius Magnus to give him what he had taken from Glabrio. Sulla might (for example)
have given Scaurus's daughter to his own nephew, Publius Sulla, or to the
much-favored Lucullus.

Pompey had set his heart against belonging to the Senate, but it was no
part of his plans to alienate himself from the circle of the Dictator; rather,
his dreams had taken a fresh direction, and he now saw himself becoming
the sole military hero in the history of the Republic who would seize proconsular commands without being at the very least a senator. They said it
couldn't be done. They had sneered at him, smirked at him, mocked him.
But those were dangerous activities when they were aimed at Gnaeus Pompeius Magnus! In the years to come he would make every last one of them
suffer—and not by killing them, as Marius might have—nor by proscribing
them, as Sulla would have. He would make them suffer by forcing them to
come to him, by maneuvering them into a position so invidious that the pain
of being nice to him would well-nigh kill their fine opinions of themselves.
And that was far sweeter to Pompey than seeing them die!

So it was that Pompey managed to contain his desire for this delectable
sprig of the *gens* Aemilia, contented himself with many visits to Praecia, and
consoled himself by eyeing Aemilia Scaura's belly, never again to be filled
with any but his progeny.

She was due to have her baby at some time early in December, but
toward the end of October she went into a sudden and terrible labor. Thus
far her pregnancy had been uneventful, so this very late miscarriage came as
a shock to everyone, including her doctors. The scrawny male child who

came so prematurely into the world died the day after, and was not long survived by Aemilia Scaura, who bled her way inexorably from pain to eternal oblivion.

Her death devastated Pompey. He had genuinely loved her in his proprietary, unselective fashion; if Sulla had searched Rome for the right bride for Pompey in a conscious effort to please him, he could not have chosen better than the giggly, slightly dense, completely ingenuous Aemilia Scaura. The son of a man called The Butcher and himself called Kid Butcher, Pompey's exposure to death had been lifelong, and not conditioned by impulses of compassion or mercy. A man lived, a man died. A woman lived, a woman died. Nothing was certain. When his mother died he had cried a little, but until the death of Aemilia Scaura only the death of his father had profoundly affected him.

Yet his wife's death smote Pompey almost to joining her upon her funeral pyre; Varro and Sulla were never sure afterward whether Pompey's struggle to leap into the flames was genuine or only partly genuine, so frantic and grief-stricken was he. In truth, Pompey himself didn't know. All he did know was that Fortune had favored him with the priceless gift of Scaurus's daughter, then snatched the gift away before it could be enjoyed.

Still weeping desolately, the young man quit Rome through the Colline Gate, a second time because of sudden death. First his father, now Aemilia Scaura. To a Pompeius from northern Picenum, there was only one alternative. To go home.

"Rome now has ten provinces," said Sulla in the House the day after the funeral of his stepdaughter. He was wearing the senatorial mourning, which consisted of a plain white toga and a tunic bearing the thin purple stripe of a knight rather than the senator's broad purple stripe. Had Aemilia Scaura been his blood daughter he could not easily have gone about public business for ten days, but the absence of any close blood relationship obviated that. A good thing; Sulla had a schedule.

"Let me list them for you, Conscript Fathers: Further Spain, Nearer Spain, Gaul-across-the-Alps, Italian Gaul, Macedonia together with Greece, Asia, Cilicia, Africa together with Cyrenaica, Sicily, and Sardinia together with Corsica. Ten provinces for ten men to govern. If no man remains in his province for more than one year, that will leave ten men for ten provinces at the beginning of every year—two consuls and eight praetors just coming out of office."

His gaze lighted upon Lepidus, to whom he appeared to address his next remarks—for no better reason, it seemed, than random selection. "Each governor will now routinely be assigned a quaestor except for the governor of Sicily, who will have two quaestors, one for Syracuse and one for Lilybaeum. That leaves nine quaestors for Italy and Rome out of the twenty. Ample. Each governor will also be assigned a full staff of public servants, from lictors and heralds to scribes, clerks, and accountants. It will be the duty of the Senate—acting on advice from the Treasury—to assign each governor a specific sum to be called the stipend—and this stipend will not be added to for any reason during the year. It therefore represents the governor's salary, and will be paid to him in advance. Out of it he must pay his staff and expenses of office, and must present a full and proper accounting of it at the end of his year's governorship, though he will not be obliged to refund any part of it he has not spent. It is his the moment it is paid over to him, and what he does with it is his own business. If he wishes to invest it in Rome in his own name before he leaves for his province, that is permitted. However, he must understand that no more moneys will be forthcoming! A further word of warning is necessary. As his stipend becomes his personal property the moment it is paid over, it can legally be attached by lien if the new governor is in debt. I therefore advise all potential governors that their public careers will be jeopardized if they get themselves into debt. A penniless governor going out to his province will be facing heavy criminal charges when he returns home!''

A glare around the chamber, then Sulla went back to business. ''I am removing all say in the matters of wars, provinces and other foreign affairs from the Assemblies. From now on the Assemblies will be forbidden to so much as discuss wars, provinces and other foreign affairs, even in *contio*. These matters will become the exclusive prerogative of the Senate.'' Another glare. ''In future, the Assemblies will pass laws and hold elections. Nothing else. They will have no say in trials, in foreign affairs, or in any military matter.''

A small murmur started as everyone took this in. Tradition was on Sulla's side, but ever since the time of the Brothers Gracchi the Assemblies had been used more and more to obtain military commands and provinces—or even to strip men appointed by the Senate of their military commands and provinces. It had happened to the Piglet's father when Marius had taken the command in Africa off him, and it had happened to Sulla when Marius had taken the command against Mithridates off him. So this new legislation was welcome.

Sulla transferred his gaze to Catulus. ''The two consuls should be sent to the two provinces considered most volatile or endangered. The consular provinces and the praetorian ones will be apportioned by the casting of lots. Certain conventions must be adhered to if Rome is to keep her good name abroad. If ships or fleets are levied from provinces or client kingdoms, the cost of such levies must be deducted from the annual tribute. The same law applies to the levying of soldiers or military supplies.''

Marcus Junius Brutus, so long a mouse, took courage. ''If a governor is heavily committed to a war in his province, will he be obliged to give up his province at the end of one year?''

''No,'' said Sulla. He was silent for a moment, thinking, then said, ''It may even be that the Senate will have no other choice than to send the consuls of the year to a foreign war. If Rome is assailed on all sides, it is hard to see how this can be avoided. I only ask the Senate to consider its alternatives very carefully before committing the consuls of the year to a foreign campaign, or before extending a governor's term of office.''

When Mamercus lifted up his hand to speak, the senators pricked up their ears; by now he was so well known as Sulla's puppet asker-of-questions that everyone knew this meant he was going to ask something which Sulla thought best to introduce via the medium of a question.

''May I discuss a hypothetical situation?'' Mamercus asked.

''By all means!'' said Sulla genially.

Mamercus rose to his feet. As he was this year's foreign praetor and therefore held curule office, he was sitting on the podium at the far end of the hall where all the curule magistrates sat, and so could be seen by every eye when he stood up. Sulla's new rule forbidding men to leave their place when they spoke made the men on the curule podium the only ones who could be seen by all.

''Say a year comes along,'' said Mamercus carefully, ''when Rome does indeed find herself assailed on all sides. Say that the consuls and as many of the praetors of the year as can be spared have gone to fight during their tenure of office—or say that the consuls of the year are not militarily skilled enough to be sent to fight. Say that the governors are depleted—perhaps one or two killed by barbarians, or dead untimely from other causes. Say that among the Senate no men can be found of experience or ability who are willing or free to take a military command or a governorship. If you have excluded the Assemblies from debating the matter and the decision as to what must be done rests entirely with the Senate, what ought the Senate to do?''

''Oh, what a splendid question, Mamercus!'' Sulla exclaimed, just as if he hadn't worded it himself. He ticked the points off on his fingers. ''Rome is assailed on all sides. No curule magistrates are available. No consulars or ex-praetors are available. No senator of sufficient experience or ability is available. But Rome needs another military commander or governor. Is that right? Have I got it right?''

"That is right, Lucius Cornelius," said Mamercus gravely.

"Then," said Sulla slowly, "the Senate must look outside its ranks to find the man, must it not? What you are describing is a situation beyond solution by normal means. In which case, the solution must be found by abnormal means. In other words, it is the duty of the Senate to search Rome for a man of known exceptional ability and experience, and give that man all the legal authorities necessary to assume a military command or a governorship."

"Even if he's a *freedman*?" asked Mamercus, astonished.

"Even if he's a freedman. Though I would say he was more likely to be a knight, or perhaps a centurion. I knew a centurion once who commanded a perilous retreat, was awarded the Grass Crown, and afterward given the purple-bordered toga of a curule magistrate. His name was Marcus Petreius. Without him many lives would have been lost, and that particular army would not have been able to fight again. He was inducted into the Senate and he died in all honor during the Italian War. His son is among my own new senators."

"But the Senate is not legally empowered to give a man outside its own ranks imperium to command or govern!" objected Mamercus.

"Under my new laws the Senate will be legally empowered to do so—and ought to do so, in fact," said Sulla. "I will call this governorship or military command a 'special commission,' and I will bestow the necessary authority upon the Senate to grant it—with whatever degree of imperium is considered necessary!—to *any* Roman citizen, even a freedman."

"What is he up to?" muttered Philippus to Flaccus Princeps Senatus. "I've never heard the like!"

"I wish I knew, but I don't," said Flaccus under his breath.

But Sulla knew, and Mamercus guessed; this was one more way to bind Gnaeus Pompeius Magnus, who had refused to join the Senate, but because of all those veterans of his father's was still a military force to be reckoned with. It was no part of Sulla's plan to allow any man to lead an army on Rome; he would be the last, he had resolved on that. Therefore if times changed and Pompey became a threat, a way had to be open for Pompey's considerable talents to be legally harnessed by the legal body responsible—the Senate. Sulla intended to legislate what amounted to pure common sense.

"It remains for me to define treason," the Dictator said a few days later. "Until my new law courts came into being some time ago, there were several different kinds of treason, from *perduellio* to *maiestas minuta*—big treasons, little treasons, and treasons in between. And what all of these treasons lacked was true specificity. In future all charges of treason will be tried in the *quaestio de maiestate,* my standing treason court. A charge of treason, as you will shortly see, will be largely limited to men given provincial governorships or commands in foreign wars. If a civilian Roman generates treason within Rome or Italy, then that man will be the object of the only trial process I will allow an Assembly to conduct. Namely, that man will be tried *perduellio* in the Centuries, and will in consequence face the old penalty—death tied to a cross suspended from an unlucky tree.''

He let that sink in a little, then continued. ''Any and all of the following will be treasonable:

''A provincial governor may not leave his province.

''A provincial governor may not permit his armies to march beyond the provincial frontier.

''A provincial governor may not start a war on his own initiative.

''A provincial governor may not invade the territory of a client king without formal permission from the Senate.

''A provincial governor may not intrigue with a client king or any body of foreign nationals in order to change the status quo of any foreign country.

''A provincial governor may not recruit additional troops without the consent of the Senate.

''A provincial governor may not make decisions or issue edicts within his own province that will alter his province's status without the formal consent of the Senate.

''A provincial governor may not remain in his province for more than thirty days after the arrival in that province of his Senate-appointed successor.

''That is all.'' Sulla smiled. ''On the positive side of things, a man with imperium will continue to hold that imperium until he crosses the sacred boundary of Rome. This has always been so. I now reaffirm it.''

''I do not see,'' said Lepidus angrily, ''why all these specific rules and regulations are necessary!''

''Oh come, Lepidus,'' said Sulla wearily, ''you're sitting here looking straight at *me. Me!* A man who did almost every 'may not' on my list! *I* was justified! *I* had been illegally deprived of my imperium and my command. But I am here now passing laws which will make it impossible for any man to deprive another of his imperium and his command! Therefore the situation I was in cannot happen again. Therefore those men who break any of my 'may nots' will be guilty of treason. No man can be permitted to so much as toy with the idea of marching on Rome or leading his army out of his province in the direction of Rome. Those days are over. And I am sitting here to prove it.''

* * *

On the twenty-sixth day of October, Sulla's nephew, Sextus Nonius Sufenas (who was Sulla's sister's younger boy) put on the first performance of what were to become annual victory games, the *ludi Victoriae;* they culminated at the Circus Maximus on the first day of November, which was the anniversary of the battle at the Colline Gate. They were good but not magnificent games, save that for the first time in a dozen decades the Trojan Game was performed. The crowd loved it because of its novelty—a complex series of maneuvers on horseback carried out by youths who had to be of noble birth. Greece, however, was not amused. Sufenas had combed Greece for athletes, dancers, musicians and entertainers, so that the Olympic Games in Olympia, celebrated at about the same time of year, were an absolute disaster. And—juicy scandal!—the younger son of Antonius Orator, Gaius Antonius Hybrida, utterly disgraced himself by driving a chariot in one of the races; if it was a social cachet for a nobleman to participate in the Trojan Game, it was an horrific solecism for a nobleman to drive a chariot.

On the Kalends of December, Sulla announced the names of the magistrates for the coming year. He would be senior consul himself, with Quintus Caecilius Metellus Pius the Piglet as his junior. Loyalty was rewarded at last. The elder Dolabella received Macedonia as his province, and the younger Dolabella was given Cilicia. Though well provided by the lots with a quaestor in the person of Gaius Publicius Malleolus, the younger Dolabella insisted upon taking none other than Gaius Verres along as his senior legate. Lucullus remained in the east serving under Thermus, the governor of Asia, but Gaius Scribonius Curio came home to a praetorship.

It was now time for Sulla to begin the most massive undertaking of all— the awarding of land to his veterans. During the next two years the Dictator intended to demobilize one hundred and twenty thousand men belonging to twenty-three legions. During his first consulship at the end of the Italian War he had handed over the rebel lands of Pompeii, Faesulae, Hadria, Telesia, Grumentum and Bovianum to his Italian War veterans, but that had been a tiny task compared to the present one.

The program was meticulously worked out, and incorporated graduations of reward according to the length of a man's service, his rank, and his personal valor. *Primus pilus* centurions in his Mithridatic legions (they all had many decorations into the bargain) were each given five hundred *iugera* of prime land, whereas the ranker soldiers of Carboan legions which had deserted to Sulla received the smallest pensions, ten *iugera* of less desirable land.

He began with the confiscated lands of Etruria in the areas which had belonged to Volaterrae and Faesulae, punished yet again. Because Etruria had by now established what amounted to a tradition of opposition to Sulla, he did not at first concentrate his veterans in enclosed soldier-communities; instead he scattered them far and wide, thinking thereby to contain future rebellion. This turned out to be a mistake. Volaterrae rose almost at once, shut its gates after lynching many of Sulla's veterans, and prepared to withstand a siege. As the town lay in a deep ravine yet was raised up on a very high, flat-topped hill in the middle of the ravine, Volaterrae looked forward to a long defiance. Sulla went there in person to establish his blockade, stayed for three months, then went back to Rome when he saw how long and wearisome a job reducing Volaterrae was going to be.

He learned from this lesson, however, and changed his mind about how his veterans would be settled on their lands; his later colonies were just that, cohesive nuclei of ex-soldiers able to stick together in the face of bitter local opposition. His one overseas experiment occurred on Corsica, where he set up two separate soldier colonies, thinking to civilize the place and eliminate the Corsican curse, banditry. A futile hope.

The new law courts settled down well, providing the perfect arena for a new legal star, the young man Marcus Tullius Cicero. Quintus Hortensius (who had thriven in the trial atmosphere of the Assemblies) took time to telescope his act down to the intimate size of the open-air courtroom; whereas Cicero found it ideal. At the end of the old year Cicero appeared alone for the defendant in a preliminary hearing before the younger Dolabella, who was *praetor urbanus*. The object of the hearing was to decide whether the sum of money known as *sponsio* should be lodged, or whether the case could proceed without it. Cicero's advocate opponents were formidable—Hortensius and Philippus. But he won, Hortensius and Philippus lost, and Cicero embarked upon a forensic career which was to have no equal.

It was in June of the year that Sulla was senior consul with Metellus Pius as his junior consul that a twenty-six-year-old nobleman of patrician family, Marcus Valerius Messala Niger, appealed to his good friend, the twenty-six-year-old Marcus Tullius Cicero, to act on behalf of a man who was Niger's friend as well as his client.

"Sextus Roscius Junior, from Ameria," said Messala Niger to Cicero. "He's charged with murdering his father."

"Oh!" said Cicero, astonished. "You're a good advocate, my dear Niger. Why not defend him yourself? Murder is juicy, but very easy, you know. No political overtones."

"That's what you think," said Messala Niger grimly. "This case has more political pitfalls than a ditch has sharpened stakes! There is only one man who has a chance of winning, and that man is you, Marcus Tullius. Hortensius recoiled in horror.''

Cicero sat up straighter, a gleam of interest in his dark eyes; he used one of his favorite tricks, dipping his head and shooting Messala Niger a keen glance from under his brows. "A murder case so complicated? How?''

"Whoever takes on the defense of Roscius of Ameria will be taking on Sulla's whole system of proscription,'' said Messala Niger. "In order to get Roscius off, it will be necessary to prove that Sulla and his proscriptions are utterly corrupt.''

The generous mouth with the full lower lip pursed into a soundless whistle. "Ye gods!''

"Ye gods, indeed. Still interested?''

"I don't know. . . . '' Cicero frowned, at war with himself; preservation of his skin was mandatory, and yet a case so difficult had the potential to win him legal laurels no other kind of case could. "Tell me about it, Niger. Then I'll see.''

Niger settled down to tell his story cleverly enough that Cicero's interest would be stimulated further. "Sextus Roscius is my own age, and I've known him since we were at school together. We both served in our six campaigns under Lucius Caesar and then Sulla in Campania. Roscius's father owned most of Ameria, including no less than thirteen river frontage properties along the Tiber—*fabulously* rich! Roscius is his only son. But there are also two cousins, sons of his brother, who are the real villains of the piece. Old Roscius went to Rome on a visit at the beginning of the year, and was murdered in Rome. I don't know whether the cousins did it, nor does Roscius. Probable, but not necessary.'' Messala Niger grimaced. "The news of the father's murder came to Ameria through an agent of the cousins, certainly. And the most suspicious part about it is that this agent didn't tell poor Roscius at all! Instead he told the cousins, who hatched a plot to filch all the property off my friend Roscius.''

"I think I begin to see,'' said Cicero, whose mind was razor-keen when it came to the criminal perfidies of men.

"Volaterrae had just revolted, and Sulla was there conducting the initial stages of the siege. With him was Chrysogonus.''

There was no need to inform Cicero who was this Chrysogonus; all of Rome knew the infamous bureaucrat in charge of the lists, the books, and all the data pertaining to Sulla's proscriptions.

"The cousins rode to Volaterrae and were granted an interview with Chrysogonus, who was willing to make a deal with them—but for a huge price. He agreed to forge Roscius's dead father's name on one of the old proscription lists. He would then 'happen to see' a routine report on the murder, and pretend to 'remember' that this name was a proscribed one. That is what transpired. Roscius's father's properties—worth a cool six million— were immediately put up for auction by Chrysogonus, who bought them all himself—for two thousand, if you please.''

"I love this villain!" cried Cicero, looking as alert as a huntsman's hound.

"Well, I do not! I loathe the man!" said Messala Niger.

"Yes, yes, he's loathsome! But what happened next?"

"All of this occurred before Roscius even knew his father was dead. The first intimation he had was when Cousin Two appeared bearing Chrysogonus's proscription order, and evicted Roscius from his father's properties. Chrysogonus kept ten of the thirteen estates for himself and installed Cousin Two on them as his live-in manager and agent. The other three estates Chrysogonus signed over to Cousin One as outright payment. The blow for poor Roscius was a twin one, of course—not only did he learn that his father had been proscribed months before, but also that he was murdered.''

"Did he believe this tissue of lies?" asked Cicero.

"Absolutely. Why should he not have? Everyone with two sesterces to rub together expected to find himself named on a proscription list, whether he lived in Rome or in Ameria. Roscius just believed! And got out."

"Who smelled the rotten carcass?"

"The elders of the town," said Messala Niger. "A son is never as sure of his father's worth and nature as his father's friends are, which is not illogical. A man's friends know him without the concomitant emotional distortions suffered by his son.''

"True," said Cicero, who didn't get on with his own father.

"So the friends of the old man held a conference, and agreed that there had not been a Marian, Cinnan or Carboan bone in the old man's entire body. They agreed to ride to Volaterrae and seek an audience with Sulla himself, beg him to reverse the proscription and allow Roscius to inherit. They gathered up masses of evidence and set off at once.''

"Accompanied by which cousin?" asked Cicero shrewdly.

"Quite correct," said Messala Niger, smiling. "They were joined by Cousin One, who actually had the temerity to assume command of the mission! In the meantime Cousin Two rode at the gallop for Volaterrae to warn Chrysogonus what was in the wind. Thus it was that the deputation never got to see Sulla. It was waylaid by Chrysogonus, who took all the details—and all the masses of evidence!—from them, and promised them that he would see the Dictator reversed his proscription. Don't worry! was his cry. Everything will be right and Roscius will inherit.''

"Did no one suspect that he was talking to the real owner of ten of the thirteen estates?'' asked Cicero incredulously.

"Not a one, Marcus Tullius.''

"It's a sign of the times, isn't it?''

"I fear so.''

"Go on, please.''

"Two months went by. At the end of them old man Roscius's friends realized that they had been neatly tricked, for no order rescinding the proscription came through, and Cousin One and Cousin Two were now known to be living on the confiscated property as if they owned it. A few enquiries revealed that Cousin One was the outright owner of three, and Chrysogonus of the other ten. That terrified everyone, as everyone assumed Sulla was a part of the villainy.''

"Do you believe he was?'' asked Cicero.

Messala Niger thought long, finally shook his head. "No, Cicero, I doubt it.''

"Why?'' asked the born lawyer.

"Sulla is a hard man. Frankly, he terrifies me. They say that in his youth he murdered women for their money, that he got into the Senate over their bodies. Yet I knew him slightly when I was in the army—too junior to be on close terms, of course, but he was always around, always busy, always in control of the job—and he struck me as aristocratically scrupulous. Do you know what I mean by that?''

Cicero felt a tinge of red creeping under his skin, but pretended he was at ease. Did he know what the patrician nobleman Marcus Valerius Messala Niger meant by aristocratic scrupulousness? Oh, yes! No one understood better than Cicero, who was a New Man, and envied patricians like Messala Niger and Sulla very much.

"I think so,'' he said.

"He has a dark side to him, Sulla. He'd probably kill you or me without a qualm if it suited him. But he would have a patrician's reasons for killing us. He wouldn't do it because he coveted thirteen lush properties on the banks of the Tiber. If it occurred to him to go to an auction of proscribed property and he was able to pick up some very cheap estates, he would. I don't say he wouldn't. But conspire to enrich himself or his freedman in a dishonorable way when nothing as vital as his career was at stake? No. I don't think so. His honor matters to him. I see it in his laws, which I think are honorable laws. I may not agree with him that the tribunes of the plebs must be legislated out of all their power, but he's done it legally and openly. He's a Roman patrician.''

"So Sulla doesn't know," said Cicero thoughtfully.

"I believe that to be the truth.''

"Pray continue, Marcus Valerius.''

"About the time that the elders of Ameria began to think that Sulla was a part of the conspiracy, my friend Roscius became more vocal. The poor fellow really was utterly flattened for months, you know. It took a long time for him to say anything. But the moment he did begin to say things, there were several attempts on his life. So two months ago he fled to Rome and sought shelter with his father's old friend, the retired Vestal Metella Balearica. You know, the sister of Metellus Nepos. His other sister was the wife of Appius Claudius Pulcher—she died giving birth to that frightful monster of a child, Publius Clodius.''

"Get on with it, Niger," said Cicero gently.

"The fact that Roscius knew such powerful people as Metellus Nepos and a retired Vestal Virgin of the Caecilii Metelli gave the two cousins some sleepless nights, it would appear. They began to believe that Roscius just might manage to see Sulla in person. But they didn't dare murder Roscius, not without risking being found out if the Caecilii Metelli insisted upon an enquiry. So they decided it was better to destroy Roscius's reputation, by fabricating evidence that he had murdered his own father. Do you know a fellow called Erucius?''

Cicero's face twisted in contempt. "Who doesn't? He's a professional accusator.''

"Well, he came forward to charge Roscius with the murder of his father. The witnesses to old Roscius's death were his slaves, and of course they had been sold along with the rest of his estate to Chrysogonus. Therefore there was no likelihood that they would appear to tell the real story! And Erucius is convinced that no advocate of ability will take on Roscius's defense because every advocate will be too afraid of Sulla to dare say damning things about the proscription process.''

"Then Erucius had better look to his laurels," said Cicero briskly. "I'll defend your friend Roscius gladly, Niger.''

"Aren't you worried that you'll offend Sulla?''

"Pooh! Rubbish! Nonsense! I know *exactly* how to do it—and do it, I will! I predict, in fact, that Sulla will thank me," said Cicero blithely.

Though other cases had been heard in the new Murder Court, the trial of Sextus Roscius of Ameria on a charge of parricide created a huge stir.

Sulla's law stipulated that it be presided over by an ex-aedile, but in that year it was under the presidency of a praetor, Marcus Fannius. Fearlessly Cicero aired the story of Roscius in his *actio prima,* and left no juror or spectator in any doubt that his main defense was the corruption behind Sulla's proscriptions.

Then came the final day of the trial, when Cicero himself was to give his final address to the jury. And there, seated on his ivory curule chair to one side of the president's tribunal, was Lucius Cornelius Sulla.

The presence of the Dictator dismayed Cicero not a jot; instead, it pushed him to hitherto undreamed-of heights of eloquence and brilliance.

"There are three culprits in this hideous affair," he said, declaiming not to the jury, but to Sulla. "The cousins Titus Roscius Capito and Titus Roscius Magnus are obvious, but actually secondary. What they did, they could not have done without the proscriptions. Without Lucius Cornelius . . . . . . Chrysogonus," he said, pausing so long between the second and the third names that even Messala Niger began to think he might say, "Sulla."

On went Cicero. "Who exactly is this 'golden child'? This Chrysogonus? Let me tell you! He is a Greek. There is no disgrace in that. He is an exslave. There is no disgrace in that. He is a freedman. There is no disgrace in that. He is the client of Lucius Cornelius Sulla. There is no disgrace in that. He is rich. There is no disgrace in that. He is powerful. There is no disgrace in that. He is the administrator of the proscriptions. There is no disgrace in that—ooops! Ooops, ooops! I *beg* your collective pardons, Conscript Fathers! You see what happens when one bumps along in a rhetorical rut for too long? I got carried away! I could have gone on saying 'There is no disgrace in that' for hours! And oh, *what* a rhetorical ravine I would have dug for myself!"

Fairly launched, Cicero paused to revel consciously in what he was doing. "Let me say it again. He is the administrator of the proscriptions. And in that there is a monumental, a gigantic, an *Olympian* disgrace! Do all of you see this splendid man on his curule chair—this model of every Roman virtue, this general without rival, this lawmaker who has broken new bounds of statesmanship, this brilliant jewel in the crown of the illustrious *gens* Cornelia? Do all of you see him? Sitting so calmly, Zeus-like in his detachment? Do all of you see him? Then look well!"

Now Cicero turned away from Sulla to glare at the jury from under his brows, a rather sticklike figure, so thin was he even in his toga; and yet he seemed to tower, to have the thews of Hercules and the majesty of Apollo.

"Some years ago this splendid man bought himself a slave. To be his steward. An excellent steward, as things turned out. When this splendid man's late wife was forced to flee from Rome to Greece, his steward was there to help and console. His steward was there in complete charge of this splendid man's dependents—wife and children and grandchildren and servants—while our great Lucius Cornelius Sulla strode up the Italian peninsula like a titan. His steward was trusted, and did not betray that trust. So he was freed, and took for himself the first two parts of a mighty name—Lucius Cornelius. As is the custom, for his third name he kept his own original name—Chrysogonus. The golden child. Upon whose head was heaped honor after honor, trust after trust, responsibility after responsibility. He was now not merely the freedman steward of a great household, but also the director, the administrator, the executor of that process which was designed to fulfill two aims: the first, to see a just and rightful punishment meted out to all those traitors who followed Marius, who followed Cinna, who even followed an insect as small as Carbo; and the second, to use the property and estates of traitors as fuel to fan poor impoverished Rome into the flame of prosperity again.''

Back and forth across the open space left in front of Marcus Fannius's tribunal did Cicero stride, his left arm raised to hold his toga at its left shoulder, his right arm limply by his side. No one moved. Every eye was fixed upon him, men breathed in shallow gasps thinking they didn't breathe at all.

"So what did he do, this Chrysogonus? All the while keeping his oily smiling bland face toward his employer, his patron, he slithered to exact his revenge on this one who had insulted him, on that one who had impeded him—he toiled mightily in the secret marches of the night with forger's pen and patron's trust to slip in this name and that name whose property he slavered for, to conspire with worms and vermin to enrich himself at the expense of his patron, at the expense of Rome. Ah, members of the jury, but he was cunning! How he plotted and schemed to cover his tracks, how he smarmed and greased in the presence of his patron, how he manipulated his little army of pimps and panders—how *industriously* he worked to make sure that his noble and illustrious patron could have no idea of what was really going on! For that is what happened. Given trust and authority, he abused both in the vilest and most despicable ways.''

The tears began to flow; Cicero sobbed aloud, wrung his hands, stood hunched over in a paroxysm of pain. "Oh, I cannot look at you, Lucius Cornelius Sulla! That it should be I—a mean and simple man from the Latin countryside—a hick, a hayseed, a bucolic shyster—that it should have to be *I* who must draw the wool from your eyes, who must open them to the—the—what adjective can I find adequate to describe the level of the treachery of your most esteemed client, Lucius Cornelius Chrysogonus? Vile treachery!

Disgusting treachery! Despicable treachery! But none of those adjectives is low enough!''

The easy tears were dashed away. ''Why did it have to be me? Would that it could have been anybody else! Would that it had been your Pontifex Maximus or your Master of the Horse—great men both, and hung about with honors! But instead the lot has fallen to me. I do not want it. But I must accept it. Because, members of the jury, which do you think I would rather do? Spare the great Lucius Cornelius Sulla this agony by saying nothing about the treachery of Chrysogonus, or spare the life of a man who, though accused of murdering his own father, has actually done nothing to warrant the charge? Yes, you are right! It must be the embarrassment, the public mortification of an honorable and distinguished and legendary man—because it *cannot* be the unjust conviction of an innocent man.'' He straightened, drew himself up. ''Members of the jury, I now rest my case.''

The verdict, of course, was a foregone conclusion: ABSOLVO. Sulla rose to his feet and strolled toward Cicero, who found the crowd around him melting away.

''Well done, my skinny young friend,'' the Dictator said, and held out his hand. ''What an actor you would have made!''

So exhilarated that he felt as if his feet were floating free in air, Cicero laughed, clasped the hand fervently. ''What an actor I am, you mean! For what is superlative advocacy except acting out one's own words?''

''Then you'll end the Thespis of Sulla's standing courts.''

''As long as you forgive me for the liberties I had to take in this case, Lucius Cornelius, I will be anything you like.''

''Oh, I forgive you!'' said Sulla airily. ''I think I could forgive almost anything if it meant I sat through a good show. And with only one exception, I've never seen a better amateur production, my dear Cicero. Besides, I've been wondering how to get rid of Chrysogonus for some time—I'm not entirely a fool, you know. But it can be ticklish.'' The Dictator looked around. ''Where is Sextus Roscius?''

Sextus Roscius was produced.

''Sextus Roscius, take back your lands and your reputation, and your dead father's reputation,'' said Sulla. ''I am very sorry that the corruption and venality of one I trusted has caused you so much pain. But he will answer for it.''

''Thanks to the brilliance of my advocate, Lucius Cornelius, it has ended well,'' said Sextus Roscius shakily.

''There is an epilogue yet to play,'' said the Dictator, jerked his head at his lictors, and walked away in the direction of the steps which led up onto the Palatine.

The next day Lucius Cornelius Chrysogonus, who was a Roman citizen of the tribe Cornelia, was pitched headlong from the Tarpeian Rock.

"Think yourself lucky," said Sulla to him beforehand. "I could have stripped you of your citizenship and had you flogged and crucified. You die a Roman death because you cared so well for my womenfolk when times were hard. I can do nothing more for you than that. I hired you originally because I knew you were a toad. What I didn't count on was becoming so busy that I was unable to keep an eye on you. But sooner or later it comes out. Bye-bye, Chrysogonus."

The two cousins Roscius—Capito and Magnus—disappeared from Ameria before they could be apprehended and brought to trial; no further trace of them was ever discovered. As for Cicero, he was suddenly a great name and a hero besides. No one else had taken on the proscriptions and won.

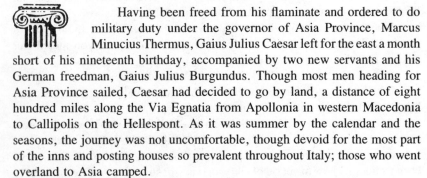 Having been freed from his flaminate and ordered to do military duty under the governor of Asia Province, Marcus Minucius Thermus, Gaius Julius Caesar left for the east a month short of his nineteenth birthday, accompanied by two new servants and his German freedman, Gaius Julius Burgundus. Though most men heading for Asia Province sailed, Caesar had decided to go by land, a distance of eight hundred miles along the Via Egnatia from Apollonia in western Macedonia to Callipolis on the Hellespont. As it was summer by the calendar and the seasons, the journey was not uncomfortable, though devoid for the most part of the inns and posting houses so prevalent throughout Italy; those who went overland to Asia camped.

Because the *flamen Dialis* was not allowed to travel, Caesar had been obliged to travel in his mind, which had devoured every book set in foreign parts, and imagined what the world might look like. Not, he soon learned, as it really was; but the reality was so much more satisfying than imagination! As for the act of travel—even Caesar, so eloquent, could not find the words to describe it. For in him was a born traveler, adventurous, curious, insatiably eager to sample everything. As he went he talked to the whole world, from shepherds to salesmen, from mercenaries looking for work to local chieftains. His Greek was Attic and superlative, but all those odd tongues he had picked up from infancy because his mother's insula contained a polyglot mixture of tenants now stood him in good stead; not because he was lucky enough to find people who spoke them as he went along, but because his intelligence was attuned to strange words and accents, so he was able to hear the Greek in some strange patois, and discern foreign words in basic Greek. It made him a good traveler, in that he was never lost for means of communication.

It would have been wonderful to have had Bucephalus to ride, of course, but young and trusty Flop Ears the mule was not a contemptuous steed in any way save appearance; there were times when Caesar fancied it owned claws rather than hooves, so surefooted was it on rough terrain. Burgundus rode his Nesaean giant, and the two servants rode very good horses—if he himself was on his honor not to bestride any mount except Flop Ears, then the world would have to accept this as an eccentricity, and understand from the caliber of his servants' horses that he was not financially unable to mount himself well. How shrewd Sulla was! For that was where it hurt—Caesar liked to make a good appearance, to dazzle everyone he encountered. A little difficult on a mule!

The first part of the Via Egnatia was the wildest and most inhospitable, for the road, unpaved but well surveyed, climbed the highlands of Candavia, tall mountains which probably hadn't changed much since well before the time of Alexander the Great. A few flocks of sheep, and once in the distance a sight of mounted warriors who might have been Scordisci, were all the evidence of human occupation the travelers saw. From Macedonian Edessa, where the fertile river valleys and plains offered a better livelihood, men became more numerous and settlements both larger and closer together. In Thessalonica, Caesar sought and was given accommodation in the governor's palace, a welcome chance to bathe in hot water—ablutions since leaving Apollonia had been in river or lake, and very cold, even in summer. Though invited to stay longer, Caesar remained only one day there before journeying on.

Philippi—the scene of several battles of fame and recently occupied by one of the sons of King Mithridates—he found interesting because of its history and its strategic position on the flanks of Mount Pangaeus; though even more interesting was the road to the east of it, where he could see the military possibilities inherent in the narrow passes before the countryside flattened a little and the terrain became easier again. And finally there lay before him the Gulf of Melas, mountain-ringed but fertile; a crust of ridge beyond it and the Hellespont came into view, more than merely a narrow strait. It was the place where Helle tumbled from the back of the Golden Ram and gave her name to the waters, it was the site of the Clashing Rocks which almost sank the Argo, it was the place where armies of Asiatic kings from Xerxes to Mithridates had poured in their thousands upon thousands from

Asia into Thrace. The Hellespont was the true crossroads between East and West.

In Callipolis, Caesar took ship at last for the final leg of his journey, aboard a vessel which had room to accommodate the horses, the mule and the pack animals, and which was sailing direct to Pergamum. He was hearing now of the revolt of Mitylene and the siege which was under way, but his orders were to report in Pergamum; he could only hope he would be posted to a war zone.

But the governor, Marcus Minucius Thermus, had other duties in mind for Caesar. "It's vital that we contain this rebellion," he said to this new junior military tribune, "because it's caused by the new system of taxation the Dictator has put into Asia Province. Island states like Lesbos and Chios were very well off under Mithridates, and they'd love to see the end of Rome. Some cities on the mainland feel much the same. If Mitylene succeeds in holding out for a year, we'll have other places thinking they can revolt too. One of the difficulties in containing Mitylene is its double harbor, and the fact that we don't have a proper fleet. So you, Gaius Julius, are going to see King Nicomedes in Bithynia and levy a fleet from him. When you've gathered it, I want you to sail it to Lesbos and put it at the disposal of my legate, Lucullus, who is in charge of the investment."

"You'll have to forgive my ignorance, Marcus Minucius," said Caesar, "but how long does it take to gather a fleet, and how many vessels of what kind do you want?"

"It takes forever," said Thermus wearily, "and you'll get whatever the King can scrape together—or it might be more accurate to say that you'll get as little as the King can escape with. Nicomedes is no different from any other oriental potentate."

The nineteen-year-old frowned, not pleased at this answer, and proceeded to demonstrate to Thermus that he owned a great deal of natural—though not unattractive—arrogance. "That's not good enough," he said. "What Rome wants, Rome must have."

Thermus couldn't help himself; he laughed. "Oh, you have a lot to learn, young Caesar!" he said.

That didn't sit well. Caesar compressed his lips and looked very like his mother (whom Thermus didn't know, or he might have understood Caesar better). "Well, Marcus Minucius, why don't you tell me your ideal delivery date and your ideal fleet composition?" he asked haughtily. "Then I will take it upon myself to deliver your ideal fleet on your ideal date."

Thermus's jaw dropped, and for a moment he genuinely didn't know how best to answer. That this superb self-confidence did not provoke a fit of anger in him, he himself found interesting; nor this time did the young man's arrogance provoke laughter. The governor of Asia Province actually found himself believing that Caesar truly thought himself capable of doing what he said. Time and King Nicomedes would rectify the mistake, but that Caesar could make it was indeed interesting, in view of the letter from Sulla which Caesar had presented to him.

He has some claim on me through marriage, this making him my nephew, but I wish to make it abundantly clear that I do not want him favored. In fact, *do not* favor him! I want him given difficult things to do, and difficult offices to occupy. He owns a formidable intelligence coupled with high courage, and it's possible he'll do extremely well.

However, if I exclude Caesar's conduct during the course of two interviews with me, his history to date has been uninspiring, thanks to his being the *flamen Dialis*. From this he is now released, legally and religiously. But it means that he has not done military service, so his valor may simply be verbal.

Test him, Marcus Minucius, and tell my dear Lucullus to do the same. If he breaks, you have my full permission to be as ruthless as you like in punishing him. If he does not break, I expect you to give him his due.

I have a last, if peculiar, request. If at any time you witness or learn that Caesar has ridden a better animal than his mule, send him home at once in disgrace.

In view of this letter, Thermus, recovering from his utter stupefaction, said in even tones, "All right, Gaius Julius, I'll give you a time and a size. Deliver the fleet to Lucullus's camp on the Anatolian shore to the north of the city on the Kalends of November. You won't stand a chance of prising one vessel out of old Nicomedes by then, but you asked for a delivery date, and the Kalends of November would be ideal—we'd be able to cut off both harbors before the winter—and give them a hard one. As to size: forty ships, at least half of which should be decked triremes or larger. Again, you'll be lucky if you get thirty ships, and of those, about five decked triremes."

Thermus looked stern. "However, young Caesar, since you opened your mouth, I feel it my duty to warn you that if you are late or if the fleet is less than ideal, it will go against you in my report to Rome."

"As it should," said Caesar, undismayed.

"You may have rooms here in the palace for the time being," said

Thermus cordially; despite Sulla's giving him permission, it was no part of Thermus's policy to antagonize someone related to the Dictator.

"No, I'm off to Bithynia today," said Caesar, moving toward the door.

"There's no need to overdo it, Gaius Julius!"

"Perhaps not. But there's every need to get going," said Caesar, and got going.

It was some time before Thermus went back to his endless paperwork. What an extraordinary fellow! Very well mannered, but in that inimitable way only patricians of the great families seemed to own; the young man left it in no doubt that he liked all men and felt himself superior to none, while at the same time knowing himself superior to all save (perhaps) a Fabius Maximus. Impossible to define, but that was the way they were, especially the Julians and the Fabians. So good-looking! Having no sexual liking for men, Thermus pondered about Caesar in that respect; looks of Caesar's kind very often predisposed their possessors toward a sexual liking for men. Yet, he decided, Caesar had not behaved preciously at all.

The paperwork reproached silently and Thermus went back to it; within moments he had forgotten all about Gaius Julius Caesar and the impossible fleet.

Caesar went overland from Pergamum without permitting his tiny entourage a night's rest in a Pergamum inn. He followed the course of the Caicus River to its sources before crossing a high ridge and coming down to the valley of the Macestus River, known as the Rhyndacus closer to the sea; the latter, it seemed from talking to various locals, he would do better not to aim for. Instead he turned off the Rhyndacus parallel to the coast of the Propontis and went to Prusa. There was, he had been told, just a chance that King Nicomedes was visiting his second-largest city. Prusa's position on the flanks of an imposing snow-covered massif appealed to Caesar strongly, but the King was not in residence. On went Caesar to the Sangarius River, and, after a short ride to the west of it, came to the principal royal seat of Nicomedia dreaming upon its long, sheltered inlet.

So different from Italy! Bithynia, he had discovered, was soft in climate rather than hot, and amazingly fertile thanks to its series of rivers, all flowing more strongly at this time of year than Italian rivers. Clearly the King ruled a prosperous realm, and his people wanted for nothing. Prusa had contained no poverty-stricken inhabitants; nor, it turned out, did Nicomedia.

The palace stood upon a knoll above the town, yet within the formidable walls. Caesar's initial impression was of Greek purity of line, Greek colors, Greek design—and considerable wealth, even if Mithridates had ruled here for several years while the Bithynian king had retreated to Rome. He never remembered seeing the King in Rome, but that was not surprising; Rome allowed no ruling king to cross the *pomerium,* so Nicomedes had rented a prohibitively expensive villa on the Pincian Hill and done all his negotiating with the Senate from that location.

At the door of the palace Caesar was greeted by a marvelously effeminate man of unguessable age who eyed him up and down with an almost slavering appreciation, sent another effeminate fellow off with Caesar's servants to stable the horses and the mule, and conducted Caesar to an anteroom where he was to wait until the King had been informed and his accommodation decided upon. Whether Caesar would succeed in obtaining an immediate audience with the King, the steward (for so he turned out to be) could not say.

The little chamber where Caesar waited was cool and very beautiful, its walls unfrescoed but divided into a series of panels formed by plaster moldings, the cornices gilded to match the panel borders and pilasters. Inside the panels the color was a soft shell-pink, outside them a deep purplish-red. The floor was a marble confection in purples and pinks, and the windows—which looked onto what seemed to be the palace gardens—were shuttered from the outside, thus loomed as framed landscapes of exquisite terraces, fountains, blooming shrubs. So lush were the flowers that their perfumes seeped into the room; Caesar stood inhaling, his eyes closed.

What opened them was the sound of raised voices coming from beyond a half-opened door set into one wall: a male voice, high and lisping, and a female voice, deep and booming.

"Jump!" said the woman. "Upsy-daisy!"

"Rubbish!" said the man. "You degrade it!"

"Oozly-woozly-soozly!" said the woman, and produced a huge whinny of laughter.

"Go away!" from the man.

"Diddums!" from the woman, laughing again.

Perhaps it was bad manners, but Caesar didn't care; he moved to a spot from which his eyes could see what his ears were already hearing. The scene in the adjacent chamber—obviously some sort of private sitting room—was fascinating. It involved a very old man, a big woman perhaps ten years younger, and an elderly, roly-poly dog of some smallish breed Caesar didn't recognize. The dog was performing tricks—standing on its hind legs to beg, lying down and squirming over, playing dead with all four feet in the air. Throughout its repertoire it kept its eyes fixed upon the woman, evidently its owner.

The old man was furious. "Go away, go away, *go away!*" he shouted. As he wore the white ribbon of the diadem around his head, the watcher in the other room deduced he was King Nicomedes.

The woman (the Queen, as she also wore a diadem) bent over to pick up the dog, which scrambled hastily to its feet to avoid being caught, ran round behind her, and bit her on her broad plump bottom. Whereupon the King fell about laughing, the dog played dead again, and the Queen stood rubbing her buttock, clearly torn between anger and amusement. Amusement won, but not before the dog received her well-aimed foot neatly between its anus and its testicles. It yelped and fled, the Queen in hot pursuit.

Alone (apparently he didn't know the next-door room was occupied, nor had anyone yet told him of Caesar's advent), the King's laughter died slowly away. He sat down in a chair and heaved a sigh, it would seem of satisfaction.

Just as Marius and Julia had experienced something of a shock when they had set eyes upon this king's father, so too did Caesar absorb King Nicomedes the Third with considerable amazement. Tall and thin and willowy, he wore a floor-length robe of Tyrian purple embroidered with gold and sewn with pearls, and flimsy pearl-studded golden sandals which revealed that he gilded his toenails. Though he wore his own hair—cut fairly short and whitish-grey in color—he had caked his face with an elaborate maquillage of snow-white cream and powder, carefully drawn in soot-black brows and lashes, artificially pinkened his cheeks, and heavily carmined his puckered old mouth.

"I take it," said Caesar, strolling into the room, "that Her Majesty got what she deserved."

The King of Bithynia goggled. There before him stood a young Roman, clad for the road in plain leather cuirass and kilt. He was very tall and wide-shouldered, but the rest of him looked more slender, except that the calves of his legs were well developed above finely turned ankles wrapped around with military boots. Crowned by a mop of pale gold hair, the Roman's head was a contradiction in terms, as its cranium was so large and round that it looked bulbous, whereas its face was long and pointed. What a face! All bones—but such *splendid* bones, stretched over with smooth pale skin, and illuminated by a pair of large, widely spaced eyes set deep in their sockets. The fair brows were thinnish, the fair lashes thick and long; the eyes themselves could be, the King suspected, disquieting, for their light blue irises were ringed with a blue so dark it appeared black, and gave the black pupils a piercing quality softened at the moment by amusement. To the individual taste of the King, however, all else was little compared to the young man's mouth, full yet disciplined, and with the most kissable, dented corners.

"Well, *hello!*" said the King, sitting upright in a hurry, his pose one of bridling seductiveness.

"Oh, stop that!" said Caesar, inserting himself into a chair opposite the King's.

"You're too beautiful not to like men," the King said, then looked wistful. "If only I were even ten years younger!"

"How old are you?" asked Caesar, smiling to reveal white and regular teeth.

"Too old to give you what I'd like to!"

"Be specific—about your age, that is."

"I am eighty."

"They say a man is never too old."

"To look, no. To do, yes."

"Think yourself lucky you can't rise to the occasion," said Caesar, still smiling easily. "If you could, I'd have to wallop you—and that would create a diplomatic incident."

"Rubbish!" scoffed the King. "You're far too beautiful to be a man for women."

"In Bithynia, perhaps. In Rome, certainly not."

"Aren't you even tempted?"

"No."

"What a disgraceful waste!"

"I know a lot of women who don't think so."

"I'll bet you've never loved one of them."

"I love my wife," said Caesar.

The King looked crushed. "I will never understand Romans!" he exclaimed. "You call the rest of the world barbarian, but it is you who are not civilized."

Draping one leg over the arm of his chair, Caesar swung its foot rhythmically. "I know my Homer and Hesiod," he said.

"So does a bird, if you teach it."

"I am not a bird, King Nicomedes."

"I rather wish you were! I'd keep you in a golden cage just to look at you."

"Another household pet? I might bite *you.*"

"Do!" said the King, and bared his scrawny neck.

"No, thanks."

"This is getting us nowhere!" said the King pettishly.

"Then you have absorbed the lesson."

"Who *are* you?"

"My name is Gaius Julius Caesar, and I'm a junior military tribune attached to the staff of Marcus Minucius Thermus, governor of Asia Province."

"Are you here in an official capacity?"

"Of course."

"Why didn't Thermus notify me?"

"Because I travel faster than heralds and couriers do, though why your own steward hasn't announced me I don't know," said Caesar, still swinging his foot.

At that moment the steward entered the room, and stood aghast to see the visitor sitting with the King.

"Thought you'd get in first, eh?" asked the King. "Well, Sarpedon, abandon all hope! He doesn't like men." His head turned back to Caesar, eyes curious. "Julius. Patrician?"

"Yes."

"Are you a relative of the consul who was killed by Gaius Marius? Lucius Julius Caesar?"

"He and my father were first cousins."

"Then you're the *flamen Dialis*!"

"I was the *flamen Dialis*. You've spent time in Rome."

"Too much of it." Suddenly aware the steward was still in the room, the King frowned. "Have you arranged accommodation for our distinguished guest, Sarpedon?"

"Yes, sire."

"Then wait outside."

Bowing severally, the steward eased himself out backward.

"What are you here for?" asked the King of Caesar.

The leg was returned to the floor; Caesar sat up squarely. "I'm here to obtain a fleet."

No particular expression came into the King's eyes. "Hmm! A fleet, eh? How many ships are you after, and what kind?"

"You forgot to ask when by," said this awkward visitor.

"Add, when by."

"I want forty ships, half of which must be decked triremes or larger, all collected in the port of your choice by the middle of October," said Caesar.

"Two and a half months away? Oh, why not just cut off both my legs?" yelled Nicomedes, leaping to his feet.

"If I don't get what I want, I will."

The King sat down again, an arrested look in his eyes. "I remind you, Gaius Julius, that this is my kingdom, not a province of Rome," he said, his ridiculously carmined mouth unable to wear such anger appropriately. "I will give you whatever I can whenever I can! You *ask*! You don't demand."

"My dear King Nicomedes," said Caesar in a friendly way, "you are a mouse caught in the middle of a path used by two elephants—Rome and Pontus." His eyes had ceased to smile, and Nicomedes was suddenly hideously reminded of Sulla. "Your father died at an age too advanced to permit you tenure of this throne before you too were an old man. The years since your accession have surely shown you how tenuous your position is—you've spent as many of them in exile as you have in this palace, and you are only here now because Rome in the person of Gaius Scribonius Curio put you back. If Rome, which is a great deal further away from Pontus than you are, is well aware that King Mithridates is far from finished—and far from being an old man!—then you too must know it. The land of Bithynia has been called Friend and Ally of the Roman People since the days of the second Prusias, and you yourself have tied yourself inextricably to Rome. Evidently you're more comfortable ruling than in exile. That means you must co-operate with Rome and Rome's requests. Otherwise, Mithridates of Pontus will come galumphing down the path toward Rome galumphing the opposite way—and you, poor little mouse, will be squashed flat by one set of feet—or the other."

The King sat without a thing to say, crimson lips agape, eyes wide. After a long and apparently breathless pause, he took air into his chest with a gasp, and his eyes filled with tears. "That isn't fair!" he said, and broke down completely.

Exasperated beyond endurance, Caesar got to his feet, one hand groping inside the armhole of his cuirass for a handkerchief; he walked across to the King and thrust the piece of cloth at him. "For the sake of the position you hold, compose yourself! Though it may have commenced informally, this is an audience between the King of Bithynia and Rome's designated representative. Yet here you sit bedizened like a *saltatrix tonsa,* and snivel when you hear the unvarnished truth! I was not brought up to chastise venerable grandfathers who also happen to be Rome's client kings, but you invite it! Go and wash your face, King Nicomedes, then we'll begin again."

Docile as a child, the King of Bithynia got up and left.

In a very short time he was back, face scrubbed clean, and accompanied by several servants bearing trays of refreshments.

"The wine of Chios," said the King, sitting down and beaming at Caesar without, it seemed, resentment. "Twenty years old!"

"I thank you, but I'd rather have water."

"*Water?*"

The smile was back in Caesar's eyes. "I am afraid so. I have no liking for wine."

"Then it's as well that the water of Bithynia is renowned," said the King. "What will you eat?"

Caesar shrugged indifferently. "It doesn't matter."

King Nicomedes now bent a different kind of gaze upon his guest; searching, unaffected by his delight in male beauty. So he looked beyond what had previously fascinated him in Caesar, down into the layers below. "How old are you, Gaius Julius?"

"I would prefer that you call me Caesar."

"Until you begin to lose your wonderful head of hair," said the King, betraying the fact that he had been in Rome long enough to learn at least some Latin.

Caesar laughed. "I agree it is difficult to bear a cognomen meaning a fine head of hair! I'll just have to hope that I follow the Caesars in keeping it into old age, rather than the Aurelians in losing it." He paused, then said, "I'm just nineteen."

"Younger than my wine!" said the King in a voice of wonder. "You have Aurelius in you too? Orestes or Cotta?"

"My mother is an Aurelia of the Cottae."

"And do you look like her? I don't see much resemblance in you to Lucius Caesar or Caesar Strabo."

"I have some characteristics from her, some from my father. If you want to find the Caesar in me, think not of Lucius Caesar's younger brother, but his older one—Catulus Caesar. All three of them died when Gaius Marius came back, if you remember."

"Yes." Nicomedes sipped his Chian wine pensively, then said, "I usually find Romans are impressed by royalty. They seem in love with the philosophy of being Republican, but susceptible to the reality of kingship. You, however, are not a bit impressed."

"If Rome had a king, sire, I'd be it," said Caesar simply.

"Because you're a patrician?"

"Patrician?" Caesar looked incredulous. "Ye gods, no! I am a *Julian*! That means I go back to Aeneas, whose father was a mortal man, but whose mother was Venus—Aphrodite."

"You are descended from Aeneas's son, Ascanius?"

"We call Ascanius by the name Iulus," said Caesar.

"The son of Aeneas and Creusa?"

"Some say so. Creusa died in the flames of Troy, but her son did escape with Aeneas and Anchises, and did come to Latium. But Aeneas also had a son by Lavinia, the daughter of King Latinus. And he too was called Ascanius, and Iulus."

"So which son of Aeneas *are* you descended from?"

"Both," said Caesar seriously. "I believe, you see, that there was only one son—the puzzle lies in who mothered him, as everyone knows his father was Aeneas. It is more romantic to believe that Iulus was the son of Creusa, but more likely, I think, that he was the son of Lavinia. After Aeneas died and Iulus grew up, he founded the city of Alba Longa on the Alban Mount— uphill from Bovillae, you might say. Iulus died there, and left his family behind to continue to rule—the Julii. We were the Kings of Alba Longa, and after it fell to King Servius Tullius of Rome, we were brought into Rome as her foremost citizens. We are still Rome's foremost citizens, as is demonstrated by the fact that we are the hereditary priests of Jupiter Latiaris, who is older by far than Jupiter Optimus Maximus."

"I thought the consuls celebrated those rites," said King Nicomedes, revealing more knowledge of things Roman.

"Only at his annual festival, as a concession to Rome."

"Then if the Julii are so august, why haven't they been more prominent during the centuries of the Republic?"

"Money," said Caesar.

"Oh, money!" exclaimed the King, looking enlightened. "A terrible problem, Caesar! For me too. I just haven't the money to give you your fleet—Bithynia is broke."

"Bithynia is not broke, and you *will* give me my fleet, O king of mice! Otherwise—splosh! You'll be spread as thin as a wafer under an elephant's foot."

"*I haven't got it to give you!*"

"Then what are we doing sitting wasting time?" Caesar stood. "Put down your cup, King Nicomedes, and start up the machinery!" A hand went under the King's elbow. "Come on, up with you! We will go down to the harbor and see what we can find."

Outraged, Nicomedes shook himself free. "I wish you would stop telling me what to do!"

"Not until you do it!"

"I'll do it, I'll do it!"

"Now. There's no time like the present."

"Tomorrow."

"Tomorrow might see King Mithridates appear over the hill."

"Tomorrow will *not* see King Mithridates! He's in Colchis, and two thirds of his soldiers are dead."

Caesar sat down, looking interested. "Tell me more."

"He took a quarter of a million men to teach the savages of the Caucasus a lesson for raiding Colchis. Typical Mithridates! Couldn't see how he could lose fielding so many men. But the savages didn't even need to fight. The cold in the high mountains did the work for them. Two thirds of the Pontic soldiers died of exposure," said Nicomedes.

"Rome doesn't know this." Caesar frowned. "Why didn't you inform the consuls?"

"Because it's only just happened—and anyway, it is not *my* business to tell Rome!"

"While you're Friend and Ally, it most definitely is. The last we heard of Mithridates, he was up in Cimmeria reshaping his lands at the north of the Euxine."

"He did that as soon as Sulla ordered Murena to leave Pontus alone," nodded Nicomedes. "But Colchis had been refractory with its tribute, so he stopped off to rectify that and found out about the barbarian incursions."

"Very interesting."

"So as you can see, there is no elephant."

Caesar's eyes twinkled. "Oh yes there is! An even larger elephant. It's called Rome."

The King of Bithynia couldn't help it; he doubled up with laughter. "I give in, I give in! You'll have your fleet!"

Queen Oradaltis walked in, the dog at her heels, to find her ancient husband without his face painted, and crying with laughter. Also decently separated by some feet from a young Roman who looked just the sort of fellow who would be sitting in much closer proximity to one like King Nicomedes.

"My dear, this is Gaius Julius Caesar," said the King when he sobered a little. "A descendant of the goddess Aphrodite, and far better born than we are. He has just maneuvered me into giving him a large and prestigious fleet."

The Queen (who had no illusions whatsoever about Nicomedes) inclined her head regally. "I'm surprised you haven't just given him the whole kingdom," she said, pouring herself a goblet of wine and taking up a cake before she sat down.

The dog bumbled over to Caesar and dumped itself on his feet, gazing up adoringly. When Caesar bent to give it a resounding pat, it collapsed, rolled over, and presented its fat belly to be scratched.

"What's his name?" asked Caesar, who clearly liked dogs.

"Sulla," said the Queen.

A vision of her sandaled toe administering a kick to Sulla's private parts rose up before Caesar's inner gaze; it was now his turn to double up with laughter.

Over dinner he learned of the fate of Nysa, only child of the King and Queen, and heir to the Bithynian throne.

"She's fifty and childless," said Oradaltis sadly. "We refused to allow Mithridates to marry her, naturally, but that meant he made it impossible for us to find a suitable husband for her elsewhere. It is a tragedy."

"May I hope to meet her before I leave?" asked Caesar.

"That is beyond our power," sighed Nicomedes. "When I fled to Rome the last time Mithridates invaded Bithynia, I left Nysa and Oradaltis here in Nicomedia. So Mithridates carried our girl off as a hostage. He still has her in his custody."

"And did he marry her?"

"We think not. She was never a beauty, and she was even then too old to have children. If she defied him openly he may have killed her, but the last we heard she was alive and being held in Cabeira, where he keeps women like the daughters and sisters he won't permit to marry," said the Queen.

"Then we'll hope that when next the two elephants collide on that path, King Nicomedes, the Roman elephant wins the encounter. If I'm not personally a part of the war, I'll make sure whoever is in command knows whereabouts Princess Nysa is."

"By then I hope I'll be dead," said the King, meaning it.

"You can't die before you get your daughter back!"

"If she should ever come back it will be as a Pontic puppet, and that is the reality," said Nicomedes bitterly.

"Then you had better leave Bithynia to Rome in your will."

"As the third Attalus did with Asia, and Ptolemy Apion with Cyrenaica? Never!" declared the King of Bithynia.

"Then it will fall to Pontus. And Pontus will fall to Rome, which means Bithynia will end up Roman anyway."

"Not if I can help it."

"You can't help it," said Caesar gravely.

The next day the King escorted Caesar down to the harbor, where he was assiduous in pointing out the complete absence of ships rigged for fighting.

"You wouldn't keep a navy here," said Caesar, not falling for it. "I suggest we ride for Chalcedon."

"Tomorrow," said the King, more enchanted with his difficult guest in every passing moment.

"We'll start today," said Caesar firmly. "It's—what? Forty miles from here? We won't do it in one ride."

"We'll go by ship," said the King, who loathed traveling.

"No, we'll go overland. I like to get the feel of terrain. Gaius Marius— who was my uncle by marriage—told me I should always journey by land if possible. Then if in future I should campaign there, I would know the lie of the land. Very useful."

"So both Marius and Sulla are your uncles by marriage."

"I'm extraordinarily well connected," said Caesar solemnly.

"I think you have everything, Caesar! Powerful relatives, high birth, a fine mind, a fine body, and beauty. I am very glad I am not you."

"Why?"

"You'll never not have enemies. Jealousy—or envy, if you prefer to use that term to describe the coveting of characteristics rather than love— will dog your footsteps as the Furies did poor Orestes. Some will envy you the beauty, some the body or its height, some the birth, some the mind. Most will envy you all of them. And the higher you rise, the worse it will become. You will have enemies everywhere, and no friends. You will be able to trust neither man nor woman."

Caesar listened to this with a sober face. "Yes, I think that is a fair comment," he said deliberately. "What do you suggest I do about it?"

"There was a Roman once in the time of the Kings. His name was Brutus," said the King, displaying yet more knowledge of Rome. "Brutus was very clever. But he hid it under a facade of brutish stupidity, hence his cognomen. So when King Tarquinius Superbus killed men in every direction, it never once occurred to him to kill Brutus. Who deposed him and became the first consul of the new Republic."

"And executed his own sons when they tried to bring King Tarquinius Superbus back from exile and restore the monarchy to Rome," said Caesar. "Pah! I've never admired Brutus. Nor will I emulate him by pretending I'm stupid."

"Then you must take whatever comes."

"Believe me, I intend to take whatever comes!"

"It's too late to start for Chalcedon today," said the King slyly. "I feel like an early dinner, then we can have some more of this wonderfully stimulating conversation, and ride at dawn."

"Oh, we'll ride at dawn," said Caesar cheerfully, "but not from here.

I'm leaving for Chalcedon in an hour. If you want to come, you'll have to hurry.''

Nicomedes hurried, for two reasons: the first was that he knew he had to keep a strict eye on Caesar, who was high-handed; and the second that he was fathoms deep in love with the young man who continued to profess that he had no weakness for men.

He found Caesar being thrown up into the saddle of a mule.

"A mule?"

"A mule," said Caesar, looking haughty.

"Why?"

"It's an idiosyncrasy."

"You're on a mule, and your freedman rides a Nesaean?"

"So your eyes obviously tell you."

Sighing, the King was helped tenderly into his two-wheeled carriage, which followed Caesar and Burgundus at a steady walk. However, when they paused for the night under the roof of a baron so old he had never expected to see his sovereign again, Caesar apologized to Nicomedes.

"I'm sorry. My mother would say I didn't stop to think. You're very tired. We ought to have sailed."

"My body is devastated, that's true," said Nicomedes with a smile. "However, your company makes me young again."

Certainly when he joined Caesar to break his fast on the morning after they had arrived in Chalcedon (where there was a royal residence), he was bright and talkative, seemed well rested.

"As you can see," he said, standing on the massive mole which enclosed Chalcedon's harbor, "I have a neat little navy. Twelve triremes, seven quinqueremes, and fourteen undecked ships. Here, that is. I have more in Chrysopolis and in Dascylium."

"Doesn't Byzantium take a share of the Bosporan tolls?"

"Not these days. The Byzantines used to levy the tolls—they were very powerful, used to have a navy almost the equal of the Rhodians. But after the fall of Greece and then Macedonia, they had to keep a large land army to repel the Thracian barbarians, who still raid them. Simply, Byzantium couldn't afford to keep a navy as well as an army. So the tolls passed to Bithynia.''

"Which is why you have several neat little navies."

"*And* why I have to retain my neat little navies! I can donate Rome ten triremes and five quinqueremes altogether, from what is here and what is elsewhere. And ten undecked ships. The rest of your fleet I'll hire."

"Hire?" asked Caesar blankly.

"Of course. How do you think we raise navies?"

"As we do! By building ships."

"Wasteful—but then you Romans are that," said the King. "Keeping your own ships afloat when you don't need them costs money. So we Greek-speaking peoples of Asia and the Aegean keep our fleets down to a minimum. If we need more in a hurry, we hire them. And that is what I'll do."

"Hire ships from where?" asked Caesar, bewildered. "If there were ships to be had along the Aegean, I imagine Thermus would have commandeered them already."

"Of course not from the Aegean!" said Nicomedes scornfully, delighted that he was teaching something to this formidably knowledgeable youth. "I'll hire them from Paphlagonia and Pontus."

"You mean King Mithridates would hire ships to his enemy?"

"Why would he not? They're lying idle at the moment, and costing him money. He doesn't have all those soldiers to fill them, and I don't think he plans an invasion of Bithynia or the Roman Asian province this year—or next year!"

"So we will blockade Mitylene with ships belonging to the kingdom Mitylene so badly wants to ally itself with," said Caesar, shaking his head. "Extraordinary!"

"Normal," said Nicomedes briskly.

"How do you go about the business of hiring?"

"I'll use an agent. The most reliable fellow is right here in Chalcedon."

It occurred to Caesar that perhaps if ships were being hired by the King of Bithynia for Rome's use, it ought to be Rome paying the bill, but as Nicomedes seemed to regard the present situation as routine, Caesar wisely held his tongue; for one thing, he had no money, and for another, he wasn't authorized to find the money. Best then to accept things as they were. But he began to see why Rome had problems in her provinces, and with her client kings. From his conversation with Thermus, he had assumed Bithynia would be paid for this fleet at some time in the future. Now he wondered exactly how long Bithynia would have to wait.

"Well, that's all fixed up," said the King six days later. "Your fleet will be waiting in Abydus harbor for you to pick it up on the fifteenth day of your October. That is almost two months away, and of course you will spend them with me."

"It is my duty to see to the assembling of the ships," said Caesar, not because he wished to avoid the King, but because he believed it ought to be so.

"You can't," said Nicomedes.

"Why?"

"It isn't done that way."

Back to Nicomedia they went, Caesar nothing loath; the more he had to do with the old man, the more he liked him. And his wife. And her dog.

Since there were two months to while away, Caesar planned to journey to Pessinus, Byzantium, and Troy. Unfortunately the King insisted upon accompanying him to Byzantium, and upon a sea journey, so Caesar never did get to either Pessinus or Troy; what ought to have been a matter of two or three days in a ship turned into almost a month. The royal progress was tediously slow and formal as the King called into every tiny fishing village and allowed its inhabitants to see him in all his glory—though, in deference to Caesar, without his maquillage.

Always Greek in nature and population, Byzantium had existed for six hundred years upon the tip of a hilly peninsula on the Thracian side of the Bosporus, and had a harbor on the horn-shaped northern reach as well as one on the southern, more open side. Its walls were heavily fortified and very high, its wealth manifest in the size and beauty of its buildings, private as well as public.

The Thracian Bosporus was more beautiful than the Hellespont—and more majestic, thought Caesar, having sailed through the Hellespont. That King Nicomedes was the city's suzerain became obvious from the moment the royal barge was docked; every man of importance came flocking to greet him. However, it did not escape Caesar that he himself got a few dark looks, or that there were some present who did not like to see the King of Bithynia on such good terms with a Roman. Which led to another dilemma. Until now Caesar's public associations with King Nicomedes had all been inside Bithynia, where the people knew their ruler so well that they loved his whole person, and understood him. It was not like that in Byzantium, where it soon became obvious that everyone assumed Caesar was the King of Bithynia's boyfriend.

It would have been easy to refute the assumption—a few words here and there about silly old fools who made silly old fools of themselves, and what a nuisance it was to be obliged to dicker for a fleet with a silly old fool. The trouble was, Caesar couldn't bring himself to do that; he had grown to love Nicomedes in every way except the one way Byzantium assumed he did, and he couldn't hurt the poor old man in that one place he himself was hurting most—his pride. But there were cogent reasons why he ought to make the true situation clear, first and foremost because his own future was involved.

He knew where he was going—all the way to the top. Bad enough to attempt that hard climb hiding a part of his nature which was real; but worse by far to attempt it knowing that the inference was quite unjustified. If the King had been younger he might have decided upon a direct appeal, for though Nicomedes condemned the Roman intolerance of homosexuality as un-Hellenic, barbarian even, he would out of his naturally warm and affectionate nature have striven to dispel the illusion. But at his advanced age, Caesar couldn't be sure that the hurt this request would produce would not also be too severe. In short, life, Caesar was discovering after that enclosed and sheltered adolescence he had been forced to endure, could hand a man conundrums to which there were no adequate answers.

Byzantine resentment of Romans was due, of course, to the occupation of the city by Fimbria and Flaccus four years earlier, when they—appointed by the government of Cinna—had decided to head for Asia and a war with Mithridates rather than for Greece and a war with Sulla. It made little difference to the Byzantines that Fimbria had murdered Flaccus, and Sulla had put paid to Fimbria; the fact remained that their city had suffered. And here was their suzerain fawning all over another Roman.

Thus, having arrived at what decisions he could, Caesar set out to make his own individual impression on the Byzantines, intending to salvage what pride he could. His intelligence and education were a great help, but he was not so sure about that element of his nature that his mother so deplored—his charm. It did win over the leading citizens of the city and it did much to mollify their feelings after the singular boorishness and brutishness of Flaccus and Fimbria, but he was forced in the end to conclude that it probably strengthened their impressions of his sexual leanings—male men weren't supposed to be charming.

So Caesar embarked upon a frontal attack. The first phase of this consisted in crudely rebuffing all the overtures made to him by men, and the second phase in finding out the name of Byzantium's most famous courtesan, then making love to her until she cried enough.

"He's as big as a donkey and as randy as a goat," she said to all her friends and regular lovers, looking exhausted. Then she smiled and sighed, and stretched her arms voluptuously. "Oh, but he's wonderful! I haven't had a boy like him in years!"

And that did the trick. Without hurting King Nicomedes, whose devotion to the Roman youth was now seen for what it was. A hopeless passion.

Back to Nicomedia, to Queen Oradaltis, to Sulla the dog, to that crazy palace with its surplus of pages and its squabbling, intriguing staff.

"I'm sorry to have to go," he said to the King and Queen at their last dinner together.

"Not as sorry as we are to see you go," said Queen Oradaltis gruffly, and stirred the dog with her foot.

"Will you come back after Mitylene is subdued?" asked the King. "We would so much like that."

"I'll be back. You have my word on it," said Caesar.

"Good!" Nicomedes looked satisfied. "Now, please enlighten me about a Latin puzzle I have never found the answer to: why is *cunnus* masculine gender, and *mentula* feminine gender?"

Caesar blinked. "I don't know!"

"There must surely be a reason."

"Quite honestly, I've never thought about it. But now that you've drawn it to my attention, it is peculiar, isn't it?"

"*Cunnus* should be *cunna*—it's the female genitalia, after all. And *mentula* should be *mentulus*—it's a man's penis, after all. Below so much masculine bluster, how hopelessly confused you Romans are! Your women are men, and your men, women." And the King sat back, beaming.

"You didn't choose the politest words for our private parts," said Caesar gravely. "*Cunnus* and *mentula* are obscenities." He kept his face straight as he went on. "The answer is obvious, I would have thought. The gender of the equipment indicates the sex it is intended to mate with—the penis is meant to find a female home, and a vagina is meant to welcome a male home."

"Rubbish!" said the King, lips quivering.

"Sophistry!" said the Queen, shoulders shaking.

"What do you have to say about it, Sulla?" asked Nicomedes of the dog, with which he was getting on much better since the advent of Caesar— or perhaps it was that Oradaltis didn't use the dog to tease the old man so remorselessly these days.

Caesar burst out laughing. "When I get home, I will most certainly ask him!"

The palace was utterly empty after Caesar left; its two aged denizens crept around bewildered, and even the dog mourned.

"He is the son we never had," said Nicomedes.

"No!" said Oradaltis strongly. "He is the son we could never have had. Never."

"Because of my family's predisposition?"

"Of course not! Because we aren't Romans. *He* is Roman."

"Perhaps it would be better to say, he is himself."

"Do you think he will come back, Nicomedes?"

A question which seemed to cheer the King up. He said very firmly, "Yes, I believe he will."

When Caesar arrived in Abydus on the Ides of October, he found the promised fleet riding at anchor—two massive Pontic sixteeners, eight quinqueremes, ten triremes, and twenty well-built but not particularly warlike galleys.

"Since you wish to blockade rather than pursue at sea," said part of the King's letter to Caesar, "I have given you as your minor vessels broad-beamed, decked, converted merchantmen rather than the twenty undecked war galleys you asked for. If you wish to keep the men of Mitylene from having access to their harbor during the winter, you will need sturdier vessels than lightweight galleys, which have to be drawn up on shore the moment a storm threatens. The converted merchantmen will ride out all but gales so terrible no one will be on the sea. The two Pontic sixteeners I thought might come in handy, if for no other reason than they *look* so fearsome and daunting. They will break any harbor chain known, so will be useful when you attack. Also, the harbor master at Sinope was willing to throw them in for nothing beyond food and wages for their crews (five hundred men apiece), as he says the King of Pontus can find absolutely no work for them to do at the moment. I enclose the bill on a separate sheet."

The distance from Abydus on the Hellespont to the Anatolian shore of the island of Lesbos just to the north of Mitylene was about a hundred miles, which, said the chief pilot when Caesar applied to him for the information, would take between five and ten days if the weather held and every ship was genuinely seaworthy.

"Then we'd better make sure they all are," said Caesar.

Not used to working for an admiral (for such, Caesar supposed, was his status until he reached Lesbos) who insisted that his ships be gone over thoroughly before the expedition started, the chief pilot assembled Abydus's three shipwrights and inspected each vessel closely, with Caesar hanging over their shoulders badgering them with ceaseless questions.

"Do you get seasick?" asked the chief pilot hopefully.

"Not as far as I know," said Caesar, eyes twinkling.

Ten days before the Kalends of November the fleet of forty ships sailed out into the Hellespont, where the current—which always flowed from the Euxine into the Aegean—bore them at a steady rate toward the southern mouth of the strait at the Mastusia promontory on the Thracian side, and the estuary of the Scamander River on the Asian side. Not far down the Scamander lay Troy—fabled Ilium, from the burning ruins of which his ancestor Aeneas had fled before Agamemnon could capture him. A pity that he hadn't had a chance to visit this awesome site, Caesar thought, then shrugged; there would be other chances.

The weather held, with the result that the fleet—still keeping well together—arrived off the northern tip of Lesbos six days early. Since it was no part of Caesar's plan to get to his destination on any other day than the Kalends of November, he consulted the chief pilot again and put the fleet snugly into harbor within the curling palm of the Cydonian peninsula, where it could not be seen from Lesbos. The enemy on Lesbos did not concern him: he wanted to surprise the besieging Roman army. And cock a snook at Thermus.

"You have phenomenal luck," said the chief pilot when the fleet put out again the day before the Kalends of November.

"In what way?"

"I've never seen better sailing conditions for this time of the year—and they'll hold for several days yet."

"Then at nightfall we'll put in to whatever sheltering bay we can find on Lesbos. At dawn tomorrow I'll take a fast lighter to find the army," said Caesar. "There's no point in bringing the whole fleet down until I find out whereabouts the commander wants to base it."

Caesar found his army shortly after the sun had risen on the following day, and went ashore to find Thermus or Lucullus, whoever was in command. Lucullus, as it turned out. Thermus was still in Pergamum.

They met below the spot where Lucullus was supervising the construction of a wall and ditch across the narrow, hilly spit of land on which stood the city of Mitylene.

It was Caesar of course who was curious; Lucullus was just testy, told no more than that a strange tribune wanted to see him, and deeming all unknown junior officers pure nuisances. His reputation in Rome had grown over the years since he had been Sulla's faithful quaestor, the only legate who had agreed to the march on Rome that first time, when Sulla had been consul. And he had remained Sulla's man ever since, so much so that Sulla had entrusted him with commissions not usually given to men who had not been praetor; he had waged war against King Mithridates and he had stayed in Asia Province after Sulla went home, holding it for Sulla while the governor, Murena, had busied himself conducting an unauthorized war against Mithridates in the land of Cappadocia.

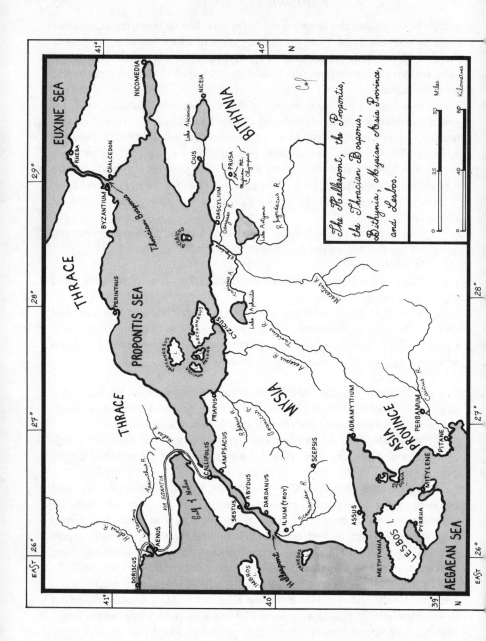

The Hellespont, the Propontis,
the Thracian Bosporus,
Bithynia, Mysian Asia Province,
and Lesbos.

Caesar saw a slim, fit-looking man of slightly more than average height, a man who walked a little stiffly—not, it seemed, because there was anything wrong with his bones, but rather because the stiffness was in his mind. Not a handsome man—but definitely an interesting-looking one—he had a long, pale face surmounted by a thatch of wiry, waving hair of that indeterminate color called mouse-brown. When he came close enough to see his eyes, Caesar discovered they were a clear, light, frigid grey.

The commander's brows were knitted into a frown. "Yes?"

"I am Gaius Julius Caesar, junior military tribune."

"Sent from the governor, I presume?"

"Yes."

"So? Why did you have to ask for me? I'm busy."

"I have your fleet, Lucius Licinius."

"My fleet?"

"The one the governor told me to obtain from Bithynia."

The cold regard became fixed. "Ye gods!"

Caesar stood waiting.

"Well, that *is* good news! I didn't realize Thermus had sent two tribunes to Bithynia," said Lucullus. "When did he send you? In April?"

"As far as I know, I'm the only one he sent."

"Caesar—Caesar . . . You can't be the one he sent at the end of Quinctilis, surely!"

"Yes, I am."

"And you have a fleet *already*?"

"Yes."

"Then you'll have to go back, tribune. King Nicomedes has palmed you off with rubbish."

"This fleet contains no rubbish. I have forty ships I have personally inspected for seaworthiness—two sixteeners, eight quinqueremes, ten triremes, and twenty converted merchantmen the King said would be better for a winter blockade than light undecked war galleys," said Caesar, hugging his delight inside himself so secretly not a scrap of it showed.

"Ye gods!" Lucullus now inspected this junior military tribune as minutely as he would a freak in a sideshow at the circus. A faint turn began to work at tugging the left corner of his mouth upward, and the eyes melted a little. "How did you manage that?"

"I'm a persuasive talker."

"I'd like to know what you said! Nicomedes is as tight as a miser's clutch on his last sestertius."

"Don't worry, Lucius Licinius, I have his bill."

"Call me Lucullus, there are at least six Lucius Liciniuses here." The general turned to walk toward the seashore. "I'll bet you have the bill! What is he charging us for sixteeners?"

"Only the food and wages of their crews."

"Ye gods! Where is this magical fleet?"

"About a mile upshore toward the Hellespont, riding at anchor. I thought it would be better to come ahead myself and ask you whether you want it moored here, or whether you'd rather it went straight on to blockade the Mitylene harbors."

Some of the stiffness had gone from Lucullus's gait. "I think we'll put it straight to work, tribune." He rubbed his hands together. "What a shock for Mitylene! Its men thought they'd have all winter to bring in extra provisions."

When the two men reached the lighter and Lucullus stepped nimbly on board, Caesar hung back.

"Well, tribune? Aren't you coming?"

"If you wish. I'm a little new to military etiquette, so I don't want to make any mistakes," said Caesar frankly.

"Get in, man, get in!"

It was not until the twenty oarsmen, ten to a side, had turned the open boat into the north and commenced the long, easy strokes which ate up distance that Lucullus spoke again.

"New to military etiquette? You're well past seventeen, tribune, are you not? You didn't say you were a *contubernalis*."

Stifling a sigh (he could see that he would be tired of explaining long before explanations were no longer necessary), Caesar said in matter-of-fact tones, "I am nineteen, but this is my first campaign. Until June I was the *flamen Dialis*."

But Lucullus never wanted lavish details; he was too busy and too intelligent. So he nodded, taking for granted all the things most men wanted elaborated. "Caesar . . . Was your aunt Sulla's first wife?"

"Yes."

"So he favors you."

"At the moment."

"Well answered! I am his loyalest follower, tribune, and I say that as a warning I owe to you, considering your relationship to him. I do not permit anyone to criticize him."

"You'll hear no criticisms from me, Lucullus."

"Good."

A silence fell, broken only by the uniform grunt of twenty oarsmen dipping simultaneously into the water. Then Lucullus spoke again, with some amusement.

"I would still like to know how you prised such a mighty fleet out of King Nicomedes."

And that secret delight suddenly popped to the surface in a manner Caesar had not yet learned to discipline; he said something indiscreet to someone he didn't know. "Suffice it to say that the governor annoyed me. He refused to believe that I could produce forty ships, half of them decked, by the Kalends of November. I was injured in my pride, and undertook to produce them. And I have produced them! The governor's lack of faith in my ability to live up to my word demanded it."

This answer irritated Lucullus intensely; he loathed having cocksure men in his army at any level, and he found the statement detestably arrogant. He therefore set out to put this cocksure child in his place. "I know that painted old trollop Nicomedes extremely well," he said in a freezing voice. "Of course you *are* very pretty, and he *is* very notorious. Did he fancy you?" But, as he had no intention of permitting Caesar to reply, he went on immediately. "Yes, *of course* he fancied you! Oh, well done for you, Caesar! It isn't every Roman who has the nobility of purpose to put Rome ahead of his chastity. I think we'll have to call you the face that launched forty ships. Or should that be arse?"

The anger flared up in Caesar so quickly that he had to drive his nails into his palms to keep his arms by his sides; in all his life he had never had to fight so hard to keep his head. But keep it he did. At a price he was never to forget. His eyes turned to Lucullus, wide and staring. And Lucullus, who had seen eyes like that many times before, lost his color. Had there been anywhere to go he would have stepped back out of reach; instead he held his ground. But not without an effort.

"I had my first woman," said Caesar in a flat voice, "at about the time I had my fourteenth birthday. I cannot count the number I have had since. This means I know women very well. And what you have just accused me of, Lucius Licinius Lucullus, is the kind of trickery only women need employ. Women, Lucius Licinius Lucullus, have no other weapon in their arsenal than to use their *cunni* to get what they want—or what some man wants them to get for him. The day I need to resort to sexual trickery to achieve my ends, Lucius Licinius Lucullus, is the day that I will put my sword through my belly. You have a proud name. But compared to mine it is less than the dust. You have impugned my *dignitas*. I will not rest until I have extirpated that stain. How I obtained your fleet is not your affair. Or Thermus's! You may rest assured, however, that it was obtained honorably and without my needing to bed the King—or the Queen, for that matter. The sex of the one being exploited is of little moment. I do not reach my goals by such methods. I reach them by using my intelligence—a gift which, it seems to me, few men own. I should therefore go far. Further, probably, than you.''

Having finished, Caesar turned his back and looked at the receding siegeworks which were making a ruin of the outskirts of Mitylene. And Lucullus, winded, could only be thankful that the verbal exchange had taken place in Latin; otherwise the oarsmen would have spread its gist far and wide. Oh, thank you, Sulla! What a hornet you have sent to enliven our placid little investment! He will be more trouble than a thousand Mitylenes.

The rest of the trip was accomplished in a stony silence, Caesar withdrawn into himself and Lucullus cudgeling his brains to think of a way by which he could retrieve his position without sacrificing his good opinion of himself—for it was absolutely inconceivable that he, the commanding officer of this war, could lower himself to apologize to a junior military tribune. And, as a satisfactory solution continued to elude him, at the end of the short journey he scaled the ladder up onto the deck of the nearest sixteener having to pretend Caesar didn't exist.

When he was standing firmly on the deck he held his right hand, palm outward, to halt Caesar's progress up the ladder.

''Don't bother, tribune,'' he said coldly. ''Return to my camp and find your quarters. I don't want to see you.''

''Am I at liberty to find my servants and horses?''

''Of course.''

If Burgundus, who knew his master as well as anyone, was sure that something had gone very wrong during the time Caesar had been away from the fleet, he was wise enough not to remark upon Caesar's pinched, glazed expression as they set off by land toward Lucullus's camp.

Caesar himself remembered nothing of the ride, nor of the layout of the camp when he rode into it. A sentry pointed down the *via principalis* and informed the new junior military tribune that he would find his quarters in the second brick building on the right. It was not yet noon, but it felt as if the morning had contained a thousand hours, and the kind of weariness Caesar now found in himself was entirely new—dark, frightful, blind.

As this was a permanent camp not expected to be struck before the next spring, its inhabitants were housed more solidly and comfortably than under leather. For the rankers, endless rows of stout wooden huts, each containing eight soldiers; for the noncombatants, bigger wooden huts each containing eighty men; for the general, a proper house almost big enough to be called a mansion, built of sun-dried bricks; for the senior legates, a similar house; for the middle rank of officers, a squarer mud-brick pile four storeys in height; and for the junior military tribunes, the same kind of edifice, only smaller.

The door was open and voices issued from within when Caesar loomed there, hesitating, his servants and animals waiting in the road behind him.

At first he could see little of the interior, but his eyes were quick to respond to changes in the degree of available light, so he was able to take in the scene before anyone noticed him. A big wooden table stood in the middle of the room, around which, their booted feet on its top, sat seven young men. Who they were he didn't know; that was the penalty for being the *flamen Dialis*. Then a pleasant-faced, sturdily built fellow on the far side of the table glanced at the doorway and saw Caesar.

"Hello!" he said cheerfully. "Come in, whoever you are."

Caesar entered with far more assurance than he felt, the effect of Lucullus's accusation still lingering in his face; the seven who stared at him saw a deadly Apollo, not a lyrical one. The feet came down slowly. After that initial welcome, no one said a word. Everyone just stared.

Then the pleasant-faced fellow got to his feet and came round the table, his hand outstretched. "Aulus Gabinius," he said, and laughed. "Don't look so haughty, whoever you are! We've got enough of those already."

Caesar took the hand, shook it strongly. "Gaius Julius Caesar," he said, but could not answer the smile. "I think I'm supposed to be billeted here. A junior military tribune."

"We knew they'd find an eighth somewhere," said Gabinius, turning to face the others. "That's all we are—junior military tribunes—the scum of the earth and a thorn in our general's side. We do occasionally work! But since we're not paid, the general can't very well insist on it. We've just eaten dinner. There's some left. But first, meet your fellow sufferers."

The others by now had come to their feet.

"Gaius Octavius." A short young man of muscular physique, Gaius Octavius was handsome in a rather Greek way, brown of hair and hazel of eye—except for his ears, which stuck straight out like jug handles. His handshake was nicely firm.

"Publius Cornelius Lentulus—plain Lentulus." One of the haughty ones, obviously, and a typical Cornelian—brown of coloring, homely of face. He looked as if he had trouble keeping up, yet was determined to keep up—insecure but dogged.

"The fancy Lentulus—Lucius Cornelius Lentulus Niger. We call him Niger, of course." Another of the haughty ones, another typical Cornelian. More arrogant than plain Lentulus.

"Lucius Marcius Philippus Junior. We call him Lippus—he's such a snail." The nickname was an unkindness, as Lippus did not have bleary eyes; rather, his eyes were quite magnificently large and dark and dreamy, set in a far better-looking face than Philippus owned—from his Claudian grandmother, of course, whom he resembled. He gave an impression of easygoing placidity and his handshake was gentle, though not weak.

"Marcus Valerius Messala Rufus. Known as Rufus the Red." Not one of the haughty ones, though his patrician name was very haughty. Rufus the Red was a red man—red of hair and red of eye. He did not, however, seem to be red of disposition.

"And, last as usual because we always seem to look over the top of his head, Marcus Calpurnius Bibulus."

Bibulus was the haughtiest one of all, perhaps because he was by far the smallest, diminutive in height and in build. His features lent themselves to a natural expression of superiority, for his cheekbones were sharp, as was his bumpy Roman nose; the mouth was discontented and the brows absolutely straight above slightly prominent, pale grey eyes. Hair and brows were white-fair, having no gold in them, which made him seem older than his years, numbering twenty-one.

Very occasionally two individuals upon meeting generate in that first glance a degree of dislike which has no foundation in fact or logic; it is instinctive and ineradicable. Such was the dislike which flared between Gaius Julius Caesar and Marcus Calpurnius Bibulus in their first exchange of glances. King Nicomedes had spoken of enemies—here was one, Caesar was sure.

Gabinius pulled the eighth chair from its position against the wall and set it at the table between his own and Octavius's.

"Sit down and eat," he said.

"I'll sit, gladly, but forgive me if I don't eat."

"Wine, you'll have some wine!"

"I never touch it."

Octavius giggled. "Oh, you'll love living here!" he cried. "The vomit is usually wall to wall."

"You're the *flamen Dialis*!" exclaimed Philippus's son.

"I was the *flamen Dialis*," said Caesar, intending to say no more. Then he thought better of that, and went on, "If I give you the details now, no one need ever ask about it again." He told the story crisply, his words so well chosen that the rest of them—no scholars, any—soon realized the new tribune was an intellectual, if not a scholar.

"Quite a tale," said Gabinius when it was over.

"So you're still married to Cinna's daughter," said Bibulus.

"Yes."

"And," said Octavius, giving a whoop of laughter, "we are now hopelessly locked in the ancient combat, Gabinius! Caesar makes it four patricians! War to the death!"

The rest gave him withering glances, and he subsided.

"Just come out from Rome, have you?" asked Rufus.

"No, from Bithynia."

"What were you doing in Bithynia?" asked plain Lentulus.

"Gathering a fleet for the investment of Mitylene."

"I'll bet that old pansy Nicomedes liked you," sneered Bibulus. Knowing that it was a breach of manners calculated to offend most of those in the room, he had tried not to say it; but somehow his tongue could not resist.

"He did, as a matter of fact," said Caesar coolly.

"Did you get your fleet?" Bibulus pressed.

"Naturally," said Caesar with a haughtiness Bibulus could never have matched.

The laughter was sharp, like Bibulus's face. "Naturally? Don't you mean, *un*-naturally?"

No one actually saw what happened next. Six pairs of eyes only found focus after Caesar had moved around the table and picked Bibulus up bodily, holding him at arm's length, feet well clear of the floor. It looked ridiculous, comedic; Bibulus's arms were swinging wildly at Caesar's smiling face but were too short to connect—a scene straight out of an inspired mime.

"If you were not as insignificant as a flea," said Caesar, "I would now be outside pounding your face into the cobbles. Unfortunately, Pulex, that would be tantamount to murder. You're too insignificant to allow me to beat you to a pulp. So stay out of my way, fleabite!" Still holding Bibulus clear of the floor, he looked about until he found something that would do—a cabinet six feet tall. Without seeming to exert much effort, he popped Bibulus on top, gracefully avoiding the boot Bibulus aimed at him. "Kick your feet up there for a while, Pulex."

Then he was gone, out into the road.

"Pulex really suits you, Bibulus!" said Octavius, laughing. "I shall call you Pulex from now on, you deserve it. How about you, Gabinius? Going to call him Pulex?"

"I'd rather call him Podex!" snapped Gabinius, red-faced with anger. "What possessed you to say that, Bibulus? It was utterly uncalled for, and it makes every one of us look bad!" He glared at the others. "I don't care what the rest of you do, but I'm going out to help Caesar unload."

"Get me down!" said Bibulus from the top of the cabinet.

"Not I!" said Gabinius scornfully.

In the end no one volunteered; Bibulus had to drop cleanly to the floor, for the flimsy unit was too unstable to permit of his lowering himself by his hands. In the midst of his monumental rage he also knew bewilderment and mortification—Gabinius was right. What *had* possessed him? All he had succeeded in doing was making a churl of himself—he had lost the esteem of his companions and could not console himself that he had won the encounter, for he had not. Caesar had won it easily—and with honor—not by striking a man smaller than himself, but rather by showing that man's smallness up. It was only natural that Bibulus should resent size and muscularity in others, as he had neither; the world, he well knew, belonged to big and imposing men. Just the look of Caesar had been enough to set him off—the face, the body, the height—and then, to cap those physical advantages, the fellow had produced a spate of fluent, beautifully chosen words! Not fair!

He didn't know whom he hated most—himself, or Gaius Julius Caesar. The man with everything. Bellows of mirth were floating in from the road, too intriguing for Bibulus to resist. Quietly he crept to the side of the doorway and peered around it furtively. There stood his six fellow tribunes holding their sides, while the man who had everything sat upon the back of a *mule*! Whatever he was saying Bibulus could not hear, but he knew the words were witty, funny, charming, likable, irresistible, fascinating, interesting, superbly chosen, spellbinding.

"Well," he said to himself as he slunk toward the privacy of his room, "he will never, never, never be rid of this flea!"

As winter set in and the investment of Mitylene slowed to that static phase wherein the besiegers simply sat and waited for the besieged to starve, Lucius Licinius Lucullus finally found time to write to his beloved Sulla.

I hold out high hopes for an end to this in the spring, thanks to a very surprising circumstance about which I would rather tell you a little further down the columns. First, I would like you to grant me a favor. If I do manage to end this in the spring, may I come home? It has been so long, dear Lucius Cornelius, and I need to set eyes on Rome—not to mention you. My brother, Varro Lucullus, is now old enough and experienced enough to be a curule aedile, and I have a fancy to share the curule aedileship with him. There is no other office a pair of brothers can share and earn approbation. Think of the games we will give! Not to mention the pleasure. I am thirty-eight now, my brother is thirty-six—almost praetor time, yet we have not been aediles. Our name demands

that we be aediles. Please let us have this office, then let me be praetor
as soon afterward as possible. If, however, you feel my request is not
wise or not deserved, I will of course understand.

Thermus seems to be managing in Asia Province, having given me
the siege of Mitylene to keep me busy and out of his hair. Not a bad
sort of fellow, really. The local peoples all like him because he has the
patience to listen to their tales of why they can't afford to pay the tribute,
and I like him because after he's listened so patiently, he insists they
pay the tribute.

These two legions I have here are composed of a rough lot of fellows.
Murena had them in Cappadocia and Pontus, Fimbria before him. They
have an independence of mind which I dislike, and am busy knocking
out of them. Of course they resent your edict that they never be allowed
to return to Italy because they condoned Fimbria's murder of Flaccus,
and send a deputation to me regularly asking that it be lifted. They get
nowhere, and by this know me well enough to understand that I will
decimate them if they give me half an excuse. They are Rome's soldiers,
and they will do as they are told. I become very testy when rankers and
junior tribunes think they are entitled to a say—but more of that anon.

It seems to me at this stage that Mitylene will have softened to a
workable consistency by the spring, when I intend a frontal assault. I
will have several siege towers in place, so it ought to succeed. If I can
beat this city into submission before the summer, the rest of Asia Province
will lie down tamely.

The main reason why I am so confident lies in the fact that I have
the most superb fleet from—you'll never guess!—Nicomedes! Thermus
sent your nephew by marriage, Gaius Julius Caesar, to obtain it from
Nicomedes at the end of Quinctilis. He did write to me to that effect,
though neither of us expected to see the fleet before March or even April
of next year. But apparently, if you please, Thermus had the audacity
to laugh at young Caesar's confidence that he would get the fleet together
quickly. So Caesar pokered up and demanded a fleet size and delivery
date from Thermus in the most high-handed manner possible. Forty ships,
half of them decked quinqueremes or triremes, delivered on the Kalends
of November. Such were Thermus's orders to this haughty young fellow.

But would you believe it, Caesar turned up in my camp on the
Kalends of November with a far better fleet than any Roman could ever
have expected to get from the likes of Nicomedes? Including two sixteeners, for which I have to pay no more than food and wages for their
crews! When I saw the bill, I was amazed—Bithynia *will* make a profit,

but not an outrageous one. Which makes me honor-bound to return the fleet as soon as Mitylene falls. *And* to pay up. I hope to pay up out of the spoils, of course, but if these should fail to be as large as I expect, is there any chance you could persuade the Treasury to make me a special grant?

I must add that young Caesar was arrogant and insolent when he handed the fleet over to me. I was obliged to put him in his place. Naturally there is only one way he could possibly have extracted such a magnificent fleet in such a short time from old pansy Nicomedes—he slept with him. And so I told him, to put him in his place. But I doubt there is any way in the world to put Caesar in his place! He turned on me like a hooded snake and informed me that he didn't need to resort to women's tricks to obtain anything—and that the day he did was the day he would put his sword through his belly. He left me wondering how to discipline him—not usually a problem I have, as you know. In the end I thought perhaps his fellow junior military tribunes might do it for me. You remember them—you must have seen them in Rome before they set out for service. Gabinius, two Lentuli, Octavius, Messala Rufus, Bibulus, and Philippus's son.

I gather tiny Bibulus did try. And got put up on top of a tall cabinet for his pains. The ranks in the junior tribunes' quarters have been fairly split since—Caesar has acquired Gabinius, Octavius, and Philippus's son—Rufus is neutral—and the two Lentuli and Bibulus loathe him. There is always trouble among young men during siege operations, of course, because of the boredom, and it's difficult to flog the young villains to do any work. Even for me. But Caesar spells trouble above and beyond the usual. I detest having to bother myself with people on this low level, but I have had no choice on several occasions. Caesar is a handful. Too pretty, too self-confident, too aware of what is, alas, a very great intelligence.

However, to give Caesar his due, he's a worker. He never stops. How I don't quite know, but almost every ranker in the camp seems to know him—and like him, more's the pity. He just takes charge. My legates have taken to avoiding him because he won't take orders on a job unless he approves of the way the job is being done. And unfortunately his way is always the better way! He's one of those fellows who has it all worked out in his mind before the first blow is struck or the first subordinate ordered to do a thing. The result is that all too often my legates end up with red faces.

The only way so far that I have managed to prick his confidence is in referring to how he obtained his wonderful fleet from old Nicomedes at such a bargain price. And it does work, to the extent that it angers him hugely. But will he do what I want him to do—physically attack me and give me an excuse to court-martial him? No! He's too clever and too self-controlled. I don't like him, of course. Do you? He had the impudence to inform me that my birth compared to his is less than the dust!

Enough of junior tribunes. I ought to find things to say about grander men—senior legates, for example. But I am afraid that about them I can think of nothing.

I hear that you have gone into the matchmaking business, and have found Pompeius Kid Butcher a wife far above his own standing. You might, if you have the time, find *me* a bride. I have been away since my thirtieth birthday, now I am almost of praetor's age and have no wife, let alone son to succeed me. The trouble is that I prefer good wine, good food and good times to the sort of woman a Licinius Lucullus must marry. Also, I like my women very young, and who is so hard up that he would give me his thirteen-year-old? If you can think of anyone, let me know. My brother absolutely refuses to act as a matchmaker, so you can imagine how happy I was to learn that you have gone into the business.

I love you and miss you, dear Lucius Cornelius.

Late in March, Marcus Minucius Thermus arrived from Pergamum, and agreed that Lucullus should attack. When he heard all the details about Caesar's Bithynian fleet he roared with laughter, though Lucullus was still unable to see the funny side of it; he was too plagued by complaints passed up the command chain about his unruly, scrapping junior military tribunes.

There was, however, a very old and unwritten army law: if a man is a constant source of trouble, put him somewhere in the battle sure to see him dead by the end of it. And, making his plans for the assault on Mitylene, Lucullus resolved to abide by this ancient army law. Caesar would have to die. Full command in the coming battle had been left with him; Thermus would be present only as an observer.

It was not extraordinary for a general to call all ranks of his officers to a final council, but rare enough in the case of Lucullus to cause some comment. Not that anyone thought it odd to see the junior military tribunes present; they were inordinately troublesome, and clearly the general did not trust them. Normally they served, chiefly as messengers, under his legionary tribunes, and it was as such that he appointed them when he came to the fine details at the end of his war council. Except for Caesar, to whom he said coldly,

"You are a pain in the *podex*, but I note that you like to work hard. I have therefore decided to give you command of a special cohort composed of all the worst elements in the Fimbriani. This cohort I will hold in reserve until I see whereabouts the fiercest resistance is. Then I will order it into that section of the battle. It will be your job as their commander to see that they reverse the situation."

"You're a dead man," said Bibulus complacently as they sat in their quarters after the council.

"Not I!" said Caesar cheerfully, splitting a hair from his head with his sword, and another with his dagger.

Gabinius, who liked Caesar enormously, looked worried. "I wish you weren't such a prominent sort of *mentula*," he said. "If you would only pipe down and make yourself inconspicuous, you wouldn't be singled out. He's given you a job he ought not to have given to a junior, especially one who has never served in a campaign before. All of his own troops are Fimbriani and under permanent sentence of exile. He's gathered together the ones who resent it most, then put you in charge of them! If he was going to give you command of a cohort, it ought to have been of men from Thermus's legions."

"I know all that," said Caesar patiently. "Nor can I help it if I'm a prominent sort of *mentula*—ask any of the camp women."

That provoked a chuckle from some, dark looks from others; those who loathed him might have forgiven him more easily had he not, over the course of the winter, earned an enviable reputation among the female camp followers—made more novel and amusing by his insistence that the lucky woman be so clean she shone.

"Aren't you worried at all?" asked Rufus the Red.

"No," said Caesar. "I have luck as well as talent. Wait and see." He slid sword and dagger into their scabbards carefully, then prepared to carry them to his room. As he passed by Bibulus he tickled him under the chin. "Don't be afraid, little Pulex," he said, "you're so small the enemy will never notice you."

"If he wasn't so sure of himself, I might find him more bearable," said plain Lentulus to Lentulus Niger as they trod together up the stairs to their rooms.

"Something will cut him down to size," said Niger.

"Then I hope I'm there to see it," said plain Lentulus, and shivered. "It's going to be nasty tomorrow, Niger."

"Most of all for Caesar," said Niger, and smiled with sour satisfaction. "Lucullus has thrown him to the arrows."

There were six siege towers drawn close to the walls of Mitylene, each big enough to permit the passage of hundreds of troops through them and onto the top of the walls quickly enough to meet the defenders and hurl them down. Unfortunately for Lucullus, the defenders were well aware that their chances of withstanding such an assault were less than their chances of winning a pitched battle outside their walls.

Halfway through the night Lucullus was woken with the news that the city's gates were all open and that sixty thousand men were pouring out to take up stations in the space between Mitylene's walls and the ditch and siege wall Lucullus had built.

Bugles blew, drums rolled, horns blared: the Roman camp became a scene of frenzied activity as Lucullus summoned his soldiers to arms. He now had all four of Asia's legions, as Thermus had brought the other two with him; these had not been a part of Fimbria's army and so would be entitled to return to Rome with Thermus at the conclusion of his term in office. Thus their presence in the siege camp at Mitylene had served to remind the Fimbriani of their permanent exile, and stirred up fresh discontent. Now that a pitched battle was inevitable, Lucullus feared that the Fimbriani would not stand and fight. Which made it more imperative than ever that Caesar's cohort of the most aggressive malcontents be separated from the rest of the army.

Lucullus had twenty-four thousand men, against Mitylene's sixty thousand. But among the seasoned Mitylene warriors would be many old men and little boys—as there always were when a city marshaled its people to fight a force of besiegers.

"I'm a fool, I should have thought of this!" said an angry Lucullus to Thermus.

"What's more to the point, how did they know we were going to attack today?" asked Thermus.

"Spies, probably among the camp women," said Lucullus. "I will have all of them killed later." He returned to the business at hand. "The worst of it is that it's still too dark to see how they've drawn themselves up. I'll have to keep them at bay until I've worked out a plan."

"You're a brilliant tactician, Lucullus," said Thermus. "It will go well, despite this."

At dawn Lucullus stood at the top of one of the towers along his own walls, examining the massed formations of enemy; his troops were already in No Man's Land, clustered along the edge of his ditch, from the bottom of which the hundreds of thousands of sharpened stakes had been hastily removed. Lucullus wanted no impaled Roman soldiers if his army should be forced back. One good thing, it would have to be a fight to the death. Lucullus's wall would prevent his own troops fleeing the field. Not that he anticipated this; the Fimbriani—when they were in the mood to fight—were as good as any troops he had ever commanded.

Before the sun rose he was in No Man's Land himself, with his command chain around him receiving their orders.

"I can't address the army, it would never hear me," he said, tight-lipped. "So everything depends on your hearing me now, and on your absolute obedience. As your orientation point you will use the great north gate of Mitylene, as it is right in the center of our sphere of operation. My army will be drawn up in the shape of a crescent moon, with the wings forward of the center. But in the middle of the hollow exactly opposite the gate I want a forward-thrusting peak. This peak will advance ahead of all other units at a walk, its objective the gate. My tactic is to use the peak to divide the enemy host in two, and to enclose each half within the loops of my crescent. That means the men must keep the shape of their formation, the wing tips almost level with the peak. I have no cavalry, so I must ask the men at the ends of the crescent to behave like cavalry wings. Fast and heavy."

Perhaps seventy men were gathered around him as he stood on a small box to give him sufficient height to see everyone; the cohort centurions were there as well as the officers. His frowning gaze rested upon Caesar and the *pilus prior* centurion who commanded that cohort of rebels he had originally intended as arrow fodder. Lucullus had no trouble in remembering the name of the *pilus prior*—Marcus Silius—an aggressive, ill-mannered upstart who was always the ringleader of the deputations the men of the Fimbriani sent regularly to petition him. This was no time to exact revenge; what he needed was to make a decision based firmly in good sense. And what he had to decide was whether this cohort ought to form the spearhead of that central peak—a cohort sure to die almost to its last man—or be buried at the back of one of the two crescent curves where it could do little save form a rein-forcement. He made up his mind.

"Caesar and Silius—you will take your cohort to the head of the peak and drive toward the gate. Once you reach the gate, hold your ground no matter what they throw at you." And he went on to make the rest of his dispositions.

"The gods help me, that *cunnus* Lucullus has given me a pretty baby to lead us,'' growled Silius to Caesar out of the side of his mouth as they waited for Lucullus to end.

From a seasoned centurion Caesar took the slur without so much as a flicker of irritation. Instead, he laughed. ''Would you rather be led by a pretty baby who sat at Gaius Marius's knee for two years hearing how to fight, or by some ostensibly skilled legate who doesn't know his military arse from his military elbow?''

Gaius Marius! That was the one name echoed in the heart of every Roman soldier like a joy-bell. The gaze Marcus Silius bent upon his commander was searching, even a little mollified. ''And what was you to Gaius Marius?'' he asked.

''He was my uncle. And he believed in me,'' said Caesar.

''But this is your first campaign—and your first battle!'' Silius objected.

''Know everything, Silius, don't you? Then you'd better add this. I won't let you or your men down. But if you let me down, I'll have the lot of you flogged,'' said Caesar.

''You got a deal,'' said Silius promptly, and slipped off to tell his junior centurions what to do.

Lucullus was not the kind of general who wasted time. The moment his officers knew what was expected of them and had put their men into formation, he sounded the advance. It was clear to him that the enemy had no actual plan of battle, for they simply waited in a huge mass spread along the ground under their walls, and when the Roman army began to walk, made no attempt to charge it. They would take its assault on their shields and then fight. Their numbers, they were sure, would win the day.

As shrewd as he was truculent, Silius spread the word from one end of his six hundred men to the other: their commander was a pretty baby who also happened to be Gaius Marius's nephew—and Gaius Marius had believed in him.

Caesar walked alone in front of the standard, his big rectangular shield on his left arm, his sword still in its metal scabbard; Marius had told him that it must not be drawn until the last moment before the enemy was engaged, because,

''You can't afford to look down at the ground, whether you're advancing at a run or a walk,'' he had mumbled out of the unparalyzed corner of his mouth. ''If you're carrying the thing unsheathed in your right hand and you stumble into a hole or trip over a rock, you'll end in wounding yourself.''

Caesar was not afraid, even in the most secret corner of himself, and it never occurred to him for one moment that he might be killed. Then he became aware that his men were singing:

"We—are—the Fim—bri—ani!
Be—ware—the Fim—bri—ani!
We—trapped—the King—of—Pontus!
We—are—the best—there—is!"

Fascinating, mused Caesar as the waiting hordes of Mitylene came closer and closer. It must be four years since Fimbria died, four years in which they've fought for two Licinii, Murena and then Lucullus. He was a wolfshead, Fimbria. But they still think of themselves as his men. They are not—and I suspect they never will be—the Liciniani. How they felt about Murena, I don't know. But they loathe Lucullus! Well, who doesn't? He's such a stiffrumped aristocrat. And he doesn't believe it's useful to have his soldiers love him. How wrong he is.

At exactly the correct moment Caesar signaled the bugler to play "launch spears," and kept cool enough not to duck when over a thousand of them whistled above his head in two volleys which sorely distressed and unsettled the men of Mitylene. Now follow up!

He drew his sword and flashed it in the air, heard the peculiar scrape of six hundred swords being pulled out of their sheaths, and then he walked calmly into the enemy like a senator into a Forum crowd, shield round and not a thought in his head for what was happening at his back. Short, double-edged and razor-sharp, the *gladius* was not a weapon to swing about one's head and slash downward; Caesar used it as it was meant to be used, held at groin level with its blade a hypoteneuse and its wicked point upward, outward. Stab and thrust, thrust and stab.

The enemy didn't like this form of attack, aimed at precious loins, and the cohort of Fimbriani troublemakers just kept on advancing, which gave the men of Mitylene scant room to wield their longer swords above their heads. Shock hurled them back, the pressure of the Romans kept them back for long enough to see Lucullus's peak at the hollow middle of his crescent bury itself deep in the enemy ranks.

After that they took courage and stood to fight by any means they could, all haters of Rome, and determined to die before their beloved Mitylene would fall once more into Roman hands.

A big part of it, Caesar soon discovered, was bluff. When a man came at you, you displayed no terror nor gave ground; for if you did, you lost the encounter mentally and your chances of dying were far greater. Attack, attack, always attack. Look invincible, then it was the enemy soldiers who gave ground. He reveled in it, blessed with fine reflexes and a phenomenally accurate eye, and for a long time he fought on without pausing to think what was happening behind him.

Then, he discovered, there was room even in the hottest contest for intelligence; he was the cohort's commander, and he had almost forgotten its existence. But how to turn about and see what was going on without being cut down? How to gain a vantage spot from which he could assess the situation? His arm was tiring a little, though the low sword stance and the light weight of the sword staved off the kind of fatigue the enemy were obviously suffering as they waved their far heavier weapons around; their swings were becoming progressively wilder and their slashes less enthusiastic.

A heap of enemy dead lay to one side of where he stood, pushed there by the eddying movements of those who still lived and fought. Caesar put everything he had into a sudden flurry of aggression and seized the opportunity this gave him to spring up onto the mound of bodies. His legs were vulnerable, but nothing higher, and the pile was wide enough once he gained its summit to turn around without guarding his legs.

A cheer went up from his men when they saw him, and that gladdened him. But he could see that his cohort was now cut off; Lucullus's spearhead had done its work, yet had not been backed up strongly enough. We are an island in the midst of enemy, he thought. Thanks to Lucullus. But we will stand, and we will not die! Coming down in a series of savage leaps which confused the enemy, he ranged himself beside Marcus Silius, soldiering on.

"We're cut off—blow 'form square,' " he said to the cohort bugler, who fought alongside the standard-bearer.

It was done with formidable precision and speed—oh, these were good troops! Caesar and Silius worked their way inside the square and went around its perimeter cheering the men on and seeing that any weak spots were strengthened.

"If only I had my mule, I could find out what was going on all over the field," said Caesar to Silius, "but junior military tribunes in charge of mere cohorts don't ride. That's a mistake."

"Easy fixed!" said Silius, who now looked at Caesar with great respect. He whistled up a dozen reserves standing nearby. "We'll build you a tribunal out of men and shields."

A short time later Caesar was standing at full stretch on top of four men who held their shields over their heads, having attained this lofty height by a series of human steps.

"Watch out for enemy spears!" shouted Silius to him.

It now became apparent that the outcome of the battle was still hotly disputed, but that Lucullus's tactics were basically sound; the enemy looked as if it might find itself rolled up by the Roman wings, closing inexorably.

"Give me our standard!" Caesar yelled, caught it when the bearer flung it into the air, and waved it on high in the direction of Lucullus, clearly visible on a white horse. "There, that should at least inform the general that we're alive and holding our ground as ordered," he said to Silius when he jumped down, having given two thwarted spearmen a rude gesture with his hand as he did so. "My thanks for providing the tribunal. Hard to know who'll win."

Not long after that the men of Mitylene launched an all-out offensive on Caesar's square.

"We'll never hold," said Silius.

"We'll hold, Silius! Squeeze everybody up as tight as a fish's anus," said Caesar. "Come on, Silius, *do it!*"

He forced his way to where the brunt of the attack was falling, Silius with him, and there laid about left and right, sensing the enemy's desperation. This marooned cohort of Romans must die to serve as an example to the rest of the field. Someone loomed beside him; Caesar heard Silius gasp, and saw the saber coming down. How he managed to fend his own opponent off with his shield and deflect the blow which would have cleaved Silius's head in two, Caesar never afterward understood—only that he did it, and then killed the man with his dagger, though that arm still carried his shield.

The incident seemed to form a kind of watershed, for after it the cohort slowly found the enemy pressure lessening, and was able some time later to continue its advance. The barred gate was reached; in its shelter the Fimbriani turned to face the far-distant Roman wall, exultant—nothing would dislodge them now!

Nothing did. At about an hour before sunset Mitylene gave up the fight, leaving thirty thousand dead soldiers upon the field, mostly old men and little boys. Mercilessly just, Lucullus then executed every woman of Lesbos in the Roman camp, while at the same time he allowed the women of Mitylene to visit the shambles of the battlefield to gather in their dead for proper burial.

It took, Caesar learned, a full month to tidy up the aftermath of battle, and was harder work than preparing for the fray. His cohort—with whom he now associated himself at all times—had decided that he was worthy of Gaius Marius's favor (of course he didn't tell them that Gaius Marius's favor had manifested itself in the form of a flaminate), and that it was Caesar's to command. Several days before the ceremony at which the general, Lucullus, and the governor, Thermus, awarded military decorations to those who had earned them, the *pilus prior* centurion Marcus Silius had gone to Lucullus and Thermus and formally sworn that Caesar had personally saved his life in battle, then held the ground on which it happened until after the contest was over; he also swore that it was Caesar who saved the cohort from certain death.

"If it had been a full legion you would have won the Grass Crown," said Thermus as he fitted the chaplet of oak leaves on Caesar's big golden head by pulling its open ends further apart, "but as only a cohort was involved, the best Rome can do is to give you the *corona civica*." After a moment's thought, he went on to say, "You realize, Gaius Julius, that winning the Civic Crown automatically promotes you to the Senate, and entitles you to other distinctions under the Republic's new laws. It would certainly seem that Jupiter Optimus Maximus is determined to have you in the Senate! The seat you lost when you ceased to be the *flamen Dialis* is now returned to you."

Caesar was the only man at the battle of Mitylene so honored, and his the only cohort given *phalerae* to adorn its *vexillum;* Marcus Silius was awarded a full set of nine golden *phalerae,* which he proudly strapped on the front of his leather cuirass. He already had nine silver *phalerae* (now switched to adorn the back of his cuirass), five broad silver *armillae,* and two gold torcs suspended from his front shoulder straps.

"I'll give Sulla this," said Silius to Caesar as they stood together among the other decorated soldiers on the tribunal while the army saluted them, "he may have denied us the chance to go home, but he was too fair a man to take our decorations off us." He eyed Caesar's oak leaf chaplet admiringly. "You're a real soldier, pretty baby," he said. "I never saw a better."

And that, said Caesar to himself afterward, was worthier praise than all the platitudes and congratulations Lucullus and Thermus and the legates heaped upon him during the banquet they gave in his honor. Gabinius, Octavius, Lippus and Rufus were very pleased for him, and the two Lentuli very quiet. Bibulus, who was not a coward but had not won anything because he had done routine messenger service throughout the battle, could not stay quiet.

"I might have known it," he said bitterly. "You did not one thing any of us could not have done, were we lucky enough to have found ourselves in the same situation. But you, Caesar, have all the luck. In *every* way."

Caesar laughed merrily as he chucked Bibulus under the chin, a habit he had fallen into; it was Gabinius who protested.

"That is to deny a man the proper merit of his actions," he said angrily. "Caesar shamed every last one of us with the amount of work he did during the winter, and he shamed every last one of us on the battlefield by doing more hard work! *Luck?* Luck, you small-minded, envious fool, had nothing to do with it!''

"Oh, Gabinius, you shouldn't let him irk you," said Caesar, who could afford to be gracious—and knew it annoyed Bibulus almost to a fit of tears. "There is always an element of luck. Special luck! It's a sign of Fortune's favor, so it only belongs to men of superior ability. Sulla has luck. He's the first one to say it. But you wait and see! Caesar's luck will become proverbial.''

"And Bibulus's nonexistent," said Gabinius more calmly.

"Probably," said Caesar, his tone indicating that this was a matter which neither interested nor provoked him.

Thermus, Lucullus, their legates, officials and tribunes returned to Rome at the end of June. The new governor of Asia Province, Gaius Claudius Nero, had arrived in Pergamum and taken over, and Sulla had given Lucullus permission to come home, at the same time informing him that he and his brother, Varro Lucullus, would be curule aediles the next year.

"By the time you come home," ended Sulla's letter, "your election as curule aedile will be over. Please excuse me from the role of matchmaker—I seem not to have my usual luck in that particular area. You will by now have heard that Pompeius's new wife has died. Besides, if your taste runs to little girls, my dear Lucullus, then you're better off doing your own dirty work. Sooner or later you'll find some impoverished nobleman willing to sell you his underaged daughter. But what happens when she grows up a bit? They all do!''

It was Marcus Valerius Messala Rufus who arrived in Rome to find a marriage in the making. His sister—of whom he was very fond—had, as he knew from her tear-stained letters, been summarily divorced by her husband. Though she continued to vow that she loved him with every breath she took, the divorce made it plain that he did not love her at all. Why, no one understood. Valeria Messala was beautiful, intelligent, well educated and not boring in any way; she didn't gossip, she wasn't spendthrift, nor did she ogle other men.

One of the city's wealthiest plutocrats died late in June, and his two sons put on splendid funeral games to his memory in the Forum Romanum. Twenty pairs of gladiators clad in ornamental silver were to fight; not one after the other, as was customary, but in two conflicts of ten pairs each—a Thracian pitted against a Gaul. These were styles, not nationalities—the only two styles practiced at that time—and the soldiers of the sawdust had been hired from the best gladiatorial school in Capua. Pining for a little diversion, Sulla was eager to go, so the brothers mourning their dead father were careful to install a comfortable enclosure in the middle of the front row facing north wherein the Dictator could dispose himself without being crushed up against people on either side.

Nothing in the *mos maiorum* prevented women from attending, nor from sitting among the men; funeral games were held to be a kind of circus, rather than a theatrical performance. And her cousin Marcus Valerius Messala Niger, fresh from his triumph of having engaged Cicero to defend Roscius of Ameria, thought that it might cheer poor divorced Valeria Messala up if he took her to see the gladiators fight.

Sulla was already ensconced in his place of honor when the cousins arrived, and the seating was almost filled; the first ten pairs of men were already in the sawdust-cushioned ring, going through their exercises and flexing their muscles as they waited for the bereaved brothers to decide the games should start with the prayers and the sacrifice carefully chosen to please the dead man. But at such affairs it was very useful to have highborn friends, and especially to have an aunt who was both an ex-Vestal and the daughter of Metellus Balearicus. Sitting with her brother, Metellus Nepos, his wife, Licinia, and their cousin Metellus Pius the Piglet (who was consul that year, and hugely important), the ex-Vestal Caecilia Metella Balearica had saved two seats which no one quite had the courage to usurp.

In order to reach them, Messala Niger and Valeria Messala had to work their way past those already sitting in the second row, and therefore directly behind the Dictator. He was, everyone noted, looking rested and well, perhaps because Cicero's tact and skill had enabled him to quash a great deal of lingering feeling about the proscriptions—and eliminate a problem—by throwing Chrysogonus off the Tarpeian Rock. All of the Forum was thronged, the ordinary people perched on every roof and flight of steps, and those with clout in the wooden bleachers surrounding the ring, a roped-off square some forty feet along a side.

It wouldn't have been Rome had not the latecomers been subjected to considerable abuse for pushing their way past those already comfortably seated; though Messala Niger didn't care a hoot, poor Valeria found herself muttering a series of apologies as she pressed on. Then she had to pass directly behind Rome's Dictator; terrified that she might bump him, she fixed her eyes on the back of his head and his shoulders. He was wearing his silly wig, of course, and a purple-bordered *toga praetexta,* his twenty-four lictors crouched on the ground forward of the front row. And as she passed Valeria noticed a fat and fleecy sausage of purple wool adhering to the white folds of toga across Sulla's left shoulder; without stopping to think, she picked it off.

He never showed a vestige of fear in a crowd, always seemed above that, oblivious to danger. But when he felt the light touch Sulla flinched, leaped out of his chair and turned around so quickly that Valeria stepped back onto someone's toes. The last ember of terror still dying out of his eyes, he took in the sight of a badly frightened woman, red-haired and blue-eyed and youthfully beautiful.

"I beg your pardon, Lucius Cornelius," she managed to say, wet her lips, sought for some explanation for her conduct. Trying to be light, she held out the sausage of purple fluff and said, "See? It was on your shoulder. I thought if I picked it off, I might also pick off some of your luck." Her eyes filled with quick tears, resolutely blinked away, and her lovely mouth shook. "I need some luck!"

Smiling at her without opening his lips, he took her outstretched hand in his and gently folded her fingers around the innocent cause of so much fear. "Keep it, lady, and may it bring you that luck," he said, and turned away to sit down again.

But all through the gladiatorial games he kept twisting around to look at where Valeria sat with Messala Niger, Metellus Pius and the rest of that party; and she, very conscious of his searching scrutiny, would smile at him nervously, then blush and look away.

"Who *is* she?" he asked the Piglet as the crowd, well pleased with the magnificent display, was slowly dispersing.

Of course the whole party had noticed (along with a lot of other people), so Metellus Pius did not dissimulate. "Valeria Messala," he said. "Cousin of Niger and sister of Rufus, who is at the moment returning from the siege of Mitylene."

"Ah!" said Sulla, nodding. "As wellborn as she is truly beautiful. Recently divorced, isn't she?"

"Most unexpectedly, and for no reason. She's very cut up about it, as a matter of fact."

"Barren?" asked the man who had divorced one wife for that.

The Piglet's lip curled contemptuously. "I doubt it, Lucius Cornelius. More likely lack of use."

"Hmm!" Sulla paused to think, then said briskly, "She must come to dinner tomorrow. Ask Niger and Metellus Nepos too—and yourself, of course. But not the other women."

* * *

So it was that when the junior military tribune Marcus Valerius Messala Rufus arrived in Rome he found himself summoned to an audience with the Dictator, who didn't mince matters. He was in love with Rufus's sister, he said, and wished to marry her.

"What could I say?" asked Rufus of his cousin Niger.

"I hope you said, delighted," said Niger dryly.

"I said, delighted."

"Good!"

"But how does poor Valeria feel? He's so old and ugly! I wasn't even given a chance to ask her, Niger!"

"She'll be happy enough, Rufus. I know he's nothing much to look at, but he's the unofficial King of Rome—*and* he's as rich as Croesus! If it doesn't do anything else for her, it will be balm to the wound of her undeserved divorce," said Niger strongly. "Not to mention how advantageous the marriage will be for us! I believe he's arranging for me to be a pontifex, and you an augur. Just hold your tongue and be thankful."

Rufus took his cousin's sound advice, having ascertained that his sister genuinely thought Sulla attractive and desirable, and did want the marriage.

Invited to the wedding, Pompey found a moment to have some private speech with the Dictator.

"Half your luck," said that young man gloomily.

"Yes, you haven't had too much luck with wives, have you?" asked Sulla, who was enjoying his wedding feast immensely, and feeling kindly disposed toward most of his world.

"Valeria is a very nice woman," Pompey vouchsafed.

Sulla's eyes danced. "Left out, Pompeius?"

"By Jupiter, yes!"

"Rome is absolutely stuffed with beautiful noblewomen. Why not pick one out and ask her *tata* for her hand?"

"I'm no good at that sort of warfare."

"Rubbish! You're young—rich—handsome—and famous," said Sulla, who liked to tick things off. "Ask, Magnus! *Just ask!* It would be a fussy father who turned you down."

"I'm no good at that sort of warfare," Pompey repeated.

The eyes which had been dancing now surveyed the young man shrewdly; Sulla knew perfectly well why Pompey wouldn't ask. He was too afraid of being told that his birth wasn't good enough for this or that patrician young lady. His ambition wanted the best and his opinion of himself insisted he have the best, but that niggling doubt as to whether a Pompeius from Picenum would be considered good enough held him back time after time. In short, Pompey wanted someone's *tata* to ask him. And nobody's *tata* had.

A thought popped into Sulla's mind, of the sort which had led him to dower Rome with a stammering Pontifex Maximus.

"Do you mind a widow?" he asked, eyes dancing again.

"Not unless she's as old as the Republic."

"I believe she's about twenty-five."

"That's acceptable. The same age as me."

"She's dowerless."

"Her birth concerns me a lot more than her fortune."

"Her birth," said Sulla happily, "is absolutely splendid on both sides. Plebeian, but magnificent!"

"Who?" demanded Pompey, leaning forward. *"Who?"*

Sulla rolled off the couch and stood looking at him a little tipsily. "Wait until I've had my nuptial holiday, Magnus. Then come back and ask me again."

For Gaius Julius Caesar his return had been a kind of triumph he thought perhaps the real thing later on might never equal. He was not only free, but vindicated. He had won a major crown.

Sulla had sent for him at once, and Caesar had found the Dictator genial; the interview took place just before his wedding—which all of Rome was talking about, but not officially. Thus Caesar, bidden seat himself, did not mention it.

"Well, boy, you've outdone yourself."

What did one say? No more candor after Lucullus! "I hope not, Lucius Cornelius. I did my best, but I can do better."

"I don't doubt it, it's written all over you." Sulla directed a rather sly glance at him. "I hear that you succeeded in assembling a fleet of unparalleled excellence in Bithynia."

Caesar couldn't help it; he flushed. "I did as I was told. *Exactly,*" he said, teeth shut.

"Smarting about it, eh?"

"The accusation that I prostituted myself to obtain that fleet is unjustified."

"Let me tell you something, Caesar," said the Dictator, whose lined and sagging face seemed softer and younger than it had when Caesar had last seen him over a year ago. "We have both been the victims of Gaius Marius, but you at least are fully freed of him at—what age? Twenty?"

"Just," said Caesar.

"I had to suffer him until I was over fifty years old, so think yourself lucky. And, if it's any consolation, I don't give a rush who a man sleeps with if he serves Rome well."

"No, it is no consolation!" snapped Caesar. "Not for Rome—not for you—not for Gaius Marius!—would I sell my honor."

"Not even for Rome, eh?"

"Rome ought not to ask it of me if Rome is who and what I believe her to be."

"Yes, that's a good answer," said Sulla, nodding. "A pity it doesn't always work out that way. Rome—as you will find out—can be as big a whore as anyone else. You've not had an easy life, though it hasn't been as hard as mine. But you're like me, Caesar. I can see it! So can your mother. The slur is present. And you will have to live with it. The more famous you become, the more eminent your *dignitas,* the more they'll say it. Just as they say I murdered women to get into the Senate. The difference between us is not in nature, but in ambition. I just wanted to be consul and then consular, and perhaps censor. My due. The rest was foisted on me, mostly by Gaius Marius."

"I want no more than those things," said Caesar, surprised.

"You mistake my meaning. I am not talking about actual offices, but about ambition. You, Caesar, want to be perfect. Nothing must happen to you that makes you less than perfect. It isn't the unfairness of the slur concerns you—what rankles is that it detracts from your perfection. Perfect honor, perfect career, perfect record, perfect reputation. *In suo anno* all the way and in every way. And because you require perfection of yourself, you will require perfection from all around you—and when they prove imperfect, you'll cast them aside. Perfection consumes you as much as gaining my birthright did me."

"I do not regard myself as perfect!"

"I didn't say that. Listen to me! I said you *want* to be perfect. Scrupulous to the highest mathematical power. It won't change. You won't change. But when you have to you will do whatever you have to do. And every time you fall short of perfection, you'll loathe it—and yourself." Sulla held up a piece of paper. "Here is a decree which I will post on the rostra tomorrow. You have won the Civic Crown. According to my laws that entitles you to a seat in the Senate, a special place at the theater and in the circus, and a standing ovation on every occasion when you appear wearing your Civic Crown. You will be required to wear it in the Senate, at the theater and in the circus. The next meeting of the Senate is half a month away. I will expect to see you in the Curia Hostilia."

And the interview was over. But when Caesar reached home he found one more accolade from Sulla. A very fine and leggy young chestnut stallion with a note clipped to its mane that said: "There is no need to ride a mule any longer, Caesar. You have my full permission to ride this beast. He is, however, not quite perfect. Look at his feet."

When Caesar looked, he burst out laughing. Instead of neat uncloven hooves, the stallion's feet were each divided into two toes, a little like a cow's.

Lucius Decumius shivered. "You better have him cut!" he said, not seeing any joke. "Don't want no more like him around!"

"On the contrary," said Caesar, wiping his eyes. "I can't ride him much, he can't be shod. But young Toes here is going to carry me into every battle I fight! And when he isn't doing that, he'll be covering my mares at Bovillae. Lucius Decumius, he's *luck*! I must always have a Toes. Then I'll never lose a battle."

His mother saw the changes in him instantly, and wondered why he sorrowed. Everything had gone so well for him! He had come back with the *corona civica* and had been glowingly mentioned in dispatches. He had even been able to inform her that the drain on his purse had not been as drastic as she had feared; King Nicomedes had given him gold, and his share of the spoils of Mitylene had been the greater because of his Civic Crown.

"I don't understand," said Gaius Matius as he sat in the garden at the bottom of the light well, hands linked about his knees as he stared at Caesar, similarly seated on the ground. "You say your honor has been impeached, and yet you took a bag of gold from the old king. Isn't that wrong?"

From anyone else the question would not have been tolerated, but Gaius Matius was a friend since infancy.

Caesar looked rueful. "Had the accusation come before the gold, yes," he said. "As it was, when the poor old man gave me the gold it was a simple guest-gift. Exactly what a client king ought to give to an official envoy from his patron, Rome. As he gives tribute, what he bestows upon Rome's envoys is free and clear." Caesar shrugged. "I took it with gratitude, Pustula. Life in camp is expensive. My own tastes are not very grand, but one is forever obliged to contribute to the common mess, to special dinners and banquets, to luxuries which everyone else asks for. The wines have to be of the best, the foods ridiculous—and it doesn't matter that I eat and drink plain. So the gold made a big difference to me. After Lucullus had said what he did to me, I thought about sending the gold back. And then I realized that if I did, I would hurt the King. I can't possibly tell him what Lucullus and Bibulus said."

"Yes, I see." Gaius Matius sighed. "You know, Pavo, I am so glad I don't have to become a senator or a magistrate. It's much nicer being an ordinary knight of the *tribuni aerarii*!"

But that Caesar could not even begin to comprehend, so he made no comment about it. Instead, he returned to Nicomedes. "I am honor bound to go back," he said, "and that will only add fuel to the rumors. During the days when I was *flamen Dialis* I used to think that nobody was interested in the doings of people like junior military tribunes. But it isn't so. Everyone gossips! The gods know among how many people Bibulus has been busy, tattling the story of my affair with King Nicomedes. I wouldn't put it past Lucullus either. Or the Lentuli, for that matter. Sulla certainly knew all the juicy details."

"He has favored you," said Matius thoughtfully.

"He has. Though I can't quite understand why."

"If you don't know, I have no chance!" An inveterate gardener, Matius noticed two tiny leaves belonging to a just-germinated weed, and busied himself digging this offender out of the grass. "Anyway, Caesar, it seems to me you'll just have to live the story down. In time it will die. All stories do."

"Sulla says it won't."

Matius sniffed. "Because the stories about him haven't died? Come, Caesar! He's a bad man. You're not. You couldn't be."

"I'm capable of murder, Pustula. All men are."

"I didn't say you weren't, Pavo. The difference is that Sulla is a bad man and you are not."

And from that stand Gaius Matius would not be budged.

Sulla's wedding came and went; the newlywed pair left Rome to enjoy a holiday in the villa at Misenum. But the Dictator was back for the next meeting of the Senate, to which Caesar had been commanded. He was now, at twenty years of age, one of Sulla's new senators. A senator for the second time at twenty!

It ought to have been the most wonderful day of his life, to walk into the filled Senate chamber wearing his chaplet of oak leaves and find the House risen to its feet—including consulars as venerable as Flaccus Princeps Senatus and Marcus Perperna—with hands vigorously applauding in this one permissible infraction of Sulla's new rules of conduct for the Senate.

Instead, the young man found his eyes studying face after face for any hint of amusement or contempt, wondering how far the story had spread, and who despised him. His progress was an agony, not helped when he ascended to the back row wherein the *pedarii* sat—and wherein he fully expected he himself would sit—to find Sulla shouting at him to sit with the men of the middle tier, wherein soldier heroes were located. Of course some men chuckled; it was kindly laughter, and meant to approve of his embarrassment. But of course he took it as derision and wanted to crawl into the furthest, darkest corner.

Through all of it, he had never wept.

When he came home after the meeting—a rather boring one—he found his mother waiting in the reception room. Such was not her habit; busy always, she rarely left her office for very long during the day. Now, stomach roiling, she waited for her son in a stilled patience, having no idea of how she could broach a subject he clearly did not wish to discuss. Had she been a talker it would have been easier for her, of course. But words came hard to Aurelia, who let him divest himself of his toga in silence. Then when he made a movement toward his study she knew she had to find *something* to say or he would leave her; the vexed subject would remain unbroached.

"Caesar," she said, and stopped.

Since he had put on his toga of manhood it had been her custom to address him by his cognomen, mostly because to her "Gaius Julius" was her husband, and his death had not changed the file of references in her mind. Besides which, her son was very much a stranger to her, the penalty she paid for all those years of keeping him at a distance because she feared for him and could not allow herself to be warm or kind.

He halted, one brow raised. "Yes, Mater?"

"Sit down. I want to talk to you."

He sat, expression mildly enquiring, as if she could have nothing of great moment to say.

"Caesar, what happened in the east?" she asked baldly.

The mild enquiry became tinged with a mild amusement. "I did my duty, won a Civic Crown, and pleased Sulla," he said.

Her beautiful mouth went straight. "Prevarication," she said, "does not suit you."

"I wasn't prevaricating."

"You weren't telling me what I need to know either!"

He was withdrawing, eyes chilling from cool to cold. "I can't tell you what I don't know."

"You can tell me more than you have."

"About what?"

"About the trouble."

"What trouble?"

"The trouble I see in your every movement, your every look, your every evasion."

"There is no trouble."

"I do not believe that."

He rose to go, slapping his thighs. "I can't help what you believe, Mater. There is no trouble."

"*Sit down!*"

He sat down, sighing softly.

"Caesar, I will find out. But I would much rather it came from you than from someone else."

His head went to one side, his long fingers locked around themselves, his eyes closed. Then he sighed again, and shrugged. "I obtained a splendid fleet from King Nicomedes of Bithynia. Apparently this was a deed of absolute uniqueness. It was said of me that I obtained it by having sexual relations with the King. So I have returned to Rome the owner of a reputation not for bravery or efficiency or even cunning, but for having sold my body in order to achieve my ends," he said, eyes still closed.

She didn't melt into sympathy, exclaim in horror, or wax indignant. Instead, she sat without saying anything until her son was obliged to open his eyes and look at her. It was a level exchange of glances, two formidable people finding pain rather than consolation in each other, but prepared to negotiate.

"A grave trouble," she said.

"An undeserved slur."

"That, of course."

"I cannot contend with it, Mater!"

"You have to, my son."

"Then tell me how!"

"You know how, Caesar."

"I honestly don't," he said soberly, his face uncertain. "I've tried to ignore it, but that's very difficult when I know what everyone is thinking."

"Who is the source?" she asked.

"Lucullus."

"Oh, I see. . . . He would be believed."

"He *is* believed."

For a long moment she said nothing more, eyes thoughtful. Her son, watching her, marveled anew at her self-containment, her ability to hold herself aloof from personal issues. She opened her lips and began to speak very slowly and carefully, weighing each word before she uttered it.

"You must ignore it, that is first and foremost. Once you discuss it with anyone, you place yourself on the defensive. And you reveal how much it matters to you. Think for a little, Caesar. You know how serious an allegation it is in the light of your future political career. But you *cannot* let anybody else see that you appreciate its seriousness! So you must ignore it for the rest of your days. The best thing is that it has happened now, rather than ten years further on—a man of thirty would find the allegation far harder to contend with than a man of twenty. For that you must be grateful. Those ten years will see many events. But never a repetition of the slur. What you have to do, my son, is to work very hard to dispel the slur.'' The ghost of a smile lit her remarkable eyes. ''Until now, your philanderings have been restricted to the ordinary women of the Subura. I suggest, Caesar, that you lift your gaze much higher. Why, I have no idea, but you do have an extraordinary effect on women! So from now on, your peers must know of your successes. That means you must concentrate upon women who matter, who are well known. Not the courtesans like Praecia, but noblewomen. Great ladies.''

''Deflower lots of Domitias and Licinias, you mean?'' he asked, smiling broadly.

''No!'' she said sharply. ''Not unmarried girls! Never, never unmarried girls! I mean the wives of important men.''

''*Edepol!*'' cried her son.

''Fight fire with fire, Caesar. There is no other way. If your love affairs are not public knowledge, everyone will assume you are intriguing with men. So they must be as scandalous and generally known as possible. Establish a reputation as Rome's most notorious womanizer. But choose your quarry very carefully.'' She shook her head in puzzlement. ''Sulla used to be able to cause women to make absolute fools of themselves over him. On at least one occasion he paid a bitter price—when Dalmatica was the very young bride of Scaurus. He avoided her scrupulously, but Scaurus punished him anyway by preventing his being elected praetor. It took him six years to be elected, thanks to Scaurus.''

''What you're trying to say is that I'll make enemies.''

''Am I?'' She considered it. ''No, what I think I mean to say is that Sulla's trouble arose out of the fact that he did *not* cuckold Scaurus. Had he, Scaurus would have found it much harder to be revenged—it's impossible for a man who is a laughingstock to appear admirable. Pitiable, yes. Scaurus won that encounter because Sulla allowed him to appear noble—the forgiving husband, still able to hold his head up. So if you choose a woman, you must always be sure that it's her husband is the goose. Don't choose a woman who might tell you to jump in the Tiber—and *never* choose one clever enough to lead you on until she is able to tell you to jump in the Tiber absolutely publicly.''

He was staring at her with a kind of profound respect as new on his face as it was inside his mind. ''Mater, you are the most extraordinary woman! How do you know all this? You're as upright and virtuous as Cornelia the Mother of the Gracchi, yet here you are giving your own son the most dreadful advice!''

''I have lived a long time in the Subura,'' she said, looking pleased. ''Besides, that is the point. You are my son, and you have been maligned. What I would do for you I would not do for anyone else, even for my daughters. If I had to, I would kill for you. But that wouldn't solve our problem. So instead I am very happy to kill a few reputations. Like for like.''

Almost he scooped her into his arms, but the old habits were too strong; so he got to his feet and took her hand, kissed it. ''I thank you, Mater. I would kill for you with equal ease and pleasure.'' A thought struck him, made him shiver with glee. ''Oh, I can't wait for Lucullus to marry! And that turd Bibulus!''

The following day brought women into Caesar's life again, though not in a philandering context.

''We are summoned by Julia,'' said Aurelia before her son left to see what was going on in the Forum Romanum.

Aware he had not yet found the time to see his beloved aunt, Caesar made no protest.

The day was fine and hot but the hour early enough to make the walk from the Subura to the Quirinal an enjoyable one. Caesar and Aurelia stepped out up the Vicus ad Malum Punicum, the street which led to the temple of Quirinus on the Alta Semita. There in the lovely precinct of Quirinus stood the Punic apple tree itself, planted by Scipio Africanus after his victory over Carthage. Alongside it grew two extremely ancient myrtle trees, one for the patricians and one for the plebeians. But in the chaotic events which had followed the Italian War the patrician myrtle had begun to wither; it was now quite dead, though the plebeian tree flourished still. It was thought that this meant the death of the Patriciate, so sight of its bare dry limbs brought Caesar no pleasure. Why hadn't someone planted a new patrician myrtle?

The hundred talents Sulla had permitted Julia to retain had provided her with quite a comfortable private dwelling in a lane running between the Alta Semita and the Servian Walls. It was fairly large and had the virtue of being newly built; Julia's income was sufficient to provide enough slaves to run it, and more than enough to permit her life's necessities. She could even afford to support and house her daughter-in-law, Mucia Tertia. Scant comfort to Caesar and Aurelia, who mourned her sadly changed circumstances.

She was almost fifty years old, but nothing seemed to change Julia herself. Having moved to the Quirinal, she took not to weaving on her loom or spinning wool, but to doing good works. Though this was not a poor district—nor even closely settled—she still found families in need of help, for reasons which varied from an excessive intake of wine to illness. A more presumptuous, tactless woman might have been rebuffed, but Julia had the knack; the whole of the Quirinal knew where to go if there was trouble.

There were no good deeds today, however. Julia and Mucia Tertia were waiting anxiously.

"I've had a letter from Sulla," said Mucia Tertia. "He says I must marry again."

"But that contravenes his own laws governing the widows of the proscribed!" said Aurelia blankly.

"When one makes the laws, Mater, it isn't at all difficult to contravene them," said Caesar. "A special enactment for some ostensible reason, and the thing is done."

"Whom are you to marry?" asked Aurelia.

"That's just it," said Julia, frowning. "He hasn't told her, poor child. We can't even decide from his letter whether he has someone in mind, or whether he just wants Mucia to find her own husband."

"Let me see it," said Caesar, holding out his hand. He read the missive at a glance, gave it back. "He gives nothing away, does he? Just orders you to marry again."

"I don't want to marry again!" cried Mucia Tertia.

A silence fell, which Caesar broke. "Write to Sulla and tell him that. Make it very polite, but very firm. Then see what he does. You'll know more."

Mucia shivered. "I couldn't do that."

"You could, you know. Sulla likes people to stand up to him."

"Men, maybe. But not the widow of Young Marius."

"What do you want me to do?" asked Caesar of Julia.

"I have no idea," Julia confessed. "It's just that you're the only man left in the family, so I thought you ought to be told."

"You genuinely don't want to marry again?" he asked Mucia.

"Believe me, Caesar, I do not."

"Then as I am the *paterfamilias,* I will write to Sulla."

At which moment the old steward, Strophantes, shuffled into the room. "*Domina,* you have a visitor," he said to Julia.

"Oh, bother!" she exclaimed. "Deny me, Strophantes."

"He asked specifically to see the lady Mucia."

"Who asked?" Caesar demanded sharply.

"Gnaeus Pompeius Magnus."

Caesar looked grim. "The prospective husband, I presume!"

"But I've never so much as met Pompeius!" cried Mucia Tertia.

"Nor have I," said Caesar.

Julia turned to him. "What do we do?"

"Oh, we see him, Aunt Julia." And Caesar nodded to the old man. "Bring him in."

Back went the steward to the atrium, where the visitor stood oozing impatience and attar of roses.

"Follow me, Gnaeus Pompeius," said Strophantes, wheezing.

Ever since Sulla's wedding Pompey had waited for further news of this mysterious bride the Dictator had found for him. When he heard that Sulla had returned to Rome after his nuptial holiday he expected to be summoned, but was not. Finally, unable to wait a moment longer, he went to Sulla and demanded to know what was happening, what had eventuated.

"About what?" asked Sulla innocently.

"You know perfectly well!" snarled Pompey. "You said you had thought of someone for me to marry!"

"So I did! So I did!" Sulla chuckled gleefully. "My, my, the impatience of youth!"

"Will you *tell* me, you malicious old tormentor?"

"Names, Magnus! Don't call the Dictator names!"

"*Who is she?*"

Sulla gave in. "Young Marius's widow, Mucia Tertia," he said. "Daughter of Scaevola Pontifex Maximus and Crassus Orator's sister, Licinia. There's far more Mucius Scaevola in her than genuine Licinius Crassus because her maternal grandfather was really the brother of her paternal grandfather. And of course she's closely related to Scaevola the Augur's girls called Mucia Prima and Mucia Secunda—hence her given name of Mucia Tertia, even though there's fifty years in age between her and the other two. Mucia Tertia's mother is still alive, of course. Scaevola divorced her for adultery with Metellus Nepos, whom she married afterward. So Mucia Tertia has two Caecilius Metellus half brothers—Nepos Junior and Celer. She's extremely well connected, Magnus, don't you agree? Too well connected to remain the widow of a proscribed man for the rest of her life! My dear Piglet, who is her cousin, has been making these noises at me for some time." Sulla leaned back in his chair. "Well, Magnus, will she do?"

"Will she do?" gasped Pompey. *"Rather!"*

"Oh, splendid." The mountain of work on his desk seemed to beckon; Sulla put his head down to study some papers. After a moment he lifted it to look at Pompey in apparent bewilderment. "I wrote to tell her she was to marry again, Magnus, so there's no impediment," he said. "Now leave me alone, will you? Just make sure I get an invitation to the wedding."

And Pompey had rushed home to bathe and change while his servants chased in a panic to find out whereabouts Mucia Tertia was living these days, then Pompey rushed straight to Julia's house blinding all those he encountered with the whiteness of his toga, and leaving a strong aroma of attar of roses in his wake. Scaevola's daughter! Crassus Orator's niece! Related to the most important Caecilii Metelli! That meant that the sons she would give him would be related by blood to everyone! Oh, he didn't care one iota that she was Young Marius's widow! He would not even care if she was as ugly as the Sibyl of Cumae!

Ugly? She wasn't ugly at all! She was very strange and very beautiful. Red-haired and green-eyed, but both on the dark side, and skin both pale and flawless. *And what about those eyes?* No others like them anywhere! Oh, she was a honey! Pompey fell madly in love with her at first glance, before a word was spoken.

Little wonder, then, that he hardly noticed the other people in the room, even after introductions were made. He drew up a chair beside Mucia Tertia's and took her nerveless hand in his.

"Sulla says that you are to marry me," he said, smiling at her with white teeth and brilliantly shining blue eyes.

"This is the first I know about it," she said, unaccountably feeling her antipathy begin to fade; he was so patently happy—and really very attractive.

"Oh well, that's Sulla for you," he said, catching his breath on a gasp of sheer delight. "But you have to admit that he does have everyone's best interests at heart."

"Naturally *you* would think so," said Julia in freezing tones.

"What are you complaining about? He didn't do too badly by you compared to all the other proscribed widows," said the tactless man in love, gazing at his bride-to-be.

Almost Julia answered that Sulla had been responsible for the death of her only child, but then she thought better of it; this rather silly fellow was too well known to belong to Sulla to hope that he would see any other side.

And Caesar, sitting in a corner, took in his first experience of Gnaeus Pompeius Magnus unobserved. To look at, not a true Roman, that was certain; the Picentine taint of Gaul was all too obvious in his snub nose, his broad face, the dent in his chin. To listen to, not a true Roman, *that* was certain; his total lack of subtlety was amazing. Kid Butcher. He was well named.

"What do you think of him?" asked Aurelia of Caesar as they trudged back to the Subura through the noon heat.

"More germane to ask, what does Mucia think of him?"

"Oh, she likes him enormously. Considerably more than ever she liked Young Marius."

"That wouldn't be hard, Mater."

"No."

"Aunt Julia will find it lonely without her."

"Yes. But she'll just find more to do."

"A pity she has no grandchildren."

"For which, blame Young Marius!" said Aurelia tartly.

They had almost reached the Vicus Patricius before Caesar spoke again. "Mater, I have to go back to Bithynia," he said.

"*Bithynia?* My son, that isn't wise!"

"I know. But I gave the King my word."

"Isn't it one of Sulla's new rules for the Senate that any senator must seek permission to leave Italy?"

"Yes."

"Then that's good," said Aurelia, sounding pleased. "You must be absolutely candid about where you're going to the whole House. And take Eutychus with you as well as Burgundus."

"Eutychus?" Caesar stopped to stare at her. "But he's your steward! You won't manage easily without him. And why?"

"I'll manage without him. He's from Bithynia, my son. You must tell the Senate that your freedman who is still your steward is obliged to travel to Bithynia to see to his business affairs, and that you must accompany him, as is the duty of any proper patron."

Caesar burst out laughing. "Sulla is absolutely right! You ought to have been a man. And so Roman! Subtle. Hit them in the face with my destination instead of pretending I'm going to Greece and then being discovered in Bithynia. One always is discovered in a lie, I find." A different thought occurred to him. "Speaking of subtlety, that fellow Pompeius is not, is he?

I wanted to hit him when he said what he did to poor Aunt Julia. And ye gods, can he brag!''

"Incessantly, I suspect," said Aurelia.

"I'm glad I met him," said her son soberly. "He showed me an excellent reason why the slur upon my reputation might prove a good thing."

"What do you mean?"

"Nothing has served to put him in his place. He has one—but it is not as high or as inviolate as he thinks. Circumstances have conspired to inflate his opinion of himself to insufferable heights. What he's wanted so far has always been given to him. Even a bride far above his merits. So he's grown into the habit of assuming it will be forever thus. But it won't, of course. One day things will go hideously wrong for him. He will find the lesson intolerable. At least I have already had the lesson."

"You really think Mucia is above his merits?"

"Don't you?" asked Caesar, surprised.

"No, I don't. Her birth is immaterial. She was the wife of Young Marius, and she was that because her father knowingly gave her to the son of a complete New Man. Sulla doesn't forget that kind of thing. Nor forgive it. He's dazzled that gullible young man with her birth. But he's neglected to expound upon all his reasons for giving her away to someone beneath her."

"Cunning!"

"Sulla is a fox, like all red men since Ulysses."

"Then it's as well I intend to leave Rome."

"Until after Sulla steps down?"

"Until after Sulla steps down. He says that will be after he superintends the election of the year after next's consuls—perhaps eleven months from now, if he holds his so-called elections in Quinctilis. Next year's consuls are to be Servilius Vatia and Appius Claudius. But who he intends for the year after, I don't know. Catulus, probably."

"Will Sulla be safe if he steps down?"

"Perfectly," said Caesar.

PART FOUR

from OCTOBER 80 B.C.
until MAY 79 B.C.

LUCIUS LICINIUS LUCULLUS

"You'll have to go to Spain," said Sulla to Metellus Pius. "Quintus Sertorius is rapidly taking the whole place over."

Metellus Pius gazed at his superior somewhat reprovingly. "Surely not!" he said in reasonable tones. "He has fruh-fruh-friends among the Lusitani and he's quite strong west of the Baetis, buh-buh-but you have good governors in both the Spanish provinces."

"Do I really?" asked Sulla, mouth turned down. "Not anymore! I've just had word that Sertorius has trounced Lucius Fufidius after that fool was stupid enough to offer him battle. Four legions! Yet Fufidius couldn't beat Sertorius in command of seven thousand men, only a third of whom were Roman!"

"He bruh-bruh-brought the Romans with him from Mauretania last spring, of course," said Metellus Pius. "The rest are Lusitani?"

"Savages, dearest Piglet! Not worth one hobnail on the sole of a Roman *caliga*! But quite capable of beating Fufidius."

"Oh . . . *Edepol!*"

For some reason beyond the Piglet, this delightfully mild expletive sent Sulla into paroxysms of laughter; some time elapsed before the Dictator could compose himself sufficiently to speak further upon the vexing subject of Quintus Sertorius.

"Look, Piglet, I know Quintus Sertorius of old. So do you! If Carbo could have kept him in Italy, I might not have won at the Colline Gate because I may well have found myself beaten long before then. Sertorius is at least Gaius Marius's equal, and Spain is his old stamping ground. When Luscus drove him out of Spain last year, I'd hoped to see the wretched fellow degenerate into a Mauretanian mercenary and trouble us never again. But I ought to have known better. First he took Tingis off King Ascalis, then he killed Paccianus and stole his Roman troops. Now he's back in Further Spain, busy turning the Lusitani into crack Roman troops. It will have to be you who goes to govern Further Spain—and at the start of the New Year, not in spring." He picked up a single sheet of paper and waved it at Metellus Pius gleefully. "You can have eight legions! That's eight less I have to find land for. And if you leave late in December, you can sail direct to Gades."

"A great command," said the Pontifex Maximus with genuine satisfaction, not at all averse to being out of Rome on a long campaign—even if that meant he had to fight Sertorius. No religious ceremonies to perform, no sleepless nights worrying as to whether his tongue would trip him up. In fact, the moment he got out of Rome, he knew his speech impediment would disappear—it always did. He bethought himself of something else. "Whom will you send to govern Nearer Spain?"

"Marcus Domitius Calvinus, I think."

"Not Curio? He's a guh-guh-guh-good general."

"I have Africa in mind for Curio. Calvinus is a better man to support you through a major campaign, Piglet dear. Curio might prove too independent in his thinking," said Sulla.

"I do see what you mean."

"Calvinus can have a further six legions. That's fourteen altogether. Surely enough to tame Sertorius!"

"In no time!" said the Piglet warmly. "Fuh-fuh-fear not, Lucius Cornelius! Spain is suh-suh-safe!"

Again Sulla began to laugh. "Why do I care? I don't know why I care, Piglet, and that's the truth! I'll be dead before you come back."

Shocked, Metellus Pius put out his hands in protest. "No! Nonsense! You're still a relatively young man!"

"It was foretold that I would die at the height of my fame and power," said Sulla, displaying no fear or regret. "I shall step down next Quinctilis, Pius, and retire to Misenum for one last, glorious fling. It won't be a long fling, but I am going to enjoy every single moment!"

"Prophets are un-Roman," said Metellus Pius austerely. "We both know they're more often wrong than right."

"Not this prophet," said Sulla firmly. "He was a Chaldaean, and seer to the King of the Parthians."

Deeming it wiser, Metellus Pius gave the argument up; he settled instead to a discussion of the coming Spanish campaign.

In truth, Sulla's work was winding down to inertia. The spate of legislation was over and the new constitution looked as if it would hold together even after he was gone; even the apportioning of land to his veterans was beginning to arrive at a stage where Sulla himself could withdraw from the business, and Volaterrae had finally fallen. Only Nola—oldest and best foe among the cities of Italy—still held out against Rome.

He had done what he could, and overlooked very little. The Senate was docile, the Assemblies virtually impotent, the tribunes of the plebs mere figureheads, his courts a popular as well as a practical success, and the future governors of provinces hamstrung. The Treasury was full, and its bureaucrats mercilessly obliged to fall into proper practices of accounting. If the Ordo Equester didn't think the loss of sixteen hundred knights who had fallen victim to Sulla's proscriptions was enough of a lesson, Sulla drove it home by stripping the knights of the Public Horse of all their social privileges, then directed that all men exiled by courts staffed by knight juries should come home.

He had crotchets, of course. Women suffered yet again when he forbade any female guilty of adultery to remarry. Gambling (which he abhorred) was forbidden on all events except boxing matches and human footraces, neither of which drew a crowd, as he well knew. But his chief crotchet was the public servant, whom he despised as disorganized, slipshod, lazy, and venal. So he regulated every aspect of the working lives of Rome's secretaries, clerks, scribes, accountants, heralds, lictors, messengers, the priestly attendants called *calatores,* the men who reminded other men of yet other men's names—*nomenclatores*—and general public servants who had no real job description beyond the fact that they were *apparitores.* In future, none of these men would know whose service they would enter when the new magistrates came into office; no magistrate could ask for public servants by name. Lots would be drawn three years in advance, and no group would consistently serve the same sort of magistrate.

He found new ways to annoy the Senate, having already banned every noisy demonstration of approbation or disapproval and changed the order in which senators spoke; now he put a law on the tablets which severely affected the incomes of certain needy senators by limiting the amount of money provincial delegations could spend when they came to Rome to sing the praises of an ex-governor, which meant these delegations could not (as they had in the past) give money to certain needy senators.

It was a full program of laws which covered every aspect of Roman public life as well as much Roman life hitherto private. Everyone knew the parameters of his lot—how much he could spend, how much he could take, how much he paid the Treasury, who he could marry, whereabouts he would be tried, and what he would be tried for. A massive undertaking executed, it seemed, virtually single-handed. The knights were down, but military heroes were up, up, up. The Plebeian Assembly and its tribunes were down, but the Senate was up, up, up. Those closely related to the proscribed were down, but men like Pompey the Great were up, up, up. The advocates who had excelled in the Assemblies (like Quintus Hortensius) were down, but the advocates who excelled in the more intimate atmosphere of the courts (like Cicero) were up, up, up.

"Little wonder that Rome is reeling, though I don't hear a single voice crying Sulla nay," said the new consul, Appius Claudius Pulcher, to his colleague in the consulship, Publius Servilius Vatia.

"One reason for that," said Vatia, "lies in the good sense behind so much of what he has legislated. He is a wonder!"

Appius Claudius nodded without enthusiasm, but Vatia didn't misinterpret this apathy; his colleague was not well, had not been well since his return from the inevitable siege of Nola which he seemed to have supervised on and off for a full ten years. He was, besides, a widower burdened with six children who were already notorious for their lack of discipline and a distressing tendency to conduct their temptestuous and deadly battles in public.

Taking pity on him, Vatia patted his back cheerfully. "Oh, come, Appius Claudius, look at your future more brightly, do! It's been long and hard for you, but you've finally arrived."

"I won't have arrived until I restore my family's fortune," said Appius Claudius morosely. "That vile wretch Philippus took everything I had and gave it to Cinna and Carbo—and Sulla has not given it back."

"You should have reminded him," said Vatia reasonably. "He has had a great deal to do, you know. Why didn't you buy up big during the proscriptions?"

"I was at Nola, if you remember," said the unhappy one.

"Next year you'll be sent to govern a province, and that will set all to rights."

"If my health holds up."

"Oh, Appius Claudius! Stop glooming! You'll survive!"

"I can't be sure of that" was the pessimistic reply. "With my luck, I'll be sent to Further Spain to replace Pius."

"You won't, I promise you," soothed Vatia. "If you won't ask Lucius Cornelius on your own behalf, *I* will! And I'll ask him to give you Macedonia. That's always good for a few bags of gold and a great many important local contracts. Not to mention selling citizenships to rich Greeks."

"I didn't think there were any," said Appius Claudius.

"There are always rich men, even in the poorest countries. It is the nature of some men to make money. Even the Greeks, with all their political idealism, failed to legislate the wealthy man out of existence. He'd pop up in Plato's Republic, I promise you!"

"Like Crassus, you mean."

"An excellent example! Any other man would have plummeted into obscurity after Sulla cut him dead, but not our Crassus!"

They were in the Curia Hostilia, where the New Year's Day inaugural meeting of the Senate was being held because there was no temple of Jupiter Optimus Maximus, and the size of the Senate had grown sufficiently to render places like Jupiter Stator and Castor's too small for a comfortable meeting that was to be followed by a feast.

"Hush!" said Appius Claudius. "Sulla is going to speak."

"Well, Conscript Fathers," the Dictator commenced, voice jovial, "basically it is all done. It was my avowed intention to set Rome back on her feet and make new laws for her that fulfilled the needs of the *mos maiorum*. I have done so. But I will continue as Dictator until Quinctilis, when I will hold the elections for the magistrates of next year. This you already know. However, I believe some of you refuse to credit that a man endowed with such power would ever be foolish enough to step down. So I repeat that I will step down from the Dictatorship after the elections in Quinctilis. This means that next year's magistrates will be the last personally chosen by me. In future years all the elections will be free, open to as many candidates as want to stand. There are those who have consistently disapproved of the Dictator's choosing his magistrates, and putting up only as many names for voting as there are jobs to fill. But—as I have always maintained!—the Dictator must work with men who are prepared to back him wholeheartedly. The electorate cannot be relied upon to return the best men, nor even the men who are overdue for office and entitled to that office by virtue of their rank and experience. So as the Dictator I have been able to ensure I have both the men I wish to work with and to whom office was morally and ethically owed. Like my dear absent Pontifex Maximus, Quintus Caecilius Metellus Pius. He continues to be worthy of my favor, for he is already on the way to Further Spain, there to contend with the outlawed felon, Quintus Sertorius.''

"He's rambling a bit," said Catulus clinically.

"Because he has nothing to say," said Hortensius.

"Except that he *will* stand down in Quinctilis."

"And I am actually beginning to believe that."

But that New Year's Day, so auspiciously begun, was to end with some long-delayed bad news from Alexandria.

Ptolemy Alexander the Younger's time had finally come at the beginning of the year just gone, the second year of Sulla's reign. Word had arrived then from Alexandria that King Ptolemy Soter Chickpea was dead and his daughter Queen Berenice now ruling alone. Though the throne came through her, under Egyptian law she could not occupy it without a king. Might, the embassage from Alexandria humbly asked, Lucius Cornelius Sulla grant Egypt a new king in the person of Ptolemy Alexander the Younger?

"What happens if I deny you?" asked Sulla.

"Then King Mithridates and King Tigranes will win Egypt," said the leader of the delegation. "The throne must be occupied by a member of the Ptolemaic dynasty. If Ptolemy Alexander is not made King and Pharaoh, then we will have to send to Mithridates and Tigranes for the elder of the two bastards, Ptolemy Philadelphus who was called Auletes because of his piping voice.''

"I can see that a bastard might be able to assume the title of King, but can he legally become Pharaoh?" asked Sulla, thus revealing that he had studied the Egyptian monarchy.

"Were he the son of a common woman, definitely not" was the answer. "However, Auletes and his younger brother are the sons of Ptolemy Soter and Princess Arsinoë, the royal concubine who was the eldest legitimate daughter of the King of Nabataea. It has long been the custom for all the small dynasts of Arabia and Palestina to send their oldest daughters to the Pharaoh of Egypt as his concubines, for that is a more august and respectable fate than marriage to other small dynasts—and brings greater security to their fathers, who all need Egyptian co-operation to carry on their trading activities up the Sinus Arabicus and across the various deserts."

"So you're saying that Alexandria *and* Egypt would accept one of the Ptolemaic bastards because his mother was royal?"

"In the event that we cannot have Ptolemy Alexander, that is inevitable, Lucius Cornelius."

"Mithridatid and Tigranic puppets," said Sulla thoughtfully.

"As their wives are the daughters of Mithridates, that too is inevitable. Tigranes is now too close to the Egyptian border for us to insist the Ptolemy bastards divorce these girls. He would invade in the name of Mithridates. And Egypt would fall. We are not militarily strong enough to deal with a war of that magnitude. Besides which, the girls have sufficient Ptolemaic blood to pass on the throne. In the event," said the delegation's leader suavely, "that the child of Ptolemy Soter and his concubine the daughter of the King of Idumaea fails to grow up and provide Auletes with a wife of half-Ptolemaic blood."

Sulla looked suddenly brisk and businesslike. "Leave it with me, I'll attend to the matter. We can't have Armenia and Pontus in control of Egypt!"

His own deliberations were already concluded long since, so without delay Sulla set off for the villa on the Pincian Hill and an interview with Ptolemy Alexander.

"Your day has arrived," said the Dictator to his hostage, no longer such a very young man; he had turned thirty-five.

"Chickpea is dead?" asked Ptolemy Alexander eagerly.

"Dead and entombed. Queen Berenice rules alone."

"Then I must go!" Ptolemy Alexander squawked, agitated. "I must go! There is no time to be wasted!"

"You can go when I say you can go, not a moment before," said Sulla harshly. "Sit down, Your Majesty, and listen to me."

His Majesty sat with his draperies flattening limply around him like a pricked puffball, his eyes very strange between the solid lines of *stibium* he had painted on both upper and lower lids, extended out toward the temples in imitation of the antique Eye of Egypt, the *wadjet;* as he had also painted in thick black brows and whitened the area between them and the black line of the upper lids, Sulla found it absolutely impossible to decide what Ptolemy Alexander's real eyes held. The whole effect, he decided, was distinctly sinister—and probably intended to be.

"You cannot talk to a king as to an inferior," said His Majesty stiffly.

"There is no king in all the world who is not my inferior," Sulla answered contemptuously. "I rule Rome! That makes me the most powerful man between the Rivers of Ocean and Indus. So you will listen, Your Majesty— and without interrupting me! You may go to Alexandria and assume the throne. But only upon certain conditions. Is that understood?"

"What conditions?"

"That you make your will and lodge it with the Vestal Virgins here in Rome. It need only be a simple will. In the event that you die without legitimate issue, you will bequeath the Kingdom of Egypt to Rome."

Ptolemy Alexander gasped. "I can't do that!"

"You can do anything I say you must do—if you want to rule in Alexandria. That is my price. Egypt to fall to Rome if you die without legitimate issue."

The unsettling eyes within their embossed ritual framework slid from side to side, and the richly carmined mouth—full and self-indulgent—worked upon itself in a way which reminded Sulla of Philippus. "All right, I agree to your price." Ptolemy Alexander shrugged. "I don't subscribe to the old Egyptian religion, so what can it matter to me after I'm dead?"

"Excellently reasoned!" said Sulla heartily. "I brought my secretary with me so you'd be able to make out the document here and now. With every royal seal and your personal cartouche attached, of course. I want no arguments from the Alexandrians after you're dead." He clapped for a Ptolemaic servant, and asked that his own secretary be summoned. As they waited he said idly, "There is one other condition, actually."

"What?" asked Ptolemy Alexander warily.

"I believe that in a bank at Tyre you have a sum of two thousand talents of gold deposited by your grandmother, the third Queen Cleopatra. Mithridates got the money she left on Cos, but not what she left at Tyre. And King Tigranes has not yet managed to subdue the cities of Phoenicia. He's too busy with the Jews. You will leave those two thousand talents of gold to Rome."

One look at Sulla's face informed His Majesty that there could be no argument; he shrugged again, nodded.

Flosculus the secretary came, Ptolemy Alexander sent one of his own slaves for his seals and cartouche, and the will was soon made and signed and witnessed.

"I will lodge it for you," said Sulla, rising, "as you cannot cross the *pomerium* to visit Vesta."

Two days later Ptolemy Alexander the Younger departed from Rome with the delegation, and took ship in Puteoli for Africa; it was easier to cross the Middle Sea at this point and then to hug the African coast from the Roman province to Cyrenaica, and Cyrenaica to Alexandria. Besides which, the new King of Egypt wanted to go nowhere near Mithridates or Tigranes, and did not trust to his luck.

In the spring an urgent message had come from Alexandria, where Rome's agent (a Roman ostensibly in trade) had written that King Ptolemy Alexander the Second had suffered a disaster. Arriving safely after a long voyage, he had immediately married his half sister cum first cousin, Queen Berenice. For exactly nineteen days he had reigned as King of Egypt, nineteen days during which, it seemed, he conceived a steadily increasing hatred of his wife. So early on the nineteenth day of his reign, apparently considering this female creature a nonentity, he murdered his forty-year-old wife/sister/cousin/queen. But she had reigned for a long time in conjunction with her father, Chickpea; the citizens of Alexandria adored her. Later during the nineteenth day of his reign the citizens of Alexandria stormed the palace, abducted King Ptolemy Alexander the Second, and literally tore him into small pieces—a kind of free-for-all fun-for-all celebration staged in the agora. Egypt was without king or queen, and in a state of chaos.

"Splendid!" cried Sulla as he read his agent's letter, and sent off an embassage of Roman senators led by the consular and ex-censor Marcus Perperna to Alexandria, bearing King Ptolemy Alexander the Second's last will and legal testament. His ambassadors were also under orders to call in at Tyre on the way home, there to pick up the gold.

From that day to this New Year's Day of the third year of Sulla's reign, nothing further had been heard.

"Our entire journey has been dogged by ill luck," said Marcus Perperna. "We were shipwrecked off Crete and taken captive by pirates—it took two months for the cities of Peloponnesian Greece to raise our ransoms, and then we had to finish the voyage by sailing to Cyrene and hugging the Libyan coast to Alexandria."

"In a pirate vessel?" asked Sulla, aware of the gravity of this news, but nonetheless inclined to laugh; Perperna looked so old and shrunken—and terrified!

"As you so shrewdly surmise, in a pirate vessel."

"And what happened when you reached Alexandria?"

"Nothing good, Lucius Cornelius. Nothing good!" Perperna heaved a huge sigh. "We found the Alexandrians had acted with celerity and efficiency. They knew exactly whereabouts to send after King Ptolemy Alexander was murdered."

"Send for what, Perperna?"

"Send for the two bastard sons of Ptolemy Soter Chickpea, Lucius Cornelius. They petitioned King Tigranes in Syria to give them both young men—the elder to rule Egypt, and the younger to rule Cyprus."

"Clever, but not unexpected," said Sulla. "Go on."

"By the time we reached Alexandria, King Ptolemy Auletes was already on the throne, and his wife—the daughter of King Mithridates—was beside him as Queen Cleopatra Tryphaena. His younger brother—whom the Alexandrians have decided to call Ptolemy the Cyprian—was sent to be regent of Cyprus. His wife—another daughter of Mithridates—went with him."

"And her name is?"

"Mithridatidis Nyssa."

"The whole thing is illegal," said Sulla, frowning.

"Not according to the Alexandrians!"

"Go on, Perperna, go on! Tell me the worst."

"Well, we produced the will, of course. And informed the Alexandrians that we had come formally to annex the Kingdom of Egypt into the empire of Rome as a province."

"And what did they say to that, Perperna?"

"They laughed at us, Lucius Cornelius. By various methods their lawyers proceeded to prove that the will was invalid, then they pointed to the King and Queen upon their thrones and showed us that they had found legitimate heirs."

"But they're *not* legitimate!"

"Only under Roman law, they said, and denied that it applied to Egypt. Under Egyptian law—which seems to consist largely of rules made up on the spur of the moment to support whatever the Alexandrians have in mind—the King and Queen are legitimate."

"So what did you do, Perperna?"

"What *could* I do, Lucius Cornelius? Alexandria was crawling with soldiers! We thanked our Roman gods that we managed to get out of Egypt alive, and with our persons intact."

"Quite right," said Sulla, who did not bother venting his spleen upon unworthy objects. "However, the fact remains that the will is valid. Egypt now belongs to Rome." He drummed his fingers on his desk. "Unfortunately there isn't much Rome can do at the present time. I've had to send fourteen legions to Spain to deal with Quintus Sertorius, and I've no wish to add to the Treasury's expenses by mounting another campaign at the opposite end of the world. Not with Tigranes riding roughshod over most of Syria and no curb in the vicinity now that the Parthian heirs are so embroiled in civil war. Have you still got the will?"

"Oh yes, Lucius Cornelius."

"Then tomorrow I'll inform the Senate what's happened and give the will back to the Vestals against the day when Rome can afford to annex Egypt by force—which is the only way we're going to come into our inheritance, I think."

"Egypt is fabulously rich."

"That's no news to me, Perperna! The Ptolemies are sitting on the greatest treasure in the world, as well as one of the world's richest countries." Sulla assumed the expression which indicated he was finished, but said, it appeared as an afterthought, "I suppose that means you didn't obtain the two thousand talents of gold from Tyre?"

"Oh, we got that without any trouble, Lucius Cornelius," said Perperna, shocked. "The bankers handed it over the moment we produced the will. On our way home, as you instructed."

Sulla roared with laughter. "Well done for you, Perperna! I can almost forgive you the debacle in Alexandria!" He got up, rubbing his hands together in glee. "A welcome addition to the Treasury. And so the Senate will see it, I'm sure. At least poor Rome didn't have to pay for an embassage without seeing an adequate financial return."

All the eastern kings were being troublesome—one of the penalties Rome was forced to endure because her internecine strife had made it impossible for Sulla to remain in the east long enough to render both Mithridates and Tigranes permanently impotent. As it was, no sooner had Sulla sailed home than Mithridates was back intriguing to annex Cappadocia, and Lucius Licinius Murena (then governor of Asia Province and Cilicia) had promptly gone to war against him—without Sulla's knowledge or permission, and in contravention of the Treaty of Dardanus. For a while Murena had done amazingly well, until self-confidence had led him into a series of disastrous encounters with Mithridates on his own soil of Pontus. Sulla had been obliged to send the elder Aulus Gabinius to order Murena back to his own provinces.

It had been Sulla's intention to punish Murena for his cavalier behavior, but then had come the confrontation with Pompey; so Murena had had to be allowed to return and celebrate a triumph in order to put Pompey in *his* place.

In the meantime, Tigranes had used the six years just gone by to expand his kingdom of Armenia southward and westward into lands belonging to the King of the Parthians and the rapidly disintegrating Kingdom of Syria. He had begun to see his chance when he learned that old King Mithradates of the Parthians was too ill to proceed with a projected invasion of Syria—and too ill to prevent the barbarians called Massagetae from taking over all his lands to the north and east of Parthia itself, as well as to prevent one of his sons, Gotarzes, from usurping Babylonia.

As Tigranes himself had once predicted, the death of King Mithradates of the Parthians had provoked a war of succession complicated by the fact that the old man had had three official queens—two his paternal half sisters, and the third none other than a daughter of Tigranes called Automa. While various sons of various mothers fought over what remained, yet another vital satrapy seceded—fabulously rich Elymais, watered by the eastern tributaries of the Tigris, the rivers Choaspes and Pasitigris; the silt-free harbors to the east of the Tigris-Euphrates delta were lost, as was the city of Susa, one of the Parthian royal seats. Uncaring, the sons of old King Mithradates warred on.

So did Tigranes. His first move (in the year Gaius Marius died) was to invade in succession the petty kingdoms of Sophene, Gordyene, Adiabene, and finally Osrhoene. These four little states conquered, Tigranes now owned all the lands bordering the eastern bank of the Euphrates from above Tomisa all the way down to Europus; the big cities of Amida, Edessa and Nisibis were now also his, as were the tolls levied along the great river. But rather than entrust such commercial enterprises as toll collecting to his own Armenians, Tigranes wooed and won over the Skenite Arabs who controlled the arid regions between the Euphrates and the Tigris south of Osrhoene, and exacted tolls on every caravan which passed across their territory. Nomad Bedouins though they were, Tigranes moved the Skenite Arabs into Edessa and Carrhae and appointed them the collectors of Euphrates tolls at Samosata and Zeugma. Their king—whose royal title was Abgar—was now the client of Tigranes, and the Greek-speaking populations of all the towns the King of Armenia had overcome were forced to emigrate to those parts of Armenia where the Greek language was hitherto unknown. Tigranes desperately wanted to be the civilized ruler of a Hellenized kingdom—and what better way to Hellenize it than to implant colonies of Greek speakers within its borders?

As a child Tigranes had been held hostage by the King of the Parthians

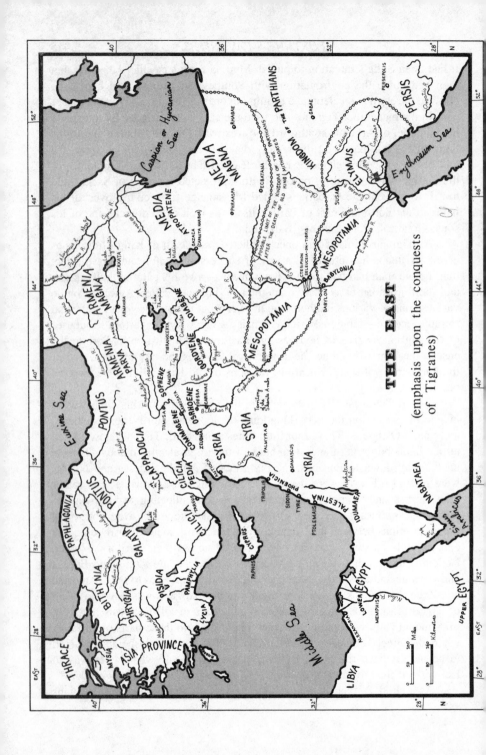

THE EAST

(emphasis upon the conquests of Tigranes)

and had lived in Seleuceia-upon-Tigris, far away from Armenia. At the time of his father's death he was the only living son, but the King of the Parthians had demanded a huge price for releasing the youth Tigranes—seventy valleys in the richest part of Armenia, which was Media Atropatene. Now Tigranes marched into Media Atropatene and took back the seventy valleys, stuffed with gold, lapis lazuli, turquoise and fertile pastures.

He now found, however, that he lacked sufficient Nesaean horses to mount his growing numbers of cataphracts. These strange cavalrymen were clad from head to foot in steel-mesh armor—as were their horses, which needed to be large to carry the weight. So in the following year Tigranes invaded Media itself, the home of the Nesaean horse, and annexed it to Armenia. Ecbatana, summer royal seat of the Kings of the Parthians—and before them, the summer royal seat of the Kings of Media and Persia, including Alexander the Great—was burned to the ground, and its magnificent palace sacked.

Three years had gone by. While Sulla marched slowly up the Italian peninsula, Tigranes had turned his attention to the west and crossed the Euphrates into Commagene. Unopposed, he occupied all the lands of northern Syria between the Amanus Mountains and the Libanus Mountains, including mighty Antioch and the lower half of the valley of the Orontes River. Even a part of Cilicia Pedia fell to him, around the eastern shore of the Sinus Issicus.

Syria was genuine Hellenized territory, its populace a fully Greek-speaking one powerfully under the influence of Greek customs. No sooner had he established his authority in Syria than Tigranes uplifted whole communities of these hapless Greek-speakers and sent them and their families to live in his newly built capital of Tigranocerta. Most favored were the artisans, not one of whom was allowed to remain in Syria. However, the King understood the need to protect his Greek imports from his Median-speaking native peoples, who were directed under pain of death to treat the new citizens with care and kindness.

And while Sulla was legislating to have himself appointed Dictator of Rome, Tigranes formally adopted the title he had hungered for all his life—King of Kings. Queen Cleopatra Selene of Syria—youngest sister and at one time wife of Ptolemy Soter Chickpea—who had managed to rule Syria through several Seleucid husbands, was taken from Antioch and made to live in the humblest circumstances in a tiny village on the Euphrates; her place in the palace at Antioch was taken by the satrap Magadates, who was to rule Syria in the name of Tigranes, King of Kings.

King of Kings, thought Sulla cynically; all those eastern potentates thought themselves King of Kings. Even, it seemed, the two bastard sons of Ptolemy Soter Chickpea, who now ruled in Egypt and Cyprus with their Mithridatid wives. But the will of the dead Ptolemy Alexander the Second *was* genuine; no one knew that better than Sulla did, for he was its witness. Sooner or later Egypt *would* belong to Rome. For the moment Ptolemy Auletes must be allowed to reign in Alexandria; but, vowed Sulla, that puppet of Mithridates and Tigranes would never know an easy moment! The Senate of Rome would send regularly to Alexandria demanding that Ptolemy Auletes step down in favor of Rome, the true owner of Egypt.

As for King Mithridates of Pontus—interesting, that he had lost two hundred thousand men in the freezing cold of the Caucasus—he would have to be discouraged yet again from trying to annex Cappadocia. Complaining by letter to Sulla that Murena had plundered and burned four hundred villages along the Halys River, Mithridates had proceeded to take the Cappadocian bank of the Halys off poor Cappadocia; to make this ploy look legitimate, he had given King Ariobarzanes of Cappadocia a new bride, one of his own daughters. When Sulla discovered that the girl was a four-year-old child, he sent yet another messenger to see King Mithridates and order him in Rome's name to quit Cappadocia absolutely, bride or no bride. The messenger had returned very recently, bearing a letter from Mithridates promising to do as he was told—and informing Sulla that the King of Pontus was going to send an embassage to Rome to ratify the Treaty of Dardanus into watertight legality.

"He'd better make sure his embassage doesn't dawdle," said Sulla to himself as he terminated all these thoughts of eastern kings by going to find his wife. It was in her presence—for she wasn't very far away—that he ended his audible reflections by saying, "If they do dawdle, they won't find me here to dicker with them—and good luck dickering with the Senate!"

"I beg your pardon, my love?" asked Valeria, startled.

"Nothing. Give me a kiss."

Her kisses were nice enough. Just as she was nice enough, Valeria Messala. So far Sulla had found this fourth marriage a pleasant experience. But not a stimulating one. A part of that was due to his age and his illnesses, he was aware; but a larger part of it was due to the seductive and sensuous shortcomings of aristocratic Roman women, who just could not relax sufficiently in bed to enter into the kind of sexual cavorting the Dictator hankered after. His prowess was flagging: he *needed* to be stimulated! Why was it that women could love a man madly, yet not enter wholeheartedly into his sexual wants?

"I believe," said Varro, who was the hapless recipient of this question, "that women are passive vessels, Lucius Cornelius. They are made to hold things, from a man's penis to a baby. And the one who holds things is passive. Must be passive! Otherwise the hold is not stable. It is the same with animals. The male is the active participant, and must rid himself of his excessive desires by rutting with many different females."

He had come to inform Sulla that Pompey was coming to Rome on a brief visit, and to enquire whether Sulla would like to see the young man. Instead of being given an audience, however, he found himself the audience, and had not yet managed to find the right moment to put his own query forward.

The darkened brows wriggled expressively. "Do you mean, my dear Varro, that a decently married man must rut with half of female Rome?"

"No, no, of course not!" gasped Varro. "*All* females are passive, so he could not find satisfaction!"

"Then do you mean that if a man wants his fleshly urges gratified to complete satiation, he ought to seek his sexual partners among men?" Sulla asked, face serious.

"Ooh! Ah! Um!" squeaked Varro, writhing like a centipede pinned through its middle. "No, Lucius Cornelius, of course not! Definitely not!"

"Then what is a decently married man to do?"

"I am a student of natural phenomena, I know, but these are questions I am not qualified or skilled enough to answer!" babbled Varro, wishing he had not decided to visit this uncomfortable, perplexing man. The trouble was that ever since the months during which he, Varro, had anointed Sulla's disintegrating face, Sulla had displayed a great fondness for him, and tended to become offended if Varro didn't call to pay his respects.

"Calm down, Varro, I'm teasing you!" said Sulla, laughing.

"One never knows with you, Lucius Cornelius." Varro wet his lips, began to formulate in his mind the words which would put his announcement of Pompey's advent in the most favorable light; no fool, Varro was well aware that the Dictator's feelings toward Pompey were ambivalent.

"I hear," said Sulla, unconscious of all this mental juggling of a simple sentence, "that Varro Lucullus has managed to get rid of his adoptive sister—your cousin, I believe."

"Terentia, you mean?" Varro's face lit up. "Oh, yes! A truly wonderful stroke of luck!"

"It's a long time," said the smiling Sulla, who adored all sorts of gossip these days, "since a woman as rich as Terentia has had so much trouble finding a husband."

"That's not *quite* the situation," said Varro, temporizing. "One can

always find a man willing to marry a rich woman. The trouble with Terentia—
who is Rome's worst shrew, I grant you!—has forever been that she refused
to look at any of the men her family found for her.''

Sulla's smile had become a grin. ''She preferred to stay at home and
make Varro Lucullus's life a misery, you mean.''

''Perhaps. Though she likes him well enough, I think. Her nature is at
fault—and what can she do about that, since it was given to her at her birth?''

''Then what happened? Love at first sight?''

''Certainly not. The match was proposed by our swindling friend, Titus
Pomponius who is now called Atticus because of his affection for Athens.
Apparently he and Marcus Tullius Cicero have known each other for many
years. Since you regulated Rome, Lucius Cornelius, Atticus visits Rome at
least once a year.''

''I am aware of it,'' said Sulla, who didn't hold Atticus's financial
flutterings against him any more than he did Crassus's—it was the way Crassus
had manipulated the proscriptions for his own gain caused his fall from Sulla's
grace.

''Anyway, Cicero's legal reputation has soared. So have his ambitions.
But his purse is empty. He needed to marry an heiress, though it looked as
if she would have to be one of those abysmally undistinguished girls our less
salubrious plutocrats seem to produce in abundance. Then Atticus suggested
Terentia.'' Varro stopped to look enquiringly at Sulla. ''Do you know Marcus
Tullius Cicero at all?'' he asked.

''Quite well when he was a lad. My late son—who would be about the
same age had he lived—befriended him. He was thought a prodigy then. But
between my son's death and the case of Sextus Roscius of Ameria, I saw
him only as a *contubernalis* on my staff in Campania during the Italian War.
Maturity hasn't changed him. He's just found his natural milieu, is all. He's
as pedantic, talkative, and full of his own importance as he ever was. Qualities
which stand him in good stead as an advocate! However, I admit freely that
he has a magnificent turn of phrase. And he *does* have a mind! His worst
fault is that he's related to Gaius Marius. They're both from Arpinum.''

Varro nodded. ''Atticus approached Varro Lucullus, who agreed to press
Cicero's suit with Terentia. And much to his surprise, she asked to meet
Cicero! She had heard of his courtroom prowess, and told Varro Lucullus
that she was determined to marry a man who was capable of fame. Cicero,
she said, might be such a one.''

''How big is her dowry?''

''Enormous! Two hundred talents.''

''The line of her suitors must stretch right round the block! And must contain some very pretty, smooth fellows. I begin to respect Terentia, if she's been proof against Rome's most expert fortune hunters,'' said Sulla.

''Terentia,'' said her cousin deliberately, ''is ugly, sour, cantankerous and parsimonious. She is now twenty-one years old, and still single. I know girls are supposed to obey their *paterfamilias* and marry whomsoever they are told to marry, but there is no man—alive or dead!—who could order Terentia to do anything she didn't want to do.''

''And poor Varro Lucullus is such a nice man,'' said Sulla, highly entertained.

''Precisely.''

''So Terentia met Cicero?''

''She did indeed. And—you could have bowled all of us over with a feather!—consented to marry him.''

''Lucky Cicero! One of Fortune's favorites. Her money will come in very handy.''

''That's what you think,'' said Varro grimly. ''She's made up the marriage contract herself and retained complete control of her wealth, though she did agree to dower any daughters she might have, and contribute toward funding the careers of any sons. But as for Cicero—he's not the man to get the better of Terentia!''

''What's he like as a person these days, Varro?''

''Pleasant enough. Soft inside, I think. But vainglorious. Insufferably conceited about his intellect and convinced it has no peer. An avid social climber . . . Hates to be reminded that Gaius Marius is his distant relative! If Terentia had been one of those abysmally undistinguished daughters of our less salubrious plutocrats, I don't think he would have looked at her. But her mother was a patrician and once married to Quintus Fabius Maximus, which means Fabia the Vestal Virgin is her half sister. Therefore Terentia was 'good enough,' if you know what I mean.'' Varro pulled a face. ''Cicero is an Icarus, Lucius Cornelius. He intends to fly right up into the realm of the sun—a dangerous business if you're a New Man without a sestertius.''

''Whatever is in the air of Arpinum, it seems to breed such fellows,'' said Sulla. ''As well for Rome that this New Man from Arpinum has no military skills!''

''Quite the opposite, I have heard.''

''Oh, I know it! When he was my *contubernalis* he acted as my secretary. The sight of a sword made him ashen. But I've never had a better secretary! When is the wedding?''

''Not until after Varro Lucullus and his brother celebrate the *ludi Romani* in September.'' Varro laughed. ''There's no room in their world at the moment for anything except planning the best games Rome has seen in a century—if at all!''

"A pity I won't be in Rome to see them," said Sulla, who did not look brokenhearted.

A small silence fell, which Varro took advantage of before Sulla could think of some other subject. "Lucius Cornelius, I wondered if you knew that Gnaeus Pompeius Magnus is coming to Rome shortly?" he asked diffidently. "He would like to call to see you, but understands how busy you are."

"Never too busy to see Magnus!" said Sulla cheerfully. He directed a keen look at Varro. "Still running round after him with a pen and paper to record his every fart, Varro?"

A deep red suffused Varro's skin; when dealing with Sulla one didn't always know how he would see even the most innocent things. Did he, for example, think that Varro's time would be better spent recording the deeds (or farts) of Lucius Cornelius Sulla? So he said, very humbly, "I do from time to time. It started as an accident because we were together when war broke out, and I was not proof against Pompeius's enthusiasm. He said I should write history, not natural history. And that is what I do. I am *not* Pompeius's biographer!''

"Very well answered!''

Thus it was that when Varro left the Dictator's house on the Palatine, he had to pause to wipe the sweat from his face. They talked endlessly about the lion and the fox in Sulla; but personally Varro thought the worst beast he harbored was a common cat.

He had done well, however. When Pompey arrived in Rome with his wife and took up residence in his family's house on the Carinae, Varro was able to say that Sulla would be glad to see Pompey, and would allocate him sufficient time for a cozy chat. That was Sulla's phrase—but uttered with tongue in cheek, Varro knew. A cozy chat with Sulla could turn out to be a walk along a tightrope above a pit of burning coals.

Ah, but the self-confidence and conceit of youth! Pompey, still some months short of his twenty-seventh birthday, breezed off to see Sulla with no misgivings whatsoever.

"And how's married life?" asked the Dictator blandly.

Pompey beamed. "Wonderful! Glorious! What a wife you found for me, Lucius Cornelius! Beautiful—educated—sweet. She's pregnant. Due to drop my first son later this year."

"A son, eh? Are you sure it will be a son, Magnus?"

"Positive."

Sulla chuckled. "Well, you're one of Fortune's favorites, Magnus, so

I suppose it will be a son. Gnaeus Junior . . . The Butcher, Kid Butcher, and Baby Butcher.''

"I like that!'' exclaimed Pompey, not at all offended.

"You're establishing a tradition,'' said Sulla gravely.

"We certainly are! Three generations!''

Pompey sat back, pleased. Then, noted the watching Sulla, a different look came into the wide blue eyes; the happiness fled, replaced by a wary and thoughtful calculation as Pompey turned something over in his mind. Sulla waited without speaking until it came out.

"Lucius Cornelius . . .''

"Yes?''

"That law you promulgated—the one about making the Senate look outside of its own ranks if no military commander could be found among the senators . . .''

"The special commission, you mean?''

"That's the one.''

"What about it?''

"Would it apply to me?''

"It could do.''

"But only if no one within the Senate volunteered.''

"It doesn't quite say that, Magnus. It says if no *capable and experienced commander* within the Senate volunteers.''

"And who decides that?''

"The Senate.''

Another silence fell. Then Pompey said, idly it seemed, "It would be nice to have lots of clients within the Senate.''

"It is always nice to have those, Magnus.''

At which point Pompey transparently decided to change the subject. "Who will be the consuls for next year?'' he asked.

"Catulus, for one. Though I haven't decided yet whether he's to be senior or junior consul. A year ago, it seemed a clear-cut decision. Now I'm not so sure.''

"Catulus is like Metellus Pius—a stickler.''

"Perhaps. Neither as old nor as wise, unfortunately.''

"Do you think Metellus Pius can beat Sertorius?''

"At first, probably not,'' said Sulla, smiling. "However, don't hold my Piglet too lightly, Magnus. It takes him a while to get into stride. But once he finds his stride he's very good.''

"Pah! He's an old woman!'' said Pompey contemptuously.

"I've known some doughty old women in my time, Magnus.''

Back to the changed subject: "Who else will be consul?"

"Lepidus."

"*Lepidus?*" Pompey gaped.

"Don't you approve?"

"I didn't say I didn't approve, Lucius Cornelius. As a matter of fact, I think I do! I just didn't think your mind was inclined his way. He hasn't been obsequious enough."

"Is that what you believe? That I give the big jobs only to men willing to wash my arse?"

Give Pompey his due, he was never afraid. So, much to Sulla's secret amusement, he continued. "Not really. But you certainly haven't given the big jobs to men who have made it as obvious as Lepidus has that he doesn't approve of you."

"Why should I?" asked Sulla, looking amazed. "I'm not fool enough to give the big jobs to men who might undermine me!"

"Then why Lepidus?"

"I'm due to retire before he takes office. And Lepidus," said Sulla deliberately, "is aiming high. It has occurred to me that it might be better to make him consul while I'm still alive."

"He's a good man."

"Because he questioned me publicly? Or despite that?"

But "He's a good man" was as far as Pompey was prepared to go. In truth, though he found the appointment of Lepidus not in character for Sulla, he was only mildly interested. Of far more interest was Sulla's provision for the special commission. When he had heard of it he had wondered what he himself might have had to do with it, but it had been no part of Pompey's plans at that stage to ask Sulla. Now, almost two years since the law had been passed, he thought it expedient to enquire rather than ask. The Dictator was right, of course. A man found it hard enough to gain his objectives as a member of the Senate; but seeking his objectives from that body when a man was not a member of it would prove extremely difficult indeed.

Thus after Pompey took his leave of Sulla and commenced the walk home, he strolled along deep in thought. First of all, he would have to establish a faction within the Senate. And after that he would have to create a smaller group of men willing—for a price, naturally—to intrigue actively and perpetually on his behalf, even engage in underhand activities. Only—where to begin?

Halfway down the Ringmakers' Stairs, Pompey halted, turned, took them lithely two at a time back up onto the Clivus Victoriae, no mean feat in a toga. Philippus! He would begin with Philippus.

Lucius Marcius Philippus had come a long way since the day he had paid a visit to the seaside villa of Gaius Marius and told that formidable man that he, Philippus, had just been elected a tribune of the plebs, and what might he do for Gaius Marius?—for a price, naturally. How many times inside his mind Philippus had turned his toga inside out and then back again, only Philippus knew for certain. What other men knew for certain was that he had always managed to survive, and even to enhance his reputation. At the time Pompey went to see him, he was both consular and ex-censor, and one of the Senate's elders. Many men loathed him, few genuinely liked him, but he was a power nonetheless; somehow he had succeeded in persuading most of his world that he was a man of note as well as clout.

He found his interview with Pompey both amusing and thought-provoking, never until now having had much to do with Sulla's pet, but well aware that in Pompey, Rome had spawned a young man who deserved watching. Philippus was, besides, financially strapped again. Oh, not the way he used to be! Sulla's proscriptions had proven an extremely fruitful source of property, and he had picked up several millions' worth of estates for several thousands. But, like a lot of men of his kind, Philippus was not a handy manager; money seemed to slip away faster than he could gather it in, and he lacked the ability to supervise his rural money-making enterprises—as well as the ability to choose reliable staff.

"In short, Gnaeus Pompeius, I am the opposite of men like Marcus Licinius Crassus, who still has his first sestertius and now adds them up in millions upon millions. *His* people tremble in their shoes whenever they set eyes on him. Mine smile slyly."

"You need a Chrysogonus," said the young man with the wide blue gaze and the frank, open, attractive face.

Always inclined to run to fat, Philippus had grown even softer and more corpulent with the years, and his brown eyes were almost buried between swollen upper lids and pouched lower ones. These eyes now rested upon his youthful adviser with startled and wary surprise: Philippus was not used to being patronized.

"Chrysogonus ended up impaled on the needles below the Tarpeian Rock!"

"Chrysogonus had been extremely valuable to Sulla in spite of his fate," said Pompey. "He died because he had enriched himself from the proscriptions—not because he enriched himself by stealing directly from his patron. Over the many years he worked for Sulla, he worked indefatigably. Believe me, Lucius Marcius, you do need a Chrysogonus."

"Well, if I do, I have no idea how to find one."

"I'll undertake to find one for you if you like."

The buried eyes now popped out of their surrounding flesh. "Oh? And why would you be willing to do that, Gnaeus Pompeius?"

"Call me Magnus," said Pompey impatiently.

"Magnus."

"Because I need your services, Lucius Marcius."

"Call me Philippus."

"Philippus."

"How can I possibly serve you, Magnus? You're rich beyond most rich men's dreams—even Crassus's, I'd venture! You're—what?—in your middle twenties somewhere?—and already famous as a military commander, not to mention standing high in Sulla's favor—and that is hard to achieve. I've tried, but I never have."

"Sulla is going," said Pompey deliberately, "and when he goes I'll sink back into obscurity. Especially if men like Catulus and the Dolabellae have anything to do with it. I'm not a member of the Senate. Nor do I intend to be."

"Curious, that," said Philippus thoughtfully. "You had the opportunity. Sulla put your name at the top of his first list. But you spurned it."

"I have my reasons."

"I imagine you do!"

Pompey got up from his chair and strolled across to the open window at the back of Philippus's study, which, because of the peculiar layout of Philippus's house (perched as it was near the bend in the Clivus Victoriae) looked not onto a peristyle garden but out across the lower Forum Romanum to the cliff of the Capitol. And there above the pillared arcade in which dwelt the magnificent effigies of the Twelve Gods, Pompey could see the beginnings of a huge building project; Sulla's Tabularium, a gigantic records house in which would repose all of Rome's accounts and law tablets. Other men, thought Pompey contemptuously, might build a basilica or a temple or a porticus, but Sulla builds a monument to Rome's bureaucracy! He has no wings on his imagination. That is his weakness, his patrician practicality.

"I would be grateful if you could find a Chrysogonus for me, Magnus," said Philippus to break the long silence. "The only trouble is that I am not a Sulla! Therefore I very much doubt that I would succeed in controlling such a man."

"You're not soft in anything except appearance, Philippus," said the Master of Tact. "If I find you just the right man, you will control him. You just can't pick staff, that's all."

"And why should you do this for me, Magnus?"

"Oh, that's not all I intend to do for you!" said Pompey, turning from the window with a smile all over his face.

"Really?"

"I take it that your chief problem is maintaining a decent cash flow. You have a great deal of property, as well as several schools for gladiators. But nothing is managed efficiently, and therefore you do not enjoy the income you ought. A Chrysogonus will go far toward fixing that! However, it's very likely that—as you're a man of famously expensive habits—even an expanded income from all your estates and schools will not always prove adequate for your needs."

"Admirably stated!" said Philippus, who was enjoying this interview, he now discovered, enormously.

"I'd be willing to augment your income with the gift of a million sesterces a year," said Pompey coolly.

Philippus couldn't help it. He gasped. *"A million?"*

"Provided you earn it, yes."

"And what would I have to do to earn it?"

"Establish a Gnaeus Pompeius Magnus faction within the Senate of sufficient power to get me whatever I want whenever I want it." Pompey, who never suffered from bashfulness or guilt or any kind of self-deprecation, had no difficulty in meeting Philippus's gaze when he said this.

"Why not join the Senate and do it for yourself? Cheaper!"

"I refuse to belong to the Senate, so that's not possible. Besides which, I'd still have to do it. Much better then to do it behind the scenes. I won't be sitting there to remind the senators that I might have any interest in what's going on beyond the interest of a genuine Roman patriot-knight."

"Oh, you're deep!" Philippus exclaimed appreciatively. "I wonder does Sulla know all the sides to you?"

"Well, I'm why, I believe, he incorporated the special commission into his laws about commands and governorships."

"You believe he invented the special commission because you refused to belong to the Senate?"

"I do."

"And that is why you want to pay me fatly to establish a faction for you within the Senate. Which is all very well. But to build a faction will cost you far more money than what you pay me, Magnus. For I do not intend to disburse sums to other men out of my own money—and what you pay me is my own money."

"Fair enough," said Pompey equably.

"There are plenty of needy senators among the *pedarii*. They won't cost you much, since all you need them for is a vote. But it will be necessary to buy some of the silver-tongues on the front benches too, not to mention a few more in the middle.'' Philippus looked thoughtful. ''Gaius Scribonius Curio is relatively poor. So is the adopted Cornelius Lentulus—Gnaeus Cornelius Lentulus Clodianus. They both itch for the consulship, but neither has the income to attain it. There are a number of Lentuli, but Lentulus Clodianus is the senior of the branch. He controls the votes of those backbenchers in the Lentulus clientele. Curio is a power within himself—an interesting man. But to buy them will take a considerable amount of money. Probably a million each. *If* Curio will sell himself. I believe he will for enough, but not blindly, and not completely. Lucius Gellius Poplicola would sell his wife, his parents and his children for a million, however.''

''I'd rather,'' said Pompey, ''pay them an annual income, as I will you. A million now might buy them, yes, but I think they would be happier if they knew that there was a regular quarter million coming in every year. In four years, that's the million. But I am going to need them for longer than four years.''

''You're generous, Magnus. Some might say foolishly so.''

''I am never foolish!'' snapped Pompey. ''I will expect to see a return for my money in keeping with the amount of it!''

For some time they discussed the logistics of payments and the amounts necessary to people the back benches with willing—nay, eager!—Pompeian voters. But then Philippus sat back with a frown, and fell silent.

''What is it?'' asked Pompey a little anxiously.

''There's one man you can't do without. The trouble is he's already got more money than he knows what to do with. So he can't be bought and he makes great capital out of that fact.''

''You mean Cethegus.''

''I do indeed.''

''How can I get him?''

''I haven't the faintest idea.''

Pompey rose, looking brisk. ''Then I'd better see him.''

''No!'' cried Philippus, alarmed. ''Cethegus is a patrician Cornelian, and such a smooth and syrupy sort of man that you'd make an enemy out of him—he can't deal with the direct approach. Leave him to me. I'll sound him out, find what he wants.''

Two days later, Pompey received a note from Philippus. It contained only one sentence: ''Get him Praecia, and he's yours.''

Pompey held the note within the flame of a lamp until it kindled, shaking with anger. Yes, that was Cethegus! His payment was his future patron's humiliation! He required that Pompey should become his pimp.

Pompey's approach to Mucia Tertia was very different from his tactics in dealing with Aemilia Scaura—or Antistia, for that matter. This third wife was infinitely above numbers one and two. First of all, she had a mind. Secondly, she was enigmatic; he could never work out what she was thinking. Thirdly, she was quite wonderful in bed—what a surprise! Luckily he hadn't made a fool of himself at the outset by calling her his wee pudding or his delectable honeypot; such terms had actually teetered on the tip of his tongue, but something in her face had killed them before he articulated them. Little though he had liked Young Marius, she had been Young Marius's wife, and that had to count for much. And she was Scaevola's daughter, Crassus Orator's niece. Six years of living with Julia had to count for something too. So all Pompey's instincts said Mucia Tertia must be treated more like an equal, and not at all like a chattel.

Therefore when he sought Mucia Tertia out, he did as he always did; gave her a lingering tongue-seeking kiss accompanied by a light and appreciative fondling of one nipple. Then—going away to sit where he could see her face, a smile of enslaved love and devotion. And after that—straight to the subject.

"Did you know I used to have a mistress in Rome?" he asked.

"Which one?" was her answer, solemn and matter-of-fact; she rarely smiled, Mucia Tertia.

"So you know of them all," he said comfortably.

"Only of the two most notorious. Flora and Praecia."

Clearly Pompey had forgotten Flora ever existed; he looked perfectly blank for several moments, then laughed and held his hands out. "*Flora?* Oh, she was forever ago!"

"Praecia," said Mucia Tertia in a level voice, "was my first husband's mistress too."

"Yes, I knew that."

"Before or after you approached her?"

"Before."

"You didn't mind?"

He could be quick, as he was now: "If I haven't minded his widow, why should I mind his ex-mistress?"

"True." She drew several skeins of finest woolen thread further into the light, and inspected them carefully. Her work, a piece of embroidery, lay in her swelling lap. Finally she chose the palest of the various purplish shades, broke off a length, and after sucking it to moisten it and rolling it between her fingers, held it up to ease it through the large eye of a needle. Only when the chore was done did she return her attention to Pompey. "What is it you have to say about Praecia?"

"I'm establishing a faction in the Senate."

"Wise." The needle was poked through the coarse fabric on which a complicated pattern of colored wools was growing, from wrong side to right side, then back again; the junction, when it was finished, would be impossible to detect. "Who have you begun with, Magnus? Philippus?"

"Absolutely correct! You really are wonderful, Mucia!"

"Just experienced," she said. "I grew up surrounded by talk of politics."

"Philippus has undertaken to give me that faction," Pompey went on, "but there's one person he couldn't buy."

"Cethegus," she said, beginning now to fill in the body of a curlique already outlined with deeper purple.

"Correct again. Cethegus."

"He's necessary."

"So Philippus assures me."

"And what is Cethegus's price?"

"Praecia."

"Oh, I see." The curlique was filling in at a great rate. "So Philippus has given you the job of acquiring Praecia for the King of the Backbenchers?"

"It seems so." Pompey shrugged. "She must speak well of me, otherwise I imagine he'd have given the job to someone else."

"Better of you than of Gaius Marius Junior."

"Really?" Pompey's face lit up. "Oh, that's good!"

Down went work and needle; the deep green eyes, so far apart and doelike, regarded their lord and master inscrutably. "Do you still visit her, Magnus?"

"No, of course not!" said Pompey indignantly. His small spurt of temper died, he looked at her uncertainly. "Would you have minded if I had said yes?"

"No, of course not." The needle went to work again.

His face reddened. "You mean you wouldn't be jealous?"

"No, of course not."

"Then you don't love me!" he cried, jumping to his feet and walking hastily about the room.

"Sit down, Magnus, do."

"You don't love me!" he cried a second time.

She sighed, abandoned her embroidery. "Sit down, Gnaeus Pompeius, do! Of course I love you."

"If you did you'd be jealous!" he snapped, and flung himself back into his chair.

"I am not a jealous person. Either one is, or one is not. And why should you want me to be jealous?"

"It would tell me that you loved me."

"No, it would only tell you that I am a jealous person," she said with magnificent logic. "You must remember that I grew up in a very troubled household. My father loved my mother madly, and she loved him too. But he was always jealous of her. She resented it. Eventually his moods drove her into the arms of Metellus Nepos, who is not a jealous person. So she's happy."

"Are you warning me not to become jealous of you?"

"Not at all," she said placidly. "I am not my mother."

"*Do* you love me?"

"Yes, very much."

"Did you love Young Marius?"

"No, never." The pale purple thread was all used up; a new one was broken off. "Gaius Marius Junior was not uxorious. You are, delightfully so. Uxoriousness is a quality worthy of love."

That pleased him enough to return to the original subject. "The thing is, Mucia, how do I go about something like this? I am a procurer—oh, why dress it up in a fancy name? I am a pimp!"

She chuckled. Wonder of wonders, she chuckled! "I quite see how difficult a position it puts you in, Magnus."

"What ought I to do?"

"As is your nature. Take hold of it and do it. You only lose control of events when you stop to think or worry how you'll look. So don't stop to think—and stop worrying about how you'll look. Otherwise you'll make a mess of it."

"Just go and see her and ask her."

"Exactly." The needle was threaded again, her eyes lifted to his with another ghost of a smile in them. "However, there is a price for this advice, my dear Magnus."

"Is there?"

"Certainly. I want a full account of how your meeting with Praecia goes."

* * *

The timing of this negotiation, it turned out, was exactly right. No longer possessed of either Young Marius or Pompey, Praecia had fallen into a doldrums wherein both stimulus and interest were utterly lacking. Comfortably off and determined to retain her independence, she was now far too old to be a creature of driving physical passions. As was true of so many of her less well-known confederates in the art of love, Praecia had become an expert in sham. She was also an astute judge of character and highly intelligent. Thus she went into every sexual encounter from a superior position of power, sure of her capacity to please, and sure of her quarry. What she loved was the meddling in the affairs of men that normally had little or nothing to do with women. And what she loved most was political meddling. It was balm to intellect and disposition.

When Pompey's arrival was announced to her, she didn't make the mistake of automatically assuming he had come to renew his liaison with her, though of course it crossed her mind because she had heard that his wife was pregnant.

"My dear, dear Magnus!" she said with immense affability when he entered her study, and held out her hands to him.

He bestowed a light kiss on each before retreating to a chair some feet away from where she reclined on a couch, heaving a sigh of pleasure so artificial that Praecia smiled.

"Well, Magnus?" she asked.

"Well, Praecia!" he said. "Everything as perfect as ever, I see—has anyone ever found you and your surroundings less than perfect? Even if the call is unexpected?"

Praecia's *tablinum*—she gave it the same name a man would have— was a ravishing production in eggshell blue, cream, and precisely the right amount of gilt. As for herself—she rose every day of her life to a toilet as thorough as it was protracted, and she emerged from it a finished work of art. Today she wore a quantity of tissue-fine draperies in a soft sage-green, and had done up her pale gold hair like Diana the Huntress, in disciplined piles with straying tendrils which looked absolutely natural rather than the result of much tweaking with the aid of a mirror. The beautiful cool planes of her face were not obviously painted; Praecia was far too clever to be crude when Fortune had been so kind, even though she was now forty.

"How have you been keeping?" Pompey asked.

"In good health, if not in good temper."

"Why not good temper?"

She shrugged, pouted. "What is there to mollify it? *You* don't come anymore! Nor does anyone else interesting."

"I'm married again."

"To a very strange woman."

"Mucia, strange? Yes, I suppose she is. But I like her."

"You would."

He searched for a way into saying what he had to say, but could find no trigger and thus sat in silence, with Praecia gazing at him mockingly from her half-sitting, half-lying pose. Her eyes—which were held to be her best feature, being very large and rather blindly blue—positively danced with this derision.

"I'm tired of this!" Pompey said suddenly. "I'm an emissary, Praecia. Not here on my own behalf, but on someone else's."

"How intriguing!"

"You have an admirer."

"I have many admirers."

"Not like this one."

"And what makes him so different? Not to mention how he managed to send *you* to procure my services!"

Pompey reddened. "I'm caught in the middle, and I hate it! But I need him and he doesn't need me. So I'm here on his behalf."

"You've already said that."

"Take the barb out of your tongue, woman! I'm suffering enough. He's Cethegus."

"Cethegus! Well, well!" said Praecia purringly.

"He's very rich, very spoiled, and very nasty," said Pompey. "He could have done his own dirty work, but it amuses him to make me do it for him."

"It's his price," she said, "to make you act as his pimp."

"It is indeed."

"You must want him very badly."

"Just give me an answer! Yes or no?"

"Are you done with me, Magnus?"

"Yes."

"Then my answer to Cethegus is yes."

Pompey rose to his feet. "I thought you'd say no."

"In other circumstances I would have loved to say no, but the truth is that I'm bored, Magnus. Cethegus is a power in the Senate, and I enjoy being associated with men of power. Besides, I see a new kind of power in it for me. I shall arrange it so that those who seek favors from Cethegus will have to do so through cultivating me. Very nice!"

"Grr!" said Pompey, and departed.

He didn't trust himself to see Cethegus; so he saw Lucius Marcius Philippus instead.

"Praecia is willing," he said curtly.

"Excellent, Magnus! But why look so unhappy?"

"He made me pimp for him."

"Oh, I'm sure it wasn't personal!"

"Not much it wasn't!"

In the spring of that year Nola fell. For almost twelve years that Campanian city of Samnite persuasion had held out against Rome and Sulla, enduring one siege after another, mostly at the hands of this year's junior consul, Appius Claudius Pulcher. So it was logical that Sulla ordered Appius Claudius south to accept Nola's submission, and logical too that Appius Claudius took great pleasure in telling the city's magistrates the details of Sulla's unusually harsh conditions. Like Capua, Faesulae and Volaterrae, Nola was to keep no territory whatsoever; it all went to swell the Roman *ager publicus*. Nor were the men of Nola to be given the Roman citizenship. The Dictator's nephew, Publius Sulla, was given authority in the area, an added gall in view of last year's mission to sort out the tangled affairs of Pompeii, where Publius Sulla's brand of curt insensitivity had only ended in making a bad situation worse.

But to Sulla the submission of Nola was a sign. He could depart with his luck intact when the place where he had won his Grass Crown was no more. So the months of May and June saw a steady trickle of his possessions wending their way to Misenum, and a team of builders toiled to complete certain commissions at his villa there—a small theater, a delightful park complete with sylvan dells, waterfalls and many fountains, a huge deep pool, and several additional rooms apparently designed for parties and banquets. Not to mention six guest suites of such opulence that all Misenum was talking: who could Sulla be thinking of entertaining, the King of the Parthians?

Then came Quinctilis, and the last in the series of Sulla's mock elections. To Catulus's chagrin, he was to be the junior consul; the senior was Marcus Aemilius Lepidus, a name no one had expected to hear in the light of his independent line in the Senate since Sulla had assumed the Dictatorship.

At the beginning of the month Valeria Messala and the twins left for the Campanian countryside; everything at the villa was ready. In Rome, no one anticipated surprises. Sulla would go—as he had come and as he had prevailed—in an aura of dense respectability and ceremony. Rome was about to lose her first dictator in a hundred and twenty years, and her first-ever dictator who had held the office for longer than six months.

The *ludi Apollinares*, games first staged by Sulla's remote ancestor, came and went; so did the elections. And the day after the curule elections a huge crowd gathered in the lower Forum Romanum to witness Sulla's laying down of his self-inflicted task. He was going to do this in public rather than within the Curia Hostilia of the Senate—from the rostra, an hour after dawn.

He did it with dignity and an impressive majesty, first dismissing his twenty-four lictors with extreme courtesy and (for Sulla) costly gifts, then addressing the crowds from the rostra before going with the electors to the Campus Martius, where he oversaw the repeal of Flaccus Princeps Senatus's law appointing him Dictator. He went home from the Centuriate Assembly a private citizen, shorn of imperium and official *auctoritas*.

"But I should like some of you to see me leave Rome," he said to the consuls Vatia and Appius Claudius, to Catulus, Lepidus, Cethegus, Philippus. "Be at the Porta Capena an hour after dawn tomorrow. Nowhere else, mind! Watch me say goodbye to Rome."

They obeyed him to the letter, of course; Sulla might now be a *privatus* stripped of all magisterial power, but he had been the Dictator for far too long for any man to believe he truly lacked power. Sulla would be dangerous as long as he lived.

Everyone bidden to the Porta Capena therefore came, though the three most favored Sullan protégés—Lucullus, Mamercus and Pompey—were not in Rome. Lucullus was on business for his games in September and Mamercus was in Cumae, while Pompey had gone back to Picenum to await the birth of his first child. When Pompey later heard of the events at the Capena Gate, he was profoundly thankful for his absence; Lucullus and Mamercus felt exactly the opposite.

The marketplace inside the gate was jammed with busy folk going about their various activities—selling, buying, peddling, teaching, strolling, flirting, eating. Of course the party in uniformly purple-bordered togas was eyed with great interest; the usual volley of loud, anti-upper-class, derogatory insults was thrown from every direction, but the curule senators had heard it all before, and took absolutely no notice. Positioning themselves close to the imposing arch of the gate, they waited, talking idly.

Not long afterward came the strains of music—pipes, little drums, tuneful flutes, outlining and filling in an unmistakably Bacchic lay. A flutter ran through the marketplace throng, which separated, stunned, to permit the progress of the procession now appearing from the direction of the Palatine.

First came flower-decked harlots in flame-colored togas, thumping their wrists against jingling tambourines, dipping their hands into the swollen sinuses of their togas to strew the route with drifts of rose petals. Then came freaks and dwarves, faces pugged or painted, some in horn-bedecked masks sewn with bells, capering on malformed legs and clad in the motley of *centunculi,* vividly patched coats like fragmented rainbows. After them came the musicians, some wearing little more than flowers, others tricked out like prancing satyrs or fanciful eunuchs. In their midst, hedged about by giggling, dancing children, staggered a fat and drunken donkey with its hooves gilded, a garland of roses about its neck and its mournful ears poking out of holes in a wide-brimmed, wreathed hat. On its purple-blanketed back sat the equally drunken Sulla, waving a golden goblet which slopped an endless rain of wine, robed in a Tyrian purple tunic embroidered with gold, flowers around his neck and atop his head. Beside the donkey walked a very beautiful but obviously male woman, his thick black hair just sprinkled with white, his unfeminine physique draped in a semi-transparent saffron woman's gown; he bore a large golden flagon, and every time the goblet in Sulla's right hand descended in his direction he topped up its splashing purple contents.

Since the slope toward the gate was downward the procession gained a certain momentum it could not brake, so when the archway loomed immediately before it and Sulla started shouting blearily for a halt, everyone fell over squealing and shrieking, the women's legs kicking in the air and their hairy, red-slashed pudenda on full display. The donkey staggered and cannoned into the wall of a fountain; Sulla teetered but was held up by the travestied flagon-bearer alongside him, then toppled slowly into those strong arms. Righted, the Dictator commenced to walk toward the stupefied party of curule senators, though as he passed by one wildly flailing pair of quite lovely female legs, he bent to puddle his finger inside her *cunnus,* much to her hilarious and apparently orgasmic delight.

As the escort regained its feet and clustered, singing and playing music and dancing still—to the great joy of the gathering crowd—Sulla arrived in front of the consuls to stand with his arm about his beautiful supporter, waving the cup of wine in an expansive salute.

"Tacete!" yelled Sulla to the dancers and musicians. They quietened at once. But no other voices filled the silence.

"Well, it's here at last!" he cried—to whom, no one could be sure: perhaps to the sky. "My first day of freedom!"

The golden goblet described circles in the air as the richly painted mouth bared its gums in the broadest and happiest of smiles. His whole face beneath the absurd ginger wig was painted as white as the patches of intact skin upon it, so that the livid areas of scar tissue were gone. But the effect was not what perhaps he had hoped, as the red outline of his mouth had run up into the many deep fissures starting under nose and on chin and foregathering at the lips; it looked like a red gash sewn loosely together with wide red stitches. But it smiled, smiled, smiled. Sulla was drunk, and he didn't care.

"For thirty years and more," he said to the slack-featured Vatia and Appius Claudius, "I have denied my nature. I have denied myself love and pleasure—at first for the sake of my name and my ambition, and later—when these had run their course—for the sake of Rome. But it is over. Over, over, over! I hereby give Rome back to you—to all you little, cocksure, maggot-minded men! You are at liberty once more to vent your spleen on your poor country—to elect the wrong men, to spend the public moneys foolishly, to think not beyond tomorrow and your own gigantic selves. In the thirty years of one generation I predict that you and those who succeed you will bring ruin beyond redemption upon Rome's undeserving head!"

His hand went up to touch the face of his supporter, very tenderly and intimately. "You know who this is, of course, any of you who go to the theater. Metrobius. My boy. Always and forever my boy!" And he turned, pulled the dark head down, kissed Metrobius full upon the mouth.

Then with a hiccough and a giggle he allowed himself to be helped back to his drunken ass, and hoisted upon it. The tawdry procession re-formed and weaved off through the gate down the common line of the Via Latina and the Via Appia, with half the people from the marketplace following and cheering.

No one in the senatorial party knew where to look, especially after Vatia burst into noisy tears. So for want of firmer guidance they drifted off in ones and twos, Appius Claudius trying to give comfort to the devastated Vatia.

"I don't believe it!" said Cethegus to Philippus.

"I think we must," said Philippus. "That's why he invited us to this parade of travesties. How else could he begin to shake us loose from his bonds?"

"Shake us loose? What do you mean?"

"You heard him. For thirty years and more he has denied his nature. He fooled me. He fooled everyone who matters. And what an exquisite revenge this day has been for a ruined childhood! Rome has been controlled, directed and healed by a deviate. We've been diddled by a mountebank. *How* he must have laughed!"

He did laugh. He laughed all the way to Misenum, carried in a flower-decked litter with Metrobius by his side and accompanied by his Bacchic revelers, all invited to stay in his villa as his guests for as long as they wanted. The party had been augmented by Roscius the comedian and Sorex the archmime, as well as many lesser theatrical lights.

They descended upon the newly renovated villa which once had been a fitting home for Cornelia the Mother of the Gracchi and teemed irreverently through its hallowed portals, Sulla in their midst still riding upon his inebriated ass.

"Liber Pater!" they called him, saluting him with blown kisses and little trills on their pipes; and he, so drunk he was only half conscious, chuckled and whinnied and whooped.

The party went on for a market interval, notable mainly for the enormous amounts of food and wine that were consumed and the number of uninvited guests who poured in from all the surrounding villas and villages. Their host, rollicking and carousing, took them to his heart and introduced them to sexual high jinks most of them had never even heard of.

Only Valeria was left out of things, entirely of her own choice; she had taken one look at the arrival of her husband and fled to her own rooms, there to lock herself in and weep. But, said Metrobius after he had persuaded her to open her door,

"It won't always be so unbearable, lady. He's been looking forward to this for so long that you must give him his head. In a few days' time he'll pay for it—he'll be terribly ill and not at all inclined to be the life of the party."

"You're his lover," she said, feeling nothing beyond a black, despairing confusion.

"I have been his lover for more years than you have seen the sun," said Metrobius gently. "I belong to him. I always have. But so do you belong to him."

"Love between men is disgusting!"

"Nonsense. That's your father and your brother and all of those cousins talking. How do you know? What have you seen of life, Valeria Messala, beyond the dismally confined isolation of a Roman noblewoman's lot? My presence doesn't mean you're not necessary to him, any more than your presence means I'm not necessary to him. If you want to stay, you're going to have to accept the fact that there have been—and still are!—many loves in Sulla's life."

"I don't have much choice, really," she said, almost to herself. "Either I go back to my brother's house, or I learn to get on amid this riotous assemblage."

"That is so," he said, smiled at her with understanding and considerable affection, then leaned across to caress the back of her neck, which somehow he seemed to know ached from the effort of holding up her proud patrician head.

"You're far too good for him," she said, surprising herself.

"All that I am, I owe to him," said Metrobius gravely. "If it had not been for him I would be nothing more than an actor."

"Well, there seems no alternative other than to join this circus! Though if you don't mind, not at its height. I have not the sinews or the training for such revelry. When you think he needs me, tell me."

And so they left it. As Metrobius had predicted, some eight days after the commencement of his binge Sulla's underlying ailments asserted themselves and the revelers were sent home. The arch-mime, Sorex, and Roscius the comedian slunk away to their suites and hid, while Valeria and Metrobius and Lucius Tuccius dealt with the ravages his breakout had inflicted upon Sulla. Who was sometimes grateful, and sometimes very difficult to help.

But, returned eventually to some vestige of tranquillity and health, the ex-Dictator applied himself to the writing of his memoirs; a paean, he informed Valeria and Metrobius, to Rome and men like Catulus Caesar—as well as to himself—besides being a metaphorical assassination of Gaius Marius, Cinna, Carbo, and their followers.

By the end of the old year and the end of the consulships of Vatia and Appius Claudius, Sulla's regimen at Misenum was so well established that the whole villa oscillated through his cycles in a fairly placid way. For a while he would scribble away at his memoirs, chuckling whenever his pen produced a particularly apt and vitriolic phrase at Gaius Marius's expense; while writing his book on the war against Jugurtha he was delirious with pleasure at the thought that now in his own words he admitted it was his personal feat in capturing Jugurtha won the war—and that Marius had deliberately suppressed this fact. Then the pen and paper would be put away and Sulla would embark upon an orgy of privately staged comedies and mimes, or else would throw a gigantic party lasting a whole market interval. He varied all these activities with others as they occurred to his ever-fertile imagination, including mock hunts with naked young boys and girls the quarry, competitions to see who could come up with the most bizarre posture for sexual intercourse, elaborate charades wherein the participants were able to requisition almost anything by way of costume or trapping. He held joke parties, nude parties by moonlight, daytime parties beside his vast white marble swimming pool while the revelers watched, enraptured, the sport of naked youths and maidens in the water. There seemed no end to his invention, nor an end to his passion for novelties of every sexual kind; though it was noticed that he indulged in no practices involving cruelty or animals, and that upon discovering one guest so inclined, he had the man driven from his house.

There could be no doubt, however, that his physical well-being was deteriorating. After the New Year had come and gone, his own sexual prowess flagged badly; by the end of February nothing had the power to stimulate him. And when this happened, his mood and temper took a turn for the worse.

Only one of his highborn Roman friends sought out Sulla's company after the move to Misenum. Lucullus. Who had been in Africa with his brother during Quinctilis, personally supervising the capture of beasts for their games at the beginning of September. When he returned to Rome halfway through Sextilis he found the city still in an uproar constantly fueled by reports of the newest extravagances at the villa in Misenum, and was subjected to scandalized litanies of Sulla's behavior.

"All you who judge him, look first to yourselves," Lucullus said stiffly. "He is entitled to do whatever he chooses."

But it was not until several days after the conclusion of the *ludi Romani* in September that Lucullus could spare time to visit Sulla, whom he found in one of his more lucid intervals, at work on the memoirs and full of glee at what he was doing to the reputation and deeds of Gaius Marius.

"You're the only one, Lucullus," he said, a trace of the old Sulla flickering in his rheumy, pain-racked eyes.

"No one has any right to criticize you!" Lucullus said, nostrils pinched. "You gave up everything for Rome."

"True, I did. And I don't deny it was hard. But my dear boy, if I hadn't denied myself for all those years I wouldn't be enjoying this present excess half so much!"

"I can see where it might have its attractions," Lucullus said, eyes following the gyrations of an exquisite female child just budding into puberty as she danced naked for Sulla in the sun outside his window.

"Yes, you like them young, don't you?" Sulla chuckled, leaned forward to grasp Lucullus by the arm. "You'd better stay to see the end of her dance. Then you can take her for a walk."

"What have you done with their mothers?"

"Nothing. I buy them from their mothers."

Lucullus stayed. And came back often.

But in March, his fires dead, Sulla became extremely hard to handle, even for Metrobius and Valeria, who had learned to work as a team. Somehow—she didn't quite know how—Valeria had found herself pregnant.

By Sulla, she hoped. But couldn't tell him, and dreaded the day when her condition became apparent. It had happened about the turn of the year, when Lucullus had produced some peculiar fungi he said he had found in Africa and the inner circle of friends had eaten of them, including Valeria. In some nightmarish dream she half-remembered every man present enjoying her, from Sulla to Sorex and even Metrobius. It was the only incident she could blame, and fear ruled her after she realized its appalling outcome.

Sulla's temper tantrums were terrible, endless hours of screaming and ranting during which he had to be restrained from doing harm to all who strayed across his path, from the children he used as playthings for his friends to the old women who did most of the laundering and cleaning up; as he kept a company of his Sullani always by him, those who did restrain him understood full well that they imperiled themselves.

"He cannot be allowed to kill people!" cried Metrobius.

"Oh, I wish he'd reconcile himself to what's happening!" said Valeria, weeping.

"You're not well yourself, lady."

An imprudent thing to say in a kind voice; out tumbled the story of the pregnancy, and Metrobius too remembered.

"Who knows?" he laughed, delighted, "I might still produce a child! The chance is one in four."

"Five."

"Four, Valeria. The child cannot be Sulla's."

"He'll kill me!"

"Take each day as it comes and say nothing to Sulla," the actor said firmly. "The future is impenetrable."

Shortly after this Sulla developed a pain in the region of his liver that gave him no peace. Up and down the long expanse of the atrium he shuffled day and night, unable to sit, unable to lie, unable to rest. His sole comfort was the white marble bath near his room, in which he would float until the whole cycle began again with the pacing, pacing, pacing, up and down the atrium. He whinged and whimpered, would get himself to the wall and have to be dissuaded from beating his head against it, so great was his torment.

"The silly fellow who empties his chamber pot started to spread a story that Lucius Cornelius is being eaten up by worms," said Tuccius the doctor to Metrobius and Valeria, his face a study in contempt. "Honestly, the ignorance of most people about the way bodies work and what constitutes a disease almost drives me to the wineskin! Until this pain began, Lucius Cornelius availed himself of the latrine. But now he's forced to use a chamber pot, and its contents are busy with worms. Do you think I can convince the servants that worms are natural, that everyone has them, that they live inside our bowels in a lifelong companionship? No!''

"The worms don't eat?'' whispered Valeria, chalk-white.

"Only what we have already eaten,'' said Tuccius. "No doubt the next time I visit Rome, I'll hear the story there too. Servants are the most efficient gossips in the world.''

"I think you've relieved my mind,'' said Metrobius.

"I do not intend to, only to disabuse you of servants' tales should you hear them. The reality is serious enough. His urine,'' Lucius Tuccius went on, "tastes sweeter than honey, and his skin smells of ripe apples.''

Metrobius grimaced. "You actually tasted his urine?''

"I did, but only after I performed an old trick that was shown to me by a wisewoman when I was a child. I put some of his urine in a dish outside, and every kind of insect swarmed to drink it. Lucius Cornelius is pissing concentrated honey.''

"And losing weight almost visibly,'' said Metrobius.

Valeria gasped, gagged. "Is he *dying*?''

"Oh, yes,'' said Lucius Tuccius. "Besides the honey—I do not know what that means save that it is mortal—his liver is diseased. Too much wine.''

The dark eyes glistened with tears; Metrobius winked them away. His lip quivered, he sighed. "It is to be expected.''

"What will we do?'' asked the wife.

"Just see it out, lady.'' Together they watched Lucius Tuccius patter away to deal with the patient. Then Metrobius said sad words in a voice which held no trace of sadness. "So many years I have loved him. Once a very long time ago I begged him to keep me with him, even though it would have meant I exchanged a comfortable life for a hard one. He declined.''

"He loved you too much,'' said Valeria sentimentally.

"No! He was in love with the idea of his patrician birth. He knew where he was going, and where he was going mattered more than I did by far.'' He turned to look down into her face, brows up. "Haven't you yet realized that love always means different things to different people, and that love given is not always returned in like measure? I have never blamed him. How could I when I am not inside his skin? And at the last, having sent me away so many times, he acknowledged me before his colleagues. 'My boy!' I would endure it all again to hear him say those words to men like Vatia and Lepidus.''

"He won't see my child.''

"I doubt he'll see you increase, lady.''

The dreadful bout of pain passed away, to be succeeded by a fresh crotchet. This was the financial plight of the city of Puteoli. Not very far from Misenum, Puteoli was dominated by the family Granius, who for generations had been its bankers and shipping magnates, and who considered themselves its owners. Unaware of the magnitude of Sulla's excesses—let alone his many illnesses—one of the city officials came begging an audience. His complaint, the message he gave the steward said, was that a Quintus Granius owed the town treasury a vast sum of money but refused to pay it, and could Sulla help?

No worse name than Granius could have sounded in Sulla's ears, unless it were Gaius Marius. And indeed there were close ties of blood and marriage between the Marii and Gratidii and Tullii of Arpinum and the Granii of Puteoli; Gaius Marius's first wife had been a Grania. For this reason several Granii had found themselves proscribed, and those Granii who were not proscribed kept very still in case Sulla remembered their existence. Among the lucky escapees was this Quintus Granius. Who now found himself taken into custody by a troop of Sullani, and haled before Sulla in his villa at Misenum.

"I do not owe these sums," said Quintus Granius sturdily, his whole stance proclaiming that he would not be budged.

Seated on a curule chair, Sulla in *toga praetexta* and full Roman majesty glared. "You will do as the magistrates of Puteoli direct! You will pay!" he said.

"No I will not pay! Let Puteoli prosecute me in a court of law and test their case as it must be tested," said Quintus Granius.

"Pay, Granius!"

"No!"

That uncertain temper, shredded as easily these days as a dandelion airball, disintegrated. Sulla came to his feet shaking with rage, both hands bunched into fists. "Pay, Granius, or I will have you strangled her and now!"

"You may have been Dictator of Rome," said Quintus Granius contemptuously, "but these days you have no more authority to order me to do anything than I have to order you! Go back to your carousing and leave Puteoli to sort out its own messes!"

Sulla's mouth opened to scream the command that Granius be strangled, but no sound came out; a wave of faintness and horrible nausea assailed him, he reeled a little. Righting himself cost him dear, but he managed it, and his eyes turned to the captain of the waiting Sullani. "Strangle this fellow!" he whispered.

Before the captain could move, Sulla's mouth opened again. A great gout of blood came flying out of it to land in far-flung splatters many feet from where Sulla stood making a cacophony of ghastly noises, the last of the blood dripping down his snowy folded front. Then the next wave took hold of him, he retched hideously and puked another dark red fountain, sinking slowly to his knees as men ran in all directions crying out in horror—all directions, that is, save toward Sulla, whom they were convinced was being eaten up by worms.

Within moments Lucius Tuccius was there, and Metrobius, and a white-faced Valeria. Sulla lay in terrible straits still vomiting blood while his lover held his head and his wife crouched in a fever of trembling, not knowing what to do. A barked command from Tuccius and servants brought armloads of towels, eyes distended as they took in the condition of the room and the worse condition of their master, choking and retching, trying to speak, both hands fastened like a vise upon Metrobius's blood-covered arm.

Forgotten, Quintus Granius stayed no longer. While the Sullani huddled terrified and their captain tried to get some spirit into them, the banker from Puteoli walked out of the room, out of the house, down the path to where his horse still stood. He mounted, turned its head, and rode away.

Much time went by before Sulla ceased his awful activity, before he could be lifted from the floor and carried, a surprisingly light weight, away from the blood-ruined room in the arms of Metrobius. The Sullani fled too, leaving the shaken servants to make order out of a dreadful chaos.

The worst of it, Sulla found—for he was quite conscious and aware of what was happening—was that the blood kept trying to choke him; it welled up his gullet constantly, even when he was not retching. Appalling! Terrifying! In a frenzy of fear and helplessness he clung to Metrobius as to a chunk of cork in the midst of the sea, his eyes staring up into that dark beloved face with desperate intensity and so much anguished appeal, all he had left to communicate with while the tide of blood kept on rising out of him. On the periphery of his vision he could see Valeria's white frightened skin in which the blue of her eyes was so vivid it was startling, and the set features of his doctor.

Is this dying? he asked himself, and knew that it was. But I don't want to die this way! Not spewing and airless, soiled and incapable of disciplining my unruly body to get the business over and done with in admirable control and a decent meed of Roman dignity. I was the uncrowned King of Rome. I was crowned with the grass of Nola. I was the greatest man between the Rivers of Ocean and Indus. Let my dying be worthy of all these things! Let it not be a nightmare of blood, speechlessness, *fear*!

He thought of Julilla, who had died alone in a welter of blood. And of Nicopolis, who had died with less blood but more agony. And of Clitumna, who had died with broken neck and broken bones. Metellus Numidicus, scarlet in the face and choking—I did not know how awful that is! Dalmatica, crying out his name in Juno Sospita. His son, the light of his life, Julilla's boy who had meant more to him than anyone else ever, ever, ever . . . He too had died an airless death.

I am afraid. So afraid! I never thought I would be. It is inevitable, it cannot be avoided, it is over soon enough, and I will never see or hear or feel or think again. I will be no one. Nothing. There is no pain in that fate. It is the fate of a dreamless ignorance. It is eternal sleep. I, Lucius Cornelius Sulla, who was the uncrowned King of Rome yet crowned with the grass of Nola, will cease to be except in the minds of men. For that is the only immortality, to be remembered in the world of the living. I had almost finished my memoirs. Only one more little book left to write. More than enough for future historians to judge me. And more than enough to kill Gaius Marius for all of time. He did not live to write his memoirs. I did. So I will win. I *have* won! And of all my victories, victory over Gaius Marius means the most to me.

For perhaps an hour the bleeding continued remorselessly, made Sulla suffer horribly; but then it went away, and he could rest more easily. Consciousness clung, he was able to look upon Metrobius and Valeria and Lucius Tuccius with a clarity of vision he had not enjoyed in many moons, as if at the last this greatest of senses was given back to him to mirror his own going in the faces he knew best. He managed to speak.

"My will. Send for Lucullus, he must read it after I am dead. He is my executor and the guardian of my children."

"I have already sent for him, Lucius Cornelius," said the Greek actor softly.

"Have I given you enough, Metrobius?"

"Always, Lucius Cornelius."

"I do not know what love is. Aurelia used to say that I knew it but did not perceive my knowledge. I am not so sure. I dreamed the other night of Julilla and our son. He came to me and begged me to join his mother. I should have known then. I didn't. I just wept. Him, I did love. More than I loved myself. Oh, how I have missed him!"

"That is about to be healed, dear Lucius Cornelius."

"One reason to look forward to death, then."

"Is there anything you want?"

"Only peace. A sense of . . . Fulfillment."

"You are fulfilled."

"My body."

"Your body, Lucius Cornelius?"

"The Cornelians are inhumed. But not me, Metrobius. It is in my will, but you must assure Lucullus I mean it. If my body is laid in a tomb, some speck of Gaius Marius's ashes might come and rest upon it. I threw them away. I ought not to have done that. Who knows where they lurk, waiting to defile me? They went floating down the Anio, I saw them smother the eddies like powdered cobwebs. But a wind came, and the unwetted bits on top flew away. So I cannot be sure. I must be burned. You will tell Lucullus that I meant it, that I must be burned and my ashes gathered beneath a tight canopy to shut out the air, and then sealed with wax inside a jar where Gaius Marius cannot get at them. I will be the only Cornelian to be burned."

"It will be done, I promise."

"Burn me, Metrobius! Make Lucullus burn me!"

"I will, Lucius Cornelius. I will."

"I wish I knew what love was!"

"But you do, of course you do! Love made you deny your nature and give yourself to Rome."

"Is that love? It cannot be. Dry as dust. Dry as my ashes. The only Cornelian to be burned, not buried."

The engorged, ruptured blood vessels at the bottom of his gullet had not done with bleeding; a fresh spate of vomiting gore assailed Sulla soon after, and lasted for many hours with little let. He was sinking, having lost over half his life-force, and the lucid intervals within his mind dwindled. Over and over when he was able he begged Metrobius to make sure no atom of Gaius Marius could ever touch his own remains, and then would ask what love was, and why he didn't know it.

Lucullus arrived in time to see him die, though no speech had Sulla left, nor even any awareness. The strange bleached eyes with the outer ring of darkness and the black, black pupils had quite lost their usual menace, just looked washed out and overcome with weariness. His breathing had become too shallow to detect by all save a mirror held to his lips, and the white skin could look no whiter because of loss of blood than it normally did. But the mulberry-colored scar tissue blazed, the hairless scalp had lost tension and was wrinkled like a wind-buffeted sea, and the mouth lay sagging against the bones of jaw and chin. Then a change came over the eyes; the pupils began to expand, to blot out the irises and join up the outer edges of darkness. Sulla's light went out, the watchers saw it go, and stared in disbelief at the sheen of gold spread across his wide-open eyes.

Lucius Tuccius leaned over and pushed down the lids and Metrobius put the coins upon them to keep them closed, while Lucullus slid the single denarius inside Sulla's mouth to pay for Charon's boat ride.

"He died hard," said Lucullus, rigidly controlled.

Metrobius wept. "Everything came hard to Lucius Cornelius. To have died easily would not have been fitting."

"I will escort his body to Rome for a State funeral."

"He would want that. As long as he is cremated."

"He will be cremated."

Numbed with grief, Metrobius crept away after that to find Valeria, who had not proven strong enough to wait for the end.

"It is all over," he said.

"I did love him," she said, small-voiced. "I know all Rome thought I married him for convenience, to see him dower my family with honors. But he was a great man and he was very good to me. I loved him, Metrobius! I did truly love him!"

"I believe you," Metrobius said, sat down near her and took her hand, began to stroke it absently.

"What will you do now?" she asked.

Roused from his reverie, he looked down at her hand, fine and white and long-fingered. Not unlike Sulla's hand. Well, they were both patrician Romans. He said, "I will go away."

"After the funeral?"

"No, I can't attend that. Can you imagine Lucullus's face if I turned up among the chief mourners?"

"But Lucullus knows what you meant to Lucius Cornelius! He knows! No one better!"

"This will be a State funeral, Valeria. Nothing can be allowed to diminish its dignity, least of all a Greek actor with a well-used arse." That came out sounding bitter; then Metrobius shrugged. "Frankly, I don't think Lucius Cornelius would like me there. As for Lucullus, he's a great aristocrat. What went on here in Misenum permitted him to indulge some of his own less admirable impulses. He likes to deflower children." The dark face looked suddenly sick. "At least Sulla's vices were the usual ones! He condoned it in Lucullus, but he didn't do it himself."

"Where are you going?"

"To Cyrenaica. The golden backwater of the world."

"When?"

"Tonight. After Lucullus has started Sulla on his last journey and the house is quiet."

"How do you get to Cyrenaica?"

"From Puteoli. It's spring. There will be ships going to Africa, to Hadrumetum. From there I'll hire my own transport."

"Can you afford to?"

"Oh, yes. Sulla could leave me nothing in his will, but he gave me more than enough in life. He was odd, you know. A miser except to those he loved. That's the saddest thing of all, that even at the end he doubted his capacity to love." He lifted his gaze from her hand to her face, his eyes shadowing as certain thoughts began to swim in the mind they reflected. "And you, Valeria? What about you?"

"I must go back to Rome. After the funeral I will return to my brother's house."

"That," said Metrobius, "may not be a good idea. I have a better one."

The drowned blue eyes were innocent of guile; she looked at him in genuine bewilderment. "What?"

"Come to Cyrenaica with me. Have your child and call me its father. Whichever one of us quickened you—Lucullus, Sorex, Roscius or I—makes no difference to me. It has occurred to me that Lucullus was one of the four of us and he knows as well as I do that Sulla could not have been your child's father. I think Rome spells disaster for you, Valeria. Lucullus will denounce you. It is a way of discrediting you. Don't forget that alone among Lucullus's equals in birth, you can indict him for practices his colleagues would condemn."

"Ye gods!"

"You must come with me."

"They wouldn't let me!"

"They'll never know. I'll inform Lucullus that you're too ill to travel with Sulla's cortege, that I'll send you to Rome before the funeral. Lucullus is too busy at the moment to remember his own frail position, and he doesn't know about your child. So if you are to escape him it must be now, Valeria."

"You're right. He would indeed denounce me."

"He might even have you killed."

"Oh, Metrobius!"

"Come with me, Valeria. As soon as he's gone you and I will walk out of this house. No one will see us go. Nor will anyone ever find out what happened to you." Metrobius smiled wryly. "After all, I was just Sulla's boy. You, a Valeria Messala, were his wife. Far above me!"

But she didn't think she was above him at all. Months ago she had fallen in love with him, even though she understood it was not in him to return that love. So she said, "I will come."

The hand he still held was patted gladly, then placed in her lap. "Good! Stay here for the present. Lucullus must not set eyes on you. Get a few things together, but nothing more than will fit on the back of a pack mule. Make sure you take only dark plain gowns, and that your cloaks have hoods. You must look like *my* wife, not the wife of Lucius Cornelius Sulla.''

Off he went, leaving Valeria Messala to look at a future vastly different from the one she had contemplated would be hers after Sulla's obsequies were over. Never having understood the threat she posed to Lucullus, she knew she had cause to be very grateful to the actor. To go with Metrobius might mean the pain of seeing him love men when she longed for him to love her; but he would regard the child as his own, and she could offer him a family life he might in time come to appreciate more than the tenuous affairs he had enjoyed with men other than Sulla. Yes, better that by far than the agony of never seeing him again! Or the finality of death. Without, she had thought until now, good reason, she had feared the cold and haughty Lucullus. Rightly so.

Rising, she began to sort through her many chests of rich garments, choosing the plainest and darkest things. Of money she had none, but her jewels were glorious. Apparently Metrobius had plenty of money, so the jewels could be her dowry. A hedge against hard times in the future. Cyrenaica! The golden backwater of the world. It sounded wonderful.

Sulla's funeral reduced his triumph to utter insignificance. Two hundred and ten litters loaded down to creaking point with myrrh, frankincense, cinnamon, balsam, nard and other aromatics—the gift of Rome's women—were carried by black-garbed bearers. And because Sulla's corpse was so shrunken and mummified by loss of blood that it could not be displayed, a group of sculptors had set to work and fashioned out of cinnamon and frankincense an effigy of Sulla sitting on his bier, preceded by a lictor made from the same spices. There were floats depicting every aspect of his life except the first thirty-three disreputable years and the last few disreputable months. There he was before the walls of Nola receiving his Grass Crown from the hands of a centurion; there he was standing sternly over a cowering King Mithridates making sure the Treaty of Dardanus was signed; there he was winning battles, legislating laws, capturing Jugurtha, executing the Carboan prisoners after the Colline Gate. A special vehicle displayed the more than two thousand chaplets and wreaths made from pure gold which had been given to him by towns and tribes and kings and countries everywhere. His ancestors rode, clad in black, in black-and-gilt chariots drawn by splendid black horses, and his chubby little five-year-old twins Faustus and Fausta walked amid the chief mourners.

The day was suffocating and overcast, the air exuded unshed rain. But the biggest funeral procession Rome had ever seen got under way from the house overlooking the Circus Maximus, wended its way down through the Velabrum to the Forum Romanum, where Lucullus—a powerful and famous speaker—gave the eulogy from the top of the rostra, standing alongside the cunning bier on which the frankincense and cinnamon Sulla sat upright behind his spicy lictor and the horrible wizened old corpse lay below in a special compartment. For the second time in three years Rome wept to see his twins deprived of a parent, and broke into applause when Lucullus told Rome that he was the children's guardian, and would never see them want. Sentiment clouded every watering eye; had it not, Rome would have perceived that Faustus and Fausta were now old enough to reveal that in physique and faces and coloring they were going to take after their maternal great-uncle, the awesome but unhandsome Quintus Caecilius Metellus Numidicus. Whom their father had called Piggle-wiggle. And murdered in a fit of rage after Aurelia had repudiated him.

As if under the spell of some enchantment, the rain held off as the procession got under way again, this time up the Clivus Argentarius, through the Fontinalis Gate beyond which lay the mansion which had once belonged to Gaius Marius, and down to the Campus Martius. There Sulla's tomb already waited in sumptuous isolation on the Via Lata adjacent to the ground on which met the Centuriate Assembly. At the ninth hour of daylight the bier was deposited on top of the huge, well-ventilated pyre, its kindling and logs interspersed with the contents of those two hundred and ten litters of spices. Never would Sulla smell sweeter than when, according to his wishes, his mortal remains burned.

Just as the torches licked at the kindling all around the base of the pyre, a huge wind arose; the miniature mountain went up with a roar, and blazed so fiercely the mourners gathered around it had to move away, shielding their faces. Then as the fire died down it began to rain at last, a solid downpour which quenched and cooled the coals so quickly that Sulla's ashes were collected a few short moments after the holocaust. Into an exquisite alabaster jar ornamented with gold and gems all that was left of Sulla went; Lucullus dispensed with the canopy Sulla had asked for to shelter his remains from contamination by a stray granule of Gaius Marius, for the rain continued unabated, and no stray granules of any dust floated on the air.

The jar was deposited carefully inside the tomb, built and masoned and sculpted within four days out of multicolored marbles, round in shape and supported by fluted columns crowned with the new kind of capital Sulla had brought back from Corinth and had made so popular—delicate sprays of acanthus leaves. His name and titles and deeds were carved upon a panel

facing the road, and beneath them was his simple epitaph. He had composed
it himself, and it said:

NO BETTER FRIEND · NO WORSE ENEMY

"Well, I'm very glad that's over," said Lucullus to his brother as they
trudged home through the tempest, soaked to their skins and shivering with
cold.

He was a worried man: Valeria Messala had not arrived in Rome. Her
brother, Rufus, her cousins Niger and Metellus Nepos, and her great-aunt the
retired Vestal were all beginning to ask agitated questions; Lucullus had been
obliged to inform them that he had sent to Misenum for her, only to be told
by an exhausted messenger on a winded horse that she had disappeared.

Almost a month went by before Lucullus called off the now frantic search,
which had included a careful combing of the shore for some miles north and
south of the villa, and of every wood and grove between Neapolis and Sinuessa. Sulla's last wife had vanished. And so had her jewels.

"Robbed and murdered," said Varro Lucullus.

His brother (who kept some things even from this beloved person) made
no answer. His luck, he told himself, bade fair to be as good as Sulla's, for
he had not got as far as the day of the funeral before he realized how dangerous
Valeria Messala might be. She knew too much about him, whereas he knew
virtually nothing about her. He would have had to kill her. How providential
therefore that someone had done it for him! Fortune favored him.

The disappearance of Metrobius concerned him not at all—if indeed he
had bothered to think about it, which he did not. Rome had more than enough
tragedy queens to stop up the gap; her theater world was stuffed with them.
Of more moment to Lucullus by far was the fact that he no longer had access
to unlimited supplies of motherless little girls. Oh, how he would miss Misenum!

PART FIVE

from SEXTILIS (AUGUST) 80 B.C.
until SEXTILIS (AUGUST) 77 B.C.

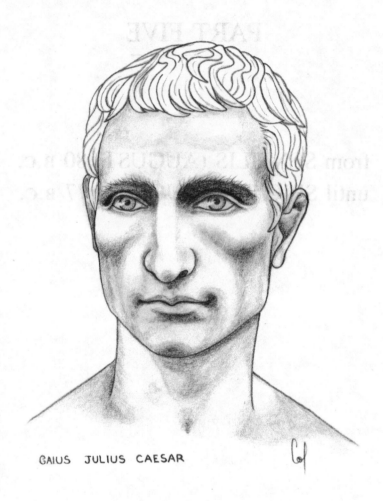

GAIUS JULIUS CAESAR

This time, Caesar sailed to the east. His mother's steward, Eutychus (really his steward, but Caesar never made the mistake of thinking that), soft and semi-sedentary for years, discovered that traveling with Gaius Julius Caesar was no leisurely progress. On land—particularly when the road was as respectable as the Via Appia—he would cover forty miles in a day, and anyone who did not keep up was left behind. Only dread of disappointing Aurelia enabled Eutychus to hang on, especially during the first few days, when the steward's fat smooth legs and pampered bottom dissolved into one enormous pain.

"You're saddlesore!" laughed Caesar unsympathetically when he found Eutychus weeping miserably after they stopped at an inn near Beneventum.

"It's my legs hurt the worst," sniffled Eutychus.

"Of course they do! On a horse they're unsupported weight, they just dangle off the end of your behind and flop about—particularly true of yours, Eutychus! But cheer up! By the time we get to Brundisium they'll feel much better. So will you. Too much easy Roman living."

The thought of reaching Brundisium did nothing to elevate the steward's mood; he burst into a fresh spate of tears at the prospect of a heaving Ionian Sea.

"Caesar's a beggar," said Burgundus, grinning, after Caesar had departed to make sure their accommodation was clean.

"He's a monster!" wailed Eutychus. *"Forty miles a day!"*

"You're lucky. This is just the beginning. He's going easy on us. Mostly because of you."

"I want to go home!"

Burgundus reached out to give the steward's shoulder a clumsy pat. "You can't go home, Eutychus, you know that." He shivered, grimaced, his wide and slightly vacant-looking eyes filled with horror. "Come on, dry your face and try to walk a bit. It's better to suffer with him than go back to face his mother—brrr! Besides, he's not as unfeeling as you think he is. Right at this moment he's arranging for a nice hot bath for your nice sore arse."

Eutychus survived, though he wasn't sure he would survive the sea crossing. Caesar and his small entourage took nine days to cover the three hundred and seventy miles between Rome and Brundisium, where the relentless young man shepherded his hapless flock onto a ship before any of them could find the breath to petition him for a few days' rest first. They sailed to the lovely island of Corcyra, took another ship there for Buthrotum in Epirus, and then rode overland through Acarnania and Delphi to Athens. This was a Greek goat path, not a Roman road; up and down the tall mountains, through wet and slippery forests.

"Obviously even we Romans don't move armies along this route," Caesar observed when they emerged into the awesome vale of Delphi, more a gardened lap on a seated massif. The idea had to be finished before he could gaze about and admire; he said, "That's worth remembering. An army could move along it if the men were stouthearted. And no one would know because no one would believe it. Hmmm."

Caesar liked Athens, and Athens liked him. In contrast to his noble contemporaries, he had nowhere solicited hospitality from the owners of large houses or estates, contenting himself with hostelries where available, and a camp beside the road where they were not. So in Athens he had found a reasonable-looking inn below the Acropolis on its eastern side, and taken up residence. Only to find himself summoned immediately to the mansion of Titus Pomponius Atticus. He didn't know the man, of course, though (like everyone else in Rome) he knew the history of the famous financial disaster Atticus and Crassus had suffered the year after Gaius Marius died.

"I insist you stay with me," said the urbane man-of-the-world, who (despite that earlier miscalculation) was a very shrewd judge of his peers. One look at Caesar told him what reports had hinted; here was someone who was going to matter.

"You are too generous, Titus Pomponius," Caesar said with a wide smile. "However, I prefer to remain independent."

"Independence in Athens will only give you food poisoning and dirty beds," Atticus answered.

The cleanliness fanatic changed his mind. "Thank you, I will come. I don't have a large following—two freedmen and four servants, if you have room for them."

"More than enough room."

And so it was arranged. As were dinner parties and tourist expeditions; Caesar found an Athens suddenly opened to him that demanded a longer stay than expected. Epicurean and lover of luxury though Atticus was reputed to be, he was not soft, so there were plenty of opportunities to engage in some rough scrambling up cliffs and mountain shoulders of historical note, and good hard gallops across the flats at Marathon. They rode down to Corinth, up to Thebes, looked at the marshy foreshores of Lake Orchomenus where Sulla had won the two decisive battles against the armies of Mithridates, explored the tracks which had enabled Cato the Censor to circumvent the enemy at Thermopylae—and the enemy to circumvent the last stand of Leonidas.

"Stranger, go tell the Spartans that here we lie, obedient to their command," Caesar read off the stone commemorating that valiant last stand. He

turned to Atticus. "The whole world can quote this inscription, but it has a resonance here on the spot that it doesn't when read off a piece of paper."

"Would you be content to be so remembered, Caesar?"

The long, fair face closed up. "Never! It was a stupid and futile gesture, a waste of brave men. I *will* be remembered, Atticus, but not for stupidity or futile gestures. Leonidas was a Spartan king. I am a patrician Roman of the Republic. The only real meaning his life had was the manner in which he threw it away. The meaning of my life will lie in what I do as a living man. How I die doesn't matter, provided I die like a Roman."

"I believe you."

Because he was a natural scholar and very well educated, Caesar found himself with much in common with Atticus, whose tastes were intellectual and eclectic. They found themselves with a similar taste in literature and works of art, and spent hours poring over a Menander play or a Phidias statue.

"There are not, however, very many good paintings left in Greece," Atticus said, shaking his head sadly. "What Mummius didn't carry off to Rome after he sacked Corinth—not to mention Aemilius Paullus after Pydna!—have successfully vanished in the decades since. If you want to see the world's best paintings, Caesar, you must go to the house of Marcus Livius Drusus in Rome."

"I believe Crassus owns it now."

Atticus's face twisted; he disliked Crassus, colleagues in speculation though they had been. "And has probably dumped the paintings in a dusty heap somewhere in the basement, where they will lie until someone drops a hint to him that they're worth more than tutored slaves on the market or insulae bought up cheap."

Caesar grinned. "Well, Atticus my friend, we can't all be men of culture and refinement! There's room for a Crassus."

"Not in my house!"

"You're not married," said Caesar toward the end of his time in Athens. He had his ideas as to why Atticus had avoided the entanglements of matrimony, but the statement as he put it was not insulting because the answer did not need to be revealing.

Atticus's long, ascetic and rather austere face produced a faint moue of disgust. "No, Caesar. Nor do I intend to marry."

"Whereas I have been married since I was thirteen. And to a girl who is still not old enough to take to my bed. That is a strange fate."

"Stranger than most. Cinna's younger daughter. Whom you would not divorce, even for Jupiter Optimus Maximus."

"Even for Sulla, you mean," said Caesar, laughing. "It was very fortunate. I escaped Gaius Marius's net—with Sulla's active connivance!—and ceased to be the *flamen Dialis*."

"Speaking of marriages, are you acquainted with Marcus Tullius Cicero?" asked Atticus.

"No. I've heard of him, of course."

"You ought to get on well together, but I suspect you may not," said Atticus thoughtfully. "Cicero is touchy about his intellectual abilities, and dislikes rivals. You may well be his intellectual superior."

"What has this to do with marriage?"

"I've just found him a wife."

"How splendid," said Caesar, uninterested.

"Terentia. Varro Lucullus's adoptive sister."

"A dreadful woman, I hear."

"Indeed. But socially better than he could have hoped for."

Caesar made up his mind; time to go, when one's host was reduced to aimless conversation. Whose fault that was, the guest knew. His reading of this Roman plutocrat in self-imposed exile was that Atticus's sexual preferences were for young boys, which imposed upon Caesar a degree of reserve normally foreign to his outgoing nature. A pity. There might otherwise have grown out of this first meeting a deep and lasting friendship.

From Athens, Caesar took the Roman-built military road north from Attica through Boeotia and Thessaly and the pass at Tempe, with a casual salute to Zeus as they rode at Caesar's remorseless pace past the distant peak of Mount Olympus. From Dium just beyond the party took ship again and sailed from island to island until it reached the Hellespont. From there to Nicomedia was a voyage of three days.

His reception in the palace at Nicomedia was ecstatic. The old King and Queen had quite given up hope of ever seeing him again, especially after word had come from Mitylene that Caesar had gone back to Rome in company with Thermus and Lucullus. But it was left to Sulla the dog to express the full extent of the joy Caesar's advent provoked. The animal tore about the palace yelping and squealing, would leap up at Caesar, race over to the King and Queen to tell them who was here, then back to Caesar; its antics quite paled the royal hugs and kisses into insignificance.

"He almost talks," said Caesar when the dog finally let him sink into a chair, so winded that it contented itself with sitting on his feet and producing a series of strangled noises. He leaned down to give the dog's belly a rub. "Sulla, old man, I never thought I'd be so glad to see your ugly face!"

*　*　*

His own parents, Caesar reflected much later that evening, when he had retired to his room and lay unclothed upon his bed, had always been rather distant figures. A father rarely home who when he was home seemed more intent upon conducting some sort of undeclared war upon his wife than in establishing a rapport with any of his children; and a mother who was unfailingly just, unsparingly critical, unable to give physical affection. Perhaps, thought Caesar from his present vantage point, that had been a large part of his father's inexplicable but patent disapproval of his mother—her fleshly coolness, her aloofness. What the young man could not see, of course, was that the real root of his father's dissatisfaction had lain in his wife's unstinting love for her work as landlady—work he considered utterly beneath her. Because they had never not known Aurelia the landlady, Caesar and his sisters had no idea how this side of her had galled their father. Instead, they had equated their father's attitude with their own starvation for hugs and kisses; for they could not know how pleasurable were the nights their parents spent together. When the dreadful news had come of the father's death—borne as it had been by the bearer of his ashes—Caesar's immediate reaction had been to take his mother in his arms and comfort her. But she had wrenched herself away and told him in clipped accents to remember who he was. It had hurt until the detachment he had inherited from her asserted itself, told him that he could have expected no other behavior from her.

And perhaps, thought Caesar now, that was no more than a sign of something he had noticed all around him—that children always wanted things from their parents that their parents were either not willing to give, or incapable of giving. His mother was a pearl beyond price, he knew that. Just as he knew how much he loved her. And how much he owed her for pointing out to him perpetually where the weaknesses lay within him—not to mention for giving him some wonderfully worldly and unmaternal advice.

And yet—and yet . . . How lovely it was to be greeted with hugs and kisses and unquestioning affection, as Nicomedes and Oradaltis had greeted him today. He didn't go so far as to wish consciously that his own parents had been more like them; he just wished that they had been his parents.

This mood lasted until he broke the night's fast with them on the next morning, and the light of day revealed the wish's manifest absurdity. Sitting looking at King Nicomedes, Caesar superimposed his own father's face upon the King's (in deference to Caesar, Nicomedes had not painted himself), and wanted to laugh. As for Oradaltis—a queen she might be, but not one-tenth as royal as Aurelia. Not parents, he thought then: grandparents.

It was October when he had arrived in Nicomedia and he had no plans to move on quickly, much to the delight of the King and Queen, who strove to fall in with all their guest's wishes, be it to visit Gordium, Pessinus, or the marble quarries on the island of Proconnesus. But in December, when Caesar had been in Bithynia two months, he found himself asked to do something very difficult and passing strange.

In March of that year the new governor of Cilicia, the younger Dolabella, had started out from Rome to go to his province in the company of two other Roman noblemen and a retinue of public servants. The more important of his two companions was his senior legate, Gaius Verres; the less important was his quaestor, Gaius Publicius Malleolus, apportioned to his service by the lots.

One of Sulla's new senators through election as quaestor, Malleolus was by no means a New Man; there had been consuls in his family, there were *imagines* in his atrium. Of money, however, there was little; only some lucky buys in the proscriptions had enabled the family to pin their hopes on the thirty-year-old Gaius, whose duty was to restore the family's old status by rising to the consulship. Knowing how small Gaius's salary would be and how expensive maintaining the younger Dolabella's life-style was going to be, his mother and sisters sold their jewels to plump out Malleolus's purse, which he intended to plump out further when he reached his province. And the women had eagerly pushed on him the greatest family treasure left, a magnificent collection of matching gold and silver plate. When he gave a banquet for the governor, the ladies said, it would increase his standing to use the family plate.

Unfortunately Gaius Publicius Malleolus was not as mentally capable as earlier men of his clan had been; he possessed a degree of gullible naïveté that did not bode well for his survival in the forefront of the younger Dolabella's retinue. No slouch, the senior legate Gaius Verres had assessed Malleolus accurately before the party had got as far as Tarentum, and cultivated the quaestor with such charm and winning ways that Malleolus deemed Verres the best of good fellows.

They traveled together with another governor and his party going to the east: the new governor of Asia Province, Gaius Claudius Nero; a patrician Claudius, he had more wealth but far less intelligence than that prolific branch of the patrician Claudii cognominated Pulcher.

Gaius Verres was hungry again. Though he had (thanks to prior knowledge of the area) done very well out of proscribing major landowners and magnates around Beneventum, he owned a genuine passion for works of art which Beneventum had not assuaged. The proscribed of Beneventum had been on the whole an untutored lot, as content with a mawkish Neapolitan copy of some sentimental group of nymphs as with a Praxiteles or a Myron. At first Verres had watched and waited for the proscription of the grandson of the notorious Sextus Perquitienus, whose reputation as a connoisseur was quite unparalleled among the knights, and whose collection thanks to his activities as a tax-farmer in Asia was perhaps even better than the collection of Marcus Livius Drusus. Then the grandson had turned out to be Sulla's nephew; the property of Sextus Perquitienus was forever safe.

Though his family was not distinguished—his father was a *pedarius* on the back benches of the Senate, the first Verres to belong to that body—Gaius Verres had done remarkably well thanks to his instinct for being where the money was and his ability to convince certain important men of his worth. He had easily fooled Carbo but had never managed to fool Sulla, though Sulla had not scrupled to use him to ruin Samnium. Unfortunately Samnium was as devoid of great works of art as Beneventum; that side of Verres's insatiably avaricious character remained unappeased.

The only place to go, decided Verres, was to the east, where a Hellenized world had scattered statues and paintings literally everywhere from Alexandria to Olympia to Pontus to Byzantium. So when Sulla had drawn the lots for next year's governors, Verres had weighed up his chances and opted for cultivating the younger Dolabella. His cousin the elder Dolabella was in Macedonia—a fruitful province when it came to works of art—but the elder Dolabella was a hard man, and had his own aims. Gaius Claudius Nero, going to Asia Province, was a bit of a stickler for the right thing. Which left the next governor of Cilicia, the younger Dolabella. Exactly the material for a Gaius Verres, as he was greedy, unethical, and a secret participant in vices which involved dirty smelly women of the most vulgar kind and substances capable of enhancing sensuous awareness. Long before the journey to the east actually began, Verres had made himself indispensable to Dolabella in pursuing his secret vices.

Luck, thought Verres triumphantly: he had Fortune's favor! Men like the younger Dolabella were not many, nor on the whole did they usually rise so high. Had not the elder Dolabella proven militarily helpful to Sulla, the younger would never have gained praetorship and province. Of course praetorship and province had been grabbed at, but the younger Dolabella lived in constant fear; so when Verres showed himself as sympathetic as he was resourceful, Dolabella sighed in relief.

While the party had traveled in conjunction with Claudius Nero, Verres had metaphorically bound his itching hands to his sides and resisted the impulse to snatch this work from a Greek sanctuary and that work from a

Greek agora. In Athens especially it had been difficult, so rich was the treasure trove all around; but Titus Pomponius Atticus sat like a huge spider at the center of the Roman web which enveloped Athens. Thanks to his financial acumen, his blood ties to the Caecilii Metelli, and his many gifts to Athens, Atticus was not a man to offend, and his condemnation of the kind of Roman who plundered works of art was well known.

But when they left Athens by ship there came the parting of the ways with Claudius Nero, who was anxious to reach Pergamum and not by nature a Grecophile. So Claudius Nero's ship sped as fast as it could to Asia Province, while Dolabella's ship sailed to the tiny island of Delos.

Until Mithridates had invaded Asia Province and Greece nine years earlier, Delos had been the epicenter of the world's slave trade. There all the bulk dealers in slaves had set up shop, there came the pirates who provided the eastern end of the Middle Sea with most of its slaves. As many as twenty thousand slaves a day had changed hands in the old Delos, though that had not meant an endless parade of slave-filled vessels choking up the neat and commodious Merchant Harbor. The trading was done with bits of paper, from transfers of ownership of slaves to the moneys paid over. Only special slaves were transported to Delos in person; the island was purely for middlemen.

There had used to be a large Italo-Roman population there, as well as many Alexandrians and a considerable number of Jews; the largest building on Delos was the Roman agora, wherein the Romans and Italians who conducted business on Delos had located their offices. These days it was windswept and almost deserted, as was the western side of the isle, where most of the houses clustered because the weather was better. In terraces up the slopes of Mount Cynthus were the precincts and temples of those gods imported to Delos during the years when it had lain under the patronage of the Ptolemies of Egypt and the Seleucids of Syria. A sanctuary of Artemis, sister of Apollo, lay closest to the smaller of the two harbors, the Sacred Harbor, in which only the ships of pilgrims anchored. Beyond this, going north, was the mighty and wonderful precinct of Apollo—huge, beautiful, stuffed with some of the greatest works of art known. And between Apollo's temple and the Sacred Lake lay the white Naxian marble lions which flanked the Processional Way linking the two.

Verres went wild with delight, could not be prised from his explorations. He flitted from one temple to another, marveling at the image of Ephesian Artemis loaded down with bulls' testicles like sterile pendulous breasts, astonished at the goddess Ma from Comana, at Sidonian Hecate, at Alexandrian Serapis, literally drooling at images in gold and chryselephantine, at gem-studded oriental thrones on which, it seemed, the original occupants must have sat cross-legged. But it was inside the temple of Apollo that he found the two statues he could not resist—a group of the satyr Marsyas playing his rustic pipes to an ecstatic Midas and an outraged Apollo, and an image in gold and ivory of Leto holding her divine babies said to have been fashioned by Phidias, master of chryselephantine sculpture. Since these two works of art were small, Verres and four of his servants stole into the temple in the middle of the night before Dolabella was due to sail, removed them from their plinths, wrapped them tenderly in blankets, and stowed them in that part of the ship's hold wherein were deposited the belongings of Gaius Verres.

"I'm glad Archelaus sacked this place, and then Sulla after him," said a pleased Verres to Malleolus at dawn. "If the slave trade still made a hive of activity out of Delos, it would be far harder to walk about undetected and do a little acquiring, even in the night marches."

A little startled, Malleolus wondered what Verres meant, but a look at that perversely beautiful honey-colored face did not encourage him to ask. Not half a day later, he knew. For a wind had risen suddenly which prevented Dolabella's sailing, and before it had blown itself out the priests of Apollo's precinct had come to Dolabella crying that two of the god's most prized treasures had been stolen. And (having remarked for how long Verres had prowled about them, stroking them, rocking them on their bases, measuring them with his eyes) they accused Verres of the deed. Horrified, Malleolus realized that the allegation was justified. Since he liked Verres, it went hard with Malleolus to go to Dolabella and report what Verres had said, but he did his duty. And Dolabella insisted that Verres return the works.

"This is Apollo's birthplace!" he said, shivering. "You can't pillage here. We'll all die of disease."

Balked and in the grip of an overmastering rage, Verres "returned" the works by tossing them over the side of the ship onto the stony shore. Vowing that Malleolus would pay. But only to himself; much to Malleolus's surprise, Verres came to thank him for preventing the deed.

"I have such a lust for works of art that it is a great trouble to me," said Verres, golden eyes warm and moist. "Thank you, thank you!"

His lust was not to be thwarted again, however. In Tenedos (which Dolabella had a fancy to visit because of the part the isle had played in the war against Troy) Verres appropriated the statue of Tenes himself, a beautiful wooden creation so old it was only remotely humanoid. His new technique was candid and unapologetic: "I want it, I must have it!" he would say, and into the ship's hold it would go while Dolabella and Malleolus sighed and shook their heads, unwilling to cause a rift in what was going to be a long and necessarily closely knit association. In Chios and in Erythrae the looting occurred again; so did Verres's services to Dolabella and Malleolus, the latter now being steadily drawn into a corruption which Verres had already made irresistible to Dolabella. So when Verres decided to remove every work of art from the temple and precinct of Hera in Samos, he was able to persuade Dolabella to hire an extra ship—and to order the Chian admiral Charidemus, in command of a quinquereme, to escort the new governor of Cilicia's flotilla on the rest of its journey to Tarsus. No pirates must capture the swelling number of treasures! Halicarnassus lost some statues by Praxiteles—the last raid Verres made in Asia Province, now buzzing like an angry swarm of wasps. But Pamphylia lost the wonderful Harper of Aspendus and most of the contents of the temple of Artemis at Perge—here, deeming the statue of the goddess a poorly executed thing, Verres contented himself with stripping its coat of gold away and melting it down into nicely portable ingots.

And so at last they came to Tarsus, where Dolabella was glad to settle into his palace and Verres glad to commandeer a villa for himself wherein the treasures he had pillaged could be put on display for his delectation. His appreciation of the works was genuine, he had no intention of selling a single one; simply, in Gaius Verres the obsessions and amoralities of the fanatical collector reached a height hitherto unknown.

Gaius Publicius Malleolus too was glad to find himself a nice house beside the river Cydnus; he unpacked his matching gold and silver plate and his moneybags, for he intended to augment his fortune by lending money at exorbitant rates of interest to those who could not borrow from more legitimate sources. He found Verres enormously sympathetic—and enormously helpful.

By this time Dolabella had sunk into a torpor of gratified sensuality, his thought processes permanently clouded by the Spanish fly and other aphrodisiac drugs Verres supplied him, and content to leave the governing of his province to his senior legate and his quaestor. Displaying sufficient sense to leave the art of Tarsus alone, Verres concentrated upon revenge. It was time to deal with Malleolus.

He introduced a subject close to the hearts of all Romans—the making of a will.

"I lodged my new one with the Vestals just before I left," said Verres, looking particularly attractive with the light of a chandelier turning his softly curling hair into old gold. "I presume you did the same, Malleolus?"

"Well, no," Malleolus answered, flustered. "I confess the thought never occurred to me."

"My dear fellow, that's insanity!" cried Verres. "Anything can happen to a man away from home, from pirates to illnesses to shipwreck—look at the Servilius Caepio who drowned on his way home twenty-five years ago—

he was a quaestor, just like you!'' Verres slopped more fortified wine into Malleolus's beautiful vermeil cup. "You *must* make a will!''

And so it went while Malleolus grew drunker and drunker—and Verres appeared to. When the senior legate decided Dolabella's foolish quaestor was too befuddled to read what he was signing, Verres demanded paper and pen, wrote out the dispositions Gaius Publicius Malleolus dictated, and then assisted him to sign and seal. The will was tucked into a pigeonhole in Malleolus's study and promptly forgotten by its author. Who, not four days later, died of an obscure malady the Tarsian physicians finally elected to call food poisoning. And Gaius Verres, producing the will, was surprised and enchanted to discover that his friend the quaestor had left him everything he owned, including the family plate.

"Dreadful business,'' he said to Dolabella sadly. "It's a very nice legacy, but I'd rather poor Malleolus was still here.''

Even through his aphrodisiac-induced haze Dolabella sensed a touch of hypocrisy, but confined his words to wondering how he was going to get another quaestor from Rome in a hurry.

"No need!'' said Verres cheerfully. "I was Carbo's quaestor, and good enough at the job to be prorogued as his proquaestor when he went to govern Italian Gaul. Appoint me proquaestor.''

And so the affairs of Cilicia—not to mention Cilicia's public purse—passed into the hands of Gaius Verres.

All through the summer Verres worked industriously, though not for the good of Cilicia; it was his own activities benefited, particularly the money-lending he had taken over from Malleolus. However, the art collection remained static. Even Verres at that point in his career was not quite confident enough to foul his own nest by stealing from towns and temples in Cilicia itself. Nor could he—at least while Claudius Nero remained its governor—begin again to plunder Asia Province; the island of Samos had sent an angry deputation to Pergamum to complain to Claudius Nero about the pillaging of Hera's sanctuary, only to be told regretfully that it was not in Claudius Nero's power to punish or discipline the legate of another governor, so the Samians would have to refer their complaint to the Senate in Rome.

It was late in September that Verres had his inspiration; he then lost no time in turning fancy into fact. Both Bithynia and Thrace abounded in treasures, so why not increase his art collection at the expense of Bithynia and Thrace? Dolabella was persuaded to appoint him ambassador-at-large and issue him with letters of introduction to King Nicomedes of Bithynia and King Sadala of the Thracian Odrysiae. And off Verres set at the start of October, overland from Attaleia to the Hellespont. This route avoided Asia

Province and might besides yield a little gold from temples along the way, even if no desirable art.

It was an embassage composed entirely of villains; Verres wanted no honest, upright characters along. Even the six lictors (to whom as an ambassador with propraetorian status Verres was entitled) he chose with great care, sure they would aid and abet him in all his nefarious undertakings. His chief assistant was a senior clerk on Dolabella's staff, one Marcus Rubrius; Verres and Rubrius had already had many dealings together, including the procurement of Dolabella's dirty smelly women. His slaves were a mixture of big fellows to heft heavy statues around and little fellows to wriggle into locked rooms, and his scribes were only there to catalogue whatever he purloined.

The journey overland was disappointing, as Pisidia and that part of Phrygia he traversed had been thoroughly looted by the generals of Mithridates nine years before. He debated swinging wider onto the Sangarius to see what he could filch at Pessinus, but in the end elected to head straight for Lampsacus on the Hellespont. Here he could commandeer one of Asia Province's warships to act as escort, and sail along the Bithynian coast loading whatever he found and fancied onto a good stout freighter.

The Hellespont was a small slice of No Man's Land. Technically it belonged to Asia Province, but the mountains of Mysia cut it off on the landward side, and its ties were more with Bithynia than with Pergamum. Lampsacus was the chief port on the Asian side of the narrow straits, almost opposite to Thracian Callipolis; here the various armies which crossed the Hellespont made their Asian landfall. In consequence Lampsacus was a big and busy port, though a great measure of its economic prosperity lay in the abundance and excellence of the wine produced in the Lampsacan hinterland.

Nominally under the authority of the governor of Asia Province, it had long enjoyed independence, Rome being content with a tribute. There was— as always in every prosperous settlement on every shore of the Middle Sea—a contingent of Roman merchants who lived there permanently, but the government and the major wealth of Lampsacus rested with its native Phocaean Greeks, none of whom held the Roman citizenship; they were all *socii*, allies.

Verres had diligently researched every likely place along his route, so when his embassage arrived in Lampsacus he was well aware of its status and the status of its leading citizens. The Roman cavalcade which rode into the port city from the hills behind it caused an immediate stir almost verging on a panic; six lictors preceded the important Roman personage, who was also accompanied by twenty servants and a troop of one hundred mounted

Cilician cavalry. Yet no warning of its advent had been received, and no one knew what its purpose in Lampsacus might be.

One Ianitor was chief *ethnarch* that year; word that a full Roman embassage was awaiting him in the agora sent Ianitor flying there posthaste, together with some of the other city elders.

"I'm not sure how long I'll be staying," said Gaius Verres, looking handsome, imperious, and not a little arrogant, "but I require fitting lodgings for myself and my people."

It was impossible, Ianitor explained hesitantly, to find a house large enough to take everyone, but he himself would of course accommodate the ambassador, his lictors and body servants, while the rest were boarded with other households. Ianitor then introduced his fellow elders, including one Philodamus, who had been chief *ethnarch* of Lampsacus during Sulla's time there.

"I hear," said the clerk Marcus Rubrius low-voiced to Verres as they were being escorted to the mansion of Ianitor, "that the old man Philodamus has a daughter of such surpassing beauty and virtue that he keeps her shut away. Name of Stratonice."

Verres was no Dolabella when it came to bodily appetites. As with his statues and paintings, he liked his women to be pure and perfect works of art, Galateas come to life. In consequence he tended when not in Rome to go for long periods without sexual satisfaction, since he would not content himself with inferior types of women, even famous courtesans like Praecia. As yet he was unmarried, intending when he did to own a bride of splendid lineage and peerless beauty—a modern Aurelia. This trip to the east was going to cement his fortune and make it possible to negotiate a suitable marital alliance with some proud Caecilia Metella or Claudia Pulchra. A Julia would have been the best, but all the Julias were taken.

Thus it was months since Verres had enjoyed a sexual flutter, nor had he expected to find one in Lampsacus. But Rubrius had made it his business to find out the weaknesses of Verres—aside from inanimate works of art— and had done a little whispering in any gossipy-looking ears as soon as the embassage had ridden into town. To find that Philodamus had a daughter, Stratonice, who was quite the equal of Aphrodite herself.

"Make further enquiries," said Verres curtly, then put on his most charmingly false smile as he came to Ianitor's door, where the chief *ethnarch* waited in person to welcome him.

Rubrius nodded and went off in the wake of the slave to his own quarters, less august by far; he was, after all, a very minor official with no ambassadorial status.

After dinner that afternoon Rubrius reappeared at the house of Ianitor and sought a private interview with Verres.

"Are you comfortable here?" asked Rubrius.

"More or less. Not like a Roman villa, however. A pity none of the Roman citizens in Lampsacus ranks among the richest. I hate making do with Greeks! They're too simple for my taste. This Ianitor lives entirely on fish—didn't even produce an egg or a bird for dinner! But the wine was superb. How have you progressed in the matter of Stratonice?"

"With great difficulty, Gaius Verres. The girl is a paragon of every virtue, it seems, but perhaps that's because her father and brother guard her like Tigranes the women in his harem."

"Then I'll have to go to dinner at Philodamus's place."

Rubrius shook his head emphatically. "I'm afraid that won't produce her, Gaius Verres. This town is Phocaean Greek to its core. The women of the family are not shown to guests."

The two heads drew together, honey-gold and greying black, and the volume of the conversation dropped to whispers.

"My assistant Marcus Rubrius," said Verres to Ianitor after Rubrius had gone, "is poorly housed. I require better quarters for him. I hear that after yourself, the next man of note is one Philodamus. Please see that Marcus Rubrius is relocated in the house of Philodamus first thing tomorrow."

"I won't have the worm!" snapped Philodamus to Ianitor when Ianitor told him what Verres wanted. "Who is this Marcus Rubrius? A grubby little Roman clerk! In my days I've housed Roman consuls and praetors—even the great Lucius Cornelius Sulla when he crossed the Hellespont that last time! In fact, I've never housed anyone as unimportant as Gaius Verres himself! Who is *he* after all, Ianitor? A mere assistant to the governor of Cilicia!"

"Please, Philodamus, please!" begged Ianitor. "For my sake! For the sake of our city! This Gaius Verres is a nasty fellow, I feel it in my bones. *And* he has a hundred mounted troopers with him. In all Lampsacus we couldn't raise half that many competent professional soldiers."

So Philodamus gave in and Rubrius transferred his lodgings. But it had been a mistake to give in, as Philodamus soon discovered. Rubrius hadn't been inside the house for more than a few moments before he was demanding to see the famous beautiful daughter, and, denied this privilege, immediately began to poke and pry through Philodamus's spacious dwelling in search of her. This proving fruitless, Rubrius summoned Philodamus to him in his own house as if he had been a servant.

"You'll give a dinner for Gaius Verres this afternoon—and serve something other than course after course of fish! Fish is fine in its place, but a man can't live on it. So I want lamb, chicken, other fowls, plenty of eggs, and the very best wine.''

Philodamus kept his temper. "But it wasn't easy," he said to his son, Artemidorus.

"They're after Stratonice," said Artemidorus, very angry.

"I think so too, but they moved so quickly in foisting this Rubrius clod on me that I had no opportunity to get her out of the house. And now I can't. There are Romans creeping round our front door and our back door.''

Artemidorus wanted to be present at the banquet for Verres, but his father, looking at that stormy face, understood that his presence would worsen the situation; after much cajoling, the young man agreed to hie himself off and eat elsewhere. As for Stratonice, the best father and son could do was to lock her in her own room and put two strong servants inside with her.

Gaius Verres arrived with his six lictors, who were posted on duty in front of the house while a party of troopers was sent to watch the back gate. And no sooner was the Roman ambassador comfortable upon his couch than he demanded that Philodamus fetch his daughter.

"I cannot do that, Gaius Verres," said the old man stiffly. "This is a Phocaean town, which means our womenfolk are never put in the same room as strangers.''

"I'm not asking that she eat with us, Philodamus," said Verres patiently. "I just want to see this paragon all of your Phocaean town talks about.''

"I do not know why they should, when they have never seen her either,'' Philodamus said.

"No doubt your servants gossip. Produce her, old man!''

"I cannot, Gaius Verres.''

Five other guests were present, Rubrius and four fellow clerks; no sooner had Philodamus refused to produce his child than they all shouted to see her. The more Philodamus denied them, the louder they shouted.

When the first course came in Philodamus seized the chance to leave the room, and sent one of his servants to the house where Artemidorus was eating, begging that he come home to help his father. No sooner had the servant gone than Philodamus returned to the dining room, there to continue obdurately refusing to show the Romans his daughter. Rubrius and two of his companions got up to look for the girl; Philodamus stepped across their path. A pitcher of boiling water had been set upon a brazier near the door, ready to be poured into bowls in which smaller bowls of food might be reheated after the trip from the kitchen. Rubrius grabbed the pitcher and tipped boiling water all over Philodamus's head. While horrified servants fled precipitately, the old man's screams mingled with the shouts and jeers of the Romans, forming up to go in search of Stratonice.

Into this melee the sounds of another intruded. Artemidorus and twenty of his friends had arrived outside his father's door, only to find Verres's lictors barring their entry. The prefect of the decury, one Cornelius, had all the lictor's confidence in his own inviolability; it never occurred to him for a moment that Artemidorus and his band would resort to force to remove them from before the door. Nor perhaps would they have, had Artemidorus not heard the frightful screams of his scalded father. The Lampsacans moved in a mass. Several of the lictors sustained minor hurts, but Cornelius died of a broken neck.

The banquet participants scattered when Artemidorus and his friends ran into the dining room, clubs in their hands and murder on their faces. But Gaius Verres was no coward. Pushing them contemptuously to one side, he quit the house in company with Rubrius and his fellow clerks to find one dead lictor sprawled in the road surrounded by his five frightened colleagues. Up the street the ambassador hustled them, the body of Cornelius lolling in their midst.

By this the whole town was beginning to stir, and Ianitor himself stood at his open front door. His heart sank when he saw what the Romans carried, yet he admitted them to his house—and prudently barred the gate behind them. Artemidorus had stayed to tend to his father's injuries, but two of his friends led the rest of the band of young men to the city square, calling on others to meet them as they marched. All the Greeks had had enough of Gaius Verres, and even a fervent speech from Publius Tettius (the town's most prominent Roman resident) could not dissuade them from retaliation. Tettius and his houseguest Gaius Terentius Varro were swept aside, and the townspeople surged off in the direction of Ianitor's house.

There they demanded entry. Ianitor refused, after which they battered at the gate with a makeshift ram to no effect, and decided instead to burn the place down. Kindling and logs of wood were piled against the front wall and set alight. Only the arrival of Publius Tettius, Gaius Terentius Varro and some other Roman residents of Lampsacus prevented disaster; their impassioned pleading cooled the hottest heads down sufficiently to see that immolation of a Roman ambassador would end in worse than the violation of Stratonice. So the fire (which had gained considerable hold on the front part of Ianitor's house) was put out, and the men of Lampsacus went home.

A less arrogant man than Gaius Verres would have fled from the seething

Greek city as soon as he deemed it safe to leave, but Gaius Verres had no intention of running; instead he sat down calmly and wrote to Gaius Claudius Nero, the governor of Asia Province, steeled in his resolve not to be beaten by a pair of dirty Asian Greeks.

"I demand that you proceed forthwith to Lampsacus and try the two *socii* Philodamus and Artemidorus for the murder of a Roman ambassador's chief lictor," he said.

But swift though the letter's journey to Pergamum was, it was still slower than the detailed report Publius Tettius and Gaius Terentius Varro had jointly provided to the governor.

"I will certainly not come to Lampsacus," said Claudius Nero's reply to Verres. "I have heard the real story from my own senior legate, Gaius Terentius Varro, who considerably outranks you. A pity perhaps that you weren't burned to death. You are like your name, Verres—a pig."

The rage in which Verres wrote his next missive added venom and power to his pen; this one was to Dolabella in Tarsus and it reached Tarsus in a scant seven days, couriered by a petrified trooper who was so afraid of what Verres might do to him if he tarried that he was fully prepared to do murder in order to obtain a fresh horse every few hours.

"Go to Pergamum at once, and at a run," Verres instructed his superior without formal salute or evidence of respect. "Fetch Claudius Nero to Lampsacus without a moment's delay to try and execute the *socii* who murdered my chief lictor. If you don't, I will have words to say in Rome about certain debaucheries and drugs. I mean it, Dolabella. And you may tell Claudius Nero that if he does not come to Lampsacus and convict these Greek *fellatores,* I will accuse him of sordid practices as well. And I'll make the charges stick, Dolabella. Don't think I won't. If I die for it, I'll make the charges stick."

When word of the events in Lampsacus reached the court of King Nicomedes, matters had arrived at an impasse; Gaius Verres was still living in the house of Ianitor and moving freely about the city, Ianitor had been ordered to notify the Lampsacan elders that Verres would remain right where he was, and everyone knew Claudius Nero was coming from Pergamum to try the father and son.

"I wish there was something I could do," said the worried King to Caesar.

"Lampsacus falls within Asia Province, not Bithynia," said Caesar. "Anything you did do would have to be in diplomatic guise, and I'm not convinced it would help those two unfortunate *socii*."

"Gaius Verres is an absolute wolfshead, Caesar. Earlier in the year he robbed sanctuaries of their treasures all over Asia Province, then went on to steal the Harper of Aspendus and the golden skin of Artemis at Perge."

"How to endear Rome to her provinces," said Caesar, lifting his lip contemptuously.

"Nothing is safe from the man—including, it seems, virtuous daughters of important Greek *socii*."

"What is Verres doing in Lampsacus, anyway?"

Nicomedes shivered. "Coming to see me, Caesar! He carries letters of introduction to me and to King Sadala in Thrace—his governor, Dolabella, has endowed him with ambassadorial status. I imagine his true purpose is to steal our statues and paintings."

"He won't dare while I'm here, Nicomedes," soothed Caesar.

The old king's face lit up. "That is what I was going to say. Would you go to Lampsacus as my ambassador so that Gaius Claudius Nero understands Bithynia is watching carefully? I daren't go myself—it might be seen as an armed threat, even if I went without a military escort. My troops are much closer to Lampsacus than are the troops of Asia Province."

Caesar saw the difficulties this would mean for him before Nicomedes had finished speaking. If he went to Lampsacus to observe events on official behalf of the King of Bithynia, the whole of Rome would assume he was indeed on intimate terms with Nicomedes. Only how could he avoid going? It was, on the surface, a very reasonable request.

"I mustn't appear to be acting for you, King," he said seriously. "The fate of the two *socii* is firmly in the hands of the governor of Asia Province, who would not appreciate the presence of a twenty-year-old Roman *privatus* claiming to be the representative of the King of Bithynia."

"But I need to know what happens in Lampsacus from someone detached enough not to exaggerate and Roman enough not to side with the Greeks automatically!" Nicomedes protested.

"I didn't say I wouldn't go. I will go. But as a Roman *privatus* pure and simple—a fellow who chanced to be in the vicinity and whose curiosity got the better of him. That way the hand of Bithynia will not be seen at all, yet I'll be able to provide you with a full report when I return. Then if you feel it necessary, you can lodge a formal complaint with the Senate in Rome, and I will testify."

Caesar departed the next day, riding overland with no one for company save Burgundus and four servants; he might then have come from anywhere and be on the road to anywhere. Though he wore a leather cuirass and kilt, his favored apparel for riding, he had taken care to pack toga and tunic and senatorial shoes, and to take with him the slave whom he employed to make new Civic Crowns for him out of oak leaves. Unwilling though he was to flaunt himself in the name of King Nicomedes, he fully intended to flaunt himself in his own name.

It was the very end of December when he rode into Lampsacus on the same road Verres had used, to find himself unnoticed; the whole town was down at the quay watching Claudius Nero and Dolabella tie up their considerable fleet. Neither governor was in a good mood, Dolabella because he writhed in the grip of Verres permanently, and Claudius Nero because Dolabella's indiscreet activities now threatened to compromise him also. Their grim faces did not lighten when they learned that suitable lodgings were not to be had, as Ianitor still housed Verres and the only other commodious mansion in Lampsacus belonged to Philodamus, the accused. Publius Tettius had solved the problem by evicting a colleague from his establishment and offering it to Claudius Nero and Dolabella to share between them.

When Claudius Nero received Verres (who was already waiting at the commandeered dwelling when the governor arrived), he learned that he was expected to preside over the court—and to accept Verres as organizer of the prosecution, as a witness, as a member of the jury, and as an ambassador whose official propraetorian status was unimpaired by the events in Lampsacus.

"Ridiculous!" he said to Verres in the hearing of Dolabella, Publius Tettius, and the legate Gaius Terentius Varro.

"What do you mean?" Verres demanded.

"Roman justice is famous. What you propose is a travesty. I have acquitted myself well in my province! As things stand at the moment, I am likely to be replaced in the spring. The same can be said of your superior, Gnaeus Dolabella. I can't speak for him"—Claudius Nero glanced toward the silent Dolabella, who avoided his gaze—"but for myself, I intend to quit my province with a reputation as one of its better governors. This case will probably be my last major one, and I won't condone a travesty."

The handsome face of Verres grew flintlike. "I want a quick conviction!" he cried. "I want those two Greek *socii* flogged and beheaded! They murdered a Roman lictor in the course of his duty! If they are allowed to get away with it, Rome's authority is further undermined in a province which still hankers to be ruled by King Mithridates."

It was a good argument, but it was not the reason why Gaius Claudius Nero ended in yielding. He did that because he had not the strength or the backbone to resist Verres in a face-to-face confrontation. With the exception of Publius Tettius and his houseguest Gaius Terentius Varro, Verres had succeeded in winning over the entire Roman contingent who lived in Lamp-sacus, and had worked their feelings into a state which threatened the town's peace for many moons to come. It was Roman versus Greek with a vengeance; Claudius Nero was just not capable of resisting the pressures now exerted upon him.

In the meantime Caesar had managed to find accommodation in a small hostelry adjacent to the wharves. As dirty as it was mean, it catered mainly to sailors, and was the only place willing to take him in: he was a detested Roman. Had it not been so cold he would gladly have camped; were he not determined to maintain his independence, he might have sought shelter in a Roman resident's house. As it was, the harborside inn it must be. Even as he and Burgundus took a stroll before what they suspected was going to be a bad supper, the town heralds were abroad crying that the trial of Philodamus and Artemidorus was to be held on the morrow in the marketplace.

The morrow saw Caesar in no hurry; he wanted everyone assembled for the hearing before he made his grand entrance on the scene. And when he did arrive he created a small sensation—a Roman nobleman, a senator, a war hero—and owning no loyalty to any of the Roman participants. None of these knew his face well enough to assign it a name, especially now Caesar was clad not in *laena* and *apex,* but in a snowy toga with the broad purple stripe of the senator on the right shoulder of his tunic and the maroon leather shoes of the senator on his feet. Added to which, he wore a chaplet of oak leaves upon his head, so every Roman including both governors was obliged to get to his feet and applaud Caesar's advent.

"I am Gaius Julius Caesar, nephew of Lucius Cornelius Sulla the Dictator," he said to Claudius Nero guilelessly, holding out his right hand. "Just passing through when I heard about this fuss! Thought I'd better turn up to see if you needed an extra man on the jury."

The name brought instant recognition, of course, more due to *flamen Dialis* than siege of Mitylene; these men had not been in Rome when Lucullus returned, did not know the fine details of Mitylene's surrender. Caesar's offer of jury duty was declined, but he was accommodated on a chair hastily found for one who was not only a war hero, but also the Dictator's nephew by marriage.

The trial began. Of Roman citizens to serve as jurors there was no lack, for Dolabella and Claudius Nero had brought a large number of minor officials with them as well as a full cohort of Roman soldiers from Pergamum—Fimbriani who recognized Caesar at once, and hailed him joyfully. Yet another reason why neither governor was pleased to have him sitting there.

Though Verres had organized the prosecution, the actual role of prosecutor was taken by a local Roman resident, a usurer who needed Claudius Nero's lictors to extract money from delinquent clients—and was aware that if he did not consent to prosecute, the lictors would cease to be forthcoming. All of Greek Lampsacus congregated about the perimeter of the court, muttering, glaring, shaking an occasional fist. Despite which, no one among them had volunteered to plead for Philodamus and Artemidorus, who were therefore obliged to conduct their own case under an alien system of law.

It was, thought the expressionless Caesar, a complete travesty. Claudius Nero, the titular president of the court, made no attempt to run it; he sat mumchance and let Verres and Rubrius do that. Dolabella was on the jury and kept making pro-Verres comments in a loud voice, as did Verres himself, also on the jury. When the Greek onlookers realized that Philodamus and Artemidorus were not going to be allowed the proper amount of court time to conduct their defense, some among them began to shout abuse; but there were five hundred armed Fimbriani stationed in the square, more than a match for any rioting crowd.

The verdict when it came was no verdict: the jury ordered a retrial, this being the only way the majority of them could register their disapproval of the cavalier proceedings without bringing down a Verrine storm about their heads.

And when he heard the retrial ordered, Verres panicked. If Philodamus and Artemidorus did not die, he suddenly realized, they could indict him in Rome with a whole indignant town to back them up—and possibly a Roman senator war hero to testify for them; Verres had gained the distinct impression that Gaius Julius Caesar was not on his side. The young man had given nothing away by look or comment, but that in itself indicated opposition. *And* he was related to Sulla, the Dictator of Rome! It was also possible that Gaius Claudius Nero would regain his courage were Verres to be tried in a Roman court inside Rome; any allegations Verres might make about Claudius Nero's personal conduct would then sound like a smear campaign to discredit an important witness.

That Claudius Nero was thinking along the same lines became apparent when he announced that he would schedule the retrial for early summer, which probably meant a new governor in Asia Province—and a new governor in Cilicia. Despite the death of a Roman lictor, Philodamus and Artemidorus suddenly had an excellent chance of going free. And if they went free, they would come to Rome to prosecute Gaius Verres. For, as Philodamus had said when he had addressed the jury,

"We *socii* know that we are under the care of Rome and that we must answer to the governor, to his legates and officials, and through him to the

Senate and People of Rome. If we are not willing to lie down under Roman rule, we understand that there must be reprisals, and that many of us will suffer. But what are we alien subjects of Rome to do when Rome permits a man who is no greater than a governor's assistant to lust after our children and snatch them from us for his own evil purposes? My son and I did no more than defend his sister and my daughter from a wicked lout! No one intended that any man should die, and it was not a Greek hand struck the first blow. I was scalded by boiling water in my own house while I tried to prevent the companions of Gaius Verres from carrying my child off to pain and dishonor. Had it not been for the arrival of my son and his friends, my daughter would indeed have been carried off to pain and dishonor. Gaius Verres did not behave like a civilized member of a civilized people. He behaved like the barbarian he is.''

The verdict of a retrial, delivered as it had been by an all-Roman jury loudly urged by Dolabella and Verres throughout the trial to do its duty and convict, emboldened the Greek crowd to speed Claudius Nero and his court out of the marketplace with jeers, boos, hisses, angry gestures.

"You'll schedule the retrial for tomorrow," said Verres to Claudius Nero.

"Next summer," said Claudius Nero faintly.

"Not if you want to be consul, my friend," said Verres. "I will pull you down with great pleasure—never doubt that for a moment! What goes for Dolabella goes for you. Do as I say in this or be prepared to take the consequences. For if Philodamus and Artemidorus live to indict me in Rome, I will have to indict you and Dolabella in Rome long before the Greeks can get there. I will make sure you're both convicted of extortion. So neither of you would be on hand to testify against me."

The retrial occurred the day following the trial. Between bribing those members of the jury willing to take a bribe and threatening those who were not, Verres got no sleep; nor did Dolabella, compelled to accompany Verres on his rounds.

That hard night's work tipped the balance. By a small majority of the jurors, Philodamus and Artemidorus were convicted of the murder of a Roman lictor. Claudius Nero ordered their immediate dispatch. Kept at a distance by the cohort of Fimbriani, the Greek crowd watched helplessly as father and son were stripped and flogged. The old man was unconscious when his head was lopped from his shoulders, but Artemidorus retained his faculties until his end, and wept not for his own fate or for his father's, but for the fate of his orphaned sister.

At the end of it Caesar walked fearlessly into the densely packed mass of Greek Lampsacans, all weeping with shock, beyond anger now. No other Roman went near them; escorted by Fimbriani, Claudius Nero and Dolabella were already shifting their belongings down to the quay. But Caesar had a purpose. It had not taken him long to decide who in the crowd were the influential ones, and these men he sought out.

"Lampsacus isn't big enough to stage a revolt," he said to them, "but revenge is possible. Don't judge all Romans by this sorry lot, and hold your tempers. I give you my word that when I return to Rome, I will prosecute the governor Dolabella and make sure that Verres is never elected a praetor. Not for gifts or for honors. Just for my own satisfaction."

After that he went to the house of Ianitor, for he wanted to see Gaius Verres before the man quit Lampsacus.

"Well, if it isn't the war hero!" cried Verres cheerfully when Caesar walked in.

He was overseeing his packing.

"Do you intend to take possession of the daughter?" Caesar asked, disposing himself comfortably in a chair.

"Naturally," said Verres, nodding at a slave who brought in a little statue for him to inspect. "Yes, I like it. Crate it." His attention returned to Caesar. "Anxious to set eyes on the cause of all this fuss, are you?"

"Consumed with curiosity. She ought to outdo Helen."

"So I think."

"Is she blonde, I wonder? I've always thought Helen must have been blonde. Yellow hair has the edge."

Verres eyed Caesar's thatch appreciatively, lifted a hand to pat his own. "You and I ought to know!"

"Where do you intend to go from Lampsacus, Gaius Verres?"

The tawny brows rose. "To Nicomedia, of course."

"I wouldn't," said Caesar gently.

"Really? And why not?" asked Verres, deceptively casual.

Caesar bent his gaze to study his own nails. "Dolabella will bite the dust as soon as I return to Rome, which will be in the spring of this year or the next. I will prosecute him myself. And I will prosecute you. Unless, that is, you return to Cilicia now."

Caesar's blue eyes lifted; the honeyed eyes of Verres met them. For a long moment neither man moved.

Then Verres said, "I know who you remind me of. Sulla."

"Do I?"

"It's your eyes. Not as washed out as Sulla's, but they have the same look. I wonder will you go as far as Sulla?"

"That is on the laps of the gods. *I* would rather say, I hope no one forces me to go as far as Sulla."

Verres shrugged. "Well, Caesar, I am no Gaius Marius, so it won't be me."

"You are certainly no Gaius Marius," Caesar agreed calmly. "He was a great man until his mind gave way. Where are you going from Lampsacus, have you decided?"

"To Cilicia with Dolabella," said Verres with another shrug.

"Oh, very wise! Would you like me to send someone down to the port to inform Dolabella? I'd hate to see him sail off and leave you behind."

"If you wish," said Verres indifferently.

Off went Caesar to find Burgundus and instruct him what to tell Dolabella. As he returned to the room through an inner door, Ianitor brought in a muffled form through the door onto the street.

"This is Stratonice?" asked Verres eagerly.

Ianitor brushed the tears from his cheeks. "Yes."

"Leave us alone with her, Greek."

Ianitor fled.

"Shall I unveil her for you while you stand at a suitably remote distance to take all of her in at once?" asked Caesar.

"I prefer to do it myself," said Verres, moving to the girl's side; she had made no sound, no attempt to run away.

The hood of her heavy cloak fell forward over her face, impossible to see. Like Myron anxious to check the result of a bronze casting, Verres twitched the cloak from her with a trembling hand. And stared, and stared.

It was Caesar broke the silence; he threw back his head and laughed until he cried. "I had a feeling!" he said when he was able, groping for a handkerchief.

The body she owned was shapeless, poor Stratonice. Her eyes were slits, her snub nose spread across her face, the reddish hair atop her flat-backed skull was sparse to the point of semi-baldness, her ears were vestigial and she had a badly split harelip. Of reasoning mentality she had very little, poor Stratonice.

Face scarlet, Verres turned on his heel.

"Don't miss your ship!" Caesar called after him. "I'd hate to have to spread the end of this story all over Rome, Verres!"

The moment Verres had gone Caesar sobered. He came across to the mute and immobile creature, picked up her cloak from the floor and draped it about her tenderly.

"Don't worry, my poor girl," he said, not sure she could even hear him. "You're quite safe." He called then for Ianitor, who came in immediately. "You knew, *ethnarch,* didn't you?"

"Yes."

"Then why in the name of Great Zeus didn't you speak out if they wouldn't? They died for nothing!"

"They died because they elected death as the preferable alternative," said Ianitor.

"And what will become of the wretched creature now?"

"She will be well looked after."

"How many of you knew?"

"Just the city's elders."

Unable to find anything to say in answer to that, Caesar left Ianitor's house, and left Lampsacus.

Gaius Verres hurried down to the port, stumbling. How dared they, those stupid, stupid Greeks? Hiding her away as if she was Helen of Troy, when all the time she was a gorgon.

Dolabella was not pleased at having to delay his departure while various crates and trunks belonging to Verres were loaded; Claudius Nero had already gone, and the Fimbriani with him.

"Quin taces!" snarled Verres when his superior asked where was the beauteous Stratonice. "I left her behind in Lampsacus. They deserve each other."

His superior was feeling the pinch of some time without the stimulating sexual sessions he had grown to rely upon; Verres soon found himself back in Dolabella's good graces, and spent the voyage from Lampsacus to Pergamum planning. He would return Dolabella to his usual condition and spend the rest of his term in Tarsus using up the gubernatorial stipend. So Caesar thought he'd prosecute, did he? Well, he wouldn't get the chance. He, Verres, would get in first! The moment Dolabella returned to Rome, he, Verres, would find a prosecutor with a prestigious name and testify Dolabella into permanent exile. Then there would be no one to contest the set of account books Verres intended to present to the Treasury. A pity that he hadn't managed to get to Bithynia and Thrace, but he had really done very nicely.

"I believe," he said to Dolabella after they left Pergamum behind, "that Miletus has some of the finest wool in the world, not to mention rugs and tapestries of rare quality. Let's stop in at Miletus and look at what's available."

"I can't get over the fact that those two *socii* died for nothing," said Caesar to Nicomedes and Oradaltis. "Why? Tell me why they just didn't produce the girl and show Verres what she was? That would have been the end of the affair! Why did they insist upon turning what ought to have been a comedy with Verres the butt into a tragedy as great as anything Sophocles dreamed of?''

"Pride, mostly," said Oradaltis, tears in her eyes. "And perhaps a sense of honor."

"It might have been understandable if the girl had looked presentable when she was a baby, but from the moment of her birth they would have known what she was. Why didn't they expose her? No one would have condemned them for it."

"The only person who might have been able to enlighten you, Caesar, died in the marketplace of Lampsacus," said Nicomedes. "There must have been a good reason, at least inside the mind of Philodamus. A vow to some god—a wife and mother determined to keep the child—a self-inflicted pain—who can tell? If we knew all the answers, life would hold no mysteries. And no tragedies."

"I could have wept when I saw her. Instead I laughed myself sick. She couldn't tell the difference, but Verres could. So I laughed. He'll hear it inside his head for years, and fear me."

"I'm surprised we haven't seen the man," said the King.

"You won't see him," said Caesar with some satisfaction. "Gaius Verres has folded his tents and slunk back to Cilicia."

"Why?"

"I asked him to."

The King decided not to probe this remark. Instead he said, "You wish you could have done something to avert the tragedy."

"Of course. It's an actual agony to have to stand back and watch idiots wreak havoc in Rome's name. But I swear to you, Nicomedes, that I will never behave so myself when I have the age and the authority!"

"You don't need to swear. I believe you."

This report had been given before Caesar went to his rooms to remove the ravages of his journey, these being unusually trying. Each of the three nights he had spent in the harborside inn he had woken to find a naked whore astride him and the traitor inside the gates of his body so lacking in discernment that, freed by sleep from his mind's control, it enjoyed itself immensely. With the result that he had picked up an infestation of pubic lice. The discovery of his crop of tiny vermin had induced a horror and disgust so great that he had been able to keep no food down since, and only a sensible sensitivity about the effects of questionable substances upon his genitalia had prevented his seizing anything offered to kill the things. So far they had defied him by living through a dip in every freezing body of water he had encountered between Lampsacus and Nicomedia, and all through his talk with the old King he had been aware of the dreadful creatures prowling through the thickets of his body hair.

Now, clenching teeth and fists, he rose abruptly to his feet. "Please excuse me, Nicomedes. I have to rid myself of some unwelcome visitors," he said, attempting a light tone.

"Crab lice, you mean?" asked the King, who missed very little, and could speak freely because Oradaltis and her dog had departed some time before.

"I'm driven mad! Revolting, sickening things!"

Nicomedes strolled from the room with him.

"There is really only one way to avoid picking up vermin when you travel," said the King. "It's painful, especially the first time you have it done, but it does work."

"I don't care if I have to walk on hot coals, tell me and I'll do it!" said Caesar with fervor.

"There are those in your peculiar society who will condemn you as effeminate!" Nicomedes said wickedly.

"No fate could be worse than these pests. Tell me!"

"Have all your body hair plucked, Caesar. Under the arms and in the groin, on the chest if you have hair there. I will send the man who attends to me and Oradaltis to you if you wish."

"At once, King, at once!" Up went Caesar's hand to his head. "What about my hair hair?"

"Have you visitors there too?"

"I don't think so, but I itch everywhere."

"They're different visitors, and can't survive in a bed. I wouldn't think you'll ever play host to them because you're so tall. They can't crawl upward, you see, so the people who pick them up from others are always the same height or shorter than the original host." Nicomedes laughed. "You'd catch them from Burgundus, but from few others. Unless your Lampsacan whores slept with you head to head."

"My Lampsacan whores attacked me in my sleep, but I can assure you that they got short shrift the moment I woke!"

An extraordinary conversation, but one Caesar was to thank his luck for many times in the years to come. If plucking out his body hair would keep these clinging horrors away, he would pluck, pluck, pluck.

The slave Nicomedes sent to him was an expert; under different circumstances Caesar would have banished him from such an intimate task, for he was a perfect pansy. Under the prevailing circumstances, however, Caesar found himself eager to experience his touch.

"I'll just take a few out every day," lisped Demetrius.

"You'll take the lot out today," said Caesar grimly. "I've drowned all I could find in my bath, but I suppose their eggs stick. That seems to be why I haven't managed to get rid of all of them so far. Pah!"

Demetrius squealed, appalled. "That isn't possible!" he cried. "Even when *I* do it, it's hideously painful!"

"The lot today," said Caesar.

So Demetrius continued while Caesar lay naked, apparently in no distress. He had self-discipline and great courage, and would have died rather than flinch, moan, weep, or otherwise betray his agony. And when the ordeal was over and sufficient time had passed for the pain to die down, he felt wonderful. He also liked the look of his hairless body in the big silver mirror King Nicomedes had provided for the palace's principal guest suite. Sleek. Unashamed. Amazingly naked. And somehow more masculine rather than less. How odd!

Feeling like a man released from slavery, he went to the dining room that evening with his new pleasure in himself adding a special light to face and eyes; King Nicomedes looked, and gasped. Caesar responded with a wink.

For sixteen months he remained in or around about Bithynia, an idyll he was to remember as the most wonderful period of his life until he reached his fifty-third year and found an even more wonderful one. He visited Troy to do homage to his ancestor Aeneas, he went to Pessinus several times, and back to Byzantium, and anywhere, it seemed, save Pergamum and Tarsus, where Claudius Nero and Dolabella remained an extra year after all.

Leaving aside his relationship with Nicomedes and Oradaltis, which remained an enormously satisfying and rewarding experience for him, the chief joy of that time lay in his visit to a man he hardly remembered: Publius Rutilius Rufus, his great-uncle on his mother's side.

Born in the same year as Gaius Marius, Rutilius Rufus was now seventy-nine years old, and had been living in an honorable exile in Smyrna for many years. He was as active as a fifty-year-old and as cheerful as a boy, mind as sharp as ever, sense of humor as keenly developed as had been that of his friend and colleague, Marcus Aemilius Scaurus Princeps Senatus.

"I've outlived the lot of them," Rutilius Rufus said with gleeful satisfaction after his eyes and mind had approved the look of this fine young great-nephew.

"That doesn't cast you down, Uncle?"

"Why should it? If anything, it cheers me up! Sulla keeps writing to beg me to return to Rome, and every governor and other official he sends out here comes to plead in person."

"But you won't go."

"I won't go. I like my *chlamys* and my Greek slippers much more than I ever liked my toga, and I enjoy a reputation here in Smyrna far greater than any I ever owned in Rome. It's a thankless and savage place, young Caesar— what a look of Aurelia you have! How is she? My ocean pearl found on the mud flats of Ostia . . . That was what I always called her. And she's widowed, eh? A pity. I brought her and your father together, you know. And though you may not know it, I found Marcus Antonius Gnipho to tutor you when you were hardly out of diapers. They used to think you a prodigy. And here you are, twenty-one years old, a senator twice over, and Sulla's most prized war hero! Well, well!"

"I wouldn't go so far as to say I'm his most prized war hero," said Caesar, smiling.

"Oh, but you are! I know! I sit here in Smyrna and hear everything. Sulla writes to me. Always did. And when he was settling the affairs of Asia Province he visited me often—it was I gave him his model for its reorganization. Based it on the program Scaurus and I evolved years ago. Sad, his illness. But it hasn't seemed to stop him meddling with Rome!"

He continued in the same vein for many days, hopping from one subject to another with the lightness of an easy heart and the interest of a born gossip, a spry old bird the years had not managed to strip of plumage or the ability to soar. If he had a favorite topic, that was Aurelia; Caesar filled in the gaps in his knowledge of her with gracefully chosen words and evident love, and learned in return many things about her he had not known. Of her relationship with Sulla, however, Rutilius Rufus had little to tell and refused to speculate, though he had Caesar laughing over the confusion as to which of his nieces had borne a red-haired son to a red-haired man.

"Gaius Marius and Julia were convinced it was Aurelia and Sulla, but it was Livia Drusa, of course, with Marcus Cato."

"That's right, your wife was a Livia."

"And the older of my two sisters was the wife of Caepio the Consul, who stole the Gold of Tolosa. You are related to the Servilii Caepiones by blood, young man."

"I don't know the family at all."

"A boring lot no amount of Rutilian blood could leaven. Now tell me about Gaius Marius and the flaminate he wished upon you."

Intending to remain only a few days in Smyrna, Caesar ended in staying for two months; there was so much Rutilius Rufus wanted to know, and so much Rutilius Rufus wanted to tell. When finally he took his leave of the old man, he wept.

"I shall never forget you, Uncle Publius."

"Just come back! And write to me, Caesar, do. Of all the pleasures my life still holds, there is none to equal a rich and candid correspondence with a genuinely literate man."

But every idyll must end, and Caesar's came to a conclusion when he received a letter from Tarsus in April of the year Sulla died; he was in Nicomedia.

"Publius Servilius Vatia, who was consul last year, has been sent to govern Cilicia," Caesar said to the King and Queen. "He requests my services as a junior legate—it seems Sulla has personally recommended me to him."

"Then you don't *have* to go," said Oradaltis eagerly.

Caesar smiled. "No Roman *has* to do anything, and that is really true from highest to lowest. Service in any institution is voluntary. But there are certain considerations which do tend to influence our decisions, voluntary in name though the duty may be. If I want a public career, I must serve in my ten campaigns, or else steadily for a full six years. No one is ever going to be able to accuse me of circumventing our unwritten laws."

"But you're already a senator!"

"Only because of my military career. And that in turn means I must continue my military career."

"Then you're definitely going," said the King.

"At once."

"I'll see about a ship."

"No. I shall ride overland through the Cilician Gates."

"Then I'll provide you with a letter of introduction to King Ariobarzanes in Cappadocia."

The palace began to stir, and the dog to mourn; poor Sulla knew the signs that Caesar was about to depart.

And once more Caesar found himself committed to return. The two old people pestered him until he agreed he would, then disarmed him by bestowing Demetrius the hair-plucker upon him.

However, before he left Caesar tried yet again to convince King Nicomedes that the best course for Bithynia after his death would be as a Roman province.

"I'll think about it" was as far as Nicomedes would go.

Caesar now cherished little hope that the old King would decide in favor of Rome; the events in Lampsacus were too fresh in every non-Roman mind—and who could blame the King if he could not face the idea of bequeathing his realm to the likes of Gaius Verres?

The steward Eutychus was sent back to Aurelia in Rome; Caesar traveled with five servants (including Demetrius the hair-plucker) and Burgundus, and traveled hard. He crossed the Sangarius River and rode first to Ancyra, the largest town in Galatia. Here he met an interesting man, one Deiotarus, leader of the segment Tolistobogii.

"We're all quite young these days," said Deiotarus. "King Mithridates murdered the entire Galatian thanehood twenty years ago, which left our people without chieftains. In most countries that would have led to the disintegration of the people, but we Galatians have always preferred a loose confederation. So we survived until the young sons of the chieftains grew up."

"Mithridates won't trap you again," said Caesar, who thought this Gaul was as cunning as he was clever.

"Not while I'm here, anyway," said Deiotarus grimly. "I at least have had the advantage of spending three years in Rome, so I'm more sophisticated than my father ever was—he died in the massacre."

"Mithridates *will* try again."

"I don't doubt it."

"You won't be tempted?"

"Never! He's still a vigorous man with many years left to rule, but he seems incapable of learning what I know for a fact—that Rome must win in the end. I would rather be in a position where Rome was calling me Friend and Ally."

"That's right thinking, Deiotarus."

On Caesar went to the Halys River, followed its lazy red stream until Mount Argaeus dominated the sky; from here to Eusebeia Mazaca was only forty miles northward across the wide shallow slope of the Halys basin.

Of course he remembered Gaius Marius's many tales of this country, of the vividly painted town lying at the foot of the gigantic extinct volcano, of the brilliant blue palace and that meeting with King Mithridates of Pontus. But these days Mithridates skulked in Sinope and King Ariobarzanes sat more or less firmly on the Cappadocian throne.

Less rather than more, thought Caesar after meeting him. For some reason no one could discover, the kings of Cappadocia had been as weak a lot as the kings of Pontus had been strong. And Ariobarzanes was no exception to the rule. He was patently terrified of Mithridates, and pointed out to Caesar how Pontus had stripped the palace and the capital of every treasure, down to the last golden nail in a door.

"But surely," said Caesar to the timid king, a small and slightly Syrian-looking man, "the loss of those two hundred thousand soldiers in the Caucasus will strap Mithridates for many years to come. No proprietor of armies can afford the loss of such a huge number of men—especially men who were not only fully trained, but veterans of a good campaign. For they were, isn't that right?"

"Yes. They had fought to regain Cimmeria and the northern reaches of the Euxine Sea for Mithridates the summer before."

"Successfully, one hears."

"Indeed. His son Machares was left in Panticapaeum to be satrap. A good choice. I believe his chief task is to recruit a new army for his father."

"Who prefers Scythian and Roxolanian troops."

"They are superior to mercenaries, certainly. Both Pontus and Cappadocia are unfortunate in that the native peoples are not good soldiers. I am still forced to rely upon Syrian and Jewish mercenaries, but Mithridates has had hordes of warlike barbarians at his disposal now for almost thirty years."

"Have you no army at the moment, King Ariobarzanes?"

"At the moment I have no need of one."

"What if Mithridates marches without warning?"

"Then I will be off my throne once more. Cappadocia, Gaius Julius, is very poor. Too poor to afford a standing army."

"You have another enemy. King Tigranes."

Ariobarzanes twisted unhappily. "Do not remind me! His successes in Syria have robbed me of my best soldiers. All the Jews are staying home to resist him."

"Then don't you think you should at least be watching the Euphrates as well as the Halys?"

"There is no money," said the King stubbornly.

Caesar rode away shaking his head. What could be done when the sovereign of a land admitted himself beaten before the war began? His quick eyes noticed many natural advantages which would give Ariobarzanes untold opportunities to pounce upon an invader, for the countryside when not filled with towering snowcapped peaks was cut up into the most bizarre gorges, just as Gaius Marius had described. Wonderful places militarily as well as scenically, yet perceived by the King as no more than ready-made housing for his troglodytes.

"How do you feel now that you've seen a great deal more of the world,

Burgundus?'' Caesar asked his hulking freedman as they picked their way down into the depths of the Cilician Gates between soaring pines and roaring cascades.

"That Rome and Bovillae, Cardixa and my sons are grander than any waterfall or mountain,'' said Burgundus.

"Would you rather go home, old friend? I will send you home gladly,'' said Caesar.

But Burgundus shook his big blond head emphatically. "No, Caesar, I'll stay.'' He grinned. "Cardixa would kill me if I let anything happen to you.''

"But nothing is going to happen to me!''

"Try and tell her that.''

Publius Servilius Vatia was installed in the governor's palace at Tarsus so comfortably by the time Caesar arrived before the end of April that he looked as if he had always been there.

"We are profoundly glad to have him,'' said Morsimus, captain of the Cilician governor's guard and a Tarsian *ethnarch*.

Dark hair grizzled by the passage of twenty years since he had accompanied Gaius Marius to Cappadocia, Morsimus had been on hand to welcome Caesar, to whom the Cilician felt more loyalty than ever he could to a mere Roman governor; here was the nephew by marriage of both his heroes, Gaius Marius and Lucius Cornelius Sulla, and he would do whatever he could to assist the young man.

"I gather Cilicia suffered greatly under Dolabella and Verres,'' said Caesar.

"Terribly. Dolabella was out of his mind on drugs most of the time, which left Verres to do precisely what he fancied.''

"Nothing was done to eject Tigranes from eastern Pedia?''

"Nothing at all. Verres was too preoccupied with usury and extortion. Not to mention the pilfering of temple artifacts he considered wouldn't be missed.''

"I shall prosecute Dolabella and Verres as soon as I go home, so I shall need your help in gathering evidence.''

"Dolabella will probably be in exile by the time you get home,'' Morsimus said. "The governor had word from Rome that the son of Marcus Aemilius Scaurus and the lady Dalmatica is assembling a case against Dolabella even now, and that Gaius Verres is covering himself in glory by supplying young Scaurus with all his evidence—and that Verres will testify in court.''

"The slippery *fellator*! That means I won't be able to touch him. And I don't suppose it matters who prosecutes Dolabella, as long as he gets his just deserts. If I'm sorry it won't be me, that's because I'm late into the courts thanks to my priesthood, and victory against Dolabella and Verres would have made me famous." He paused, then said, "Will Vatia move against King Tigranes?"

"I doubt it. He's here specifically to eliminate pirates."

A statement confirmed by Vatia himself when Caesar sought an interview. An exact contemporary of Metellus Pius the Piglet (who was his close cousin into the bargain), Vatia was now fifty years old. Originally Sulla had intended that Vatia be consul with Gnaeus Octavius Ruso nine years earlier, but Cinna had beaten him in that election, and Vatia, like Metellus Pius, had had to wait a long time for the consulship which was his by birthright. His reward for unswerving loyalty to Sulla had been the governorship of Cilicia; he had preferred this province to the other consular province, Macedonia, which had in consequence gone to his colleague in the consulship, Appius Claudius Pulcher.

"Who never got to Macedonia," said Vatia to Caesar. "He fell ill in Tarentum on his way, and returned to Rome. Luckily this happened before the elder Dolabella had left Macedonia, so he's been instructed to stay there until Appius Claudius is well enough to relieve him."

"What's the matter with Appius Claudius?"

"Something long-standing, is all I know. He wasn't a fit man during our consulship—never cheered up no matter what I said! But he's so impoverished he has to govern. If he doesn't, he won't be able to repair his fortune."

Caesar frowned, but kept his thoughts to himself. These dwelt upon the limitations inherent in a system which virtually forced a man sent to govern a province into a career of clerical crime; tradition had hallowed the right of a governor to sell citizenships, contracts, immunities from taxation and tithe, and pop the proceeds into his own hungry purse. Senate and Treasury unofficially condoned these activities in order to keep Rome's costs down, one of the reasons why it was so hard to get a jury of senators to convict a governor of extortion in his province. But exploited provinces meant hatred of Rome, a rolling reckoning for the future.

"I take it we are to go to war against the pirates, Publius Servilius?" Caesar asked.

"Correct," said the governor, surrounded by stacks of paper; clearly he enjoyed the clerical side of his duties, though he was not a particularly avaricious man and did not need to augment his fortune by provincial exploitation. Particularly when he was to go to war against the pirates, whose ill-gotten gains would give the governor of Cilicia plenty of legitimate spoils.

"Unfortunately," Vatia went on, "I will have to delay my campaign because of the straits to which my province has been reduced by the activities of my predecessor in this office. This year will have to be devoted to internal affairs."

"Then do you need me?" asked Caesar, too young to relish the idea of a military career spent at a desk.

"I do need you," said Vatia emphatically. "It will be your business to raise a fleet for me."

Caesar winced. "In that I do have some experience."

"I know. That's why I wanted you. It will have to be a superior fleet, large enough to split into several flotillas if necessary. The days when pirates skipped round in open little *hemioliai* and *myoparones* have almost gone. These days they man fully decked triremes and biremes—even quinqueremes!—and are massed in fleets under the command of admirals—*strategoi* they call these men. They cruise the seas like navies, their flagships encrusted in gilt and purple. In their hidden bases they live like kings, employing chained gangs of free men to serve their wants. They have whole arsenals of weapons and every luxury a rich man in Rome might fancy. Lucius Cornelius made sure the Senate understood why he was sending me to a remote, unimportant place like Cilicia. It is here the pirates have their main bases, so it is here we must begin to clear them out."

"I could make myself useful by discovering whereabouts the pirate strongholds are—I'm sure I'd have no trouble managing that as well as the raising of a fleet."

"That won't be necessary, Caesar. We already know the location of the biggest bases. Coracesium is notorious—though so well fortified by nature and by men that I doubt whether I or any other man will ever succeed in taking it. Therefore I intend to begin at the far end of my territory—in Pamphylia and Lycia. There is a pirate king called Zenicetes who controls the whole of the Pamphylian gulf, including Attaleia. It is he who will first feel Rome's wrath."

"Next year?" asked Caesar.

"Probably," said Vatia, "though not before the late summer, I think. I cannot start to war against the pirates until Cilicia is properly regulated again and I am sure I have the naval and military strength to win."

"You expect to be prorogued for several years."

"The Dictator and the Senate have assured me I will not be hurried. I am to have however many years prove necessary. Lucius Cornelius is now retired, of course, but I do not believe the Senate will go against his wishes.''

Off went Caesar to raise a fleet, but not with enthusiasm; it would be more than a year before he saw action, and his assessment of Vatia's character was that when war did come, Vatia would lack the speed and initiative the campaign called for. In spite of the fact that Caesar bore no love for Lucullus, there was no doubt in his mind that this second general he was serving under was no match in mind or ability for Lucullus.

It was, however, an opportunity to do more traveling, and that was some compensation. The naval power without rival at this eastern end of the Middle Sea was Rhodes, so to Rhodes did Caesar betake himself in May. Always loyal to Rome (it had successfully defied King Mithridates nine years before), Rhodes could be relied upon to contribute vessels, commanders and crews to Vatia's coming campaign, though not marine troops; the Rhodians did not board enemy ships and turn a naval engagement into a land-style fight.

Luckily Gaius Verres had not had time to visit Rhodes, so Caesar found himself welcomed and the island's war leaders willing to talk. Most of the dickering revolved around whether Rome was to pay Rhodes for its participation, which was unfortunate. Vatia felt none of the allied cities, islands and communities called upon to provide ships was entitled to any sort of payment in moneys; his argument was that every contributor would directly benefit from removal of the pirates, so ought to donate its services free of charge. Therefore Caesar was obliged to negotiate within his superior's parameters.

"Look at it this way," he said persuasively. "Success means enormous spoils as well as relief from raids. Rome isn't in a position to pay you, but you will share in the division of the spoils, and these will pay for your participation—and give you something over as profit. Rhodes is Friend and Ally of the Roman People. Why jeopardize that status? There are really only two alternatives—participation or nonparticipation. And you must decide now which it is going to be."

Rhodes yielded. Caesar got his ships, promised for the summer of the following year.

From Rhodes he went to Cyprus, unaware that the ship he passed sailing into the harbor of Rhodus bore a precious Roman cargo; none other than Marcus Tullius Cicero, worn down by a year of marriage to Terentia and the delicate negotiations he had brought to a successful conclusion in Athens when his younger brother, Quintus, married the sister of Titus Pomponius Atticus. Cicero's own union had just produced a daughter, Tullia, so he had been able to depart from Rome secure in the knowledge that his wife was fully occupied in mothering her babe. On Rhodes lived the world's most famous teacher of rhetoric, Apollonius Molon, and to his school was Cicero going. He needed a holiday from Rome, from the courts, from Terentia and from his life as it was. His voice had gone, and Apollonius Molon was known to preach that an orator's vocal and physical apparatus had to equal his mental skills. Though he loathed travel and feared that any absence from Rome would undermine his forensic career, Cicero was looking forward very much to this self-imposed exile far from his friends and family. Time for a *rest*.

For Caesar there was to be no rest—not that one of Caesar's temperament needed a rest. He disembarked in Paphos, which was the seat of Cyprus's ruler, Ptolemy the Cyprian, younger brother of the new King of Egypt, Ptolemy Auletes. More a wastrel than a nonentity, the regent Ptolemy's long residence at the courts of Mithridates and Tigranes showed glaringly during Caesar's first interview with him. Not merely did he understand nothing; he wasn't interested in understanding anything. His education seemed to have been entirely overlooked and his latent sexual preferences had asserted themselves the moment he left the custody of the kings, so that his palace was not unlike the palace of old King Nicomedes. Except that Ptolemy the Cyprian was not a likable man. The Alexandrians, however, had accurately judged him when he had first arrived in Alexandria with his elder brother and their wives; though the Alexandrians had not opposed his appointment as regent of Cyprus, they had sent a dozen efficient bureaucrats to Cyprus with him. It was these men, as Caesar discovered, who really ruled Cyprus on behalf of the island's owner, Egypt.

Having artfully evaded the advances of Ptolemy the Cyprian, Caesar devoted his energies to the Alexandrian bureaucrats. Not easy men to deal with—and no lovers of Rome—they could see nothing for Cyprus in Vatia's coming campaign, and clearly had taken umbrage because Vatia had sent a junior legate twenty-one years old as his petitioner.

"My youth," said Caesar haughtily to these gentlemen, "is beside the point. I am a decorated war hero, a senator at an age when routine admission to the Senate is not permitted, and Publius Servilius Vatia's chief military assistant. You ought to think yourselves lucky I deigned to drop in!"

This statement was duly taken note of, but bureaucratic attitudes did not markedly change for the better. Argue like a politician though he did, Caesar could get nowhere with them.

"Cyprus is affected by piracy too. Why can't you see that the pirate menace will be eliminated only if *all* the lands which suffer from their depredations club together to eliminate them? Publius Servilius Vatia's fleet has to be large enough to act like a net, sweeping the pirates before it into some place from which there is no way out. There will be enormous spoils, and Cyprus will be able to rejoin the trading markets of the Middle Sea. As you well know, at present the Cilician and Pamphylian pirates cut Cyprus off.''

"Cyprus does not need to join the trading markets of the Middle Sea," said the Alexandrian leader. "Everything Cyprus produces belongs to Egypt, and goes there. We tolerate no pirates on the seas between Cyprus and Egypt.''

Back to the regent Ptolemy for a second interview. This time, however, Caesar's luck asserted itself; the regent was in the company of his wife, Mithridatidis Nyssa. Had Caesar known what was the physical style of the Mithridatidae he would have seen that this young lady was a typical member of her house—large in frame, yellow of hair, eyes a greenish gold. Her charms were of coloring and voluptuousness rather than in any claim to true beauty, but Caesar instantly appreciated her charms. So, she made it obvious, did she appreciate Caesar's charms. And when the silly interview with Ptolemy the Cyprian was over, she strolled out with her husband's guest on her arm to show him the spot where the goddess Aphrodite had risen from the foam of the sea to embark upon her divine course of earthly havoc.

"She was my thirty-nine-times great-grandmother," said Caesar, leaning on the white marble balustrade which fenced the official site of the goddess's birth off from the rest of the shore.

"Who? Not Aphrodite, surely!''

"Surely. I am descended from her through her son, Aeneas.''

"Really?'' The slightly protuberant eyes studied his face as if searching for some sign of this staggeringly august lineage.

"Very much really, Princess.''

"Then you belong to Love,'' purred the daughter of Mithridates, and put out one long, spatulate finger to stroke Caesar's sun-browned right arm.

The touch affected him, though he did not show it. "I've never heard it put that way before, Princess, but it makes sense,'' he said, smiling, looking out to the jewel of the horizon where the sapphire of the sea met the aquamarine of the sky.

"Of course you belong to Love, owning such an ancestress!''

He turned his head to gaze at her, eyes almost at the same level as hers, so tall was she. "It is remarkable,'' he said in a soft voice, "that the sea produces so much foam at this place yet at no other, though I can see nothing to account for it.'' He pointed first to the north and then to the south. "See? Beyond the limits of the fence there is no foam!''

"It is said she left it to be here always.''

"Then the bubbles are her essence." He shrugged off his toga and bent to unbuckle his senatorial shoes. "I must bathe in her essence, Princess."

"If you were not her thirty-nine-times great-grandson, I would tell you to beware," said the Princess, watching him.

"Is it religiously forbidden to swim here?"

"Not forbidden. Only unwise. Your thirty-nine-times great-grandmother has been known to smite bathers dead."

He returned unsmitten from his dip to find she had made a sheet out of her robe to cover the spiky shore grasses, and lay waiting for him upon it. One bubble was left, clinging to the back of his hand; he leaned over to press it gently against her virginally smooth nipple, laughed when it burst and she jumped, shivered uncontrollably.

"Burned by Venus," he said as he lay down with her, wet and exhilarated from the caress of that mysterious sea-foam. For he had just been anointed by Venus, who had even arranged for this superb woman to be on hand for his pleasure, child of a great king and (as he discovered when he entered her) his alone. Love and power combined, the ultimate consummation.

"Burned by Venus," she said, stretching like a huge golden cat, so great was the goddess's gift.

"You know the Roman name of Aphrodite," said the goddess's descendant, perfectly poised on a bubble of happiness.

"Rome has a long reach."

The bubble vanished, but not because of what she said; the moment was over, was all.

Caesar got to his feet, never enamored of lingering once the lovemaking was done. "So, Mithridatidis Nyssa, will you use your influence to help me get my fleet?" he asked, though he did not tell her why this request caused him to chuckle.

"How very handsome you are," she said, lying on her elbow, head propped on her hand. "Hairless, like a god."

"So are you, I note."

"All court women are plucked, Caesar."

"But not court men?"

"No! It hurts."

He laughed. Tunic on, he dealt with his shoes, then began the difficult business of arranging his toga without assistance. "Up with you, woman!" he said cheerfully. "There's a fleet to be obtained, and a hairy husband to convince that all we've been doing is looking at the sea-foam."

"Oh, him!" She started to dress. "He won't care what we've been doing. Surely you noticed that I was a virgin!"

"Impossible not to."

Her green-gold eyes gleamed. "I do believe," she said, "that if I were not in a position to help you raise your fleet, you would have spared me hardly a glance."

"I have to deny what you say," he stated, but tranquilly. "I was once accused of doing exactly that to raise a fleet, and what I said then is still true—I would rather put my sword through my belly than employ women's tricks to achieve my ends. But you, dear and lovely Princess, were a gift from the goddess. And that is a very different thing."

"I have not angered you?"

"Not in the least, though you're a sensible girl to have assumed it. Do you get your good sense from your father?"

"Perhaps. He's a clever man. But he's a fool too."

"In what way?"

"His inability to listen to advice from others." She turned to walk with him toward the palace. "I'm very glad you came to Paphos, Caesar. I was tired of being a virgin."

"But you were a virgin. Why then with me?"

"You are the descendant of Aphrodite, therefore you are more than a mere man. I am the child of a king! I can't give myself to a mere man, only to one of royal and divine blood."

"I am honored."

The negotiations for the fleet took some time, time Caesar didn't grudge. Every day he and Ptolemy the Cyprian's unenjoyed wife made a pilgrimage to the birthplace of Aphrodite, and every day Caesar bathed in her essence before expending some of his own essence in Ptolemy the Cyprian's greatly enjoyed wife. Clearly the Alexandrian bureaucrats had a great deal more respect for Mithridatidis Nyssa than for her husband—which may have had something to do with the fact that King Tigranes was just across the water in Syria. Egypt was remote enough to consider itself safe, but Cyprus was a different matter.

He parted from the daughter of King Mithridates amicably, and with a regret which haunted him for a long time. Aside from his physical pleasure in her, he found that he liked and esteemed her unselfconscious assurance, her knowledge that she was any man's equal because she was the child of a great king. A man could not exactly wipe his feet upon a Roman woman, Caesar reflected, but a Roman woman was nonetheless no man's equal. So upon leaving Paphos, he gave Mithridatidis Nyssa an exquisitely carved cameo of the goddess, though he could ill afford the rare and costly striated stone it was worked upon.

Understanding much of this, she was immensely pleased, as she wrote to her elder sister, Cleopatra Tryphaena, in Alexandria:

> I suppose I will never see him again. He is not the kind of man who goes anywhere or does anything without an excellent reason, and by reason, I mean a man's reason. I think he might have loved me a little. But that would never draw him back to Cyprus. No woman will ever come between him and his purpose.
>
> I had not met a Roman before, though I understand that in Alexandria they are to be met fairly frequently, so you probably know quite a few. Is his difference because he is a Roman? Or because he is himself alone? Perhaps you can tell me. Though I think I know what you will answer.
>
> I liked best the unassailable quality he owned; and his calmness, which was not matter-of-fact. Admittedly with my help, he got his fleet. I know, I know, he used me! But there are times, dear Tryphaena, when one does not mind being used. He loved me a little. He prized my birth. And there is not a woman alive who could resist the way he laughs at her.
>
> It was a very pleasant interlude. I miss him, the wretch! Do not worry about me. To be on the safe side, I took the medicine after he left. Was I married in truth rather than in name only, I might have been tempted not to—Caesar blood is better blood than Ptolemy. As it is, there will never be children for me, alas.
>
> I am sorry for your difficulties, and sorry too that we were not reared to understand the situation in Egypt. Not, mind you, that our father, Mithridates, and our uncle, Tigranes, would have cared about these difficulties. We are simply their way to obtain an interest in Egypt, since we do have the necessary Ptolemaic blood to establish our claims. But what we could not know was this business about the priests of Egypt and their hold upon the common people, those of true Egyptian blood rather than Macedonian. It is almost as if there were two countries called Egypt, the land of Macedonian Alexandria and the Delta, and the land of the Egyptian Nile.
>
> I do think, dearest Tryphaena, that you ought to proceed to make your own negotiations with the Egyptian priests. Your husband Auletes is not a man for men, so you do have hope of children. You *must* bear

children! But that you cannot do under Egyptian law until after you are crowned and anointed, and you cannot be crowned and anointed until the Egyptian priests agree to officiate. I know the Alexandrians pretended to the embassage from Rome that you were crowned and anointed—they had the security of knowing that Marcus Perperna and his other ambassadors are ignorant of Egyptian laws and ways. But the people of Egypt *know* you have not been confirmed in the monarchy. Auletes is a silly man, somewhat deficient in true intellect and quite without political acumen. Whereas you and I are our father's daughters, and better blessed.

Go to the priests and begin to negotiate. In your own name. It is clear to me that you will achieve nothing—even children—until the priests are brought around. Auletes chooses to believe that he is more important than they, and that the Alexandrians are powerful enough to end in defeating the priests. He is wrong. Or perhaps it might be best to say, Auletes believes it is more important to be the Macedonian King than the Egyptian Pharaoh—that if he is King, he must also end in becoming Pharaoh. From your letters to me, I am aware that *you* have not fallen into this trap. But it is not enough. You must also negotiate. The priests understand that our husbands are the last of the line, and that to establish rival dynasts of Egyptian blood after almost a thousand years of foreign invasions and foreign rulers would be more perilous than sanctioning the last of the Ptolemies. So I imagine that what they really want is to be deferred to rather than ignored or held lightly. Defer to them, dearest Tryphaena. And make your husband defer to them! After all, they have custody of the Pharaoh's treasure labyrinths, of Nilotic income, and of the Egyptian people. The fact that Chickpea succeeded in sacking Thebes seven years ago is beside the point. He *was* crowned and anointed, he *was* Pharaoh. And Thebes is not the whole of the Nile!

In the meantime continue to take the medicine and do not antagonize either your husband or the Alexandrians. As long as they remain your allies, you have a basis for your negotiations with the priests in Memphis.

By the end of Sextilis, Gaius Julius Caesar had returned to Vatia in Tarsus and could present him with agreements to provide ships and crews at his demand from all the important naval cities and territories in Vatia's bailiwick. Clearly Vatia was pleased, especially at the agreement with Cyprus. But he had no further military duties for his young subordinate, and was besides the harbinger of the news that Sulla was dead in Rome.

"Then, Publius Servilius," said Caesar, "with your leave I would like to return home."

Vatia frowned. "Why?"

"For several reasons," said Caesar easily. "First—and most importantly—I am of little use to you—unless, that is, you intend to mount an expedition to eject King Tigranes from eastern Pedia and Euphratic Cappadocia?"

"Such are not my orders, Gaius Julius," said Vatia stiffly. "I am to concentrate upon governing my province and eliminating the pirate menace. Cappadocia and eastern Pedia must wait."

"I understand. In which case, you have no military duties for me in the near future. My other reasons for wishing to return home are personal. I have a marriage to consummate and a career in the law courts to embark upon. My time as *flamen Dialis* has meant that I am already long in the tooth to begin as an advocate. I mean to become consul in my year. It is my birthright. My father was praetor, my uncle consul, my cousin Lucius consul. The Julii are once more in the forefront."

"Very well, Gaius Julius, you may go home," said Vatia, who was sensitive to these arguments. "I will be happy to commend you to the Senate, and to classify your gathering of my fleet as campaign duty."

The death of Sulla had marked the end of amicable relations between the consuls Lepidus and Catulus. Not a pair who by nature were intended to get on together, the actual passing of the Dictator saw the first instance of their falling out; Catulus proposed that Sulla be given a State funeral, whereas Lepidus refused to countenance the expenditure of public funds to bury one whose estate could well afford to bear this cost. It was Catulus who won the ensuing battle in the Senate; Sulla was interred at the expense of the Treasury he had, after all, been the one to succeed in filling.

But Lepidus was not without support, and Rome was starting to see those return whom Sulla had forced to flee. Marcus Perperna Veiento and Cinna's son, Lucius, were both in Rome shortly after the funeral was over. Somehow Perperna Veiento had succeeded in evading actual proscription despite his tenure of Sicily at the advent of Pompey—probably because he had not stayed to contest possession of Sicily with Pompey, and had not enough money to make him an alluring proscription prospect. Young Cinna, of course, was penniless. But now that the Dictator was dead both men formed the nucleus of factions secretly opposed to the Dictator's policies and laws, and naturally preferred to side with Lepidus rather than with Catulus.

Not only the senior consul but also armed with a reputation of having stood up to Sulla in the Senate, Lepidus considered himself in an excellent position to lessen the stringency of some of Sulla's legislation now that the Dictator was dead, for his senatorial supporters actually outnumbered those who were for Catulus.

"I want," said Lepidus to his great friend Marcus Junius Brutus, "to go down in the history books as the man who regulated Sulla's laws into a form more acceptable to *everyone*—even to his enemies."

Fortune had favored both of them. Sulla's last handpicked list of magistrates had included as a praetor the name of Brutus, and when the consuls and praetors had assumed office on the previous New Year's Day, the lots to determine which provinces would go to which executives had been good to both Lepidus and Brutus; Lepidus had drawn Gaul-across-the-Alps and Brutus Italian Gaul, their terms as governors to commence at the end of their terms in office—that is, on the next New Year's Day. Gaul-across-the-Alps had not recently been a consul's province, but two things had changed that: the war in Spain against Quintus Sertorius (not going well) and the state of the Gallic tribes, now stirring into revolt and thus threatening the land route to Spain.

"We'll be able to work our provinces as a team," Lepidus had said eagerly to Brutus once the lots were drawn. "I'll wage war against rebellious tribes while you organize Italian Gaul to send me supplies and whatever other support I might need."

Thus both Lepidus and Brutus looked forward to a busy and rewarding time as governors next year. Once Sulla was buried, Lepidus had gone ahead with his program to soften the harshest of Sulla's laws, while Brutus, president of the Violence court, coped with the amendments to Sulla's laws for that court instituted in the previous year by Sulla's praetor Gnaeus Octavius. Apparently with Sulla's consent, Gnaeus Octavius had legislated to compel some of the proscription profiteers to give back property obtained by violence, force, or intimidation—which of course also meant removing the names of the original owners from the lists of the proscribed. Approving of Gnaeus Octavius's measure, Brutus had continued his work with enthusiasm.

In June, Sulla's ashes now enclosed in the tomb on the Campus Martius, Lepidus announced to the House that he would seek the House's consent to a *lex Aemilia Lepida* giving back some of the land Sulla had sequestrated from towns in Etruria and Umbria in order to bestow it upon his veterans.

"As you are all aware, Conscript Fathers," Lepidus said to an attentive Senate, "there is considerable unrest to the north of Rome. It is my opinion—and the opinions of many others!—that most of this unrest stems out of our late lamented Dictator's fixation upon punishing the communities of Etruria and Umbria by stripping from them almost every last *iugerum* of town land. That the House was not always in favor of the Dictator's measures, the House clearly showed when it opposed the Dictator's wish to proscribe every citizen in the towns of Arretium and Volaterrae. And it is to our credit that we did manage to dissuade the Dictator from doing this, even though the incident occurred when he was at the height of his power. Well, do not think that my new law has anything good to offer Arretium and Volaterrae! They actively supported Carbo, which means they will get nothing from me. No, the communities I am concerned about were at most involuntary hosts to Carbo's legions. I speak about places like Spoletium and Clusium, at the moment seething with resentment against Rome because they have lost their town lands, yet were never traitorous! Just the hapless victims of civil war, in the path of someone's army.''

Lepidus paused to look along the tiers on both sides of the Curia Hostilia, and was satisfied at what his eyes saw. A little more feeling in his voice, he continued.

''Any place which actively supported Carbo is not at issue here, and the lands of these traitors are more than enough to settle Sulla's soldiers upon. I must emphasize that. With very few exceptions, Italy is now Roman to the core, its citizens enfranchised and distributed across the full gamut of the thirty-five tribes. Yet many of the districts of Etruria and Umbria in particular are still being treated like rebellious old-style Allies, for during those times it was always Roman practice to confiscate a district's public lands. But how can Rome usurp the lands of proper, legal Romans? It is a contradiction! And we, Conscript Fathers of Rome's senior governing body, cannot continue to condone such practices. If we do, there will be yet another rebellion in Etruria and Umbria—and Rome cannot afford to wage another war at home when she is so pressed abroad! At the moment we have to find the money to support fourteen legions in the field against Quintus Sertorius. And obviously this is where our precious money must go. My law to give back their lands to places like Clusium and Tuder will calm the people of Etruria and Umbria before it is too late.''

The Senate listened, though Catulus spoke out strongly against the measure and was followed by the most pro-Sullan and conservative elements, as Lepidus had expected.

''This is the thin end of the wedge!'' cried Catulus angrily. ''Marcus Aemilius Lepidus intends to pull down our newly formed constitution a piece at a time by starting with measures he knows will appeal to this House! But *I* say it cannot be allowed to happen! Every measure he succeeds in having

sent to the People with a *senatus consultum* attached will embolden him to
go further!''

But when neither Cethegus nor Philippus came out in support of Catulus,
Lepidus felt he was going to win. Odd perhaps that they had not supported
Catulus; yet why question such a gift? He therefore went ahead with another
measure in the House before he had succeeded in obtaining a *senatus consultum* of approval for his bill to give back the sequestrated lands.

"It is the duty of this House to remove our late lamented Dictator's
embargo upon the sale of public grain at a price below that levied by the
private grain merchants," he said firmly, and with the doors of the Curia
Hostilia opened wide so that those who listened outside could hear. "Conscript
Fathers, I am a sane, decent man! I am not a demagogue. As senior consul
I have no need to woo our poorest citizens. My political career is at its
zenith—I am not a man on the rise. I can afford to pay whatever the private
grain merchants ask for their wheat. Nor do I mean to imply that our late
lamented Dictator was wrong when he fixed the price of public grain to the
price asked by the private grain merchants. I think our late lamented Dictator
did not realize the consequences, is all. For what in actual fact has happened?
The private grain merchants have raised their prices because there is now no
governmental policy to oblige them to keep their prices down! After all,
Conscript Fathers, what businessman can resist the prospect of greater profits?
Do kindness and humanity dictate his actions? Of course not! He's in business
to make a profit for himself and his shareholders, and mostly he is too myopic
to see that when he raises the price of his product beyond the capacity of his
largest market to pay for it, he begins to erode his whole profit basis.

"I therefore ask you, members of this House, to give my *lex Aemilia
Lepida frumentaria* your official stamp of approval, enabling me to put it
before the People for ratification. I will go back to our old, tried-and-true
method, which is to have the State offer public grain to the populace for the
fixed price of ten sesterces the *modius*. In years of plenty that price still
enables the State to make a good profit, and as years of plenty outnumber
years of scarcity, in the long run the State cannot suffer financially."

Again the junior consul Catulus spoke in opposition. But this time support
for him was minimal; both Cethegus and Philippus were in unequivocal favor
of Lepidus's measure. It therefore got its *senatus consultum* at the same session
as Lepidus brought it up. Lepidus was free to promulgate his law in the
Popular Assembly, and did. His reputation rose to new heights, and when he
appeared in public he was cheered.

But his *lex agraria* concerning the sequestrated lands was a different
matter; it lingered in the House, and though he put it to the vote at every

meeting, he continued to fail to secure enough votes to obtain a *senatus consultum*—which meant that under Sulla's constitution he could not take it to an Assembly.

"But I am not giving up," he said to Brutus over dinner at Brutus's house.

He ate at Brutus's house regularly, for in truth he found his own house unbearably empty these days. At the time the proscriptions had begun, he, like most of Rome's upper classes, had very much feared he would be proscribed; he had remained in Rome during the years of Marius, Cinna and Carbo—and he was married to the daughter of Saturninus, who had once attempted to make himself King of Rome. It had been Appuleia herself who had suggested that he divorce her at once. They had three sons, and it was of paramount importance that the family fortunes remain intact for the younger two of these boys; the oldest had been adopted into the ranks of Cornelius Scipio and was bound to prosper, that family being closely related to Sulla and uniformly in Sulla's camp. Scipio Aemilianus (namesake of his famous ancestor) was fully grown at the time Appuleia suggested the divorce, and the second son, Lucius, was eighteen. The youngest, Marcus, was only nine. Though he loved Appuleia dearly, Lepidus had divorced her for the sake of their sons, thinking that at some time in the future when it was safe, he would remarry her. But Appuleia was not the daughter of Saturninus for nothing; convinced that her presence in the lives of her ex-husband and her sons would always place them in jeopardy, she committed suicide. Her death was a colossal blow to Lepidus, who never really recovered emotionally. And so whenever he could he spent his private hours in the house of another man: especially the house of his best friend, Brutus.

"Exactly right! You must never give up," said Brutus. "A steady perseverance will wear the Senate down, I'm sure of it."

"You had better hope that senatorial resistance crumbles quickly," said the third diner, seated on a chair opposite the *lectus medius*.

Both men looked at Brutus's wife, Servilia, with a concern tempered by considerable respect; what Servilia had to say was always worth hearing.

"What precisely do you mean?" asked Lepidus.

"I mean that Catulus is girding himself for war."

"How did you find that out?" asked Brutus.

"By keeping my ears pricked," she said with expressionless face. Then she smiled in her secretive, buttoned-up way. "I popped around to visit Hortensia this morning, and she's not the sister of our greatest advocate for no reason—like him, she's an inveterate talker. Catulus adores her, so he talks to her too much—and she talks to anyone with the skill to pump her."

"And you, of course, have that skill," said Lepidus.

"Certainly. But more importantly I have the interest to pump her. Most of her female visitors are more fascinated by gossip and women's matters, whereas Hortensia would far rather talk politics. So I make it my business to see her often."

"Tell us more, Servilia," said Lepidus, not understanding what she was saying. "Catulus is girding himself for what war? Nearer Spain? He's to go there as governor next year, complete with a new army. So I suppose it's not illogical that he's—er, girding himself for war, as you put it."

"This war has nothing to do with Spain or Sertorius," said Brutus's wife. "Catulus is talking of war in Etruria. According to Hortensia, he's going to start persuading the Senate to arm more legions to deal with the unrest there."

Lepidus sat up straight on the *lectus medius.* "But that's insanity! There is only one way to keep the peace in Etruria, and that's to give its communities back a good proportion of what Sulla took away from them!"

"Are you in touch with any of the local leaders in Etruria?" asked Servilia.

"Of course."

"The diehards or the moderates?"

"The moderates, I suppose, if by diehards you mean the leaders of places like Volaterrae and Faesulae."

"That's what I mean."

"I thank you for your information, Servilia. Rest assured, I will redouble my efforts to settle matters in Etruria."

Lepidus did redouble his efforts, but could not prevent Catulus from exhorting the house to start recruiting the legions he believed would be necessary to put down the brewing revolt in Etruria. Servilia's timely warning, however, enabled Lepidus to canvass support among the *pedarii* and the senior backbenchers like Cethegus; the House, listening to Catulus's impassioned diatribe, was lukewarm.

"In fact, Quintus Lutatius," said Cethegus to Catulus, "we are more concerned about the lack of amity between you and our senior consul than we are about hypothetical revolts in Etruria. It seems to us that you have adopted an inflexible policy of opposing whatever our senior consul wants. I find that sad, especially so soon after Lucius Cornelius Sulla went to so much trouble to forge new bonds of co-operation between the various members and factions within the Senate of Rome."

Squashed, Catulus subsided. Not, as it turned out, for very long. Events conspired to make him seem right and to kill any chance Lepidus had of obtaining that elusive *senatus consultum* for his law giving back much of the sequestrated lands. For at the end of June the dispossessed citizens of Faesulae attacked the soldier settlements all around it, threw the veterans off their allotments, and killed those who resisted.

The deaths of several hundred loyal Sullan legionaries could not be ignored, nor could Faesulae be allowed to get away with outright rebellion. At a moment when the Senate should have been turning its attention toward preparing for the elections to be held in Quinctilis, the Senate forgot all about elections. The lots had been cast to determine which consul would conduct the curule balloting (they fell upon Lepidus), this being a new part of Sulla's constitution, but nothing further was done. Instead, the House instructed both consuls to recruit four new legions each and proceed to Faesulae to put the insurrection down.

The meeting was preparing to break up when Lucius Marcius Philippus rose and asked to speak. Lepidus, who held the *fasces* for the month of Quinctilis, made his first major mistake: he decided to allow Philippus to have his say.

"My dear fellow senators," said Philippus in stentorian tones, "I *beg* you not to put an army into the hands of Marcus Aemilius Lepidus! I do not request. I do not ask. *I beg!* For it is plain to me that our senior consul is plotting revolution—has been plotting revolution ever since he was inaugurated! Until our beloved Dictator died, he did and said nothing. But the moment our beloved Dictator died, it started. He refused to countenance the voting of State funds to bury Sulla! Of course he lost—but I for one never believed he thought he could win! He used the funeral debate as a signal to all his supporters that he was about to legislate treasonous policies. And he proceeded to legislate treasonous policies! He proposed to give back sequestrated lands to people who had *deserved* to lose them! And when this body stalled, he sought the adulation of every Class lower than the Second by a trick every demagogue has used, from Gaius Gracchus to Lepidus's father-in-law Saturninus—he legislated cheap State grain! Rome was not supposed to vote money to honor the dead body of her greatest citizen—oh, no! But Rome was supposed to spend far more of her public money to dower her worthless *proletarii* with cheap grain—oh, yes!"

Lepidus was not the only man stunned by this attack; the whole House was sitting bolt upright in shock. Philippus swept on.

"Now, my fellow senators, you want to give this man four legions and send him off to Etruria? Well, I refuse to let you do that! For one thing, the curule elections are due to be held shortly and the lot fell upon him to hold them. Therefore he must remain in Rome to do his duty, not go haring off to raise an army! I remind you that we are about to hold our first free elections in some years, and that it is imperative we hold them on time and with due legality. Quintus Lutatius Catulus is perfectly capable of recruiting and waging war against Faesulae and any other Etrurian communities which may choose to side with Faesulae. It is against Sulla's laws for both consuls to be absent from Rome in order to wage war. Indeed, it was to prevent that from happening that our beloved Dictator incorporated his clause about the specially commissioned command into his opus! We have been provided with the constitutional means to give command in our wars to the most competent man available, even if he is not a member of the Senate. Yet here I find you giving a vital command to a man who has no decent war record! Quintus Lutatius is tried and true, we know him to be competent in military matters. But Marcus Aemilius Lepidus? He's unversed and unproven! He is also, I maintain, a potential revolutionary. You *cannot* give him legions and send him to wage war in an area where the words out of his own mouth have indicated a treasonous interest in favoring that area over Rome!''

Lepidus had listened slack-jawed to the opening sentences of this speech, but then with sudden decision had turned to his clerk and snatched the wax tablet and stylus from those hands; for the remainder of the time Philippus spoke he took notes. Now he rose to answer, the tablet held where he could refer to it.

''What is your motive in saying these things, Philippus?'' he asked, not according Philippus the courtesy of his full name. ''I confess myself at a loss to divine your motive—but you have one, of that I am sure! When the Great Tergiversator rises in this House to deliver one of his magnificently worded and delivered speeches, rest assured there is always a hidden motive! Some fellow is paying him to turn his toga yet again! How rich he has become!— how fat!—how contented!—how sunk in a private mire of voluptuousness!— and always in the pay of some creature who needs a senatorial mouthpiece!''

The wax tablet was lifted a little; Lepidus glared sternly across its top at the silent senators. Even Catulus, a glance in his direction showed, was flabbergasted by Philippus's speech. Whoever was behind him, it was definitely not Catulus or any member of his faction.

''I will deal with Philippus's points in order, Conscript Fathers. One, my passivity before the Dictator died. That is not true! As everyone here knows! Cast your minds back!

''Two, the voting of public funds to pay for the Dictator's funeral. Yes, I was opposed. So were many other men. And why not? Are we to have no voices?

"As for—three—my opposition being a signal to my—do I have any?—supporters that I would undo everything Lucius Cornelius Sulla knitted up—what absolute rubbish! I have attempted to have two laws enacted and succeeded with one alone. But have I given the slightest indication to anybody that I intend to overturn Sulla's entire body of laws? Have you heard me criticizing the new court system? Or the new regulations governing the public servants? The Senate? The election process? The new treason laws restraining the actions of provincial governors? The restricted functions of the Assemblies? Even the severely curtailed tribunate of the plebs? No, Conscript Fathers, you have not! *Because I do not intend to tamper with these provisions!*"

The last sentence was thundered out, so much so that not a few of the men who listened jumped. He paused to allow everyone to recover, then pressed on.

"Four, the allegation that my law returning *some* sequestrated lands—some, not all!—to their original owners is a treasonous one. That too is rubbish. My *lex Aemilia Lepida* does not say that any confiscated lands belonging to genuinely treasonous towns or districts should be given back. It concerns only lands belonging to places whose participation in the war against Carbo was innocent or involuntary."

Lepidus dropped his voice, put much feeling into it. "My fellow senators, stop to think for a moment, please! If we are to see a truly united and properly Roman Italy, we must cease to inflict the old penalties we imposed upon the Italian Allies upon men who under the law are now as Roman as we are ourselves! If Lucius Cornelius Sulla erred anywhere, it was in that. In a man of his age it was perhaps understandable. But it is unpardonable for the majority of us, at least twenty years his junior, to think along the same lines he did. I remind you that Philippus here is also an old man, with an old man's outmoded prejudices. When he was censor he displayed his prejudices flagrantly by refusing to do what Sulla in actual fact did do—distribute the new Roman citizens right across the thirty-five tribes."

He was beginning to sway them, for indeed this was a much younger body than it had been ten years ago. Feeling the worst of his anxiety lift, Lepidus continued.

"Five, my grain law. That too righted a very manifest wrong. I believe that had Lucius Cornelius Sulla stayed on as the Dictator for a longer period of time, he would have seen this for himself and done what I did—legislated to return cheap grain to the lower classes. The grain merchants were greedy. None can deny it! And indeed this body was wise enough to see the good sense behind my grain law, for you authorized its passage, and thus removed the likelihood that with this coming harvest Rome might have seen violence and riots. *For you cannot take away from the common people a privilege that has been with them long enough for them to assume it is a right!*

"Six, my function as the consul chosen by lot to supervise the curule elections. Yes, the lot did fall upon me, and under our new constitution that means I alone can officiate at the curule elections. But, Conscript Fathers, it was not I who asked to be directed to take four legions and put down the revolt at Faesulae as my first order of business! It was you directed me! *Of your own free will!* Unsolicited by me! It did not occur to you—nor did it occur to me!—that business of the nature of the curule elections should take precedence over open revolt within Italy. I confess that I assumed I was first to help put down open revolt, and only then hold the curule elections. There is plenty of time before the end of the year for elections. After all, it is only the beginning of Quinctilis.

"Seven, it is *not* expressly against the laws of Sulla that both consuls should be absent from Rome in order to wage war. Even to wage war outside Italy. According to Lucius Cornelius Sulla, the first duty of the consuls is to care for Rome and Italy. Neither Quintus Lutatius Catulus nor I will be exceeding his authority. The clause providing for the specially commissioned non-senatorial commander can only be brought into being if the legally elected magistrates *and all other competent senators* are not available to wage war.

"And finally, point number eight," said Lepidus. "How am I less qualified to command in a war than Quintus Lutatius Catulus? Each of us last saw service during the Italian War, as legates. Neither of us left Rome during the years of Cinna and Carbo. Both of us maintained an honest and obdurate neutrality which Lucius Cornelius Sulla most definitely did not punish us for—after all, here we are, his last pair of personally chosen consuls! Our military experience is much of a muchness. There is nothing to say which of us may shine the brighter in the field against Faesulae. It is in Rome's interests to hope that both of us shine with equal brightness, is it not? Normal Roman practice says that if the consuls are willing to assume the mantle of military command at the directive of the Senate, then the consuls must do so. The consuls were so directed by the Senate. The consuls have done so. There is no more to be said."

But Philippus was not done. Displaying neither frustration nor anger, smoothly and reasonably he turned the debate around into a lament against the obvious enmity which had flared between the consuls, and labored this point through what seemed like half a hundred concrete examples from mere asides to major clashes. The sun had set (which meant that technically the Senate had to end its deliberations), but both Catulus and Lepidus were unwilling to postpone a decision until the following day, so the clerks of the House kindled torches and Philippus droned on. It was very well done. By the time that Philippus reached his peroration, the senators would have agreed to practically anything to be allowed to go home for food and sleep.

"What I propose," he said at last, "is that each of the consuls swears an oath to the effect that he will not turn his army into an instrument of personal revenge against the other. Not a very big thing to ask! But I for one would rest easier if I knew such an oath had been taken."

Lepidus rose to his feet wearily. "My personal opinion of your proposal, Philippus, is that it is without a doubt the silliest thing I have ever heard of! However, if it will make the House any happier and allow Quintus Lutatius and me to go about our tasks more expeditiously, then I for one am willing to swear."

"I am in full accord, Marcus Aemilius," said Catulus. "Now may we all go home?"

"What *do* you think Philippus was up to?" asked Lepidus of Brutus over dinner the following day.

"Truly I do not know," said Brutus, shaking his head.

"Have you any idea, Servilia?" the senior consul asked.

"Not really, no," she answered, frowning. "My husband gave me a general outline of what had been said last night, but I might be able to learn more if you could possibly provide me with a copy of the verbatim proceedings—that is, if the clerks took them down."

So high had Lepidus's opinion of Servilia's political acumen become that he saw nothing untoward in this request, and agreed to give her the document on the morrow before he left Rome to recruit his four legions.

"I am beginning to think," said Brutus, "that you stand no chance to improve the lot of the Etrurian and Umbrian towns which weren't directly involved in Carbo's war. There are just too many men like Philippus in the Senate, and they don't want to hear what you have to say."

The pacifying of at least some of the Umbrian districts mattered to Brutus, who was the largest landowner in Umbria after Pompey; he wanted no soldier settlements adjoining his own lands. These were mostly around Spoletium and Iguvium, two areas already sequestrated. That they had not yet received any veteran settlers was due to two factors: the torpor of the commissions set up to deal with apportionment, and the departure of fourteen of Sulla's old legions for service in the Spains twenty months ago. It was only this second factor had enabled Lepidus to bring on his legislation; had all twenty-three of Sulla's legions remained in Italy to be demobilized as originally planned, then Spoletium and Iguvium would have seen their full complement of vet-. erans already.

"What Philippus had to say yesterday was an absolute shock," said Lepidus, flushing with anger at the memory of it. "I just can't believe those idiots! I truly thought that when I answered Philippus, I would win them around—I spoke good sense, Servilia, plain good sense! And yet they let Philippus bluff them into extracting that ridiculous oath we all had to swear this morning up in Semo Sancus Dius Fidius!"

"Which means they're ready to be swayed even more," she said. "What worries me is that you won't be in the House to counter the old mischief-maker the next time he speaks—and speak, he will! He's hatching something."

"I don't know why we call him old," said Brutus, who was prone to digress. "He isn't really that old—fifty-eight. And though he looks as if he might be carried off tomorrow by an apoplexy, it's my guess he won't be. That would be too good to be true!"

But Lepidus was tired of digressions and speculations, and suddenly got down to serious business. "I'm off to Etruria to recruit," he said, "and I'd like you to join me as soon as possible, Brutus. We had planned to work as a team next year, but I think it behooves us to start now. There's nothing coming up in your court which won't wait until next year and a new judge, so I shall ask that you be seconded to me as my senior legate immediately."

Servilia looked concerned. "Is it wise to recruit your men in Etruria?" she asked. "Why not go to Campania?"

"Because Catulus got in ahead of me and took Campania for himself. Anyway, my own lands and contacts are in Etruria, not south of Rome. I'm comfortable there, I know many more people."

"But that's what perturbs me, Lepidus. I suspect Philippus might make much of it, continue to throw doubts into everyone's minds as to your ultimate intentions. It doesn't look good to be recruiting in an area seething with potential revolt."

"Let Philippus!" said Lepidus scornfully.

The Senate let Philippus. As Quinctilis passed into Sextilis and recruitment proceeded at a great rate, Philippus made it his duty to keep a watchful eye upon Lepidus through, it seemed, an amazingly large and efficient network of agents. No time did he waste upon watching Catulus in Campania; *his* four legions were filling up rapidly with Sulla's oldest retainers, bored with civilian life and farming, eager for a new campaign not too far from home.

The trouble was that the men enlisting in Etruria were not Sulla's veterans. Rather they were green young men of the region, or else veterans who had fought for Carbo and his generals and managed to be missing from the ranks when surrender occurred. Most of Sulla's men resettled in Etruria elected to remain on their allotments to protect them, or else hied themselves off to Campania to enlist in the legions of Catulus.

All through September did Philippus roar in the House while both Catulus and Lepidus, their enlistments filled, bent their energies to training and refining their armies. Then at the very beginning of October, Philippus managed to weary the Senate into demanding that Lepidus return to hold the curule elections in Rome. The summons went north to Lepidus's camp outside Saturnia, and Lepidus's answer came back by the same courier.

"I cannot leave at this juncture," it said baldly. "You must either wait for me or appoint Quintus Lutatius in my stead."

Quintus Lutatius Catulus was ordered to return from Campania—but not to hold the elections; it was no part of Philippus's plan to allow Lepidus this grace, and Cethegus had allied himself with Philippus so firmly that whatever Philippus wanted was assented to by three quarters of the House.

In all this no move had yet been made against Faesulae, which had locked its gates and sat back to see what happened, very pleased that Rome could not seem to agree upon what to do.

A second summons was dispatched to Lepidus demanding that he return to Rome at once to hold the elections; again Lepidus refused. Both Philippus and Cethegus now informed the senators that Lepidus must be considered to be in revolt, that they had proof of his dealings and agreements with the refractory elements in Etruria and Umbria—and that his senior legate, the praetor Marcus Junius Brutus, was equally involved.

Said Servilia in a letter to Lepidus:

> I believe I have finally managed to work out what is behind Philippus's conduct, though I have been able to find no definite proof of my suspicions. However, you may take it that whatever and whoever is behind Philippus is also behind Cethegus.
>
> I studied the verbatim text of that first speech Philippus made over and over again, and had many a cozy chat with every woman in a position to know something. Except for the loathsome Praecia, who is now queening it in the Cethegus ménage, it would appear exclusively. Hortensia knows nothing because I believe Catulus her husband knows nothing. However, I finally obtained the vital clue from Julia, the widow of Gaius

Marius—you perceive how far I have extended my net pursuing my
enquiries!

Her once-upon-a-time daughter-in-law, Mucia Tertia, is now married to that young upstart from Picenum, Gnaeus Pompeius who has the
temerity to call himself Magnus. *Not* a member of the Senate, but very
rich, very brash, very anxious to excel. I had to be extremely careful
that I did not give Julia any impression that I might be sniffing for
information, but she is a frank person once she reposes her trust in
someone, and she was inclined to do so from the outset because of my
husband's father's loyalty to Gaius Marius—whom, you might remember, he accompanied into exile during Sulla's first consulship.

It turns out too that Julia has detested Philippus ever since he sold
himself to Gaius Marius many years ago; apparently Gaius Marius despised the man even as he used him. So when at my third visit (I thought
it wise to establish Julia's full trust before mentioning Philippus in more
than a passing fashion) I drew the conversation around to the present
situation and Philippus's possible motives in making you his victim,
Julia mentioned that she thought from something Mucia Tertia had said
to her during her last visit to Rome that Philippus is now in the employ
of *Pompeius*! As is none other than Cethegus!

I enquired no further. It really wasn't necessary. From the time of
that initial speech, Philippus has harped tirelessly upon Sulla's special
clause authorizing the Senate to look outside its own ranks for a military
commander or a governor should a good man not be available within its
own ranks. Still puzzled as to what this could have to do with the present
situation? I confess I was! Until, that is, I sat and mentally reviewed
Philippus's conduct over the past thirty-odd years.

I concluded that Philippus is simply working for his master, if his
master be in truth Pompeius. Philippus is not a Gaius Gracchus or a
Sulla; he has no grand strategy in mind whereby he will manipulate the
Senate into dismissing all of you currently embroiled in this campaign
against Faesulae and appointing Pompeius in your stead. He probably
knows quite well that the Senate will not do that under any circumstances—there are too many capable military men sitting on the Senate's
benches at the moment. If both the consuls should fail—and at this stage
it is difficult to see why either of you should—there is none other than
Lucullus ready to step into the breach, and he is a praetor this year, so
has the imperium already.

No, Philippus is merely making as big a fuss as he can in order to
have the opportunity to remind the Senate that Sulla's special commission

clause does exist. And presumably Cethegus is willing to support him because he too somehow is caught in Pompeius's toils. Not from want of money, obviously! But there are other reasons than money, and Cethegus's reasons could be *anything*.

Therefore, my dear Lepidus, it seems to me that you are to some extent an incidental victim, that your courage in speaking up for what you believe even though it runs counter to most of the Senate has presented Philippus with a target he can use to justify whatever colossal amount it is that Pompeius is paying him. He's simply lobbying for a man who is not a senator but deems it worthwhile to have a strong faction within the Senate against the day when his services might be needed.

In fairness, I could be completely wrong. However, I do not think I am.

"It makes a great deal more sense than anything else I've heard," said Lepidus to his correspondent's husband after he had read her letter out loud for Brutus's benefit.

"And I agree with Servilia," said Brutus, awed. "I doubt she's wrong. She rarely is."

"So, my friend, what do I do? Return to Rome like a good boy, hold the curule elections and pass then into obscurity—or do I attempt what the Etrurian leaders want of me and lead them against Rome in open rebellion?"

It was a question Lepidus had asked himself many times since he had reconciled himself to the fact that Rome would never permit him to restore Etruria and Umbria to some semblance of normality and prosperity. Pride was in his dilemma, and a certain driving need to stand out from the crowd, albeit that crowd be composed of Roman consulars. Since the death of his wife the value of his actual life had diminished in his own eyes to the point where he held it of scant moment; he had quite lost sight of the real reason for her suicide, which was that their sons should be freed from political reprisals at any time in the future. Scipio Aemilianus and Lucius were with him wholeheartedly and young Marcus was still a child; he it was who fulfilled the Lepidus family's tradition by being the male child born with a caul over his face, and everyone knew that phenomenon meant he would be one of Fortune's favorites throughout a long life. So why ought Lepidus worry about any of his sons?

For Brutus the dilemma was somewhat different, though he did not fear defeat. No, what attracted Brutus to the Etrurian scheme was the culmination of eight years of marriage to the patrician Servilia: the knowledge that she considered him plain, humdrum, unexciting, spineless, contemptible. He did not love her, but as the years went by and his friends and colleagues esteemed her opinions on political matters more and more, he came to realize that in her woman's shell there resided a unique personage whose approval of him *mattered*. In this present situation, for instance, she had written not to him but to the consul, Lepidus. Passing him over as unimportant. And that shamed him. As he now understood it shamed her also. If he was to retrieve himself in her eyes, he would have to do something brave, high-principled, distinctive.

Thus it was that Brutus finally answered Lepidus's question instead of evading it. He said, "I think you must attempt what the elders want of you and lead Etruria and Umbria against Rome."

"All right," said Lepidus, "I will. But not until the New Year, when I am released from that silly oath."

When the Kalends of January arrived, Rome had no curule magistrates; the elections had not been held. On the last day of the old year Catulus had convened the Senate and informed it that on the morrow it would have to send the *fasces* to the temple of Venus Libitina and appoint the first *interrex*. This temporary supreme magistrate called the *interrex* held office for five days only as custodian of Rome; he had to be patrician, the leader of his decury of senators, and in the case of the first *interrex,* the senior patrician in the House. On the sixth day he was succeeded as *interrex* by the second most senior patrician in the House also leader of his decury; the second *interrex* was empowered to hold the elections.

So at dawn on New Year's Day the Senate formally appointed Lucius Valerius Flaccus Princeps Senatus the first *interrex* and those men who intended to stand for election as consuls and praetors went into a flurry of hasty canvassing. The *interrex* sent a curt message to Lepidus ordering him to leave his army and return to Rome forthwith, and reminding him that he had sworn an oath not to turn his legions upon his colleague.

At noon on the third day of Flaccus Princeps Senatus's term, Lepidus sent back his reply.

> I would remind you, Princeps Senatus, that I am now proconsul, not consul. And that I kept my oath, which does not bind me now I am proconsul, not consul. I am happy to give up my consular army, but would remind you that I am now proconsul and was voted a proconsular army, and will not give up this proconsular army. As my consular army consisted of four legions and my proconsular army also consists of four legions, it is obvious that I do not have to give up anything.

However, I am willing to return to Rome under the following circumstances:

that I am re-elected consul;

that every last *iugerum* of sequestrated land throughout Italy be returned to its original owner;

that the rights and properties of the sons and grandsons of the proscribed be restored to them;

and that their full powers be restituted to the tribunes of the plebs.

"And that," said Philippus to the members of the Senate, "should tell even the densest senatorial dunderhead what Lepidus intends! In order to give him what he demands, we would have to tear down the entire constitution Lucius Cornelius Sulla worked so hard to establish, and Lepidus knows very well we will not do that. This answer of his is tantamount to a declaration of war. I therefore beseech the House to pass its *senatus consultum de re publica defendenda.*"

But this required impassioned debate, and so the Senate did not pass its Ultimate Decree until the last day of Flaccus's term as first *interrex*. Once it was passed the authority to defend Rome against Lepidus was formally conferred upon Catulus, who was ordered to return to his army and prepare for war.

On the sixth day of January, Flaccus Princeps Senatus stood down and the Senate appointed its second *interrex*, who was Appius Claudius Pulcher, still lingering in Rome recovering from his long illness. And since Appius Claudius was actually feeling much better, he flung himself into the task of convening the Centuriate Assembly and holding the curule elections. These would occur, he announced, within the Servian Walls on the Aventine in two days' time, this site being outside the *pomerium* but adequately protected from any military action by Lepidus.

"It's odd," said Catulus to Hortensius just before he left for Campania, "that after so many years of not enjoying the privilege of free choice in the matter of our magistrates, we should find it so difficult to hold an election at all. Almost as if we were drifting into the habit of allowing someone to do everything for us, like a mother for her babies."

"That," said Hortensius in freezing tones, "is sheer fanciful claptrap, Quintus! The most I am prepared to concede is that it is an extraordinary coincidence that our first year of free choice in the matter of our magistrates should also throw up a consul who ignored the tenets of his office. We are now conducting these elections, I must point out to you, and the governance of Rome will proceed in future years as it was always intended to proceed!"

"Let us hope then," said Catulus, offended, "that the voters will choose at least as wisely as Sulla always did!"

But it was Hortensius who had the last word. "You are quite forgetting, my dear Quintus, that it was Sulla chose Lepidus!"

On the whole the leaders of the Senate (including Catulus and Hortensius) professed themselves pleased with the wisdom of the electors. The senior consul was an elderly man of sedentary habit but known ability, Decimus Junius Brutus, and the junior consul was none other than Mamercus. Clearly the electors held the same high opinion of the Cottae as Sulla had, for last year Sulla had picked Gaius Aurelius Cotta as one of his praetors, and this year the voters returned his brother Marcus Aurelius Cotta among the praetors; the lots made him *praetor peregrinus*.

Having remained in Rome to see who was returned, Catulus promptly offered supreme command in the war against Lepidus to the new consuls. As he expected, Decimus Brutus refused on the grounds of his age and lack of adequate military experience; it was Mamercus was bound to accept. Just entering his forty-fourth year, Mamercus had a fine war record and had served under Sulla in all his campaigns. But unforeseen events and Philippus conspired against Mamercus. Lucius Valerius Flaccus the Princeps Senatus, colleague in the second-last consulship of Gaius Marius, dropped dead the day after he stepped down from office as first *interrex,* and Philippus proposed that Mamercus be appointed as a temporary Princeps Senatus.

"We cannot do without a Leader of the House at this present time," Philippus said, "though it has always been the task of the censors to appoint him. By tradition he is the senior patrician in the House, but legally it is the right of the censors to appoint whichever patrician senator they consider most suitable. Our senior patrician senator is now Appius Claudius Pulcher, whose health is not good and who is proceeding to Macedonia anyway. We need a Leader of the House who is young and robust—*and* present in Rome! Until such time as we elect a pair of censors, I suggest that we appoint Mamercus Aemilius Lepidus Livianus as a caretaker Princeps Senatus. I also suggest that he should remain within Rome until things settle down. It therefore follows that Quintus Lutatius Catulus should retain his command against Lepidus."

"But I am going to Nearer Spain to govern!" cried Catulus.

"Not possible," said Philippus bluntly. "I move that we direct our good Pontifex Maximus Metellus Pius, who is prorogued in Further Spain, to act as governor of Nearer Spain also until we can see our way clear to sending a new governor."

As everyone was in favor of any measure which kept the stammering

Pontifex Maximus a long way from Rome and religious ceremonies, Philippus got his way. The House authorized Metellus Pius to govern Nearer Spain as well as his own province, made Mamercus a temporary Princeps Senatus, and confirmed Catulus in his command against Lepidus. Very disappointed, Catulus took himself off to form up his legions in Campania, while an equally disappointed Mamercus remained in Rome.

Three days later word came that Lepidus was mobilizing his four legions and that his legate Brutus had gone to Italian Gaul to put its two garrison legions at Bononia, the intersection of the Via Aemilia and the Via Annia, where they would be perfectly poised to reinforce Lepidus. Still toying with revolt because they had suffered the loss of all their public lands, Clusium and Arretium could be expected to offer Brutus every assistance in his march to join Lepidus—and to block any attempt by Catulus to prevent his joining up with Lepidus.

Philippus struck.

"Our supreme commander in the field, Quintus Lutatius Catulus, is still to the south of Rome—has not in fact yet left Campania. Lepidus is moving south from Saturnia already," said Philippus, "and will be in a position to stop our commander-in-chief sending any of his troops to deal with Brutus in Italian Gaul. Besides which, I imagine our commander-in-chief will need all four of his legions to contain Lepidus himself. So what can we possibly do about Brutus, who holds the key to Lepidus's success in his hands? Brutus must be dealt with—and dealt with smartly! *But how?* At the moment we have no other legions under the eagles in Italy, and the two legions of Italian Gaul belong to Brutus. Not even a Lucullus—were he still in Rome instead of on his way to govern Africa Province—could assemble and mobilize at least two legions quickly enough to confront Brutus."

The House listened gloomily, having finally been brought to realize that the years of civil strife were not over just because Sulla had made himself Dictator and striven mightily with his laws to stop another man from marching on Rome. With Sulla not dead a year yet, here was another man coming to impose his will upon his hapless country, here were whole tracts of Italy in arms against the city the Italians had wanted to belong to so badly in every way. Perhaps there were some among the voiceless ranks who were honest enough to admit that it was largely their own fault Rome was brought to this present pass; but if there were, not one of them spoke his thoughts aloud. Instead, everyone gazed at Philippus as if at a savior, and trusted to him to find a way out.

"There is *one* man who can contain Brutus at once," said Philippus,

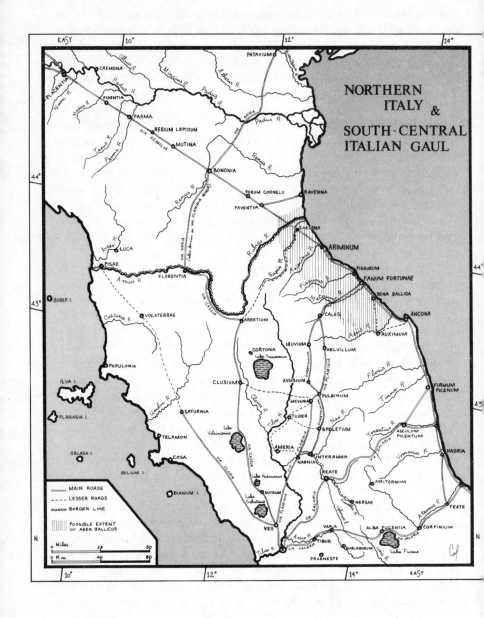

NORTHERN
ITALY &
SOUTH-CENTRAL
ITALIAN GAUL

sounding smug. "He has his father's old troops—and indeed his own old troops!—working for him on his estates in northern Picenum and Umbria. A *much* shorter march to Brutus than from Campania! He has been Rome's loyal servant in the past, as was his father Rome's loyal servant before him. I speak, of course, of the young knight Gnaeus Pompeius Magnus. Victor at Clusium, victor in Sicily, victor over Africa and Numidia. It was not for nothing that Lucius Cornelius Sulla permitted this young knight to triumph! This young knight is our brightest hope! And he is in a position to contain Brutus within days!"

The newly appointed temporary Princeps Senatus and junior consul shifted on his curule chair, frowning. "Gnaeus Pompeius is not a member of the Senate," Mamercus said, "and I cannot like the idea of giving any kind of command to someone outside our own."

"I agree with you completely, Mamercus Aemilius!" said Philippus instantly. "No one could *like* it. But can you offer a better alternative? We have the constitutional power in times of emergency to look outside the Senate for our military answer, and this power was given to us by none other than Sulla himself. No more conservative man than Sulla ever lived, nor a man more attached to the perpetuation of the *mos maiorum*. Yet he it was who foresaw just this present situation—and he it was who provided us with an answer."

Philippus stayed by his stool (as Sulla had directed all speakers must), but he turned around slowly in a circle to look at the tiers of senators on both sides of the House. As orator and presence he had grown in stature since the time when he had set out to ruin Marcus Livius Drusus; these days there were no ludicrous temper tantrums, no storms of abuse.

"Conscript Fathers," he said solemnly, "we have no time to waste in debate. Even as I speak, Lepidus is marching on Rome. May I respectfully ask the senior consul Decimus Junius Brutus to put a motion before the House? Namely, that this body authorize the knight Gnaeus Pompeius Magnus to raise his old legions and march to contend with Marcus Junius Brutus in the name of the Senate and People of Rome. Further, that this body confer a propraetorian status upon the knight Gnaeus Pompeius Magnus."

Decimus Brutus had opened his mouth to consent when Mamercus prevented him, one hand on the senior consul's arm. "I will agree to your putting that motion before the House for a vote, Decimus Junius," he said, "but not until Lucius Marcius Philippus has clarified one phrase he used in wording his motion! He said, 'to raise his old legions' instead of specifying *how many* legions! No matter how stellar Gnaeus Pompeius's military record might be, he is not a member of the Senate! He cannot be given the authority to raise legions in Rome's name to however many he may himself consider enough. I say that the motion must specify the exact number of legions this House authorizes Gnaeus Pompeius to raise, and I say further that the number of legions be limited to two. Brutus the governor of Italian Gaul has two legions of relatively inexperienced soldiers, the permanent garrison of that province. It ought not to take more than two legions of hoary old Pompeian veterans to deal with Brutus.''

This perceptive opposition did not please Philippus, but he deemed it wise to accede; Mamercus was of that slow and steady kind who somehow always managed to accumulate a lot of senatorial clout—and he was married to Sulla's daughter.

"I beg the House's pardon!" cried Philippus. "How sloppy of me! And I thank our esteemed Princeps Senatus and junior consul for his timely intervention. I meant to say two legions, of course. Let the motion be put to the House, Decimus Junius, with that exact number of legions.''

The motion was put, and the motion was passed without one single dissenting voice. Cethegus had raised his arms above his head in a stretch and a yawn, the signal to all his followers on the back benches that they were to vote in the affirmative. And because the motion dealt with war, the senatorial resolution carried the force of law with it; in war and in foreign matters the various Assemblies of the Roman People no longer had a say.

It was, after all that political maneuvering, a hasty and pathetic little war, hardly deserving of the name. Even though Lepidus had started out to march on Rome considerably earlier than Catulus left Campania, still Catulus beat him to Rome and occupied the Campus Martius. When Lepidus did appear across the river in Transtiberim (he had come down the Via Aurelia), Catulus barred and garrisoned all the bridges, and thereby forced Lepidus to march north to the Mulvian Bridge. Thus it was that the two armies came to grips on the northeastern side of the Via Lata under the Servian Walls of the Quirinal; in that place most of the fighting occurred. Some fierce clashes of arms elevated the battle beyond a rout, but Lepidus turned out to be a hopeless tactician, incapable of deploying his men logically and quite incapable of winning.

An hour after the two sides met Lepidus was in full retreat back to the Mulvian Bridge, with Catulus in hot pursuit. North of Fregenae he turned and fought Catulus again, but only to secure his flight to Cosa. From Cosa he managed to escape to Sardinia, accompanied by twenty thousand of his foot soldiers and fifteen hundred cavalry troopers. It was his intention to restructure his army in Sardinia, then return to Italy and try again. With him went his middle son, Lucius, the Carboan ex-governor Marcus Perperna Veiento, and Cinna's son. But Lepidus's eldest son, Scipio Aemilianus, declined to leave Italy. Instead he barricaded himself and his legion inside the old and formidable fortress on the Alban Mount above Bovillae, and there withstood siege.

The much-publicized return to Italy from Sardinia never came to pass. The governor of Sardinia was an old ally of Lucullus's, one Lucius Valerius Triarius, and he resisted Lepidus's occupation bitterly. Then in April of that unhappy year Lepidus died still in Sardinia; his troops maintained that what killed him was a broken heart, mourning for his dead wife. Perperna Veiento and Cinna's son took ship from Sardinia to Liguria, and thence marched their twenty thousand foot and fifteen hundred horse along the Via Domitia to Spain and Quintus Sertorius. With them went Lucius, Lepidus's middle son.

The eldest son, Scipio Aemilianus, proved the most militarily competent of the rebels, and held out in Alba Longa for some time. But eventually he was forced to surrender; following orders from the Senate, Catulus executed him.

If ignominy was to set the standard of events, Brutus fared far the worst. While ever he heard nothing from Lepidus he held his two legions in Italian Gaul at the major intersection of Bononia; and thus allowed Pompey to steal a march on him. That young man (now some twenty-eight years old) had of course already been mobilized when Philippus secured him his special commission from the Senate. But instead of bringing his two legions up from Picenum to Ariminum and then inland along the Via Aemilia, Pompey chose to go down the Via Flaminia toward Rome. At the intersection of this road with the Via Cassia north to Arretium and thence to Italian Gaul, he turned onto the Via Cassia. By doing this he prevented Brutus from joining Lepidus—had Brutus ever really thought he might.

When he heard of Pompey's approach up the Via Cassia, Brutus retreated into Mutina. This big and extremely well-fortified town was stuffed with clients of the Aemilii, Lepidus as well as Scaurus. It therefore welcomed Brutus gladly. Pompey duly arrived; Mutina was invested. The city held out until Brutus heard of the defeat and flight of Lepidus, and his death in Sardinia. Once it became clear that Lepidus's troops were now absolutely committed to Quintus Sertorius in Spain, Brutus despaired. Rather than put Mutina through any further hardship, he surrendered.

"That was sensible," said Pompey to him after Pompey had entered the city.

"Both sensible and expedient," said Brutus wearily. "I fear, Gnaeus Pompeius, that I am not by nature a martial man."

"That's true."

"I will, however, go to my death with grace."

The beautiful blue eyes opened even wider than usual. "To your death?" asked Pompey blankly. "There is no need for that, Marcus Junius Brutus! You're free to go."

It was Brutus's turn to open his eyes wide. "Free? Do you mean it, Gnaeus Pompeius?"

"Certainly!" said Pompey cheerfully. "However, that does not mean you're free to raise fresh resistance! Just go home."

"Then with your permission, Gnaeus Pompeius, I will proceed to my own lands in western Umbria. My people there need calming."

"That's fine by me! Umbria is my patch too."

But after Brutus had ridden out of Mutina's western gate, Pompey sent for one of his legates, a man named Geminius who was a Picentine of humble status and inferior rank; Pompey disliked subordinates whose station in life was equal to his own.

"I'm surprised you let him go," said Geminius.

"Oh, I had to let him go! My standing with the Senate is not yet so high that I can order the execution of a Junius Brutus without overwhelming evidence. Even if I do have a propraetorian imperium. So it's up to you to find that overwhelming evidence."

"Only tell me what you want, Magnus, and it will be done."

"Brutus says he's going to his own estates in Umbria. Yet he's chosen to head *northwest* on the Via Aemilia! I would have said that was the wrong way, wouldn't you? Well, perhaps he's heading cross-country. Or perhaps he's looking for more troops. I want you to follow him at once with a good detachment of cavalry—five squadrons ought to be enough," said Pompey, picking his teeth with a thin sliver of wood. "I suspect he's looking for more troops, probably in Regium Lepidum. Your job is to arrest him and execute him the moment he seems treasonous. That way there can be no doubt that he's a double traitor, and no one in Rome can object when he dies. Understood, Geminius?"

"Completely."

What Pompey did not explain to Geminius was the ultimate reason for this second chance for Brutus. Kid Butcher was aiming for the command in Spain against Sertorius, and his chances of getting it were much greater if he could find an excuse for not demobilizing. Could he make it appear that Italian Gaul was potentially rebellious right along the length of the Via Aemilia, then he had every excuse for lingering there with his army now that the war was over. He would be far enough away from Rome not to seem to present any threat to the Senate, yet he would still be under arms. Ready to march for Spain.

Geminius did exactly as he was told. When Brutus arrived in the township of Regium Lepidum some distance to the northwest of Mutina, he was welcomed joyfully. As the name of the place indicated, it was populated by clients of the Aemilii Lepidi, and naturally it offered to fight for Brutus if he wished. But before Brutus could answer, Geminius and his five squadrons of cavalry rode in through the open gates. There in the forum of Regium Lepidum, Geminius publicly adjudged Marcus Junius Brutus an enemy of Rome, and cut his head off.

Back went the head to Pompey in Mutina, together with a laconic message from Geminius to the effect that he had surprised Brutus in the act of organizing a fresh insurrection, and that in Geminius's opinion Italian Gaul was unstable.

Off went Pompey's report to the Senate:

> For the time being I consider it my duty to garrison Italian Gaul with my two legions of veterans. The troops Brutus commanded I disbanded as disloyal, though I did not punish them beyond removing their arms and armor. And their two eagles of course. I consider the conduct of Regium Lepidum a symptom of the general unrest north of the border, and hope this explains my decision to stay.
>
> I have not dispatched the head of the traitor Brutus with this record of my deeds because he was at the time of his death a governor with a propraetorian imperium, and I don't think the Senate would want to pin it up on the rostra. Instead, I have sent the ashes of body and head to his widow for proper interment. In this I hope I have not erred. It was no part of my intentions to execute Brutus. He brought that fate upon himself.
>
> May I respectfully request that my own imperium be permitted to stand for the time being? I can perform a useful function here in Italian Gaul by holding the province for the Senate and People of Rome.

The Senate under Philippus's skillful guidance pronounced those men who had taken part in Lepidus's rebellion *sacer,* but because the horrors of the proscriptions still lingered, did not exact any reprisals against their families; the crude pottery jar containing his ashes in her lap, the widow of Marcus Junius Brutus could relax. Her six-year-old son's fortune was safe, though it would be up to her to ensure that he did not suffer political odium when he grew up.

Servilia told the child of his father's death in a way which gave him to understand that he was never to admire or assist his father's murderer, Gnaeus Pompeius Magnus, the Picentine upstart. The boy listened, nodding solemnly. If the news that he now had no father upset him or grieved him, he gave no sign.

He had not yet sprung into speedy growth, but remained a weedy, undersized little boy with spindly legs and a pouting face. Very dark of hair and eye and olive of skin, he had produced a certain juvenile prettiness which his besotted mama saw as permanent beauty, and his tutor spoke highly of his ability to read and write and calculate (what the tutor did not say, however, was that little Brutus entirely lacked an original bent, and imagination). Naturally Servilia had no intention of ever sending Brutus to school with other boys; he was too sensitive, too intelligent, too precious—someone might pick on him!

Only three members of her family had come to pay their condolences to Servilia, though two of those were, strictly speaking, not close relatives. After the last of their various parents, grandparents and others had died, the only surviving person linked to them by blood, Uncle Mamercus, had placed the six orphaned children of his brother and sister in the charge of a Servilius Caepio cousin and her mother. These two women, Gnaea and Porcia Liciniana, now came to call—a courtesy Servilia could well have done without. Gnaea remained the dour and silent subordinate of her overpowering mother; at almost thirty years of age, she was even plainer and flatter of chest than she had been in her late adolescence. Porcia Liciniana dominated the conversation. As she had done all of her life.

"Well, Servilia, I never thought to see you a widow at such an early age, and I'm sorry for you," said this formidable lady. "It always seemed remarkable to me that Sulla spared your husband and his father from the proscription lists, though I assumed that was because of you. It might have been awkward—even for Sulla!—to proscribe the father-in-law of his own son-in-law's niece, but he really ought to have done so. Old Brutus stuck to Gaius Marius and then Carbo like a moth melted into a wax candle. It had to have been his son's marriage to you saved them both. And you would think the son would have learned, wouldn't you? But no! Off he went to serve an idiot like Lepidus! Anyone with any sense could have seen *that* business would never prosper."

"Quite so," said Servilia colorlessly.

"I'm sorry too," said Gnaea gruffly, contributing her mite.

But the glance Servilia bestowed upon this poor creature held neither love nor pity; Servilia despised her, though she did not loathe her as she did the mother.

"What will you do now?" asked Porcia Liciniana.

"Marry again as soon as I can."

"Marry again! That is not fitting for one of your rank. *I* did not remarry after *I* was widowed."

"I imagine no one asked you," said Servilia sweetly.

Thick-skinned though she was, Porcia Liciniana nonetheless felt the sting of the acid in this statement, and rose majestically to her feet. "I've done my duty and paid my condolences," she said. "Come, Gnaea, it's time to go. We mustn't hinder Servilia in her search for a new husband."

"And good riddance to you, you old *verpa!*" said Servilia to herself after they had gone.

Quite as unwelcome as Porcia Liciniana and Gnaea was her third visitor, who arrived shortly afterward. The youngest of the six orphans, Marcus Porcius Cato was Servilia's half brother through their common mother, sister to Drusus and Mamercus.

"My brother Caepio would have come," said young Cato in his harsh and unmelodic voice, "except that he's out of Rome with Catulus's army— a *contubernalis,* if you know that term."

"I know it," said Servilia gently.

But the thickness of Porcia Liciniana's skin was as air compared to Marcus Porcius Cato's, so this sally was ignored. He was now sixteen years old and a man, but he still lived in the care of Gnaea and her mother, as did his full sister, Porcia. Mamercus had sold Drusus's house as too large some time ago; they all occupied Cato's father's house these days.

Though the massive size of his blade-thin eagle's nose would never allow him to be called handsome, Cato was actually a most attractive youth, clear-skinned and wide-shouldered. His large and expressive eyes were a soft grey, his closely cropped hair an off-red that shaded to chestnut, and his mouth quite beautiful. To Servilia, however, he was an absolute monster—loud, slow to learn, insensitive, and so pugnaciously quarrelsome that he had been a thorn in the side of his older siblings from the time he began to walk and talk.

Between them lay ten years of age and different fathers, but more than that; Servilia was a patrician whose family went back to the time of the Kings of Rome, whereas Cato's branch of his family went back to a Celtiberian slave, Salonia, who had been the second wife of Cato the Censor. To Servilia, this slur her mother had brought upon her own and her husband's families was an intolerable one, and she could never set eyes upon any of her three younger siblings without grinding her teeth in rage and shame. For Cato these feelings were undisguised, but for Caepio, supposed to be her own full brother (she knew he was not), what she felt had to be suppressed. For decency's sake. *Rot* decency!

Not that Cato felt any social stigma; he was inordinately proud of his great-grandfather the Censor, and considered his lineage impeccable. As noble Rome had forgiven Cato the Censor this second marriage (founded as it had been in a sly revenge against his snobbish son by his first wife, a Licinia), young Cato could look forward to a career in the Senate and very likely the consulship.

"Uncle Mamercus turned out to have picked you an unsuitable husband," said Cato.

"I deny that," said Servilia in level tones. "He suited me well. He was, after all, a Junius Brutus. Plebeian, perhaps, but absolutely noble on *both* sides."

"Why can you never see that ancestry is far less important than a man's deeds?" demanded Cato.

"It is not less important, but more."

"You're an insufferable snob!"

"I am indeed. I thank the gods for it."

"You'll ruin your son."

"That remains to be seen."

"When he's a bit older I'll take him under *my* wing. That will knock all the social pretensions out of him!"

"Over my dead body."

"How can you stop me? The boy can't stay plastered to your skirts forever! Since he has no father, I stand *in loco parentis.*"

"Not for very long. I shall remarry."

"To remarry is unbecoming for a Roman noblewoman! I would have thought *you* would have set out to emulate Cornelia the Mother of the Gracchi."

"I am too sensible. A Roman noblewoman of patrician stock must have a husband to ensure her pre-eminence. A husband, that is, who is as noble as she is."

He gave vent to a whinnying laugh. "You mean you're going to marry some overbred buffoon like Drusus Nero!"

"It's my sister Lilla who is married to Drusus Nero."

"They dislike each other."

"My heart bleeds for them."

"*I* shall marry Uncle Mamercus's daughter," said Cato smugly.

Servilia stared, snorted. "You will not! Aemilia Lepida was contracted to marry Metellus Scipio years ago, when Uncle Mamercus was with his father, Pius, in Sulla's army. And compared to Metellus Scipio, Cato, you're a complete mushroom!"

"It makes no difference. Aemilia Lepida might be engaged to Metellus Scipio, but she doesn't love him. They fight all the time, and who does she turn to when he makes her unhappy? To me, of course! I shall marry her, be sure of it!"

"Is there nothing under the sun that can puncture your unbelievable complacence?" she demanded.

"If there is, I haven't met it," he said, unruffled.

"Don't worry, it's lying in wait somewhere."

Came another of those loud, neighing laughs. "You hope!"

"I don't hope. *I know.*"

"My sister Porcia is all settled," Cato said, not wanting to change the subject, simply imparting fresh information.

"To an Ahenobarbus, no doubt. Young Lucius?"

"Correct. To young Lucius. I like him! He's a fellow with the right ideas."

"He's almost as big an upstart as you are."

"I'm off," said Cato, and got up.

"Good riddance!" Servilia said again, but this time to its object's face rather than behind his back.

Thus it was that Servilia went to her empty bed that night plunged into a mixture of gloom and determination. So they did not approve of her intention to remarry, did they? So they all considered her finished as a force to be reckoned with, did they?

"They're wrong!" she said aloud, then fell asleep.

In the morning she went to see Uncle Mamercus, with whom she had always got on very well.

"You are the executor of my husband's will," she said. "I want to know what becomes of my dowry."

"It's still yours, Servilia, but you won't need to use it now you're a widow. Marcus Junius Brutus has left you sufficient money in your own right to live comfortably, and his son is now a very wealthy young boy."

"I wasn't thinking of continuing to live alone, Uncle. I want to remarry if you can find me a suitable husband."

Mamercus blinked. "A rapid decision."

"There is no point in delaying."

"You can't marry again for another nine months, Servilia."

"Which gives you plenty of time to find someone for me," said the widow. "He must be at least as wellborn and wealthy as Marcus Junius, but preferably somewhat younger."

"How old are you now?"

"Twenty-seven."

"So you'd like someone about thirty?"

"That would be ideal, Uncle Mamercus."

"Not a fortune-hunter, of course."

She raised her brows. "*Not* a fortune-hunter!"

Mamercus smiled. "All right, Servilia, I'll start making enquiries on your behalf. It ought not to be difficult. Your birth is superlative, your dowry is two hundred talents, and you have proven yourself fertile. Your son will not be a financial burden for any new husband, nor will you. Yes, I think we ought to be able to do quite well for you!"

"By the way, Uncle," she said as she rose to go, "are you aware that young Cato has his eye on your daughter?"

"What?"

"Young Cato has his eye on Aemilia Lepida."

"But she's ready engaged—to Metellus Scipio!"

"So I told Cato, but he seems not to regard this engagement as an impediment. I don't think, mind you, that Aemilia Lepida has any idea in her mind of exchanging Metellus Scipio for Cato. But I would not be doing my duty to you, Uncle, if I failed to inform you what Cato is going around saying."

"They're good friends, it's true," said Mamercus, looking perturbed, "but he's exactly Aemilia Lepida's age! That usually means girls aren't interested."

"I repeat, I don't know that she is interested. All I'm saying is that *Cato* is interested. Nip it in the bud, Uncle—nip it in the bud!"

And that, said Servilia to herself as she emerged into the quiet street on the Palatine where Mamercus and Cornelia Sulla lived, will put *you* in your place, Marcus Porcius Cato! How dare you look as high as Uncle Mamercus's daughter! Patrician on both sides!

Home she went, very pleased with herself. In many ways she was not sorry that life had served this turn of widowhood upon her; though at the time she married him Marcus Junius Brutus had not seemed too old, eight years of marriage had aged him in her eyes, and she had begun to despair of bearing other children. One son was enough, but there could be no denying several girls would contribute much; if well dowered they would find eligible husbands who would prove of use politically to her son. Yes, the death of Brutus had been a shock. But a grief it was not.

Her steward answered the door himself.

"What is it, Ditus?"

"Someone has called to see you, *domina*."

"After all these years, you Greek idiot, you ought to know better than to phrase your announcement that way!" she snapped, enjoying his involuntary shiver of fear. "*Who* has called to see me?"

"He said he was Decimus Junius Silanus, lady."

"He *said* he was Decimus Junius Silanus. Either he is who he says he is, or he is not. Which is it, Epaphroditus?"

"He is Decimus Junius Silanus, lady."

"Did you put him in the study?"

"Yes, lady."

Off she went still wrapped in her black *palla*, frowning as she strove to place a face together with the name Decimus Junius Silanus. The same Famous Family as her late husband, but of the branch cognominated Silanus because the original bearer of that nickname had been, not ugly like the leering Silanus face which spouted water into every one of Rome's drinking and washing fountains, but apparently too handsome. Owning the same reputation as the Memmii, the Junii Silani men continued to be too handsome.

He had called, he said, extending his hand to the widow, to give her his condolences and offer her whatever assistance he might. "It is very difficult for you, I imagine," he ended a little lamely, and blushed.

Certainly from his face he could not be mistaken for any but a Junius Silanus, for he was fair of hair and blue of eye and quite startlingly handsome. Servilia liked blond men who were handsome. She placed her hand in his for exactly the proper length of time, then turned and shed her *palla* upon the back of her late husband's chair, revealing herself clad in more black. The color suited her because her skin was clear and pale, yet her eyes and hair were as jet as her widow's weeds. She also had a sense of style which meant she dressed smartly as well as becomingly, and she looked to the dazzled man as elegantly perfect in the flesh as she had in his memory.

"Do I know you, Decimus Junius?" she asked, gesturing that he sit on the couch, and herself taking up residence on a chair.

"You do, Servilia, but it *was* some years ago. We met at a dinner party in the house of Quintus Lutatius Catulus in the days before Sulla became Dictator. We didn't talk for long, but I do remember that you had recently given birth to a son."

Her face cleared. "Oh, of course! Please forgive me for my rudeness."

She put a hand to her head, looked sad. "It's just that so much has happened to me since then."

"Think nothing of it," he said warmly, then sat without a thing to say, his eyes fixed upon her face.

She coughed delicately. "May I offer you some wine?"

"Thank you, no."

"I see you have not brought your wife with you, Decimus Junius. Is she well?"

"I have no wife."

"Oh!"

Behind her closed and alluringly secretive face, the thoughts were racing. He fancied her! There could be no doubt about it, he fancied her! For some years, it seemed. An honorable man too. Knowing she was married, he had not ventured to increase his acquaintance with her or with her husband. But now that she was a widow he intended to be the first and stave off competition. He was very wellborn, yes—but was he wealthy? The eldest son, since he bore the first name of Decimus: Decimus was the first name of the eldest son in the Junii Silani. He looked to be about thirty, and that was right also. But was he wealthy? Time to fish.

"Are you in the Senate, Decimus Junius?"

"This year, actually. I'm a city quaestor."

Good, good! He had at least a senatorial census. "Where are your lands, Decimus Junius?"

"Oh, all over the place. My chief country estate is in Campania, twenty thousand *iugera* fronting onto the Volturnus between Telesia and Capua. But I have river frontage lands on the Tiber, a very big place on the Gulf of Tarentum, a villa at Cumae and another at Larinum," he said eagerly, keen to impress her.

Servilia leaned back infinitesimally in her chair and exhaled very cautiously. He was rich. Extremely rich.

"How is your little boy?" he asked.

That obsession she could not conceal, it flamed behind her eyes and suffused her face with a passion that sat ill upon her naturally enigmatic features. "He misses his father, but I think he understands."

Decimus Junius Silanus rose to his feet. "It is time I went, Servilia. May I come again?"

Her creamy lids fell over her eyes, the black lashes fanning upon her cheeks. A faint pink came into them, a faint smile turned up the corners of her little folded mouth. "Please do, Decimus Junius. It would please me greatly," she said.

And so much for you, Porcia Liciniana! she said to herself exultantly as she let her visitor personally out of her house. I have found my next husband, though I have not yet been a widow for a month! Wait until I tell Uncle Mamercus!

Said Lucius Marcius Philippus to Gnaeus Pompeius Magnus in a letter written a month after the death of Marcus Junius Brutus:

It is true that we are into the second half of the year, but things are proceeding quite well, all considered. I had hoped to tie Mamercus permanently to Rome, but after word came that Brutus as well as Lepidus was dead, he refused to believe that his role as Princeps Senatus tied him to Rome any longer, and asked the Senate for permission to prepare for the war against Sertorius. Our senatorial goats promptly turned into sheep and gave Mamercus the four legions belonging to Catulus, these still being under arms in Capua waiting for discharge. Catulus, I hasten to add, is well satisfied with his little campaign against Lepidus; he (undeservedly) earned an imposing military reputation without needing to venture further from Rome than the Campus Martius, and urged the Senate to give Mamercus the governance of Nearer Spain and the command against Sertorius.

It is possible that Mamercus might be what Spain needs. Therefore I must ensure that he never gets there. For I must procure for you a special commission in Spain before Lucullus can come back from Africa. Fortunately I think the right tool to foil Mamercus's ambitions has just come into my hand. He—yes, naturally it is a man—is one of this year's crop of twenty quaestors, by name Gaius Aelius Staienus. *And* he was assigned by lot to the army of the consul, no less! In other words he has been in Capua working for Catulus since the beginning of his term, and in future he will be working for Mamercus.

A trustier, bigger villain you are unlikely to meet, my dear Magnus! Quite up there with Gaius Verres—who, having secured the conviction and exile of the younger Dolabella by testifying against him in the prosecution brought by young Scaurus, now struts around Rome engaged to a Caecilia Metella, if you please! The daughter of Metellus Caprarius the Billy-goat, and sister of those three up-and-coming young men who are, alas, the best the Caecilii Metelli have produced in this generation. Quite a comedown.

Anyway, my dear Magnus, I have approached our villain Gaius Aelius Staienus and secured his services. We didn't get around to precise amounts of money, but he won't come cheap. He will, however, do whatever has to be done. Of that I am sure. His idea is to foment a mutiny among the troops as soon as Mamercus has been in Capua long enough for it to appear that Mamercus is the reason for the mutiny. I did venture to say that these were Sulla's veterans and I didn't think they'd turn on their beloved Sulla's son-in-law, but Staienus just laughed at my doubts. My misgivings quite melted away, it was such a hearty and confident laugh. Not to mention that one cannot but expect great things from a man who arranged his own adoption into the Aelii, and tries to have people call him Paetus rather than Staienus! He impresses all sorts of men, but particularly those of low class, who approve of his style of oratory and are easily enflamed by it.

Thus having until I found Staienus opposed the Mamercus command, I have now changed my tune and press for it eagerly. Every time I see the dear fellow I ask him why he's still lingering in Rome instead of taking himself off to Capua to train his troops. I think we can be sure that by September at the latest Mamercus will be the victim of a massive mutiny. And the moment I hear of it, I will start urging the Senate to turn its mind toward the special commission clause.

Luckily things continue to go from bad to worse in the Spains, which will make my task easier. So be patient and sanguine, my dear Magnus, do! It *will* happen, and it will happen early enough in the year for you to cross the Alps before the snows close the passes.

The mutiny when it came a little after the beginning of the month Sextilis was very cleverly engineered by Gaius Aelius Staienus, for it was neither bloody nor bitter, and smacked of such sincerity that its victim, Mamercus, found himself unwilling to discipline the men. A deputation had come to him and announced with absolute firmness that the legions would not go to Spain under any general save Gnaeus Pompeius Magnus because they believed no one except Gnaeus Pompeius Magnus could beat Quintus Sertorius.

"And perhaps," said Mamercus to the House when he came to Rome to report—he was shaken enough to speak honestly—"they are quite right! I confess I do not blame them. They were very properly respectful. Enlisted men of their experience have a nose for such matters, and it is not as if they do not know me. If they think I cannot deal with Quintus Sertorius, then I too must wonder if I can. If they think Gnaeus Pompeius is the only man for the job, then I must wonder if they are not right."

Those quiet and frank words had a profound effect upon the senators, who found themselves—even in their front ranks—bereft of indignation and the inclination to debate. Which made it easy for Philippus to be heard.

"Conscript Fathers," he commenced with love in his voice, "it is high time we took stock of the situation in Spain with no passion and no prejudices. What a sober and uplifting experience it has been for me to listen to our very dear and very intelligent junior consul, our Princeps Senatus, Mamercus Aemilius Lepidus Livianus! Let me therefore continue in that same measured and thoughtful vein."

Round he went in a circle, looking into every face he could manage to see from his position in the front row on the left side.

"The early successes of Quintus Sertorius after he re-entered Spain to join the Lusitani three and a half years ago were fairly easy to understand. Men like Lucius Fufidius held him lightly and offered battle precipitately. But by the time that our Pontifex Maximus, Quintus Caecilius Metellus Pius, arrived to govern Further Spain, and his colleague Marcus Domitius Calvinus arrived to govern Nearer Spain, we knew Quintus Sertorius was going to be hard to beat. And then in that first campaigning summer Sertorius's legate Lucius Hirtuleius attacked Calvinus's six legions *with a mere four thousand men!*—and trounced him. Calvinus died on the field. So did most of his troops. Sertorius himself moved against Pius, though he preferred to concentrate upon Pius's valued legate, Thorius. Thorius died on the field and his three legions were badly mauled. Our beloved Pius was forced to retreat for the winter into Olisippo on the Tagus, with Sertorius on his tail.

"The following year—which was last year—saw no big battles. But no big successes either! Pius spent the time trying to stay out of Sertorius's clutches while Hirtuleius overran central Spain and established Sertorius's ascendancy among the Celtiberian tribes. Sertorius already had the Lusitani in the palm of his hand, and now almost all of Spain bade fair to being his— save for the lands between the Baetis River and the Orospeda Mountains, where Pius concentrated himself too strongly to tempt Sertorius.

"But last year's governor of Gaul-across-the-Alps, Lucius Manlius, thought *he* could deal a blow at Sertorius. So he crossed the Pyrenees into Nearer Spain with four good legions. Hirtuleius met him on the Iberus River and beat him so soundly Lucius Manlius was forced to retreat immediately back into his own province. Where, he soon discovered, he was no longer safe! Hirtuleius followed him and inflicted a second defeat.

"This year has been no better for us, Conscript Fathers. Nearer Spain has not yet received a governor and Further Spain remains with the prorogued Pius, who has not moved west of the Baetis nor north of the Orospeda.

Unopposed, Quintus Sertorius marched through the pass at Consabura into Nearer Spain and has set up a capital at Osca—for he has actually had the audacity to organize his occupation of Rome's territories along Roman lines! He has an official capital city and a senate—even a school in which he intends to have the children of barbarian chieftains taught Latin and Greek so that they will be able to take their places as the leaders of Sertorian Spain! His magistrates bear Roman titles, his senate consists of three hundred men. And now he has been joined by Marcus Perperna Veiento and the forces of Lepidus that managed to escape from Sardinia.''

None of this was new, all of it was well known. But no one had drawn it all together and condensed it into a few moments of crisp, dispassionate speech. The House heaved a collective sigh and huddled down on its stools, defenseless.

"Conscript Fathers, we *have* to send Nearer Spain a governor! We did try, but Lepidus made it impossible for Quintus Lutatius to go, and a mutiny has made it impossible for our Princeps Senatus to go. It is obvious to me that this next governor will have to be a very special man. His duties must be first to make war, and only after that to govern. In fact, almost his sole duty will be to make war! Of the fourteen legions which went with Pius and Calvinus two and a half years ago, it seems perhaps seven are left, and all of these are with Pius in Further Spain. Nearer Spain *is* garrisoned—by Quintus Sertorius. There is no one in the province to oppose him.

"Whoever we send to Nearer Spain will have to bring an army with him—we cannot take troops off Pius. And we have the nucleus of that army sitting in Capua, four good legions mostly composed of Sullan veterans. Who have steadfastly refused to go to Spain under the command of any other man than Gnaeus Pompeius Magnus. Who is not a senator, but a knight.''

Philippus paused for a long time, unmoving, to let this sink in. When he resumed his voice was brisker, more practical.

"So there, my fellow senators, we have one suggestion, courtesy of the Capuan army—Gnaeus Pompeius Magnus. However, the law as Lucius Cornelius Sulla wrote it stipulates that command must go first to someone who is a member of the Senate, who is willing to take the command, and who is militarily qualified to take the command. I intend to discover now if there is such a man in the Senate.''

He turned to the curule podium and looked at the senior consul. "Decimus Junius Brutus, do you want the command?''

"No, Lucius Marcius, I do not. I am too old, too untalented.''

"Mamercus?''

"No, Lucius Marcius, I do not. My army is disaffected.''

"Urban praetor?"

"Even if my magistracy permitted me to leave Rome for more than ten days, I do not," said Gnaeus Aufidius Orestes.

"Foreign praetor?"

"No, Lucius Marcius, I do not," said Marcus Aurelius Cotta.

After which six more praetors declined.

Philippus turned then to the front rows and began to ask the consulars.

"Marcus Tullius Decula?"

"No."

"Quintus Lutatius Catulus?"

"No."

And so it went, one nay after another.

Philippus presumed to ask himself, and answered: "No, I do not! I am too old, too fat—and too militarily inept."

He turned then from one side of the House to the other. "Is there *any* man present who feels himself qualified to take this high command? Gaius Scribonius Curio, what about you?"

Nothing would Curio have liked better than to say yes: but Curio had been bought, and honor dictated his reply. "No."

There was one very young senator in attendance who had to sit on both his hands and bite his itching tongue to remain still and silent, but he managed it because he knew Philippus would never countenance his appointment. Gaius Julius Caesar was not going to draw attention to himself until he stood at least an outside chance of winning.

"So then," said Philippus, "it comes back to the special commission and to Gnaeus Pompeius Magnus. With your own ears you have heard man after man disqualify himself. Now it may be that among those senators and promagistrates at this moment on duty abroad, there is a suitable man. But we cannot afford to wait! The situation must be dealt with now or we will lose the Spains! And it is very clear to me that the only man available and suitable is Gnaeus Pompeius Magnus! A knight rather than a senator. But he has been under arms since his sixteenth year, and since his twentieth year he has led his own legions into battle after battle! Our late lamented Lucius Cornelius Sulla preferred him over all other men. Rightly so! Young Pompeius Magnus has experience, talent, a huge pool of veteran soldiers, and Rome's best interests at heart.

"We own the constitutional means to appoint this young man governor of Nearer Spain with a proconsular imperium, to authorize him to command however many legions we see fit, and to overlook his knight status. However, I would like to request that we do not word his special commission to suggest that we deem him to have already served as consul. *Non pro consule, sed pro consulibus*—not as a consul after his year in office, but rather on behalf of the consuls of the year. That way he is permanently reminded of his special commission.''

Philippus sat down; Decimus Junius Brutus the senior consul stood up. ''Members of this house, I will see a division. Those in favor of granting a special commission with a proconsular imperium and six legions to Gnaeus Pompeius Magnus, knight, stand to my right. Those opposed, stand to my left.''

No one stood to Decimus Brutus's left, even the very young senator Gaius Julius Caesar.

PART SIX

from SEPTEMBER 77 B.C.
until WINTER 72–71 B.C.

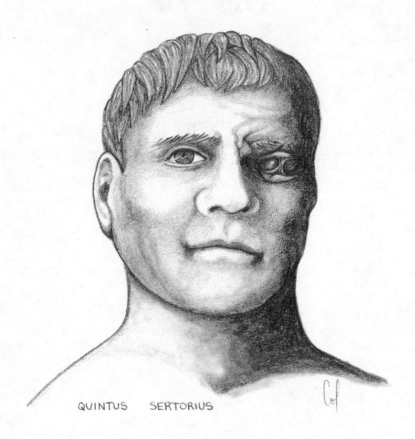

QUINTUS   SERTORIUS

There was no one with whom Pompey could share the news when Philippus's letter arrived in Mutina, and no one when the Senate's decree came through on the Ides of Sextilis. He was still trying to persuade Varro that the expedition to Spain would be as interesting as it was beneficial to an up-and-coming author of natural and man-made phenomena, but Varro's responses to his many missives were lukewarm. Varro's children had arrived at an age he found delightful and he had no wish to absent himself from Rome for what might be a long time.

The new proconsul who had never been consul was very well prepared, and knew exactly how he intended to proceed. First, he wrote to the Senate and informed it that he would take three of the four legions which had belonged to Catulus and then to Mamercus, and three legions made up of his own veterans. However, he said, the kind of war Metellus Pius was waging in Further Spain did not seem to be an attacking one, and the emphasis had shifted from the Further to the Nearer province since Metellus Pius's early days; therefore he requested that the Senate instruct Metellus Pius to give up one of his seven legions to Pompey. That worthy's brother-in-law, Gaius Memmius, was now a tribune of the soldiers with Metellus Pius, but the following year would see him old enough to stand for quaestor; would it be possible that Gaius Memmius be allowed to stand for quaestor *in absentia,* and then join Pompey's staff as quaestor for Nearer Spain?

The Senate's assent (it was now clay in Philippus's hands) came back before Pompey quit Mutina, bolstering his conviction that whatever he wanted would be given to him. Now the father of a son almost two years old and a daughter born earlier in this year, Pompey had left Mucia Tertia at his stronghold in Picenum and issued firm orders that she was not to visit Rome in his absence. He expected a long campaign and could see no virtue in exposing his beautiful and enigmatic wife to temptation.

Though he had already raised a thousand horse-troopers from among his old cavalry units, it was Pompey's intention to add to their number by recruiting in Gaul-across-the-Alps, one good reason why he preferred to go to Spain by the land route. He was also a poor sailor, dreaded the sea, and did not trust it as a way of reaching his new province, though the winter winds favored it.

Every map had been studied, every trader and frequenter of the land route to Spain had been interviewed. The Via Domitia was, however, fraught with difficulties: as Pompey now knew. After Marcus Perperna Veiento had crossed with the remnants of Lepidus's army from Sardinia to Liguria and headed off in the direction of Spain, he had taken great delight in working as much mischief for Rome along the way as he could. The result was that

all the principal tribes of Gaul-across-the-Alps were in revolt—Helvii, Vocontii, Salluvii, Volcae Arecomici.

The worst aspect of tribal unrest in the further Gallic province lay in the
delays Pompey would suffer as he fought his way to Spain through territory
full of hostile and formidably warlike peoples. Of eventual success he had
no doubt, but he desperately wanted to arrive in Nearer Spain before this
coming winter cracked down; if he was to make sure that he and not Metellus
Pius won the war against Sertorius, he could not afford to spend a whole year
getting to Spain, and that seemed a likely prospect given the unrest in Gaul-
across-the-Alps. All the passes through the Alps were in the custody of one
or another of the tribes at present in revolt; the headhunting Salluvii controlled
the lofty ranges of the Alpes Maritimae closest to the sea, the Vocontii
occupied the valley of the Druentia River and the Mons Genava Pass, the
Helvii guarded the middle reaches of the Rhodanus Valley, and the Volcae
Arecomici lay athwart the Via Domitia to Spain below the central massif of
the Cebenna.

It would add laurels to his brow if he suppressed all these barbarian
insurrections, of course—but not laurels of high enough quality. They lay in
the purlieu of Sertorius. Therefore—how to avoid a long and costly transit
of Gaul-across-the-Alps?

The answer had occurred to Pompey before he marched from Mutina in
the first part of September: he would avoid the usual roads by blazing a new
one. The largest of the northern tributaries which fed into the Padus River
was the Duria Major, which came down rushing and roaring from the highest
alps of all, those towering between the bowl of western Italian Gaul and the
lakes and rivers feeding eastern Gallia Comata—Lake Lemanna, the upper
Rhodanus River, and the mighty Rhenus River which divided the lands of
the Gauls from the lands of the Germans. The beautiful cleft carved out of
the mountains by the Duria Major was always known as the Vale of the Salassi
because it was inhabited by a Gallic tribe called the Salassi; when a generation
ago gold had been found in the stream as an alluvium and Roman prospectors
had begun to cull it, the Salassi had so strenuously resisted this Roman
intrusion that no one any longer tried to retrieve the gold much further up
the Vale than the town of Eporedia.

But at the very top of the Vale of the Salassi there were said to be two
passes across the Alpes Penninae. One was a literal goat track which led over
the very highest mountains and down to a settlement of the tribe Veragri
called Octodurum, and then followed the source-stream of the Rhodanus until
it entered the eastern end of Lake Lemanna; because of its ten-thousand-foot
altitude this pass was only open during summer and early autumn, and was

too treacherous to permit the passage of an army. The second pass lay at an altitude of about seven thousand feet and was wide enough to accommodate wagons, though its road was not paved or Roman-surveyed; it led to the northern sources of the Isara River and the lands of the Allobroges, then to the Rhodanus about halfway down its course to the Middle Sea. The German Cimbri had fled through this pass after their defeat by Gaius Marius and Catulus Caesar at Vercellae, though their progress had been slow and most of them had been killed by the Allobroges and the Ambarri further west.

During the first interview Pompey conducted with a group of tamed Salassi he abandoned any thought of the higher pass; but the lower one interested him mightily. A path wide enough for wagons—no matter how rough or perilous it might prove to be—meant that he could traverse it with his legions—and, he hoped, his cavalry. The season was about a month behind the calendar, so he would cross the Alpes Graiae in high summer if he got going by early September, and the chances of snow even at seven thousand feet were minimal. He decided not to cart any baggage by wagon, trusting that he would be able to find his heavier provisions and equipment around Narbo in the far Gallic province, and thus commandeered every mule he could find to serve as a pack animal.

"We're going to move fast, no matter how difficult the terrain," he told his assembled army at dawn on the day he marched. "The less warning the Allobroges have of our advent, the better our chances of not becoming bogged down in a war I'd much rather not fight. Nothing must be allowed to prevent us reaching the Pyrenees before the lowest pass into Spain is closed! Gaul-across-the-Alps morally belongs to the Domitii Ahenobarbi—and as far as I'm concerned, they can keep it! We want to be in Nearer Spain by winter. And be in Nearer Spain by winter we will be!"

The army crossed the lower of the two passes at the top of the Vale of the Salassi at the end of September and encountered surprisingly little opposition from either the route itself or the people who lived along it. When Pompey descended into the Isara valley and the lands of the fierce Allobroges, he caught them so much by surprise that they brandished their spears in the direction of his dust and never succeeded in catching up with him. It was not until he reached the Rhodanus itself that he chanced upon organized opposition. This came from the Helvii, who lived on the great river's western bank and in part of the Cebenna massif behind. But they proved easy meat for Pompey, who defeated several contingents of Helvii warriors sent against him, then demanded and took hostages against future good behavior. The Vocontii and Salluvii courageous enough to venture down onto the Rhodanus plains met the same fate, as did the Volcae Arecomici after Pompey's army

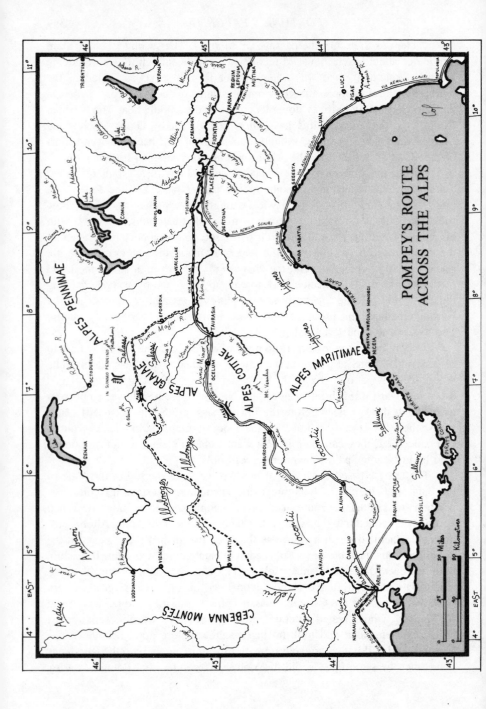

had crossed the causeway through the marshes between Arelate and Nemausus. Past the last danger, Pompey then bundled up his cache of several hundred child hostages and sent them to Massilia for custody.

Before winter he had crossed the Pyrenees and found himself an excellent campsite among the civilized Indigetes around the township of Emporiae. Pompey was into Nearer Spain, but barely. The proconsul who had never been a senator—let alone a consul—sat down to write to the Senate of his adventures since leaving Italian Gaul, with heavy emphasis upon his own courage and daring in blazing a new way across the Alps, and upon the ease with which he had defeated Gallic opposition.

Missing the finishing touches Varro had always applied to his bald and fairly limited prose, Pompey then wrote to the other proconsul, Metellus Pius the Piglet in Further Spain.

I have arrived at Emporiae and gone into winter camp. I intend to spend the winter toughening my troops for next year's campaigns. I believe the Senate has ordered you to give me one of your legions. By now my brother-in-law Gaius Memmius will have been elected quaestor. He is to be my quaestor, and can lead your donated legion to me.

Obviously the best way to defeat Quintus Sertorius is for us to work in concert. That is why the Senate did not appoint one of the two of us senior to the other. We are to be co-commanders and work together.

Now I have spent a great deal of time talking to men who know Spain, and I have devised a grand strategy for us in this coming year. Sertorius does not care to penetrate the Further province east of the Baetis because it is so densely settled and Romanized. There are not enough savages there to make it receptive to Sertorius.

It behooves you, Quintus Caecilius, to look after your Further province and do nothing which might provoke Sertorius to invade your lands east of the Baetis. *I* will eject him from coastal Nearer Spain this year. It will not be an arduous campaign from the point of view of supplies, as this coastal area contains excellent forage growing on good terrain. I will march south in the spring, cross the Iberus River and head for New Carthage, which I ought to reach comfortably by midsummer. Gaius Memmius will take the one legion you owe me and march from the Baetis via Ad Fraxinum and Eliocroca to New Carthage, which of course is still our town. Just isolated from the rest of the Nearer province by Sertorius's forces. After I join up with Gaius Memmius in New Carthage we will return to winter at Emporiae, strengthening the various coastal towns as we go.

The following year I will eject Sertorius from inland Nearer Spain and drive him south and west into the lands of the Lusitani. In the third year, Quintus Caecilius, we will combine our two armies and crush him on the Tagus.

When Metellus Pius received this communication midway through January he retired to his study in the house he occupied in the town of Hispalis, there to peruse it in private. He didn't laugh; its contents were too serious. But smile sourly he did, unaware that Sulla had once got a letter not unlike this one, full of airy information about a country Sulla knew far better than Pompey did. Ye gods, the young butcher was sure of himself! And so patronizing!

Three years had now gone by since Metellus Pius and his eight legions had arrived in Further Spain, three years which had seen Sertorius outgeneral and outthink him. No one had a more profound respect for Quintus Sertorius and his legate Lucius Hirtuleius than did Metellus Pius the Piglet. And no one knew better than he how hard it would be—even for a Pompey—to beat Sertorius and Hirtuleius. As far as he was concerned, the tragedy lay in the fact that Rome had not given him long enough. According to Aesop slow but steady won the race, and Metellus Pius was the embodiment of slow but steady. He had licked his wounds and reorganized his forces to absorb the loss of one legion, then skulked in his province without provoking Sertorius. Very deliberately. For while he waited and assembled the intelligence reports detailing Sertorius's movements, he thought. He did not believe it impossible to beat Sertorius; rather, he believed Sertorius could not be beaten by orthodox military methods. And, he had become convinced, the answer lay at least partly in establishing a more cunning and devious intelligence network—the kind of intelligence network which would make it impossible for Sertorius to anticipate his troop movements. On the surface, a tall order, as the natives were the key to intelligence for both himself and Sertorius. But not an insuperable task! Metellus Pius was working out a way.

Now Pompey had entered upon the Spanish stage, empowered by the Senate (or rather, by Philippus) with an equal imperium, and quite sure his own talents far outshone Sertorius, Hirtuleius and Metellus Pius combined. Well, time would teach Pompey what Metellus Pius knew full well Pompey was not at the moment willing to hear; time and a few defeats. Oh, there could be no doubt that the young man was as brave as a lion—but the Piglet had known Sertorius since his eighteenth year, and knew that Sertorius too was as brave as a lion. What was more important by far, he was Gaius Marius's military heir; he understood the art of war as few in the history of

Rome ever had. However, Metellus Pius had begun to sniff out Sertorius's weakness, and was *almost* sure it lay in his ideas about himself. Could those royal and magical ideas be undermined, Sertorius might unravel.

But Sertorius would not unravel, Metellus Pius decided, because a Gnaeus Pompeius Magnus opposed him on a battlefield.

His son came in, having knocked and been bidden to enter; Metellus Pius was a stickler for the correct etiquette. Known to everyone as Metellus Scipio (though in private his father addressed him as Quintus), the son's full name was majestic: Quintus Caecilius Metellus Pius Cornelianus Scipio Nasica. Now nineteen years old, he had traveled out the year before to join his father's staff as a *contubernalis*, very pleased that—as his own father had done before him—he could serve his military training under his father. The paternal bond was not a close blood tie, for Metellus Pius had adopted the eldest son of his wife Licinia's sister, married to Scipio Nasica. Why the elder Licinia was fertile enough to have produced many children and the younger Licinia barren, the Piglet did not know. These things happened, and when they did a man either divorced his barren wife or—if he loved her, as the Piglet did his Licinia—adopted.

On the whole the Piglet was pleased at the result of this adoption, though he might perhaps have wished that the boy was ever so slightly more intelligent and considerably less naturally arrogant. But the latter could be expected; Scipio Nasica was arrogant. Tall and well built, Metellus Scipio owned a certain haughtiness of expression which had to serve as a substitute for good looks, of which he had none. His eyes were blue-grey and his hair quite light, so he didn't look at all like his adoptive father. And if some of his contemporaries (like young Cato) had been heard to say that Metellus Scipio always walked around as if he had a bad smell under his nose, it was generally agreed that he did have something to turn up his nose about. Since his tenth birthday he had been contracted in betrothal to the daughter of Mamercus and his first wife, a Claudia Pulchra, and though the two young people did a great deal of squabbling, Metellus Scipio was genuinely very attached to Aemilia Lepida, as she was to him.

"A letter from Gnaeus Pompeius Magnus in Emporiae," said Metellus Pius to his son, waving it in the air but showing no inclination to allow his son to read it.

The superior expression on Metellus Scipio's face increased; he sniffed contemptuously. "It is an outrage, Father," he said.

"In one way yes, Quintus my son. However, the contents of his letter have cheered me up considerably. Our brilliant young military prodigy obviously deems Sertorius a military dunce—no equal for himself!"

"Oh, I see." Metellus Scipio sat down. "Pompeius thinks he'll wrap Sertorius up in one short campaign, eh?"

"No, no, my son! Three campaigns," said the Piglet gently.

Sertorius had spent the winter in his new capital of Osca together with his most valued legate, Lucius Hirtuleius, another extremely capable legate, Gaius Herennius, and the relative newcomer, Marcus Perperna Veiento.

When Perperna had first arrived things had not gone well, for Perperna had automatically assumed that his gift of twenty thousand infantry and fifteen hundred cavalry would remain in his own personal command.

But, "I cannot allow that," had Sertorius said.

Perperna had reacted with outrage. "They are *my* men, Quintus Sertorius! It is *my* prerogative to say what happens to them and how they should be used! And *I* say they still belong to me!"

"Why are you trying to emulate Caepio the Consul before the battle of Arausio?" asked Sertorius. "Don't even think of it, Veiento! In Spain there is only one commander-in-chief and one consul—me!"

This had not ended the matter. Perperna maintained to all and sundry that Sertorius did not have the right to refuse him an equal status or take his army off him.

Then Sertorius had aired it before his senate. "Marcus Perperna Veiento wishes to make war against the Roman presence in Spain as a separate entity and with a rank equal to mine," he said. "He will not take orders from me or follow my strategies. I ask you, Conscript Fathers, to inform this man that he must subordinate himself to me or leave Spain."

Sertorius's senate was happy so to inform Perperna, but still Perperna had refused to accept defeat. Sure that right and custom were on his side, he appealed to his army in assembly. And was told by his men in no uncertain terms that Sertorius was in the right of it. They would serve Quintus Sertorius, not Perperna.

So Perperna had finally subsided. It had seemed to everyone (including Sertorius) that he gave in with good grace and held no grudges. But underneath his placid exterior Perperna smouldered still, keeping the coals of his outrage from dying out. As far as he was concerned, in Roman terms he ranked exactly with Quintus Sertorius: both of them had been praetors, neither consul.

Unaware that Perperna still boiled, Sertorius proceeded that winter Pompey had arrived in Spain to draw up his plans for the coming year's campaign.

"I don't know Pompeius at all," said the commander-in-chief without undue concern. "However, after looking at his career, I don't think he'll be hard to beat. Had I deemed Carbo capable of winning against Sulla, I would have remained in Italy. He had some good men in Carrinas, Censorinus and Brutus Damasippus, but by the time he himself deserted—which is really when we might have seen what Pompeius was made of—he left an utterly demoralized command and soldiery behind. Even if one goes back to Pompeius's earliest battles it becomes obvious that he has never faced a truly able general or an army with an indestructable spirit.''

"All that will change!" said Hirtuleius, grinning.

"It certainly will. What do they call him? Kid Butcher? Well, I don't think I'll glorify him to that extent—I'll just call him a kid. He's cocksure and conscienceless, and he has no respect for Roman institutions. If he did, he wouldn't be here with an imperium equal to the old woman's in Further Spain. He manipulated the Senate into giving him this command when he has absolutely no right to it, no matter what special clauses Sulla might have incorporated into his laws. So it's up to me to show him his proper place. Which is not nearly as high as he thinks.''

"What will he do, any idea?" asked Herennius.

"Oh, the logical thing," said Sertorius cheerfully. "He'll march down the east coast to take it off us.''

"What about the old woman?" asked Perperna, who had adopted Sertorius's name for Metellus Pius with glee.

"Well, he hasn't exactly shone so far, has he? Just in case Pompeius's advent has emboldened him, however, we'll pin him down in his province. I'll mass the Lusitani on his western borders. That will oblige him to leave the Baetis and take up residence on the Anas, an extra hundred miles on the march from the coast of Nearer Spain if he's tempted to aid Pompeius. I don't think he will be tempted, mind you. The old woman is unadventurous and cautious. And why would he strain at the bit to help a kid who has managed to prise identical imperium out of the Senate? The old woman is a stickler, Perperna. He'll do his duty to Rome no matter who has been given identical imperium. But he won't do one iota more. With the Lusitani swarming on the far side of the Anas, he'll see his first duty as containing them.''

The meeting broke up and Sertorius went to feed his white fawn. This creature, magical enough by virtue of its rare color, had assumed enormous importance in the eyes of his native Spanish followers, who regarded it as evidence of Sertorius's divinely bestowed magical powers. He had not lost his knack with wild animals over the years, and by the time he arrived in Spain the second time he was well aware of the profound effect his ability to snap his fingers and call up wild creatures to him had on the native peoples. The white fawn, apparently motherless, had come to him two years ago out of the mountains in central Spain, tiny and demure; dazzled by its beauty,

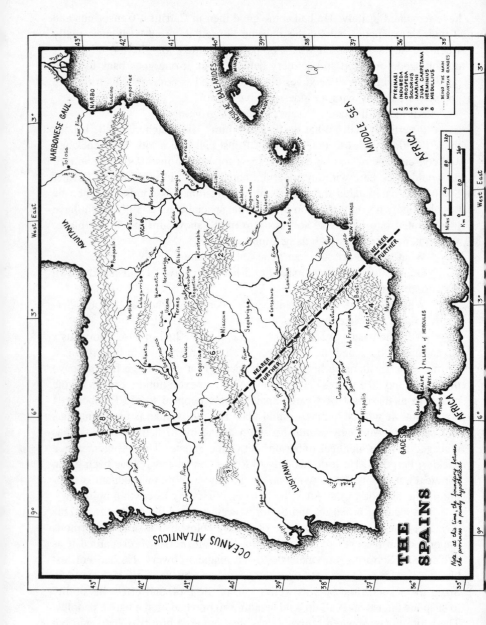

THE SPAINS

Note: at this time, the boundary between the provinces is purely hypothetical.

he had gone down on his knees to it without pausing to think what he was doing, only concerned to put his arms around it and comfort it. But his Spaniards had murmured in awe and looked at him quite differently from that day forward. For the white fawn, they were convinced, was no one less than a personification of their chief goddess, Diana, who was showing Sertorius her special favor and raising him above all other men. And he had known who the white fawn was! For he had gone down on his knees in humble worship.

The white fawn had been with him ever since, followed him about like a dog. No other man or woman would it permit to go near it; only Sertorius. And—more magical still!—it had never grown, remained a dainty ruby-eyed mite which frisked and cavorted around Sertorius begging to be hugged and kissed, and slept on a sheepskin at the side of his bed. Even when he campaigned it was with him. During battles he tied it to a post in some safe place, for if he left it free it would always try to reach him in the fray, and he could not afford the risk of its dying; did it die, his Spaniards would deem him deserted by the goddess.

In truth he had begun to think himself that the white fawn was a sign of divine blessing, and believed in it more and more; he called it, of course, Diana, and referred to himself when he spoke to it as Daddy.

"Daddy's here, Diana!" he called.

And Diana came to him eagerly, asking to be kissed. He knelt down to its level and put his arms about its shivering form, put his lips to the soft sleekness of its head, one hand pulling on its ear in rhythmic caresses it loved. He always excluded it from his house when he conferred with his legates, and it would mope, sure it had in some inexplicable way offended Daddy. The frenzy of guilt and contrition with which it greeted him afterward had to be dealt with in extra hugs and many murmured words of love; only then would it eat. Perhaps understandably, he thought more of Diana than he did of his German wife and his half-German son—there was nothing god-given about them. Only his mother did he love more than he did Diana, and her he had not seen in seven years.

The white fawn nosing contentedly at its rich dried grasses (for winter in Osca meant snow and ice, not grazing), Sertorius sat down on a boulder outside his back door and tried to insert himself inside Pompey's mind. A kid! Did Rome truly believe that a kid from Picenum could defeat *him*? By the time he rose he had concluded that Rome and the Senate had been tricked by the shell game Philippus performed so well. For of course Sertorius maintained contact with certain people inside Rome—and they were neither humble nor obscure. Beneath Sulla's blanket many malcontents moved invisibly, and some of them had made it their business to keep Sertorius informed. Since the appointment of Pompey the tenor of these communications had changed a little; a few important men were beginning to hint that if Quintus Sertorius could defeat the new champion of the Senate, Rome might be glad to welcome him home as the Dictator.

But he had thought of something else too, and privately summoned Lucius Hirtuleius to see him.

"We'll make absolutely sure the old woman stays in Further Spain," he said to Hirtuleius, "for it may be that the Lusitani won't be discouragement enough. I want you and your brother to take the Spanish army to Laminium in the spring and station yourselves there. Then if the old woman does decide to try to help the kid, you'll contain him. Whether he attempts to break out of his province via the headwaters of the Anas or the Baetis, you'll be in his way."

The Spanish army was just that, forty thousand Lusitanian and Celtiberian tribesmen whom Sertorius and Hirtuleius had painfully but successfully trained to fight like Roman legions. Sertorius had other Spanish forces which he had retained in their native guise, superb at ambush and guerrilla warfare; but he had known from the beginning that if he was to beat Rome in Spain, he must also have properly trained Roman legions at his disposal. Many men of Roman or Italian nationality had drifted to enlist under him since Carbo's final defeat, but not enough. Thus had Sertorius generated his Spanish army.

"Can you do without us against Pompeius?" asked Hirtuleius.

"Easily, with Perperna's men."

"Then don't worry about the old woman. My brother and I will make sure he stays in Further Spain."

"Now remember," said Metellus Pius to Gaius Memmius as that worthy prepared to march for New Carthage, "that your troops are more precious than your own skin. If things should take a turn for the worse—that is, if Pompeius should not do as well as he thinks he will—get your men into shelter strong enough to keep them safe from attack. You're a good reliable fellow, Memmius, and I'm sorry to lose you. But don't forget your men."

Handsome face solemn, Pompey's new quaestor who happened to be his brother-in-law as well led his single legion eastward across country commonly held to be the richest and most fertile on earth—richer than Campania, richer than Egypt, richer than Asia Province. With exactly the right summer and winter climates, lavish water from rivers fed by perpetual snow and deep alluvial soils, Further Spain was a breadbasket, green in spring and early summer, golden at the bountiful harvest. Its beasts were fat and productive, its waters teemed with fish.

With Gaius Memmius there journeyed two men who were neither Roman nor Spanish; an uncle and nephew of almost the same age, both named Kinahu Hadasht Byblos. By blood they were Phoenician and by nationality citizens of the great city port of Gades, which had been founded as a Phoenician colony nearly a thousand years before and still kept its Punic roots and customs very much in the foreground of Gadetanian life. The rule of the Carthaginians had not been difficult to accept, as the Carthaginians were also of Punic stock. Then had come the Romans, who proved to suit the people of Gades too; Gades prospered, and gradually the noble Gadetani had come to understand that the destiny of their city was inextricably bound to Rome's. Any civilized people of the Middle Sea was preferable to domination by the barbarian tribesmen of eastern and central Spain, and the chief fear of the Gadetani remained that Rome would eventually deem Spain not worth the keeping, would withdraw. It was for that reason that the uncle and nephew named Kinahu Hadasht Byblos traveled with Gaius Memmius and his single legion to make themselves useful in any way they could. Memmius had gladly handed them the responsibility for procuring supplies, and used them also as interpreters and sources of information. Because he could not comfortably pronounce their Punic name, and because they spoke Latin (quite well, both of them!) with a lisp emerging from their own lisping language, Pompey's new quaestor had nicknamed them Balbus, which indicated a speech impediment; though he couldn't work out why, Memmius had learned that they were enormously pleased to be dowered with a Latin cognomen.

"Gnaeus Pompeius has instructed me to proceed through Ad Fraxinum and Eliocroca," said Memmius to the elder Balbus. "Is that really the way we ought to go?"

"I think so, Gaius Memmius," said the foreign-looking Balbus, whose hooked nose and high cheekbones proclaimed his Semitic blood, as did his very large dark eyes. "It means we'll follow the Baetis almost all the way to its western sources, then cross the Orospeda Mountains where they are narrowest. It is a watershed, but if we march from Ad Fraxinum to Basti we can pick up a road leading across the watershed to Eliocroca on the far side. From Eliocroca we descend rapidly onto the Campus Spartarius. That is what the Romans call the plains of the Contestani around New Carthage. There are no advantages to going any other way."

"How much opposition are we likely to encounter?"

"None until we cross the Orospeda. Beyond that, who knows?"

"Are the Contestani for us or against us?"

Balbus shrugged in a very foreign way. "Can one be sure of any Spanish tribe? The Contestani have always dwelt in proximity to civilized men, which ought to count for something. But one must call Sertorius a civilized man too, and all the Spanish admire him very much."

"Then we shall see what we shall see," said Memmius, and worried no more about it; first reach Eliocroca.

Until Gaius Marius had opened up the mines in the ranges between the Baetis and the Anas (called the Marian Mountains after him), the Orospeda Mountains had been the chief source of lead and silver exploited by Rome. As a result the southern part of the ranges was thin of forest, and that included Memmius's line of march. Altogether he had a distance of three hundred miles to negotiate, two hundred less than Pompey, but because the terrain was more difficult Memmius had started out somewhat earlier than Pompey, in mid-March. At the end of April, not having hurried at all, he came down from the Orospeda to the little town of Eliocroca on a southern branch of the Tader River; the Campus Spartarius stretched before him.

Having been in Spain too long to trust any native people, Memmius tightened his ranks up and marched defensively toward New Carthage, some thirty miles away to the southwest. Wisely, as he soon discovered. Not far down the good mining road from Eliocroca he found the Contestani lying in wait for him, and promised an offering to Jupiter Optimus Maximus of a bull calf if he kept his legion intact until he could reach safety. Safety obviously was New Carthage itself; Gaius Memmius wasted no time thinking about remaining anywhere outside its island peninsula.

They were a very long twenty-five miles, but the two hundred Gallic cavalry he had with him he sent ahead to guard the approach to the bridge between the mainland and the city, deeming his plight hopeless only if the Contestani cut him off at that one narrowest point. He had started at a brisk pace from Eliocroca at dawn, encountered the massed tribesmen five miles further on, then fought his way crablike with his cohorts in square on the road, the men forming its sides within the moving column spelling the men on its exposed sides. Foot soldiers themselves and unused to pitched battle, the Contestani could not break his formation. When he reached the bridge he found it uncontested and passed across to safety, his legion intact.

The elder Balbus he sent to Gades aboard a dowdy ship which reeked of *garum*, the malodorous fish paste so prized by every cook in the world; the letter Balbus carried to Metellus Pius was a whiffy one, but no less important for that. It explained the situation, asked for help, and warned Metellus Pius that New Carthage could not last out until winter unless it got food. The younger Balbus he sent on a more perilous mission, to penetrate the boiling tribes north of New Carthage and try to reach Pompey.

Pompey left the vicinity of Emporiae fairly early in April, his local advisers having informed him that the volume of the Iberus would be low enough by the end of April to allow him to ford it comfortably.

He had satisfactorily solved the problem of his legates by commissioning none but Picentines or Italians and investing as his two senior legates Lucius Afranius and Marcus Petreius, both *viri militares* from Picenum who had been under Pompeian eagles for some years. Caesar's messmate from Mitylene, Aulus Gabinius, came from a Picentine family; Gaius Cornelius was not one of the patrician Cornelii, nor was Decimus Laelius related to the Laelii who had risen into prominence under Scipio Africanus and Scipio Aemilianus. Militarily all had proven themselves or showed promise, but socially none of them save perhaps Aulus Gabinius (whose father and uncle were senators) could hope to advance in Rome without large rations of Pompey's patronage.

Things went very well. Advancing rapidly down the coast, Pompey and his six legions and his fifteen hundred cavalrymen actually reached Dertosa on the north bank of the Iberus before encountering any opposition at all. As Pompey began to ford the Iberus some two legions commanded by Herennius attempted to thwart him, but were easily beaten off; Pompey's chest swelled and he proceeded south in optimistic mood. Not far down the road Herennius reappeared, this time reinforced by two legions under Perperna, but when the soldiers in their vanguard began to fall, they drew off southward in a hurry.

Pompey's scouts were excellent. As he moved steadily further from the Iberus they brought him word that Herennius and Perperna had gone to earth in the big enemy town of Valentia, almost a hundred miles to the south of Pompey's position. As Valentia lay on the Turis River and the wide alluvial plains of the Turis were rich and intensively farmed, Pompey increased his speed. When he reached Saguntum—near the mouth of a small, short river which lay in the midst of fairly poor country—he learned from his trusty scouts that Sertorius himself was completely out of range, could not possibly assist Herennius and Perperna to hold Valentia. Apparently afraid that Metellus Pius was going to invade northern Spain from the headwaters of the Tagus, Sertorius had positioned his own army on the upper reaches of the Salo at Segontia, where he would be able to intercept the Piglet as he emerged from the narrow bridge of mountains which separated the Tagus from the Iberus. Crafty, thought Pompey smugly, but you really ought to be within hailing distance of Herennius and Perperna, Sertorius!

It was now the middle of May, and Pompey was learning how cruelly hot the long summer of the Spanish lowlands could be. He was also learning how much water his men could drink in one short day, and how quickly they could devour his food supplies. With the harvest still several months off, foraging for grain had yielded little from the granaries of what towns he had passed through once he left the Iberus. This coast—which had looked so rich on his maps and sounded so rich when his advisers spoke of it—was no Italy; if he had always thought of the Adriatic coast as poor and underpopulated, it was fairer and denser by far than the littoral of eastern Spain.

Protesting itself loyal to Rome, Saguntum was unable to give him grain. Pirates had raided its storage silos, the people of the town would eat sparingly until their crops came in. Thus Valentia and the plains of the Turis beckoned; Pompey struck camp and marched.

If the sight of the formidable crags inland gave even a remote promise of how tortuous and difficult it would be for any army to march through central Spain, then Sertorius, sitting in Segontia in early May, could not hope to relieve Valentia before the end of June—and that, his scouts assured Pompey, only if Sertorius learned to fly! Unable to credit that any general could lead men faster than he could, Pompey believed his scouts, who may have been genuinely of that opinion—or who more likely were secretly working for Sertorius. Be that as it may, not one day south of Saguntum, Pompey learned that Sertorius and his army were already between him and Valentia— and busy attacking the loyal Roman town of Lauro!

What Pompey could not have been brought to understand was that Sertorius knew every kink, every valley, every pass and every track between the Middle Sea and the mountains of western Spain—and that he could move through them at seemingly incredible speed because each village and hamlet he encountered would if asked give him all its food, would push him onward with a love which amounted to adulation. No Celtiberian or Lusitanian welcomed the Roman presence in Spain; every Celtiberian and Lusitanian realized that Rome was in Spain only to exploit the country's riches. That this bright white hope, Sertorius, was himself a Roman the native Spanish peoples saw as a special gift from their gods. For who knew how to fight the Romans better than a Roman?

When the scouts reported back that Sertorius led but two small legions, Pompey gasped. The cheek of it! The gall of it! To lay siege to a Roman town not far from six crack Roman legions and fifteen hundred horse—! It beggared description! Off went Pompey to Lauro in a fever of anticipation, exultant because Fortune had given him Sertorius as his adversary so early in the war.

A cool dispassionate look at Lauro and Sertorius's lines from atop a vantage point to the north of the little plain was more than enough to reinforce Pompey's confidence. A mile to the east of Lauro's walls lay the sea, while to the west there reared a high but flat-topped hill. To one looking down on the situation from Pompey's superior height, the hill to the west was the ideal base from which to conduct operations. Yet Sertorius had quite ignored it! Mind made up, Pompey hustled his army west of the city walls intent upon occupying the hill, and sure that the hill was already his. Riding upon his big white bedizened Public Horse, the twenty-nine-year-old general led his troops and cavalry himself—and at the double—striding out in front so that those who were massed atop Lauro's walls would be sure to see him in person.

Though he was looking at the hill all the way to its foot, Pompey had actually arrived there before he saw its flat top bristling with spears. And suddenly the air was rent by boos, jeers, catcalls: Sertorius and his men were shouting down to Pompey that he'd have to be speedier than that if he wanted to take a hill from Quintus Sertorius!

"Did you think I wouldn't realize you'd make for it, kid?" came one lone voice from the top. "You're too slow! Think you're as clever as Africanus and as brave as Horatius Cocles, don't you, kid? Well, Quintus Sertorius says you're an amateur! You don't know what real soldiering is! But stay in the vicinity, kid, and let a professional show you!"

Not foolish enough to attempt to storm Sertorius in such an impregnable position, Pompey had no other choice than to retreat. Eyes straight ahead, aware that his face was burning, he wheeled his horse and ploughed straight through the ranks of his own men and did not stop until he stood once more upon his original vantage point. By now the sun was past its zenith, but the day was long enough to fit one more maneuver into the hours left, and pride dictated that Pompey should fit it in.

Chest heaving as he fought to discipline his emotions, he surveyed the scene again. Below him his own army stood at ease, gulping the last of the water from shrinking, wrinkled skins athwart each water donkey, and all too obviously talking to each other as they exposed their steaming heads to the drying rays of the sun and leaned upon their spears or shields. Talking about their lovely young general and his humiliation, wondering if this was going to be the first campaign their lovely young general couldn't win. Wishing they had made their wills, no doubt.

He hadn't wanted Afranius or Petreius with him, couldn't even bear the thought of the younger ones, especially Aulus Gabinius. But now he beckoned to Afranius and Petreius to ride up to him, and when they had ranged themselves one on either side of his Public Horse, he pointed with a stick at the scene in the distance. Not one word did his senior legates say, just waited dumbly to be told what Pompey wanted to do next.

"See where Sertorius is?" Pompey asked, but rhetorically only; he didn't expect a reply. "He's busy along the walls, I think sapping them. His camp is right there. He's come down from his hill, I see! He doesn't really want it, he's interested in taking the town. But I won't fall for that trick again!" This was said through clenched teeth. "The distance we have to march before we engage him is about a mile, and the length of his line is about half that—he's spread awfully thin, which is to our advantage. If he's to stand any chance at all he'll have to tighten up when he sees us coming—and we have to presume that he thinks he stands a chance, or he wouldn't be there. He can scatter either west or east, or in both directions at once. I imagine he'll go both ways—I would." That popped out; Pompey reddened, but went on smoothly. "We'll advance on him with our wings projecting ahead of our center, cavalry distributed equally between them on their tips, infantry—one legion to each wing—forming the densest part of the wings closest to the center, where I'll put my other four legions. When an army is approaching across flat ground it's hard to tell how far ahead of the center the wings are, and we'll extend them further forward the closer we get. If he holds me light—and he seems to hold me light!—he won't believe me capable of military guile. Until my wings enfold him on both sides and prevent his escaping to either the west or the east. We'll roll him up against the walls, which leaves him nowhere to go."

Afranius ventured a remark. "It will work," he said.

Petreius nodded. "It will work," he said.

That was all the confirmation Pompey needed. At the foot of his vantage point he had the buglers blow "form ranks and fall into line," and left Afranius and Petreius to issue his orders to the other legates and the leading centurions. Himself he busied in summoning six mounted heralds.

Thus it was that by the time Afranius and Petreius returned to him it was too late and too public to dissuade him from what he had done; appalled, Afranius and Petreius watched the heralds ride away, hoping desperately that for Pompey's sake Pompey's new maneuver worked.

While the army moved out, the heralds under a flag of truce rode right up to the outer defenses of Sertorius's camp. There they brayed their message to the inhabitants of Lauro standing on top of Lauro's walls.

"Come out, all you people of Lauro!" they bellowed. "Come out! Line your battlements and watch while Gnaeus Pompeius Magnus teaches this renegade wolfshead who calls himself a Roman what being a true Roman is!

Come out and watch Gnaeus Pompeius Magnus inflict absolute defeat upon
Quintus Sertorius!''

It was going to work! thought Pompey, smarting enough to ride once
again in the forefront of his army. His wings extended further and further
forward as the legions advanced, and still Sertorius made no move to order
his men to flee east and west. They would be enclosed! Sertorius and all his
soldiers would die, die, *die*! Oh, Sertorius would learn in the most painful
and final way what it was like to anger Gnaeus Pompeius Magnus!

The six thousand men Sertorius had held in reserve completely hidden
from Pompey's scouts as well as from Pompey's high vantage point had fallen
on Pompey's unprotected rear and were tearing it into pieces before Pompey
in the vanguard even knew. When he was apprised of it, there was nothing
he could do to avert disaster. His wings were now so far forward that he was
powerless to reverse their thrust, and they had turned inward, were busy
engaging Sertorius's men under Lauro's walls—their battlements now black
with observers of the debacle, thanks to Pompey's heralds. When attempt
after attempt to wheel failed, the most Pompey and his legates could do was
to struggle frantically to form the four legions of the center into square. To
make matters worse, squadrons of Sertorian cavalry were riding into view
from behind Lauro and falling upon Pompey's horse from the rear of his wing
tips. Disaster piled upon disaster.

But they were good men and ably served by good centurions, those
veteran Roman legions Pompey led; they fought back bravely, though their
mouths gaped from lack of water and a terrible dismay had filled their hearts
because someone had outgeneraled their lovely young man, and they hadn't
thought there was anyone alive could do that. So Pompey and his legates
managed in the end to form their square, and somehow even to pitch a camp.

At dusk Sertorius drew off, left them to finish the camp amid mountainous
heaps of dead. And amid jeers and boos which now came not only from
Sertorius's soldiers, but also from the citizens of Lauro. Pompey couldn't
even escape to weep in private, found himself too mortified to throw his
scarlet general's cape over his head and weep beneath its cover. Instead he
forced himself to move here and there with smiles and encouraging words,
cheering the parched men up, trying to think where he might find water,
unable to think how he might extricate himself from shame.

In the first light of dawn he sent to Sertorius and asked for time to dispose
of his dead. His request was granted with sufficient generosity to enable him
to shift his camp clear of the reeking field, and to a site well provided with
potable water. But then a black depression descended upon him and he left

it to his legates to count and bury the dead in deep pits and trenches; there
was no timber nearby for burning, no oil either. As they toiled he withdrew
to his command tent while his uninjured men—terribly, terribly few—constructed a stout camp around him to keep Sertorius at bay after the armistice
was ended. Not until sunset, the battle now a day into the past, did Afranius
venture to seek an audience. He came alone.

"It will be the *nundinae* before we're finished with the burial details,"
said the senior legate in a matter-of-fact voice.

The general spoke, equally matter-of-fact. "How many dead are there,
Afranius?"

"Ten thousand foot, seven hundred horse."

"Wounded?"

"Five thousand fairly seriously, almost everybody else with cuts or
bruises or scratches. Those troopers who lived are all right, but they're short
of mounts. Sertorius preferred to kill their horses."

"That means I'm down to four legions of foot—one legion of which is
seriously wounded—and eight hundred troopers who cannot all be provided
with horses."

"Yes."

"He whipped me like a cur."

Afranius said nothing, only looked at the leather wall of the tent with
expressionless eyes.

"He's Gaius Marius's cousin, isn't he?"

"That's right."

"I suppose that accounts for it."

"I suppose it does."

Nothing more was said for quite a long time. Pompey broke the silence.
"How can I explain this to the Senate?" It came out half whisper, half
whimper.

Afranius transferred his gaze from the tent wall to his commander's face,
and saw a man a hundred years old. His heart smote him, for he genuinely
did love Pompey, as friend and overlord. Yet what alarmed him more than
his natural grief for friend and overlord was his sudden conviction that if
Pompey was not shored up, not given back his confidence and his inborn
arrogance, the rest of him would waste away and die. This grey-faced old
man was someone Afranius had never met.

So Afranius said, "If I were you, I'd blame it on Metellus Pius. Say he
refused to come out of his province to reinforce you. I'd triple the number
of men in Sertorius's army too."

Pompey reared back in horror. "No, Afranius! No! I could not possibly do that!"

"Why?" asked Afranius, amazed; a Gnaeus Pompeius Magnus in the throes of moral or ethical dilemmas was an utter unknown.

"Because," said Pompey in a patient voice, "I am going to need Metellus Pius if I am to salvage *anything* out of this Spanish commission. I have lost nearly a third of my forces, and I cannot ask the Senate for more until I can claim at least one victory. Also because it is possible someone who lives in Lauro will escape to Rome. His story will have credence when he tells it. And because, though I am not a sage, I do believe that truth will out at exactly the worst moment."

"Oh, I understand!" cried Afranius, enormously relieved; Pompey was not experiencing moral or ethical scruples, he was just seeing the facts as the facts were. "Then you already know what you have to explain to the Senate," he added, puzzled.

"Yes, yes, I *know!*" snapped Pompey, goaded. "I simply don't know *how* to explain it! In words, I mean! Varro isn't here, and who else is there with the right words?"

"I think," said Afranius delicately, "that your own words are probably the right words for news like this. The connoisseurs of literature in the Senate will just assume that you've chosen a plain style for the plain truth—that's how their minds work, if you ask me. As for the rest of them—they're not connoisseurs, so they won't see anything wrong with your words anyway."

This splendidly logical and pragmatic analysis went far toward cheering Pompey up, superficially at least. The deeper and more cruelly lacerated layers, incorporating as they did pride, *dignitas,* confidence, and many complicated images of self, would be slow to mend; some layers would mend maimed, some layers would perhaps not mend at all.

Thus Pompey sat down to begin his report to the Senate with his nostrils assailed by the perpetual stench of rotting flesh, and did not spare himself even by omitting his rashness in sending heralds to cry to the citizens of Lauro, let alone his mistaken tactics on the battlefield itself. He then sent the draft, written with a stylus upon wax smeared and gouged by many erasures, to his secretary, who would copy it in fair script (with no spelling or grammatical errors) in ink upon paper. Not that he finished the missive; Lauro wasn't finished.

Sixteen days went by. Sertorius continued his investment of Lauro while Pompey did not move out of his camp. That this inertia could not last Pompey was well aware; he was rapidly running out of food, and his mules and horses were growing thinner almost as one looked at them. Yet he couldn't retreat—not with Lauro under siege and Sertorius doing exactly as he liked. He had no choice but to forage. Upon pain of threatened torture his scouts swore to him that the fields to the north were entirely free of Sertorian patrols, so he ordered a large and well-armed expedition of cavalry to forage in the direction of Saguntum.

The men had not been gone for two hours when a frantic message for help came: Sertorius's men were swarming everywhere, picking off the troopers one by one. Pompey sent a full legion to the rescue, then spent the next hours pacing up and down the ramparts of his camp looking anxiously northward.

Sertorius's heralds gave him the verdict at sunset.

"Go home, kid! Go back to Picenum, kid! You're fighting real men now! You're an amateur! How does it feel to run up against a professional? Want to know where your foraging party is, kid? Dead, kid! Every last one of them! But you needn't worry about burying them this time, kid! Quintus Sertorius will bury them for you, free of charge! He's got their arms and armor in payment for the service, kid! Go home! Go home!"

It had to be a nightmare. It could not truly be happening! Where had the Sertorian forces come from when none of those who had fought on the battlefield, even the hidden cavalry, had moved from the siegeworks before Lauro?

"These were not his legionaries or his regular cavalry, Gnaeus Pompeius," said the chief scout, shivering in dread. "These were his guerrillas. They come out of nowhere, they ambush, they kill, they vanish again."

Thoroughly disenchanted with his Spanish scouts, Pompey had all of them executed and vowed that in future he would use his own Picentines as scouts; better to use men he trusted who didn't know the countryside than men he couldn't trust even if they did know the countryside. That was the first lesson of warfare in Spain he had really absorbed, though it was not to be the last. For he was *not* going home to Picenum! He was going to stay in Spain and have it out with Sertorius if he died in the effort! He would fight fire with fire, stone with stone, ice with ice. No matter how many blunders he made, no matter how many times that brilliant personification of anti-Roman evil might run tactical rings around him, he would not give up. Sixteen thousand of his soldiers were dead and almost all his cavalry. But he would not give up until the last man and the last horse were dead.

The Gnaeus Pompeius Magnus who retreated slowly from Lauro at the end of Sextilis with the screams of the dying city echoing in his ears was a very different one from the man who had strutted south in the spring so full of his own importance, so confident, so *careless*. The new Gnaeus Pompeius could even listen with a look of alert interest on his face to the stentorian voices of the Sertorian heralds who dogged his footsteps detailing to his soldiers the hideous fate in store for the women of Lauro when they reached their new owners in far-western Lusitania. No other Sertorian personnel even bothered about his footsteps as he hastened north past Saguntum, past Sebelaci, past Intibili, across the Iberus. In less than thirty days Pompey brought his exhausted, half-starved men into their winter camp at Emporiae, and moved no more that awful year. Especially after he heard that Metellus Pius had won the only battle he had been called upon to fight—and won it brilliantly.

It was after Metellus Pius had seen Balbus Senior and read Memmius's letter that he began to think about how he might extricate Memmius from his incarceration in New Carthage. There had been changes in the man Sertorius dismissed as an old woman too, changes wrought by the crushing blow to his pride the Senate had dealt him in bestowing an equal imperium upon Kid Butcher, of all people. Perhaps nothing less than this monumental insult could have stripped away sufficient layers of the Piglet's defensive armor to allow the metal inside to show, for the Piglet had been cursed—or blessed—with an autocratic father of superb courage, incredible haughtiness and a stubbornness that had sometimes amounted to intellectual imbecility. Metellus Numidicus had been cheated of his war against Jugurtha by Gaius Marius, cheated time and time again—or so he had seen it—by that same New Man. And in turn cheated his son of anything more than a reputation for filial devotion in piously striving to have his hugely admired father recalled from an exile inflicted by Gaius Marius. Then just when the son might have congratulated himself that he stood highest in Sulla's estimation, along came the twenty-two-year-old Pompey with a bigger and better army to offer.

His punctilious attention to what was the proper thing for a Roman nobleman to do forbade Metellus Pius the satisfaction of trying to make his tormentor, Pompey, look insignificant by any underhanded means. And so without his realizing it a new and better general was busy jerking and tugging himself free of the Piglet's tired old stammering skin. To make Pompey look small by winning more battles more decisively was unimpeachable, a fitting revenge because it emerged out of what a Roman nobleman could be when he was pushed to it by a Picentine upstart. Or an upstart from Arpinum, for that matter!

Having learned that particular lesson very early on, he chose his scouts from among the ranks of his own Roman men and the men of Phoenician

Gades who feared the Spanish barbarians far more than they did the Romans. So it was that Metellus Pius had learned the whereabouts of Lucius Hirtuleius and his younger brother not very long after they had sat themselves down with the Spanish army in the neighborhood of Laminium, in south-central Spain. With one of his new sour smiles, the Piglet leaned back and appreciated this strategy to the full before flicking a mental obscene gesture in the direction of Laminium and vowing that ten years would not see him fool enough to venture up the headwaters of either Anas or Baetis. Let Hirtuleius rot from sheer inactivity!

He had ensconced himself on the Anas fairly close to its mouth, thinking that it was wiser to let the Lusitani see how well prepared he was to deal with them than to reside more comfortably along the Baetis, a hundred miles to the east. But he had busied himself to such purpose by June that he felt the defenses of his province were in good enough state to resist the wall of waiting Lusitani without his personal presence on the Anas—and without more than two of his six remaining legions to garrison his fortifications.

By now the old woman of the Further province knew perfectly well who were Sertorius's informants; so he proceeded to put his new policies about intelligence into practice, and leaked in the most innocent way to these men the news that he was moving away from his position on the lower Anas. Not up the headwaters of the Anas or the Baetis—and thus into the arms of Lucius Hirtuleius at Laminium—but to relieve Gaius Memmius in New Carthage. He would (the informants were telling Hirtuleius not many days later) cross the Baetis from Italica to Hispalis, then move up the Singilis River toward the massif of the Solorius, cross it on its northwestern flank at Acci, proceed thence to Basti, and so down onto the Campus Spartarius through Eliocroca.

In actual fact this was the way Metellus Pius might have gone; but what was important to him was that Hirtuleius should believe it. The Piglet was well aware that Herennius, Perperna and Sertorius himself were thoroughly absorbed in teaching Pompey a much-needed lesson, and that Sertorius reposed full confidence in the ability of Hirtuleius and the Spanish army to pen the Piglet up inside his own provincial sty. But New Carthage was a way out of his own provincial sty that could possibly lead to a northward march from New Carthage to relieve Pompey at Lauro; the five legions the Piglet would have were a possible tipping of the balance from Sertorius's way to Pompey's. The march of Metellus Pius could therefore not be allowed to happen.

What Metellus Pius hoped was that Hirtuleius would decide to leave Laminium and come down onto the easy terrain between the Anas and the Baetis. Away from the crags in which any Sertorian general was likely to be victorious, Hirtuleius would be easier to beat. No Sertorian general trusted the peoples of the Further province east of the Baetis, which was why Sertorius had never attempted to invade that area. So when Hirtuleius heard the news of Metellus Pius's projected march, he would have to intercept it before Metellus Pius could cross the Baetis into safe territory. Of course Hirtuleius's most prudent course would have been to travel well to the north of the Further province and wait to intercept Metellus Pius on the Campus Spartarius itself, this certainly being country friendly to Sertorius. But Hirtuleius was too canny to make this logical move; if he left central Spain for a place so far away, all the Piglet had to do was to double back and romp through the pass at Laminium, then choose the quickest line of march to join Pompey at Lauro.

There was only one thing Hirtuleius could do: move down onto the easy terrain between the Anas and the Baetis, and stop Metellus Pius before he crossed the Baetis. But Metellus Pius marched more quickly than Hirtuleius thought he could, was already close to Italica and the Baetis when Hirtuleius and the Spanish army were still a hard day's slog away. So Hirtuleius hurried, unwilling to let his prey slip across the broad deep river.

The month was Quinctilis and southern Spain was in the grip of that summer's first fierce heat wave; the sun sprang up from behind the Solorius Mountains fully armed to smite lands not yet recovered from the previous day's onslaught—and only slightly relieved by the breathless, humid night. With extraordinary solicitude for his troops, Metellus Pius gently inserted them into big, airy, shady tents, encouraged them to hold cloths soaked in cold spring water to brows and napes of necks, made sure they had drunk well of that same cold spring water, then issued each man with a novel item of extra equipment to carry into battle—a skin full of cold water strapped to his belt.

Even when the merciless sun was glinting off the forest of Hirtuleius's spears rapidly approaching down the road from the north, Metellus Pius kept his men in the shade of their tents and made sure there were enough tubs of cold water to keep the cold compresses coming. At the very last moment he moved, his soldiers fresh and keen, chattering cheerfully to each other as they marched into position about how they would manage to help each other snatch a much-needed drink in the middle of the fight.

The Spanish army had tramped ten hard miles in the sun already. Though it was well provided with water donkeys, it had not the time to pause and drink before battle was joined. His men wilting, Hirtuleius stood no chance of winning. At one time he and Metellus Pius actually fought hand-to-hand— a rare occurrence in any conflict since the days of Homer—and though Hirtuleius was younger and stronger, his well-watered and well-cooled opponent got the better of him. The struggle carried them apart before the contest came to an end, but Hirtuleius bore a wound in his thigh and Metellus Pius the glory. Within an hour it was over. The Spanish army broke and fled into the west, leaving many dead or exhausted upon the field; Hirtuleius had to cross the Anas into Lusitania before he could allow his men to stop.

"Isn't that *nice*?" asked Metellus Pius of his son as they stood surveying the diminishing dust to the west of Italica.

"*Tata,* you were wonderful!" cried the young man, forgetting that he was too grown up to use the diminutive of childhood.

The Piglet swelled, huffed. "And now we'll all have a good swim in the river and a good night's sleep before we march tomorrow for Gades," he said happily, composing letters in his mind to the Senate and to Pompey.

Metellus Scipio stared. "Gades? Why Gades?"

"Certainly Gades!" Metellus Pius shoved his son between the shoulder blades. "Come on, lad, into the shade! I'll have no man down with sunstroke, I need every last one of you. Don't you fancy a long sea voyage to escape this heat?"

"A long sea voyage? To where?"

"To New Carthage, of course, to relieve Gaius Memmius."

"Father, you are absolutely beyond a doubt *brilliant*!"

And that, reflected the Piglet as he drew his son into the shade of the command tent, was every bit as thrilling to hear as the rousing volley of cheers and the shouts of "Imperator!" with which his army had greeted him after the battle was over. He had done it! He had inflicted a decisive defeat upon Quintus Sertorius's best general.

The fleet which put out from Gades was a very big one, and formidably guarded by every warship the governor could commandeer. The transports were loaded with wheat, oil, salt fish, dried meat, chickpea, wine, even salt— all intended to make sure New Carthage did not starve because of the Contestani blockade from land and the pirate blockade from sea.

And having revictualed New Carthage, Metellus Pius loaded Gaius Memmius's legion aboard the empty transports, then sailed at a leisurely pace up the eastern coast of Nearer Spain, amused to see the pirate craft his fleet encountered scuttle out of the way. The pirates may have defeated Gaius Cotta in a fleet-to-fleet engagement several years before in these same waters, but they had little appetite for salt Piglet.

The Piglet was going, of course—exemplary Roman nobleman that he was—to deliver Gaius Memmius and the legion to Pompey in Emporiae: and if he was also going to crow a little and to be just a trifle too sympathetic about Pompey's ignominious summer in the field, well . . . The Piglet considered Pompey owed him that for trying to steal his thunder.

Just after the fleet passed the great pirate stronghold of Dianium it put in to a deserted cove to anchor for the night; a small boat came stealing out of Dianium and made for the Roman ships. In it was the younger Balbus, full of news.

"Oh, how good it is to be back among friends!" he said in his soft, lisping Latin to Metellus Pius, Metellus Scipio and Gaius Memmius (not to mention his uncle, very pleased to see him safe and well).

"I take it that you didn't manage to make contact with my colleague Gnaeus Pompeius," said Metellus Pius.

"No, Quintus Caecilius. I got no further than Dianium. The whole coast from the mouth of the Sucro to the Tader is just boiling with Sertorius's men, and I look too much like a man of Gades—I would have been captured and tortured for sure. In Dianium there are many Punic-looking fellows, however, so I thought it wiser to lie low there and hear whatever I could hear."

"And what did you hear, Balbus Minor?"

"Oh, I not only heard! I also *saw*! Something extremely interesting," said Balbus the nephew, eyes shining. "Not two market intervals ago a fleet sailed in. It had come all the way from Pontus, and it belonged to King Mithridates."

The Romans tensed, leaned forward.

"Go on," said Metellus Pius softly.

"On board the flagship were two envoys from the King, both Roman deserters—I think they had been legates commanding some of Fimbria's troops. Lucius Magius and Lucius Fannius."

"I've seen their names," said Metellus Pius, "on Sulla's proscription lists."

"They had come to offer Quintus Sertorius—he arrived in person to confer with them four days after they sailed in—three thousand talents of gold and forty big warships."

"What was the price?" growled Gaius Memmius.

"That when Quintus Sertorius becomes the Dictator of Rome, he confirms Mithridates in all the possessions he already has and allows him to expand his kingdom further."

"*When Sertorius is Dictator of Rome?*" gasped Metellus Scipio, staggered. "That will never happen!"

"Be quiet, my son! Let the good Balbus Minor continue," said his father, who kept his own outrage concealed.

"Quintus Sertorius agreed to the King's terms, with one proviso—that Asia Province and Cilicia remain Rome's."

"How did Magius and Fannius take that?"

"Very well, according to my source. I suppose they expected it, as Rome is not to lose any of her provinces. They consented on the King's behalf, though they said the King would have to hear from them in person before confirming it formally."

"Is the Pontic fleet still in Dianium?"

"No, Quintus Caecilius. It stayed only nine days, then it sailed away again."

"Did any gold or ships change hands?"

"Not yet. In the spring. However, Quintus Sertorius did send the King evidence of his good faith."

"In what form?"

"He presented the King with a full century of crack Spanish guerrilla troops under the command of Marcus Marius, a young man he esteems highly."

The Piglet frowned. "Marcus *Marius*? Who is he?"

"An illegitimate son of Gaius Marius got on a woman of the Baeturi when he was governor *propraetore* of the Further province forty-eight years ago."

"Then this Marcus Marius is not so young," said Gaius Memmius.

"True. I am sorry, I misled you." Balbus looked abject.

"Ye gods, man, it's not a prosecutable offense!" said the Piglet, amused. "Go on, go on!"

"Marcus Marius has never left Spain. Though he speaks good Latin and was properly educated—Gaius Marius knew of him, and had left him well provided for—his inclinations are toward the Spanish barbarian cause. He has been, as a matter of fact, Quintus Sertorius's most successful guerrilla commander—he specializes in the guerrilla attack."

"So Sertorius has sent him off to teach Mithridates how to ambush and raid," said Metellus Scipio. "Thank you, Sertorius!"

"And will the money and ships be delivered to Dianium?" asked Metellus Pius.

"Yes. In the spring, as I have said."

This amazing piece of news provided food for thought and for Metellus Pius's pen all the way to Emporiae. Somehow he had never considered that Sertorius's ambitions extended further than setting himself up as a Romanized King of All Spain; his cause had seemed absolutely inseparable from the native Spanish cause.

"But," he said to Pompey when he reached Emporiae, "I think it's high time we looked at Quintus Sertorius more closely. The conquest of Spain is only his first step. Unless you and I can stop him, he's going to arrive on Rome's doorstep with his nice white diadem all ready to tie round his head. King of Rome! And ally of Mithridates and Tigranes."

After all that purring anticipation, it had not proven possible for Metellus Pius to twist his own thin knife in Pompey's glaringly obvious wounds. He had taken one look at the erstwhile Kid Butcher's empty face and empty eyes and understood that instead of reminding him of his shortcomings, he would have to subject him to extensive spiritual and mental repairs. Numidicus the father would have said that his own honor demanded that the knife be twisted anyway, but Pius the son had lived too long in his father's shadow to have quite such a rarefied idea of his honor.

With the object of effecting extensive repairs to Pompey's shattered image of himself, the Piglet craftily sent his tactless and haughty son off into Narbonese Gaul with Aulus Gabinius, there to recruit cavalry and horses; he had a talk to Gaius Memmius to enlist him as an ally, and sent Afranius and Petreius to start reorganizing Pompey's skeletal army. For some days he kept conversation and thoughts away from the last season's campaigns, glad that the news from Dianium had given conversation and thoughts such a dynamic fresh turn.

Finally, with December almost upon him and a pressing need to return to his own province, the old woman from Further Spain got down to business.

"I do not think it necessary to dwell upon events already in the past," he said crisply. "What ought to concern both of us is next year's campaigns."

Pompey had always liked Metellus Pius well enough, though he now found himself wishing his colleague had rubbed him raw, crowed and exulted; he might then have been able to dismiss his opinions as worthless and healthily hated his person. As it was, the genuine kindness and consideration only drove his own inadequacy home harder. Clearly the Piglet did not deem him important enough to despise. He was just another junior military tribune who had come a cropper on his first lone mission, had to be picked up, dusted off, and set astride his horse again.

However, at least this attitude meant they could sit together amicably. In pre-Sertorian times Pompey would have taken over what was obviously going to be a war conference; but the post-Sertorian Pompey simply sat and waited for Metellus Pius to produce a plan.

"This time," said the Piglet, "we will both march for the Sucro and Sertorius. Neither of us has a big enough army to do the job unassisted. However, I can't move through Laminium because Hirtuleius and the Spanish army will be back there lying in wait for me. So I will have to go by a very devious route indeed, and with as much stealth as possible. Not that word of my coming won't reach Sertorius, and therefore Hirtuleius. But Hirtuleius will have to move from Laminium to contain me, and he won't do that until Sertorius orders him to. Sertorius is a complete autocrat in all matters military.''

"So what way can you go?" asked Pompey.

"Oh, far to the west, through Lusitania," said the Piglet cheerfully. "I shall fetch up eventually at Segovia."

"Segovia! But that's at the end of the earth!"

"True. It will throw sand in Sertorius's eyes beautifully, however, as well as avoiding Hirtuleius. Sertorius will think I am about to move into the upper Iberus and try to take it off him while he's busy dealing with you. He'll send Hirtuleius to stop me because Hirtuleius at Laminium will be more than a hundred miles closer to Segovia than he."

"What do you want me to do, precisely?" asked this new and much humbler Pompey.

"Stay in camp here in Emporiae until May. It will take me two months to reach Segovia, so I'll be moving long before you. When you do march, proceed with extreme caution. The most vital part of the whole strategy is that you look as if you're moving with purpose and completely independently of me. But that you do not reach the Turis and Valentia until the end of June.''

"Won't Sertorius try to stop me at Saguntum or Lauro?"

"I doubt it. He doesn't work the same territory twice. You are now in a position to know Saguntum and Lauro well."

Pompey turned dull red in the face, but said nothing.

The Piglet went on as if he noticed no change in Pompey's complexion. "No, he'll let you reach the Turis and Valentia this time. They will be new to you, you see. Herennius and the traitor Perperna are still occupying Valentia, but I don't think they'll stay to let you besiege them—Sertorius doesn't like making his stand in coastal cities, he prefers his mountain strongholds— they are impossible to take."

Metellus Pius paused to study Pompey's face, faded back to its new pinched whiteness, and was profoundly thankful to see that his eyes were interested. Good! He was taking it in.

"From Segovia I will march for the Sucro, where I expect Sertorius will maneuver you into battle."

Frowning, Pompey turned this over in his mind, which, the Piglet now realized, was still functioning well; it was just that Pompey no longer possessed the confidence to make his own plans. Well, a couple of victories and that would come back! Pompey's nature was formed, couldn't be unformed. Just battered.

"But a march from Segovia to the Sucro will take you right down the middle of the driest country in Spain!" Pompey protested. "It's an absolute desert! And until you reach the Sucro itself you'll be crossing ridge after ridge instead of following valley floors. An awful march!"

"That's why I shall make it," said Metellus Pius. "No one has ever chosen the route voluntarily before, and Sertorius will certainly not expect *me* to do so. What I hope is to reach the Sucro before his scouts sniff my presence." His brown eyes surveyed Pompey with pleasure. "You've studied your maps and reports intensively, Pompeius, to know the lay of the land so well."

"I have, Quintus Caecilius. It can't substitute for actual experience, but it's the best one can do until the experience is accumulated," said Pompey, pleased at this praise.

"You're already accumulating experience, don't worry about that!" said Metellus Pius heartily.

"Negative experience," muttered Pompey.

"No experience is negative, Gnaeus Pompeius, provided it leads to eventual success."

Pompey sighed, shrugged. "I suppose so." He looked down at his hands. "Where do you want me when you reach the Sucro? And when do you think that will be?"

"Sertorius himself won't move north from the Sucro to the Turis," said Metellus Pius firmly. "Herennius and Perperna may try to contain you at Valentia or on the Turis somewhere, but I think their orders will be to fall back to Sertorius on the Sucro. I shall aim to be in Sertorius's vicinity at the end of Quinctilis. That means that if you reach the Turis by the end of June, you must find a good excuse to linger there for one month. Whatever happens, don't keep marching south to find Sertorius himself until the end of Quinctilis! If you do, I won't be there to reinforce you. Sertorius's aim is to remove you and your legions from the war completely—that would leave him with vastly superior numbers to deal with me. I would go down."

"Last year saw you come up, Quintus Caecilius."

"That might have been a freak occurrence, and I hope that is what Sertorius will call it. Rest assured that if I meet Hirtuleius and am victorious again, I will endeavor to conceal my success from Sertorius until I can join my forces to yours."

"In Spain, difficult, I'm told. Sertorius hears everything."

"So they maintain. But I too have been in Spain for some years now, and Sertorius's advantages are melting away. Be of good cheer, Gnaeus Pompeius! We *will* win!"

To say that Pompey was in a better frame of mind after the old woman from the Further province left to take his fleet back to Gades was perhaps a slight exaggeration, but there certainly had been a stiffening in his spine. He removed himself from his quarters to join Afranius, Petreius and the more junior legates in putting the finishing touches to his restructured army. As well, he thought, that he had insisted on taking one of the Piglet's legions away from him! Without it, he could not have campaigned. The exact number of his soldiers offered him two alternatives: five under-strength legions, or four normal strength. Since he was far from being a military dunce, Pompey elected five under-strength legions because five were more maneuverable than four. It came hard to look his surviving troops in the eye—this being the first time he had really done so since his defeat—but to his gratified surprise, he learned that none of them held the deaths of so many of their comrades against him. Instead they seemed to have settled into a dour determination that Sertorius would not prosper, and were as willing as always to do whatever their lovely young general wanted.

As the winter in the lowlands was a mild and unusually dry one, Pompey welded his new units together by leading them up the Iberus a little way and reducing several of Sertorius's towns—Biscargis and Celsa fell with satisfying thumps. At this point, it being the end of March, Pompey withdrew again to Emporiae and began to prepare for his expedition down the coast.

A letter from Metellus Pius informed him that after taking delivery of his forty warships and three thousand talents of gold in Dianium, Sertorius himself had departed into Lusitania with Perperna to help Hirtuleius train more men to fill the reduced ranks of the Spanish army, leaving Herennius in charge of Osca.

Pompey's own intelligence network had markedly improved, thanks to the efforts of uncle and nephew Balbus (now in his service), and his Picentine scouts were faring better than he had expected.

Not until after the beginning of May did he move, and then he proceeded with extreme caution. A man of the land himself, he noted automatically as he crossed the Iberus at Dertosa that this rich and extensively farmed valley looked very dry for the time of year, and that the wheat coming up in the fields was sparser than it ought to be, was not yet eared.

Of the enemy there was no sign, but that fact did not fill Pompey with pleasure on this second march into the south. It merely made him more

cautious still, his column defensive. Past Saguntum and Lauro he hurried
with averted face; Saguntum stood, but Lauro was a blackened ruin devoid
of life. At the end of June, having sent a message he hoped would reach
Metellus Pius in Segovia, he reached the wider and more fertile valley of the
Turis River, on the far bank of which stood the big, well-fortified city of
Valentia.

Here, drawn up on the narrow flats between the river and the city, Pompey
found Herennius and Perperna waiting for him. In number, his Picentine
scouts informed him, they were stronger than he, but had the same five legions;
some thirty thousand men to Pompey's twenty thousand. Their greatest advantage was in cavalry, which his scouts estimated at a thousand Gallic horse.
Though Metellus Scipio and Aulus Gabinius had tried strenuously to recruit
cavalry in Narbonese Gaul during the early winter, Pompey's troopers numbered only four hundred.

At least he could be sure that what his Picentine scouts told him was
reliable, and when they assured him that there was little difference between
scouting in Italy and scouting in Spain, he believed them. So, secure in the
knowledge that no Sertorian cohorts lurked behind him ready to outflank him
or fall upon his rear, Pompey committed his army to the crossing of the Turis.
And to battle on its southern bank.

The river was more a declivity than a steep-sided trench, thus presented
no obstacle even when battle was joined; its bed was rock-hard, its waters
ankle deep. There was no particular tactical advantage to be seized by either
side, so what developed was a conventional clash which the army with better
spirit and strength would win. The only innovation Pompey used had arisen
out of his deficiency in cavalry; correctly assuming that Perperna and Herennius would use their superiority in horse to roll up his flanks, Pompey had
put troops bearing old-fashioned phalanx spears on the outside of his wings
and ordered these men to use the fearsome fifteen-foot-long weapons against
mounts rather than riders.

The struggle was hotly contested and very drawn out. By no means as
gifted a general as either Sertorius or Hirtuleius, Herennius did not see until
it was too late that he was getting the worst of it; Perperna, to his west, was
ignoring his every order. The two men had, in fact, not been able before the
battle began to agree upon how it should be conducted; they ended in fighting
as two separate entities, though this Pompey could not discern, only learned
of later.

The end of it was a heavy defeat for Herennius, but not for Perperna.
Deciding that it was better to die if Sertorius insisted he must continue the
war in tandem with this treacherous, odious man Perperna, Herennius threw

his life away on the field, and the heart went out of the three legions and the cavalry directly under his command. Twelve thousand men died, leaving Perperna and eighteen thousand survivors to retreat to Sertorius on the Sucro.

Mindful of Metellus Pius's warning that he must not reach the Sucro until the end of Quinctilis, Pompey did not attempt to pursue Perperna. The victory, so decisive and complete, had done his wounded self the world of good. How wonderful it was to hear his veterans cheering him again! And to wreath the eagles and the standards in well-earned laurels!

Valentia of course was now virtually defenseless, only its walls between the inhabitants and Roman vengeance. So Pompey sat down before it and subjected it to a merciless inspection which revealed more than enough weaknesses to suit his purpose. A few mines—a fire along a section made of wood—finding and cutting off the water supply—and Valentia surrendered. With some of his newly learned caution, Pompey removed every morsel of food from the city and hid the lot in an abandoned quarry beneath a carpet of turf; he then sent the entire citizenry of Valentia to the slave market in New Carthage—by ship, as the Roman fleet of Further Spain just happened (thanks to the foresight of a certain Roman Piglet) to be cruising in those waters, and no one had seen a sign of the forty Pontic triremes Sertorius now possessed. And six days before the end of Quinctilis did Pompey march for the Sucro, where he found Sertorius and Perperna enclosed in two separate camps on the plain between him and the river itself.

Pompey now had to contend with a distressing dilemma. Of Metellus Pius he had heard nothing, and could not therefore assume that reinforcements were nearby. Like the situation on the Turis, the lay of the land bestowed no tactical advantage upon Sertorius; no hills, big forests, handy groves or ravines lay in even remote proximity, which meant that Sertorius had nowhere to hide cavalry or guerrillas. The closest town was little Saetabis five miles to the south of the river, which was wider than the Turis and notorious for quicksands.

If he delayed battle until Metellus Pius joined him—always provided that Metellus Pius was coming—then Sertorius might retreat to more suitably Sertorian country—or divine that Pompey was stalling in the expectation of reinforcements. On the other hand, if he engaged Sertorius he was grossly outnumbered, almost forty thousand against twenty thousand. Neither side now had many horse, thanks to Herennius's losses.

In the end it was fear Metellus Pius would not come that decided Pompey to commit himself to battle—or so he told himself, refusing to admit that his old greedy self was whispering inside his head that if he did fight now, he wouldn't have to share the laurels with a Piglet. The clash with Herennius and Perperna was only a prelude to this engagement with Sertorius, and Pompey burned to expunge the memory of Sertorius's taunts. Yes, his confidence had returned! So at dawn on the second-last day of Quinctilis, having constructed a formidable camp in his rear, Gnaeus Pompeius Magnus marched his five legions and four hundred horse onto the plain opposite Sertorius and Perperna, and deployed them for battle.

On the Kalends of April, Quintus Caecilius Metellus Pius the Piglet had left his comfortable quarters outside Italica on the western bank of the Baetis and headed for the Anas River. With him went all six of his legions—a total of thirty-five thousand men—and a thousand Numidian light horse. Since the aristocratic fluid coursing through his veins was undiluted by any good farming blood, he failed to notice as he went that the cultivated lands he traversed did not look as verdant, nor the sprouting crops as lush, as in other years. He had abundant grain in his supply column, and all the other foodstuffs necessary to vary the diet of his men and maintain their good health.

There was no waiting wall of Lusitani on the Anas when he reached it some hundred and fifty miles from its mouth; that pleased him, for it meant no word had come to them of his whereabouts, that they still waited for him by the sea. Though big settlements were nonexistent this far upstream, there were small hamlets, and the soil of the river valley was being tilled. Word of his arrival would certainly go downstream to the massed tribesmen; but by the time they got here, he intended to be far away from the Anas. They could pursue him, but they would not catch him!

The Roman snake wound on through the rolling uplands at a good pace, heading now for the Tagus at Turmuli. Occasional skirmishes of a purely local nature did happen, but were swished away like flies from a horse's rump. As Segovia was his penultimate destination, the Piglet did not attempt to follow the Tagus further upstream but continued to march cross-country instead, somewhere to the north of northwest.

The road he was following throughout was nothing more than a primitive wagon trail, but in the manner of such things it took the line of least resistance across this western plateau; its altitude varied only in the hundreds of feet, and never got above two thousand five hundred. As the region was unknown to him, the Piglet gazed about in fascination, exhorting his team of cartographers and geographers to chart and describe everything minutely. Of people there were few; any the Romans chanced upon were immediately killed.

Onward they pressed through beautiful mixed forests of oak, beech, elm and birch, sheltered from the increasing heat of the sun. The victory against Hirtuleius last year had put marvelous heart into the men, and had also endowed their general with a new attitude toward their comfort. Resolved that they must not suffer any more than possible—and aware too that he was well on time—the old woman of the Further province made sure the pace he set did not tire his soldiers to the point whereat a good meal and a good night's rest had not the power to restore them.

The Roman column passed between two much higher ranges and emerged into the lands which ran down to the Durius, the least well known to the Romans of all Spain's major rivers. Ahead of him had he continued on the same course was big and prosperous Salamantica, but Metellus Pius now turned to the northeast and hugged the slopes of the mountains on his right, unwilling to provoke the tribe of Vettones whose gold workings had caused the great Hannibal to sack Salamantica one hundred and forty-five years before. And on the Kalends of June, Quintus Caecilius Metellus Pius brought his army to a halt outside Segovia.

Hirtuleius had beaten him to Segovia nonetheless—not very surprising. Laminium lay only two hundred miles away, whereas Metellus Pius had needed to cover a distance of six hundred miles. Presumably someone at Turmuli on the Tagus had sent a message to Sertorius that the Romans were passing through—but not up the Tagus. Sertorius had (as the old woman of the Further province had surmised) assumed that the Roman objective was the upper Iberus, a ploy to lure Sertorius away from the east coast and Pompey, or else a genuine attempt to strike at Sertorius's loyalest heartlands. Hirtuleius had been ordered to intercept the old woman before he could reach Sertorius's heartlands. Of one thing Metellus Pius was sure: they had not guessed whereabouts he was *really* going. To have guessed that, Sertorius would have had to hold a much higher opinion of the old woman's ability—and subtlety!—than he did.

The first thing was to get the army into a very strongly fortified camp. As prudent as always, Metellus Pius made his men dig and build clad in their armor—an extra burden no legionary welcomed—but, as their centurions told them, Hirtuleius was in the neighborhood. They worked in a frenzy, burrowing and raising mounds like a vast colony of insects. The wagons, oxen, mules and horses had been brought in while the red flags were being planted and the surveying was still going on, then were left under the care of a skeleton crew because noncombatants were also being pressed into service. Thirty-five thousand men labored with such logic and organization that the camp was finished in one day, though each side measured one mile in length, the timber-reinforced ramparts were twenty-five feet high, there were towers every two hundred paces, and the ditch in front of the walls was twenty feet deep. Only when the four gates made of solid logs were slammed shut and the sentries posted did the general heave a sigh of relief; his army was safe from attack.

The day had not passed without incident, however. Lucius Hirtuleius had found the idea of the old woman from the Further province cozily ensconced behind trenches, walls and palisades too much to stomach, so he had launched a cavalry sortie from his own camp aimed at forcing the old woman to break off his construction. But Metellus Pius had not been in Spain for three and a half years for nothing; he was learning to think like his enemy. Deliberately paring away six hundred Numidian light horse from his column many miles before he reached Segovia, he instructed them to follow on with great stealth, then position themselves where a potential attacker could not see them. No sooner was the sortie under way than out they came from under the nearby trees and chased Hirtuleius back to his own camp.

For the full eight days of a *nundinum* nothing further happened. The men had to rest, to feel as if no enemy forces would dare to disturb their tranquillity, to sleep the nights away and spend the long hours of sunlight in a mixture of exercise and recreation. From where his command tent stood at the junction of the *via praetoria* and the *via principalis* (it occupied a knoll within the flat expanse of the camp so the general could see over the tops of its buildings to all four walls), the general walked the length of both main streets, dived off into the alleyways lined by oiled cowhide tents or slab huts, and everywhere talked to his men, explained to them carefully what he was going to do next, let them see that he was superbly confident.

He was not a warm man, nor one who felt comfortable when dealing with his subordinates or inferiors, yet nor was he so cold that he could render himself proof against overt affection. Ever since the battle on the Baetis when he had cared for his soldiers so scrupulously, they had looked at him differently; shyly at first, then more and more openly. And they looked at him with love, and told him how grateful they were to him for giving them the chance of that victory with his care, his forethought. Nor did it make any difference to them that his motives for this care had been entirely practical, founded not in love for them but in the desire to beat Hirtuleius. They knew better. He had fussed and clucked like the old woman Sertorius called him so derisively; he had betrayed a personal interest in their well-being.

Since then they had sailed with him from Gades to Emporiae and back again, and they had marched six hundred miles through unknown country riddled with barbarians; and always he had kept them safe. So by the time that Quintus Caecilius Metellus Pius walked the streets and alleys of his camp at Segovia, he had thawed in the glow of this extraordinary affection, and understood that time, his own mind and a properly Roman attitude to detail had dowered him with an army he would weep to part from. They were his. What he did not quite come to terms with was the fact that he was also theirs. His son never did come to terms with this last fact, and found it difficult to accompany his father on these strolls around what was a veritable town. Metellus Scipio was more snob than stickler, incapable by nature of eliciting or accepting the affection of those who were not his peers—even, it might be said, of those who were not directly related to him through blood or adopted blood.

By the time that their general led them out to tempt Lucius Hirtuleius into battle, his men knew why he had crammed six full legions and a thousand horse into a camp considerably smaller than it ought to have been. He wanted Hirtuleius to think that there were only five under-strength legions with him, and to think too that he had built his camp so stoutly because his army had been obliged to travel without all the adjuncts it needed; some of the Numidian cavalry troopers had been heard to pass remarks to this effect while they chased Hirtuleius's cavalry away during the sortie.

Taking a deliberate leaf out of Scipio Africanus's book, he chose the kind of ground to form up on that a general in command of ill-equipped troops in cheerless spirits would choose—cut up by tiny watercourses, a trifle uneven, impeded by bushes and small trees. And it was plain to Hirtuleius that in order to cover the front presented by forty thousand superbly armed Spanish soldiers in top condition, Metellus Pius had been obliged to thin out his center. To compensate for this his wings straggled too far forward, with the Numidian cavalry at their tips behaving as if they were commanded by someone who could not control them. In two minds as to whether he would fight that day when his scouts had come to tell him that the old woman's army was marching out of its camp, Hirtuleius surveyed the opposition and the ground, grunted contemptuously, and elected to give battle after all.

The old woman's wings engaged Hirtuleius first, which was exactly what he wanted. Forward he charged for that thin center, intent upon punching a hole in it through which he would pull three legions in a hurry, then turn and fall upon its rear. But the moment the Spanish army inserted itself between those unruly wings, Metellus Pius sprang his trap. His best men were hidden within the wings; some suddenly moved to reinforce his center, others turned to fight on the flanks. Before he could attempt to extricate himself, Lucius Hirtuleius found himself rolled neatly into a milling mass of bewildered men, and lost the battle. He and his younger brother died on the field, and the soldiers of Metellus Pius, singing a victory paean, cut the beloved Spanish army of Sertorius into pieces. Very few of its men survived; those who did fled into Lusitania howling the awful news of defeat, and came no more to fight for Quintus Sertorius. Their fellow tribesmen, cheated of their quarry at the mouth of the Anas, had followed the Romans at first, then decided to invade the Further province, even to cross the Baetis. But when the word spread of the fate of the Spanish army, they keened a terrible dirge at the passing of their great chance, then melted away into the forests.

Little more than a village perched atop a crag high above the plateau, Segovia could not hold out against Metellus Pius for one single day. Its people were put to the sword and its buildings went up in flames. Metellus Pius wanted no one left alive to fly eastward to warn Sertorius that his Spanish army was dead.

As soon as his centurions pronounced the men fit and rested enough to leave, Metellus Pius commenced his march to the mouth of the Sucro River. Time dictated that he should cross the formidable massif behind Segovia without trying to find a way around it: the Juga Carpetana (as it was called) proved difficult but not impossible to conquer even for the ox-drawn wagons, and the passage was a short one, some twenty-five miles. Miaccum followed Segovia, and Sertobriga followed Miaccum; Metellus Pius and his army passed far enough to the south of them to delude their inhabitants into thinking they saw Hirtuleius and the Spanish army returning to Laminium.

After that it was a weary trek through country so arid even the sheep seemed to avoid it, but there were riverbeds at regular intervals which yielded water below the ground, and the distance to the upper Sucro, still flowing, was not so great that the army of Further Spain stood in any danger. The heat of course was colossal, and of shade there was none. But Metellus Pius marched only by night, as the moon was full enough, and by day made his men sleep in the shade of their tents.

What instinct caused him to cross the Sucro to its northern bank the moment he encountered that river he never afterward knew, for lower down its course the bed turned out to be a shifting mire of sandy gravel which would have proven time-consuming to ford. As it was, his legions were on the northern side of the stream when, stirring into activity just before sunset, he and his men heard in the distance the unmistakable sounds of battle. It was the second-last day of Quinctilis.

From dawn until an hour before sunset Quintus Sertorius watched Pompey's legions drawn up in battle formation, wondering as the day dragged on if Pompey would stay the course, or whether he would commence to march away. It was this latter alternative Sertorius wanted; the moment Pompey's back was turned, he would have found out soon enough that he had made a terrible blunder. As it was, either the kid was smart enough to know what he was doing, or else some lucky divinity stood by his shoulder and persuaded him to wait on for hour after hour in the frightful sun.

Things were not going well for Sertorius, despite the many advantages he enjoyed—the superior ability of his troops to endure the heat, plenty of water to drink and splash around, an intimate knowledge of the surrounding countryside. For one thing, he had heard nothing from Lucius Hirtuleius once he had reached Segovia beyond a curt note saying Metellus Pius was not there, but that he would wait for thirty days to see whether the old woman turned up before he proceeded as ordered to join Sertorius. For another, his scouts posted on the highest hills in the district had discerned no column of dust coming down the dry valley of the Sucro to indicate that Hirtuleius was on his way. And—by far the biggest worry of all!—Diana had disappeared.

The little white fawn had been with him all the way from Osca, unperturbed by the scuffle and chaos of an army on the march, unperturbed too by the summer sun (which ought to have burned her, as she was albino, but never did—one more sign of her divine origins). And then when he had located himself here by the Sucro, with Herennius and Perperna in good position near Valentia to soften Pompey up, Diana disappeared. One night he had gone to sleep in his command tent knowing the animal was curled up on its sheepskin rug beside his pallet, only to find when he awoke at dawn that it had vanished.

At first he had not fretted about its absence. Beautifully trained, it never soiled the interior of any building with urine or droppings, so Sertorius had simply assumed that it had gone off to do its business. But while he broke his fast it also broke its fast, and during the summer it was always hungriest after the respite of darkness. Yet it did not come back to eat.

That had been thirty-three days ago. His alarm growing, Sertorius had quietly searched further and further afield without result, then finally had needed to ask other people if they had seen it. Immediately the news had spread—it seemed like a fire in tinder-dry scrub—until the whole camp had scattered panic-stricken to look for Diana; Sertorius had been driven to issue a harsh order that discipline must be maintained even if *he* disappeared.

The creature meant so much, especially to the Spaniards. When day succeeded day without a sign of it, morale plummeted, the decline fueled by that stupid disaster at Valentia which Perperna had brought on when he refused to work with poor loyal Gaius Herennius. Sertorius knew well enough that the fault lay with Perperna, but his people were convinced the fault lay in Diana's disappearance. The white fawn was Sertorius's luck, and now his luck was gone.

It was almost sunset when Sertorius committed his army to battle, secure in the knowledge that his troops were in much better condition to fight than Pompey's, obviously suffering from the long wait under the summer sun. Pompey himself was commanding his right with Lucius Afranius on the left and the center under some legate Sertorius suspected was new to Spain, as no one among his scouts could put a name to the face. Their encounter outside Lauro the previous year had given Sertorius a profound contempt for Pompey's generalship, so he elected to fight opposite Pompey himself, which left Perperna to deal with Afranius; his center belonged to Sertorius as well.

Things went excellently for Sertorius from the beginning, and looked even better when Pompey was carried from the field just as the sun set, one thigh scoured to ribbons by a barbed spear. Behind him he left his big white Public Horse, dead by the same spear. Despite the valiant attempts of young Aulus Gabinius to rally it, Pompey's rudderless right began to retreat.

Unfortunately Perperna was not doing nearly as well against Afranius, who punched a hole in his lines and reached Perperna's camp. Sertorius was forced to go to Perperna's rescue in person, and only contrived to eject Afranius from the camp after sustaining heavy losses. Darkness had fallen as the full moon rose, but the battle went on by moonlight and torchlight despite the dust; Sertorius was determined that he would not break off the engagement until he stood in a strong enough position to win on the morrow.

Thus it was that when hostilities did cease, Sertorius had good cause to look forward to the next dawn.

"I'll string the kid's carcass from a tree and leave it for the birds," he said, smiling nastily. Then, with an eager yet despairing look: "I don't suppose Diana has come back?"

No, Diana had not come back.

As soon as it was light enough to see battle was joined again. Pompey was still in command, lying on a stretcher held at shoulder height by some of his tallest men. Formed anew during the night, his army was drawn together tightly and had obviously been ordered to minimize its losses by not incurring any risks—just the sort of enemy Sertorius detested most.

And then a little after sunrise a fresh face and a fresh army strolled onto the battlefield: Quintus Caecilius Metellus Pius, marching out of the west and through Perperna's ranks as if they did not exist. For the second time in less than a day Perperna's camp fell. Metellus Pius pressed on toward the camp of Sertorius. Time to go.

As he and Perperna beat a hasty retreat, Sertorius was heard to wail desolately, "If that wretched old woman had not arrived, I would have kicked the kid all the way back to Rome!"

The retreat ended in the foothills to the west of Saetabis. Here order began once more to emerge from disorder as Sertorius, trying to ignore Perperna, counted his losses—perhaps four thousand men all told—and put the men (mostly Perperna's) from badly mauled cohorts among cohorts in need of a few extra men. It had been Perperna's intention to make a formal protest about this, to complain loudly that Sertorius was deliberately undermining his authority, but one look at the set face with the maimed orbit decided him to leave well enough alone. For the time being.

Here too Sertorius finally got the news that Lucius and Gaius Hirtuleius had been killed at Segovia, together with the entire Spanish army. A crushing blow, and one Sertorius had never expected. Not when the enemy had been the old woman from the Further province! And how *cunning,* to march so circuitously that his real intentions had never even been suspected, to hustle himself past Miaccum and Sertobriga in the distance pretending to be Hirtuleius, to march then by the light of the moon and raise no dust to give his presence away as he came down the Sucro!

My Spaniards are right, he thought. When Diana disappeared I lost my luck. Fortune no longer favors me. If Fortune ever did.

The kid and the old woman, he was informed, had evidently decided there was no point in continuing to march southward; after they had cleaned up the field and looted hapless Saetabis of all its food, their armies had turned into the north. Well, that was good thinking. Sextilis was upon them and they had a long way to go before the kid could insert himself into winter camp. Only what did the old woman intend to do? Was he going back to Further Spain, or was he marching all the way north with the kid? Aware of an awful lassitude he did not know how to shake off, Quintus Sertorius decided his wounds were now licked sufficiently to heal; he would follow the old woman and the kid as they headed north, do what damage he could without risking another outright confrontation.

His camp was dismembered and his army moving out, its guerrilla units in the lead, when two little children of the area came to him shyly, their bare feet even browner than their naked bodies, nostrils and ears pierced by shining balls of gold. In between them, a precious strand of family rope around its neck, was a dirt-encrusted brown fawn. The tears sprang unbidden to Quintus Sertorius's remaining eye—how nice, how kind! They had heard of the loss of his beautiful goddess-given white fawn, and come to offer him their own pet as a replacement.

He squatted down to their level, his face turned away so that they only saw its good side, would not be frightened by its bad side. To his great surprise, the creature they led began to leap and struggle at his advent; animals never shied away from Quintus Sertorius!

"Did you bring me your pet?" he asked gently. "Thank you, thank you! But I can't take it, you know. I'm off to fight the Romans, and I'd much rather you kept it safe with you."

"But it's yours," said the girl-child.

"Mine? Oh no! Mine was white."

"It's white," she said, spat on her hand, and rubbed the juice into its coat. "See?"

At this moment the fawn managed to pull its neck free of the rope and launched itself at Sertorius. Tears pouring down the right side of his face—the good side—he took it into his arms, hugged it, kissed it, could not let it go. "Diana! My Diana! Diana, Diana!"

When the children had been sent off with their precious bit of family rope put into a big bag of gold carried by a slave under instructions to deliver everything to their parents, Quintus Sertorius bathed his fawn in the nearby spring and looked it over, crooning and clucking. Whatever the reason for its original disappearance might have been, it had clearly not prospered in the wild. Some large cat had attacked it, for it bore the deep and half-healed marks of vicious claws on both sides of its rump, as if it had been pounced on from behind and dragged down. How it had managed to escape only the Goddess knew—or had contrived at. Its poor little trotters were worn and bloodied, its ears shredded along their edges, its muzzle torn. The children had found it when they took the family sheep out to graze, and it had come straight up to them, put its nose in the girl-child's grimy hands and sighed in shivering relief.

"Well, Diana," said Sertorius as he put it into a box upon the tray of a wagon, "I hope you've learned that the wilds are for the wild. Did you smell a stag, was that it? Or did the camp dogs bait you? In future, my girl, you'll travel like this. I can't bear the thought of losing you again."

Word had flown swifter than birds on the wing; Diana was back! And so was Quintus Sertorius's luck.

Pompey and Metellus Pius left Valentia behind, continuing north to Saguntum. The food they had plundered from Saetabis (there was nothing else to plunder) was a welcome addition to their dwindling supplies, and so was Pompey's cache in the disused quarry outside Valentia. They had agreed that both would march together up the east coast to Emporiae, and that Metellus Pius would winter that year in Narbonese Gaul; though his men had not voiced any complaint at their thousand-mile detour to reinforce Pompey, the Piglet thought that another five-hundred-mile walk would do them for the year. Besides, he wanted to be in the thick of the action in the spring, and he knew that the annihilation of the Spanish army would keep the Further province safe from any raiding Lusitani.

Saguntum had sent them an embassage to inform them that it would do whatever possible to assist them, and was still stoutly Roman in sentiment. Not surprising: it had been Saguntum's Roman (and Massiliote) affiliations which had caused the outbreak of the second Punic war against Carthage a century and a half earlier. Of food, however, the town had little to offer, and this the two generals believed. The harvest was poor because the rains of winter had not come to give the crops their best drink of the growing season, nor had the late spring rains come to send them shooting up heavy with ears of grain.

It was therefore imperative that the two armies move as swiftly as possible to the Iberus, where the harvest was later and richer. If they could reach it by the end of Sextilis it would be theirs, not Sertorius's. The embassage from Saguntum had therefore been thanked and sent home; Metellus Pius and Pompey would not be staying.

Pompey's leg wound was healing, but slowly; the barbs of the spear which had inflicted it had torn chunks out of sinews and tendons as well as muscles, and much tissue had to grow and reknit before he would be able to bear any weight on it. The loss of his Public Horse he seemed to feel, thought the Piglet, more than he did the use of his leg or the loss of its beauty. Well, a horse was more beautiful than a man's leg. Pompey wouldn't find one to match it this side of the *rosea rura* in Sabine country. Spanish horses were small and underbred.

His spirits were down again, not unnaturally. Not only had Metellus Pius been the sole reason for the victory on the Sucro, but Metellus Pius had also slaughtered Sertorius's best general and best army. Even Lucius Afranius, Marcus Petreius and Pompey's new legate, Lucius Titurius Sabinus, had fared better than poor Pompey himself. All very well to say that it was upon Pompey personally that the brunt of Sertorius's venom had fallen; Pompey knew he hadn't met the test. And now, his scouts told him, the renegade Marian was dogging their footsteps as they marched north, no doubt waiting for his next opportunity. His guerrilla units were already in evidence, harrying what foraging parties were sent out, but Pompey had learned as much wisdom as the Piglet in this respect, so the two armies suffered very little. On the other hand, they obtained very little in the way of food.

Then—apparently quite by accident—they ran into the army of Quintus Sertorius on the plains of the coast just after they had passed Saguntum. And Sertorius decided to engage them, making sure that he and his own legions faced Pompey. Pompey was the weak link, not Metellus Pius.

The strategy was a mistake. Sertorius would have done far better to have contained Metellus Pius himself and left Pompey to Perperna; Pompey appeared on the field on his stretcher, unwilling to have it said that, like Achilles, he skulked in his tent while his allies got on with the battle. Hostilities began in the early afternoon, and it was all over by nightfall. Though he had sustained a slight wound on his arm, Metellus Pius had carried the day. He inflicted losses of five thousand upon Perperna but experienced few himself. Poor Pompey's ill luck continued to dog him; his cavalry was killed to the last man and his casualties stood at six thousand— a legion and a half. That they could claim the engagement as a victory for Rome was due to Perperna's losses plus the three thousand men who died fighting for Sertorius.

"He'll be back at dawn," said the Piglet cheerfully when he came to see how Pompey was.

"He'll withdraw, surely," said Pompey. "It didn't go well for him, but it went disastrously for Perperna."

"He'll be back, Gnaeus Pompeius. I know him."

Oh, the pain! Oh, the gall! The wretched Piglet *knew him*!

And he was right, of course. Sertorius was back in the morning, determined to win. This time he rectified his mistake and concentrated his own energies upon Metellus Pius, whose camp he attacked as soon as it was light enough to see. But the old woman was ready for him. He had put Pompey and his men in the camp as well, and trounced Sertorius. Looking a lot younger and fitter these days, Metellus Pius chased Sertorius into Saguntum, while Pompey on his stretcher was carried back to his tent.

But the action had brought Pompey a personal grief, despite its success. Gaius Memmius—brother-in-law, friend, quaestor—was killed, the first of Pompey's legates to perish.

While he wept huddled in the back of a mule-drawn cart, Metellus Pius commanded the march north, leaving Sertorius and Perperna to do whatever they wanted, which was probably to exact reprisals on the inhabitants of Saguntum. They wouldn't stay long, of that Metellus Pius was sure; Saguntum could hardly feed itself, let alone an army.

At the end of Sextilis the two Roman armies reached the Iberus only to find the harvest—such as it was—safely in the granaries of Sertorius's formidable mountain strongholds, and the earth burned to a uniformly black desert. Sertorius had not stayed long in Saguntum. He had outmaneuvered them and got to the Iberus first, there to wreak devastation.

Emporiae and the lands of the Indigetes were in little better condition;

two winters of Pompey's occupation had made the purses of the people fat, but their harvest was lean.

"I shall send my quaestor Gaius Urbinius to the Further province to recruit enough troops to keep my lands safe," said the Piglet, "but if we are to break Sertorius's back, then I have to be close to you in spring. So, as we thought, it will have to be Narbonese Gaul for me."

"The harvest isn't good there either."

"True. But they haven't had an army quartered on them for many years, so they'll have enough to spare for me." The Piglet frowned. "What worries me more is what you're going to do. I don't think there's enough here to fatten your men up—and if you can't fatten them up in winter, they'll stay very thin."

"I'm off to the upper Durius," said Pompey calmly.

"Ye gods!"

"Well, it's a good way west of Sertorius's towns, so it ought to be easier to reduce the local fortresses than it would be places like Calagurris or Vareia. The Iberus belongs to Sertorius from end to end. But the Durius doesn't. The few native Spaniards I trust tell me that the country isn't as high nor the cold as perishing as it is nearer to the Pyrenees."

"The Vaccei inhabit the region, and they're warlike."

"Oh, tell me what Spanish tribe isn't?" asked Pompey wearily, shifting his aching leg.

The Piglet was nodding thoughtfully. "You know, Pompeius, the more I think about it, the better I like it," he said. "You go there! Just make sure you start before winter makes it too hard to cross the watershed at the top end of the Iberus."

"Don't worry, I'll beat the winter. But first," he said grimly, "I have a letter to write."

"To Rome and the Senate."

"That's right, Pius. To Rome and the Senate." The blue eyes, older and warier these days, stared into the Piglet's brown ones. "The thing is, will you let me write and speak for you too?"

"You most definitely can," said Metellus Pius.

"You're sure you wouldn't rather write for yourself?"

"No, it's better that it comes from you. You're the one those couch-fat experts gave the special commission. I'm just an ordinary old governor in the throes of a frightful war. They won't take any notice of me, they know perfectly well that I'm one of the old retainers. It's you they don't know, Magnus. You they probably don't quite trust. You're not one of *them*. Write to them! And give them a fright, Magnus!"

"Don't worry, I will."

The Piglet got up. "Well, I'll take myself off to Narbo first thing to-morrow. Every day less I'm here means less of your food I eat."

"Won't you at least polish up my prose? Varro used to."

"No, not I!" said the Piglet, and laughed. "They know my literary style. Give them something they've never seen before."

Pompey gave them something they had never seen before.

To the Senate and People of Rome:

I write this from Emporiae on the Nones of October in the consulship of Lucius Octavius and Gaius Aurelius Cotta. On the Ides of October I commence my march up the Iberus River to the Durius River and its confluence with the Pisoraca River, where there is a town called Septimanca in the middle of a fertile highland. There I hope to winter my men in enough comfort to keep their bellies full. Luckily I do not have nearly as many men as I did two years ago when I arrived in Emporiae. I am down to four legions of less than four thousand men each, and I have no cavalry.

Why do I have to march my fourteen thousand men some five hundred miles through hostile territory to winter them? Because there is nothing to eat in eastern Spain. That is why. Then why do I not buy in food from Gaul or Italian Gaul since the winds at this time of year favor shipping it in my direction? Because I have no money. No money for food and no money for ships. That is why. I have no other choice than to rob food from Spanish tribesmen who will, I hope, prove weak enough to let themselves be robbed by fourteen thousand hungry Roman men. That is why I have to march so far, to find tribesmen I hope will prove weak enough. There is no food to be had on the Iberus without reducing one of Sertorius's strongholds, and I am not in a position to do that. How long did it take Rome to reduce Numantia? And Numantia is a hen coop of a place compared to Calagurris or Clunia. Nor was Numantia commanded by a Roman.

You know from my dispatches that I have not had a good two years in the field, though my colleague Quintus Caecilius Metellus Pius Pontifex Maximus has had more success. Quintus Sertorius takes some getting used to. This is *his* country. He knows it and he knows the people. I do not. I did my best. I do not believe that anyone else you might have sent could have done better. My colleague Pius took three years to hatch his first victory. I at least have collaborated in two victories in my second year, when my colleague Pius and I combined our forces and beat Sertorius on the Sucro River, then again near Saguntum.

My colleague Pius and I believe we will win. I do not just say that. We will win. But in order to win, we need a bit of help from home. We need more legions. We need money. I do not say "*more* money" because I for one have not received any money at all. Nor I believe has my colleague Pius received any money beyond his stipend for his first year as governor. Yes, I can hear you now: win a few victories and sack a few cities and there is your money. Well, Spain is not like that. There is no money in Spain. The best I or anyone else can hope for when we take a town is a bit of food. There is no money. In case you are having a bit of trouble reading this, I will say that again. THERE IS NO MONEY. When you sent me here you gave me six legions and fifteen hundred cavalry and enough money to pay everyone and find my supplies for about half a year. That was two years ago. My war chest was empty in half a year. That was a year and a half ago. But no more money. No more troops either.

You know—I know you know because my colleague Pius and I both reported it in our dispatches—that Quintus Sertorius has made a pact with King Mithridates of Pontus. He has agreed to confirm King Mithridates in all his conquests and allow Pontus more conquests when he is *Dictator of Rome*. Now that should tell you that Quintus Sertorius is not going to stop when he is King of Spain. He intends to be King of Rome too, no matter what title he likes to award himself. There are only two people who can stop him. My colleague Pius and I. I say that because we are here on the spot and we have the chance to stop him. But we cannot stop him with what we have. He has all the manpower Spain can offer and he has the Roman skills to turn barbarian Spaniards into good Roman soldiers. If he had not these two things, he would have been stopped years ago. But he is still here and still recruiting and training. My colleague Pius and I cannot recruit in Spain. No one in his right mind would join our armies. We cannot pay our men. We cannot even keep their bellies full. And the gods be my witness, there are no spoils to share.

I can beat Sertorius. If I cannot do it any other way, then I will be the drop of water that wears down the hardest stone to a hollow shell a child can break with a toy hammer. My colleague Pius feels the same. But I cannot beat Sertorius unless I am sent more soldiers and more cavalry AND SOME MONEY. My soldiers here have not been paid in a year and a half, and I owe the dead as well as the living. I did bring a lot of my own money with me, but I have spent it all buying supplies. I do not apologize for my troop losses. They were the result of a miscalculation not helped by the information I received in Rome. Namely, that six legions and fifteen hundred horse were more than enough to deal with Sertorius. I ought to have had ten legions and three thousand cavalry. Then I would have beaten him in the first year and Rome would be the richer in men and money. You ought to think about that, you miserly lot.

And here is something else for you to think about. If I am not able to stay in Spain and my colleague Pius is therefore unable to come out of his little corner of Spain, what do you think will happen? I will go back to Italy. Dragging Quintus Sertorius and his armies along in my wake like the tail on a comet. Now you think about that long and hard. And send me some legions and some cavalry AND SOME MONEY.

By the way, Rome owes me a Public Horse.

The letter reached Rome at the end of November, a time of flux in Sulla's reorganized Senate. The consuls of the year were drawing to the end of their tenure in office and the consuls-elect were feeling their coming power. Because of Lucius Octavius's state of chronic ill health, only one consul, Gaius Aurelius Cotta, occupied the curule chair. Mamercus Princeps Senatus read Pompey's letter to the silent senators, as this was one privilege Sulla had not stripped from the Leader of the House.

It was Lucius Licinius Lucullus, senior consul-elect for the next year, who rose to reply; his junior colleague was the present consul's middle brother, Marcus Aurelius Cotta, and neither of the Cottae wanted to answer that bald, comfortless letter.

"Conscript Fathers, you have just listened to a soldier's report rather than the meretricious missive of a politician."

"A soldier's report? I'd rather call it as incompetently written as its author is an incompetent commander!" said Quintus Hortensius, holding his nose with his fingers as if to shut out a bad smell.

"Oh, pipe down, Hortensius!" said Lucullus wearily. "I do not need to have what I am about to say punctuated by the smart remarks of a stay-at-home general! When you can leap off your dining couch and abandon your pretty fish to outsoldier Quintus Sertorius, I'll not only give you the floor, I'll strew rose petals before your pudgy flat feet! But until your sword is as sharp as your tongue, keep your tongue where it belongs—behind your gourmandizing teeth!''

Hortensius subsided, looking sour.

''It is not the meretricious missive of a politician. Nor does it spare us politicians. On the other hand it does not spare its writer either. It isn't full of excuses, and the statement about battles won and lost is fully supported by the dispatches we have received regularly from Quintus Caecilius Metellus Pius.

''Now I have never been to Spain. Some of you sitting here do know the place, but many more of you are in my boat, and know it not at all. In the old days the Further province always had the reputation of being good pickings for a governor—rich, well ordered, peaceful, yet amply provided with barbarians on two frontiers so that the wars a governor might feel free to wage were fairly easily managed. The Nearer province has never enjoyed the same reputation—the pickings are lean and the native peoples in a perpetual state of unrest. Therefore the governor of Nearer Spain could only look forward to an empty purse and much aggravation from the mountain-dwelling tribesmen.

''However, all that changed when Quintus Sertorius arrived. He already knew Spain well, from his missions for Gaius Marius to a military tribunate under Titus Didius—during which, I remind you, he won the Grass Crown, though still a youngster. And when this remarkable and absolutely formidable man arrived back in Spain as a Marian rebel fleeing retribution, the Nearer province became literally ungovernable, and the Further province ungovernable west of the Baetis. As Gnaeus Pompeius's letter says, it took the excellent governor of Further Spain almost three years to win a battle against one of Sertorius's adherents, Hirtuleius—not against Sertorius himself. What the letter does not reproach us with is the fact that due to strife inside Italy, we neglected to send Nearer Spain a governor at all for nearly two years. That, Conscript Fathers, was tantamount to handing Sertorius the Nearer province as a gift!''

Lucullus paused to look directly at Philippus, who was leaning forward on his stool and smiling broadly. It galled Lucullus to be doing Philippus's work for him; but he was a fair man, and it came better from the consul-elect than from one even the stupidest senator now realized was Pompey's lobbyist.

''When, Conscript Fathers, you gave your special commission to Gnaeus Pompeius Magnus, I was governing Africa Province and you could find no capable senator willing to undertake the task of uprooting Quintus Sertorius. You sent Gnaeus Pompeius off with six legions and fifteen hundred cavalry.

I tell you frankly that I would not have consented to go with less than ten full legions and three thousand cavalry—the figures Gnaeus Pompeius gives in his letter as adequate for the job. The correct figures!

"If one examines Gnaeus Pompeius's military record, it is impressive. And Pompeius is young enough to be flexible, adaptable, all the qualities men lose along with their youthful enthusiasm. Against any other enemy of Rome, six legions and fifteen hundred cavalry would probably have been sufficient. But Quintus Sertorius is a very special case. We have not seen his like since Gaius Marius, and I personally rank him a better general than Marius. So the initial defeats of Pompeius are not so very surprising. His luck was out, was all. For he ran up against one of the best military minds Rome has ever produced. Do you doubt that? You ought not! It is the truth.

"However, even the finest military minds think in a certain way. The governor of the Further province, our good Pius, has now been in Spain long enough to have begun to understand the way Sertorius thinks. I congratulate Pius for that. Frankly, I did not think he had it in him! Yet he cannot beat Sertorius alone. The theater of war is too vast—it is Italy during the Italian War all over again. One man cannot be north and south at the same time, and between the two regions is a dry and mountainous barrier.

"You sent the second man—a mere knight upon whom you put a kind of unnamed military crown—to govern the Nearer province. How did you phrase it, Philippus?—*non proconsule, sed pro consulibus*. You gave him to understand that you were sending him adequately staffed and adequately remunerated. Oh, make no mistake, he was eager for the job! At twenty-nine years of age and already a hoary veteran, which one of us military fellows would not have been? He was eager for the job, and may well have been eager enough to have gone off even less well provided! You might have got him as cheaply as four legions and five hundred cavalry!"

"A pity we didn't," said Catulus. "He's lost more men than that since he's been there."

"Hear, hear!" cried Hortensius.

"And that," said Lucullus, ignoring the brothers-in-law this time, "brings me to the crux of the matter. How can Rome hope to stop a man like Quintus Sertorius when Rome is not willing to send the money or the men to Spain that would ensure he was stopped? Not even a Quintus Sertorius could have coped with the war Pompeius and Pius might have brought to bear on him on two fronts had each of them commanded ten legions and three thousand horse! Pompeius's letter accuses *this body* of losing the war—and I agree with that judgement! How can this body expect miracles when it will not pay the magicians to work them? No money, no reinforcements—it *cannot* go on! This body must find the money to pay the woefully inadequate legions of Pompeius and Pius, and it must also find the money to give Pompeius at least two more legions. Four would be better."

Gaius Cotta spoke from the curule chair. "I agree with every last thing you've said, Lucius Licinius. But we do not have the money, Lucius Licinius. We just do not have the money."

"Then we have to find it," said Lucullus.

"Find it from where?" asked Gaius Cotta. "It is three years since we saw any significant revenues from Spain, and since the Contestani rose up we have seen no revenues at all. The Further province cannot mine the Marian Mountains or the southern Orospeda, and the Nearer province now cannot mine around New Carthage. The days when the Treasury's share of the gold, silver, lead and iron from Spain amounted to twenty thousand talents are gone, as are the mines themselves. Added to which, the events of the last fifteen years have reduced our income from Asia Province to its lowest level since we inherited the place over fifty-five years ago. We are at war in Illyricum, Macedonia and Gaul-across-the-Alps. We even hear rumors that King Mithridates is rising again, though no one can be sure. And should Nicomedes of Bithynia die, the situation in the east will become more precarious still."

"To deny our governors in Spain money and troops because we foresee events at the other end of Our Sea that may well not come to pass, Gaius Cotta, is absolute idiocy," said Lucullus.

"No, Lucius Lucullus!" Cotta snapped, angered. "I do not need to foresee anything to know that we do not have the money to send to Spain, let alone the troops! Gnaeus Pompeius and Quintus Pius must put up with things the way they are!"

The long face grew flintlike. "Then," said Lucullus in freezing tones, "there will be a new comet in Rome's sky. Its head will be loyal enough, for that will be a bankrupt Gnaeus Pompeius hurrying home with his tatterdemalion army. But the tail—ah, the tail! The tail will be Quintus Sertorius and the barbarians of Spain he holds in utter thrall. Joined along the way by Volcae, Salluvii, Vocontii, Allobroges, Helvii—and no doubt by the Boii and Insubres of Italian Gaul—not to mention the Ligures and Vagienni!"

Absolute silence greeted this Parthian shot.

Deciding it was time to break Sulla's rule, Philippus got to his feet and walked deliberately into the middle of the Curia Hostilia floor. There he looked at everybody in turn, from an ashen Cethegus to the flinching figures of Catulus and Hortensius. Then he turned to the curule podium and gazed at the discomfited Gaius Cotta, whose face reflected his state of mind.

"I suggest, Conscript Fathers," Philippus said, "that we summon the heads of the Treasury and the tax experts and see how we can find a considerable sum of money the honorable consul says we do not have. I also suggest that we find some legions and a squadron or two of cavalry."

When Pompey arrived before Septimanca in the lands of the Vaccei he found it smaller than his informants had thought, though it looked prosperous enough. It was situated on a bluff above the Pisoraca River, but not invulnerably so; at Pompey's advent the whole district surrendered without a fight. Surrounded by interpreters, he endeavored to soothe Septimancan fears and convince the chieftains of the region that he would eventually pay in full for what he took, and that his men would behave.

Clunia, some miles to the north of the sources of the Durius, was the westernmost of Sertorius's strongholds, but some of the settlements to the south of the same reach of that river had heard of the fate of Segovia and sent to Pompey at Septimanca the moment he arrived there, fervently assuring him of their loyalty to Rome and offering him whatever he needed. So after a conference with his legates, interpreters and locals, he dispatched Lucius Titurius Sabinus and fifteen cohorts to winter at Termes, Celtiberian in populace but no longer keen to serve Sertorius.

In fact (as Pompey told Metellus Pius in a letter sent to wish him felicitations for the New Year) the ground swell was now beginning. If in the next campaign season they could damage Sertorius so badly he visibly reeled, places like Septimanca and Termes anxious to submit would increase. The war would go on in Sertorius's heartland of the Iberus; there would be no more expeditions to the lower east coast.

The spring came early to the upper Durius, and Pompey did not linger. Leaving the people of Septimanca and Termes to plant their crops (with something extra in case the Romans came back next winter), the reunited four very under-strength legions set off up the Pisoraca to Pallantia, which had declared for Sertorius, apparently for no other reason than that the rival Septimanca had declared for Rome.

Metellus Pius pulled up stakes in Narbonese Gaul early as well, and marched up the Iberus with the intention of eventually joining Pompey marching down. His most important task, however, was to open the route between the Iberus and central Spain to Roman use, so when he reached the Salo—a big tributary of the Iberus flowing from the Juga Carpetana—he turned up it and one by one subdued the Sertorian towns along it. At the end of this crisp campaign he now had a quick way home to his own province, and had cut Sertorius off from the headwaters of both the Tagus and the Anas, which meant isolation from the tribes of Lusitania.

Pallantia turned out to be a hard nut to crack, so Pompey settled down to besiege it in the manner of Scipio Aemilianus before Numantia—as he informed the town through a relentless barrage of heralds. To retaliate, Pallantia sent to Sertorius in Osca, and Sertorius responded by bringing his own army to besiege the besiegers. It was clear that he wanted nothing to do with the old woman of the Further province, whose efforts up the Salo he chose to ignore as he passed by; Sertorius was as certain as ever that Pompey was the weak link in the Roman chain.

Neither side was interested in a direct confrontation at Pallantia, where Pompey concentrated upon reducing the town and Sertorius upon reducing Pompey's ranks. So while Pompey piled logs and tinder against Pallantia's stout wooden walls, Sertorius picked off Pompey's men a few at a time. And at the beginning of April Pompey withdrew, leaving Sertorius to help the town repair its burned section of fortifications before setting off in pursuit.

A month later Pompey and Metellus Pius met before one of Sertorius's strongest towns, Calagurris on the upper Iberus.

With the Piglet came a chest of money for Pompey and two more legions plus six thousand extra men formed into cohorts to plump out his existing legions to full strength. And with all that largesse from Rome came his new proquaestor, none other than Marcus Terentius Varro.

Oh, how glad he was to see that shiny pate with the fringe of dark hair above its ears! Pompey wept unashamedly.

"I'd gone before Varro and your reinforcements reached Narbo," said the Piglet as the three of them sat in Pompey's tent over a much-needed goblet of watered wine, "but I picked him up when I came out of the Salo valley into the Iberus. And I'm pleased to say he handed me a full war chest too, Magnus."

Pompey's chest expanded; he exhaled a huge sigh of relief. "I take it then that my letter worked," he said to Varro.

"*Worked?*" Varro laughed. "I'd rather say it lit a fire under the Senate hotter than any since Saturninus declared that he was King of Rome! I wish you could have seen everybody's faces when Lucullus started itemizing the number of Gallic tribes which were sure to tack themselves on to Sertorius's comet tail when he followed you toward Rome!"

"Lucullus?" asked Pompey, astonished.

"Oh, he was your champion, Magnus!"

"Why? I didn't think he was fond of me."

"He probably isn't. But I think he was afraid someone might suggest sending him to replace you in Spain. He's a very good military man, but the last thing he wants is to be sent to Spain. Who in full possession of his wits would want Spain?"

"Who indeed," said the Piglet, smiling.

"So I now have six legions, and both of us can issue some pay," said Pompey. "How much did we get, Varro?"

"Enough to give the living and the dead their back pay, and to pay the living for a part of this year. But unfortunately not enough to keep on paying them. I'm sorry, Magnus. It was the best Rome could do."

"I wish I knew where Sertorius kept his treasure! I'd make sure it was the next town I attacked, and I wouldn't rest until his moneybags were in my war chest," said Pompey.

"I doubt Sertorius has any funds either, Magnus," said the Piglet, shaking his head.

"Rubbish! He got three thousand talents of gold from King Mithridates not more than a year ago!"

"Swallowed up already, is my guess. Don't forget that he has no provinces to bring in a regular income, and he hasn't the slaves to work the mines. Nor do the Spanish tribes have money."

"Yes, I suppose you're right."

A small and comfortable silence fell. Metellus Pius broke it suddenly, as if reaching a decision he had mulled over in his mind for some time. He drew a breath of sufficient dimension to make Pompey and Varro look at him.

"Magnus, I have an idea," he said.

"I'm listening."

"We've just agreed Spain is impoverished, Spaniards and Romans alike. Even the Punic Gadetanians are suffering. Wealth is an unattainable dream to most men who live in Spain. Now I happen to have a tiny treasure which belongs to the Further province, and has sat in a trunk in the governor's residence at Castulo since Scipio Africanus put it there. I have no idea why none of our more avaricious governors took it, but they didn't take it. It amounts to one hundred talents of gold coins minted by Hannibal's brother-in-law, Hasdrubal."

"That's why they didn't take it," said Varro, grinning. "How could any Roman get rid of Carthaginian gold coins without someone asking questions?"

"You're right."

"So, Pius, you have a hundred talents in Carthaginian gold coins," said Pompey. "What do you intend to do with them?"

"I have a little more than that, actually. I also have twenty thousand *iugera* of prime river frontage land on the Baetis which a Servilius Caepio took off some local nobleman in payment for tax arrears. It too has been sitting there in Rome's name for decades, bringing in a little in lease money."

Pompey saw the point. "You're going to offer the gold and the land as a reward to anyone who turns Quintus Sertorius in."

"Absolutely correct."

"That's a brilliant idea, Pius! Whether we like it or not, it seems to me that we'll never manage to crush Sertorius on a battlefield. He's just too clever. He also has enormous reserves of men to draw on, and they don't mind whether he pays them or not. All they want is to see the end of Rome. But there are a few greedy men around any army camp or national capital. If you offer a reward you bring the war right inside Sertorius's palace walls. And you make it a war of nerves. Do it, Pius! Do it!"

Pius did it. The proclamations went out within a market interval from one end of Spain to the other: a hundred talents of gold coins and twenty thousand *iugera* of prime river frontage land on the Baetis to the lucky man who laid information directly leading to the death or capture of Quintus Sertorius.

That it smote Sertorius hard was made apparent to Metellus Pius and Pompey very soon, for they heard that when Sertorius learned of the reward he immediately dismissed his bodyguard of Roman troops and replaced it with a detachment of his loyalest Oscan Spaniards, then removed himself from the company of his Roman and Italian adherents. Actions which wounded the Romans and Italians to the quick. How dared Quintus Sertorius assume it would be a Roman or an Italian to betray him! Chief among the offended Romans and Italians was Marcus Perperna Veiento.

Amid this war of nerves the actual war ground on inexorably. Working now as a team, Pompey and Metellus Pius reduced some of Sertorius's towns, though Calagurris had not fallen; Sertorius and Perperna had turned up with thirty thousand men and sat back to pick off the Roman besiegers in much the same way as Sertorius had dealt with Pompey before Pallantia. In the end lack of supplies forced Pompey and Metellus Pius to pull out of the investment of Calagurris, not Sertorius's harassment; their twelve legions just could not be fed.

Supplies were a perpetual problem, thanks to the previous year's poor harvest. And as spring turned into summer and summer blazed on toward the coming harvest, a freakish disaster played havoc with the war of attrition Pompey and Metellus Pius were intent upon waging. The whole of the western end of the Middle Sea underwent a frightful shortage of food when scanty rains in winter and late spring were succeeded, just as the crops struggled to mature, by a deluge which stretched from Africa to the Alps, from Oceanus Atlanticus to Macedonia and Greece. The harvest did not exist: not in Africa, in Sicily, in Sardinia, in Corsica, in Italy, in Italian Gaul, in Gaul-across-the-Alps, or in Nearer Spain. Only in Further Spain did some crops survive, though not with the usual abundance.

"The only comfort," said Pompey to the Piglet at the end of Sextilis, "is that Sertorius will run short of food too."

"His granaries are full from earlier years," said the Piglet gloomily. "He'll survive far more easily than we will."

"I can go back to the upper Durius," said Pompey doubtfully, "but I don't think the area can feed six full legions."

Metellus Pius made up his mind. "Then I am going back to my province, Magnus. Nor do I think you will need me next spring. What has still to be done in Nearer Spain, you can do for yourself. There won't be food for *my* men in Nearer Spain, but if you can get inside some of Sertorius's bigger strongholds you'll manage to provision your own men. I can take two of your legions to Further Spain with me and winter them there. If you want them back in the spring I'll send them to you—but if you think you won't be able to feed them, I'll keep them. It will be difficult, but the Further province is not as badly hit as every other place west of Cyrenaica. Rest assured, whoever stays with me will be well fed."

Pompey accepted the offer, and Metellus Pius marched with eight legions for his own province far earlier in the year than he had planned or wanted to. The four legions Pompey kept were sent at once to Septimanca and Termes, while Pompey, lingering with Varro and the cavalry on the lower Iberus (thanks to the deluge grazing for horses was no longer a problem, so Pompey was sending his troopers to Emporiae to winter under the command of Varro), sat down to write to the Senate in Rome for the second time. And even though he now had Varro, he kept the prose his own.

To the Senate and People of Rome:

I am aware that the general shortage of grain must be affecting Rome and Italy as badly as it is affecting me. I have sent two of my legions to the Further province with my colleague Pius, who is in better case than Nearer Spain.

This letter is not to ask for food. I will manage to keep my men alive somehow, just as I will manage to wear Quintus Sertorius down. This letter is to ask for money. I still owe my men about one year of pay, and am tired of never catching up for the future.

Now although I am at the western end of the earth, I do hear what is going on elsewhere. I know that Mithridates invaded Bithynia in early summer, following on the death of King Nicomedes. I know that the tribes to the north of Macedonia are boiling from one end of the Via Egnatia to the other. I know that the pirates are making it impossible for Roman fleets to bring grain from eastern Macedonia and Asia Province back to Italy to help overcome the present food crisis. I know that the consuls of this year, Lucius Lucullus and Marcus Cotta, have been compelled to go out to fight Mithridates during their consulship. I know that Rome is pressed for money. But I also know that you offered the consul Lucullus seventy-two millions of sesterces to pay for a fleet—and that he declined your offer. So you do have at least seventy-two millions of sesterces under a flagstone in the Treasury floor, don't you? That's what really annoys me. That you value Mithridates higher than you do Sertorius. Well, I don't. One is an eastern potentate whose only real strength is in numbers. The other is a *Roman*. His strength is in that. And I know which man I'd rather be fighting. In fact, I wish you'd offered the job of putting Mithridates down to me. I might have jumped at it after this thankless business in Spain, an address no one remembers.

I cannot continue in Spain without some of those seventy-two millions of sesterces, so I suggest you lever up that flagstone in the Treasury floor and scoop a few bags of money out. The alternative is simple. I will discharge my soldiers here in Nearer Spain—all the men of the four legions I still have with me—and leave them to fend for themselves. It is a long way home. Without the structure of command and the comfort of knowing they are led, I believe few of them will elect to march home. The majority of them will do what I would myself in the same situation. They will go to Quintus Sertorius and offer to enlist in his armies because he will feed them and he will pay them regularly. It is up to you. Either send me money, or I will discharge my troops on the spot.

By the way, I have not been paid for my Public Horse.

Pompey got his money; the senators understood an ultimatum when it was put to them in such downright, forthright language. The whole country groaned, but was in no condition to deal with an invasion by Quintus Sertorius, especially reinforced by four legions of Pompeian troops. So salutary was the shock of Pompey's letter that Metellus Pius also received money. It only remained for the two Roman generals to find food.

Back came Pompey's two legions from Further Spain, bringing a huge column of supplies with them, and back to his war of attrition went Gnaeus Pompeius Magnus. He took Pallantia at last, then moved on to Cauca, where he begged the townspeople to take in his sick and wounded and succor them. The townspeople agreed; but Pompey disguised his best soldiers as sick and wounded, and took Cauca from within. One after the other Sertorius's strongholds fell, yielding their stores of grain to Pompey. When winter came, only Calagurris and Osca still held out.

Pompey received a letter from Metellus Pius.

I am delighted, Pompeius. This year's campaigning by you and you alone has broken Sertorius's back. Perhaps the victories in the field were mine, but the determination has been all yours. At no time did you give up, at no time did you allow Sertorius the room to breathe. And always it was you Sertorius himself attacked, whereas I had the luck to face first Hirtuleius—a good man, but not in Sertorius's class—and then Perperna—a pure mediocrity.

However, I would like to commend the soldiers of our legions. This has been the most thankless and bitter of all Rome's wars, and our men have had to endure hideous hardships. Yet neither of us has experienced discontent or mutiny, though the pay has been years late and the booty nonexistent. We have sacked cities to scrabble like rats for the last grain of wheat. Yes, two wonderful armies, Gnaeus Pompeius, and I wish I was confident that Rome will reward them as they ought to be rewarded. But I am not. Rome cannot be defeated. Battles she may lose, wars she does not. Perhaps our gallant troops are the reason for that, if one takes their loyalty, their good behavior and their absolute determination to grind on into account. We generals and governors can only do so much; in the end, I believe the credit must go to Rome's soldiers.

I do not know when you plan to go home. It may be, I suppose, that as the Senate gave you your special command, the Senate will take it away. For myself, I am the Senate's governor in the Further province, and in no hurry to return home. It is easier for the Senate at the moment to prorogue me if I request it than to find Further Spain a new governor. So I will request that I be prorogued for at least two more years. Before I leave I would like to set my province on its feet properly, and make it safe from the Lusitani.

I do not look forward upon my eventual return to Rome to engaging in a fresh conflict—a clash with the Senate to procure lands on which to settle my veterans. Yet I refuse to see my men go unrewarded. Therefore what I plan to do is to settle my men in Italian Gaul, but on the far side of the Padus, where there are tremendous expanses of good tilling soil and rich pastures at present in the hands of Gauls. It is not Roman land per se so the Senate will not be interested, and I will back my veterans against a pack of Insubres any day. I have already discussed this with my centurions, who profess themselves well pleased. My soldiers will not have to mill about aimlessly for up to several years waiting for a committee of land commissioners and bureaucrats to survey and chat and cull lists and chat and apportion and chat, and end in accomplishing nothing. The more I see of committees, the more convinced I am that the only thing a committee can organize is a catastrophe.

I wish you well, dear Magnus.

Pompey wintered that year among the Vascones, a powerful tribe which occupied the western end of the Pyrenees, and whose men were now thoroughly disenchanted with Sertorius. Because they were good to his soldiers, Pompey kept his army busy in building a stronghold for them, having elicited an oath from them to the effect that Pompaelo (as he called this new focus for a town) would always remain loyal to the Senate and People of Rome.

That winter was a bitter one for Quintus Sertorius. Perhaps he had always known that his was a lost cause; certainly he knew he had never been one of Fortune's favorites. But he could not consciously admit these facts to himself in so many words. Instead he told himself that things had gone all his way as long as he had managed to delude his Roman adversaries that they could win against him in the field. His downfall had arrived when the old woman and the kid saw through the ploy and adopted a policy of trying to avoid battle. Fabian strategy.

The offer of a reward for betrayal had cut him to the heart, for Quintus Sertorius was a Roman, and understood the cupidity which lived somewhere inside the most reasonable and decent of men. He could no longer trust any of his Roman or Italian confederates, brought up in the same traditions as he, whereas his Spanish people were as yet innocent of that particular fault civilization brought along with it. Always alert now for a hand stealing toward a knife or a certain look on a face, his temper began to shred under the strain. Aware that this new behavior must seem peculiar and atypical to his Spaniards, he strove mightily to control his moods; and in order to control them, he began to use wine as a pacifier.

Then—cruelest blow of his life—word came from Nersae that his mother was dead. The ultimate betrayal. Not if the bloodied bodies of his German wife and the son he had deliberately excluded from a Roman education had been laid at his feet would he have mourned as he mourned for his mother, Maria. For days he shut himself in his darkened room, only Diana the white fawn and an endless number of wine flagons for company. The years of absence, the loss! The loss! The guilt.

When he finally emerged a strange iron had entered into him. Hitherto the epitome of courtesy and kindness, he now revealed a Sertorius who was surly and suspicious even of his Spaniards, and quick to insult even his closest friends. Physically could he seem to feel Pompey prising apart the hold he had kept on Spain as Pompey pursued his policy of attrition with smooth efficiency, physically could he seem to feel his world disintegrating. And then, fed by the insidious phantoms in his wine, the paranoia in him erupted. When he heard that some of his Spanish chieftains were surreptitiously removing their sons from his famous school in Osca, he descended with his bodyguards upon its light-filled and peaceful colonnades and killed many of the children who remained. It was the beginning of his end.

Marcus Perperna Veiento had never forgotten or forgiven the way Sertorius had wrested control of his army from him, nor could he cope with the natural superiority in this Marian renegade from the Sabine mountains. Every time they fought a battle it was brought home to Perperna anew that he had neither the talent nor the devotion of his soldiers that Sertorius possessed in such abundance. Oh, but it came hard to admit that he could not surpass Sertorius in anything! Except, as it turned out, in treachery.

From the moment he learned of the reward being offered by Metellus Pius, his course was set. That Sertorius would make it so easy for him by lashing out in all directions was a piece of luck he hadn't counted on, but seized nonetheless.

Perperna threw a feast—to relieve the monotony of life in wintry Osca, he explained lightly, inviting his Roman and Italian cronies. And inviting Sertorius, of course. He wasn't sure Sertorius would come until he actually saw that familiar bulk and divided face come through his door, but then he rushed forward and eagerly ushered his principal guest to the *locus consularis* upon his own couch, and made sure his slaves plied the man with undiluted fortified wine.

Everyone present was a party to the plot; the atmosphere crackled with emotions. Chiefly fear, apprehension. So the wine flowed unwatered down every throat until Perperna began to think that no one would remain sober enough to do the deed. The little white fawn had come with its master, of course—he never stirred without it these days—and settled itself on the couch between him and Perperna, an affront which angered Perperna with a peculiar intensity considering the real purpose of the gathering. So as soon as he could he removed himself from the *lectus medius,* thrust the part-Roman, part-Spanish Marcus Antonius down in his place. A low fellow got on some peasant by one of the great Antonii, he had never been acknowledged by his father, let alone been showered with the usual openhanded Antonian generosity.

The conversation grew coarser, the roistering more vulgar, with Antonius at its forefront. Sertorius, who detested obscene language and jokes, took no part in the banter. He cuddled Diana and drank, the readable side of his face aloof, withdrawn. Then one of the others made a particularly crude remark which appealed to everybody except Sertorius, who threw himself backward on the couch with a grimace of disgust. Fearing that he would get up and leave, Perperna in a panic gave the signal, though the noise was so uproarious he didn't know whether it would be heard.

Down onto the floor he threw his silver goblet, so hard that it gave forth a ringing clatter and bounced high into the air. Absolute silence fell immediately. But Antonius was quicker by far than the unsuspecting, wine-soaked Sertorius; he drew a Roman legionary's big dagger from under his tunic, hurled himself upon Sertorius and stabbed him in the chest. Diana squealed and scrabbled away, Sertorius began to struggle upright. All the company surged forward to pin the stricken man down by arms and legs, while Antonius plied his dagger up and down, up and down. Sertorius had made no outcry, but had he cried out no one would have come to help him; his Spanish bodyguards waiting outside Perperna's door had been murdered earlier in the night.

Still squealing, the white fawn jumped up on the couch as the assassins drew back, satisfied; it began to nose frantically at its master, covered in blood, perfectly still. Now this was a task Perperna felt himself qualified to do! Seizing the knife Marcus Antonius had dropped, he plunged it into Diana's left side just behind the foreleg. The white fawn collapsed in a tangle athwart the dead Sertorius, and when the jubilant party picked him up to throw him out the door of Perperna's house like a piece of unwanted furniture, they pitched Diana after him.

Pompey heard the news in what, he decided afterward, was actually a predictable way, though at the time it struck him as noisome, disgusting. For Marcus Perperna Veiento sent him Sertorius's head as fast as a horse and rider could gallop from Osca to Pompaelo. With the gruesome trophy came a note which informed Pompey that he and Metellus Pius owed Perperna one hundred talents of gold and twenty thousand *iugera* of land. A second letter to the same effect had been dispatched to Metellus Pius, Perperna said.

Pompey replied on his own behalf, and sent a courier in a hurry to Metellus Pius bearing a copy:

> It brings me no joy to learn that Quintus Sertorius died at the hands of a worm like you, Perperna. He was *sacer,* but he deserved a better fate at nobler hands.
>
> I take great pleasure in denying you the reward, which was not offered for a head. It was offered to anyone willing to *lay information* leading to *our* apprehending or killing Quintus Sertorius. If the copy of our reward poster you happened to see did not specify the laying of information, then blame the scribe. But I certainly did not see any poster neglecting to say the laying of information. You, Perperna, come from a consular family, belonged to the Senate of Rome and were a praetor. You ought to have known better.
>
> As I presume you will succeed Quintus Sertorius in the command, it gives me great pleasure to *lay information* with you that the war will go on until the last traitor is dead and the last insurgent has been sold into slavery.

When Spain learned of the death of Quintus Sertorius, his Spanish adherents vanished into Lusitania and Aquitania; even some of his Roman and Italian soldiers deserted Perperna's cause. Undeterred, Perperna marshaled all those who had elected to remain and in May ventured out of Osca to give battle to Pompey, whose curt reply to his petition for the reward had angered him greatly. Who did the Picentine upstart think he was, to answer on behalf of a Caecilius Metellus? Though the Caecilius Metellus had not answered at all.

The battle was no contest. Perperna stumbled upon one of Pompey's legions foraging in the country south of Pompaelo; its men were scattered, and hampered too by several dozen oxcarts. Seeing the last army of Sertorius bearing down on them, Pompey's men fled into the confines of a steep gulch. Perperna, elated, followed them. Only when every last man was inside the gulch did Pompey spring his trap; down from its sides thousands of his soldiers leaped out of concealment, and massacred the last army of Quintus Sertorius.

Some soldiers found Perperna hiding in a thicket and brought him to Aulus Gabinius, who at once brought him to Pompey. Grey with terror,

Perperna tried to bargain for his life by offering Pompey all of Quintus Sertorius's private papers—which, he whimpered, would confirm the fact that there were many important men in Rome who were anxious to see Sertorius win, reconstruct Rome on Marian principles.

"Whatever they might be," said Pompey, face wooden, blue eyes expressionless.

"What might be?" asked Perperna, shivering.

"Marian principles."

"Please, Gnaeus Pompeius, I beg of you! Only let me give you these papers, and you'll see for yourself how right I am!"

"Very well, give them to me," said Pompey laconically.

Looking immensely relieved, Perperna told Aulus Gabinius whereabouts to look for the papers (he had carried them along with him, fearing to leave them in Osca), and waited with scarcely concealed impatience until the detail came back again. Two of the men bore a large chest between them, and put it on the ground at Pompey's feet.

"Open it," said Pompey.

He squatted down and rustled through the packed scrolls and papers inside for a very long time, occasionally spreading a sheet out to read it, nodding to himself as he muttered. The vaster bulk of what the chest contained he merely glanced at, but some of the shorter papers he also merely glanced at caused him to raise his brows. He stood up when the chest was empty and a huge pile of documents lay higgledy-piggledy on the trampled grass.

"Push all that rubbish together and burn it here and now in front of me," said Pompey to Aulus Gabinius.

Perperna gasped, but said nothing.

When the contents of the chest were blazing fiercely, Pompey thrust his chin toward Gabinius, a look of profound satisfaction on his face. "Kill this worm," he said.

Perperna died under a Roman legionary's sword, and the war in Spain was over in the moment his head rolled and jumped across the blood-soaked ground.

"So that's that," said Aulus Gabinius.

Pompey shrugged. "Good riddance," he said.

Both of them had been standing looking down at Perperna's disembodied face, its eyes goggling in horrified surprise; now Pompey turned away and began to walk back to the rest of his legates, who had known better than to intrude themselves when they had not been summoned.

"Did you have to burn the papers?" asked Gabinius.

"Oh, yes."

"Wouldn't it have been better to have brought them back to Rome? Then all the traitors would have been flushed out."

Pompey shook his head, laughed. "What, keep the Treason Court busy for the next hundred years?" he asked. "Sometimes it is wiser to keep one's own counsel. A traitor does not cease to be a traitor because the papers which would have indicted him have gone up in smoke."

"I don't quite understand."

"I mean they'll keep, Aulus Gabinius. They'll keep."

Though the war was over, Pompey was too meticulous a man to pack up and march home bearing Perperna's head on a spear. He liked to clean up his messes, which principally meant killing anyone he thought might prove a threat or a danger in the future. Among those who perished were Sertorius's German wife and son, whom Pompey found in Osca when he accepted the capitulation of that frowning fortress in June. The thirty-year-old man who was pointed out to him as Sertorius's son looked enough like him to make the tale credible, though he spoke no Latin and conducted himself like a Spaniard of the Illergetes.

On hearing of Sertorius's death, Clunia and Uxama repented of their submissions to Pompey, shut their gates and prepared to withstand siege. Pompey was happy to oblige them. Clunia fell. Uxama fell. So eventually did Calagurris, where the appalled Romans discovered that the men of the town had eaten their own women and children rather than surrender; Pompey had every living Calagurrian executed, then put not only the town but the entire district to the torch.

Of course all through this, communications had flown back and forth between the victorious general and Rome. Not all the letters were official ones, nor all the documents for public dissemination; chief among Pompey's correspondents was Philippus, who was crowing mightily in the Senate. The consuls of the year were two of Pompey's secret clients, Lucius Gellius Poplicola and Gnaeus Cornelius Lentulus Clodianus, which meant that Pompey was able to petition them to secure the Roman citizenship for those Spaniards who had assisted him significantly. At the top of Pompey's list was the same outlandish name, twice written; Kinahu Hadasht Byblos, uncle and nephew, aged thirty-three and twenty-eight respectively, citizens in good standing of Gades, Punic merchant princes. But they did not assume Pompey's name, for it was no part of Pompey's plan to let loose a flood of Spanish Gnaeus Pompeius This and That upon Rome. The Gadetanian uncle and nephew were put in the clientship of one of Pompey's more recent legates, Lucius Cornelius Lentulus, a cousin of the consul. So they entered into Roman life and annals as Lucius Cornelius Balbus Major and Lucius Cornelius Balbus Minor.

Still Pompey refused to hurry. The mines around New Carthage were reopened, the Contestani punished for attacking dear, dead Gaius Memmius: his sister was now a widow. He would have to do something about *that* when he returned to Rome! Slowly the province of Nearer Spain was carefully pieced together, given a properly organized bureaucracy, a tax structure, succinct rules and laws, and all the other adjuncts necessary to pronounce a place Roman.

Then in the autumn Gnaeus Pompeius Magnus bade farewell to Spain, devoutly hoping he would never need to return. He had quite recovered his self-confidence and his good opinion of himself, though never again would he face any military adversary without a premonitory shudder, never again would he enter into any war unless he knew he outnumbered the enemy by several legions at least. And never again would he fight another Roman!

At the crest of the pass through the Pyrenees the victorious general set up trophies, including armor which had belonged to Quintus Sertorius and the armor in which Perperna had lost his head. They hung sturdily stapled to tall poles with crossarms, *pteryges* flapping in the mournful mountain wind, a mute reminder to all who crossed from Gaul into Spain that it did not pay to go to war with Rome. Alongside the various trophies Pompey erected a cairn which bore a tablet on which he set forth his name, his title, his commission, the number of towns he had taken and the names of the men who had been rewarded with the Roman citizenship.

After which he descended into Narbonese Gaul and spent the winter there feasting on shrimps and dug-mullets. Like his war, that year had seen a turn for the better; the harvests were good in both the Spains—but bountiful in Narbonese Gaul.

He did not plan to reach Rome until the middle of the year at the earliest, though not because he came home feeling any sense of failure. Simply, he didn't know what to do next, where to go next, what pillar of Roman tradition and veneration to tumble. On the twenty-eighth day of September he would turn thirty-five years old, no longer the fresh-faced darling of the legions. Thus it behooved him to find a goal suitable for a man, not a boy. But *what* goal? Something the Senate would hate to give him, of that there could be no doubt. He could feel the answer lurking in the mazes of that part of his mind he shrank from exploring, but still it eluded him.

Then he shrugged, cast all those thoughts away. There were more immediate things to do, such as opening up the new road he had pioneered across the Alps—survey it, pave it, make it—what? The Via Pompeia? That sounded good! But who wanted to die leaving the name of a road as his monument to glory? No, better to die leaving just the name itself. Pompey the Great. Yes, *that* said it all.

PART SEVEN

from SEPTEMBER 78 B.C.
until JUNE 71 B.C.

MARCUS LICINIUS CRASSUS

Caesar had seen no reason to hurry home after he left the service of Publius Servilius Vatia; rather, his journey was a tour of exploration of those parts of Asia Province and Lycia he had not yet visited. However, he was back in Rome by the end of September in the year Lepidus and Catulus were consuls to find Rome acutely apprehensive about the conduct of Lepidus, who had left the city to recruit in Etruria before doing what he was supposed to do—hold the curule elections. Civil war was in the air, everyone talked it.

But civil war—real or imagined—was not high on Caesar's list of priorities. He had personal matters to attend to.

His mother seemed not to have aged at all, though there had been a change in her; she was very sad.

"Because Sulla is dead!" her son accused, a challenge in his voice that went back to the days when he had thought Sulla was her lover.

"Yes."

"*Why?* You owed him nothing!"

"I owed him your life, Caesar."

"Which *he* put in jeopardy in the first place!"

"I am sorry he is dead," said Aurelia flatly.

"I am not."

"Then let us change the subject."

Sighing, Caesar leaned back in his chair, acknowledging himself defeated. Her chin was up, a sure sign that she would not bend no matter what brilliant arguments he used.

"It is time I took my wife into my bed, Mater."

Aurelia frowned. "She's barely sixteen."

"Too young for a girl to marry, I agree. But Cinnilla has been married for nine years, and that makes her situation quite different. When she greeted me I could see in her eyes that she is ready to come to my bed."

"Yes, I think you're right, my son. Though your grandfather would have said that the union of two patricians is fraught with peril in childbirth. I would have liked to see her just a little more grown up before she dealt with that."

"Cinnilla will be fine, Mater."

"Then when?"

"Tonight."

"But there should be some sort of reinforcement of marriage first, Caesar. A family dinner—both your sisters are in Rome."

"There will be no family dinner. And no fuss."

Nor was there. Having been told no fuss, Aurelia didn't mention the coming change in her status to her daughter-in-law, who, when she went to go to her own little room, found herself detained by Caesar in a suddenly empty *triclinium*.

"It's this way today, Cinnilla," Caesar said, taking her by the hand and leading her toward the master's sleeping cubicle.

She went pale. "Oh! But I'm not ready!"

"For this, no girl ever is. A good reason to get it over and done with. Then we can settle down together comfortably."

It had been a good idea to give her no time to spend in thinking about what was to come, though of course she had thought of little else for four long years. He helped her off with her clothes, and because he was incurably neat folded them carefully, enjoying this evidence of feminine occupation of a room that had known no mistress since Aurelia had moved out after his father died. Cinnilla sat on the edge of the bed and watched him do this, but when he began to divest himself of his own clothes she shut her eyes.

Done, he sat beside her and took both her hands in his, resting them upon his bare thigh.

"Do you know what will happen, Cinnilla?"

"Yes," she said, eyes still closed.

"Then look at my face."

The big dark eyes opened, fixed themselves painfully on his face, which was smiling and, she fancied, full of love.

"How pretty you are, wife, and how nicely made." He touched her breasts, full and high, with nipples almost the color of her tawny skin. Her hands came up to caress his, she sighed.

Arms about her now, he kissed her, and this she found just wonderful, so long dreamed of, so much better than the dreams. She opened her lips to him, kissed him back, caressed him, found herself lying alongside him on the bed, her body responding with delicious flinches and shivers to this full-length contact with his. His skin, she discovered, was quite as silky as her own, and the pleasure it gave her to feel it warmed her to the quick.

Though she had known exactly what would happen, imagination was no substitute for reality. For so many years she had loved him, made him the focus of her life, that to be his wife in flesh as well as at law was glorious. Worth the wait, the wait which had become a part of her state of exaltation. In no hurry, he made sure she was absolutely ready for him, and did nothing to her that belonged to more sophisticated realms than the dreams of virgin girls. He hurt her a little, but not nearly enough to spoil her spiraling excitement; to feel him within her was best of all, and she held him within her until some magical and utterly unexpected spasm invaded every part of her. That, no one had told her about. But that, she understood, was what made women want to remain married.

When they rose at dawn to eat bread still hot from the oven and water cold from the stone cistern in the light-well garden, they found the dining room filled with roses and a flagon of light sweet wine on the sideboard. Tiny dolls of wool and ears of wheat hung from the lamps. Then came Aurelia to kiss them and wish them well, and the servants one by one, and Lucius Decumius and his sons.

"How nice it is to be properly married at last!" said Caesar.

"I quite agree," said Cinnilla, who looked as beautiful and fulfilled as any bride ought to look after her wedding night.

Gaius Matius, last to arrive, found the little celebratory breakfast enormously touching. None knew better than he how many women Caesar had enjoyed; yet this woman was his wife, and how wonderful it was to see that he was not disappointed. For himself, Gaius Matius doubted that he could have gratified a girl of Cinnilla's age after living with her as a sister for nine long years. But evidently Caesar was made of sterner stuff.

It was at the first meeting of the Senate Caesar attended that Philippus succeeded in persuading that body to summon Lepidus back to Rome to hold the curule elections. And at the second meeting he heard Lepidus's curt refusal read out, to be followed by the senatorial decree ordering Catulus back to Rome.

But between that meeting and the third one Caesar had a visit from his brother-in-law, Lucius Cornelius Cinna.

"There will be civil war," young Cinna said, "and I want you to be on the winning side."

"Winning side?"

"Lepidus's side."

"He won't win, Lucius. He can't win."

"With all of Etruria and Umbria behind him he can't lose!"

"That's the sort of thing people have been saying since the beginning of the world. I only know one person who can't lose."

"And who might that be?" Cinna demanded, annoyed.

"Myself."

A statement Cinna saw as exquisitely funny; he rolled about with laughter. "You know," he said when he was able, "you really are an odd fish, Caesar!"

"Perhaps I'm not a fish at all. I might be a fowl, which would certainly make an odd-looking fish. Or I might be a side of mutton on a hook in a butcher's stall."

"I never know when you're joking," said Cinna uncertainly.

"That's because I rarely joke."

"Rubbish! You weren't serious when you said you were the only man who couldn't lose!"

"I was absolutely serious."

"You won't join Lepidus?"

"Not if he were poised at the gates of Rome, Lucius."

"Well, you're wrong. I'm joining him."

"I don't blame you. Sulla's Rome beggared you."

And off went young Cinna to Saturnia, where Lepidus and his legions lay. Issued this time by Catulus on behalf of the Senate, the second summons went to Lepidus, and again Lepidus refused to return to Rome. Before Catulus went back to Campania and his own legions, Caesar asked for an interview.

"What do you want?" asked the son of Catulus Caesar coldly; he had never liked this too-beautiful, too-gifted young man.

"I want to join your staff in case there's war."

"I won't have you on my staff."

Caesar's eyes changed, assumed the deadly look Sulla's used to get. "You don't have to like me, Quintus Lutatius, to use me."

"How would I use you? Or to put it better, what use would you be to me? I hear you've already applied to join Lepidus."

"That's a lie!"

"Not from what I hear. Young Cinna went to see you before he left Rome and the two of you fixed it all up."

"Young Cinna came to wish me well, as is the duty of a brother-in-law after his sister's marriage has been consummated."

Catulus turned his back. "You may have convinced Sulla of your loyalty, Caesar, but you'll never convince me that you're anything other than a troublemaker. I won't have you because I won't have any man on my staff whose loyalty is suspect."

"When—and if! Lepidus marches, *cousin,* I will fight for Rome. If not as a member of your staff, then in some other capacity. I am a patrician Roman of the same blood family as you, and nobody's client or adherent." Halfway to the door, Caesar paused. "You would do well to file me in your mind as a man who will always abide by Rome's constitution. I will be consul in my year—but not because a loser like Lepidus has made himself Dictator of Rome. Lepidus doesn't have the courage or the steel, Catulus. Nor, I might add, do you.''

Thus it was that Caesar remained in Rome while events ran at an ever-accelerating rate toward rebellion. The *senatus consultum de re publica defendenda* was passed, Flaccus Princeps Senatus died, the second *interrex* held elections, and finally Lepidus marched on Rome. Together with several thousand others of station high and low and in between, Caesar presented himself in full armor to Catulus on the Campus Martius; he was sent as a part of a group of several hundred to garrison the Wooden Bridge from Transtiberim into the city. Because Catulus would sanction no kind of command for this winner of the Civic Crown, Caesar did duty as a man in the ranks. He saw no action, and when the battle under the Servian Walls of the Quirinal was over, he betook himself home without bothering to volunteer for the chase after Lepidus up the coast of Etruria.

Catulus's arrogance and spite were not forgotten. But Gaius Julius Caesar was a patient hater; Catulus's turn would come when the time was right. Until then, Catulus would wait.

Much to Caesar's chagrin, when he had arrived in Rome he found the younger Dolabella already in exile and Gaius Verres strutting around oozing virtue and probity. Verres was now the husband of Metellus Caprarius's daughter—and very popular with the knight electors, who thought his giving evidence against the younger Dolabella was a great compliment to the disenjuried Ordo Equester—*here* was a senator who was not afraid to indict one of his fellow senators!

However, Caesar let it be known through Lucius Decumius and Gaius Matius that he would act as advocate for anyone in the Subura, and busied himself during the months which saw the downfall of Lepidus and Brutus—and the rise of Pompey—with a series of court cases humble enough, yet highly successful. His legal reputation grew, connoisseurs of advocacy and rhetoric began to attend whichever court it was he pleaded before—mostly the urban or foreign praetor's, but occasionally the Murder Court. Contrive to smear him though Catulus did, people listened to Catulus less and less because they liked what Caesar had to say, not to mention how he said it.

When some of the cities of Macedonia and central Greece approached him to prosecute the elder Dolabella (back from his extended governorship because Appius Claudius Pulcher had finally arrived in his province), Caesar consented. This was the first really important trial he had undertaken, for it was to be heard in the *quaestio de repetundae*—the Extortion Court—and involved a man of highest family and great political clout. He knew little of the circumstances behind this elder Dolabella's governorship, but proceeded to interview possible witnesses and gather evidence with meticulous care. His *ethnarch* clients found him a delight; scrupulously considerate of their rank, always pleasant and easy to get on with. Most amazing of all did they find his memory—what he had heard he never forgot, and would often seize upon some tiny, inadvertent statement which turned out to be far more important than anyone had realized.

"However," he said to his clients on the morning that the trial opened, "be warned. The jury is composed entirely of senators, and senatorial sympathies are very much on Dolabella's side. He's seen as a good governor because he managed to keep the Scordisci at bay. I don't think we can win."

They didn't win. Though the evidence was so strong only a senatorial jury hearing the case of a fellow senator could have ignored it—Caesar's oratory was superb—the verdict was ABSOLVO. Caesar didn't apologize to his clients, nor were they disappointed in his performance. Both the forensic presentation and Caesar's speeches were hailed as the best in at least a generation, and men flocked to ask him to publish his speeches.

"They will become textbooks for students of rhetoric and the law," said Marcus Tullius Cicero, asking for copies for himself. "You shouldn't have lost, of course, but I'm very glad I got back from abroad in time to hear you best Hortensius and Gaius Cotta."

"I'm very glad too, Cicero. It's one thing to be gushed over by Cethegus, quite another to be asked crisply by an advocate of *your* standing for copies of my work," said Caesar, who was indeed pleased that Cicero should ask.

"You can teach me nothing about oratory," said Cicero, quite unconsciously beginning to demolish his compliment, "but rest assured, Caesar, that I shall study the way you investigated your case and presented your evidence very closely." They strolled up the Forum together, Cicero still talking. "What fascinates me is how you've managed to project your voice. In normal conversation it's so deep! Yet when you speak to a crowd you pitch it high and clear, and it carries splendidly. Who taught you that?"

"No one," said Caesar, looking surprised. "I just noticed that men with deep voices were harder by far to hear than men with higher voices. So since I like to be heard, I turned myself into a tenor."

"Apollonius Molon—I've been studying with him for the last two years—says it all depends on the length of a man's neck what sort of voice he has. The longer the neck, the deeper the voice. And you do have a long, scraggy neck! Luckily," he added complacently, "my neck is exactly the right length."

"Short," said Caesar, eyes dancing.

"Medium," said Cicero firmly.

"You look well, and you've put on some much-needed weight."

"I am well. And itching to be back in the courts. Though," said Cicero thoughtfully, "I do not think I will match my skills against yours. Some titans should never clash. I fancy the likes of Hortensius and Gaius Cotta too."

"I expected better of them," said Caesar. "If the jury hadn't made up its mind before the trial began instead of paying attention to my case, they would have lost, you know. They were sloppy and clumsy."

"I agree. Gaius Cotta is your uncle, is he not?"

"Yes. Not that it matters. He and I enjoy a clash."

They stopped to buy a pasty from a vendor who had been selling his famous savory snacks for years outside the State House of the *flamen Dialis*.

"I believe," said Cicero, wolfing his pasty down (he liked his food), "that there is still considerable legal doubt about your erstwhile flaminate. Aren't you tempted to use it and move into that commodious and very nice house behind Gavius's stall there? I understand you live in an apartment in the Subura. *Not* the right address for an advocate with your style, Caesar!"

Caesar shuddered, threw the remainder of his turnover in the direction of a begging bird. "Not if I lived in the meanest hovel on the Esquiline, Cicero, would I be tempted!" he declared.

"Well, I must say I'm glad to be on the Palatine these days," Cicero said, starting on his second pasty. "My brother, Quintus, has the old family house on the Carinae," he said grandly, just as if his family had owned it for generations rather than bought it when he had been a boy. He thought of something, and giggled. "Speaking of acquittals and the like, you heard what Quintus Calidius said after a jury of his peers convicted him in the Extortion Court, didn't you?"

"I'm afraid I missed it. Do enlighten me."

"He said he wasn't surprised he lost, because the going rate to bribe a jury in these days of Sulla's all-senatorial courts is three hundred thousand sesterces, and he just couldn't lay his hands on that kind of cash."

Caesar saw the funny side too, and laughed. "Then I must remember to stay out of the Extortion Court!"

"Especially when Lentulus Sura is foreman of the jury."

As Publius Cornelius Lentulus Sura had been the foreman of the elder Dolabella's jury, Caesar's brows rose. "That *is* handy to know, Cicero!"

"My dear fellow, there is absolutely nothing I can't tell you about our law courts!" said Cicero, waving one hand in a magnificent gesture. "If you have any questions, just ask me."

"I will, be sure of it," said Caesar. He shook hands with Cicero and walked off in the direction of the despised Subura.

Quintus Hortensius ducked out from behind a convenient column to join Cicero while he was still watching Caesar's tall form diminishing in the distance.

"He was very good," said Hortensius. "Give him a few more years of experience, my dear Cicero, and you and I will have to look to our laurels."

"Give him an honest jury, my dear Hortensius, and your laurels would have been off your head this morning."

"Unkind!"

"It won't last, you know."

"What?"

"Juries composed entirely of senators."

"Nonsense! The Senate is back in control forever."

"*That* is nonsense. There's a swell in the community to have their powers restored to the tribunes of the plebs. And when they have their old powers back, Quintus Hortensius, the juries will be made up of knights again."

Hortensius shrugged. "It makes no difference to me, Cicero. Senators or knights, a bribe is a bribe—when necessary."

"I do not bribe my juries," said Cicero stiffly.

"I know you don't. Nor does he." Hortensius flapped his hand in the direction of the Subura. "But it's an accepted custom, my dear fellow, an accepted custom!"

"A custom which can afford an advocate no satisfaction. When *I* win a case I like to know I won it on my merits, not on how much money my client gave me to dole out in bribes."

"Then you're a fool and you won't last."

Cicero's good-looking but not classically handsome face went stiff. The brown eyes flashed dangerously. "I'll outlast you, Hortensius! Never doubt it!"

"I am too strong to move."

"That was what Antaeus said before Hercules lifted him off the ground. *Ave,* Quintus Hortensius."

At the end of January in the following year, Cinnilla gave birth to Caesar's daughter, Julia, a frost-fair and delicate mite who pleased father and mother enormously.

"A son is a great expense, dearest wife," said Caesar, "whereas a daughter is a political asset of infinite value when her lineage is patrician on both sides and she has a good dowry. One can never know how a son will turn out, but our Julia is perfect. Like her grandmother Aurelia, she will have her pick of dozens of suitors."

"I can't see much prospect for the good dowry," said the mother, who had not had an easy time of it during labor, but was now recovering well.

"Don't worry, Cinnilla my lovely! By the time Julia is old enough to marry, the dowry will be there."

Aurelia was in her element, having taken charge of the baby and fallen head-over-heels in love with this grandchild. She had four others by now, Lia's two sons by their different fathers and Ju-Ju's daughter and son, but none of *them* lived in her house. Nor were they the progeny of her son, the light of her life.

"She will keep her blue eyes, they're very pale," said Aurelia, delighted baby Julia had thrown to her father's side, "and her hair has no more color than ice."

"I'm glad you can see hair," said Caesar gravely. "To me she looks absolutely bald—and that, since she's a Caesar and therefore supposed to have a thick head of hair, is not welcome."

"Rubbish! Of course she has hair! Wait until she's one year old, my son, and then you'll see that she has a thick head of hair. It will never darken much. She'll be silver rather than gold, the precious little thing."

"She looks as homely as poor Gnaea to me."

"Caesar, Caesar! She's newborn! And she's going to look very like you."

"What a fate," said Caesar, and departed.

He proceeded to the city's most prestigious inn, on the corner of the Forum Romanum and the Clivus Orbius; he had received a message that his clients who had commissioned him to prosecute the elder Dolabella were back in Rome, and anxious to see him.

"We have another case for you," said the leader of the Greek visitors, Iphicrates of Thessalonica.

"I'm flattered," said Caesar, frowning. "But who is there you could be interested in prosecuting? Appius Claudius Pulcher hasn't been governor long enough to bring a case against him, surely, even if you could persuade the Senate to consent to trying a governor still in office."

"This is an odd task which has nothing to do with Macedonian governors," said Iphicrates. "We want you to prosecute Gaius Antonius Hybrida for atrocities he committed while he was a prefect of cavalry under Sulla ten years ago.''

"Ye gods! After all this time, why?"

"We do not expect to win, Caesar. That is not the object of our mission. Simply, our experiences under the elder of the two Dolabellae has brought home to us forcibly that there are some Romans put over us who are little better than animals. And we think it high time that the city of Rome was made aware of this. Petitions are useless. No one bothers to read them, least of all the Senate. Charges of treason or extortion are rarefied businesses in courts only the upper classes of Rome bother to attend. What we want is to attract the attention of the knights, and even of the lower classes. So we thought of a trial in the Murder Court, a juicy arena all classes attend. And when we cast around for a suitable subject, the name of Gaius Antonius Hybrida leaped to every mind immediately.''

"What did he do?" Caesar asked.

"He was the prefect of cavalry in charge of the districts of Thespiae, Eleusis and Orchomenus during the time when Sulla or some of his army lived in Boeotia. But he did very little soldiering. Instead he found delight in terrible pleasures—torture, maiming, rape of women and men, boys and girls, murder.''

"Hybrida?"

"Yes, Hybrida.''

"Well, I always knew he was a typical Antonian—drunk more than sober, incapable of keeping any money in his purse, avid for women and food in enormous excess." An expression of distaste appeared on Caesar's face. "But torture? Even for an Antonian, that's not usual. I'd believe it quicker of an Ahenobarbus!''

"Our evidence is absolutely unassailable, Caesar.''

"I suppose he must get it from his mother. She wasn't a Roman, though I always heard she was a decent enough woman. An Apulian. But the Apulians are not barbarians, and what you describe is pure barbarism. Even Gaius Verres didn't go so far!''

"Our evidence is absolutely unassailable," said Iphicrates again. He looked a little sly. "Now perhaps you understand our plight: who in Rome's highest circles will believe us unless all of Rome is talking, and all of Rome sees our evidence with its own eyes?''

"You have victims for witnesses?"

"Dozens of them if necessary. People of unimpeachable virtue and standing. Some without eyes, some without ears, some without tongues, some without hands—or feet—or legs—or genitals—or wombs—or arms—or skin—or noses—or combinations of these. The man was a beast. So were his cronies, though they do not matter, as they were not of the high nobility.''

Caesar looked sick. "His victims lived, then.''

"Most of them lived, that is true. Antonius, you see, thought that what he did was an art. And the art lay in inflicting the most pain and dismemberment without death ensuing. Antonius's greatest joy was to ride back into one of his towns months later to see that his victims still lived.''

"Well, it will be awkward for me, but I will certainly take the case,'' said Caesar sternly.

"Awkward? How, awkward?''

"His elder brother, Marcus, is married to my first cousin once removed— the daughter of Lucius Caesar, who was consul and later murdered by Gaius Marius. There are three little boys—Hybrida's nephews—who are my first cousins twice removed. It is not considered good form to prosecute members of one's own family, Iphicrates.''

"But is the actual relationship one which extends to Gaius Antonius Hybrida? Your cousin is not married to him.''

"True, and it is for that reason I will take the case. But many will disapprove. The blood does link in Julia's three sons.''

It was Lucius Decumius he chose to talk to, rather than to Gaius Matius or someone else closer to his rank.

"You hear everything, dad. But have you heard of this?''

Having been dowered with a physical apparatus incapable of looking older when he was younger and younger when he was older, Lucius Decumius remained ever the same; Caesar was hard put to calculate his age, which he guessed at around sixty.

"A bit, not much. His slaves don't last beyond six months, yet you never sees them buried. I always gets suspicious when I never sees them buried. Usually means all sorts of nasty antics.''

"Nothing is more despicable than cruelty to a slave!''

"Well, you'd think so, Caesar. You got the world's best mother, you been brought up right.''

"It should not have to do with how one is brought up!'' said Caesar angrily. "It surely has to do with one's innate nature. I can understand such atrocities when they're perpetrated by barbarians—their customs, traditions and gods ask things of them which we Romans outlawed centuries ago. To think of a Roman nobleman—one of the Antonii!—taking *pleasure* in inflicting such suffering—oh, dad, I find it hard to believe!''

But Lucius Decumius merely looked wise. "It's all around you, Caesar, and you knows it is. Maybe not quite so horrible, but that's mostly because people is afraid of getting caught. You just consider for a moment! This Antonius Hybrida, he's a Roman nobleman just like you say. The courts protects him and his own sort protects him. What's he got to be afraid of, once he starts? All what stops most people starting, Caesar, is the fear of getting caught. Getting caught means punishment. And the higher a man is, the further he's got to fall. But just sometimes you finds a man with the clout to be whatever he wants to be who goes ahead and *is* what he wants to be. Like Antonius Hybrida. Not many like him in any place. *Not many!* But there's always some, Caesar. Always some.''

"Yes, you're right. Of course you're right.'' The eyelids fell tiredly, blocked out Caesar's thoughts. "What you're saying is that such men must be brought to book. Punished.''

"Unless you wants a lot more of the same. Let one off and two more gets daring.''

"So I must bring him to book. That won't be easy.''

"It won't be easy.''

"Aside from dark rumors of disappearing slaves, what else do you know about him, dad?''

"Not much, except that he's hated. Tradesmen hates him. So do ordinary people. When he pinches a sweet little girl as he walks down the street, he pinches too hard, makes her cry.''

"And where does my cousin Julia fit into all this?''

"Ask your mother, Caesar, not me!''

"I can't ask my mother, Lucius Decumius!''

Lucius Decumius thought about that, and nodded. "No, you can't, right enough.'' He paused to ponder. "Well, that Julia's a silly woman—not one of your smarter Julias for sure! *Her* Antonius is a bit of a lad, if you follows me, but not cruel. Thoughtless. Don't know when to give his boys a good kick up the arse, little beggars.''

"You mean his boys run wild?''

"As a forest boar.''

"Let me see. . . . Marcus, Gaius, Lucius. Oh, I wish I knew more about family matters! I don't listen to the women talking, is the trouble. My mother could tell me in an instant. . . . But she's too clever, dad, she'd want to know why I'm interested, and then she'd try to persuade me not to take the case. After which we'd quarrel. Far better that when she does learn I'm taking the case, it's an accomplished fact.'' He sighed, looked rueful. "I think I'd better hear more about Hybrida's brother's boys, dad.''

Lucius Decumius screwed up his eyes, pursed his lips. "I sees them about the Subura—shouldn't be scampering in the Subura with no pedagogue or servant, but they does. Steal food from the shops, more to torment than because they wants it.''

"How old are they?"

"Can't tell you exactly, but Marcus looks about twelve in size and acts five in mind, so put him at seven or eight. The other two is littler.''

"Yes, they're hulking brutes, all the Antonii. I take it the father of these boys hasn't much money.''

"Always on the edge of disaster, Caesar.''

"I won't do him or his boys any good if I prosecute, then.''

"You won't.''

"I have to take the case, dad.''

"Well, I knows that!''

"What I need are some witnesses. Preferably free men—or women—or children—who are willing to testify. He *must* be doing it here too. And his victims won't all be vanished slaves.''

"I'll go looking, Caesar.''

His womenfolk knew the moment he came in the front door that some trouble had come upon him, but neither Aurelia nor Cinnilla tried to discover its nature. Under more normal circumstances Aurelia certainly would have, but the baby occupied her attention more than she would have cared to admit, so she missed the significance of Caesar's mood. And therefore the chance to talk him out of prosecuting Gaius Antonius Hybrida, whose nephews were Caesar's close cousins.

The Murder Court was the logical venue, but the more Caesar thought about the case the less he liked the idea of a trial in the Murder Court. For one thing, the president was the praetor Marcus Junius Juncus, who resented his allocation to an ex-aedile's court, but no ex-aediles had volunteered this year; Caesar had already clashed with him during a case he had pleaded in January. The other great difficulty was the un-Roman litigants. It was very difficult indeed in any court to get a favorable verdict when the plaintiffs were foreign nationals and the defendant a Roman of high birth and standing. All very well for his clients to say that they didn't mind losing the case, but Caesar knew a judge like Juncus would ensure the proceedings were kept quiet, the court shoved away somewhere designed to discourage a large audience. And the worst of it was that the tribune of the plebs Gnaeus Sicinius was monopolizing Forum audiences by agitating ceaselessly for a full restoration of all the powers which had used to belong to the tribunes of the plebs. Nobody was interested in anything else, especially after Sicinius had come out with a witticism already going down in the collection of every literary dilettante who amassed political witticisms.

"Why," the consul Gaius Scribonius Curio had asked him, exasperated, "is it that you harass me and my colleague Gnaeus Octavius, you harass the praetors, the aediles, your fellow tribunes of the plebs, Publius Cethegus, all our consulars and great men, bankers like Titus Atticus, even the poor quaestors!—and yet you never say a word against Marcus Licinius Crassus? Isn't Marcus Crassus worthy of your venom? Or is it Marcus Crassus who is putting you up to your antics? Go on, Sicinius, you yapping little dog, tell me why you leave Crassus alone!"

Well aware that Curio and Crassus had had a falling-out, Sicinius pretended to give the question serious consideration before answering.

"Because Marcus Crassus has hay wrapped around *both* his horns," he said gravely.

The very large audience had collapsed on the ground laughing, appreciating every nuance. The sight of an ox with hay wrapped around one horn was common enough; the hay was a warning that the animal might look placid, but it would suddenly gore with the hayed horn. Oxen with hay wrapped around both horns were avoided like lepers. Had Marcus Crassus not possessed the unruffled, bovine look and build of an ox, the remark would not have been so apt; but what made it so hilarious was the inference that Marcus Crassus was such a prick he had two of them.

Therefore, how to attract away some of Sicinius's devoted following? How to give the case the audience it deserved? And while Caesar chewed these matters over, his clients journeyed back to Boeotia to gather evidence and witnesses in the exact way Caesar had instructed; the months went on, the clients returned, and still Caesar had not applied to Juncus to hear the case.

"I do not understand!" cried Iphicrates, disappointed. "If we do not hurry, we may not be heard at all!"

"I have a feeling there's a better way," said Caesar. "Be patient with me a little longer, Iphicrates. I promise I will make sure you and your colleagues don't have to wait in Rome for more months. Your witnesses are well hidden?"

"Absolutely, just as you ordered. In a villa outside Cumae."

And then one day early in June, the answer came. Caesar had paused by the tribunal of the *praetor peregrinus*, Marcus Terentius Varro Lucullus. The younger brother of the man most of Rome deemed her brightest man of the future was very like Lucullus—and very devoted to him. Separated as children by the vicissitudes of fortune, the bond had not weakened; rather, it had grown much stronger. Lucullus had delayed his climb up the *cursus honorum* so that he could be curule aedile in tandem with Varro Lucullus, and together they had thrown games of such brilliance that people still talked about them. It was commonly believed that both the Luculli would achieve the consulship in the near future; they were as popular with the voters as they were aristocratic.

"How goes your day?" Caesar asked, smiling; he liked the foreign praetor, in whose court he had pleaded many little cases with a confidence and freedom few other judges engendered. Varro Lucullus was extremely knowledgeable about law, and a man of great integrity.

"My day goes boringly," said Varro Lucullus, answering the smile with one of his own.

Somehow Caesar's brilliant idea was born and reached full maturity between his question and Varro Lucullus's answer; that was usually what happened, the lightning perception of how to go about some difficult thing after months of puzzling.

"When are you leaving Rome to hear the rural assizes?"

"It's traditional for the foreign praetor to pop up on the Campanian seaside just as summer reaches its most unendurable pitch," said Varro Lucullus, and sighed. "However, it looks as if I'll be tied down in Rome for at least another month."

"Then don't cut it short!" said Caesar.

Varro Lucullus blinked; one moment he had been talking to a man whose legal acumen and ability he prized highly, the next moment he was gazing at the space where Caesar had been.

"I know how to do it!" Caesar was saying shortly afterward to Iphicrates in the private parlor he had hired at his inn.

"How?" asked the important man of Thessalonica eagerly.

"I *knew* I was right to delay, Iphicrates! We're not going to use the Murder Court, nor will we lay criminal charges against Gaius Antonius Hybrida."

"Not lay criminal charges?" gasped Iphicrates. "But that is the whole object!"

"Nonsense! The whole object is to create a huge stir in Rome. We won't do that in Juncus's court, nor will his court enable us to steal Sicinius's Forum audiences. Juncus will tuck himself away in the smallest, most airless corner of the Basilica Porcia or Opimia, everyone compelled to be present will faint from the heat, and no one who is not compelled to be present will be there at all. The jury will hate us and Juncus will gallop through the proceedings, egged on by jurors and advocates.''

''But what other alternative is there?''

Caesar leaned forward. ''I will lay this case before the foreign praetor as a civil suit,'' he said. ''Instead of charging Hybrida with murder, I will sue him for damages arising out of his conduct while a prefect of cavalry in Greece ten years ago. And you will lodge an enormous *sponsio* with the foreign praetor—a sum of money far greater than Hybrida's whole fortune. Could you raise two thousand talents? And be prepared if something goes wrong to lose them?''

Iphicrates drew a breath. ''The sum is indeed enormous, but we came prepared to spend whatever it takes to make Rome see that she must cease to plague us with men like Hybrida—and the elder Dolabella. Yes, Caesar,'' said Iphicrates deliberately, ''we will raise two thousand talents. It will take some doing, but we will find it here in Rome.''

''All right, then we lodge two thousand talents in *sponsio* with the foreign praetor in the civil suit against Gaius Antonius Hybrida. That will create a sensation in itself. It will also demonstrate to the whole of Rome that we are serious.''

''Hybrida won't be able to find a quarter of that sum.''

''Absolutely right, Iphicrates, he won't. But it is in the jurisdiction of the foreign praetor to waive the lodgement of *sponsio* if he considers there is a case to be answered. And if there's one thing about Varro Lucullus, it's that he is fair. He will waive Hybrida's matching sum, I'm sure of it.''

''But if we win and Hybrida has not lodged two thousand talents as his matching *sponsio,* what happens?''

''Then, Iphicrates, he has to find it! Because he has to pay it! That's how a civil suit works under Roman law.''

''Oh, I see!'' Iphicrates sat back and linked his arms about his knees, smiling gently. ''Then if he loses, he's a beggar. He will have to leave Rome a bankrupt—and he will never be able to return, will he?''

''He will never be able to return.''

''On the other hand, if we lose, he takes our two thousand?''

''That's right.''

''Do you think we will lose, Caesar?''

''No.''

''Then why are you warning me that something could go wrong? Why do you say we must be prepared to forfeit our money?''

Frowning, Caesar tried to explain to this Greek what he, a Roman through and through, had absorbed from infancy. "Because Roman law is not as watertight as it seems. A lot depends on the judge, and the judge under Sulla's law cannot be Varro Lucullus. In that respect, I pin my faith upon Varro Lucullus's integrity, that he will choose a judge prepared to be dispassionate. And then there is another risk. Sometimes a brilliant advocate will find a hole in the law that can let in an entire ocean—Hybrida will be defended by the best advocates in Rome." Caesar tensed, held his hands like claws. "If *I* can be inspired to find an answer to our problem, do you think there is no one else capable of being inspired to find an answer to Hybrida's problem? That is why men like me enjoy legal practice, Iphicrates, when judge and process are free from taint or bias! No matter how conclusive and watertight we think our case is, beware of the bright fellow on the other side. What if Cicero defends? Formidable! Mind you, I don't think he'll be tempted when he learns the details. But Hortensius wouldn't be so fussy. You must remember too that one side *has* to lose. We are fighting for a principle, and that is the most dangerous reason of all for going to law."

"I will consult with my colleagues and give you our answer tomorrow," said Iphicrates.

The answer was that Caesar should proceed to ask the foreign praetor to hear a civil suit against Gaius Antonius Hybrida. Down to Varro Lucullus's tribunal went Caesar with his clients, there to apply to lodge a *sponsio* of two thousand talents, the sum in damages being demanded from Hybrida.

Varro Lucullus sat mute, deprived of breath, then shook his head in wonder and held out his hand to examine the bank draft. "This is real and you are serious," he said to Caesar.

"Absolutely, *praetor peregrinus*."

"Why not the Extortion Court?"

"Because the suit does not involve extortion. It involves murder—but more than murder! It involves torture, rape, and permanent maiming. After so many years, my clients do not wish to seek criminal justice. They are seeking damages on behalf of the people of Thespiae, Eleusis and Orchomenus whom Gaius Antonius Hybrida damaged. These people are incapable of working, of earning their livings, of being parents or husbands or wives. To support them in comfort and with kindness is costing the other citizens of Thespiae, Eleusis and Orchomenus a fortune that my clients consider Gaius Antonius Hybrida should be paying. This is a civil suit, *praetor peregrinus*, to recover damages."

"Then present your evidence in brief, advocate, so that I may decide whether there is a case to be answered."

"I will offer before your court and the judge you appoint the testimony of eight victims or witnesses of atrocities. Six of these will be residents of the towns of Thespiae, Eleusis and Orchomenus. The other two are residents of the city of Rome, one a freedman citizen, the other a Syrian national.''

''Why do you offer Roman testimony, advocate?''

''To show the court that Gaius Antonius Hybrida is still indulging in his atrocious practices, *praetor peregrinus*.''

Two hours later Varro Lucullus accepted the suit in his court and lodged the Greek *sponsio*. A summons was issued against Gaius Antonius Hybrida to appear to answer the charges on the morrow. After which Varro Lucullus appointed his judge. Publius Cornelius Cethegus. Keeping his face straight, Caesar cheered inside. Brilliant! The judge was a man so wealthy he based his whole power upon the claim that he could not be bought, a man so cultivated and refined that he wept when a pet fish or a lapdog died, a man who covered his head with his toga so he couldn't see a chicken being decapitated in the marketplace. And a man who had no love whatsoever for the Antonii. Would Cethegus consider that a fellow senator must be protected, no matter what the crime? Or the civil suit? No, not Cethegus! After all, there was no possibility of loss of Roman citizenship or of exile. This was civil litigation, only money at stake.

Word ran round the Forum Romanum quicker than feet could run; a crowd began to gather within moments of Caesar's appearance before the foreign praetor's tribunal. As Caesar stimulated interest by enlarging upon the injuries Hybrida's victims had sustained, the crowd grew, hardly able to wait for the case to begin on the morrow—could there truly be such awful sights to be seen as a flayed man and a woman whose genitalia had been so cut up she couldn't even urinate properly?

News of the case beat Caesar home, as he could see from his mother's face.

''What is this I hear?'' she demanded, bristling. ''You're acting in a case against Gaius Antonius Hybrida? That is not possible! There is a blood tie.''

''There is no blood tie between Hybrida and me, Mater.''

''His nephews are your cousins!''

''They are his brother's children, and the blood tie is from their mother. Consanguinity could only matter if it were Hybrida's sons—did he have any, that is!—who were my cousins.''

''You can't do this to a Julia!''

''I dislike the family implication, Mater, but there is no direct involvement of a Julia.''

"The Julii Caesares have allied themselves in marriage with the Antonii! That is reason enough!"

"No, it is not! And more fool the Julii Caesares for seeking an alliance with the Antonii! They're boors and wastrels! For I tell you, Mater, that I would not let a Julia of my own family marry any Antonius," said Caesar, turning his shoulder.

"Reconsider, Caesar, please! You will be condemned."

"I will not reconsider."

The result of this confrontation was an uncomfortable meal that afternoon. Helpless to contend with two such steely opponents as her husband and her mother-in-law, Cinnilla fled back to the nursery as soon as she could, pleading colic, teething, rashes, and every other baby ailment she could think of. Which left Caesar, chin up, to ignore Aurelia, chin up.

Some did voice disapproval, but Caesar was by no means setting a precedent in taking this case; there had been many others in which consanguinity was in much higher degree than the technical objections men like Catulus raised in the prosecution of Gaius Antonius Hybrida.

Of course Hybrida could not ignore the summons, so he was waiting at the foreign praetor's tribunal with a retinue of famous faces in attendance, including Quintus Hortensius and Caesar's uncle, Gaius Aurelius Cotta. Of Marcus Tullius Cicero there was no sign, even in the audience; until, Caesar noticed out of the corner of his eye, the moment in which Cethegus opened the hearing. Trust Cicero not to miss such scandalous goings-on! Especially when the legal option of a civil suit had been chosen.

Hybrida was uneasy, Caesar saw that at once. A big, muscular fellow with a neck as thick as a corded column, Hybrida was a typical Antonius; the wiry, curly auburn hair and red-brown eyes were as Antonian as the aquiline nose and the prominent chin trying to meet across a small, thick mouth. Until he had heard about Hybrida's atrocities Caesar had dismissed the brutish face as that of a lout who drank too much, ate too much, and was overly fond of sexual pleasures. Now he knew better. It was the face of a veritable monster.

Things got off to a bad start for Hybrida when Hortensius elected to take a high hand and demanded that the suit forthwith be dismissed, alleging that if the matter was one-tenth as serious as the suit indicated, it should be heard before a criminal court. Varro Lucullus sat expressionless, unwilling to intervene unless his judge asked for his advice. Which Cethegus was not about to do. Sooner or later his turn would have come up to preside over this court, and he had not looked forward to some monotonous argument about a purse of moneys. Now here he was with a veritable plum of a case—one which might repel him, but would at least not bore him. So he dealt smartly with Hortensius and got things under way with smooth authority.

By noon Cethegus was ready to hear the witnesses, whose appearance created a sensation. Iphicrates and his companions had chosen the victims they had brought all the way from Greece with an eye to drama as well as to pity. Most moving was a man who could not testify on his own behalf at all; Hybrida had removed most of his face—and his tongue. But his wife was as articulate as she was filled with hatred, and a damning witness. Cethegus sat listening to her and looking at her poor husband green-faced and sweating. After their testimony concluded he adjourned for the day, praying he got home before he was sick.

But it was Hybrida who tried to have the last word. As he left the area of the tribunal he grasped Caesar by the arm and detained him.

"Where did you collect this sorry lot?" he asked, assuming an expression of pained bewilderment. "You must have had to comb the world! But it won't work, you know. What are they, after all? A handful of miscreant misfits! That's all! A mere handful anxious to take hefty Roman damages instead of existing on piddling Greek alms!"

"*A mere handful?*" roared Caesar at the top of his voice, and stilling the noise of the dispersing crowd, which turned to hear what he said. "Is that all? I say to you, Gaius Antonius Hybrida, that *one* would be too many! Just one! Just one man or woman or child despoiled in this frightful way is one too many! Just one man or woman or child plundered of youth and beauty and pride in being alive is one too many! Go away! Go home!"

Gaius Antonius Hybrida went home, appalled to discover that his advocates had no wish to accompany him. Even his brother had found an excuse to go elsewhere. Though he did not walk alone; beside him trotted a small plump man who had become quite a friend in the year and a half since he had joined the Senate. This man's name was Gaius Aelius Staienus, and he was hungry for powerful allies, hungry to eat free of charge at someone else's table, and very hungry for money. He had had some of Pompey's money last year, when he had been Mamercus's quaestor and incited a mutiny—oh, not a nasty, bloody mutiny! And it had all worked out extremely well in the end, with not a whiff of suspicion stealing his way.

"You're going to lose," he said to Hybrida as they entered Hybrida's very nice mansion on the Palatine.

Hybrida was not disposed to argue. "I know."

"But wouldn't it be nice to win?" asked Staienus dreamily. "Two thousand talents to spend, that's the reward for winning."

"I'm going to have to *find* two thousand talents, which will bankrupt me for more years than I have left to live."

"Not necessarily," said Staienus in a purring voice. He sat down in Hybrida's cliental chair, and looked about. "Have you any of that Chian wine left?" he asked.

Hybrida went to a console table and poured two undiluted goblets from a flagon, handed one to his guest, and sat down. He drank deeply, then gazed at Staienus. "You've got something boiling in your pot," he said. "What is it?"

"Two thousand talents is a vast sum. In fact, one thousand talents is a vast sum."

"That's true." The gross little mouth peeled its thick lips back to reveal Hybrida's small and perfect white teeth. "I am not a fool, Staienus! If I agree to split the two thousand talents equally with you, you'll guarantee to get me off. Is that right?"

"That's right."

"Then I agree. You get me off, and one thousand of those Greek talents are yours."

"It's simple, really," said Staienus thoughtfully. "You have Sulla to thank for it, of course. But he's dead, so he won't care if you thank me instead."

"Stop tormenting me and tell me!"

"Oh, yes! I forgot that you prefer to torment others than be tormented yourself." Like many small men suddenly given a position of power, Staienus was incapable of concealing his pleasure at owning power, even though this meant that when the affair was over, so was his friendship with Hybrida. No matter how successful his ploy. But he didn't care. A thousand talents was reward enough. What was friendship with a creature like Hybrida anyway?

"Tell me, Staienus, or get out!"

"The *ius auxilii ferendi*," was what Staienus said.

"Well, what about it?"

"The original function of the tribunes of the plebs, and the only function Sulla didn't take off them—to rescue a member of the plebs from the hands of a magistrate."

"The *ius auxilii ferendi*!" cried Hybrida, amazed. For a moment his pouting face lightened, then darkened again. "They wouldn't do it," he said.

"They might," said Staienus.

"Not Sicinius! Never Sicinius! All it takes is one veto within the college and the other nine tribunes of the plebs are powerless. Sicinius wouldn't stand for it, Staienus. He's a wretched nuisance, but he's not bribable."

"Sicinius," said Staienus happily, "is not popular with any of his nine colleagues. He's made such a thorough nuisance of himself—and stolen their thunder in the Forum!—that they're sick to death of him. In fact the day before yesterday I heard two of them threaten to throw him off the Tarpeian Rock unless he shut up about restoring their rights."

"You mean Sicinius could be intimidated?"

"Yes. Definitely. Of course you'll have to find a goodly sum of cash between now and tomorrow morning, because none of them will be in it unless they're well rewarded. But you can do that—especially with a thousand talents coming in because of it."

"How much?" asked Hybrida.

"Nine times fifty thousand sesterces. That's four hundred and fifty thousand. Can you do it?"

"I can try. I'll go to my brother, he doesn't want scandal in the family. And there are a few other sources. Yes, Staienus, I believe I can do it."

And so it was arranged. Gaius Aelius Staienus had a busy evening bustling from the house of one tribune of the plebs to another—Marcus Atilius Bulbus, Manius Aquillius, Quintus Curius, Publius Popillius, and on through nine of the ten. He did not go near the house of Gnaeus Sicinius.

The hearing was due to recommence two hours after dawn; by then the Forum Romanum had already experienced high drama, so it promised to be quite a day for the Forum frequenters, who were ecstatic. Just after dawn his nine fellow tribunes of the plebs had ganged up on Gnaeus Sicinius and physically hauled him to the top of the Capitol, where they beat him black and blue, then held him over the end of the overhanging ledge called the Tarpeian Rock and let him look down at the needle-sharp outcrop below. No more of this perpetual agitating to see the powers of the tribunate of the plebs restored! they cried to him as he dangled, and got an oath from him that he would in future do as his nine colleagues told him. Sicinius was then packed off home in a litter.

And not more than a very few moments after Cethegus opened the second day's proceedings in the suit against Hybrida, nine tribunes of the plebs descended upon Varro Lucullus's tribunal shouting that a member of the plebs was being detained against his will by a magistrate.

"I appeal to you to exercise the *ius auxilii ferendi*!" cried Hybrida, arms extended piteously.

"Marcus Terentius Varro Lucullus, we have been appealed to by a member of the plebs to exercise the *ius auxilii ferendi*!" said Manius Aquillius. "I hereby notify you that we so exercise it!"

"This is a manifest outrage!" Varro Lucullus shouted, leaping to his feet. "I refuse to allow you to exercise that right! Where is the tenth tribune?"

"At home in bed, very sick," sneered Manius Aquillius, "but you can send to him if you like. He won't veto us."

"You transgress justice!" yelled Cethegus. "An outrage! A shame! A scandal! How much has Hybrida paid you?"

"Release Gaius Antonius Hybrida, or we will take hold of every last man who objects and throw him from the Tarpeian Rock!" cried Manius Aquillius.

"You are obstructing justice!" said Varro Lucullus.

"There can be no justice in a magistrate's court, as you well know, Varro Lucullus," said Quintus Curius. "One man is not a jury! If you wish to proceed against Gaius Antonius, then do so in a criminal court, where the *ius auxilii ferendi* does not apply!"

Caesar stood without moving, nor did he try to object. His clients huddled in his rear, shivering. Face stony, he turned to them and said softly, "I am a patrician, and not a magistrate. We must let the *praetor peregrinus* deal with this. Say nothing!"

"Very well, take your member of the Plebs!" said Varro Lucullus, hand on Cethegus's arm to restrain him.

"And," said Gaius Antonius Hybrida, standing in the midst of nine tribunes of the plebs bent on war, "Since I have won the case, I will take the *sponsio* lodged by our Greek-loving Caesar's clients here."

The reference to Greek love was a deliberate slur which brought back to Caesar in one red flash all the pain of that accusation concerning King Nicomedes. Without hesitating, he walked through the ranks of the tribunes of the plebs and took Hybrida's throat between his hands. Hybrida had always considered himself a Hercules among men, but he could neither break the hold nor manage to come at his taller assailant, whose strength he would not have believed were he not its victim. It took Varro Lucullus and his six lictors to drag Caesar off him, though some men in the crowd wondered afterward at the inertia of the nine tribunes of the plebs, who made no move to help Hybrida at all.

"This case is dismissed!" bawled Varro Lucullus at the top of his lungs. "There is no suit! I, Marcus Terentius Varro Lucullus, so declare it! Plaintiffs, take back your *sponsio*! And every last mother's son of you go home!"

"The *sponsio*! The *sponsio* belongs to Gaius Antonius!" cried another voice: Gaius Aelius Staienus.

"It does not belong to Hybrida!" Cethegus yelled. "The case has been dismissed by the *praetor peregrinus,* in whose jurisdiction it lies! The *sponsio* returns to its owners, there is no wager!"

"Will you take your member of the plebs and quit my tribunal!" said Varro Lucullus through his teeth to the tribunes of the plebs. "Go, get out of here, all of you! And I take leave to tell you that you have done the cause of the tribunate of the plebs no good by this scandalous miscarriage of its original purpose! I will do my utmost to keep you muzzled forever!"

Off went the nine men with Hybrida, Staienus trailing after them howling for the lost *sponsio,* Hybrida tenderly feeling his bruised throat.

While the excited crowd milled, Varro Lucullus and Caesar looked at each other.

"I would have loved to let you strangle the brute, but I hope you understand that I could not," said Varro Lucullus.

"I understand," said Caesar, still shaking. "I thought I was well in control! I'm not a hot man, you know. But I don't care for excrement like Hybrida calling me a deviate."

"That's obvious," said Varro Lucullus dryly, remembering what his brother had had to say on the subject.

Caesar too now paused to recollect whose brother he was with, but decided that Varro Lucullus was quite capable of making up his own mind.

"Do you believe," said Cicero, rushing up now that the violence appeared to be at an end, "the gall of that worm? To demand the *sponsio,* by all the gods!"

"It takes a lot of gall to do *that,*" said Caesar, pointing to the mutilated man and his spokeswoman wife.

"Disgusting!" cried Cicero, sitting down on the steps of the tribunal and mopping his face with his handkerchief.

"Well," said Caesar to Iphicrates, who hovered uncertainly, "at least we managed to save your two thousand talents. And I would say that if what you wanted was to create a stir in Rome, you have succeeded. I think the Senate will be very careful in future whom it sends to govern Macedonia. Now go back to your inn, and take those poor unfortunates with you. I'm just sorry that the citizens of their towns will have to continue supporting them. But I did warn you."

"I am sorry about only one thing," said Iphicrates, moving away. "That we failed to punish Gaius Antonius Hybrida."

"We didn't succeed in ruining him financially," said Caesar, "but he will have to leave Rome. It will be a long time before he dares to show his face in this city again."

"Do you think," asked Cicero, "that Hybrida actually bribed nine tribunes of the plebs?"

"I for one am sure of it!" snapped Cethegus, whose anger was slow to cool. "Apart from Sicinius—little though I love that man!—this year's tribunes of the plebs are a shabby lot!"

"Why should they be splendid?" asked Caesar, whose anger had cooled completely. "There's no glory to be had in the office these days. It's a dead end."

"I wonder," asked Cicero, loath to abandon the direction of his thoughts, "how much nine tribunes of the plebs cost Hybrida?"

Cethegus pursed his lips. "About forty thousand each."

Varro Lucullus's eyes danced. "You speak with such absolute authority, Cethegus! How do you know?"

The King of the Backbenchers set his ire aside; it did not become his style, though, he assured himself, it was excusable. He proceeded to answer the foreign praetor with raised brows and the customary drawl in his voice. "My dear *praetor peregrinus,* there is nothing I do not know about the cupidity of senators! I could give you every bribable senator's price down to the last sestertius. And for that shabby lot, forty thousand each."

And that, as Hybrida was busy discovering, was what Gaius Aelius Staienus had paid; he had kept ninety thousand sesterces for himself.

"Give them back!" said the man who loved to torture and mutilate his fellow men. "Give the extra money back, Staienus, or I'll tear your eyes out with my own fingers! I'll be three hundred and sixty thousand sesterces out of purse as it is—you and your two thousand talents!"

"Don't forget," said the uncowed Staienus, looking vicious, "that it was my idea to use the *ius auxulii ferendi.* I'll keep the ninety thousand. As for you—thank all the gods that you're not stripped of your whole fortune!"

The sensation of the almost-hearing took some time to die away, and there were several long-lasting results of it. One was that that year's College of Tribunes of the Plebs went down in the annals of political diarists as the most shameful ever; one other was that Macedonia did remain in the hands of responsible—if warlike—governors; Gnaeus Sicinius spoke no more in the Forum about restoring its full powers to the tribunate of the plebs; Caesar's fame as an advocate soared; and Gaius Antonius Hybrida absented himself from Rome and the places Romans frequented for several years. In fact, he went on a little trip to the island of Cephallenia in the Ionian Sea, where he found himself the only civilized man (if such he could be called) in the whole region, and discovered too several incredibly ancient grave mounds filled with treasure—exquisitely chased and inlaid daggers, masks made of pure gold, electrum flagons, rock-crystal cups, heaps of jewelry. Greater by far in value than two thousand talents. Great enough to assure him the consulship when he returned home, if he had to buy every single vote.

No stirring incidents enlivened the next year for Caesar, who remained in Rome and practiced as an advocate with resounding success. Cicero was not in Rome that year, however. Elected quaestor, he drew the lot for Lilybaeum in western Sicily, where he would work under the governor, Sextus Peducaeus. As his quaestorship meant he was now a member of the Senate, he was willing to leave Rome (though he had hoped for a job within Italy, and cursed his luck in the lots) and plunge himself enthusiastically into his work, which was mostly to do with the grain supply. It was a poor year, but the consuls had dealt with the coming shortage in an effective way; they bought huge quantities of grain still in storage in Sicily, and sold it cheaply in Rome by enacting a *lex frumentaria*.

Like almost everyone else literate, Cicero adored both to write and receive letters, and had been an avid correspondent for many years before this one, his thirty-first. But it was to this time in western Sicily that the enduring focus of his epistolary efforts was to date; that is, the steady flow of letters between him and the erudite plutocrat, Titus Pomponius Atticus. Thanks to Atticus, the loneliness of those many months in insular Lilybaeum was alleviated by a steady flow of information and gossip about everything and everyone in Rome.

Said Atticus in a missive sent toward the end of Cicero's Sicilian exile:

> The expected food riots never happened, only because Rome is fortunate in her consuls. I had a few words with Gaius Cotta's brother, Marcus, who is now consul-elect for next year. In this nation of clever men, I asked, why are the common people still obliged from time to time to subsist on millet and turnips? It is high time, I said, that Rome levied against the private growers of Sicily and our other grain provinces and forced them to sell to the State rather than hang on for higher prices from the private grain merchants, for all too often that simply means the grain sits ensiloed in Sicily when it ought to be feeding the common people. I disapprove of stockpiling for profit when that affects the well-being of a nation full of clever men. Marcus Cotta listened to me with great attention, and promised to do something about it next year. As I do not have shares in grain, I can afford to be patriotic and altruistic. And stop laughing, Marcus Tullius.

Quintus Hortensius, our most self-important plebeian aedile in a generation, has given magnificent games. Along with a free distribution of grain to the populace. *He* intends to be consul in his year! Of course your absence has meant he is enjoying a high time of it in the law courts, but young Caesar always manages to give him a fright, and often filches his laurels. He doesn't like it, and was heard to complain the other day that he wished Caesar would depart from Rome too. But those bits of Hortensical nonsense are as nothing compared to the banquet he gave on the occasion of his (yes, it has finally happened!) inauguration as an augur. He served roast peacock. You read aright: *roast peacock*. The birds (six of them all told) had been roasted and carved down to the eunuch's nose, then the cooks somehow reassembled all the feathers over the top, so that they were carried in head-high on golden platters in all their fine plumage, tails fanned out and crests nodding. It created a sensation, and other gourmets like Cethegus, Philippus and the senior consul-elect, Lucullus, sat there contemplating suicide. However, dear Marcus, the actual eating of the birds was an anticlimax. An old army boot would have tasted—and chewed!—better.

The death of Appius Claudius Pulcher in Macedonia last year has led to a most amusing situation. That family never seems to have much luck, does it? First, nephew Philippus when he was censor stripped Appius Claudius of everything, then Appius Claudius wasn't enterprising enough to buy up big at the proscription auctions, then he became too ill to govern his province, then he caps a bitter life by getting to his province at last, doing very well in military terms, and expiring before he could fix his fortune.

The six children he has left behind we all know only too well, of course. Frightful! Especially the youngest members. But Appius Claudius, the oldest son, is turning out to be very clever and enterprising. First, the moment his father's back was turned he gave the oldest girl, Claudia, to Quintus Marcius Rex, though she had no dowry whatsoever. I believe Rex paid through the nose for her! Like all the Claudii Pulchri she is a ravishing piece of goods, and that certainly helped. We expect that Rex will fare reasonably well as *her* husband, as she is reputed to be the only one of the three girls with a nice disposition.

Three boys are a difficulty, no one denies that. And adoption is out of the question. The youngest boy (who calls himself plain Publius Clodius) is so repulsive and wild that no one can be found willing to adopt him. Gaius Claudius, the middle boy, is an oaf. Unadoptable too. So there is young Appius Claudius, just twenty years of age, obliged to fund not only his own career in the Senate, but the careers of two younger brothers as well. What Quintus Marcius Rex was compelled to contribute can be but a drop in the empty Claudius Pulcher bucket.

Yet he has done remarkably well, dear Marcus Tullius. Knowing that he would be refused by every *tata* with a grain of sense, he looked around for a rich bride and went a-wooing—guess who? None other than that dismally plain spinster, Servilia Gnaea! You know who I mean— she was, you might say, hired by Scaurus and Mamercus to live with Drusus's six orphans. Had no dowry and the most terrifying mother in Rome, a Porcia Liciniana. But it appears Scaurus and Mamercus dowered Gnaea with a full two hundred talents to be paid to her the moment Drusus's orphans were all grown. And they are grown! Marcus Porcius Cato, the youngest of the brood, aged eighteen at the moment, lives in his father's house and has declared his independence.

When the twenty-year-old Appius Claudius Pulcher came a-wooing, Servilia Gnaea grabbed him. She is, they say, all of thirty-two years old now, and an old maid to her core. I do *not* believe the rumor that she shaves! Her mother does, but that everybody knows. The best part about Appius Claudius's bargain is that his mother-in-law, the aforementioned Porcia Liciniana, has retired to a commodious seaside villa which, it seems, Scaurus and Mamercus bought against this day at the time they hired the daughter. So Appius Claudius does not have to live with his mother-in-law. The two hundred talents will come in handy.

But that is not the best of it, Marcus. The best is that Appius Claudius has married off his youngest sister, Clodilla, to none other than *Lucullus*! All of fifteen years old—he and Lucullus say. I'd make her fourteen, but I might be wrong. What a match! Thanks to Sulla, Lucullus is fabulously rich, and has besides control of the fortunes of The Heavenly Twins. Oh, I am not implying that our upright, downright Lucullus would embezzle from Faustus and Fausta—but what is to stop him popping the interest in his purse?

Thus due to the amazing energy and enterprise of this twenty-year-old youth, the fortunes of the family Appius Claudius Pulcher have taken an astonishing turn for the better. All of Rome is laughing, but not without sincere admiration. He is worth watching, our Appius Claudius! Publius Clodius, aged fourteen—then Clodilla *is* fifteen—is already a menace, and his big brother will do nothing to discipline him. He's very good-looking and precocious, he's dangerous with girls and up to all kinds of mischief. I believe, however, that he is intellectually brilliant, so he may settle down in time and become a model of the patrician Roman nobleman.

And what else have I got to tell you? Oh, yes. That famous pun of Gnaeus Sicinius's about Marcus Crassus—you will not have forgotten the hay on *both* Crassus's horns!—is even cleverer than we thought at the time. It has just come out that Sicinius has been heavily in debt to Crassus for years. So the pun contained yet another nuance. *Faenum* is "hay" and *faenerator* is "moneylender." The hay wrapped round Crassus's horns is loan money! Rome learned of the additional nuance because Sicinius is a ruined man and cannot pay Crassus back. I wasn't aware that Crassus lent money, but his nose is clean, alas. He lends only to senators and does not levy interest. His way of building up a senatorial clientele. I think it will pay to watch friend Crassus. Do *not* borrow money from him, Marcus! Interest-free is a great temptation, but Crassus calls in his debts whenever he feels like it—no notice whatsoever—and he expects to be paid at once. If he isn't paid, you're ruined. And there is not a thing the censors (if we had censors) could do about it, because he charges no interest. *Quod erat demonstrandum:* he cannot be called a usurer. He's just a thoroughly nice fellow busy helping his senatorial friends out.

And I believe that is all. Terentia is well, as is little Tullia. What a nice child your daughter is! Your brother is much as always. How I wish he could learn to get on better with my sister! But I think both you and I have given up on that. Pomponia is a termagant, Quintus is a real country squire. By that I mean he is stubborn, frugal, and proud. And wants to be master of his house.

Keep well. I will write again before I leave Rome to go back to Epirus, where my cattle ranch is thriving. Too wet for sheep, of course—their feet rot. But everyone is so keen to grow wool that they forget how much cowhide the world consumes. Cattle as an investment are underestimated.

At the end of Sextilis, Caesar received an urgent summons from Bithynia. King Nicomedes was dying, and asking for him. This was exactly what Caesar needed; Rome was growing daily more suffocating, the courts duller. And though the news from Bithynia was not happy, it was to be expected. Within one day of reading Oradaltis's note, he was packed and ready to go.

Burgundus would be with him as always, Demetrius who plucked his body hair could not be left behind nor could the Spartan Brasidas, who made his Civic Crowns out of oak leaves. In fact, this time Caesar traveled with more state than of yore; his importance was increasing, and he now found himself in need of a secretary, several scribes, several personal servants, and a small escort of his own freedmen. Therefore it was with twenty persons in his entourage that he left for the east. An expensive exercise. He was now twenty-five years old, and he had been in the Senate for five of those years.

"But don't think," said Burgundus to the new members of the party, "that you're going to travel in comfort. When Gaius Julius moves, he moves!"

Nicomedes was still alive when Caesar reached Bithynia, though he could not recover from this illness.

"It's really nothing more nor less than plain old age," said Queen Oradaltis, weeping. "Oh, I shall miss him! I have been his wife since I was fifteen. How will I manage without him?"

"You will because you have to," said Caesar, drying her eyes. "I see that dog Sulla is still brisk enough, so you'll have his company. From what you tell me, Nicomedes will be glad to go. I for one dread the idea of lingering beyond my usefulness."

"He took to his bed for good ten days ago," said Oradaltis, pattering down a marble corridor, "and the physicians say he may go at any time—today, tomorrow, next month—no one knows."

When he set eyes on the wasted figure in the big carven bed, Caesar could not believe he would last beyond that day. Little was left save skin and bone, and nothing at all of the King's physical individuality; he was dry and wrinkled as a winter apple. But when Caesar spoke his name he opened his eyes at once, held out his hands and smiled gummily, the tears falling.

"You came!" he cried, voice surprisingly strong.

"How could I not?" asked Caesar, sitting down on the edge of the bed to take both skeletal claws in a firm grip. "When you ask me to come, I come."

With Caesar there to carry him from bed to couch and couch to chair somewhere in the sun and out of the wind, Nicomedes brightened, though the use of his legs was gone permanently and he would drop into a light doze halfway through a sentence, then wake up long moments later with no memory of what he had been saying. His ability to eat solid foods had gone; he existed upon beakers of goat's milk mixed with fortified wine and honey, and dribbled more of them down his outside than he managed to drink. It is interesting, thought the fastidious and immaculate Caesar, that when this is happening to someone so beloved, the usual reactions are not present. I am not repelled. I am not tempted to command a servant to clean him up. Rather, it is a pleasure to care for him. I would empty his chamber pot gladly.

"Have you heard from your daughter?" Caesar asked him on one of his better days.

"Not directly. However, it seems she is still alive and well at Cabeira."

"Can't you negotiate with Mithridates to bring her home?"

"At the price of the kingdom, Caesar, you know that."

"But unless she comes home there is no heir anyway."

"Bithynia has an heir right here," said Nicomedes.

"In Nicomedia? Who?"

"I thought of leaving Bithynia to you."

"Me?"

"Yes, you. To be King."

"No, my dear old friend, that isn't possible."

"You would make a great king, Caesar. Wouldn't you like to rule your own land?"

"My own land is Rome, Nicomedes, and like all Romans, I was brought up to believe in the Republic."

The King's bottom lip trembled. "Can't I tempt you?"

"No."

"Bithynia needs someone young and very strong, Caesar. I can think of no one but you!"

"There is Rome herself."

"And Romans like Gaius Verres."

"That's true. But there are also Romans like me. Rome is the only answer, Nicomedes. Unless you want to see Pontus rule."

"Anything is preferable to that!"

"Then leave Bithynia to Rome."

"Can you draw up my testament in a properly Roman fashion?"

"Yes."

"Then do so, Caesar. I will leave my kingdom to Rome."

Halfway through December, King Nicomedes III of Bithynia died. One hand was given to Caesar and the other to his wife, though he did not wake from his long dream to say goodbye.

The will had been couriered to Rome soon enough that Caesar had received a reply from the Senate before the eighty-five-year-old King died, to the effect that the governor of Asia Province, Marcus Junius Juncus, was being notified, and would journey to Bithynia to begin incorporating Bithynia into Asia Province after the King was dead; as Caesar intended to stay until this happened, Caesar was to inform Juncus when it had.

That was a disappointment; Bithynia's first governor would not be a nice or understanding man.

"I want every treasure and work of art in the whole kingdom catalogued," said Caesar to the widowed queen, "also the contents of the treasury, the size of the fleets, the size of the army, and every suit of armor, sword, spear, piece of artillery and siege engine you have."

"It will be done, but why?" asked Oradaltis, frowning.

"Because if the governor of Asia Province thinks to enrich his own purse by appropriating as much as one spear or one drachma, I want to know," said Caesar grimly. "I will then make it my business to prosecute him in Rome, and I'll secure a conviction too! Because while you're cataloguing everything, you will make sure you have at least six of the most important Romans in your land as witnesses that the catalogue is correct. That will render the document hard evidence even a senatorial jury cannot ignore."

"Oh, dear! Will I be safe?" asked the Queen.

"In person, quite safe. However, if you can bear to uproot yourself and move into a private house—preferably not here in Nicomedia or in Chalcedon or Prusa—taking everything you want with you, then you ought to survive in peace and comfort for the rest of your life."

"You dislike this Marcus Junius Juncus very much."

"I dislike him very much."

"Is he a Gaius Verres?"

"I doubt that, Oradaltis. Just ordinarily venal. Thinking himself the first official representative of Rome on the scene, I imagine he'll steal whatever he decides Rome will let him get away with," said Caesar calmly. "Rome will demand a catalogue of everything from him, but it's my guess that the list you make and the list he makes won't tally. Then we'll have him!"

"Won't he suspect the existence of a catalogue?"

Caesar laughed. "Not he! Eastern realms are not prone to be so precise—precision is Roman. Of course knowing I'm here he'll think I've skimmed the place first, so it won't even cross his mind that I might have conspired with you to trap him."

By the end of December it was all done. The Queen shifted her residence to the little fishing village of Rheba, around the corner of the Bosporus on the Euxine shore. Here Nicomedes had maintained a private villa which his queen thought an ideal place for a retired ruler to occupy.

"When Juncus demands to annex your villa, you will show him a copy of the deed of ownership and inform him that the original is in the hands of your bankers. Where will you bank?''

"I had thought Byzantium. It will be closest to me.''

"Excellent! Byzantium is not a part of Bithynia, so Juncus won't be able to get a look at your accounts—or his hands on your funds. You will also inform Juncus that the contents of your villa are yours, a part of your dowry. That will prevent his taking anything away from you. So don't list anything you do take with you in the catalogue! If anyone is entitled to skim the place, it's you.''

"Well, I must think of Nysa too,'' said the old woman wistfully. "Who knows? Perhaps one day before I am dead, my daughter will be returned to me.''

Word came that Juncus had sailed into the Hellespont and would arrive in Nicomedia some days hence; he intended to pause en route to inspect Prusa, said his messenger. Caesar established the Queen in her villa, made sure that the treasury yielded her enough to provide her with an adequate income, lodged Oradaltis's funds and the catalogue with her chosen bankers in Byzantium, and then took ship from Byzantium with his retinue of twenty. He would hug the Thracian coast of the Propontis all the way to the Hellespont, and thus avoid encountering Marcus Junius Juncus, the governor of Asia Province—and the governor now of Bithynia.

Caesar was not going back to Rome. Instead he planned to sail to Rhodes, and there study with Apollonius Molon for a year or two. Cicero had convinced him that this would put an additional polish on his oratory, though he was well aware how good his oratory already was. He didn't miss Rome as Cicero always did, nor did he miss his family. Very pleasant and reassuring though possession of that family was, his wife and child and mother were there to wait for him, and would be there when eventually he returned. It never occurred to him that one or more of them might be snatched from him by death while he was away.

This trip, he was discovering, was an expensive one, and he had refused to allow Nicomedes or Oradaltis to give him money. He had asked for a keepsake only, and been given a genuine emerald from Scythia rather than the much paler, cloudier stones from the Sinus Arabicus; a flattish cabochon the size of a hen's egg, it had the King and Queen of Bithynia engraved in profile upon it. Not for sale at any price, nor for any need. However, Caesar never worried about money. For the time being he had sufficient, and the future, he was convinced, would look after itself; an attitude which drove his careful mother to distraction. But retinues of twenty and hired ships did multiply by a factor of ten those early journeys he had made!

In Smyrna he spent time with Publius Rutilius Rufus again, and was highly entertained by the old man's stories of Cicero, who had visited him on his way back to Rome from Rhodes.

"An amazing kind of mushroom!" was Rutilius Rufus's verdict to Caesar. "He'll never be happy in Rome, you know, though he worships the place. I would call him the salt of the earth—a decent, warmhearted and old-fashioned fellow."

"I know what you mean," nodded Caesar. "The trouble is, Uncle Publius, that he has a superbly able mind and much ambition."

"Like Gaius Marius."

"No," said Caesar firmly. "*Not* like Gaius Marius."

In Miletus he learned how Verres had stolen the finest wools and tapestries and rugs the city owned, and advised the *ethnarch* to lodge a complaint with the Senate in Rome.

"Though," he said, preparing to embark for the voyage to Halicarnassus, "you were lucky he didn't pilfer your art and despoil your temples as well. That was what he did elsewhere."

The ship he had hired in Byzantium was a neat enough cargo vessel of some forty oars, high in the poop where the two great rudder oars resided, and having a cabin for his use on the deck amidships. Thirty assorted mules and horses—including the Nesaean and his own beloved Toes—were accommodated in stalls between his cabin and the poop. As they never sailed more than fifty miles without putting in at another port, readying to sail again was something of a fussy ordeal as horses and mules were brought back on board and settled down.

Miletus was no different from Smyrna, Pitane, half a dozen earlier ports of call; everyone in the harborside area knew that this particular ship was on hire to a Roman senator, and everyone was hugely interested. Look, there he was! The lovely young man in the pristine toga who walked as if he owned the world! Well, and didn't he own the world? He was a Roman senator. Of course the lesser lights in his retinue contributed to the talk, so that all the habitual loiterers around the Miletus harborfront knew that he was a high aristocrat, a brilliant man, and single-handedly responsible for persuading King Nicomedes of Bithynia to leave his realm to Rome when he died. Little wonder then that Caesar himself was always glad when the gangplanks were away, the anchors up, and the ship cast off to put out to sea again.

But it was a beautiful day and the water was calm, a good breeze blew to fill the great linen sail and spare the oarsmen, and Halicarnassus, the captain assured Caesar as they stood together on the poop, would be reached on the following day.

Some seven or eight miles down the coast, the tip of a promontory jutted into the sea; Caesar's ship sailed placidly between it and a looming island.

"Pharmacussa," said the captain, pointing to the island.

They passed it close inshore with Iasus on the mainland much further away, on a course which would skirt the next peninsula on that dissected coast. A very small place, Pharmacussa was shaped like a lopsided pair of woman's breasts, the southernmost mound being the bigger of the two.

"Does anyone live there?" asked Caesar idly.

"Not even a shepherd and his sheep."

The island had almost slid by when a low, sleek war galley emerged from behind the bigger breast, moving very fast, and on a course to intercept Caesar's ship.

"Pirates!" squawked the captain, face white.

Caesar, who had turned his head to look down their wake, nodded. "Yes, and another galley coming up our rear. How many men aboard the one in front?" he asked.

"Fighting men? At least a hundred, armed to the teeth."

"And on the one behind?"

The captain craned his neck. "It's a bigger ship. Perhaps one hundred and fifty."

"Then you do not recommend that we resist."

"Ye gods, Senator, no!" the man gasped. "They would kill us as soon as look at us! We must hope they're looking for a ransom, because they know from our lie in the water that we're not carrying cargo."

"Do you mean they're aware there's someone aboard us who will fetch a good ransom?"

"They know everything, Senator! They have spies in every port around the Aegean. It's my guess the spies rowed out from Miletus yesterday with a description of my vessel and the news that she carries a Roman senator."

"Are the pirates based on Pharmacussa, then?"

"No, Senator. It would be too easy for Miletus and Priene to scour them out. They've just been hiding there for a few days—on the lookout for a likely victim. It's never necessary to wait more than a few days. Something juicy always comes along. We're unlucky. This being winter and usually stormy, I'd hoped to escape pirates. But the weather has been too good, alas!"

"What will they do with us?"

"Take us back to their base and wait for the ransom."

"Whereabouts is their base likely to be?"

"Lycia, probably. Somewhere between Patara and Myra."

"Quite a long way from here."

"Several days' sail."

"Why so far away?"

"It's absolutely safe there—a haven for pirates! Hundreds of hidden coves and valleys—there are at least thirty big pirate settlements in the area."

Caesar looked unperturbed, though the two galleys were now closing on his ship very quickly; he could see the armed men lining each gunwale, and hear their shouts. "What's to stop me sailing back with a fleet after I've been ransomed and capturing the lot of them?"

"You'd never find the right cove, Senator. There are hundreds, and they all look exactly the same. A bit like the old Knossus labyrinth, only linear rather than square."

Summoning his body servant, Caesar asked calmly for his toga, and when the terrified man came back bearing an off-white armful, Caesar stood while he draped it.

Burgundus appeared. "Do we fight, Caesar?"

"No, of course not. It's one thing to fight when the odds are even remotely favorable, quite another when the odds indicate that to fight is suicide. We'll go tamely, Burgundus. Hear me?"

"I hear."

"Then make sure you tell everyone—I want no foolhardy heroes." Back he turned to the captain. "So I'd never locate the right cove again, eh?"

"Never, Senator, believe me. Many have tried."

"In Rome we were led to believe Publius Servilius Vatia got rid of the pirates when he conquered the Isauri. He was even let call himself Vatia Isauricus, so great was his campaign."

"Pirates are like swarming insects, Caesar. Smoke them out all you like, but as soon as the air is clear again, they're back."

"I see. Then when Vatia put—ooops, Vatia *Isauricus!*—put an end to the reign of King Zenicetes of the pirates, he only scraped the scum off the surface. Is that correct, Captain?"

"Yes and no. King Zenicetes was just one pirate chieftain. As for the Isauri"—the captain shrugged—"none of us who sail these waters could ever understand why a great Roman general went to war against an inland tribe of Pisidian savages thinking he was striking a blow at piracy! Perhaps a few Isauric grandsons have joined the pirates, but the Isauri are too far from the sea to be concerned with piracy and pirates."

Both warships were now alongside, and men were pouring on board the merchantman.

"Ah! Here comes the leader," said Caesar coolly.

A tall, youngish man clad in a Tyrian purple tunic heavily embroidered with gold pushed his way between the milling hordes on the deck and mounted the plank steps to the poop. He was not armed, nor did he look at all martial.

"Good day to you," said Caesar.

"Am I mistaken in thinking that you are the Roman senator Gaius Julius Caesar, winner of the Civic Crown?"

"No, you are not mistaken."

The pirate chieftain's light green eyes narrowed; he put a manicured hand up to his carefully curled yellow hair. "You're very collected, Senator," the pirate said, his Greek indicating that perhaps he came from one of the isles of the Sporades.

"I see no point in being anything else," said Caesar, lifting his brows. "I presume you will allow me to ransom myself and my people, so I have little to fear."

"That's true. But it doesn't stop my captives from shitting themselves in terror."

"Not this captive!"

"Well, you're a war hero."

"What happens now—er—I didn't quite catch the name?"

"Polygonus." The pirate turned to look at his men, who had gathered the merchantman's crew into one group and Caesar's twenty attendants into another.

Like their chief, the rest of the pirates were dandies; some sported wigs, some used hot tongs to produce rolling curls in their long locks, some were painted like whores, some preferred exquisitely close shaves and the masculine look, and all were very well dressed.

"What happens now?" Caesar repeated.

"Your crew is put aboard my ship, I put a crew of my own men at the oars of your ship, and we all row south as fast as we can, Senator. By sunset we'll be off Cnidus, but we'll keep on going. Three days from now you'll be safe in my home, where you will live as my guest until your ransom is paid."

"Won't it be easier to allow some of my servants to leave the ship here? A lighter could take them back to Miletus—that is a rich city, it ought not to have too much difficulty raising my ransom. How much is my ransom, by the way?"

The chieftain ignored the second question for the moment; he shook his head emphatically. "No, we've had our last ransom from Miletus for a while. We distribute the burden around because sometimes the ransomed men are slow to pay it back to whichever community scraped it together. It's the turn of Xanthus and Patara—Lycia. So we'll let you send your servants off when we get to Patara." Polygonus tossed his head to make his curls float. "As for the sum—twenty silver talents."

Caesar reared back in horror. "Twenty silver talents?" he cried, outraged. "Is *that* all I'm worth?"

"It's the going rate for senators, all pirates have agreed. You're too young to be a magistrate."

"*I* am Gaius Julius Caesar!" said the captive haughtily. "Clearly, fellow, you fail to understand! I am not only a patrician, I am also a Julian! And what does being a Julian mean, you ask? It means that I am descended from the goddess Aphrodite through her son, Aeneas. I come from consular stock, and I will be consul in my year. I am not a *mere* senator, fellow! I am the winner of a Civic Crown—I speak in the House—I sit on the middle tier— and when I enter the House every man—including consulars and censors!— must rise to his feet and applaud me. Twenty silver talents? *I* am worthy fifty silver talents!"

Polygonus had listened fascinated to all this; his captives were *never* like this one! So sure of himself, so unafraid, so—arrogant! Yet there was something in the handsome face Polygonus liked—could that be a twinkle in the eyes? Was this Gaius Julius Caesar mocking him? But why should he mock in a way which meant he was going to have to pay back more than double his proper ransom? He was serious—he had to be serious! However . . . *Surely* that was a twinkle in his eyes!

"All right, Your Majesty, fifty silver talents it is!" said Polygonus, his own eyes twinkling.

"That's better," said Caesar. And turned his back.

Three days later—having encountered no Rhodian or other city fleet patrolling the empty seas—Caesar's staff were put ashore opposite Patara. Polygonus had sailed aboard his own galley; Caesar had seen no more of him. But he came to supervise the off-loading of Caesar's staff into a lighter.

"You can keep the lot except for one if you like," said the pirate leader. "One's enough to raise a ransom."

"One is not appropriate for a man of my importance," said Caesar coldly. "I will keep three men only—my body servant Demetrius and two scribes. If I have to wait a long time I shall need someone to copy out my poetry. Or perhaps I'll write a play. A comedy! Yes, I should have *plenty* of material for a comedy. Or perhaps a farce.''

"Who will lead your people?"

"My freedman, Gaius Julius Burgundus."

"The giant? What a man! He'd fetch a fortune as a slave."

"He did in his day. He'll have to have his Nesaean horse," Caesar went on, tones fussy, "and the others must have their mounts too. They will have to keep some state, I insist upon that."

"You can insist all you like, Your Majesty. The horses are good ones. I'll keep them."

"You will not!" snapped Caesar. "You're getting fifty talents in ransom, so you can hand the horses over. I'll just keep Toes for myself—unless your roads are paved? Toes isn't shod, so he can't be ridden on sealed roads."

"You," said Polygonus, awed, "are beyond a joke!"

"Put the horses ashore, Polygonus," said Caesar.

The horses went ashore. Burgundus was acutely unhappy at leaving Caesar so poorly attended in the custody of these villains, but knew better than to argue. His job was to find the ransom.

And then it was onward into eastern Lycia, hugging a coast as lonely and desolate as any in the world. No roads, hamlets or fishing villages, only the mighty mountains of the Solyma plunging from permanently snowcapped heights all the way into the water. The coves were upon them before their presence could be spied out, and then were only tiny indentations in some mountain flank, a sliver of reddish-yellow sand running up against a reddish-yellow cliff. But never a sign of a pirate settlement! Intriguing! Caesar remained without moving from the poop from the time his ship sailed past the river on which stood Patara and Xanthus, watching the coast slide by hour after hour.

At sunset the two galleys and the merchantman they escorted veered inshore toward one of innumerable similar-looking coves, and were run up on the sand until they beached. Only when he had leaped down and was walking on the shifting ground did Caesar see what no one could have from the water; the cliff at the back of the cove was actually two cliffs, a flange of one concealing the gap between them, and in behind them a big hollow bowl of low-lying land. The pirate lair!

"It's winter, and the fifty talents we'll get for you means we can afford to have a lovely holiday instead of sailing in the early spring storms," said Polygonus, joining Caesar as he strolled through the gap in the cliffs.

His men were already rigging rollers beneath the prows of the galleys and the cargo vessel; while Caesar and Polygonus watched the three ships were pulled up from the sand and between the cliffs, then brought to permanent rest propped on struts inside the hidden valley.

"Do you always do this?" asked Caesar.

"Not if we're going out again, but that would be unusual. While we're out on the prowl we don't come home."

"A very nice arrangement you have here!" said Caesar, voice full of appreciation.

The hollow bowl was perhaps a mile and a half in width and about half that in length, more or less oval in shape. At its terminus furthest from the cove, a thin waterfall tumbled from hidden heights above into a pool; the pool turned into a stream and meandered down to the cove, though it could not be seen from the water. The pirates (or Mother Earth) had gouged a thin channel for it at the very end of the sands, below the cliff.

A well-built and properly organized town filled most of the valley. Stone houses three and four storeys high lined gravel streets, several very large stone silos and warehouses stood opposite the place where the ships were grounded, and a marketplace with a temple provided a focus for communal life.

"How many people do you have?" asked Caesar.

"Including wives and mistresses and children—and lovers for some of the men!—about—oh, a thousand plus five hundred. Then there are the slaves."

"How many slaves?"

"Two thousand, or thereabouts. We don't lift a finger for ourselves," said Polygonus proudly.

"I'm surprised there's not an insurrection when the men are absent. Or are the women and the male lovers fearsome warriors?"

The pirate chieftain laughed scornfully. "We're not fools, Senator! Every slave is chained permanently. And since there is no escape, why rise?"

"That wouldn't stop me," said Caesar.

"You'd be caught when we came back. There are no spare ships here to sail away in."

"Perhaps it's I who would catch you when you came back."

"Then I'm very glad that all of us will be here until your ransom arrives, Senator! You'll do no rising."

"Oh!" said Caesar, looking disappointed. "Do you mean to say I am to provide you with fifty talents and not even be offered a little feminine diversion while I wait? I don't rise for men, but I'm rather famous with women."

"I'll bet you are, if such is your preference," Polygonus said, chuckling. "Never fear! If you want women, we have them."

"Do you have a library in this wonderful little haven?"

"There are a few books around, though we're not scholars."

The two men arrived outside a very large house. "This is my place. You'll stay here—I prefer to keep you under my eye, I think. You'll have your own suite of rooms, of course."

"A bath would be most welcome."

"Since I have all the comforts of the Palatine, a bath you shall have, Senator."

"I wish you'd call me Caesar."

"Caesar it is."

The suite of rooms was big enough to accommodate Demetrius and the two scribes as well as Caesar, who was soon luxuriating in a bath of exactly the right temperature, a little above tepid.

"You'll have to shave me as well as pluck me for however many days we're here, Demetrius," said Caesar, combing the slight waves of his pale hair downward from the crown. He put down the mirror, made of chased gold encrusted with gems, shaking his head. "There's a fortune in this house."

"They have stolen many fortunes," said Demetrius.

"And no doubt stored much of the loot away in some of these many buildings. They're not all inhabited." And off drifted Caesar to join Polygonus in the dining room.

The food was excellent and varied, the wine superb.

"You keep a good cook," said Caesar.

"I see you eat abstemiously and drink no wine," said Polygonus.

"I am passionate about nothing except my work."

"What, not your women?"

"Women," said Caesar, washing his hands, "are work."

"I've never heard them called that before!" laughed Polygonus. "You're an odd fish, Caesar, to save your passions for work." He patted his belly and sniffed appreciatively at the contents of his rock-crystal goblet. "For myself, the only thing I like about piracy is the delightful life it brings me when I'm not sailing the sea. But most of all, I love good wine!"

"I don't dislike the taste," said Caesar, "but I detest the sensation of losing my wits, and I notice that even half a cup of watered wine takes the edge off them."

"But when you wake up, that's as good as you're going to feel all day!" cried Polygonus.

Caesar grinned. "Not necessarily."

"What do you mean?"

"For instance, my dear fellow, I will wake completely sober and in my normal robust health on the morning of the day I sail in here with a fleet at my command, capture this place, and take all of you into my custody. I can assure you that when I look at you in chains, I will feel infinitely better than I did when I woke up! But even that is relative. For on the day I crucify you, Polygonus, I will feel as I have never felt before!"

Polygonus roared with laughter. "Caesar, you are the most entertaining guest I've ever housed! I love your sense of humor!"

"How terribly nice of you to say so. But you won't laugh when I crucify you, my friend."

"It can't happen."

"It will happen."

A vision of gold and purple, hands loaded down with rings and chest flashing with necklaces, Polygonus lay back on his couch and laughed again. "Do you think I didn't see you standing on your ship watching the shore? Rubbish, Caesar, rubbish! No one can find his way back!"

"You do."

"That's because I've done it a thousand times. For the first hundred times I lost myself over and over again."

"I can believe that. You're not nearly as intelligent as I."

That cut: Polygonus sat up. "Clever enough to have captured a Roman senator! And to bleed him of fifty talents!"

"Your egg isn't hatched yet."

"If this egg doesn't hatch, it will sit here and rot!"

Shortly after this spirited exchange Polygonus flounced off, leaving his prisoner to find his own way back to his rooms. There a very pretty girl waited for him, a gift very much appreciated—after Caesar sent her to Demetrius to make sure she was clean.

For forty days he remained in the pirate hideout; no one restricted his freedom to wander where he willed, talk to whomsoever he fancied. His fame spread from one end of the place to the other, and soon everyone knew that he believed he would sail back after he had been ransomed, would capture and crucify them all.

"No, no, only the men!" said Caesar, smiling with great charm at a party of women come to quiz him. "How could I crucify beauty such as I see here?"

"Then what will you do with us?" the most forward female asked, eyes inviting.

"Sell you. How many women and children are here?"

"A thousand."

"A thousand. If the average price you fetch in whatever slave market I send you to is one thousand three hundred sesterces each, then I will have repaid my ransom to those obliged to find it, and made them a small profit. But you women and children are far more beautiful than one usually finds in a small town, so I expect an average price of two thousand sesterces each. That will give my ransomers a fat profit."

The women dissolved into giggles; oh, he was lovely!

In fact, everyone liked him enormously. He was so pleasant, so jolly and good-humored, and he never displayed the slightest sign of fear or depression. He would joke with everyone, and joked so often about crucifying the men and selling the women and children into slavery that it became almost a constant entertainment. His eyes twinkled, his lips twitched, he thought it as hugely funny as they did. The first girl talked of his prowess as a lover, which meant that many of the women cast lures in his direction; but it didn't take the men long to find out that he was scrupulous about the women he selected—never a woman belonging permanently to someone else.

"The only men I cuckold are my peers," he would say in a lordly voice, looking every inch the aristocrat.

"Friends?" they would ask, guffawing.

"Enemies," Caesar would answer.

"Well, and aren't we your enemies?"

"My enemies, yes. But not my peers, you low collection of absolute scum!" he would say.

At which point everybody would fall about laughing, loving the way he insulted them with such affectionate good humor.

And then one afternoon as he dined with Polygonus, the pirate chieftain sighed.

"I'll be sorry to lose you, Caesar."

"Ah! The ransom has been found."

"It will arrive with your freedman tomorrow."

"How do you arrange that? I must presume he will be guided here, since you say the place cannot be found."

"Oh, he has had some of my men with him the whole time. When the last talent was in the last bag, I received a message. They'll be here tomorrow about noon."

"And then I can go?"

"Yes."

"What about my hired ship?"

"It too."

"The captain? His sailors?"

"They'll be on board. You'll sail at dusk, westward."

"So you included my hired ship in your price."

"Certainly not!" said Polygonus, astonished. "The captain raised ten talents to buy back his ship and crew."

"Ah!" breathed Caesar. "Another debt I must in honor pay."

As predicted, Burgundus arrived at noon the following day, the fortieth of Caesar's imprisonment.

"Cardixa will allow me to continue being the father of her sons," said Burgundus, wiping the tears from his eyes. "You look very well, Caesar."

"They were considerate hosts. Who raised the ransom?"

"Patara half, Xanthus half. They weren't happy, but they didn't dare refuse. Not so soon after Vatia."

"They'll get their money back, and sooner than they think."

The whole pirate town turned out to see Caesar off, some of the women openly weeping. As did Polygonus.

"I'll never have another captive like you!" he sighed.

"That's very true," said Caesar, smiling. "Your career as a pirate is over, my friend. I'll be back before the spring."

As always, Polygonus found this exquisitely funny, and was still sniggering as he stood on the sandy little beach to watch the captain of Caesar's hired ship maneuver its bow into the west. Of light there was little.

"Don't stop, Captain!" the pirate leader shouted. "If you do, you'll have my escort up your arse!"

And out from behind the mountain flank to the east it came, a *hemiolia* capable of keeping up with any craft that sailed.

But by dawn it wasn't there, and the river upon which stood Patara lay ahead.

"Now to soothe some financial fears," said Caesar. He looked at the captain. "By the way, I will repay you the ten talents you had to outlay to ransom your ship and crew."

Obviously the captain didn't believe it lay in Caesar's power to do this. "An unfortunate voyage!" he mourned.

"I predict that when it's over you'll sail back to Byzantium a very happy man," said Caesar. "Now get me ashore."

His visit was very quickly over, he was back and waiting to leave on the following day before all the horses and mules had been loaded aboard. With him was the rest of his entourage. He looked brisk. "Come, Captain, hustle yourself!"

"To Rhodus?"

"To Rhodus, of course."

That voyage took three days, calling at Telmessus on the first night and Caunus on the second. Caesar refused to allow his animals to be off-loaded in either place.

"I'm in too big a hurry—they'll survive," he said. "Oh, my luck! Favored by Fortune as always! Thanks to my career as a raiser of fleets, I know exactly where to go and whom to see when we reach Rhodus!"

He did indeed, with the result that he had collected the men he wanted to see not two hours after his ship had tied up.

"I need a fleet of ten triremes and about five hundred good men," he said to the group of Rhodians congregated in the offices of the harbormaster.

"For what reason?" asked the young admiral Lysander.

"To accompany me back to the headquarters of the pirate chief Polygonus. I intend to capture the place."

"Polygonus? You'll never find his lair!"

"I'll find it," said Caesar. "Come, let me have the fleet! There will be some rich pickings for Rhodes."

Neither his enthusiasm nor his confidence persuaded the men of Rhodes to agree to this wild scheme; it was Caesar's authority earned him his ten triremes and five hundred soldiers. They knew him of old, and some of Vatia's clout still clung to him. Though King Zenicetes had burned his eyrie on top of Mount Termessus when Vatia arrived to capture it, Rhodian respect for Vatia had grown a thousandfold; unperturbed at what seemed the loss of untold plunder, Vatia had simply waited for the ashes to cool, then sieved the lot, and so retrieved the melted precious metals. If Vatia could do that, then his erstwhile legate, Caesar, might be likely to have some of Vatia's style. Therefore, the men of Rhodes concluded, Caesar was worth a bet.

At the mouth of Patara's river the fleet moored on the last night before the search for Polygonus's lair would begin; Caesar went into the city and commandeered every empty merchantman to follow in the Rhodian wake. And all the next day he stood on the poop of his hired ship, eyes riveted on the cove-scalloped coast sliding by for hour after hour.

"You see," he said to his captain, "before Polygonus left Patara I knew enough from listening to the pirates talk to have an idea what the coves were going to look like. So in my mind I set a definition of what I was going to call a cove, and what I would not. Then I simply counted every cove.''

"I was looking for landmarks—rocks in the sea shaped like this or that, an oddly shaped mountain—that sort of thing,'' said the captain, and sighed. "I am lost already!''

"Landmarks are deceptive, a man's memory of them treacherous. Give me numbers any day,'' said Caesar, smiling.

"What if you've missed your count?''

"I haven't.''

Nor had he. The cove wherein the five hundred soldiers from Rhodes landed looked exactly like every other. The fleet had lain all night to the west of it, undetected, though as it turned out Polygonus had set no watches. All four of his war galleys were drawn up inside the hidden bowl; he deemed himself safe. But the sun had scarcely risen before he and his men were standing in the chains they had used to confine their slaves.

"You can't say I didn't warn you,'' said Caesar to Polygonus, wearing a stout set of manacles.

"I'm not crucified yet, Roman!''

"You will be. You will be!''

"How did you find this place?''

"Arithmetic. I counted every cove between Patara and here.'' Caesar turned, beckoning to the Rhodian admiral Lysander. "Come, let's see what sort of fortune Polygonus has salted away.''

Many fortunes, as it turned out. Not only were the granaries almost full, but of other foodstuffs there were enough to feed all of Xanthus and Patara for the rest of that winter and spring. One big building was crammed with priceless fabrics and purples, with citrus-wood tables of rarest grain, with golden couches and the finest of chairs. Another building contained chest after chest of coins and jewelry. Much of the jewelry was Egyptian in make, rich with faience, beryl, carnelian, sard, onyx, lapis lazuli and turquoise. One small chest when opened revealed several thousand ocean pearls, some of them as big as pigeon's eggs, others in rare colors.

"I'm not truly surprised,'' said Lysander. "Polygonus has been raiding these sea-lanes for twenty years, and he's a well-known hoarder. What I didn't realize was that he must also have been raiding the shipping between Cyprus and Egypt.''

"Because of the ocean pearls and the jewelry?''

"One doesn't see such stuff elsewhere.''

"And the Alexandrians on Cyprus had the gall to tell me that their shipping was safe!''

"They dislike outsiders knowing their weaknesses, Caesar."

"That, I soon understood." Caesar huffed, pleased. "Well, Lysander, let's divide the spoils."

"Strictly speaking, Caesar, we are your agents. Provided you pay us for the hire of men and ships, the spoils belong to you," said Lysander.

"Some but by no means all, my friend. I want no questions asked of me in the House that I cannot answer with an unmistakable ring of truth. So I will take a thousand talents in coin for the Treasury of Rome, five hundred talents more in coin for myself, and a handful of these pearls if I may choose whichever ones I fancy. I suggest that the few remaining coins and all the jewelry go to Rhodes as her share. The warehouse of furniture and fabrics you can sell, but I would like the sum realized used to build a temple in Rhodus to honor my ancestress, Aphrodite."

Lysander blinked. "Most generous, Caesar! Why not take the whole chest of pearls for yourself? It would keep you free from money worries for the rest of your life."

"No, Lysander, I'll take just one handful. I like wealth as much as the next man, but too much might turn me into a miser." Caesar bent to run his hands through the pearls, picking out this one and that: twenty the dark and iridescent colors of the scum on the Palus Asphaltites in Palestina; a pearl the size of a strawberry that was the same color and shape as a strawberry; a dozen the color of the harvest moon; one giant with purple in it; and six perfect silver-cream ones. "There! I can't sell them, you know, without all of Rome wondering where they came from. But I can give them away to certain women when I need to."

"Your fame will spread, to be so unavaricious."

"I want no word of it spoken, Lysander, and I do mean that! My continence has absolutely nothing to do with lack of avarice. It has to do with my reputation in Rome, and with a vow I made that I would never lay myself open to charges of extortion or the theft of Rome's property." He shrugged. "Besides, the more money I have, the faster I'll throw it away."

"And Patara and Xanthus?"

"Receive the women and children to sell into slavery, plus all the food stored here. They should get back far more than they had to find to ransom me from the slave sales, and the food is a bonus. But with your permission I will take ten more talents for the captain of my ship. He too had to pay a ransom." One hand on Lysander's shoulder, Caesar guided him out of the building. "The ships from Xanthus and Patara will be here by dusk. May I suggest that you put Rhodus's share on board your galleys before they arrive?

I'll have my clerks catalogue everything. Send the money for Rome to Rome under escort.''

"What do you want done with the pirate men?''

"Load them on board Pataran or Xanthian ships, and give them to me to take to Pergamum. I'm not a curule magistrate, so I have not the power to execute in the provinces. That means I must take the men to the governor in Pergamum and ask him for permission to do what I promised I would do—crucify them.''

"Then I'll put Rome's share on board my own galleys. It's a small enough cargo. The moment the seas are safe—early summer, perhaps—I'll send the money to Rome from Rhodus.'' Lysander thought of something else. "I'll send four of my ships with you to Pergamum as an escort. You've brought Rhodes so much wealth that Rhodes will be delighted to oblige you in everything.''

"Just remember that I did! Who knows? One day I may need to call in the favor,'' said Caesar.

The pirates were being led off toward the beach; Polygonus, last in the endless line, gave Caesar a grave salute.

"What luxury-loving fellows they were,'' said Caesar, shaking his head. "I had always thought of pirates as dirty, unschooled and in love with fighting. But these men were soft.''

"Of course,'' said Lysander. "Their savagery is overrated. How often do they need to fight for what they pillage, Caesar? Rarely. When they do fight it is under the supervision of their own admirals, who are remarkably skilled. The smaller pirates like Polygonus don't attack convoys. They prey on unescorted merchantmen. The pirates who sail in fleets are mostly to be found around Crete. But when you live behind the walls of the Solyma like Polygonus, you tend to regard yourself as permanently secure—literally an independent kingdom.''

"Rhodes could do more than it does to arrest the pirate menace,'' said Caesar.

But Lysander shook his head, chuckled. "Blame Rome for that! It was Rome insisted we reduce the size of our fleets when Rome took on the burden of ruling the eastern end of our great sea. She thought she could police everything, including the shipping lanes. But she's too parsimonious to spend the necessary money. Rhodes is under her direction these days. So we do as we are bidden. If we were to strike out independently with sufficient naval power to eradicate the pirates, Rome would begin to think that she was hatching her own Mithridates.''

And that, reflected Caesar, was inarguable.

* 　 * 　 *

Marcus Junius Juncus was not in Pergamum when Caesar reached the river Caicus and moored in the city port; it was nearing the end of March by Roman reckoning, which meant that winter was not yet over, though the voyage up the coast had been uneventful. The city of Pergamum looked magnificent upon its lofty perch, but even from the lowlands of the river traces of snow and ice could be seen upon temple roofs and palace eaves.

"Where is the governor? In Ephesus?" asked Caesar when he found the proquaestor, Quintus Pompeius (closer by blood to the branch Rufus than to Pompey's branch).

"No, he's in Nicomedia," said Pompeius curtly. "I was just on my way to join him, actually. You're lucky to catch any of us here, we've been so busy in Bithynia. I came back to fetch some cooler clothes for the governor—we didn't expect Nicomedia to be warmer than Pergamum."

"Oh, it always is," said Caesar gravely, and managed to refrain from asking the proquaestor of Asia Province did he not have more urgent things to do than fetch cooler clothing for Juncus? "Well, Quintus Pompeius," he went on affably, "if you like, I'll carry the governor's clothing. I'm giving you a little work to do before you can leave. See those ships there?"

"I see them," said Pompeius, none too pleased at being told by a younger man that he would have to do this, and not do that.

"There are some five hundred pirates on board who need to be incarcerated somewhere for a few days. I'm off to Bithynia to obtain formal permission from Marcus Junius to crucify them."

"Pirates? Crucify?"

"That's right. I captured a pirate stronghold in Lycia—with the aid of ten ships of the Rhodian navy, I hasten to add."

"Then you can stay here and look after your own wretched prisoners!" snapped Pompeius. "*I'll* ask the governor!"

"I'm very sorry, Quintus Pompeius, but that's not the way it's done," said Caesar gently. "I am a *privatus,* and I was a *privatus* when I captured the men. I must see the governor in person. Lycia is a part of his province, so I must explain the circumstances myself. That is the law."

The tussle of wills was prolonged a few moments more, but there was never any doubt as to who would win; off went Caesar in a fast Rhodian galley to Nicomedia, leaving Pompeius behind to deal with the pirate prisoners.

And, thought Caesar sadly as he cooled his heels in a small palace anteroom until the busy Marcus Junius Juncus had time to see him, things had already changed almost beyond recognition. The gilding was still there, the frescoes and other objects of art which could not be removed without leaving obvious damage behind, but certain familiar and beloved statues were gone from hallways and chambers, as were several paintings.

The light was fading when Juncus flounced into the room; evidently he had paused to eat dinner before releasing a fellow senator from his long wait.

"Caesar! How good to see you! What is it?" the governor asked, holding out his hand.

"*Ave,* Marcus Junius. You've been busy."

"That's right, you know this palace like the look of your hand, don't you?" The words were smooth enough, but the inference was plain.

"Since it was I sent you word when King Nicomedes died, you must know that."

"But you didn't have the courtesy to wait here for me."

"I am a *privatus,* Marcus Junius, I would only have been in your way. A governor is best left to his own devices when he has a task to do as important as incorporating a new province into Rome's flock," said Caesar.

"Then what are you doing here now?" Juncus eyed his visitor with intense dislike, remembering their little exchanges in the Murder Court—and who had mostly won them.

"I was captured by pirates off Pharmacussa two months ago."

"Well, that happens to many. I presume that you managed to ransom yourself, since you're standing before me. But there's nothing I can do to help you recover the ransom, Caesar. However, if you insist I will have my staff enter a complaint with the Senate in Rome."

"I am able to do that myself," said Caesar pleasantly. "I am not here to complain, Marcus Junius. I'm here to request your permission to crucify five hundred captured pirates."

Juncus stared. "What?"

"As you so perceptively perceived, I ransomed myself. Then in Rhodus I requisitioned a small fleet and some soldiers, went back to the pirate stronghold, and captured it."

"You had no right to do that! I am the governor, it was my job!" snapped Juncus.

"By the time I had sent word to Pergamum—I have just come from Pergamum, where I left my prisoners—and a message had been forwarded to you here in Nicomedia, Marcus Junius, the winter would have been over, and Polygonus the pirate vanished from his base to do his campaigning. I may be a *privatus,* but I acted as all members of the Senate of Rome are expected to—I proceeded to ensure that Rome's enemies did not escape Rome's retribution."

This swift retort gave Juncus pause; he had to search for the proper answer. "Then you are to be commended, Caesar."

"So I think."

"And you're asking me for permission to crucify five hundred good strong men? I can't do that! Your captives are now mine. I shall sell them into slavery."

"I pledged them my word that they would be crucified," said Caesar, lips tightening.

"You pledged *them* your word?" asked Juncus, genuinely aghast. "They're outlaws and thieves!"

"It would not matter to me if they were barbarians and apes, Marcus Junius! I swore that I would crucify them. I am a Roman and my word is my bond. I must fulfill my word."

"The promise was not yours to give! As you've pointed out, you're a *privatus*. I do agree that you acted correctly in moving to ensure that Rome's enemies did not escape retribution. But it is my prerogative to say what will happen to prisoners in my sphere of *auctoritas*. They will be sold as slaves. And that is my last word on the subject."

"I see," said Caesar, eyes glassy. He got up.

"Just a moment!" cried Juncus.

Caesar faced him again. "Yes?"

"I presume there was booty?"

"Yes."

"Then where is it? In Pergamum?"

"No."

"You can't keep it for yourself!"

"I did not. Most of it went to the Rhodians, who provided the manpower and seapower for the exercise. Some went to the citizens of Xanthus and Patara, who provided the fifty talents for my ransom. My share I donated to Aphrodite, asking that the Rhodians build a temple in her honor. And Rome's share is on its way to Rome."

"And what about my share?"

"I wasn't aware you were entitled to one, Marcus Junius."

"I am the governor of the province!"

"The haul was rich, but not that rich. Polygonus was no King Zenicetes."

"How much did you send to Rome?"

"A thousand talents in coin."

"Then there was enough."

"For Rome, yes. For you, no," said Caesar gently.

"As governor of the province, it was my job to send Rome's share to the Treasury!"

"Minus how much?"

"Minus the governor's share!"

"Then I suggest," said Caesar, smiling, "that you apply to the Treasury for the governor's share."

"I will! Never think I will not!"

"I never would, Marcus Junius."

"I will complain to the Senate about your arrogance, Caesar! You have taken the governor's duties upon yourself!"

"That is true," said Caesar, walking out. "And just as well. Otherwise the Treasury would be a thousand talents the poorer."

He hired a horse and rode overland to Pergamum through a melting landscape, Burgundus and Demetrius hard put to keep up. On and on without pausing to rest he rode, his anger fueling his tired head and aching muscles. Just seven days after leaving Pergamum he was back—and two full days ahead of the Rhodian galley, still traversing the Hellespont.

"All done!" he cried cheerfully to the proquaestor Pompeius. "I hope you've made the crosses! I haven't any time to waste."

"Made the crosses?" asked Pompeius, astonished. "Why would I cause crosses to be made for men Marcus Junius will sell?"

"He was inclined that way at first," said Caesar lightly, "but after I had explained that I had given my word they would be crucified, he understood. So let's start making those crosses! I was due to commence studying with Apollonius Molon two months ago. Time flies, Pompeius, so up and into it!"

The bewildered proquaestor found himself hustled as Juncus never did, but could not move quickly enough to satisfy Caesar, who ended in buying timber from a yard and then set the pirates to making their own crosses.

"And make them properly, you scum, for hang on them you will! There's no worse fate than lingering for days because a cross is not well made enough to hasten death."

"Why didn't the governor elect to sell us as slaves?" asked Polygonus, who was unhandy with tools and therefore not progressing in his cross making. "I was sure he would."

"Then you were wrong," said Caesar, taking the bolts from him and beginning to fasten crosspiece to tree. "How did you ever manage to forge a successful career as a pirate, Polygonus? You are hopelessly incompetent!"

"Some men," said Polygonus, leaning on a spade, "make very successful careers out of being incompetent."

Caesar straightened, cross bolted. "Not I!" he said.

"I realized that some time ago," said Polygonus, sighing.

"Go on, start digging!"

"What are those for?" Polygonus asked, allowing Caesar to take his spade while he himself pointed at a pile of wooden pins.

"Wedges," grunted Caesar, soil flying. "When this hole is deep enough to take the weight of cross and man together, your cross will be dropped in it. But the earth here is too loose to fix it firmly upright, so we'll hammer wedges into the ground all around the base. Then when the job's done and you're dead, your cross will come out easily the moment the wedges are removed. That way, the governor can save all these wonderful instruments of an ignominious death for the next lot of pirates I capture."

"Don't you get out of breath?"

"I have sufficient breath to work and talk at the same time. Come, Polygonus, help me drop your final resting place in the hole. . . . There!" Caesar stood back. "Now shove one of the wedges into the hole—the cross is leaning." He put down the spade and picked up a mallet. "No, no, on the other side! Toward the lean! You're no engineer, are you?"

"I may not be an engineer," said Polygonus, grinning, "but I have engineered my executioner into making my cross!"

Caesar laughed. "Do you think I'm not aware of that, friend? However, there is a price to pay. As any good pirate should know."

Amusement fled; Polygonus stared. "A price?"

"The rest will have their legs broken. They'll die quickly. You, on the other hand, I will provide with a little rest for your feet so there's not too much weight dragging you down. It is going to take you *days* to die, Polygonus!"

When the Rhodian galley which had followed Caesar from Nicomedia rowed into the river leading to the port of Pergamum, the oarsmen gaped and shivered. Men died—even by execution—in Rhodes, but Roman-style justice was not a part of Rhodian life; Rhodes was Friend and Ally, not part of a Roman province. So the sight of five hundred crosses in a field lying fallow between the port and the sea was as strange as it was monstrous. A field of dead men—all save one, the leader, whose head was adorned with the irony of a diadem. He still moaned and cried out.

Quintus Pompeius had remained in Pergamum, unwilling to leave until Caesar was gone. It was the sight of those crosses, as if a forest had been devised wherein no tree differed from its fellows in the slightest degree.

Crucifixions happened—this was the death meted out to a slave, never to a free man—but never en masse. Yet there in neat rows, uniformly spaced apart, stood a regimented death. And the man who could organize and achieve it in such a short time was not a man to ignore. Or leave in charge of Pergamum, however unofficially. Therefore Quintus Pompeius waited until Caesar's fleet sailed for Rhodes and Patara.

The proquaestor arrived in Nicomedia to find the governor elated; Juncus had found a cache of gold bullion in a dungeon beneath the palace and appropriated it for himself, unaware that Caesar and Oradaltis had put it there to trap him.

"Well, Pompeius, you've worked very hard to incorporate Bithynia into Asia Province," said Juncus magnanimously, "so I shall accede to your request. You may call yourself Bithynicus."

As this raised Pompeius (Bithynicus) to a state of exaltation almost equal to the governor's, they reclined to eat dinner in a positive glow of well-being.

It was Juncus who brought up the subject of Caesar, though not until the last course had been picked over.

"He's the most arrogant *mentula* I've ever encountered," he said, lips peeled back. "Denied me a share of the spoils, then had the temerity to ask for my permission to crucify five hundred hale and hearty men who will at least fetch me some compensation when I sell them in the slave market!"

Pompeius stared at him, jaw dropped. "Sell them?"

"What's the matter?"

"But you ordered the pirates crucified, Marcus Junius!"

"I did not!"

Pompeius (Bithynicus) shriveled visibly. *"Cacat!"*

"What's the matter?" Juncus repeated, stiffening.

"Caesar arrived back in Pergamum seven days after he had gone to see you and told me that you had consented to his crucifying the men. I admit I was a bit surprised, but it never occurred to me that he was lying! Marcus Junius, he crucified the lot of them!"

"He wouldn't dare!"

"He *did* dare! With such complete assurance—so relaxed! He pushed me around like a bond servant! I even said to him that I was surprised to hear you'd consented, and did he look uncomfortable or guilty? No! Truly, Marcus Junius, I believed every word he said! Nor did you send a message to the contrary," he added craftily.

Juncus was beyond anger; he wept. "Those men were worth two million sesterces on the market! Two million, Pompeius! And he sent a thousand talents to the Treasury in Rome without even reporting to me first, or offering me a share! Now I'm going to have to apply to the Treasury for a share, and you know what a circus that is! I'll be lucky if the decision comes through before my first great-grandchild is born! While he—the *fellator!*—must have appropriated thousands of talents for himself! Thousands!''

"I doubt it," said Pompeius (Bithynicus), trying to look anywhere but at the desolate Juncus. "I had some speech with the senior captain of the Rhodian ships, and it appears that Caesar really did give all the loot to Rhodes, Xanthus and Patara. The haul was rich, but not an Egyptian treasure. The Rhodian believed Caesar took very little for himself, and that seems to be the common belief among all those concerned. One of his own freedmen said Caesar liked money well enough, but was too clever to prize it ahead of his political skin, and informed me with a sly smile that *Caesar* would never find himself arraigned in the Extortion Court. It also appears that the man had pledged the pirates he would crucify them while he was living at their stronghold waiting to be ransomed. It may be difficult to prove he took a thing from the pirate spoils, Marcus Junius."

Juncus dried his eyes, blew his nose. "I can't prove he took anything in Nicomedia or elsewhere in Bithynia, either. But he did! He *must* have! I've known virtuous men in my time, and I would swear he isn't among them, Pompeius! He's too sure of himself to be virtuous. And far too arrogant. He acts as if he owns the world!''

"According to the pirate leader—who thought Caesar very strange—he acted as if he owned the world while he was held a prisoner. Used to sweep around insulting everybody with high good humor! The ransom was levied at twenty talents, which apparently outraged Caesar! He was worth at least *fifty* talents, he said—and made them set the ransom at fifty talents!''

"So that's why he said fifty talents! I noticed it at the time, but I was too angry with him to take him up on it, and then I forgot." Juncus shook his head. "That probably explains him, Pompeius. The man's mad! Fifty talents is a censor's ransom. Yes, I believe the man is mad.''

"Or perhaps he wanted to frighten Xanthus and Patara into paying up quickly," said Pompeius.

"No! He's mad, and the madness comes out in self-importance. He's never been any different." A bitter look descended upon Juncus's countenance. "But his motives are irrelevant. All I want is to make him pay for what he's done to me! Oh, I don't believe it! *Two million sesterces!''*

If Caesar suffered any misgivings about the accumulating enmity his activities were provoking, he concealed them perfectly; when his ship finally docked in Rhodus he paid off the captain with a most generous bonus, hired a comfortable but not pretentious house on the outskirts of the city, and settled to studying with the great Apollonius Molon.

Since this big and independent island at the foot of Asia Province was a crossroads for the eastern end of the Middle Sea, it was constantly bombarded with news and gossip, so there was no need for any visiting Roman student to feel cut off from Rome or from developments in any part of the Roman world. Thus Caesar soon learned of Pompey's letter to the Senate and the Senate's reaction—including the championship of Lucullus; and he learned that last year's senior consul, Lucius Octavius, had died in Tarsus soon after he had arrived there early in March to govern Cilicia. It was too soon to know what the Senate planned to do about a replacement. The testamentary gift of Bithynia had pleased everyone in Rome from highest to lowest, but, Caesar learned in Rhodes, not everyone had wanted this new land to be a part of Asia Province, and the battle was not over just because Juncus had been ordered to go ahead with incorporation. Both Lucullus and Marcus Cotta, now the consuls, were in favor of making Bithynia a separate province with a separate governor, and Marcus Cotta had his eye on the post in the following year.

Of more interest to the Rhodians, however, was more local news; what was happening in Pontus and Cappadocia held an importance for them that Rome and Spain could not. It was said that after King Tigranes had invaded Cappadocia four years ago, not one citizen had been left in Eusebeia Mazaca, so many had the King deported to resettle in Tigranocerta; the Cappadocian king who had not impressed Caesar when he saw him had been living in exile in Alexandria since the invasion, giving as his reason for this peculiar choice of location the fact that Tarsus was too close to Tigranes, and Rome too expensive for his purse.

There were plenty of rumors that King Mithridates was busy mobilizing a new and vast army in Pontus, so angry had the King been at the news that Bithynia had fallen to Rome's lot in a will; but no one had any details, and Mithridates was still definitely well within his own borders.

Marcus Junius Juncus came in for his share of gossip too. About him it was being said that he had alienated some of the most important Roman citizens in Bithynia—particularly those resident in Heraclea on the Euxine—and that formal complaints had been sent off to the Senate in Rome alleging that Juncus was plundering the country of its greatest treasures.

Then at the beginning of June the whole of Asia Province jolted, shuddered; King Mithridates was on the march, had overrun Paphlagonia and reached Heracleia, just on the Bithynian border. Word had flown to Rome that the King of Pontus intended to take Bithynia for himself. Blood, birth and proximity all dictated that Bithynia belonged to Pontus, not to Rome, and King Mithridates would not lie down while Rome usurped Bithynia! But at Heracleia the vast Pontic horde stopped short, and there remained; as usual, having thrown down the challenge to Rome, Mithridates had balked and now lay still, waiting to see what Rome would do.

Marcus Junius Juncus and Quintus Pompeius (Bithynicus) fled back to Pergamum, where they spent more time writing lengthy reports to the Senate than attempting to ready Asia Province for another war against the King of Pontus. With no governor in Cilicia thanks to the death of Lucius Octavius, the two legions stationed in Tarsus made no move to march to the aid of Asia Province, and Juncus did not summon them. The two legions of the Fimbriani stationed in Ephesus and Sardes were recalled to Pergamum, but were moved no closer to Bithynia than Pergamum. Speculation had it that Juncus intended to defend his own skin, not Bithynia.

In Rhodus, Caesar listened to the gossip but made no effort to journey to Pergamum, more concerned, it seemed, at the talk that Asia Province wanted no more truck with Mithridates but was not willing to fight him either—unless the governor issued firm orders. And the governor made no attempt to issue firm orders about a thing. The harvest would begin in Quinctilis in the southern part of the province and by Sextilis the northern parts would also be reaping. Yet Juncus did nothing, made no move to commandeer grain against the possibility of war.

Word came during Sextilis that both the consuls, Lucullus and Marcus Cotta, had been authorized by the Senate to deal with Mithridates; suddenly Bithynia was a separate province and given to Marcus Cotta, while Cilicia went to Lucullus. No one could say what the fate of Asia Province would be, its governor only a praetor and caught between the two consuls of the year. Outranked by Lucullus and Marcus Cotta, Juncus would have to do as he was told. But he was not a Lucullus man; he wasn't efficient nor beyond reproach. Things boded ill for Juncus.

Not many days later Caesar received a letter from Lucullus's brother, Varro Lucullus.

> Rome is in an uproar, as you can imagine. I write to you, Caesar, because you are out of things at the moment, because I need to air my thoughts on paper and am not a diarist, and because I can think of no one I would rather write to. I am doomed to remain here in Rome no matter what happens short of the deaths of both the consuls, and since the senior consul is my brother and the junior consul is your uncle,

neither of us will want that. Why am I doomed to remain in Rome? I have been elected senior consul for next year! Isn't that excellent? My junior colleague is Gaius Cassius Longinus—a good man, I think.

Some local news first. You have probably heard that our mutual friend Gaius Verres succeeded in smarming up to the electorate and the lot officials so successfully that he is urban praetor. But have you heard how he managed to turn that usually thankless job into a profit-making one? After the plutocrat Lucius Minucius Basilus died without leaving a will behind him, Verres had to hear the plea of his closest relative to inherit. This closest relative is a nephew, one Marcus Satrius. But guess who contested? None other than Hortensius and Marcus Crassus, each of whom had rented a rich property from Basilus during his lifetime. They now came before Verres and alleged that Basilus would have left them these properties had he made a will! And Verres upheld their claims! Off went Hortensius and Marcus Crassus the richer, off went wretched Satrius the poorer. As for Gaius Verres—well, you don't think he found for Hortensius and Marcus Crassus out of the goodness of his heart, do you?

Of course we have the annual nuisance among our ten tribunes of the plebs. This year's specimen is a peculiar man, Lucius Quinctius. Fifty years old and self-made, likes to dress when not obliged to be togate in a full-length robe of Tyrian purple, and full of detestable affectations of speech and manner. The college had not been in office for one full day before Quinctius was haranguing the Forum crowds about restoring the full powers of the tribunate, and in the House he concentrated his venom upon my brother.

Quinctius is now very quiet and well behaved. My dear brother Lucullus dealt with him beautifully, using a two-pronged attack (as he put it). The first prong consisted in throwing last year's tribune of the plebs, Quintus Opimius, to the dogs—the dogs being Catulus and Hortensius, who prosecuted Opimius for constantly exceeding his authority and succeeded in having him fined a sum exactly equal to his whole fortune. Opimius has been obliged to retire from public life, a ruined man. The second prong consisted in Lucullus's sweetly reasonable and relentless whispering in Quinctius's ear, to the effect that if Quinctius didn't shut up and would not tone down his behavior, he too would be thrown to Catulus and Hortensius, and he too would be fined a sum exactly equal to his whole fortune. The exercise took some time, but it worked.

In case you think you are gone and absolutely forgotten, you are not, my dear Caesar. All of Rome is talking about the little flirtation you had with some pirates, and how you crucified them against the orders of the governor. What, I hear you ask, it's known in Rome already? Yes, it is! And no, Juncus didn't talk. His proquaestor, that Pompeius who has actually had the effrontery to add Bithynicus to his utterly undistinguished name, wrote the story to everyone. Apparently his intention was to make Juncus the hero, but such is popular caprice that everyone—even Catulus!—deems you the hero. In fact, there was some talk about giving you a Naval Crown to add to your Civic Crown, but Catulus was not prepared to go that far, and reminded the Conscript Fathers that you were a *privatus,* therefore were not eligible for military decorations.

Pirates have been the subject of much discussion in the House this year, but please put your mental emphasis on the word discussion. Whether it is because Philippus seems in the grip of a permanent lethargy, or because Cethegus has largely absented himself from meetings, or because Catulus and Hortensius are more interested in the courts than in the Senate these days, I do not know: but the fact remains that this year's House has proven itself a slug. Make a decision? Oh, impossible! Speed things up? Oh, impossible!

Anyway, in January our praetor Marcus Antonius agitated to be given a special commission to eradicate piracy from Our Sea. His chief reason for demanding that this job be given to him appears to lie in the fact that his father, the Orator, was given a similar command thirty years ago. There can be no doubt that piracy has grown beyond a joke, and that in this time of grain shortages we must protect shipments of grain from the east to Italy. However, most of us were inclined to laugh at the thought of Antonius—not a monster like brother Hybrida, admittedly, but an amiable and feckless idiot, certainly—being given a huge command like eradicating piracy from one end of Our Sea to its other.

Beyond interminable discussion, nothing happened. Save that Metellus the eldest son of the Billy-goat Caprarius (he is a praetor this year) also thought it a good idea, and began to lobby for the same job. When Metellus's lobbying became a threat to Antonius, Antonius went to see— guess who? Give up? Praecia! You know, the mistress of Cethegus. She has Cethegus absolutely under her dainty foot—so much so that when the lobbyists need Cethegus these days, they rush round to pay court to Praecia. One can only assume that Praecia must harbor a secret craving for big, beefy cretins—more *mentula* than *mente*—because it ended in Antonius's getting the job! Little Goat retired from the arena maimed in self-esteem, but will live to fight again another day, I predict. Cethegus was so lavish in his support that Antonius got an unlimited imperium on the water and a regular proconsular imperium on the land. He was told to recruit one legion of land troops—though his fleets, he was told, he would have to requisition from the port cities in whatever area he happens to be cruising unlimitedly. This year, the western end of Our Sea.

If the complaints the House is beginning to get from the port cities of the west is anything to go by, then it would seem that Marcus Antonius is better at raising sums of money than eradicating pirates. So far, his pirate tally is considerably less than yours! He fought an engagement off the coast of Campania which he claimed as a great victory, but we have seen no proof like ship's beaks or prisoners. I believe he has shaken his fist at Lipara and roared lustily at the Baleares, but the east coast of Spain remains firmly in the hands of Sertorius's pirate allies, and Liguria is untamed. Most of his time and energy (according to the complaints) is expended upon riotous and luxurious living. Next year, he informs the Senate in his latest dispatch, he will transfer himself to the eastern end of Our Sea, to Gytheum in the Peloponnese. From this base he says he will tackle Crete, where all the big pirate fleets harbor. My thought is that Gytheum is reputed to have an unparalleled climate and some very beautiful women.

Now to Mithridates.

The news that King Nicomedes had actually died failed to reach Rome until March—delayed by winter storms, it seems. Of course the will was safely lodged with the Vestals and Juncus had already received his instructions to proceed with incorporation of Bithynia into the Asia Province the moment you informed him the King was dead, so the House presumed all was in train. But hard on the heels of this news came a formal letter from King Mithridates, who said that Bithynia belonged to Nysa, the aged daughter of King Nicomedes, and that he was marching to put Nysa on the throne. No one took it seriously; the daughter hadn't been heard of in years. We sent Mithridates a stiff note refusing to countenance any pretender on the Bithynian throne, and ordering him to stay within his own borders. Usually when we prod him he behaves like a snail, so no one thought any more about the matter.

Except for my brother, that is. His nose, refined by all those years of living and fighting in the east, sniffed coming war. He even tried to speak about the possibility in the House, but was—not howled down—more snored out. His province for next year was Italian Gaul.

When he drew it in the New Year's Day lots he was delighted; his worst fear until that moment had been that the Senate would take Nearer Spain off Pompeius and give it to him! Which was why he always spoke up so vigorously for Pompeius in the House—oh, he didn't want Nearer Spain!

Anyway, when at the end of April we learned that Lucius Octavius had died in Tarsus, my brother asked that he be given Cilicia as his province, and that Italian Gaul be given to one of the praetors. There was going to be war with King Mithridates, he insisted. And what was senatorial reaction to these forebodings? Lethargy! Smothered yawns! You would have thought that Mithridates had never massacred eighty thousand of us in Asia Province not fifteen years ago! *Or* taken the whole place over until Sulla threw him out. The Conscript Fathers discussed, discussed, discussed. . . . But could come to no conclusions.

When the news came that Mithridates was on the march and had arrived at Heracleia with three hundred thousand men, you'd think *something* would have happened! Well, nothing did. The House couldn't agree what ought to be done, let alone who ought to be sent east—at one stage Philippus got up and suggested the command in the east should be given to Pompeius Magnus! Who (to give him his due) is far more interested in retrieving his tattered reputation in Spain.

Finally my poor Lucullus did something he despised himself for doing—he went to see Praecia. As you can quite imagine, his approach to the woman was very different from Marcus Antonius's! Lucullus is far too stiff-necked to smarm, and far too proud to beg. So instead of expensive presents, languishing sighs, or protestations of undying love and lust, he was very crisp and businesslike. The Senate, he said, was comprised of fools from one back tier clear to the other, and he was fed up wasting his breath there. Whereas he had always heard that Praecia was as formidably intelligent as she was well educated. Did *she* see why it was necessary that someone be sent to deal with Mithridates as soon as possible—and did she see that the best person for the job was Lucius Licinius Lucullus? If she did see both of these facts, would she please kick Cethegus up the arse to do something about the situation? Apparently she *loved* being told she was more intelligent and better educated than anyone in the Senate (one presumes she lumped Cethegus in with the rest!), for she must have given Cethegus a thundering great kick up the arse—things happened in the House *immediately*!

Italian Gaul was put aside to be given to a praetor (as yet not named), and Cilicia awarded to my brother. With orders to proceed to the east during his consulship, and to take over as governor of Asia Province on the first day of next year without relinquishing Cilicia. Juncus was supposed to stay on in Asia Province, prorogued yet again, but that was canceled. He is to come home at the end of the year; there have been so many complaints about his conduct in poor Bithynia that the House agreed unanimously to recall him.

There is only one legion of troops in Italy. Its men were being recruited and trained to be sent to Spain, but will now go east with Lucullus. The kick Praecia administered to Cethegus was so hard that the Conscript Fathers voted Lucullus the sum of seventy-two million sesterces to assemble fleets, whereas Marcus Antonius wasn't offered any money at all. Marcus Cotta was appointed governor of the new Roman province of Bithynia, but he has Bithynia's navy at his disposal, so is quite well off for ships—*he* wasn't offered any money either! What have we come to, Caesar, when a *woman* has more power than the consuls?

My dear brother covered himself in glory by declining the seventy-two millions. He said that the provisions Sulla had made in Asia Province would be adequate for his needs—he would levy his fleets upon the various cities and districts of Asia Province, then deduct the cost from the tributes. Since money is almost nonexistent, the Conscript Fathers voted my brother their sincere thanks.

It is now the end of Quinctilis, and Lucullus and Marcus Cotta will be leaving for the east in less than a month. Luckily under Sulla's constitution the consuls-elect outrank the urban praetor, so Cassius and I basically will be in charge of Rome, rather than the awful Gaius Verres.

The expedition will sail all the way—not so huge an undertaking with only one legion to transport—because it is faster in summer than marching across Macedonia. I think too that my brother doesn't want to get bogged down in a campaign west of the Hellespont, as Sulla did. He believes that Curio is well and truly capable of dealing with a Pontic invasion of Macedonia—last year Curio and Cosconius in Illyricum worked as a team to such effect that they rolled up the Dardani and the Scordisci, and Curio is now making inroads on the Bessi.

Lucullus ought to arrive in Pergamum around the end of September, though what will happen after that I do not know. Nor, I suspect, does my brother Lucullus.

And that, Caesar, brings you up to date. Please write whatever news you hear—I do not think Lucullus will have the time to keep me informed!

The letter made Caesar sigh; suddenly breathing exercises and rhetoric were not very stimulating. However, he had received no summons from Lucullus, and doubted he ever would. Especially if the tale of his pirate coup was all over Rome. Lucullus would have approved the deed—but not the doer. He liked things bureaucratically tidy, officially neat. A *privatus* adventurer usurping the governor's authority would not sit well with Lucullus, for all he would understand why Caesar had acted.

I wonder, thought Caesar the next day, if the wish is father to the actuality? Can a man influence events by the power of his unspoken desires? Or is it rather the workings of Fortune? I have luck, I am one of Fortune's favorites. And here it is yet again. The chance! And offered while there is no one to stop me. Well, no one except the likes of Juncus, who doesn't matter.

Rhodus now insisted that King Mithridates had launched not one invasion, but three, each originating at Zela in Pontus, where he had his military headquarters and trained his vast armies. The main thrust he was definitely heading himself, three hundred thousand foot and horse rolling down the coast of Paphlagonia toward Bithynia, and supported by his general-cousins Hermocrates and Taxiles—as well as a fleet of one thousand ships, a good number of them pirate craft, under the command of his admiral-cousin Aristonicus. But a second thrust commanded by the King's nephew Diophantus was proceeding into Cappadocia, its eventual target Cilicia; there were a hundred thousand troops involved. Then there was a third thrust, also one hundred thousand strong, under the command of a general-cousin, Eumachus, and the bastard son of Gaius Marius sent to the King by Sertorius, Marcus Marius. This third force was under orders to penetrate Phrygia and try to enter Asia Province by the back door.

A pity, sighed Caesar, that Lucullus and Marcus Cotta would not hear this news soon enough; the two legions which belonged to Cilicia were already on their way by sea to Pergamum at the command of Lucullus, which left Cilicia unprotected against an invasion by Diophantus. So there was nothing to do there except hope that events contrived to slow Diophantus down; he would meet little opposition in Cappadocia, thanks to King Tigranes.

The two legions of Fimbriani were already in Pergamum with the craven governor, Juncus, and there was no likelihood that Juncus would send them south to deal with Eumachus and Marcus Marius; he would want them where they could ensure his own escape when Asia Province fell to Mithridates for the second time in less than fifteen years. And with no strong Roman to command them, the people of Asia Province would not resist. Could not resist. It was now the end of Sextilis, but Lucullus and Marcus Cotta were at sea for at least another month—and that month, thought Caesar, would prove the vital one as far as Asia Province was concerned.

"There is no one else," said Caesar to himself.

The other side of Caesar answered: "But I will get no thanks if I am successful."

"I don't do it for thanks, but for satisfaction."

"Satisfaction? What do you mean by satisfaction?"

"I mean I must prove to myself that I *can* do it."

"They won't adore you the way they adore Pompeius Magnus."

"Of course they won't! Pompeius Magnus is a Picentine of no moment, he could never be a danger to the Republic. He has not the blood. Sulla had the blood. And so do I."

"Then why put yourself at risk? You could end in being had up for treason—and it's no use saying there is no treason! There doesn't have to be. Your actions will be open to interpretation, and who will be doing the interpreting?"

"Lucullus."

"Exactly! He's already got you marked as a born troublemaker and he'll see this in the same light, even if he did award you a Civic Crown. Don't congratulate yourself because you were sensible enough to give most of the pirate spoils away—you still kept a fortune that you didn't declare, and men like Lucullus will always suspect you of keeping that fortune."

"Even so, I must do it."

"Then try to do it like a Julius, not a Pompeius! No fuss, no fanfares, no shouting, no puffing yourself up afterward, even if you are completely successful."

"A quiet duty for the sake of satisfaction."

"Yes, a quiet duty for the sake of satisfaction."

He summoned Burgundus.

"We're off to Priene at dawn tomorrow. Just you, me, and the two most discreet among the scribes. A horse and a mule each—Toes and a shod horse for me, however, as well as a mule. You and I will need our armor and weapons."

Long years of serving Caesar had insulated Burgundus against surprise, so he displayed none. "Demetrius?" he asked.

"I won't be away long enough to need him. Besides, he's best left here. He's a gossip."

"Do I seek passage for us, or hire a ship?"

"Hire one. Small, light, and very fast."

"Fast enough to outdistance pirates?"

Caesar smiled. "Definitely, Burgundus. Once is enough."

The journey occupied four days—Cnidus, Myndus, Branchidae, Priene at the mouth of the Maeander River. Never had Caesar enjoyed a sea voyage more, whipping along in a sleek undecked boat powered by fifty oarsmen who rowed to the beat of a drum, their chests and shoulders massively developed by years of this same exercise; the boat carried a second crew equally good, and they spelled each other before real tiredness set in, eating and drinking hugely in between bouts of rowing.

They reached Priene early enough on the fourth day for Caesar to seek out the *ethnarch,* a man of Aethiopian name, Memnon.

"I presume you wouldn't be an *ethnarch* so soon after the reign of Mithridates in Asia Province if you had sympathized with his cause," said Caesar, brushing aside the customary courtesies. "Therefore I must ask you— do you welcome the idea of another term under Mithridates?"

Memnon flinched. "No, Caesar!"

"Good. In which case, Memnon, I require much of you, and in the shortest period of time."

"I will try. What do you require?"

"Call up the militia of Priene yourself and send to every town and community from Halicarnassus to Sardes to call up its militia. I want as many men as you can find as quickly as you can. Four legions, and all under their usual officers. The assembly point will be Magnesia-by-the-Maeander eight days from now."

Light broke; Memnon beamed. "The governor has acted!"

"Oh, absolutely," said Caesar. "He's placed me in command of the Asian militia, though unfortunately he can spare no other Roman staff. That means, Memnon, that Asia Province will have to fight for itself instead of sitting back and letting Roman legions take all the glory."

"Not before time!" said Memnon, a martial spark in his eye.

"I feel the same way. Good local militia, Roman-trained and Roman-equipped, are much underestimated. But after this I can assure you they won't be."

"Whom do we fight?" asked Memnon.

"A Pontic general named Eumachus and a renegade Spaniard named Marcus Marius—no relation to my uncle the great Gaius Marius," lied Caesar, who wanted his militia full of confidence, not awed by that name.

So off went Memnon to organize the calling up of the Asian militia, without asking to see an official piece of paper or even pausing to wonder if Caesar was who and what he said he was. When Caesar was doing the pushing, nobody thought to question him.

That night after he retired to his rooms in Memnon's house, Caesar conferred with Burgundus.

"You won't be with me on this campaign, old friend," he said, "and there's no use protesting that Cardixa wouldn't speak to you again if you weren't on hand to protect me. I need you to do something far more important than standing on the sidelines of a battle wishing you were a Roman legionary—or a militiaman. I need you to ride for Ancyra to see Deiotarus."

"The Galatian thane," said Burgundus, nodding. "Yes, I remember him."

"And he's bound to remember you. Even among the Gauls of Galatia, men don't come as big as you. I'm sure he knows more about the movements of Eumachus and Marcus Marius than I do, but it isn't to warn him that I'm sending you. I want you to tell him that I'm organizing an army of Asian militia and will try to lure the Pontic forces down the Maeander. Somewhere along the Maeander I hope to trap and defeat them. If I do, they'll retreat back into Phrygia before re-forming their ranks and then trying to invade again. I want you to tell Deiotarus that he will never have a better opportunity to wipe this Pontic army out than if he catches it in Phrygia attempting to reform. In other words, tell him, he will be acting in concert with me. If I in Asia Province and he in Phrygia both do our jobs well, then there will be no invasion of Asia Province or Galatia this year."

"How do I travel, Caesar? I mean, looking like what?"

"I think you ought to look like a war god, Burgundus. Put on the gold armor Gaius Marius gave you, stuff the biggest purple feathers you can find in the marketplace into the crest of your helmet, and sing some frightful German song as loudly as you can. If you encounter Pontic soldiers, ride right through the middle of them as if they didn't exist. Between you and the Nesaean, you'll be the personification of martial terror."

"And after I've seen Deiotarus?"

"Return to me along the Maeander."

The hundred thousand Pontic men who had set out with Eumachus and Marcus Marius from Zela in the spring were under orders to concentrate upon infiltrating Asia Province as their first priority, but to travel in a more or less direct line between Zela in Pontus and any Phrygian backwater meant traversing Galatia, and Mithridates was not sure about Galatia. A new generation of chieftains had arisen to replace those he had murdered at a feast almost thirty years ago, and Pontic authority over Galatia was at best a tenuous thing. Eventually it would be necessary to deal with this odd outcrop of misplaced Gauls, but not first of all. His best men Mithridates had reserved for his own divisions, so the soldiers under the command of Eumachus and Marcus Marius were not properly seasoned. A campaign down the Maeander against disorganized communities of Asian Greeks would stiffen the troops, endow them with confidence.

As a result of these cogitations, the King of Pontus kept Eumachus and Marcus Marius and their army with him as he marched into Paphlagonia. He was, he congratulated himself, superbly well equipped for this sally against Rome; in Pontic granaries there lay two million *medimni* of wheat, and one *medimnus* produced two one-pound loaves of bread a day for thirty days. Therefore in wheat alone he had sufficient in storage to feed all his people and all his armies for several years. Therefore it mattered to him not at all that he carried an extra hundred thousand men with him into Paphlagonia. Petty details about how these enormous quantities of grain and other foodstuffs were to be transported he did not concern himself with; that lay in the domain of underlings, whom he simply assumed would wave their conjuring sticks and transport. In reality these hirelings had neither the training nor the practical imagination to do what came naturally to a Roman *praefectus fabrum*—though no Roman general would have dreamed of moving an army over long distances if it numbered more than ten legions all told.

Consequently by the time that Eumachus and Marcus Marius split their hundred thousand men away from the three hundred thousand belonging to Mithridates, supplies were running so short that the King was obliged to send snakelike trails of men back many miles to struggling oxcarts and make these men carry heavy loads of foods on their shoulders to feed the army. Which in turn meant a percentage of the soldiers were always exhausted from having to work as porters. The fleet was bringing supplies to Heracleia, the King was told; in Heracleia all would be set to rights, the King was told.

However, Heracleia was scant comfort to Eumachus and Marcus Marius, who left the main forces to march inland down the Billaeus River, crossed a range of mountains and emerged in the valley of the Sangarius. In this fertile part of Bithynia they ate well at the expense of the local farmers, but soon were heading into heavily forested uplands where only small vales and pockets lay under cultivation.

Thus what brought Eumachus and Marcus Marius to the parting of their ways was their inability to feed one hundred thousand Pontic soldiers.

"You won't need the whole army to deal with a few Asian Greeks," said Marcus Marius to Eumachus, "and certainly you won't need cavalry.

So I'm going to remain on the Tembris River with some of the foot and all the horse. We'll farm and we'll forage, and wait for news of you. Just make sure you're back by winter—and that you're marching half the people of Asia Province with you as food porters! It isn't far from the upper Tembris to the lands of the Galatian Tolistobogii, so in the spring we'll fall on them and annihilate them. Which will give us plenty of Galatian food to eat next year.''

''I don't think the King my cousin would like to hear you belittle his glorious military venture by speaking of it in terms of food,'' said Eumachus, not fiercely or haughtily; he was too afraid of Mithridates ever to feel fierce or haughty.

''The King your cousin is in bad need of some good Roman training, then he'd appreciate how hard it is to feed so many men on a march,'' said Marcus Marius, unimpressed. ''I was sent to teach you lot the art of ambush and raid, but so far all I've done is general an army. I'm not a professional at it. But I do have common sense, and common sense says half of this force has to stay somewhere on a river where there's enough flat land to farm and yield sustenance. Hard luck if speaking of a campaign in terms of food upsets the King! If you want my opinion, he doesn't even live on the same earth the rest of us do.''

More time was wasted while Marcus Marius relocated himself, for Eumachus refused to leave until he was sure whereabouts he would find Marius on his return. Thus it was the beginning of September before he and some fifty thousand infantrymen crossed the Dindymus Mountains and picked up one of the tributaries of the Maeander. Naturally the further downstream the army moved the better foraging and food became, a stimulus to continue until the whole of this rich part of the world belonged once more to King Mithridates of Pontus.

Because most of the biggest towns along the ever-winding river lay on its south bank, Eumachus marched on its north bank, following a paved road which had started in the town of Tripolis. Promising the soldiers that they would be allowed to sack when Asia Province was secured, Eumachus bypassed Nysa, the first big city they encountered, and continued downstream in the direction of Tralles. It was impossible to keep the men entirely together on the march, since food had constantly to be found, and sometimes attractions like a flock of succulent young sheep or fat geese would send several hundred men whooping and chasing until every last animal was caught and slaughtered, by which time troop unrest had spread.

In fact, the pleasant and placid progress through rich land had produced an element of festival. The scouts Eumachus sent out reported back twice a day, always with the same news: no sign of opposition. That, thought Eumachus scornfully, was because no focus of resistance existed south of Pergamum! All the Roman legions (even those of Cilicia) were garrisoned on the outskirts of Pergamum to protect the governor's precious person; this had been known to every Pontic general for some time, and Marcus Marius had confirmed it by sending scouts to the Caicus.

So lulled and secure was Eumachus that he was not concerned when one evening his scouts failed to report back at their usual time, an hour before sunset. The city of Tralles was now somewhat closer than Nysa was behind, and the gently tilting undulations of the river valley which threw the Maeander into so many wandering, winding turns were flushed gold, long light upon harvest stubble. Eumachus gave the order to halt for the night. No fortifications were thrown up, no organized routine went into the making of a general camp; what happened resembled starlings settling, a process fraught with chatter, squabbles, relocations.

There was just enough light to see by when out of the dim shadows four legions of Asian militia in properly Roman rank and file fell upon the supping Pontic army and slaughtered its unprepared soldiers piecemeal. Though they outnumbered the Asian militiamen by more than two to one, the Pontic troops were so taken unaware that they could put up no resistance.

Provided with horses and by sheer chance located on the far side of the Pontic camp from Caesar's attack, Eumachus and his senior legates managed to get away, rode without caring about the fate of the army for the Tembris River and Marcus Marius.

But luck was not with King Mithridates that year. Eumachus arrived back at the Tembris just in time to see Deiotarus and the Galatian Tolistobogii descend upon Marcus Marius's half of the invasion force. This was a cavalry battle in the main, but it never developed into a bitter contest; the largely Sarmatian and Scythian levies which had enlisted with Mithridates fought best on open steppe, could not maneuver in the steep-sided valley of the upper Tembris, and fell in thousands.

By December, the remnants of the Phrygian army had struggled back to Zela under the command of Eumachus; Marcus Marius himself had set out to find Mithridates, preferring to tell the King in person what had happened than detail it in a report.

The Asian militia was jubilant, and joined with the whole population of the Maeander valley in victory celebrations which lasted for many days.

In his speech to the troops before the battle Caesar had harped upon the fact that Asia Province was defending itself, that Rome was far away and incapable of helping, that for once the fate of Asia Province depended wholly upon the Asian Greeks of that land. Speaking in the colloquial Greek of the region, he worked upon the feelings of patriotism and self-help to such effect that the twenty thousand men of Lydia and Caria whom he led to ambush the camping Eumachus were so fired that the battle was almost an anticlimax. For four *nundinae* he had drilled and disciplined them, for four *nundinae* he had imbued them with a consciousness of their own worth, and the results were everything that he could possibly have hoped for.

"No more Pontic armies will come this year," he said to Memnon at the victory feast in Tralles two days after the defeat of Eumachus, "but next year you may see more. I have taught you what to do and how to do it. Now it's up to the men of Asia Province to defend themselves. Rome, I predict, will be so caught up on other fronts that there won't be legions or generals available for duty anywhere in Asia Province. But you know now that you *can* look after yourselves."

"That we do, Caesar, and we owe it to you," said Memnon.

"Nonsense! All you really needed was someone to get you started, and it was my good fortune that I was to hand."

Memnon leaned forward. "It is our intention to build a temple to Victory as close to the site of the battle as the floodplain permits—there is talk of a small hill upon the outskirts of Tralles. Would you allow us to erect a statue of you within the temple so that the people never forget who led them?"

Not if Lucullus had been present to veto the request would Caesar have declined this singular honor. Tralles was a long way from Rome and not one of Asia Province's biggest cities; few if any Romans of his own class would ever visit a temple to Victory which could claim no distinctions of age or (probably) great art. But to Caesar this honor meant a great deal. At the age of twenty-six he would have a life-sized statue of himself in full general's regalia inside a victory temple. For at twenty-six he had led an army to victory.

"I would be delighted," he said gravely.

"Then tomorrow I will send Glaucus to see you and take all the measurements. He's a fine sculptor who works out of the studios in Aphrodisias, but since he is in the militia he's here with us now. I'll make sure he brings his painter with him to make some colored sketches. Then you need not stay for further sittings if you have things to do elsewhere."

Caesar did have things to do elsewhere. Chief among these was a journey to see Lucullus in Pergamum before news of the victory near Tralles reached him by other means. As Burgundus had come back from Galatia seven days before the battle, he was able to send the German giant to Rhodes escorting the two scribes and his precious Toes. The journey to Pergamum he would make alone.

He rode the hundred and thirty miles without stopping for longer than it took to change horses, which he did often enough to get ten miles an hour out of those he rode during daylight, and seven miles an hour out of those he rode during the night. The road was a good Roman one, and though the moon was thin, the sky was cloudless; his luck. Having started out from Tralles at dawn the day after the victory feast had ended, he arrived in Pergamum three hours after dark on the same day. It was the middle of October.

Lucullus received him at once. Caesar found it significant that he did so unaccompanied by Caesar's uncle Marcus Cotta, who was also in the governor's palace; in the consul's favor, however, of Juncus there was no sign either.

Caesar found his outstretched hand ignored. Nor did Lucullus bid him sit down; the interview was conducted throughout with both men on their feet.

"What brings you so far from your studies, Caesar? Have you encountered more pirates?" Lucullus asked, voice cold.

"Not pirates," said Caesar in a businesslike manner, "but an army belonging to Mithridates. It came down the Maeander fifty thousand strong. I heard about its advent before you arrived in the east, but I thought it pointless to notify the governor, whose access to information was better than mine, but who had made no move to defend the Maeander valley. So I had Memnon of Priene call up the Asian militia—which, as you know, he is authorized to do provided he has been so instructed by Rome. And he had no reason to assume I was not acting for Rome. By the middle of September the local city leaders of Lydia and Caria had assembled a force of twenty thousand men, which I put through drills and exercises in preparation for combat. The Pontic army entered the province in the latter part of September. Under my command, the Asian militia defeated Prince Eumachus near the city of Tralles three days ago. Almost all the Pontic soldiers were killed or captured, though Prince Eumachus himself got away. I understand that another Pontic army under the Spaniard Marcus Marius will be dealt with by the *tetrarch* Deiotarus of the Tolistobogii. You should receive word as to whether Deiotarus has succeeded within the next few days. That is all," Caesar ended.

The long face with the chilly grey eyes did not thaw. "I think that is quite enough! Why *didn't* you notify the governor? You had no way of knowing what he planned."

"The governor is an incompetent and venal fool. I have already experienced his quality. Had he been willing to take control—which I doubt—nothing would have been done quickly enough. I knew that. And that is why I didn't notify him. I didn't want him underfoot because I knew I could do what had to be done far better than he could."

"You exceeded your authority, Caesar. In fact, you had no authority to exceed."

"That's true. Therefore I exceeded nothing."

"This is not a contest in sophistry!"

"Better perhaps if it was. What do you want me to say? I am not very old, Lucullus, but I have already seen more than enough of these fellows Rome sends to her provinces endowed with imperium, and I do not believe that Rome is better served by blind obedience to the likes of Juncus, the Dolabellae or Verres than it is by men of my kind, imperium or not. I saw what had to be done and I did it. I might add, I did it knowing I would get no thanks. I did it knowing I would be reprimanded, perhaps even put on trial for a little treason."

"Under Sulla's laws, there is no little treason."

"Very well then, a big treason."

"Why have you come to see me? To beg for mercy?"

"I'd sooner be dead!"

"You don't change."

"Not for the worse, anyway."

"I cannot condone what you've done."

"I didn't expect you to."

"Yet you came to see me. Why?"

"To report to the magistrate in command, as is my duty."

"I presume you mean your duty as a member of the Senate of Rome," said Lucullus, "though that was surely owed to the governor as much as to me. However, I am not unjust, and I see that Rome has cause to be grateful for your swift action. In similar circumstances I might have acted in a similar way—could I have assured myself I was not flouting the governor's imperium. To me, a man's imperium is far more important than his quality. I have been blamed by some for the fact that King Mithridates is at large to commence this third war against Rome because I refused to aid Fimbria in capturing Mithridates at Pitane, and—it is commonly said—thereby allowed Mithridates the room to escape. *You* would have collaborated with Fimbria on the premise that the end justifies the means. But I did not see my way clear to acknowledging the outlawed representative of an illegal Roman government. I stand by my refusal to help Fimbria. I stand by every Roman man endowed with imperium. And to conclude, I find you far too much like the other youth with big ideas, Gnaeus Pompeius who calls himself Magnus. But you, Caesar, are infinitely more dangerous than any Pompeius. You are born to the purple.''

"Odd," Caesar interrupted. "I said the same thing myself."

Lucullus gave him a withering look. "I will not prosecute you, Caesar, but nor will I commend you. The battle fought at Tralles will be reported very briefly in my dispatches to Rome, and described as conducted by the Asian militia under local command. Your name will not be mentioned. Nor will I appoint you to my staff, nor will I permit any other governor to appoint you to his staff."

Caesar had listened to this with wooden face and distant eyes, but when Lucullus indicated by an abrupt gesture that he was finished, Caesar's expression changed, became mulish.

"I do not insist that I be mentioned in dispatches as the commander of the Asian militia, but I do *absolutely* insist that I be named in dispatches as present for the entire duration of the campaign on the Maeander. Unless I am listed, I will not be able to claim it as my fourth campaign. I am determined to serve in ten campaigns before I stand for election as quaestor."

Lucullus stared. "You don't have to stand as quaestor! You are already in the Senate."

"According to Sulla's law, I must be quaestor before I can be praetor or consul. And before I am quaestor, I intend to have ten campaigns listed."

"Many men elected quaestor have never served in the obligatory ten campaigns. This isn't the time of Scipio Africanus and Cato the Censor! No one is going to bother to count up how many campaigns you've served in when your name goes up for the quaestorian elections."

"In my case," said Caesar adamantly, "someone will make it his business to count up my campaigns. The pattern of my life is set. I will get nothing as a favor and much against bitter opposition. I stand above the rest and I will outdo the rest. But never, I swear, unconstitutionally. I will make my way up the *cursus honorum* exactly as the law prescribes. And if I am listed as having served in ten campaigns, in the first of which I won a Civic Crown, then I will come in at the top of the quaestor's poll. Which is the only place I would find acceptable after so many years a senator."

Eyes flinty, Lucullus looked at the handsome face with its Sullan eyes and understood he could go so far, no further. "Ye gods, your arrogance knows no bounds! Very well, I will list you in dispatches as present for the duration of the campaign and also present at the battle."

"Such is my right."

"One day, Caesar, you will overextend yourself."

"Impossible!" said Caesar, laughing.

"It's remarks like that make you so detestable."

"I fail to see why when I speak the truth."

"One further thing."

About to go, Caesar stayed. "Yes?"

"This winter the proconsul Marcus Antonius is moving his theater of command against the pirates from the western end of Our Sea to its eastern end. I believe he means to concentrate upon Crete. His headquarters will be at Gytheum, where some of his legates are already working hard—Marcus Antonius has to raise a vast fleet. You, of course, are our best gatherer of ships, as I know from your activities in Bithynia and Vatia Isauricus from your activities in Cyprus. Rhodes has obliged you twice! If you wish to add another campaign to your count, Caesar, then report to Gytheum at once. Your rank, I will inform Marcus Antonius, will be junior military tribune, and you will board with Roman citizens in the town. If I hear that you have set up your own establishment or exceeded your junior status in any way, I swear to you, Gaius Julius Caesar, that I will have you tried in Marcus Antonius's military court! And do *not* think I can't persuade him! After you— a relative!—prosecuted his brother, he doesn't love you at all. Of course you can refuse the commission. Such is your right as a Roman. But it's the only military commission you'll get anywhere after I write a few letters. I am the consul. That means my imperium overrules every other imperium, including the junior consul's—so don't look for a commission there, Caesar!"

"You forget," said Caesar gently, "that the aquatic imperium of Marcus Antonius is unlimited. On water, I believe he would outrank even the senior consul of the year."

"Then I'll make sure I'm never upon the same piece of water as the one where Antonius is bobbing up and down," said Lucullus tiredly. "Go and see your uncle Cotta before you leave."

"What, no bed for the night?"

"The only bed I'd give you, Caesar, belonged to Procrustes."

Said Caesar to his uncle Marcus Aurelius Cotta some moments later: "I knew dealing with Eumachus would land me in hot water, but I had no idea Lucullus would go as far as he has. Or perhaps I ought to say that I thought either I would be forgiven or tried for treason. Instead, Lucullus has concentrated upon personal retaliations aimed at hampering my career."

"I have no genuine influence with him," said Marcus Cotta. "Lucullus is an autocrat. But then, so are you."

"I can't stay, Uncle. I'm ordered to leave at once for—oh, Rhodes I suppose, preparatory to relocating myself at Gytheum—in a boardinghouse which has to be run by a Roman citizen! Truly, your senior colleague's conditions are extraordinary! I will have to send my freedmen home, including Burgundus—I am not to be allowed to live in any kind of state."

"Most peculiar! Provided his purse is fat enough, even a *contubernalis* can live like a king if he wants. And I imagine," said Marcus Cotta shrewdly, "that after your brush with the pirates, you can afford to live like a king."

"No, I've been strapped. Clever, to pick on Antonius. I am not beloved of the Antonii." Caesar sighed. "Fancy his giving me junior rank! I ought at least to be a *tribunus militum,* even if of the unelected kind."

"If you want to be loved, Caesar—oh, rubbish! What am I doing, advising you? You know more answers than I know questions, and you know perfectly well how you want to conduct your life. If you're in hot water, it's because you stepped into the cauldron of your own free will—and with both eyes wide open."

"I admit it, Uncle. Now I must go if I'm to find a bed in the town before all the landlords bolt their doors. How is my uncle Gaius?"

"Not prorogued for next year in Italian Gaul, despite the fact it needs a governor. He's had enough. And he expects to triumph."

"I wish you luck in Bithynia, Uncle."

"I suspect I'm going to need it," said Marcus Cotta.

It was the middle of November when Caesar arrived in the small Peloponnesian port city of Gytheum, to find that Lucullus had wasted no time; his advent was anticipated and the terms of his junior military tribunate spelled out explicitly.

"What on earth have you done?" asked the legate Marcus Manius, who was in charge of setting up Antonius's headquarters.

"Annoyed Lucullus," said Caesar briefly.

"Care to be more specific?"

"No."

"Pity. I'm dying of curiosity." Manius strolled down the narrow, cobbled street alongside Caesar. "I thought first I'd show you where you'll be lodging. Not a bad place, actually. Two old Roman widowers named Apronius and Canuleius who share a huge old house. Apparently they were married to sisters—women of Gytheum—and moved in together after the second sister died. I thought of them immediately when the orders came through because they have lots of room to spare, and they'll spoil you. Funny old codgers, but very nice. Not that you'll be in Gytheum much. I don't envy you, chasing ships from the Greeks! But your papers say you're the best there is, so I daresay you'll manage."

"I daresay I will," agreed Caesar, smiling.

Collecting warships in the Peloponnese was not entirely unenjoyable, however, for one soaked in the Greek classics: did sandy describe Pylos, did titans build the walls of Argos? There was a certain quality of ageless dreaming about the Peloponnese that rendered the present irrelevant, as if the gods themselves were mere nurselings compared to the generations of men who had lived here. And while he was very good at incurring the enmity of the Roman great, when Caesar dealt with humbler men he found himself much liked.

The fleets grew slowly through the winter, but at a rate Caesar thought Antonius would find hard to criticize. Instead of accepting promises, the best gatherer of ships in the world would commandeer any warlike vessels he saw on the spot, then tie the towns down to signed contracts guaranteeing delivery of newly built galleys to Gytheum in April. Marcus Antonius, Caesar thought, would not be ready to move before April, as he wasn't expected to sail from Massilia until March.

In February the Great Man's personal entourage began to dribble in, and Caesar—brows raised, mouth quivering—got a far better idea of how Marcus Antonius campaigned. When Gytheum did not prove to own a suitable residence, the entourage insisted that one be built on the shore looking down the Laconian Gulf toward the beautiful island of Cythera; it had to be provided with pools, waterfalls, fountains, shower baths, central heating and imported multicolored marble interiors.

"It can't possibly be finished until summer," said Caesar to Manius, eyes dancing, "so I was thinking of offering the Great Man room and board with Apronius and Canuleius."

"He won't be happy when he finds his house unfinished," said Manius, who thought the situation as funny as Caesar did. "Mind you, the locals are adopting a praiseworthily Greek attitude toward sinking their precious town funds into that vast sybaritic eyesore—they're planning on renting it for huge sums to all sorts of would-be potentates after Antonius has moved on."

"I shall make it my business to spread the fame of the vast sybaritic eyesore far and wide," said Caesar. "After all, this is one of the best climates in the world—ideal for a long rest cure or a secret espousal of unmentionable vices."

"I'd like to see them get their money back," said Manius. "What a waste of everyone's resources! Though I didn't say that."

"Eh?" shouted Caesar, hand cupped around his ear.

When Marcus Antonius did arrive, it was to find Gytheum's commodious and very safe harbor filling up with ships of all kinds (Caesar had not been too proud to accept merchantmen, knowing that Antonius had a legion of land troops to shunt about), and his villa only half finished. Nothing, however, could dent his uproariously jolly mood; he had been drinking unwatered wine to such effect that he had not been sober since leaving Massilia. As far as his fascinated legate Marcus Manius and his junior military tribune Gaius Julius Caesar could see, Antonius's idea of a campaign was to assault the private parts of as many women as he could find with what, so rumor had it, was a formidable weapon. A victory was a howl of feminine protest at the vigor of the bombardment and the size of the ram.

"Ye gods, what an incompetent sot!" said Caesar to the walls of his pleasant and comfortable room in the house of Canuleius and Apronius; he dared not say it to any human listener.

He had, of course, seen to it that Marcus Manius mentioned his fleet-gathering activities in dispatches, so when his mother's letter arrived at the end of April not many days after Antonius, the news it contained presented a merciful release from duty in Gytheum without the loss of a campaign credit.

Caesar's eldest uncle, Gaius Aurelius Cotta, returned from Italian Gaul early in the new year, dropped dead on the eve of his triumph. Leaving behind him—among many other things—a vacancy in the College of Pontifices, for he had been in length of years the oldest serving pontifex. And though Sulla had laid down that the college should consist of eight plebeians and seven patricians, at the time of Gaius Cotta's death it contained nine plebeians and only six patricians, due to Sulla's need to reward this man and that with pontificate or augurship. Normally the death of a plebeian priest meant that the college replaced him with another plebeian, but in order to arrange the membership as Sulla had laid down, the members of the college decided to co-opt a patrician. And their choice had fallen upon Caesar.

As far as Aurelia could gather, Caesar's selection hinged upon the fact that no Julian had been a member of the College of Pontifices or the College of Augurs since the murders of Lucius Caesar (an augur) and Caesar Strabo (a pontifex) thirteen years before. It had been generally accepted that Lucius Caesar's son would fill the next vacancy in the College of Augurs, but (said Aurelia) no one had dreamed of Caesar for the College of Pontifices. Her informant was Mamercus, who had told her that the decision had not been reached with complete accord; Catulus opposed him, as did Metellus the eldest son of the Billy-goat. But after many auguries and a consultation of the prophetic books, Caesar won.

The most important part of his mother's letter was a message from Mamercus, that if he wanted to make sure of his priesthood, Caesar had better get back to Rome for consecration and inauguration as soon as he possibly could; otherwise it was possible Catulus might sway the college to change its mind.

His fifth campaign recorded, Caesar packed his few belongings with no regrets. The only people he would miss were his landlords, Apronius and Canuleius, and the legate Marcus Manius.

"Though I must confess," he said to Manius, "that I wish I could have seen the vast sybaritic eyesore standing on the cove in all its ultimate glory."

"To be pontifex is far more important," said Manius, who had not realized quite how important Caesar was; to Manius he had always seemed a down-to-earth and unassuming fellow who was very good at everything he did and a glutton for work. "What will you do after you've been inducted into the college?"

"Try to find some humble propraetor with a war on his hands he can't handle," said Caesar. "Lucullus is proconsul now, which means he can't order the other governors about."

"Spain?"

"Too prominent in dispatches. No, I'll see if Marcus Fonteius needs a bright young military tribune in Gaul-across-the-Alps. He's a *vir militaris,* and they're always sensible men. He won't care what Lucullus thinks of me as long as I can work." The fair face looked suddenly grim. "But first things first, and first is Marcus Junius Juncus. I shall prosecute him in the Extortion Court."

"Haven't you heard?" asked Manius.

"Heard what?"

"Juncus is dead. He never got back to Rome. Shipwrecked."

He was a Thracian who was not a Thracian. In the year that Caesar left Gytheum to assume his pontificate, this Thracian who was not a Thracian turned twenty-six, and entered upon the stage of history.

His birth was respectable, though not illustrious, and his father, a Vesuvian Campanian, had been one of those who applied within sixty days to a praetor in Rome under the *lex Plautia Papiria* passed during the Italian War, and had been awarded the Roman citizenship because he had not been one of those Italians who had borne arms against Rome.

Nothing in the boy's farming background could explain the boy's passion for war and everything military, but it was obvious to the father that when this second son turned seventeen he would enlist in the legions. However, the father was not without some influence, and was able to procure the boy a cadetship in the legion Marcus Crassus had recruited for Sulla after he landed in Italy and began his war against Carbo.

The boy thrived under a martial regimen and distinguished himself in battle before he had his eighteenth birthday; he was transferred to one of Sulla's veteran legions, and in time was promoted to junior military tribune. Offered a discharge at the end of the last campaign in Etruria, he elected instead to join the army of Gaius Cosconius, sent to Illyricum to subdue the tribes collectively called Delmatae.

At first he had found the locale and the style of warfare exhilarating, and added *armillae* and *phalerae* to his growing number of military decorations. But then Cosconius had become mired in a siege which lasted over two years; the port city of Salonae refused to yield or to fight. For the boy who was by now becoming a young man, the investment of Salonae was an intolerably boring and uneventful waste of his time. His course was set: he intended to espouse a career in the army as a *vir militaris*—a Military Man. Gaius Marius had started out as a Military Man, and look where he ended! Yet here he was sitting for month after month outside an inert mass of brick and tile, doing nothing, going nowhere.

He asked for a transfer to Spain because (like many of his companions) he was fascinated by the exploits of Sertorius, but the legate in command of his legion was not sympathetic, and refused him. Boredom piled upon boredom; he applied a second time for a transfer to Spain. And was refused a second time. After that blow his conduct deteriorated. He gained a name for insubordination, drinking, absence from camp without permission. All of which disappeared when Salonae fell and the general Cosconius began to collaborate with Gaius Scribonius Curio, governor of Macedonia, in a massive sweep aimed at subduing the Dardani. Now this was more like it!

The incident which brought about the young man's downfall was classified as insurrection, and the unsympathetic legate turned out to be a secret enemy. The young man—along with a number of others—was arraigned in Cosconius's military court and tried for the crime of mutiny. The court found against him. Had he been an auxiliary or any kind of non-Roman, his sentence would automatically have consisted of flogging and execution. But because he was a Roman and an officer with junior tribunician status—and was the owner of many decorations for valor—the young man was offered two alternatives. He would lose his citizenship, of course; but he could choose to be flogged and exiled permanently from Italy, or he could choose to become a gladiator. Understandably he chose to be a gladiator. That way, he could at least go home. Being a Campanian, he knew all about gladiators; the gladiatorial schools were concentrated around Capua.

Shipped to Aquileia along with some seven other men convicted in the same mutiny who had also elected a gladiatorial fate, he was acquired by a dealer and sent to Capua for auction. However, it was no part of his intentions to advertise his erstwhile Roman citizen status. His father and older brother did not like the sport of gladiatorial combat and never went to funeral games; he could live in fairly close proximity to his father's farm without their ever knowing it. So he picked a ring name for himself, a good, short, martial-sounding name with splendid fighting connotations: Spartacus. Yes, it rolled off the tongue well: Spartacus. And he vowed that Spartacus would become a famous gladiator, be asked for up and down the length of Italy, turn into a local Capuan hero with girls hanging off his arm and more invitations to dinner than he could handle.

In the Capuan market he was sold to the *lanista* of a famous school owned by the consular and ex-censor Lucius Marcius Philippus, for the look of him was wonderfully appealing: he was tall, had magnificently developed calves, thighs, chest, shoulders and arms, a neck like a bull, skin like a sun-drenched girl's except for a few interesting-looking scars; and he was handsome in a fair-haired, grey-eyed way; and he moved with a certain princely grace, bore himself regally. The *lanista* who paid one hundred thousand sesterces for him on behalf of Philippus (who naturally was not present—Philippus had never set eyes on any of the five hundred gladiators he owned and rented out so profitably) thought from the look of him that Spartacus was a born gladiator. Philippus couldn't lose.

There were only two styles of gladiator, the Thracian and the Gaul. Looking at Spartacus, the *lanista* was hard put to decide which kind he ought to be trained as; usually the man's physique dictated the answer, but Spartacus was so splendid he could be either. However, Gauls bore more scars and ran a slightly higher risk of permanent maiming, and the price had been a long one. Therefore the *lanista* elected to make Spartacus a Thracian. The more beautiful he remained in the ring, the higher his hiring price would be after he began to gain a reputation. His head was noble, would look better bare. A Thracian wore no helmet.

Training began. A cautious man, the *lanista* made sure that Spartacus's athletic prowess was the equal of his looks before commissioning his armor, which was silver-plated and embossed with gold. He wore a scarlet loincloth held at the waist by a broad black leather sword belt, and carried the curved saber of a Thracian cavalryman. His shins were protected by greaves which extended well up each thigh, which meant he moved more awkwardly and slowly than his opponent, the Gaul—and needed more intelligence and co-ordination to manage these contraptions. Upon his right arm he wore a leather sleeve encrusted with metal scales, held in place by straps across neck and chest; it projected down over the back of his right hand to the knuckles. His outfit was completed by a small, round shield.

It all came easily to Spartacus. Of course he was a bit of a mystery (his seven fellow convicts had gone elsewhere from Aquileia) as he would never speak of his military career, and what the Aquileian agent had said in his letter was sketchy in the extreme. But he spoke Campanian Latin as well as Campanian Greek, he was modestly literate, and he knew his way around an army. All of which began to disturb the *lanista,* who foresaw complications. Spartacus was too much the warrior, even in the practice ring with wooden sword and leather buckler. The first arm he broke in several places might have been a mistake, but when his tally of badly broken bones had put five *doctores* out of commission for some months, the *lanista* sent for Spartacus.

"Look," the man said in a reasonable voice, "you must learn to think of soldiering in the ring as a game, not a war. What you're doing is a sport! The Etrusci invented it a thousand years ago, and it's been passed down the ages as an honorable and highly skilled profession. It doesn't exist anywhere in the world outside of Italy. Some man dies and his relatives put on—not the games Achilles celebrated for Patroclus, running and jumping, boxing and wrestling—but a solemn contest of athletic ability in the guise of warrior sport."

The fair young giant stood listening with expressionless face, but the *lanista* noticed that the fingers of his right hand kept opening and closing, as if wishing for the feel of a sword.

"Are you listening to me, Spartacus?"

"Yes, *lanista.*"

"The *doctor* is your trainer, not your enemy. And let me tell you, a good *doctor* is hard to come by! Thanks to your misguided enthusiasm I'm five *doctores* poorer than I was a month ago, and I can't replace them with men anything like as good as they were. Oh, they'll all live! But two of them are permanently out of a job! Spartacus, you are not fighting the enemies of Rome, and shedding buckets of blood is not the object of the game! People come to see a sport—a physical activity of thrust and parry, power and grace, skill and intelligence. The nicks and cuts and slashes all gladiators sustain bleed quite freely enough to thrill the audience, which doesn't come to see two men kill each other—or cut off arms! It comes to see a sport. A sport, Spartacus! A contest of athletic prowess. If the audience wanted to see men kill and maim each other, it would go to a battlefield—the gods know we've had more than our share of battlefields in Campania!" He stopped to eye Spartacus. "Now did that sink in? Do you understand better?"

"Yes, *lanista*," said Spartacus.

"Then go away and train some more, like a good boy! Take out your ardor on the bolsters and the swinging wooden men—and next time you face a *doctor* with your toy sword, put your mind on making a beautiful movement through the air with it, not a nasty crunchy sound of bones breaking!"

As Spartacus was quite intelligent enough to understand what the *lanista* had tried to explain to him, for some time after their chat he did turn his mind to the rituals and ceremonies of pure movement—even found it a challenge he could enjoy. The wary and apprehensive *doctores* who faced him were gratified to see that he did not try to break their limbs, but instead concentrated upon the various traceries of movement which so thrilled a crowd. It took the *lanista* a longer time to believe that Spartacus was cured of his bloodthirstiness, but at the end of six months he put his problem gladiator on a list of five pairs who were to fight at the funeral games of one of the Guttae of Capua. Because it was a local performance the *lanista* could attend it himself, see for himself how Spartacus shaped up in the ring.

The Gaul who faced Spartacus (they were the third pair on) was a good match for him; a little taller, equally splendid of body. Naked except for a small patch of cloth covering his genitalia, the Gaul fought with a very long, slightly curved shield and a straight, two-edged sword. The chief glory of his apparel was his helmet, a splendid silver cap with cheek flaps and a neck guard, and surmounted by a leaping enameled fish larger than a conventional plume would have been.

Spartacus had never seen the Gaul before, let alone spoken to him; in a huge establishment like Philippus's school the only men one got to know were one's *doctores,* the *lanista,* and fellow pupils at the same stage of development. But he had been told beforehand that this first opponent was an experienced fighter of some fourteen bouts who had gained much popularity in Capua, the arena he usually occupied.

It went well for a few moments as Spartacus in his clumsier gear moved in slow circles just out of the Gaul's reach. Looking upon his handsome face and Herculean body, some of the women in the crowd sighed audibly, made kissing sounds; Spartacus was forming the nucleus of a future band of devoted female followers. But as the *lanista* did not allow a new man access to women until he had earned this bonus in the ring, the kissing sounds affected Spartacus, took his mind off the Gaul just a little. He raised his small round shield a foot too high, and the Gaul, moving like an eel, chopped a neat gash in his left buttock.

That was the end of it. And the end of the Gaul. So fast that no one in the crowd saw more than a blur, Spartacus whirled on his left heel and brought his curved saber down against the side of his opponent's neck. The blade went in far enough to sever the spinal column; the Gaul's head fell over sideways, flopped against his shoulder and hung there with horrified eyes still blinking their lids and mouth aping the kissing sounds thrown to Spartacus. There were screams, shouts, tremendous ripples and eddies in the crowd as some fainted and some fled and some vomited.

Spartacus was marched back to the barracks.

"That does it!" said the *lanista*. "You'll never, never make a gladiator!"

"But he wounded me!" protested Spartacus.

The *lanista* shook his head. "How can someone so clever be so stupid?" he asked. "Stupid, stupid, stupid! With your looks and your natural ability, you could have been the most famous gladiator in all of Italy—earned yourself an easy competence, me a pat on the back, and Lucius Marcius Philippus a huge fortune! But you haven't got it in you, Spartacus, because you're so stupid! So clever and so stupid! You're out of here today."

"Out of here? Where to?" the Thracian demanded, still angry. "I have to serve my time as a gladiator!"

"Oh, you will," said the *lanista*. "But not here. Lucius Marcius Philippus owns another school further out of Capua, and that's where I'm sending you. It's a cozy little establishment—about a hundred gladiators, ten or so *doctores,* and the best-known *lanista* in the business. Gnaeus Cornelius Lentulus Batiatus. Old Batiatus the barbarian. He's from Illyricum. After me, Spartacus, you'll find Batiatus a cup of pure poison."

"I'll survive," said Spartacus, unimpressed. "I have to."

At dawn the next day a closed box-cart came for the deportee, who entered it quickly, then discovered when the bolt on the door slammed home that the only other communication between interior and exterior was narrow gaps between the ill-fitting planks. He was a prisoner who couldn't even see where he was going! A *prisoner!* So alien and horrific was the concept to a Roman that by the time the cart turned in through the enormously high and formidably barred gates of the gladiatorial school run by Gnaeus Cornelius Lentulus Batiatus, the prisoner was bruised, grazed and half senseless from beating himself against the planks.

That had been a year ago. His twenty-fifth birthday had passed at the other school, and his twenty-sixth inside the walls of what its inmates referred to as the Villa Batiatus. No pampering at the Villa Batiatus! The exact number of men held there varied slightly from time to time, but the record books usually said one hundred gladiators—fifty Thracians and fifty Gauls. To Batiatus they were not individuals, just Thracians and Gauls. All of them had come from other schools after some kind of offense—mostly associated with violence or rebellion—and they lived like mine slaves except that when inside the Villa Batiatus they were not chained, and they were well fed, comfortably bedded, even provided with women.

But it was genuine slavery. Each man knew he was inside the Villa Batiatus until he died, even if he survived the ring; once too old to fight, a man was put to work as a *doctor* or a servant. They were not paid, nor were their bouts spaced far enough apart to allow wounds to heal when business for Batiatus was brisk—and business for Batiatus was almost always brisk. For he was the bottom-price man; anyone who had a few sesterces to rub together and a wish to honor a dead relative with funeral games could hire a couple of Batiatus's men. Because of the low price, most of the engagements were fairly local.

Escape from the Villa Batiatus was virtually impossible. Its interior was divided into many small areas each walled and barred off from every other area, and no part wherein gladiators moved was actually adjacent to the immensely high outside walls, all of which were topped by inward-angled iron spikes. Escape on the outside (they were often outside on engagements) was also virtually impossible; each man was chained at wrists and ankles, wore an iron collar around his neck, traveled in a windowless prison cart, and when on foot was escorted everywhere by a party of archers carrying small composite bows, arrows at the ready. Only in the moment a man entered the ring was he freed from his chains, and then the archers were stationed nearby.

How different from the kind of life an ordinary soldier of the sawdust lived! *He* was free to come and go from his barracks, was coddled and made much of, the idol of a good many women, and aware he was banking a sizable nest egg. He fought no more than five or six bouts in a year, and after five years or thirty bouts—whichever came first—he retired. Even free men sometimes elected to become gladiators, though the bulk were deserters or mutineers from the legions, and a very few were sent to the schools already enslaved. All this care and cosseting arose out of the fact that a trained gladiator was a very expensive investment, had to be preserved and kept happy to earn the owner of his school a nice fat profit.

At the school of Batiatus things were different. He didn't care whether a man bit the sawdust during his first bout or fought regularly for ten years. Men much over twenty were not accepted as gladiators, and ring life lasted ten years at the most; it was a young man's sport. Even Batiatus didn't send grizzled men into the ring; the crowd (and the bereaved doing the hiring) liked its combatants supple, unset. Once retired from the ring, a man in the Villa Batiatus simply went on existing and enduring there. A desperate fate considering that when an ordinary gladiator retired, he was free to do what he liked where he liked; usually he went to Rome or some other big city, and hired himself out as a bouncer, a bodyguard, or a bully-boy.

The Villa Batiatus was a place of unyielding routines which were heralded by the clanging of an iron bar on an iron circle and rotated according to a schedule painted too high on the main exercise yard wall to be defaced. The hundred or however many men were locked at sunset into barred stone cells holding between seven and eight, each having no communication with its neighbors—even sound did not penetrate the walls. No man remained with the same group; sleeping arrangements were staggered so that each man moved each evening to six or seven new companions. After ten days he was shuffled yet again, and so crafty were the permutations Batiatus had worked out that a new man had to wait for a year before he succeeded in getting to know every other man. The cells were clean and equipped with big comfortable beds as well as an anteroom which contained a bath, running water and plenty of chamber pots. Warm in winter and cool in summer, the cells were used only between sunset and sunrise. They were serviced during the day by domestic slaves with whom the men had no contact.

At sunrise the men were roused by the sound of bolts sliding back, and commenced the day's routines. For all that day a gladiator would associate with the men he had shared a cell with on the previous night, though talk was forbidden. Each group broke its fast in the walled-off yard directly in front of its cell; if it was raining, a hide shelter was rigged overhead. Then the group would work together in the practice drills, after which a *doctor* would divide them, Gaul against Thracian if that were possible, and put them to dueling with wooden swords and leather shields. This was followed by the main meal of the day—cooked meats, plenty of fresh bread, good olive oil, fruit and vegetables in season, eggs, salt fish, some sort of pulse porridge sopped up with bread, and all the water a man could drink. Wine, even sparse enough to be a mere flavoring, was never served. After the meal they rested in silence for two hours before being set to polishing armor, working leather, repairing boots, or some other gladiatorial maintenance; any tools were scrupulously logged and collected afterward, and archers watched. A third and lighter meal followed a hard exercise workout, then it was time for each man to move to his new set of companions.

Batiatus kept forty women slaves whose only duty aside from soft work in the kitchens was to assuage the sexual appetites of the gladiators, who were visited by these women every third night. Again, a man took his turn with all forty; in numbered order, the seven or eight women deputed to a cell would file into the cell under escort and each go straight to an assigned bed— nor could she remain in that bed once intercourse had taken place. Most of the men were capable of at least three or four sexual encounters during the night, but each time had to be with a different woman. Well aware that in this activity lay the greatest danger of some form of affection growing up, Batiatus set a watch on the lucky cells (a duty no servant minded, as the cells were lit for the night) and made sure the women moved on and the men did not try to strike up conversations.

Not all hundred gladiators were in residence at once. From one third to one half of them were on the road—an existence all of them loathed, as conditions were not as comfortable as inside the Villa Batiatus, and of women there were none. But the absence of a group allowed the women days of rest (strictly rostered—Batiatus had a passion for rosters and tricky permutations) and also gave those who were heavily pregnant time to have their babies before returning to duty. Duty was excused them only during the last month before labor and the first month after it, which meant that the women strove not to fall pregnant, and that many who did immediately procured abortions. Every baby born was removed from its mother at once; if a female it was thrown away on the Villa Batiatus rubbish heap, and if a male was taken to Batiatus himself for inspection. He always had a few women clients anxious to purchase a male baby.

The leader of the women was a genuine Thracian by name of Aluso. She was a priestess of the Bessi, she was warlike, she had been one of Batiatus's whores for nine years, and she hated Batiatus more fiercely than any gladiator in the school. The female child she had borne during her first year at the Villa Batiatus would under her tribal culture have been her successor as priestess, but Batiatus had ignored her frenzied pleas to be allowed to keep the baby, who had been thrown out with the rubbish. After that Aluso had taken the medicine and no other babies followed. But she nursed her outrage, and swore by terrible gods that Batiatus would die a piece at a time.

All of this meant that Gnaeus Cornelius Lentulus Batiatus was one of the most efficient and meticulous men the city of gladiators had ever known. Nothing escaped him—no precaution was overlooked—no detail left unattended to. And in that side of him lay a part of the reason why this school for unsatisfactory gladiators was so successful. The other part of the reason lay in Batiatus's personal skill as a *lanista*. He trusted no one, he deputed nothing better done himself. So he kept the only key to the stone fortress wherein the armor and weapons were stored; he took all the bookings; he made all the travel arrangements; he picked every archer, slave, armorer, cook, laundress, whore, *doctor* and assistant personally; he kept the accounts; and he alone ever saw the school's owner, Lucius Marcius Philippus—who never visited his establishment, but rather made Batiatus come to Rome. Batiatus was also the only one of Philippus's old employees who had survived the colossal shaking up Pompey had instituted some years before; in fact, so impressed was Pompey by Batiatus that he asked him to take over as Philippus's general manager. But Batiatus had smiled and declined; he loved his work.

Yet the end of the Villa Batiatus was in sight when Spartacus and seven other gladiators returned from an engagement in Larinum at the end of the month Sextilis in the year Caesar left Gytheum and the service of Marcus Antonius to assume his pontificate.

Larinum had been a fascinating experience, even for eight men kept cooped up in a prison cart and chained for every moment save those spent fighting in the ring. At the end of the previous year one of Larinum's most prominent men, Statius Albius Oppianicus, had been prosecuted by his stepson, Aulus Cluentius Habitus, for attempting to murder him. The trial had taken place in Rome, and a horrific story of mass murder going back over twenty years had tumbled out. Oppianicus, the whole of Rome had learned, was responsible for the murders of his wives, sons, brothers, in-laws, cousins, and others, each killing committed or commissioned in order to accumulate money and power. A friend of the fabulously rich aristocrat Marcus Licinius Crassus, Oppianicus had nearly been acquitted; the tribune of the plebs Lucius Quinctius became involved, and a huge sum of money had been set aside to bribe the jury of senators. That Oppianicus had ended in being convicted was due to the avarice of his appointed briber, the same Gaius Aelius Staienus who had proven so useful to Pompey a few years earlier—and kept ninety thousand sesterces for himself when Gaius Antonius Hybrida had hired him to bribe nine tribunes of the plebs. For Staienus was incapable of honorably fulfilling the most dishonorable commissions; he kept the money Oppianicus gave him to bribe the jury and let Oppianicus be condemned.

Larinum could still find little to talk about except the perfidy of Oppianicus, even when gladiators were in town to stage funeral games—there had been too many funeral games in Larinum, was the trouble. So while they ate chained up to a table in the courtyard of a local inn, the gladiators had listened to the four archers marveling, and looked interested. Though they were not allowed to speak to each other, of course they did. Time and much practice had enabled them to carry on snatches of shortened conversation, and mass murder among the upper classes of Larinum was wonderful cover.

Despite the huge obstacles the obsessive meticulousness of Batiatus had thrown up everywhere, Spartacus—now the veteran of more than twelve months as a resident of the Villa Batiatus—was gathering together the threads of a plot aimed at a mass escape—and a mass murder. He finally knew everybody and had learned how to communicate with people he couldn't see daily—or even monthly. If Batiatus had created a complicated web which kept his whores and his gladiators from getting to know each other well, Spartacus had constructed an equally complicated web which enabled whores and gladiators to pass on ideas and information and pass back comments, favorable or critical. In fact, the Batiatus system had allowed Spartacus to make positive use of this enforced indirect contact; it meant personalities were not thrown together often enough to clash—or to contemplate supplanting Spartacus as the leader of the coming insurrection.

He had started to send out feelers at the beginning of the summer, and now at the end of it his plans were in place. Every gladiator without exception had agreed that if Spartacus could engineer a breakout, he would be a part of it, and the whores—a vital part of Spartacus's scheme—had also agreed.

There were two Roman deserters whose understanding of military discipline and methods were almost the equal of Spartacus's, and through the whisper network he had appointed them his deputies in the escape. They fought as Gauls and had adopted the ring names of Crixus and Oenomaus because the audiences disliked Latin names which reminded them that most of their sawdust heroes were Roman military outlaws. As chance would have it, both Crixus and Oenomaus were with Spartacus in Larinum, a boon for Spartacus, who had been able to move the date of his projected breakout forward in time.

They would go eight days after the return from Larinum, no matter how many or how few gladiators were actually at the Villa Batiatus. As this was the day after the *nundinae* the number was likely to be higher than lower, enhanced by the fact that Batiatus curtailed his show bookings during September, when he was accustomed to take his annual vacation and pay his annual visit to Philippus.

The Thracian priestess Aluso had become Spartacus's most fervid ally; after the plot had been agreed to by everyone, whichever men were in the same cell as Spartacus contrived with the aid of the other women to ensure that Spartacus and Aluso were able to spend the whole night together if Aluso was one of the women's detail. In voices more breath than noise they had gone over the innumerable factors involved, and Aluso vowed that through the agency of her women, she would keep all the men in a fever of enthusiasm. She had been stealing kitchen implements for Spartacus since early summer, so cunningly that when they were finally missed one of the cooks was blamed; no one suspected a gladiators' revolt. A cleaver—a small carving knife—a hank of stout twine—a glass jar since smashed to slivers—a meat hook. A modest haul, but enough for eight men. All of these were held in the women's quarters, which the women cleaned themselves. But on the night before the breakout the women delegated to visit Spartacus's cell carried the implements concealed within their scanty clothing; Aluso was not among them.

Morning dawned. The eight men left their cell to eat in their enclosure. Clad only in loincloths, they carried nothing, but tucked inside the V of scarlet cloth each man wore was a section of twine about three feet long. The archer, an assistant *doctor* and two ex-gladiators who now served as yardsmen were garroted so quickly that the iron door of the cell still gaped open; Spartacus and his seven companions grabbed the weapons from their beds and were scattering along the row of cells using a key found on the archer before anyone knew what was happening. Each group of gladiators had dallied and grumbled on rising, shuffled and delayed, so that none had finished moving from cell to yard before eight silent athletes were among them. A cleaver flashed, a knife was plunged into a chest, a wicked chunk of broken glass sliced through a throat, and the eight pieces of twine were passed on.

It was done without a word, a shout, a warning; Spartacus and the other gladiators now held the row of cells and the yards leading from them. Some of the dead men carried keys, more gates leading further into the labyrinth were unlocked, and the seventy men who were imprisoned in the Villa Batiatus at the time streamed silently onward, outward. There was a shed in which axes and tools were kept; a muffled jangle, and anything useful was in a gladiator's hand. Another flaw in Batiatus's ground plan now lay revealed, for the high internal walls kept what was going on limited to the immediate vicinity. Batiatus ought to have erected watchtowers and put his archers in them.

The alarm was given when the men reached the kitchens, but that was far too late. Possessed now of every sharp instrument the kitchens owned, the gladiators used pot lids to ward off arrows and went after everyone left alive. Including Batiatus, who had meant to leave on his vacation the previous day but instead had stayed because he had found a discrepancy in his books.

The men kept him alive until they had liberated the women, who tore him apart a little at a time under the clinical supervision of Aluso; she ate his heart with relish.

And by the time the sun had risen Spartacus and his sixty-nine companions had taken the Villa Batiatus. The weapons were removed from storage and every cart was yoked up to oxen or to mules. The food from the kitchens and all the spare armaments were piled into the wagons, the main gates were thrown open, and the little expedition marched bravely out into the world.

Knowing Campania of old, Spartacus's planning had not been confined to the taking of the Villa Batiatus. It stood beside the route from Capua to Nola some seven miles out of the city; Spartacus turned away from Capua and headed in the direction of Nola. Not far along the road they encountered another wagon train and attacked it, for no other reason than that they wanted no one alive to report which way they had gone. To the delight of all, the wagons turned out to be loaded with weapons and armor for another gladiatorial school. There were now more items useful for a war than people to wear or wield them.

Soon the cavalcade left the main road to take a deserted track which headed west of south toward Mount Vesuvius.

Clad in an archer's scaly jacket and carrying a Thracian's saber, Aluso moved to join Spartacus at the front of the column. She had washed off Batiatus's blood, but still licked her chops with the purring content of a cat every time she thought of how she had eaten his heart.

"You look like Minerva," said Spartacus, smiling; he had found nothing to criticize in Aluso's treatment of Batiatus.

"I feel like myself for the first time in ten years." And she jiggled the big leather bag dangling from her waist; it held the head of Batiatus, which she intended to scarify and transform its skull into her drinking cup, as was the custom of her tribe.

"You'll be my woman only, if that pleases you."

"It pleases me if I can be a part of your war councils."

They spoke in Greek since Aluso knew no Latin, and spoke with the ease of those who had enjoyed each other's bodies without any emotional clouding of simple passion, united in the pleasure of being free, of walking unchained and unsupervised.

Vesuvius was impressively different from other peaks. It stood alone amid the rolling plenty of Campania not far from the shores of Crater Bay, sloping upward in easy planes for three thousand feet neatly patched with vineyards, orchards, vegetable and wheat fields; the soil was deep and rich.

For several thousand more feet above the tilled slopes there reared a rocky, dissected tower dotted with trees hardy enough to dig their knobby toes into crevices, but devoid of habitation or cultivation.

Spartacus knew every inch of the mountain. His father's farm lay on its western flank, and he and his older brother had played for years amid the crags of the upper peak. So he led his train with purpose ever upward until he reached a bowl-shaped hollow high among the rocks on the northern side. The edges of the hollow were steep and it was difficult getting the carts inside it, but in its bottom grew lush grass, and there was room for a much larger collection of people and animals than Spartacus owned. Yellow smears of sulphur stained the escarpment and the smells which a mound in the middle exhaled were noisome; yet that meant the grasses had never been grazed and shepherds never brought their flocks here. The place was thought to be haunted, a fact Spartacus did not impart to his followers.

For several hours he concentrated upon getting his camp organized, shelters built out of the planks dismembered from prison wagons, women set to preparing food, men deputed to this task and that. But when the sun had sunk lower than the western rim of the round hollow, he called everyone together.

"Crixus and Oenomaus, stand one to each side of me," he said, "and Aluso, as chieftain of the women, as our priestess and as my woman, sit at my feet. The rest of you will face us."

He waited until the group had sorted itself out, then raised himself higher than Crixus and Oenomaus by jumping upon a rock.

"We are free for the moment, but we must never forget that under the law we are slaves. We have murdered our keepers and our owner, and when the authorities find out we will be hunted down. Never before have we been able to gather as a people and discuss our purposes, our fate, our future."

He drew a deep breath. "First of all, I will keep no man or no woman against his or her will. Those of a mind to seek their own ways separate from mine are at liberty to go at any time. I ask for no vows, no oaths, no ceremonies swearing fidelity to me. We have been prisoners, we have felt chains, we have been given no privileges accorded to free men, and the women have been forced into harlotry. So I will do nothing to bind you.

"This here"—he waved his hand about to indicate the camp—"is a temporary shelter. Sooner or later we will have to leave it. We were seen climbing the mountain, and the news of our deed will soon follow us."

A gladiator squatting on his haunches in the front row—Spartacus didn't know his name—raised a hand to speak.

"I see that we will be pursued and hunted down," said the fellow, frowning. "Would it not be better to disband now? If we scattered in a hundred directions, some of us at least will manage to escape. If we stay together, we will be captured together."

Spartacus nodded. "There is truth in what you say. However, I'm not in favor of it. Why? Chiefly because we have no money, no clothes other than what Batiatus issued us—and they brand us for what we are—and nothing to help us except weapons, which would be dangerous if we were scattered. Batiatus had no money on the premises, not one single sestertius. But money is a vital necessity, and I think we have to stay together until we find it."

"How can we do that?" asked the same fellow.

The smile Spartacus gave him was rueful but charming. "I have no idea!" he said frankly. "If this were Rome we could rob someone. But this is Campania, and full of careful farmers who keep everything in a bank or buried where we'd never find it." He spread his hands in an appeal. "Let me tell you what I would like us to do, then everyone can think about it. Tomorrow at this same time we'll meet and vote."

No more enlightened than the rest, Crixus and Oenomaus nodded vigorously.

"Tell us, Spartacus," said Crixus.

The light was dying little by little, but Spartacus atop his rock seemed to concentrate the last rays of the sun upon himself, and looked like a man worth following. Determined, sure, strong, reliable.

"You all know the name Quintus Sertorius," he said. "A Roman in revolt against the system which produces men like Batiatus. He has gathered Spain to himself, and soon he will be marching to Rome to be the Dictator and found a new style of Republic. We know that because we heard people talking whenever we were sent somewhere to fight. We learned too that many in Italy want Quintus Sertorius at the head of Rome. Especially the Samnites."

He paused, wet his lips. "I know what I am going to do! I am going to Spain to join Quintus Sertorius. But if it is at all possible I would bring him another army—an army which would already have struck blows against the Rome of Sulla and his heirs. I am going to recruit among the Samnites, the Lucanians, and all the others in Italy who would rather see a new Rome than watch their heritage run away to nothing. I will recruit among the slaves of Campania too, and offer them full citizenship rights in the Rome of Quintus Sertorius. We have more weapons than we can use—unless we recruit more men. And when Rome sends troops against us we will defeat them and take their gear too!"

He shrugged. "I have nothing to lose but my life, and I have vowed that never again will I endure the kind of existence Batiatus forced upon me.

A man—even a man enslaved!—must have the right to associate freely with his fellows, to move in the world. Prison is worse than death. I will *never* go back to any prison!''

He broke down, wept, dashed the tears away impatiently. "I am a man, and I will make my mark! But all of you should be saying that too! If we stay together and form the nucleus of an army, then we stand a chance to defend ourselves and make a great mark. If we scatter in a hundred directions, every last one of us will have to run, run, run. Why run like deer if we can march like men? Why not carve ourselves a place in the Rome of Quintus Sertorius by softening up Italy for him, then marching to join him as he comes? Rome has few troops in Italy, we know that. Which of us hasn't heard the Capuans complaining that their livelihood is dwindling because the legionary camps are empty? Who is there to stop us? I was a military tribune once. Crixus, Oenomaus, and many of you here belonged to Rome's legions. Is there anything that the likes of Lucullus or Pompeius Magnus knows about forming and running an army that I do not, or Crixus, or Oenomaus, or any of you? It isn't a difficult business to run an army! So why don't we become an army? We can win victories! There are no veteran legions in Italy to stop us, just cohorts of raw recruits. It is we who will attract experienced soldiers, the Samnites and Lucanians who fought to be free of Rome. And between us we will train the inexperienced who join us—does it follow that a slave is necessarily a man without martial ability or valor? Servile armies have brought Rome to the brink of ruin several times, and only fell because they were not led by men who understand how Rome fights. They were not led by Romans!''

Both mighty arms went up above his head; Spartacus closed his hands into fists and shook them. "*I* will lead our army! And I will lead it to victory! I will bring it to Quintus Sertorius wreathed in laurels and with Rome in Italy beneath its foot!'' Down came the arms. "Think about what I have said, I ask nothing more.''

The little band of gladiators and women said nothing when Spartacus jumped down, but the looks directed at him were glowing and Aluso was smiling at him fiercely.

"They will vote for you tomorrow,'' she said.

"Yes, I think they will.''

"Then come with me now to the spring of water. It needs to be purified if it is to give life to many.''

Quite how she understood what she was doing Spartacus did not know, but was awed to discover that after she had muttered her incantations and dug with the severed hand of Batiatus at the crumbling walls to one side of the hot, smelly fountain which gushed out of a cleft, a second spate of water appeared—cool, sweet, quenching.

"It is an omen," said Spartacus.

In twenty days a thousand volunteers had accumulated inside the hollow near the top of Vesuvius, though it remained a mystery to Spartacus how word had flown around when he had as yet sent no messengers or recruiting teams into the surrounding countryside. Perhaps a tenth of those who arrived to join the gladiators were escaped slaves, but by far the majority were free men of Samnite nationality. Nola wasn't far away, and Nola hated Rome. So did Pompeii, Neapolis, and all the other partisans of Italy who had fought to the death against Sulla, first in the Italian War, then for Pontius Telesinus. Rome might delude herself that she had crushed Samnium; but that, thought Spartacus as he entered Samnite name after Samnite name on his recruitment list, would never happen until the last Samnite was no more. Many of them arrived wearing armor and carrying weapons, hoary veterans who spat at the mention of Sulla's name or made the sign to ward off the Evil Eye at the mention of Cethegus and Verres, the two who had scorched the Samnite heartlands.

"I have something to show you," said Crixus to Spartacus, voice eager; it was the morning of the last day of September.

Drilling a century of slaves, Spartacus handed the task to another gladiator and moved off with Crixus, who was dragging anxiously at his arm. "What is it?" he asked.

"Better to see for yourself," said Crixus as he led Spartacus to a gap in the crater wall which allowed a far and sweeping view of Vesuvius's northern slopes.

Two Samnites were on sentry duty, and turned excited faces toward their leader. "Look!" said one.

Spartacus looked. Below him for a thousand feet the crags and pockets of the upper mountain presented an inhospitable mien; below that lay ordered fields. And through the wheat stubble there wound a column of Roman soldiers led by four mounted men in the Attic helmets and contoured cuirasses of high officers, the man riding alone behind three riding abreast wearing the looped and ritually knotted scarlet sash of high imperium around his glittering chest.

"Well, well! They've sent a praetor against us at the very least!" said Spartacus with a chuckle.

"How many legions?" asked Crixus, looking worried.

Spartacus stared, astonished. "Legions? You were in them, Crixus, you ought to be able to tell!"

"That's just it! I was *in* them. When you're *in* them, you never get to see what you look like."

Spartacus grinned, ruffled Crixus's hair. "Rest easy, there's no more than half a legion's worth down there—five cohorts of the greenest troops I've ever seen. Notice how they straggle, can't keep a straight line or an even distance apart? What's more important, they're being led by someone just as green! See how he rides behind his legates? Sure sign! A confident general is always out in front."

"Five cohorts? That's at least two and a half thousand men."

"Five cohorts that have never been in a legion, Crixus."

"I'll sound general quarters."

"No, stay here with me. Let them think we haven't noticed them. If they hear bugles and shouting, they'll stop and camp down there on the slopes. Whereas if they think they've stolen a march on us, that idiot leading them will keep on coming until he's among the rocks and realizes he can't make a camp. By then it will be too late to re-form and march down again—the whole lot will have to doss down in little groups wherever they can find the room. Idiots! If they'd gone round to the south, they could have used the track right up to our hollow."

By the time darkness fell Spartacus had established beyond doubt that the punitive expedition was indeed composed of raw recruits, and that the general was a praetor named Gaius Claudius Glaber; the Senate had ordered him to pick up five cohorts in Capua as he passed through—and keep on marching until he found the rebels and flushed them out of their Vesuvian hole.

By dawn the punitive expedition no longer existed. Throughout the night Spartacus had sent silent raiding parties down into the crags, some even lowered on ropes, to kill swiftly and noiselessly. So green indeed were these recruits that they had shed their armor and piled their arms together before cuddling up to campfires which betrayed where every pocket of them slept, and so green was Gaius Claudius Glaber that he thought the lie of the land a greater protection than a proper camp. Closer to dawn than to dusk some of the more wakeful soldiers began to understand what was going on, and gave the alarm. The stampede began.

Spartacus struck then in force, using his women followers as torchbearers to light his way. Half Glaber's troops died, the other half fled—but left their arms and armor behind them. Chief among the fugitives were Glaber and his three legates.

Two thousand eight hundred sets of infantry equipment went to swell the cache in the hollow; Spartacus stripped his growing army of its gladiatorial

accoutrements in favor of legionary gear and added Glaber's baggage train
to his carts and animals. Volunteers were now streaming in, most of them
trained soldiers; when his tally grew to five thousand, Spartacus decided the
hollow on Vesuvius had outlived its usefulness and moved his legion out.

He knew exactly where he was going.

Thus it was that when the praetors Publius Varinius and Lucius Cossinius
marched two legions of recruits out of camp in Capua and headed off along
the Nola road, they encountered a well laid out Roman fortification not far
from the devastated Villa Batiatus. Varinius, the senior in command, was
experienced. So was Cossinius, his second-in-command. One look at the men
of their two legions had horrified them; so raw were these recruits that their
basic training had only just begun! To add to the praetors' difficulties the
weather was cold, wet, and windy, and some kind of virulent respiratory
infection was raging through the ranks. When Varinius saw the workmanlike
structure beside the Nola road he knew at once that it belonged to the rebels—
but also knew that his own men were not capable of attacking it. Instead he
put the two legions into a camp alongside the rebels.

No one knew a name then, nor any details about the rebels save that
they had extirpated the gladiatorial school of Gnaeus Cornelius Lentulus
Batiatus (who appeared on its books as the proprietor), gone to earth on Mount
Vesuvius, and had been joined by some thousands of discontented Samnites,
Lucanians, and slaves. From the disgraced Glaber had come the news that
the rebels now owned every scrap of his gear, and that they were well enough
led to have gone about destroying Glaber's five cohorts like experts.

However, some thorough scouting revealed to Varinius and Cossinius
that the force inside the rebel camp numbered only about five thousand, and
that a certain proportion were women. Heartened, Varinius deployed his two
legions for battle the next morning, secure in the knowledge that even with
sick raw troops he had the numbers to win. It was still raining hard.

When the battle was over Varinius didn't know whether to blame his
defeat upon the sheer terror the sight of the rebels had inspired in his men,
or upon the illness which caused so many of his legionaries to lay down their
arms and refuse to fight, pleading that they couldn't, they just couldn't. Worst
blow of all was that Cossinius had been killed trying to rally a group of
would-be deserters—and that a great deal of equipment had been spirited off
the field by the rebels. There was no point in pursuing the rebels, who had
marched off through the rain in the direction of their camp. Varinius wheeled
his bedraggled and demoralized column about and went back to Capua, where
he wrote to the Senate frankly, not sparing himself—but not sparing the Senate

either. There were no experienced troops in Italy, he said, except for the rebels.

He did have a name to illuminate his report: Spartacus, a Thracian gladiator.

For six market intervals Varinius concentrated upon the training of his miserable soldiers, most of whom had survived the battle, but seemed less likely to survive the respiratory disease which still raged through their ranks. He commandeered the services of some old Sullan veteran centurions to help him train, though he couldn't persuade them to enlist. The Senate thought it prudent to begin recruiting four more legions, and assured Varinius that he had its support in whatever measures he felt called upon to execute. A fourth praetor out of that year's group of eight was dispatched from Rome to act as Varinius's senior legate: Publius Valerius. One fled, one dead, one vanquished; the fourth was not a happy man.

Varinius thought his men sufficiently well trained to begin operations at the end of November, and led them out of Capua to attack Spartacus's camp. Only to find it deserted. Spartacus had stolen away, yet one more indication that, Thracian or no, he was a military man in the Roman manner. Illness still dogged poor Varinius. As he led his two under-strength legions south he had to watch helplessly as whole cohorts were forced to abandon the march, their centurions promising to catch up with him as soon as the men felt better. Near Picentia, just before the ford across the Silarus River, he caught up with the rebels at last; only to see in horror that Spartacus's legion had mushroomed into an army. Five thousand less than two months ago—twenty-five thousand now! Not daring to attack, Varinius was obliged to watch this suddenly great force cross the Silarus and march off along the Via Popillia into Lucania.

When the sick cohorts caught up and the stricken men still with him showed signs of recovering, Varinius and Valerius held a conference. Did they follow the rebels into Lucania or return to Capua to spend the winter training a bigger army?

"What you really mean," said Valerius, "is whether we would do better to give battle now, even though outnumbered badly, or whether we can raise enough extra men during the winter to make delaying a confrontation until the spring a wiser move."

"I don't think there is a decision to make," said Varinius. "We have to follow them now. By the spring they're likely to be doubled in strength— and every man they add to their ranks will be a Lucanian veteran."

So Varinius and Valerius followed, even when the evidence told them that Spartacus had departed from the Via Popillia and was moving steadily into the wilds of the Lucanian mountains. For eight days they followed without seeing more than old signs, pitching a stout camp each and every night. Taxing work, but the prudent alternative.

On the ninth evening the same process was begun amid the grumbles of men who had not been legionaries long enough to understand the necessity or the advantages of a safe camp. And while the earth walls were being piled up out of the refuse thrown from the ditches, Spartacus attacked. Outnumbered and outgeneraled, Varinius had no choice other than to retreat, though he left his beautifully caparisoned Public Horse behind along with most of his soldiers. Of the eighteen cohorts he had started with from Capua, only five returned out of Lucania; having crossed the Silarus into Campania again, Varinius and Valerius left these five cohorts to guard the ford under the command of a quaestor, Gaius Toranius.

The two praetors journeyed back to Rome, there to exhort the Senate to train more men as quickly as possible. The situation was undeniably growing more serious every day, but between Lucullus and Marcus Cotta in the east and Pompey in Spain, many of the senators felt that the recruiting process was a waste of time. The Italian well was dry. Then in January came the news that Spartacus had issued out of Lucania with *forty thousand* men organized into eight efficient legions. The rebels had rolled over poor Gaius Toranius at the Silarus, killed him and every man in his five cohorts. Campania lay at the mercy of Spartacus, who, said the report, was busy trying to persuade towns of Samnite population to come over to his side, declare for a free Italy.

The tribunes of the Treasury were told very succinctly to cease their noises of complaint and start finding the money to lure veterans out of retirement. The praetor Quintus Arrius (who had been scheduled to replace Gaius Verres as governor of Sicily) was instructed to hustle himself to Capua and begin organizing a proper consular army of four legions, stiffened as much as possible with veteran intakes. The new consuls, Lucius Gellius Poplicola and Gnaeus Cornelius Lentulus Clodianus, were formally given the command in the war against Spartacus.

All of this Spartacus gradually discovered from the time he had re-entered Campania. As his army was still growing, he had learned to weld it on the march, forming and drilling new cohorts as he went. It had been a grief when Oenomaus was killed during the successful attack on the camp of Varinius and Valerius, but Crixus was still very much alive and other capable legates were rising to the surface. The Public Horse which had belonged to Varinius made a wonderful mount for a supreme commander! Showy. Every morning Spartacus kissed its nose and stroked its flowing silvery mane before leaping upon its back; he called it Batiatus.

Certain that towns like Nola and Nuceria would rally behind him, he had sent his ambassadors to see their magistrates at once, explaining that he was intent upon helping Quintus Sertorius establish a new Italian Republic, and asking for donations of men, matériel, money. Only to be told firmly that no city of Campania or any other region in Italy would support the cause of Quintus Sertorius—or of Spartacus the gladiator general.

"We do not love the Romans," said the magistrates of Nola, "and we are proud of the fact that we held out longer against Rome than any other place in all of Italy. But no more. Never again. Our prosperity is gone, all our young men are dead. We will not join you against Rome."

When Nuceria returned the same answer Spartacus held a small conference with Crixus and Aluso.

"Sack them," said the Thracian priestess. "Teach them that it is wiser to join us."

"I agree," said Crixus, "though my reason is different. We have forty thousand men, enough equipment to outfit every last one, and plenty to eat. But we have nothing else, Spartacus. It is all very well to promise our troops lives of distinction and wealth under the government of Quintus Sertorius, but it might be better to give them some of that wealth right now. If we sack any town which refuses to join us, we will terrify the towns we have still to reach—*and* we will please our legions. Women, plunder—there's not a soldier born who doesn't love a sack!"

His temper frayed by what he saw as unappreciative rejection, Spartacus made up his mind more quickly than the old Spartacus of pregladiatorial days would have; that had been a different life, he a different sort of man. "Very well. We attack Nuceria and Nola. Tell the men to have no mercy."

The men had no mercy. Looking at the results, Spartacus decided that there was much merit in sacking towns. Nuceria and Nola had yielded treasure as well as money, food, women; if he continued to sack, he would be able to present Quintus Sertorius with a huge fortune as well as an army! And if he did, then it seemed likely that Quintus Sertorius the Dictator of Rome would make Spartacus the Thracian gladiator his Master of the Horse.

Therefore the huge fortune had to be obtained before he left Italy. Requests were still pouring in from whole districts of men anxious to join him, and telling of rich pickings in parts of Lucania, Bruttium and Calabria which had not been touched by the Italian War. So from Campania the rebels journeyed south to sack Consentia in Bruttium and then Thurii and Metapontum on the Gulf of Tarentum. Much to Spartacus's delight, all three towns were possessed of staggering wealth.

When Aluso had finished scarifying the skull of Batiatus, he had given her a sheet of silver with which to line it; but after Consentia, Thurii and Metapontum, he told her to throw the silver on the nearest rubbish heap, replace it with gold. And there was a certain seduction in all this—as well as the ever-present seduction of Aluso, who thought like a barbarian but had terrible magic and stood to him as the talisman of his luck. As long as he had Aluso by his side, he was one of Fortune's favorites.

Yes, she was wonderful. She could find water, she sensed when disaster was looming, she always gave him the right advice. Growing heavy with his child, her rich red mouth a perfect foil for flaxen hair and wild white wolf's pallid eyes, ankles and wrists clashing with the gold she loaded upon them, he thought her perfect, not the least because she was a Thracian and he had become a Thracian. They belonged together; she was the personification of this strange new life.

Early in April he was marching into eastern Samnium, sure that here at least the towns would join him. But Asernia, Bovianum, Beneventum and Saepinum all rejected his overtures—we won't join you, we don't want you, go away! Nor were they worth sacking. Verres and Cethegus had left nothing. However, individual Samnites kept flocking to join his army, which had now swelled to ninety thousand men.

So many people, Spartacus was finding out, were difficult to manage. Though the troops were organized into proper Roman legions and were armed in Roman style, he could never seem to find enough capable legates and tribunes to keep an iron control over soldierly impulses, wine, the hideous strife the female camp followers provoked. Time, he decided, to march for Italian Gaul, Gaul-across-the-Alps, and Quintus Sertorius in Nearer Spain. Not to the west of the Apennines—he had no desire to venture anywhere near the city of Rome. He would proceed up the Adriatic littoral through regions which had fought bitterly against Roman control of the peninsula—Marrucini, Vestini, Frentani, southern Picentines. Many of their men would join him!

But Crixus didn't want to go to Nearer Spain. Nor did the thirty thousand men in his division of the army.

"Why go so far?" he asked. "If what you say about Quintus Sertorius is true, then one day he will arrive in Italy. It's better that he finds us in Italy still, with our foot on Rome's neck. The distance from here to Spain is half as far again as a thousand miles, and we'd be marching the whole way through barbarian tribes who would see us as just another lot of Romans. My men and I are against the idea of leaving Italy."

"If you and your men are against the idea of leaving Italy," said Spartacus angrily, "then don't leave Italy! What do I care? I've close to a hundred thousand men to look after, and that's far too many! So off you go, Crixus—the further, the better! Take your thirty thousand idiots, stay in Italy!''

So when Spartacus and seventy thousand soldiers—together with a vast baggage train and forty thousand women, not to mention babies and young children—turned north to cross the Tifernus River, Crixus and his thirty thousand followers turned south in the direction of Brundisium. It was the end of April.

At about the same moment, the consuls Gellius and Clodianus left Rome to pick up their troops from Capua, Quintus Arrius the ex-praetor having told the Senate that the four legions of new soldiers assembled in Capua were as good as they were ever going to be; he could not guarantee that they were battleworthy, but he hoped they were.

When the consuls reached Capua they were informed of the split between Spartacus and Crixus, and of the new direction into the north that Spartacus himself was taking. A plan was developed; Quintus Arrius would take one legion south to deal with Crixus at once, Gellius would take the second legion and shadow Spartacus from behind until Arrius could rejoin him, while Clodianus took the other two legions on a rapid march past Rome, then east on the Via Valeria to emerge on the Adriatic coast well to the north of Spartacus. The two consuls would then have Spartacus between them and could close the jaws of their pincer.

Some days later came splendid news from Quintus Arrius. Though out-numbered five to one, he had concealed himself in ambush on Mount Garganus in Apulia and fallen upon the undisciplined, jostling mass of men Crixus led into the trap. Crixus himself and all thirty thousand of his followers were killed, those who survived the ambush by execution afterward; Quintus Arrius had no intention of leaving live enemy in his wake.

Gellius was not so lucky. What Arrius had done to Crixus, Spartacus did to him. The troops of the single legion Gellius possessed scattered in wild panic the moment they saw a vast force descending upon them—a good thing, as it turned out, for those who stayed were slaughtered. And at least they fled without abandoning arms or armor, so that when the reunited Arrius and Gellius managed to round them up they still had their equipment and could (theoretically, anyway) fight again without needing to return to Capua.

The course Arrius and Gellius took after their defeat was of no moment to Spartacus; he marched immediately into the north to deal with Clodianus, of whose ploy he had been informed by a captured Roman tribune. At Hadria on the Adriatic coast the two armies met with much the same result for

Clodianus as for Gellius. The troops of Clodianus dispersed in panic. Victor on both fields, Spartacus continued his northward progress unopposed.

Nothing daunted, Gellius, Clodianus and Arrius collected their men and tried again at Firmum Picenum. Again they were defeated. Spartacus marched into the Ager Gallicus. He crossed the Rubico into Italian Gaul at the end of Sextilis and started up the Via Aemilia toward Placentia and the western Alps. Quintus Sertorius, here we come!

The valley of the Padus was lush, rich countryside which provided forage aplenty and towns with granaries full to overflowing. As he now systematically sacked towns likely to yield good plunder, Spartacus did not endear himself or his army to the citizens of Italian Gaul.

At Mutina, halfway to the Alps, the vast army encountered the governor of Italian Gaul, Gaius Cassius Longinus, who tried valiantly to block their progress with a single legion. Gallant though the action was, it could not but fail; Cassius's legate Gnaeus Manlius came up two days later with Italian Gaul's other legion and suffered the same fate as Cassius. On both occasions the Roman troops had stayed to fight, which meant that Spartacus collected over ten thousand sets of arms and armor on the field.

The last Roman to whom Spartacus had personally spoken—and if he spoke to none, then nor did anyone else in that vast and terrifying horde—had been the tribune captured during the first defeat of Gellius months before. Neither at Hadria nor at Firmum Picenum did he so much as see Gellius, Clodianus or Arrius at close quarters. But now at Mutina he had two high-ranking Roman prisoners, Gaius Cassius and Gnaeus Manlius, and he fancied the idea of speaking with them: time to let a couple of members of the Senate see the man of whom all Italy and Italian Gaul was talking! Time to let the Senate know who he was. For he had no intention of killing or detaining Cassius and Manlius; he wanted them to return to Rome and report in person.

He had, however, loaded his prisoners down with chains, and made sure that when they were brought into his presence he was seated on a podium and wearing a plain white toga. Cassius and Manlius stared, but it was when Spartacus addressed them in good, Campanian-accented Latin that they realized what he was.

"You're an Italian!" said Cassius.

"I'm a Roman," Spartacus corrected him.

No Cassius was easily cowed; the clan was warlike and very fierce, and if an occasional Cassius committed a military blunder, no Cassius had ever run away. So this Cassius proved himself a true member of his family by lifting one manacled arm and shaking his fist at the big, handsome fellow on the podium.

"Free me from the indignity of these bonds and you'll soon be a dead Roman!" he snarled. "A deserter from the legions, eh? Put in the ring as a Thracian!"

Spartacus flushed. "I'm no deserter," he said stiffly. "In me you see a military tribune who was unjustly convicted of mutiny in Illyricum. And you find your bonds an indignity? Well, how do you think I found my bonds when I was sent to the kind of school run by a worm like Batiatus? One set of chains deserves another, Cassius the proconsul!"

"Kill us and get it over and done with," said Cassius.

"Kill you? Oh, no, I have no intention of doing that," said Spartacus, smiling. "I'm going to set you free now that you've felt the *indignity* of bonds. You will go back to Rome and you will tell the Senate who I am, and where I'm going, and what I intend to do when I get there—and what I will be when I come back."

Manlius moved as if to answer; Cassius turned his head and glared; Manlius subsided.

"Who you are—a mutineer. Where you're going—to perdition. What you're going to do when you get there—rot. What you'll be when you come back—a mindless shade without substance or shadow," sneered Cassius. "I'd be glad to tell the Senate all of that!"

"Then tell the Senate this while you're about it!" snapped Spartacus, rising to his feet and ripping off the immaculate toga; he raked his feet on it with the relish of a dog raking its hind legs after defecation, then kicked it off the podium. "In my train I have eighty thousand men, all properly armed and trained to fight like Romans. Most of them are Samnites and Lucanians, but even the slaves who enlisted under me are brave men. I have thousands of talents in plunder. And I am on my way to join Quintus Sertorius in Nearer Spain. Together he and I will inflict total defeat upon Rome's armies and generals in both the Spains, and then Quintus Sertorius and I will march back to Italy. *Your* Rome doesn't stand a chance, proconsul! Before the next year has passed, Quintus Sertorius will be the Dictator of Rome, and I will be his Master of the Horse!"

Cassius and Manlius had listened to this with a series of expressions chasing each other across their faces—fury, awe, anger, bewilderment, amazement—and finally, when they were sure Spartacus had ended, *amusement*! Both men threw their heads back and roared with unfeigned laughter while Spartacus stood feeling a slowly rising tide of red suffuse his cheeks. What had he said that they found so funny? Did they laugh at his temerity? Did they think him mad?

"Oh, you fool!" said Cassius when he was able, the tears of hilarity running like a freshet. "You great bumpkin! You booby! Don't you have an intelligence network? Of course you don't! You're not a Roman commander's anus! What's the difference between this horde of yours and a horde of barbarians? Nothing, and that is the simple truth! I can't believe you don't know, but you really don't know!"

"Know what?" asked Spartacus, his color gone. There had been no room for rage at the derision in Cassius's voice, at the epithets he hurled; all that filled Spartacus's mind was fear.

"Sertorius is *dead*! Assassinated by his own senior legate Perperna last winter. There is no rebel army in Spain! Just the victorious legions of Metellus Pius and Pompeius Magnus, who will soon be marching back to Italy to put paid to you and your whole horde of barbarians!" And Cassius laughed again.

Spartacus didn't stay to hear, he fled from the room with his hands clapped against his ears and sought out Aluso.

Now the mother of Spartacus's son, Aluso could find nothing to say to console him; he covered his head in folds of his scarlet general's cape snatched from the couch, and wept, wept, wept.

"What can I do?" he asked her, rocking back and forth. "I have an army with no objective, a people with no home!"

Hair hanging in strings over her face, knees wide apart as she squatted with her blood-cup and her knucklebones and the grisly tattered hand of Batiatus, Aluso whipped the bones with the hand, stared and muttered.

"Rome's great enemy in the west is dead," she said at last, "but Rome's great enemy in the east still lives. The bones say we must march to join Mithridates."

Oh, why hadn't he thought of that for himself? Spartacus threw away the general's cape, looked at Aluso with wide, tear-blurred eyes. "Mithridates! Of course Mithridates! We will march across the eastern Alps into Illyricum, cross Thrace to the Euxine and join ourselves to Pontus." He wiped his nose with the back of his hand, snuffled, gazed at Aluso wildly. "In Thrace is your homeland, woman. Would you rather stay there?"

She snorted scornfully. "My place is with you, Spartacus. Whether they know it or not, the Bessi are a defeated people. No tribe in the world is strong enough to resist Rome forever, only a great king like Mithridates. No, husband, we will not stay in Thrace. We will join ourselves to King Mithridates."

One of the many problems about an army as huge as that one belonging to Spartacus was the sheer impossibility of direct communication with all its members. He gathered the vast crowd together as best he could and did his utmost to make sure that all his men and their women understood why they

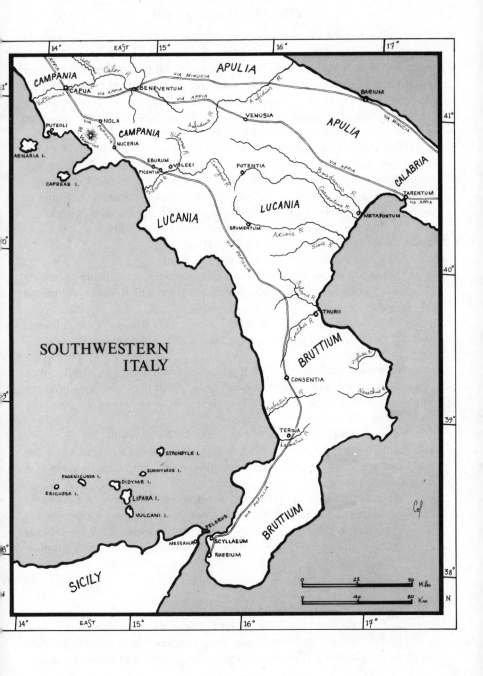

were going to turn in their tracks and march back down the Via Aemilia toward Bononia, where they would take the Via Annia northeast to Aquileia and Illyricum. Some did understand, but many did not, either because they hadn't heard Spartacus himself and so had received a garbled version of what he said, or because they owned all an Italian's fear and detestation of the eastern potentate. Quintus Sertorius was *Roman*. Mithridates was a savage who ate Italian babies and would enslave everyone.

The march resumed, this time eastward, but as Bononia came closer discontent among the soldiers and their camp followers grew. If Spain was an eternity away, what was Pontus? Many of the Samnites and Lucanians— and they were a majority in the army—spoke Oscan and Latin, but little or no Greek; how would they get on in a place like Pontus without Greek?

At Bononia a hundred-strong deputation of legates, tribunes, centurions and men from the ranks came to see Spartacus.

"We will not leave Italy" was what they said.

"Then I will not desert you," said Spartacus, swallowing a terrible disappointment. "Without me you will disintegrate. The Romans will kill all of you."

When the deputation left he turned as always to Aluso. "I am defeated, woman, but not by an external enemy, even Rome. They are too afraid. They do not understand."

Her bones were not lying happily. She scattered them angrily, then scooped them up and put them in their pouch. What they said she would not tell him; some things were better left in the minds and hearts of women, who were closer to the earth.

"Then we will go to Sicily," she said. "The slaves of that place will rise for us, as they have risen twice before. Perhaps the Romans will leave us to occupy Sicily in peace if we promise to sell them enough grain at a cheap enough price."

The uncertainty in her she could not disguise; sensing it, for one wild moment Spartacus toyed with the idea of deflecting his army south onto the Via Cassia and marching on the city of Rome. But then the reason in what Aluso suggested won out. She was right. She was always right. Sicily it must be.

 To become a pontifex was to enter the most exclusive enclave of political power in Rome; the augurship came a close second and there were some families whose augurships were as jealously guarded and prized as any family guarded and prized its pontificate, but always the pontificate came out that little bit ahead. So when Gaius Julius Caesar was inducted into the College of Pontifices he knew that he had moved more surely toward his ultimate goal, the consulship, and that this inauguration more than made up for his failure as the *flamen Dialis*. No one would ever be able to point the finger at him and imply that his status was in doubt, that perhaps he ought to be the *flamen Dialis* in fact; his position as a co-opted pontifex told everybody he was firmly ensconced at the very core of the Republic.

His mother, he learned, had befriended Mamercus and his wife Cornelia Sulla, and moved these days more freely among the high nobles her exile to an insula in the Subura had driven away; she was so enormously respected, so admired. The odium of her marriage to Gaius Marius had removed his Aunt Julia from the position she might otherwise have come to occupy with increasing age—that of the modern Cornelia the Mother of the Gracchi. And it now seemed as if his mother might inherit the title! These days she dined with women like Catulus's wife, Hortensia, and Hortensius's wife, Lutatia, with young matrons like Servilia—the widow of a Brutus and the wife of Decimus Junius Silanus (by whom she now had two little girls to add to Brutus's son)—and with several Licinias, Marcias, Cornelia Scipiones and Junias.

"It's wonderful, Mater, but why?" he asked, eyes twinkling.

Her beautiful eyes gleamed, the creases at the corners of her mouth compressed until little dimples popped up in her cheeks. "Why do you expect answers to rhetorical questions?" she asked. "You know as well as I do, Caesar. Your career is accelerating, and I am helping." She gave a slight cough. "Besides, most of these women seem to me to be utterly lacking in common sense. So they tend to come to me with their problems." She thought about that statement, amended it: "All, that is, except Servilia. Now *she* is a very structured woman! Knows exactly where she's going. You ought to meet her, Caesar."

He looked indescribably bored. "Thank you, Mater, but no. I am extremely grateful for every little bit of help you can give me, but that does not mean I'll join the sweet-watered-wine-and-little-cakes circle. The only women aside from you and Cinnilla who interest me are the wives of men I intend to cuckold. As I have no quarrel with Decimus Junius Silanus, I fail to see why I should cultivate his wife. The patrician Servilii are insufferable!"

"This one isn't insufferable," said Aurelia, but not in the tone of voice which suggested she had an end to pursue. Instead she changed the subject. "I haven't seen any evidence that you intend to settle back into city life."

"That's because I don't. I have just enough time to join Marcus Fonteius in Gaul-across-the-Alps for a quick campaign, so that's where I'm off to. I'll be back by next June—I'm going to stand for election as one of the tribunes of the soldiers."

"Sensible," she approved. "I'm told that you're a superlative soldier, so you'll do well in an *official* capacity."

He winced. "Unkind and unfair, Mater!"

Fonteius, who like most of the Transalpine governors had based himself in Massilia, was perfectly willing to keep Caesar busy for ten months. He had sustained a bad leg wound fighting the Vocontii, and chafed at the thought of watching all his work go for nothing because he could not ride. So when Caesar arrived Fonteius handed him the province's two legions and told him to finish the campaign up the Druentia River; Fonteius would occupy himself dealing with the supply lines to Spain. After the news of the death of Sertorius came, the governor breathed a sigh of relief and embarked in tandem with Caesar upon a sweeping campaign up the Rhodanus valley into the lands of the Allobroges.

Born soldiers both, Fonteius and Caesar got on famously together, and admitted freely to each other at the end of the second campaign that there was no joy quite like working with a man of eminent military sense. So when Caesar returned to Rome in his habitual headlong fashion, he rode in the knowledge that his record now stood at seven campaigns—only three to go! He had loved his time in Gaul, never having ventured west of the Alps before, and found it considerably easier dealing with the Gauls themselves because (thanks to his old tutor, Marcus Antonius Gnipho, to Cardixa and to some of his mother's tenants) he spoke several Gallic dialects fluently. Deeming no Roman conversant with their tongues, the Salluvian and Vocontian scouts tended to slip into Gallic whenever they wished to exchange information not for Roman ears; but Caesar understood very quickly, learned much he wasn't supposed to—and never gave himself away.

It was a good time to be standing for election as a tribune of the soldiers. The presence of Spartacus meant that his duty in the consuls' legions would be within Italy. But first he had to get himself elected—don the specially chalked, snow-white toga of the candidate and move among the electors in every marketplace and basilica in Rome, not to mention arcades and colonnades, guilds and colleges, the porticus and the portico. Since there were twenty-four tribunes of the soldiers elected annually by the Assembly of the People, it was not a particularly difficult feat to be voted in, but Caesar had set himself a much harder task than mere election: he was resolved to be the candidate who polled the highest number of votes in every election he would

contest as he climbed the *cursus honorum*. Thus he put himself through much
that the average candidate for that lowest of all magistracies deemed super-
fluous effort. Nor would he avail himself of the services of a privately employed *nomenclator,* that arch-recollector of people's names; Caesar would
be his own *nomenclator,* never forget a face or the name associated with it.
A man flattered by instant placing of his name with his face after some years
had elapsed since the last meeting was very prone to think highly of such a
brilliant, courteous, capable fellow—and vote for him. Curiously most candidates forgot the Subura, just looked blank and dismissed it as a low-life
infestation Rome would be better without; but Caesar, who had lived in the
Subura all his life, knew that it abounded with men of the lowest end of the
First Class and the upper end of the Second Class. Not one of whom was
unknown to him. Not one of whom would refuse to vote for him.

He was returned at the head of the poll, and like the twenty quaestors
elected at the same convocation of the Assembly of the People, he would
commence his duties on the fifth day of December rather than on New Year's
Day. The lots which would give him his legion placement (with five others,
he would be assigned to one of the consuls' four legions) would not be drawn
until he took office, nor could he make a nuisance of himself by visiting a
consular legion ahead of his time; even Capua was off-limits. Distressing,
considering the disastrous military events of that particular year!

By the end of Quinctilis it was glaringly obvious even to the most obtuse
senator that the consuls Gellius and Clodianus were incapable of halting
Spartacus. With Philippus leading the chorus (difficult for him, since Gellius
and Clodianus belonged to Pompey as much as he did himself), the Senate
tactfully told the consuls that they were being removed from command in the
war against Spartacus; they were needed in Rome to govern, and it was now
clear that the war should go to a man endowed with a full proconsular
imperium—a man who had personal access to retired veterans and the clout
to inspire them to return to the eagles. A man with a good war record, and
preferably of Sullan convictions. A man who not only belonged to the Senate,
but had been at the least a praetor.

Of course everyone inside the Senate and outside it knew that there was
only one candidate for the job, only one candidate sitting idle in Rome without
province abroad or war of some kind already on his hands, only one candidate
with the necessary veteran resources and war record: Marcus Licinius Crassus.
Urban praetor the year before, he had declined to take a governorship, pleading
as his excuse the fact that Rome needed him more at home than in some
foreign place. In anyone else such lethargy and lack of true political zeal
would have been instantly condemned; but Marcus Crassus was allowed his

foibles. Had to be allowed them! Most of the Senate was in debt to him for some trifling loan or another.

Not that he agitated for the job. That was not his style. Instead he sat back in his suite of offices behind the Macellum Cuppedenis and waited. A suite of offices sounded most imposing—until the curious man visited Crassus's establishment. No expensive pictures hung on its walls, no comfortable couches were positioned around, no spacious halls permitted clients to cluster and chat, no servants hovered to offer Falernian wine or rare cheeses. Such was known to happen: Titus Pomponius Atticus, for instance—that ex-partner of Crassus's who now so loathed him—conducted his multifarious businesses in exquisite premises. Crassus, however, did not even begin to understand the need a harried businessman's *animus* might have to surround itself with beautiful comfortable things. To Crassus wasted space was wasted money, money spent on pretty offices was wasted money. When he was in his suite of rooms he occupied a desk in one corner of a crowded hall, shoved about or sidled around by all the toiling accountants, scribes and secretaries who shared the same area; it may have been just a trifle inconvenient, but it meant his staff was permanently under his eye—and his eye missed nothing.

No, he didn't agitate for the job, and he had no need to buy himself a senatorial lobby. Let Pompeius Magnus waste his money on that sort of exercise! Not necessary when one was willing to lend a needy senator whatever amount of cash he wanted—and interest-free. Pompeius would never see his money back. Whereas Crassus could call in his loans at any time and not be out of purse.

In September the Senate finally acted. Marcus Licinius Crassus was asked if he would assume a full proconsular imperium, take unto himself eight legions, and command in the war against the Thracian gladiator Spartacus. It took him several days to reply, which he finally did in the House with all his customary brevity and deliberateness. To Caesar, watching appreciatively from his seat on the opposite side of the Curia Hostilia, it was a lesson in the power of presence and the powerful stench of money.

Crassus was quite tall but never looked it, so wide was he. Not that he was fat. Rather, he was built like an ox, with thick wrists and big hands, a mighty neck and shoulders. In a toga he was sheer bulk until one saw the muscles in the exposed right forearm, felt the solid oak of it in a handshake. His face was big and broad, expressionless but not unpleasantly so, and the light grey eyes had a habit of resting upon their objective with a mild kindness. Hair and brows were pale brown, not quite mouse-colored, and his skin went dark in the sun quickly.

He spoke now in his normal voice, which was surprisingly high (Apollonius of Molon would have said that was because his neck was short, reflected Caesar), and said, "Conscript Fathers, I am sensible of the honor you accord me in offering me this high command. I would *like* to accept, but . . ."

He paused, gaze ambling affably from one face to another. "I am a humble man, and I am very aware that whatever influence I have is due to a thousand men of the knightly order who cannot make their presence directly felt inside this House. I could not accept this high command without being sure that they consented to it. Therefore I humbly ask this House to present a *senatus consultum* to the Assembly of the People. If that body votes me my command, I will be happy to accept."

Clever Crassus! applauded Caesar.

If the Senate gave, the Senate could take away. As it had in the case of Gellius and Clodianus. But if the Assembly of the People was asked to ratify a decree handed down from the Senate—and did ratify it—then only the Assembly of the People could unmake it. Not impossible, by any means. But between the tribunes of the plebs drawn claw and fang by Sulla and the general apathy of the House in making decisions, a law passed in the Assembly of the People would put Crassus in a very strong position. Clever, clever Crassus!

No one was surprised when the House obediently handed down its *senatus consultum,* nor when the Assembly of the People voted overwhelmingly to ratify it. Marcus Licinius Crassus was more solidly commander in the war against Spartacus than Pompey in Nearer Spain; Pompey's imperium was bestowed by Senate alone, it was not a law on Rome's tablets.

With the same efficiency that had made a huge success out of an enterprise as dubious as training dirt-cheap slaves in expensive skills, Marcus Crassus went to work at once upon this new challenge.

The first thing he did was to announce the names of his legates: Lucius Quinctius, that fifty-two-year-old nuisance to consuls and law courts; Marcus Mummius, almost of praetor's age; Quintus Marcius Rufus, somewhat younger but in the Senate; Gaius Pomptinus, a young Military Man; and Quintus Arrius, the only veteran of the war against Spartacus whom Crassus cared to keep.

He then declared that as the consuls' legions were reduced from four to two by casualties and desertions, he would use only the top twelve of the twenty-four tribunes of the soldiers, but not the present year's tribunes of the soldiers; their term was almost expired, and he thought nothing would be worse for these unsatisfactory legions than to change their immediate commanders scarcely a month into the campaign. Therefore he would call up next year's tribunes of the soldiers early. He also asked for one of next year's quaestors by name—Gnaeus Tremellius Scrofa, of an old praetorian family.

In the meantime he removed himself to Capua and sent out agents among his veteran soldiers from the days when he fought Carbo and the Samnites. He needed to enlist six legions very quickly. Some of his critics remembered that his soldiers hadn't liked his reluctance to share the spoils of towns like Tuder, and predicted that he would get few volunteers. But whether it was memories or hearts the years had softened, his veterans flocked to Crassus's eagles. By the beginning of November, when word had come that the Spartacani had turned around and were heading back down the Via Aemilia again, Crassus was almost ready to move.

First, however, it was time to deal with the remnants of the consuls' legions, who had never been shifted from the camp at Firmum Picenum after the combined defeat of Gellius and Clodianus. They comprised twenty cohorts (which were the number of cohorts in two legions) but were the survivors of four legions, so few of them had fought together as a legionary unit. It had not been possible to transfer them to Capua until Crassus's own six legions were formed and organized; so few legions had been raised during the past years that half of the camps around Capua had been closed and dismantled.

When Crassus sent Marcus Mummius and the twelve tribunes of the soldiers to pick up these twenty cohorts from Firmum Picenum, he was aware that Spartacus and his Spartacani were drawing close to Ariminum. Mummius was issued strict orders. He was to avoid any sort of contact with Spartacus, thought to be still well to the north of Firmum Picenum. Unfortunately for Mummius, Spartacus had moved his troops independently of his camp followers and his baggage train once he reached Ariminum, knowing that a threat to his rear was nonexistent. Thus it was that at about the same moment as Mummius arrived at the camp built by Gellius and Clodianus, so did the leading echelons of the Spartacani.

A clash was inevitable. Mummius did his best, but there was little either he or his tribunes of the soldiers (Caesar was among them) could do. None of them knew the troops, the troops had never been properly trained, and they feared Spartacus the way children feared nursery bogeys. To call what ensued a battle was impossible; the Spartacani just rolled through the camp as if it didn't exist, while the panicked soldiers of the consuls' legions scattered in all directions. They threw down their weapons and pulled off their shirts of mail and helmets, anything which would slow their flight; the tardy perished, the fleet of foot got away. Not bothering to pursue, the Spartacani streamed onward, merely pausing to pick up abandoned arms and armor and strip the corpses of those who had not escaped.

"There was nothing you could have done to avert this," said Caesar to Mummius. "The fault lay in our intelligence."

"Marcus Crassus will be furious!" cried Mummius, despairing.

"I'd call that an understatement," said Caesar grimly. "But the Spartacani are an undisciplined lot, all the same."

"Over a hundred thousand!"

They were camped atop a hill not far from the vast collection of people still rolling southward; Caesar, whose eyes saw into far distances, pointed.

"Of soldiers he has not more than eighty thousand, maybe less. What we're looking at now are camp followers—women, children, even men who don't seem to be bearing arms. And there are at least fifty thousand of them. Spartacus has a millstone around his neck. He has to drag the families and personal effects of his soldiers with him. You're looking at a homeless people, not an army, Mummius."

Mummius turned away. "Well, there's no reason to linger here. Marcus Crassus has to be informed what happened. The sooner, the better."

"The Spartacani will be gone in a day or two. Might I suggest that we remain here until they are gone, then gather up the men of the consuls' legions? If they're let, they'll disappear forever. I think Marcus Crassus would be better pleased to see them, whatever their state of disarray," said Caesar.

Arrested, Mummius looked at his senior tribune of the soldiers. "You're a thinking sort of fellow, Caesar, aren't you? You're quite right. We should round the wretches up and bring them back with us. Otherwise our general's fury will know no bounds."

Five cohorts lay dead among the ruins of the camp, as did most of the centurions. Fifteen cohorts had survived. It took Mummius eleven days to track them down and muster them, not as difficult a task as Mummius for one had feared; their wits were more scattered than their persons.

Clad only in tunics and sandals, the fifteen cohorts were marched to Crassus, now in camp outside Bovianum. He had caught a detachment of Spartacani which had wandered off to the west of the main body and killed six thousand, but Spartacus himself was now well on his way toward Venusia, and Crassus had not deemed it clever to follow him into country unfavorable to a much smaller force. It was now the beginning of December, but as the calendar was forty days ahead of the seasons, winter was yet to come.

The general listened to Mummius in an ominous silence. Then: "I do not hold you to blame, Marcus Mummius,'' he said, ''but what am I to do with fifteen cohorts of men who cannot be trusted and have no stomach for a fight?''

No one answered. Crassus knew exactly what he was going to do, despite his question. Every man present understood that, but no man present other than Crassus knew what he was going to do.

Slowly the mild eyes traveled from one face to another, lingered upon Caesar's, moved on.

''How many are they by head?'' he asked.

''Seven thousand five hundred, Marcus Crassus. Five hundred soldiers to the cohort,'' said Mummius.

''I will decimate them,'' said Crassus.

A profound silence fell; no one moved a muscle.

''Parade the whole army tomorrow at sunrise and have everything ready. Caesar, you are a pontifex, you will officiate. Choose your victim for the sacrifice. Ought it to be to Jupiter Optimus Maximus, or to some other god?''

''I think we should offer to Jupiter Stator, Marcus Crassus. He is the stayer of fleeing soldiers. And to Sol Indiges. And Bellona. The victim ought to be a black bull calf.''

''Mummius, your tribunes of the soldiers will see to the lots. Except for Caesar.''

After which the general dismissed his staff, who moved out of the command tent without finding a single word to say to each other. *Decimation!*

At sunrise Crassus's six legions were assembled side by side in their ranks; facing them, paraded in ten rows each of seven hundred and fifty men, stood the soldiers who were to be decimated. Mummius had worked feverishly to devise the quickest and simplest method of procedure, as the most important numerical division for decimation was the decury of ten men; it went without saying that Crassus himself had been an enormous help with the logistics.

They stood as Mummius and his tribunes of the soldiers had rounded them up, clad only in tunics and sandals, but each man held a cudgel in his right hand and had been numbered off from one to ten for the lots. Branded cowards, they looked cowards, for not one among them could stand without visibly shaking, every face was a study in terror, and the sweat rolled off them despite the early morning chill.

''Poor things,'' said Caesar to his fellow tribune of the soldiers, Gaius Popillius. ''I don't know which appalls them more—the thought of being the one to die, or the thought of being one of the nine who must kill him. They're not warlike.''

''They're too young,'' said Popillius, a little sadly.

"That's usually an advantage," said Caesar, who wore his pontifical toga today, a rich and striking garment composed entirely of broad scarlet and purple stripes. "What does one know at seventeen or eighteen? There are no wives and children at home to worry about. Youth is turbulent, in need of an outlet for violent impulses. Better battle than wine and women and tavern brawls—in battle, the State at least gets something out of them that's useful to the State."

"You're a hard man," said Popillius.

"No. Just a practical one."

Crassus was ready to begin. Caesar moved to where the ritual trappings were laid out, drawing a fold of toga over his head. Every legion carried its own priest and augur, and it was one of the military augurs who inspected the black bull calf's liver. But because decimation was confined to the imperium of a proconsular general, it required a higher religious authority than legionary Religious, which was why Caesar had been deputed, and why Caesar had to verify the augur's findings. Having announced in a loud voice that Jupiter Stator, Sol Indiges and Bellona were willing to accept the sacrifice, he then said the concluding prayers. And nodded to Crassus that he could begin.

Assured of divine approval, Crassus spoke. A tall tribunal had been erected to one side of the guilty cohorts, on which stood Crassus and his legates. The only tribune of the soldiers who was a part of this group was Caesar, the officiating priest; the rest of them were clustered around a table in the middle of the space between the veteran legions and the cohorts to be decimated, for it was their duty to apportion the lots.

"Legates, tribunes, cadets, centurions and men of the ranks," cried Crassus in his high, carrying voice, "you are gathered here today to witness a punishment so rare and so severe that it is many generations since it was last exacted. Decimation is reserved for soldiers who have proven themselves unworthy to be members of Rome's legions, who have deserted their eagles in the most craven and unpardonable fashion. I have ordered that the fifteen cohorts standing here in their tunics shall be decimated for very good reason: since they were inducted into military service at the beginning of this year they have consistently fled from the scene of every battle they were asked to fight. And now in their last debacle they have committed the ultimate soldier's crime—they abandoned their weapons and armor on the field for the enemy to pick up and use. None of them deserves to live, but it is not within my power to execute every single man. That is the prerogative of the Senate, and the Senate alone. So I will exercise my right as the proconsular commander-in-chief to decimate their ranks, hoping that by doing so, I will inspire those men left alive to fight in future like Roman soldiers—and to show the rest of you, my loyal and constant followers, that I *will not* tolerate cowardice! And may all our gods bear witness that I will have avenged the good name and honor of every Roman soldier!''

As Crassus reached his peroration, Caesar tensed. If the men of the six legions assembled to watch cheered, then Crassus had the army's consent; but if his speech was greeted by silence, he was going to be in for a mutinous campaign. No one ever liked decimation. That was why no general practiced it. Was Crassus, so shrewd in business and politics, as shrewd in his judgement of Rome's veteran soldiers?

The six legions cheered wholeheartedly. Watching him closely, Caesar saw a tiny sagging of relief in Crassus; so even he had not been sure!

The dispersal of the lots began. There were seven hundred and fifty decuries, which meant that seven hundred and fifty men would die. A very long drawn-out procedure which Crassus and Mummius had speeded up with some excellent organization. In a huge basket lay seven hundred and fifty tablets—seventy-five of them were numbered I, seventy-five were numbered II, and so on, up to the number X. They had been thrown in at random, then shuffled well. The tribune of the soldiers Gaius Popillius had been deputed to count seventy-five of these jumbled little two-inch squares of thin wood into each of ten smaller baskets, one of which he gave to each of the ten remaining tribunes of the soldiers to disperse.

That was why the guilty cohorts had been arranged in ten well-spaced rows, seventy-five well-spaced decuries to the row. A tribune of the soldiers simply walked from one end of his row to the other, stopping before each decury and pulling a tablet from his basket. He called out the number, the man allocated it stepped forward, and he then passed on to the next decury.

Behind him the slaughter began. Even in this was order, meticulousness. Centurions from Crassus's own six legions who did not know any of the men in the guilty cohorts had been ordered to supervise the actual executions. Few of the centurions who had belonged to the fifteen cohorts had lived, but those who did live had not been excused the punishment, so they took their chances with the rankers. Death was meted out to the man who had drawn the lot by the other nine men of his decury, who were required to beat him to death with their cudgels. In that way no one escaped suffering, be they the nine who lived or the one who died.

The supervising centurions knew how it should be done, and said so. ''You, kneel and don't flinch,'' to the condemned man. ''You, strike his head to kill,'' to the man farthest left. ''You, strike to kill,'' to the next man, and so along the nine, who were all forced to bring down their knob-headed sticks upon the back of the kneeling man's defenseless cranium. That was as kind as the punishment could be, and at least stripped it of any element of the mindless mob beating wildly at all parts of the victim's body. Because none of these men had the heart to kill, not every blow was a killing one, and some blows missed entirely. But the supervising centurions kept on barking, barking, barking to strike hard and strike accurately, and as the process proceeded down the line of decuries it became more workmanlike, quicker. Such is repetition combined with resignation to the inevitable.

In thirteen hours the decimation was done, the last of it in darkness lit by torches. Crassus dismissed his footsore and bored army, obliged to stand until the last man was dead. The seven hundred and fifty corpses were distributed across thirty pyres and burned; instead of being sent home to the relatives, the ashes were tipped into the camp latrine trenches. Nor would their wills be honored. What money and property they left was forfeit to the Treasury, to help pay for all those abandoned weapons, helmets, shields, shirts of mail and legionary gear.

Not one man who had witnessed the first decimation in long years was left untouched by it; on most its effect was profound. Now fourteen somewhat under-strength cohorts, the wretched men who had lived through it swallowed both fear and pride to work frantically at becoming the kind of legionaries Crassus demanded. Seven more cohorts of properly trained recruits came from Capua before the army moved on and were incorporated into the fourteen to make two full-strength legions. As Crassus still referred to them as the consuls' legions, the twelve tribunes of the soldiers were appointed to command them, with Caesar, the senior, at the head of Legio I.

While Marcus Crassus decimated the ranks of those who could not screw up the courage to face the Spartacani, Spartacus himself was holding funeral games for Crixus outside the city of Venusia. It was not his custom to take prisoners, but he had plucked three hundred men of the consuls' legions (and some others he intended to keep alive for the moment) from their camp at Firmum Picenum; all the way to Venusia he trained them as gladiators, half as Gauls, half as Thracians. Then dressing them in the finest equipment, he made them fight to the death in honor of Crixus. The ultimate victor he dispatched in an equally Roman way—he had the man first flogged and then beheaded. Having drunk the blood of three hundred enemy men, the shade of Crixus was eminently satisfied.

The funeral games of Crixus had served another purpose; as his enormous host feasted and relaxed, Spartacus went among them in a more personal way than he had outside Mutina, and persuaded everyone that the answer to the vexed question of a permanent and fruitful home lay in Sicily. Though he had stripped every granary and silo bare along the route of his march, and laid in great stores of cheeses, pulses, root vegetables and durable fruits, and drove with him thousands of sheep, pigs, hens and ducks, keeping his people from starving haunted him far more than the specter of any Roman army. Winter was coming; they must, he resolved, be established in Sicily before the very cold weather descended.

So in December he moved south again to the Gulf of Tarentum, where the hapless communities of that rich plain of many rivers suffered the loss of autumn harvest and early winter vegetables. At Thurii—a city he had already sacked on his first visit to the area—he turned his host inland, marched up the valley of the Crathis and emerged onto the Via Popillia. No Roman troops lay in wait; using the road to cross the Bruttian mountains comfortably, he came down to the small fishing port of Scyllaeum.

And there across the narrow strait it loomed—Sicily! One tiny sea voyage and the long travels were over. But what a hideous voyage it was! Scylla and Charybdis inhabited those perilous waters. Just outside the Bay of Scyllaeum, Scylla lashed and gnashed her triple sets of teeth in each of her six heads, while the dogs' heads girdling her loins slavered and howled. And if a ship was lucky enough to sneak by her as she slept, yet there remained Sicilian Charybdis, roaring round and round and round in a huge, sucking whirlpool of greed.

Not, of course, that Spartacus himself believed in such tall tales; but without his realizing it he was losing whole layers of his Romanness, peeling them away like onion scales down to a kernel more primitive, more childlike. His life had not been lived in a truly Roman fashion since he had been expelled from the legions of Cosconius, and that was almost five years ago. The woman he had taken up with believed implicitly in Scylla and Charybdis, so did many of his followers, and sometimes—just *sometimes!*—he saw the frightful creatures in his dreams.

As well as harboring a big fishing fleet which pursued the migrating tunny twice a year, Scyllaeum accommodated pirates. The proximity of the Via Popillia and Roman legions passing to and from Sicily prohibited to any large pirate fleets a haven there, but the few small-scale freebooters who used Scyllaeum were in the act of beaching their trim, undecked little vessels for the winter when that huge tumult of people descended upon the place.

Leaving his army to gorge itself on fish, Spartacus sought out the leader of the local pirates at once and asked him if he knew any pirate admirals who had command of big numbers of big ships. Why yes, several! was the answer.

"Then bring them to see me," said Spartacus. "I need an immediate

THE WANDERINGS OF
SPARTACUS

73-71 B.C.

WITH LOCATION OF THE MAIN
BATTLEFIELDS X
(NAMED FOR THE DEFEATED)

———— PERTINENT ROADS NOT TRAVELED
BY SPARTACUS

.... THE INITIAL FORAY — 73 B.C.
CAPUA-VESUVIUS-FICENTIA-WILDS
OF LUCANIA

- - - - THE TREK TO SERTORIUS — 72 B.C.
LUCANIAN MOUNTAINS — NOLA —
CONSENTIA-THURII — METAPONTUM-
SAMNIUM — ADRIATIC COAST — VIA
AEMILIA — MUTINA

⟶⟶⟶ THE TREK TO SICILY — 72 B.C.
MUTINA — BONONIA (DO I MARCH ON ROME?)
ADRIATIC COAST — VENUSIA — THURII —
VIA POPILLIA — SCYLLAEUM

———— THE FLIGHT FROM CRASSUS — 71 B.C.
SCYLLAEUM — VIA POPILLIA —
SILARUS RIVER — EBURUM (CASTUS &
BANNICUS) — FINAL DEFEAT NEAR
POTENTIA — SPARTACUS DISAPPEARS

Miles
0   50   100

Kilometres
0   100   200

To Thrace, Anatolia &
Mithridates ⟶

To Spain & Sertorius ⟵

AQUILEIA

Via Postumia

Padus River

Via Aemilia

PLACENTIA

MUTINA
Defeat of
Cassius & Manlius X

BONONIA

Via Annia

Rubico R.

Via Aemilia

Arnus R.

Via Cassia

Via Cassia

Defeat of the
Two Consuls X

FIRMUM PICENUM

Tiber R.

Defeat of
Clodianus X

HADRIA

Via Valeria

ROMA

BUCA

Via Appia

Defeat of
Gellius X

Defeat of
Crixus X

CAPUA

Defeat of
Spartacus

VENUSIA

Defeat of
Castus &
Gannicus

Via Popillia

METAPONTUM

THURII

CONSENTIA

Via Popillia

PELORUS

Via Popillia

MESSANA

SCYLLAEUM

SICILY

SYRACUSE

Col

passage to Sicily for some thousands of my best soldiers, and I'm willing to pay a thousand talents of silver to any men who guarantee to ship us over within the month."

Though Crixus and Oenomaus were dead, two replacements had risen to the surface of the polyglot collection of men Spartacus used as his legates and tribunes. Castus and Gannicus were both Samnites who had fought with Mutilus during the Italian War and Pontius Telesinus during the war against Sulla; they were martial by nature and had some experience of command. Time had taught Spartacus that his host refused to march as an army unless the enemy threatened—many men had women, quite a few children, some even parents in the train. It was therefore impossible for one man to control or direct such wayward masses; instead, Spartacus had split the host into three divisions with three separate baggage columns, commanding the largest and foremost himself, and giving the other two to Castus and Gannicus.

When word came that two pirate admirals were coming to see him, Spartacus summoned Aluso, Castus and Gannicus.

"It looks as if I'll have ships enough to transport twenty thousand men across to Pelorus very soon," he said, "but it's the vast bulk of my people I'm going to have to leave behind who concern me. Some months might go by before I can bring them to Sicily. What do you think about leaving them here in Scyllaeum? Is there food enough? Or ought I to send everyone left behind back to Bradanus country? The local farmers and fishermen are saying it's going to be a cold winter."

Castus, who was older and more seasoned than Gannicus, gave this some deliberate thought before answering.

"Actually, Spartacus, it's not bad pickings hereabouts. West of the harbor is a little sort of promontory, flat and fertile. I reckon the whole lot of us could last there without digging too deep into the supplies for—oh, a month, maybe two months. And if twenty thousand of the biggest eaters are in Sicily, three months."

Spartacus made up his mind. "Then everyone will stay here. Move the camps to the west of the town and start the women and children growing things. Even cabbages and turnips will help."

When the two Samnites had gone, Aluso turned her wild wolf's eyes upon her husband and growled in the back of her throat. It always made his hackles rise, that eerie animalistic way she had whenever the prophetic spirit invaded her.

"Beware, Spartacus!" she said.

"What is there to beware of?" he asked, frowning.

She shook her head and growled again. "I do not know. Something. Someone. It is coming through the snow."

"It won't snow for at least a month, perhaps longer," he said gently. "By then I'll be in Sicily with the pick of my men, and I doubt the campaign in Sicily will extend us. Is it those who will wait here ought to beware?"

"No," she said positively, "it is you."

"Sicily is soft and not well defended. I won't stand in any danger from militiamen and grain barons."

She stiffened, then shivered. "You will never get there, Spartacus," she said. "You will never get to Sicily."

But the morrow gave the lie to that, for two pirate admirals arrived in Scyllaeum, and both were so famous he even knew their names: Pharnaces and Megadates. They had commenced their pirate careers far to the east of Sicily, in the waters of the Euxine Sea. For the last ten years, however, they had controlled the seas between Sicily and Africa, raiding anything smaller than a well-guarded Roman grain fleet. When they felt like it they even sailed into the harbor of Syracuse—right under the nose of the governor!—to pick up provisions and vintage wine.

Both of them, thought the astonished Spartacus, looked like sleekly successful merchants—pallid, plump, finicky.

"You know who I am," he said bluntly. "Will you do business with me despite the Romans?"

They exchanged sly smiles.

"We do business everywhere and with everyone despite the Romans," said Pharnaces.

"I need passage for twenty thousand of my soldiers between here and Pelorus."

"A very short journey, but one winter makes hazardous," said Pharnaces, evidently the spokesman.

"The local fishermen tell me it's quite possible."

"Indeed, indeed."

"Then will you help me?"

"Let me see. . . . Twenty thousand men at two hundred and fifty per ship—it's only a matter of miles, they won't care if they're packed in like figs in a jar—is eighty ships." Pharnaces grimaced slightly. "That many of large enough size we do not have, Spartacus. Twenty ships between us."

"Five thousand at a time," said Spartacus, brow wrinkled. "Well, it will have to be four trips, that's all! How much, and when can you start?"

Like twin lizards, they blinked in perfect unison.

"My dear fellow, don't you haggle?" asked Megadates.

"I don't have time. How much, and when can you start?"

Pharnaces took over again. "Fifty silver talents per ship per voyage—four thousand in all," he said.

It was Spartacus's turn to blink. "Four thousand! That's just about all the money I've got."

"Take it or leave it," said the admirals in perfect unison.

"If you guarantee to have your ships here within five days I'll take it," said Spartacus.

"Give us the four thousand in advance and we guarantee it," said Pharnaces.

Spartacus looked cunning. "Oh no you don't!" he exclaimed. "Half now, the other half when the job's finished."

"Done!" said Pharnaces and Megadates in perfect unison.

Aluso had not been allowed to attend the meeting. For reasons he wasn't sure of, Spartacus found himself reluctant to tell her what had transpired; perhaps what she saw for him was a watery grave, if he was never to reach Sicily. But of course she got it out of him, and to his surprise nodded happily.

"A good price," she said. "You'll recoup your money when you reach Sicily."

"I thought you said I wasn't going to reach Sicily!"

"That was yesterday, and the vision lied. Today I see with clarity, and all is well."

So two thousand talents of silver were dug out of the carts and loaded aboard the beautiful gilded quinquereme with the purple and gold sail that had brought Pharnaces and Megadates to Scyllaeum. Its mighty oars beating the water, it crawled out of the bay.

"Like a centipede," said Aluso.

Spartacus laughed. "You're right, a centipede! Perhaps that's why it doesn't fear Scylla."

"It's too big for Scylla to chew."

"Scylla is a clump of wicked rocks," said Spartacus.

"Scylla," said Aluso, "is an entity."

"In five days' time I will know for sure."

Five days later the first five thousand men were assembled in Scyllaeum port itself, each man with his gear beside him, his armor on his back, his helmet on his head, his weapons at his side, and a ghastly fear in his chest. He was to sail between Scylla and Charybdis! Only the fact that most of the men had talked to the fishermen gave them the courage to go through with it; the fishermen swore Scylla and Charybdis existed, but knew the charms to soothe them to sleep and promised to use them.

Though the weather had been good for all five days and the sea calm, the twenty pirate ships didn't come. Brow knotted, Spartacus conferred with Castus and Gannicus and decided to keep his five thousand men where they were overnight. Six days, seven days, eight days. Still the pirate ships didn't come. Ten days, fifteen days. The five thousand men had long since been sent back to their camps, but every day Spartacus was to be seen standing on the high point at the harbor entrance, hand shading his eyes, peering into the south. They would come! *Must* come!

"You have been swindled," said Aluso on the sixteenth day, when Spartacus showed no sign of going to his lookout.

The tears welled up, he swallowed convulsively. "I have been swindled," he said.

"Oh, Spartacus, the world is full of cheats and liars!" she cried. "At least what we have done has been done in good faith, and you are a father to these poor people! I see a home for us there across the water, I see it so clearly I can almost touch it! And yet we will never reach it. The first time I read the bones I saw that, but later the bones too lied to me. Cheats and liars, cheats and liars!" Her eyes glowed, she growled. "But beware of him who comes out of the snow!"

Spartacus didn't hear. He was weeping too bitterly.

"I am a laughingstock," said Spartacus to Castus and Gannicus later in the day. "They sailed off with our money knowing they wouldn't come back. Two thousand talents for a few moments' work."

"It wasn't your fault," said Gannicus, usually the silent one. "Even in business there's supposed to be honor."

Castus shrugged. "They're not businessmen, Gannicus. All they do is take. A pirate is an undisguised thief."

"Well," said Spartacus, sighing, "it's done. What matters now is our own future. We must continue to exist in Italy until the summer, when we will commandeer every fishing boat between Campania and Rhegium and take ourselves across to Sicily."

The existence of a new Roman army in the peninsula was known, of course, but Spartacus had wandered the land with virtual impunity for so long now that he took little notice of Roman military efforts. His scouts had grown lazy, and he himself not so much lazy as indifferent. Over the time that he had shepherded his vast flock, he had come to see his purpose in an unmartial light. He was the patriarch in search of a home for his children, neither king nor general. And now he would have to start them moving again. But where to? They ate so much!

When Crassus began his own march into the south, he went at the head of a military organization dedicated to one end—the extirpation of the Spartacani. Nor for the moment was he in any hurry. He knew exactly whereabouts his quarry was, and had guessed that its objective was Sicily. Which made no difference to Crassus. If he had to fight the Spartacani in Sicily, all the better. He had been in touch with the governor (still Gaius Verres) and been assured that the slaves of Sicily were in no condition to foment a third uprising against Rome even if the Spartacani came. Verres had put the militia on alert and stationed them around Pelorus, conserving his Roman troops for whatever shape a campaign might assume, and sure that Crassus would arrive hard on the heels of the Spartacani to take the brunt of the action.

But nothing happened. The whole enormous mass of Spartacani continued to camp around Scyllaeum, it seemed because no shipping was available. Then Gaius Verres wrote.

I have heard a curious tale, Marcus Crassus. It seems that Spartacus approached the pirate admirals Pharnaces and Megadates and asked them to ferry twenty thousand of his best troops from Scyllaeum to Pelorus. The pirates agreed to do this for a price of four thousand talents—two thousand to be paid as a deposit, the other two thousand upon completion of the job.

Spartacus gave them two thousand talents and off they sailed. Laughing their heads off! For no more than a promise they had enriched themselves mightily. While some may say that they were fools for not proceeding with the scheme and thereby earning themselves another two thousand talents, it appears Pharnaces and Megadates preferred the fortune they had got for doing no work at all. They had formed a poor opinion of Spartacus himself, and foresaw a risk in trying to earn the other two thousand.

My own personal opinion is that Spartacus is a rank amateur, a hayseed. Pharnaces and Megadates gulled him as easily as a Roman trickster can gull an Apulian. Had there been a decent army in Italy last year it would have rolled him up, I am sure of it. All he has on his side are sheer numbers. But when he faces you, Marcus Crassus, he will not prosper. Spartacus has no luck, whereas you, dear Marcus Crassus, have proven yourself one of Fortune's favorites.

When he read that final sentence, Caesar burst out laughing. "What does he want?" he asked, handing the note back to Crassus. "Is he in need of a loan? Ye gods, that man eats money!"

"I wouldn't lend to him," said Crassus. "Verres won't last."

"I hope you're right! How does he know so much about what happened between the pirate *strategoi* and Spartacus?"

Crassus grinned; it worked a small miracle upon his big smooth face, which suddenly looked young and naughty. "Oh, I daresay they told him all about it when he applied for his cut of the two thousand talents."

"Do you think they gave him a cut?"

"Undoubtedly. He lets them use Sicily as their base."

They were sitting alone in the general's command tent, in a stout camp pitched beside the Via Popillia outside Terina, a hundred miles from Scyllaeum. It was the beginning of February, and winter had begun; two braziers produced a glow of heat.

Just why Marcus Crassus had settled upon the twenty-eight-year-old Caesar as his particular friend was a source of great debate among his legates, who were more puzzled than jealous. Until Crassus had begun to share his leisure moments with Caesar he had owned no friends at all, therefore no legate felt himself passed over or supplanted. The conundrum arose out of the incongruity of the relationship, for there were sixteen years between them in age, their attitudes to money lay at opposite poles, they looked inappropriate when seen together, and no mutual literary or artistic leaning existed. Men like Lucius Quinctius had known Crassus for years, and had had close dealings with him both political and commercial without ever being able to claim a deep-seated friendship. Yet from the time Crassus had co-opted this year's tribunes of the soldiers two months too early, he had sought Caesar out, made overtures and found them reciprocated.

The truth was actually very simple. Each man had recognized in the other someone who was going to matter in the future, and each man nursed much the same political ambitions. Had this recognition not taken place, the friendship could not have come about. But once it existed other factors came into play to bind them more tightly. The streak of hardness which was so evident in Crassus also lay in the smoother, utterly charming Caesar; neither man cherished illusions about his noble world; both had burrowed deeply into mines of common sense and neither cared very much about personal luxuries.

The differences between them were superficial, though they were blinding: Caesar the handsome rake developing a formidable reputation as a womanizer versus Crassus the absolutely faithful family man; Caesar the brilliant intellectual with style and flair versus Crassus the plodding pragmatist. An odd couple. That was the verdict among the fascinated observers, who all from that time on began to see Caesar as a force to be reckoned with; for if he was not, why would Marcus Crassus have bothered with him?

"It will snow tonight," said Crassus. "In the morning we'll march. I want to use the snow, not become hampered by it."

"It would make so much sense," said Caesar, "if our calendar and the seasons coincided! I can't abide inaccuracy!"

Crassus stared. "What provoked that remark?"

"The fact that it's February and we're only beginning to feel winter."

"You sound like a Greek. Provided one knows the date and waggles a hand outside the door to feel the temperature, what can it matter?"

"It matters because it's slipshod and untidy!" said Caesar.

"If the world was too tidy it would be hard to make money."

"Harder to hide it, you mean," said Caesar with a grin.

When Scyllaeum drew near the scouts reported that Spartacus still camped within the little promontory beyond the port, though there were signs that he might move fairly soon. His Spartacani had eaten the region out.

Crassus and Caesar rode ahead with the army's engineers and an escort of troopers, aware that Spartacus owned no cavalry; he had tried to train some of his foot soldiers to ride, and for a while had attempted to tame the wild horses roaming the Lucanian forests and mountains, but had had no success with either men or mounts.

The snow was falling steadily in a windless afternoon when the two Roman noblemen and their company began to prowl the country just behind the triangular outthrust wherein lay the Spartacani; if any watch had been set it was a halfhearted one, for they encountered no other men. The snow of course was a help, it muffled noise and coated horses and riders in white.

"Better than I hoped," said Crassus with much satisfaction as the party turned to ride back to camp. "If we build a ditch and a wall between those two ravines, we'll shut Spartacus up in his present territory very nicely."

"It won't hold them for long," said Caesar.

"Long enough for my purposes. I want them hungry, I want them cold, I want them desperate. And when they break out, I want them heading north into Lucania."

"You'll accomplish the last, at any rate. They'll try at our weakest point, which won't be to the south. No doubt you'll want the consuls' legions doing most of the digging."

Crassus looked surprised. "They can dig, but alongside everybody else. Ditch and wall have to be finished within one market interval, and that means the hoariest old veterans will be plying spades too. Besides, the exercise will keep them warm."

"I'll engineer it for you," Caesar offered, but without expectation of assent.

Sure enough, Crassus declined. "I would rather you did, but it isn't possible. Lucius Quinctius is my senior legate. The job has to go to him."

"A pity. He's got too much office and oratory in him."

Office and oratory or no, Lucius Quinctius tackled the job of walling the Spartacani in with huge enthusiasm. Luckily he had the good sense to lean on the expertise of his engineers; Caesar was right in thinking him no fortification architect.

Fifteen feet wide and fifteen feet deep, the ditch dived into the ravines at either end, and the earth removed from it was piled up into a log-reinforced wall topped with a palisade and watchtowers. From ravine to ravine, the ditch, wall, palisade and watchtowers extended for a distance of eight miles, and were completed in eight days despite constant snow. Eight camps—one for each legion—were spaced at regular intervals beneath the wall; the general would have ample soldiers to man his eight miles of fortifications.

Spartacus became aware that Crassus had arrived the moment activity began—if he had not been aware earlier—but seemed almost uninterested. All of a sudden he bent the energies of his men toward constructing a huge fleet of rafts which apparently he intended should be towed behind Scyllaeum's fishing boats. To the watching Romans it appeared that he pinned his faith on an escape across the strait, and thought the scheme foolproof enough to ignore the fact that his landward escape route was rapidly being cut off. Came the day when this mass exodus by water began; those Romans not obliged by duty to be elsewhere climbed the flank of nearby Mount Sila for the best view of what happened in Scyllaeum harbor. A disaster. Those rafts which remained afloat long enough to load with people could not negotiate the entrance, let alone the open strait beyond; the fishing boats were not built to tow such heavy, unwieldy objects.

"At least it doesn't seem as if many of them drowned," said Caesar to Crassus as they watched from Mount Sila.

"That," said Crassus, voice detached, "Spartacus probably thinks a pity. Fewer mouths to feed."

"*I* think, said Caesar, "that Spartacus loves them. The way a self-appointed king might love his people."

"Self-appointed?"

"Kings who are born to rule care little for their people," said Caesar, who had known a king born to rule. He pointed to where the shores of the bay were scenes of frenzied activity. "I tell you, Marcus Crassus, that man loves every last ungrateful individual in his vast horde! If he didn't, he would have cut himself off from them a year ago. I wonder who he really is?"

"Starting with what Gaius Cassius had to say, I'm having that question investigated," said Crassus, and prepared to descend. "Come on, Caesar, you've seen enough. *Love!* If he does, then he's a fool."

"Oh, he's definitely that," said Caesar, following. "What have you found out?"

"Almost everything except his real name. That may not come to light. Some fool of an archivist, thinking Sulla's Tabularium would hold military records as well as everything else, didn't bother to put them in a waterproof place. They're indecipherable, and Cosconius doesn't remember any names. At the moment I'm chasing his minor tribunes."

"Good luck! They won't remember any names either."

Crassus gave a grunt which might have been a short laugh. "Did you know there's a myth about him running around Rome—that he's a Thracian?"

"Well, everybody knows he's a Thracian. Thracian or Gaul—there are only the two kinds." Caesar's laugh rang out joyously. "However, I take it that this myth is being assiduously disseminated by the Senate's agents."

Crassus stopped, turned to gaze back and up at Caesar, a look of startled surprise on his face. "Oh, you are clever!"

"It's true, I am clever."

"Well, and doesn't it make sense?"

"Certainly," said Caesar. "We've had quite enough renegade Romans of late. We'd be fools to add one more to a list that includes such military luminaries as Gaius Marius, Lucius Cornelius Sulla and Quintus Sertorius, wouldn't we? Better by far to have him a Thracian."

"Huh!" Crassus emitted a genuine grunt.

"I'd dearly love to set eyes on him!"

"You may when we bring him to battle. He rides a very showy dappled grey horse tricked out with red leather tack and every kind of knightly knob and medallion. It used to belong to Varinius. Besides, Cassius and Manlius saw him at close quarters, so we have a good description. And he's a distinctive kind of fellow—very big, tall, and fair."

A grim duel began which went on for over a month, Spartacus trying to break through Crassus's fortifications and Crassus throwing him back. The Roman high command knew that food must be running very short in the Spartacani camps when every soldier Spartacus possessed—Caesar had estimated the total at seventy thousand—attacked along the entire eight-mile front, trying to find the Roman weak point. It seemed to the Spartacani that they had found it toward the middle of the wall, where the ditch appeared to have crumbled under an onslaught of spring water; Spartacus poured men across and over the wall, only to run them into a trap. Twelve thousand Spartacani died, the rest receded.

After that the Thracian who was not a Thracian tortured some prisoners he had saved from the consuls' legions, scattering his teams of men with red-hot pincers and pokers where he thought the maximum number of Roman soldiers would see the atrocity and hear the screams of their comrades. But after experiencing the horror of decimation Crassus's legions feared him a great deal more than they pitied the poor fellows being ripped and burned, and coped with it by electing not to watch, stuffing their ears with wool. Desperate, Spartacus produced his most prestigious prisoner, the *primus pilus* centurion of Gellius's old second legion, and nailed him to a cross through wrist and ankle joints without according him the mercy of broken limbs to help him die. Crassus's answer was to set his best archers along the top of his wall; the centurion died in a blizzard of arrows.

As March came in Spartacus sent the woman Aluso to sue for terms of surrender. Crassus saw her in his command hut, in the presence of his legates and tribunes of the soldiers.

"Why hasn't Spartacus come himself?" asked Crassus.

She gave him a compassionate smile. "Because without my husband the Spartacani would disintegrate," she said, "and he does not trust you, Marcus Crassus, even under truce."

"Then he's cleverer these days than he was when he let the pirates swindle him out of two thousand talents."

But Aluso was not the kind to rise to any bait, so she did not answer, even with a look. Her appearance was, Caesar thought, deliberately contrived to unsettle a civilized reception committee; she appeared the archetypal barbarian. Her flaxen hair streamed wild and stringy over back and shoulders, she wore some kind of blackish felt tunic with long sleeves, and beneath it tight-legged trousers. Over the clothing of arms and ankles she blazed with golden chains and bracelets, had loaded the long lobes of her ears with more gold, and her henna-stained fingers with rings. Around her neck she wore several loops of tiny bird skulls strung together, and from the solid gold belt at her trim waist there dangled grisly trophies—a severed hand still owning some nails and shreds of skin, a child's skull, the backbone of a cat or dog complete with tail. The whole was finished with a magnificent wolf pelt, paws knotted on her chest, the head with bared teeth and jewels for eyes perched above her brow.

With all this, she was not unattractive to the silent men who watched her, though none would have called her beautiful; her kind of face with its light, mad-looking eyes was too alien.

On Crassus, however, she failed to make the impression she had striven for. Crassus was proof against any attraction save money. So he stared at her in exactly the same way as he stared at everyone, with what seemed a gentle calmness.

"Speak, woman," he said.

"I am to ask you for terms of surrender, Marcus Crassus. We have no food left, and the women and children are starving in order that our soldiers may eat. My husband is not the kind of man who can bear to see the helpless suffer. He would rather give himself and his army up. Only tell me the terms and I will tell him. And then tomorrow I will come back with his answer."

The general turned his back. Over his shoulder he said, his Greek far purer than hers, "You may tell your husband that there are no terms under which I would accept his surrender. I will not permit him to surrender. He started this. Now he can see it through to the bitter end."

She gasped, prepared for every contingency but that one. "I cannot tell him that! You must let him surrender!"

"No," said Crassus, back still turned. His right hand moved, its fingers snapped. "Take her away, Marcus Mummius, and see her through our lines."

It was some time later before Caesar could catch Crassus on his own, though he burned to discuss the interview.

"You handled it brilliantly," he said. "She was so sure she would unsettle you."

"Silly woman! My reports say she's a priestess of the Bessi, though I'd rather call her a witch. Most Romans are superstitious—I've noticed you are, Caesar!—but I am not. I believe in what I can see, and what I saw was a female of some slight intelligence who had got herself up as she imagined a gorgon might look." He laughed spontaneously. "I remember being told that when he was a young man Sulla went to a party dressed as Medusa. On his head he wore a wig of living snakes, and he frightened the life out of everyone there. But you know, and I know, that it wasn't the snakes frightened the life out of anyone. It was—simply Sulla. Now if she had *that* quality, I might have quaked in my boots."

"I agree. But she does have the second sight."

"Many people have the second sight! I've known dear old grannies as dithery and fluffy as lambs who had the second sight, and grand-looking advocates you wouldn't think had a single corner of their minds that wasn't solid law. Anyway, what makes you think she has the second sight?"

"Because she came to the interview more frightened of you than you could ever have been of her."

For a month the weather had been "set," as the mother of Quintus Sertorius might have put it—nights well below freezing point, days not much warmer, blue skies, snow turned to ice underfoot. But after the Ides of March had gone there came a terrible storm which started as sleet and ended with snow piling up and up. Spartacus seized his chance.

Where the wall and ditch fused into the ravine closest to Scyllaeum—and the oldest of Crassus's veteran legions had its camp—the whole one hundred thousand Spartacani left alive hurled themselves into a frantic struggle to bridge the ditch and climb over the wall. Logs, stones, the dead bodies of humans and animals, even large pieces of loot were flung into the trench, heaped up to surmount the palisade. Like the shades of the dead the enormous mass of people rolled in wave after wave across this makeshift passage and fled into the teeth of the storm. No one opposed them; Crassus had sent the legion a message not to take up arms, but to remain quietly inside its camp.

Disorganized and haphazard, the flight unraveled what little structure the Spartacani host had owned beyond hope of knitting it up again. While the fighting men—better led and disciplined—floundered north on the Via Popillia with Spartacus, Castus and Gannicus, the bulk of the women, children, aged and noncombatants became so lost they entered the forests of Mount Sila; amid the tangles of low branches, rocks, undergrowth, most of them lay down and died, too cold and too hungry to struggle on. Those who did survive to see better weather came eventually upon Bruttian settlements, were recognized for what they were, and killed at once.

Not that the fate of this segment of the Spartacani held any interest for Marcus Licinius Crassus. When the snow began to lessen he struck camp and moved his eight legions out onto the Via Popillia in the wake of the Spartacani soldiers. His progress was as plodding as an ox, for he was always methodical, always in possession of his general's wits. There was no use in chasing; cold, hunger and lack of real purpose would combine to slow the Spartacani down, as would the size of their army. Better to have the baggage train in the middle of the legionary column than run the risk of losing it. Sooner or later he would catch up.

His scouts, however, were very busy, very swift. As March ground to its end they reported to Crassus that the Spartacani, having reached the river Silarus, had divided into two forces. One, under Spartacus, had continued up the Via Popillia toward Campania, while the other, under Castus and Gannicus, had struck east up the valley of the middle Silarus.

"Good!" said Crassus. "We'll leave Spartacus alone for the moment and concentrate on getting rid of the two Samnites."

The scouts then reported that Castus and Gannicus had not gone very far; they had encountered the prosperous little town of Volcei and were eating well for the first time in two months. No need to hurry!

When the four legions preceding Crassus's baggage train came up, Castus and Gannicus were too busy feasting to notice. The Spartacani had spread without making more than an apology for a camp on the foreshores of a little lake which at this time of the year contained sweet, potable water; by autumn the same locale would have held few charms. Behind the lake was a mountain. Crassus saw immediately what he had to do, and decided not to wait for the four legions which followed the baggage train.

"Pomptinus and Rufus, take twelve cohorts and sneak around the far side of the mountain. When you're in position, charge downhill. That will take you right into the middle of their—camp? As soon as I see you I'll attack from the front. We'll squash them between us like a beetle."

The plan should have worked. It *would* have worked, except for the vagaries of chance the best scouts could not divine. For when they saw how much food Volcei could provide, Castus and Gannicus sent word to Spartacus to retrace his footsteps, join the revelry. Spartacus duly retraced his footsteps and appeared on the far side of the lake just as Crassus launched his attack. The men belonging to Castus and Gannicus bolted into the midst of the newcomers, and all the Spartacani promptly vanished.

Some generals would have clawed the air, but not Crassus. "Unfortunate. But eventually we'll succeed," he said, unruffled.

A series of storms slowed everybody down. The armies of both sides lingered around the Silarus, though it appeared that it was now Spartacus's turn to leave the Via Popillia, while Castus and Gannicus used the road to march into Campania. Crassus lurked well in the rear, a fat spider bent on getting fatter. He too had decided to split his forces now that his eight legions were reunited; the baggage train, he knew, was safe. Two legions of infantry and all the cavalry were put under the command of Lucius Quinctius and Tremellius Scrofa, and ordered to be ready to follow whichever segment of Spartacani left the Via Popillia, while Crassus himself would pursue the segment on the road.

Like a millstone he ground on; as his legion was attached to the general's division, Caesar could only marvel at the absolute tenacity and method of this extraordinary man. At Eburum, not far north of the Silarus, he caught Castus and Gannicus at last, and annihilated their army. Thirty thousand died on the field, tricked and trapped; only a very few managed to slip through the Roman lines and flee inland to find Spartacus.

Greatest pleasure of all to every soldier in the victorious army was what Crassus discovered among the tumbled heaps of Spartacani baggage after the battle; the five eagles which had been taken when various Roman forces had been defeated, twenty-six cohort standards, and the *fasces* belonging to five praetors.

"Look at that!" cried Crassus, actually beaming. "Isn't it a wonderful sight?"

The general now displayed the fact that when he needed to, he could move very fast indeed. Word came from Lucius Quinctius that he and Scrofa had been ambushed—though without grievous losses—and that Spartacus was still nearby.

Crassus marched.

The grand undertaking had foundered. Left in the possession of Spartacus was the part of the army marching with him up to the sources of the Tanagrus River; that, and Aluso, and his son.

When his defeat of Quinctius and Scrofa proved indecisive because their cavalry—fleeter by far than infantry—mustered and allowed the Roman foot to withdraw, Spartacus made no move to leave the area. Three little towns had provided his men with ample food for the moment, but what the next valley and the one after that held, he no longer had any idea. It was approaching spring; granaries were low, no vegetables had yet formed and plumped after the hard winter, the hens were scrawny, and the pigs (crafty creatures!) had gone into hiding in the woods. An obnoxious local from Potentia, the closest town, had taken great pleasure in journeying out to see Spartacus in order to tell him that Varro Lucullus was expected any day to land in Brundisium from Macedonia, and that the Senate had ordered him to reinforce Crassus immediately.

"Your days are numbered, gladiator!" said the local with glee. "Rome is invincible!"

"I should cut your throat," said the gladiator wearily.

"Go ahead! I expect you to! And I don't care!"

"Then I won't give you the satisfaction of a noble death. Just go home!"

Aluso was listening. After the fellow had taken himself off (very disappointed that his lifeblood had not streamed out upon the ground) she moved close to Spartacus and put her hand gently upon his arm.

"It finishes here," she said.

"I know, woman."

"I see you fall in battle, but I cannot see a death."

"When I fall in battle I'll be dead."

He was so very tired, and the catastrophe at Scyllaeum still haunted him. How could he look his men in the face knowing that it had been his own misguided carelessness which had ended in their being penned in by Crassus? The women and children were gone and he knew they would not reappear. They had all died from starvation somewhere in the wild Bruttian countryside.

With no idea whether what the man from Potentia had told him about Varro Lucullus was true or not, he knew that it cut him off from Brundisium nonetheless. Crassus controlled the Via Popillia; the news of Castus and Gannicus had reached him even before he ambushed Quinctius and Scrofa. Nowhere to go. Nowhere, that is, except one last battlefield. And he was glad, glad, glad. . . . Neither birth nor ability had tailored him for such an enormous responsibility, the lives and welfare of a whole people. He was just an ordinary Roman of Italian family who had been born on the slopes of Mount Vesuvius, and ought to have spent his life there alongside his father and his brother. Who did he think he was, to attempt to give birth to a new nation? Not noble enough, not educated enough, not grand enough. But there was some honor in dying a free man on a battlefield; he would never go back to a prison. Never.

When word came that Crassus and his army were approaching, he took Aluso and his son and put them in a wagon harnessed to six mules far enough away from where he intended to make his last stand to ensure that they would elude pursuit. He would have preferred that they leave immediately, but Aluso refused, saying she must wait for the outcome of the conflict. In the covered rear of the vehicle lay gold, silver, treasures, coin; a guarantee that his wife and child would prosper. That they might be killed he understood. Yet their fates were on the laps of the gods, and the gods had been passing strange.

Some forty thousand Spartacani formed up to meet Crassus. Spartacus made no speech to them before the battle, but they cheered him deafeningly as he rode down their ranks on beautiful dappled grey Batiatus. He took his place beneath the standard of his people—the leaping enameled fish of a Gaul's fighting helmet—turned in the saddle to raise both hands in the air, fists clenched, then slid out of the horse's saddle. His sword was in his right hand, the curved saber of a Thracian gladiator; he closed his eyes, raised it, and brought it down into Batiatus's neck. Blood sprayed and gushed, but the lovely creature made no protest. Like a sacrificial victim it went down on its knees, rolled over, died.

There. No need for a speech. To kill his beloved horse told his followers everything. Spartacus did not intend to leave the field alive; he had dispensed with his means of escape.

As battles went it was straight, uncomplicated, extremely bloody. Taking their example from Spartacus, most of his men fought until they dropped, some in death, some in utter exhaustion. Spartacus himself killed two centurions before an unknown in the struggling mass cut the hamstrings in one leg. Unable to stand, he fell to his knees, but fought on doggedly until a huge pile of bodies by his side tumbled over and buried him.

Fifteen thousand Spartacani survived to flee the field; six thousand went in the direction of Apulia, the rest south toward the Bruttian mountains.

"Over in just six months, and a winter campaign at that," said Crassus to Caesar. "I've lost very few men all considered, and Spartacus is dead. Rome has her eagles and *fasces* back, and a lot of the plunder will prove impossible to return to its original owners. We'll all do quite well out of it."

"There is a difficulty, Marcus Crassus," said Caesar, who had been delegated to inspect the field for men still alive.

"Oh?"

"Spartacus. He isn't there."

"Rubbish!" said Crassus, startled. "I saw him fall!"

"So did I. I even memorized exactly where the spot was. I can take you straight to it—in fact, come with me now and I will! But he isn't there, Marcus Crassus. He isn't there."

"Odd!" The general huffed, pursed his lips, thought for a moment, then shrugged. "Well, what does it really matter? His army's gone, that's the main thing. I can't celebrate a triumph over an enemy classified as slave. The Senate will give me an ovation, but it's not the same. Not the same!" He sighed. "What about his woman, the Thracian witch?"

"We haven't found her either, though we did round up quite a few camp followers who had huddled together out of the way. I questioned them about her—and found out that her name is Aluso—but they swore she had climbed into a red-hot, sizzling chariot drawn by fiery snakes and driven off into the sky."

"Shades of Medea! I suppose that makes Spartacus Jason!" Crassus turned to walk with Caesar toward the heap of dead that had buried the fallen Spartacus. "I think somehow the pair of them got away. Don't you?"

"I'm sure they did," said Caesar.

"Well, we'll have to scour the countryside for Spartacani anyway. They might come to light."

Caesar made no reply. His own opinion was that they would never come to light. He was clever, the gladiator. Too clever to try to raise another army. Clever enough to become anonymous.

All through the month of May the Roman army tracked down Spartacani in the fastnesses of Lucania and Bruttium, ideal locations for brigandry which made it imperative that every surviving Spartacanus be captured. Caesar had estimated those who escaped southward at about nine or ten thousand, but all he and the other hunting details managed to find were some six thousand six hundred all told. The rest would probably become brigands, contribute to the perils of journeying down the Via Popillia to Rhegium without an armed escort.

"I can keep on going," he said to Crassus on the Kalends of June, "though the catch will become progressively smaller and harder to snare."

"No," said Crassus with decision. "I want my army back in Capua by the next market day. Including the consuls' legions. The curule elections are due next month and I intend to be back in Rome in plenty of time to stand for the consulship."

That was no surprise; Caesar in fact did not consider it worthy of comment. Instead he continued on the subject of the fugitive Spartacani. "What about the six thousand or so who fled northeast into Apulia?"

"They got as far as the border of Italian Gaul, actually," said Crassus. "Then they ran into Pompeius Magnus and his legions returning from Spain. You know Magnus! He killed the lot."

"So that only leaves the prisoners here. What do you want to do with them?"

"They'll go with us as far as Capua." The face Crassus turned upon his senior tribune of the soldiers was its usual phlegmatic self, but the eyes held an obdurate coldness. "Rome doesn't need these futile slave wars, Caesar. They're just one more drain on the Treasury. Had we not been lucky, five eagles and five sets of *fasces* might have been lost forever, a stain on Rome's honor I for one would have found unendurable. In time men like Spartacus might be blown up out of all proportion by some enemy of Rome's. Other men might strive to emulate him, never knowing the grubby truth. You and I know that Spartacus was a product of the legions, far more a Quintus Sertorius than a maltreated slave. Had he not been a product of the legions he could never have gone as far as he did. I do not want him turning into some sort of slave hero. So I will use Spartacus to put a stop to the whole phenomenon of slave uprisings."

"It was far more a Samnite than a slave uprising."

"True. But the Samnites are a curse Rome will have to live with forever. Whereas slaves must learn their place. I have the means to teach them their place. And I will. After I finish with the remnants of the Spartacani, there will be no more slave uprisings in our Roman world."

Used to thinking so quickly and summing men up so well that he had arrived at the answer long before anyone else, Caesar found himself absolutely unable to guess what Crassus was up to.

"How will you accomplish that?" he asked.

The accountant took over. "It was the fact that there are six thousand six hundred prisoners gave me the idea," Crassus said. "The distance between Capua and Rome is one hundred and thirty-two miles, each of five thousand feet. That is a total of six hundred and sixty thousand feet. Divided by six thousand six hundred, a distance of one hundred feet. I intend to crucify one Spartacanus every hundred feet between Capua and Rome. And they will remain hanging from their crosses until they rot away to bare bones."

Caesar drew a breath. "A terrible sight."

"I have one question," said Crassus, his smooth and unlined brow creasing. "Do you think I ought to put all the crosses on one side of the road, or alternate between both sides?"

"One side of the road," said Caesar instantly. "Definitely on one side of the road only. That is, provided by road you mean the Via Appia rather than the Via Latina."

"Oh yes, it has to be the Via Appia. Straight as an arrow for miles and miles, and not as many hills."

"Then one side of the road. The eye will take the sight in better that way." Caesar smiled. "I have some experience when it comes to crucifixion."

"I heard about that," said Crassus seriously. "However, I can't give you the job. It's not a fitting one for a tribune of the soldiers. He's an elected magistrate. By rights it belongs to the *praefectus fabrum*."

As the *praefectus fabrum*—the man who looked after all the technical and logistic factors involved in army supply—was one of Crassus's own freedmen and brilliant at his work, neither Caesar nor Crassus doubted that it would be a smooth operation.

Thus it was that at the end of June when Crassus, his legates, his tribunes of the soldiers and his own appointed military tribunes rode up the Via Appia from Capua escorted by a single cohort of troops, the left-hand side of the ancient and splendid road was lined with crosses all the way. Every hundred feet another Spartacanus slumped from the ropes which cruelly bound arms at the elbow and legs below the knees. Nor had Crassus been kind. The six thousand six hundred Spartacani died slowly with unbroken limbs, a soughing of moans from Capua to the Capena Gate of Rome.

Some people came to sightsee. Some brought a recalcitrant slave to look upon Crassus's handiwork and point out that this was the right of every master, to crucify. But many upon looking turned immediately to go home again, and those who were obliged to travel on the Via Appia anywhere between Capua and Rome were grateful that the crosses adorned only one side of the road. As the distance rendered the sight more bearable, the popular spot for those who lived in Rome to see was from the top of the Servian Walls on either side of the Capena Gate; the view extended for miles, but the faces were blurs.

They hung there for eighteen months enduring the slow cycle of decay that took them from living skin and muscle to clacking bones, for Crassus would not permit that they be taken down until the very last day of his consulship.

And, thought Caesar in some wonder, surely no other military campaign in the whole history of Rome had been so rounded, so neat, so finite: what had begun with a decimation had ended with a crucifixion.

PART EIGHT

from MAY 71 B.C.
until MARCH 69 B.C.

THE CONSUL POMPEY

Col

When Gnaeus Pompeius Magnus reached the border at the Rubico River, he didn't halt his army. That part of the Ager Gallicus he owned lay in Italy, and to Italy he would go, no matter what Sulla's laws said. His men were starved to see their homes, and there were still more among them who were his Picentine and Umbrian veterans than there were others. Outside Sena Gallica he put them into a vast camp under orders not to stray without leave from a tribune and proceeded then to Rome with a cohort of foot to escort him down the Via Flaminia.

The answer had come to him shortly after he began the long march from Narbo to his new pass across the Alps, and he wondered then at his denseness in not seeing it sooner. Three times he had been given a special commission: once by Sulla, twice by the Senate; twice with propraetorian status, once with proconsular status. He was, he knew, undoubtedly the First Man in Rome. But he also knew that no one who mattered would ever admit the fact. So he would have to prove it to everyone, and the only way he could do that was to bring off some coup so staggering in its audacity and so glaringly unconstitutional that after it was done all men would *have* to accord him his rightful title of the First Man in Rome.

He who was still a knight would force the Senate to make him consul.

His opinion of the Senate grew progressively lower, and his liking for that body remained nonexistent. The members of it could be bought as easily as cakes from a bakery, and its inertia was so monumental that it could hardly move out of the way of its own downfall. When he had begun to march his men from Tarentum to Rome in order to force Sulla to give him a triumph, Sulla had backed down! At the time he hadn't seen it that way—such was Sulla's effect on people—but he now understood that indeed the affair had been a victory for Magnus, not for Sulla. And Sulla had been a far more formidable foe than ever the Senate could be.

During his last year in the west he had followed the news about the successes of Spartacus with sheer disbelief; even though he owned the consuls Gellius and Clodianus, still he found it impossible to credit the degree of their incompetence in the field—and all they could do to excuse themselves was to harp about the poor quality of their soldiers! It had been on the tip of his pen to write and tell them that *he* could have generaled an army of eunuchs better, but he had refrained; there was no point in antagonizing men one had paid a long price for.

The two further items he had learned about in Narbo only served to reinforce his incredulity. The first item came in letters from Gellius and Clodianus: the Senate had stripped them of the command in the war against Spartacus. The second item came from Philippus: after blackmailing the

Senate into procuring a law from the Assembly of the People, Marcus Licinius Crassus had deigned to accept the command, together with eight legions and a good amount of cavalry. Having campaigned with Crassus, Pompey deemed him mediocre in the extreme, and his troops mediocre too. So Philippus's news only served to make him shake his head in a quiet despair. Crassus wouldn't defeat Spartacus either.

Just as he left Narbo there arrived the final verification of his impression of the war against Spartacus—so poor was the quality of Crassus's troops that he had *decimated* them! And that, as every commander knew from history and his manuals of military method, was a last measure doomed to failure— it utterly destroyed morale. *Nothing* could stiffen the backbones of men so cowardly that they had earned the punishment of decimation. Yet wasn't it just like big, lumbering Crassus to believe decimation could cure his army's ailments?

He began to toy with the thought of arriving back in Italy in time to clean up Spartacus, and out of that like a thunderclap had burst THE IDEA. Of course the Senate would beg him on bended knee to accept yet another special commission—the extirpation of the Spartacani. But this time he would insist that he be made consul before he took on the job. If Crassus could blackmail the Conscript Fathers into a command legalized by the People, then what hope did the Conscript Fathers have of withstanding Gnaeus Pompeius Magnus? Proconsul (*non pro consule, sed pro consulibus*) was just not good enough anymore! Was he to become the Senate's perpetual workhorse per- petually palmed off with an imperium outside of true senatorial power? No! Never again! He didn't at all mind the idea of entering the Senate if he could do so as consul. To the best of his recollection, no one had ever managed to do that. It was a first, a mighty big first—and it would demonstrate to the whole world that he was the First Man in Rome.

Right across the miles of the Via Domitia he had indulged in one fantasy after another, so happy and affable that Varro (to name only one) couldn't understand what was going through his mind. At times Pompey had been tempted to say something, then would sheer away, resolve to hug this delicious scheme to himself. Varro and the rest would find out soon enough.

The mood of joyous anticipation continued to prevail after the new pass had been surveyed and paved and the army descended the Vale of the Salassi into Italian Gaul. Down the Via Aemilia, and still Pompey whistled and chirped blithely. Then at the little town of Forum Popillii, well inside Italy, the awful blow fell. He and his six legions literally ran into a jostling mob of draggled men armed in a nonissue manner which betrayed that they were Spartacani. To round them up and kill them all was easy; what came hard was to learn that Marcus Crassus had annihilated the army of Spartacus in a battle fought less than a month before. The war against Spartacus was over.

His chagrin was obvious to every last one of his legates, who all assumed that he had whistled and chirped his way down the Via Aemilia because he had expected to go straight into another campaign. That he had planned to demand to be made consul because of this campaign occurred to no one. For several days he gloomed; even Varro avoided his company.

Oh, Pompey was thinking, why didn't I hear this while I was still in Gaul-across-the-Alps? I will have to use the threat of my undischarged army, but I have brought that army inside the borders of Italy contrary to Sulla's constitution. And Crassus still has an army in the field. If I was in Gaul-across-the-Alps I could skulk there until Crassus celebrated his ovation and his troops returned to civilian life. I could have used my tame senators to block the curule elections until I made my move. As it is, I'm in Italy. So it will have to be the threat of my army.

Those several gloomy days, however, were succeeded by a new mood; Pompey led his men into their camp at Sena Gallica not whistling and chirping exactly, but not glooming either. Reflection had led him to ask himself a very important question: what were the men of Crassus's army anyway? Answer: the scum of Italy, too craven to stand and fight. Why should the fact that Crassus had won change that? The six thousand fugitives he had encountered at Forum Popillii were pathetic. So perhaps decimation had stiffened the backbones of Crassus's men a bit—but could it last? Could it match the splendid courage and perseverance of men who had slogged through the Spanish heat and cold for years without pay, without booty, without decent food, without thanks from the precious Senate? No. The final answer was a loud and definite NO!

And as Rome grew closer Pompey's mood gradually soared back toward its earlier happiness.

"What exactly are you thinking?" Varro demanded as he and Pompey rode together down the middle of the road.

"That I am owed a Public Horse. The Treasury never paid me for my dear dead Snowy."

"Isn't that your Public Horse?" asked Varro, pointing at the chestnut gelding Pompey bestrode.

"This nag?" Pompey snorted contemptuously. "My Public Horse has to be white."

"Actually it's not a nag, Magnus," said the owner of part of the *rosea rura,* an acknowledged expert on horseflesh. "It's really an excellent animal."

"Just because it belonged to Perperna?"

"Just because it belongs to itself!"

"Well, it's not good enough for me."

"Was that really what you were thinking about?"

"Yes. What did you think I was thinking about?"

"That's my question! *What?*"

"Why don't you hazard a guess?"

Varro wrinkled his brow. "I thought I had guessed when we ran across those Spartacani outside Forum Popillii—I thought you were planning on another special commission and were very disappointed when you discovered Spartacus was no more. Now—I just don't know!"

"Well, Varro, wonder on. I think in this I will keep my counsel for the present," said Pompey.

The cohort Pompey had chosen to escort him to Rome was one made up of men whose homes were in Rome. This kind of common sense was typical of Pompey—why haul men off to Rome who would rather be elsewhere? So after he had got them into a small camp on the Via Recta, Pompey allowed them to don civilian garb and go into the city. Afranius, Petreius, Gabinius, Sabinus and the other legates quickly drifted off in their wake, as did Varro, anxious to see his wife and children.

That left Pompey alone in command of the Campus Martius—or at least his segment of it. To his left as he looked in the direction of the city but closer to it was another small camp. The camp of Marcus Crassus. Also, it would appear, escorted by about one cohort. Like Pompey, Crassus flew a scarlet flag outside his command tent to indicate that the general was in residence.

Unfortunate, unfortunate . . . Why did there have to be another army inside Italy? Even an army of cowards? It was no part of Pompey's plans actually to fight a civil war; somehow he could never feel comfortable with that idea. It wasn't loyalty or patriotism made him reject the idea, it was more that he did not feel inside himself the emotions men like Sulla felt. To Sulla there had been absolutely no alternative. Rome was the citadel inside which dwelt his heart, his honor, his very source of life. Whereas Pompey's citadel always had been and always would be Picenum. No, he wouldn't fight a civil war. But he had to make it look as if he would.

He sat down to draft his letter to the Senate.

To the Senate of Rome:

I, Gnaeus Pompeius Magnus, received a special commission from you six years ago to put down the revolt of Quintus Sertorius in Nearer

Spain. As you know, in conjunction with my colleague in the Further province, Quintus Caecilius Metellus Pius, I succeeded in putting that revolt down, and in bringing about the death of Quintus Sertorius. Also of his various legates, including the vile Marcus Perperna Veiento.

I am not the bearer of great spoils. There were no great spoils to be had in a country devastated by a long series of catastrophes. The war in Spain has been one war Rome has had to fight at a loss. Nevertheless I ask for a triumph, secure in the knowledge that I did as you commanded, and that many thousands of Rome's enemies are dead through me. I ask for this triumph to be awarded to me without any delay so that I can put myself up as a candidate for the consulship in the curule elections to be held in Quinctilis.

He had intended to draft the letter so that Varro could look it over and compose something fairer, more diplomatic. But after reading this very short note through several times, Pompey came to the conclusion that it could not be bettered. Hit 'em *hard*!

Philippus arrived just as he was sitting back, satisfied.

"Good!" cried Pompey, rising to his feet and shaking Philippus by the hand (a limp and sweaty exercise). "I have a letter for you to read. You can take it to the Senate for me."

"Requesting your well-deserved triumph?" Philippus asked, sitting down with a sigh; he had walked out to the Via Recta because litters were so slow, but he had forgotten how far it was and how hot a June day could be, even if by the seasons it was still spring.

"A little more than that," said Pompey, handing over his wax tablet with a grin.

"Something to drink first, my dear fellow, please?"

It took Philippus some time to decipher Pompey's dreadful schoolboy writing; he got the gist of the last sentence at exactly the same moment as he took his first big, thirsty gulp of well-watered wine, and choked. He was coughing and spluttering so badly that Pompey had to get up and thump him on the back, and it was some time before Philippus could compose himself sufficiently to comment.

But he didn't comment. Instead he looked at Pompey as if he had never seen him before. It was a genuinely exploratory gaze that took in the muscular frame still clad in cuirass and kilt, the fair and faintly freckled skin, the enormously attractive face with its dented chin and thatch of bright gold Alexandrian hair. And the eyes—wide, candid, eager, such a vivid blue! Pompeius Magnus, the New Alexander. Where did it come from, the gall which must have fueled this demand? The father had been a very strange man, yet the son always contrived to convince people that he was not strange at all. Oh, but the son was far stranger than the father! Few things came as a surprise to Lucius Marcius Philippus. But this was more than a mere surprise. This was the kind of shock could carry a man off!

"You're surely not serious?" he asked faintly.

"Why shouldn't I be serious?"

"Magnus, what you ask cannot be done! It—is—just—not—possible! It goes against every law, written and unwritten! No one can be consul without being in the Senate! Even Young Marius and Scipio Aemilianus were not elected consul until after they were in the Senate! You could I suppose argue that Scipio Aemilianus set a precedent by being consul before he was praetor, and Young Marius had never been so much as quaestor. But he was put into the Senate well ahead of the elections! And Sulla has absolutely eliminated all such precedents! Magnus, I beg of you, don't send that letter!"

"I *want* to be consul!" said Pompey, his small mouth growing thin and ringed with white.

"The gale of laughter it will provoke will waft your letter straight back to you! It cannot be done!"

Pompey sat down, swung one shapely leg over the arm of his chair and jiggled its booted foot. "Of course it can be done, Philippus!" he said sweetly. "I have six legions of the best and toughest troops in the world to say it can be done."

The breath went out of Philippus with an audible whoof! He began to shake. "You wouldn't!" he cried.

"I would, you know."

"But Crassus has eight legions sitting in Capua! It would be another civil war!"

"Pah!" said Pompey, still jiggling his foot. "Eight legions of cowards. I'd eat them for dinner."

"That's what you said about Quintus Sertorius."

The foot stopped. Pompey went pale, stiffened. "Don't ever say that to me again, Philippus."

"Oh, *cacat*!" groaned Philippus, wringing his hands. "Magnus, Magnus, I beg you, don't do this! Where did you get the idea that Crassus is commanding an army of cowards? Because of the consuls' legions, the decimation? Well, disabuse yourself! He forged himself a splendid army, as loyal to him as yours is to you. Marcus Crassus is no Gellius or Clodianus! Haven't you heard what he did on the Via Appia between Capua and Rome?"

"No," said Pompey, beginning to look just the slightest bit uncertain. "What did he do?"

"There are six thousand six hundred Spartacani hanging on six thousand six hundred crosses along the Via Appia between Capua and Rome—that's one cross every hundred feet, Magnus! He decimated the survivors of the consuls' legions to show them what he thought of craven troops, and he crucified the survivors of Spartacus's army to show every slave in Italy what happens to slaves who rebel. Those are not the actions of a man you can dismiss lightly, Magnus! Those are the actions of a man who might deplore civil war—it doesn't do his businesses any good!—but who, if the Senate so commands him, would take up arms against you. And stand a very good chance of destroying you!"

The uncertainty passed; Pompey's face set mulishly. "I will have my scribe make a fair copy of my letter, Philippus, and you will read it out in the House tomorrow."

"You'll ruin yourself!"

"I won't."

The interview was clearly at an end; Philippus got up. He wasn't out of the tent before Pompey was busy writing again. This time he addressed Marcus Licinius Crassus.

Greetings and a thousand congratulations, my old friend and colleague of the days fighting Carbo. While I was pacifying Spain, I hear that you have been pacifying Italy. They tell me you have welded a fine body of fighting men out of consular cravens and taught all of us how best to deal with rebellious slaves.

Once again, a thousand congratulations. If you are planning to be in your quarters this evening, may I pop in for a nice chat?

"Now what does he want?" demanded Crassus of Caesar.

"Interesting," said Caesar, handing Pompey's letter back. "I don't think much of his literary style."

"He doesn't have a literary style! He's a barbarian."

"And do you plan to be in this evening so our friend can pop in for his 'nice chat'? I wonder is that phrase innocent, or is it full of guile?"

"Knowing Pompeius, he thinks the phrase is the correct one. And yes, I certainly plan to be in this evening," said Crassus.

"With me or without me?" Caesar asked.

"With you. Do you know him?"

"I met him once a long time ago, but I very much doubt he'll remember me or the occasion."

A statement Pompey confirmed when he arrived several hours later. "*Have* I met you, Gaius Julius? I don't remember."

Caesar's laughter was spontaneous, but not mocking. "I'm not surprised, Gnaeus Pompeius. You only had eyes for Mucia."

Light dawned. "Oh! You were there in Julia's house when I went to meet my wife! Of course!"

"How is she? I've not seen her in years."

"I keep her in Picenum," said Pompey, unaware that this way of putting the matter might sound odd. "We have a boy and a girl these days—and more soon, I hope. I haven't seen her in years either, Gaius Julius."

"Caesar. I prefer to be called Caesar."

"That's good, because I much prefer being called Magnus."

"I imagine you do!"

Crassus decided it was time he got a word in. "Sit down, Magnus, please. You look very brown and fit for an old man—is it thirty-five now?"

"Not until the second-last day of September."

"That's to split hairs. You've packed more into your first thirty-five years than most men do into twice that many, so I dread to think what seventy will bring for *you*. Spain all tidy?"

"Beautifully tidy. But," said Pompey magnanimously, "I had some extremely competent help, you know."

"Yes, he surprised everyone, old Pius. Never did a thing until he went out to Spain." Crassus got up. "A drop of wine?"

Pompey laughed. "Not unless the vintage has improved, you incurable tightpurse!"

"It never varies," said Caesar.

"Vinegar."

"Just as well I don't drink wine, spending a whole campaign with him, isn't it?" asked Caesar, smiling.

"You don't drink wine? Ye gods!" At a loss, Pompey turned to Crassus. "Have you applied for your triumph yet?" he asked.

"No, I don't qualify for a triumph. The Senate prefers to call the war against Spartacus a slave war, so all I qualify for is an ovation." Crassus cleared his throat, looked a little cast down. "However, I have applied for an ovation. To be held as soon as possible. I want to lay down my imperium in time to stand for the consular elections."

"That's right, you were praetor two years ago, so there's no impediment, is there?'' Pompey looked cheerful. ''I doubt you'll have trouble getting in, after your resounding victory. Ovation one day, consul the next, I daresay.''

''That's the idea,'' said Crassus, who hadn't smiled yet. ''I have to persuade the Senate to grant me land for at least half of my troops, so being consul will be a help.''

''That it will,'' said Pompey cordially, and got up. ''Well, I must go. I like to get in a decent walk, keeps me from seizing up—getting to be an old man, as you say!''

And off he went, leaving Crassus and Caesar looking at each other blankly.

''What *was* all that about?'' asked Crassus.

''I have a funny feeling,'' said Caesar thoughtfully, ''that we are going to find out.''

As a messenger had delivered the scribe-copied, neat and tidy version of Pompey's letter early in the afternoon, Philippus did not expect any further word from Pompey until after he had read the letter out in the Senate. But he had only just risen from the dinner couch late that same afternoon when another messenger arrived from Pompey to summon him back to the Campus Martius. For a wild moment Philippus contemplated sending a curt refusal; then he thought of the wonderful annual lump sum Pompey still paid him, sighed, and ordered a litter. No more walking!

''If you've changed your mind about my reading out your letter tomorrow, Magnus, all you had to do was notify me! Why am I here for the second time in one day?''

''Oh, don't worry about the letter!'' said Pompey impatiently. ''Just read the thing out and let them have their laugh. They'll be laughing on the other side of their faces soon enough. No, it's not for that I wanted to see you. I have a job for you that's far more important, and I want you to get started on it at once.''

Philippus frowned. ''What job?'' he asked.

''I'm going to drive Crassus onto my side,'' said Pompey.

''Oho! And how do you plan to do that?''

''*I* won't be doing it. You and the rest of my lobby will. I want you to swing the Senate away from granting land to Crassus for his troops. But you have to do it now, before he's allowed his ovation, and well before the curule elections. You have to maneuver Crassus into a position which will prevent his offering the use of his army to the Senate if the Senate decides it must squash me with force. I didn't know how to go about it until I went to see

Crassus a short time ago. And he let it drop that he's running for consul because he believes as consul he'll be in a better position to demand land for his veterans. You know Crassus! There's not a chance in the world that he'd pay for land himself, but he can't discharge his soldiers without some sort of settlement. He probably won't ask for much—after all, it was a short campaign. And that's the tack you're going to adopt—that a six months' campaign isn't worth giving away the *ager publicus* for, especially as the enemy was servile. If the booty was worth his army's while, then it might be content with that. But I know Crassus! Most of the booty won't be entered on the list for the Treasury. He can't help himself—he *has* to try to keep the lot. And get compensation for his men out of the State.''

"As a matter of fact I heard the booty wasn't great," said Philippus, smiling. "Crassus declared that Spartacus paid out almost everything he had to the pirates when he tried to hire them to take his men to Sicily. But from other sources I've heard this wasn't so, that the sum he paid was half what he had *in cash*."

"That's Crassus!" said Pompey with a reminiscent grin. "I tell you, he can't help himself. How many legions has he got? Eight? Twenty percent to the Treasury, twenty percent to Crassus, twenty percent to his legates and tribunes, ten percent to the cavalry and centurions, and thirty percent to the foot soldiers. That would mean each foot soldier would get about a hundred and eighty-five sesterces. Wouldn't pay the rent for long, would it?''

"I didn't realize you were so good at arithmetic, Magnus!''

"Always better at that than reading and writing.''

"How much will your men get from booty?''

"About the same. But the tally's honest, and they know it is. I always have a few representatives from the ranks present when I tot up booty. Makes them feel better, not so much to know their general's honest as because they think themselves honored. Those of mine who don't already have land will get land. From the State, I hope. But if not from the State, I'll give them some of my land.''

"That's remarkably generous of you, Magnus.''

"No, Philippus, it's just forethought. I'm going to need these men—and their sons!—in the future, so I don't mind being generous now. But when I'm an old man and I've fought my last campaign, I can assure you I won't be willing to stand the damage myself.'' Pompey looked determined. "My last campaign is going to bring in more money than Rome has seen in a hundred years. I don't know what campaign it's going to be, except that I'll pick a rich one. Parthia's what I'm thinking of. And when I bring the wealth of Parthia back to Rome, I expect Rome to give my veterans land. My career so far has put me badly out of purse—well, *you* know how much I pay out each and every year to you and the rest of my lobby in the Senate!''

Philippus hunched himself defensively in his chair. "You'll get your money's worth!"

"You're not wrong about that, my friend. And you can start tomorrow," said Pompey cheerfully. "The Senate must refuse to give Crassus land for his troops. I also want the curule elections delayed. And I want my application to be allowed to run for the consulship tabled in the House and kept tabled. Is that clear?"

"Perfectly." The hireling got up. "There's only one real difficulty, Magnus. Crassus has a great many senators in debt to him, and I doubt we can turn them onto our side."

"We can—if we give those men who don't owe Crassus much the money to pay him back. See how many owe him forty thousand sesterces or less. If they're our creatures or might be willing to be our creatures, instruct them to pay Crassus back immediately. If nothing else tells him how serious his situation is, that will," said Pompey.

"Even so, I wish you'd let me postpone your letter!"

"You will read my letter out tomorrow, Philippus. I don't want anyone deluded about my motives. I want the Senate and Rome to know here and now that I am going to be consul next year."

Rome and the Senate knew by the following noon, for at that hour Varro erupted into Pompey's tent, breathless and disheveled.

"You're not serious!" Varro gasped, throwing himself into a chair and flapping a hand in front of his flushed face.

"I am."

"Water, I need water." With a huge effort Varro pulled himself out of the chair and went to the table where Pompey kept his liquid refreshments. He downed a goodly draft, refilled his beaker and went back to his chair. "Magnus, they'll swat you like a moth!"

Pompey dismissed this with a contemptuous gesture, staring at Varro eagerly. "How did they take it, Varro? I want to hear every last detail!"

"Well, Philippus lodged an application to speak with the consul Orestes—who has the *fasces* for June—before the meeting, and as it was he who had requested the meeting be convened in the first place, he spoke as soon as the auguries were over. He got up and read out your letter."

"Did they laugh?"

Startled, Varro lifted his head from his water. "*Laugh?* Ye gods, no! Everyone sat there absolutely stunned. Then the House began to buzz, softly at first, then louder and louder until the place was in an uproar. The consul

Orestes finally managed to establish order, and Catulus asked to speak. I imagine you know pretty much what he had to say.''

"Out of the question. Unconstitutional. An affront to every legal and ethical precept in the history of Rome.''

"All that, and a great deal more. By the time he finished he was literally foaming at the mouth.''

"What happened after he finished?''

"Philippus gave a really magnificent speech—one of the best I've ever heard him give, and he's a great orator. He said you'd earned the consulship, that it was ridiculous to ask a man who had been propraetor twice and proconsul once to crawl into the House under a vow of silence. He said you'd saved Rome from Sertorius, you'd turned Nearer Spain into a model province, you'd even opened up a new pass across the Alps, and that all of those things—plus a lot more—proved that you had always been Rome's loyalest servant. I can't go into all his flights of fancy—ask him for a copy of his speech, he read it out—but he made a profound impression, I can tell you that.

"And then," Varro went on, looking puzzled, "he changed horses! It was very odd! One moment he was talking about letting you run for consul, the next moment he was talking about the habit we had got into of doling out little pieces of Rome's precious *ager publicus* to appease the greed of common soldiers, who thanks to Gaius Marius now expected as a matter of course to be rewarded with public land after the smallest and meanest campaign. How this land was being given to these soldiers not in Rome's name, but in the general's name! The practice would have to stop, he said. The practice was creating private armies at the expense of Senate and People, because it gave soldiers the idea that they belonged to their general first, with Rome coming in a bad second.''

"Oh, good!" purred Pompey. "Did he stop there?''

"No, he didn't," said Varro sipping his water. He licked his lips, a nervous reaction; the idea was beginning to occur to him that Pompey was behind all of it. "He went on to refer specifically to the campaign against Spartacus, and to Crassus's report to the House. Mincemeat, Magnus! Philippus made mincemeat out of Crassus! How dared Crassus apply for land for the veterans of a six months' campaign! How dared Crassus apply for land to reward soldiers who had had to be decimated before they found the courage to fight! How dared Crassus apply for land to give to men who had only done what any loyal Roman was expected to do—put down an enemy threatening the homeland! A war against a foreign power was one thing, he said, but a war against a felon leading an army of slaves conducted on Italian soil was quite another. No man was entitled to ask for rewards when he had literally been defending his home. And Philippus ended by begging the House not to tolerate Crassus's impudence, nor encourage Crassus to think he could buy personal loyalty from his soldiers at the expense of Rome.''

"Splendid Philippus!" beamed Pompey, leaning forward. "So what happened after that?''

"Catulus got up again, but this time he spoke in support of Philippus. How right Philippus was to demand that this practice started by Gaius Marius of giving away State land to soldiers should stop. It *must* stop, said Catulus! The *ager publicus* of Rome had to stay in the public domain, it could not be used to bribe common soldiers to be loyal to their commanders.''

"And did the debate end there?''

"No. Cethegus was given leave to speak, and he backed both Philippus and Catulus without reservation, he said. After him, so did Curio, Gellius, Clodianus, and a dozen others. After which the House worked itself into such a state that Orestes decided to terminate the meeting," Varro ended.

"Wonderful!" cried Pompey.

"This is your doing, Magnus, isn't it?''

The wide blue eyes opened even wider. "*My* doing? Whatever can you mean, Varro?''

"You know what I mean," said Varro, tight-lipped. "I confess I've only just seen it, but I have seen it! You're using all your senatorial employees to drive a wedge between Crassus and the House! And if you succeed, you will have succeeded in removing Crassus's army from the Senate's command. And if the Senate has no army to command, Rome cannot teach you the lesson you so richly deserve, Gnaeus Pompeius!''

Genuinely hurt, Pompey gazed beseechingly at his friend. "Varro, Varro! I *deserve* to be consul!''

"You deserve to be crucified!''

Opposition always hardened Pompey; Varro could see the ice forming. And, as always, it unmanned him. So he said, trying to retrieve his lost ground, "I'm sorry, Magnus, I spoke in anger. I retract that. But surely you can see what a terrible thing you are doing! If the Republic is to survive, every man of influence in it must avoid undermining the constitution. What you have asked the Senate to allow you to do goes against every principle in the *mos maiorum*. Even Scipio Aemilianus didn't go so far—and *he* was directly descended from Africanus and Paullus!''

But that only made matters worse. Pompey got up, stiff with outrage. "Oh, go away, Varro! I see what you're saying! If a prince of the blood didn't go so far, how dare a mere mortal from Picenum? I *will* be consul!''

* * *

The effect the doings of that meeting of the Senate had on Marcus Terentius Varro was as nothing compared to the effect it had on Marcus Licinius Crassus. His report came from Caesar, who had restrained Quintus Arrius and the other senatorial legates after the meeting concluded, though Lucius Quinctius took some persuading.

"Let me tell him," Caesar begged. "You're all too hot, and you'll make him hot. He has to remain calm."

"We never even got a chance to speak our piece!" cried Quinctius, smacking his fist into the palm of his other hand. "That *verpa* Orestes let everyone talk who was in favor, then closed the meeting before a single one of us could answer!"

"I know that," said Caesar patiently, "and rest assured, we'll all get our chance at the next meeting. Orestes did the sensible thing. Everyone was in a rage. And we'll have the floor first next time. Nothing was decided! So let me tell Marcus Crassus, please."

And so, albeit reluctantly, the legates had gone to their own homes, leaving Caesar to stride out briskly for the Campus Martius and Crassus's camp. Word of the meeting had flown about like a wind; as he slipped neatly through the crowds of men in the lower Forum Romanum on his way to the Clivus Argentarius, Caesar heard snatches of talk which all revolved around the prospect of yet another civil war. Pompey wanted to be consul—the Senate wouldn't have it—Crassus wasn't going to get his land—it was high time Rome taught these presumptuous generals a much-needed lesson—what a terrific fellow Pompey was—and so on.

" . . . And there you have it," Caesar concluded.

Crassus had listened expressionless to the crisp and succinct summary of events Caesar presented to him, and now that the tale was over he maintained that expressionless mask. Nor did he say anything for some time, just gazed out of the open aperture in his tent wall at the quiet beauty of the Campus Martius. Finally he gestured toward the scene outside and said without turning to face Caesar, "Lovely, isn't it? You'd never think a cesspool like Rome was less than a mile down the Via Lata, would you?"

"Yes, it is lovely," said Caesar sincerely.

"And what do you think about the not so lovely events in the Senate this morning?"

"I think," said Caesar quietly, "that Pompeius has got you by the balls."

That provoked a smile, followed by a silent laugh. "You are absolutely correct, Caesar." Crassus pointed in the direction of his desk, where piles of filled moneybags lay all over its surface. "Do you know what those are?"

"Money, certainly. I can't guess what else."

"They represent every small debt a senator owed me," said Crassus. "Fifty repayments altogether."

"And fifty fewer votes in the House."

"Exactly." Crassus heaved his chair around effortlessly and put his feet up among the bags atop his desk, leaned back with a sigh. "As you say, Caesar, Pompeius has got me by the balls."

"I'm glad you're taking it calmly."

"What's the point in ranting and raving? That wouldn't help. Couldn't change a thing. More importantly, is there anything will change the situation?"

"Not from a testicular aspect, for sure. But you can still work within the parameters Pompeius has set—it's possible to move about, even with someone's hairy paw wrapped around your poor old balls," said Caesar with a grin.

Crassus answered it. "Quite so. Who would have thought Pompeius had that kind of brilliance?"

"Oh, he's brilliant. In an untutored way. But it was not a *politic* ploy, Crassus. He hit you with the stunning hammer first and then stated his terms. If he owned any political sense, he would have come to you first and told you what he intended to do. Then it might have been arranged in peace and quiet, without all of Rome stirred into a fever pitch at the prospect of another civil war. The trouble with Pompeius is that he has no idea how other people think, or how they're going to react. Unless, that is, their thoughts and reactions are the same as his own."

"You are probably right, but I think it has more to do with Pompeius's self-doubt. If he absolutely believed he could force the Senate to let him be consul, he would have come to me before he moved. But I'm less important to him than the Senate, Caesar. It's the Senate he has to sway. I'm just his tool. So what can it matter to him if he stuns me first? He's got me by the balls. If I want land for my veterans, I have to inform the Senate that it can't rely on me or my soldiers to oppose Pompeius." Crassus shifted his booted feet; the bags of money chinked.

"What do you intend to do?"

"I intend," said Crassus, swinging his feet off the desk and standing up, "sending you to see Pompeius right now. I don't need to tell you what to say. Negotiate, Caesar."

Off went Caesar to negotiate.

One of the few certainties, he thought wryly, was that he would find each general at home; until triumph or ovation was held, no general could

cross the *pomerium* into the city, for to do so was to shed imperium automatically, thereby preventing triumph or ovation. So while legates and tribunes and soldiers could come and go as they pleased, the general himself
was obliged to remain on the Campus Martius.

Sure enough, Pompey was at home—if a tent could be called a home.
His senior legates Afranius and Petreius were with him, looked at Caesar
searchingly; they had heard a little about him—pirates and the like—and knew
that he had won the Civic Crown at twenty years of age. All things which
made *viri militares* like Afranius and Petreius respect a man mightily; and
yet this dazzling fellow, immaculate enough to be apostrophized a dandy,
didn't look the type. Togate rather than clad in military gear, nails trimmed
and buffed, senatorial shoes without a scuff or a smear of dust, hair perfectly
arranged, he surely could not have walked from Crassus's quarters to Pompey's through wind and sun!

"I remember you said you didn't drink wine. Can I offer you water?"
asked Pompey, gesturing in the direction of a chair.

"Thank you, I require nothing except a private conversation," said
Caesar, seating himself.

"I'll see you later," said Pompey to his legates.

He waited until he saw the two disappointed men well out of hearing
down the path toward the Via Recta before he directed his attention at Caesar.
"Well?" he asked in his abrupt manner.

"I come from Marcus Crassus."

"I expected to see Crassus himself."

"You're better off dealing with me."

"Angry, is he?"

Caesar's brows lifted. "Crassus? Angry? Not at all!"

"Then why can't he come to see me himself?"

"And set all of Rome chattering even harder than it already is?" asked
Caesar. "If you and Marcus Crassus are to do business, Gnaeus Pompeius,
better that you do so through men like me, who are the soul of discretion
and loyal to our superiors."

"So you're Crassus's man, eh?"

"In this matter, yes. In general I am my own man."

"How old are you?" asked Pompey bluntly.

"Twenty-nine in Quinctilis."

"Crassus would call that splitting hairs. You'll be in the Senate soon,
then."

"I'm in the Senate now. Have been for almost nine years."

"Why?"

"I won a Civic Crown at Mitylene. Sulla's constitution says that military heroes enter the Senate," said this dandy.

"Everyone always refers to Rome's constitution as Sulla's constitution," said Pompey, deliberately ignoring unwelcome information like a Civic Crown. He had never won a major crown himself, and it hurt. "I'm not sure I'm grateful to Sulla!"

"You ought to be. You owe him your various special commissions," said Caesar, "but after this little episode, I very much doubt that the Senate will ever be willing to award another special commission to a knight."

Pompey stared. "What do you mean?"

"Just what I say. You can't force the Senate into letting you become consul and expect the Senate to forgive you, Gnaeus Pompeius. Nor can you expect to control the Senate forever. Philippus is an old man. So is Cethegus. And when they go, who will you use in their stead? The seniors in the Senate will all be men of Catulus's persuasion—the Caecilii Metelli, the Cornelii, the Licinii, the Claudii. So a man wanting a special commission will have to go to the People, and by the People I do not mean patricians and plebeians combined. I mean the Plebs. Rome used to work almost exclusively through the Plebeian Assembly. I predict that in the future, that is how she will work again. Tribunes of the plebs are so enormously useful—but only if they have their legislating powers." Caesar coughed. "It's also cheaper to buy tribunes of the plebs than it is the high fliers like Philippus and Cethegus."

All of that sank in; impassively Caesar watched it vanish thirstily below Pompey's surface. He didn't care for the fellow, but wasn't sure exactly why. Having had much childhood exposure to Gauls, it was not the Gaul in him Caesar objected to. So what was it? While Pompey sat there digesting what he had said, Caesar thought about the problem, and came to the conclusion that it was simply the man he didn't care for, not what he represented. The conceit, the almost childish concentration on self, the lacunae in a mind which obviously held no respect for the Law.

"What does Crassus have to say to me?" demanded Pompey.

"He'd like to negotiate a settlement, Gnaeus Pompeius."

"Involving what?"

"Wouldn't it be better if you put forward your requirements first, Gnaeus Pompeius?"

"I do wish you'd stop calling me that! I hate it! I am Magnus to the world!"

"This is a formal negotiation, Gnaeus Pompeius. Custom and tradition demand that I address you by *praenomen* and *nomen*. Are you not willing to put forward your requirements first?"

"Oh, yes, yes!" snapped Pompey, not sure exactly why he could feel his temper fraying, except that it had to do with this smooth, polished fellow Crassus had sent as his representative. Everything Caesar had said so far made eminent good sense, but that only made the situation more maddening. He, Magnus, was supposed to be calling the tune, but this interview wasn't coming up to expectation. Caesar behaved as if it were he had the power, he the upper hand. The man was prettier than dead Memmius and craftier than Philippus and Cethegus combined—and yet he had won the second highest military decoration Rome could award—and from an incorruptible like Lucullus, at that. So he had to be very brave, a very good soldier. Had Pompey also known the stories about the pirates, the will of King Nicomedes and the battle on the Maeander, he might have decided to conduct this interview along different lines; Afranius and Petreius had heard some of it, but—typical Pompey!—he had heard nothing. Therefore the interview proceeded with more of the real Pompey on display than would otherwise have been the case.

"Your requirements?" Caesar was prompting.

"Are purely to persuade the Senate to pass a resolution that will let me run for consul."

"Without membership in the Senate?"

"Without membership in the Senate."

"What if you do persuade the Senate to allow you to run for consul, and then lose at the elections?"

Pompey laughed, genuinely amused. "I couldn't lose if I tried!" he said.

"I hear the competition is going to be fierce. Marcus Minucius Thermus, Sextus Peducaeus, Lucius Calpurnius Piso Frugi, Marcus Fannius, Lucius Manlius—as well as the two leading contenders at this stage, Metellus Little Goat and Marcus Crassus," said Caesar, looking amused.

None of the names meant much to Pompey except the last one; he sat up straight. "You mean he still intends to run?"

"If, as seems likely, Gnaeus Pompeius, you are going to ask him to withhold the use of his army from the Senate, then he *must* run for consul— and *must* be elected," said Caesar gently. "If he isn't consul next year, he'll be prosecuted for treason before January has run its course. As consul, he cannot be made to answer for any action until his consulship and any proconsulship which follows are over and he is once more a *privatus*. So what he has to do is to succeed in being elected consul, and then succeed in restoring full powers to the tribunate of the plebs. After that he will have to persuade one tribune of the plebs to pass a law validating his action in withholding his army from the Senate's use—and persuade the other nine not to veto. Then when he does become a *privatus* again, he can't be prosecuted for the treason you are asking him to commit.''

A whole gamut of expressions chased each other across Pompey's face— puzzlement, enlightenment, bewilderment, total confusion, and finally fear. "What are you trying to say?" he cried, out of his depth and beginning to feel an awful sense of suffocation.

"I am saying—and very clearly, I think!—that if either of you is to avoid prosecution for treason due to the games you intend to play with the Senate and two armies which actually belong to Rome, *both* of you will have to be consul next year, and *both* of you will have to work very hard to restore the tribunate of the plebs to its old form," said Caesar sternly. "The only way *either* of you can escape the consequences is by procuring a plebiscite from the Plebeian Assembly absolving *both* of you from any guilt in the matter of armies and senatorial manipulation. Unless, that is, Gnaeus Pompeius, you have not brought your own army across the Rubico into Italy?"

Pompey shuddered. "I didn't think!" he cried.

"Most of the Senate," Caesar said in conversational tones, "is composed of sheep. No one is unaware of that fact. But it does blind some people to another fact—that the Senate has a certain number of wolves in its fold. I do not number Philippus among the senatorial wolves. Nor Cethegus, for that matter. But Metellus Little Goat should rightly be cognominated Big Wolf, and Catulus has fangs for tearing, not molars for ruminating. So does Hortensius, who might not be consul yet, but whose clout is colossal and whose knowledge of the law is formidable. Then we have my youngest and brightest uncle, Lucius Cotta. You might say even I am a senatorial wolf! Any one of the men I've named—but more likely all of them combined—is quite capable of prosecuting you and Marcus Crassus for treason. And you will have to stand your trial in a court juried by *senators*. Having thumbed your nose at a great many senators. Marcus Crassus might get off, but you won't, Gnaeus Pompeius. I'm sure you have a huge following in the Senate, but can you hold it together after you've dangled the threat of civil war in its face and forced it to accede to your wishes? You may hold your faction together while you're consul and then proconsul, but not once you're a *privatus* again. Not unless you keep your army under its eagles for the rest of your life—and that, since the Treasury won't pay for it, would not be possible, even for a man with your resources.''

So many ramifications! The awful sense of suffocation was increasing; for a moment Pompey felt himself back on the field at Lauro, helpless to prevent Quintus Sertorius from running rings around him. Then he rallied, looked tough and absolutely determined. ''How much of what you've said does Marcus Crassus himself understand?''

''Enough,'' said Caesar tranquilly. ''He's been in the Senate a long time, and in Rome even longer. He's in and out of the law courts, he knows the constitution backward. It's all there in the constitution! Sulla's *and* Rome's.''

''So what you're saying is that I have to back down.'' Pompey drew a breath. ''Well, I won't! I want to be consul! I deserve to be consul, and I *will* be consul!''

''It can be arranged. But only in the way I've outlined,'' Caesar maintained steadily. ''Both you and Marcus Crassus in the curule chairs, restoration of the tribunate of the plebs and an exculpatory plebiscite, followed by another plebiscite to give land to the men of both armies.'' He shrugged lightly. ''After all, Gnaeus Pompeius, you have to have a colleague in the consulship! You can't be consul *without* a colleague. So why not a colleague laboring under the same disadvantages and suffering the same risks? Imagine if Metellus Little Goat were to be voted in as your colleague! His teeth would be fixed in the back of your neck from the first day. And he would marshal every reserve he could to make sure you didn't succeed in your attempts to restore the tribunate of the plebs. Two consuls in a very close collaboration are extremely difficult for the Senate to resist. Especially if they have ten united, rejuvenated tribunes of the plebs to back them up.''

''I see what you're saying,'' said Pompey slowly. ''Yes, it would be a great advantage to have an amenable colleague. All right. I will be consul with Marcus Crassus.''

''Provided,'' said Caesar pleasantly, ''that you don't forget the second plebiscite! Marcus Crassus must get that land.''

''No problem! I can get land for my men too, as you say.''

''Then the first step has been taken.''

Until this shattering discussion with Caesar, Pompey had assumed that Philippus would mastermind his candidacy for the consulship, would do whatever was necessary; but now Pompey wondered. Had Philippus seen *all* the consequences? Why hadn't he said anything about prosecutions for treason and the necessity to restore the tribunate of the plebs? Was Philippus perhaps a little tired of being a paid employee? Or was he past his prime?

''I'm a dunce about politics,'' said Pompey with what he tried to make engaging frankness. ''The trouble is, politics don't fascinate me. I'm far more interested in command, and I was thinking of the consulship as a sort of huge civilian command. You've made me see it differently. And you make sense,

Caesar. So tell me this—how do I go about it? Should I just keep on lodging letters through Philippus?''

"No, you've done that, you've thrown down your challenge," said Caesar, apparently not averse to acting as Pompey's political adviser. "I presume you've given Philippus orders to delay the curule elections, so I won't go into that. The Senate's next move will be aimed at trying to get the upper hand. It will give you and Marcus Crassus firm dates—you for your triumph, Marcus Crassus for his ovation. And of course the senatorial decree will instruct each of you to disband your army the moment your celebrations are over. That's quite normal.''

He sat there, thought Pompey, not a scrap differently from the way he had the moment he arrived; he displayed no thirst, no discomfort in that vast toga from the heat of the day, no sign of a sore behind from the hard chair or a sore neck from looking at Pompey slightly to one side. And the words which gave voice to the thoughts were as well chosen as the thoughts were well organized. Yes, Caesar definitely bore watching.

Caesar continued. "The first move will have to come from you. When you get the date for your triumph, you must throw up your hands in horror and explain that you've just remembered you can't triumph until Metellus Pius comes home from Further Spain, because you and he agreed to share one triumph between the two of you—no spoils worth speaking of, and so forth. But the moment you give this excuse for not disbanding your army, Marcus Crassus will throw *his* hands up in horror and protest that he cannot disband *his* army if that leaves only one fully mobilized army inside Italy— yours. You can keep this farce going until the end of the year. It won't take the Senate many moons to realize that neither of you has any intention of disbanding his army, but that both of you are to some extent legalizing your positions. Provided neither of you makes a militarily aggressive move in Rome's direction, you both look fairly good.''

"I like it!" said Pompey, beaming.

"I'm so glad. It's less strain to preach to the converted. Now where was I?" Caesar frowned, pretended to think. "Oh, yes! Once the Senate understands that neither army is going to be disbanded, it will issue the appropriate *consulta* to allow both of you to stand for the consulship *in absentia*—for of course neither of you can enter Rome to lodge your candidacies in person to the election officer. Only the lots will show whether the election officer will be Orestes or Lentulus Sura, but I can't see much difference between them.''

"How do I get around the fact that I'm not in the Senate?" asked Pompey.

"You don't. That's the Senate's problem. It will be solved with a *senatus consultum* to the Assembly of the People allowing a knight to seek election as consul. I imagine the People will pass it happily—all those knights will consider it a tremendous win!''

''And Marcus Crassus and I can disband our armies when we've won election,'' said Pompey, satisfied.

''Oh, no,'' said Caesar, shaking his head gently. ''You keep your armies under their eagles until the New Year. Therefore you won't celebrate triumph and ovation until the latter half of December. Let Marcus Crassus ovate first. Then you can triumph on the last day of December.''

''It all makes perfect sense,'' said Pompey, and frowned. ''Why didn't Philippus explain things properly?''

''I haven't any idea,'' said Caesar, looking innocent.

''I think I do,'' said Pompey grimly.

Caesar rose, pausing to arrange the folds of his toga just so, utterly absorbed in the task. Finished, he walked with his graceful, straight-shouldered gait to the flap of the tent. In the entrance he paused, looked back, smiled. ''A tent is a most impermanent structure, Gnaeus Pompeius. It looks good for the general awaiting his triumph to set up an impermanent structure. But I don't think it's quite the impression you should be striving to make from now on. May I suggest that you hire an expensive villa on the Pincian Hill for the rest of the year? Bring your wife down from Picenum? Entertain? Breed a few pretty fish? I will make sure Marcus Crassus does the same. You'll both look as if you're prepared to live on the Campus Martius for the rest of your lives if necessary.''

Then he was gone, leaving Pompey collecting composure and thoughts. The military holiday was over; he would have to sit down with Varro and read law. Caesar seemed to know every nuance, yet he was six years younger. If the Senate had its share of wolves, was Gnaeus Pompeius Magnus going to be a sheep? Never! By the time New Year's Day came around, Gnaeus Pompeius Magnus would know his law *and* his Senate!

''Ye gods, Caesar, you're clever!'' said Crassus feebly when Caesar had ended his tale of Pompey. ''I didn't think of half that! I don't say I wouldn't have worked it all out eventually, but you must have done it between my tent and his. A villa on the Pincian, indeed! I have a perfectly good house on the Palatine I've just spent a fortune redecorating—why spend money on a villa on the Pincian? I'm comfortable in a tent.''

''What an incurable cheeseparer you are, Marcus Crassus!'' said Caesar, laughing. ''You'll rent a villa on the Pincian at least as expensive as Pompeius's and move Tertulla and the boys into it at once. You can afford it.

Look on it as a necessary investment. It is! You and Pompeius are going to have to seem like bitter opponents for the next almost six months.''

"And what are you going to do?" asked Crassus.

"I'm going to find myself a tribune of the plebs. Preferably a Picentine one. I don't know why, but men from Picenum are attracted to the tribunate of the plebs, and make very good ones. It shouldn't be difficult. There are probably half a dozen members of this year's college who hail from Picenum.''

"Why a Picentine?''

"For one thing, he'll be inclined to favor Pompeius. They're a clannish lot, the Picentines. For another, he'll be a fire-eater. They're born breathing fire in Picenum!''

"Take care you don't end up with burned hands," said Crassus, already thinking about which of his freedmen would drive the hardest bargain with the agents who rented villas on the Pincian Hill. What a pity he'd never thought of investing in real estate there! An ideal location. All those foreign kings and queens looking for Roman palaces—no, he wouldn't rent! He'd *buy*! Rent was a disgraceful waste; a man never saw a sestertius's return.

In November the Senate gave in. Marcus Licinius Crassus was informed that he would be allowed to stand *in absentia* for the consulship. Gnaeus Pompeius Magnus was informed that the Senate had sent a decree to the Assembly of the People asking that body to waive the usual requirements—membership in the Senate, the quaestorship and praetorship—and legislate to allow him to stand for the consulship. As the Assembly of the People had passed the necessary law, the Senate was pleased to inform Gnaeus Pompeius Magnus that he would be allowed to stand *in absentia* for the consulship, et cetera, et cetera.

When a candidate stood for office *in absentia,* canvassing was difficult. He couldn't cross the *pomerium* into the city to meet the voters, chat to everyone in the Forum, pose modestly nearby when some tribune of the plebs called a *contio* of the Plebeian Assembly to discuss the merits of this favored candidate—and lambaste his rivals. Because *in absentia* required special permission from the House, it was rarely encountered, but never before had two candidates for the consulship both stood *in absentia*. However, as things turned out the usual disadvantages mattered not a bit. Debate in the Senate—even under the threat of those two undischarged armies—had been as feverishly hot as it had been protracted; when the House gave in at last, every other candidate for the consulship had withdrawn from the contest as a protest against the blatant illegality of Pompey's candidature. If there were no other candidates, Pompey and Crassus would look what they were: dictators in disguise.

Many and varied were the threats called down upon Pompey's head and Crassus's head, mostly in the form of prosecution for treason the moment imperium was lost; so when the tribune of the plebs Marcus Lollius Palicanus (a man from Picenum) called a special meeting of the Plebeian Assembly in the Circus Flaminius on the Campus Martius, every senator who had turned his back on Pompey and Crassus sat up with a shock of realization. They were going to wriggle out of treason charges by bringing back the full powers of the tribunate of the plebs and having ten grateful tribunes of the plebs legislate them immunity from the consequences of their actions!

Many in Rome wanted to see the restoration, most people because the tribunate of the plebs was a hallowed institution in proper harmony with the *mos maiorum,* and not a few people because they missed the vigor and buzz of the old days in the lower Forum Romanum when some militant demagogue fired up the Plebs until fists swung and hired ex-gladiators waded into the fray. So Lollius Palicanus's meeting, widely advertised as being to discuss the restoration of the tribunate of the plebs, was bound to attract crowds. But when the news got round that the consular candidates Pompey and Crassus were going to speak in support of Palicanus, enthusiasm reached heights unknown since Sulla had turned the Plebeian Assembly into a rather attenuated men's club.

. Used for the less well patronized games, the Circus Flaminius held a mere fifty thousand people; but on the day of Palicanus's meeting every bleacher was full. Resigned to the fact that no one save those lucky enough to be within a couple of hundred feet would hear a word, most of those who had streamed out along the bank of the Tiber had only come so that they could tell their grandchildren that they had been there on the day two consular candidates who were also military heroes had promised to restore the tribunate of the plebs. Because they would do it! They would!

Palicanus opened the meeting with a rousing speech aimed at procuring the most possible votes for Pompey and Crassus at the curule elections; those close enough to hear were those high enough in the classes to have a worthwhile vote. All Palicanus's nine colleagues were present, and all spoke in support of Pompey and Crassus. Then Crassus appeared to great applause and spoke to great applause. A nice series of preliminary entertainments before the main performance. And here he came, Pompey the Great! Clad in glittering golden armor as bright as the sun, looking absolutely gorgeous. He did not have to be an orator; for all the crowd cared, he might have recited gibberish.

The crowd had come to *see* Pompey the Great, and went home deliriously satisfied.

No surprise then that when the curule elections took place on the day before the Nones of December, Pompey was voted in as senior consul and Crassus as his junior. Rome was going to have a consul who had never been a member of the Senate—and Rome had preferred him to his more elderly and orthodox colleague.

"So Rome has her first consul who was never a senator," said Caesar to Crassus after the election gathering had dispersed. He was sitting with Crassus on the loggia of the Pincian villa where once King Jugurtha of Numidia had sat plotting; Crassus had bought the property after he saw the long list of illustrious foreign names who had rented it over the years. Both of them were looking at the public slaves clearing up the enclosures, bridges and voting platforms from the Saepta.

"For no other reason than that he *wanted* to be consul," said Crassus, aping the peevish note Pompey put into his voice whenever he was thwarted. "He's a big baby!"

"In some ways, yes." Caesar turned his head to glance at Crassus's face, which bore its usual placid expression. "It's you who'll have to do the governing. He doesn't know how."

"Oh, don't I know! Though he must have absorbed something by now from Varro's handy little instant manual on senatorial and consular conduct," said Crassus, and grunted. "I ask you! The senior consul having to peruse a manual of behavior! I have these wonderful visions of what Cato the Censor would say."

"He's asked me to draft the law returning all its powers to the tribunate of the plebs, did he tell you?"

"When does he ever tell me anything?"

"I declined."

"Why?"

"First of all, because he assumed he'd be senior consul."

"He *knew* he'd be senior consul!"

"And secondly, you're perfectly capable of drafting any law the pair of you might want to promulgate—you were urban praetor!"

Crassus shook his huge head, put his hand on Caesar's arm. "Do it, Caesar. It will keep him happy. Like all spoiled big babies, he has a gift for using the right people to achieve his ends. If you decline because you don't care to be used, that's all right by me. But if you'd like the challenge and you think it would add to your legislative experience, then do it. No one is going to know—he'll make sure of that.''

"How right you are!'' laughed Caesar, then sobered. ''I would like to do it, as a matter of fact. We haven't had decent tribunes of the plebs since I was a boy—Sulpicius was the last. And I can foresee a time when all of us might need tribunician laws. It has been very interesting for a patrician to associate with the tribunes of the plebs the way I have been lately. Palicanus has a replacement ready for me, by the way.''

"Who?''

"A Plautius. Not one of the old family Silvanus. This one is from Picenum and seems to go back to a freedman. A good fellow. He's prepared to do whatever I need done through the newly revitalized Plebeian Assembly.''

"The tribunician elections haven't been held yet. Plautius may not get in,'' said Crassus.

"He'll get in,'' said Caesar confidently. ''He can't lose—he's Pompeius's man.''

"And isn't that an indictment of our times?''

"Pompeius is lucky having you for a colleague, Marcus Crassus. I keep seeing Metellus Little Goat there instead. A disaster! But I am sorry that you haven't the distinction of being senior consul.''

Crassus smiled, it seemed without rancor. ''Don't worry, Caesar. I am reconciled.'' He sighed. ''However, it would be nice to see Rome mourn my passing more than she does Pompeius's passing when we leave office.''

"Well,'' said Caesar, rising, ''it's time I went home. I have devoted little time to the women of my family since I came back to Rome, and they'll be dying to hear all the election news.''

But one glance at his reception room caused Caesar to rue his decision to go home; it appeared to be full of women! A count of heads reduced full to six—his mother, his wife, his sister Ju-Ju, his Aunt Julia, Pompey's wife, and another woman closer inspection placed as his cousin Julia called Julia Antonia because she was married to Marcus Antonius, the pirate eradicator. Everyone's attention was focused on her, not surprising: she was perched on the edge of a chair with her legs stretched out rigidly before her, and she was bawling.

Before Caesar could move any further, someone gave him a tremendous buffet in the small of the back, and he whipped around to see a big, unmistakably Antonian child standing there grinning. Not for long! Caesar's hand went out to grasp the boy painfully by his nose, dragged him forward. Howls quite as loud as those his mother was producing erupted from his gaping mouth, but he wasn't about to curl into a helpless ball; he lashed out with one big foot at Caesar's shins, doubled his hands into fists and swung with both of them. At the same time two other, smaller boys dived on Caesar too, pummeling his sides and chest, though the immense folds of toga prevented this triple assault from inflicting any real damage.

Then too quickly for anyone to see how it was done, all three boys were rendered *hors de combat*. The two smaller ones Caesar dealt with by banging their heads together with an audible crack and throwing them heavily against the wall; the biggest boy got a wallop on the side of the face that made his eyes water, and was marched to join his brothers in a jerking progress punctuated by resounding kicks on his backside.

The bawling mother had ceased her plaints when all this had begun, and now leaped from her chair to descend upon the tormentor of her darling precious sons.

"*Sit down, woman!*" roared Caesar in a huge voice.

She tottered back to her chair and collapsed, bawling.

He turned back to where the three boys half-lay, half-sat against the wall, blubbering as lustily as their mother.

"If any one of you moves, he'll wish he'd never been born. This is my house, not the Pincian menagerie, and while you're guests in it you'll behave like civilized Romans, not Tingitanian apes. Is that quite clear?"

Holding the crumpled disorder of dirty toga around him, he walked through the midst of the women to the door of his study. "I am going to rectify the damage," he said in the deceptively quiet tones his mother and wife recognized as temper reined in by an iron hold, "and when I return, I expect to see a beautiful peace descended. Shut that wretched woman up if you have to gag her, and give her sons to Burgundus. Tell Burgundus he has my full permission to strangle them if necessary."

Caesar was not gone long, but when he returned it was to find the boys vanished and the six women sitting bolt upright in utter silence. Six pairs of enormous eyes followed him as he went to sit between his mother and his wife.

"Well, Mater, what's the trouble?" he asked pleasantly.

"Marcus Antonius is dead," Aurelia explained, "by his own hand, in Crete. You know that he was defeated by the pirates twice on the water and once on the land, and lost all his ships and men. But you may not know that the pirate *strategoi* Panares and Lasthenes literally forced him to sign a treaty between Rome and the Cretan people. The treaty has just arrived in Rome, accompanied by poor Marcus Antonius's ashes. Though the Senate hasn't had time to meet about it, they are already saying around the city that Marcus

Antonius has disgraced his name forever—people are even beginning to refer to him as Marcus Antonius *Creticus*! But they don't mean Crete, they mean Man of Chalk.''

Caesar sighed, his face betraying exasperation rather than sorrow. ''He wasn't the right man for that job,'' he said, not willing to spare the feelings of the widow, a vastly silly woman. ''I saw it when I was his tribune in Gytheum. However, I confess I didn't see precisely what the end would be. But there were plenty of signs.'' He looked at Julia Antonia. ''I'm sorry for you, lady, but I fail to see what I can do for you.''

''Julia Antonia came to see if you would organize Marcus Antonius's funeral rites,'' said Aurelia.

''But she has a brother. Why can't Lucius Caesar do it?'' asked Caesar blankly.

''Lucius Caesar is in the east with the army of Marcus Cotta, and your cousin Sextus Caesar refuses to have anything to do with it,'' said Aunt Julia. ''In the absence of Gaius Antonius Hybrida, we are the closest family Julia Antonia has in Rome.''

''In that case I will organize the obsequies. It would be wise, however, to make it a very quiet funeral.''

Julia Antonia rose to go, shedding handkerchiefs, brooches, pins, combs in what seemed an endless cascade; she seemed now to hold no umbrage against Caesar for his summary treatment of her sons—or for his dispassionate appraisal of her late husband's ability. Evidently she liked being roared at and told to behave, reflected Caesar as he escorted her toward the door. No doubt the late Marcus Antonius had obliged her! A pity he hadn't also disciplined his children, as the mother was incapable of it. Her boys were fetched from Burgundus's quarters, where they had undergone a salutary experience; the sons of Cardixa and Burgundus had dwarfed them completely. Like their mother they seemed not to have taken permanent offense. All three eyed Caesar warily.

''There's no need to be afraid of me unless you've stepped over the mark of common decent behavior,'' said Caesar cheerfully, his eyes twinkling. ''If I catch you doing that—watch out!''

''You're very tall, but you don't look all that strong to me,'' said the oldest boy, who was the handsomest of the three, though his eyes were too close together for Caesar's taste. However, they stared at him straightly enough, and their expression did not lack courage or intelligence.

''One day you'll encounter a tiny little fellow who slaps you flat on your back before you can move a finger,'' said Caesar. ''Now go home and look after your mother. And do your homework instead of prowling through the

Subura getting up to mischief and stealing from people who've done you no harm. Homework will benefit you more in the long run.''

Mark Antony blinked. ''How do you know about that?''

''I know *everything*,'' said Caesar, shutting the door on them. He returned to the rest of the women and sat down again. ''The invasion of the Germans,'' he said, smiling. ''What a frightful tribe of little boys! Does no one supervise them?''

''No one,'' said Aurelia. She heaved a sigh of pure pleasure. ''Oh, I did enjoy watching you dispose of them! My hand had been itching to administer a good spanking ever since they arrived.''

Caesar's eyes were resting on Mucia Tertia, who looked, he thought, marvelously attractive; marriage to Pompey obviously agreed with her. Mentally he added her name to his list of future conquests—Pompey had more than asked for it! But not yet. Let the abominable Kid Butcher first climb even higher. Caesar had no doubt he could succeed with Mucia Tertia; he had caught her staring at him several times. No, not yet. She needed more time to ripen on Pompey's vine before he snipped her off. At the moment he had enough on his plate dealing with Metella Little Goat, who was the wife of Gaius Verres. Now ploughing *her* furrow was one exercise in horticulture he found enormously gratifying!

His sweet little wife was watching him, so he removed his eyes from Mucia Tertia and focused them on her instead. When he dropped one lid in a wink Cinnilla had to suppress a giggle, and demonstrated that she had inherited one characteristic from her father; she blushed scarlet. A dear lady. Never jealous, though of course she heard the rumors—and probably believed them. After all these years she must surely know her Caesar! But she was too shaped by Aurelia ever to bring up the subject of his philanderings, and naturally he did not. They had nothing to do with her.

With his mother he was not so circumspect—it had been her idea in the first place to seduce the wives of his peers. Nor was he above asking her advice from time to time, when some woman proved difficult. Women were a mystery he suspected would always remain a mystery, and Aurelia's opinions were worth hearing. Now that she mixed with her peers from Palatine and Carinae she heard all the gossip and faithfully reported it to him free of embellishments. What he liked of course was to drive his women out of their minds for love of him before dropping them; it rendered them useless to their cuckolded husbands ever after.

''I suppose all of you gathered to console Julia Antonia,'' he said, wondering if his mother would have the gall to offer him sweet watered wine and little cakes.

"She arrived at my house trailing trinkets and those awful boys," said Aunt Julia, "and I knew I couldn't cope with all four of them. So I brought them here."

"And you were visiting Aunt Julia?" asked Caesar of Mucia Tertia, his smile devastating.

She drew a breath, caught it, coughed. "I visit Julia a lot, Gaius Julius. The Quirinal is very close to the Pincian."

"Yes, of course." He gave much the same smile to Aunt Julia, who was by no means impervious to it, but naturally saw it in a different way.

"I suspect I'll see a great deal more of Julia Antonia in the future, alas," said Aunt Julia, sighing. "I wish I had your technique with her sons!"

"Her visits won't go on for long, Aunt Julia, and I'll make it my business to have a little word with the boys, don't worry. Julia Antonia will be married again in no time."

"No one would have her!" said Aurelia, snorting.

"There are always men peculiarly susceptible to the charms of utterly helpless women," said Caesar. "Unfortunately she's a bad picker. So whoever she marries will prove no more satisfactory a husband than did Marcus Antonius the Man of Chalk."

"In that, my son, you are definitely right."

He turned his attention to his sister Ju-Ju, who had said not one word so far; she had always been the silent member of the family, despite owning a lively disposition. "I used to accuse Lia of being a bad picker," he said, "but I didn't give you a chance to show me what sort of picker you were, did I?"

She gave him back his own smile. "I am very well content with the husband you picked for me, Caesar. However, I'm quite prepared to admit that the young men I used to fancy before I married have all turned out rather disappointing."

"Then you'd better let Atius and me pick your daughter's husband when the time comes. Atia is going to be very beautiful. And intelligent, which means she won't appeal to everyone."

"Isn't that a pity?" asked Ju-Ju.

"That she's intelligent, or that men don't appreciate it?"

"The latter."

"*I* like intelligent women," said Caesar, "but they're few and far between. Don't worry, we'll find Atia someone who does appreciate her qualities."

Aunt Julia rose. "It will be dark soon, Caesar—I know you prefer to be called that, even by your mother. But it still comes hard to me! I must go.''

"I'll ask Lucius Decumius's boys to find you a litter and escort you,'' said Caesar.

"I have a litter,'' said Aunt Julia. "Mucia isn't allowed to go out on foot, so we traveled between the Quirinal and the Subura in extreme comfort— or we would have had we not shared the conveyance with Julia Antonia, who nearly washed us away. We also have some stout fellows to escort us.''

"And I came by litter too,'' said Ju-Ju.

"Degenerate!'' sniffed Aurelia. "You'd all do better to walk.''

"I'd love to walk,'' said Mucia Tertia softly, "but husbands don't see things the way you do, Aurelia. Gnaeus Pompeius thinks it unseemly for me to walk.''

Caesar's ears pricked. Aha! Some faint discontent! She was feeling constricted, too hedged about. But he said nothing, simply waited and chatted to everyone while a servant ran up to the crossroads square to summon the litters.

"You don't look well, Aunt Julia'' was the last subject he broached, and leaving it until he was handing her into her side of the roomy conveyance Pompey had provided for Mucia Tertia.

"I'm growing old, Caesar,'' she said in a whisper, giving his hand a squeeze. "Fifty-seven. But there's nothing the matter except that my bones ache when the weather's cold. I'm beginning to dread winters.''

"Are you warm enough up there on the outer Quirinal?'' he asked sharply. "Your house is exposed to the north wind. Shall I have your cellar fitted with a *hypocausis*?''

"Save your money, Caesar. If I need it, I can afford to install a furnace myself,'' she said, and shut the curtains.

"She isn't well, you know,'' he said to his mother as they went back into the apartment.

Aurelia thought about that, then gave measured judgement. "She'd be well enough, Caesar, if she had more to live for. But husband and son are both dead. She has no one except us and Mucia Tertia. And we are not enough.''

The reception room was ablaze with the little flames of lamps and the shutters had been closed against the chill wind percolating down the light well. It looked warm and cheery, and there on the floor with Cinnilla was Caesar's daughter, almost six years old. An exquisite child, fine-boned and graceful, so fair she had a silver look.

When she saw her father her great blue eyes sparkled; she held out her arms. *"Tata, tata!"* she cried. "Pick me up!"

He picked her up, pressed his lips against her pale pink cheek. "And how's my princess today?"

And while he listened with every sign of fascination to a litany of small and girlish doings, Aurelia and Cinnilla watched them both. Cinnilla's thoughts got no further than the fact that she loved them, but Aurelia's dwelt upon that word, princess. She is exactly that, a princess. Caesar will go far, and one day he will be very rich. The suitors will be unnumbered. But he won't be as kind to her as my mother and stepfather/uncle were to me. He will give her to the man he needs the most no matter how she feels about it. So I must train her to accept her fate, to go to it gracefully and in good spirits.

On the twenty-fourth day of December, Marcus Crassus finally celebrated his ovation. Since there had been an undeniable Samnite element in Spartacus's army, he had won two concessions from the Senate: instead of going afoot he was allowed to ride a horse; and instead of wearing the lesser crown of myrtle he was allowed to wear the triumphator's crown of laurel. A good crowd turned out to cheer him and his army, marched up from Capua for the occasion, though there were broad winks and many digs in the ribs at sight of the spoils, a poor collection. The whole of Rome knew Marcus Crassus's besetting sin.

The numbers who attended Pompey's triumph on the last day of December were much greater, however. Somehow Pompey had managed to endear himself to the people of Rome, perhaps because of his relative youth, his golden beauty, that fancied resemblance to Alexander the Great, and a certain happy cast to his features. For the love they felt for Pompey was not of the same kind as the love they had used to feel for Gaius Marius, who continued (despite all Sulla's efforts) to remain the favorite person in living memory.

At about the same time that the curule elections were being held in Rome early in December, Metellus Pius finally crossed the Alps into Italian Gaul with his army, which he proceeded to disband before settling its troops in the wide rich lands to the north of the Padus River. Whether because he had sensed something in Pompey toward the end of their period together in Spain that had caused him to suspect that Pompey would not be content with a return to obscurity, the Piglet had remained obdurately aloof from the troubles in Rome. When written to in appeal by Catulus, Hortensius and the other prestigious Caecilii Metelli, he had refused to discuss matters which, he maintained, his long absence in Spain disqualified him from commenting upon. And when he did reach Rome at the end of January he celebrated a modest triumph with those troops who had accompanied him to Rome for the occasion, and took his seat in a Senate supervised by Pompey and Crassus as if nothing whatsoever was amiss. It was an attitude which spared him much pain, though it also meant he never did receive as much credit for the defeat of Quintus Sertorius as he deserved.

The *lex Pompeia Licinia de tribunicia potestate* was tabled in the House early in January under the aegis of Pompey, who held the *fasces* as senior consul. The popularity of this law, restoring as it did full powers to the tribunate of the plebs, flattened senatorial opposition. All those whom Pompey and Crassus had thought to hear roaring against it in the House contented themselves with a few bleats; the *senatus consultum* recommending to the Assembly of the People that the law be passed was obtained by a near unanimous vote. Some had quibbled that it should by rights have gone to the Centuriate Assembly for ratification, but Caesar, Hortensius and Cicero all asserted firmly that only a tribal assembly could ratify measures involving the tribes. Within the three stipulated market days, the *lex Pompeia Licinia* passed into law. Once more the tribunes of the plebs could veto laws and magistrates, bring forward plebiscites having the force of law in their Plebeian Assembly without the senatorial blessing of a *senatus consultum,* and even prosecute for treason, extortion and other gubernatorial transgressions.

Caesar was speaking in the House on a regular basis now; since he was always worth listening to—witty, interesting, brief, pungent—he soon gathered a following, and was asked with ever increasing frequency to publish his speeches, considered every bit as good as Cicero's. Even Cicero had been heard to say that Caesar was the best orator in Rome—after himself, that is.

Anxious to utilize some of his newly restored powers, the tribune of the plebs Plautius announced in the Senate that he was going to legislate in the Plebeian Assembly to give back their citizenships and rights to those condemned with Lepidus and with Quintus Sertorius. Caesar rose at once to speak in favor of the law, and pleaded with very moving eloquence to extend this measure to include all those proscribed by Sulla. Yet when the Senate refused to grant the extension and endorsed the Plautian law only in respect of those outlawed for following Lepidus and Sertorius, Caesar looked strangely cheerful, not at all put out.

"The House turned you down, Caesar," said Marcus Crassus, puzzled, "yet here I find you positively purring!"

"My dear Crassus, I knew perfectly well they'd never sanction a pardon for Sulla's proscribed!" said Caesar, smiling. "It would mean too many important men who got fat off the proscriptions must give everything back.

No, no! However, it looked very much as if the Catulus rump was going to succeed in blocking pardons for the Lepidans and Sertorians, so I made that measure look modest enough to seem inviting by harping on Sulla's proscribed. If you want something done and you think it's going to be opposed, Marcus Crassus, always go much further than what you want. The opposition becomes so incensed by the additions that it quite loses sight of the fact that it originally opposed the lesser measure.''

Crassus grinned. "You're a politician to the core, Caesar. I hope some of your opponents don't study your methods too closely, or you'll find life harder than it is."

"I love politics," said Caesar simply.

"You love everything you do, so you jump in boots and all. That's your secret. Well, that and the size of your mind."

"Don't flatter me, Crassus, my head is quite large enough," said Caesar, who loved to pun on the fact that "head" meant what resided on a man's shoulders—and also meant what resided between a man's legs.

"Too big, if you ask me," said Crassus, laughing. "You'd better be a little more discreet in your dealings with other men's wives, at least for the time being. I hear our new censors are going to examine the senatorial rolls the way a sedulous nursemaid looks for nits."

There were censors for the first time since Sulla had cut that office from the list of magistracies; an unlikely, peculiar pair in Gnaeus Cornelius Lentulus Clodianus and Lucius Gellius Poplicola. Everyone knew they were Pompey's hirelings, but when Pompey had mooted their names in the House, the more appropriate men who had planned to run for censor—Catulus and Metellus Pius, Vatia Isauricus and Curio—all withdrew, leaving the field clear for Clodianus and Gellius.

Crassus's prediction was right. It was normal censorial practice to let all the State contracts first, but after letting the sacred contracts for feeding the Capitoline geese and chickens and other religious matters, Clodianus and Gellius proceeded to the senatorial rolls. Their findings were read out at a special *contio* they called from the rostra in the lower Forum Romanum, and created a huge stir. No less than sixty-four senators were expelled, most of them for being under suspicion of having taken bribes (or given out bribes) when on jury duty. Many of the jurors at the trial of Statius Albius Oppianicus were expelled, and the successful prosecutor of Oppianicus, his stepson Cluentius, was demoted by being transferred from his rural tribe to urban Esquilina. But more sensational by far were the expulsions of one of last year's quaestors,

Quintus Curius, last year's senior consul, Publius Cornelius Lentulus Sura, and Gaius Antonius Hybrida, the Monster of Lake Orchomenus.

It was not impossible for an expelled senator to re-enter the House, but he could not expect to do it through the offices of the censors who had expelled him; he had to stand for election as either a quaestor or a tribune of the plebs. A wearisome business for Lentulus Sura, who had already been consul! And not one he contemplated immediately, for Lentulus Sura was in love, and didn't care very much about the Senate. Shortly after his expulsion he married the feckless Julia Antonia. Caesar had been right. Julia Antonia was a poor picker of husbands, and Lentulus Sura a worse choice than Marcus Antonius the Man of Chalk.

The Senate finished with, Clodianus and Gellius went back to contract letting, this time civilian rather than sacred. These mostly concerned the farming of provincial taxes and tithes, though they also covered the erection or restoration of numerous State-owned buildings and public facilities, from the refurbishment of latrines to circus bleachers, bridge making, basilicae. Again there was a huge stir; the censors announced that they were abandoning the system of taxation Sulla had brought in to relieve Asia Province.

Lucullus and Marcus Cotta had pursued their war against King Mithridates to what seemed a successful conclusion, though the laurels definitely belonged to Lucullus. The year of the Pompey and Crassus consulship saw Mithridates obliged to flee to the court of his son-in-law Tigranes of Armenia (where Tigranes refused to see him), and Lucullus just about in full possession of Pontus as well as Cappadocia and Bithynia; only Tigranes remained to be dealt with. His hands free to bury themselves in some much-needed administrative work, Lucullus promptly began to see to the tangled financial affairs of Asia Province, which he had been governing in tandem with Cilicia for three years. And cracked down on the tax-farming *publicani* so hard that on two occasions he exercised his right within his province to execute and had several of these men beheaded, as had Marcus Aemilius Scaurus some years earlier.

The squeals of outrage in Rome were enormous, especially when Lucullus's reforms made it even more difficult for the tax-farmers to operate at a maximum profit than had Sulla's. A member of the arch-conservative senatorial rump, Lucullus had never been popular in high business circles, which meant that men like Crassus and Atticus loathed him. Perhaps because alone among the current crop of generals Lucullus bade fair to eclipsing him, Pompey too disliked Lucullus.

It was therefore no surprise when Pompey's pair of tame censors announced that Sulla's system in Asia Province was to be abandoned; things would go back to the way they had been in the old pre-Sullan days.

But all of this made no difference to Lucullus, who ignored the censorial directives. While ever he was governor of Asia Province, he said, he would continue with Sulla's system, which was a model and ought to be implemented in every one of Rome's provinces. The hastily shaped companies which had marshaled men to go out to Asia Province faltered, voices were raised in Forum and Senate, and all the most powerful knights thundered that Lucullus must be dismissed as governor.

Still Lucullus continued to ignore directives from Rome, and to ignore his precarious position. More important to him by far was the tidying up which always followed in the wake of big wars; by the time he left his two provinces they would be *proper*.

Though he was not by nature or inclination attracted to arch-conservative senators like Catulus and Lucullus, Caesar nonetheless had cause to be grateful to Lucullus; he had received a letter from Queen Oradaltis of Bithynia.

My daughter has come home, Caesar. I'm sure you know that Lucius Licinius Lucullus has had great success in his war against King Mithridates, and that for a year now he has been campaigning in Pontus itself. Among the many fortresses the King maintained, Cabeira had always been thought to be his strongest. But this year it fell to Lucullus, who found all sorts of horrible things—the dungeons were full of political prisoners and potentially dangerous relatives who had been tortured, or used as specimens by the King in his constant experimentations with poison. I will not dwell upon such hideous matters, I am too happy.

Among the women Lucullus found in residence was Nysa. She had been there for nearly twenty years, and has come home to me a woman of more than sixty. However, Mithridates had treated her well according to his lights—she was held to be no different from the small collection of minor wives and concubines he kept in Cabeira. He also kept some of his sisters there whom he didn't wish to see marry or have any opportunity to bear children, so my poor girl had plenty of spinsterly company. For that matter, the King has so many wives and concubines that those in Cabeira had also been living like spinsters for years! A colony of old maids.

When Lucullus opened up their prison he was very kind to all the women he found, and took exquisite care that there should be no masculine offense offered to them. The way Nysa tells it, he behaved as did Alexander the Great toward the mother, wives and other harem members of the third King Darius. I believe Lucullus sent the Pontic women to his ally in Cimmeria, the son of Mithridates called Machares.

Nysa he freed completely the moment he discovered who she was. But more than that, Caesar. He loaded her down with gold and presents and sent her back to me under an escort of troops sworn to honor her. Can you imagine this aged, never very beautiful woman's pleasure at journeying through the countryside as free as any bird?

Oh, and to see her again! I knew nothing until she walked through the front door of my villa in Rheba, glowing like a young girl. She was so happy to see me! My last wish has come true, I have my daughter back.

She came just in time. My dear old dog, Sulla, died of antiquity a month before her advent, and I despaired. The servants tried desperately to persuade me to get another dog, but you know how it is. You think of all the special wonders and laughable antics that beloved pet has owned, his place in your family life, and it seems such a betrayal to bury him, then hurry some other creature into his basket. I'm not saying it's wrong to do so, but a little time has to go by before the new pet takes on characteristics special to him, and I very much fear I would have been dead before any new pet became a person in his own right.

No need for dying now! Nysa wept to find her father gone, of course, but we have settled down here together in such harmony and delight—we both handline fish from the jetty and stroll through the village for our constitutional. Lucullus did invite us to live in the palace at Nicomedia, but we have decided to remain where we are. And we have a dear little pup named Lucullus.

Please, Caesar, try to find the time to journey to the east again! I would so much like you to meet Nysa, and I miss you dreadfully.

It was last year's tribune of the plebs, Marcus Lollius Palicanus, whom the delegates from all the cities of Sicily except Syracuse and Messana approached to prosecute Gaius Verres. But Palicanus referred them to Pompey, and Pompey in turn referred them to Marcus Tullius Cicero as the ideal man for that particular job.

Verres had gone to Sicily as its governor after his urban praetorship, and—mostly thanks to Spartacus—remained its governor for three years. He had only just returned to Rome when the Sicilian delegation sought out Cicero during January. Both Pompey and Palicanus were personally concerned; Palicanus had gone to the assistance of some of his clients when Verres persecuted them, and Pompey had amassed a considerable number of clients in Sicily during his occupation of it on Sulla's behalf.

Quaestor in Lilybaeum under Sextus Peducaeus the year before Verres arrived to govern Sicily in Peducaeus's place, Cicero had developed an enormous fondness for Sicily too. Not to mention having amassed a nice little retinue of clients. Yet when the Sicilians came to see him, he backed away.

"I never prosecute," he explained. "I defend."

"But Gnaeus Pompeius Magnus recommended you! He said you were the only man who could win. Please, we beg of you, break your rule and prosecute Gaius Verres! If we do not win Sicily could well rise up against Rome."

"Raped the place, did he?" asked Cicero clinically.

"Yes, he raped it. But having raped it, Marcus Tullius, he then dismembered it. We have nothing left! All our works of art are gone from every temple, paintings and statues both, and any valuables in the hands of private owners—what can we say about a man who actually had the temerity to enslave a *free woman* famous for her tapestry work and make her run a factory for his profit? He stole the moneys the Treasury of Rome gave him to purchase grain, then commandeered the grain from the growers without paying for it! He has stolen farms, estates, even inheritances. The list is endless!"

This catalogue of perfidies startled Cicero greatly, but still he shook his head. "I'm sorry, but I do not prosecute."

The spokesman drew a breath. "Then we will go home," he said. "We had thought that a man so knowledgeable about Sicily's history that he went to great trouble to rediscover the whereabouts of the tomb of Archimedes would see our plight, and help. But you have lost your affection for Sicily, and clearly you do not value Gnaeus Pompeius as he values you."

To be reminded of Pompey and of a famous coup—he had indeed rediscovered the lost tomb of Archimedes outside the city of Syracuse—was too much. Prosecution in Cicero's opinion was a waste of his talents, for the (highly illegal) fees were always far less than the inducements offered by some sweating ex-governor or *publicanus* in danger of losing everything. Nor (such was the mentality of men) was it popular to prosecute! The prosecuting advocate was always seen as a nasty piece of work determined to make a ruin out of some hapless individual's life, whereas the defending advocate who got the hapless individual off was a popular hero. It made not the slightest difference that most of these hapless individuals were cunning, avaricious and guilty to the extreme; any threat to a man's right to conduct his life as he saw fit was bound to be considered an infringement of his personal entitlements.

Cicero sighed. ''Very well, very well, I will take the case!'' he said. ''But you must remember that the defending attorneys speak after the prosecuting team, so that the jury has clean forgotten every word the prosecution said by the time it is given the directive to find a verdict. You must also remember that Gaius Verres is very highly connected. His wife is a Caecilia Metella, the man who should have been consul this year is his brother-in-law, he has another brother-in-law who is the present governor of Sicily—you'll get no help from that quarter, and nor will I!—and every other Caecilius Metellus will be on his side. If I prosecute, then Quintus Hortensius will defend, and other advocates almost as famous will join him as his juniors. I said I will take the case. That does not mean I think I can win.''

The delegation had hardly left his house before Cicero was regretting his decision; who needed to offend every Caecilius Metellus in Rome when his chances of becoming consul rested on the slender base of personal ability in the law courts? He was as much a New Man as his detested fellow man from Arpinum, Gaius Marius, but he didn't have a soldiering bone in his body and a New Man's progress was harder if he could not earn fame on the battlefield.

Of course he knew why he had accepted; that absurd loyalty he felt he owed to Pompey. The years might be many and the legal accolades multiple, but how could he ever forget the careless kindness of a seventeen-year-old cadet toward the cadet his father despised? As long as he lived Cicero would be grateful to Pompey for helping him through that ghastly, miserable military experience in the ranks of Pompey Strabo's cadets; for shielding him from Pompey Strabo's indifferent cruelties and terrifying rages. No other hand had been raised to assist him, yet young Pompey, the general's son, had raised his hand. He had been warm that winter thanks to Pompey, he had been given clerical duties thanks to Pompey, he had never needed to lift a sword in battle thanks to Pompey. And he could never, never forget it.

So off to the Carinae he betook himself to see Pompey.

''I just wanted to tell you,'' he said in a voice of doom, ''that I have decided to prosecute Gaius Verres.''

''Oh, splendid!'' said Pompey heartily. ''A lot of Verres's victims are— or sometimes *were*—my clients. You can win, I know you can. And name your favors.''

''I need no favors from you, Magnus, and you can never be in any doubt that it is I who owe you.''

Pompey looked startled. ''You do? On what account?''

''You made my year with your father's army bearable.''

"Oh, that!" Laughing, Pompey shook Cicero by the arm. "I hardly think that's worth a lifetime's gratitude."

"To me it is," said Cicero, tears in his eyes. "We shared a lot during the Italian War."

Perhaps Pompey was remembering less palatable things they had shared, like the search for his father's naked and insulted body, for he shook his head as if to banish the Italian War from his mind, and gave Cicero a beaker of excellent wine. "Well, my friend, you just let me know what I can do to assist you now."

"I will," said Cicero gratefully.

"All those Little Goat men of the Caecilii Metelli will be against this prosecution, of course," said Pompey thoughtfully. "So will Catulus, Hortensius, others."

"And you've just mentioned the main reason why I have to get this case heard early enough in the year. I daren't run the risk of having the case bound over until next year—Little Goat and Hortensius will be consuls then, everyone seems to be saying."

"A pity in a way," said Pompey. "Next year there may well be knight juries again, and that would go against Verres."

"Not if the consuls rig the court behind the scenes, Magnus. Besides, there's no guarantee our praetor Lucius Cotta will find in favor of knight juries. I was talking to him the other day—he thinks his enquiries into the composition of court juries are going to take months—and he's not convinced knight juries will be any better than senatorial ones. Knights can't be prosecuted for taking bribes."

"We can change the law," said Pompey, who, having no respect for the law, thought that whenever it became inconvenient it should be changed— to suit himself, naturally.

"That could prove difficult."

"I don't see why."

"Because," said Cicero patiently, "to change that law would mean enacting another law in one of the two tribal Assemblies—both dominated by knights."

"They've indemnified Crassus and me against our action last year," said Pompey, unable to distinguish the difference between one law and another.

"That is because you've been very nice to them, Magnus. And they want you to go on being very nice to them. A law making them culpable for accepting bribes is quite a separate pot of stew."

"Oh, well, perhaps as you say Lucius Cotta won't find in favor of knight juries. It was just a thought."

Cicero rose to go. "Thank you again, Magnus."

"Keep me informed."

One month later Cicero notified the urban praetor, Lucius Cotta, that he would be prosecuting Gaius Verres in the Extortion Court on behalf of the cities of Sicily, and that he would be asking for the sum of forty-two and a half million sesterces—one thousand seven hundred talents—in damages, as well as for the restoration of all works of art and valuables stolen from Sicily's temples and citizens.

Though he had come back from Sicily swaggering, confident that his position as the brother-in-law of Metellus Little Goat would be adequate protection against possible prosecution, when Gaius Verres heard that Cicero—Cicero, who *never* prosecuted!—had lodged an intention to prosecute, he panicked. Word was sent immediately to his brother-in-law Lucius Metellus the governor of Sicily to bury any evidence Verres himself might have overlooked in his rush to remove his plunder from the island. Significantly, neither Syracuse nor Messana had joined with the other cities to press charges; that was due to the fact that Syracuse and Messana had aided and abetted Verres, and shared in the proceeds of his nefarious activities. But how fortunate that the new governor was his wife's middle brother!

The two brothers left in Rome, Quintus called Little Goat (who was certain to be consul next year) and the youngest of the three sons of Metellus Caprarius, Marcus, hastily conferred with Verres to see what could be done to avert the disaster of a trial, and agreed to bring Quintus Hortensius into the case. Certainly Hortensius would lead the defense if the matter came to court, but at this stage what was needed was a ploy aimed at averting a trial, especially one conducted by Cicero.

In March, Hortensius lodged a complaint with the urban praetor; Cicero, he alleged, was not the proper man to prosecute any case against Gaius Verres. Instead of Cicero, Hortensius nominated Quintus Caecilius Niger, a relative of the Little Goats who had been Verres's quaestor in Sicily during the middle one of his three years as governor. The only way Cicero's fitness to prosecute could be determined was to hold a special hearing called a *divinatio*—guess-work (so named because the judges at this special hearing reached a conclusion without hard evidence being presented—that is, they arrived at a finding by guesswork). Each prospective prosecutor was required to tell the judges why he ought to be the chief prosecutor, and after listening to Caecilius Niger, who spoke poorly, and Cicero, the judges found in favor of Cicero and directed that the case be heard quickly.

Verres, the two Metellus Little Goats and Hortensius had to think again.

"You'll be praetor next year, Marcus," said the great advocate to the youngest brother, "so we'll have to make sure the lots fall on you to become president of the Extortion Court. This year's president, Glabrio, loathes Gaius Verres. And if for no other reason than that he loathes you, Verres, Glabrio won't allow the slightest breath of scandal to touch his court—yes, what I'm saying is that if the case is heard this year and Glabrio is court president, we won't be able to bribe the jury. And don't forget that this year Lucius Cotta will be watching every important jury like a cat a mouse. Because this case will attract a lot of attention, I think Lucius Cotta is going to base much of his opinion about the fitness of all-senator juries on it. As for Pompeius and Crassus—they don't love us at all!"

"You mean," said Gaius Verres, whose brass-colored beauty was looking a little tarnished these days, "that we have to get my case held over until next year, when Marcus will be president of the Extortion Court."

"Exactly," said Hortensius. "Quintus Metellus and I will be the consuls next year—a great help! It won't be difficult for us to rig the lots to give Marcus the Extortion Court, and it makes no difference whether next year's juries are senatorial or equestrian—we'll bribe!"

"But it's only April," said Verres gloomily. "I don't see how we can stall proceedings until the end of the year."

"Oh, we can," said Hortensius confidently. "In these cases where evidence has to be gathered at a far distance from Rome—*and* up and down a country as big as Sicily!—it takes any prosecutor six to eight months to prepare his case. I know Cicero hasn't begun because he's still here in Rome, and hasn't sent any agents out to Sicily yet. Naturally he'll hope to pull in evidence and witnesses fast, and that's where Lucius Metellus comes in—as the governor of Sicily, he will put every obstacle possible in the path of Cicero or his agents."

Hortensius beamed. "I predict that Cicero won't be ready before October, if then. Of course that's time enough for a trial. But we won't let it be! Because we will apply to try another case in Glabrio's court ahead of yours, Gaius Verres. The victim will have to be someone who has left a trail of hard evidence behind him that we can gather very quickly. Some poor wretch who extorted in a minor way, not an important fish like the governor of a province. We should choose the prefect of an administrative district in—say, Greece. I have a victim in mind—we will have enough evidence to satisfy the urban praetor that we have a case by the end of Quinctilis. Cicero can't possibly be ready by then. But we will be!''

"Which victim are you thinking of?'' asked Metellus Little Goat, looking relieved; naturally he and his brothers had shared in Gaius Verres's profits, but that didn't mean he was willing to suffer a brother-in-law exiled and disgraced for extortion.

"I'm thinking of that Quintus Curtius who was Varro Lucullus's legate, and was prefect of Achaea while Varro Lucullus was governor of Macedonia. If Varro Lucullus hadn't been so busy in Thrace conquering the Bessi and taking boat rides down the Danubius all the way to the sea, he would have ensured that Curtius was prosecuted himself. But by the time he came home and found out about Curtius's little peculations he deemed it too late and too minor to bother about, so he never instituted proceedings. But the evidence is there for the gathering, and Varro Lucullus would be delighted to help land our little fish. I'll lodge an application with the urban praetor to have the case against Quintus Curtius heard this year in the Extortion Court,'' said Hortensius.

"Which means,'' said Verres eagerly, "that Lucius Cotta will direct Glabrio to hear whichever of the two cases is ready first, and as you say, it will be Curtius. Then once you're in court you'll drag the proceedings out until the end of the year! Cicero and my trial will have to wait. Brilliant, Quintus Hortensius, absolutely brilliant!''

"Yes, I think it's pretty cunning,'' said Hortensius smugly.

"Cicero will be furious,'' said Metellus Little Goat.

"I'd *adore* to see that!'' said Hortensius.

But they didn't see Cicero worked into a fury after all. The moment he heard that Hortensius had applied to try an ex-prefect of Achaea in the Extortion Court, he understood exactly what Hortensius was aiming at. Dismay smote him, followed by despair.

His beloved cousin Lucius Cicero was visiting from Arpinum, and saw the instant that Cicero entered his study how disturbed he was. "What's wrong?'' asked Lucius Cicero.

"Hortensius! He's going to have another case ready to be heard in the Extortion Court before I can assemble my evidence to try Gaius Verres.'' Cicero sat down, the picture of depression. "We'll be held over until next year—and I'd be willing to bet my entire fortune that the Metelli Little Goats have already cooked it up with Hortensius to make sure Marcus Little Goat is the praetor in charge of next year's Extortion Court.''

"And Gaius Verres will be acquitted,'' said Lucius Cicero.

"Bound to be! Can't not be!"

"Then you'll have to be ready first," said Lucius Cicero.

"What, before the end of Quinctilis? That's the date our friend Hortensius has asked the urban praetor to put aside. I can't be ready by then! Sicily is huge, the present governor is Verres's brother-in-law and will impede me wherever I go—I can't, can't, *can't* do it, I tell you!"

"Of course you can," said Lucius Cicero, standing up and looking brisk. "Dear Marcus Tullius, when you sink your teeth into a case no one is smoother or better organized. You're so orderly and logical, you have such method! And you know Sicily very well, you have friends there—including many who suffered at the hands of the frightful Gaius Verres. Yes, the governor will try to slow you down, but all those people Verres injured will be trying even harder to speed you up! It is the end of April now. Get your work in Rome finished within two market intervals. While you do that I will arrange for a ship to take us to Sicily, and to Sicily the pair of us will go by the middle of May. Come on, Marcus, you can do it!"

"Would you really come with me, Lucius?" asked Cicero, face lightening. "You're almost as well organized as I am, you'd be the most tremendous help to me." His natural enthusiasm was returning; suddenly the task didn't seem quite so formidable. "I'll have to see my clients. I don't have enough money to hire fast ships and gallop all over Sicily in two-wheeled gigs harnessed to racing mules." He slapped one hand on his desk. "By Jupiter, Lucius, I'd love to do it! If only to see the look on Hortensius's face!"

"Then do it we will!" cried Lucius, grinning. "Fifty days from Rome to Rome, that's all the time we'll be able to spare. Ten days to travel, forty days to gather evidence."

And while Lucius Cicero went off to the Porticus Aemilia in the Port of Rome to talk to shipping agents, Cicero went round to the house on the Quirinal where his clients were staying.

He knew the senior of them well—Hiero of Lilybaeum, who had been *ethnarch* of that important western Sicilian port city when Cicero had been quaestor there.

"My cousin Lucius and I are going to have to gather all our Sicilian evidence within fifty days," Cicero explained, "if I am to beat Hortensius's case into court. We *can* do it—but only if you're willing to bear the expense." He flushed. "I am not a rich man, Hiero, I can't afford speedy transport. There may be some people I have to pay for information or items I need, and there will certainly be witnesses I'll have to bring to Rome."

Hiero had always liked and admired Cicero, whose time in Lilybaeum had been a joy for every Sicilian Greek doing business with Rome's quaestor, for Cicero was quick, brilliant, innovative when it came to account books and fiscal problems, and a splendid administrator. He had also been liked and admired because he was such a rarity: an honest man.

"We are happy to advance you whatever you need, Marcus Tullius," said Hiero, "but I think now is a good time to discuss the matter of your fee. We have little to give except cash moneys, and I understand Roman advocates are averse to accepting cash moneys—too easy for the censors to trace. Art works and the like are the customary donatives, I know. But we have nothing left worthy of you."

"Oh, don't worry about that!" said Cicero cheerfully. "I know exactly what I want as a fee. I intend to run for plebeian aedile for next year. My games will be adequate, but I cannot compete with the really rich men who are usually aediles. Whereas I can win a great deal of popularity if I distribute cheap grain. Pay me in grain, Hiero—it is the one thing made of gold that springs out of the ground each and every year as a fresh crop. I will buy it from you out of my aedilician fines, but they won't run to more than two sesterces the *modius*. If you guarantee to sell me grain for that price to the amount I require, I will ask no other fee of you. Provided, that is, I win your case."

"Done!" said Hiero instantly, and turned his attention to making out a draft on his bank for ten talents in Cicero's name.

Marcus and Lucius Cicero were away exactly fifty days, during which time they worked indefatigably gathering their evidence and witnesses. And though the governor, various pirates, the magistrates of Syracuse and Messana (and a few Roman tax-farmers) tried to slow their progress down, there were far more people—some of great influence—interested in speeding them up. While the quaestorian records in Syracuse were either missing or inadequate, the quaestorian records in Lilybaeum yielded mines of evidence. Witnesses came forward, so did accountants and merchants, not to mention grain farmers. Fortune favored Cicero too; when it came time to go home and only four days of the fifty were left, the weather held so perfectly that he, Lucius and all the witnesses and records were able to make the voyage to Ostia in a sleek, light, open boat. They arrived in Rome on the last day of June, with a month left in which to get the case organized.

In the course of that month Cicero stood as a candidate for plebeian aedile as well as working on the lawsuit. How he fitted everything in was afterward a mystery to him; but the truth was that Cicero never functioned better than when his desk was so loaded with work that he could hardly see over the top of it. Decisions flickered like shafts of lightning, everything fell into place, the silver tongue and the golden voice produced wit and wisdom spontaneously, the fine-looking head, so massive and bulbous, struck everyone who saw it as noble, and the striking person who sometimes cowered inside Cicero's darkest corner was on full display. During the course of that month he even devised a completely new technique for conducting a trial, a technique which would do what so far Roman legal procedures had never managed to do—get an overwhelming mass of hard and damning evidence in front of a jury so quickly and effectively that it left the defense with no defense.

His reappearance from Sicily after what seemed an absence of scant days had Hortensius gasping, especially as gathering a case against the hapless Quintus Curtius had not proven as easy as Hortensius had surmised—even with the willing assistance of Varro Lucullus, Atticus and the city of Athens. However, a moment's cool reflection served to convince Hortensius that Cicero was bluffing. He couldn't possibly be ready to go before September at the earliest!

Nor had Cicero found everything in Rome to his satisfaction upon his return. Metellus Little Goat and his youngest brother had put in some excellent work on Cicero's Sicilian clients, who were now certain that Cicero had lost interest in the case—he had accepted an enormous bribe from Gaius Verres, whispered the Metelli Little Goats through carefully chosen agents. It took Cicero several interviews with Hiero and his colleagues to learn why they were all atwitter. Once he did find out, to allay their fears was not difficult.

Quinctilis brought the three sets of elections, with the curule Centuriate Assembly ones held first. As far as Cicero's case was concerned, the results were dismal; Hortensius and Metellus Little Goat were next year's consuls and Marcus Little Goat was successfully returned as one of the praetors. Then came the elections in the Assembly of the People; the fact that Caesar was elected a quaestor at the top of the poll hardly impinged upon Cicero's consciousness. After which the twenty-seventh day of Quinctilis rolled round, and Cicero found himself elected plebeian aedile together with a Marcus Caesonius (no relation to the Julii with the cognomen of Caesar); they thought they would deal well together, and Cicero was profoundly glad that his colleague was a very wealthy man.

Thanks to the present consuls, Pompey and Crassus, so many things were going on in Rome that summer that elections were of no moment; instead of deliberately puffing them up into the position of prime importance, the electoral officers and the Senate wanted everything to do with elections over and done with. Therefore on the day following the Plebeian Assembly elections—the last of the three—the lots were cast to see what everyone was going to do next year. No surprise whatsoever then that the lots magically bestowed the Extortion Court on Marcus Little Goat! Everything was now set up to exonerate Gaius Verres early in the New Year.

On the last day of Quinctilis, Cicero struck. As no comitia meetings had been scheduled, the urban praetor's tribunal was open and Lucius Aurelius Cotta in personal attendance. Forth marched Cicero with his clients in tow, announced that he had completely prepared his case against Gaius Verres, and demanded that Lucius Cotta and the president of the Extortion Court, Manius Acilius Glabrio, should schedule a day to begin the trial as soon as they saw fit. Preferably very quickly.

The entire Senate had watched the duel between Cicero and Hortensius with bated breath. The Caecilius Metellus faction was in a minority, and neither Lucius Cotta nor Glabrio belonged to it; in fact, most of the Conscript Fathers were dying to see Cicero beat the system set up by Hortensius and the Metelli Little Goats to get Verres off. Lucius Cotta and Glabrio were therefore delighted to oblige Cicero with the earliest possible hearing.

The first two days of Sextilis were *feriae*—which did not preclude the hearing of criminal trials—but the third day was more difficult—on it was held the procession of the Crucified Dogs. When the Gauls had invaded Rome and attempted to establish a bridgehead on the Capitol four hundred years earlier, the watchdogs hadn't barked; what woke the consul Marcus Manlius and enabled him to foil the attempt was the cackling of the sacred geese. Ever since that night, on the anniversary day a solemn cavalcade wound its way around the Circus Maximus. Nine dogs were crucified on nine crosses made of elder wood, and one goose was garlanded and carried on a purple litter to commemorate the treachery of the dogs and the heroism of the geese. Not a good day for a criminal trial, dogs being chthonic animals.

So the case against Gaius Verres was scheduled to begin on the fifth day of Sextilis, in the midst of a Rome stunned by summer and stuffed with visitors agog to see all the special treats Pompey and Crassus had laid on. Stiff competition, but no one made the mistake of thinking that the trial of Gaius Verres would attract no onlookers, even if it continued through Crassus's public feast and Pompey's victory games.

Under Sulla's laws governing his new standing courts the general trial procedure originated by Gaius Servilius Glaucia was preserved, though considerably refined—refined to the detriment of speed. It occurred in two sections, the *actio prima* and the *actio secunda,* with a break in between the two *actiones* of several days, though the court president was at liberty to make the break much longer if he so desired.

The *actio prima* consisted of a long speech from the chief prosecutor followed by an equally long speech from the chief of the defense, then more long speeches alternating between the prosecution and the defense until all the junior advocates were used up. After that came the prosecution's witnesses, each one being cross-examined by the defense and perhaps re-examined by the prosecution. If one side or the other filibustered, the hearing of witnesses could become very protracted. Then came the witnesses for the defense, with the prosecution cross-examining each one, and perhaps the defense re-examining. After that came a long debate between the chief prosecutor and the chief defender; these long debates could also occur between each witness if either side desired. The *actio prima* finally ended with the last speech delivered by the chief defense counsel.

The *actio secunda* was more or less a repetition of the *actio prima*, though witnesses were not always called. Here there occurred the greatest and most impassioned orations, for after the concluding speeches of prosecution and defense the jury was required to give its verdict. No time for discussion of this verdict was allowed to the jury, which meant that the verdict was handed down while the jurors still had the words of the chief defense counsel ringing in their ears. This was the principal reason why Cicero loved to defend, hated to prosecute.

But Cicero knew how to win the case against Gaius Verres: all he needed was a court president willing to accommodate him.

"Praetor Manius Acilius Glabrio, president of this court, I wish to conduct my case along different lines than are the custom. What I propose is not illegal. It is novel, that is all. My reasons lie in the extraordinary number of witnesses I will call, and in the equally extraordinary number of different offenses with which I am going to charge the defendant Gaius Verres," said Cicero. "Is the president of the court willing to listen to an outline of what I propose?"

Hortensius rushed forward. "What's this, what's this?" he demanded. "I ask again, what *is* this? The case against Gaius Verres must be conducted on the usual lines! I insist!"

"I will listen to what Marcus Tullius Cicero proposes," said Glabrio, and added gently, "without interruptions."

"I wish to dispense with the long speeches," said Cicero, "and concentrate upon one offense at a time. The crimes of Gaius Verres are so many and so varied that it is vital the members of the jury keep each crime straight in their heads. By dealing with one crime at a time, I wish to assist the court in keeping everything straight, that is all. So what I propose to do is briefly to outline one particular crime, then present each of my witnesses plus my evidence to do with that crime. As you see, I intend to work alone—I have absolutely no assistant advocates. The *actio prima* in the case of Gaius Verres should not contain any long speeches by either the prosecution or the defense. It is a waste of the court's time, especially in light of the fact that there is at least one more case for this court to hear before this year is ended—that of Quintus Curtius. So I say, let the *actio secunda* contain all the magnificent speeches! It is only after all the magnificent speeches of the *actio secunda* have been given that the jury hands down its verdict, so I do not see how my colleague Quintus Hortensius can object to my asking for an *actio prima* procedure which will enable the jury to listen to our impassioned oratory during the *actio secunda* as if it had never heard any of what we said before! Because it won't have heard any of it! Oh, the freshness! The anticipation! The pleasure!''

Hortensius was now looking a little uncertain; there was sound sense in what Cicero was saying. After all, Cicero hadn't asked for anything which might detract from the defense's entitlement to the last word, and Hortensius found himself very much liking the idea of being able to deliver his absolute best as a shock of juridical surprise at the end of the *actio secunda*. Yes, Cicero was right! Get the boring stuff over as quickly as possible in the *actio prima,* and save the Alexandrian lighthouse stuff for the grand finale.

Thus when Glabrio looked at him enquiringly, Hortensius was able to say smoothly, ''Pray ask Marcus Tullius to enlarge further.''

''Enlarge further, Marcus Tullius,'' said Glabrio.

''There is little more to say, Manius Acilius. Only that the defending advocates be allowed not one drip more of time to speak than I spend speaking—during the *actio prima* only, of course! I am willing to concede the defense as much time as they wish during the *actio secunda*. Since I see a formidable array of defending advocates, whereas I alone staff the prosecution, that will give the defense as much of an advantage as I think they ought to have. I ask only this: that the *actio prima* be conducted as I have outlined it.''

''The idea has considerable merit, Marcus Tullius,'' said Glabrio. ''Quintus Hortensius, how do you say?''

''Let it be as Marcus Tullius has outlined,'' said Hortensius.

Only Gaius Verres looked worried. ''Oh, I wish I knew what he was up to!'' he whispered to Metellus Little Goat. ''Hortensius ought not to have agreed!''

''By the time the *actio secunda* comes around, Gaius Verres, I can assure you that the jury will have forgotten everything the witnesses said,'' his brother-in-law whispered back.

"Then why is Cicero insisting on these changes?"

"Because he knows he's going to lose, and he wants to make some sort of splash. How else than by innovation? Caesar used the same tack when he prosecuted the elder Dolabella—insisted on innovations. He got a great deal of praise, but he lost the case. Just as Cicero will. Don't worry! Hortensius *will* win!"

The only remarks of a general nature Cicero made before he plunged into an outline of the first category of Gaius Verres's crimes were to do with the jury.

"Remember that the Senate has commissioned our urban praetor, Lucius Aurelius Cotta, to enquire into the composition of juries—and has agreed to recommend his findings to the Assembly of the People to be ratified into law. Between the days of Gaius Gracchus and our Dictator, Lucius Cornelius Sulla, the Senate completely lost control of a hitherto uncontested right—to staff the juries of Rome's criminal courts. That privilege Gaius Gracchus handed to the knights—and we all know the result of *that*! Sulla handed the new standing courts back to the Senate. But as the sixty-four men our censors have expelled have shown, we senators have not honored the trust Sulla reposed in us. Gaius Verres is not the only person on trial here today. The Senate of Rome is also on trial! And if this senatorial jury fails to conduct itself in an honorable and honest way, then who can blame Lucius Cotta if he recommends that jury duty be taken off us Conscript Fathers? Members of this jury, I beseech you not to forget for one moment that you carry an enormous responsibility on your shoulders—and the fate!—and the reputation!—of the Senate of Rome."

And after that, having neatly confined the defense to the same time span as he used himself, Cicero plunged into hearing his witnesses and presenting his inanimate evidence. One by one they testified: grain thefts to the amount of three hundred thousand *modii* in just one year from just one small district, let alone the amounts looted from other districts; thefts of property which reduced the farmers of just one district from two hundred and fifty to eighty in three years, let alone the thefts of property from many other districts; embezzlement of the Treasury's moneys intended for the purchase of grain; usury at twenty-four and more percent; the destruction or alteration of tithe records; the looting of statues and paintings from temples; the dinner guest who in front of his host prised the jewels out of ornamented cups; the dinner guest who on his way out scooped up all the gold and silver plate and popped it in bags the easier to carry it away; the building of a ship free of charge in which to carry back some of his loot to Rome; the condoning of pirate bases and cuts of pirate profits; the overturning of wills; and on, and on, and on.

Cicero had records, documents, wax tablets with the changed figures still visible—and witnesses galore, witnesses who could not be intimidated or discredited during cross-examination. Nor had Cicero produced witnesses to grain thefts within just one district, but within many districts, and the catalogue of works by Praxiteles, Phidias, Polyclitus, Myron, Strongylion and every other famous sculptor which Verres had looted was supported by bills of "sale" that saw the owner of a Praxiteles Cupid obliged virtually to give it away to Verres. The evidence was massive and absolutely damning. It came like a flood, one category of theft or misuse of authority or exploitation after another for nine full days; the *actio prima* concluded on the fourteenth day of Sextilis.

Hortensius was shaking when he left the court, but when Verres tried to speak to him he shook his head angrily. "At your place!" he snapped. "And bring your brothers-in-law!"

The house of Gaius Verres lay in the best part of the Palatine; though it was actually one of the biggest properties on that hill, the amount of art crammed into it made it look as small and overcrowded as the yard of a sculptural mason in the Velabrum. Where no statues could stand or paintings hang there were cupboards in which resided vast collections of gold and silver plate, or jewelry, or folded lengths of gloriously worked embroidery and tapestry. Citrus-wood tables of rarest grain supported on pedestals of ivory and gold jostled against gilded chairs or collided with fabulous couches. Outside in the peristyle garden were jammed the bigger statues, mostly bronzes, though gold and silver glittered there too. A clutter representing fifteen years of plundering and many fortunes.

The four men gathered in Verres's study, no less a jumble, and perched wherever the precious objects allowed them.

"You'll have to go into voluntary exile," said Hortensius.

Verres gaped. "You're joking! There's the *actio secunda* still to come! Your speeches will get me off!"

"You fool!" roared Hortensius. "Don't you understand? I was tricked, bamboozled, hoodwinked, gulled—any word you like to describe the fact that Cicero has ruined any chance I ever had to win this wretched case! A year could go by between *actio prima* and *actio secunda,* Gaius Verres, I and my assistants could deliver the world's best oratory for a month, Gaius Verres— and still the jury would not have forgotten that utter landslide of evidence! I tell you straight, Gaius Verres, that if I had known a *tithe* of your crimes before I started, I would never have agreed to defend you! You make Mummius or Paullus look like a tyro! And what have you done with so much money? Where is it, for Juno's sake? How could any man have spent it when that man pays a pittance for a Praxiteles Cupid and mostly doesn't pay at all? I've defended a lot of unmitigated villains in my time, but you win all the prizes! Go into voluntary exile, Gaius Verres!''

Verres and the Metelli Little Goats had listened to this tirade with jaws dropped.

Hortensius rose to his feet. "Take what you can with you into exile, but if you want my advice, leave the art works you looted from Sicily behind. You'll never be able to carry more than you stole from Hera of Samos anyway. Concentrate on paintings and small stuff. And ship your money out of Rome at dawn tomorrow—don't leave it a moment longer.'' He walked to the door, threading his way through the precious artifacts. "I will take my ivory sphinx by Phidias, however. Where is it?''

"Your what?'' gasped Verres. "I don't owe you anything—you didn't get me off!''

"You owe me one ivory sphinx by Phidias,'' said Hortensius, "and you ought to be thanking your good luck I didn't make it more. If nothing else is worth it to you, the advice I've just given you most definitely is. My ivory sphinx, Verres. *Now!*''

It was small enough for Hortensius to tuck under his left arm, hidden by folds of toga; an exquisite piece of work that was perfect down to the last detail in a feathered wing and the minute tufts of fur protruding between the clawed toes.

"He's cool,'' said Marcus Little Goat after Hortensius went.

"Ingrate!'' snarled Verres.

But the consul-elect Metellus Little Goat frowned. "He's right, Gaius. You'll have to leave Rome by tomorrow night at the latest. Cicero will have the court seal this place as soon as he hears you're moving things out—why on earth did you have to keep it all here?''

"It isn't all here, Quintus. These are just the pieces I can't bear not to see every day. The bulk of it is stored on my place at Cortona.''

"Do you mean there's *more*? Ye gods, Gaius, I've known you for years, but you never cease to surprise me! No wonder our poor sister complains you ignore her! So this is only the stuff you can't bear not to see every day? And I've always thought you kept this place looking like a curio shop in the Porticus Margaritaria because you didn't even trust your slaves!''

Verres sneered. "Your sister complains, does she? And what right does she have to complain, when Caesar's been keeping her *cunnus* well lubricated for months? Does she think I'm a fool? Or so blind I can't see beyond a Myron bronze?" He got up. "I ought to have told Hortensius where most of my money went—your face would have been mighty red, wouldn't it? The three Little Goats are expensive in-laws, but you most of all, Quintus! The art I've managed to hang on to, but who gobbled up the proceeds from sales of grain, eh? Well, now's the end of it! I'll take my sphinx-stealing advocate's advice and go into voluntary exile, where with any luck what I manage to take with me will stay mine! No more money for the Little Goats, including Metella Capraria! Let Caesar keep her in the style to which she's accustomed—and I wish you luck prising money out of that man! Don't expect to see your sister's dowry returned. I'm divorcing her today on grounds of her adultery with Caesar."

The result of this speech was the outraged exit of both his brothers-in-law; for a moment after they had gone Verres stood behind his desk, one finger absently caressing the smooth painted planes of a marble cheek belonging to a Polyclitus Hera. Then, shrugging, he shouted for his slaves. Oh, how could he bear to part with one single item contained in this house? Only the salvation of his skin and the knowledge that keeping some was better than losing all enabled him to walk with his steward from one precious object to the next. Go, stay, go, go, stay . . .

"When you've hired the wagons—and if you blab about it to anyone, I'll crucify you!—have them brought round to the back lane at midnight tomorrow. And everything had better be properly crated, hear me?"

As Hortensius had predicted, Cicero had Glabrio seal the abandoned house of Gaius Verres on the morning after his secret departure, and sent to his bank to stop the transfer of funds. Too late, of course; money was the most portable of all treasures, requiring nothing more than a piece of paper to be presented at the other end of a man's journey.

"Glabrio is empaneling a committee to fix damages, but I'm afraid they won't be huge," said Cicero to Hiero of Lilybaeum. "He's cleaned his money out of Rome. However, it looks as if most of what he stole from Sicily's temples has been left behind—not so with all the jewels and plate he stole from individual owners, alas, though even that he couldn't entirely spirit away, there was so much of it. The slaves he left behind—a poor lot, but their hatred of him has proven useful—say that what is in his house here in Rome is minute compared to what he has hidden away on his estate near Cortona. I imagine that's where the brothers Metelli have gone, but I borrowed a tactic from my friend Caesar, who travels faster than anyone else I know. The court's expedition will reach Cortona first, I predict. So we may find more belonging to Sicily there.''

"Where has Gaius Verres gone?" asked Hiero, curious.

"It seems he's heading for Massilia. A popular place for the art lovers among our exiles," said Cicero.

"Well, we are delighted to have our national heritage back," said Hiero, beaming. "Thank you, Marcus Tullius, thank you!"

"I believe it will be I who ends in thanking you—that is," said Cicero delicately, "if you are pleased enough with my conduct of the case to honor our agreement about the grain next year? The Plebeian Games will not be held until November, so your price need not come from this year's harvest."

"We are happy to pay you, Marcus Tullius, and I promise you that your distribution of grain to the people of Rome will be magnificent."

"And so," said Cicero later to his friend Titus Pomponius Atticus, "this rare venture into the realm of prosecution has turned out to be a bonus I badly needed. I'll buy my grain at two sesterces the *modius,* and sell it for three sesterces. The extra sestertius will more than pay for transportation."

"Sell it for four sesterces the *modius,"* said Atticus, "and pop a bit of money into your own purse. It needs fattening."

But Cicero was shocked. "I couldn't do that, Atticus! The censors could say I had enriched myself by illegally taking fees for my services as an advocate."

Atticus sighed. "Cicero, Cicero! You will never be rich, and it will be entirely your own fault. Though I suppose it's true that you can take the man out of Arpinum, but you can never take Arpinum out of the man. You think like a country squire!"

"I think like an honest man," said Cicero, "and I'm very proud of that fact."

"Thereby implying that I am not an honest man?"

"No, no!" cried Cicero irritably. "You're a businessman of exalted rank and Roman station—what rules apply to you are not the rules apply to me. I'm not a Caecilius, but you are!"

Atticus changed the subject. "Are you going to write the case against Verres up for publication?" he asked.

"I had thought of doing so, yes."

"Including the great speeches of an *actio secunda* that never happened? Did you compose anything ahead of time?"

"Oh yes, I always have rough notes of my speeches months before their delivery dates. Though I shall modify the *actio secunda* speeches to incorporate a lot of the things I discussed during the *actio prima*. Titivated up, naturally.''

"Naturally," said Atticus gravely.

"Why do you ask?''

"I'm thinking of establishing a hobby for myself, Cicero. Business is boring, and the men I deal with even more boring than the business I do. So I'm opening a little shop with a big workshop out back—on the Argiletum. Sosius will have some competition, because I intend to become a publisher. And if you don't object, I would like the exclusive right to publish all your future work. In return to you of a payment of one tenth of what I make on every copy of your works I sell.''

Cicero giggled. "How delicious! Done, Atticus, done!''

 It was in April, shortly after the newly elected censors had confirmed Mamercus as Princeps Senatus, that Pompey announced he would celebrate votive victory games commencing in Sextilis and ending just before the *ludi Romani* were due to begin on the fourth day of September. His satisfaction in making this announcement was apparent to all, though not every scrap of it was due to the victory games themselves; Pompey had brought off a marital coup of enormous significance to a man from Picenum. His widowed sister, Pompeia, was to wed none other than the dead Dictator's nephew, Publius Sulla *sive* Sextus Perquitienus. Yes, the Pompeii of northern Picenum were rising up in the Roman world! His grandfather and father had had to make do with the Lucilii, whereas he had allied himself with the Mucii, the Licinii, and the Cornelii! Tremendously satisfying!

But Crassus didn't care a scrap whom Pompey's sister chose as her second husband; what upset him was the victory games.

"I tell you," Crassus said to Caesar, "he intends to keep the countryfolk spending up big in Rome for over two months, and right through the worst of summer! The shopkeepers are going to put up statues to him all over the city—not to mention old grannies and daddies who love to take in lodgers during summer and earn a few extra sesterces!''

"It's good for Rome. And good for money.''

"Yes, but where am *I* in all this?" asked Crassus, squeaking.

"You'll just have to create a place for yourself.''

"Tell me how—and when? Apollo's games last until the Ides of Quinctilis, then there are three sets of elections five days apart—curule, People, Plebs. On the Ides of Quinctilis he intends to hold his wretched parade of the Public Horse. And after the plebeian elections there's an ocean of time for shopping—but not enough time to go home to the country and come back again!—until his victory games begin in the middle of Sextilis. They last for *fifteen days*! What conceit! And after they end it's straight into the Roman games! Ye gods, Caesar, his public entertainments are going to keep the bumpkins in town for closer to three months than two! And has *my* name been mentioned? No! *I* don't exist!''

Caesar looked tranquil. ''I have an idea,'' he said.

''What?'' demanded Crassus. ''Dress me up as Pollux?''

''And Pompeius as Castor? I like it! But let's be serious. Anything you do, my dear Marcus, is going to have to cost more than Pompeius is outlaying for his entertainments. Otherwise whatever you do won't eclipse him. Are you willing to spend a huge fortune?''

''I'd be willing to pay almost anything to go out of office looking better than Pompeius!'' Crassus snorted. ''After all, I am the richest man in Rome— have been for two years now.''

''Don't delude yourself,'' said Caesar. ''You just talk about your wealth, and no one has come up with a bigger figure. But our Pompeius is a typical landed rural nobleman—*very* closemouthed about what he's worth. And he's worth a lot more than you are, Marcus, so much I guarantee. When the Ager Gallicus was officially brought within the boundary of Italy, the price of it soared. He owns—owns, not leases or rents!—several million *iugera* of the best land in Italy, and not only in Umbria and Picenum. He inherited all that magnificent property the Lucilii used to own on the Gulf of Tarentum, and he came back from Africa in time to pick up some very nice river frontage on the Tiber, the Volturnus, the Liris and the Aternus. You are not the richest man in Rome, Crassus. I assure you that Pompeius is.''

Crassus was staring. ''That's not possible!''

''It is, you know. Just because a man doesn't shout to the world how much he's worth doesn't mean he's poor. You shout about your money to everyone because you started out poor. Pompeius has never been poor in his life—and never will be poor. When he gives his land to his veterans he looks glamorous, but I'd be willing to bet that all he really gives them is tenure of it, not title to it. *And* that everyone pays him a tithe of what their land produces. Pompeius is a kind of king, Crassus! He didn't choose to call himself Magnus for no reason. His people regard him as their king. Now that he's senior consul, he just believes his kingdom has grown.''

''I'm worth ten thousand talents,'' said Crassus gruffly.

''Two hundred and fifty million sesterces to an accountant,'' said Caesar, smiling and shaking his head. "Would you draw ten percent of that in annual profits?"

"Oh, yes."

"Then would you be willing to forgo this year's profits?"

"You mean spend a thousand talents?"

"I mean exactly that."

The idea hurt; Crassus registered his pain visibly. "Yes—if in so doing I can eclipse Pompeius. Not otherwise."

"The day before the Ides of Sextilis—which is four days before Pompeius's victory games begin—is the feast of Hercules Invictus. As you remember, Sulla dedicated a tenth of his fortune to the god by giving a public feast on five thousand tables."

"Who could forget that day? The black dog drank the first victim's blood. I'd never seen Sulla terrified before. Nor after, for that matter. His Grass Crown fell in the defiled blood."

"Forget the horrors, Marcus, for I promise you there will be no black dogs anywhere near when you dedicate a tenth of *your* fortune to Hercules Invictus! You'll give a public banquet on *ten* thousand tables!" said Caesar. "Those who might otherwise have preferred the comfort of a seaside holiday to watching one spectacle after another will all stay in Rome—a free feast is top of everyone's priorities."

"Ten thousand tables? If I heaped every last one of them feet high in licker-fish, oysters, freshwater eels and dug-mullets by the cartload, it would still not cost me more than two hundred talents," said Crassus, who knew the price of everything. "And besides, a full belly today might make a man think he'll never be hungry again, but on the morrow that same man will be hungry. Feasts vanish in a day, Caesar. So does the memory of them."

"Quite right. However," Caesar went on dreamily, "those two hundred talents leave eight hundred still to be spent. Let us presume that in Rome between Sextilis and November there will be about three hundred thousand Roman citizens. The normal grain dole provides each citizen with five *modii*—that is, one *medimnus*—of wheat per month, at a price of fifty sesterces. A cheap rate, but not as cheap as the actual price of the grain, of course. The Treasury makes at least a little profit, even in the lean years. This year, they tell me, will not be lean. Nor—such is your luck!—was last year a lean one. Because it is out of last year's crop you will have to buy."

"Buy?" asked Crassus, looking lost.

"Let me finish. Five *modii* of wheat for three months . . . Times three hundred thousand people . . . Is four and a half million *modii*. If you buy now instead of during summer, I imagine you could pick up four and a half million *modii* of wheat for five sesterces the *modius*. That is twenty-two and a half million sesterces—approximately eight hundred talents. And that, my dear Marcus,'' Caesar ended triumphantly, ''is where the other eight hundred talents will go! Because, Marcus Crassus, you are going to distribute five *modii* of wheat per month for three months to every Roman citizen free of charge. Not at a reduced price, my dear Marcus. *Free!*''

''Spectacular largesse,'' said Crassus, face expressionless.

''I agree, it is. And it has one great advantage over every ploy Pompeius has devised. His entertainments will have finished over two months before your final issue of free grain. If memories are short, then you have to be the last man left on the field. Most of Rome will eat free bread thanks to Marcus Licinius Crassus between the month when the prices soar and the time when the new harvest brings them down again. You'll be a hero! And they'll love you forever!''

''They might stop calling me an arsonist,'' grinned Crassus.

''And there you have the difference between your wealth and Pompeius's,'' said Caesar, grinning too. ''Pompeius's money doesn't float as cinders on Rome's air. It really is high time that you smartened up your public image!''

As Crassus chose to go about purchasing his vast quantity of wheat with stealth and personal anonymity and said not a word about intending to dedicate a tenth of his wealth to Hercules Invictus on the day before the Ides of Sextilis, Pompey proceeded with his own plans in sublime ignorance of the danger that he would find himself eclipsed.

His intention was to make all of Rome—and Italy—aware that the bad times were over; and what better way to do that than to give the whole country over to feasting and holidaymaking? The consulship of Gnaeus Pompeius Magnus would live in the memory of the people as a time of prosperity and freedom from anxiety—no more wars, no more famines, no more internal strife. And though the element of self spoiled his intentions, they were genuine enough. The ordinary people, who were not important and therefore did not suffer during the proscriptions, spoke these days with wistful longing for the time when Sulla had been the Dictator; but after the consulship of Gnaeus Pompeius Magnus was over, Sulla's reign would not loom so large in memory.

At the beginning of Quinctilis Rome began to fill up with country people, most of whom were looking for lodgings until after the middle of September. Nor did as many as usual leave for the seashore, even among the upper classes. Aware that crime and disease would both be on the increase, Pompey

devoted some of his splendid organizational talents to diminishing crime and
disease by hiring ex-gladiators to police the alleys and byways of the city,
by making the College of Lictors keep an eye on the shysters and tricksters
who frequented the Forum Romanum and other major marketplaces, by enlarging the swimming holes of the Trigarium, and plastering vacant walls
with warning notices about good drinking water, urinating and defaecating
anywhere but in the public latrines, clean hands and bad food.

Unsure how many of these countryfolk understood how amazing it was
that Rome's senior consul had been a knight at the time he was elected (and
did not become a senator until he was inaugurated on New Year's Day),
Pompey had resolved to use the parade of the Public Horse to reinforce this
fact. Thus had his tame censors Clodianus and Gellius revived the *transvectio*,
as the parade was called, though it had not been held after the time of Gaius
Gracchus. Until the consulship of Gnaeus Pompeius Magnus, who wanted to
make a public splash with his Public Horse.

It began at dawn on the Ides of Quinctilis in the Circus Flaminius on
the Campus Martius, where the eighteen hundred holders of the Public Horse
offered to Mars Invictus—Undefeated Mars—whose temple lay within the
Circus. The offering made, the knights mounted their Public Horses and rode
in solemn procession, century by century, through the gate in the vegetable
markets, along the Velabrum into the Vicus Iugarius, and thence into the
lower Forum Romanum. They turned to ride up the Forum to where, on a
specially erected tribunal in front of the temple of Castor and Pollux, the
censors sat to review them. Each man when he drew close to the tribunal
was expected to dismount and lead his Public Horse up to the censors, who
minutely inspected it and him. Did it or he not measure up to the ancient
equestrian standards, then the censors were at liberty to strip the knight of
his Public Horse and expel him from the eighteen original Centuries. It had
been known to happen in the past; Cato the Censor had been famous for the
stringency of his inspections.

So novel was the *transvectio* that most of Rome tried to jam into the
Forum Romanum to watch it, though many had to content themselves with
seeing the parade pass by between the Circus Flaminius and the Forum. Every
vantage point was solid with people—roofs, plinths, porticoes, steps, hills,
cliffs, trees. Vendors of food, fans, sunshades and drinks scrambled through
the masses in the most precarious way crying their wares, banging people on
the head with the corners of their neck-slung open boxes, giving back as
much abuse as they collected, each one with a slave in attendance to replenish
the box or keep some sticky-fingered member of the crowd from pilfering
the goods or the proceeds. Toddlers were held out to piss on those below

them, babies howled, children dived this way and that through the masses, gravy dribbled down tunics in a nice contrast to custard cascades, fights broke out, the susceptible fainted or vomited, and everybody ate nonstop. A typical Roman holiday.

The knights rode in eighteen Centuries, each one preceded by its ancient emblem—wolf, bear, mouse, bird, lion, and so on. Because of the narrowness of some parts of the route they could ride no more than four abreast, which meant that each Century held twenty-five rows, and the whole procession stretched for nearly a mile. Each man was clad in his armor, some suits of incredible antiquity and therefore bizarre appearance; others (like Pompey's, whose family had nudged into the eighteen original Centuries and did not own ancient armor they would have cared to try to pass off as Etruscan or Latin) magnificent with gold and silver. But nothing rivaled the Public Horses, each a splendid example of horseflesh from the *rosea rura,* and mostly white or dappled grey. They were bedizened with every medallion and trinket imaginable, with ornate saddles and bridles of dyed leather, fabulous blankets, brilliant colors. Some horses had been trained to pick up their feet in high-stepping prances, others had manes and tails braided with silver and gold.

It was beautifully staged, and all to show off Pompey. To have examined every man who rode, no matter how rapid the censors were, was manifestly impossible; the parade would have taken thirty summer hours to ride past the tribunal. But Pompey's Century had been placed as one of the first, so that the censors solemnly went through the ritual of asking each of some three hundred men in turn what his name was, his tribe, his father's name, and whether he had served in his ten campaigns or for six years, after which his financial standing (previously established) was approved, and he led his horse off to obscurity.

When the fourth Century's first row dismounted, Pompey was in its forefront; a hush fell over the Forum specially induced by Pompey's agents in the crowd. His golden armor flashing in the sun, the purple of his consular degree floating from his shoulders mixed with the scarlet of his general's degree, he led his big white horse forward trapped in scarlet leather and golden *phalerae,* his own person liberally bedewed with knight's brasses and medallions, and the scarlet plumes in his Attic helmet a twinkling mass of dyed egret's feathers.

"Name?" asked Clodianus, who was the senior censor.

"Gnaeus Pompeius Magnus!" hollered Pompey.

"Tribe?"

"Clustumina!"

"Father?"

"Gnaeus Pompeius Strabo, consul!"

"Have you served in your ten campaigns or for six years?"

"Yes!" screamed Pompey at the top of his voice. "Two in the Italian War, one defending the city at the Siege of Rome, two with Lucius Cornelius Sulla in Italy, one in Sicily, one in Africa, one in Numidia, one defending Rome from Lepidus and Brutus, six in Spain, and one cleaning up the Spartacani! They are sixteen campaigns, and every one of them beyond cadet status took place under my own generalship!"

The crowd went berserk, shouting, cheering, applauding, feet drumming, arms flailing; wave after wave of acclamation smote the stunned ears of the censors and the rest of the parade, setting horses plunging and some riders on the cobbles.

When the noise finally died down—it took some time to do so, because Pompey had walked out into the center of the open space in front of Castor's, his bridle looped over his arm, and turned in slow circles applauding the crowds—the censors rolled up their screeds and sat regally nodding while the sixteen Centuries behind Pompey's rode past at a trot.

"A splendid show!" snarled Crassus, whose Public Horse was the property of his elder boy, Publius, now twenty. He and Caesar had watched from the loggia of Crassus's house, this having originally belonged to Marcus Livius Drusus, and owning a superb view of the lower Forum. "What a farce!"

"But brilliantly staged, Crassus, brilliantly staged! You must hand Pompeius top marks for inventiveness and crowd appeal. His games should be even better."

"Sixteen campaigns! And all beyond his cadetship he claims he generaled himself! Oh yes, for about a market interval after his daddy died at the Siege of Rome and during which he did nothing except ready his daddy's army to march back to Picenum—and Sulla generaled him in Italy, so did Metellus Pius—and Catulus was the general against Lepidus and Brutus—and what do you think about that last claim, that he 'cleaned up the Spartacani'? Ye gods, Caesar, if we interpreted our own careers as loosely as he's interpreted his, we're all generals!"

"Console yourself with the fact that Catulus and Metellus Pius are probably saying much the same thing," said Caesar, who hurt too. "The man's a parvenu from an Italian backwater."

"I hope my ploy with the free grain works!"

"It will, Marcus Crassus, I promise you it will."

* * *

Pompey went home to his house on the Carinae exultant, but the mood didn't last. On the following morning Crassus's heralds began proclaiming the news that on the feast of Hercules Invictus, Marcus Licinius Crassus the consul would dedicate a tenth of everything he owned to the god, that there would be a public feast laid out on ten thousand tables, and that the bulk of the donation would be used up in giving every Roman citizen in Rome five free *modii* of wheat during September, October and November.

"How dared he!" gasped Pompey to Philippus, who had come to compliment him upon his performance at the *transvectio*—and to see how the Great Man would swallow Crassus's ploy.

"It's very clever," said Philippus in an apologetic voice, "especially because Romans are so quick at reckoning up how much anything costs. Games are too abstruse, but food is common knowledge. They know the price of everything from a licker-fish to a salt sprat. Even when they can't afford the salt sprat, they'll ask its cost in the market. Human curiosity. They'll all know how much Crassus paid for his wheat too, not to mention how many *modii* he's had to buy. We'll be deafened by clicking abacuses."

"What you're trying to say without actually saying it is that they'll conclude Crassus has spent more on them than I have!" said Pompey, a red glint in his blue eyes.

"I am afraid so."

"Then I'll have to set my agents to gossiping about how much games cost." Pompey glanced at Philippus from under his lids. "How much will Crassus lay out? Any idea?"

"A thousand talents or thereabouts."

"*Crassus? A thousand talents?*"

"Easily."

"He's too much the miser!"

"Not this year, Magnus. Your generosity and showmanship have evidently stung our big ox into goring with both his horns."

"What can I do?"

"Very little except turn on absolutely wondrous games."

"You're holding something back, Philippus."

The fat jowls wobbled, the dark eyes flickered. Then he sighed, shrugged. "Oh well, better it comes from me than from one of your enemies. It's the free grain will win for Crassus."

"What do you mean? Because he's filling empty bellies? There are no empty bellies in Rome this year!"

"He'll distribute five *modii* of free grain to every Roman citizen in Rome during September, October and November. Count up! That's two one-pound loaves a day for ninety days. And the vast majority of those ninety days will occur long after your entire gamut of entertainment is over. Everyone will have forgotten you and what you did. Whereas until the end of November, every Roman mouth taking a bite out of a loaf of bread will make an invocation of thanks to Marcus Licinius Crassus. He can't lose, Magnus!'' said Philippus.

It had been a long time since Pompey had last thrown a tantrum, but the one he threw for the sole edification of Lucius Marcius Philippus was one of his best. The hair came out in hanks, the cheeks and neck were raw with scratches, the body covered in bruises where he had dashed various parts of his anatomy against the floor or the walls. Tears ran like rain, he broke furniture and art into small pieces, his howls threatened to lift the roof. Mucia Tertia, hurrying to see what had happened, took one look and fled again. So did the servants. But Philippus sat in a fascinated appreciation until Varro arrived.

''Oh, Jupiter!'' whispered Varro.

''Amazing, isn't it?'' asked Philippus. ''He's a lot quieter now. You ought to have seen him a few moments ago. Awesome!''

''I've seen him before,'' said Varro, edging around the prone figure on the black-and-white marble tiles to join Philippus on his couch. ''It's the news about Crassus, of course.''

''It is. When have you seen him like this?''

''When he couldn't fit his elephants through the triumphal gate,'' said Varro, voice too low for the supine Pompey to hear; he was never sure how much of a Pompey tantrum was contrived, how much an actual travail which really did blot out conversation and action around him. ''Also when Carrinas slipped through his siege at Spoletium. He can't bear to be thwarted.''

''The ox gored with both horns,'' said Philippus pensively.

''The ox,'' said Varro tartly, ''has three horns these days, and the third is—so feminine rumor has it!—far the biggest.''

''Ah! It has a name, then.''

''Gaius Julius Caesar.''

Pompey sat up immediately, clothing shredded, scalp and face bleeding. ''I heard that!'' he said, answering Varro's unspoken debate about his tantrums. ''What about Caesar?''

''Only that he masterminded Crassus's campaign to win huge popularity,'' said Varro.

''Who told you?'' Pompey climbed lithely to his feet and accepted Philippus's handkerchief.

''Palicanus.''

"He'd know, he was one of Caesar's tame tribunes," said Philippus, wincing as Pompey blew his nose productively.

"Caesar's thick with Crassus, I know," said Pompey, tones muffled; he emerged from the handkerchief and tossed it to a revolted Philippus. "It was he did all the negotiating last year. *And* suggested that we restore the tribunate of the plebs." This was said with an ugly look at Philippus, who had not suggested it.

"I have enormous respect for Caesar's ability," said Varro.

"So does Crassus—and so do I." Pompey still looked ugly. "Well, at least I know where Caesar's loyalties lie!"

"Caesar's loyalties lie with Caesar," said Philippus, "and you should never forget that. But if you're wise, Magnus, you'll keep Caesar on a string despite his ties to Crassus. You'll never not need a Caesar, especially after I'm dead—and that can't be far off. I'm too fat to see seventy. *Lucullus* fears Caesar, you know! Now that takes some doing. I can think of only one other man whom Lucullus feared. Sulla. You look at Caesar closely. *Sulla!*"

"If you say I ought to keep him on a string, Philippus, then I will," said Pompey magnanimously. "But it will be a long time before I forget that he spoiled my year as consul!"

Between the end of Pompey's victory games (which were a great success, chiefly because Pompey's tastes in theater and circus were those of a common man) and the beginning of the *ludi Romani,* the Kalends of September intervened, and on the Kalends of September the Senate always held a meeting. It was always a significant session, and this year's session followed that tradition; Lucius Aurelius Cotta revealed his findings at it.

"I have acquitted myself of the commission which you laid upon me early in the year, Conscript Fathers," Lucius Cotta said from the curule dais, "I hope in a manner you will approve. Before I go into details, I will briefly outline what I intend to ask you to recommend into law."

No scrolls or papers resided in his hands, nor did his urban praetor's clerk seem to have documents. As the day was exceedingly hot (it still being midsummer by the seasons), the House breathed a faint sigh of relief; he was not going to make it a long-drawn meeting. But then, he was not a long-drawn person; of the three Cottae, Lucius was the youngest and the brightest.

"Candidly, my fellow members of this House," Lucius Cotta said in his clear, carrying voice, "I was not impressed by the record of either senators *or* knights in the matter of jury duty. When a jury is composed entirely of senators, it favors those of the senatorial order. And when a jury is composed of knights who own the Public Horse, it favors the equestrian order. Both kinds of jurors are susceptible to bribes, chiefly because, I believe, all a man's fellow jurors are of his own kind—either senatorial or equestrian.

"What I propose to do," he said, "is to divide jury duty up more equitably than ever before. Gaius Gracchus took juries off the Senate and gave them to the eighteen Centuries of the First Class who own a Public Horse and a census of at least four hundred thousand sesterces per annum in income. Now it is incontrovertible that with few exceptions every senator comes from a family within the ranks of the eighteen Centuries at the top end of the First Class. What I am saying is that Gaius Gracchus did not go far enough. Therefore I propose to make every jury a three-way forum by having each jury composed of one-third senators, one-third knights of the Public Horse, and one-third *tribuni aerarii*—the knights who comprise the bulk of the First Class, and have a census of at least three hundred thousand sesterces per annum in income."

A hum began, but not of outrage; the faces turned like flowers toward the sun of Lucius Cotta were astonished, but in a thoughtful way.

Lucius Cotta grew persuasive. "It seems to me," he said, "that we of the Senate grew sentimental over the years which elapsed between Gaius Gracchus and the dictatorship of Lucius Cornelius Sulla. We remembered with longing the privilege of jury duty without remembering the reality of jury duty. Three hundred of us to staff every jury, against fifteen hundred knights of the Public Horse. Then Sulla gave us back our beloved jury duty, and even though he enlarged the Senate to cope with this, we soon learned that each and every one of us resident in Rome was perpetually chained to some jury or other. Because, of course, the standing courts have greatly added to jury duty. Trial processes were far less numerous when most trial processes had to be individually enacted by an Assembly. I think Sulla had reasoned out that the smaller size of each jury and the greater size of the Senate itself would overcome the vexations of perpetual jury duty, but he underestimated the problem.

"I entered upon my enquiry convinced of that one fact only—that the Senate, even in its enlarged condition, is not a body numerous enough to provide juries for every trial. And yet, Conscript Fathers, I was loath to hand the courts back to the knights of the eighteen Public Horse Centuries. To do that, I felt, would have been a betrayal of two things—my own senatorial order, and the truly excellent system of justice which Sulla gave us in his permanent standing courts."

Everyone was leaning forward now, rapt: Lucius Cotta was speaking absolute sense!

"At first, then, I thought of dividing jury duty equally between the Senate and the eighteen senior Centuries, with each jury composed of fifty percent senators and fifty percent knights. However, a few calculations showed me that the onus of duty for senators was still too heavy.''

Face very serious, eyes shining, both hands out, Lucius Cotta changed his thrust slightly. ''If a man is to come to sit in judgement on his fellow man,'' he said quietly, ''no matter what his rank or status might be, then he should come fresh, eager, interested. That is not possible when a man has to serve on too many juries. He grows jaded, skeptical, disinterested—and more prone to accept bribes. For what other compensation, he might ask himself, can he obtain except a bribe? The State does not pay its jurors. Therefore the State ought not to have the right to suck up huge quantities of any man's time.''

There were nods and murmurs of approval; the House liked where Lucius Cotta was going very much.

''I am aware that many of you were thinking along these lines, that jury duty ought to be given to a larger body of men than the Senate. I am aware, naturally, that for a short time once before the juries were divided between the two orders. But, as I have said already, none of the solutions which had occurred to us until now went far enough. If there are eighteen hundred minus the membership of the Senate in the eighteen senior Centuries, then the knight pool is reasonably wide, and one knight might perhaps sit on one jury in any year.''

Lucius Cotta paused, well satisfied with what his eyes saw. He went on more briskly. ''A man of the First Class, my fellow senators, is just that. A man of the First Class. A prominent citizen of means, with an income of no less than three hundred thousand sesterces per annum. Yet because Rome is now ancient, some things have not changed, or else have continued in the old way but with extra people or functions tacked on. Like the First Class. At the very beginning we had only the eighteen senior Centuries, but because we doggedly kept those eighteen Centuries to only one hundred men in each, we had to expand the First Class by tacking on more Centuries. When we got to seventy-three extra Centuries tacked on, we decided to expand the First Class in a different way—not by keeping on adding more Centuries, but by increasing the number of men in each Century beyond the old one hundred. So we ended up with what I might call a top-light First Class! Just one thousand eight hundred men in the senior eighteen Centuries, and many thousands of men in the seventy-three other Centuries.

''So why not, I asked myself, offer public duty to these many, many thousands of men of the First Class who are not senior enough in family or name to belong to the eighteen Centuries of the Public Horse? If these more junior men were to form one third of each and every jury empaneled, the burden of duty for one man would be extremely light, yet a great incentive for the vast body of more junior knights we call the *tribuni aerarii*. Imagine if you will a jury of, say, fifty-one men: seventeen senators, seventeen knights of the Public Horse, and seventeen *tribuni aerarii*. The seventeen senators have the clout of experience, legal knowledge and long association with jury duty. The seventeen knights of the Public Horse have the clout of distinguished family and great wealth. And the seventeen *tribuni aerarii* have the clout of freshness, a new and different experience, membership in the First Class of Roman citizens, and at least considerable wealth.''

Both the hands went out again; Lucius Cotta dropped the right one and extended the left toward the massive bronze doors of the Curia Hostilia. "That is my solution, Conscript Fathers! A tripartite jury of equal numbers of men from all three orders within the First Class. If you award me a *senatus consultum*, I will draft my measure in properly legal fashion and present it to the Assembly of the People."

Pompey held the *fasces* for the month of September, and sat upon his curule chair at the front of the dais. Beside him was an empty chair—that of Crassus.

"How says the senior consul-elect?" Pompey asked correctly of Quintus Hortensius.

"The senior consul-elect commends Lucius Cotta for this splendid piece of work," said Hortensius. "Speaking as a curule magistrate-elect *and* as an advocate in the courts, I applaud this eminently sensible solution to a vexed problem."

"The junior consul-elect?" asked Pompey.

"I concur with my senior colleague," said Metellus Little Goat, who had no reason to oppose the measure now that the case of Gaius Verres was in the past and Verres himself vanished.

And so it went through the ranks of those asked to speak; no one could find fault. There were some who were tempted to find fault, of course, but every time they thought of how much jury duty finding fault was likely to let them in for, they shuddered and ended in saying nothing.

"It really is splendid," said Cicero to Caesar as the exodus from the House drew them together. "We're both men who like to work with honest juries. How cunning Lucius Cotta was! Two segments of the jury would have to be bribed to secure the right verdict—which is more expensive by far than half!—and what one segment accepted, the other two would be inclined to deny. I predict, my dear Caesar, that while jury bribery may not entirely disappear, there will be considerably less of it. The *tribuni aerarii* will regard it as a matter of honor to behave decently and justify their incorporation. Yes indeed, Lucius Cotta has been very clever!''

Caesar took great pleasure in reporting this to his uncle over dinner in his own *triclinium*. Neither Aurelia nor Cinnilla was present; Cinnilla was into her fourth month of pregnancy and suffering an almost constant sickness of the stomach, and Aurelia was caring for little Julia, who was also ailing in a minor way. So the two men were alone, and not ungrateful for it.

''I admit that the bribery aspect did occur to me,'' said Lucius Cotta, smiling, ''but I couldn't very well be blunt in the House when I wanted the measure approved.''

''True. Nonetheless it has occurred to most, and as far as Cicero and I are concerned, it's a terrific bonus. On the other hand, Hortensius may well privately deplore it. Bribery aside, the best part about your solution is that it will preserve Sulla's standing courts, which I believe are the greatest advance in Roman justice since the establishment of trial and jury.''

''Oh, very nice praise, Caesar!'' Lucius Cotta glowed for a moment, then put his wine cup on the table and frowned. ''You're in Marcus Crassus's confidence, Caesar, so perhaps you can allay my fears. In many ways this has been a halcyon year—no wars on the horizon we're not winning comfortably, the Treasury under less stress than it has been in a very long time, a proper census being taken of all the Roman citizens in Italy, a good harvest in Italy and the provinces, and something like a nice balance struck between old and new in government. If one leaves aside the unconstitutionality of Magnus's consulship, truly this year has been a good one. As I walked here through the Subura, I got a feeling that the ordinary Roman people— the sort who rarely get to exercise a vote and find Crassus's free grain a genuine help in stretching their income—are happier than they have been in at least a generation. I agree that they're not the ones who suffer when heads roll and the gutters of the Forum run with blood, but the mood that kind of thing engenders infects them too, even though their own heads are not in jeopardy.''

Pausing for breath, Lucius Cotta took a mouthful of wine.

''I think I know what you're going to say, Uncle, but say it anyway,'' said Caesar.

''It's been a wonderful summer, especially for the lowly. A host of entertainments, food enough to eat to bursting point and take home sackloads to feed every member of the family to bursting point, lion hunts and performing elephants, chariot races galore, every farce and mime known to the Roman stage—and free wheat! Public Horses on parade. Peaceful elections held on time for once. Even a sensational trial wherein the villain got his just deserts

and Hortensius a smack in the eye. Cleaned up swimming holes in the Trigarium. Not nearly as much disease as everyone expected, and no outbreak
of the summer paralysis. Crimes and confidence tricks quite depressed!''
Lucius Cotta smiled. ''Whether they deserve it or not, Caesar, most of the
credit—and the praise!—is going to the consuls. People's feelings about them
are as romantic as they are fanciful. You and I, of course, know better.
Though one cannot deny that they've been excellent consuls—legislated only
to save their necks, and for the rest, left well enough alone. And yet—and
yet—there are rumors growing, Caesar. Rumors that all is not amicable
between Pompeius and Crassus. That they're not speaking to each other. That
when one is obliged to be present somewhere, the other will be absent. And
I'm concerned, because I believe that the rumors are true—and because I
believe that we of the upper class owe the ordinary people one short little
perfect year.''

"Yes, the rumors are true," said Caesar soberly.

"Why?"

"Chiefly because Marcus Crassus stole Pompeius's thunder and Pompeius cannot bear to be eclipsed. He thought that between the Public Horse
farce and his votive games, he'd be everyone's hero. Then Crassus provided
three months of free grain. *And* demonstrated to Pompeius that he's not the
only man in Rome with an absolutely vast fortune. So Pompeius has retaliated
by cutting Crassus out of his life, consular and private. He should, for instance,
have notified Crassus that there was a meeting of the Senate today—oh,
everyone knows there's always a meeting on the Kalends of September, but
the senior consul calls it, and must notify his juniors.''

"He notified me," said Lucius Cotta.

"He notified everyone except Crassus. And Crassus interpreted that as
a direct insult. So he wouldn't go. I tried to reason with him, but he refused
to budge.''

"Oh, *cacat!*" cried Lucius Cotta, and flopped back on his couch in
disgust. "Between the pair of them, they'll ruin what would otherwise be a
year in a thousand!''

"No," said Caesar, "they won't. I won't let them. But if I do manage
to patch up a peace between them, it won't last long. So I'll wait until the
end of the year, Uncle, and bring some Cottae into my schemes. At the end
of the year we'll force them to stage some sort of public reconciliation that
will bring tears to every eye. That way, it's *exeunt omnes* on the last day of
the year with everybody singing their lungs out—Plautus would be proud of
the production.''

"You know," said Lucius Cotta thoughtfully, straightening up, "when you were a boy, Caesar, I had you in my catalogue of men as what Archimedes might have called a prime mover—you know, 'Give me a place to stand, and I will shift the whole globe!' That was genuinely how I saw you, and one of the chief reasons why I mourned when you were made *flamen Dialis*. So when you managed to wriggle out of it, I put you back where I used to have you in my catalogue of men. But it hasn't turned out the way I thought it would. You move through the most complicated system of gears and cogs! For such a young man, you're very well known at many levels from the Senate to the Subura. But not as a prime mover. More in the fashion of a lord high chamberlain in an oriental court—content to be the mind behind events, but allowing other men to enjoy the glory.'' He shook his head. ''I find that so odd in you!''

Caesar had listened to this with tight mouth and two spots of color burning in his normally ivory cheeks. ''You didn't have me wrongly catalogued, Uncle,'' he said. ''But I think perhaps my flaminate was the best thing could have happened to me, given that I did manage to wriggle out of it. It taught me to be subtle as well as powerful, it taught me to hide my light when showing it might have snuffed it out, it taught me that time is a more valuable ally than money or mentors, it taught me the patience my mother used to think I would never own—and it taught me that *nothing* is wasted! I am still learning, Uncle. I hope I never stop! And Lucullus taught me that I could continue to learn by developing ideas and launching them through the agency of other men. I stand back and see what happens. Be at peace, Lucius Cotta. My time to stand forth as the greatest prime mover of them all will come. I will be consul in my year, even. But that will only be my beginning.''

November was a cruel month, even though its weather was as fair and pleasant as any May when season and calendar coincided. Aunt Julia suddenly began to sicken with some obscure complaint none of the physicians including Lucius Tuccius could diagnose. It was a syndrome of loss—weight, spirit, energy, interest.

''I think she's tired, Caesar,'' said Aurelia.

''But not tired of living, surely!'' cried Caesar, who couldn't bear the thought of a world without Aunt Julia.

''Oh yes,'' answered Aurelia. ''That most of all.''

''She has so much to live for!''

''No. Her husband and her son are dead, so she has nothing to live for. I've told you that before.'' And, wonder of wonders, the beautiful purple eyes filled with tears. ''I half understand. My husband is dead. If you were to die, Caesar, that would be my end. I would have nothing to live for.''

"It would be a grief, certainly, but not an end, Mater," he said, unable to believe he meant that much to her. "You have grandchildren, you have two daughters."

"That is true. Julia does not, however." The tears were dashed away. "But a woman's life is in her men, Caesar, not in the women she has borne or the children they bear. No woman truly esteems her lot, it is thankless and obscure. Men move and control the world, not women. So the intelligent woman lives her life through her men."

He sensed a weakening in her, and struck. "Mater, just what did Sulla mean to you?"

And, weakened, she answered. "He meant excitement and interest. He esteemed me in a way your father never did, though I never longed to be Sulla's wife. Or his mistress, for that matter. Your father was my true mate. Sulla was my dream. Not because of the greatness in him, but because of the agony. Of friends he had none who were his peers. Just the Greek actor who followed him into retirement, and me, a woman." The weakness left her, she looked brisk. "But enough of that! You may take me to see Julia."

Julia looked and sounded a shadow of her old self, but sparked a little when she saw Caesar, who understood a little better what his mother had told him: the intelligent woman lived through men. Should that be? he wondered. Ought not women have more? But then he envisioned the Forum Romanum and the Curia Hostilia filled half with women, and shuddered. They were for pleasure, private company, service, and usefulness. Too bad if they wanted more!

"Tell me a Forum story," said Julia, holding Caesar's hand.

Her own hand, he noted, grew more and more to resemble a talon, and his nostrils, so attuned to that exquisite perfume she had always exuded, these days sensed a sourness in it, an underlying odor it could not quite disguise. Not exactly age. The word death occurred to him; he pushed it away and glued a smile to his face.

"Actually I do have a Forum story to tell you—or rather, a basilica story," he said lightly.

"A basilica? Which one?"

"The first basilica, the Basilica Porcia which Cato the Censor built a hundred years ago. As you know, one end of its ground floor has always been the headquarters of the College of Tribunes of the Plebs. And perhaps because the tribunes of the plebs are once more enjoying their full powers, this year's lot decided to improve their lot. Right in the middle of their space is a huge column which makes it just about impossible for them to conduct a meeting of more than their ten selves. So Plautius, the head of the college, decided to get rid of the pillar. He called in our most distinguished firm of architects, and asked it if there was any possibility the column could be dispensed with. And after much measuring and calculating, he got his answer: yes, the column could be dispensed with and the building would remain standing comfortably.''

Julia lay on her couch with her body fitted around Caesar, sitting on its edge; her big grey eyes, sunk these days into bruised-looking orbits, were fixed on his face. She was smiling, genuinely interested. ''I cannot imagine where this story is going,'' she said, squeezing his hand.

''Nor could the tribunes of the plebs! The builders brought in their scaffolds and shored the place up securely, the architects probed and tapped, everything was ready to demolish the pillar. When in walked a young man of twenty-three—they tell me he will be twenty-four in December—and announced that he forbade the removal of the pillar!

'' 'And who might you be?' asked Plautius.

'' 'I am Marcus Porcius Cato, the great-grandson of Cato the Censor, who built this basilica,' said the young man.

'' 'Good for you!' said Plautius. 'Now shift yourself out of the way before the pillar comes down on top of you!'

''But he wouldn't shift, and nothing they could do or say would make him shift. He set up camp right there beneath the offending obstacle, and harangued them unmercifully while ever there was someone present to harangue. On and on and on, in a voice which, says Plautius—and I agree with him, having heard it for myself—could shear a bronze statue in half.''

Aurelia now looked as interested as Julia, and snorted. ''What rubbish!'' she said. ''I hope they vetoed him!''

''They tried. He refused to accept the veto. He was a full member of the Plebs and his great-grandfather built the place, they would disturb it over his dead body. I give him this—he hung on like a dog to a rat! His reasons were endless, but mostly all revolved around the fact that his great-grandfather had built the Basilica Porcia in a certain way, and that certain way was sacred, hallowed, a part of the *mos maiorum*.''

Julia chuckled. ''Who won?'' she asked.

''Young Cato did, of course. The tribunes of the plebs just couldn't stand that voice anymore.''

''Didn't they try force? Couldn't they throw him off the Tarpeian Rock?'' asked Aurelia, looking scandalized.

''I think they would have loved to, but the trouble was that by the time they might have been driven to use force, word had got around, and so many people had gathered every day to watch the struggle that Plautius felt it would do the tribunes of the plebs more harm in the eyes of the populace to use real force than any good removal of the column might have brought them. Oh, they threw him out of the building a dozen times, but he just came back! And it became clear that he would never give up. So Plautius held a meeting and all ten members of the college agreed to suffer the continued presence of the pillar," said Caesar.

"What does this Cato look like?" asked Julia.

Caesar wrinkled his brow. "Difficult to describe. He's as ugly as he is pretty. Perhaps the closest description is to say that he reminds me of a highly bred horse trying to eat an apple through a latticework trellis."

"All teeth and nose," said Julia instantly.

"Exactly."

"I can tell you another story about him," said Aurelia.

"Go ahead!" said Caesar, noting Julia's interest.

"It happened before young Cato turned twenty. He had always been madly in love with his cousin Aemilia Lepida—Mamercus's daughter. She was already engaged to Metellus Scipio when Metellus Scipio went out to Spain to serve with his father, but when he came back some years before his father, he and Aemilia Lepida fell out badly. She broke off the engagement and announced that she was going to marry Cato instead. Mamercus was furious! Especially, it seems, because my friend Servilia—she's Cato's half sister—had warned him about Cato and Aemilia Lepida. Anyway, it all turned out fine in the end, because Aemilia Lepida had no intention of marrying Cato. She just used him to make Metellus Scipio jealous. And when Metellus Scipio came to her and begged to be forgiven, Cato was out, Metellus Scipio was in again. Shortly afterward they were married. Cato, however, took his rejection so badly that he tried to kill both Metellus Scipio and Aemilia Lepida, and when that was frustrated, he tried to sue Metellus Scipio for alienating Aemilia Lepida's affections! His half brother Servilius Caepio—a nice young man, just married to Hortensius's daughter—persuaded Cato that he was making a fool of himself, and Cato desisted. Except, apparently, that for the next year he wrote endless poetry I am assured was all very bad."

"It's funny," said Caesar, shoulders shaking.

"It wasn't at the time, believe me! Whatever young Cato may turn out to be like later on, his career to date indicates that he will always have the ability to irritate people intensely," said Aurelia. "Mamercus and Cornelia Sulla—not to mention Servilia!—detest him. So these days, I believe, does Aemilia."

"He's married to someone else now, isn't he?" asked Caesar.

"Yes, to an Attilia. Not a terribly good match, but then, he doesn't have a great deal of money. His wife bore a little girl last year."

And that, decided Caesar, studying his aunt, was as much diverting company as she could tolerate for the moment.

"I don't want to believe it, but you're right, Mater. Aunt Julia is going to die," he said to Aurelia as soon as they left Julia's house.

"Eventually, but not yet, my son. She'll last well into the new year, perhaps longer."

"Oh, I hope she lasts until after I leave for Spain!"

"Caesar! That's a coward's hope," said his remorseless mother. "You don't usually shirk unpleasant events."

He stopped in the middle of the Alta Semita, both hands out and clenched into fists. "Oh, leave me alone!" he cried, so loudly that two passersby glanced at the handsome pair curiously. "It's always duty, duty, duty! Well, Mater, to be in Rome to bury Aunt Julia is one duty I don't want!" And only custom and courtesy kept him at his mother's side for the rest of that uncomfortable walk home; he would have given almost anything to have left her to find her own way back to the Subura.

Home wasn't the happiest of places either. Now into her sixth month of pregnancy, Cinnilla wasn't very well. The "all day and all night sickness" as Caesar phrased it, trying to make a joke, had disappeared, only to be succeeded by a degree of swelling in the feet and legs which both distressed and alarmed the prospective mother. Who was obliged to spend most of her time in bed, feet and legs elevated. Not only was Cinnilla uncomfortable and afraid; she was cross too. An attitude of mind the whole household found difficult to cope with, as it did not belong in Cinnilla's nature.

Thus it was that for the first time during his periods of residence in Rome, Caesar elected to spend his nights as well as his days elsewhere than the apartment in the Subura. To stay with Crassus was not possible; Crassus could only think of the cost of feeding an extra mouth, especially toward the end of the most expensive year of his life. And Gaius Matius had recently married, so the other ground-floor apartment of Aurelia's insula (which would have been the most convenient place to stay) was also not available. Nor was he in the mood for dalliance; the affair with Caecilia Metella Little Goat had been abruptly terminated when Verres decamped to Massilia, and no one had yet appealed to him as a replacement. Truth to tell, the frail state of physical well-being in both his aunt and his wife did not encourage dalliance. So he ended in renting a small four-roomed apartment down the Vicus Patricius from his home, and spent most of his time there with Lucius Decumius for company. As the neighborhood was quite as unfashionable as his mother's insula, his political acquaintances would not have cared to visit him there, and the secretive side of him liked that anyway. The forethought in him also saw its possibilities when the mood for dalliance returned; he began to take an interest in the place (it was in a good building) and acquire a few nice pieces of furniture and art. Not to mention a good bed.

At the beginning of December he effected a most touching reconciliation. The two consuls were standing together on the rostra waiting for the urban praetor Lucius Cotta to convene the Assembly of the People; it was the day upon which Cotta's law reforming the jury system was to be ratified. Though Crassus held the *fasces* for December and was obliged to attend, Pompey was not about to permit a public occasion of such moment to pass without his presence. And as the consuls could not very well stand one to either end of the rostra without provoking much comment from the crowd, they stood together. In silence, admittedly, but at least in apparent amity.

Along to attend the meeting came Caesar's first cousin, young Gaius Cotta, the son of the late consul Gaius Cotta. Though he was not yet a member of the Senate, nothing could have prevented his casting his vote in the tribes; the law belonged to his Uncle Lucius. But when he saw Pompey and Crassus looking more like a team than they had done in months, he cried out so loudly that the noise and movement around him stilled. Everyone looked his way.

"Oh!" he cried again, more loudly still. "My dream! My dream has come true!"

And he bounded onto the rostra so suddenly that Pompey and Crassus automatically stepped apart. Young Gaius Cotta planted himself between them, one arm around each, and gazed at the throng in the well of the Comitia with tears streaming down his face.

"*Quirites!*" he shouted, "last night I had a dream! Jupiter Optimus Maximus spoke to me out of cloud and fire, soaked me and burned me! Far below where I stood I could see the two figures of our consuls, Gnaeus Pompeius Magnus and Marcus Licinius Crassus. But they were not as I saw them today, standing together. Instead they stood one to the east and one to the west, stubbornly looking in opposite directions. And the voice of the Great God said to me out of the cloud and the fire, 'They must not leave their consular office disliking each other! They must leave as friends!' "

An utter silence had fallen; a thousand faces looked up at the three men. Gaius Cotta let his arms fall from about the consuls and stepped forward, then turned to face them.

"Gnaeus Pompeius, Marcus Licinius, will you not be friends?" the young man asked in a ringing voice.

For a long moment no one moved. Pompey's expression was stern, so was Crassus's.

"Come, shake hands! Be friends!" shouted Gaius Cotta.

Neither consul moved. Then Crassus rotated toward Pompey and held out one massive hand.

"I am delighted to yield first place to a man who was called Magnus before he so much as had a beard, and celebrated not one but two triumphs before he was a senator!" Crassus yelled.

Pompey emitted a sound somewhere between a squeal and a yelp, grabbed at Crassus's paw and wrung both it and his forearm, face transfigured. They stepped toward each other and fell on each other's necks. And the crowd went wild. Soon the news of the reconciliation was speeding into the Velabrum, into the Subura, into the manufactories beyond the swamp of the Palus Ceroliae; people came running from everywhere to see if it was true that the consuls were friends again. For the rest of that day the two of them walked around Rome together, shaking hands, allowing themselves to be touched, accepting congratulations.

"There are triumphs, and then again, there are triumphs," said Caesar to his uncle Lucius and his cousin Gaius. "Today was the better kind of triumph. I thank you for your help."

"Was it hard to convince them that they had to do it?" asked the young Gaius Cotta.

"Not really. If that pair understand nothing else, they always understand the importance of popularity. Neither of them is an adept at the art of compromise, but I split the credit equally between them, and that satisfied them. Crassus had to swallow his pride and say all those nauseating things about dear Pompeius. But on the other hand he reaped the accolades for being the one to hold out his hand first and make the concessions. So, as in the duel about pleasing the people, it was Crassus won. Luckily Pompeius doesn't see that. He thinks *he* won because he stood aloof and forced his colleague to admit his superiority."

"Then you had better hope," said Lucius Cotta, "that Magnus doesn't find out who really won until after the year is over."

"I'm afraid it disrupted your meeting, Uncle. You'll never keep a crowd still enough to vote now."

"Tomorrow will do just as well."

The two Cottae and Caesar left the Forum Romanum via the Vestal Stairs onto the Palatine, but halfway up Caesar stopped and turned to look back. There they were, Pompey and Crassus, surrounded by hordes of happy Romans. And happy themselves, the breach forgotten.

"This year has been a watershed," said Caesar, beginning to ascend the rest of the steps. "All of us have crossed some kind of barrier. I have the oddest feeling that none of us will enjoy the same life again."

"Yes, I know what you mean," said Lucius Cotta. "My stab at the history books happened this year, with my jury law. If I ever decide to run for consul, I suspect it will be an anticlimax."

"I wasn't thinking along the lines of anticlimax," said Caesar, laughing.

"What will Pompeius and Crassus do when the year is ended?" asked young Gaius Cotta. "They say neither of them wants to go out to govern a province."

"That's true enough," said Lucius Cotta. "Both of them are returning to private life. Why not? They've each had great campaigns recently—they're both so rich they don't need to stuff provincial profits in their purses—and they crowned their dual consulship with laws to exonerate them from any suspicion of treason and laws to grant their veterans all the land they want. I wouldn't go to govern a province if I were in their boots!"

"You'd find their boots more uncomfortable than they're worth," said Caesar. "Where can they go from here? Pompeius says he's returning to his beloved Picenum and will never darken the doors of the Senate again. And Crassus is absolutely driven to earn back the thousand talents he spent this year." He heaved a huge and happy sigh. "And I am going to Further Spain as its quaestor, under a governor I happen to like."

"Pompeius's ex-brother-in-law, Gaius Antistius Vetus," said young Cotta with a grin.

Caesar didn't mention his most devout wish: that he leave for Spain before Aunt Julia died.

But that was not to be. He was summoned to her bedside on a blustery night midway through February; his mother had been staying in Julia's house for some days.

She was conscious, and could still see; when he entered the room her eyes lit up a little. "I waited for you," she said.

His chest ached with the effort of keeping his emotions under control, but he managed to smile as he kissed her, then sat upon the edge of her bed, as he always did. "I wouldn't have let you go," he said lightly.

"I wanted to see you," she said; her voice was quite strong and distinct.

"You see me, Aunt Julia. What can I do for you?"

"What would you do for me, Gaius Julius?"

"Anything in the world," he said, and meant it.

"Oh, that relieves me! It means you will forgive me."

"Forgive you?" he asked, astonished. "There's nothing to forgive, absolutely nothing!"

"Forgive me for not preventing Gaius Marius from making you the *flamen Dialis,"* she said.

"Aunt Julia, no one could stop Gaius Marius from doing what he wanted to do!" Caesar cried. "Rome's outskirts are ornamented with the tombs of the men who tried! It never for one moment occurred to me to blame you! And you mustn't blame yourself."

"I won't if you don't."

"I don't. You have my word on it."

Her eyes closed, tears oozed from beneath their lids. "My poor son," she whispered. "It is a terrible thing to be the son of a great man. . . . I hope you have no sons, for you will be a very great man."

His gaze met his mother's, and he suddenly saw a tinge of jealousy in her face.

The response was savage and immediate; he gathered Julia into his arms and put his cheek to hers. "Aunt Julia," he said into her ear, "what will I do without your arms around me and all your kisses?" And there! his eyes were saying to his mother, *she* was the source of my juvenile hugs and kisses, not you! Never you! How can I live without Aunt Julia?

But Aunt Julia didn't answer, nor did she lift her lids to look at him. She neither spoke nor looked again, but died still clasped in his arms several hours later.

Lucius Decimius and his sons were there, so was Burgundus; he sent his mother home with them, and himself walked through the bustling crowds of day without seeing a single person. Aunt Julia was dead, and no one save he and his family knew of it. The wife of Gaius Marius was dead, and no one save he and his family knew of it. Just when the tears should have come this thought came, and the tears were driven inward forever. Rome should know of her death! And Rome would know of her death!

"A quiet funeral," said Aurelia when he entered her apartment at the going down of the sun.

"Oh no!" said Caesar, who looked enormously tall, filled with light and power. "Aunt Julia is going to have the biggest woman's funeral since the death of Cornelia the Mother of the Gracchi! And all the ancestral masks will come out, including the masks of Gaius Marius and his son."

She gasped. "Caesar, you can't! Hortensius and Metellus Little Goat are consuls, Rome has gone conservative with a vengeance! Some Hortensian tribune of the plebs will have you thrown from the Tarpeian Rock if you display the *imagines* of two men their Rome brands as traitors!''

''Let them try,'' said Caesar scornfully. ''I will send Aunt Julia to the darkness with all the honor and public acclaim she ought to have.''

And that resolution of course made the grief easier to bear; Caesar had something concrete to do, an outlet he found worthier of that lovely lady than bouts of tears and a constant feeling of irreplaceable loss. Keep busy, keep working. Work for *her*.

He knew how he was going to get away with it, of course. Which was to make it impossible for any of the magistrates to foil him or prosecute him, no matter how they tried. But preferably to make it impossible for them to try at all. The funeral was arranged with Rome's most prestigious undertakers, and the price agreed upon was fifty talents of silver; for this huge amount of money everyone agreed to participate despite the fact that Caesar intended to display the masks of Gaius Marius and Young Marius for all of Rome to see. Actors were hired, chariots for them to ride in: the ancestors would include King Ancus Marcius, Quintus Marcius Rex, Iulus, that early Julian consul, Sextus Caesar and Lucius Caesar, and Gaius Marius and his son.

But that was not the most important arrangement; he would trust no one except Lucius Decumius and his Brethren of the crossroads college to do that. Which was to spread the word as far and wide as possible through Rome that the great Julia, widow of Gaius Marius, had died and would be buried at the third hour in two days' time. Everyone who wanted to come must come. For Gaius Marius there had been no public funeral, and for his son only the sight of a head rotting away on the rostra. Therefore Julia's obsequies would be splendid, and Rome could do her long overdue mourning for the Marii by attending Julia's rites.

He caught all the magistrates napping, for no one informed them what was going to happen, and none of the magistrates had planned to be present at Julia's funeral. But Marcus Crassus came, and so did Varro Lucullus, and Mamercus with Cornelia Sulla, and none other than Philippus. So too did Metellus Pius the Piglet come. Plus the two Cottae, of course. All of them had been warned; Caesar wanted no one unwillingly compromised.

And Rome turned out en masse, thousands upon thousands of ordinary people who cared nothing for interdictions and decrees of outlawry or sacrilege. Here was a chance at last to mourn for Gaius Marius, to see that beloved fierce face with its gigantic eyebrows and its stern frown worn by a man who was as tall and as broad as Gaius Marius had been. And Young Marius too, so comely, so impressive! But more impressive still was Gaius

Marius's living nephew, robed in a mourning toga as black as the coats of the horses which drew the chariots, his golden hair and pale face a striking contrast to the pall of darkness around him. So good-looking! So godlike! This was Caesar's first appearance before a huge crowd since the days when he had supported crippled old Marius, and he needed to ensure that the people of Rome would not forget him. He was the only heir Gaius Marius had left, and he intended that every man and woman who came to Julia's funeral would know who he was: Gaius Marius's heir.

He gave her eulogy from the rostra; it was the first time he had spoken from that lofty perch, the first time he had looked down upon a sea of faces whose eyes were all directed at him. Julia herself had been exquisitely prepared for her last and most public appearance, so artfully made up and padded that she looked like a young woman; her beauty alone made the crowd weep. Three other very beautiful women were near her on the rostral platform, one in her fifties whom Lucius Decumius's agents were busy whispering here and there was Caesar's mother, one of about forty whose red-gold hair proclaimed her Sulla's daughter, and a very pregnant little dark girl sitting in a black sedan chair who turned out to be Caesar's wife. On her lap there sat the most ravishing silver-fair child perhaps seven years old; it was not difficult to tell that this was Caesar's daughter.

"My family," cried Caesar from the rostra in his high-pitched orator's voice, "is one of women! There are no men of my father's generation left alive, and of the men in my own generation, I am the only one here in Rome today to mourn the passing of my family's most senior woman. Julia, whose name was never shortened or added to, for she was the eldest of her Julian peers, and graced the name of her *gens* so incomparably that Rome knows no other woman like her. She had beauty, a gentle disposition, all the loyalty a man could ask for in a wife or mother or aunt, the warmth of a loving nature, the kindness of a generous spirit. The only other woman to whom I might compare her also lost her husband and her children long before she died—I mean, of course, another great patrician woman, Cornelia the Mother of the Gracchi. Their careers were not unalike in that Cornelia and Julia both suffered the loss of a son whose head was removed from his body, and neither of whom was allowed burial. And who can tell which woman's sorrows were the greater, when one suffered the deaths of all her sons but knew not the disgrace of a dishonored husband, and the other suffered the death of her only child but knew the disgrace of a dishonored husband and poverty in her old age? Cornelia lived into her eighties, Julia expired in her fifty-ninth year. Was that lack of courage on Julia's part, or an easier life on Cornelia's? We will never know, people of Rome. Nor should we ever ask. They were two great and illustrious women.

"But I am here to honor Julia, not Cornelia. Julia of the Julii Caesares, whose lineage was greater than any other Roman woman's. For in her were joined the Kings of Rome and the founding Gods of Rome. Her mother was Marcia, the youngest daughter of Quintus Marcius Rex, the august descendant of the fourth King of Rome, Ancus Marcius, and who is remembered every day in this great city with gratitude and praise, for he it was who brought Rome fresh sweet water to gush out of fountains in every public square and crossroads. Her father was Gaius Julius Caesar, the younger son of Sextus Julius Caesar. Patricians of the tribe Fabia, once the Kings of Alba Longa, and descended from Iulus, who was the son of Aeneas, who was the son of the goddess Venus. In her veins there ran the blood of a mighty and powerful goddess, and the blood of Mars and Romulus too—for who was Rhea Silvia, the mother of Romulus and Remus? She was Julia! Thus in my blood-aunt Julia the supreme mortal power of kings conjoined with the immortal power of the gods who hold even the greatest kings in thrall.

"When she was eighteen years old, she married a man of whom every last one of you knows, and many of you knew as a living man. She married Gaius Marius, consul of Rome an unprecedented seven times, called the Third Founder of Rome, the conqueror of King Jugurtha of Numidia, the conqueror of the Germans, and winner of the earliest battles in the Italian War. And until this indisputably mighty man died at the height of his power, she remained his loyal and faithful wife. By him she had her only child, Gaius Marius Junior, who was senior consul of Rome at the age of twenty-six.

"It is not her fault that neither husband nor son kept his reputation untarnished after death. It is not her fault that an interdiction was placed upon her and that she was forced to move from her home of twenty-eight years to a far meaner house exposed to the bitter north winds which whistle across the outer Quirinal. It is not her fault that Fortune left her little to live for save to help the people of her new district in their troubles. It is not her fault that she died untimely. It is not her fault that the life-masks of her husband and son were forbidden ever to be displayed again.

"When I was a child I knew her well, for I was Gaius Marius's boy during that terrible year when his second stroke left him a helpless cripple. Every day I went to her house to do my duty to her husband and to receive her sweet thanks. From her I had a love I have known from no other woman, for my mother had to be my father too, and could not permit herself the luxury of hugs and kisses, for they are not the province of a father. But I had Aunt Julia for those, and though I live to be a thousand years old, I will never forget a single hug, a single kiss, a single loving glance from her beautiful grey eyes. And I say to you, people of Rome, mourn for her! Mourn for her as I do! Mourn for her fate and for the sadness of an undeservedly sad life. And mourn too for the fates of her husband and her son, whose *imagines* I show you on this unhappy day. They say I am not allowed to show you the Marian masks, that I can be stripped of my rank and my citizenship for committing this outrageous crime of displaying here in the Forum—which knew both men so well!—two inanimate things made of wax and paint and someone else's hair! And I say to you that if it be so ordered, if I be stripped of my rank and my citizenship for displaying the Marian masks, *then so be it*! For I will honor this aunt of my blood as she ought to be honored, and that honor is all wrapped up in her devotion to the Marii, who were husband and son. I show these *imagines* for Julia's sake, and I will permit no magistrate in this city to remove them from her funeral procession! Step forward, Gaius Marius, step forward, Gaius Marius Junior! Honor your wife and mother, Julia of the Julii Caesares, daughter of kings and gods!''

The crowd had wept desolately, but when the actors wearing the masks of Gaius Marius and Young Marius stepped forward to make their obeisances to the stiff still figure on the bier, a murmuring began that swelled into a chorus of exclamations and then exploded into a full-throated roar. And Hortensius and Metellus Little Goat, watching appalled from the top of the Senate House steps, turned away in defeat. Gaius Julius Caesar's crime would have to be suffered in legal and disciplinary silence, for Rome wholeheartedly approved.

"It was brilliant," said Hortensius to Catulus a little later. "Not only did he defy Sulla's and the Senate's laws, but he used the opportunity to remind every last face in that crowd that *he* is descended from kings and gods!"

"Well, Caesar, you got away with it," said Aurelia at the end of that very long day.

"I knew I would," he said, dropping his black toga on the floor with a sigh of sheer weariness. "The conservative rump of the Senate may be in power this year, but not one member of it can be sure that next year's electors will feel the same way. Romans like a change of government. And Romans like a man with the courage of his convictions. Especially if he elevates old Gaius Marius to the pedestal from which the people of this city have never torn him down, no matter how many of his statues toppled."

Moving like an ancient dropsical woman, Cinnilla dragged herself into the room and went to sit at Caesar's side on the couch. "It was wonderful," she said, pushing her hand into his. "I am glad I felt well enough to attend the eulogy, even if I couldn't get any further. And how well you spoke!"

Turning side on, he cupped her face in his fingers and pushed a stray strand of hair away from her brow. "My poor little one," he said tenderly, "not much longer to go now." He swept her feet from the floor and placed them in his lap. "You ought not to sit with your legs dangling, you know that."

"Oh, Caesar, it has been so long! I carried Julia with no trouble whatsoever, yet here I am this second time in such a mess! I don't understand it," she said, eyes filling with tears.

"I do," said Aurelia. "This one is a boy. I carried both my girls without trouble, but you, Caesar, were a burden."

"I think," said Caesar, putting Cinnilla's feet on the couch beside him and rising, "that I'll go to my own apartment to sleep tonight."

"Oh, please, Caesar, don't!" begged his wife, face puckering. "Stay here tonight. I promise we won't talk of babies and women's troubles. Aurelia, you must stop or he'll leave us."

"Pah!" said Aurelia, getting up from her chair. "Where is Eutychus? What all of us need is a little food."

"He's settling Strophantes in," said Cinnilla sadly, her face clearing when Caesar, resigned, sank back onto the couch. "Poor old man! They're all gone."

"So will he be soon," said Caesar.

"Oh, don't say that!"

"It's in his face, wife. And it will be a mercy."

"I hope," said Cinnilla, "that I don't live to be the last one left. That is the worst fate of all, I think."

"A worse fate," said Caesar, who didn't want to be reminded of painful things, "is to speak of nothing except gloom."

"It's just Rome," she said, smiling to reveal that little pink crease of inner lip. "You'll be better when you get to Spain. You're never really as happy in Rome as you are when you're traveling."

"Next *nundinus,* wife, by sea at the start of winter. You are quite right. Rome isn't where I want to be. So how about having this baby anytime between now and the next *nundinus*? I'd like to see my son before I leave."

He saw his son before he left at the next *nundinus,* but the child when finally the midwife and Lucius Tuccius managed to remove it from the birth canal had obviously been dead for several days. And Cinnilla, swollen and convulsing, one side paralyzed from a massive stroke, died at almost the same moment as she put forth her stillborn boy.

No one could believe it. If Julia had been a shock and a grief, the loss of Cinnilla was unbearable. Caesar wept as he never had in his life before, and cared not who saw him. Hour after hour, from the moment of that first horrible convulsion until it was time to bury her too. One was possible. Two was a nightmare from which he never expected to awaken. Of the dead child he had neither room nor inclination to think; Cinnilla was dead, and she had been a part of his family life from his fourteenth year, a part of the pain of his flaminate, the chubby dark mite whom he had loved as a sister for as long as he has loved her as a wife. Seventeen years! They had been children together, the only children in that house.

Her death smote Aurelia as Julia's could not, and that iron woman wept as desolately as her son did. A light had gone out that would dim the rest of her life. Part grandchild, part daughter-in-law, a sweet little presence left only in echoes, an empty loom, half of an empty bed. Burgundus wept, Cardixa wept, their sons wept, and Lucius Decumius, Strophantes, Eutychus, all the servants who scarcely remembered Aurelia's apartment without Cinnilla there. The tenants of the insula wept, and a great many people in the Subura.

This funeral was different from Julia's. That had been a glory of sorts, a chance for the orator to show off a great woman and his own family. There were similarities; Caesar extracted the Cornelius Cinna *imagines* from the storage room in which he had hidden them alongside the masks of the two Marii, and they were worn by actors to scandalize Hortensius and Metellus Little Goat anew; and though it was not accepted practice to eulogize a young woman from the rostra, Caesar went through that public ordeal too. But not in a kind of glory. This time he spoke softly, and confined his remarks to the pleasure he had known in her company and the years during which she had consoled him for the loss of his boy's freedom. He talked about her smile and those dismal hairy garments she had dutifully woven for her destiny as *flaminica Dialis*. He talked about his daughter, whom he held in his arms while he spoke. He wept.

And he ended by saying, "I know nothing of grief beyond what I feel inside myself. That is grief's tragedy—that each of us must always deem his or her own grief greater than anyone else's. But I am prepared to confess to you that perhaps I am a cold, hard man whose greatest love is for his own *dignitas*. So be it. Once I refused to divorce Cinna's daughter. At the time I thought I refused to obey Sulla's command to divorce her for my own private benefit and the possibilities it opened up. Well, I have explained to you what grief's tragedy is. But that tragedy is as *nothing* to the tragedy of never knowing how much someone has meant to you until after that someone is dead."

No one cheered the *imago* of Lucius Cornelius Cinna, nor those of his ancestors. But Rome wept so deeply that for the second time in two *nundinae,* Caesar's enemies found themselves rendered impotent.

His mother was suddenly years older, absolutely heartbroken. A difficult business for the son, whose attempts to comfort her with hugs and kisses were still repulsed.

Am I so cold and hard because she is so cold and hard? But she isn't cold and hard with anyone except me! Oh, why does she do this to me? Look how she grieves for Cinnilla. And how she grieved for awful old Sulla.

If I were a woman, my child would be such a consolation. But I am a Roman nobleman, and a Roman nobleman's children are at best on the periphery of his life. How many times did I see my father? And what did I ever have to talk to him about?

"Mater," he said, "I give you little Julia to be your own. She's almost exactly the same age now as Cinnilla was when she came to live here. In time she'll fill the largest part of your vacant space. I won't try to suborn her away from you."

"I've had the child since she was born," said Aurelia, "and I know all that."

Old Strophantes shuffled in, looked rheumily at mother and son, shuffled out again.

"I must write to Uncle Publius in Smyrna," Aurelia said. "He's another one who has outlived everybody, poor old man."

"Yes, Mater, you do that."

"I don't understand you, Caesar, when you behave like the child who cries because he's eaten all his honey cake yet thinks it ought never to diminish."

"And what has provoked that remark?"

"You said it during Julia's funeral oration. That I had to be both mother and father to you, which meant I couldn't give you the hugs and kisses Julia did. When I heard you say that, I was relieved. You understood it at last. But now I find you just as bitter as ever. Accept your lot, my son. You mean more to me than life, than little Julia, than Cinnilla, than anyone. You mean more to me than your father did. And more by far than Sulla ever could have, even had I weakened. If there cannot be peace between us, can't we at least declare a truce?"

He smiled wryly. "Why not?" he asked.

"You'll come good once you get out of Rome, Caesar."

"That's what Cinnilla said."

"She was right. Nothing will ever blow away your grief at this death, but a brisk sea voyage will blow away the rubbish cluttering up your mind. It will function again. It can't not."

It can't not, echoed Caesar, riding the short miles between Rome and Ostia, where his ship waited. That is a truth. My spirit might be bruised to pulp, but my mind is unharmed. New things to do, new people to meet, a new country to explore—and no sign of Lucullus! I will survive.

AUTHOR'S AFTERWORD

Fortune's Favorites, though by no means the last book in this series, does mark the end of that period of Roman history wherein the ancient sources are a little thin, due to the absence of Livy and Cassius Dio, not to mention Cicero at his most prolific. In effect, this has meant that in the first three books I have been able to encompass almost all the historical events from one end of the Mediterranean to the other. So *Fortune's Favorites* also marks a turning point in how I treat my subject, which is the fall of the Roman Republic. The books still to come will have to concentrate upon fewer aspects than the full sweep of the history of the time, which I think will be an advantage to both reader and writer.

However, even *Fortune's Favorites* is enriched by increasing ancient source material, as marked by the appearance as characters of two animals—the dog belonging to the wife of King Nicomedes of Bithynia, and the famous pet fawn of Quintus Sertorius. Both are attested; the dog by Strabo, the fawn by Plutarch.

Fortune's Favorites also arrives at the beginning of a period of Roman history flirted with by Hollywood, to the detriment of history, if not Hollywood. The reader will find a rather different version of Spartacus than the celluloid one. I have neither the room nor the inclination to argue here why

I have chosen to portray Spartacus in the way I have; scholars will be able to see the why—and the who—of my argument in the text.

The glossary has been completely rewritten specifically to suit this book; please note that some of the general articles, like **steel** and **wine,** have been lifted out. As the books go on, I would have to keep increasing the size of the glossary did I not cull the entries, and time and space dictate the impossibility of a glossary which would eventually be longer than the book.

For those interested readers, the glossaries of the earlier books if combined with this one will yield information on most things. The entries on the governmental structure of Republican Rome will always be incorporated, though in a changing form as various laws and men worked upon it. Only those places and/or peoples about which the reader might want to refresh his or her knowledge are included. The most interesting new entries concern ships, which are now becoming more important. Hence find **bireme, hemiolia, merchantman, myoparo, quinquereme, sixteener** and **trireme** in the glossary of *Fortune's Favorites.*

Of the drawings, both the "youthened" young Pompey and the Pompey in his thirties are taken from authenticated busts. The young man Caesar is a "youthened" drawing taken from a bust of the middle-aged man—a somewhat easier exercise than with Pompey, as Caesar kept his figure. The drawing of Sulla is taken from a bust. Dissension rages as to which of two extant busts is actually Sulla: one is of a handsome man in his late thirties, the other is of an old man. I think *both* are Sulla. Ears, nose, chin, face shape and face folds are identical. But the handsome mature man is now wearing a wig of tight curls (that it is a wig is confirmed by two tongues of absolutely straight hair projecting down in front of the ears), has lost his teeth (a phenomenon which lengthens the chin, of course), and at some time in the recent past has lost a great deal of weight. As Sulla was at most sixty-two when he died, illness must have taken a terrible toll—a fact quite consistent with what Plutarch has to say. Lucius Licinius Lucullus is also an authenticated bust.

Which leaves Metellus Pius, Quintus Sertorius, and Crassus, all drawn from unidentified portrait busts of Republican date. In *The First Man in Rome,* I "youthened" an anonymous bust to suit the young Sertorius; that bust is now drawn as it was, except that I have removed the left eye and replaced it with scar tissue (taken from a photograph in one of my medical textbooks).

Alone among the really great men of that time, Marcus Licinius Crassus has no authenticated likeness passed down to our time. So I chose an unidentified bust of a thickset, placid-looking man to portray, as what we know of Crassus strongly suggests that he was a heavy, phlegmatic individual—at least on his surface. Otherwise the jokes about oxen would have had little point.

King Nicomedes is not an authenticated likeness; though there are coin profiles, debate still rages as to whether there were two kings after Nicomedes II (the King Nicomedes whom Marius met in 97 B.C.), Nicomedes III and Nicomedes IV, or whether the two reigns separated by an exile in Rome were both Nicomedes III. I think the last Nicomedes to reign was Nicomedes III. Be that as it may, I chose to draw from an unidentified bust of Republican date which in profile looks somewhat Nicomedian, though the bust wears no diadem, therefore cannot have been a king. Chiefly I wanted my readers to see what the diadem looked like when worn.

To save people the trouble of writing to me, I am aware that Suetonius describes Caesar's eyes as *"nigris vegetisque oculis,"* usually translated as "keen black eyes" or "piercing black eyes" or "lively black eyes." However, Suetonius also calls him fair, and was writing a hundred and fifty years after Caesar's death; a length of time which could well have meant those portrait busts kept up by repainting no longer reflected the true eye color. To be both fair and black-eyed is very rare. Caesar's great-nephew, Augustus, was also fair; his eyes are said to have been grey, a color more in keeping with fairness. Pale eyes with a dark ring around the outside of the iris always have a piercing quality, so I elected to depart from Suetonius's eye color rather than from his general description of a fair man; Plutarch, disappointingly unforthcoming about Caesar's looks, does mention Caesar's white skin. Velleius Paterculus says Caesar "surpassed all others in the beauty of his person." It is from Suetonius that one discovers he was tall and slender, but excellently built. I wouldn't like any of my readers to think that I have succumbed to the temptations of a lady novelist and endowed a major historical character with a physical appeal he did not in fact have! Poor Caesar really did have everything—brains, beauty, height, and a good body.

One further comment and I will desist from the portrait busts: the drawings are rendered exactly to scale, so those faces with preternaturally large eyes simply reflect the whim of the original sculptor, who perhaps chose to flatter his sitter by making the eyes too large. Big eyes were the greatest mark of beauty to a Roman.

To enlighten those who may scratch their heads because Pompey's letters to the Senate differ markedly from Sallust, and Cicero's court speeches from the published speeches which have come down to us: there is considerable doubt about the veracity of Sallust on the subject of Pompey's correspondence, and Cicero rewrote his speeches for publication. I have therefore elected to stay with my own words. On the subject of elephants, it must be borne in mind that the Romans were acquainted with African pachyderms, not Indian ones, and that the African species was both larger and far less amenable to taming.

Those who would like a bibliography are welcome to write to me care of my publishers.

The next book in the series will be called *Caesar's Women*.

GLOSSARY

ABSOLVO   The term employed by a jury when voting for the acquittal of the accused. It was used in the courts, not in the Assemblies.

aedile   There were four Roman magistrates called aediles; two were plebeian aediles, two were curule aediles. Their duties were confined to the city of Rome. The plebeian aediles were created first (in 494 B.C.) to assist the tribunes of the plebs in their duties, but, more particularly, to guard the rights of the Plebs to their headquarters, the temple of Ceres in the Forum Boarium. The plebeian aediles soon inherited supervision of the city's buildings as a whole, as well as archival custody of all plebiscites passed in the Plebeian Assembly, together with any senatorial decrees (*consulta*) directing the passage of plebiscites. They were elected by the Plebeian Assembly. Then in 367 B.C. two curule aediles were created to give the patricians a share in custody of public buildings and archives; they were elected by the Assembly of the People. Very soon, however, the curule aediles were as likely to be plebeians by status as patricians. From the third century B.C. downward, all four were responsible for the care of Rome's streets, water supply, drains and sewers, traffic, public buildings, monuments and facilities, markets, weights and measures (standard sets of these were housed in the basement of the temple of Castor and Pollux), games, and the public grain supply. They had the power to fine citizens and non-citizens alike for infringements of any regulation appertaining to any of the above, and deposited the moneys in their coffers to help fund the games. Aedile—plebeian or curule—was not a part of the *cursus honorum,* but because of its association with the games was a valuable magistracy for a man to hold just before he stood for office as praetor.

Aeneas   Prince of Dardania, in the Troad. He was the son of King Anchises and the goddess Aphrodite (Venus to the Romans). When Troy (Ilium to the Romans) fell to the forces of Agamemnon, Aeneas fled the burning city with his aged father perched upon his shoulder and the Palladium under one arm. After many adventures, he arrived in Latium and founded the race from whom true Romans implicitly believed they were descended. His son, variously called Ascanius or Iulus, was the direct ancestor of the Julian family.

aether   That part of the upper atmosphere permeated by godly forces, or the air immediately around a god. It also meant the sky, particularly the blue sky of daylight.

Ager Gallicus   Literally, Gallic land. The exact location and dimensions of the Ager Gallicus are not known, but it lay on the Adriatic shores of Italy partially within peninsular Italy and partially within Italian Gaul. Its southern border was possibly the Aesis River, its northern border not far beyond Ariminum. Originally the home of the Gallic tribe of Senones who settled there after the invasion of the first King Brennus in 390 B.C., it came into the Roman *ager publicus* when Rome took control of that part of Italy. It was distributed in 232 B.C. by Gaius Flaminius, and passed out of Roman public ownership.

ager publicus   Land vested in Roman public ownership, most of it acquired by right of conquest or confiscated from its original owners as a punishment for disloyalty. This latter was particularly common within Italy itself. Roman *ager publicus* existed in every overseas province, in Italian Gaul, and inside the Italian peninsula. Responsibility for its disposal (usually in the form of large leaseholds) lay in the purlieus of the censors, though much of the foreign *ager publicus* lay unused.

Agger   An *agger* was a double rampart bearing formidable fortifications. *The* Agger was a part of Rome's Servian Walls, and protected the city on its most vulnerable side, the Campus Esquilinus.

agora   The open space, usually surrounded by colonnades or some kind of public buildings, which served any Greek or Hellenic city as its public meeting place and civic center. The Roman equivalent was a forum.

ague   The old name for the rigors of malaria.

Allies   Any nation or people or individual formally invested with the title "Friend and Ally of the Roman People" was an Ally. The term usually carried with it certain privileges in trade, commerce and political activities. (See also **Italian Allies,** *socii*).

AMOR   Literally, "love." Because it is "Roma" spelled backward, the Romans of the Republic commonly believed it was Rome's vital secret name, never to be uttered aloud in that context.

Anatolia   Roughly, modern Asian Turkey. It incorporated the ancient regions of Bithynia, Mysia, Asia Province, Phrygia, Pisidia, Pamphylia, Cilicia, Paphlagonia, Galatia, Pontus, Cappadocia, and Armenia Parva.

Ancus Marcius   The fourth King of Rome, claimed by the family Marcius (particularly that branch cognominated Rex) as its founder-ancestor; unlikely, since the Marcii were plebeians. Ancus Marcius is said to have colonized Ostia, though there is some doubt as to whether he did this, or whether he took the salt pits at the mouth of the Tiber from their Etruscan owners by force of arms. Rome under his rule flourished. His one lasting public work was the building of the Wooden Bridge, the Pons Sublicius. He died in 617 B.C., leaving sons who did not inherit the throne—a source of later trouble.

animus   The *Oxford Latin Dictionary* has the best definition, so I will quote it: "The mind as opposed to the body, the mind or soul as constituting with the body the whole person." There are further definitions, but this one is pertinent to the way *animus* is used herein. One must be careful, however, not to attribute belief in the immortality of the soul to Romans.

arcade   A long line of shops on both sides of a narrow walkway within a roofed building. The Covered Bazaar in Istanbul is probably very like (if much larger than) an ancient arcade.

Armenia Magna   In ancient times, Armenia Magna extended from the southern Caucasus to the Araxes River, east to the corner of the Caspian Sea, and west to the sources of the Euphrates. It was immensely mountainous and very cold.

Armenia Parva   Though called Little Armenia, this small land occupying the rugged and mountainous regions of the upper Euphrates and Arsanius Rivers was not a part of the Kingdom of Armenia. Until taken over by the sixth King Mithridates of Pontus, it was ruled by its own royal house, but always owed allegiance to Pontus, rather than to Armenia proper.

armillae   The wide bracelets, of gold or of silver, awarded as prizes for valor to Roman legionaries, centurions, cadets and military tribunes of more junior rank.

Arvernian   Pertaining to the Gallic tribe Arverni, who occupied lands in and around the northern half of the central massif of the Cebenna, in Gaul-across-the-Alps.

Assembly *(comitia)*   Any gathering of the Roman People convoked to deal with governmental, legislative, judicial, or electoral matters. In the time of Sulla there were three true Assemblies—the Centuries, the People, and the Plebs.

The **Centuriate Assembly** *(comitia centuriata)* marshaled the People, patrician and plebeian, in their Classes, which were filled by a means test and were economic in nature. As this was originally a military assemblage, each Class gathered in the form of Centuries (which, excepting for the eighteen senior Centuries, by the time of Sulla numbered far in excess of one hundred men per century, as it had been decided to limit the number of Centuries). The Centuriate Assembly met to elect consuls, praetors, and (every five years usually) censors. It also met to hear charges of major treason *(perduellio)*, and could pass laws. Because of its originally military nature, the Centuriate Assembly was obliged to meet outside the *pomerium,* and normally did so on the Campus Martius at a place called the *saepta.* It was not usually convoked to pass laws or hear trials.

The **Assembly of the People** *(comitia populi tributa)* allowed the full participation of patricians, and was tribal in nature. It was convoked in the thirty-five tribes into which all Roman citizens were placed. Called together by a consul or praetor, it normally met in the lower Forum Romanum, in the Well of the Comitia. It elected the curule aediles, the quaestors, and the tribunes of the soldiers. It could formulate and pass laws, and conduct trials until Sulla established his standing courts.

The **Plebeian Assembly** *(comitia plebis tributa* or *concilium plebis)* met in the thirty-five tribes, but did not allow the participation of patricians. The only magistrate empowered to convoke it was the tribune of the plebs. It had the right to enact laws (strictly, plebiscites) and conduct trials, though the latter more or less disappeared after Sulla established his standing courts. Its members elected the plebeian aediles and the tribunes of the plebs. The normal place for its assemblage was in the Well of the Comitia. (See also **voting** and **tribe**.)

atrium   The main reception room of a Roman *domus,* or private house. It mostly contained an opening in the roof (the *compluvium*) above a pool (the *impluvium*) originally intended as a water reservoir for domestic use. By the time of the late Republic, the pool had become ornamental only.

auctoritas   A very difficult Latin term to translate, as it meant far more than the English word "authority" implies. It carried nuances of pre-eminence, clout, public importance and—above all—the ability to influence events through sheer public reputation. All the magistracies possessed *auctoritas* as an intrinsic part of their nature, but *auctoritas* was not confined to

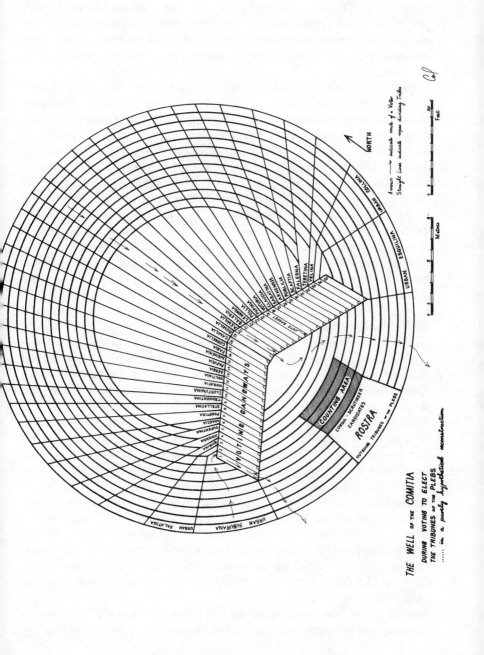

THE WELL OF THE COMITIA

DURING VOTING TO ELECT
THE TRIBUNES OF THE PLEBS
..... in a purely hypothetical reconstruction

NORTH

Arrows → indicate route of a Voter
Straight Lines indicate ropes dividing Tribes

Metres

Feet

VOTING GANGWAYS

COUNTING AREA

ROSTRA

CONSUL · SCRUTINEER
CANDIDATES
OUTGOING TRIBUNES of the PLEBS

VOTE BASKET

URBAN COLLINA
URBAN ESQUILINA
URBAN SUBURANA
URBAN PALATINA

those who held magistracies; the Princeps Senatus, Pontifex Maximus, other priests and augurs, consulars, and even some private individuals outside the ranks of the Senate also owned *auctoritas*. Though the King of the Backbenchers, Publius Cornelius Cethegus, never held a magistracy, his *auctoritas* was formidable.

augur   A priest whose duties concerned divination. He and his fellow augurs comprised the College of Augurs, an official State body which had numbered twelve members (usually six patricians and six plebeians) until in 81 B.C. Sulla increased it to fifteen members, always intended thereafter to contain at least one more plebeian than patrician. Originally augurs were co-opted by their fellow augurs, but in 104 B.C. Gnaeus Domitius Ahenobarbus brought in a law compelling election of future augurs by an assembly of seventeen tribes chosen from the thirty-five by lot. Sulla removed election in 81 B.C., going back to co-optation. The augur did not predict the future, nor did he pursue his auguries at his own whim; he inspected the proper objects or signs to ascertain whether or not the projected undertaking was one meeting with the approval of the gods, be the undertaking a *contio* (q.v.), a war, a new law, or any other State business, including elections. There was a standard manual of interpretation to which the augur referred: augurs "went by the book." The augur wore the *toga trabea* (see that entry), and carried a curved staff called the *lituus*.

auxiliary   A legion of non-citizens incorporated into a Roman army was called an auxiliary legion; its soldiers were also known as auxiliaries, and the term extended to cover cavalry units as well. By the time of Sulla's dictatorship, auxiliary infantry had more or less disappeared, whereas auxiliary cavalry was still very much in evidence.

Bacchic   Pertaining to the god Bacchus (in Greek, Dionysos), who was the patron of wine, and therefore by extension the patron of carousing. During the early and middle Republic excesses of a Bacchic nature were frowned upon, and even legislated against; by the time of Sulla, however, some degree of tolerance had crept in.

barbarian   Derived from a Greek word having strong onomatopoeic overtones; on first hearing these peoples speak, the Greeks thought they sounded "bar-bar," like animals barking. It was not a word used to describe any people settled around the Mediterranean Sea, but referred to races and nations deemed uncivilized, lacking in an admirable or desirable culture. Gauls, Germans, Scythians, Sarmatians and other peoples of the Steppes were considered barbarian.

basilica   A large building devoted to public activities such as courts of law, and also to commercial activities in shops and offices. The basilica was two-storeyed and clerestory-lit, and incorporated an arcade of shops under what we might call verandah extensions along either length side. Though the aediles looked after these buildings once erected, their actual building was undertaken at the expense of a prominent Roman nobleman. The first basilica was put up by Cato the Censor on the Clivus Argentarius next door to the Senate House, and was known as the Basilica Porcia; as well as accommodating banking institutions, it was also the headquarters of the College of the Tribunes of the Plebs. At the time of this book, there also existed the Basilica Aemilia, the Basilica Sempronia, and the Basilica Opimia, all on the borders of the lower Forum Romanum.

Bellona   The Italian goddess of war. Her temple lay outside the *pomerium* of Rome on the Campus Martius, and was vowed in 296 B.C. by the great Appius Claudius Caecus. A group of special priests called *fetiales* conducted her rituals. A large vacant piece of land lay in front of the temple, known as Enemy Territory.

bireme   A ship constructed for use in naval warfare, and intended to be rowed rather than sailed (though it was equipped with a mast and sail, usually left ashore if action was likely). Some biremes were decked or partially decked, but most were open. It seems likely that the oarsmen did sit in two levels at two banks of oars, the upper bank and its oarsmen accommodated in an outrigger, and the lower bank's oars poking through ports in the galley's sides. Built of fir or another lightweight pine, the bireme could be manned only in fair weather, and fight battles only in very calm seas. It was much longer than it was wide in the beam (the ratio was about 7:1), and probably averaged about 100 feet (30 meters) in length. Of oarsmen it carried upward of one hundred. A bronze-reinforced beak made of oak projected forward of the bow just below the waterline, and was used for ramming and sinking other vessels. The bireme was not designed to carry marines or grapple to engage other vessels in land-style combat. Throughout Greek, Republican Roman and Imperial Roman times, all ships were rowed by professional oarsmen, *never* by slaves. The slave oarsman was a product of Christian times.

Boreas   The north wind.

Brothers Gracchi   See **Gracchi.**

caelum grave et pestilens   Malaria.

Calabria   Confusing for modern Italians! Nowadays Calabria is the toe of the boot, but in ancient times Calabria was the heel. Brundisium was its most important city, followed by Tarentum. Its people were the Illyrian Messapii.

Campus Esquilinus   The area of flattish ground outside the Servian Walls and the double rampart of the Agger. It lay between the Porta Querquetulana and the Colline Gate, and was the site of Rome's necropolis.

Campus Lanatarius   An area of flattish ground inside the Servian Walls on that part of the Aventine adjacent to the walls. It lay between the Porta Raudusculana and the Porta Naevia. Here were extensive stockyards and slaughtering yards.

Campus Martius   The Field of Mars. Situated north of the Servian Walls, the Campus Martius was bounded by the Capitol on its south and the Pincian Hill on its east; the rest of it was enclosed by a huge bend in the Tiber River. In Republican times it was not inhabited as a suburb, but was the place where triumphing armies bivouacked, the young were trained in military exercises, horses engaged in chariot racing were stabled and trained, the Centuriate Assembly met, and market gardening vied with public parklands. At the apex of the river bend lay the public swimming holes called the Trigarium, and just to the north of the Trigarium were medicinal hot springs called the Tarentum. The Via Lata (Via Flaminia) crossed the Campus Martius on its way to the Mulvian Bridge, and the Via Recta bisected it at right angles to the Via Lata.

Capena Gate   The Porta Capena. One of Rome's two most important gates in the Servian Walls (the other was the Porta Collina, the Colline Gate). It lay beyond the Circus Maximus, and outside it was the common highway which branched into the Via Appia and the Via Latina about half a mile from the gate.

capite censi   Literally, the **Head Count.** See that entry.

carcer   A dungeon. The other name for the Tullianum was simply Carcer.

Carinae   One of Rome's more exclusive addresses. Incorporating the Fagutal, the Carinae was the northern tip of the Oppian Mount on its western side; it extended between the Velia and the Clivus Pullius. Its outlook was southwestern, across the swamps of the Palus Ceroliae toward the Aventine.

cartouche   The personal hieroglyphs peculiar to each individual Pharaoh of Egypt, enclosed within an oval (or rectangular with rounded corners) framing line. The practice continued through to rulers of the Ptolemaic dynasty.

Cassiterides   The Tin Isles. Now known as the Scilly Isles, off the southwestern tip of Cornwall, England. The tin mined in Cornwall was shipped to the Cassiterides, which was used as a way station. Crassus's father voyaged there in 95 B.C.

Castor   The never-forgotten Heavenly Twin. Though the imposing temple in the Forum Romanum was properly the temple of Castor and Pollux (also called the Dioscuri), it was always referred to by Romans as Castor's. This led to many jokes about dual enterprises in which one of the two prime movers was consistently overlooked. Religiously, Castor and Pollux were among the principal deities worshipped by Romans, perhaps because, like Romulus and Remus, they were twins.

cavalry   Horse-mounted soldiers. By the time of the late Republic, all cavalry incorporated into Roman armies was auxiliary in nature: that is, composed of non-citizens. Germans, Gauls, Thracians, Galatians and Numidians commonly formed Roman cavalry units, as these were all peoples numbering horse-riding tribes among them. There seems at most times to have been adequate volunteers to fill cavalry ranks; Gauls and Numidians apparently were the most numerous. The cavalry was formed into regiments of five hundred horsemen, each regiment divided into ten squadrons of fifty troopers. They were led by officers of their own nationality, but the overall commander of cavalry was always Roman.

cavea   See the entry on **theaters.**

cella   A room without a specific name (or function, in domestic dwellings). A temple room was always just a *cella.*

Celtiberian   The general term covering the tribes inhabiting northern and north-central Spain. As the name suggests, racially they were an admixture of migratory Celts from Gaul and the more ancient indigenous Iberian stock. Their towns were almost all erected upon easily fortified crags, hills or rocky outcrops, and they were past masters at guerrilla warfare.

censor   The censor was the most august of all Roman magistrates, though he lacked imperium and was therefore not entitled to be escorted by lictors. Two censors were elected by the Centuriate Assembly to serve for a period of five years (called a *lustrum*); censorial activity was, however, mostly limited to the first eighteen months of the *lustrum,* which was ushered in by a special sacrifice, the *suovetaurilia,* of pig, sheep and ox. No man could stand for censor unless he had been consul first, and usually only those consulars of notable *auctoritas* and *dignitas* bothered to stand. The censors inspected and regulated membership in the Senate and the Ordo Equester, and conducted a general census of Roman citizens throughout the Roman world. They had the power to transfer a citizen from one tribe to another as well as one Class to another. They applied the means test. The letting of State contracts for everything from the farming of taxes to public works was also their responsibility. In 81 B.C. Sulla abolished the office, apparently as a temporary measure.

census   Every five years the censors brought the roll of the citizens of Rome up to date. The name of every Roman citizen male was entered on these rolls, together with information about his tribe, his economic class, his property and means, and his family. Neither women nor children were formally registered as being Roman citizens, though there are cases documented in the ancient sources that clearly show some women awarded the Roman citizenship in their own right. The city of Rome's census was taken on the Campus Martius at a special station erected for the purpose; those living elsewhere in Italy had to report to the authorities at the nearest municipal registry, and those living abroad to the provincial governor. There is some evidence, however, that the censors of 97 B.C., Lucius Valerius Flaccus and Marcus Antonius Orator, changed the manner in which citizens living outside Rome but inside Italy proper were enrolled.

centunculus　　A coat or quilt made out of patches in many colors.

Centuriate Assembly　　See the entry under **Assembly.**

centurion　　The regular professional officer of both Roman citizen and auxiliary infantry legions. It is a mistake to equate him with the modern noncommissioned officer; centurions enjoyed a relatively exalted status uncomplicated by modern social distinctions. A defeated Roman general hardly turned a hair if he lost even senior military tribunes, but tore his hair out in clumps if he lost centurions. Centurion rank was graduated; the most junior commanded an ordinary century of eighty legionaries and twenty noncombatant assistants, but exactly how he progressed in what was apparently a complex chain of progressive seniority is not known. In the Republican army as reorganized by Gaius Marius, each cohort had six *centuriones* (singular, *centurio*), with the most senior man, the *pilus prior,* commanding the senior century of his cohort as well as the entire cohort. The ten men commanding the ten cohorts which made up a full legion were also ranked in seniority, with the legion's most senior centurion, the *primus pilus* (this term was later reduced to *primipilus*), answering only to his legion's commander (either one of the elected tribunes of the soldiers, or one of the general's legates). During Republican times promotion to centurion was up from the ranks. The centurion had certain easily recognizable badges of office: he wore greaves on his shins, a shirt of scales rather than chain links, a helmet crest projecting sideways rather than front-to-back, and carried a stout knobkerrie of vine wood. He also wore many decorations.

century　　Any grouping of one hundred men. Most importantly, the Roman legion was organized in basic units of one hundred men called centuries. The Classes of the Centuriate Assembly were also organized in centuries, but with steadily increasing population these centuries came eventually to contain far more than one hundred men.

chlamys　　The cloaklike outer garment worn by Greek men.

chryselephantine　　A work of art fashioned in gold and ivory.

chthonic　　Pertaining to the Underworld, and ill-omened.

Cimbri   A Germanic people originally inhabiting the upper or northern half of the Jutland peninsula (modern Denmark). Strabo says that a sea-flood drove them out in search of a new homeland about 120 B.C. In combination with the Teutones and a mixed group of Germans and Celts (the Marcomanni-Cherusci-Tigurini) they wandered Europe in search of this homeland until they ran foul of Rome. In 102 and 101 B.C. Gaius Marius utterly defeated them, and the migration disintegrated.

Circus Flaminius   The circus situated on the Campus Martius not far from the Tiber and the Forum Holitorium. It was built in 221 B.C., and sometimes served as a place for a comitial meeting, when the Plebs or the People had to meet outside the *pomerium*. It seems to have been well used as a venue for the games, but for events pulling in smaller attendances than the Circus Maximus. It held about fifty thousand spectators.

Circus Maximus   The old circus built by King Tarquinius Priscus before the Republic began. It filled the whole of the Vallis Murcia, a declivity between the Palatine and Aventine Mounts. Even though its capacity was about one hundred and fifty thousand spectators, there is ample evidence that during Republican times freedman citizens were classified as slaves when it came to admission to the Circus Maximus, and were thus denied. Just too many people wanted to go to the circus games. Women were permitted to sit with men.

citizenship   For the purposes of this series of books, the Roman citizenship. Possession of it entitled a man to vote in his tribe and his Class (if he was economically qualified to belong to a Class) in all Roman elections. He could not be flogged, he was entitled to the Roman trial process, and he had the right of appeal. The male citizen became liable for military service on his seventeenth birthday. After the *lex Minicia* of 91 B.C., the child of a union between a Roman citizen of either sex and a non-Roman was forced to assume the citizenship of the non-Roman parent.

citocacia   A mild Latin profanity, meaning "stinkweed."

citrus wood   The most prized cabinet wood of the Roman world. It was cut from vast galls on the root system of a cypresslike tree, *Callitris quadrivavis vent.*, which grew in the highlands of North Africa all the way from the Oasis of Ammonium and Cyrenaica to the far Atlas of Mauretania. Though termed citrus, the tree was not botanically related to orange or lemon. Most citrus wood was reserved for making tabletops (usually mounted upon a single chryselephantine pedestal), but it was also turned as bowls. No tabletops have survived to modern times, but enough bowls have for us to see that citrus wood was certainly the most beautiful timber of all time.

Classes   These were five in number, and represented the economic divisions of property-owning or steady-income-earning Roman citizens. The members of the First Class were the richest, the members of the Fifth Class the poorest. Those Roman citizens who belonged to the *capite censi* or Head Count were too poor to qualify for a Class status, and so could not vote in the Centuriate Assembly. In actual fact, it was rare for the Third Class to be called upon to vote in the Centuriate Assembly, let alone members of the Fourth or Fifth Class!

client   In Latin, *cliens*. The term denoted a man of free or freed status (he did not have to be a Roman citizen) who pledged himself to a man he called his patron. In the most solemn and binding way, the client undertook to serve the interests and obey the wishes of his patron. In return he received certain favors—usually gifts of money, or a job, or legal assistance. The freed slave was automatically the client of his ex-master until discharged of this obligation—if he ever was. A kind of honor system governed the client's conduct in relation to his patron, and was adhered to with remarkable consistency. To be a client did not necessarily mean that a man could not also be a patron; more that he could not be an ultimate patron, as technically his own clients were also the clients of his patron. During the Republic there were no formal laws concerning the client-patron relationship because they were not necessary—no man, client *or* patron, could hope to succeed in life were he known as dishonorable in this vital function. However, there were laws regulating the foreign client-patron relationship; foreign states or client-kings acknowledging Rome as patron were legally obliged to find the ransom for any Roman citizen kidnapped in their territories, a fact that pirates relied on heavily for an additional source of income. Thus, not only individuals could become clients; whole towns and even countries often were.

client-king   A foreign monarch might pledge himself as a client in the service of Rome as his patron, thereby entitling his kingdom to be known as a Friend and Ally of the Roman People. Sometimes, however, a foreign monarch pledged himself as the client of a Roman individual, as did certain rulers to Lucullus and Pompey.

clivus   A hilly street.

cognomen   The last name of a Roman male anxious to distinguish himself from all his fellows possessed of an identical first (*praenomen*) and family (*nomen*) name. He might adopt one for himself, as did Pompey with the *cognomen* Magnus, or simply continue to bear a *cognomen* which had been in the family for generations, as did the Julians cognominated Caesar. In some families it became necessary to have more than one *cognomen*: for example, Quintus Caecilius Metellus Pius Cornelianus Scipio Nasica, who was the adopted son of Metellus Pius the Piglet. Quintus was his first name (*praenomen*); Caecilius his family name (*nomen*); Metellus Pius were *cognomina* belonging to his adoptive father; Cornelianus indicated that he was by blood a Cornelian; and Scipio Nasica were the *cognomina* of his blood father. As things turned out, he was always known as Metellus Scipio, a neat compromise to both blood and adoptive family.

The *cognomen* often pointed up some physical characteristic or idiosyncrasy—jug ears, flat feet, hump back, swollen legs—or else commemorated some great feat—as in the Caecilii Metelli who were cognominated Dalmaticus, Balearicus, Macedonicus, Numidicus, these being related to a country each man had conquered. The best *cognomina* were heavily sarcastic—Lepidus, meaning a thoroughly nice fellow, attached to a right bastard—or extremely witty—as with the already multiple-cognominated Gaius Julius Caesar Strabo Vopiscus, who earned an additional name, Sesquiculus, meaning he was more than just an arsehole, he was an arsehole and a half.

cohort   The tactical unit of the legion. It comprised six centuries, and each legion owned ten cohorts. When discussing troop movements, it was more customary for the general to speak of his army in terms of cohorts than legions, which perhaps indicates that, at least until the time of Caesar, the general deployed or peeled off cohorts in battle. The maniple, formed of two centuries (there were three maniples to the cohort), ceased to have any tactical significance from the time of Marius.

college   A body or society of men having something in common. Rome owned priestly colleges (such as the College of Pontifices), political colleges (as the College of Tribunes of the Plebs), civil colleges (as the College of Lictors), and trade colleges (for example, the Guild of Undertakers). Certain groups of men from all walks of life, including slaves, banded together in what were called crossroads colleges to look after the city of Rome's major crossroads and conduct the annual feast of the crossroads, the Compitalia.

colonnade   A roofed walkway flanked by one row of outer columns when attached to a building in the manner of a verandah, or, if freestanding (as a colonnade often was), by a row of columns on either side.

comitia   See the entry under **Assembly.**

Comitia   The large round well in which meetings of the *comitia* were held. It was located in the lower Forum Romanum adjacent to the steps of the Senate House and the Basilica Aemilia, and proceeded below ground level in a series of steps, forming tiers upon which men stood; comitial meetings were never conducted seated. When packed, the well could hold perhaps three thousand men. The rostra, or speaker's platform, was grafted into one side.

CONDEMNO The word employed by a jury to deliver a verdict of "guilty." It was a term confined to the courts; both courts and Assemblies had their own vocabularies.

confarreatio The oldest and strictest of the three forms of Roman marriage. By the time of Sulla, the practice of *confarreatio* was confined to patricians, and then was not mandatory. One of the chief reasons why *confarreatio* lost much popularity lay in the fact that the *confarreatio* bride passed from the hand of her father to the hand of her husband, and thus had far less freedom than women married in the usual way; she could not control her dowry or conduct business. The other main reason for the unpopularity of *confarreatio* lay in the extreme difficulty of dissolving it; divorce (*diffarreatio*) was so legally and religiously arduous that it was more trouble than it was worth unless the circumstances left no alternative.

Conscript Fathers When it was established by the Kings of Rome (traditionally by Numa Pompilius), the Senate consisted of one hundred patricians entitled *patres*—"fathers." Then when plebeian senators were added during the first years of the Republic, they were said to be *conscripti*—"chosen without a choice." Together, the patrician and plebeian members were said to be *patres et conscripti;* gradually the once-distinguishing terms were run together, and all members of the Senate were simply the Conscript Fathers.

consul The consul was the most senior Roman magistrate owning imperium, and the consulship (modern scholars do not refer to it as the "consulate" because a consulate is a modern diplomatic institution) was the top rung on the *cursus honorum*. Two consuls were elected each year by the Centuriate Assembly, and served for one year. They entered office on New Year's Day (January 1). One was senior to the other; he was the one who had polled his requisite number of Centuries first. The senior consul held the *fasces* (q.v.) for the month of January, which meant his junior colleague looked on. In February the junior consul held the *fasces,* and they alternated month by month throughout the year. Both consuls were escorted by twelve lictors, but only the lictors of the consul holding the *fasces* that month shouldered the actual *fasces* as they preceded him wherever he went. By the last century of the Republic, a patrician or a plebeian could be consul, though never two patricians together. The proper age for a consul was forty-two, twelve years after entering the Senate at thirty, though there is convincing evidence that Sulla in 81 B.C. accorded patrician senators the privilege of standing for consul two years ahead of any plebeian, which meant the patrician could be consul at forty years of age. A consul's imperium knew no bounds; it operated not only in Rome and Italy, but throughout the provinces as well, and overrode the imperium of a proconsular governor. The consul could command any army.

consular The name given to a man after he had been consul. He was held in special esteem by the rest of the Senate, and until Sulla became dictator was always asked to speak or give his opinion in the House ahead of the praetors, consuls-elect, etc. Sulla changed that, preferring to exalt magistrates in office and those elected to coming office. The consular, however, might at any time be sent to govern a province should the Senate require the duty of him. He might also be asked to take on other duties, like caring for the grain supply.

consultum The term for a senatorial decree, though it was expressed more properly as a *senatus consultum*. It did not have the force of law. In order to become law, a *consultum* had to be presented by the Senate to any of the Assemblies, tribal or centuriate, which then voted it into law—*if* the members of the Assembly requested felt like voting it into law. Sulla's reformations included a law that no Assembly could legislate a bill unless it was accompanied by a *senatus consultum*. However, many senatorial *consulta* (plural) were never submitted to any Assembly, therefore were never voted into law, yet were accepted as laws by all of Rome; among these *consulta* were decisions about provincial governors, declaration and conduct of wars, and all to do with foreign affairs. Sulla in 81 B.C. gave these senatorial decrees the formal status of laws.

contio This was a preliminary meeting of a comitial Assembly in order to discuss the promulgation of a projected law, or any other comitial business. All three Assemblies were required to debate a measure in *contio,* which, though no voting took place, had nonetheless to be convoked by the magistrate empowered.

contubernalis A military cadet: a subaltern of lowest rank and age in the hierarchy of Roman military officers, but excluding the centurions. No centurion was ever a cadet, he was an experienced soldier.

corona civica Rome's second-highest military decoration. A crown or chaplet made of oak leaves, it was awarded to a man who had saved the lives of fellow soldiers and held the ground on which he did this for the rest of the duration of a battle. It could not be awarded unless the saved soldiers swore a formal oath before their general that they spoke the truth about the circumstances. L. R. Taylor argues that among Sulla's constitutional reforms was one relating to the winners of major military crowns; that, following the tradition of Marcus Fabius Buteo, he promoted these men to membership in the Senate, which answers the vexed question of Caesar's senatorial status (complicated as it was by the fact that, while *flamen Dialis,* he had been a member of the Senate from the time he put on the *toga virilis*). Gelzer agreed with her—but, alas, only in a footnote.

corona graminea or ***obsidionalis***   Rome's highest military decoration. Made of grass (or sometimes a cereal such as wheat, if the battle took place in a field of grain) taken from the battlefield and awarded "on the spot," the Grass Crown conferred virtual immortality on a man, for it had been won on very few occasions during the Republic. The man who won it had to have saved a whole legion or army by his personal efforts. Both Quintus Sertorius and Sulla were awarded Grass Crowns.

cubit   A Greek and Asian measurement of length not popular among Romans; it was normally held to be the distance between a man's elbow and the tips of his fingers, and was probably about 18 inches (450mm).

cuirass   Armor encasing a man's upper body without having the form of a shirt. It consisted of two plates of bronze, steel, or hardened leather, the front one protecting thorax and abdomen, the other the back from shoulders to lumbar spine. The plates were held together by straps or hinges at the shoulders and along each side under the arms. Some cuirasses were exquisitely tailored to the contours of an individual's torso, while others fitted any man of a particular size and physique. The men of highest rank—generals and legates—wore cuirasses tooled in high relief and silver-plated (sometimes, though rarely, gold-plated). Presumably as an indication of imperium, the general and perhaps the most senior of his legates wore a thin red sash around the cuirass about halfway between the nipples and waist; the sash was ritually knotted and looped.

cultarius   Scullard's spelling: the O.L.D. prefers *cultrarius*. He was a public servant attached to religious duties, and his only job appears to have been to cut the sacrificial victim's throat. However, in Republican Rome this was undoubtedly a full-time job for several men, so many were the ceremonies requiring sacrifice of an animal victim. He probably also helped dispose of the victim and was custodian of his tools.

cunnus   An extremely offensive Latin profanity—"cunt."

Cuppedenis Markets   Specialized markets lying behind the upper Forum Romanum on its eastern side, between the Clivus Orbius and the Carinae/ Fagutal. In it were vended luxury items like pepper, spices, incense, ointments and unguents and balms; it also served as the flower market, where a Roman (all Romans loved flowers) could buy anything from a bouquet to a garland to go round the neck or a wreath to go on the head. Until sold to finance Sulla's campaign against King Mithridates, the actual land belonged to the State.

Curia Hostilia   The Senate House. It was thought to have been built by the shadowy third king of Rome, Tullus Hostilius, hence its name: "the meeting-house of Hostilius."

cursus honorum   See the entry on **magistrates.**

curule chair   The *sella curulis* was the ivory chair reserved exclusively for magistrates owning imperium: at first I thought only the curule aedile sat in one, but it seems that at some stage during the evolution of the Republic, imperium (and therefore the curule chair) was also conferred upon the two plebeian aediles. Beautifully carved in ivory, the chair itself had curved legs crossing in a broad X, so that it could be folded up. It was equipped with low arms, but had no back.

DAMNO   The word employed by a comitial Assembly to indicate a verdict of "guilty." It was not used in the courts, perhaps because the courts did not have the power to execute a death penalty.

decury   A group of ten men. The tidy-minded Romans tended to subdivide groups containing several hundred men into tens for convenience in administration and direction. Thus the Senate was organized in decuries (with a patrician senator as the head of each decury), the College of Lictors, and probably all the other colleges of specialized public servants as well. It has been suggested that the legionary century was also divided into decuries, ten men messing together and sharing a tent, but evidence points more to eight soldiers. As a legionary century contained eighty soldiers, not one hundred, this would give ten groups of eight soldiers. But perhaps each eight legionaries were given two of the century's twenty noncombatants as servants and general factotums, thus bringing each octet up to a decury.

demagogue   Originally a Greek concept, the demagogue was a politician whose chief appeal was to the crowds. The Roman demagogue (almost inevitably a tribune of the plebs) preferred the arena of the Comitia well to the Senate House, but it was no part of his policy to "liberate the masses," nor on the whole were those who flocked to listen to him composed of the very lowly. The term simply indicated a man of radical rather than ultra-conservative bent.

denarius   Plural, denarii. Save for a very rare issue or two of gold coins, the denarius was the largest denomination of coin under the Republic. Of pure silver, it contained about 3.5 grams of the metal, and was about the size of a dime—very small. There were 6,250 denarii to one silver talent. Of actual coins in circulation, there were probably more denarii than sesterces.

diadem   This was not a crown or a tiara, but simply a thick white ribbon about one inch (25mm) wide, each end embroidered and often finished with a fringe. It was the symbol of the Hellenic sovereign; only King and/or Queen could wear it. The coins show that it was worn either across the forehead or behind the hairline, and was knotted at the back below the occiput; the two ends trailed down onto the shoulders.

dies religiosi   Days of the year regarded as ill-omened. On them nothing new ought to be done, nor religious ceremonies conducted. Some *dies religiosi* commemorated defeats in battle, on three *dies religiosi* the *mundus* (underworld gate) was left open, on others certain temples were closed, on yet others the hearth of Vesta was left open. The days after the Kalends, Nones and Ides of each month were *dies religiosi,* and thought so ill-omened that they had a special name: Black Days.

diffarreatio   See the entry on ***confarreatio.***

dignitas   Like ***auctoritas*** (q.v.), the Latin *dignitas* has connotations not conveyed by the English word derived from it, "dignity." It was a man's personal standing in the Roman world rather than his public standing, though his public standing was enormously enhanced by great *dignitas.* It gave the sum total of his integrity, pride, family and ancestors, word, intelligence, deeds, ability, knowledge, and worth as a man. Of all the assets a Roman nobleman possessed, *dignitas* was likely to be the one he was most touchy about, and protective of. I have elected to leave the term untranslated in my text.

diverticulum   In the two earlier books, I used this term to mean only the "ring roads" around the city of Rome that linked all the arterial roads together. In *Fortune's Favorites* it is also used to indicate sections where an arterial road bifurcated to connect with important towns not serviced by the arterial road itself, then fused together again, as with the two *diverticula* on the Via Flaminia which must have already existed by the late Republic, though not generally conceded to exist until imperial times. Did the *diverticulum* to Spoletium not exist, for example, neither Carrinas nor Pompey would have been able to fetch up there so quickly.

divinatio   Literally, guesswork. This was a special hearing by a specially appointed panel of judges to determine the fitness of a man to prosecute another man. It was not called into effect unless a man's fitness was challenged by the defense. The name referred to the fact that the panel of judges arrived at a decision without the presentation of hard evidence—that is, they arrived at a conclusion by guesswork.

doctor   The man who was responsible for the training and physical fitness of gladiators.

drachma   The name I have elected to use when speaking of Hellenic currency rather than Roman, because the drachma most closely approximated the denarius in weight at around 4 grams. Rome, however, was winning the currency race because of the central and uniform nature of Roman coins; during the late Republic, the world was beginning to prefer to use Roman coins rather than Hellenic.

Ecastor! Edepol! The most genteel and inoffensive of Roman exclamations of surprise or amazement, roughly akin to "Gee!" or "Wow!" Women used "Ecastor!" and men "Edepol!" The roots suggest they invoked Castor and Pollux.

electrum An alloy of gold and silver. In times dating back to before the Republic electrum was thought to be a metal in itself, and like the electrum rod in the temple of Jupiter Feretrius on the Capitol, it was left as electrum. By the time of the Republic, however, it was known to be an alloy, and was separated into its gold and silver components by cementation with salt, or treatment with a metallic sulphide.

Epicurean Pertaining to the philosophical system of the Greek Epicurus. Originally Epicurus had advocated a kind of hedonism so exquisitely refined that it approached asceticism on its left hand, so to speak; a man's pleasures were best sampled one at a time, and strung out with such relish that any excess defeated the exercise. Public life or any other stressful work was forbidden. These tenets underwent considerable modification in Rome, so that a Roman nobleman could call himself an Epicure yet still espouse his public career. By the late Republic, the chief pleasure of an Epicurean was food.

epulones A minor order of priests whose business was to organize senatorial banquets after festivals of Jupiter Optimus Maximus, and also to arrange the public banquets during games and some feast days.

equestrian Pertaining to the knights.

ethnarch The general Greek word for a city or town magistrate. There were other and more specific names in use, but I do not think it necessary to compound confusion in readers by employing a more varied terminology.

Euxine Sea The modern Black Sea. Because of the enormous number of major rivers which flowed into it (especially in times before water volume was regulated by dams), the Euxine Sea contained less salt than other seas; the current through Thracian Bosporus and Hellespont always flowed from the Euxine toward the Mediterranean (the Aegean)—which made it easy to quit the Euxine, but hard to enter it.

exeunt omnes Literally, "Everybody leave!" It has been a stage direction employed by playwrights since drama first came into being.

faction The following of a Roman politician is best described as a faction; in no way could a man's followers be described as a political party in the modern sense. Factions formed around men owning *auctoritas* and *dignitas,* and were purely evidence of that individual's ability to attract and hold followers. Political ideologies did not exist, nor did party lines. For that reason I have avoided (and will continue to avoid) the terms Optimate and Popularis, as they give a false impression of Roman political solidarity to a party-acclimatized modern reader.

Faesulae Modern Fiesole. Possibly because it was settled by the Etruscans before Rome became a power, it was always deemed a part of Etruria; in actual fact it lay north of the Arnus River, in what was officially Italian Gaul.

fasces The *fasces* were bundles of birch rods ritually tied together in a crisscross pattern by red leather thongs. Originally an emblem of the Etruscan kings, they passed into the customs of the emerging Rome, persisted in Roman life throughout the Republic, and on into the Empire. Carried by men called **lictors** (q.v.), they preceded the curule magistrate (and the propraetor and proconsul as well) as the outward symbol of his imperium. Within the *pomerium* only the rods went into the bundles, to signify that the curule magistrate had the power to chastise, but not to execute; outside the *pomerium* axes were inserted into the bundles, to signify that the curule magistrate or promagistrate did have the power to execute. The only man permitted to insert the axes into the midst of the rods inside the *pomerium* was the dictator. The number of *fasces* indicated the degree of imperium: a dictator had twenty-four, a consul and proconsul twelve, a praetor and propraetor six, and the aediles two. Sulla, incidentally, was the first dictator to be preceded by twenty-four lictors bearing twenty-four *fasces;* until then, dictators had used the same number as consuls, twelve.

fasti The *fasti* were originally days on which business could be transacted, but came to mean other things as well: the calendar, lists relating to holidays and festivals, and the list of consuls (this last probably because Romans preferred to reckon up their years by remembering who had been the consuls in any given year). The entry in the glossary to *The First Man in Rome* contains a fuller explanation of the calendar than space permits me here—under *fasti,* of course.

fellator *Mea culpa, mea culpa, mea maxima culpa!* My fault entirely that in the two previous volumes of this series, I managed to give the man on the receiving end the wrong name! It does happen that one becomes confused, as I do by opposites, left and right, and clockwise versus anticlockwise. A cerebral aberration of sorts. The fact remains that I was wrong. The *fellator* was the man sucking the penis, the *irrumator* the man whose penis was being sucked. *Fellator* sucker, *irrumator* suckee.

feriae Holidays. Though attendance at public ceremonies on such holidays was not obligatory, *feriae* traditionally demanded that business, labor and lawsuits not be pursued, and that quarrels, even private ones, should be avoided. The rest from normal labors on *feriae* extended to slaves and also some animals, including oxen but excluding equines of all varieties.

fetiales   A special college of priests whose duties were to serve Bellona, the goddess of war. Though it was an honor to be appointed a *fetialis*, during the late Republic the rites of making war or peace as pertaining to Bellona were much neglected; it was Caesar's great-nephew, Augustus, who brought the college back to full practice.

filibuster   A modern word for a political activity at least as old as the Senate of Rome. It consisted, then as now, of "talking a motion out": the filibusterer droned on and on about everything from his childhood to his funeral plans, thus preventing other men from speaking until the political danger had passed. And preventing the taking of a vote!

flamen   The *flamines* (plural) were probably the oldest of Rome's priests in time, dating back at least as far as the Kings. There were fifteen *flamines*, three major and twelve minor. The three major flaminates were *Dialis* (Jupiter Optimus Maximus), *Martialis* (Mars), and *Quirinalis* (Quirinus). Save for the poor *flamen Dialis*—his nature is discussed fully in the text—none of the *flamines* seemed terribly hedged about with prohibitions or taboos, but all three major *flamines* qualified for a public salary, a State house, and membership in the Senate. The wife of the *flamen* was known as the *flaminica*. The *flamen* and *flaminica Dialis* had to be patrician in status, though I have not yet discovered whether this was true of the other *flamines*, major or minor. To be on the safe side, I elected to stay with patrician appointments.

Fortuna   One of Rome's most worshipped and important deities. Generally thought to be a female force, Fortuna had many different guises; Roman godhead was usually highly specific. Fortuna Primigenia was Jupiter's firstborn, Fors Fortuna was of particular importance to the lowly, Fortuna Virilis helped women conceal their physical imperfections from men, Fortuna Virgo was worshipped by brides, Fortuna Equestris looked after the knights, and Fortuna Huiusque Diei ("the fortune of the present day") was the special object of worship by military commanders and prominent politicians having military backgrounds. There were yet other Fortunae. The Romans believed implicitly in luck, though they did not regard luck quite as we do; a man *made* his luck, but was—even in the case of men as formidably intelligent as Sulla and Caesar—very careful about offending Fortuna, not to mention superstitious. To be favored by Fortuna was considered a vindication of all a man stood for.

forum   The Roman meeting place, an open area surrounded by buildings, many of which were of a public nature.

Forum Boarium   The meat markets, situated at the starting-post end of the Circus Maximus, below the Germalus of the Palatine. The Great Altar of Hercules and several different temples to Hercules lay in the Forum Boarium, which was held to be peculiarly under his protection.

Forum Holitorium   The vegetable markets, situated on the bank of the Tiber athwart the Servian Walls between the river and the flank of the Capitoline Mount. There were three gates in the walls at the Forum Holitorium— the Porta Triumphalis (used only to permit the triumphal parade into the city), the Porta Carmentalis, and the Porta Flumentana. It is generally thought that the Servian Walls of the Forum Holitorium were crumbled away to nothing by the late Republic, but I do not believe this; the threat of the Germans alone caused many repairs to the Servian Walls.

Forum Romanum   'This long open space was the center of Roman public life, and was largely devoted, as were the buildings around it, to politics, the law, business, and religion. I do not believe that the free space of the Forum Romanum was choked with a permanent array of booths, stalls and barrows; the many descriptions of constant legal and political business in the lower half of the Forum would leave little room for such apparatus. There were two very large market areas on the Esquiline side of the Forum Romanum, just removed from the Forum itself by one barrier of buildings, and in these, no doubt, most freestanding stalls and booths were situated. Lower than the surrounding districts, the Forum was rather damp, cold, sunless—but very much alive in terms of public human activity.

freedman   A manumitted slave. Though technically a free man (and, if his former master was a Roman citizen, himself a Roman citizen), the freedman remained in the patronage of his former master, who had first call on his time and services. He had little chance to exercise his vote in either of the two tribal Assemblies, as he was invariably placed into one of two vast urban tribes, Suburana or Esquilina. Some slaves of surpassing ability or ruthlessness, however, did amass great fortunes and power as freedmen, and could therefore be sure of a vote in the Centuriate Assembly; such freedmen usually managed to have themselves transferred into rural tribes as well, and thus exercised the complete franchise.

free man   A man born free and never sold into outright slavery, though he could be sold as a *nexus* or debt slave. The latter was rare, however, inside Italy during the late Republic.

games   In Latin, *ludi*. Games were a Roman institution and pastime which went back at least as far as the early Republic, and probably a lot further. At first they were celebrated only when a general triumphed, but in 336 B.C.

the *ludi Romani* became an annual event, and were joined later by an ever-increasing number of other games throughout the year. All games tended to become longer in duration as well. At first games consisted mostly of chariot races, then gradually came to incorporate animal hunts, and plays performed in specially erected temporary theaters. Every set of games commenced on the first day with a solemn but spectacular religious procession through the Circus, after which came a chariot race or two, and then some boxing and wrestling, limited to this first day. The succeeding days were taken up with theatricals; comedy was more popular than tragedy, and eventually the free-wheeling Atellan mimes and farces most popular of all. As the games drew to a close, chariot racing reigned supreme, with animal hunts to vary the program. Gladiatorial combats did *not* form a part of Republican games (they were put on by private individuals, usually in connection with a dead relative, in the Forum Romanum rather than in the Circus). Games were put on at the expense of the State, though men ambitious to make a name for themselves dug deeply into their private purses while serving as aediles to make "their" games more spectacular than the State-allocated funds permitted. Most of the big games were held in the Circus Maximus, some of the smaller ones in the Circus Flaminius. Free Roman citizen men and women were permitted to attend (there was no admission charge), with women segregated in the theater but not in the Circus; neither slaves nor freedmen were allowed admission, no doubt because even the Circus Maximus, which held 150,000 people, was not large enough to contain freedmen as well as free men.

Gaul, Gauls　　A Roman rarely if ever referred to a Celt as a Celt; he was known as a Gaul. Those parts of the world wherein Gauls lived were known as some kind of Gaul, even when the land was in Anatolia (Galatia). Before Caesar's conquests, Gaul-across-the-Alps—that is, Gaul west of the Italian Alps—was roughly divided into two parts: Gallia Comata or Long-haired Gaul, neither Hellenized nor Romanized, and a coastal strip with a bulging extension up the valley of the river Rhodanus which was known as The Province, and both Hellenized as well as Romanized. The name Narbonese Gaul (which I have used in this book) did not become official until the principate of Augustus, though Gaul around the port of Narbo was probably always known as that. The proper name for Gaul-across-the-Alps was Trans-alpine Gaul. That Gaul more properly known as Cisalpine Gaul because it lay on the Italian side of the Alps I have elected to call Italian Gaul. It too was divided into two parts by the Padus River (the modern Po); I have called them Italian Gaul-across-the-Padus and Italian Gaul-this-side-of-the-Padus. There is also no doubt that the Gauls were racially closely akin to the Romans, for their languages were of similar kind, as were many of their technologies. What enriched the Roman at the ultimate expense of the Gaul was his centuries-long exposure to other Mediterranean cultures.

gens A man's clan or extended family. It was indicated by his *nomen*, such as Cornelius or Julius, but was feminine in gender, hence they were the *gens Cornelia* and the *gens Julia*.

gig A two-wheeled vehicle drawn by either two or four animals, more usually mules than horses. Within the limitations of ancient vehicles—springs and shock absorbers did not exist—the gig was very lightly and flexibly built, and was the vehicle of choice for a Roman in a hurry because it was easy for a team to draw, therefore speedy. However, it was open to the elements. In Latin it was a *cisia*. The *carpentum* was a heavier version of the gig, having a closed coach body.

gladiator There is considerable wordage within the pages of this book about gladiators, so I will not enlarge upon them here. Suffice it to say that during Republican times there were only two kinds of gladiator, the Thracian and the Gaul, and that gladiatorial combat was not usually "to the death." The thumbs-up, thumbs-down brutality of the Empire crowds did not exist, perhaps because the State did not own or keep gladiators under the Republic, and few of them were slaves; they were owned by private investors, and cost a great deal of money to acquire, train and maintain. Too much money to want them dead or maimed in the ring. Almost all gladiators during the Republic were Romans, usually deserters or mutineers from the legions. It was very much a voluntary occupation.

governor A very useful English term to describe the promagistrate— proconsul or propraetor—sent to direct, command and manage one of Rome's provinces. His term was set at one year, but very often it was prorogued, sometimes (as in the case of Metellus Pius in Further Spain) for many years.

Gracchi The Brothers Gracchi, Tiberius Sempronius Gracchus and his younger brother, Gaius Sempronius Gracchus. They were the sons of Cornelia (daughter of Scipio Africanus and Aemilia Paulla) and Tiberius Sempronius Gracchus (consul in 177 and 163 B.C., censor in 169 B.C.), and the consulship, high military command and the censorship were thus their birthright. Neither man advanced beyond the tribunate of the plebs, due to a peculiar combination of high ideals, iconoclastic thinking, and a tremendous sense of duty to Rome. Tiberius Gracchus, a tribune of the plebs in 133 B.C., set out to right the wrongs he saw in the way the Roman State was administering its *ager publicus;* his aim was to give it to the civilian poor of Rome, thus encouraging them by dowering them with land to breed sons and work hard. When the end of the year saw his work still undone, Tiberius Gracchus flouted custom by attempting to run for the tribunate of the plebs a second time. He was clubbed to death on the Capitol.

Gaius Gracchus, ten years Tiberius's junior, was elected a tribune of the plebs in 123 B.C. More able than his brother, he had also profited from his mistakes, and bade fair to alter the whole direction of the ultra-conservative Rome of his time. His reforms were much wider than Tiberius's, and embraced not only the *ager publicus,* but also cheap grain for the populace (a measure aimed not only at the poor, for he adopted no means test), regulation of service in the army, the founding of Roman citizen colonies abroad, public works throughout Italy, removal of the courts from the Senate, a new system to farm the taxes of Asia Province, and an enhancement of citizen status for Latins and Italians. When his year as a tribune of the plebs finished, Gaius Gracchus emulated his brother and ran for a second term. Instead of being killed for his presumption, he got in. At the end of his second term he determined to run yet again, but was defeated in the elections. Helpless to intervene, he had to see all his laws and reforms begin to topple. Prevented from availing himself of peaceful means, Gaius Gracchus resorted to violence. Many of his partisans were killed when the Senate passed its first-ever "ultimate decree," but Gaius Gracchus himself chose to commit suicide before he could be apprehended.

The glossary attached to *The Grass Crown* contains a much fuller article on the Gracchi.

guild   An organized body of professionals, tradesmen, or slaves. One of the purposes behind the organization of guilds lay in protective measures to ensure the members received every advantage in business or trade practices, another to ensure the members were cared for properly in their places of work, and one interesting one, to ensure that the members had sufficient means at their deaths for decent burial.

Head Count   The *capite censi* or *proletarii:* the lowly of Rome. Called the Head Count because at a census all the censors did was to "count heads." Too poor to belong to a Class, the urban Head Count usually belonged to an urban tribe, and therefore owned no worthwhile votes. This rendered them politically useless beyond ensuring that they were fed and entertained enough not to riot. Rural Head Count, though usually owning a valuable tribal vote, rarely could afford to come to Rome at election time. Head Count were neither politically aware nor interested in the way Rome was governed, nor were they particularly oppressed in an Industrial Revolution context. I have sedulously avoided the terms "the masses" or "the proletariat" because of post-Marxist preconceptions not applicable to the ancient lowly. In fact, they seem to have been busy, happy, rather impudent and not at all servile people who had an excellent idea of their own worth and scant respect for the Roman great. However, they had their public heroes; chief among them seems to have been Gaius Marius—until the advent of Caesar, whom they adored. This in turn might suggest that they were not proof against military might and the concept of Rome as The Greatest.

Hellenic, Hellenized   Terms relating to the spread of Greek culture and customs after the time of Alexander the Great. It involved life-style, architecture, dress, industry, government, commercial practices and the Greek language.

hemiolia   A very swift, light bireme of small size, much favored by pirates in the days before they organized themselves into fleets and embarked upon mass raiding of shipping and maritime communities. The *hemiolia* was not decked, and carried a mast and sail aft, thus reducing the number of oars in the upper bank to the forward section of the ship.

herm   A stone pedestal designed to accommodate a bust or small sculpture. It was chiefly distinguished by possessing male genitals on its front side, usually erect.

horse, Nesaean   The largest kind of horse known to the ancients. How large it was is debatable, but it seems to have been at least as large as the mediaeval beast which carried an armored knight, as the Kings of Armenia and the Parthians both relied on Nesaeans to carry their cataphracts (cavalry clad in chain mail from head to foot, as were the horses). Its natural home was to the south and west of the Caspian Sea, in Media, but by the time of the late Republic there were some Nesaean horses in most parts of the ancient world.

Horse, October   On the Ides of October (this was about the time the old campaigning season finished), the best war-horses of that year were picked out and harnessed in pairs to chariots. They then raced on the sward of the Campus Martius, rather than in one of the Circuses. The right-hand horse of the winning team was sacrificed to Mars on a specially erected altar adjacent to the course of the race. The animal was killed with a spear, after which its head was severed and piled over with little cakes, while its tail and genitalia were rushed to the Regia in the Forum Romanum, and the blood dripped onto the altar inside the Regia. Once the ceremonies over the horse's cake-heaped head were concluded, it was thrown at two competing crowds of people, one comprising residents of the Subura, the other residents of the Via Sacra. The purpose was to have the two crowds fight for possession of the head. If the Via Sacra won, the head was nailed to the outside wall of the Regia; if the Subura won, the head was nailed to the outside wall of the Turris Mamilia (the most conspicuous building in the Subura). What was the reason behind all this is not known; the Romans of the late Republic may well not have known themselves, save that it was in some way connected with the close of the campaigning season. We are not told whether the war-horses were Public Horses or not, but we might be pardoned for presuming they were Public Horses.

Horse, Public   A horse which belonged to the State—to the Senate and People of Rome. Going all the way back to the Kings of Rome, it had been governmental policy to provide the eighteen hundred knights of the eighteen most senior Centuries with a horse to ride into battle—bearing in mind the fact that the Centuriate Assembly had originally been a military gathering, and the senior Centuries cavalrymen. The right of these senior knights to a Public Horse was highly regarded and defended.

hubris   The Greek word for overweening pride in self.

hypocausis   In English, hypocaust. A form of central heating having a floor raised on piles and heated from a furnace (the early ones were wood-fired) below. The hypocaust began to heat domestic dwellings about the time of Gaius Marius, and was also used to heat the water in baths, both public and domestic.

ichor   The fluid which coursed through the veins of the gods; a kind of divine blood.

Ides   The third of the three named days of the month which represented the fixed points of the month. Dates were reckoned backward from each of these points—Kalends, Nones, Ides. The Ides occurred on the fifteenth day of the long months (March, May, July and October), and on the thirteenth day of the other months. The Ides were sacred to Jupiter Optimus Maximus, and were marked by the sacrifice of a sheep on the Arx of the Capitol by the *flamen Dialis*.

Ilium   The Latin name for Homer's city of Troy.

Illyricum   The wild and mountainous lands bordering the Adriatic Sea on its eastern side. The native peoples belonged to an Indo-European race called Illyrians, were tribalized, and detested first Greek and then Roman coastal incursions. Republican Rome bothered little about Illyricum unless boiling tribes began to threaten eastern Italian Gaul, when the Senate would send an army to chasten them.

imago, imagines   An *imago* was a beautifully tinted mask made of refined beeswax, outfitted with a wig, and startlingly lifelike (anyone who has visited a waxworks museum will understand how lifelike wax images can be made, and there is no reason to think a Roman *imago* was very much inferior to a Victorian wax face). When a Roman nobleman reached a certain level of public distinction, he acquired the *ius imaginis,* which was the right to have a wax image made of himself. Some modern authorities say the *ius imaginis* was bestowed upon a man once he attained curule office, which would mean aedile. Others plump for praetor, still others for consul. I plump for consul, also the Grass or Civic Crown, a major flaminate, and Pontifex Maximus. All the *imagines* belonging to a family were kept in painstakingly wrought miniature temples in the atrium of the house, and were regularly sacrificed to. When a prominent man or woman of a family owning the *ius imaginis* died, the wax masks were brought out and worn by actors selected because they bore a physical resemblance in height and build to the men the masks represented. Women of course were not entitled to the *ius imaginis*—even Cornelia the Mother of the Gracchi.

imperator   Literally, the commander-in-chief or general of a Roman army. However, the term (first attested to in the career of Lucius Aemilius Paullus) gradually came to be given only to a general who won a great victory; his troops had to have hailed him imperator on the field before he qualified for a triumph. Imperator is the root of the word "emperor."

imperium   Imperium was the degree of authority vested in a curule magistrate or promagistrate. It meant that a man owned the authority of his office, and could not be gainsaid provided he was acting within the limits of his particular level of imperium and within the laws governing his conduct. Imperium was conferred by a *lex curiata,* and lasted for one year only. Extensions for prorogued governors had to be ratified by the Senate and/or People. Lictors shouldering *fasces* indicated a man's imperium; the more lictors, the higher the imperium.

in absentia   In the context used in these books, a candidacy for office approved of by Senate (and People, if necessary) and an election conducted in the absence of the candidate himself. He may have been waiting on the Campus Martius because imperium prevented his crossing the *pomerium,* as with Pompey and Crassus in 70 B.C., or he may have been on military service in a province, as with Gaius Memmius when elected quaestor.

in loco parentis   Still used today, though in a somewhat watered-down sense. To a Republican Roman, *in loco parentis* (literally, in the place of a parent) meant a person assumed the full entitlements of a parent as well as the inherent responsibilities.

insula   An island. Because it was surrounded on all sides by streets, lanes or alleyways, an apartment building was known as an insula. Roman insulae were very tall (up to one hundred feet—thirty meters—in height) and most were large enough to incorporate an internal light well; many were so large they contained multiple light wells. The insulae to be seen today at Ostia are not a real indication of the height insulae attained within Rome; we know

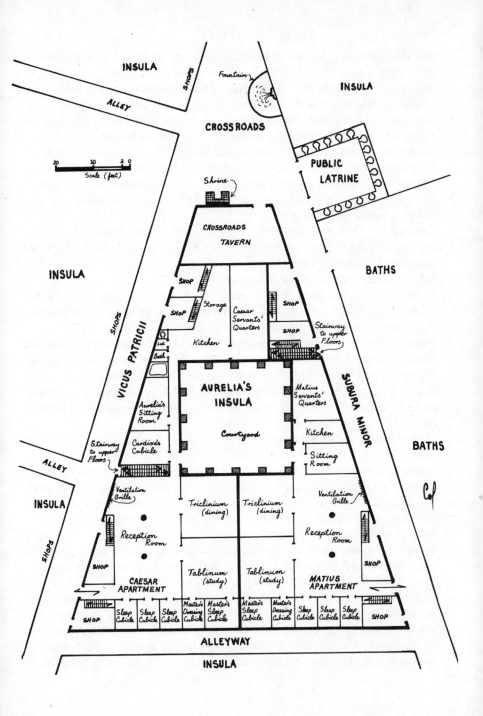

that Augustus tried fruitlessly to limit the height of Roman city insulae to one hundred feet.

in suo anno   Literally, in his year. The phrase was used of men who attained curule office at the exact age the law and custom prescribed for a man holding that office. To be praetor and consul *in suo anno* was a great distinction, for it meant that a man gained election at his first time of trying— many consuls and not a few praetors had to stand several times before they were successful, while others were prevented by circumstances from seeking office at this youngest possible age. Those who bent the law to attain office at an age younger than that prescribed were also not accorded the distinction of being *in suo anno*.

interrex   "Between the kings." The patrician senator, leader of his decury, appointed to govern for five days when Rome had no consuls. The term is more fully explained in the text.

Iol   Modern Cherchel, in Algeria.

Italia   The name given to all of peninsular Italy. Until Sulla regulated the border with Italian Gaul east of the Apennines by fixing it at the Rubico River, the Adriatic side probably ended at the Metaurus River.

Italian Allies   Certain states and/or tribes within peninsular Italy were not gifted with the Roman citizenship until after they rose up against Rome in 91 B.C. (a war detailed in *The Grass Crown*). They were held to be *socii*, that is, allies of Rome. It was not until after Sulla became dictator at the end of 82 B.C. that the men of the Italian Allies were properly regulated as Roman citizens.

Italian Gaul   See the entry under **Gaul.**

iudex   The Latin term for a judge.

iugerum, iugera   The Roman unit of land measurement. In modern terms the *iugerum* consisted of 0.623 (five eighths) of an acre, or 0.252 (one quarter) of a hectare. The modern reader used to acres will get close enough by dividing the number of *iugera* in two; if more accustomed to hectares, divide the number of *iugera* by four.

Iulus   Strictly speaking, the Latin alphabet owned no *J*. The equivalent was consonantal *I*, pronounced more like the English *Y*. If rendered in English, Iulus would be Julus. Iulus was the son of **Aeneas** (q.v.) and was believed by the members of the *gens Julia* to be their direct ancestor. The identity of his mother is of some import. Virgil says Iulus was actually Ascanius, the son of Aeneas by his Trojan wife, Creusa, and had accompanied Aeneas on all his travels. On the other hand, Livy says Iulus was the son of Aeneas by his Latin wife, Lavinia. What the Julian family of Caesar's day believed is not known. I shall go with Livy; Virgil was too prone to tamper with history in order to please his patron, Augustus.

ius   In the sense used in this book, an incontrovertible right or entitlement at law and under the *mos maiorum*. Hence the *ius auxilii ferendi* (q.v.), the *ius imaginis* (see **imago**), and so forth.

ius auxilii ferendi   The original purpose of the tribunate of the plebs was to protect members of the Plebs from discriminatory actions by the Patriciate, this latter group of aristocrats then forming both the Senate and the magistracy. The *ius auxilii ferendi* was the right of any plebeian to claim to the tribunes of the plebs that he must be rescued from the clutches of a magistrate.

Jupiter Stator   That aspect of Jupiter devoted to halting soldiers who were fleeing the field of battle. It was a military cult of generals. The chief temple to Jupiter Stator was on the corner of the Velia where the Via Sacra turned at right angles to run down the slope toward the Palus Ceroliae; it was large enough to be used for meetings by the Senate.

Kalends   The first of the three named days of each month which represented the fixed points of the month. Dates were reckoned backward from each of these points—Kalends, Nones, Ides. The Kalends always occurred on the first day of the month. They were sacred to Juno, and originally had been timed to coincide with the appearance of the New Moon.

knights   The *equites,* the members of what Gaius Gracchus named the Ordo Equester. Under the Kings of Rome, the *equites* had formed the cavalry segment of the Roman army; at this time horses were both scarce and expensive, with the result that the eighteen original Centuries comprising the knights were dowered with the Public Horse by the State. As the Republic came into being and grew, the importance of Roman knight cavalry diminished, yet the number of knight Centuries in the Classes increased. By the second century B.C., Rome no longer fielded horse of her own, and the knights became a social and economic group having little to do with military matters. The knights were now defined by the censors in economic terms alone, though the State continued to provide a Public Horse for each of the eighteen hundred most senior *equites*. The original eighteen Centuries were kept at one hundred men each, but the rest of the knights' Centuries (between seventy-one and seventy-three) swelled within themselves to contain many more than one hundred men apiece.

Until 123 B.C., all senators were knights as well, but in that year Gaius Gracchus split the Senate off as a separate body of three hundred men. It was at best an artificial kind of process; all non-senatorial members of senatorial families were still classified as knights, and the senators were not put into three senator-only Centuries, but left for voting purposes in whatever Centuries they had always occupied.

The insoluble puzzle is: who were the *tribuni aerarii*? A knight's census was 400,000 sesterces, presumably income, and the *tribunus aerarius* had a census of 300,000 sesterces. At first I thought they were possibly senior public servants—Treasury supervisors and the like—but I have swung round to thinking that Mommsen was right. He suggested that there were at least two echelons of knight of the First Class: those with a census of 400,000 sesterces, and those with a census of 300,000 sesterces; and that the lesser-incomed knights were the *tribuni aerarii*. Does that mean only the eighteen hundred knights owning the Public Horse possessed a census of 400,000 sesterces or more? I would doubt that too. There were many thousands of very rich men in Rome, and no census could so neatly divide one income group from another at a round-figure cutoff point. Perhaps it went more that a senior knight dowered with the Public Horse *had* to have at least 400,000 sesterces income for census purposes. Whereas the other seventy-plus Centuries of the First Class contained a mixture of full knights and *tribuni aerarii*. The Centuries of juniors, one imagines, contained more census-rated *tribuni aerarii* than the Centuries of seniors. But no one knows for certain!

There was nothing to stop a knight who qualified for the (entirely unofficial) senatorial means test of one million sesterces becoming a senator under the old system, wherein the censors filled vacancies in the Senate; that by and large knights did not aspire to the Senate was purely because of the knightly love of trade and commerce, forbidden fruit for senators, who could only dabble in land and property. When Sulla reorganized senatorial admission by regulating it through election to the quaestorship, presumably the electoral officers (whose duty it was to accept or deny a candidacy) inspected the candidate's means. But I also suspect that quite a few men firmly ensconced in the Senate did *not* have one million sesterces income!

Lake Nemi   A small volcanic lake in the Via Appia flank of the Alban Hills. In a grove of sacred trees on its shore stood Diana's temple, served by a priest called Rex Nemorensis. He was an escaped slave who succeeded to the priesthood by first defiling the grove by breaking off a bough from a tree, then killing the existing Rex Nemorensis in combat.

lanista   The proprietor of a gladiatorial school, though not necessarily its actual owner. It was the *lanista* who saw to the overall running of the school; he may sometimes have supervised the training of the men, but that was more properly the duty of the men called *doctores*.

Lar, Lares   These were among the most Roman of all gods, having no form, shape, sex, number, or mythology. They were *numina*. There were many different kinds of Lares, who might function as the protective spirits or forces of a locality (as with crossroads and boundaries), a social group (as with the family's private Lar, the Lar Familiaris), sea voyages (the Lares Permarini), or a whole nation (Rome had public Lares, the Lares Praestites). By the late Republic, however, people had come to think of the Lares as two young men accompanied by a dog; they were depicted in this way in statues. It is doubtful, however, whether a Roman actually believed that there were only two of them, or that they owned this form and sex; more perhaps that the increasing complexity of life made it convenient to tag them.

latifundia   Large tracts of public land leased by one person and run as a single unit in the manner of a modern ranch. The activity was pastoral rather than agricultural. *Latifundia* were usually staffed by slaves who tended to be chained up in gangs and locked at night into barracks called *ergastula*.

Latium   That region of Italy in which Rome was situated; it received its name from the original inhabitants, the Latini. Its northern boundary was the Tiber River, its southern a point extending inland from the seaport of Circeii; on the east it bordered the more mountainous lands of the Sabines and the Marsi. When the Romans completed the conquest of the Volsci and the Aequi around 300 B.C., Latium became purely Roman.

lectus funebris   The imposing couch upon which the corpse of a man or woman of family rich enough to afford a proper funeral was arranged after the undertakers had dressed and improved the looks of the corpse. It possessed legs, was painted black or made of ebony, trimmed with gilt, and covered in black quilts and cushions.

legate   A *legatus*. The most senior members of a Roman general's staff were his legates. All men classified as legates were members of the Senate; they answered only to the general, and were senior to all types of military tribune. Not every legate was a young man, however. Some were consulars who apparently volunteered for some interesting war because they hankered after a spell of army life, or were friends of the general.

legion   *Legio*. The legion was the smallest Roman military unit capable of fighting a war on its own, though it was rarely called upon to do so. It was complete within itself in terms of manpower, equipment, facilities to make war. Between two and six legions clubbed together constituted an army; the times when an army contained more than six legions were unusual. The total number of men in a full-strength legion was about six thousand, of whom perhaps five thousand were actually soldiers, and the rest were classified as noncombatants. The internal organization of a legion consisted of ten cohorts of six centuries each; under normal circumstances there was a modest cavalry unit attached to each legion, though from the time of Sulla downward the cavalry tended more to be grouped together as a whole body separate from the infantry. Each legion was in charge of some pieces of artillery, though artillery was not employed on the field of battle; its use was limited to siege operations. If a legion was one of the consuls' legions it was commanded by up to six elected tribunes of the soldiers, who spelled each other. If a legion belonged to a general not currently a consul, it was commanded by one of the general's legates, or else by the general himself. Its regular officers were the centurions, of whom it possessed some sixty. Though the troops belonging to a legion camped together, they did not live together en masse; they were divided into units of eight men who tented and messed together. See also **cohort.**

legionary This is the correct English word to describe an ordinary soldier (*miles gregarius*) in a Roman legion. "Legionnaire," which I have sometimes seen used, is more properly applied to a soldier in the French Foreign Legion, or to a member of the American Legion.

lex, leges A law or laws. The word *lex* also came to be applied to the plebiscite (*plebiscitum*), passed by the Plebeian Assembly. A *lex* was not considered valid until it had been inscribed on bronze or stone and deposited in the vaults below the temple of Saturn. However, residence therein must have been brief, as space was limited and the temple of Saturn also housed the Treasury. After Sulla's new Tabularium was finished, laws were deposited there instead of (probably) all over the city. A law was named after the man or men who promulgated it and then succeeded in having it ratified, but always (since *lex* is feminine gender) with the feminine ending to his name or their names. This was then followed by a general description of what the law was about. Laws could be—and sometimes were—subject to repeal at a later date.

lex Caecilia Didia There were actually two laws, but only one is of relevance to this volume. Passed by the consuls of 98 B.C., the relevant one stipulated that three *nundinae* or market days had to elapse between the first *contio* to discuss a law in any of the Assemblies and the day of its ratification by vote of the Assembly. There is some debate as to whether the period consisted of twenty-four or seventeen days; I have elected seventeen.

lex Domitia de sacerdotiis Passed in 104 B.C. by Gnaeus Domitius Ahenobarbus, later Pontifex Maximus. It specified that new pontifices and augurs must be elected by a tribal Assembly comprising seventeen of the thirty-five tribes chosen by lot. Until this law, pontifices and augurs were co-opted by the college members. Sulla once dictator repealed it.

lex frumentaria The general term for a grain law. There were many such, commencing with Gaius Gracchus. All grain laws pertained to the public grain supply—that is, the grain bought by the State and distributed by the aediles. Most such laws provided cheap grain, but some took cheap grain away.

lex Genucia   Passed in 342 B.C. by the tribune of the plebs Lucius Genucius. It stipulated that a period of ten years must elapse between one man's holding the same office twice. There were two other *leges Genuciae,* not referred to in this book.

lex Minicia de liberis   Passed about 91 B.C. There is some doubt as to whether its author was a Minicius or a Minucius. It laid down that the children of a marriage between a Roman citizen and a non-Roman citizen, irrespective of which parent was the Roman citizen, must take the citizen status of the non-Roman parent.

lex Plautia Papiria   Passed in 89 B.C. as a supplementary measure to Lucius Caesar's law granting the Roman citizenship to Italian *socii* not directly embroiled in the war between Rome and the Italian Allies. This supplementary law laid down that an Italian resident within peninsular Italy but not in his original *municipium* who had not taken up arms against Rome could be granted the full citizenship if he applied to a praetor in Rome within sixty days of the law's ratification. Phew!

lex rogata   A law promulgated in an Assembly by direct co-operation between the presiding magistrate and the members of the Assembly. In other words, the law was not presented to the Assembly in a cut-and-dried, fully drafted state, but was drafted during *contio* in the Assembly.

lex sumptuaria   Any law regulating the purchase and consumption of luxuries. They were popular laws among magistrates who deplored luxury-loving tendencies, but rarely worked in practice. The most common articles legislated against were spices, peppers, perfumes, incenses, imported wines, and genuine Tyrian purple. Sulla's sumptuary law even stipulated how much a family could spend on a funeral or a banquet.

lex Villia annalis   Passed in 180 B.C. by the tribune of the plebs Lucius Villius. It stipulated certain minimum ages at which the curule magistracies could be held (presumably thirty-nine for praetors and forty-two for consuls), and apparently also stipulated that two years must elapse between a man's holding the praetorship and the consulship.

LIBERO   The word used in Assembly trials to register a verdict of acquittal.

Liber Pater   The original Italian fertility god who looked after the sperm of men and the germination of crops. He became identified with wine and good times, with Bacchus and with Dionysos, but he does not appear to have been held lightly. The Italian Allies when pursuing their war against Rome adopted Liber Pater as their tutelary god.

licker-fish   A freshwater bass of the Tiber River. The creature was to be found only between the Wooden Bridge and the Pons Aemilius, where it lurked around the outflows of the great sewers and fed upon what they disgorged. Apparently it was so well fed that it was notoriously hard to catch. This may have been why it was so prized as a delicacy by Rome's Epicureans.

lictor   The man who formally attended a curule magistrate as he went about his official business by preceding him in single file to clear a way, or by being on hand as he conducted his business in case he needed to employ restraint or chastise. The lictor had to be a Roman citizen and was a State employee, though he does not seem to have been of high social status, and was probably so poorly paid that he relied upon his magistrate's generosity with gratuities. On his left shoulder he bore the bundle of rods called *fasces* (q.v.). Within the city of Rome he wore a plain white toga, changing to a black toga for funerals; outside Rome he wore a scarlet tunic cinched by a broad black leather belt bossed in brass, and inserted the axes into the *fasces*.

There was a College of Lictors, though the site of lictorial headquarters is not known. I placed it behind the temple of the Lares Praestites on the eastern side of the Forum Romanum adjacent to the great inn on the corner of the Clivus Orbius, but there is no factual evidence of any kind to support this location. Within the college the lictors (there must have been at least three hundred of them) were organized into decuries of ten men, each headed by a prefect, and the decuries were collectively supervised by several college presidents.

litter   A covered cubicle equipped with legs upon which it rested when lowered to the ground. A horizontal pole on each corner projected forward and behind the conveyance; it was carried by four to eight men who picked it up by means of these poles. The litter was a slow form of transport, but it was by far the most comfortable known in the ancient world. I imagine it was considerably more comfortable than most modern transport!

ludi   The games. See that entry.

Lusitani   The peoples of far western and northwestern Spain. Less exposed to Hellenic and Roman culture than the Celtiberians, the Lusitani were probably somewhat less Celtic than Iberian in racial content, though the two strains were mixed in them. Their organization was tribal, and they seem to have farmed as well as grazed.

macellum   A market.

magistrates   The elected representatives of the Senate and People of

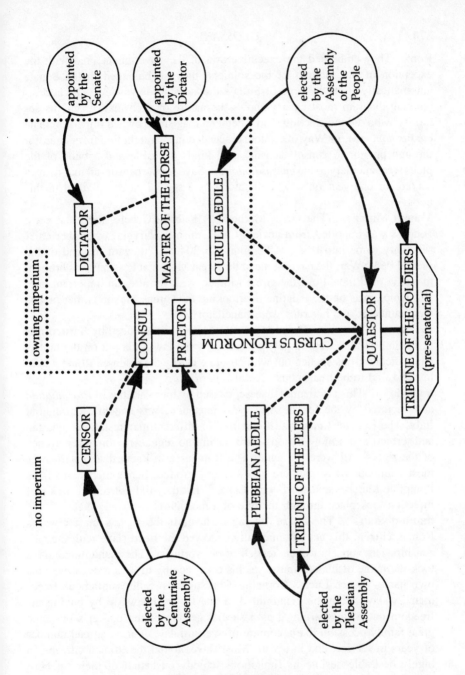

Roman Magistrates

Rome. They embodied the executive arm of the government, and with the exception of the tribunes of the soldiers, they all belonged to the Senate automatically from the time of Sulla's dictatorship downward. The accompanying diagram most clearly shows the nature of each magistracy, its seniority, who did the electing, and whether a magistrate owned imperium. The *cursus honorum,* or Way of Honor, proceeded in a straight line from quaestor through praetor to consul; censor, both kinds of aedile and tribune of the plebs were ancillary to the *cursus honorum.* Save for the censor, all magistrates served for one year only. The dictator was a special case explained in this book.

Magna Mater   The Great Mother. As Kubaba Cybele, the great earth goddess was imported from ancient Carchemish to Phrygia, where her chief sanctuary came into being at Pessinus. In 204 B.C., toward the end of the second Punic War, the navel stone of the Great Mother at Pessinus was brought to Rome, and the cult of the Great Mother was ever after an important one. Her temple was on the Palatine overlooking the Circus Maximus, her priests were eunuchs, and her rites were flagellatory.

maiestas   Treason. The refinements of treason introduced by **Saturninus** (q.v.) in 103 B.C. were largely cancelled by the law Sulla put on the tablets when dictator; this spelled out with absolute clarity the offenses Rome would hitherto find to be treasonous. See also *perduellio.*

malaria   This pestilential disease, caused by four varieties of *Plasmodium* and vectored by the female *Anopheles* mosquito, was endemic throughout Italy. The Romans knew that it occurred in different manifestations: quartan and tertian, and a more serious form having no regular rhythmic recurrence of the rigors. All were the ague. The Romans also knew that malaria was most common wherever there was swampy ground, hence their fear of the Pomptine Marshes and the Fucine Lake. What they did not realize was that infection took place through the bite of a mosquito.

manumission   The act of freeing a slave. If the slave's master was a Roman citizen, this act automatically endowed the freed slave with the citizenship. His vote, however, tended to be worthless. The manumitted slave took the name of his old master as his own, adding to it as a *cognomen* his own name—hence Lucius Cornelius Chrysogonus, Sulla's infamous freedman. A slave might be manumitted in one of several ways: by buying his freedom out of his earnings; as a special gesture of the master's on some great family occasion like a coming-of-age birthday; after an agreed number of years in service; and in a will. Most slaves found the Roman citizenship highly desirable despite its limitations, chiefly on behalf of their freeborn descendants. It was not at all uncommon for men with skills to sell themselves into slavery, particularly among the Greeks. For the rest of his life the freed slave had to wear a slightly conical skullcap on the back of his head—the Cap of Liberty. See also **freedman.**

Marsi   One of the most important Italian peoples. The Marsi lived around the shores of the Fucine Lake, which belonged to them, and their territory extended into the high Apennines. Their history indicates that until the time of the Italian War they had always been loyal to Rome. The Marsi worshipped snakes, and were famous as snake charmers.

measures and weights   Most measurements were based upon body parts, hence the foot, the hand, the pace. The Roman foot at 296mm was just slightly short of 12 inches, and it was divided into 12 inches. 5 feet made up a pace, and the Roman mile at 1,000 paces was about 285 feet short of the English mile, thus there were 20 Roman miles for every 19 English—too small a difference to make it necessary in my text to specify miles (or feet) as Roman.

Area was measured in *iugera* (see that entry).

Grains such as wheat were dry-measured rather than weighed, as they poured like fluids; the dry measures were the *medimnus* and the *modius* (see those entries).

The bulk container was the *amphora,* which held about 25 liters (6 American gallons), and was the volume of a Roman cubic foot. Ships' cargoes were always expressed in *amphorae.*

The Roman pound, or *libra,* weighed about 7/10ths of an English pound at 327 grams, and was divided into 12 ounces (*unciae*). Heavy weights were measured in the **talent** (see that entry).

medimnus   A dry measure for grains and other pourable solids. It equalled 5 *modii* and occupied a volume of 10 U.S. gallons, and weighed about 65 Roman pounds (47.5 English pounds). This provided sufficient grain for two one-Roman-pound loaves of bread per day for about 30 days, given that the waste husked off the grain in grinding was replaced by water and other ingredients. The ordinary Roman who lived in one or two rooms in an insula did not normally grind his flour and bake his bread at home; he came to an arrangement with his local baker (as indeed was done in many parts of Europe until relatively recently), who took a cut of the grain ration as his price. Perhaps the final result was that one *medimnus* of wheat provided the ordinary Roman with one large loaf per day for 30 days?

mentula   A choice Latin obscenity for the penis.

merchantman   A cargo ship. Much shorter in length and broader in the beam than a war galley (the ratio was about 4:1), it was stoutly built of some *pinus* like fir, and was designed to be sailed more than rowed, though it was always equipped with a bank of oars for use when becalmed or being chased by pirates. The single sail was cross-rigged; sometimes a smaller sail was rigged forward of the mainsail on a foremast. Steerage was usually in the form of two large rudder oars, one on either side at the stern. High in the poop, it was decked to protect its cargo, and usually had a cabin amidships as well as a cabin aft. Cargo was loaded in *amphorae* if grain or wine; these large earthenware jars with pointed bottoms were stowed in the hold embedded in sawdust to prevent their shifting in heavy seas. The average merchantman seems to have carried about 100 tons of cargo. Though able to stay at sea night and day—and in the hands of a good captain able to sail across open sea—the merchantman when possible hugged the coast, and its captain was more likely to want to put into port at dusk than to sail on. Perhaps the only merchantmen which regularly stayed at sea and crossed open waters were the ships of large grain fleets. These often doubled as troop transports.

Middle Sea   The name I have used for the Mediterranean Sea. My observant readers will notice a new term now creeping into the narrative: Our Sea. *Mare nostrum* (our sea) is what it came to be called as the Republic neared its end.

miles gloriosus   *Miles* means soldier, and at first glance *gloriosus* might seem to mean glorious. But it commonly meant boastful or vainglorious, as it did in the hands of the playwright.

Military Man   The *vir militaris*. What might be called a "career soldier." His whole life revolved around the army, and he continued to serve in the army after his obligatory number of years or campaigns had expired. If he entered the Roman political arena he relied upon his military reputation to catch votes, but many Military Men never bothered to enter the political arena at all. However, if a Military Man wanted to general an army, he had no choice but to attain the praetorship, which was the lowest magistracy carrying command of an army with it. Gaius Marius, Quintus Sertorius, Titus Didius, Gaius Pomptinus, Publius Ventidius were all Military Men; but Caesar the Dictator, the greatest military man of them all, was never a Military Man.

minim   A bright vermilion pigment made from cinnabar (mercuric sulphide) which the triumphing general painted on his face, apparently to ape the terracotta face of the statue of Jupiter Optimus Maximus in his temple on the Capitol.

Minutus   Meager in size.

modius   The customary measure of grain. A *modius* occupied 2 U.S. gallons or 8 liters, and weighed about 13 (presumably Roman) pounds. The public grain was doled out in increments of 5 *modii* per month, this equaling one *medimnus* (see this entry also for information about bread).

mos maiorum   The established order of things, used to describe the habits and customs of government and public institutions. Perhaps the best definition is to say that the *mos maiorum* was Rome's unwritten constitution. *Mos* meant established custom; and in this context *maiores* meant ancestors or forebears. To sum up, the *mos maiorum* was how things had always been done—and how they should always be done in the future too!

mundus   A beehive-shaped pit which was divided into two parts and normally kept covered. Its exact purpose is a mystery, but it seems to have been believed in late Republican times to be an entranceway to the Underworld. The lid was removed thrice in the year on *dies religiosi* (q.v.) in order to allow the shades of the dead to walk the city.

myoparo   A small war galley much favored by pirates before they began to band together in much larger ships to sail as properly admiraled fleets capable of attacking and beating professional navies. The *myoparo* is somewhat mysterious as to its size and type, but it seems to have been an improvement upon the *hemiolia* (q.v.) and preferred to the *hemiolia*. The only drawing of it is not informative, though it does seem to indicate that the *myoparo* had only one bank of oars rowed over the top of the gunwale rather than through ports, and also possessed mast and sail.

nefas   Sacrilege; an impious or sacrilegious act.

Nesaean horse   See **horse, Nesaean.**

nobleman   *Nobilis*. A man and his descendants were described as noble once he had achieved the consulship. This was an artificial aristocracy invented by the plebeians in order to cut the inarguably noble patricians down to size; once the first century of the Republic was over, more plebeians reached the consulship than did patricians. Nobility mattered enormously.

nomen   The family, clan, or gentilicial name—the name of the *gens* in (for men) masculine form. Cornelius, Julius, Domitius, Licinius were all *nomina* (plural).

Nones   The second of the three named days of the month which represented the fixed points of the month. Dates were reckoned backward from each of these points—Kalends, Nones, Ides. The Nones occurred on the seventh day of the long months (March, May, July and October), and on the fifth day of the other months. The Nones were sacred to Juno.

non pro consule, sed pro consulibus   The famous phrase of Lucius Marcius Philippus when proposing that Pompey be given command of Nearer Spain in the war against Quintus Sertorius. As a piece of hair-splitting it was brilliant, and reconciled many in the Senate to Pompey who were obdurately against a proconsular command going to a man outside the Senate. It said, more or less, "not as a man after his consulship, but as a man acting on behalf of the consuls of the year."

***numen, numina,* numinous**   Pertaining to gods who were absolutely spirits or forces, having no bodies, faces, sex, or mythology. See the glossary of *The First Man in Rome* for much fuller explanation.

nundinum   The interval between one market day and the next; the eightday Roman week. Save for the Kalends, Nones and Ides, the days of the Roman calendar were not named; on the calendars themselves they are allocated a letter between A and H, with A (presumably) being the market day. When the Kalends of January coincided with the market day, the whole year was considered to be unlucky, but this did not happen regularly because of intercalations and the fact that the eight-day round of letters was continued on without an interruption between last day of the old year and first (Kalends) day of the new year.

nundinus, nundinae (plural)   The market day, occurring every eighth day; the singular, *nundinus,* was less used than the plural, *nundinae.* Under normal circumstances the courts were open on *nundinae,* but the Assemblies were not.

October Horse   See **Horse, October.**

Olympia   The famous temple and precinct of Zeus was nowhere near Mount Olympus in Thessaly; it lay on the Alpheus River in the district of Elis, in the western Peloponnese.

opus incertum   The oldest of several ways in which the Romans built their walls. A facing of irregular small stones mortared together was constructed with a hollow interior or cavity; this was filled with a mortar composed of black pozzolana and lime mixed through an aggregate of rubble and small stones (*caementa*). Even in the time of Sulla, *opus incertum* was still the most popular way to build a wall. It was probably also cheaper than brick.

Ordo Equester   The name given to the knights by Gaius Gracchus. See the entry on **knights.**

Oscan   The language spoken by the Samnites, Campani, Lucani, Apuli, Bruttii and other Italian peoples of the more southern part of the Italian peninsula; it was the chief language of central Italy even during the latter decades of the Republic. It was Indo-European, but not closely allied to Latin; some of the peoples who spoke Oscan used a Latin alphabet to write it, but more (including the widest group of Oscan speakers, the Samnites) used an alphabet derived from Etruscan. Many Romans could speak and understand

Oscan. The Atellan mimes were sometimes staged in Rome with the cast speaking in Oscan.

paean A song or hymn of praise, sometimes composed in honor of a living man, more often relating to the gods.

pantheon The word used nowadays to encompass collectively the whole array of gods in a polytheistic system of religious belief.

Parvus So small as to be of no account.

paterfamilias The head of the family unit. His right to do as he pleased with the various members of his family was rigidly protected at law.

patrician, Patriciate The Patriciate was the original Roman aristocracy. To an ancestor-revering, birth-conscious people like the Romans, the importance of belonging to patrician stock can hardly be overestimated. The older among the patrician families were aristocrats before the Kings of Rome, the youngest among them (the Claudii) apparently emerging at the very beginning of the Republic. All through the Republic they kept the title of patrician, as well as a prestige unattainable by any plebeian—and this in spite of the nobility, the "new aristocracy" ennobled above mere plebeian status by having consuls in the family. However, by the last century of the Republic a patrician owned little distinction beyond his blood; the wealth and energy of the great plebeian families had steadily eroded original patrician rights. Sulla, a patrician himself, seems to have tried in small ways to elevate the patrician above his plebeian brothers, but did not dare legislate major privileges. Yet entitlement and privilege under the constitution mattered not a scrap to most Romans: they knew the patrician was better. During the last century of the Republic the following patrician families were still producing senators, and some praetors and consuls: Aemilius, Claudius, Cornelius, Fabius (but through adoption only), Julius, Manlius, Pinarius, Postumius, Sergius, Servilius, Sulpicius, and Valerius.

patron, patronage Republican Roman society was organized into a system of patronage and clientship (see also **client**). Though perhaps the smallest businessmen and the lowly of Rome were not always participants in the system, it was nevertheless prevalent at all levels in society, and not all patrons were from the upper echelons of society. The patron undertook to offer protection and favors to those who acknowledged themselves his clients. Freed slaves were in the patronage of their ex-masters. No woman could be a patron. Many patrons were clients of patrons more powerful than themselves, which technically made their clients also the clients of their patron. The patron might do nothing for years to obtain help or support from a client, but one day the client would be called upon to do his patron a favor—vote for him, or lobby for him, or perform some special task. It was customary for the patron to see his clients at dawn in his house on "business" days in the calendar; at these matinées the clients would ask for help or favor, or merely attend to offer respect, or offer services. A rich or generous patron often bestowed gifts of money upon his clients when they assembled at such times. If a man became the client of another man whom in earlier days he had hated to the point of implacable enmity, that client would thereafter serve his erstwhile enemy, now his patron, with complete fidelity, even to death (*vide* Caesar the Dictator and Curio the Younger).

Pavo   A peacock.

pedarius   A senatorial backbencher (see entry on the **Senate**).

People of Rome   This term embraced every single Roman who was not a member of the Senate; it applied to patricians as well as plebeians, and to the Head Count as well as to the First Class.

perduellio   High treason. Until first Saturninus and then Sulla redefined treason and passed new treason laws, *perduellio* was the only form treason had in Roman law. Old enough to be mentioned in the **Twelve Tables** (q.v.), it required a trial process in the Centuriate Assembly, a most cumbersome affair. It carried an automatic death penalty, of crucifixion on a cross tied to an unlucky tree (that is, a tree which had never borne fruit).

peristyle   An enclosed garden or courtyard which was surrounded by a colonnade and formed the outdoor area of a house.

phalerae   Round, chased, ornamented silver or gold discs about 3 to 4 inches (75 to 100mm) in diameter. Originally they were worn as insignia by Roman knights, and also formed a part of the trappings of a knight's horse. Gradually they came to be military decorations awarded for exceptional bravery in battle. Normally they were given in sets of nine (three rows of three each) upon a decorated leather harness of straps designed to be worn over the mail shirt or cuirass.

piaculum   A sacrifice made as atonement for some offense.

Picenum   That part of the eastern Italian peninsula roughly occupying the area of the Italian leg's calf muscle. Its western boundary formed the crest of the Apennines; Umbria lay to the north, and Samnium to the south. The original inhabitants were of Italiote and Illyrian stock, but there was a tradition that Sabines had migrated east of the Apennine crest and settled in Picenum, bringing with them as their tutelary god Picus, the woodpecker, from which the region got its name. A tribe of Gauls called the Senones also settled in the area at the time Italy was invaded by the first King Brennus in 390 B.C. Politically Picenum fell into two parts: northern Picenum, closely allied to southern Umbria, was under the sway of the great family called Pompeius;

and Picenum south of the Flosis or Flussor River was under the sway of peoples allied to the Samnites.

pilum, pila   The Roman infantry spear, especially as modified by Gaius Marius. It had a very small, wickedly barbed head of iron and an upper shaft of iron; this was joined to a shaped wooden stem which fitted the hand comfortably. Marius modified it by introducing a weakness into the junction between iron and wooden sections, so that when the *pilum* lodged in an enemy shield or body, it broke apart, and thus could not be hurled back by the enemy. After a battle all the broken *pila* were collected from the field; they were easily mended by the artificers.

plebeian, Plebs   All Roman citizens who were not patricians were plebeians; that is, they belonged to the Plebs (the *e* is short, so that *Plebs* rhymes with *webs,* not *glebes*). At the beginning of the Republic no plebeian could be a priest, a magistrate, or even a senator. This situation lasted only a very short while; one by one the exclusively patrician institutions crumbled before the onslaught of the Plebs, who far outnumbered the patricians—and several times threatened to secede. By the late Republic there was very little if any advantage to being a patrician—except that everyone knew patrician was better.

Plebeian Assembly   See the entry under **Assemblies.**

podex   An impolite word for the posterior fundamental orifice: an arsehole rather than an anus.

Pollux   The ever-forgotten Heavenly Twin. See **Castor.**

pomerium   The sacred boundary enclosing the city of Rome. Marked by white stones called *cippi,* it was reputedly inaugurated by King Servius Tullius, and remained without change until Sulla's dictatorship. The *pomerium* did not exactly follow the Servian Walls, one good reason why it is doubtful that the Servian Walls were built by King Servius Tullius—who would certainly have caused his walls to follow the same line as his *pomerium.* The whole of the ancient Palatine city of Romulus was enclosed within the *pomerium,* whereas the Aventine lay outside it. So too did the Capitol. Tradition held that the *pomerium* might be enlarged, but only by a man who significantly increased the size of Roman territory. In religious terms, Rome herself existed only inside the *pomerium;* all outside it was merely Roman territory.

pontifex   Many Latin etymologists think that in very early times the pontifex was a maker of bridges (*pons:* bridge), and that the making of bridges was considered a mystical art putting the maker in close touch with the gods. Be that as it may, by the time the Republic came along the pontifex was a priest. Incorporated into a special college, he served as an adviser to Rome's magistrates and comitia in all religious matters—and would inevitably himself become a magistrate. At first all pontifices had to be patrician, but a *lex Ogulnia* of 300 B.C. stipulated that half the College of Pontifices had to be plebeian. During periods when the pontifices (and augurs) were co-opted into the college by other members, new appointees tended to be well under senatorial age; the early twenties were common. Thus the appointment of Caesar at twenty-seven years of age was not at all unusual or remarkable.

Pontifex Maximus   The head of Rome's State-administered religion, and most senior of all priests. He seems to have been an invention of the infant Republic, a typically masterly Roman way of getting round an obstacle without demolishing it and ruffling feelings. In the time of the Kings of Rome, the Rex Sacrorum had been the chief priest, this being a title held by the King himself. Apparently considering it unwise to abolish the Rex Sacrorum, the anti-monarchical rulers of the new Republic of Rome simply created a new priest whose role and status were superior to the Rex Sacrorum. This new priest was given the title of Pontifex Maximus. To reinforce his statesmanlike position, it was laid down that he should be elected, not co-opted (the other priests were all co-opted). At first he was probably required to be a patrician, but soon could as easily be a plebeian. He supervised all the members of the various priestly colleges—and the Vestal Virgins. The State gave him its most imposing house as his residence, but in Republican times he shared this residence with the Vestal Virgins, apparently on a half-and-half basis. His official headquarters had the status of an inaugurated temple: the little old Regia in the Forum Romanum just outside his State house.

popa   He was a public servant attached to religious duties, and his only job appears to have been to wield the big stunning hammer; the cutting of the beast's throat was the province of the *cultarius* (see that entry).

population of Rome   A vexed question upon which much ink has been expended by modern scholars. I think there is a tendency to underestimate the number of people who actually dwelt inside Rome herself, few if any of the scholars admitting to a number as great as one million. The general consensus seems to be half a million. However, we do know the dimensions of the Republican city inside the Servian Walls: in width, one-plus kilometers, in length, two-plus kilometers. Then as now, Rome was a city of apartment dwellers, and that is a strong clue to the actual population. Of Roman citizens—that is, males on the census rolls—there were perhaps a quarter of a million; plus wives and children; and plus slaves. It was an absolutely penurious household which did not have at least one slave in service; the Head Count seem to have owned slaves too. Then there were the non-citizens, of whom Rome had hordes: Jews, Syrians, Greeks, Gauls, all sorts. With wives, children, and slaves. Rome teemed with people, its insulae were multitudinous. Non-citizens, wives, children and slaves must have pushed that quarter-million well above a million. Otherwise the insulae would have been half empty and the city smothered in parks. I think two million is closer to the mark.

porta   A city or town gate. Rome's gates were all equipped with mighty oak doors and portcullises.

portico   The word I have chosen to indicate a large covered porch forming an entrance to a building or temple.

porticus   Not a porch, but a whole building incorporating some sort of large central courtyard. The actual building was usually longer than wide, and constructed on a colonnade principle. The Porticus Margaritaria in the upper Forum Romanum was a squarer version of the *porticus,* and housed Rome's most expensive shops. The Porticus Aemilia in the Port of Rome was a very long building which housed firms and agents dealing with shipping, import and export.

praefectus fabrum   One of the most important men in a Roman army, technically the *praefectus fabrum* was not even a part of it; he was a civilian appointed to the post by the general. The *praefectus fabrum* was responsible for equipping and supplying the army in all respects, from its animals and their fodder to its men and their food. Because he let out contracts to businessmen and manufacturers for equipment and supplies, he was a very powerful figure—and unless he was a man of superior integrity, in a perfect position to enrich himself. The evidence of Caesar's *praefectus fabrum,* the Gadetanian banker Lucius Cornelius Balbus, indicates just how important and powerful these suppliers of armies were.

praenomen   A Roman man's first name. There were very few *praenomina* (plural) in use, perhaps twenty, and half of them were not common, or else were confined to the men of one particular *gens,* as with Mamercus, confined to the Aemilii Lepidi, and Appius, confined to the patrician Claudii. Each *gens* or clan favored certain *praenomina* only, perhaps two or three out of the twenty. A modern scholar can often tell from a man's *praenomen* whether he was a genuine member of the *gens:* the Julii, for instance, favored Sextus, Gaius and Lucius only, with the result that a man called Marcus Julius is highly suspect. The Licinii favored Publius, Marcus and Lucius; the Pompeii favored Gnaeus, Sextus and Quintus; the Cornelii favored Publius, Lucius and Gnaeus; the Servilii of the patrician *gens* favored Quintus and Gnaeus. One of the great puzzles for modern scholars concerns that Lucius Claudius who was Rex Sacrorum during the late Republic; Lucius was not a patrician Claudian *praenomen,* yet the Rex Sacrorum was certainly a patrician Claudius. I have postulated that there was a certain branch of the Claudii bearing the *praenomen* Lucius which always traditionally provided Rome with her Rex Sacrorum. The whole subject of *praenomina* has me in stitches whenever I watch one of those Hollywood Roman epics; they always get it wrong!

praetor This magistracy ranked second in the hierarchy of Roman magistrates. At the very beginning of the Republic, the two highest magistrates of all were known as praetors. By the end of the fourth century B.C., however, the term consul had come into being for the highest magistrates, and praetors were relegated to second-best. One praetor was the sole representative of this position for many decades thereafter; he was obviously the *praetor urbanus,* as his duties were confined to the city of Rome, thus freeing up the two consuls for duties as war leaders outside the city. In 242 B.C. a second praetor, the *praetor peregrinus,* was created to cope with matters relating to foreign nationals and Italy rather than Rome. As Rome acquired her overseas provinces more praetors were created to govern them, going out to do so in their year of office rather than afterward as propraetors. By the last century of the Republic there were six praetors elected in most years, eight in others, depending upon the State's needs. Sulla brought the number of praetors up to eight during his dictatorship, and limited duty during their year in actual office to his law courts.

praetor peregrinus I have chosen to translate this as the foreign praetor because he dealt with non-citizens. By the time of Sulla his duties were confined to litigation and the dispensation of legal decisions; he traveled all over Italy as well as hearing cases involving non-citizens within Rome herself.

praetor urbanus The urban praetor, whose duties by the late Republic were almost all to do with litigation. Sulla further refined this by confining the urban praetor to civil rather than criminal suits. His imperium did not extend beyond the fifth milestone from Rome, and he was not allowed to leave Rome for longer than ten days at a time. If both the consuls were absent from Rome, he was Rome's senior magistrate, therefore empowered to summon the Senate, make decisions about execution of government policies, even organize the defenses of the city under threat of attack.

Princeps Senatus The Leader of the House. He was appointed by the censors according to the rules of the *mos maiorum:* he had to be a patrician, the leader of his decury, an *interrex* more times than anyone else, of unimpeachable morals and integrity, and have the most *auctoritas* and *dignitas.* The title Princeps Senatus was not given for life, but was subject to review by each new pair of censors. Sulla stripped the Leader of the House of a considerable amount of his *auctoritas,* but he continued to be prestigious.

privatus Used within the pages of this book to describe a man who was a senator but not currently a magistrate.

proconsul   One serving the State with the imperium of a consul but not in office as consul. Proconsular imperium was normally bestowed upon a man after he finished his year as consul and went to govern a province *proconsule*. A man's tenure of a proconsulship was usually for one year only, but it was very commonly **prorogued** (q.v.), sometimes for several years; Metellus Pius was proconsul in Further Spain from 79 to 71 B.C. Proconsular imperium was limited to the proconsul's province or command, and was lost the moment he stepped across the *pomerium* into Rome.

Procrustes   A mythological Greek gentleman of dubious tastes. In his stronghold somewhere in Attica (said to be on the road to the Isthmus of Corinth) he kept two beds, one too short for the average man, and one too long. Having lured the traveler into his lair, he overpowered his victim and then popped the poor fellow on whichever of the two beds fitted least. If the victim was too short for the long bed, Procrustes stretched him out until he did measure up; if the victim was too tall for the short bed, Procrustes lopped bits off his extremities until he did measure up. Theseus killed him by treating him as he had treated all his victims.

proletarii   Those Roman citizens who were too poor to give the State anything by way of taxes, duties, or service. The only thing they could give the State was *proles*—children. See **Head Count.**

promagistrate   One serving the State in a magisterial role without actually being a magistrate. The offices of quaestor, praetor and consul (the three magistracies of the formal *cursus honorum*) were the only three relevant.

propraetor   One serving the State with the imperium of a praetor but not in office as a praetor. Propraetorian imperium was normally bestowed upon a man after he had finished his year as praetor and went to govern a province *propraetore*. Tenure of a propraetorship was usually for one year, but could be prorogued.

proquaestor   One serving the State as a quaestor but not in office as a quaestor. The office did not carry imperium, but under normal circumstances a man elected to the quaestorship would, if asked for personally by a governor who ended in staying in his province for more than one year, remain in the province as proquaestor until his superior went home.

prorogue   This meant to extend a man's tenure of promagisterial office beyond its normal time span of one year. It affected proconsuls and propraetors, but also quaestors. I include the word in this glossary because I have discovered that modern English language dictionaries of small or even medium size neglect to give this meaning in treating the word "prorogue."

province   Originally this meant the sphere of duty of a magistrate or promagistrate holding imperium, and therefore applied as much to consuls and praetors in office inside Rome as it did to those abroad. Then the word came to mean the place where the imperium was exercised by its holder, and finally was applied to that place as simply meaning it was in the ownership (or province) of Rome.

pteryges   The leather straps which depended from the waist to the knees as a kilt, and from the shoulders to the upper arms as sleeves; they were sometimes fringed at their ends, and ornamented with metallic bosses as well as tooling. The traditional mark of the senior officers and generals of the Roman army, they were not worn by the ranks.

publicani   Tax-farmers, or contracted collectors of Rome's public revenues. Such contracts were let by the censors about every five years, though it would seem that Sulla when dictator suspended this when he terminated the office of censor. No doubt he provided some other means of letting contracts.

Public Horse   See **Horse, Public.**

public servants   The more research I do, the more I come to see that Rome had many public servants. However, the Senate and Assemblies—that is, government—traditionally abominated public servants, and many of Rome's public transactions were conducted by firms and/or individuals in the private business sector. This privatization was an ongoing thing throughout the Republic, and was usually effected through the censors, praetors, aediles and quaestors. Contracts were let, a price for the particular service was agreed to. All this notwithstanding, of public servants there were many—clerks, scribes, secretaries, accountants, general factotums, religious attendants, public slaves, electoral officers, comitial officers, lictors—not to mention the legions. Cavalry might be considered to be "on hire." Pay and conditions were probably not good, but aside from the public slaves all public servants seem to have been Roman citizens. The bulk of clerical employees were apparently Greek freedmen.

Pulex   A flea.

Punic   Pertaining to Carthage and the Carthaginians. It derives from the original homeland of the Carthaginians—Phoenicia.

Pusillus   Absolutely infinitesimal in size.

Pythagorean   Pertaining to the philosophical system originated by Pythagoras. In Rome of the late Republic he had a reputation as a bit of a ratbag—that is, eccentric enough to be considered slightly potty. He taught that the soul was doomed to transmigrate from one kind of organism to another (even plants) for all eternity unless when imprisoned within a man that man espoused a way of life designed to free the soul: he preached rules of silence, chastity, contemplation, vegetarianism, etc. Women were as welcome to participate in the way of life as men. The Neopythagorean cult practiced in Rome had departed from true Pythagoreanism, but the preoccupation with numbers and a way of life was still strong. Unfortunately among the foods Pythagoreans advocated consuming in large quantities were beans; the result was a great deal of methane in the air around a Pythagorean. He or she was therefore very often the butt of unsympathetic wits. A medical friend of mine maintains that excessive amounts of fava beans can promote excessive bleeding in childbirth.

quaestio   A court of law or judicial investigatory panel.

quaestor   The lowest rung on the senatorial *cursus honorum*. It was always an elected office, but until Sulla laid down during his dictatorship that in future the quaestorship would be the only way a man could enter the Senate, it was not necessary for a man to be quaestor in order to be a senator. Sulla increased the number of quaestors from perhaps twelve to twenty, and laid down that a man could not be quaestor until he was thirty years of age. The chief duties of a quaestor were fiscal. He might be (chosen by the lots) seconded to Treasury duty within Rome, or to collecting customs, port dues and rents elsewhere in Italy, or serve as the manager of a provincial governor's moneys. A man going to govern a province could ask for a quaestor by name. The quaestor's year in office began on the fifth day of December.

Quinctilis   Originally the fifth month when the Roman New Year had begun in March, it retained the name after January New Year made it the seventh month. We know it, of course, as July; so did the Romans—after the death of the great Julius.

quinquereme   A very common and popular form of ancient war galley: also known as the "five." Like the **bireme** and the **trireme** (q.v.), it was much longer than it was broad in the beam, and was designed for no other purpose than to conduct war at sea. It used to be thought that the quinquereme had five banks of oars, but it is now almost universally agreed that no galley ever had more than three banks of oars, and more commonly perhaps had only two banks. The "five" was most likely called a "five" because it had five men on each oar, or else if it had two banks of oars put three men on the upper oars and two men on the lower. If there were five men on an oar, only the man on the tip or end of the oar had to be highly skilled; he guided the oar and did the really hard work, while the other four provided little beyond muscle-power. However, five men on an oar meant that at the commencement of the sweep the rowers had to stand, falling back onto the seat as they pulled. A "five" wherein the rowers could remain seated would have needed three banks of oars as in the trireme, two men on each of the two upper banks, and one man on the lowest bank. It seems that all three kinds of quinqueremes were used, each community or nation having its preference. For the rest, the quinquereme was decked, the upper oars lay within an outrigger, and a mast and sail were part of the design, though usually left ashore if battle was expected. The oarsmen numbered about 270, the sailors perhaps 30, and if the admiral believed in boarding rather than or as well as ramming, some 120 marines could be carried along with fighting towers and catapults. Like its smaller sister galleys, the "five" was rowed by professional oarsmen, never slaves.

Quirites   Roman citizens of civilian status.

quod erat demonstrandum   "That was the thing to be proved."

Regia   The ancient little building in the Forum Romanum, oddly shaped and oriented toward the north, that served as the offices of the Pontifex Maximus and the headquarters of the College of Pontifices. It was an inaugurated temple and contained shrines or altars or artifacts of some of Rome's oldest and most shadowy gods—Opsiconsiva, Vesta, Mars of the sacred shields and spears. Within the Regia the Pontifex Maximus kept his records. It was *never* his residence.

Republic   The word was originally two words—*res publica*—meaning the thing which constitutes the people as a whole: that is, the government.

Rex Sacrorum   During the Republic, he was the second-ranking member of the College of Pontifices. A relic of the days of the Kings of Rome, the Rex Sacrorum had to be a patrician, and was hedged around with as many taboos as the *flamen Dialis*.

rhetoric   The art of oratory, something the Greeks and Romans turned into a science. An orator was required to speak according to carefully laid out rules and conventions which extended far beyond mere words; body language and movements were an intrinsic part of it. There were different styles of rhetoric; the Asianic was florid and dramatic, the Attic more restrained and intellectual in approach. It must always be remembered that the audience which gathered to listen to public oration—be it concerned with politics or with the law courts—was composed of connoisseurs of rhetoric. The men who watched and listened did so in an extremely critical way; they had learned all the rules and techniques themselves, and were not easy to please.

Ria   Plutarch (writing in Greek almost two hundred years later) gives the name of Quintus Sertorius's mother as Rhea; but this is not a Latin gentilicial name. However, even today "Ria" is a diminutive commonly used in Europe for women named "Maria." It was some years before I discovered that my Dutch housekeeper, Ria, was actually Maria. Maria would be the name of a female member of the Marii, Gaius Marius's *gens*.

The attachment of Quintus Sertorius to Gaius Marius from his earliest days in military service right through to the end which saw even his loyalest adherents recoil in horror makes me wonder about that name, Rhea. Sertorius, says Plutarch also, was very devoted to his mother. Why then should not Sertorius's mother have been a Maria called Ria for short, and a close blood relative of Gaius Marius's? To have her this answers many questions. As part of my novelist's license I have chosen to assume that Sertorius's mother was a blood relative of Marius's. However, this is pure speculation, albeit having some evidence to support it. In this Roman series I have severely limited my novelist's imagination, and do not allow it to contradict history.

Roma   The proper title in Latin of Rome. It is feminine.

Romulus and Remus   The twin sons of Rhea Silvia, daughter of the King of Alba Longa, and the god Mars. Her uncle Amulius, who had usurped the throne, put the twins in a basket made of rushes and set it adrift on the Tiber (shades of Moses?). They were washed up beneath a fig tree at the base of the Palatine Mount, found by a she-wolf, and suckled by her in a cave nearby. Faustulus and his wife Acca Larentia rescued them and raised them to manhood. After deposing Amulius and putting their grandfather back on his throne, the twins founded a settlement on the Palatine. Once its walls were built and solemnly blessed, Remus jumped over them—apparently an act of horrific sacrilege. Romulus put him to death. Having no people to live in his Palatine town, Romulus then set out to find people, which he did by establishing an asylum in the depression between the two humps of the Capitol. This asylum attracted criminals and escaped slaves, which says something about the original Romans! However, he still had no women. These were obtained by tricking the Sabines of the Quirinal into bringing their women to a feast; Romulus and his desperadoes kidnapped them. Romulus ruled for a long time. Then one day he went hunting in the Goat Swamps of the Campus Martius and was caught in a terrible storm; when he didn't come home, it was believed he had been taken by the gods and made immortal.

rosea rura   The most fertile piece of ground in Italy lay outside the Sabine city of Reate. It was called the *rosea rura*. Apparently it was not tilled, perhaps because it grew a wonderful kind of grass which regenerated so quickly it was very difficult to overgraze. Many thousands of mares grazed on it, and stud donkeys which fetched huge prices at auction; the object of the pastoral *rosea rura* activities was the breeding of mules, these being the best mules available.

rostra   A *rostrum* (singular) was the reinforced oak beak of a war galley used to ram other ships. When in 338 B.C. the consul Gaius Maenius attacked the Volscian fleet in Antium harbor, he defeated it completely. To mark the end of the Volsci as a rival power to Rome, Maenius removed the beaks of the ships he had sent to the bottom or captured and fixed them to the Forum wall of the speaker's platform, which was tucked into the side of the Well of the Comitia. Ever after, the speaker's platform was known as the rostra—the ships' beaks. Other victorious admirals followed Maenius's example, but when no more beaks could be put on the wall of the rostra, they were fixed to tall columns erected around the rostra.

Roxolani   A people inhabiting part of the modern Ukraine and Rumania, and a sept of the Sarmatae. Organized into tribes, they were horse-people who tended to a nomadic way of life except where coastal Greek colonies of the sixth and fifth centuries B.C. impinged upon them sufficiently to initiate them into agriculture. All the peoples who lived around the Mediterranean despised them as barbarians, but after he conquered the lands around the Euxine Sea, King Mithridates VI used them as troops, mostly cavalry.

Sabines   The Oscan-speaking people of unknown racial origin who lived to the north and east of Rome between the Quirinal Hill inside Rome and the crest of the Apennines. Their ties to Rome went back to the apocryphal "rape," and they resisted Roman incursions into their lands for several centuries. The chief Sabine towns were Reate, Nersae and Amiternum. Sabines were famous for their integrity, bravery, and independence.

sacer   Though it more usually meant sacred to a god, *sacer* in the sense used in this book meant one whose person and property had been forfeited to a god because some divine law had been profaned; Sulla used the term in his proscriptions because Roma was a goddess.

saepta   "The sheepfold." During the Republic this was simply an open area on the Campus Martius not far from the Via Lata. Here the Centuriate Assembly met. The *saepta* was divided up for the occasion by temporary fences so that the five Classes could vote in their Centuries.

salii   A college of priests in service to Mars; the name meant "leaping dancers." There were twenty-four of them in two colleges of twelve. They had to be patrician.

saltatrix tonsa   This delicious political slur was most famously used by Cicero to describe Lucius Afranius, a Picentine adherent of Pompey's. It translates as a "barbered dancing-girl": that is, a male homosexual who dressed as a woman and sold his sexual favors. In a day when slander and defamation were not charges pursuant at law, anything went in the political slur department!

Samnites, Samnium   Rome's most obdurate enemies among the peoples of Italy lived in lands lying between Latium, Campania, Apulia, Picenum and the Adriatic, though as a people the Samnites spilled into southern Picenum and southern Campania. The area was largely mountainous and not particularly fertile; its towns tended to be poor and small, and numbered among them Caieta, Aeclanum and Bovianum. The two really prosperous cities, Aesernia and Beneventum, were Latin Rights colonies seeded by Rome. Besides the true Samnites, peoples called Frentani, Paeligni, Marrucini and Vestini inhabited parts of Samnium.

Several times during Rome's history the Samnites inflicted hideous defeats upon Roman armies; no Roman general thought of them lightly. Whenever there seemed a chance that some insurgent movement might overthrow Rome, the Samnites enlisted in its ranks.

Sarmatians   A people, probably of Germanic stock, the Sarmatians occupied the steppelands on the northwestern side of the Euxine Sea—the modern Ukraine—though originally they had lived to the east of the Tanais (the Don). They were nomadic in habit and all rode horses. The tribal culture permitted a rare equality of women with men; the women attended councils and fought as warriors. By the last century B.C. they had lost several subgroups which became nations in themselves, principally the **Roxolani** (q.v.) and the Iazyges, who settled further south. Mithridates used Sarmatae as cavalry troops in his armies.

satrap   The title given by the Kings of Persia to their provincial or territorial governors. Alexander the Great seized upon the term and employed it, as did the later Arsacid Kings of the Parthians and the Kings of Armenia. The region administered by a satrap was called a satrapy.

Saturninus   Lucius Appuleius Saturninus, tribune of the plebs in 103, 100 and 99 B.C. His early career was marred by an alleged grain swindle while he was quaestor of the grain supply at Ostia, and the slur remained with him throughout the rest of his life. During his first term as a tribune of the plebs he allied himself with Gaius Marius and succeeded in securing lands in Africa for resettlement of Marius's veteran troops. He also defined a new kind of treason, *"maiestas minuta"* or "little treason," and set up a special court to try cases of it. His second term as a tribune of the plebs in 100 B.C. was also in alliance with Marius, for whom he obtained more land for veterans from the German campaign. But eventually Saturninus became more of an embarrassment to Marius than a help, so Marius repudiated him publicly; Saturninus then turned against Marius.

Toward the end of 100 B.C., Saturninus began to woo the Head Count, as there was a famine at the time, and the Head Count was restless. He passed a grain law which he could not implement, as there was no grain to be had. When the elections were held for the tribunate of the plebs for 99 B.C., Saturninus ran again, only to be defeated. His boon companion, Gaius Servilius Glaucia, arranged the murder of one of the lucky candidates, and Saturninus took the dead man's place. He was tribune of the plebs for the third time. Stirred by the famine and Saturninus's oratory, the Forum crowds became dangerous enough to force Marius and Scaurus Princeps Senatus into an alliance which resulted in the passing of the Senate's Ultimate Decree. Apprehended after the water supply to the Capitol was cut off, Saturninus and his friends were imprisoned in the Senate House until they could be tried. But before the trials could take place, they were killed by a rain of tiles from the Senate House roof. All of Saturninus's laws were then annulled. It was said ever after that Saturninus had aimed at becoming King of Rome. His daughter, Appuleia, was married to the patrician Marcus Aemilius Lepidus.

For a fuller narration of the career of Saturninus, see the entry in the glossary of *The Grass Crown*.

Scipio Africanus   Publius Cornelius Scipio Africanus was born in 236 B.C. and died around the end of 184 B.C. A patrician of august family, he distinguished himself as a very young man in battle, then at the age of twenty-six, still a private citizen, he was invested with a proconsular imperium by the People rather than the Senate, and dispatched to fight the Carthaginians in Spain. Here for five years he did brilliantly, winning for Rome her two Spanish provinces. Consul at the early age of thirty-one, he ignored senatorial opposition and invaded Africa via Sicily. Both Sicily and Africa eventually fell, and Scipio was invited to assume the *cognomen* Africanus. He was elected censor and appointed Princeps Senatus in 199 B.C., and was consul again in 194 B.C. As farsighted as he was brilliant, Scipio Africanus warned Rome that Antiochus the Great of Syria would invade Greece; when it happened he went as his brother Lucius's legate to fight the invader. But Cato the Censor, a rigid moralist, had always condemned the Scipiones for running a morally loose army, and embarked upon a persecution of Africanus and his brother which seems to have caused Africanus's early death. Scipio Africanus was married to Aemilia Paulla, the sister of the conqueror of Macedonia. One of his two daughters was Cornelia the Mother of the Gracchi. His two sons failed to prosper.

Scythians   A nomadic, horse-mounted people of probable Germanic stock who lived in the Asian steppelands to the east of the Tanais River (the Don), and extended as far south as the Caucasus. They were socially well organized enough to have kings, and were famous goldsmiths.

secret name of Rome   Rome, presumably in the guise of goddess Roma, had a secret name. This secret name was apparently guarded by a special goddess, Diva Angerona, whose statue (located on the altar in the shrine of Volupia) had a bandage across its mouth. There were arcane rites celebrated in which the name was uttered, but the taboo was strictly enforced and the danger of uttering the secret name was believed in even by the most sophisticated people. It seems most thought the secret name was Amor, which is Roma spelled backward. *Amor* means "love."

sedan chair   An open chair on a frame designed to be carried by two to four men. A sedan chair could probably be hired like a taxi.

Seleucid   The adjective of lineage attached to the royal house of Syria, whose sovereigns were descended from Seleucus Nicator, one of Alexander the Great's companions, though not one of his known generals. After Alexander's death he cemented a kingdom which eventually extended from Syria and Cilicia to Media and Babylonia, and had two capitals, Antioch and Seleuceia-on-Tigris, and two wives, the Macedonian Stratonice and the Bactrian Apama. By the last century B.C. the Kingdom of the Parthians had usurped the eastern lands, and Rome most of Cilicia; the kingdom of the Seleucids was then purely Syria.

Senate   Properly, *senatus*. This was originally a patricians-only body which first contained one hundred members and then three hundred. Because of its antiquity the legal definitions of its rights, powers and duties were mostly nonexistent. Membership in the Senate was for life (unless a man was expelled by the censors for inappropriate behavior or impoverishment), which predisposed it to the oligarchical form it acquired. Throughout its history, its members fought strenuously to preserve their pre-eminence in government. Until Sulla prevented access to the Senate save by the quaestorship, appointment was in the purlieus of the censors, though from the middle Republic down the quaestorship if held before admission to the Senate was soon followed by admission to the Senate; the *lex Atinia* provided that tribunes of the plebs should automatically enter the Senate upon election. There was a means test of entirely unofficial nature; a senator was supposed to enjoy an income of a million sesterces.

Senators alone were entitled to wear the *latus clavus* on their tunics; this was a broad purple stripe down the right shoulder. They wore closed shoes of maroon leather, and a ring which had originally been made of iron, but later came to be gold. Senatorial mourning consisted of wearing the knight's narrow stripe on the tunic. Only men who had held a curule magistracy wore a purple-bordered toga; ordinary senators wore plain white.

Meetings of the Senate had to be held in properly inaugurated premises; the Senate had its own *curia* or meeting-house, the Curia Hostilia, but was prone also to meet elsewhere at the whim of the man convening the meeting— presumably he always had well-founded reasons for choosing a venue other than the Senate House, like a necessity to meet outside the *pomerium*. The ceremonies and meeting and feast on New Year's Day were always held in the temple of Jupiter Optimus Maximus. Sessions could go on only between sunrise and sunset, and could not take place on days when any of the Assemblies met, though were permissible on comitial days if no Assembly did meet.

Until Sulla reorganized this as he did so much else, the rigid hierarchy of who spoke in what turn had always placed the Princeps Senatus and consulars ahead of men already elected to office but not yet in office, whereas after Sulla consuls-elect and praetors-elect spoke ahead of these men; under both systems a patrician always preceded a plebeian of exactly equal rank in the speaking hierarchy. Not all members of the house were accorded the privilege of speaking. The *senatores pedarii* (I have used a British parliamentary term, backbenchers, to describe them, as they sat behind the men allowed to speak) could vote, but were not called upon in debate. No restrictions were placed upon the time limit or content of a man's speech, so filibustering was common. If an issue was unimportant or everyone was obviously in favor of it, voting might be by voice or a show of hands, but a formal vote took place by the division of the House, meaning that the senators left their stations and grouped themselves to either side of the curule dais according to their yea or nay, and were then physically counted. Always an advisory rather than a true legislating body, the Senate issued its *consulta* or decrees as requests to the various Assemblies. If the issue was serious, a quorum had to be present before a vote could be taken, though we do not know what precise number constituted a quorum. Certainly most meetings were not heavily attended, as there was no rule which said a man appointed to the Senate had to attend meetings, even on an irregular basis.

In some areas the Senate reigned supreme, despite its lack of legislating power: the *fiscus* was controlled by the Senate, as it controlled the Treasury; foreign affairs were left to the Senate; and the appointment of provincial governors, the regulation of provincial affairs, and the conduct of wars were left for the sole attention of the Senate.

senatus consultum de re publica defendenda   The Senate's Ultimate Decree, so known because Cicero shortened its proper title to *senatus consultum ultimum*. Dating from 121 B.C., when Gaius Gracchus resorted to violence to prevent the overthrow of his laws, in civil emergencies the Senate overrode all other governmental bodies by passing the *senatus consultum de re publica defendenda*. This Ultimate Decree proclaimed the Senate's sovereignty and established what was, in effect, martial law. It was really a way to sidestep appointing a dictator.

Servian Walls   *Murus Servii Tullii*. Republican Romans believed that the formidable walls enclosing the city of Rome had been erected in the time of King Servius Tullius. However, evidence suggests that they were not built until after Rome was sacked by the Gauls in 390 B.C. Down to the time of Caesar the Dictator they were scrupulously kept up.

sesterces   The Latin singular is *sestertius,* the Latin plural is *sestertii.* Roman accounting practices were established in sesterces, though the denarius seems to have been a more common coin. In Latin writing, sesterces were abbreviated as *HS*. A small silver coin, the sestertius was worth a quarter of a denarius.

Sextilis   Originally the sixth month when the Roman New Year had begun in March, it kept its name after January New Year made it the eighth month. We know it, of course, as August; so too did the Romans—but not until the reign of Augustus.

Sibylline Books   The Roman State possessed a series of prophecies written in Greek and called the Sibylline Books. Legend had it that the famous Sibyl at Cumae offered to sell the books to King Tarquinius Priscus of Rome, and he refused. So she burned one of the books (they were written on palm leaves). He refused again, she burned another book. Eventually he bought the remainder, which were placed in the care of a special college of minor priests, and only consulted when Senate or People commanded it, usually in the face of some major crisis. Sulla raised the number of priests in the college from ten to fifteen; they were thereafter known as the *quindecimviri sacris faciundis*. The books, however, were lost in the fire which destroyed Jupiter's temple on July 6 of 83 B.C. Sulla ordered that a search of the world's sibyls be made and the books reassembled. This was done.

sive   Either, or.

sixteener   With the sixteener we enter the world of the ancient dreadnoughts, the supergalleys. That there were more than three banks of oars is now not believed possible: two arrangements were feasible, namely a bireme of two banks and eight men per oar, or a trireme of three banks with six men to each of the upper banks of oars and four men on the lowest bank. One bank of oars is equally as impossible as four because the sweep and angle of an oar prevents its being operated by more than eight men. If the oar were designed to be operated by eight men, it would have been about 57 feet long; a six-man oar measured about 45 feet long. With a length growing close to 200 feet, the beam of a sixteener was probably about 25 to 28 feet, which enabled the deck to accommodate a large body of marines and several pieces of artillery, as well as several tall towers. There seems evidence to suggest that the sixteener owned fewer oars than a smaller galley, number of oars being compensated for by the increased power of each oar. The number of oarsmen probably lay in the vicinity of 500 to 800, and the sixteener may have been able to accommodate 400 marines.

The supergalley was not of any use in genuine naval warfare; her size and unseaworthiness made her useful only for boarding or for firing missiles, though even the vastest galleys were equipped with rams. King Mithridates VI was enormously fond of sixteeners, as is recounted in *The First Man in Rome*.

For those perusers of the glossary whose curiosity is piqued as to how big the ancient naval architects and shipwrights could make galleys, wait for later books in this series! I might have Cleopatra dig Ptolemy IV's "forty" river barge out of mothballs.

socius, socii　　A *socius* was a man of a citizenship having allied status with Rome.

Sol Indiges　　One of the most ancient Italian gods, apparently (as the Sun) the husband of Tellus (the Earth). Though little is known of his cult, he was apparently enormously reverenced. Oaths sworn by him were very serious affairs.

spelt　　A very fine, soft white flour used for making cakes, never bread. It was ground from the variety of wheat now known as *Triticum spelta*.

sponsio　　In cases of civil litigation where judgement was arrived at by one man rather than by a jury, the urban or foreign praetor could only allow the case to be heard after a sum of money called *sponsio* was lodged with him before the hearing began. This was either the sum being asked for in damages, or the sum of money in dispute. In bankruptcy or nonpayment of debts cases, the sum owed became the *sponsio*. Until Sulla was dictator, if the sum concerned could not be found by either the plaintiff or the defendant, the praetor could not allow the case to be heard. This meant many cases which ought to have been heard were not. Sulla fixed this by allowing the urban or foreign praetor to waive the lodgement of *sponsio*. He had first done this, incidentally, in 88 B.C. when he tried to shore up the constitution before leaving for the war against Mithridates; but these laws were quickly repealed. The law he put on the tablets as dictator remained in effect.

stibium　　The ancient version of mascara. A black antimony-based powder soluble in water, *stibium* was used to darken the brows and/or lashes, or to draw a line around the perimeter of the eye. It would be interesting to know just how recently a more benign substance than *stibium* replaced it, but, alas, no work of reference tells me.

stimulus, stimuli　　To the Romans a *stimulus* was a sharpened wooden stake placed in the bottom of a trench or ditch as part of defense fortifications. It could also mean a sharp instrument used to goad an animal. And by extension, a *stimulus* was something causing acute mental pain or worry.

strategoi　　A Greek word in the plural. A military commander or general.

Subura   The poorest and most densely populated part of the city of Rome. It lay to the east of the Forum Romanum in the declivity between the Oppian spur of the Esquiline Mount and the Viminal Hill. Its people were notoriously polyglot and independent of mind; many Jews lived in the Subura, which at the time of Sulla contained Rome's only synagogue. Suetonius says Caesar the Dictator lived in the Subura.

Sulpicius   Publius Sulpicius Rufus had been a conservative and moderate sort of man throughout his time in the Senate, and including the first part of his tribunate of the plebs in 88 B.C. It would seem that the news that King Mithridates had not distinguished between Italians and Romans when he murdered 80,000 of them in Asia Province caused Sulpicius to change his views about many things, including the limitations conservative and anti-Italian elements in Rome were placing upon the admission of the newly enfranchised Italians into the Roman rolls. Sulpicius turned militant radical, allying himself with Gaius Marius. He passed four laws, the most important of which stipulated that all the new Roman citizens must be distributed equally across the whole thirty-five tribes, but the most disturbing of which took the command of the war against Mithridates away from Sulla; he gave it to Marius instead. This provoked Sulla into marching on Rome that first time. Together with Marius, Old Brutus and some others, Sulpicius fled from the city after Sulla took it over. The rest of the refugees escaped overseas, probably because it was no part of Sulla's intentions to apprehend them, but Sulpicius was taken in the Latin port of Laurentum and killed on the spot. His head was sent to Rome; Sulla fixed it to the rostra in an attempt to cow the newly elected consul Cinna. All four of Sulpicius's laws were repealed by Sulla.

sumptuary law   Any law attempting to regulate the purchase or consumption of luxuries.

tabled   Of a law, and used in the British parliamentary sense. When a drafted proposed law or amendment or paper is tabled, it is "put on the table" for inspection, discussion, and thought. It then remains tabled until passed or rejected.

talent   This was the load a man could carry. Bullion and very large sums of money were expressed in talents, but the term was not confined to precious metals and money. In modern terms the talent weighed about 50 to 55 pounds (25 kilograms). A talent of gold weighed the same as a talent of silver, but was far more valuable, of course.

Tarpeian Rock   Its precise location is still hotly debated, but we do know that it was quite visible from the lower Forum Romanum, as people being thrown off it could be seen from the rostra. Presumably it was an overhang at the top of the Capitoline cliffs, but since the drop was not much more than eighty feet, the Tarpeian Rock must have been located directly over some sort of jagged outcrop—we have no evidence that anyone ever survived the fall. It was the traditional place of execution for Roman citizen traitors and murderers, who were either thrown from it or forced to jump from it. The tribunes of the plebs were particularly fond of threatening to throw obstructive senators from the Tarpeian Rock. I have located it on a line from the temple of Ops.

tata   The Latin diminutive for "father"—akin to our "daddy." I have, by the way, elected to use the almost universal "mama" as the diminutive for "mother," but the actual Latin was "*mamma*."

Tellus   The Roman earth goddess, of undeniably Italian origin. After the navel stone of Magna Mater was imported from Pessinus in 205 B.C., worship of Tellus was neglected. Tellus had a big temple on the Carinae, in earlier days imposing; by the last century B.C. it was dilapidated.

tergiversator   Thank you, Professor Erich Gruen! You have given me much valued information and much food for thought—but "tergiversator" I especially prize, even if it is a small point. "Tergiversator" is a very imposing word for a political turncoat.

tetrarch   The chief of a fourth section of any state or territory. The three tribes of Galatia—Tolistobogii, Trocmi, and Volcae Tectosages—were each divided into four parts, and each of the four parts was headed by a tetrarch.

Teutones   See the entry entitled **Cimbri.**

theaters   Republican Rome owned no permanent structures devoted to the staging of plays. Whenever the games included theatricals, temporary wooden structures had to be built for the occasion, and dismantled after the games were over. The old conviction that theater was morally degrading, a corrupting force, never quite died. A reflection of this can be seen in the fact that women were not allowed to sit with men, and were relegated to the very back rows of the audience. Only public pressure had obliged the magistrates to include plays in the public entertainments put on during games; the Roman people adored comedy, farces and mimes. The wooden theaters were built like permanent stone ones— amphitheatrical in shape, with a raised stage, wings, flies, and concealed entrances and exits for the actors. The *scenae* (backdrops) were as high as the top tier of the *cavea* (auditorium). The *cavea* was a semicircle of stepped tiers, which left a semicircular vacant space called the orchestra between the front row of the audience and the stage.

Thrace   Loosely, that part of Balkan Europe between the Hellespont and a line just east of Philippi; it had coasts on both the Aegean and the Euxine Seas, and extended north as far as the mouth of the Danubius (the Danube). The Romans considered that its western boundary was the river Nestus. Thrace never really got itself organized, and remained until Roman occupation a place of partially allied Germano-Illyrian-Celtic tribes long enough settled in the area to warrant the name Thracian. Both the Greeks and the Romans considered the Thracians utterly barbaric. After 129 B.C. the strip of Thrace along the Aegean seaboard was governed by Rome as a part of Macedonia. For Rome had built the Via Egnatia, the great highway between the Adriatic and the Hellespont, and needed to protect this quickest way to move her soldiers between west and east. Thrace's largest city by far was the old Greek colony of Byzantium, on the Thracian Bosporus, but it of course was not inhabited by Thracians; nor was any other seaport. The Bessi constituted the most warlike and Roman-hating tribal confraternity, but the Odrysiae were slightly more Hellenized, and had a king who strove to placate Rome.

Tingitanian ape   The Barbary ape, a macaque, terrestrial and tailless. Monkeys and primates were not common around the Mediterranean, but the macaque still found on Gibraltar was always present in North Africa.

toga   The garment only a full citizen of Rome was entitled to wear. Made of lightweight wool, it had a peculiar shape (which is why the togate "Romans" in Hollywood movies never look right). After exhaustive and brilliant experimentation, Dr. Lillian Wilson of Johns Hopkins worked out a size and shape which produced a perfect-looking toga. To fit a man 5 feet 9 inches (175cm) tall having a waist of 36 inches (89.5cm), the toga was about 15 feet (4.6m) wide, and 7 feet 6 inches (2.25m) long. The length measurement is draped on the man's height axis and the much bigger width measurement is wrapped around him. However, the shape was far from being a simple rectangle! It looked like this:

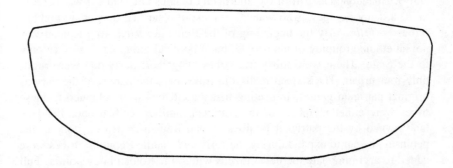

Unless the toga is cut as illustrated, it will absolutely refuse to drape the way it does on the togate men of the ancient statues. The Republican toga of the last century B.C. was very large (the size varied considerably during the thousand years it was the customary garb of the Roman). And a man draped in his toga could *not* have worn a loincloth or other undergarment!

toga candida The specially whitened toga worn by those seeking office as an elected magistrate. Its stark whiteness was achieved by bleaching the garment in the sun for many days, then working finely powdered chalk through it.

toga praetexta The purple-bordered toga of the curule magistrate. It continued to be worn by these men after their term in office was over. It was also the toga worn by children of both sexes.

toga trabea Cicero's "particolored toga." It was the striped toga of the augur, and very likely of the pontifex also. Like the *toga praetexta*, it had a purple border all the way around it, but it was also striped in broad bands of alternating red and purple down its length.

toga virilis The plain white toga of a Roman male. It was also called the *toga alba*, or the *toga pura*.

togate The correct English-language term to describe a man clad in his toga.

torc A thick round necklace or collar, usually of gold. It didn't quite form a full circle, as it had a gap about an inch wide interrupting it; this was worn at the front. The torc was the mark of a Gaul or Celt, though some Germans wore it also. The ends of the torc at the gap were normally finished in some decorative way, with knobs, animal heads, twists, swirls. Smaller versions of the torc were awarded as Roman military decorations and worn on the shoulders of the shirt or cuirass.

transvectio The parade of the Public Horse held on the Ides of Quinctilis (July). Abandoned as part of the aftermath of Gaius Gracchus, it was revived in 70 B.C. by Pompey, who wanted to make it clear that he was a knight.

tribe *Tribus*. By the beginning of the Republic, *tribus* to a Roman was not an ethnic grouping of his people, but a political grouping of service only to the State. There were thirty-five tribes altogether; thirty-one were rural, only four urban. The sixteen really old tribes bore the names of the various original patrician *gentes*, indicating that the citizens who belonged to these tribes were either members of the patrician families, or had once lived on land owned by the patrician families. When Roman-owned territory in the peninsula began to expand during the early and middle Republic, tribes were added to accommodate the new citizens within the Roman body politic. Full Roman citizen colonies also became the nuclei of fresh tribes. The four urban tribes were supposed to have been founded by King Servius Tullius, though they probably originated somewhat later. The last tribe of the thirty-five was created in 241 B.C. Every member of a tribe was entitled to register one vote in a tribal Assembly, but his vote counted only in helping to determine which way the tribe as a whole voted, for a tribe delivered just one vote, the majority of its members. This meant that in no tribal Assembly could the huge number of citizens enrolled in the four urban tribes sway the vote, as the urban tribes delivered only four of the thirty-five ultimate votes. Members of rural tribes were not disbarred from living in Rome, nor were their progeny obliged to be enrolled in an urban tribe. Most senators and knights of the First Class belonged to rural tribes. It was a mark of distinction.

tribune, military   Those on the general's staff who were not elected tribunes of the soldiers but who ranked above cadets and below legates were called military tribunes. If the general was not a consul in office, military tribunes might command legions. Otherwise they did staff duties for the general. Military tribunes also served as cavalry commanders.

tribune of the plebs   These magistrates came into being early in the history of the Republic, when the Plebs was at complete loggerheads with the Patriciate. Elected by the tribal body of plebeians formed as the *concilium plebis* or *comitia plebis tributa* (the Plebeian Assembly), they took an oath to defend the lives and property of members of the Plebs, and to rescue a member of the Plebs from the clutches of a (patrician in those days) magistrate. By 450 B.C. there were ten tribunes of the plebs. A *lex Atinia de tribunis plebis in senatum legendis* in 149 B.C. provided that a man elected to the tribunate of the plebs automatically entered the Senate. Because they were not elected by the People (that is, by the patricians as well as by the plebeians), they had no power under Rome's unwritten constitution and were not magistrates in the same way as tribunes of the soldiers, quaestors, curule aediles, praetors, consuls, and censors; their magistracies were of the Plebs and their power in office resided in the oath the whole Plebs took to defend the sacrosanctity—the inviolability—of its elected tribunes. The power of the office also lay in the right of its officers to interpose a veto (*intercessio*) against almost any aspect of government: a tribune of the plebs could veto the actions or laws of his nine fellow tribunes, or any—or all!—other magistrates, including consuls and censors; he could veto the holding of an election; he could veto the passing of any law; and he could veto any decrees of the Senate, even those dealing with war and foreign affairs. Only a dictator (and perhaps an *interrex*) was not subject to the tribunician veto. Within his own Plebeian Assembly, the tribune of the plebs could even exercise the death penalty if his right to proceed about his duties was denied him.

The tribune of the plebs had no imperium, and the authority vested in the office did not extend beyond the first milestone outside the city of Rome. Custom dictated that a man should serve only one term as a tribune of the plebs, but Gaius Gracchus put an end to that; even so, it was not usual for a man to stand more than once. As the real power of the office was vested in negative action—the veto—tribunician contribution to government tended to be more obstructive than constructive. The conservative elements in the Senate loathed the tribunate of the plebs.

The College of Tribunes of the Plebs entered office on the tenth day of December each year, and had its headquarters in the Basilica Porcia. Sulla as dictator in 81 B.C. stripped the tribunate of the plebs of all its powers save the right to rescue a member of the Plebs from the clutches of a magistrate, but the consuls Pompey and Crassus restored all the powers of the office in 70 B.C. It was too important to do without. See also the entry under *ius auxilii ferendi.* And **Plebs,** of course.

tribune of the soldiers   Two dozen young men aged between twenty-five and twenty-nine years of age were elected each year by the Assembly of the People to serve as the *tribuni militum,* or tribunes of the soldiers. They were true magistrates, the only ones too young to belong to the Senate, and were the governmental representatives of the consuls' legions (the four legions which belonged to the consuls in office). Six tribunes of the soldiers were allocated to each of the four legions, and normally commanded them. The command was shared in such a way that there was always a tribune of the soldiers on duty as commander, but apparently one of the six (probably by lot or by his number of votes) was senior to the others.

tribuni aerarii   These were men of knight's status whose census at 300,000 sesterces made them junior to the knights of a 400,000 sesterces census. See the entry on **knights** for further information.

triclinium   The dining room of a Roman house or apartment. By preference it was square in shape, and possessed three couches arranged to form a U. Standing in the doorway one looked into the hollow of the U; the couch on the left was called the *lectus summus,* the couch forming the middle or bottom of the U was the *lectus medius,* and the couch on the right was the *lectus imus.* Each couch was very broad, perhaps 4 or 5 feet, and at least twice that long. One end of the couch had a raised arm forming a head, the other end did not. In front of the couches (that is, inside the hollow of the U) was a narrow table also forming a U. The male diners reclined on their left elbows, supported by bolsters; they were not shod, and could call for their feet to be washed. The host of the dinner reclined at the left end of the *lectus medius,* which was the end having no arm; the guest of honor reclined at the other end of the same couch, in the spot called the *locus consularis.* At the time of these books it was rare for women to recline alongside the men unless the dinner party was a men's affair and the female guests were of low virtue. Respectable women sat on upright chairs inside the double U of couches and tables; they entered the room with the first course and left as soon as the last course was cleared away. Normally they drank only water, as women drinking wine were thought of low moral virtue. See the illustration.

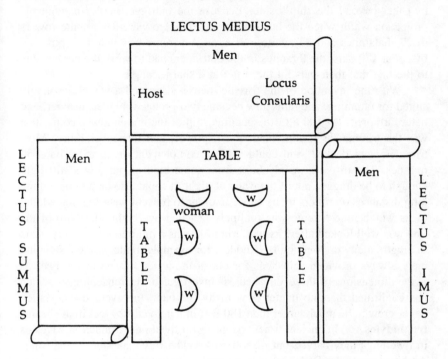

trireme With the bireme, the commonest and most favored of all the ancient war galleys. By definition a trireme had three banks of oars, and with the advent of the trireme about 600 B.C came the invention of the projecting box above the gunwale called an outrigger (later galleys, even biremes, often were fitted with outriggers). In a trireme every oar was much the same length at about 15 feet (5m), this being relatively short; only one rower manned an oar. The average trireme was about 130 feet long, and the beam was no wider than 13 feet (excluding the outrigger): the ratio was therefore about 10:1. The rower in the lowest bank the Greeks called a thalamite; he worked his oar through a port in the hull so close to the water line that it was fitted with a leather cuff to keep the sea out. There were about 27 thalamites per side, giving a total of 54 thalamite oars. The rower in the middle bank was called a zygite; he worked his oar through a port just below the gunwale. Zygites equaled thalamites in number. The outrigger rower was a thranite; he sat above and outboard of the zygite on a special bench within the outrigger housing. His oar projected from a gap in the bottom of the outrigger perhaps two feet beyond the ship's side. Because the outrigger could maintain its projection width when the hull narrowed aft, there were 31 thranite rowers to 27 thalamites and 27 zygites per side. A trireme was therefore powered by about 170 oars; the thranites in the outriggers had to work the hardest due to the fact that their oars hit the water at a sharper angle.

With the invention of the trireme there had arrived a vessel absolutely suited for ramming, and rams now became two-pronged, bigger, heavier, and better armored. By 100 B.C. the genuine ship of the line in a war-going fleet was the trireme, as it combined speed, power, and maneuverability. Most triremes were decked, and could carry a complement of up to perhaps 50 marines. The trireme, mainly built from some kind of pine, was still light enough to be dragged out of the water at night; it could also be portaged quite long distances on rollers by its crew. In order to prevent waterlogging adding to its weight, the trireme was routinely beached overnight. If a ship of the line was well looked after, its warfaring life was a minimum of twenty years in length; a city or community (Rhodes, for example) maintaining a standing navy always provided shipsheds for out-of-the-water storage of the fleet. It is the dimensions of these shipsheds as investigated by archaeologists which has confirmed that, no matter how many the oars, the average war galley never grew to be much larger than 180 feet in length and 20 feet in the beam.

troglodytes   In ancient times, people who lived not so much in caves as in dwellings they carved out of soft rocks. The Egyptian side of the Sinus Arabicus (now the Red Sea) was reputed to have troglodytes, and the soft tufa stone of the Cappadocian gorges provided homes for the local peoples from times before recorded history.

trophy   Captured enemy gear of sufficiently imposing appearance or repute. It was the custom of the Roman general to set up trophies (usually suits of armor, standards) if he won a significant victory. He might choose to do so on the actual field of battle as a memorial, or as Pompey did on the crest of a mountain pass, or else inside a temple he vowed and built in Rome.

tunic   The ubiquitous article of clothing for all the ancient Mediterranean peoples, including the Greeks and the Romans. A Roman tunic tended to be rather loose and shapeless, made without darts to give it a waisted look; it covered the body from the shoulders and upper arms to the knees. Sleeves were probably set in (the ancients knew how to sew, cut cloth, and make clothing comfortable), and sometimes long. The tunic was usually belted with a cord or with buckled leather, and the Romans wore theirs longer at the front than at the back by about three inches. Upper-class Roman men were probably togate if outside the doors of their own homes, but there is little doubt that men of lower classes only wore their togas on special occasions, such as the games or elections. If the weather was wet, a cloak of some kind was preferred to a toga. The knight wore a narrow purple stripe down the right (bared to show the tunic) shoulder called the *angustus clavus;* the senator's purple stripe, the *latus clavus,* was wider. Anyone on a census lower than 300,000 sesterces could not wear a stripe at all. The customary material for a tunic was wool.

Twelve Tables   A bit like the Ten Commandments. These twelve tablets (the originals were perhaps made of wood, but the later version was certainly of bronze) were a codified system of laws drawn up about 450 B.C. during the early Republic by a committee called the *decemviri legibus scribundis;* from them all Roman law descended. They covered most aspects of law, civil as well as criminal, but in a rather small-town way, and must often have amused the schoolboys of the last century B.C. as they learned their XII Tables off by heart. Law by then had become far more sophisticated.

Venus Erucina   That aspect of Venus which ruled the act of love, particularly in its freest and least moral sense. On the feast of Venus Erucina prostitutes offered to her, and the temple of Venus Erucina outside the Colline Gate of Rome was accustomed to receive gifts of money from successful prostitutes.

Venus Libitina   That aspect of Venus (the goddess of the life-force) which ruled the extinction of the life-force. An underworld deity of great importance in Rome. Her temple was sited beyond the Servian Walls more or less at the central point of Rome's vast necropolis (cemetery) on the Campus Esquilinus. Its exact location is not known. The temple precinct was large and had a grove of trees, presumably cypresses, as they are associated with death. In this precinct Rome's undertakers and funeral directors had their headquarters, operating, it would seem likely, from stalls or booths. The temple itself contained a register of Roman citizen deaths and was rich thanks to the accumulation of the coins which had to be paid to register a death. Should Rome for whatever reason cease to have consuls, the *fasces* of the consuls were deposited on a special couch inside the temple; the axes which were only inserted into the consuls' *fasces* outside Rome were also kept in the temple. I imagine that Rome's burial clubs, of which there were many, were in some way connected with Venus Libitina.

vermeil   Silver plated with gold.

verpa   A Latin obscenity used more in verbal abuse than as a sign of contempt. It referred to the penis—apparently in the erect state only, when the foreskin is drawn back—and had a homosexual connotation. Note Servilia's choice of this epithet to hurl at another woman—the bossy, overpowering Porcia Liciniana.

Vesta, Vestal Virgins   Vesta was a very old and numinous Roman goddess having no mythology and no image. She was the hearth, the center of family life, and Roman society was cemented in the family. Her official public cult was personally supervised by the Pontifex Maximus, but she was so important that she had her own pontifical college, the six Vestal Virgins. The Vestal Virgin was inducted at about seven or eight years of age, took vows of complete chastity, and served for thirty years, after which she was released from her vows and sent back into the general community still of an age to bear children. Few retired Vestals ever did marry; it was thought unlucky to do so. The chastity of the Vestal Virgins was Rome's public luck: a chaste college was favored by Fortune. When a Vestal was accused of unchastity she was formally brought to trial in a specially convened court; her alleged lover or lovers were tried in a separate court. If convicted, she was cast into an underground chamber dug for the purpose; it was sealed over, and she was left there to die. In Republican times the Vestal Virgins shared the same residence as the Pontifex Maximus, though sequestered from him and his family. The temple of Vesta was near this house, and was small, round, and very old. It was adjacent to the Regia of the Pontifex Maximus and to the well of Juturna, which in early days had supplied the Vestals with water they had to draw from the well each day in person; by the late Republic this ritual was a ritual only. A fire burned permanently inside Vesta's temple to symbolize the hearth; it was tended by the Vestals, and could not be allowed to go out for any reason.

vexillum   A flag or banner. The study of flags nowadays is called vexillology.

via   A main thoroughfare or highway.

vicus   A good-sized street.

Villa Publica   A parklike piece of land on the Campus Martius; it fronted onto the Vicus Pallacinae, and was the place where the various components and members of the triumphal parade forgathered before the parade commenced.

viri capitales   The three young men of presenatorial age who were deputed to look after Rome's prisons and asylums. As Rome was a society which did not imprison save on a purely temporary basis, this was not a very onerous task. The *viri capitales,* however, seem to have lingered in the lower Forum Romanum on days when there were no public or Senate meetings and the praetors' tribunals were not open, apparently so some sort of public figure of authority was available for citizens in need of protection or help. This Cicero reveals in his *pro Cluentio*.

vir militaris   See the entry under **Military Man**.

voting   Roman voting was timocratic, in that the power of the vote was powerfully influenced by economic status, and in that voting was not "one man, one vote" style. Whether an individual was voting in the Centuries or in the Tribes, his own personal vote could only influence the verdict of the Century or Tribe in which he polled. Election outcomes were determined by the number of Century or Tribal votes going a particular way: thus in the Centuries of the First Class there were only 91 votes all told, the number of Centuries the First Class contained, and in the tribal Assemblies only 35 votes all told, the number of Tribes. Juridical voting was different. A juror's vote did have a direct bearing on the outcome of a trial, as the jury was supposed to have an odd number of men comprising it, and the decision was a majority one, not a unanimous one. If for some reason the jury was even in number and the vote was tied, the verdict had to be adjudged as for acquittal. Jury voting was timocratic also, however, in that a man without high economic status had no chance to sit on a jury.

Wooden Bridge   Rome's oldest bridge, the Pons Sublicius, spanned the Tiber downstream of Tiber Island, and was the only one made of wood. It was reputed to have been built in the time of King Ancus Marcius.

yoke   The yoke was the crossbeam or tie which rested upon the necks of a pair of oxen or other animals in harness to draw a load. In human terms it came to mean the mark of servility, of submission to the superiority and domination of others. There was a yoke called the Tigillum located somewhere on the Carinae inside the city of Rome; the young of both sexes were required to pass beneath it, perhaps a sign of submission to the burdens of adult life. However, it was in military terms that the yoke came to have its greatest metaphorical significance. Very early Roman (or possibly even Etruscan) armies forced a defeated enemy to pass beneath the yoke: two spears were planted upright in the ground, and a third spear was lashed from one to the other as a crosstie; the whole apparatus was too low for a man to pass under walking upright, he had to bend right over. Other people in Italy than the Romans also had the custom, with the result that from time to time a Roman army was made to pass under the yoke, as when the Samnites were victorious at the Caudine Forks. To acquiesce to passing under the yoke was regarded as an intolerable humiliation for Rome; so much so that the Senate and People usually preferred to see an army stand and fight until the last man in it was dead. That at least was honorable defeat.

Some Events in the History of Rome Prior to

THE FIRST MAN IN ROME

(Note: All dates are B.C.)

ca. 1100	A refugee from Troy, Aeneas established himself in Latium. Son, Iulus, became King of Alba Longa.
753–715	Romulus first King of Rome: built the Palatine city.
715–673	Numa Pompilius second King: created 100 senators, priestly colleges, made 10-month year a 12-month year.
673–642	Tullus Hostilius third King: built Senate House.
642–617	Ancus Marcius fourth King: built Wooden Bridge, fortified Janiculum, seized salt flats at Ostia for Rome.
616–578	Tarquinius Priscus fifth King: built Circus Maximus, sewered central Rome, enlarged Senate to 300, created Tribes and Classes, established the censu
578–534	Servius Tullius sixth King: created *pomerium*, built Agger.
534–510	Tarquinius Superbus seventh King: finished temple of Jupiter Optimus Maximus, destroyed Gabii.
509	Tarquinius Superbus expelled, monarchy abolished. THE REPUBLIC OF ROME BEGINS. Brutus and Valerius first chief magistrates (called praetors, not consuls).
508	Pontifex Maximus created to overpower Rex Sacrorum.
500	Titus Larcius the first-ever dictator.
494	First secession of Plebs: 2 tribunes of the plebs and 2 plebeian aediles create(
471	Second secession of Plebs: Plebeian Assembly made tribal.
459	Number of tribunes of the plebs raised from 2 to 10.
456	Third secession of Plebs: plebeians granted land.
451	*Decemviri* codified the XII Tables of Roman Law.
449	Fourth secession of Plebs: *lex Valeria Horatia* defined sacrosanctity of tribune of the plebs.
447	Assembly of the People created: 2 quaestors created.
445	*Leges Canuleiae:* (a) replaced consuls with military tribunes owning consular powers, (b) allowed marriage between patricians and plebeians.
443	Censors elected for the first time.
439	Maelius, would-be King of Rome, killed by Servilius Ahala.
421	Quaestors raised to 4, office opened to plebeians.
396	Introduction of pay for Rome's soldiers. It was not increased until Caesar doubled it when dictator.
390	Gauls sacked Rome, Capitol saved by warning of geese.
367	The consulship restored. 2 curule aediles created.
366	First plebeian consul. *Praetor urbanus* created.
356	First plebeian dictator. Censorship opened to plebeians.
351	First plebeian censor.
343–341	First Samnite War. Rome concludes peace.
342	*Leges Genuciae:* (a) debt relief, (b) no man to hold same office more than onc(in 10 years, (c) both consuls could be plebeian.